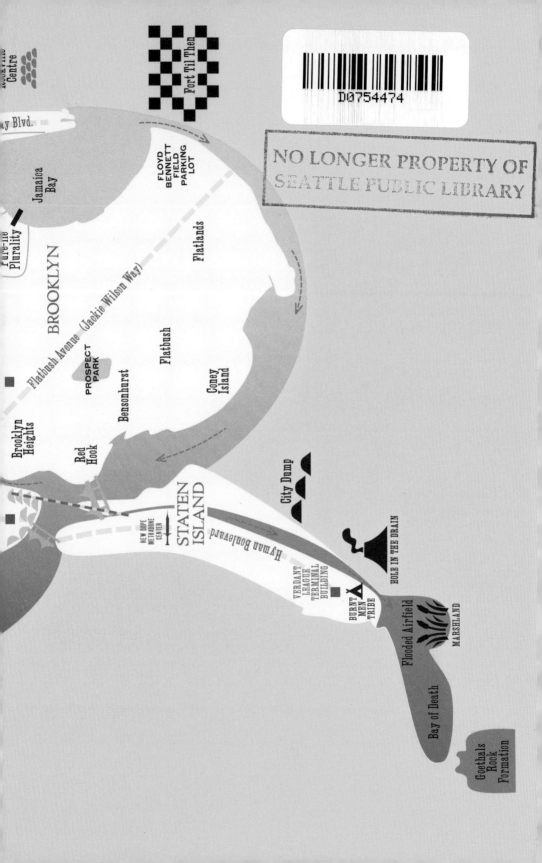

MORE CRITICAL PRAISE FOR ARTHUR NERSESIAN'S NOVELS

For *The Five Books of (Robert) Moses*

"The unquestioned authority of Robert Moses is difficult to fully grasp today—this unimaginable, outsized character whose outrageous deeds seem the stuff of novels. And that is how Nersesian is tackling him, by blending fact with fiction. Historical events and persons are interwoven with a fascinating apocalyptic story and literary license, at last revealing the tumultuous life and legacy of Robert Moses. Faced with such a daunting subject matter . . . Nersesian's narrative is masterful."
—*Brooklyn Eagle*

"Imagine Kurt Vonnegut channeling the Book of Revelations and transmitting it to the faithful of a postcataclysmic New York City and you get a glimpse of the monumental literary feat Arthur Nersesian has accomplished . . . It is imaginative, frightening, and hilarious, often all at the same time."
—Michael Imperioli, author of *The Perfume Burned His Eyes*

"Arthur Nersesian's fantastical magnum opus is both a love song to the vibrant culture of 'old' New York City and a cautionary commentary on the rampant political opportunism of the twenty-first century. As meticulously plotted as the best Stephen King novels, with world-building that might arouse jealousy in Philip K. Dick, *The Five Books of (Robert) Moses* shows us why Nersesian has established himself as one of New York City's most vital chroniclers."
—T Cooper, author of *Real Man Adventures* and the Changers YA series

For *Gladyss of the Hunt*

"The novel combines a riveting story in the hunt for a demented serial killer, a psychologically acute tale of a woman's gradual maturation, and a thoughtful meditation on New York City's sad decline into a tourist-friendly, Disneyfied version of a Gotham that has become a stranger to itself."
—*Sensitive Skin*

"A rookie cop and a rough-edged veteran pair up to stop a series of grisly murders in Manhattan . . . Nersesian revisits New York in a tale combining grit and glamour, poignancy and cynical wit."
—*Kirkus Reviews*

For *Mesopotamia*

"*Mesopotamia* is a solid, absurdist mystery. It's a vacation from the cosmopolitan, for both its heroine and its author—and, just like the tabloids it skewers, a sensationalist retreat for the reader."
—*Village Voice*

"This wild and wildly entertaining novel [is] a satirical thriller with a tabloid touch that revels in the low-rent colorfulness of its characters."
—*Library Journal*

"The immortal shadow of Elvis Presley gyrates wildly through this satiric exploration of America's fascination with tabloid journalism."　　*—Publishers Weekly*

"Thoroughly entertaining ... A quirky, hard-edged, slightly absurdist thriller from a writer who definitely bears watching."　　*—Booklist*

For *Unlubricated*

"Reading *Unlubricated* can make you feel like a commuter catapulting herself down the stairs to squeeze onto the A train before the doors close ... In his paean to the perplexities of dislocation and discovery—both in bohemian life and in life at large—Nersesian makes us eager to see what happens when the curtain finally rises."
　　—New York Times Book Review

"Nersesian's raw, smutty sensibility is perfect for capturing the gritty city artistic life, but this novel has as much substance as style ... Nersesian continuously ratchets up the suspense, always keeping the fate of the production uncertain—and at the last minute he throws a curveball that makes the previous chaos calm by comparison. Nersesian is a first-rate observer of his native New York ..."　　*—Publishers Weekly*

"Nersesian knows his territory intimately and paces the escalating chaos with a precision that would do Wodehouse proud."　　*—Time Out New York*

For *Chinese Takeout*

"Not since Henry Miller has a writer so successfully captured the trials and tribulations of a struggling artist ... A masterly image."
　　—Library Journal (starred review)

"One of the best books I've read about the artist's life. Nersesian captures the obsession one needs to keep going under tough odds ... trying to stay true to himself, and his struggle against the odds makes for a compelling read."　　*—Village Voice*

"Nersesian weaves a heartfelt, tragicomic bohemian romance with echoes of the myth of Orpheus and Eurydice ... Infused with the symbolism of Greek legend, the hip squalor of this milieu takes on a mythic charge that energizes Nersesian's lyrical celebration of an evanescent moment in the life of the city."　　*—Publishers Weekly*

"Capturing in words the energy, dynamism, and exhaustion of creating visual art is a definite achievement. Setting the act of creation amidst Lower East Side filth, degradation, and hope, and making that environment a palpable, organic character in a novel confirms Nersesian's literary artistry. His edgy exploration of the love of art and of life, and of the creative act and the sweat and toil inherent to it, is hard to put down."　　*—Booklist*

"Thoroughly validates Nersesian's rep as one of the wittiest and most perceptive chroniclers of downtown life."　　*—Time Out New York*

"Nersesian has a talent for dark comedy and witty dialogue . . . Woven throughout . . . are gems of observational brilliance . . . A vivid tour." —*American Book Review*

"A witty tour through the lowest depths of high art . . . A fast paced portrait of the joys and venalities of *la vie bohème.*" —*Kirkus Reviews*

For *Suicide Casanova*

"Sick, depraved, and heartbreaking—in other words, a great read, a great book. *Suicide Casanova* is erotic noir and Nersesian's hard-boiled prose comes at you like a jailhouse confession." —Jonathan Ames, author of *You Were Never Really Here*

"Nersesian has written a scathingly original page-turner, hilarious, tragic, and shocking—this may be his most brilliant novel yet." —Kate Christensen, author of *The Great Man*

". . . tight, gripping, erotic thriller . . ." —*Philadelphia City Paper*

"Sleek, funny, and sometimes sickening . . . a porn nostalgia novel, if you will, a weepy nod to the sleaze pond that Times Square once was." —*Memphis Flyer*

"A vivid, compelling psycho-thriller, *Suicide Casanova* confirms Nersesian's place as one of New York City's most important chroniclers. His unique psychological vision of the city rates with those of Paul Auster and Madison Smartt Bell." —Blake Nelson, author of *Girl*

"Every budding author should read this book. Stop your creative writing class on the technique of Hemingway and study the elegant gritty prose of Nersesian. Stop your literary theory class on Faulkner and read the next generation of literary genius." —*Cherry Bleeds*

For *dogrun*

"Darkly comic . . . It's Nersesian's love affair with lower Manhattan that sets these pages afire." —*Entertainment Weekly*

"A rich parody of the all-girl punk band." —*New York Times Book Review*

"Nersesian's blackly comic urban coming-of-angst tale offers a laugh in every paragraph." —*Glamour*

For *Manhattan Loverboy*

"Best Book for the Beach, Summer 2000." —*Jane Magazine*

"Best Indie Novel of 2000." —*Montreal Mirror*

"Part Lewis Carroll, part Franz Kafka, Nersesian leads us down a maze of false leads and dead ends . . . told with wit and compassion, drawing the reader into a world of paranoia and coincidence while illuminating questions of free will and destiny. Highly recommended." —*Library Journal*

"A tawdry and fantastic tale . . . Nersesian renders Gotham's unique cocktail of wealth, poverty, crime, glamour, and brutality spectacularly. This book is full of lies, and the author makes deception seem like the subtext of modern life, or at least America's real pastime . . . Love, hate, and falsehood commingle. But in the end, it is [protagonist] Joey's search for his own identity that makes this book a winner." —*Rain Taxi Review of Books*

"*MLB* sits somewhere between Kafka, DeLillo, and Lovecraft—a terribly frightening, funny, and all too possible place." —*Literary Review of Canada*

For *The Fuck-Up*

"The charm and grit of Nersesian's voice is immediately enveloping, as the down-and-out but oddly up narrator of his terrific novel, *The Fuck-Up*, slinks through Alphabet City and guttural utterances of love." —*Village Voice*

"Nersesian creates a charming everyman whose candor and sure-footed description of his physical surroundings and emotional framework help his tale flow naturally and therefore believably." —*Paper*

"For those who remember that the '80s were as much about destitute grit as they were about the decadent glitz described in the novels of Bret Easton Ellis and Jay McInerney, this book will come as a fast-paced reminder." —*Time Out New York*

"*The Fuck-Up* is *Trainspotting* without drugs, New York style." —Hal Sirowitz, author of *Mother Said*

"Fantastically alluring! I cannot recommend this book highly enough!" —*Flipside*

"Combining moments of brilliant black humor with flashes of devastating pain, it reads like a roller coaster ride . . . A wonderful book." —*Alternative Press*

"Touted as the bottled essence of early-'80s East Village living, *The Fuck-Up* is, refreshingly, nothing nearly so limited . . . A cult favorite since its first, obscure printing in 1991, I'd say it's ready to become a legitimate religion." —*Smug Magazine*

"Not since *The Catcher in the Rye*, or John Knowles's *A Separate Peace*, have I read such a beautifully written book . . . Nersesian's powerful, sure-footed narrative alone is so believably human in its poignancy . . . I couldn't put this book down." —*Grid Magazine*

THE FIVE BOOKS OF (ROBERT) MOSES

A NOVEL BY
ARTHUR NERSESIAN

BROOKLYN, NEW YORK, USA
BALLYDEHOB, CO. CORK, IRELAND

Published by Akashic Books
©2020 Arthur Nersesian

Illustrations by Lisa D. Archigian
Rescue City and Old Town maps by Sohrab Habibion

ISBN: 978-1-61775-499-9
Library of Congress Control Number: 2019943819

Printed in China

Akashic Books
Brooklyn, New York, USA
Ballydehob, Co. Cork, Ireland
Twitter: @AkashicBooks
Facebook: AkashicBooks
E-mail: info@akashicbooks.com
Website: www.akashicbooks.com

Table of Contents

Author's Note

The Five Books of (Robert) Moses is a work of fiction that embellishes and bends certain historical events and figures. Two key characters in this book are Robert Moses and his older brother Paul, who had a less-than-amicable relationship. Anyone who is interested in them should read Robert Caro's excellent nonfiction book *The Power Broker: Robert Moses and the Fall of New York*.

In the volume you are now holding, due to a single terrorist act, history is profoundly altered. As we all know, Richard Nixon didn't finish his second term, nor did Ronald Reagan win the presidency in 1976. However, if Nixon had not been forced to resign due to the Watergate scandal—as is the case in this book—Reagan might've been in the White House four years earlier. Similarly, if the leaders of the antiwar movement *had* been detained and were unable to sway public opinion against America's involvement, the war in Southeast Asia might've lasted many more years.

The Five Books of (Robert) Moses is populated with a number of actual people, the majority of whom lived in New York City in the late 1960s. In fictitiously making their hometown uninhabitable due to a harrowing sequence of events, I've also taken the liberty of reimagining how their lives and fates might have likewise been altered.

—A.N.

CAST OF CENTRAL CHARACTERS IN RESCUE CITY

THE SARKISIANS
Ulysses Sarkisian—amnesiac visitor to Rescue City
Karen Sarkisian—gangcop and council cop captain

THE MOSES FAMILY
Robert Moses*—master builder of New York City
Paul Moses*—Robert Moses's older brother
Beatrice Moses-Mayer—aide extraordinaire for the Verdant League

THE POLITICAL PARTIES OF RESCUE CITY

ALL ARE CREATED EQUAL PARTY, AKA "THE CRAPPERS"
Mallory—member of the Election Commission, later mayor
William Clayton—first Crapper mayor of Rescue City
Donald McNeill*—Mallory's campaign manager
Hector Gonzalez—council cop lieutenant, later deputy attorney general
Chuck Schuman—Karen Sarkisian's assistant, later attorney general
Tatianna—head secretary of the criminal justice department
Anthony LaCoste—gangcop and council cop lieutentant
Gaspar Stenson—gangcop captain
Caleb Straus—gangcop sergeant
Philip Kendowski—gangcop sergeant

WE THE PEOPLE PARTY, AKA "THE PIGGERS"
Horace Shub—first Pigger mayor
Newton Underwood—city council president
Chain—gangcop and council cop captain
Scouter Lewis—head of the council cops under Mayor Shub, formerly a
    detective in Old Town
Deere Flare—campaign worker for Mayor Shub
John Cross Plains—borough president of Queens, later mayor of Rescue
    City North
Ramsey Farrell—gangcop captain
Captain Polly Femus—warden of the Bronx Zoo

VERDANT LEAGUE
Adolphus Rafique—borough president of Staten Island
Timothy Leary*—Rafique's assistant
Jane Jacobs*—deputy mayor, critic of urban renewal
Roger Loveworks—police chief

ADDITIONAL CHARACTERS

THE BREAKAWAY CITY OF QUIRKLYN
Joe "the Brain" Brainard*—Verdant League–appointed field manager for the Quirklyn political campaign, former poet and graphic designer
Ondine*—an Andy Warhol Superstar, city council candidate, East New York
Jackie Curtis*—an Andy Warhol Superstar, city council candidate, Bushwick
Candy Darling*—an Andy Warhol Superstar, city council candidate, Green-Burg
Valerie Solanas* (impersonated by Bea Moses-Mayer)—an Andy Warhol Superstar, city council candidate, South Ozone Park
Cookie Mueller*—a John Waters Dreamlander
Charles Ludlam*—theatrical consultant for the Quirklyn political campaign, former playwright and actor
Jack Healy—leader of the defense militia spanning all of Quirklyn
Patrick Healy—member of the Quirklyn defense
David Wojo—head of defense, Green-Burg
Jean-Michel Gaillard—head of defense, Bushwick
Keith Bowers—head of defense, East New York
Antonio Lucas—head of defense, South Ozone Park

PURE-ILE PLURALITY
Rolland Siftwelt—head of PP
Marsha Johnson*—supervisor for Brooklyn South
Erica Allen Rudolph—member of Domination Theocracy

PROMINENT RESCUE CITY FIGURES
Jackie Wilson*—gang leader who formalized the gangocracy (aka Wovoka*)
Dianne Colder—Feedmore lobbyist
Oric—forcibly impaired psychic
Danny Varholski—Andy Warhol imitator
Akbar Del Piombo—associate of Karen Sarkisian

MKULTRA DWELLERS
Root Ginseng—outreach worker
Plato—escape planner
Scorpion Boy—Plato's son
Tim Mack—highly repressed dweller
Richard—blind head of the Streptococci basin

ADDITIONAL HISTORICAL FIGURES IN RESCUE CITY

Bernstein*—political reporter
Ted Berrigan*—poet
Philip and Daniel Berrigan*—antiwar activists
Daniel Ellsberg*—former Pentagon employee, suspected terrorist
Joe Gallo*—rogue Mafia leader
Allen Ginsberg*—subversive poet
Emmett Grogan*—director of the Lotus methadone clinic
Abbie Hoffman*—antiwar activist
Woodward*—political reporter

ADDITIONAL HISTORICAL FIGURES OUTSIDE OF RESCUE CITY

Samuel Bush*—World War I munitions lobbyist, grandfather and
    great-grandfather to two US presidents
J. Edgar Hoover*—FBI director
Anna Mae Aquash*—Native American activist

*Actual historical figure

BOOK ONE

SWING VOTER
OF
STATEN ISLAND

For Margarita Shalina

Lift up your eyes and look from the place where you are.
—The Book of Genesis

1
10/27/80

"Shoot him . . ."

He was in an office sleeping on a couch.

Focusing on handling security for the eighth annual Domestic POW Conference. "Shoot him once in the head . . ."

to Sutphin . . ." Morning sun. "Catch the Q28 to Fulton Street . . ." Low-level warehouses. "Change to the B17, take it to the East Village in Manhattan . . ." Empty truck bays. "Wait outside Cooper Union . . ." Nothing. "Until Dropt arrives . . ." No one around. "Shoot him once in the head." *Who? Where am I?* "Then grab a cab back to the airport and catch the next flight out . . ."

A sharp pinch compelled him to look down. A big hairy rat was biting him. No, it was a runty dog with protruding ribs and hips trying to angle its little jaws around his right ankle. Uli shook the small mutt off and considered hailing a cab, but the loop of words instructed him otherwise.

His thoughts started breaking through his nonstop chant.

"Walk to Sutphin, catch the Q28 to Fulton Street, change to the

B17, take it to the East Village in Manhattan, wait outside Cooper Union until Dropt arrives, shoot him once in the head, then grab a cab back to the airport . . ."

He couldn't stop chanting. In fact, Uli wasn't fully aware that he was even repeating anything aloud. He had just left JFK Airport and was shuffling like a sleepwalker up Rockaway Boulevard in Queens.

As he moved along the barren avenue, he felt it again. The small dog was calmly trying to eat Uli's leg as he walked. He kicked the little beast away, and it dashed off yelping. Looking up, Uli nearly bumped into a wooden post with three arrow-shaped signs. Each one pointed in a different direction: *Woodhaven Boulevard*, *Atlantic Avenue*, and *Sutphin Boulevard*.

"Walk to Sutphin, catch the Q28 to Fulton Street . . ." He now remembered that a white-haired man with a brown lap dog had hastily imparted the crucial instructions—the chant.

Turning left at the next corner, Uli spotted something odd half a block up the long sandy street. Raised five feet aboveground with a small ladder attached was a wooden platform that looked like a boat pier on dry land. He noticed an attractive middle-aged woman with short chestnut hair and big orange-tinted sunglasses seated at its base.

She was leaning tiredly against a post, scribbling in some phone book–sized document. As he approached, he saw a floppy-eared dog with strangely large hind legs pressed up against her.

"*Run!*" a loud voice yelled from no place visible. Something was very wrong. Uli's throat was parched and his shirt was drenched in sweat. He sensed some kind of drug was in his system, dulling his thoughts and inhibiting his flight reflexes. Suddenly, a pack of wild dogs burst out from behind a warehouse a couple hundred feet away and raced toward him.

Uli's shoes sank and slid along the sandy road, and he finally grasped that the raised wooden platform was the Q28 bus stop.

The woman saw him sprinting her way with the pack in hot pursuit. She heaved her thick document up onto the platform, then slipped her strange dog into a shoulder bag. As she climbed up the ladder onto the wooden landing, her derriere blocked Uli's frenzied escape.

He jumped up along the side of the five-foot structure, seizing onto a banner that read, MOVE 4 SHUB, just as a Doberman leaped at him. He rolled onto the wooden scaffold, winded. A large pit bull pounced up onto the first two steps of the ladder, but couldn't ascend the remaining rungs.

"They're a lot . . . quicker than . . . they look . . ." Uli said, trying to catch his breath. The dogs were barking and lunging up at them from every direction.

The woman ignored him and continued filling out her form. He saw that her pet wasn't a dog at all.

"Where'd you get the wallaby?" he asked, staring at the large-eyed marsupial peaking out of her shoulder bag.

"He was sitting on the road next to his dead mother who had been hit by a car," she finally replied, still scribbling.

"I'm sorry, I didn't get your name."

"I don't want to be rude," she said, "and I'm sure you don't either. I just have a lot of work to do before this day is done."

A half hour later, Uli began wondering how much longer he could sit still on this plywood platform, hardly bigger than a kitchen table, with an antisocial jerk and her orphaned kangaroo.

"I respect your desire for peace, but I just need to make sure the Q28 stops here."

"About a dozen buses stop here—eventually. The problem is, they all take forever and, as I'm sure you know, this is one of the most dangerous spots in the city. So if I were you, I'd get on whatever bus comes first and take it to a more populated transfer point." She immediately returned to her forms.

Over the next hour or so, whenever Uli stole a glance, he saw her flipping through her mammoth document, reading, revising, making notes. The worst aspect of this silence was the *Walk to Sutphin* chant that kept looping through his head.

"May I ask what exactly it is you're doing?" he eventually inquired.

"Filling out forms."

"I just arrived here, so I don't really know what's going on."

"You *just* got here?"

"So it seems, I can't really remember anything. What are the forms for?"

"Okay, well, there are two major political parties, or gangs: the Piggers got Bronx and Queens, and the Crappers control Manhattan and Brooklyn. They run this place."

"Why would any group name itself *Piggers* or *Crappers*?"

"The Piggers were initially called the *We the Peoplers* and the Crappers were the *All Created Equalers*. Somehow over the years those titles got corrupted. Anyway," she returned to her goliath document, "I'm doing administrative work for the Crappers."

"What kind of work?"

Letting out a big sigh, she said, "Okay, I serve on the Election Commission to Combat Citywide Voter Fraud. I have to conform the figures recorded here to the number, model, access, and quality of voting equipment and booths in the two dozen or so districts that comprise eastern Queens—which I just inspected—for next week's mayoral and presidential elections. And if it's not filled out and submitted by three o'clock tomorrow, the Crapper Party loses all rights to appeal. Any other questions?"

Though nothing she said made any sense to Uli, he nodded nervously.

"If I seem a little curt," she added, "up until about ninety minutes ago, I had a private bodyguard and a nice new car."

"What happened to them?"

"Who knows? I went into the Howard Beach polling center for five minutes, came out, and both were gone. So I'm not in the best of moods."

The baby kangaroo jerked forward in her shoulder bag and plopped down five feet to the earthen street.

"Shit!" the woman shrieked just as the Doberman snatched up the joey in its jaws. Without thinking, she jumped down off the platform. "Give it back, fucker!" she yelled, grabbing the kangaroo by its jerking legs.

A rottweiler was about to leap up on her, when Uli dropped down squarely on its broad back, stunning the canine. He pulled out the small red-handled pistol that the man at the airport had given him and put a bullet through the snarling Doberman's large skull. The woman lurched back from the blast, then scooped up the traumatized marsupial and scurried up the ladder to the platform. When a large German shepherd lunged at him, Uli tried shooting it as well, only to find that his gun was out of bullets. Dropping the weapon, he caught the animal by its long snout, then used its own momentum to fling it across the sandy roadway. Some smaller dogs barked furiously at him while backing away.

"Where the fuck did you learn to do that?" the woman asked as he climbed back up the platform.

"Haven't a clue."

"You look familiar," she said, peering at him closely for the first time. "Where are you from?"

"The airport," he replied, then absentmindedly explained, "I was told to walk to Sutphin, catch the Q28 to Fulton Street, change to the B17, take it to the East Village in Manhattan, wait outside Cooper Union until Dropt arrives, shoot him once in the head, then grab a cab back to the airport and catch the next flight—"

"Is that some sort of joke?" she snapped. "My husband was shot by an assassin. He was paralyzed from the neck down."

"I have no idea who I am or what I'm doing here," Uli said, exasperated.

"You really look familiar. You don't have a sister, do you?"

"Other than those instructions, all I remember is being on a cargo plane . . . or maybe that was a dream . . ."

"No, you probably came in on a drone. They fly them in several times a day. They drop off supplies and take off again, but people can't board them." She pointed to one circling overhead.

"I vaguely remember some chubby white-haired guy with a high voice."

"That sounds like Newton Underwood. He's commissioner of supply stock under Shub, and the city council president. Underwood probably found you in one of the drones and guinea-pigged you into an assassin. You're probably a late detainee."

Still slightly out of it, Uli watched closely as the woman resumed filling out one of her forms.

KEW GARDENS VOTING DISTRICT
23,631 registered voters

Voting Equipment
Finger ink: Y or N?

If so, how much? _____
Paper ballots: Y or N?
    If so, how many? _____
Hole-punching voting machines: Y or N?
    If so, how many?_____

_____
Signature of Inspector

—982—

After filling it in with numbers and checks, she signed her name—
Mallory.

Looking tiredly at the distant hills around him, Uli said, "I don't remember JFK as being near a mountain range."

"You're at the first designated Rescue City in Nevada. This is all federal territory."

"I thought this was Queens."

"Queens, Nevada. Actually, we're pretty close to Brooklyn." She pulled off her orange-tinted glasses.

"What do you mean by *Nevada*?"

"The army gridded up the Nevada desert and gave each massive box a number. Someone told me that this is Area 41 through 51." She pulled at her chestnut hairdo. It turned out to be a wig, which she shoved into her handbag. Then she wiped the sweat off her brow and neck. "They started building this place during the last world war. They finished it during the Cold War. There were seven or eight central target areas throughout the city. It wasn't originally designed for people, just for aerial and troop training. You'll see signs of warfare all over the place."

Glancing beyond the woman's shoulder, Uli spotted a small cloud of dust rising in the hot, wavy distance. "Mallory, is that a bus?"

"How did you know my name?" she shot back.

"I saw you sign it in your book."

"Do me a big favor and don't ever say my name again. I'm not too popular out here."

"Why?

"Long story. I used to be on the city council."

As a small bus approached, Uli could see that all of its windows, including the windshield, were bound in a wide metal mesh. It looked like a cage on wheels with a few arms branching out the windows to the roof.

"Did you hit your head?" Mallory asked, pointing to the back of his scalp. "You seem to have a little blood." Looking more carefully, she said, "Actually, you've got a square inch shaved."

"You're kidding!"

"It's not a fresh wound. It's sutured. If you comb your hair back no one'll see it."

As the bus closed in, the dogs erupted into a renewed frenzy of snarls and snaps. The pack was caught by surprise as the bus sped right into it, nearly crushing one of the bigger canines under its front wheels. The dogs scurried away, barking angrily.

The small bus flung open its door.

"You okay?" asked the driver, a large light-skinned black guy with only one arm.

"Now we are," Mallory sighed.

"Where you heading?" the driver asked Uli after Mallory paid and took a seat.

"Walk to Sutphin," Uli said calmly, "catch the Q28 to Fulton Street."

"That's this bus. It takes awhile, and our route isn't very direct, but eventually we'll make it to Fulton Street."

"Change to the B17, take it to the East Village in Manhattan, wait outside Cooper Union until Dropt arrives, shoot him once in the head—"

"I didn't ask for your freakin life story," the driver replied as he zoomed onward. A large handwritten sign said, 1/16. In his pocket, Uli found a rectangular piece of paper that had neither a number nor a president's face on it. It simply said, ONE FOOD STAMP. Uli handed it to the driver, who counted back the change—fifteen neatly sliced parts of another food stamp.

Two men—one bald and thin, the other thick with long, curly hair—and a woman were the only other passengers. Each had an arm stretched out the mesh-covered window.

"What's up with them?" Uli asked the driver.

"The solar panel's loose on the roof."

"You have photoelectric cells generating this bus?"

"They generate all the vehicles here, and if it slides off, we got no battery—ride's over."

Seated behind the driver, Mallory returned to her mega-form. Upon taking a seat toward the rear, Uli slipped his arm out the window like the others. He felt the unsteady piece of paneling on the roof and pressed his hand down on it.

"Howdy," said the thin male passenger. He had a bald head and squinty eyes. "The name's Jim Carnival." He was holding what looked like a World War II mine detector with his free hand. Between his knees was an old bucket. "This is the wife Mary and our boy Oric." The woman appeared slightly younger, but the heavyset "son" seemed to be around the same age as his father. Through Oric's shaggy curls of hair, Uli spotted a small metal cross protruding from the back of his cranium and tried not to stare.

"Is that the former First Lady?" Carnival shouted over to Mallory, who hunched forward, annoyed. "Don't worry, we'll keep it on the hush-hush, ma'am. I worked briefly for your husband."

Mallory nodded without stopping her frantic scribbling.

"So where are you from, pal?" Carnival asked Uli.

"New York, I think. I just got here." Whenever he tried to remember anything, all that came to mind was, *Walk to Sutphin, catch the Q28 to Fulton Street, change to the B17 . . .*

"Hold on," the guy said. "You just arrived from *old* New York?"

"I think so. I'm totally disoriented."

"You look familiar," the wife spoke up.

Uli shrugged.

"Howard Beach 9!" the supposed son, Oric, blurted for no apparent reason.

Amid the trash littering the floor of the bus, Uli spotted a newspaper entitled the *Daily Posted New York Times*. Picking it up and flipping through the articles, he read the last page: *Weekly Police Blotter*. A subcategory read, *Number of Car Bombings: 4*. Without listing the names of any victims or any other colorful details, the article gave bare-bone descriptions of the four harrowing bomb blasts. One car was blown up on the Little Concourse in the Bronx, killing twenty-one people and wounding fifty-four. An alleged former member of a group called SNCC was suspected. A second car bomb exploded in the Upper West Side in Manhattan, killing thirty-four and wounding twelve. A third one detonated in Brighton Beach, Brooklyn, killing four, wounding eighteen. The last bomb that week had gone off near the Chrystler Building in Queens, killing six and wounding thirteen.

Under *Conventional Crimes* some details were offered: Five former FALN suspects died in police custody in the Morrisania section of the Bronx. A family of seven was found murdered during a home invasion in Astoria, Queens. One of them had been an associate of the Black Cubs, a splinter group of the Black Bears, which in turn had splintered off from the Black Panthers. A solicar was hijacked in Staten Island and the driver, a known BMT operative, was murdered. In Sheepshead Bay, Brooklyn, ten seniors, possible fundraisers for the March 29th Army, were killed when a suspicious fire swept through their retirement home. Six former SLA suspects were shot dead during a concert in Bed-Stuy, Brooklyn. There was a massacre at a Crapper club in Boerum Hill, Brooklyn, which claimed twenty-five lives.

Underneath that, Uli read:

BOROUGH ELECTION RESULTS

MANHATTAN:
Total Pigger districts: 1
Total Crapper districts: 9
No change from last election

STATEN ISLAND:
Total Pigger districts: 0
Total Crapper districts: 0
Total Independent districts (Verdant League): 10
No change from last election

THE BRONX:
Total Pigger districts: 9
Total Crapper districts: 1
No change from last election

BROOKLYN:
Total Pigger districts: 3
Total Crapper districts: 17
No change from last election

QUEENS:
Fresh Meadows (Crapper) invaded
2,345 Crappers, 3,392 Piggers
Outcome: Pigger
Councilwoman Diana McNair (C) removed
Councilman Abraham Hodges (P) elected

Hillcrest (Pigger) invaded
6,331 Crappers, 6,323 Piggers
Outcome: Crapper
Councilman Larry Mahonney (P) removed
Councilman Earl Grims (C) elected
Total Pigger districts: 18
Total Crapper districts: 2
Two changes from last election

"It's good to see communities standing up against invading gangs once in a while," Carnival commented, staring at the paper over Uli's shoulder.

"These invasions occur every week, do they?" Uli asked.

"Just like with car bombings—every time *they* do one, *we* do one."

"And who are *we* again?" Uli asked.

"This is Crapper territory and we're Crappers," Carnival responded proudly.

"Speak for yourself," Mary murmured.

"Hey! We're losing our plate!" the driver shouted back to the passengers.

Uli pressed the solar panel harder against the roof. He peered out of the window across the barren urban landscape. On the near side of a huge lake, he spotted a cluster of tall, liver-colored buildings in the distance. He could see lines of dark-suited people filing into several buses.

"That's Pud Pullers up in Howard Beach," Carnival said. "You definitely don't want to go there."

"Pud Pullers?"

"Its real name is Pure-ile Plurality. That's the only good thing about this stinking place," his wife retorted. "It's a haven for family unity."

Carnival shook his head in disgust. The couple were clearly not of one mind.

The bus turned a corner and moved past a row of buildings with plastic garbage bags dangling from them. Down a side street Uli was surprised to see a llama sticking its long neck into one of the suspended bags, rooting for food.

"They figured that by releasing all the animals from the zoo out here we'd somehow become more lovable," Carnival said. "Instead we have mountains of strange dung."

Some of the buildings were clearly abandoned and covered with crudely painted images of male faces. Captioned underneath each one were apparent birth and death dates, as well as brief epitaphs, like *Crapper Hero* and *Killed 8 Piggers*. Doing the math, Uli realized that few of them had made it to the age of twenty. The semiabandoned neighborhood was like a large cemetery where the amateurishly rendered portraits on the collapsed structures served as large headstones.

"Flatlands," the driver announced thirty minutes later as they entered what looked like a new neighborhood.

This area was bordered by a row of four-story apartment buildings with street-level stores that had been converted into flimsy bulwarks and slapdash fortifications. Interspersed through these principal structures were poorly built garages, usually just corrugated tin roofs affixed between uncemented cinder-block walls.

"Correction! Howard Beach 9!" shouted Oric, the manlike child, rocking back and forth.

At that moment, the bus hit a bump and Carnival's old mine detector fell toward Uli, who caught the large pan base before it could brain him. A long beep sounded.

When he handed the contraption back, the man looked at him strangely, then leaned it toward Uli's head. The machine emitted a second beep.

"You know you got an electronic bug in your skull?"

"Underwood probably inserted it there," Mallory spoke up.

"What are you talking about?"

"It means someone is tracking you," Carnival said. "Go to St. Vinny's—if anyone can corkscrew that thing out of your head, they can."

Uli thanked Carnival for the advice and asked where he and his family were coming from.

"Rockaway Beach," Carnival said. "The wife and I met in old New York's Rockaway when we were kids."

"Correction! Rockaway 6, Greenpoint 22. Correction!"

"So what were you doing in Rockaway?" Uli asked.

"We were digging for clams." The man lifted the bucket between his legs and revealed a collection of rusty and sand-encrusted bullets. "These clams are worth money. Bunch of them got buried in the sand down there during the parachute drops years ago."

"Do you have guns for the bullets?"

"Everyone has guns, but no one has any ammo left. Hence, bullets are expensive. I can get about five stamps for each one."

The conversation was interrupted by the one-armed driver shouting through his window: "Get the fuck out of my way!"

Some vehicle was slowing down in front of them. The driver swung the bus onto an empty sidewalk and pulled ahead of the car. As they sped past, Uli could see a strange-looking man in the vehicle shouting upward at the bus driver.

"Fuck you!" the driver yelled back.

"What's going on?" Uli asked nervously as they sped down the sandy street.

"Some damn Flatland motherfucker is trying to hijack us."

Uli could hear the man shouting from the car behind them: "Just stop!"

"How far along are they in the cleanup anyway?" Carnival asked.

"Cleanup?" Uli replied, his confusion mounting.

As Carnival rambled on about the operation, Uli got a clear view of the guy in the car behind them. Other than his fashionable goatee and a trimmed widow's peak, the man looked uncannily like Oric.

"One way or another," Carnival said, "I'm getting back to Old Town."

Suddenly the car slammed into their rear bumper, sending Mallory and her document to the floor.

"Oh shit, he's got a gun!" Carnival's wife shrieked, seeing the man holding something out his window. A blast exploded through the rear window.

"This guy's going to kill us all!" Carnival cried out, grabbing his mine detector in both hands as if it were a rifle.

"Okay, everyone, hold onto the damn panel!" the driver shouted. All did.

Without slowing down, the bus made a sharp left turn and slid across the unswept sands of a larger road. All the buildings on the north side of it were bleached white by the Nevada sun while the structures along the south side were carbonized black by some bygone fire.

"Shit!" the driver yelled, peeking into his rearview. "That Flatlander's serious. He ain't letting up."

The pursuing car, which had now edged next to them, slammed into the side of the bus. The two vehicles drove neck and neck, scraping against each other. Carnival's wife jumped out of her seat and positioned herself next to the driver, trying to help him turn the wheel against the car, but it wasn't working. Their bus was slowing down. Pretty soon they'd be forced to a halt.

Mallory nervously pulled her chestnut wig back over her head, then grabbed a heavy flannel shirt out of her bag and slipped it on.

As Carnival's shrieking wife kept the steering wheel turned against the mad driver from Flatlands, Uli watched the bus driver reach under his seat for a bottle of liquor, which he uncorked with his teeth. With his one good hand, he calmly forced a napkin down the neck. Then flipping open a lighter, he lit the napkin and tossed the bottle out the window. It exploded along the top of the car but missed its solar panel.

"Hold on!" the bus driver shouted, grabbing the wheel from Mary and slamming on the brakes, which sent the other vehicle flying into the side of an abandoned building. The driver turned right and sped away.

"That was too damn close," Mallory muttered.

"I wonder what they wanted," Uli said.

As the bus turned up Flatbush Avenue five minutes later, the sand that had been covering the road began to thin out. The quality of the roadway was still poor, but the one-armed driver gracefully dodged potholes without having to slow down. Eventually they made a left on Church Avenue, where signs of life began returning.

"Welcome to Japtown," Carnival said with a sigh.

The neighborhood was covered with delicate wooden buildings that had tiered levels and swirling pagoda-style bamboo roofs.

"This area was designed to resemble Japan for ground and aerial training," Carnival explained.

Little shops with twirling roofs dotted the area: a tarot card psychic, a barbershop, a scratch-and-match vendor, a sushi bar, an Optimo cigar stand. When the bus turned down a side street, Uli saw a mini restaurant row—a group of food vendors toiling over smoky barbecues and hibachis. Directly across from them, a line of people gathered outside a movie theater that looked like it might originally have been a Buddhist temple.

With an apparently limited supply of red plastic letters for the marquee, the establishment had improvised: W9zT S10E StoR7.

2

After ten more blocks, the cute japanesque architecture ended, and with it, all signs of civilization. Streets were again barren, and the buildings took on a harsher, colder style. Soon they came upon a complex of larger buildings that looked like skeletons of the Soviet housing made popular under Khrushchev. The structures appeared empty and most were burned out altogether.

Six passengers who had boarded the bus along Church Avenue had already gotten off, leaving only the five original riders and the driver.

"Welcome to Borough Park," Mallory said. "Once a thriving Hasidic community."

"What happened?"

"It was a dignified Pigger neighborhood eight years ago—before the Crappers took over Brooklyn. The local residents kept supporting their own Pigger leader, Moss Leere, and the Crappers persecuted them until they couldn't take it anymore and moved to Queens."

The bus passed a partially collapsed cupola with a big Star of David on the front. It looked like something out of czarist Russia. According to Mallory, the destroyed synagogue had once been the spiritual center of the area.

"Shit!" the driver suddenly shouted. "He's back."

Turning around, they all saw it. Smoke from the burned paint on the roof was streaming off. The car from Flatlands was gaining on them. In a desperate effort to lose it, the bus driver veered off his route and sped deeper into the desolation of Borough Park. Soon, though, the Flatlander once again slammed into their rear bumper.

"I can't outrun him," the driver conceded, trying to block the car from getting around.

"Maybe we should stop and see what he wants," Uli suggested.

Carnival noticed a cinder block propped under a broken seat in front of him. He pulled open a hole in the mesh covering his window and hurled the large concrete weight onto the front of the pursuing car. The block shattered the solar panel affixed to the vehicle's hood, bringing it to a slow halt.

"Bull's-eye!" the bus driver yelled back to Carnival, then turned at the next corner to try and get back to his route. Amid the maze of sandy streets blocked by debris, they had difficulty finding their way. The driver came upon a narrow yet recently cleared street that ran loosely parallel to his route. Following it as far as he could, he eventually turned again, only to find a shiny new car blocking him. A group of burly young men were standing around it. The bus driver stomped on the brakes and tried turning his vehicle around.

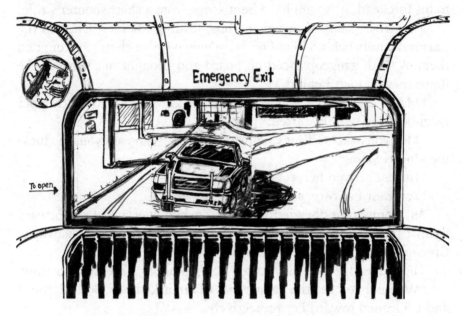

"We might be trapped! These guys are probably in cahoots with the Flatlander!"

"I don't think so," Uli said. Then he noticed Mallory desperately hoisting her thick document and official identification badge up under the solar panel above the bus.

Still in her wig disguise, she slipped contact lenses over her pupils. The driver had only completed the second part of a three-point turn when some kid raced over from the shiny car, dragging a long spike strip before the front wheels. The bus driver jammed on the brakes, causing the solar panel to shoot forward and crash to the pavement.

"Fuck!" Mallory yelled, as her huge election document tumbled to the ground as well.

The driver groaned and threw the bus into reverse, crashing into a dead fire hydrant.

The rest of the burly boys dashed over to them. Four unsynchronized bursts erupted and the bus sank down several inches—they had popped the tires.

"I'm Officer Chain! Open the goddamn door, we're Pigger gangcops!" the oldest and fattest of them shouted, flashing a gold badge. He was stocky and bald, with wire-framed glasses and a square-linked chain wrapped around his thick neck like a glittering, unknotted tie. Some strange mechanical object that Uli didn't recognize was affixed to his forehead. It resembled a bent scope from a sharpshooter's rifle.

The driver stepped out of the bus, leading Mallory, Uli, and the Carnival family behind him. Five large men with machetes surrounded them. A sixth gangcop raced on board and brought out some of the items they had left behind.

"May I ask why, if you're a Pigger officer and this is a Crapper neighborhood—" Uli started.

"May you ask?" Officer Chain cut him off. "Who are you, the fucking king of Siam?"

"He just arrived here," Mary explained.

"Sergeant LaCoste, secure your prisoners."

As a brawny redheaded gangcop pushed everyone face forward against the side of the bus, Oric nervously whispered, "Rockaway 6, Greenpoint 22, Howard Beach 9."

The redhead lecherously patted down Mallory's breasts and groin.

"Where'd you get the kangaroo?" Chain asked her. Both Carnival and Uli leaned toward her protectively.

"Found him along the side of the road."

"You look familiar as shit," Chain said, as his sharp chain swung up against her arm.

"Never had the pleasure," she responded icily.

"What's your name?"

"Frances," Carnival spoke up before she could say anything. "She's my child."

"What are your affiliations?" one of the men asked her.

"None of us are wearing any colors," Mallory answered, as though citing a key rule of engagement.

"That's right. You don't have the right to ask nothing!" the bus driver declared.

"How about you, detainee?" the bald bully said to Uli, scanning his eyes with his scopic horn. A red ray shooting out from its tip led Uli to believe it was a lie detector. "You pro-life or pro-choice?"

"He doesn't know the issues," Mallory answered for him.

When one of the interrogators edged up toward Mallory again, Uli stepped forward, compelling the man to lift his blade. Mallory raised her hand, urging restraint.

The lead cop swung his cyberhorn into Mallory's eyes, but before he could ask any questions, Carnival punched the device.

"Motherfucker!" Chain groaned, grabbing his forehead.

One of the other gangcops immediately brought his machete up against Carnival's long lean neck. Chain tapped his horn until the red light flickered back on, then leaned forward so that the scanner pointed directly in Carnival's face.

"What's your name, asshole?"

"Chad."

"Are those yours, Chad?" Chain pointed toward the old bucket and clunky mine detector.

"I found them."

"What gang are you all with?"

"We're from different parties," Mary replied.

"Not anymore you're not," Chain said. He gestured to one of his assistants, who pinned Carnival's arms behind his back.

"Don't you dare touch my husband!" Mary screamed.

"Or whatchu gonna do?"

"I used to be a Pigger councilwoman, asshole," she shot back.

Chain scanned one of her eyes with his instrument. "How do you like that? She's not lying. Well, you're lucky, honey, 'cause as you know, our party would never permit us to make a woman a widow or turn a child into an orphan."

"The family must be kept together at all costs," added one of the other gangcops.

Chain began laughing and two of his lackeys grabbed Carnival's wife and Mallory, whom they seemed to actually believe was his daughter.

"Hold on!" Mallory yelled. Her little kangaroo was struggling to get out of her arm bag. She grabbed its furry legs and asserted, "We're not related!" With her free hand, she fumbled through her purse and brought out an identity card.

Pushing his horn up against her right pupil, Chain concluded, "You don't look Jewish."

When the gangcop handed back Mallory's ID, Uli peered over and read the name on it: *Alison Lowenstein*—INDEPENDENT.

"Chad and his Pigger wife are under arrest," Chain announced. "The rest of you—scram!"

"Wait!" Mary screamed.

"They're *my* passengers," the bus driver objected. "I demand to know what you're arresting them for."

"His metal detector is a rifle." Chain kicked off the pancake base of the instrument, revealing that it was in fact disguising the barrel of a gun. Lifting the plastic bucket, he added, "And here are the rounds."

"What the hell?" Mary shouted at her spouse.

"Pa!" their idiot son cried fearfully. "Howard Beach! Correction!"

"I'm so sorry, babe," Carnival mumbled to his wife.

"This guy called that guy *Pa*," said one of the gangcops, grabbing Oric's chubby right arm. "He's in the family, let's take him too."

Uli clutched Oric's other arm. "Come on, he's mentally incompetent and obviously older than that guy. How the hell can this be his son?"

One of the gangcops pressed his machete to Uli's throat as another shoved Oric up against the bus. A third fingerprinted the fat man and ran the print through a scanning machine in the shiny car's glove compartment. A moment later, he reported back, "The guy's clean," and shoved Carnival's son toward Uli.

The driver started back toward his bus, but was stopped by Chain. "We're confiscating your vehicle."

"Officer, where can we post bail for them?" Mallory asked.

As a response, one of the gangcops grabbed the joey from Mallory's bag and tossed him to the sandy sidewalk, then shoved her back up against the bus.

"You're interrupting a vital Pigger mission," Uli said as they pinned his arm back. "I work for Council President Underwood."

"Oh sure," Chain replied with a sneer, shining his scope in Uli's eyes.

"Call Underwood. Tell him you're holding the guy who was supposed to walk to Sutphin, catch the Q28 to Fulton Street, change to the B17 to the East Village, and shoot Dropt."

Registering no lie, Chain walked back to his shiny car. He snatched the radio phone from his dashboard and made a call. After a minute, he beckoned Uli over and handed him the black phone.

Uli heard the strangely familiar high-pitched voice: "S'that you?"

"Yes sir."

"Tell me your mission again."

"Walk to Sutphin, catch the Q28 to Fulton Street, change to the B17 and take it to the East Village in Manhattan, wait outside Cooper Union for Dropt to arrive, shoot him once in the head, then grab a cab back to the airport and catch the next flight—"

"And why isn't this being carried out, soldier?"

"These guys hijacked the bus I was on and falsely arrested two people."

"I don't give a shit about that, just tell me you still have the gun I gave you."

"Yes sir, I was heading to Manhattan when these guys hijacked the bus—"

"All right, listen, I just got a call from the blond lobbyist." Uli had no idea who Underwood was talking about. "She's impatient, so she's going to help you. Proceed to Jay Street in Downtown Brooklyn and meet her at the bus stop."

"Fine, but there's this fat bald guy who illegally arrested some friends of mine—"

Chain snatched the radio phone out of Uli's hand and slammed it down. "Get walking before I change my own fat bald mind."

Uli, the bus driver, Mallory, and Oric started to move away without the Carnival parents, who were being arrested. Seeing her bulky election document amid the shards of shattered solar paneling, Mallory bent down and scooped it up, never breaking her stride.

"If they're Piggers," Uli asked softly, "why do they have jurisdiction in a Crapper borough?"

"Since they work as council cops, they have citywide jurisdiction," Mallory explained.

After several blocks down the long sandy street, the driver stopped, looked back at his hijacked bus, and groaned. Two corpses swung by their necks from a broken light post. Oric dashed about thirty feet back toward his murdered parents before Uli tackled him. The challenged man collapsed in the sand and wept.

"They're back in Old Town now," the driver said.

Mallory handed Uli her election document, then removed the billowy shirt and wig she had used as a disguise. Pausing, she quickly popped the contact lenses out of her eyes and slipped them into a tiny plastic case. She took Oric gently in her arms and helped him to his feet.

The four of them walked farther down the succession of barren streets, away from the swinging bodies. Soon they sat down near a small empty square under the long shadow of a statue that appeared to be Lenin.

Oric began mumbling, "I didn't see it coming, I didn't see it coming . . ."

"It's not your fault!" Mallory held the man-child's hand as he whimpered softly.

"If all of Queens votes for the Piggers," Uli asked, tiredly toting Mallory's giant book, "who exactly are you protecting with this document?"

"After a bunch of years in office, Shub has disappointed even most of the hard-core Piggers. Hell, he was so damn powerful that he wouldn't allow any other Piggers to run against him in the primary."

"So what exactly do you hope to do?"

"I was appointed to a bipartisan commission that sends officials to monitor the elections at different polling sites. They're the ones responsible for making sure the right equipment is available and accessible. If I can just make sure that the hardware is there, we should get a reasonably fair mayoral election, and we might actually have a shot at beating the son of a bitch."

"Do you know anything about that Chain prick?" the bus driver asked her.

"Yeah, I know him. He would've recognized me with that scope if I didn't have the contact lenses. Years ago, when my husband was mayor and Horace Shub was head of the city council, that bastard was his chief of security. Hor eventually fired Chain to appease the Crapper moderates—the man was a known sadist. A few years ago, the Slope had a mini uprising because they resented Shub's Pigger policies, and Chain was reappointed to oversee the council cops."

"What exactly is the difference between the council cops and the gangcops?"

"The council cops have jurisdiction in both the Pigger and Crapper boroughs. The gangcops are just locals."

"As I thought, which is why I was confused when Chain said he was a Pigger gangcop."

"Oh, a handful of people, who originally rose through the gangs, still hold dual posts."

3

Oric's mental limitations did not extend to his sense of love or grief. The Carnivals' adopted and orphaned son continued weeping as they headed down the middle of empty streets, passing abandoned and damaged buildings. By late afternoon, when they had crossed a desolate intersection marked *Ditmas Avenue*, they came to the outskirts of a new neighborhood that bore the sign, *BEN HUR*.

Moving into the northern end of Bensonhurst, they approached a battery of a dozen or so older blue-haired women and six male amputees working in the street. Some of the crew were digging with shovels. Others were stooped on their knees upon squares of cardboard. Each person was an arm's reach from the next. They moved in a straight line at their own slow pace, scooping sand into wheelbarrows.

"What the hell is this?" Uli asked.

"Sandstorms," Mallory replied. "They hit about twice a month this time of year. The locals dig them out—refundable sand."

"You should get your children to help you," Uli suggested to one lady who appeared to be the group leader.

"Nasty prick!" she barked.

"Didn't no one tell you 'bout the epidemic?" the bus driver asked when they were out of earshot.

"What epidemic?"

"The EGGS epidemic," the driver said. "Something in the water messed up their plumbing."

"Roughly one-third of all women of child-bearing age died within the first five years of coming here," Mallory chimed in as they labored along down the street.

MY JAW'S SORE, announced the canary-yellow T-shirt of a brightly lipsticked woman they came upon who appeared to be a malnourished hooker. She was leaning invitingly from the window of a tenement on New Utrecht Avenue.

Uli heard an emaciated man on a corner chanting in what sounded like Spanish, "Si . . . si . . ." Then he realized the scary creature was actually hustling something. "What exactly is c-c?" he asked the driver.

"There are two main drugs here: choke and croak, or methadone, which is flown in. Pigger gangsters control croak because Underwood grabs it from JFK."

"What's choke?"

"That's pot made from indigenous plants. Crappers handle the choke production in Hoboken. They harvest fields of it across from Manhattan, using the river for irrigation."

Lapsing back into silence, Uli smelled a foul odor and realized it was coming from Oric. He sped up a little and walked with Mallory, the other two trailing behind.

"You know that guy chasing us in Flatlands?" Mallory said after a while.

"What about him?"

"Did he look familiar to you?"

"Yeah, he looked like *him*," Uli said, tipping his head toward Oric.

"Did that couple, the Carnivals, seem odd to you?" she asked.

"Everything here seems odd to me. Do you think they abducted Oric?"

"Why would anyone abduct a mentally retarded man?" she asked. Uli shrugged. "In any event, there's a home for the mentally impaired run by the Verdant League down in Staten Island."

"Maybe we can drop him off," Uli suggested.

They began to hear lively carousing in the distance. A group of people were gathered around an energetic band that consisted of two youths drumming on upside-down spackle buckets, accompanied by various homemade wind and string instruments. Beautiful women twirled like dervishes with equally handsome guys. Half a block farther down, a group of older men standing around a barrel filled with greenish flames was sucking on stinky cigars. A vendor was turning chunks of skewered meats over a small flame. A sign on his cart said, *GB-ways!* Smelly, oil-bearing smoke trailed down the block. Oric paused at the food stand.

"Come on," the one-armed bus driver said, and led everyone into a small empty shop that had a large rickety table with a row of grills in the center. Against one wall was a stack of old milk crates. He went up to the worn wooden counter where there was a large can of old soup spoons, along with napkins and four plastic squirt bottles, each with a different color paste inside.

The driver took a crate and dropped it on the floor at the table's edge. Everyone followed him, taking napkins and spoons. A small Asian woman with the face of a bat appeared at the rear door smoking a corncob pipe.

"One-stamp size," the driver said, holding up his index finger for emphasis. Uli saw that there was only one item on the menu; its size was determined by the price.

The woman disappeared into the back, presumably the kitchen. Several minutes later, she reappeared wearing oven gloves and carrying an old pot filled with flat noodles in steaming water, which she carefully placed on the grill. Underneath she slid a small Sterno can. She lit the Sterno with a match, creating a small blue flame.

A boy who appeared to be her son followed her out with a cardboard box containing raw vegetables and several dull knives. He returned with a tray of sizzling chunks of meat, which he dumped into the boiling pot.

"Food here don't make you sick," the driver commented, "but you got to work a little." Since he had only the one arm, he instructed Uli to chop up the browning celery and wilted carrots. Mallory was told to dice an onion the size of a small cantaloupe and Oric was given the task of shredding lettuce, cabbage, and basil leaves. Everyone dumped their sectioned vegetables into the bubbling pot.

The driver picked up a bright red squirt container and was about to squeeze it into the pot when Mallory said she didn't like it spicy and that everyone had the right to season their own bowl.

"Fine," the driver said, putting down the hot sauce.

When the flame in the can finally burned out, Mallory began doling out hearty bowls of soup. Everyone quietly slurped down their food. Oric and the driver had another two bowls. The driver and Mallory both said they were getting low on cash, so each of them pulled out a quarter-stamp. Uli made up the difference with a half-stamp. After paying the lady, they tiredly resumed their walking.

Ten minutes later Mallory spotted a tall man with extraordinarily wide hips wearing a skipper's cap—a bus dispatcher. The official stood like a statue before the only illuminated building on the block. When Mallory asked if he knew when the next bus was coming, she was told that some driver just had his bus hijacked.

"His passengers were all hung by the neck," the dispatcher said, "so all bus service is being suspended in western Brooklyn until morning."

"They only hung two folks over in Borough Park," clarified the driver as he slowly approached. "That was my bus."

"Sorry to hear it. No more buses or cabs neither tonight," the dispatcher replied flatly. "Best chance you have is bedding down right here." He pointed his thumb behind him at a run-down building with an old sign that read, HOTEL BEDMILL. "He has several rooms available, and 'cause of your tragedy he'll probably cut the price."

Mallory led the little group inside a dim, paint-peeled lobby where several questionable characters sat on crates in the corner like human mushrooms. A large bug-eyed man wearing an old derby was stationed at a counter next to a wood-burning stove, listening to the radio.

"Half a stamp per night. You can do two per room," the clerk said. Everyone started digging through their pockets.

"Give me something quiet," the driver said, slapping a half-stamp on the worn countertop.

The clerk gave him a towel and explained that the bathroom was in the hallway. "Checkout's at nine a.m. sharp."

"You snore, boy?" the driver asked Oric, who was leaning up against him at the counter.

The heavyset man shook his head and farted. The driver asked for a second towel.

Mallory politely asked if Uli could spare some cash.

"This is it." He held up his last half-stamp.

"I thought I'd be back home by late this afternoon, or I would have . . . All I have is a quarter-stamp," she said. "Want to share?"

"Do you snore or fart?" he half joked.

"If I do, my husband never told me about it," she answered. "Then again, he was usually sleeping with some underage, overweight assistant."

Uli put his half-stamp down and said, "Keep your cash and maybe you can buy me coffee tomorrow."

The clerk handed him a key and two towels.

They marched up two flights of steps and down a corridor filled with various creaks and bangs coming from the rooms they passed, until they located their door. Inside they found a narrow, ancient bed with a ridiculously springy mattress.

Feeling sore all over, Uli didn't want to sleep on the filthy floor, especially considering he had paid for the room. Before he could prepare some suitable compromise, Mallory kicked off her shoes, unbuttoned her shirt, and said, "You want the wall or the outside?"

"Either's fine," Uli replied gratefully.

She stripped down to her bra and panties and brushed an accumulation of sand off the bed. Then she jumped on the mattress, pulling a threadbare sheet over her. For a moment there was an awkward silence as each of them listened to the other's slow breaths. Uli tried once again to remember anything about his past, but all he could think of was his assassin's mantra—*Walk to Sutphin, catch the Q28* . . . It was driving him nuts.

"So how'd you like your first day in Nevada?" Mallory murmured with her back to him.

"How did a national refugee camp turn into a sealed detainment center?"

"During the first year they talked about building a monorail connecting us to Vegas. Hell, we could even make calls off the reservation. Then, while monitoring phone calls, they discovered they had accidentally shipped half a dozen suspected terrorist cells here, but they didn't know exactly who or where they were. The US attorney general's explanation was that the baby *was* the bathwater. He eventually used it as the basis to end our right to communicate with the outside world until they could figure out who the bad guys were."

"How did they get professionals out here? Doctors, lawyers, and so on?"

"Garlic Heads, they called us—Alternative Service workers. I came with a small group from Columbia University."

"What's Alternative Service?"

"The government allowed conscientious objectors to serve here instead of Vietnam. And women like me who probably would have joined the Peace Corps."

A moment later, now feeling much more at ease, Uli yawned. Within ten minutes they were both fast asleep.

. . . a Central American mother stops her car at a light. Two large guys jump in. One puts a hand over her mouth, and a knife to her throat. They have her drive to an isolated side street. They move her to the backseat where her infant is crying. They are talking, but not in English. They move the baby to the front seat, they pull the woman's legs apart, panties aside. The space is too cramped, so the driver shoves the cold barrel of his revolver into her ▬▬▬ *A Native American woman is curled around him in bed, both of them are naked; she is whispering sweet nothings, amorous, wanting to fuck, but he's too disgusted by the car rape. When she manages to pull the sheet back and touch his cock, he's horrified to see that it has turned into a banana . . . As though there is nothing wrong, she proceeds to peel his banana . . . What the fuck! He grabs her hands and they pop off at the wrist. He's holding two cleanly severed hands . . . and he's incredibly aroused.*

Awakening, Uli found he had become intimate with Mallory— though she wasn't the woman from his dream. He was grasping her thighs and slamming himself against her.

"Oh God!" she gasped. Before he could apologize, she reached around, clutching his hips, clawing his ass cheeks, and pulled him into her. Her head turned and their lips locked together. She was plunging her tongue into his mouth. He unclasped her bra as she pulled off his boxers, then he tugged off her panties.

"No . . . I don't want you to get pregnant," he muttered, remembering that it could be a death sentence in this strange place.

"My tubes were tied long ago."

They spent the next half hour screwing. There was something incredible about this woman, maybe because Uli couldn't recall ever having sex before. Finally, in unison, they trembled into a shivering orgasm. As they held each other tightly, she fell back asleep. For him, though, it felt like falling from a great height, through infinite space.

4

█████████████████████████████████ *Walk to Sutphin*, Uli thought as soon as he woke up, *catch the Q28 to Fulton Street, change to the B17 and take it to*—he couldn't remember where. Opening his eyes, he saw that Mallory had already dressed and left the dank room. After using the filthy communal bathroom for a quick sink-bath, Uli dressed and went down to the shabby lobby. There, surrounded by prematurely old retirees and a bizarre number of amputees, he found Mallory sitting next to two frail seniors, feverishly working on her endless election form.

"I would've woken you up with a frothy cappuccino," she said without looking up, "but they don't have room service here at the Bad Smell."

"That's Bedmill!" shouted the same bulbous clerk who had checked them in the night before.

Oric and the driver appeared moments later, before either Mallory or Uli could so much as mention last night's indiscretion.

"If you're all heading up to Manhattan, the nearest bus stop is over in south Sunset Park," the driver offered. "It's not too close, so we should probably get started."

The four spent the next twenty minutes hiking alongside the drab semioccupied, Soviet-style projects of New Utrecht Avenue, which grew increasingly desolate. One demolished intersection was pockmarked with holes in the old concrete, evidence of a major gun battle. Uli couldn't tell if it was from an old military training exercise or a recent gang conflict.

Mallory, who was walking ahead of the others, abruptly froze and seemed to stare up at the blue sky. Uli saw, however, that her eyes were closed. She was smelling the air. Without warning, she bolted full speed down an empty street.

"Hey!" the driver shouted.

Fearing that she was in some kind of danger, Uli dashed after her. He seized a rusty pipe on the ground in case he needed a weapon. Mallory came to a dead halt roughly two blocks away, before a sandy field that looked like it had once been the parking lot for an old factory of some kind. There, she dropped to her knees as if she were about to be executed. Uli looked up, trying to spot the enemy, but the vast industrial complex was eerily deserted.

"What's going on?" he cried out.

Mallory signaled over to him frantically, instructing him to back away. He approached timidly, nonetheless, trying to follow her sight line. That was when he spotted it, about ten feet away, hopping slowly toward her. It was a small kangaroo, possibly the joey she had lost yesterday. It was unlikely that the baby marsupial could have hopped all the way to this neighborhood without being attacked by dogs or hit by solicars, yet the animal seemed to know Mallory. Uli watched as it tentatively sniffed her face. She picked it up and set it snugly into her bag.

"What the hell is that?" Uli asked, pointing to three stone smoke-stacks rising from a long, flat building that looked like some kind of plant. A hooded conveyor belt angled out of it in the distance.

"It was modeled after a famous steel mill in Leningrad and used for battlefield simulation."

Moments later they returned to New Utrecht Avenue, where Oric and the bus driver were waiting for them. They resumed walking.

"Is there any connection between these various military training zones?" Uli asked.

"I think they were built as three different scenarios," answered Mallory. "The Japanese architecture is back that way, and the Soviet structures are clumped here in western Brooklyn. Manhattan is largely Germanic."

"What about Bronx and Queens?"

"There were no rivers or swamps back then, so they were both long stretches of land. The Air Force did a lot of bombardment there. Because the area was so heavily blitzed, it had to be redeveloped later on from the ground up. So for the most part, those pricks got all the best houses."

"Where are the newest houses?"

"The newest are here—they were hastily built when we were still coming in—but the the best ones are up in Queens. They were built in the fall of '71."

"How do you know all this stuff?"

"Construction was still underway when we arrived. We struck up friendships with some of the workers when we got here, and they told us all about it."

"How about Staten Island?"

"They have gorgeous houses over there along the shoreline. People believe they were meant for administrators and the military. Proof that they had intended to stay and oversee Rescue City."

"And when were those built?"

"That's the funny thing. The workmen claimed they were built in '71 as well, but after the flooding, when the water went back down and some of the houses collapsed, we found newspapers behind the walls and in the floorboards that were dated from as early as 1968."

"Why is that funny?"

"Old Town was hit in 1970—why would they build housing *before* the bombing?"

"Maybe they needed an administration center back then."

"I suppose."

"So when the administrators and military pulled out, who moved in?"

"Pigger officials mainly, but that didn't last too long. When the sewer got blocked and Staten Island flooded, the homes became un-inhabitable, even after it drained. The rest of the borough is strictly third world. I stayed down there for a while after Shub came to power . . ."

The first sign of Sunset Park was a food stand where for a six-teenth-stamp the driver bought a piece of deep-fried dough covered in powdered sugar—a donut without a hole. Although Oric and the others watched him eat, no one else ordered anything.

After another block they passed a strip mall of small businesses: a body-art parlor called Tattoo You; a barbershop, Unkindest Kuts; a homemade brewery, Fine Fermentations; and a diner called Ham-burgeriffic. Lastly, there was a Chinese takeout place, operated by two scantily clad Asian women, called Food Ho's.

"They got awful versions of every major cuisine here," Mallory told Uli.

Throughout this area Uli spotted betting parlors. In addition to the council-operated OTDs—off-track dog races—Uli saw slot ma-chine and blackjack parlors, not to mention scratch-and-match tickets for sale everywhere. "This place has a serious gambling problem," he remarked.

"Joe Gallo, the black sheep of the New York crime families, runs this place. He decided it was better to be a big fish here than a dead fish in Old Town," the driver imparted as they marched westward.

"Did you lose your arm in Vietnam?" Uli asked. The two of them were now walking ahead of Mallory and Oric.

"Why, you find one there?" the driver countered. When Uli didn't laugh, he said, "I got stamped-and-amped for a crime I didn't commit."

Uli didn't ask what this meant.

The driver led the tired group to an establishment with a sign that read, SIXTEENTH-STAMP STORE. He and Oric entered.

Next door was the Sunset Park Crapper headquarters. Mallory hurried inside. Explaining her vital mission and dire situation, she was able to appropriate ten stamps for official business. Then she entered the general store and surveyed the impulse items lining the shelves. Candy, mentholated cigarettes, and various liquors—all of which fit into sample-sized wrappers or narrow containers so they could be sold for a sixteenth-stamp apiece. Mallory purchased fruit-named soft drinks for everybody.

As Uli sipped his bright-pink "strawberry" beverage out front, a beat-up minibus screeched to a halt and the driver hastily tossed out a small bundle of the *Daily Posted New York Times*.

Uli surveyed the headlines: "Big Antiwar Rally Today." A smaller article announced, "Antiwar Folksinger Fillip Ocks Hangs Self in Rockaway, CIA Involvement Strongly Suspected."

Uli read the latest listing of crimes and their terrorist links. Like in the issue he had read on the bus, they were all supplied by nameless sources. A truck bomb had blown up in Rego Park, killing eighteen. Members of the Shining Path were suspected. Six middle-aged women from Howard Beach—who had somehow pissed off members of an extremist cyclist group, the August 30th MassCritters—had been sexually assaulted and strangled. The Symbionese Liberation Army was suspected of shooting and killing a dozen people in Far Rockaway. According to the paper, the Black Liberation Army had engineered a string of jewelry heists in Staten Island. The list went on.

The single detail that the *Times* failed to mention, Uli noticed, was how these crimes—particularly the violent ones—served each of the revolutionary organizations' higher ideals. How could raping middle-aged women from Howard Beach help the cause of the notorious August 30th MassCritters? What could the BLA possibly do with cheap bracelets, paste-gem amulets, and imitation diamond tiaras to further its cause of racial equality? In a place where slander charges could probably not be pursued, Uli sensed the writer had taken wild liberties.

Also, inexplicably—since there seemed to be no official communication between the residents of Rescue City and the rest of the world—the newspaper also included a lively page of national and international news. One misspelled headline screamed, "Reagan Orders Secret Bombing of Louse and Terroran!" A second article proclaimed, "Religious Cult in Go'on'ya Commits Mass Sewercide."

Uli turned to the sports/politics page:

BOROUGH ELECTION RESULTS

MANHATTAN:
> Total Pigger districts: 1
> Total Crapper districts: 9
> No change from last election

STATEN ISLAND:
> Total Pigger districts: 0
> Total Crapper districts: 0
> Total Independent districts (Verdant League): 10
> No change from last election

THE BRONX:
> Total Pigger districts: 9
> Total Crapper districts: 1
> No change from last election

BROOKLYN:
> Greenpoint (Pigger) invaded
> 2,124 Crappers, 2,122 Piggers
> Outcome: Crapper
> Councilman Guido Basilicata (P) removed
> Councilman Antonia Basilicata (C) reelected
> Total Pigger districts: 2
> Total Crapper districts: 18
> One change from last election

QUEENS:
> Far Rockaway (Pigger) invaded

2,438 Crappers, 2,435 Piggers
Outcome: Crapper
Councilman Ted Kostiyan (P) removed
Councilwoman Carmen D. Sapio (C) reelected

Howard Beach (Pigger) invaded
1,335 Crappers, 1,332 Piggers
Outcome: Crapper
Councilman Jimmy Church (P) removed
Councilman Dwight Valone (C) elected
Total Pigger districts: 16
Total Crapper districts: 4

Two changes from last election

The Crappers had won in both Howard Beach and Far Rockaway by only three votes. And in Greenpoint, they had beaten the Piggers by two votes. All were paper-thin victories. Yet the number of people killed in those three districts, Uli realized, nearly mimicked the figures that Oric had been nervously barking out during the previous day's trip through Brooklyn.

The newspaper report set Uli's thoughts into a paranoid tailspin: if that cross-shaped object buried in the back of Oric's shaggy-haired skull was harnessing the man's psychic abilities so he could predict the slim margins of Pigger victories, then the late Jim Carnival—the overzealous Crapper—could travel into the designated neighborhoods with his hidden gun and "correct" the Pigger constituencies, disguising the casualties as typical crimes, thus altering the outcome of the local elections.

Uli reentered the sixteenth-stamp store and discreetly guided Oric out to the street. Uli carefully inspected the strange cross on the man's head and wondered if it was an antenna of some kind. Then he delicately asked, "What exactly does *correction* mean?"

Oric paused a moment, then pointed his chubby index finger at Uli and said, "*Bam!*"

"What's going on here?" Mallory asked as she came out of the store, seeing Oric shooting off an imaginary pistol. While she fed the baby kangaroo celery stalks she had just purchased, Uli filled her in on his little theory.

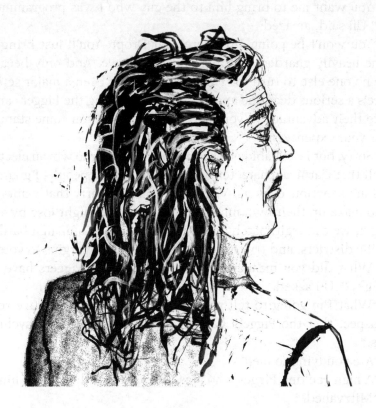

Taking a deep breath, she said, "The majority of this city is registered as Crappers, yet through strategic invasions and voter disqualifications, the Piggies under Shub have managed to stay in charge for the better part of the past decade."

Uli considered this, then said, "Share."

"Well, since you openly stated you were programmed to kill Dropt, I can't accuse you of guile. In fact, after risking your life to cover for me with Chain, and having monitored your actions over the past twenty-four hours, I think I can trust you."

"Trust me with what?"

"I have to get *back* to Kew Gardens in Queens to turn in this Affidavit of Electoral Inventories by the three o'clock deadline, so that Dropt will have a shot at getting a fair election next week." She held up her fat book. "This theory about Oric kind of changes things. See, the Piggers have their own guy."

"What kind of guy?"

"We need you to bring Oric to the Manhattan Crapper headquarters in the Lower East Side, pronto," she said without answering.

"You want me to bring him to the guy who I was programmed to kill?" Uli said, amazed.

"You won't be going anywhere near Dropt. You'll just bring Oric to the heavily guarded building and then leave. And only because I have no one else to turn to. This bus fiasco has been a major setback. There's a serious deadline approaching, something the Piggers are using to their advantage. If you help me, I can give you some stamps to cover your expenses."

"Sorry, but I can't abide by the notion of murder to win an election."

"If that Carnival character was actually killing people, I guarantee it wasn't sanctioned by us. We're the political party that wants people to make up their own minds. If we know we might lose by a slim margin, we can legitimately reallocate our funds, campaign harder in specific districts, and try to convince the wobbly margins to vote."

"What did you mean when you said that the Piggers have their own guy?" Uli asked.

"What I'm going to tell you is highly classified. We have reason to suspect that the Piggers have had their own election psychic for years."

"Are you lying to me?"

"A high-ranking Pigger who was mitzvahed told us about him."

"Mitzvahed?"

"They call him Karove. We can't locate him, but we're pretty sure he exists. Maybe with Oric we can balance the scales."

Uli let out a long sigh. "So how exactly do I get to the Manhattan Crapper headquarters?"

"I'll go with you to Fulton Street and put you on a bus to the Lower East Side."

"What do you think of that?" Uli called over to Oric. "Would Mallory lie to us?"

"Mallor— Mallor— Mallor—" The challenged man seemed to be having difficulty pronouncing her name. Finally he just blurted out, "Mayory!"

"It feels like I'm fated to go there," Uli conceded. First Underwood had tried to program him to assassinate the rival candidate there, now Mallory was begging him to take Oric there.

When the group finally reached the Sunset Park bus stop, the dispatcher there immediately reassigned their one-armed driver to a southbound route. The others waited at the end of a long line for the next northbound vehicle. Nearly an hour later, when the bus finally pulled up, it was already packed. Mallory let the baby marsupial stretch its legs and relieve itself one last time before slipping it back into her shoulder bag. Then she squeezed on board and they started north.

The new bus chugged up Fort Hamilton Parkway toward Flatbush Avenue, and here the street became pure asphalt—apparently the local assemblage of sand refunders had swept the street down earlier. When the bus made a stop on 39th Street, a cluster of seats opened up in the rear.

Uli hastily grabbed a seat next to a window, pulling Oric with him. Mallory sat across from them. The bus moved through bumper-to-bumper traffic until they came to a standstill alongside the western edge of the Green-wood Cemetery. All got an up-close view of some closed-coffin funeral in progress.

"What can I say about the passing of my own brother?" a bearded minister called out to a crowd of gray-ponytailed men and women. "From a divine point of view, we live in a devil's playground where each person's greatest and darkest temptation is truly tested. And while we live, only God can see through our meager disguises." The minister looked up and over the crowd. His gaze suddenly locked onto Uli through the bus window. "But lo! From where I presently stand, I too can see the shame and pain that a single man can inflict upon an entire nation! And that man is . . . You Lee!"

"What's that, padre?" someone yelled out from the crowd.

"He's the reason we're all here!" The minister began pointing at Uli, and called out some name that Uli didn't catch.

"Which one?" he heard someone in the crowd shriek.

"That one sitting in the back of the bus!"

The mourners turned, almost as one, and stared up at him, then started racing over to the bus. Uli slid his window shut, but their collective hands, arms, and torsos began rocking the vehicle as though it were hit by a wave.

The bus was frozen in traffic, so the many wrinkled and arthritic fingers working together were able to pop out the emergency back window. Uli tried to rise to his feet but Oric was squeezed up next to him, making a quick retreat difficult. All at once, a dozen hands and arms thrust inward and grabbed him. Uli punched back, furiously trying to defend himself, but it was too much. In another moment, overpowered, he was being yanked out headfirst, through the aluminum window frame. Before being fully extracted from the vehicle, however, something caught his ankles. Horizontally, still in the air, he exchanged punches with the elderly mob below. Oric was holding onto him, anchoring himself between Uli's legs, braced up against the bus seat. Crackling voices screamed at him:

"You monstrous son of a bitch!"

"Die in hell, you scumbag!"

Uli felt his shirt and jacket pulled from his chest, and his body flopped down against the outside of the bus just above the wheel.

"Get that cocksucker!"

While one man was whacking his cane furiously at Uli's head, pruned hands scratched at his face and tore his clothes. Just as an elderly lady was about to thrust the pointy end of a parasol into his face, someone grabbed its handle and knocked the woman down. A vaguely familiar blond man was fighting to defend Uli. The guy kicked the knee out from under another old woman clawing at Uli's exposed chest. Her fingernails felt like ten little fishhooks tearing down his flesh. Once released, Uli tried to wiggle backward.

"What the fuck are you doing here?" the blond man with a high voice screamed at him.

"I don't know!" Uli shouted back. "Who am I?"

Someone clipped Uli along the side of his skull with a small bat. The blond man grabbed the improvised weapon and yanked it away before the swinger could take a second shot. With all his might, the stranger shoved Uli upward, back into the bus.

"Get that yellow-haired fucker!" someone yelled.

A large bald man carrying a machete came running up toward Uli's protector just as the traffic jam finally opened up and the bus started moving. The blond man jumped up onto the side of the bus, folding his arm precariously inside the windowsill. Uli tried to pull him up, but he was barely inside the bus himself.

The bald man led the chase along the sidewalk, with a group of surprisingly agile seniors racing along the avenue.

"I can't hold on, my arm is slipping!" the blond man gasped.

"Who am I?" Uli groaned, but neither could say another word, investing everything in just clinging to each other as the bus picked up speed.

"Huey!" the blond guy screamed when the bus slowed to turn. "Meet me at Rockefeller Center!"

"I'll get off *now*!" Uli shouted.

"No, just meet me at Rockefeller Center at three!"

The blond man pushed away from the bus to avoid falling under its wheels and rolled onto the ground. In another moment, the bus zoomed on and Oric and Mallory pulled Uli all the way back inside. Everyone sitting around him stared in shock.

"What the hell did you do?" Mallory asked, cradling her kangaroo in her bag.

"Haven't the foggiest," he replied, trembling. He modestly folded his arms over his aching and exposed chest, which was red with scratches and welts.

Some guy pulled an old shirt from a laundry bag and said, "I was going to toss this anyways."

"Thanks," Uli said, taking the wrinkled garment and pulling it on. It read, *Rescue Me from My Rescuers.*

Upon finally calming down, Uli thanked Mallory for her concern and Oric for saving him. Slowly the other passengers stopped staring. Uli's paranoia still engaged, however, he decided not to say anything about the strangely familiar blond man. Mallory took a seat behind him and resumed working on her never-ending form. Uli sensed that the best chance of getting to the bottom of his situation was by going to Rockefeller Center at three o'clock and meeting with the blond guy.

As the bus moved steadily uphill, Uli noticed the green dome of a narrow tower peeking out in the distance. Though the building couldn't have been much taller than ten floors, with its lime-covered cap and distinct red clockface, it was the tallest building he had seen since arriving.

"What's that?" he asked Mallory, pointing to it. He was beginning to vaguely recognize some of these landmarks.

"The Williamsburgh Savings Bank," she muttered back.

"They have banks here?"

"No, it's actually the municipal building that houses the criminal justice system. It's where Shub works."

"Is Rockefeller Center the same place here that it is in old New York?"

"Yeah, Midtown Manhattan. Why?"

Uli shrugged and stared off dismally, so she didn't press. Soon the bus merged into a four-lane boulevard. Uli spotted a street sign that said, *Flatbush Avenue,* and under it, *Jackie Wilson Way.*

"Wasn't Jackie Wilson the first black baseball player?"

"That was Jackie Robinson," Mallory responded without looking up. "He was a pop singer, but this is a different Jackie Wilson."

Uli closed his eyes and tried to rest.

"Last stop!" the driver shouted after another twenty minutes, flapping open the front door. As people tumbled out, Mallory grabbed Oric's hand. She quickly led them to a line of people at a connecting stop a block away. A sign said, *B17 Bus to Lower Manhattan & Staten Island*.

"My bus is leaving in just a few minutes or I'd wait with you. Yours is leaving in twenty minutes," Mallory said, gently stroking the short snout of the joey peeking out of her bag. Handing Uli five stamps, she added, "Buy Oric some food and take him to the bathroom before boarding. Traffic in Manhattan is unbelievably slow."

"Do they know we're coming?"

"I'll call from Queens. Just ask for Dr. Adele and tell him I sent you. He'll take care of Oric." Glancing at her wristwatch, Mallory assured him she would be there as soon as she submitted the updated Affidavit of Electoral Inventories to the Election Commission in Kew Gardens, Queens, and paid a quick visit to her paralyzed husband up in a Harlem hospice. Uli wished her a safe trip. She nodded back tiredly. It was almost as if the prior night of intimacy had never occurred.

"Very hungered," said Oric soulfully, as they roamed through the chaotic Fulton Street Mall near Jackie Wilson Way.

Having survived the incident at Green-wood Cemetery, Uli now appreciated why Mallory carried a disguise. From among the racks of cheap garments and bins of sundry merchandise, Uli purchased a new shirt, a short brim hat, and sunglasses. Whoever he or Huey was, some people obviously knew and despised him.

Spotting a noisy crowd across the street mall, Uli and Oric headed over to see what all the hubbub was about. The gathering was pressed up against a rope held by two brawny security workers. Uli made out an oddly thin young woman with distinctive eyebrows, who was screaming, "Come shake hands with the protector of freedom and godliness—Horace Shub!"

Another security guard placed a microphone stand in the middle of the clearing. A moment later, a small simian-faced man with abnormally large hands walked up and tapped the mic to make sure it was on. It was indeed Shub, the Pigger mayor.

"My opponent, Dropt, remains immobile on dynamically fluid issues," the man said in a tinny meter. "He doesn't waver when you need the wavering." He made a flapping motion. "He's intractable in a business that requires a lot of tractoring!" The bugle-eared mayor issued a series of tight little gasps that Uli realized was self-satisfied laughter. Shub then started working the rope line, shaking the grimy bouquet of outstretched hands.

The extent of the mayor's animal magnetism became fully evident to Uli when Oric suddenly broke loose and dashed toward the man, knocking down others.

"Oric, no!" Uli shouted. "Wait! No!"

"Terrorist with a bomb!" someone screamed, and all hell broke loose. Within seconds everyone had retreated in panic. Shub was huddled off to his armored car and a phalanx of beefy security guards pushed forward, slamming Oric to the pavement.

"No! Please be careful, he's got something coming out of his skull," Uli called out. Oric's curly hair obscured the strange metallic cross.

A thin, young, short-haired brunette rushed over and watched as the men pinned Oric's chubby arms up against his fat back, cuffing his wrists together.

"This is what happens to those who try to interfere with God's plan!" the woman announced victoriously. "Take him away, boys!"

"No! Please!" Uli appealed to her. "He didn't mean anything. He's got the mind of a child."

A security guard took Uli into custody, checking his fingerprints and asking exactly how he knew the would-be assassin. Two other bodyguards frisked Oric, pulling his pants down and shirt up, while a third inspected his head-cross. Another fingerprinted him to verify his identity. Discovering that Oric was a registered Crapper, they rushed him into a black van to interrogate him about his gang loyalties and possible terrorist ties.

After twenty minutes of Oric continuously weeping and finally wetting himself, they realized Uli wasn't kidding and released the mentally impaired man to his custody.

"We can still have you arrested for not controlling him," the brunette threatened Uli, who noticed fresh bruises along Oric's face and neck. *REELECT SHUB!* announced a brochure now protruding from Oric's back pocket. The tagline read, *A Vote on Earth Is a Win in Heaven.*

Once they were alone, Uli apologized to Oric and led him back toward a line of food carts on Jackie Wilson Way.

"So hungered," Oric whimpered.

Some meat on a skewer called "God Be Ways" seemed to be as predominant as hot dogs in the old New York City. A maimed vendor was standing before his homemade cart with a crude sign, ONE-ARMED BANDIT, alongside a picture of a slot machine with a jackpot of hot shish kebabs. Inspecting the charred chunks of fat and muscle speared on a short wooden stick, Uli asked exactly what it was.

"*Be Ways* means *backwards*, so the question you want to ask is what's *God* spelled backwards." The vendor held up one of the barbecued meat skewers. Uli thanked him and kept walking.

The various other deep-fried objects crammed into pita pockets seemed better options than man's best friend. Uli told Oric to get what he liked most, and the oval man waddled hastily toward the corn dog cart. Uli bought four dogs on sticks and selected two baked yams with butter instead of some sugary dessert. The vendor bagged it all and handed it to him.

As they crossed the street to return to the bus stop, they passed a middle-aged Latina with a basket of bananas on her head.

"I'll take some of those, if you're selling," Uli said.

"An eighth of a stamp for three," she replied, as he selected the fruit. When he handed her the eighth-stamp, she reached up and snatched the sunglasses right off his face. "Oh shit!" She looked familiar to Uli, and stumbled backward as though she were staring at a ghost.

"Do you know me?"

Her voice became soft: "Let go."

Uli could see that she was so terrified that her diaphragm wouldn't contract. People started looking over, so Uli grabbed Oric and vanished into the crowd.

They cautiously returned to the B17 bus stop, where Uli noticed an unusual-looking blond woman across the street checking him out. In addition to a raccoon-like application of eyeliner and stiff golden hair, she wore a black miniskirt.

He casually peeled a banana as she walked over and asked if he was looking for her.

"Sure," Uli replied. She seemed too fashionable to be a prostitute.

"I'm Dianne Colder." She shook his hand with a firm grip. "I have been waiting for you since yesterday. That's when Underwood said you'd be here."

"I got stuck in Sunset Park." Oric immediately started getting fidgety, so Uli added, "Dianne, this is my pal—"

"Kid!" Oric cut him off.

"So, I heard you tried taking out the mayor, kid," she replied with a grin.

"—nap," Oric blurted.

"He wants to take a nap," Uli added weakly.

"What's that thing sticking out of the back of his skull?" Oric's hair was matted down with sweat, so the strange object was now protruding like a tiny TV antenna.

"It's a skull plate," Uli said. "He was wounded in 'Nam."

"That explains a lot." She sniffed at him and wrinkled her nose.

"Who exactly are you?" Uli inquired.

"I'm a lobbyist for the Feedmore Corporation," she said, handing him a click pen with some sort of corporate logo on it. "I come to Rescue City about once every six months to make sure everything is as it should be. That way, when I go to Washington, I can tell them all is well."

She knows the way out of here, Uli thought.

"So hungered," Oric said again.

Uli opened the bag of food and handed him a greasy corn dog. Oric gobbled it down while staring at Colder like a wild animal. When Uli took one out for himself, the woman made a disgusted expression and asked, "You're not really going to eat that, are you?"

"Manhattan—*boom!*" Oric shouted through his mouthful of corn dog.

"What?" Colder asked, startled.

"Big boom bang!"

"Hmm . . . I'll be right back," she said, then abruptly dashed down the block.

The Manhattan-bound bus immediately pulled up and opened its flapped door. It took a few minutes for everyone to board. Uli and Oric grabbed seats at the very rear. Others behind them crowded into the aisles. To Uli's relief, the driver closed the door and they began rolling.

In a few minutes the bus was crawling over a causeway supported by two narrow stone towers. Those structures, along with the faux span webbing overhead, were obviously a sad homage to the original Brooklyn Bridge.

With his first real view of multiple boroughs, Uli could see how they were graded and contoured. Brooklyn seemed to be built on one level; Manhattan was slightly lower, allowing for water to spill around it; and Staten Island, off to the southwest, was the lowest. The water level appeared oddly higher around Staten Island than Brooklyn. A lengthy wall of what appeared to be slick brown stones was constructed around the lower lip of Manhattan.

A blond head suddenly emerged through the crowd of standees. Uli's heart sank as Dianne Colder smiled at him and held up a brown paper bag.

"This is the best chow you're going to find outside of Old Town," she said as she approached.

He tried hiding his dismay. "What exactly is it?"

"A cactus burrito. I only got one since Pogo obviously relishes the shit they serve here."

The bus moved at a snail's pace over the low bridge and Colder launched into some weird tangent: "Einstein's theory of relativity, you can prove—light bends, zing! Ha ha! But Darwin's theory of evolution is a whole 'nother story! What are you gonna do? Wait around till the next monkey talks, right?"

Oric nodded nervously in agreement. To pacify him, Uli handed over the rest of the corn dogs and opened the wax paper containing the cactus burrito. The tortilla shell stuffed with local vegetables and topped with a spicy chipotle sauce was heavenly.

"Remember when the Crappers started a school in the Village? They didn't teach Johnny reading and writing, you know why? 'Cause they'd teach him *fisting*." She shoved her clawlike hand in Oric's face. "A word every bit as ugly as it sounds, ha!"

Uli tasted something acrid. Dipping his fingers into the sauce and holding it up to the light, he detected a powdery substance and felt a wave of fatigue. She must have slipped some kind of narcotic into his food.

"Blist bags!" Oric shouted furiously through the dog in his mouth.

"Big breasts?" Colder asked, modestly covering her own chest.

"Big blast! Big blast!"

Colder turned to face Oric. On the verge of passing out, Uli tossed the remainder of his burrito out the bus window.

5

Oric's fingers digging into his side awakened Uli to the fact that they were slowly descending off the cheap imitation of the Brooklyn Bridge. Rather than hooking into City Hall like the original bridge, this new one tilted onto 14th Street. After several minutes, the bus pulled up at the northeast corner of Second Avenue. The driver stood up and called to the back of the bus: "We ain't going one more stop till lil' Miss Miniskirt pays her damn fare. I couldn't pull over on the bridge, lady, but I ain't moving another inch till you pay up just like everyone else."

"Oh damn," Colder said, "I got on so quickly I forgot." She rose and angled her way through the crowd to the front of the bus.

"Come on," Uli said, and punched open the rear emergency window. He helped his heavy companion down to the pavement.

Before Uli could join him, Oric waddled toward a large pastry shop with a sign that said, *Veniero's*. The bus turned south on Second Avenue as Uli hit the ground.

Checking a wall clock through the shop window as he caught up to Oric, he saw that it was one thirty. Too late to drop off Oric first.

"Blig bast!" Oric said nervously.

"We're getting as far away from that scary lady as we can," Uli explained.

"Blast, big boom!"

"Where blast?"

"I'll never know."

"Why won't you know?"

"You know, you're me." He touched Uli's forehead.

Still concerned that they were being pursued, Uli took the challenged man's hand and hastily led him westward along 14th Street. They joined a stream of young hippie types heading in the same direction. A growing crowd was visible several blocks away.

Onion Square, declared a psychedelic hand-painted sign at the corner of Fourth Avenue. Just as Mallory had said, all the buildings in the area had a distinctly European flavor. A small German restaurant called Lüchow's was the only establishment here that triggered a distant memory from old New York, or Old Town as the locals called it.

The crowd of long-haired kids was centered around a large make-shift wooden stage in the middle of a barren field—Onion Square. Old-fashioned bullhorn speakers were blasting a speech: ". . . If these bastards aren't going to end this war, we've got to end it for them!"

All cheered.

Glancing up at the stage, Uli saw a slim Mediterranean man with a springy Afro wearing an American flag on his shirt.

"Remember, it takes two eyes to spell FBI and CIA." He spoke with a slight lisp. "And they're always watching! They're right here among us!" All cheered once again.

"Do you know where Rockefeller Center is?" Uli asked some post-adolescent with peach fuzz and pimples standing next to him.

"Up that way," the guy replied, throwing his arm northward.

"Who's that speaking?"

"Abbie Hoffman."

"What's he talking about?"

"The *war*," the kid answered.

"What war?"

"Vietnam!" the fuzzy-faced youth replied, then walked away in disgust. "It's an antiwar rally."

Something told Uli that he was in favor of the war, but he had no clue as to why.

Next, an older, wild-bearded man with black-framed glasses, a top hat, and a waistcoat took the stage. He began reciting rhymes: "Communism's / shooting jism / on top'a Asia / We'll invade ya / Napalm bomb / And all is calm / It's a mock, you see / our Democracy . . ."

"Who's that?" Uli asked another unsuspecting youth whose neck was ringed with turquoise beads.

"Ginsberg!" the kid shot back, not wanting to miss a single word of the rant.

"Beware / she's there!" Oric pointed at a thick shag of blond hair on the western edge of the crowded square.

A beat-up city bus was turning onto Park Avenue through the tangle of long-haired war protestors. Uli impulsively grabbed Oric's hand, raced across the square, and flagged it down. The driver pulled past them to the curb and opened the doors.

"You go by Rockefeller Center?"

"*Rock & Filler* Center," the driver corrected as Uli paid their fares.

"Rock and Filler?" Uli asked, taking a seat behind the driver. "Sorry, I just got to Rescue City so I don't know my way around."

"By Crapper decree, many of the names in Manhattan and Brooklyn have been corrupted."

"Why?"

"To remind us that this is not the place they want us to think it is. It's *word protest*."

"How about in Queens and the Bronx?" Uli asked.

"The Piggers are proud to be here, so they've kept most of the original names intact."

As the bus sped up Park Avenue, the talkative driver kept playing tour guide: "Many of the buildings you see around here have been rebuilt two, even three different times. The Air Force held multiple bombing exercises down here. The Army Corp of Engineers would repair buildings, like restacking bowling pins, then the Air Force would knock them down again. They were initially modeled after Gropius's Weissenhof houses. This gray building coming up on your left was bombed and rebuilt at least four times; it's based on a famous building designed by the Taut brothers."

Eventually reaching 51st Street, the bus made a left and came to a halt on a low-rent stretch of Fifth Avenue, before a small Gothic European church with a missing spire. A smattering of worshippers were entering it.

"This is the stop for Rock & Filler," the driver announced.

Uli and Oric got off along with a handful of others. Oric immediately split off and trotted into the church. Uli raced after him.

Inside, Uli was surprised to find that the house of worship was actually a hollowed-out brownstone. Its upper floorboards had been removed, revealing only unmilled crossbeams and a high, peeling ceiling. Rows of benches faced forward to a large fold-out picnic table. Behind it was a big wooden cross. Clean holes bored at the ends of the tall crucifix suggested that the Jesus had been set free.

Oric was staring at some lady photographing a colorful mural on a large wall that looked like a little girl riding a dog. On a tray in front of the image was a coffee mug that said, DONAT, behind which was a row of unlit, half-melted votive candles. Off to the side of the dog-riding girl were sketches of three homeless men, and above them, a yellow starfish.

When Uli stepped back, the tableau pieces all locked together. "Oh, it's the manger scene," he declared. The little girl was actually a boy, and the dog was a donkey. "That's God," he explained to Oric.

"Huh?"

"That's who your mom and dad are with," Uli elaborated.

"In there?" Oric said, looking at the unevenly plastered wall.

"No, they're *with* the kid in the painting—the baby Jesus." Uli reached into his pocket and took out a sixteenth-stamp. He instructed Oric to light a candle for his murdered parents, the Carnivals, then asked him to stay put. "I'll be right back."

"I wait for my brother." Oric pointed to the wall.

Uli asked someone outside where Rock & Filler Center was. He was pointed to a traffic jam of cars and people squeezing around an empty mall between two large buildings. Instead of Saks Fifth Avenue, Uli saw a six-column archway across the street. Approaching the plaque affixed to it, he found himself standing before a quarter-scale replica of the Brandenburg Gate. He figured this was one of the German sections of town.

He moved tentatively toward Rock & Filler Center, looking around for the blond stranger from the cemetery. At 50th Street, he spotted a familiar figure down by 49th, but it wasn't the blond guy. Uli's body clenched up as he realized it was the Flatlands pursuer, the one who resembled a short-haired Oric. The man's clothing was singed and wrinkled.

No sooner had Uli turned away, when he heard, "Hey! Wait a sec—"

A loud explosion knocked Uli and a dozen others backward to the ground. As Uli rose to his feet several moments later, he saw a large plume of black smoke suspended in the air before him. It appeared that the goateed pursuer, along with a cluster of others, had been blown to smithereens.

"Fuck a duck!" one of the seniors behind him shouted.

Once the ringing in his ears had subsided, Uli limped through the smoke to the edge of a small crater. Smoldering body parts from at least a dozen victims were strewn about the twisted frame of a destroyed minibus. Gasping for breath, he heard others screaming in shock, and realized that he must've seen a lot of this kind of thing, since his heart hadn't so much as skipped a beat.

With the Flatlands pursuer presumably dead, Uli continued his search for the blond stranger. Rock & Filler Center had two paved walkways on either side of a raised stone garden that ended at a drop-off. Walking to the edge, still gasping for breath, Uli found himself standing on the precipice of a large empty ditch. It was roughly thirty feet deep by thirty feet wide, with a muddy puddle at the bottom. At the far side of the hole, a man was taking a piss on a pile of white stones.

"What the hell happened over there?" the urinator called out to him.

"A truck bomb."

"Pigger faggots!"

"Yeah," Uli replied tiredly. Behind the urinator was a narrow four-story office building that looked nothing like the surrounding structures.

"Do you know what that building is?" Uli asked.

"Yeah. Number 30."

As Uli walked over, he saw that the front of the building looked like it had been chiseled down. Inside the lobby, two men in dark-blue blazers were checking people's IDs and whatever bags they carried. A sign read, *Manhattan Municipal Government Offices*—hence the bomb blast?

Uli headed back to Fifth Avenue, where arriving EMS workers triaged the injured as a growing crowd watched. Uli wondered if perhaps the goateed man had killed his nameless blond friend before being blown up. *How else would the Flatlander know I'm here?* he pondered. *I should've gotten off the bus after that cemetery in Brooklyn.* When the first gangcops finally arrived and started rounding up witnesses, Uli decided to leave before he could be detained.

He found Oric back at the church, rubbing the wall frantically, while other worshippers stared at him.

"What are you doing?" Uli asked, trying to pull him away.

"I saw him! He's with them."

"Who is?"

"My brother, but he said . . . he said they ain't mine, so . . ." Oric looked confused and then distressed.

"I think maybe you had a bad dream."

"No dreams. My brother, he just came here, see, and . . . he said you take me to him."

Uli gently led Oric outside the church and across the street. As Oric continued with his nonsense, more emergency vehicles came to take care of the wounded. Uli led him to the bus stop at the corner of 51st. Glancing eastward, he could see a row of odd towers across the slim waterway separating Manhattan from Queens. It was as though a Hollywood producer had shot a big-budget film there and left this elaborate set behind.

"What exactly are those?" Uli asked a tall man wearing a pointy bamboo hat who was also waiting for the bus.

"Just backdrops," the guy replied. "They're nicer than the ones across from Wall Street."

A southbound bus eventually pulled up. With his mission to meet the blond man a failure, Uli's next move was to drop Oric off at the Crapper headquarters.

Uli paid their fares and watched as a balding gangcop waved all traffic past the explosion site. Oric started whimpering again, and then murmured, "See you soon."

The buildings down Fifth Avenue, though occasionally singed and almost all run-down, looked occupied. Small-business owners had loaded piles of merchandise onto the cramped sidewalks, forcing pedestrians into the street, just as they had around Downtown Brooklyn.

Growing impatient, the driver angled the bus along the far right side of the street. With two tires on the edge of the curb and the other two in the gutter, she drove down a new lane of her own creation.

At 42nd Street, Uli saw a big sandy mound where he had expected the stately New York Public Library. It seemed that not all of the city's landmarks, or their German-inspired replicas, had made it into the final imitative plans.

Passing 34th Street, Uli saw a strange building soaring up six majestic flights with a sign that read, *Vampire Stake Building*. It was covered with leering gargoyles and hieroglyphics that suggested powers of the occult. A string of sightseers queued up at the front door.

At 23rd Street, when a group of people finally got off, Oric and Uli grabbed a pair of seats across from a cute young woman with curly hair and glasses. She smiled, revealing a mouthful of black teeth.

Uli greeted her with a smile of his own. "Hi, I just arrived yesterday from Old Town and I'm totally lost."

"You must be a detainee!"

"I have no clue."

"Unlike everyone else here," the young woman said with a chuckle, "I never really lived in New York. My name's Kennesy. You guys go to the rally earlier today?"

"Yeah," Uli said. "How 'bout you?"

"Yeah. Now I'm heading down to CoBs&GoBs for a benefit show." She spoke with a slight Southern twang.

"What's that?"

"A musical palace. I'm a deejay for a rock show on the local radio station."

"Where exactly are you from?" Uli asked.

"Mississippi."

"How'd you wind up here?"

"When I was a kid, we lost our place to Hurricane Camille and were offered temporary asylum in New York City. No sooner did we arrive there than the attack happened and we were offered refuge out here."

"So which gang are you with?"

"That's a rather indiscreet question," Kennesy replied coyly, "but I'm still a Crapper. At least until they fragment into half a dozen other parties."

"Why do you say that?"

"Go to the next Crapper convention and see for yourself."

"What would I see?"

"Well, recently they broadcasted the Pigger convention in Queens. It was like watching a High Mass. Everyone talks softly, one at a time, and they all applaud politely. But the Crapper convention, wow! They held it at the Coliseum on Columbus Circle last year. I did a radio show from there, and I swear, I couldn't hear myself think. Five thousand screaming voices. Fistfights in the aisles."

"Amazing that they've been able to hold two boroughs together."

"Yeah, but in the last month they've lost three Brooklyn neighborhoods and one in Manhattan. Inwood just elected its first Pigger councilperson, Julie Rudian. And it was done by internal dissent. All the Crappers just voted for her."

"Sounds pretty messed up."

"That's the wave of the future, and the Crappers don't get it," she said. "It won't be gang warfare that'll decide the future of this place, it'll be the *sentiment* of the people. Folks in Manhattan are growing more and more Piggish."

"Why do you think that is?"

"Pure-ile Plurality—they're this quasi-evangelical outreach organization." Uli remembered seeing their headquarters in southern Queens. "A lot of Piggers work for them. They're always hiring people. You know that expression, *If you win their hearts and minds* . . . Well, PP's food trucks won the stomachs of Inwood, then they went down to Harlem. Now they're going all the way down to the East Village. They start with food, then it's clothes and basic medical treatment. Soon it'll be free movies in the park."

"So is PP an arm of the Piggers?"

"Technically no. If any evidence is found showing they are swayed by any one gang, they could lose their government funding—"

"Would you mind keeping your brilliant insights to yourself?" interrupted an older woman a few seats away.

Kennesy rolled her eyes, and without lowering her voice she resumed: "The only thing I respect about the Piggers is their pro-life stand. They've accepted this as the life they are fated to, instead of always waiting for the day they get to leave—that's the pro-choice position."

"How can someone actually want to live in this hellhole?" Uli said quietly.

"Just ask anyone here what it was like being homeless. After being evacuated when Camille struck, we were given housing in Queens shelters. Then, when the bombs went off, we were moved out into a hangar at LaGuardia Airport. Try living there on cots with thousands of people and tell me this isn't better." She let out a deep sigh.

"Why couldn't they just give us subsidies and let us stay somewhere like Prospect Park?" burst the irritable woman who had just tried silencing them. "That's what they did during the San Francisco earthquake! Why the hell did they ship us out to a radioactive desert in the middle of nowhere?"

"You didn't have to come here," Kennesy replied, and explained to Uli, "I don't know about you, but everyone here *applied* to get in. There's still a lot of poor people living in Old Town."

"What do you mean a *radioactive desert*?" Uli asked the older woman.

"There's no scientific proof of radioactivity," Kennesy shot back.

"This is where they set off all the A-bombs back in the fifties," the woman explained to Uli.

"And in case you don't remember," Kennesy countered, "they *did* try subsidies. They handed out supplies in the streets of New York. Everyone got in line. Do you remember who eventually wound up with the bulk of stock?"

The older woman made a sour face.

"The Mafia, that's who. No one has ever starved or frozen here. Hell, we even got cars and other basic luxuries."

"We can't travel or have children!" the lady barked.

"People were *homeless*. They couldn't afford to travel anyway. And why the hell would someone who doesn't even have a home want to have a homeless baby?"

"So only the rich should reproduce, is that it?"

"Look, you want to blame someone for sticking us out here? How about the terrorists who hit the city!"

Before Uli could intervene, the driver called out, "Eighth Street, Crapper HQ. Last stop."

Uli and Oric got off with the cute hurricane evacuee, who bade them farewell and headed south down Lafayette Street.

Uli and Oric moved eastward to Astor Place. Almost immediately, two hands grabbed Uli's elbows from behind. A thick arm looped over his head and across his neck. Back-kicking his assailant's kneecap, Uli grabbed the arm and flung a fat bespectacled kid up over his back and onto the pavement. Just as quickly, a third and fourth pair of beefy hands grabbed at his arms. The fat kid pressed a wet rag against Uli's face. Another pair of hands grabbed his knees and lifted him. As Uli struggled, he smelled the chloroform compound and held his breath. Twisting his head around, he recognized one of his assailants as the guy from Midtown with the pointy bamboo hat. Uli struggled to free one hand, but he felt his consciousness thinning out.

"Ma! Da! Ma-Da! I miss you!" he heard Oric yell.

Dazed, Uli was now being lifted into a van. The geeky fat boy kept the rag pressed tightly over his mouth. Uli found himself fading to Oric's screams.

6

██████████████████████
█████████████████████

Sleeping on a hard wooden bench ████████████████
people bleeding ████████████████████ a hospital waiting room ████
████████████
██████████████████████████

Wake up now! Wake up! GET THE HELL UP! GO!

"What?" The sun was bright in the doorway, so it had to be the next morning. Uli was hanging upside down with his hands bound together.

She's going to torture you! You're going to have one chance and that's it!

"Help me!" Uli shouted back.

Where are you? It was the blond man. Yet the voice was female. How could this be?

"I don't know," he said aloud. Looking around, he saw that he was alone and dismissed the interaction as the afterwash of a bizarre dream.

An awful sulfuric stench pulled him to full consciousness. He appeared to be in a barnyard. His lower section was numb with pain. He could still hear Oric's shrieks nearby.

"How do you know about the blast?" Uli heard a woman's voice shouting.

During an interlude of silence, Uli figured something sinister was underway. Sure enough, Oric started screaming terribly.

"Talk, you fat fucking retard!"

"Great Neck," Oric groaned. "Little Neck. Great Neck, Little Neck!"

"What are you talking about? What's this neck shit?"

"Dark, dark," Oric heaved. "Then light!"

"You are going to tell me what that *Great Neck, Little Neck* shit means or you're going to—"

"Plague walkers!" Oric shouted. "They'll enter at lotus eaters! Spread death, water pumps!"

"What the fuck?"

Uli recognized the voice. It was Dianne Colder, the Feedmore lobbyist. He could hear her engaging in some kind of strenuous activity. Maybe she was punching Oric. It didn't last long. To the frenzied squeal of pigs across the barn, Oric was shouting, "No, please! Don't hurt Oric no more!"

Uli mustered all his strength, flexing his waist to catch a glimpse of the knot around his knees. Then he heard a loud thud.

"Shit! You fat fuck!"

"Brother, brother!" Oric screamed.

"Scat! Get out of there!" he heard Colder calling over the shrieks. "Serves you right! You should have told me!"

In a moment, her footsteps were marching toward Uli. He dropped his arms back down and hung limp, pretending to be unconscious. The lobbyist paused before him, then poked him hard in the stomach—he didn't budge. As she crouched low to inspect his lifelessness, Uli sprung his body outward and wrapped his bound wrists over her blown-out, highlighted hair.

"Wait a sec!" she screamed, immediately trying to negotiate. "Ninety-two percent of all Crappers—"

He yanked her head sharply forward, dislocating her vertebral column. With a crunch, she fell into a perfect seated position and just stared straight ahead.

"Oh my God," she slowly said. "I can't move— I—"

He had paralyzed her. Only her mouth still worked. Like a broken robot, she manically cursed at him, occasionally calling for help.

Uli twisted on his rope like a large marlin on a hook. Behind him, hanging from a nail, he saw a rusty scythe veiled under years of dusty cobwebs.

"I didn't mean to hurt him," Colder said.

Uli swung backward and caught the wheat cutter in his bound hands. He squeezed the wooden handle up between his knees. Oric's shrieks were unbearable now.

"I was only trying to scare him."

"What'd you do?" Uli asked as he frantically rubbed his knotted wrists over the rusty tool.

"He was yelling strange shit! He kept saying, *Great Neck, Little Neck*." She paused. "I guess he was talking about *my* neck!"

"He's psychic," Uli explained candidly, since the woman was clearly headed nowhere.

"Well, if he wasn't so fat, I wouldn't've dropped him in the pigpen," said the talking blond head. As Uli continued sawing away at his ropes, she added, "The average Pigger is 12.8 pounds lighter than the average Crapper. Did you know that?"

"That's obviously a lie, so you've probably been lying all along," Uli replied, cutting through the final strands.

Once free, he began sawing through the cords holding his ankles together. The dried-out rope snapped and Uli fell to the ground, collapsing on top of Dianne Colder.

"You are a truly despicable human being!" she shouted painfully.

"Even if that were true," he countered, "I'd still be a hundred percent better than you."

A car screeched to a halt outside. Uli grabbed the rusty scythe, hid against the side of the barn, and waited.

"Help! Quick!" Colder squealed, now lying flat on her back. "He's in here!"

A large man rushed inside. Uli swung the scythe deep into the front of the guy's neck. It was the man in the goofy hat who had worked with the fat boy when they kidnapped him at Astor Place. The man grabbed his neck wound, dropped to his knees, flipped over, and gurgled slowly to death. Uli removed the scythe and dashed out to the pen.

Four large hogs were chewing on the tied-up limbs and torso of Oric's bloody body. Uli could see their teeth tearing through flesh as though it were raspberry pudding. When he kicked one of the animals away, it tried to bite him. He slashed and stabbed at their fat hairy backs with the rusty weapon. When the biggest one charged him, Uli jabbed it right in the eye. The hog squealed insanely with blood shooting forth, causing the others to dash off. Uli used the opportunity to heave Oric out over the rails of the bloody pen. Among his many wounds, Oric's right shoulder was eaten clean to the bone. The hogs had chewed into his belly and bit into his head, tearing off the cross-shaped device along with the back of his scalp.

Oric was still slightly conscious. Placing him gently on his back, Uli tried to tie a tourniquet around his gnawed arm, but two of the worst bites on his torso had apparently severed major veins or arteries. The poor man was bleeding to death and there was nothing Uli could do.

"I'm so sorry, Oric."

"It's okay, friend," the dying man muttered. "The Carnivals abducted me and had some goddamn scientist shove that thought cuff into my skull."

"What . . . ? Why?"

"They knew I had some basic psychic gifts. And by retarding me they could enhance those abilities."

"Oh my God."

"You're the only one who figured it out. He was using my predictions to change the outcomes of . . ." Oric was losing it. "That was my twin brother in Flatlands trying to rescue me . . . I'll be joining him now."

"I didn't know."

Oric was gasping for breath and consciousness. "You . . . you have . . . too!"

"Have what?"

Oric moved his mouth, but nothing came out.

"DO I HAVE SOMETHING IN MY HEAD?"

Oric stared at him.

"A TWIN, DO I HAVE A TWIN?"

Oric just kept staring. It took Uli a moment to realize he was dead. He hauled the man over his shoulder and trudged out to the front yard. There he saw an old sports car with only two seats. The keys were still in the ignition.

"No, wait, please don't leave me here!" Colder cried out faintly as Uli checked Oric's pulse for the last time. He was about to drive off and just abandon the paralyzed lobbyist, but then remembered that she was the only person he had met here who had mentioned routinely leaving the place. She had to know some way off the reservation. Racing back inside the barn, Uli scooped up Colder's limp body and carried her out.

"Thank you. Bless your soul."

"We have to get you to a hospital right away," he said, loading her up on the roof of the old car so that she was lying belly-down with her head facing forward.

"There aren't any good hospitals here," she blurted. "These animals can barely handle basic bruises."

"We have to get you and Oric out of here. He's going to die."

"The retard's already dead," she spat out. "There's a phone in the barn. I'll give you a number. Call Rufus! Tell him Bambi's in trouble!"

Uli glanced around and spotted an old burlap sack slung over a laundry line running from a wooden post to the end of the barn. He pulled the cord down and grabbed the sack, which he slid under the corporate shill's skinny body. He tied the line tightly around Colder's left wrist, strung it through the windows, and knotted it to her other wrist so that she was pressed flat against the roof of the car.

"No! Call Rufus, he'll come right over—"

"Underwood sent you to kill us," Uli interrupted while securing her legs.

Letting out a deep sigh, she said, "You got it all wrong—*he* works for *me*. The only reason I'm here is to protect the company's interest—" She cut herself off now, evidently realizing in her muted agony that she was imparting too much information.

"How are you protecting its interest?"

"The same way you are," she said simply.

"I'll give you one chance," he reasoned. "If I think you're lying, I'm feeding you to the pigs. Now tell me what's *really* going on."

"Our job is to sway the election."

"The mayoral election?"

"Fuck no, the presidential election. It's tightly split along party lines. I'm here to tilt it right."

"Just how do you hope to do that?"

She didn't respond.

"If you want me to call Rufus, you better talk quickly."

"The five boroughs work almost like the electoral college. Each borough gets a single vote. Three out of five boroughs throw a single electoral college vote from Rescue City, Nevada, to the presidential election."

"Are the boroughs divided?"

"Queens and the Bronx are Pigger. These days they are generally voting for the Democratic Party. Brooklyn and Manhattan are Crapper. Right now they're going with the Republicans. Staten Island is the wild card. They went Democratic in the last election, but the Staten Island borough president has the power to ratify or veto the vote of his constituents at his own whim."

"Really?"

"Yeah, and the only reason I was sent here was to make sure Staten Island swings to the Democrats."

"So you're a Democrat?"

"I'm whatever they tell me to be!"

"How exactly did you hope to alter the vote?"

"I already did it—with a large quantity of bullets. Look, if this really matters to you—"

"It doesn't. These people can all kill each other for all I care. I just want out."

"Then call Rufus and within thirty minutes I'll have you sitting in a Jacuzzi in a Vegas hotel with two underage girls."

That was the best offer he'd had since he found himself sleepwalking near the airport two days ago.

Uli went into the barn and picked up the phone, only to find that the line was dead. When he told Colder the phone wasn't working, she cursed and said that the whole borough was probably out.

"We gotta get out of here! Take me to the hotel at the corner of 4th Street and First Avenue in Manhattan," she commanded.

Before untying the cord, Uli propped up Oric's dead body in the passenger seat. The man had rescued Uli yesterday from the geriatric mob at the funeral in Sunset Park, and now this blond bitch had brutally killed him.

Uli jumped into the car, turned the key, and hit the accelerator. In his rearview as he left the compound, he saw a sign that read, *CALYPSO PIG FARM.* Dianne Colder began screaming from the roof.

Before long, Uli realized he was in Staten Island. After twenty minutes of bouncing over dunes, following rusty signs directing him to Manhattan, crisscrossing streams of wastewater along Hyman Boulevard, he had to clamp his nose due to the stench. Driving past the rows of gorgeously designed buildings he had heard about, situated along the banks of the borough, he saw that they were indeed uninhabitable. Some were still submerged up to their roofs, just as Mallory had said. These flooded structures were evidence of how high the sewage water had risen.

Finally, he came to a major intersection: one bridge to the right, another straight ahead. "Straight!" he heard Colder yell.

He sped through an unattended tollgate onto a two-lane ramp marked, *Staten Island Ferry Bridge*. The wooden bridge swayed as he drove from submerged foundation to submerged foundation. The guardrail was a string of rotten two-by-fours. Fearing he would skid right off the aging planks into the toxic waters, Uli slowed to a crawl. To the southeast, he spotted the other bridge, a short, red arch connecting Staten Island to Brooklyn. Nearer to his right, a dark angle of land narrowed to a point, then turned into a tall, reinforced concrete wall. The liquid sewage reached almost to the top of it. Below him, the black muck oozed south from the western side of Manhattan. At the other side of the dam, the water was noticeably cleaner as it moved around Brooklyn.

Approaching Manhattan, Uli saw up close what he had spotted from the Brooklyn Bridge the day before. A tight wall of sandbags had been constructed next to the concrete dam wall running along the southeastern edge of Manhattan. The bags moved around the bottom of the borough and up its west side. Orange sentry booths that looked like giant traffic cones lined the bagged wall.

Speeding through Lower Manhattan, Uli ignored the passing motorists who gawked at the screaming blonde roped like a deer to his rooftop. He made his way onto Houston, turned left on First Avenue, and screeched to a halt at the corner of 4th Street, in front of a building with a shingle that read, *CLASS-A LADY HOTEL*.

"Is this where you live?" he asked, getting out of the sports car with Oric's motionless body still slumped forward in the passenger seat.

"What the hell's the matter with you?" Colder attempted to spit bugs out of her mouth as she spoke. "Do you want out of here or not!"

"Exactly how much are you getting paid to destroy American democracy?"

"Everything great and powerful about this nation was made . . . not in the halls of Congress, but by the laissez-faire system . . . Corporate interests *are* American interests!"

"What's your room number? What's Rufus's number?"

"I don't trust you. Untie me and carry me up there."

"Don't be absurd."

At that moment, a large man in a gangcop uniform turned the corner and moved toward them.

"HELP! Pol—" Colder started to scream.

Uli kissed her hard on her bright-red lips. The officer walked past without even noticing that the woman was strapped to the roof of the car, or that a dead man was slumped in the passenger seat.

"So what room are we in?" he asked again, as he frisked her for her room key, finding nothing.

"I'm not telling you shit, asshole!"

For the first time, Uli noticed a strange bump on the front of Colder's neck. He tapped it gently.

"What do you think you're—"

"How come I didn't see this before?"

"See what?"

"You have an Adam's apple."

"What are you talking about?"

Uli yanked up her skirt and pulled her panties aside, revealing a set of small pink testicles. He didn't know how he could have missed it before. The lobbyist was a transvestite.

"Mark my words," she spat out, "you'll never get out of here alive! I don't care who you are!"

"Who am I?" he asked.

"A dumb asshole!"

"The only way you're going to get medical help is by giving me Rufus's number."

Uli pulled the burlap sack out from under her and shoved the end of it in her mouth, slipping the rest of it over her head and torso. Ignoring her muffled cries, he entered the lobby of her grungy hotel.

"Wanna room?" asked a bored desk clerk who was listening to Elvis crooning "Viva Las Vegas" over an ancient radio.

"Actually, I'm looking for my girlfriend. I forgot her room number."

"Who is she?"

"The lobbyist—Dianne Colder."

"What a bitch," the clerk muttered. "No offense, but every time she comes here she complains about something—the smell, the view, the furniture. I'm not responsible for the whole world, you know."

"Just try dating her," Uli replied, as the man looked up her number.

"Room 2A, second floor in the back."

"Would you have the key?" Uli asked, seeing hotel keys dangling out of almost every mailbox behind the counter.

"I can only give that to her."

"Well, she's probably up there anyway," Uli said, and headed upstairs.

"Hold on, I'm not supposed to let anyone up." But the clerk was too lazy to pursue him.

The hallways had an old embossed wallpaper pattern that looked like a series of mushrooms. A funky, mildewy smell probably accounted for the hotel's vacancies, Uli thought, as he sped up the two flights. Her door was locked, but the adjacent room's door was ajar, with the bed unmade. Uli went inside. A fire escape in the back connected the two units. He opened the window and climbed over to Colder's window, which was locked. He pulled off his shirt, wrapped it around his fist, and shattered the pane. Then he reached in, unlocked her window, opened it, and climbed through. The first things he saw were several fashionable skirts and a cabinet full of mascara, along with an advance galley copy of a book entitled *Boo Hoo: Whiny Vietnam War Widows* by Dianne Colder.

Shit, he thought, *the only chance I have of getting out of here is working with this bitch!* His anger at her for killing Oric was finally calming down. He picked up the phone to try to reach the mysterious Rufus, only to discover that the line was dead. As he clicked the receiver to hopefully get an outside line, he heard a ruckus outside. Racing down the stairs and into the lobby, he found the desk clerk slumped over his radio with the red handle of a longneck screwdriver sticking out of his right eye. The cash drawer was emptied out.

The victim moaned softly when Uli leaned him backward. He was still slightly conscious.

"What happened?"

"I gave him all my stamps," the man groaned. "He didn't have to—"

"What'd he look like?"

The clerk passed out before he could say anything further. Uli laid him down to die in peace, then dashed outside. His sports car was missing.

An old guy standing on the corner asked, "Was that your two-seater?"

"Yeah, did you see where it went?"

"Some black guy just ran out of the hotel, jumped into the driver's seat, and took off."

Uli sighed. The sadistic thug who had needlessly stabbed the clerk to death had also stolen the car with an even bigger sadist still strapped to the roof and poor Oric's body inside.

Stepping around the clerk's body back inside the Class-A Lady, Uli's only regret was not giving the poor bastard a proper burial. He picked up a phone and dialed 911. It rang and rang for about five minutes before an answering machine clicked on. The message said: "*If you wish to report an emergency of some kind, please leave the nature of the crime, the location, and the time. Oh, and your name.*" A beep followed.

Uli reported that a robbery and homicide had just been committed, then hung up, failing to leave his name or the location. He went back upstairs to Dianne Colder's empty room. Looking carefully through her stylish clothes and the usual personal items, he found nothing particularly helpful. Wrapped in her sheets he discovered a possible weapon—a small black plastic item shaped like a pickle. Uli slipped it into his pocket. Just before leaving, he pulled the mattress up and found several objects dangling from the hollowed underside of the old box spring. Taped there were a face mask, eye goggles, a small tank marked *Charon*, and a plastic box containing a full syringe of some unknown substance. Uli took the four items, slipped them into an old shopping bag from the woman's room, and hit the street just as a police car turned the corner.

He started running west. From the corner of 4th Street and Third Avenue, he spotted a brown three-story building with a small clock tower—presumably Cooper Union. Through his acute amnesia, he vaguely remembered that the original one had been some kind of school and that Abe Lincoln was somehow affiliated with it, perhaps he had gone there.

Entering the large lobby of the building, he approached a group of fierce-looking guards sitting behind a long table and explained that he had an appointment with a woman named Mallory. One guard picked up the phone and called upstairs.

"You were supposed to be here yesterday," Mallory said, marching toward him five minutes later. "Where the hell is Oric?"

"We almost made it," Uli said somberly. "We were right over there, about a hundred feet away, before we got grabbed." He pointed out the big bay window to the corner of 8th and Lafayette.

"Oh my God, the Piggers got him?"

"They tortured him. I don't think they intended to, but they killed him."

"Fucking bastards!" she shouted.

The security guard rolled Uli's fingerprints on a card and slipped them into a bulky electronic scanning device. A few minutes later the results appeared on a small screen.

"He's got no record, which means he's a security risk," the head guard announced.

"This is a special situation. He's not going into any high-security areas," Mallory assured him. "I'll take full responsibility."

"We'll have to put him under escort," the guard said.

"Fine."

"What's all this?" the guard asked Uli, referring to the contents of the shopping bag from Dianne Colder's room.

Uli took out the small metal tank and the plastic case holding the hypodermic needle. "Oric's killer had them in her room. I thought maybe you could tell me what they're for."

Mallory looked at them closely before shrugging.

"You can pick them up on the way out," the guard said, putting them back in the bag and then into his desk drawer.

Uli was directed through a metal detector. Flanked by two guards, he followed Mallory upstairs into a small conference room. The guards stood outside and closed the door. Upon the table was a pot of warm coffee and a tray of Spam-and-Velveeta sandwiches from a meeting that had just broken up. Seeing Uli staring hungrily at the food, Mallory offered it to him. He gobbled down a sandwich in three bites and a cup of coffee in a single gulp.

"So, exactly what happened?"

"This blond bitch intercepted us at the Fulton Street bus station just after you left," Uli explained, cramming a second sandwich into his mouth. "Her name was Dianne Colder."

"Oh, the lobbyist abducted you?"

"Not then—she accompanied us after you left. Of course, Oric had to blurt out one of his crazy predictions, which made her suspicious as hell. But she seemed to think I was on her side, and I didn't want to alarm her, so when the bus reached Manhattan we jumped out the rear window and snuck away."

"What was Oric's final prediction?" she asked intently.

"Something like *big blast* was all he said."

"I wonder where."

"While dodging her, we went through Midtown and I saw someone blow up a vehicle in front of Rock & Filler Center. I think that was probably it. Anyway, they chloroformed me."

"*Who* chloroformed you?"

"There were at least four of them," Uli said. "One was the man I ended up killing in Staten Island—and there was also a chubby boy with bangs and glasses."

"Then what?"

"When I woke up, I was dangling upside down like a side of beef in some barnyard in Staten Island." He remembered an odd detail: "The only reason I woke up was because I heard some voice in my ear screaming at me."

"Whose voice was it?"

"I can't really describe it. It sounded so familiar. I heard it my first day here, when I was being chased by dogs. Then I thought it was this blond guy who rescued me in Brooklyn yesterday."

"This place is a little bizarre."

"Yeah, it's like everyone's a terrorist," Uli said, remembering the newspaper articles. "I'm assuming it's all embellished."

"Not entirely. I was actually in a quote-unquote terrorist group back in Old Town. Weather Bureau."

"What did you do?"

"The usual: protested the war, visited Cuba, blew up draft offices, ROTC offices, recruiting centers. Stuff like that."

"Nothing too dangerous," he kidded.

"Actually, it cost me a finger." She opened her right hand, revealing a missing finger.

"You really are a terrorist," he said.

"You have to realize that a lot of disenfranchised groups saw terrorism as a legitimate alternative. Anyway, did you get some sense of what this blond lobbyist was after?"

"She said she was here in Rescue City to bribe the borough president of Staten Island."

"Bribe him to do what?"

"To cast the swing vote to give the Democrats the one electoral college vote this place has for the upcoming presidential election."

"I'm surprised she told you this. Are you sure you're not the enemy?"

"I don't know who I am. Maybe she was lying."

"It all makes perfect sense. The Piggers are terrified of Ronald Reagan."

"The actor?" Uli asked.

"He was elected president in '76 after Nixon," Mallory said. "His reelection is our one great hope."

"Why?"

"They don't think we know. That's why the Feedmore Corporation doesn't ship in radios or TVs."

"But I've seen people using them."

"Those government-issued radios and televisions don't pick up reception beyond about two miles or so. Hell, they can barely pick up the one station transmitted here. But using parts from them, some people have managed to rig together shortwave radios, so we can occasionally catch news from the outside world."

"And what have you heard?"

"Reagan has been going head-to-head with the Russians, outspending them on defense."

"So?"

"He's cut every social program in order to come up with the cash for his arms race."

"That's awful."

"Actually, it's good for us. The money that goes into Rescue City is one of the biggest expenses in the national budget."

"What are you saying?"

"In order to pay for his military buildup, Reagan's been talking about closing this place down. It's supposed to be a close presidential election," Mallory continued. "If Reagan gets reelected and cuts funding, we'll all be repatriated with the rest of the country."

"So if the Staten Island borough president votes Democrat and Reagan loses his reelection," Uli concluded, "we're stuck here."

"It's going to be murder to try to reason with Rafique."

"Why, who is he?"

"When you were in Staten Island, did you smell anything funny?" she asked.

"Yeah, the pig farms."

"That stink isn't from pigs. It's because the river is blocked with sewage. Jackie Wilson did it years ago in order to seize control. It's a long story, but the sewage makes the borough nearly uninhabitable."

"What does this have to do with the borough president?"

"A number of years ago, Adolphus Rafique broke off from the Crappers and started this weird anarchist cult in the East Village district. He named it the Verdant League. Its members rejected the newly implemented capitalist model with the food stamp currency that the Piggers had come up with. The VL evenly distributed all food and housing in the Lower East Side among themselves. When the rest of us objected to Rafique, he and his renegade band moved out to Staten Island, becoming the new majority there since it was so underpopulated."

"How do they deal with the stench?"

"Most of those who joined his cult have had their sinuses cauterized. It knocks out a lot of the taste, but you don't smell a thing. The hard-core members call themselves the Burnt Men. Anyway, because of the deadlock between the two Pigger and two Crapper boroughs, Rafique usually becomes the tiebreaker, so he's now a major player." Mallory paused. "What could the blond lobbyist have bribed Adolphus with?"

"Bullets," Uli remembered. "That's what she said. She gave him a bunch of bullets."

"I guess that makes sense, though he supposedly has some secret weapon. Rafique is constantly under attack from both gangs, and bullets are one of the things that Feedmore doesn't provide anymore." Mallory paused again. "Jeez, you know, you might actually be the best person to help us. Help everyone here."

"Do what?"

"Try to convince Rafique not to throw his vote to the Democrats."

"Nothing personal, but I already tried to do you a favor and got poor Oric killed. I'm not even a Crapper."

"That's one of the reasons you'd be perfect." When Uli smiled dismally, Mallory explained: "Rafique won't let any party affiliates into his precious Verdant League headquarters. And you're not in the Rescue City data bank. But more importantly, it's just a matter of time before the Piggers catch up with you. Help me and I'll tell you a possible way out of here."

"What exactly am I supposed to do?"

"Rafique may be an anarchist, but he's also very smart. Just tell him that we know that the blond woman who bribed him works for the Feedmore Corporation. And tell Jane too."

"Who is Jane?"

"Jane Jacobs?"

Uli looked puzzled.

"Short middle-aged woman who wrote that famous study of urban renewal. She got shamed into coming here with the rest of the Garlic Heads—the Alternative Service workers."

"And she works with Rafique?"

"Yeah, she's his number two, but she wants to be number one."

"And this election is a big deal for them?"

"In Staten Island it is—those people are political. They *all* vote. This is the sort of thing that could cost Rafique his seat."

"I'd rather appeal to his liberalism."

"So you'll do it?"

Mallory said she'd do her best to address his concerns, but that she couldn't make any promises. She then mentioned that she had made some inquiries about Carnival and his wife. There was no record of either of them from before they arrived. While here, though, Jim had run for a city council office a number of years earlier as a Crapper candidate. "This was back when Manhattan was still bipartisan. After losing several successive elections, he finally stole an election down in East New York. In order to placate the Piggers in his district, he ended up marrying former Pigger councilwoman Mary."

"It sounded like she was a Pigger," Uli recalled.

"This was before the Piggers took orders from Feedmore."

"Did you find out anything about Oric?"

"No one ever reported them having children."

"Oh, they didn't. Oric reverted to normal when he was dying. He said the Carnivals abducted him and had some scientists turn him into an idiot savant."

"You're kidding! The CIA usually only uses those beyond help."

"Oric had help. Remember the guy chasing us in the Flatlands? He was Oric's twin."

"That explains a lot," Mallory said. "Siblings sometimes have a psychic connection here."

"What do you mean *here*?"

"I mean out here in the desert. This is a sacred Native American site. It has something to do with duality. Siblings, twins, often have certain powers."

"I'm not sure I believe this."

"It's not a coincidence that they put us all here."

"What does that mean?"

"The federal government was able to kill two birds at once—creating a refugee city along with turning this into a research lab for psychic studies."

"Sounds like conspiracy-theory stuff," he said.

"Maybe, but the Russians poured millions of rubles into trying to develop telepathic communications with their cosmonauts."

"Why do I know that?" Uli asked.

Suddenly the door flew open and a secretary with a strange unicorn-horn hairdo led a group of men into the room.

"Where is he?" someone called out.

"No, wait!" Mallory shouted. "Dropt shouldn't—"

▮▮▮▮▮▮▮▮▮▮▮▮▮▮▮▮▮▮▮▮▮▮▮▮▮▮▮▮▮▮▮▮▮

▮▮▮▮▮▮▮▮▮

It felt as if something sleeping inside of him had sprung to life. Before he knew what he was doing, he had hurled himself through the four guards and pushed himself right up to James Dropt. All he could think was, *Walk to Sutphin, catch the Q28 to Fulton Street, change to the B17, take it to the East Village in Manhattan* ▮▮▮▮▮▮▮▮▮▮▮▮▮▮▮▮

His hand, which was already in his pocket, pulled out the single-chambered pistol and pointed it at Dropt's head. He squeezed the trigger and ▮▮▮▮▮▮▮▮▮▮▮▮▮▮

7

Uli awoke to find himself on the floor in the conference room with his wrists cuffed and a squad of bodyguards standing over him.

"What the hell . . . ?"

"I had this damn room screened!" Mallory was shouting to the captain of security. "Goddamnit, I informed them downstairs that he was a risk, and no one, certainly not Dropt, was supposed to come in!"

"Help!" Uli called out with his face pressed against the floor.

"He didn't," a captain named Stenson stated. "He heard that your buddy got Underwood's Manchurian Candidate experiment, and since the subject was carrying no detectable weapon, Dropt wanted us to test their work."

"You could've told me," Mallory replied angrily.

"What did I do?" Uli asked.

"You went into a fugue state," one of the guards politely explained, "and you tried to kill Dropt with this." He held up the soft-edged oblong piece of rubbery plastic. "We initially thought it was some kind of explosive, but after doing some quick tests, we determined that it was what is commonly referred to as a *marital aid*. Where'd you get it?"

"Oh, from that lobbyist's place," he answered.

The door swung open again and a team of armed guards rushed in. Uli, still in handcuffs, watched as the real James Dropt entered. The candidate looked at Uli for an instant, testing to see if he'd revert back into his altered state. Whatever demonic possession had him a moment ago, he was free of it now.

"So," Dropt spoke directly to Uli, "we hear you were jumped, and a Crapper seer was killed."

"Yeah. I'm really sorry about it," he said earnestly.

"Did Mallory inform you that we suspect the Piggers have a secret seer of their own?"

"She did."

"Any idea why you were brought to Rescue City?"

"Not a clue. I think I had some kind of surgery done on my brain, but I don't know." Uli pointed to the sutures in the back of his scalp.

"You were probably part of the antiwar movement incarcerated for indefinite detention. Despite my service in Vietnam, that's how I got here."

"I was going to take him downstairs to see Dr. Adele, to find out if Underwood really did put a bug in his head," Mallory said.

"Oh, Adele is out sick today," Dropt said.

"Then you'll have to come back tomorrow," Mallory told Uli.

He thanked her and wished Dropt good luck with the upcoming election. Mallory escorted him out into the hall, where the guards uncuffed him.

"I'm sorry about all that," she said. "I honestly had no idea they were going to do that."

"No harm done. And if you still need my help, I'll try to get Rafique to consider throwing his vote to the Republicans. But only if you show me a way out of this place."

"Let me clarify that my offer to get you out is a little harebrained. No one has ever come back to verify that it works."

"If there's any chance at all, I'll take it," Uli said, as they passed the security detail and exited the building.

"Your mission, then, is right behind you. About a hundred yards down is the southbound M3 bus. It goes directly down Bowery, then along Water Street, and right over the Staten Island Ferry Bridge. You're going to ride down to the very bottom of Staten Island. The Verdant League headquarters is the last stop."

"Wait a second. If you're trying to extort him, why don't you just call him on the phone yourself?"

"Well, even if he takes the call, which I highly doubt since he refuses to interact with anyone affiliated with either party, a face-to-face appeal is much more persuasive. He's a gentleman, he'll give you accomodations for the night."

"Then when I come back here tomorrow, I can see this Dr. Adele?" Uli asked.

"Absolutely, and afterward I'll give you detailed instructions about a possible way out of Rescue City. You have my word."

"Fine."

"Lucky you," Mallory said, pointing up Third Avenue. "There's your bus."

He said goodbye and hurried toward the bus stop as she returned inside.

As the M3 pulled up, a loud grinding of engines compelled Uli to look back. A convoy of large trucks with *Feedmore Road Repair* stenciled on their doors was pulling up next to the Crapper headquarters.

Uli paid his fare and squeezed between an overweight woman with purple hair and a bony elderly guy.

The first blast shattered the windows of the bus, sprinkling the passengers with fine particles of glass. Two other explosions quickly followed. The final and most powerful one knocked the bus onto its side.

An incredible weight slammed into Uli's chest. For a moment he blacked out. When he came to, gasping for breath, he realized that three or four people were piled on top of him, including the large purple-haired lady. Beneath him, bent backward over a seat, was the thin older man, who appeared crushed to death. Those who were still conscious were moaning and writhing in pain. Uli wormed around bodies until he was able to climb up the side of the bus to an emergency window, which he pushed open.

One by one he started pulling people out. When the driver, some of the sturdier passengers, and a man on the street began pitching in, Uli climbed off the bus and sprinted over to the demolished Crapper headquarters.

Approaching the smoldering rubble, he could hear sections of the building still collapsing internally. Uli searched for the original entrance, but couldn't locate it. Yesterday's Midtown bombing looked like child's play by comparison. From one spot in the wreckage he heard a faint banging and muffled cries for help. Immediately, he started grabbing stones and debris and heaving them into the street.

"Over here!" he yelled. "There's a person trapped down here! Someone help me!"

Several nearby men and women joined in, pulling wood and stone from around the smoky and pulverized site. After fifteen minutes, tunneling roughly ten feet into the wreckage, they unearthed a pair of squirming legs. Uli was able to carefully free the upper torso of a shaggy-headed man.

"My buddy's trapped right there." The guy pointed into the hole he had just been pulled out from.

Uli peered in and through the dusty darkness could make out the bottom half of another man twisting in pain. After twenty more minutes of excavating, Uli and the others were finally able to pull the second man free.

"My name is Bernstein," said the first rescuee, shaken and dusty.

"I'm Woodward," coughed the second man upon catching his breath. Someone handed him a bottle of water which he gulped down. Patting the chalky dust off his clothes, he added, "Those bastards at Rikers must've done this!"

"Did you see Mallory?" Uli asked frantically, surveying the destruction around them.

"No, we were doing research in the records room on the third floor," Bernstein said. "Next thing we know, the floor is dropping below us."

Uli excused himself and walked around the smoldering block-long, block-wide mountain of rubble. Though a couple of other people had been pulled out, the vast majority were still trapped inside. Hard as he listened, Uli could hear no other muted cries or dull sounds.

Over the next hour or so, firefighters arrived from Brooklyn and Manhattan, as did gangcops, to make sure Piggers or terrorists didn't try to exploit the chaos.

Soon, the gangcops had to hold back the screaming family members of those buried inside. For fear of further collapse, the Manhattan Crapper fire chief, Mike Maloney, who had taken charge of the situation, waited for an engineer to arrive before trying to put together a comprehensive excavation plan.

Gas mains and electricity were shut off. At the engineer's recommendation, four teams were set up to start digging into the disaster from all sides at once. Council cop lieutenant Hector Gonzalez arrived with a crude diagram detailing the main Crapper offices. He needed salvage crews to work around the clock. Uli volunteered to work with the northern crew, which was focusing on Dropt's office, where he was supposed to be holding a meeting at the time with eight of the borough's twelve councilpeople. Uli believed that was where Mallory had been heading when she left him. Two rescue dogs were called in. The engineer deemed it too soon for heavier equipment, so only a small tractor was brought over.

Uli soon realized the full ramifications of the explosion. Aside from the fact that the upper echelon of the Crapper leadership, including Mallory, had probably been wiped out, gone too would be any possibility of him leaving Rescue City.

He worked feverishly with his team at the northern wall, hoping against hope that they might still find Mallory alive. Each group created a human chain of thirty or so people passing buckets of bricks, two-by-four studs, hunks of broken dry wall, and miles of electrical wiring.

The blast had occurred around two thirty. By four thirty, half an hour after his team had assembled, they located the first cluster of victims—four crushed bodies: the councilman from Chelsea, his top aide, a clerical worker, and Dropt's secretary with the unicorn-horn hairdo. By five thirty Uli had stripped down to his T-shirt and was passing the buckets from a middle-aged man named Luke to a guy named Marky behind him. Uli learned that both had come to Rescue City to fulfill Alternative Service requirements—instead of going to Vietnam—and had been working with the Crappers on social programs.

"Ten years ago we get evacuated due to a terror attack in Old Town," Luke said. "Now we're getting it here."

Over the ensuing hours, as the three became friendly, Uli explained that he suffered from acute amnesia and asked, "What exactly happened in Old Town?"

"A terrorist attack," Luke said with fatigue, handing an empty ten-gallon spackle bucket to Uli.

"A series of bombs went off in Lower Manhattan," Marky elaborated.

"Like missiles?"

"No," Marky replied, after cutting through a section of piping with a chainsaw. "A bunch of small contamination bombs dispersing radioactive stuff. Extremely low-tech, but lots of them."

"How many dead?" Uli asked.

"None immediately," Luke said. "The worst part at first was that Manhattan had to be evacuated. A lot of poorer neighborhoods in the outer boroughs were flooded overnight by the newly displaced middle class."

"Albany was quick to respond," Marky said with a smirk. "They immediately suspended all rent stabilization and control laws on newly available apartments, so that within two years almost all rents tripled, though they were still cheap by middle-class standards."

"Keep in mind the city was near bankruptcy," Luke said. "They were willing to sacrifice the poor to save their dwindling middle class."

"So everyone was just rounded up and brought here?" Uli concluded.

"There were a variety of plans that kept getting vetoed and compromised," Luke said. "Lindsay and Rockefeller appealed to Nixon for help. The federal government had a plan, but things got screwy."

"And the only reason they all agreed to come here was because they were promised that once Manhattan was scrubbed down, they'd be brought right back."

"And all the poor out here were told they would be given priority housing in Manhattan as a kind of restitution."

"Who initiated this?" Uli asked. It didn't sound like something Nixon would do.

"The Democrats started it," Luke recalled, "but then critics kept hitting on things like Kennedy's War on Poverty and LBJ's Great Society and wasting money on the poor . . . so the Republicans wound up taking the lead—"

A severed foot emerged out of the debris before them. Sifting onward, they soon located a new clump of mangled bodies. For the next twenty minutes the three of them silently pulled out limbs, torsos, two heads, three more feet, and then what appeared to be a very large mouth.

By seven thirty their group had recovered six more bodies. Along with the other three crews, the total came to twenty-eight dead. In the hands of two corpses they found scribbled goodbye notes, indicating that some people had survived the initial explosion only to bleed to death while waiting to be rescued. This made everyone work harder. Floodlights were brought in.

As it grew late, Marky, Luke, and the others on Uli's line were gradually replaced. Only Uli remained from the original group. He was intent on staying until they had located Mallory. By eleven p.m.

he started dropping his buckets and seeing double. His shift supervisor finally ordered him to get some sleep.

It was an unusually hot night for the Nevada desert. A series of food tables were unfolded on 7th Street between Second and Bowery. Outdoor showers and portable toilets were unloaded on 6th Street, as were a row of shower stalls. For volunteers who lived too far away to commute home, cots were brought in and lined up under the stars down 6th Street.

Uli dropped exhausted onto a hard cot, barely able to kick off his shoes.

8

Flashing lights, shouts, and various engines revved up. Uli awoke to the news that the dead body of mayoral candidate James Dropt had just been located. The bright lights of the Rescue City TV crew shone down on the catastrophe. Uli wandered over to Bowery just as the recovery team wheeled the gurney with Dropt's mangled body past. All four crews stopped working and quietly lined the sidewalk to catch a glimpse of their fallen leader. With Dropt's corpse found, the last vestiges of hope had vanished. Even Uli felt it—not so much sadness as a general despair from those all around. The possibility of the first Crapper victory since Mallory's husband had been shot was blown asunder.

Dropt's body was slid into the back of an ambulance, which departed slowly under a single police escort. Most of the crew workers either went back to work or returned to their narrow outdoor cots. As Uli thought about the leader he had only briefly met, he had this awful fear that if he had assassinated Dropt, maybe they wouldn't have blown up Cooper Union. He could hear men in the neighboring cots weeping. Following a shallow sleep, he arose with the first rays of the sun.

Sitting elbow to elbow, knee to knee with others at a community table over a bowl of flavorless cereal, Uli learned both good and bad news. Just an hour earlier they had discovered four people still alive, buried in the basement. Unfortunately, they had also unearthed twenty-two more crushed bodies, which included the last of the councilpeople. They had accounted for all but two people, and one of those was Mallory.

Passing by the makeshift morgue set up near the rear of the headquarters, Uli spotted something that made him cringe. It was the crushed body of the baby kangaroo that Mallory had taken such pains to rescue. Seeing the little marsupial's body, Uli knew in his heart of hearts that she was dead.

In the early afternoon, he saw a crowd gathering around a small

TV. The Honorable Horace Shub was in the middle of a speech denouncing the bombing and begging for reconciliation between the various gangs. Apparently, vengeful Crapper gangs from northern Brooklyn had ventured across the barren no-man's-land into weaker Pigger neighborhoods in Queens during the night and burned stores and slaughtered twelve Piggers before order was restored.

"James Dropt was a greatly good man," Shub said in his weirdly earnest way. "He believed in a peaceable resolution to our manifold problems. I am calling upon the councilpeople of New York, both the Created Equalers and the We the People Party, to put an end to the anger and join me in working together and bringing peace to our greatly good, God-fearing municipality . . ."

Uli didn't stick around to see how the mayor's speech was going to end. As he walked along Bowery, his thoughts reverted to Mallory. He decided that as a tribute to her, he was going to do what he had initially set out to do for personal gain: he would venture down to Staten Island, locate the borough president, and try to convince—or, if need be, extort—Adolphus Rafique to cast his decisive vote in favor of the former matinee idol Ronald Reagan.

Over the next fifteen minutes or so, exhausted young volunteers for the Crapper recovery effort gathered with Uli at the M3 bus stop. A number of them were still coughing and hawking up dust particles.

"How long is it to the very last stop?" Uli asked the driver when the bus finally arrived.

"A little over two hours, but I better warn you that Shub ordered a curfew because of the rioting, so there's only one more bus going down there. Then they're canceling service for the night."

"What time is the last bus leaving there to head back this way?"

"Six o'clock sharp."

Uli thanked the driver and took a seat, hoping to catch some shuteye. Tired as he was, though, he couldn't stop looking at the strange revisionist city passing around him.

He was able to remember more of the places from old New York that were missing here. Little Italy, SoHo, and Chinatown had all been consolidated into one tiny neighborhood—LittleHoTown. Tribeca and Wall Street, on the other hand, were gone without a trace.

As they ascended the wooden Staten Island Ferry Bridge over the sandbagged wall protecting the Battery, foul odors began to rise.

There was something depressing about the low-level skyline of buildings behind them that made up this odd simulacrum of Manhattan.

An old man slid his hand along the overhead aluminum bar as he walked down the aisle peddling something. Uli figured it was gum until he spotted a middle-aged woman with a bad dye job giving the fellow a sixteenth-stamp. In return he handed her a small padded clothespin that the woman duly clipped over her flared nostrils.

"Want a nose pin?" the solicitor asked Uli next.

Uli purchased one, and as he clipped it on, the bridge started swaying back and forth.

"Why is this thing so damn shaky?" Uli asked the pin seller, and added, "I'm new here."

"The Feedmore Corporation gave us ten old ferry boats, but Staten Island here is a lot closer than in Old Town and the water is much shallower, so the local engineer submerged the ferries, laid planks over the tops, and turned it into this ratty-ass bridge." The pin seller studied Uli's face closely.

"But the sewage level is rising, isn't it?"

"Not anymore. At its worst, the water level came right up to the bridge. That was when Rafique decided to dig the canal, and in one day the water dropped six feet."

When they reached Staten Island moments later, Uli noticed the other bridge, dull and red with an abruptly arching span shooting northeast. "Is that the Verrazano?"

"Name's been shortened like the bridge," the man replied. "Here it's just the *Zano.*"

The bus headed slowly past the row of submerged and semisubmerged luxury houses, all uninhabited. The paved street turned to packed dirt and sloped steeply downhill. A handmade sign read, *Hyman Boulevard.* It was the same street he had driven up with Dianne Colder strapped to his roof.

For the first mile or so, in the low swampy parts of the borough, more abandoned houses sprang up. They almost looked like homes on a military base. Though the land was mostly dry now, earlier floodwaters had wrecked the area.

Crossing sporadic flows of black sewage, the bus stopped at various points along the succession of tiny Staten Island communities, all of which looked more barren than anywhere else he'd been on the reservation.

The farther down they drove, the more primitive the little settlements appeared. Many of the structures were made from old packing crates and pallet wood, probably from when the old Staten Island airport had been functioning. In one instance, Uli noticed a small circle of huts with thatched roofs that looked like they had been made with grass and dried mud.

Whenever they went down a sharp incline, the smell worsened and the road would be washed out by an inlet of lumpy black water. The driver had to gun the engine to slice through the hazardous streams. Clearly the entire borough was one big environmental disaster zone.

Just like Manhattan, hand-painted planks corrupted the original names of deserted little outposts with their ramshackle huts: *Doggone Hills*, *New Dope Beach*, *Great Killers*, and so on. Large rodents, perhaps prairie dogs, sat on their haunches staring at the passing bus.

As the bus ventured to the southern tip of the borough, the road grew worse with ever fewer shanties. Occasionally, Uli saw people walking about. Most of them appeared dirty and sickly, much like the borough itself. On several occasions when people boarded the bus, Uli wondered how they could stand the smell. Looking over the swampy streams and arid dunes he kept wondering how much farther the route continued. Sometimes when the bus lumbered uphill, they'd catch a desert breeze and there would be a fleeting reprieve from the heat and smell, but then the road would slant downhill again, through the liquid shit.

When the bus finally came to its terminus, only one passenger remained on board with Uli, a skinny kid curled up in the rear. How he could sleep through such stinking turbulence was a mystery.

"Tottenville—Nut Central!" the driver shouted, as he folded open the door. Uli wished him a good day and stepped off. The kid followed, then walked away in the opposite direction.

A huge terminal that had fallen into disrepair was balanced all alone on the edge of a hill. This was the southern demarcation of Staten Island, Nevada. Below it was a dusty recreation field that looked like it might once have supported a Little League team, a haunting reminder of the absence of children. Beyond that a swamp of sewage covered the old airfield.

The oxidized copper ferry building was an homage to the old St. George landing, even though it was in a different area of the borough than in old New York. In front of the station was a big hand-painted sign: *The Dastardly Notorious VERDANT LEAGUE—Adolphus Rafique will debate with anyone at any time (subject to availability)!*

The terminal was covered with old paneled doors and large unwashed bay windows reinforced by wire netting, but there didn't seem to be anyone inside. Uli followed a faded red arrow pointing around to the back of the building, where he heard a muffled ruckus. Seminaked forms danced sweatily in the sun, chanting through plumes of smoke to the steady beats of handmade drums. They looked like a strange fusion of Native Americans and urban homeless. Uli figured they were the tribe that Mallory had mentioned—the Burnt Men. Semidomesticated barking canines dashed about and chickens squawked. A smoky bonfire burned in the center of it all. An old man in a loincloth and white face paint stopped dancing and stared at Uli. The banks of the swamp behind the dusty rec field were a honeycomb of tents and cardboard partitions.

Uli reached a set of open double doors in the rear of the terminal and came upon a heavyset security guard. He was sitting at a desk with a phone and several strange clerical-looking machines reading a worn paperback copy of Tolkien's *The Hobbit*.

"If you're here for the Turning Toxic into Organic class, it's been canceled till next week," the man said, "but if you're here for the Fantasy Literature course—"

"Actually, I was hoping to debate with Mr. Rafique."

"Do you have an appointment?"

"No, but the sign says he'll debate with anyone at any time," Uli said.

"*If* he's not out campaigning," the guard amended. "He's running for mayor and for the presidency, you know."

"Is he available?"

"That depends. Are you Pigger or Crapper?"

"I'm neither."

The security guard held his finger up asking for patience, then lifted his phone and dialed a number.

"Why does that sign say this is Tempelhof Airport?" Uli asked while waiting.

"That was the main airfield for the Berlin airlift. Before it was flooded, this was where the piloted flights landed with all the supplies, so they— Hello." The guard asked if Adolphus Rafique was available to debate "an unregistered walk-in." After another moment, he hung up and said, "Rafique's there, but you have to have your paw prints checked and get cleared here first." He took out a blank index card and an ink blotter.

"I can save you some time by telling you that there is no record of me."

"Which means you're potentially a detainee, which in turn means a possible terrorist," the guard said, pressing Uli's thumb and middle finger onto the blotter and then the card. He fanned the card till it was dry, then slipped it into the slot of a machine that looked like a black cigar box. Wires connected it to a small monitor, upon which boxy green digits appeared. "As you say, you're not registered with either party," the guard confirmed.

"That's why I want to talk to Mr. Rafique."

The guard told him he'd have to strip down to his underwear.

"Can't you just frisk me?"

"Adolphus Rafique has survived ten attempts on his life. Twice he was shot in the head. A few years ago some guy stuck a wooden spike right through his heart."

"How'd he survive?"

"The Native Americans down in the swamp claim that it's his private mana. A lifetime of losing election after election yet always coming back has made him a survivalist."

"I could use a gift like that," Uli replied, as he started peeling off his shirt and pants. After having every inch of his naked body checked, he put his clothes back on. The guard stuck an adhesive pass on his shirt pocket and told him to report to room 310.

Just inside the building, a plaque said, THE VERITAS VERDANT LEAGUE. *What you don't know* is *hurting you.*

Although most of the fluorescent bars overhead appeared to be burned out, the large bay windows running along the side of the building caught the light of the setting sun and the white marble floors made maximum use of it. Uli walked through empty halls until he spotted a young olive-skinned man dressed in loose black formal wear. He had scraggy facial hair with tortoise-shell glasses taped together over the bridge of his prominent Roman nose. Long white strings of cloth flowed from his sides.

"Excuse me!" Uli called out to him, but the man rushed away.

He continued down the hallways, from empty room to empty room, until he happened upon what appeared to be a yoga class in session. The practitioners were bent forward on one knee, arms in the air, striking warrior poses. But there was something wrong. The class looked strangely out of sync. It took Uli a moment to realize that everyone in the room was missing a limb. It was amputee yoga. Hearing more sounds down the hallway, Uli moved along and peeked into another classroom.

A young brown-skinned teacher was addressing a lecture hall of older students. Uli stepped into the doorway and tried to listen to the young man speaking in a thick unidentifiable accent: ". . . The extreme leftward gave the extreme right a chance to tip the wobbly middle, and they did it. Conned away from the crucifix retards who gave away their votes on trinket issues and working-class gestures, losing their basic well-being, not to mention the future of their dumb kiddies. Billions of bucks that could've gone to health or education were wasted in unwinnable slapdowns half a world away, so major corporations could secretly lift their little wallets. Dumbocracy is dead, and we're living proof of the need for a new criterion for voters based on a standard level of education and skepticism to protect the sentimentally feeble-minded . . . If mankind or America is to survive, we need a Smartocracy! If we can mobilize our forces, then in ten or twenty years, after we've returned to New York, we can try to instigate our own revolution to take power by—"

Turning abruptly, the man spotted Uli watching him from the doorway. Uli smiled as the foreign ideologue closed the door on him.

Uli headed on to a huge staircase at the end of the hallway and found a glass-framed directory that listed different departments:

DePartMeNt OF PRo7EcTEeS & DeTAiNEeS
DEpARtMEnT Ov EgG6 EPiDEmIc & AcUte Ammezia
Twln TeLePaTnY & ShAPeShiF7IhG
WoWoKa Profisies—CLoseD IndEflnit7Y
dePaRtMEnt oF tErRORist oRgANiZaSHUns
    & tHeIR maNY SPlIntERy gROvPs

At the bottom was listed, *STATEN ISLAND BOROUGH PRESIDENT, ROOM 310.*

Uli marched up the three flights. Checking out the tiny gold numbers on each door, he located Adolphus Rafique's room.

An overweight secretary handed Uli a clipboard with an extensive questionnaire on it. "You got to fill this out if you want to speak to him."

Uli looked over the form: *Name (both Nevada & New York), Address (Nev. & New), Birth Date, Employment, (Nev. & New).* On the back of page two, under *Personal Convictions (optional),* stranger questions appeared, starting with, *Past and Present Gang & Party Affiliations,* and moving on to, *Personal Stance on Hot-Button Issues,* including, *Pro-life or Pro-choice.* Next was *Criminal Record.*

Before he could even finish reading it, an older man with a slightly wandering eye popped his head into the waiting area. "Mr. Rafique's ready for you."

When Uli entered the borough president's office, Adolphus Rafique shook his hand and took his blank form, then asked, "Why do you look familiar?"

Uli shrugged. "I didn't have a chance to write anything—"

"My eyes are shot anyway," Rafique said. "Just have a seat and tell me about yourself." The man tossed his old suit jacket against the back of his chair.

"Well, I found myself walking outside of JFK, chanting about killing Dropt, without a clue of how I got here. Though I'm beginning to remember some things, I suffer from general amnesia—"

"I just heard over the Crapper radio station that they blew up Cooper Union," Rafique cut in. "I don't suppose *you* killed him."

"No."

"What do you want to talk about?"

"Do you remember meeting a tall blonde in a fashionable miniskirt?"

"Ahh, the lobbyist," Rafique sighed. "She gave me this." He exposed his hairy wrist—a brand-new digital watch. On it was the Feedmore logo: a brown-skinned baby suckling a light-skinned breast. "Also a big coffee mug."

"May I ask what you talked about with her?"

"It started out as an intellectual discourse on conservatism versus liberalism, and the next thing I know she's trying to unzip my trousers."

"Then what?"

"When I explained that I was a Buddhist celibate, she offered me bullets, provided I override my constituents and throw my presidential vote to the Democrats."

"It makes complete sense that she's trying to get you to vote for the Democratic Party."

"Uh, yeah, I already figured all this out," Rafique replied.

"What would you say if . . . if . . ."

"If what?" Rafique asked, glaring at him.

Uli was about to try to extort him by threatening to tell his second-in-command about his underhanded deal with Dianne Colder and the bullets, but he had forgotten the damned rival's name. "What would you say if Spencer Tracy was reelected—"

"Ronald Reagan," Rafique corrected. "Not that it matters, 'cause there's no way he's getting reelected."

"Why not?"

"I heard over a homemade radio that a bunch of Iranian students recently grabbed the staff of the American embassy in Tehran and have been holding them hostage," Rafique explained. "Reagan hasn't taken any action and the American people don't forgive things like that."

"Not true." Uli didn't know how he knew, but he knew this: "When a Democrat doesn't use military force, people regard it as weakness. When a Republican doesn't use force, it's viewed as restraint."

"We'll just see about that," Adolphus Rafique said, apparently amused by this.

"The point is, if Reagan is reelected to office, he's going to cut all excessive government spending. He's going to shut this place down and dump everyone in some Jersey ghetto—Orange or Newark, probably."

"How exactly do you know that?"

"It was Plan A," Uli answered without thinking, then froze. The dam of amnesia apparently had hairline fractures: he began remembering snippets of administrative and congressional hearings on what to do with the New York refugees. His mind flooded momentarily with flowcharts delineating costs and projecting expenses. Congress-woman Chisholm and Senator Javits from New York had cosponsored a bill. The plan was simply to transport the displaced New Yorkers to several economically distressed cities nearby in the Garden State, where housing stock was plentiful yet dilapidated. For a while it looked like the plan was going to fly. However, it required first passing a local referendum in New Jersey. That was when a coalition of lobbyists let loose a paranoid television and radio barrage demonstrating how such a plan would turn eastern New Jersey into a permanent ghetto. The referendum failed, and just as quickly the lobbyists initiated what became known as America's first Rescue City, where unfortunate people could slowly get back up on their feet without dragging down surrounding communities.

"Look," Rafique said, "you seem fairly smart, so I'll simply tell you that we Staten Islanders want to live in peace. Over the years we've had marauding gangs from both sides attack our people and use our borough as a dumping ground. We've had our food trucks hijacked and the water pipes from Jamaica Bay shut off. Hell, even after we built the canal that rescued Manhattan, we've still been attacked by the Crappers. We don't have the same resources as the others. That's why we need those bullets."

"Did you know Mallory?"

"The councilwoman who married the former mayor?"

"She died in the explosion as well."

"Too bad. I liked her."

"She asked me to speak to you before she was . . ." Uli paused. "Before she was murdered, she wanted me to try to get you to change your vote."

"If the Crappers were as honorable as they want to appear, they would've unblocked the sewer years ago." Adolphus had clearly made up his mind.

Uli had tried his best. Glancing at the wall clock above Rafique's desk, he noticed with a start that it was five minutes to six o'clock. "I don't mean to be rude, but the last bus out of Staten Island tonight is leaving in a few minutes."

"Go ahead."

Uli said goodbye and dashed down the stairs, through the halls, and out of the large and drafty terminal. He ran about a hundred feet toward the dusty road before he looked up and saw it lying on its side with its long brown tail flipping in the breeze.

A large cougar, probably down from the surrounding mountains, slowly rose to its feet and stared at Uli, then started slinking toward him. In the distance, Uli could see a rising plume of dust. The six o'clock bus was crossing the final stretch of roadway toward its terminus.

Uli took a deep breath and considered cutting across the rocky field toward the road to intercept the vehicle, but the cougar was still approaching. Keeping roughly forty feet between himself and the massive feline, Uli started retreating back to the VL headquarters. He watched helplessly as the last bus of the day reached the end of the road and, seeing no one there, drove in a big circle and slowly headed back toward Manhattan.

"Hold on!" Uli yelled out, and waved to the vehicle.

This only drew the big cat to him quicker.

"Fuck!" he muttered, as he hurried through the front door of the terminal building.

"What's up?" a security guard asked.

"A cougar is stalking me!" Uli said nervously, glancing toward the door.

The guard opened a side door and asked, "You see a cougar around here?"

"Yeah, it just took off," said a soft female voice. Uli turned to see a tall attractive woman with light-brown skin standing there.

"That was a big one," said a middle-aged man with white cream on his face, who had appeared through the same door as the tall woman.

"It kept me from catching my bus," Uli said. "Now I'm stuck out here for the damn night."

A very old hunchbacked man with a brown, cracked face, clearly blind, tapped up to all of them with a white cane. He gently placed his wrinkled palm on the tall woman's back.

"We'll put you up," offered the man with the white on his face.

"No, I can't, I have a bit of a problem." He didn't want to go into the whole amnesia mess.

"We know about your situation," said the woman, who looked to be maybe thirty. She had long, powerful legs and was barefoot.

"Besides," the man added, "the Piggers just blew up Crapper headquarters. They're rioting out there. Added to which it's a full moon. Spend the night here, and let them all kill themselves."

"Look, I just want to get the hell out of here," Uli said.

"Maybe you should be more concerned with why you were sent here," said the tall woman.

"What do you know about me?"

The ancient blind man started rocking back and forth, mumbling something incoherent.

"What's he saying?" Uli asked.

"Wovoka summoned you," she replied.

"He said that?"

"No, he's deaf, blind, and mute," the woman explained, then repeated, "But Wovoka summoned you."

"For what?" Uli asked.

The white-faced man shrugged. "We might be able to help you discover who you are, though there are no guarantees."

"I appreciate your concern, but I really don't believe in any Indian mumbo jumbo. And I should also add that I don't have any money or anything, if that's what you're after—"

"Since you're stuck out here for the night anyway, you have two choices," said the apparent chief with the cold cream on his face. "You can walk back to the city, which is a serious hike *if* you know where you're going. Or you're welcome to join us on a little trip. It might reveal some of the mystery about why you're here. Afterward, we'll have dinner and put you up for the night."

"Where exactly is this trip to?"

"A hole in the earth's skull, through which you can visit memories past and future," said the tall woman. "It's believed to be a nexus between this world and the other."

"It's also a really pretty rock formation," said the middle-aged chief.

"How far away is it?"

"About an hour each way," said the woman. "If we leave here now, we should make it back for a late dinner."

"Why are you so eager to take me to this place?"

"I was instructed to," the chief replied.

"By who?"

"Look," the woman said as if reading his thoughts, "your fear is understandable, but this is one of those moments when it really pays to have a little faith. We're under a serious time constraint, but I guarantee you'll be safe, and you might come to understand why you're here. In the meantime, we can answer all your questions in the boat."

Under any other circumstances, the idea of venturing out with a group of obvious nuts would have been simply out of the question, but it seemed unlikely that they would go through all this just to kill him. Besides, if they were going to execute him, they'd have the entire night to do it anyway.

"Let's go."

The chief gave a sharp low whistle, then led Uli downhill toward the embankment of the smelly basin. A long, leaky wooden canoe was being paddled across the fetid waters by a muscular man. The cream-faced chieftain and the tall muscular woman grabbed the sides of the boat when Uli got in. The blind elderly guy stood on the shore as the woman and man started paddling across the quagmire that had formerly been the old airfield. The putrid smell alone was almost enough to make Uli hallucinate.

Only when they were far from shore, as Uli accidentally rocked the boat, did the chief mention that this little body of water was known as the Bay of Death; if any of them fell in, they'd perish before the day was done.

"I guess a life preserver wouldn't make a difference anyway," Uli said, pinching his nostrils, then asked, "So, are you a born-again Indian tribe or something?"

"Actually, I'm a Buddhist," the man smiled. "I was formerly a Harvard professor of psychology."

"How'd you get stuck out here?"

"I experimented with some mind-expanding drugs, advocated others to do so, and finally got arrested. Nixon himself sent me here," he said almost proudly.

"How about the others in your tribe? I heard something about anarchism."

"We all care about the Great Mother, not the state," the woman spoke up, "but most of us are former Diggers from the Bay Area or Yippies from New York. My name, by the way, is Bea."

Uli shook her hand and turned back to the man. "You're the head of this shindig?"

"No way." He introduced himself as Tim Leary. "They voted a pig as the head of the tribe, kind of a joke on the Piggers, but he died a few years back."

"This place belongs to the Verdant League?"

"Actually, this area was Paiute and Shoshone. At least it was in the last century. But even before that, this part of Nevada was the site of the Sacred Caves going back thousands of years, and we're loyal to that."

"Where are they?"

"Below us, around us. Huge underground caverns, aquifers. There are long lava tubes and subterranean rivers redirected to build that damned waterway for the reservation. The Native American spirits probably blocked the drain for despoiling their holy place. There are documents that go back a hundred years foreseeing this area as the final reservation of the world's many scattered tribes."

"Who documented it?"

"A Paiute mystic who was raised by whites. He talked about a dung-filled meadow where herds of buffalo could graze while the albino man destroyed himself."

"Was it Black Elk?" Uli asked as they continued paddling over the shit-filled basin.

"No. Wovoka. But the whites gave him a Christian name, Jack Wilson." Uli remembered that as the alternative name for Flatbush Avenue. "He came back repeatedly, pretending to be one of the refugees, swearing he was from Manhattan."

"What do you mean he *came back*?"

"Actually, he was always here," Leary corrected. "Jackie Wilson was alone here for over a hundred years, waiting without aging, knowing without saying, being without hoping."

"And this is the guy who summoned me?"

"Yes."

"By name?"

"Yes, and he also gave me your face."

"So what's my name?" Uli asked, trying to get his mind off the smell.

"Ew-el-la-lee."

It sounded biblically similar to the other name he had heard two days earlier in Brooklyn—Huey. "Did he tell you why I'm here?"

"He doesn't answer questions. He shows."

After ten more minutes of being paddled through an ever-narrowing creek, Uli asked, "Where exactly are we heading?"

"This is the canal that Rafique made that drained New York Harbor," Leary replied calmly. "It leads to an old lake bed, and at the end of that is what was called the Goethals Bridge. Actually, the rock formation that once arched over the Goethals Basin collapsed, so it's really now just an overhang . . ." As the chieftain talked, it was obvious that the odors didn't bother him.

Just as Mallory had said, everyone Uli had seen since arriving at the terminal had evidently sacrificed some of their senses for surviving in Staten Island—any indication of their having an olfactory system was gone.

"So what is all that white stuff on your face?" Uli asked the chief, trying to get his mind off the stink.

"I'm Irish. It's sunscreen. This place is a melanoma nightmare," the man responded as Uli pulled out the nose pin he had bought on the bus. "You okay?"

"My nose is dying a cruel and unusual death." Tears were streaming down Uli's face. Although his sinuses were as blocked as the sewage river, the toxic vapor seemed to infiltrate every pore of his body.

"Oh! I brought this for you," Leary said, and casually pulled something out of his waistband. He handed Uli a tiny tin. "We should start preparing for your meeting with Wovoka. Lie back in the canoe, put some of this on your top lip, close your eyes, and just listen to my voice."

Opening the tin, Uli found a clear ointment and smeared some under his nose. The long and skinny claw of E. coli that had hooked up into his brain suddenly withdrew. A strong mentholated aroma liberated his sinuses. Lying back in the rear of the boat, Uli closed his eyes and listened to the chieftain, who said, "When we get to our destination, what you're going to be doing is commonly called *bilocation*. With Wovoka's help, you're going to travel out of here."

"Where?"

"You two will decide that," Leary said. "All I want you to do is try to relax, and when the time comes I want you to just let go. Do you understand?"

"Not really."

"We'll practice. I'm going to put you in a scene, and I want you to try to just lose yourself."

"Okay."

"Envision a cool November day. You are walking upon the spongy floor of soft pine needles, among rolling hills of a New England forest. I want you to think of this as you inhale and exhale. Imagine your breath is like the spirit of some bird; look and try to find your bird guide, and it will take you over the trees and gentle pastures. Just inhale, exhale, and stay focused on your guide."

9

After roughly half an hour of contemplation, imagining himself as a pigeon flying through some pastoral scene, Uli's cool inner reality came to an abrupt halt. The canoe started tipping from side to side. The woman warrior said, "Come on. We walk from here."

Nearly naked now except for scanty articles of cloth and home-made moccasins, his three companions were waiting for him.

When Uli got out, Bea and the silent paddler pulled the canoe up on the shore and flipped it over, draining the putrid water that had leaked inside. The man unknotted the long thick rope from the front of the boat and wrapped it around his bulging chest, then led the three others up along a series of stony plateaus rising like a row of massive steps.

Although moonbeams illuminated the landscape, clouds blocked Uli's view of the summit. Looking back, he could see Staten Island spread out below. The black lines of sewage water snaked over the borough like veins and arteries on an old person's hands. Manhattan and Brooklyn were barely visible in the distance.

"What is this place?"

"It's a very big, very old volcano," Leary replied. "There are only a few of them left in the world. Some are thought to be a thousand times larger than a regular volcano. And they are devastating. In fact, thousands of years ago, one of them in Africa was responsible for the near extinction of mankind. They believe that after it blew, only about seven thousand people remained."

"And this is one of those?"

"The entire reservation is built on one. The sacred caves are its lava vents and fumaroles, and someday when it blows the entire country as we know it will come to an end." Leary paused. "Strange things don't happen here simply because we pray for them or because old Native Americans say they do. They happen because this is a portal. It's literally the beginning of the end. In a few minutes, when you are lowered into the Goethals, you're going to be closer than anyone else alive to that awesome power."

"I'm not going to be bitten by snakes or anything, am I? 'Cause I'm terrified of snakes."

"No, you'll just sweat a bit."

They continued climbing upward several hundred feet until, winded, they reached the last step, a long flat plateau. Just when Uli thought the hike would get easier, the terrain started buckling into layers. He felt as though he were on the surface of a hostile planet. Trenches and precipices, vague under the moon, began appearing along with endless steam-filled ponds and geysers.

They finally reached a massive rock formation that rose like a stone rampway and jutted out over a large bubbling gorge. They walked out onto the rocky overhang about a hundred feet, until it nearly vanished into the steam.

The muscular paddler took the thick rope he was holding and began making complex knots.

"Once we lower you, I want you to close your eyes and concentrate like you did in the canoe," Leary instructed.

The muscle man told Uli to lie flat on the hot rocks as he slowly fit the knots around Uli's limbs, then wove the rope into a harness.

"What was your bird guide?" Leary asked.

"I imagined I was a pigeon."

"The flying rat of New York, perfect! Now, instead of green fields, let your winged rodent take you over a special place somewhere in New York."

"Can't we just do this here?" Uli asked, referring to the terra firma of the ridge.

"The visions over the Goethals are the strongest."

"My memories of the Big Apple aren't too good. I'm not sure I was ever even there."

"Do you remember 42nd Street?"

"I think so," Uli said, and closing his eyes he was able to recall a postcard image of Times Square.

"Just focus on that," Leary said.

Wrapping the loose ends of the thick rope around their waists, Bea and the paddler lowered Uli off the narrow overhang of rock and into the foggy breach below. Lying flat like a static Superman, Uli saw steamy plumes rising from the crater, shrouding the surface of a deep and bubbly cauldron. To push away all fear, he closed his eyes and tried to recollect the group of old buildings squeezed together by intersecting avenues around the palpitating heart of 42nd Street.

He simply couldn't remember a lot: Moderately sized buildings and low-level theaters with all the flourishes of the last century were pressed up against the cracked New York sidewalks. The strangely futuristic white structure—the Allied Chemical Building—with its lightbulbed news ticker, sat in the middle of the square.

A backfiring truck sent a flutter of pigeons high in the air. Uli watched as they descended in a dense yet complex pattern like little gray-feathered bombs flying onto the sill of a grungy office building. He now realized that he was one of them. But he wasn't in Times Square, he was in a residential community in one of the outer boroughs, he didn't know which. The backfiring wasn't a truck. It was the muffled explosion of dynamite under a steel blanket. A freeway was being built right through some neighborhood. Then, as though seeing old photographs from his past, he remembered attending an Ivy League school and traveling down to Mexico. Uli had no idea why he was seeing this, but pushing it out of his head, he directed his thoughts back to the unharmonious buildings around Times Square.

Dawn—at the intersection of 42nd and Seventh Avenue. He knew this had to be a memory, but he couldn't recognize it. Before rush hour could commence, Uli watched a tall, older figure wheeling a shopping cart. The man took an odd-looking oblong object out of his cart and waited for the light to turn green. Once a few vehicles passed, he walked out into the middle of the empty street with the long, dangling object and lobbed it high in the air. He missed whatever he was aiming at but carefully caught the object as it fell. It was two weights connected by a long string: an old pair of sneakers tied together. The man was aiming for the arching bar holding the yellow metal casing around the three circular lights. Finally, the dirty laces of the two sneakers, which were knotted together, wound several times around the end of the narrow support bar.

The old man returned to the corner, grabbed his shopping cart, and slowly wheeled it away. All that remained was the street and the sneakers dangling from the pole.

This odd act of sneaker tossing seemed to freeze time itself. It also brought Uli down onto the sidewalk. It took him a moment to realize that Times Square was completely empty. He started walking below the marquees of various run-down theaters toward Eighth Avenue.

He felt a surge of paranoia. Someone was watching him, following him. He tried to see who it could be. He suspected it might be the old man, but no one was there. Finally, Uli took shelter in one of the porn arcades, which led to a series of locked cubicles. He headed down a narrow staircase that brought him into the catacomb of tunnels that made up the Times Square subway station. He could hear footsteps close behind him. As he raced ahead, he realized his pursuer had somehow gotten in front of him. Turning a corner, he saw what looked like a black robot mechanically marching forward. When he drew nearer, he heard it ask, "Where'd our freedom go?"

"I don't know," Uli replied, surprising himself. It was then that he realized he too was a shiny black robot—a freedom fighter!

"We're losing an undeclared war!" he heard someone shout. He saw then that he was one in a long line of soldiers. Together, they all marched up a flight of stairs to the sunny sidewalk. He was in a parade.

"We're so proud of you, boy!" some flag-waver shouted.

He was a part of this brigade marching off to fight some unknown invaders.

Day and night, through rain and shine, they marched in lockstep. The first battlefields were college campuses: outside agitators and sleeper-cell subversives had organized students . . . His brigade grabbed the wispy students, chopping off their shaggy heads with what looked like gardening shears, then they headed into more protests, into rallies and gatherings, tearing apart the wispy infiltrators.

Instead of blood and guts their bodies were filled with gas; it was like cutting up a cloud.

"There really is an enemy that is trying to conquer us!" he heard.

His detachment marched south across the landscape. At one mountaintop he realized his militia had multiplied and branched into columns as far as the eye could see. Eventually they reached an Native American reservation, where they attacked a tribe.

"Don't kill what you're trying to save!" he heard one white wisp say.

When he sliced up this shiny cloud, he realized two things: first, that his robot arms and legs were malfunctioning; and second, that the clouds were just reforming. He was injured, slowing the others down. When he returned to his family, they applauded him. He was happy until he saw the young woman, an attractive brunette, who must've been close, a daughter or maybe a wife. Whoever she was, she was scared and angry. He couldn't communicate with her. She spoke another language. For some reason, he cared deeply about her. Though he tried to comfort her, he only hurt her . . . He tried talking, but only strange sounds came out of his mouth: "Ana . . . aren, Ana . . . aren . . ."

Looking in a mirror, he realized he was still clad in robotic armor. When he popped off one of his armor plates, he found, to his horror, that he too had changed from a solid to a gas. "They've infected me!" he screamed, and started weeping.

"They affected you! We're all the same!" He suddenly understood the girl.

Another voice, a somehow more real one, yelled, "Go back to Times Square!"

He looked out at the rugged Nevada terrain, and finally remembered where he was. Closing his eyes again, he heard, *Focus on Times Square, dude!* And he was back there. But everything was strobing. The earth was spinning faster and faster, day and night, day and night . . .

It was like watching a movie at high speed: One by one, the many cheap hotels and little porn theaters were evicted. Old, squat buildings were demolished and replaced with tall, shiny ones. New chain stores replaced small businesses. The decrepit and isolated men and women were transformed into pudgy jolly families from out of town. Even the sidewalks were pulled tight and clean like new gray sheets.

As though someone had changed a TV channel, a flash of a family seated around a table interrupted his vision. He now found himself in another strange place, coughing sick people in rows of beds in some large, airy tent. He was seated before an elderly woman, supine in bed, skin and bones, death rattle, only a handful of shallow breaths from the end. As if plunging into the aged woman's ear, into the brown, arid dunes of her shrunken brain, to the dusty archives of her life, he saw her reborn as young and sexy, a beautfiul young mother and bride. It was the turn of the century now. Not in America. Strange soldiers burst into their dining room where she was sitting with her husband and their two young children, in the middle of lunch.

Although he couldn't hear anything, Uli saw the family being forced outside. There they were joined by other members of their village. Something more than the rolling hills told him that they were in Asia Minor. A strange sound or word, but probably a name, popped into his head: *Gourgen Yanikian.*

Who the hell?

Again he tried to refocus, remember 42nd Street, and he was suddenly back in Midtown Manhattan. A nearly transparent force rippled and rushed like a surge of water down flooded avenues and streets. Uli sensed he was literally *seeing* time. Instead of rushing steadily forward, time pushed forth and pulled back out. One by one, the buildings shuddered, flaked, and collapsed, as though suffering heart attacks. A fluttering of architectural corrections and stylistic revisions built up and receded in each of the many buildings. Newer, sleeker, taller buildings quickly rose high in their places like rockets on launchpads. Finally, time stopped completely and the city of buildings seemed to present itself across the ages all at once. Small, ancient wooden shacks mingled with towering futuristic skyscrapers.

The walkways came alive, trembling and broadening from dirt paths into stone slabs and cement sidewalks. They carried the interplay of varied city dwellers: occasional Native Americans from hundreds of years earlier, Dutch settlers from the early seventeenth century, subjects of the Crown in tricornered hats, bearded pioneers of the midnineteenth century, top hats and waistcoats from the Gilded Age, a pageantry of turn-of-the-century immigrants. They weren't merely walking side by side, but overlayed like transparencies, occupying the same space as the Depression-era downtrodden and happy-go-lucky hippies. Like shadows breaking off from darkness, sleek figures appeared who had to be citizens from the future. The entire city was becoming one giant shimmering termite hill. Communities with different races gave way to a single group of homogenized Americans.

Uli watched as everything inexplicably grew very hot and bright. All these overlapping people and societies over time, yet occupying the singular space, proceeded to march north and eastward through the city streets, slowly and steadily. They streamed over the Queensboro Bridge. All passed above the flowing current of the East River. Once on the other side, instead of arriving in the industrial concrete space of Long Island City, underneath the old elevated trains and dirty freeways, he saw a vast desert. All kept marching under the glaring sun, marching, sleeping, waking—marching and falling slowly to the ground, some remaining there, others continuing, marching . . .

The rope suddenly snapped. Throwing his arms down to block the fall, Uli hit something wet. The pungent reek of shit filled his sinuses. He realized he was shivering in the bottom of the canoe. The others were sitting upright, gliding in the bright moonlight back over the flooded Staten Island airfield. Uli could make out the dark shape of a rusting aerial tower overhead.

A massive front-lobe headache pushed away all thoughts. Uli's entire body felt like a single aching board. At the same time, utterly exhausted, he couldn't stop shivering. He couldn't remember ever feeling so cold.

"He's freezing," Leary said, rubbing Uli's hands.

"We're almost there," said Bea.

In another minute the muscle man jumped onto the muddy banks and pulled the narrow boat ashore. Bea and Leary tried lifting Uli, but the older man had trouble holding his legs, so Bea carried him in her arms like a child. She took him inside a small army surplus tent, where she dropped him into a pile of blankets and skins and started tearing off his clothes. In another moment, semidelirious, Uli became aware that she was pressing against him, naked, rubbing and bumping her slick hard body against his quivering flesh.

"Thank . . . you . . ." he shivered out the words, then passed out.

10

Uli woke to the sound of drumbeats and distant chants. Though a great deal of time seemed to have passed, it was still the same night. Bea was lying naked, bracing him tightly in her arms. He felt so grateful to her, he wanted to kiss her, but he also knew she hadn't done anything for romantic reasons.

"You okay?" she asked.

"I don't know what happened. I thought I was going to die."

"You were down too long. Do you remember anything?"

"Yeah, but . . . it was wild."

"Do you remember anything about us returning to New York?"

"I saw things that made no sense."

"Like what?"

"Robots in dark uniforms fighting dark clouds." He didn't add that he himself had been a robot.

"And I thought I took too much acid in the sixties!"

"Maybe I inhaled too much of Bayonne, New Jersey."

"Bayonne is known to cause wild hallucinations," she said. "But seriously, you didn't see anything about closing down this shithole?"

"Actually," Uli now remembered, "I did see everyone leaving New York, but they were leaving Old Town, not here."

"Where did they go?"

"Across the 59th Street Bridge, but not into Queens."

"Where then?"

"A desert."

"Huh, we got that. What did they do in the desert?"

"Died, mainly."

"What did you see prior to them leaving?"

"I remember seeing this strange old man doing something with sneakers, I'm not sure what . . . and then I saw New York over time . . ."

"Did you find out anything about your reason for being here?"

"No, not really. But I don't know, I saw a lot of weird things." Sitting up, he yawned. "God, I'm starving."

"Me too. Let's get some chow."

A distant bonfire produced enough light for Uli to inspect her long lean body as she rose to dress. He watched her muscles ripple when she pulled on her shirt and shorts. After helping Uli dress, Bea led him outside to their large communal space, a dry patch on the former rec field, where the tribe of roughly a hundred had pitched tents behind the old terminal. For some reason the smell here wasn't as bad as the rest of Staten Island.

Lit by the full moon, several circles of Indian-fusion types were celebrating on large homemade drums, all to a single beat. A bigger group was chanting. Among them were several large topless women swaying with their hands up in a trancelike state. In the middle, a small group of oddly dressed men and women were dancing in a circle.

"What's all this? Are they on the warpath?"

"No, it's just a powwow," she explained. "They do it for purification, friendship, the wiping of tears, all that stuff."

"They have great costumes," Uli said.

"They really strive for authenticity here. That thing is called the *bustle*." She pointed out the colorful items sticking out of some of their backs: feathers and pointy quills that looked like they had been plucked from porcupines. "On their heads are warbonnets—those are optional."

"What about that guy wearing the German shepherd?" Uli asked.

"That's a coyote skin for animal medicine. Some of them are shape-shifters, but no one here is actually Native American, so in a way it's all just an homage."

"And how about the topless ladies?"

"They work for tips," Bea kidded. The only person not dressed like a Native American was the blind, deaf old man who was now seated next to the drums.

Bea led Uli to another firepit off to one side, where a collection of large cast-iron pots simmered from tripoded bars of steel over bright embers. She collected spoons and a pair of large wooden bowls and handed them to Uli, who held them out as she used a stick to remove a kettle top. With a large ladle, Bea filled the two bowls. From a small metal container, she took out a loaf of black bread, then the two of them walked over to the outer circle and sat down to watch the evening's festivities.

"What's with the old blind guy?"

"He just showed up one day. Someone said he came from across the desert, but who knows."

"He doesn't seem to be one of the tribe."

"No, we feed him and look after him, but he's locked in his own world."

Inspecting the soup in the moonlight, Uli was surprised to see that it was purple. He nervously took a sip from his spoon and was delighted to find that it was a bowl of Russian borscht. "This is wonderful," he said between slurps, ignoring the festivities.

"The cook still has her sinuses and taste buds. A few of us still do," Bea said. "She also made some kind of stew in the big pot."

The two returned to the tripods of crockery, where Bea served them several racks of what looked like lamb chops.

"This is the best food I've eaten since I got here," Uli said with a full mouth. "What the hell is it?"

"Feral pigs. They're all over the place out here."

"You're kidding."

"Nope. Sometimes they grow as large as eight hundred pounds. It's one reason I rarely go out into the desert alone."

"What did you do before you came here? Tell me about yourself."

"My life story: I was raised in the East Tremont section of the Bronx. When I was young, my mother died after a slip and fall. My father had a nervous breakdown soon afterward and vanished. I was adopted by our neighbors. Not a particularly loving childhood. When I graduated from Bronx High School of Science, I moved to the Lower East Side."

"And what'd you do there?"

"There were only a few years before Manhattan was evacuated. During that time I had some crappy low-paying jobs and did a lot of volunteer work for lost causes. That area was filled with lost causes."

"I love lost causes," Uli said. "Which ones?"

"Let's see. I worked briefly for Mary Calderone. She was the head of Planned Parenthood. She was mainly trying to get schools to develop sex education and loosen up the federal antiabortion laws."

"Yeah, that'll never happen," Uli muttered.

"She came under so much flak that she finally had to step down as president. I also volunteered for the Catholic Worker. Dorothy Day is an amazing woman. And of course I always helped whenever there were antiwar rallies, which were pretty constant."

"Anything else?" Uli sensed that he had worked on the other side of some of these causes and was hoping she might trigger some of his lost memories.

"For a week I worked for Jane Jacobs at the JCSLME before they officially disbanded."

"Jane Jacobs, the number two here?"

"Yeah."

"What was the JCS—"

"The Joint Committee to Stop the Lower Manhattan Expressway. It was a huge expressway—the LOMEX, they called it, designed to connect the bridges to the Holland Tunnel and slice up Lower Manhattan in the process. They did most of the protesting years earlier, but talk of some of these government programs lingers."

"How'd Jane Jacobs wind up out here?"

"She has two sons who were approaching draft age. She was about to move to Canada with them. But because she was a recognizable community activist, she was offered a Garlic Head deal. If she and her family came here and worked, her sons would get draft deferrals. We all figured we'd be back there in two years."

"So you really miss New York?"

"My life here is actually better, a lot better than in New York," she said. "If we were told we could return to New York tomorrow, I think I'd stay here. I really do. I mean, I've never felt so equal or powerful as I do living out here in Nevada."

"But don't you feel cut off from civilization? Don't you miss the technological advances? Men walking on the moon and all the electronic gadgetry?"

"You have no clue how much that stuff has taken from us."

"Like what?"

"Like that," Bea said, pointing up. The brilliant glow of a million constellations burned brightly in the sky. "If you stare up there for ten seconds, you'll count more shooting stars than you've seen in a lifetime. It's more amazing than any TV show could ever be. And it makes you think more about God and man than all the college classes put together."

An owl hooted nearby.

"And listening to nature is far more rewarding than most phone calls."

"I've always been a city boy myself," Uli said.

"The price of all this technology is that people aren't evolving spiritually anymore."

Uli yawned, then apologized and explained that the day had knocked him out.

"Me too," she said. "Do you want to sleep in your own tent or would you like to come back with me?"

"I was very comfortable with you."

Bea brought Uli to the line of latrines positioned at the edge of the encampment so that all waste flowed into the polluted basin. While Bea was in the bathroom, Uli heard some rustling behind a clump of nearby bushes. Expecting to see an animal, he was surprised to come face-to-face with a naked old man scurrying around on all fours. The guy hissed at Uli, then ran into the distance. Uli watched him as he sniffed a large rock and then urinated.

"What the hell is he doing?" he asked Bea upon her return.

"Oh, that's Sam. He's just prowling."

"Prowling?"

"You'd probably regard it as flaky," she said with a smile. "He's trying to become a badger."

"A badger? Have you ever seen anyone turn into an animal?"

"I don't know all the jargon, but there is worldwide documentation of shape-shifting. In Europe there are ample cases of werewolves, weredogs, werebirds . . . there are even claims of weredolphins . . ."

When they got back to Bea's tent, she dropped to her fours and crawled in through the flaps. As she pulled her shirt and pants off, Uli gave up his line of questioning. He turned away from her, took a deep breath, and removed his own clothes. Together they got in under the thick quilt. Uli immediately began gently stroking Bea's back, amazed by how muscular she was.

"What are you doing?" she asked.

"I was wondering if you wanted to—"

"Not until the third date," she said tiredly.

"Huh?"

"It's my one rule: if I date anyone three times, I'll sleep with them. And though this isn't technically a date, I'll let it count as the first."

Exhausted after the long day, both were fast asleep within minutes.

The large cougar was asleep on their legs.

"Bea," Uli softly prodded, attempting not to panic.

Still asleep, she reached out and swatted the animal's flanks. It hopped to its feet and bound out of the tent.

"We could've been killed," he complained with a sigh.

"We can always get killed," she sleepily replied, and pulled him closer.

When he kissed her she didn't stop him, but she didn't kiss back. A bright sun was just peeking up over the hills. In a moment, they both started dressing.

"This place is really beautiful," Uli commented.

"Want to go on a hike?"

"Sure."

Before the camp could become busy with activity, Bea filled a bag with shipped-in oranges, apples, homemade biscuits, and some left-over racks of pork from the night before. She offered him a nose pin, but he still had the one he'd bought on the bus. Together they went out to the basin, where she grabbed one of the four hand-carved canoes. They got in and paddled over the basin for roughly half an hour until they came to land on the far side. Bea pulled the canoe up on an isolated landing and led him on a walk through the sparse landscape. The region wasn't all desert, and the two hiked over parched salt flats with strange mineral formations until they came to a steep hill. With sweat trickling down his face, peering back over the vast, low skyline and rolling hills, Uli felt raw, endless beauty in the soaring expanse. It was as if no other humans had ever set foot here.

Upon reaching the top of a hill, he spotted a seemingly perfect curve in the wild—a long, bending concrete wall in the distance.

"That was the original end of the retaining wall where the sewage river once flowed."

"Where was it blocked?" Uli asked.

"A ways north of here. Want to see it?"

"Sure."

"We won't be back in Tottenville till later this afternoon."

"My appointment book is wide open."

Over the next few hours, as they hiked southeast, Uli recounted how he'd found himself walking along a road near JFK Airport without knowing who he was or how he got there. He had been programmed to kill Dropt, who was then murdered yesterday.

"Did your trip to the Goethals answer any questions?"

"Nothing clearly. At one point, I saw some woman and her family, and I think they might have been Armenians during the genocide."

"Maybe you're Armenian."

"Why did you guys greet me at the terminal? I mean, why me?"

"Tim only said that an important person in deep trouble would be passing through."

"I have this awful feeling that he's mistaken me for someone else. It's happened before."

"The vision you told me about . . ." she started.

"I'd call it a dream."

"Well, I've never heard of anyone being able to move through time."

"A dream's a dream," Uli opined.

"Unless, of course, you learned something in that dream that you didn't previously know."

"Since my memory is missing, I'm not sure what I know, and I have to confess right now that I think this entire Wovoka thing is a load of bullshit."

"Consider this: if it's *not* bullshit, he might've been showing you something."

As they walked, Uli contemplated his dream sequence. He remembered the tall old man tossing the pair of sneakers over the Times Square sign pole. What significance could this have?

"So, what do you want out of life?" he eventually asked.

She shrugged.

"Do you want children?"

"Not anymore. Now that no one else can have them, it doesn't really bother me."

"Have you ever committed any terrorist acts?"

"Would it bother you if I did?"

"Nothing you can do would bother me."

"Just for that, I'm gonna count this as a second date," she said with a smile.

By eleven a.m., the sulfuric odor had intensified as the land turned to marsh and seemed to fill with primordial vegetation. After another hour, Bea pointed at a hill on the horizon behind them. Large craggy rocks surrounded its top like a crown.

"Up there somewhere is the hole Jackie Wilson supposedly bore into the old sewer system when he was trying to fix the drain."

Uli felt a dull pain in his lower back and the arches of his feet. Next thing he knew, he was flat on his back, looking up. Bea was stroking his forehead.

"You fainted," she said.

Uli got up slowly. "Sorry, the heat and smell must've gotten to me." He breathed deeply. "We better start heading back."

But just looking at him, Bea knew that the long walk through the toxic landscape would take forever. "Actually, there's another canoe just up ahead," she said. "But we have to crawl through a fence and be quiet."

"Why?" he asked, trying to get his bearings.

"We just do," she said, leading the way. "Let's go."

When they were nearing the canoe, moving through a bog of tall grass, they heard something rushing toward them from several hundred feet away.

"It's probably one of those feral pigs," Uli speculated.

"No, they run off when they hear people." Bea started stepping backward, as if she'd seen something terrifying. "Get in the canoe and start paddling," she said, then suddenly dashed off in the direction of the sounds they'd just heard.

"Wait a sec!" he called out.

"Go, I'll catch up!" she yelled back. "Just do as I say!"

Uli begrudgingly got in the canoe and slowly paddled along a finger of water leading toward the Bay of Death. He wondered what to do about Bea. Suddenly, something very large plopped right into the front half of the canoe, almost catapulting him into the toxic sludge.

Uli leaned back instinctively to keep from tipping over and quickly realized it was Bea.

"Where the hell were you?" he gasped.

She was winded and covered in sweat.

"You okay?" He put his hand to her face, causing her to flinch. She seemed to be elsewhere.

"Give me a minute," she said, still panting.

"Where did you go? Why did you run off?"

"A minute," she said, still trying to catch her breath.

Uli picked up the paddle and resumed rowing them across the filthy basin.

11

As they neared Tottenville, Uli noticed someone on the far shore staring out at them. It was an older, slightly hunched man, and though Uli wasn't certain, he thought it might be Rafique. Then he saw the figure limp away. When the canoe glided onto shore, Leary and a small entourage walked stiffly over to the water's edge.

"Uh oh, I think we're in trouble."

"I can't imagine why," Bea responded.

Leary asked if he could speak to Uli alone. Getting out of the canoe, Uli watched as two of the chief's sidekicks led Bea away.

"You missed the morning bus," Leary said sternly.

"I wasn't planning on catching it."

"Well, you can't stay here."

"Why not?"

"We have strict rules about residency, so unless you have further business with Rafique . . ."

"I don't understand."

"There is a limit to the amount of people we can feed and house here. Hell, there's a long list of applicants waiting to join us. If you want to apply for residency here—"

"I was only hoping to spend a few more days here."

"There's another bus at six. Please be on it."

"Where did they take Bea?"

"This place doesn't run itself, she has chores to do like everyone else," Leary said, then walked away.

When Uli called out to Bea in the distance, a group of large men who looked like security staff walked over in tight formation.

"I just want to talk to Bea."

"Well, she doesn't want to see you," said the biggest of them. "Now please go."

"I'm not leaving until I'm convinced that she's safe."

"Then you're going to make us remove you by force," the man responded, and reached out to grab Uli. Without thinking, Uli pulled the man forward, sending him to the ground. When a second man lurched at him, Uli swooped low and flipped the guy over his back.

"Should I get Loveworks?" someone asked.

"Actually, this is Harry Blumenthal's—"

"No!" Leary interceded. "I'll tell her to speak to you when she's done with her chores."

Although Uli offered to help one of the two men to his feet, the guy got up on his own.

Realizing that he couldn't fight the entire tribe, Uli ambled over to the main road. The security team followed behind him. Uli sat up against the only tree near the bus stop and waited. The guards finally walked away.

Over the next two hours, Uli tried to figure out what could have offended the tribe. Eventually he dozed.

He was back in the parking lot, and then it was a hospital, and then he was elsewhere. By the arid and hilly landscape, Uli instantly knew he was back in Asia Minor and felt a palpable sense of dread. He noticed the young family he had seen dining earlier—minus the father. It seemed that a few days had passed. The beautiful mother, now filthy and exhausted, was clinging to the hands of her two toddlers. The three of them were standing at the rear of a bedraggled line of a hundred or so women and children—all dressed in heavy turn-of-the-century garb, covered in the dust and dirt of the unpaved road—moving tiredly under the burning noonday sun.

He watched them all shuffling along like sleepwalkers. Some in slippers, clothing torn. Others in long, heavy dresses that were frayed at the hems. Hair matted, caked in dirt and grime. White powder crusted around the sides of their chapped lips. From the scabbed wounds and bruises along their arms and faces, it was clear they had survived some sort of attack.

Uli sensed that their men had already been slaughtered. The slow line was being led by two short, fat soldiers. A third soldier was bringing up the distant rear. It appeared that they had already walked miles through the dust.

When Uli shifted positions for a better view, he could see a gang of beefy men hidden up ahead behind a mound of large rocks. As the refugees approached, some of the younger men in the gang bolted toward them.

An older man with an eye patch and walking stick took off after the younger marauders. Amid screaming and shouting, a fight broke out. Uli realized they were battling each other for the prettiest women in the group. None of the women were much younger than twenty-five; all the teenage girls must have already been taken.

When a young attacker tried to grab one of the women, she kicked him. The youth punched her hard in the face, then tried dragging her away. Before he could get very far, however, a large older woman, perhaps the young woman's mother, raced up and gouged her fingers into his eyes. She knocked him backward, but another man approached, pulled out a dagger, and calmly slashed her throat. As she fell to the ground gagging, the teenage attacker took out his penis and started urinating on the dying woman.

The daughter was too tired to even rise from the dirt. When one of the other soldiers yelled at the throat-slitter, the teenager stopped pissing and kicked the daughter in the ribs, stomping her midsection until she started to cough blood.

Uli noticed that none of the men actually had guns—they didn't need them. As the mother and her two children tried to march past the small band of now-retreating attackers, one of the men grabbed her daughter. The little girl let out a high-pitched shriek and her brother froze in terror. The mother tried to hold her daughter around the waist. Uli watched as one of the men tore off the back of the young mother's lace shirt, then ripped her corset down, exposing her breasts, before knocking her to the ground. Another older man lifted the screaming girl over his shoulder and walked off up a hill. Realizing that the man had abducted the little girl, the first attacker raced after him to recover his prize. The terrified boy ran over to his weeping mother, who tried to rise but passed out. Her screaming daughter was carried away.

Once hit, the victims either stumbled onward or simply collapsed to the ground, too exhausted to do anything else. None of the attackers finished them off. Apparently, there was no point in humiliating people who were nearly dead.

He awoke to the sensation of something trickling down his neck. At first he thought it was just sweat, but when the delicate sensation moved upward, he flinched, fearing it was a spider.

Bea was kneeling before him, stroking his head with one hand and holding a brown paper bag in the other. "Sorry," she said. "You looked so much at peace, I didn't want to wake you."

"I was having some weird, very elaborate, violent dream," he replied as he rose to his feet. The bloodred rays of the setting sun shot across the landscape and blinded him. "It was almost a continuation of something I saw at the Goethals."

"This place has another kind of reception. Dreams are far more vivid here. Some think it's a form of communication."

"Tim seemed really pissed off," Uli said, changing the subject. He didn't care for all her hocus-pocus. "Maybe we weren't supposed to talk about that thing at the Goethals."

"Actually, he asked me to help you think about it."

"Oh?"

"You have to understand. He's never had a vision about some mysterious stranger coming and rescuing us all. He's never taken a stranger out to the Goethals. He thinks you're here for a reason."

"What reason could that possibly be?"

"I don't know. Neither does he. But he does know that whatever your purpose is, it's not going to be achieved hanging around here."

"Do *you* want me to remain here?" Uli asked.

"Look, I'm sure we'll meet again, but for now I actually agree with him."

"What am I supposed to do?"

"What were you going to do twenty-four hours ago when you walked out of your meeting with Rafique?"

"Frankly, I haven't given it much thought. I don't have a home or job, I don't even know who I am."

"I promised not to counsel you. All I can say is trust your instincts," Bea said, "and be very careful. Rescue City is as divisive and ruthless as any prison yard."

"At least tell me why you ran off when we were on the other side of the basin today."

"It's a little embarrassing," she said. "I'd rather not go into it."

"I really need to know."

"I thought that animal was stalking us because of me, and I was trying to lead it away."

"It was a wild boar."

"Yeah, well, I just began menstruating. I figured he caught my scent and I was trying to draw him away from you. In case you didn't notice, I'm very fast."

"I did notice. I couldn't keep up with you."

"I went back to where we had come from, but after a while, when I realized it wasn't following me, I ran back to you."

"How did you get into the boat? I had already left the shore."

"I jumped from a big rock."

Uli decided not to ask any more questions, since she obviously didn't want to talk about it.

They chatted idly a bit more, until the six o'clock bus finally appeared in the distance. She kissed Uli gently on the lips as the vehicle came to a halt in front of them.

"Oh, this is for you," she said, handing him the paper bag she had been holding. "It's just some fruit for your trip."

He thanked her. "The next time we meet, will it count as our third date?"

"You bet," she said with a twinkle in her eye.

"Then I'll definitely see you later." Uli kissed her again and stepped inside the bus. The little door folded shut and the vehicle sped off.

"Well, looky here, it's my old traveling buddy."

It was the one-armed driver he had been hijacked with in Borough Park four days before. Uli greeted him and took a seat.

"I hate to tell you this, but the fare is still a sixteenth-stamp."

"Of course." Uli rummaged through his pockets and discovered that the few stamps he'd had yesterday were missing. "Can I owe you?"

"Nothing personal, but I don't even let my mother ride for free. What you got in there?"

Uli opened the brown bag that Bea had given him. "Apples, carrots, and bananas."

"With these old teeth, all I can eat are the 'nanas."

Uli handed them over and took a seat across from the driver. "Let me ask you something," he said. "Where would you go if you didn't have any money or a place to sleep?"

"Well, seeing how you're educated and all, there's only one place out here where you can just walk in and get an instant job and a home, but I don't particularly recommend it."

"What is it?"

"PP," the driver said. "Last stop."

"Why wouldn't you recommend it?"

"Everyone calls it *Pud Pullers*, 'cause they don't really fuck you, but they don't get you off either."

In a way it made complete sense. The dubious philanthropic organization, Pure-ile Plurality, seemed to be the hidden citadel of power behind the Piggers. Uli remembered what the girl on the bus had said—that if someone could get evidence that the organization was controlled by the Piggers, the city council would be forced to stop funding them.

"How long is the trip?"

"Long. Several hours. You're lucky 'cause we bypass Manhattan, going directly over the Zano on the way back to Brooklyn. I'll wind through Park Slope, then over toward JFK."

Uli was glad to hear it. The thought of seeing the decimated Crapper headquarters again was just too much for him.

The bus slowly headed north. No one got on at either Charleston or Rossville. When it pulled into a neighborhood called Bulls Head, a few others boarded. They drove along the eastern side of Staten Island, where a delta of shitty creeks and inlets broke off from the primary river.

Despite the cool evening air, the toxic smell intensified again, making Uli's eyes tear. The bus lumbered across another of the many long flat riverbanks where the backed-up sewage swelled out over the road. Uli tried to snooze but the smell was too much, even with his nose pin.

As they pulled up onto the Zano Bridge, they passed over a small barge heading south along the shoals of Staten Island. Since the water under the bridge was significantly less polluted and a gentle breeze was blowing down from the north, the odor virtually vanished as they crossed into Brooklyn. As soon as they arrived in the borough, the bus hit traffic. It took fifteen minutes for them to get through Red Hook.

When the bus reached a plateau at the top of Park Slope, Uli realized they were nearing Flatbush Avenue/Jackie Wilson Way. He began to smell something burning. Twenty minutes later, they were approaching the "buffer zone," a border area for the two warring boroughs.

"Shit!" the driver muttered, seeing a column of thick black smoke rising in front of them. "Everyone take a deep breath, we're going in."

Throughout the next several blocks, smoke shot out of windows and doorways of buildings on both sides of the street. Uli spotted some guy throwing a Molotov cocktail into the window of a sixteenth-stamp store. Men in blue shirts were running up the street.

"Get that fucker!" Uli heard one of them yell. "He stabbed Barnes!"

Red-shirted figures were slowly retreating. As the bus moved along, Uli saw two lines of men fighting side by side with pipes, spears, and chains—a gang war was raging.

"It's retaliation for the Manhattan bombing," the driver said. "The guys in blue are Crappers, the red shirts are Piggers."

"Actually, it's retaliation *for* the retaliation," some old voice behind Uli chimed in.

"They probably blew up the building themselves. The Crappers are always provoking things," another rider opined.

The longer the bus proceeded along the Brooklyn-Queens border, the hotter the conflagration grew. Soon, burning debris thrown from a partially collapsed building blocked the street.

Uli watched as two red shirts grabbed one of the overweight blue shirts. While one spun him to his knees, the other shoved a knife into the man's neck. Not content to simply let him die, more red shirts joined in, stabbing and kicking him.

Others on the bus looked away, but Uli found himself transfixed. Something new inside of him, some deep animalistic power, like an erection in his heart, made him yearn to join the red shirts.

In another moment, the driver zoomed through the inferno, rolling right over burned pieces of wood. Once clear, the bus sped along for several more blocks until screeching to a halt before a man sitting on a tiny traffic island with a single metal pole. A sign on the pole said, *Aqueduct Dog Track*, with an arrow pointing straight ahead. As the man rose, Uli saw he had a shirt that was half red and half blue. For a moment he wondered if it was a statement of bipartisan unity. Then he realized the guy had incurred a serious stomach wound and was bleeding badly. Mercifully, the driver let him stagger on board without paying. The wounded Crapper soldier struggled down the aisle holding his stomach. He limped to the back and dropped into a double seat. Perhaps fearing gang reprisals, no one helped.

When the bus hit a huge pothole, Uli whacked his head against the seat in front of him. The ensuing headache compelled him to sprawl out over two seats and before long he was asleep. Immediately he returned to his interrupted dream.

The mother woke to the screams of her son. They found themselves alone, but then the last of the marauders, the older man with an eye patch and walking stick, noticed them passing by. As though inspecting a farm animal, he cupped one of the young mother's exposed breasts in his hand. She kept moving as though nothing had happened. He grabbed her thick black hair, twisted it tightly around his large hand, and yanked her. Her crying son clutched her dress, refusing to let go. The boy started furiously kicking and slapping the old man with the eye patch. Without any indication of anger, the guy released the mother and stepped away as though to let them pass. Then, as the two proceeded onward, he lifted his heavy walking stick and brought it squarely down on the top of the boy's skull. The child flopped forward, convulsing and gushing blood, and his mother slumped next to his small body. The man with the eye patch calmly coiled the woman's long beautiful hair in his hand like rope and led her back up to join the rest of his band.

The last soldier, an older man whose fat head swelled out of his tight helmet, brought up the rear of the prisoners and cursed. As he stepped around the fallen elderly bodies—still alive, yet too injured to keep walking—he shouted angrily at the attackers. For a moment, Uli thought he was condemning the violent assault, but he quickly realized why the soldier was outraged: since the marauders hadn't slaughtered all the women, he now had to march them into the endless expanse of burning desert.

Suddenly Uli's vision changed. There was a black guy in the blond lobbyist's sports car. He was talking to the blond man who had rescued Uli, only the man looked different—he wasn't blond, or a he!

An intense pain shot through his body, causing him to leap to his feet and scream. Covered in sweat, still on the bus, Uli felt embarrassed. Yet something was pressing into his groin. Reaching into his pants, Uli found that his missing roll of food stamps had somehow slipped through a hole in his pocket and gotten caught in his underwear.

"Sorry," he said to no one in particular.

Aside from the weak bus headlights, the streets were now pitch black. The bus was nearly empty. The working streetlights were far and few. The sporadic buildings in this section of the reservation were mostly industrial warehouses with hurricane fences. There were no other cars or people around. Uli figured they were somewhere in outer Queens. As they rolled past blocks of darkness, haphazard piles of garbage and vandalized solicars littered the streets.

Soon the road narrowed into a tight single lane as it hugged a concrete retaining wall that went on for at least a mile. When the road lifted above the height of the wall, Uli saw a large enclosed reservoir with a sign that read, *Jamaica Bay.*

Slowly, vaguely, through the darkness, Uli recognized this moonlit basin from a few days earlier. He had come full circle. He heard a large cargo plane overhead, which reminded him that he was near JFK Airport. At a lonely, barren intersection, the bus came to a tired halt, the last stop.

The driver threw open the door and called out, "Pud Pullers! Time for everyone to get rubbed off!"

Looking out the window, Uli saw the large brownish buildings before him. He remembered spotting them from the far end of Jamaica Bay on the first day he had arrived.

"Hey, this guy's not moving," an elderly passenger said, referring to the wounded blue shirt. The guy had flopped sideways and was dripping and drooling into a pool of blood below him. Uli helped the driver carry the street fighter's body off the bus.

Some strange girl who was waiting outside came over as they laid the dead Crapper's body on the sidewalk. She took rosary beads from around her neck, dropped to her knees, and started praying: "Jesus, son of Yahweh! This man hath fought in the army of Satan. For him it is too late. Please burn his body for all eternity like the many fetuses he aborted and the countless children and virgins he doubtlessly sodomized. Amen."

Uli realized that it was the zealous Shub campaigner who had threatened him when Oric was detained. Everyone walked away from the dead man on the sidewalk.

"You're just going to leave him here?" asked Uli.

"Someone will find him before the dogs do," the driver assured him. "The local gangcops get a reward every time they bring in a body."

The driver walked around to the rear of the bus, where he pulled out a lengthy orange extension cord and plugged it into an outlet at the base of a streetlight. It was time for a recharge. He returned to his seat and pulled the visor of his hat over his eyes, instantly falling asleep. Uli followed the small crowd heading toward the complex of buildings.

At the doorway, a plaque read, *Pure-ile Plurality: How the Other Half*

Should Live. A broad walkway led into a narrow courtyard in front of a large well-lit lobby. Only through this central building could one gain access to the overpasses leading to the neighboring warehouses.

Roughly a dozen women holding infants or pushing strollers hurried past Uli, presumably to catch the bus. Uli thought perhaps he had been misinformed about the EGGS epidemic.

One straggling mother, noticing him glancing at her child's face, smiled proudly. She pulled back a small comforter, revealing a shivering Chihuahua dressed in swaddling clothes. Its moist eyes blinked delicately.

"Dat's mi bebe," she cooed.

"But it's—"

"I think I might owe you an apology," he heard from behind. It was the self-righteous campaigner who had just condemned the lost soul of the dead soldier.

"Sorry?"

"It wasn't very Christian of me, scalding your poor feeble-minded friend," she said. "I know I should be more forgiving, but you have to understand that decent people have suffered so much." Turning to the mother, who was patiently waiting for her dog baby to be adored, the young zealot said, "You better hurry, Consuela. The bus back to Manhattan is almost recharged."

"Much gracias," Consuela said, then dashed off with her pup to the bus.

"May I ask what it is you're doing here?" the zealot said to Uli.

"Actually, I was hoping to volunteer."

"Great, where you coming from?"

"I just arrived from Staten Island."

"Let's go, I'll show you the way."

The young campaigner introduced herself as Deere Flare. As she led Uli inside, she softly explained, "These ladies are here for treatment. You've got to be very careful."

"Careful how?"

"Since the EGGS epidemic, many women have been traumatized about being reproductively challenged. The man in charge here, Rolland Siftwelt, has set up a variety of workshops to help them cope with their infertility. He's also established these furry surrogates."

A security guard at the central building asked Uli to pass through a metal detector and then took his fingerprints. When Uli turned up without any kind of record at all, the guard stopped him.

"It's okay," Deere assured the man. "I'll vouch for him. Mr. Sift-welt wants to see him."

On the second floor, she silently led him down a linoleum-tiled hallway, up a short stack of steps, and through a large outer reception area with a middle-aged secretary stationed in front of a tall set of cloudy glass double doors.

"Joane, could you tell Mr. Siftwelt that a new arrival is here?" Deere said politely. Looking at her watch, she added, "Oh gosh, I'm late for a strategy meeting. I'll see you later." She abruptly ran off.

"Name?" the frumpy secretary said.

"Huey, I think."

The secretary suggested he take a seat. Looking over at a maga-zine rack, Uli saw a number of illustrated pamphlets printed on cheap grainy paper. One with a large yellow oval on it was entitled *Making Lemons out of Lemonade.* Another pleaded, *Join the Gang o' God!* Inside was a cartoon of a robust, happy creature and a puny, gloomy figure. The big fellow was pointing to a multilayered cake. Underneath, in a small font, it said, *When Unhappy—EAT!*

The intercom buzzed. The secretary smiled and nodded for Uli to go inside—Rolland Siftwelt was ready for him. Uli entered his office, but the chairman of PP was nowhere to be seen. A wide variety of trinkets and snow globes filled his shelves. Posted behind Siftwelt's big desk was a large map of New York, Nevada, divided up by red and blue borders.

Uli heard a flush, then a red-faced man with a muscular chest and huge biceps burst through a small side door that had to be his private bathroom.

"The name's Rolland Siftwelt." He gave Uli a powerful handshake and talked in a low, confiding voice: "Remember what New York City was like before we were attacked?"

"I'm suffering from acute memory loss, so . . . I don't remember much, just bits and pieces."

"It was very, very dangerous. Divided by gangs and drug dealers, the homeless roamed the streets and the average inner-city resident was incarcerated at least once before the age of twenty-five. Teen preg-nancies boomed and life expectancy dropped."

"Don't all those things still exist here?"

"We do have some drugs and two gangs, but there are fewer bul-lets and teens with every passing day."

Siftwelt's phone rang and he pardoned himself to answer it. He listened for a moment with a pinched expression on his face, then shouted, "There's a big difference between a three-foot prototype and one designed to carry people! I've got someone in my office." He slammed the phone down, took a moment to recompose himself, and asked, "Ever heard of Jack Wilson?"

"Yeah, they renamed Flatbush Avenue after him," Uli said.

"He vanished a number of years ago. Rumor has it he was killed by one of his lieutenants and his body was dumped in the desert. But lately a crazy new rumor has been surfacing—that he learned to fly."

"He could fly?"

"A plane."

"You mean . . . an airplane? He built an airplane?"

"It's absolutely ludicrous, but the rumor has all these kite flyers thinking they can be the next Wilbur and Orville Wright."

"How'd the rumor get started?" Uli asked hopefully.

"Someone supposedly found a miniature prototype. But rumors abound here. There was another rumor a few years back that Wilson was imprisoned in some sinister bunker out in the desert." Siftwelt leaned forward in his chair. "Before we go any further, let me fill you in a bit on what we're about. We started out as a religious mission that went door-to-door in many of the inner cities of this great country."

"Does that mean—"

"If you let me just make my pitch, I think it'll answer all your questions." Uli smiled and Siftwelt resumed. "For starters, we have a big dorm that most workers live in. Novices usually start with outreach. We pair them up and send them into tough neighborhoods, where they try to spread the word of a good, healthy, violence-free, community-building lifestyle. As well as the value of getting educated."

"You know, there's a rumor that the Piggers run PP."

"There's also a rumor that a group called Domination Theocracy runs us. And another that PP runs the Piggers."

"So you don't mix religion and politics?"

"Let me put it this way: even when the Crappers were in power, I was friends with Mayor Will just as I am with Shub. Could I get either man to do as I say? No."

"Are you a religious organization?"

"Everything's religious," the man replied.

Before Uli could ask any further questions, a tall, thin black woman with a wide-open face and a sweet smile entered.

"This is Marsha Johnson," Siftwelt introduced. "And this is our

newest member, Huey. Marsha is the supervisor for Brooklyn South."
Turning to her, he added, "Huey is going to be working with you.
Would you mind giving him a tour and bringing him up to speed?"

"Sure." Instead of taking a seat, Marsha led him out the door. Uli
thanked Siftwelt as he exited the office.

"This job is mainly old-fashioned street-corner work," Marsha
said. "We have to try to energize a listless people. It's very late. Why
don't you get settled? We'll talk more after you get some food."

Joane, the executive secretary, instructed Uli to fill out a batch
of forms. While he did so, she typed him a temporary ID and mentioned other perks such as a free haircut and suit, both available in
the basement. She said that the barbershop and cafeteria were often
open quite late. She concluded by giving him a dorm key to a room in
Building 4.

He thanked her and headed downstairs, where he tried to see the
tailor. A sign on the door indicated he had missed his chance for the
day. In the next room over, a bald man was sitting in a barber chair
reading a copy of *The Godfather* by Mario Puzo. Uli approached him
and asked if he could get a quick haircut. "I'd like a little taken off the
sides, but leave the top and sideburns intact."

"Sure," the barber replied.

Uli took a seat and had a large white bib buttoned around his shirt
collar. Looking straight ahead, he noticed a photo of Vice President
Spiro Agnew staring back at him in place of a mirror. He sat for ten
nervous minutes as the barber snipped away. Then, without asking,
the man applied hot lather to his face and gave Uli an extremely close
shave with a straight-edge razor. He padded him down with talcum
powder and brushed off all the snipped hair.

"Thanks," Uli said.

The guy nodded. When Uli caught a glimpse of himself in a passing window, he realized why the barber had no mirrors. The old bastard had given him a crew cut. Uli ran his hand over his quarter-inch
of bristle and sighed. For an instant, he remembered being in boot
camp.

Uli got directions to the cafeteria, which was located in Building
3. It was a large, harshly illuminated area lined with low tables and
fold-out benches. The cashier at the entrance asked to see his ID and
slowly copied the name *Huey* onto her clipboard.

Dinner that night was a choice of smoked hocks or meatloaf. There
was also a selection of green vegetables, yellow vegetables, and white

starches. Uli moved his tray along a shiny metal counter and inspected the various steamer pans through a glass case. He picked the hocks, potatoes, broccoli, soda water, and a bun. Most of those present were men missing at least one limb. They seemed to have either just completed their shifts or were coming on for the night shift. By the time Uli took a seat, he was starving.

The vegetables were mush that seemed to undergo a cellular breakdown as soon as they were taken out of their watery solvent. The hocks, which Uli strongly suspected to be reshaped Spam, retained some kind of stringy texture, perhaps protected by the grease, but they only tasted like the salt and pepper he shook on them. The stale bun and flat soda water were the highlights of the meal.

After downing what he could, Uli sat with his eyes closed and tried not to throw up. When he heard footsteps approaching, he glanced up to find Marsha Johnson standing before him with a few battered books.

"You're literate, aren't you?" she said

He nodded yes.

"I located some material about this place that might be helpful."

"Thanks." Uli noticed a film of dust on the cover of the top volume.

"Most people here are nonliterate," she said, taking a seat across from him. She flipped through one book entitled T.R.C.N.Y. Inside the title was spelled out: *Temporary Rescue City of New York, copyright 1971 by the US Army.* "This book is just about the New York contingent. It doesn't really include other protectees who wound up here over the years."

"Which other protectees?"

"Earthquake and hurricane victims. Some time ago, for instance, three people from the Love Canal area arrived. People who couldn't find perma-temp shelter anywhere else."

As Uli flipped through the pages, he glimpsed facts, figures, pie charts, and graphs on the New Yorkers shipped here around ten years earlier. Nearly a million people had initially been brought in from the city. They comprised a little less than one-eighth of all New Yorkers, mostly from the poorest rung of the city.

Judging by a shorter document entitled S.D.P., or *Supplemental Detainee Profile*—which had been issued by the Department of the Interior, copyright 1975—over the course of the next three years the core purpose of the place seemed to have shifted from a rescue location to a detention center. A hundred and fifty thousand people from around the country with questionable criminal or political backgrounds had been relocated here as well. Most of these people were well educated.

"How many doctors are there on the reservation?" Uli asked.

"Alternative Service was responsible for bringing in all the trained professionals, but they were only able to enlist about twenty-five doctors. That was ten years ago, and ten have been killed or died, so now only fifteen are still active. The good news is that a lot of residents died as well. If you're unfortunate enough to wind up in the hospital and you don't die while waiting for treatment, you'll probably be seen to by a nurse or PA. They do most of the work."

"And what exactly will I be doing here?"

"We have a budding educational system. All literates are automatically assigned to go through various parts of south Brooklyn and try to register people in our new school. We'll give you cartoon brochures for the nonliterates."

"What's the attendance now?"

"We have about fifty people currently enrolled."

"Sounds easy enough."

"If you can register one person per week, you'll be way ahead of the curve." Marsha gave him other supporting materials to review, which dealt with how to approach and treat reservation residents. "We meet at nine a.m. out front at the bus stop," she chirped. "You'll be introduced to Patricia Itt, your new outreach partner."

"Great," Uli said, as he accidentally belched out the fumes of his meal.

After Marsha left, Uli returned his food tray and tiredly crossed an overpass searching for his assigned dorm room. He paused by a window midway and looked out. Past the back half of an empty warehouse built along a pier he could see the crystal-clear waters of Jamaica Bay and the desert beyond. Scanning the building he had just exited, now across from him, he caught sight of something strange through a window a few flights down.

A muscular Siftwelt was standing forward at his desk. His shirt appeared unbuttoned and untucked. His tie was pulled loose. He was bumping repeatedly against the edge of the blotter, then he collapsed on his desktop. Uli noticed a slim, almost ghostly shape behind him. He tried to make out who this erect form was, but the person reached over and pulled a cord, dropping the blinds.

Uli walked on to a large room filled with quiet men and women seated in old cloth sofas and armchairs bordered by end tables with ugly brass lamps. There were islands of small cubicles, each with its own portable black-and-white television. In the middle was an open area with a large color TV for group viewing. Another room had a series of small tables where several men sat busily writing. Two older gentlemen discreetly played cards. Another duet was focused on some board game. Upon one table was an abandoned copy of the *Clarion Call*, which appeared to be the official PP newspaper. Uli mindlessly scooped it up.

Following the numbers stenciled on the doors, Uli walked down an ever-narrowing corridor, then up a stairway, until he came to the top floor in the rear of Building 4. There he found his door. He opened it and flipped on a light to see a boxy room, seven feet by seven feet. His new home consisted of a slot of a window, a single bed, a chest of drawers, and, like in the recreation room, an end table with an ugly lamp.

He gazed out at the courtyard and over a bordering wall to the pier that jutted out into the bay. Another large warehouse stood along the pier. He hung up his jacket, took off his shoes, and lay down on a squeaky bed with a flattened mattress. How many other bodies had passed over it? he wondered.

He cracked open the US Army–authored, xeroxed book that Marsha had loaned him and skimmed facts and figures about the reservation as recorded nine years earlier. The introduction explained what Luke, the bucket-passer at the Crapper headquarters wreckage, had told him—that the place had been created by a presidential act prompted by political haggling and private-sector wrangling. Before he was able to even turn the first page, Uli fell fast asleep.

A distant canine howl woke him some time later. He could faintly hear a bongo drum, broken by occasional barks. In the large windows of the deserted warehouse on the pier, he thought he saw a figure moving along the upper floor.

The sky was a silky shade of blue. Reading the *Clarion Call*, he learned that a suspect had already been apprehended in the bombing of the Crapper headquarters:

DROPT'S ASSASSIN ARRESTED
by Christen Soll

Daniel Ellsberg, a suspected terrorist with CIA ties, was arrested for bombing the Manhattan Crapper headquarters at Cooper Union and killing over four dozen people, including the Crapper mayoral candidate, James Dropt.

Ramsey Farrell, an up-and-coming gangcop lieutenant from Queens, arrested the man who masterminded the bombing. Ellsberg, a former Pentagon employee according to an unnamed source, has clear connections to the notorious Weather Bureau. He was apprehended early yesterday on Ditmas Boulevard and charged with twenty-two counts of murder along with a host of related charges that include the theft of four road repair trucks. According to confidential sources, Ellsberg has not revealed the identity of his coconspirators. He was sent into detention here eight years ago for allegedly stealing military secrets from the Pentagon and trying to smuggle them to his contact in Hanoi . . .

Another article also caught Uli's eye:

TERRORIST TRUCK BOMB KILLS 2 NEAR ST. PAT'S
by Harold Steward

A truck was blown up in front of Rock & Filler Center on Tuesday, killing two people and wounding three others. Sources claim that Crapper guerrillas intent on blowing up the Midtown Crapper Administration at 30 Rock & Filler Center accidentally detonated their bomb before they were able to remove it from the truck. Mike Mulligatawny, 53, and Sam Reynolds, 62, both registered Crappers, were killed. Four others were wounded. Pray for their eternal punishment.

Instead of blaming random terrorists, as had the paper he found on the bus, this publication only fingered Crappers. What bothered Uli most was that the article about Rock & Filler Center had greatly undercounted the dead and injured. The dozen or so who had been killed and the countless wounded were victims again—this time to propaganda.

Depressed by the news, Uli pulled his shoes on and walked back to the television area which was now empty. He followed the sound of deep chuckles to a small chubby man sitting alone in front of the large community TV.

"What's up?" he asked the merry viewer.

"Jackie Gleason in *The Honeymooners*," the man said, trembling with laughter. When he caught his breath, he shook his fist and said, "To the moon, Alice!"

"They broadcast this?"

"No, we get to watch the tapes." Pointing to a broom closet, the viewer added, "We have an archive next door."

In a little room lined with bookshelves, a clipboard listed all the videotapes in the library. The collection consisted of top-rated television shows, including *The Twilight Zone, The Outer Limits, The Prisoner, Have Gun—Will Travel, Naked City, Gilligan's Island, Wanted Dead or Alive, Hogan's Heroes, The Andy Griffith Show, Ben Casey, The Tonight Show,* and *Bewitched.* Uli felt too exhausted to watch anything, so he went to the communal bathroom and took a hot shower. Utilizing the free supplies, he brushed his teeth, then returned to his own little cubicle. Glancing out the skinny window, he spotted a lone figure coming out of the empty warehouse on the pier.

As soon as Uli lay down, he heard the distinct clicking of high-heeled shoes. Peering out the window again, he saw a woman exiting the warehouse as well. Uli was fairly certain it was Marsha Johnson. Her eyes were open wide though there was a strangely vacant smile on her face. He watched her vanish around a corner, then he went back to bed.

12

Uli woke to a strange synchronized chant: *"We're right, 'cause we're right, 'cause we're right, 'cause we're right . . ."*

Looking out the small window, he saw a group of roughly two hundred men and women donning gray sweats in tight formation, doing jumping jacks to the beat of the chant. Uli figured this was why all the workers here looked so trim and fit.

He shaved and showered, then slipped on his filthy clothes and jammed two food stamps into his pocket. In a corner of the room where the carpet was coming up, he hid the balance of stamps that Mallory had given him.

Down in the cafeteria, people were gathering for breakfast. Grabbing an orange tray, he moved down the food line.

"Name?" asked a large curly-haired woman monitoring everyone who entered.

"Huey."

The monitor checked under the letter *H* and told him to proceed. Uli was given a plate of reddish scrambled eggs and yellow mashed potatoes; both appeared to be made from a mix. He took two pieces of black bread, a cup of watery coffee, and an unripened apple. He found that if he ate quickly without inhaling, the food didn't taste so bad. Since he needed energy, he had two more helpings of everything. His dirty clothes made him feel self-conscious, so after stacking his tray in the dishwasher's window, he raced to the tailor. He found a short line of men and women already gathered. After twenty minutes, it was his turn. He was given a baggy suit to try on and a stool to stand upon. A woman with a mouthful of needles and a piece of chalk made notations on the cloth.

"How soon will the suit be ready?" Uli asked eagerly.

"Every morning I get the same number of people waiting for me that you saw today," she said laboriously. "There's a one-month backlog."

"A month? My clothes are literally falling off my body."

"I'm sorry, but unless you want to pay something extra—"

"How much to get it done right now?"

"Four stamps for right now."

"I've got two stamps." He held them out and she snatched them.

He waited in the hallway until five minutes to nine, an hour and a half later, when she waved to him. His suit was done. He immediately put it on. Although the polyester blend abraded his inner thighs and the fabric felt carcinogenic, it was a perfect fit. He walked proudly to the bus stop. In the half an hour or so that it took for the bus to arrive, about two dozen others joined him. The men all wore the same style and color suit as he, while the women had on long, dark-blue dresses with matching jackets.

Marsha Johnson, the Brooklyn South supervisor for educational outreach, was the last of the group to appear. "I've been waiting eight weeks for a new suit," she said to him. "How'd you get one so quickly?"

Uli shrugged innocently, then asked, "Did I see you outside last night?"

"Outside where?"

"You were coming from the abandoned building on the pier." He pointed over to it.

"No way, it's dangerous out there."

"What the heck is that place anyway?"

"They were going to convert it to a school, but then they decided they'll turn it into a giant church instead."

Marsha introduced him to his new team of coworkers: Lionel, Eileen, Harvey, Linda, Derek, and Sam. Uli knew he'd never remember their names, he wasn't even sure of his own. After a flurry of handshakes, the little group returned to their conversation about the upcoming mayoral election and how, if Shub lost, it would mark the advent of godlessness in Rescue City.

"And this is your new partner, Patricia Itt," Marsha said, leading him to a woman with goofy curls shooting out of her head like mattress springs.

His new partner didn't so much as look at him. Instead, she walked over to the bus as it pulled up and kicked its dented fender. Then she screamed up to the driver about being late. Uli looked at their supervisor with concern.

"She's a Taurus," Marsha explained. "That's what they do. They're impulsive."

"Okeydoke."

Marsha joined others boarding the bus. Uli's new coworker, however, stood before the vehicle and continued to berate the driver as everyone got on. Regarding her as a kind of angry female Oric, Uli gently took Patricia by her arm and led her onto the bus.

When the two sat down in the rear, Patricia Itt finally seemed to notice him: "I heard you're from Old Town."

"I don't really remember."

"What's it like there now?" she asked. "They were supposed to clean it up."

Uli repeated what he had just said.

"They told us that once it was cleaned up they were bringing back the evacuees and releasing most of the detainees, and I was told I was only a suspect, so I would probably be released."

"Good." Even Oric had been easier to deal with.

"I heard they elected some guy named Koch as mayor." Something shifted in Uli's memory, confirming the name. "So why hasn't he done anything to help us?"

Uli replied that he had no idea what was keeping them from containing the microscopic traces of radioactive particles from each tiny crack on the endless streets and buildings that made up Lower Manhattan. Impatient with his answer, Patricia turned around and started making barking sounds at someone behind her.

Uli noticed early-morning nomads canvassing the garbage piles in the burned-out zone between Brooklyn and Queens. Billboards along the roadway had pictures of Mayor Shub squinting earnestly, along with the slogan, *Vote Shub & Don't Look Back!*

He ain't lyin or flirtin, another campaign poster rhymed, *reelect him or you'll be hurtin!*

As the bus bounced and skidded along, it stopped every once in a while to pick up passengers.

Unlike that nightmarish bus trip on the first day, this one remained packed with PP people. It eventually passed through east Brooklyn, where Uli realized that he preferred the traditional Japanese architecture over the dreary Soviet designs.

About forty minutes later, when they reached the southern end of Brooklyn, teams of missionaries started bailing out two at a time at each stop.

"You and Patricia are going to be at the western end of Coney Island," Marsha said, giving Uli a small stack of leaflets and two full paper bags. "Hand out the pictograph flyers, and these are your lunches. I'll come at the end of the day to collect you." Uli felt like a child whose mother was depositing him at school.

The bus slowed down as they approached a miniature amusement park. The supervisor signaled to him that it was their stop.

Once on the sidewalk, Patricia raced up ahead of Uli, past the food concessions and the half dozen or so rides that made up Astroland.

"Slow down!" he shouted as she bounded over the sparsely populated walkway. Uli now felt like a geriatric father in pursuit of some hyperactive child. He stared out over the narrow man-made river to see the results of a strange catastrophe. The wreckage of four rusty roller coasters were coupled together—it was the old Cyclone ride. Two of the cars were half-buried in the sand on a little beach. The rest were submerged in the bluish-green waters.

"Wow!" Uli uttered. It appeared that at the zenith of the ride, the roller coaster had come off its track and flown out over the desert, crashing into the river.

Apparently having seen it all before, Patricia just pulled out her stack of brochures and raced over to passersby: "Hey, you! Get an education! Right here, right now—*pow!*"

Uli spent the day trying to hand out the educational pamphlets. But by lunch he had only gotten rid of three and he saw all three people toss them to the ground. Patricia kept up her effective rhyming system, and by four o'clock, when some stray youth walked by Uli, he tried to make a similarly upbeat plea: "Get an education—it's better than Claymation!"

"You fucked that up big time," Patricia said to him.

"What are you talking about?"

"You ain't suppose to tell folks to get no cremation."

"No, I said it's better than *Claymation!*"

"Well, you ain't suppose to throw big words at folks trying to make 'em feel small an' all," she said in a singsong beat.

"I was trying to convince him—"

"If you do it again, see if I don't report you to Marsha," Patricia said, then dashed off.

Uli waited a moment longer, then sank down on a bench and tried to imagine the ocean lazily lapping at the shores of the old Coney Island. Eventually, he leaned over, pulled his legs up, and nodded off to sleep.

* * *

"Lazy Jehovah's Witnesses!"

The words jolted him awake. Some old-timer, a pale giant of a man, was sitting next to him on the bench and staring at his stack of brochures. The fellow had deeply sunken eyes, floppy ears, a long narrow nose, and not a single strand of hair.

"This ain't South Ferry, but it'll have to do," the guy said as he pulled a large Danish from a brown paper bag. "That's where I used to live in Old Town."

"Would you be interested in getting an education?" Uli asked, offering him a brochure.

"I have a degree from Princeton, hotshot." The hairless man took a bite out of his pastry and continued talking: "I just couldn't get a job, that's how I wound up in the Bronx way back when. But that wasn't why I wanted to change my name. That was something else entirely . . ."

Uli still felt exhausted and decided to take advantage of the situation. To dupe Patricia, he acted as though he were listening, pretending to attempt a recruitment. While the old man's voice droned on, Uli closed his eyes.

There was something familiar about the guy's high voice—as though he were speaking at a frequency only Uli could pick up—but it didn't make complete sense: ". . . *indguessoonlytonenofeusecouldoprevail* . . ." Slowly screening out the static, Uli was eventually able to decipher what the man was saying: "The other had to eat crow and that was me . . . We were a redundancy of sorts. What he did was amazing, the great pyramid of parks, beaches, highways, bridges . . ."

Uli's awareness seemed to click off, yet he could feel his brain digesting information like a stomach filling inside his head. When he awoke again, he could still hear the old man's words flowing almost magnetically into his ears, and yet he hadn't really grasped any of it.

"I'm truly sorry, Millie! Sorry about the failed revolution! Sorry about leaving you to return to New York . . . Sorry to Teresa and the kids for all our hopes that drowned in the goddamn pool . . . Sorry, Lucretia, for being so undeserving . . . Most of all, Beatrice, I'm sorry to you, for not putting it all behind me and for abandoning you . . ."

"I'm sorry too," Uli finally joined in, yawning. "But at least it sounds like you had more than your share of women." He looked over to the million-year-old man, only to see that *he* was fast asleep. Apparently, Uli's own brain had dreamed or imagined this entire bizarre "sorry" soliloquy. He quietly rose to his feet and left the strange elderly man snoozing on the bench.

At six p.m., Marsha waved over from the street entrance to the boardwalk. Uli signaled to Patricia Itt and together the three of them returned to the bus, which collected all the outreach workers as it headed back to the PP compound.

Patricia ratted him out on the bus ride back: "He was just a lazy-bones! Spent practically the whole day with some old liver spot, not doing nothing."

Uli didn't respond.

Back in his dorm, he washed his face. Finding a pair of abandoned slippers in the communal bathroom, he put them on and came down to dinner in his former shirt and pants, not wanting to get his new suit dirty.

"So, how'd you like your first day?" Marsha asked as Uli sat staring at his inedible dinner of something brown floating in something green.

"Maybe a good night's sleep will make a difference," he replied.

"Actually, I wanted to invite you to a prayer meeting we're having downstairs."

Uli said he was experiencing indigestion, which was partly true, and he politely declined.

As he headed out of the cafeteria and up to Building 4 after the meal, his limbs felt increasingly heavy. He was simply tapped out.

Lumbering up to his distant room, he barely heard the sultry whisper: "Blow job?"

He turned to see Deere Flare, the young woman with the abrupt forehead whom he'd met yesterday getting off the bus. She was wearing a white shirt, a tight plaid skirt, dark nylon stockings, and seductive black heels.

"Did you say something?"

"Sleeping on a bench with some old mummy when you should be trying to educate the masses. Tsk, tsk," she said, moving toward him.

"Huh?"

"I spotted you today out in Coney Island, hon." Smiling she added, "I guess I'm not the only one who's seen something I oughtn't."

"I think you've confused me with someone else."

"You saw us last night," she accused. "Did you take a photo? Is that it?"

"What are you talking about?" But Uli knew exactly what she was talking about. Now he was sure he had seen Siftwelt in the middle of some vague sexual misconduct the night before.

"Why are you here, pal? Trying to dredge up the dirt, is that it?"

"I'm stuck here," Uli said. "I'm just trying to do a little good."

"Give me the film or you'll regret it."

"Give me a break."

Deere Flare turned and walked away, sternly snapping her high heels against the hard tile floor. Uli returned to his little room and found that someone had gone through his meager belongings. The little stash of money that he had hidden under the fold of his carpet was sitting on top of his chest of drawers. He was actually glad they'd searched his room. He didn't have anything to hide.

Uli was about to lie down, but thought he heard something in the distance once again. He looked out the window at the long building on the pier that Marsha had said was about to be converted into a church. Although he didn't see anyone enter or exit, a lone person passed by one of the darkened windows.

He found himself thinking about the macabre fantasy or vision he'd had at the Goethals about being a robotic warrior, and wondered what it could possibly mean. Who was the strange girl he had disappointed? Then he thought about Mallory and Oric's painful deaths and soon felt wide awake. He went downstairs and tried to exit the building. The guard on duty asked him where he thought he was going.

"Just hoping to catch some air."

"Doors close after ten p.m.," said the older man.

Uli thanked him and figured there had to be at least one unmanned exit in this four-block complex. Heading down to the basement cafeteria, he saw two workers silently piling a mountain of black plastic garbage bags into the back of a pickup truck in an adjacent garage. When the workers walked off, Uli casually grabbed two of the bags and carried them out. After loading them in the rear of the pickup, he continued down the empty street along the old brick wall. Off in the distance he could make out a large circular field. As he hiked toward it, he spotted an old sign that read, *Aqueduct Dog Track, 2 miles*. He turned back and, still wide awake, moved toward the abandoned warehouse—a two-story structure fingering out over the basin.

PP had evidently torn down a number of other buildings in the immediate area. Uli figured they could easily erect yet another connecting overpass to this one. Reaching the doorway, he found it cinder-blocked shut. The windows on the ground floor were covered by worn sheets of plywood, but he was able to easily slip one board aside and climb in. Within the dark, cavernous warehouse, he felt a chilly wind.

The ground floor was alive with the sounds of scampering and flapping. Small desert animals and birds had taken shelter in the empty structure. Above, he could hear footsteps. Uli proceeded up a set of stairs to the second floor, where the windows allowed moonlight to pass through. To his surprise, he came to a long corridor filled with silent people, like a party of spirits, buzzing to or from one of three massive rooms. Inside the first large area, Uli made out sweaty and interlocked forms in tight and repetitive motion.

As his eyes adjusted, he saw that though most of the copulators simply lowered their garments, some were completely naked. He recognized one woman, a fellow neophyte, who was orally enveloping a much older man. Some of the couples appeared to be of the same gender; all were having muted sex. No sooner did he realize this than a lean, bald man dropped to his knees before him.

Uli jumped back in shock. Until that moment, he had felt as though he were invisible. He quickly retreated to one of the other rooms. Roughly ten couples were engaged in heated states of intimacy. Near one corner, he spotted her. Marsha Johnson was gratifying two men simultaneously. Uli walked over as one of the men shot his ample emission onto the floor, then stumbled away. A moment later, the second man also disengaged from her and ejaculated.

"Marsha," he whispered, acutely aware that he hadn't heard anyone speak, "I knew I saw you."

Without responding, she reached up and started unclasping his belt.

"Wait," he whispered. Lowering his face to hers, he asked, "What are you doing?"

She wore a lusty smile, an expression uncharacteristic of the cautious person he had briefly come to know. Her eyes appeared glossy, as though she were in some far-off place. At that moment another man, skinny with an alarmingly large erection, walked right up and simply entered her without making a peep.

"Hey!" Uli said.

The guy didn't respond. As the newcomer had feverish sex with Marsha, Uli stared at the man's face. He was a member of the same outreach group—Lionel. Though they all acted as if they were sleepwalking, Uli guessed that the men were actually faking it.

After watching Marsha have intercourse with three more males, he saw her silently rise, fix her blouse, and leave the building. The smile never left her face.

Uli followed her down the steps and across the street. She headed to a service door in the rear of Building 2 that had no knob. With the tips of her fingers, she was able to pry it open. Uli caught the door before it closed and trailed her up the steps. She walked across an overpass, finally turning off at the women's dorm.

Uli continued on to Building 4 and his own room, where he lay on his bed and stared upward. As darkness was gradually replaced by the morning light, he tried to figure out what the hell was going on. Eventually, without sleep, he rose, dressed, skipped breakfast, and went back to the bus stop out front—a new work day had begun.

13

When Marsha joined the group outside, she looked thoroughly rested. Uli asked her how she had slept.

She didn't bat an eyelash. "Fine, how about you?"

"I had a weird dream."

"What kind of dream?" she asked politely.

"That a lot of people were in a large warehouse silently making love to each other."

Marsha looked away nervously and said, "I don't want to sound like a prude, but I feel really uncomfortable hearing things like that."

"I'm sorry, but you asked."

"I won't make that mistake again," she responded, then boarded the bus.

Slightly embarrassed, Uli got on last, pulling Patricia Itt in with him. Some of the men he'd seen having sex with Marsha and one another were seated calmly in the back of the vehicle as it rolled out to south Brooklyn. Like the previous day, Uli and Patricia Itt were the last to be dropped off.

Arriving on the mini boardwalk of Coney Island with the thick-headed Patricia, Uli immediately felt tired. If these people hadn't wised up while stuck in this awful Rescue City, he thought, a brochure filled with dumb cartoons and morbid statistics wasn't going to do it.

He glumly watched Patricia as she moved excitedly from person to person like a hummingbird on amphetamines. She appeared truly happy. Slowly he distilled her secrets: Reject the big picture. Be lower-brained. Stay small and vibrant. Marsha's lessons weren't bad either: follow your base urges and simply deny.

"Hey, Jehovah, want some rugelach?" It was the tall hairless Lazarus from the previous day, splayed out on the same bench, again eating a pastry out of a brown paper bag. Uli politely declined the man's offer and told him he was busy.

Uli tried to purge his own cynicism as he occasionally flung flyers toward those walking past. After a few hours, and as people grew more scarce, he looked over and saw Patricia trying to hand a flyer to a stray mutt. The dog sniffed the piece of paper and dashed off.

When Uli sat down again, the old man asked, "Do I know you, sir?"

"We both fell asleep here yesterday."

"Oh, yes! You're the parasite who crawled into my ear, and now I can't get you out of my brain."

The old man immediately resumed his cryptic ramblings from the day before. Uli tried to be polite, but the guy seemed to be gearing up for a monologue.

"At my age, everybody is just five things."

"What five things?" Uli said.

"Five fingers on the hand." The old man held his large palm open. "Five appendages on the body. Five books of the Torah. Five boroughs of this city—"

"So what five things are you?" Uli cut him short.

"I used to be a father, a son, a husband, a brother, and an uncle."

"Aren't you still?"

"Now I'm a terrorist, a traitor, a coward, a monster, and a fraud."

This is going to be a long day, Uli told himself, but simply said, "Pretty hard on yourself, aren't you?"

The old man launched into the the story of his sad life, though clearly he had a few screws loose. Uli tried to be attentive, but just like before, he began dozing. He found himself thrust into a complex dream in which he was someone else, trapped in some dark subterranean system along with a filthy tribe of bewildered half-wits fighting for leadership and a way out.

He abruptly awoke with the hideous thought that the creepy Deere woman was somewhere nearby watching him. The old man continued yammering away obliviously as Uli quietly stood back up and headed over toward the amusement park. He noticed Patricia staring at him.

"There are people down there," Uli said to her, spotting a clump of youths who had just exited the park.

"I'll come along," she said.

"No, stay here." He pointed to a dilapidated building nearby. "The seniors in that home are going to come out for an afternoon stroll. I saw them do it yesterday and we missed them."

By the time Uli made it to the amusement park entrance, the youths had vanished. Between the evenly spaced slats of wood that made up the promenade, something red caught his eye—someone had dropped a string of tickets, still unripped, on the sand below. He was about to return to Patricia, but he became transfixed by more youths getting spun around a ride as though in a huge blender. Another ride looked like a flying cup and saucer. Participants had to stand up against the inner rim of the giant cup as it whipped around at gravity-defying angles, the centrifugal force holding them in place. Uli watched a lone bumper car driver, a middle-aged man with a joyous expression, repeatedly smashing into a group of vacant bumper cars. Without thinking, Uli found himself smiling. Catching sight of the roller coaster that had crashed into the river, he thought that in one sense the doomed ride must've been a godsend. After all, where these newer ones merely teased people with a spectacular body-hurling thrill, that one had actually delivered.

Peering down the boardwalk, he saw Patricia standing alone, holding a flyer out to the empty space. She waved from the distance, and he wondered if her perkiness somehow fed off of his despair. He pointed angrily to the old-age home. When a lone figure exited the building, Patricia rushed over and Uli made his move. Scrambling underneath the boardwalk, he grabbed what turned out to be three unused tickets.

Sneaking inside so that Patricia wouldn't see him, Uli first rode the Loop the Loop, then the bumper cars, and finally the mini roller coaster.

Roughly twenty-five minutes later, feeling refreshed, he hurried back out to the boardwalk, but there was no sign of of his coworker. In the old-age home, he asked if anyone had seen a woman with a bad haircut—they hadn't.

He spent the remaining three hours searching for her. He began to suspect that the despicable young woman with the prominent forehead was somehow behind this disappearance. Deere Flare thought he had taken blackmailing photos of her with Siftwelt and had probably sworn revenge. Would she actually kidnap his partner just to make him look bad?

At six o'clock there was still no sign of the Itt girl. In a slight panic, Uli took half of the remaining brochures and shoved them into a garbage can. Then he returned to their original spot to find his supervisor waiting for him.

"Where's Patricia?"

"I don't know. I went into the amusement park to hand out some flyers." He held up the remaining stack. "When I came back, she was gone."

"You're supposed to look out for each other," Marsha said. "That's why we have partners."

"She was handing out flyers to the seniors at the home. I went away for just a moment and she was gone."

"Did you check the home?"

"Yeah," Uli responded absently. "Maybe she returned to PP alone."

"I just hope she didn't drown," Marsha said and sighed.

Uli thought she was kidding, but looking out at the narrow band of greenish water, he realized she was serious. Marsha told him she'd have to notify the local Crapper gangcops.

"She probably went home early," he said. "It was a pretty slow day."

"Let's hope."

Together the two boarded the bus back to the compound, where they found that Patricia had not returned. No one had heard from her. Uli offered to go out tomorrow and hand out flyers alone.

"That's not my primary concern right now," Marsha said, clearly agitated.

She reported Patricia Itt's disappearance to Rolland Siftwelt, who checked in with the gangcops.

To keep from worrying, Uli spent the evening in the PP library reviewing audiovisual and tape recordings of inspirational speeches by religious and secular leaders of the last forty years. In addition to stirring oratories by the Kennedy brothers and Martin Luther King Jr., he listened to George Meany, Jimmy Hoffa, and Albert Shanker all rallying their labor forces.

After several hours, he started to feel a tingling in his conscience.

He wasn't sure if it was a result of the speeches or guilt for losing his partner. All he knew was that social change seemed possible. As he walked past the cafeteria, he spotted Marsha talking to another outreach worker.

"Excuse me," he said, "have you found out anything about Patricia's disappearance?"

"I think the correct word is *recidivism*."

"What do you mean?"

"Patricia was a drug addict and prostitute. A healthy percentage of the PP labor force are former addicts. This is a rescue mission."

"Patricia is a—"

"From the first day, her pimp started sniffing around, trying to win her back. She probably returned to him. It's amazing that we even got her here in the first place. She had only been sober for about two months."

"She was an actual prostitute?"

"And a drug addict. Many of us were," Marsha replied flatly.

"You too?" That might explain her nocturnal conduct.

"Didn't you ever have any problems with crime or addiction?" Marsha asked earnestly.

Uli looked off sadly and nodded yes. As far as he knew, he had never taken drugs or had a criminal record. But just from the strange warrior guilt dreams, he knew something in his past had definitely gone awry.

"Are you okay?"

"I just feel awful about all this," Uli said. "I should've kept a closer eye on her."

"Here at PP we're great believers in forgiveness," Marsha soothed, placing her hand on his shoulder. "Everyone screws up—frequently the hardest part is forgiving ourselves."

Uli smiled weakly.

"I'm sorry for judging you earlier, when you shared your weird dream."

"I should probably keep certain things to myself."

"No, you were right. It's probably healthier to let it all out." Looking down, she added, "All we really have is each other."

Uli took her hand in his, gave it a soft shake, and returned to his room.

He lay on his bed feeling sad, until he heard something in the darkness, a kind of ecstatic bark that sounded like Patricia Itt. He got dressed and headed down the stairs to the basement cafeteria he had left through the night before. He walked across to the future house of worship and again climbed in through the ground-floor window. Inside, he scurried up the steps to the last room in the front. A number of people were copulating, yet he was glad that he didn't find Marsha among them. Although he felt sexual stirrings, he kept reminding himself that he might be in enemy territory. This could be some kind of trap, he thought, though it was intriguing to watch. As long as he didn't participate, he couldn't be accused of anything. He waited an hour, waving off a number of offers. He felt like a zoologist as he watched more people arrive, copulate, and leave.

Finally, to his thrilled disappointment, she arrived. He watched as one man made love to her, then a second, then a third and fourth simultaneously. Before a fifth man could grab her, Uli put his arm around Marsha's slim back and led her to an isolated corner. Spinning her around against a wall, he made her spread her arms and legs apart as though he were about to search her. She offered no resistance. Reaching underneath her wet dress, he gently stroked along her curly hairs and moistened lips. Then he unzipped his pants, but stopped before he fully succumbed to his burgeoning desire.

Turning Marsha back around so that she was facing him, he looked deep into her eyes. She smiled mindlessly. Her pupils didn't seem focused. He could've been anyone. He kissed her hard on the lips, but she didn't kiss back. Unbuttoning her shirt to reveal her small breasts, he was surprised to find that she was even wearing a bra. He unclasped it and suckled her until she started gently moaning. She whimpered softly as he gave her a deep crimson hickey. Then he did the same to her other breast, leaving a matching mark. She tried thrusting her hips into his, and though he was thoroughly aroused, he abruptly left the warehouse.

14

Bright and early the next morning at the bus stop, Marsha announced to everyone that it was going to be a short day. They had to return to the complex no later than six p.m.

"Forecasts show a storm brewing tonight. And I don't want anyone getting stuck outside."

As all boarded the bus, Marsha took Uli aside and suggested that he join another outreach group that was looking for new workers to rescue prostitutes in Brighton Beach.

Instead of responding, Uli posed his own question: "Did you find marks on your breasts?"

"I beg your pardon—"

"I made them," he interrupted, "but I'm sure you must've found other strange things on your body as well."

"You're crazy!"

"Late at night you go to the abandoned warehouse on the pier and you have sex with multiple partners. None of you seem conscious."

She didn't say anything, just stared at him vacantly.

"I'd like to go back to Coney Island one last time," he resumed. "I think I was getting through to some of the locals and was hoping to win them over. I guess I'm also half hoping to catch sight of Patricia."

"If you do see her with someone," Marsha finally replied, unable to make eye contact, "don't fight. Just try to find out where they're going and notify the authorities."

On the rest of the ride out to Brooklyn, she didn't so much as look at Uli.

When the bus arrived at Coney Island, Uli headed toward the boardwalk. Only the tall, hairless senior was there, sitting on his usual bench, muttering to the boundless emptiness surrounding him.

"Remember me from yesterday?" Uli greeted.

"Sure," the old man said with a smile, "you're the parasite who crawled into my ear and got lost in my brain."

Though the man seemed somewhat senile, Uli couldn't resist asking, "Do you remember the young woman who was with me yesterday? She vanished. You didn't see her, did you?"

"You know what I know," the old bird replied, then closed his eyes.

Stay on course, Uli reminded himself. *Patricia will be found. You're here to try to bring people a purpose in life.* He decided to take a different approach and looked for a crowd.

Walking a few blocks away, he spotted a group of men in the distance. There was an open-air court bracketed by ten-foot-high basketball hoops. A number of guys roughly his age were in the middle of a fierce competition. Uli waited, but the game wouldn't end.

Compelled by the urgency of his mission, he walked over to the edge of their court and shouted: "Your only way out of here is through *education!*"

Some of the men running back and forth under the hot sun glanced at him, but they continued playing. Uli attempted to be a little more confrontational, muttering, "Don't be apathetic *dolts!*" When they raced by him toward the opposite end of the court once more, Uli yelled, "You're all a bunch of stupid *motherfuckers!*"

The shooter stopped midjump, still holding the ball.

Uli took to his heels with the entire basketball team running behind. The river was three blocks away. The first block was no problem. By the end of the second block, the most athletic pursuer was right on his tail. A punch slid along his kidney, giving him a second wind.

A row of carbonized buildings lined his escape route. At the end of the street was a hurricane fence that had been clipped and rolled back. A retaining wall separated him from the waterway. Dodging singed furniture abandoned on the street, Uli jumped the wall, inhaled to the bottoms of his lungs, and speared hard into the blue-green waters.

Moments later, when his head broke the river's surface, he gasped for breath and looked back. Twenty feet behind, their heads were bobbing over the crumbling concrete wall. Not one of them cared to join him in the slow-moving river. Something whizzed by, then a host of other items kerplunked about him. Stones and sundry salvos were being thrown as he splashed away. Fortunately, he discovered that he swam well in a suit. The water was as warm as a bathtub. But just as he was taking comfort in his lead—*bang!* Something big crowned him hard. Dazed, Uli unintentionally gulped the acrid water.

Flailing, he knocked into a long rectangular object drifting past. It was an eight-foot-long wooden sign that read, *Water Hazardous—Do Not Swim.*

"Don't let us catch y'ass," one of the basketball players shouted from the distance. "'Cause when we do, you're fuckin dead!"

Uli kicked off his shoes and climbed up onto the wooden sign. Though he could've headed over to the desert side of the river on the far shore, there was nowhere for him to go from there, so he just kept floating north. He realized he never should've interrupted their game, let alone insulted them. He was simply trying to get their attention— to *help* them.

Soon he could see an even spacing of sewage pipes jutting out below the retaining wall of Brooklyn. Liquid refuse from the borough was intermittently plopping into the river. Still, the water here was nothing like the toxic muck drowning Staten Island. Before floating under the distant span of the Zano Bridge, he spotted some kind of ragtag community on the desert's edge.

Staten Island—or rather a slice of desert dividing it from Brooklyn— was on the far side, but the water was moving too rapidly to cross. The angle of land shooting out from the desert turned out to be a sharp bend in the river, sending the waters north. Drifting closer, he saw that near the bend, along the banks dead ahead, there was a row of faux skyscrapers, similar to those he had seen from Midtown. Like everything else here, these panels were an homage—an unintentional modern art installation mimicking the Wall Street skyline.

Moving along shoelessly, he saw that the bend gave rise to a long wall—a concrete dam separating the northward-flowing river of Brooklyn from the southward-oozing sewage. It extended all the way to Manhattan. On the opposite side of the bend there appeared another waterway. The waste of all five boroughs was draining somewhere south along the eastern edge of Staten Island.

Uli floated toward the base of the pseudo-skyline and finally located a small walkway next to the concrete wall where he was able to climb up onto the narrow shore between the two waterways.

The strip of land under the bridge had three small shacks, and ended at a rocky cliff that marked the beginning of Staten Island. Examining the lower panels of the skyline, Uli saw that each one was a fiberglass sheet, ten feet square. They were locked into rusty steel frames and held up by scaffolding. Sand had accumulated along the steel grid, and an array of intricate cableworks were anchored into the earth with large spikes.

In the distance, Uli could see cars rising and dipping over the creaky two-lane causeway that joined Manhattan to Richmond County—the Staten Island Ferry Bridge.

"What the fuck you think you doin?" The voice came from out of the nearest shack. A long chain whipped around his neck and pulled him backward to the ground. Three paunchy middle-aged men with mustaches moved around him. The apparent leader was short and balding with a close-cropped beard and wire-framed glasses. He held a thick lead pipe that looked perfect for breaking bones. The second man was stretching a black leather bullwhip before his huge beer belly. The last man, younger with a bushy mustache, sported an old machete with black electrical tape clumsily spooled around its handle.

"I'm sorry," Uli said, exhausted, "I was chased into the river."

"Who chase you?" asked the leader, glancing around.

"A gang upstream in Coney Island."

The leader switched to Spanish: "Faggot thinks we're idiots."

"I think no such thing," Uli replied in his own tortured Spanish.

"Look at his bullshit suit," the one with the bullwhip said.

"I'm from Pure-ile Plurality," Uli explained.

"Anyone can steal a suit," said the leader. "You a Pigger runt?"

"No," he answered, and buttoning up his shirt, he added, "I'm an outreach worker for Pure-ile Plurality. I was trying to get students to join our new educational program."

"Hey," the one with the bullwhip said, "you think you smart 'cause you speak a little Spanish? What are you doing on our monument?"

"Just admiring it, I assure you."

"He's scoping it out," the man wielding the machete opined to the others. "He's a government agent!"

"That's ridiculous."

"Look, he's bleeding," observed the guy with the whip.

Uli touched his head and found blood on his fingers.

"Prove to me you're from Pud Pullers," the leader said, giving him the benefit of the doubt. He stroked his heavy pipe.

"Call Rolland Siftwelt. He'll vouch for me."

"We're in the desert, asshole, do you see a phone anywhere?" the whippersnapper said, then kicked Uli behind his knees, sending him back to the ground in pain. The fat man snapped his whip in the air.

"Let's do the motherfucker," snorted the machete man.

"Not here. Remember the last time. We got to get him to dig his own hole."

"Oh yeah. Get up," the leader commanded.

With his knee throbbing, Uli slowly rose to his feet and was pointed to the left of the faux monstrosity.

When they moved back under the Zano Bridge, he heard the men conversing in Spanish about how to kill him.

Staring into the empty horizon, thoughts of the blond stranger from Green-wood Cemetery flashed through Uli's head. He was the only person Uli had recognized in Rescue City. Even though the blond man had missed his rendezvous, Uli deduced that this must be the reason he came to this place—to rescue that guy.

As the trio marched him forward and then knocked him to his knees, Uli thought, *Sorry, blond stranger, whoever you are.* Suddenly, a pack of miniature dogs descended upon him, snapping at his heels.

"Conchita!" a shrill female voice cried out. "Conchita! You come back here, you bad baby!"

He turned around to see the reproductively crippled woman he had met briefly his first night at Pure-ile Plurality. She was chasing after her surrogate baby, the big-eyed Chihuahua.

"Hold it!" Uli shouted. "She knows me!" Her name popped into his head. "Consuela! Remember me from Pure-ile Plurality?"

"Oh yeah, I *always* see you there. You're *always* so sweet," Consuela replied. Fortunately, her mental fuzziness went well beyond the trauma of child deprivation. She ran up to Uli and started petting his sweaty head like he was a tall dog. "He's *so* good, he's *so* right."

When Uli hugged her, she hugged back, reluctant to let him go.

"All right," the leader said, pulling Consuela off him. Picking up her dog-child and handing it back to her, the man directed her to her shack, then he just stood there staring fiercely upward.

"Man, you not gonna let him go, are you?" the fat man with the whip asked.

"You wanna know why? I tell you why," the leader answered. "'Cause we kill him and Pure-ile Plurality gonna investigate. Then iz gonna be a matter of time before Consuela starts yapping about the nice man who was here, and they add one plus one, and we each lose our right hand, and I tell you right now, I don't mind losing a hand, but I ain't ready to give up sex."

"Shit!" the bullwhipper said.

"No hard feeling, man," the leader said to Uli, and as an offer of reconciliation, he held out his hand and said, "Slap me five, dude." Tiredly, Uli slapped the man's palm. "You tell 'em. Tell 'em. We didn't mess you up or nothing, right?"

"Absolutely."

"So that's got to be worth a little something," the leader suggested.

Uli reached into his pocket and handed the man a soggy stamp. He started to ask the guy how he could navigate around the waterway to get back to Brooklyn, but the mustached leader simply shoved him backward, plunging him into the swiftly flowing current. With his knee still in pain, Uli thrashed about helplessly in the water.

"*Vaya con Dios!*" the leader called out, laughing.

Uli fought to keep his head above water. The strong current and his exhausted body did not allow for a clean swim. The best he could do was drift along on his back for what felt like forever.

Paddling to the river's edge back on the Brooklyn side once the powerful flow subsided, Uli grabbed at a narrow ledge that couldn't have been more than five inches wide. He tried climbing onto it but slipped back into the water three times before he was able to edge up slowly. Reaching over a filthy drain pipe to the top of the retaining wall, he carefully hoisted himself up, flopping onto the paved shores of Brooklyn. Eventually catching his breath, he rose to his feet and stumbled sopping wet down a wide street until he came to a hand-painted signpost that read, *Atlantic Avenue*.

Shoeless, he hobbled up the boulevard for roughly twenty minutes, dripping a trail of water behind him, until he spotted the familiar dome of the Williamsburgh Savings Bank.

After another forty-five minutes of trekking, which somewhat dried his suit out, he reached Jackie Wilson Way, then turned left toward the grand bazaar of Downtown Brooklyn. He moved amid the slow schools of bargain hunters who, like aquatic bottom-feeders, scavenged back and forth amid endless purchases. In stockinged feet and feeling clammy all over, Uli shoved his way through the market crowd. He angled along sidewalks covered with food vendors toward the Fulton Street bus stop. Nervously locked in the crush and pull of urban shoppers, he momentarily forgot that he was trapped on a small isolated colony in the middle of a desert and simply thought, *I got to move out of here.*

Irregular shoes and shoe parts, most of them with laces knotted together into asymmetrical pairs, were heaped in large orange bins. Sorting through the tumble of footwear while being elbowed by other consumers, he located a pair of shoes that was approximately his size. The fact that they were blue suede and loose in the toes didn't matter. He paid a wet half-stamp and laced them on.

As Uli continued through the packed downtown streets, he realized they were actually narrower than even the sidewalks in other parts of Rescue City. The lanes squeezed people into tight spaces, where odors, chants, and a million little conversations were exchanged amid cacophonous music and blasting business bulletins.

We're safe, the entire environment seemed to hum. *No one can hurt all of us.*

Shoving through the crowd, Uli thoughtlessly counted the maimed and blind people he passed, both men and women. Perhaps they had been injured during the endless turf wars. Even if they had only suffered slight wounds, however, he figured their conditions must have been exacerbated by the poor medical care.

"Your fly's down!" some youth barked at him. Uli checked his zipper, only to find that it was secure.

"He's just snagging you," a female called through the crowd. Looking up, he saw it was Deere Flare, the sanctimonious campaigner. She was surrounded by others from Pure-ile Plurality, but instead of their official dark-blue suits they were wearing *PRO-LIFE!* T-shirts. He listened as they shouted angry political slogans through bullhorns while handing out *Reelect Shub* brochures.

Noticing his bruises and scuffs, Deere asked, "What the fuck happened to you?"

"I did something stupid and was chased. So I jumped into the river and they threw things at me."

"That was smart," she said. "These animals don't know how to swim or even want to know. Where did you go?"

"Near that Staten Island isthmus where the Wall Street skyscrapers are. Then some Spanish-speaking gang grabbed me, but they didn't hurt me, they just tossed me back in."

"You're a regular Huck Finn. You didn't swallow the water, did you?"

"A little, why?"

"Did you go in the Brooklyn or Manhattan side?"

"Brooklyn."

"That's still not great, but if you had gone in by Manhattan, you'd probably be dead by now," she said. "When the water loops around Manhattan, it's so backed up and polluted that people immediately come down with dysentery and cholera."

"I heard," Uli said, nervous about the strange taste in his mouth.

"I'm sorry about the other day. It was wrong of me to make an insane accusation like that."

"It's all right." Nodding toward the campaign brochures, he said, "I thought PP wasn't allowed to perform religious or political acts."

"We're not PP, we're DT."

"What's that?"

"Domination Theocracy. You'd like us, we're actually against the Piggers and feel that the party should be taken over by Pure-ile Plurality." She paused, then added, "The only reason I'm telling you this is 'cause someone said you share our values."

"Sure," he said in a daze.

"If you want to join us, we're having a strategy luncheon at the Queens Pigger headquarters in about half an hour. In fact, I've got to get going right now."

"Fine, where's the bus?"

"Bus?" she laughed, letting out an unintentional snort. "Buses are for Crappers."

15

W hile speeding north in a sporty new solicar driven by Deere
Flare, Uli knew something was off. For starters, she was being
utterly charming.

"Why are we heading this far north?"

"Because we're going to Rikers Island—the political action center," she said reasonably enough.

Uli hoped that seeing him bloodied and vulnerable, perhaps she
had found a tender spot in her heart and changed her mind about him.

She drove along what seemed to be the Brooklyn-Queens Expressway through Williamsburg and Greenpoint. As they approached Long
Island City, Uli noticed men on ladders with binoculars sitting along
the side of the road, inspecting cars as they slowly entered Queens.
He imagined it was some kind of Pigger border patrol. When they
exited the two-lane road and passed through the northeastern end
of Long Island City, Uli saw a distinct change. Unlike the slums and
abandoned stretches of northern Brooklyn or the overcrowded streets
of Manhattan, this place was cleaner and well zoned. People looked
better dressed. Instead of retro-supported structures originally built
for target practice, the houses here appeared to be new single-family
dwellings. Likewise, there were fewer projects and tenement buildings. Each home had either a red Pigger flag on the porch or the statue
of a saint on the front lawn, or both.

"You see it immediately, don't you?" Deere said. "The streets here are safer, cleaner."

"What about it?"

"This is the difference between pro-life and pro-choice. Piggers aren't trying to cut and run like Crappers. They've accepted that this is their life and they're going to make the best of it."

"All politics just comes down to housing assignments," Uli joked.

"What do you mean?"

"Somebody should do a study and see if everyone who got a nice place became a Pigger and everyone who wound up in one of the dumps in Brooklyn became a Crapper."

"A healthy percentage of folks originally assigned to places up here moved down there, and vice versa," Deere countered.

They turned left on Steinway Street and sped north onto a narrow causeway over a swamp and entered a small fortified island. Remembering suddenly that this site was a jail in old New York City, Uli felt a strange chill. He recalled lying on a table in a small room in JFK Airport here in Nevada, the sounds of cargo planes whirring in the background. A man with a shaggy head of white hair who looked like a schoolyard bully (Underwood?) was holding a small dog while staring down at him as two men wearing doctor masks did some kind of work on his cranium. ▮▮▮▮▮▮▮▮ *Walk to Sutphin, catch the Q28 to Fulton Str*▮▮▮▮▮ ▮▮▮▮▮▮▮▮▮▮▮▮▮▮▮▮ *317 and take it to the East Village in Manhattan, wait outside Cooper Union until Dropt arrives, shoot him once in the head, then grab a cab back to the airport . . .* He remembered the strange words being played over and over.

"Wait a fucking second!" Uli exclaimed as they sped past a sentry before the only entranceway.

"We're here," Deere announced, as a large goon dashed to Uli's side of the car, blocking his possible escape. Two familiar faces approached. One was the shaggy-haired bastard, still holding the small brown dog in his dainty little hands. The other was Chain, the murderous bus-jacker with the telescopic horn. The goon who helped Uli out of the car was one of the gangcops he had encountered with Chain last week in Borough Park.

"What's going on?" Uli asked calmly.

"This is the Domination Theocracy welcome committee," Deere said, getting out of the car, "and we're initiating you as a new member."

"Remember me?" the white-haired man asked in his high-pitched voice.

"You were the one who programmed me."

"You were assigned to assist me," the man said earnestly.

"You're Underwood, aren't you?"

"Yeah, and for the record, sorry about the whole brain-programming thing. Apparently we were supposed to take you as close to the target as possible before releasing you. Live and learn." He pet his little dog and added, "Now, Cirrus and I just want to talk to you about a certain missing person."

"Did you put something in my head?" Uli asked.

"Just a way to get you out of here."

"Come on inside," said the gangcop he recognized. "Let's talk about the missing girl."

Uli figured they were referring to the disappearance of Patricia Itt. Since they didn't even bother handcuffing him, Uli wasn't too worried. They walked him into the large Gothic building that looked like a small medieval castle, past a guard and down a flight of steps to the basement.

"How many teams do we have on Fulton Street?" Underwood asked.

"About three," Deere replied. "Where we really need more campaigners is Bed-Stuy. Polls show we're only about twenty points behind there. If we assemble some ground forces for a door-to-door, we should be able to close the gap."

"I'm not worried about Bed-Stuy," Chain said to her calmly. "J.J. Weltblack is the head of the polling center there."

"It don't matter," Underwood said.

"To hell with their big announcement!" Deere declared. "Shub will win this one just like all the others!"

"No, he won't," Underwood said to both of them, "and we don't want him to. We got a brand-new plan and it's a beaut."

"What's their big announcement?" Uli asked as they reached the bottom landing.

Chain and Deere glanced at each other, as though surprised that Uli understood English.

"Just that your old bus buddy is running," Chain said. "She fooled me in Borough Park, but she won't fool me again."

"Running from who?"

"Running *for* mayor."

"Who's my bus buddy?" Uli pressed.

"Former councilwoman Mallory is running in Dropt's place," Deere spelled out. "She's got exactly one more day to campaign. The election is tomorrow."

"Good news is she's way ahead in the polls," Underwood said, handing his little dog off to an assistant.

They all packed into a small, stuffy, windowless room in the basement. Uli felt strangely at ease in this tight space and focused on Underwood's Brussels griffon, specifically on a small wire running from the back of its neck to a tiny bulb on its collar. He recalled seeing it before.

"They say dogs can pick up on earthquakes and stuff before they happen," Underwood said in a friendly voice. "Some pointy-head figured that if they can tap into that part of the brain, they might be able to sense other dangers before they occur. So far, knock on wood, Cirrus's lightbulb hasn't gone off."

Chain switched on his prosthetic polygraphic horn. "Does it surprise you that Mallory's ahead in the polls?"

"No, I'm just amused."

"Why?"

"'Cause it's a lie. She was crushed to death."

"Which means that you know that *we* know that you were trying to locate her body," Chain said.

"I was trying to find *anyone*," Uli replied.

"Are you glad Mallory is running?" Deere asked with a smile.

"If she really is alive and running, sure, why not?"

"'Cause that's only half the news," Deere answered, and chuckled. "The half they broadcast." She looked at Chain and Underwood with a glorious grin.

"What's the other half?" Uli asked.

"Telling him won't make a difference," Chain said smugly.

"She mysteriously vanished from St. Vinny's Hospital the other day," Deere relished in telling.

"So I guess the Crappers will run someone else," Uli speculated.

"They got no one else with the same numbers in the polls," Underwood said. "Mallory was their only real shot."

"They're still running her even though she's missing?"

"That's right, only they haven't reported her as missing," Newton Underwood explained. "Which brings us to who *you* abducted."

"I turned my back for five minutes in the amusement park and she was gone. I looked all over for her."

"In the amusement park?" Underwood said.

"Oh, he's talking about little Patsy Nitwit," Deere chimed in.

"What did you do to Dianne Colder?" Chain asked.

"The blond lobbyist?"

"That's the one."

"Nothing, why?"

"We found her head hanging in East New York. Her hair was knotted around a street post."

"Oh God!" Uli gasped, trying to sound sincere.

"Tell us everything from the meeting I set up—when you first met her in Downtown Brooklyn—until you last saw her," Underwood said, taking a seat directly in front of Uli. Before he could respond, Chain muttered something and everyone abruptly exited, leaving Uli alone in the interrogation room.

He vaguely remembered going through difficult interrogations in the past—when *he* was the interrogator. From the point of view of the prisoner, interrogations involved giving a single story that checked out, and then sticking to it under constant pressure and terror and finally torture. But eventually everyone cracked, and everything spilled out—lies, truth, piss, shit, everything.

Ultimately it all depended on how they wanted to handle him. If they were simply trying to force out a confession, it was just a matter of torture. If they were looking for the truth, though, they'd have to be more crafty, meaning he would have half a chance.

The three soon reentered. Underwood took a seat facing Uli and once again asked him to start talking about the Colder woman upon first meeting her.

"She offered to help me assassinate Dropt in the Lower East Side, but she got sidetracked," he recounted.

"By what?" Deere asked.

"She saw a retarded man named Oric who she felt was some kind of agent."

"The half-wit from the bus?" Chain said.

"Yeah."

"And I saw you with him at the Shub rally," Deere interjected.

"I got to know him on the ride from JFK and we were heading in the same direction, but we weren't together."

"Go on."

"Colder thought the guy could be a possible asset," Uli said.

"Why?"

"I'm not sure."

"Why do you think?" Chain thrust his polygraphic scope in Uli's face.

"She heard him say something that made her think he knew something about something, but I don't know what."

"Think you might remember if I remind you?" Chain asked, almost tenderly.

"I might."

"Did she say anything about the mission being in jeopardy?"

"You mean my mission to kill Dropt?"

"*Any* mission."

"As you probably remember, since you caused it, I have a memory problem. I don't even know my own name."

"What exactly do you remember?"

Uli was convinced that if Underwood knew he and Oric had eluded Colder by jumping out the bus window upon reaching Manhattan, they would be torturing him right now. So he proceeded with the assumption that they didn't know.

"I told her that I thought we should stay on track with the assassination," Uli said. "But Colder insisted that we had to abduct the retarded man."

"How?"

"We said we were going to take him to get some cake."

"Where?"

"Some pastry shop in the East Village. He had the mind of a child."

"Then what?"

"I sat with him while she called someone."

"Who?"

"I don't know."

"What was the name of the pastry shop?" Chain asked.

"I don't remember, some Italian name. He had a slice of chocolate cake."

"Then what?"

"Roughly an hour later, some guy showed up. We put the retarded man in a car and drove him down to some pig farm in northern Staten Island."

"What happened there?"

"I didn't think what was going to happen would happen."

"What happened?"

"She tortured that poor retard for hours."

"If you didn't want to help her, why did you?"

"'Cause of you," Uli said, talking directly to Underwood.

"What about me?"

"She said you worked for her and were a liar, that you had no way out of this hellhole or you would've taken it long ago. But she said if I did as she told me, she'd help me eliminate Dropt and then get me out of here herself."

"That sounds like Dianne," Chain grinned. "If she needed someone, she'd snap him right up."

"What exactly did she get out of the retard?" Underwood asked.

"No clue," Uli replied stiffly. To his surprise, Underwood whipped him across the face with some kind of hard plastic cord. When Uli lurched forward, Chain grabbed his hands.

"What did the retard say?"

"Conversation's over."

"Hell it is," said Underwood.

"You people are government officials and I have rights."

"All rights were suspended when you boarded the drone. Now what'd the retard say?"

"I don't fucking know!" Uli shouted.

"Cuff his hands," Underwood said. Chain and the other gangcop each pulled an arm behind the chair and slipped his wrists through hard plastic loops connected by a narrow band.

Uli heard the clicking of notches as it closed into the catch lock. When he struggled to get to his feet, they fastened white bands of plastic around each of his ankles, securing them to the front legs of his chair.

"Get the fuck off of me!"

The weapon in Underwood's hand turned out to be an extension cord with a plug on one side and two copper wires on the other.

"You're smart," Underwood said, as he plugged the cord into a socket and held the two wires apart. "There was a reason she was torturing the retard and I want to know what it was!"

Deere ripped open his shirt and Chain splashed a small paper cup of water on him. Underwood pressed the wires to his bare chest. The shock of electricity running through his body felt like a mashing and burning around his lungs and heart. Underwood quickly withdrew the wires.

"Okay!" Uli groaned. "I know! I know what it was!" He took a deep breath, but before he could say anything, Underwood pressed the two wire ends to his cheeks, causing him to writhe in anguish. "A seer!" he shrieked. Underwood removed the wires. "A Crapper seer, she called him."

All gasped.

"What else!"

"She intercepted him before he could get to the Crapper head-quarters."

"If he was a seer, why was he traveling alone?" Deere asked.

"He wasn't alone!" Uli shouted to Chain. "He belonged to that couple you hung in Borough Park."

"What's this?" Underwood asked Chain.

"The two Crappers I caught on the bus. One of them who called himself Chad had a rifle lodged inside a metal detector and a bucket of old bullets. I left Chad and his wife hanging out there."

"How the fuck did two know-nothing Crappers acquire a god-damned seer?" Underwood asked Uli.

"How the hell would I know?"

"Rogue NSAers?" muttered Chain.

"Actually, she might be FBI," Underwood speculated.

"FBI?" Uli asked.

"This place is overagented."

"We really should be torturing Scouter about this," Chain sighed.

"Who?" Uli asked.

"Fucking Scouter!" Underwood answered angrily. "Which brings us back to you!"

Again Underwood jabbed the charged copper wires against Uli's bare chest. The muscles in his body cramped all at once. The electricity seemed to reshape time itself, turning it into a vortex of excruciating pain. When the man pulled the wires back, Uli gasped for air. Every cell in his body hurt. Before the sadistic son of a bitch could reelectrocute him, Uli blurted, "He had a metal cross sticking out the back of his skull."

"A brain cuff," Chain said.

"That explains his retardation," Deere added, "but it doesn't explain his gifts."

As though Uli were a broken information machine, Chain grabbed the wires to fix him with another jolt.

"He was a twin! His twin was chasing us!"

"A twin?" Underwood said. "Sounds like our agents were able to secure an experiment. What happened to this twin?"

"He got blown up at Rock & Filler Center," Uli said, trying to catch his breath.

"So much for grabbing any assets," Deere said under her breath.

"Okay, now listen up," Underwood commanded, bringing his own sweaty face within inches of Uli's. "You're going to tell me exactly what that retard said. What predictions did he make?"

"Gibberish," Uli replied sternly. "He talked gibberish."

"I will fry your balls until smoke is coming out of your asshole."

"I really don't know!" Staring terrified at the copper wires, Uli tried to maintain steady breaths. "He kept saying *big bang boom* or some shit. I think he knew that the Manhattan Crapper headquarters was going to get blown up."

"What else?"

"That was it."

"We both know he said something else," Underwood seethed. "And you're going to fucking tell me what it is!"

Deere reached down and started undoing the buckle of Uli's belt. She tore his pants open, ripping the zipper down the middle. As the young sadist fumbled in his underpants, Uli yanked forward, trying to rise out of the chair. "Karove! They're going to shoot someone named Karove!" he screamed.

"I knew it!" Underwood shot back. Apparently, Uli's fabrication was exactly what he had been hoping to hear.

"Let's get rid of him," Deere said.

"We can't do that," Chain said.

"Move him to the Bronx Zoo," Underwood said. "Polly the People Eater will take care of him."

Chain dashed out of the little room.

"What else?" Deere asked, visibly disappointed.

"That's all I remember, I swear it. He died after that."

"What happened to Dianne after she killed retardo?" Underwood asked.

"We drove to Manhattan to finish the primary mission."

"Okay, now a trick question. What was the name of the Pigger worker who picked you up at the pastry shop and drove you down to Staten Island?"

"Don't remember." Uli started hyperventilating.

"What kind of car did he drive?"

"Some sporty car."

"What did he do then?"

"He drove us down to the pig farm and left."

"He drove away?"

"I guess." Uli felt utterly frazzled.

"If he drove away, how the fuck did you and Colder get to the Lower East Side?"

"I told you, in his sports car."

"But you just said he drove away!"

"I meant he *went* away. I don't know where. For all I know, he lived within walking distance. What does it matter?"

"We found him dead in the Calypso Pig Farm where you just said he left you!" Underwood shouted spittingly.

"That had to have happened after we left," Uli responded.

Underwood stormed out of the small interrogation room, leaving Uli alone with the cruel campaigner.

"Who killed him?" Deere asked, eager to take charge of the interview.

"No clue," Uli answered, collapsing back in his chair.

Deere grabbed the electrical wires. "I owe you this for Siftwelt."

"HELP!"

She slipped the needle-sharp wires through his underwear and jabbed them into the soft base of his testicles. An unbelievably searing pain coursed through the most sensitive part of his body, shooting up his thighs and midsection. Uli tried struggling back. With a fixed grin, Deere held the wires pressed to his gonads, sending more volts through him. He attempted to focus on some tiny point deep inside himself, but he couldn't get a fix. He found himself silently, manically counting to ten over and over, as though he were forcing time to move faster. But the pain intensified beyond levels he thought humanly possible. He could actually feel his flesh cooking, frying from pink to brown.

16

As soon as he blacked out, his eyes popped open elsewhere. He seemed to be in some large barren field surrounded by sandy hills. At first he thought he spotted the young Armenian mother, but then realized he was mistaken. Strangers were standing around. His heart was beating frantically; something exciting had just happened, but he didn't know what. He couldn't hear a thing. Suddenly, coming down a sandy slope before him was Bea in all her muscular beauty. She was smiling at him. He saw blood on her shirt, but he knew it wasn't hers. As she approached, he watched in slow motion as the front of her skull erupted, spraying her blood, bone, and brains into his face.

"No!" he cried.

Someone tossed a cup of water on his face, waking him to the smell of his own sizzled skin. He was still strapped to the wooden chair, but Underwood and Chain had returned and pulled Deere off of him.

"Where exactly is Colder's apartment located?" The Pigger leader had to ask the question several times before it sunk in.

"Fourth . . . and . . . First." Uli was barely able to get the words out. The pain was perfectly balanced with exhaustion.

"That's right. She liked the Class-A Lady on First," said Chain dolefully.

The burns on his scrotum and mesoderm felt like red-hot nails had been driven up through his peritoneum. But he sensed the worst was over.

"What happened there?" Underwood pressed.

Though Uli's mouth moved, nothing came out. He had pissed his pants. The surging agony made it difficult for him to breathe, let alone speak.

"Croak him up," Chain said.

A few minutes passed before a gangcop assistant produced a syringe and injected the drug into Uli's bound arm. As the glowing numbness spread, Uli passed out in joy. Another moment and he was wide awake again.

"What happened when you got to her place?" Underwood repeated.

"She went upstairs and came back down a few minutes later. Then I left her to use her bathroom and she waited in the car. When I came out, she and the car were gone."

"How long were you up there?"

"Five minutes tops."

"Why didn't you report it?" Chain asked.

"I did. I called 911 and got a recording."

"It's true," Deere chuckled. "The Crapper gangcops have a recorded announcement for 911 now."

"So the hotel clerk saw both of you together?"

"Yeah, but the guy who stole the car and kidnapped Colder killed him."

"Bullshit—you killed him and you killed her!" Underwood shouted back viciously. "You killed her and chopped off her head."

"All I've ever wanted since I got into this toilet was to leave. And she offered me a way out. I sure as hell wouldn't have killed her until after I got out of here. Keeping her safe was more important to me than to any of you." A moment of silence convinced Uli that his attempt at sincerity had stuck.

"So what'd you do next?" Chain asked.

"I thought maybe she'd gone to the Manhattan headquarters to do the job herself, so I headed over there."

"But—"

"Just as I got there, the place was blown up."

"So why didn't you return to me like you were programmed to?" Underwood asked earnestly.

"Because I had a hunch that you might do to me then what you're doing to me now."

"What'd you say to Adolphus Rafique?" Underwood asked, surprising Uli. They seemed to know almost all his movements.

"Where would I have seen Rafique?"'

"In Staten Island. You went down there after the Crapper headquarters was blown to smithereens."

"Says who?" Uli shot back.

"Says me!" yelled Deere, who had been silently basking in the sight and fumes of her work.

"She's crazy," Uli said.

"You caught me and you didn't even know it," Deere countered.

"What are you talking about?"

"I saw you sticking around afterward, digging clams out of that Crapper mud pile. When you were done, you got on the bus to Staten Island. The next day, when you got to PP, I greeted you." Deere went dead silent. A moment later she resumed, "Hell, we talked to each other when you arrived at PP."

"So what happened?" Underwood asked. "What turned you around and made you head down to Shit Island?"

Uli realized he had to switch course. "After I saw that couple get strung up out in Borough Park and their retarded son get eaten alive, only to show up at the Crapper headquarters just as it was blown to bits, do you know how much carnage I've witnessed? I spent hours digging bodies out of that wreck. Then I heard that there was an alternative to living between two warring gangs—a third group that just wanted to be left alone in Staten Island—so I went down there and discovered that they are a bunch of delusional savages who think they're Indians and elected a pig as their leader." He took a deep breath. "You're all too stupid to realize that you're captives here, and instead of joining together to escape, you fight each other and you are all going to die here."

"Pal," Chain replied sternly, "the reason we don't leave is because we are men of honor. And men of honor honor their contract."

When Uli rolled his eyes, Underwood let out a big guffaw. Chain did as well.

"Can't you just let me go?" Uli asked, changing the subject and trying to warm up his captors. "After all, I'm minding my own business just working at PP."

"And we'd be content to leave you there," Underwood said. "The only problem is, we have an informant who claims that you ditched Colder and were trying to bring the retard to Crapper headquarters yourself."

"That's completely absurd." This was the piece of the puzzle Uli feared would come out.

"Here's what we're going to do," Underwood said. "We're going to hold you until our informant gets here. If the informant says they've never seen you before, we'll put you back on a drone and get you out of here."

"Fair enough," Uli said, not at all believing him.

"Before leaving you alone, though, we're going to need your personal effects so you don't kill yourself," Deere said.

"You mean like my deep-fried balls?"

"Your belt," she said, yanking it off his pants.

In another moment, Uli was lifted to his feet, and he had to hold up the rear of his pants. They led him out of the interrogation room, down a hallway, and into a dark concrete holding cell. Chain kicked Uli hard behind the knees, sending him to the ground, then locked the large metallic door behind him.

With his wrists still cuffed together behind his back, Uli could barely move. The croak was thinning in his system and the pain from the electrocution and other injuries was returning with a vengeance. Once again, he passed out.

███████ *"What she's doing is crazy!" a male was* ████. *He seemed to be listening in on a phone conversation, tapping the call. "She's going to get herself arrested!"* ██████████████████████████████

"She's well within her rights," a female voice responded. ████████

"You're her mother! Do you real████████ *her ruin her life?"*

"You're being over████████*," the woman replie*█████████

"I'm begging you before it's to█████████████

He awoke to see the heavy door swinging open. A short girlish figure stepped forward from behind a wall of lights. He squinted and made out the cute rock-and-roll deejay he had met on the bus—the hurricane evacuee, Kennesy.

"They got you too?"

"No, silly, I got *you*." She closed the door on him before he could struggle to his feet.

Ten minutes later, he heard the bolt slide to one side and the heavy door swung open once more. Chain, Newton Underwood, and three other goons were there to collect him.

"Good news: your transfer just came through." Underwood held a form in one hand and his little dog in the other. "You're going back to Washington."

Chain, who now had a large pistol in a holster, reached down, grabbed Uli by his cuffed elbows, and lifted him to his feet. As they led him upstairs, every muscle and bone in his body ached. He could barely walk.

"Can I get more of that painkiller?"

"You're going to get the ultimate painkiller soon," Chain replied.

Once he got outside, though, Uli felt heartened just seeing the sun. It was difficult to believe that there was only one sun and that this exact same fiery ball was shining upon the real New York City.

"This is it, isn't it?" Uli asked, squinting. "You're going to kill me."

"Well, Very Special Officer Who-wee, life is just too intelligently designed for me to believe that this is all," Underwood waxed philosophical. "I like to think that the great engineer in the sky finally brings us home for a much greater purpose."

"Or, if you prefer," Chain added softly, "you're the great-grandson of a chimp and you're about to go from being to nothingness." One of the other goons chuckled.

The narrow bands of the plastic cuff dug into Uli's wrists, cutting off his circulation, as they walked him to a nearby truck. Chain and his giant assistant got in the back and Underwood sat in the driver's seat, setting his little dog in his lap. Uli was deposited next to him, with his hands still cuffed tightly behind his back.

To relieve his wrist pain he kept jerking forward in his seat. While they sped along, he noticed something flickering in the distance. It was a relatively thin building that couldn't have been more than four stories high, but it was strangely shimmering and had a sharp point at the top. A portrait of a tall armless man in a diaper adorned the front of the structure.

"What the hell?" Uli whispered as if seeing something divine.

"The Jesus Chrystler Building," Chain said. "Loosely based on the old Chrysler Building."

"How'd they get Jesus on it?" The savior looked elegantly deco.

"They can put Jesus on anything nowadays."

"Shouldn't that building be in Manhattan?"

"Yeah, but they already had this pointy little thing out here," Underwood said, almost kindly. "It was actually a radio tower that was partially destroyed during a gang fight, so some Christian developer took it over . . . Oh God, looky!" he chirped, despite the fact that he was driving, "the little red lightbulb on Cirrus's collar just flipped on—"

A heavy, older-model truck cut in front of them, forcing their vehicle off the road. Chain pulled the huge pistol out of his holster. As Underwood fumbled to get the truck started again, the first arrow shattered the side window, just missing Underwood's thick neck.

"Shit! We're under attack!"

Chain and his assistant popped open their doors. A three-pronged frog spear was immediately thrust into the younger gangcop's face. He seized the weapon, but before he could turn it back on his attacker, Chain accidentally squeezed the trigger of his pistol and blew off the back of the young cop's skull.

"Shit!" Chain groaned.

"Back in the truck!" Underwood shouted, finally getting the vehicle into reverse.

Pulling his door shut, Chain accidentally squeezed off a second round. It tore through the seat in front of him, lodging firmly into the city council president's back.

"You . . . moron!" Underwood gurgled out, grabbing his chest.

"Shit!" Chain groaned again. He opened the driver's door and tugged Underwood out of his seat, dropping him to the ground.

Uli took a deep gulp of air and swung his legs over the stick shift. As Chain flopped himself into the driver's seat, Uli kicked the man right in his telescopic horn. It cracked off, and Chain fell to the ground on top of Underwood. Before the gangcop leader could rise, a shaggy-haired assassin stabbed him in the back, then again in the side. Chain tried to crawl away on all fours, but the assassin continued jabbing the knife into him.

"WAIT! Don't kill him!" Uli shouted. "He knows where they're holding Mallory!"

Underwood's little dog huddled next to his dead master, cowering in fear. The assassin placed his bloody blade against Uli's throat and was joined by a second man, at which point Uli recognized who they were. It was Bernstein and Woodward, the two men he had pulled from the wreckage of the Manhattan Crapper headquarters.

"Hold on!" he begged. "I was the one who rescued you guys."

"Let's see the hands."

"I can't!" Uli bent forward.

"He's handcuffed," Woodward confirmed.

"What the hell are you doing with these Domination monsters?" Woodward asked.

"They kidnapped me. They were going to kill me."

Bernstein pulled out a knife and cut off Uli's plastic handcuffs.

"My heart!" Chain screamed, rolling around in a growing pool of blood. He grabbed his chest, which, ironically, seemed to be the only part of his body not stabbed.

"Where are they holding Mallory?" Uli asked him.

No response.

Bernstein grabbed the long, sharp chain dangling around the gangcop's neck and wrapped it twice around his thick throat. Then, flipping the sadist onto his belly, Woodward yanked the chain around his knees and ankles.

"She's . . . in Manhattan." He gasped for breath as the chain dug into the soft turkey gobbler of his neck. "Please, let me go—"

"Where in Manhattan?" Woodward demanded.

"Evil! Evil—" He gagged and soon throttled himself with his own chain.

The three men jumped into the old truck and pulled away. Bernstein explained, "Someone in Rikers informed us that they were holding an important Crapper prisoner. We were hoping it might be Mallory."

"Who told you that?"

"We don't reveal our sources," Woodward said, slipping on a visored hat so that he looked like an employee of a trucking company.

Wincing in agony from his recent torture, Uli asked if either of them had any painkillers.

"Actually, I just got some great choke," Bernstein said, pulling out a cellophane baggie. He also produced a small pipe, and soon Uli was deeply inhaling as much of the cannabis as he could. Within minutes, his pain became manageable.

As they drove through the clean streets of Queens, there was no sign of warfare. They could've been in Queens, New York.

"It's difficult to believe a place like this exists in America," Uli blurted.

"It started out as a wonderful thing, truly compassionate, with the very best of intentions, and then . . ." Woodward paused. "Well, we came here with the first detainees."

"Why were you detained?" Uli asked, trying to get his mind off his stinging genitals.

"Back in '72 we were covering a hot story," Woodward explained. "A burglary at the Watergate complex in Washington. Some of the criminals had ties to the CIA."

Uli vaguely remembered the incident.

"It wasn't until we started reporting on an unnamed source inside the White House that we got in trouble. Attorney General John Mitchell wanted a name," Bernstein said.

"Did Mitchell threaten to arrest you?" Uli had a strange sense that he had met this attorney general. In fact, he felt he had known the man quite well.

"No. In fact, he invited us to dinner with Martha," Woodward said. "We consulted our editor and publisher, who backed us a hundred percent. We thought we were safe 'cause Edgar Hoover had just died."

"But in the middle of the night we were awakened by knocks on our doors."

"Then what?"

"We were told that we were going to be questioned. They gave us some coffee, and the next thing I know I'm passing out."

"Me too," said Bernstein. "We woke up on one of those god-damned supply drones landing here. That was eight years ago."

"Why didn't you just stay on the plane?"

"They don't take off until they're empty. And only when they take off does the next one land. Besides, we had no idea what was going on. This entire country is in a state of denial," concluded Bernstein sadly. "To this day, I still wonder if my wife knows what happened. I have this awful fear that she thinks I ran off with another woman."

"Maybe that's what happened to me."

"They put the whole counterculture here," Woodward said.

"Were you investigating the war in some way?" Bernstein asked.

"I don't really know, I've been having memory problems." Uli didn't think he had been a reporter, or even opposed the government. "When exactly did the war start?"

"The Democrats started it slowly under Kennedy. Johnson esca-lated it. Then the antiwar movement kicked in and Nixon claimed the peaceniks were preventing the US from winning, so after New York got hit, they tied the movement to domestic terrorists and a lot of the leaders were rounded up and sent here."

"When did the war end?" Uli asked.

"It hasn't," Bernstein said. "As of two months ago, based on radio reports we've managed to pick up, over a quarter-million Americans have been killed—"

"You know what just occurred to me?" Woodward interrupted. "She could be in the East Village."

"Who?" Bernstein asked.

"Mallory."

"Why do you say that?" Uli asked.

"That Chain guy's last words."

"He called us evil," Bernstein said.

"No, we asked him where they were holding Mallory and he said *Evil*, which is an old Pigger term for the East Village."

17

After the sun had set, their old truck rolled into Downtown Brooklyn, where it immediately got stuck in bumper-to-bumper traffic. The crowd of pathological shoppers were fumbling through the latest tawdry products piled in the blue sales troughs along the sidewalk: plastic belts, unmatched flip-flops, rubbery wallets, broken flashlights, hazardous children's toys, missing pieces from board games, carcinogenic paint sets, lenseless reading glasses, dented cans of unlabeled food, half-crushed boxes of pasta, aerosol cans without spray tops, nonbiodegradable cleansing solutions, and so on. All selling for peanuts.

"What you're seeing is one of the greatest feats of Pigger ingenuity," Woodward said. "This place started out as a fully subsidized pantry of free items. By referendum, the Piggers were able to convince the majority of people here to auction off these supplies, thereby switching the system over from a charitable service to a free-market economy."

"Why?"

"They claim it's all taxed to operate the city government," Bernstein said. "But now the Pigger Party and the city government are essentially one and the same."

"Subsequently, the Piggers always have the largest war chests during election times."

"Ninety-four percent of the time the candidates with the bigger budgets win."

The engine of their truck suddenly stopped humming, and they came to a silent halt.

"Shit," Bernstein muttered, "we're out."

"Out of what?" Uli asked. Horns behind them instantly blared.

"Electricity," Woodward said. "The sun set an hour ago. We've got to run a cord to an outlet and recharge for the night."

"You better scat," Bernstein said to Uli as they got out to push.

Bernstein steered, as the other two pushed.

"We still have to find Mallory," said Uli.

"Hey! We got rid of Underwood and Chain."

"Yeah, that's it for us," said Bernstein. "We're supposed to *report* the news, not make it."

"Poor Mallory's probably dead," Woodward said. "And all those Piggers at Rikers Island know your face. Once they realize you're not dead with the others, you're going to be public enemy number one."

"Your best bet is to head down to Stink Island if you can. You can camp out in the desert. Bring a warm sleeping bag. 'Cause if you light a fire, they'll spot you."

The two men gave Uli ten stamps, all they could spare. Uli thanked them for the money and advice and helped them push their truck down a side street to a small clothing shop. A proprietor they knew allowed them to plug in their extension cord for a recharge at the discounted price of two stamps.

The reporters headed south toward Park Slope and Uli turned west to where Deere Flare had been politicking earlier, near the corner of Jackie Wilson Way and Jay Street.

Her coven of campaigners was gone. As Uli passed through the late-night throngs of consumers at the grand bazaar, he saw trucks unloading a wealth of new items. The Piggers had obviously privatized the economy for more than just the revenue to run the city. When an economy was doing well, constituents usually elected the incumbent party. By dumping cheap items on the eve of an election, the government could simulate boom conditions and get itself reelected.

Uli's only chance of not getting caught, he realized, was by radically altering his appearance. Goin Outa Biznez, a popular clothing franchise that he had seen scattered throughout Rescue City, had a line of green army surplus jackets hanging from a drop gate. Uli picked one that fit loosely and selected a flannel shirt with a flower pattern, along with a tight pair of canary-yellow bell-bottoms.

About a block away, he passed a young woman wearing a T-shirt with the apt remark, *Quit Honking—You Ain't Gettin' There No Faster*. She was selling a large box of curly black wigs. Uli pulled one over his PP crew cut and paid her.

He spotted a colorful diner near Jay Street called JR's. Inside, the food line was shorter than the line for the bathroom. Pushing to the rear, he calculated that at the ambitious rate of two minutes per person, it would take twenty minutes to get to a toilet stall.

Forty-five minutes later, Uli found himself in the filthiest, smelliest restroom he had encountered in Rescue City. With little arm and leg room, he stripped off his torn and wrinkled Pure-ile Plurality suit, shoved it in the garbage can, and pulled on his new floral shirt and flared yellow pants. The fact that he hadn't shaved in a few days accented his hippie look.

Someone started banging on the flimsy plywood door. "Hey! We gotta shit too!"

When he opened the door, he saw that the line of bowel-laden, bladder-heavy people had practically doubled. Some burly fellow screamed at him about getting high in the john, which convinced him that the hippie disguise was working.

Uli walked the few blocks to the Fulton Street bus depot. Strangely, the only person there was an older man in an official uniform, precariously balanced on a wooden milk carton, snoring loudly. Uli noticed the wording on his visored cap: *Today's Bus Info*.

"Do you know what time the Lower East Side bus comes?" Uli asked softly.

The man jolted awake. "Bus service had been suspended for the rest of the evening due to the coming storm."

"How the hell am I supposed to get home?"

"Shoulda thought of that before you became a freakin' hippie."

Uli sighed aloud.

"Take a freakin cab," the scheduler suggested.

"I don't have enough stamps."

"Where you going, Crazy Fag Island?"

"No, Manhattan."

"Oh, that dumb-ass hippie festival," the guy replied.

"What dumb-ass festival?"

"That Foul Festival celebrating the Day of the Dead. I'd shake my LSD if I were you, boy. When the sky breaks, it's going to come down like the Hoover Dam and wash you hippies clean."

Despite the foreboding clouds and the empty bus stop, the streets were still filled with people. Uli heard a bullhorn shouting deals: *"Big storm a-coming, folks, and we got nowhere to put it all, so these are end-of-the-world sales . . ."*

Feeling irritable as the choke began wearing off and the stinging in his seared scrotum worsened, Uli glanced up and observed the clouds and sky growing phosphorus one moment and mustard-colored the next. People were shopping frantically. The winds began rising. That was when he spotted the first *MALLORY FOR MAYOR* poster. It looked like it had just been put up and the storm had already pulled it partially loose. He lumbered over to a soda vendor who advertised a greenish drink called Bolt! that looked like antifreeze.

"How much?"

"A sixteenth," the vendor said.

Uli handed him the denomination and got a tiny chilled bottle. It tasted pleasantly minty, so he gulped it down and bought a second bottle.

"Don't drink too much of the root or you'll get the jitters," the merchant cautioned.

As Uli gulped it down, some bastard deliberately knocked into him, causing him to spill half the bottle on the ground. It was a member of a gang walking in tight formation through the crowd. People quickly parted for them.

Pigger gangcops must be out looking for me, he thought tensely. *Shit! They must've discovered the bodies of Underwood and Chain!*

Not aware that Bolt! was a carbonated antihistamine, Uli broke out into a feverish sweat and decided it was entirely up to him to warn the masses that the gang from the northern boroughs—who had just assassinated their candidate—had also grabbed their replacement candidate.

"The Piggers kidnapped Mallory!" he shouted into the wind. "They are stealing your election and we must fight them! Fight them in the streets, fight them in the river, fight them in the desert!" He borrowed liberally and unknowingly from Churchill, but no one reacted.

He opened his arms and grabbed a passerby. "Don't you see? The terrorist attack on Manhattan was just part of their plan! That's how they were able to put us here and gain control in the first place!" He started trembling. In a moment he fainted.

██████████████████████ *Walk to Sutphin, change to the* ██████████
██

Uli woke moments later gagging, unable to breathe or see a thing. The rain hadn't commenced, but a violent sandstorm was in full force. Leaflets were scattered everywhere. The world was a brown snow globe being shaken by a madman.

Through granular waves, Uli stumbled along with outstretched arms and fingers. A random sequence of metal gates slammed down far and near. Unable to keep his eyes open, he pulled his shirt up over his mouth so he could breathe and hobbled forth . . . Bumping into something, he fell down . . . Crawling on his knees, he was able to feel cheap merchandise that had been cast off . . . toys, appliances, clothing . . . He felt a pair of glasses, which he slipped into his pocket. Rising slowly, tripping again, bumping blindly into others bumping into him . . . the entire time hearing the sounds of negotiation . . . voices still making lowball offers . . . *"Take it for whatever's in yer pocket"* . . . Counteroffers were ping-ponged back, stormproof haggling . . . Others frantically crisscrossed like beetles, knocking over sales bins and each other . . .

A tremendous explosion blasted a hundred feet before him . . . An orange fireball under an amber veil of sand, then blackness. *"All sales are final."* Gagging, coughing through the thick burning smoke. Screams. Shouts . . . *"A car bomb sale!"* . . . Sirens. People dashing around him in panic . . . crying for others . . . *"Final sale before dying"* . . . *"Oh my God! Help me! . . . My leg! I don't have no leg!"* . . . *"Meerkat! Meerkat! What did I do? Why'd you go?!"* . . . *"Sixteen for a sixteenth-stamp!"* . . . He could hear objects crunching under endless feet . . .

Uli moved away from the blast site and sales . . . downhill into the grainy darkness . . . Looking up through the black smoke and sand, he made out the geometric rooftops of mini warehouses . . . just north of Brooklyn Heights . . . The storm simmered down just long enough for him to make out one of the narrow suspension towers . . . The overpass to Manhattan was several blocks away . . . much smaller than the original Brooklyn Bridge. Faux webbing connected to a thick cable reached upward to the top of the two stone towers. The wind kicked up again, forcing Uli to close his eyes . . . Breathing through the thin fabric of his new floral shirt, he moved blindly toward Manhattan while grazing his open palm along the railing.

When he was halfway across the waterway, the wind tapered again and he found himself facing a blockade in the center of the bridge. A group of blue-shirted men were stopping cars going in both directions, checking their trunks.

"Hands up," a uniformed guard wearing swimming goggles ordered. "We have to frisk you."

"Why?" Uli asked, as they patted him down. Without explanation, they allowed him to continue into Manhattan.

Unlike the vehicular exit he had taken with Oric, the Brooklyn Bridge walkway descended onto 14th Street farther east, at Avenue B. Uli proceeded westward, the howling winds deafening once again. The sand was now so thick he couldn't see his hand in front of his face.

Ten minutes after getting off the bridge, with the storm still raging, Uli walked smack into a building. Groping around blindly, he located a door and tried the knob—no luck. With his eyes tightly shut, he continued down the sidewalk, feeling for other doors, grabbing and turning knobs, one after the next, to no avail. After moving a couple of blocks south, he stumbled several long blocks west. He finally found his way into a courtyard, where he tried the knob of a large majestic door. It opened and Uli toppled in, quickly shoving the door shut behind him. He was in the rear of a large church. At least a hundred young people sitting quietly in rows of pews turned around to see him—reminding him that he was a fugitive.

"Sorry," he said, pulling his wig on straight. The glasses he had grabbed off the ground in Brooklyn turned out to be sunglasses, so he slipped them on too. A young red-haired man standing at a podium in the front of the room returned to a poem he was in the middle of reading: "*Having just won the nomination of his fringe party / the well-meaning candidate celebrated over an unpopular brand of herbal tea . . .*"

"Quarter-stamp admission," whispered a striking young woman with bells on her wrists and a reindeer tattoo on her shoulder. She pointed to a handmade sign that said, *Quarter-Stamp Admission.*

"What exactly is this?"

"Karl Marx Brothers Church of Political Poetical Potency."

"Is it a funeral?"

"No, the Foul Festival poetry reading."

"Is this really a celebration of the Day of the Dead?" He thought maybe the cynical bus dispatcher in Brooklyn had been kidding.

"We used to celebrate Halloween, but the Piggers accused us of Satan worship, so we moved it to All Souls' Day, which is both a Catholic and pagan holiday."

"Wasn't that yesterday?"

"Yeah, but the celebration permit just came through today." The belled beauty handed Uli a mimeographed map of the area, complete with dots showing where various artistic, theatrical, and musical happenings were taking place.

"*Zoning madness, irrational parking regulations / unscheduled bulk trash collections,*" he heard the poet rant. "*Do pigs roll in crap, or the other way around? / Soon he, she height, brings us all the way, down, down . . .*"

"Do you have anything to drink or eat?" Uli asked softly, surrendering his quarter-stamp.

The bell-jiggling lady meekly inked the back of his hand with a chicken-foot peace sign. "You're in luck," she said, pointing to a table several feet away "There's a cactus soufflé that, like the poet who made it, was unfairly neglected."

"What time does this end?" he asked, hungrily inspecting various dishes on the tabletop.

"It's an all-night marathon," she said, as another poet moved to the podium.

While the new poet read more civic-minded verses, Uli gobbled up the last squares of casserole. He gulped down several cups of bitter cactus tea until he felt bloated. Almost immediately, though, he started feeling queasy and needed to sit down. The only available seat was in the front row.

"I'm sure our next reader requires no introduction," the woman with the bells introduced. "Along with Gregory Corso and Jack Kerouac, he is one of the founders of the Beat movement. When he came here, he felt bumped out of life, so he now refers to himself as founder of a new movement—the Bump poets. I have the privilege of introducing Allen Ginsberg."

In a show of appreciation, everyone in the audience bumped their feet against the wooden floor.

"Happy belated Day of the Dead, I hope you all remember to vote tomorrow." The poet commenced reading his latest work, "Foul": "*I smelled the worst farts of my age and wondered, what do these pigs eat? / But then I remember that crap smells like perfume to none but the Crapper . . .*"

Uli brought his hands to his face. The cactus was returning with a vengeance. "Where's the bathroom?" he nervously asked the poetry aficionado sitting next to him.

"There." The youth pointed to a door behind the podium.

Uli rose to his feet and staggered three short steps toward the center aisle before he felt his entire midsection clench up. A projectile of bright-green vomit shot out of him onto the poet's beard and chest.

"Oh my God!" yelled the emcee. A neo-Victorian free-associator who thought she was witnessing a violent act tackled Uli as he was still heaving.

"Leave him alone!" Ginsberg shouted sympathetically. "The poor bastard's sick."

After a minute of regurgitating tremors, Uli finally regained gastrointestinal control. He rose, wiped his chin, and explained that he had just filled himself up at the food table.

"Take it easy, son," Ginsberg said, wiping the vomit off his own shirt. "That cactus dish was sitting in the sun way too long."

"I'll be glad to pay for the dry cleaning," Uli offered.

"It's okay," Ginsberg said, then added, "I was meaning to buy a second shirt anyway."

Most of the people had returned to their seats but were still chattering anxiously as two volunteers hastily mopped up the puke.

After a few more minutes of fidgeting from the crowd, the bell-wristed woman approached Uli with her middle and index fingers V-ing upward. "Peace, bro."

"I'm really embarrassed about all this."

"Listen, I know this sounds really uncool," she said in a whisper, "but if I refund your admission, would you mind leaving quietly?"

"But—"

"The thing is, until you're gone, it's going to be difficult for us to regain our peaceful poetical center."

Uli saw her point, but he explained that he, too, was in a bind. A fierce storm was raging and he simply had nowhere else to go.

"Down the block is Post Script 123, a gallery that's having a humongous art exhibit. I bet you can crash there for a couple of hours."

Passing on the admission refund, Uli left quietly. Outside, the sandstorm had turned into a thick, windy rain, which at least served to rinse off his filthy clothes. In a doorway, he took out the event map that the woman had given him. Sure enough, the group art show of the Foul Festival was taking place just a few blocks away. Through the wet darkness, Uli navigated a couple blocks east to First Avenue and 9th Street.

He spotted it nearby—Post Script 123 was located in a former municipal building. He walked past a group of men unloading five coffin-like boxes into the rear of the large structure.

In the alcove of the gallery entrance, Uli dried off as best as he could, then stepped in and began inspecting the art. Few artists had more than two pieces on the wall. What was lacking in technical skill was generously made up for in daring conception. Stick figures sheepishly performed deviant sexual acts and other base biological functions. Childishly drawn gang members wearing red and blue shirts were locked in mortal combat, complete with chopped-off limbs and eviscerated intestines. Seeing a portrait of a Pigger warrior murdered in his sleep, Uli realized that all he really wanted was a place to rest until morning.

In order to avoid drawing attention to himself, he kept looking at the art. Drawn in crayon, packs of dogs with ferocious yellow teeth were barking at blue and red people on yellow bus platforms. In acrylic, unmanned supply planes circled overhead. One series of paintings really captured the spirit of the place: watercolor renditions of points at which the city bordered the limitless expanse of desert. Six vibrant silk-screened posters of Pigger and Crapper politicians were mounted side by side.

With no more artwork to peruse, most art lovers gone, and the snack bowl of pretzel crumbs empty, Uli decided to make his move and snuck out into the end corridor. There, he tried turning the knobs of four doors before he finally caught one that was unlocked—a custodian's closet with a large marble sink. Pushing aside an old mop bucket, he created just enough space to lie down in a fetal position. He removed the wiry wet wig that had become itchy and cold on his head and hung it on a hot overhead pipe to dry. With a dry mop as a pillow, he rested his head.

18

"**W**hat the fuck?" was the phrase that woke him the next morning. An old man with a stubby cigar—the janitor—had just opened the door and caught him sleeping under the sink. Exhausted and achy, Uli lay perfectly still. His seared groin was in slightly less pain.

"Get the fuck out before I drag you out!" the mop jockey barked.

Uli slowly rose, yawned leisurely, and grabbed his now dried-out, shrunken wig. He heard it rip when he yanked it over his scalp.

As the custodian led him back through the large gallery toward the front doors, Uli saw that the art had been removed from the walls and the spacious room had been transformed into a local bastion of gangocracy. Five large accordion-like outhouses—antiquated voting booths—were stationed at equal intervals around the space. Uli realized that this was what the men had been unloading the previous night. Next to each one was a small registration table. It all served to remind him that even though his candidate of choice was missing, this was the big day of both the mayoral and the national presidential elections.

He stepped outside to find a line of roughly fifty young people waiting for the polling place to open.

"Anyone heard anything about Mallory?" Uli called out. No one responded. "Anyone know where the Manhattan Pigger headquarters is?"

"Go back to Queens, asshole," one shabbily dressed rebel yelled.

To the east, Uli caught sight of a single-humped Arabian camel rolling across Avenue A. He headed in that direction and came to an empty lot stretching three blocks south and one block east. A handmade sign strung to a gate said, *THOMPSON SQUARE PARK.*

The dromedary camel was grazing on one of the few trees in the north end of the park. Uli figured it was one of the animals that had been set loose when they liberated the Bronx Zoo. Peering south, he saw a line of ragged kids. As he drew closer, he discovered they were waiting for food being doled out from the back of a stylish gray minibus. The small Styrofoam bowls of steaming lentil beans on white rice with a side of shredded Spam looked surprisingly appetizing. Jumping to the back of the long line, Uli could hear the thumping of music coming from inside the little gravel park. Some band was performing from a wooden makeshift platform. A kid with bright orange hair got in line behind him. As the music poured from the loudspeakers, Uli thoughtlessly rocked back and forth.

"Can you believe this sellout shit?"

"Sellout shit?" Uli thought the youth was talking about the free food.

"Yeah, bunch of faggots think they're the Beatles."

Behind the orange-haired kid stood a green-haired kid. In another minute, blue-haired and yellow-haired kids also beaded the line.

"You want a glimpse into the future of rock music, come see us perform this afternoon," the orange-headed one suggested.

"Who exactly are you?"

"We're Fuck the Rainbow. I don't suppose you're important or nothing?"

"Important, how?"

"Like the music critic for *Rolling Bone* magazine?" said the green head.

Instead of pointing out that he was waiting in a free-food line because he was impoverished, Uli just smiled.

"We'll put you on the guest list anyway. One o'clock at CoBs&GoBs over on Bowery."

The line was inching forward and Uli eventually found himself at the minibus's side window. It wasn't until he was being served that he realized this was a Pure-ile Plurality service. He didn't recognize the woman handing him the plastic spoon, napkin, and carton of milk. But the fellow who gave him a bowl of rice with shredded Spam and lentils was the same one who had been laughing to *The Honeymooners* in the TV room. Uli's hippie disguise seemed to do its job as he took the steaming food, thanked the guy, and walked solemnly into Thompson Square Park. He slipped down the long walkway toward the center of the lot. Joining the youthful audience, he squatted on a rocky field dotted with camel dung.

Uli ate his food while an ugly man in a skimpy dress with pancake makeup sang "The Tracks of My Tears" by Smokey Robinson & the Miracles. The cross-dressing crooner covered another four songs before being forced off the stage by an emcee with a blond halo cut named Jonathan Sexual.

"Folks, as you know, today is erection day, so when you go into those little booths, be sure you pull the right lever. And just remember that Mallory is the only candidate who came out against the war. Now please join me in welcoming our next performer, Taboo!"

Another cross-dresser came onstage and began singing a string of campy folk songs in a tinny falsetto. People kept flooding into the little field of stones, forcing those sitting in the rear to stand in order to see.

Then, *BOOM!* A car bomb exploded on the east end of the park. Wild screams and black smoke, thick as wool, rose from the site. Most of the crowd hurried over to see the carnage.

"Folks, please clear the area so we can get an ambulance in there!" the emcee shouted, to little avail.

More people on Avenue A rushed forward until *BOOM!* This time Uli actually saw bodies flying through the air. An even bigger car bomb went off twenty feet in front of the first one. The dense crowd crushed along the east end of the park broke out in pandemonium.

From the painful shrieks and panicky shouts that rose up a block away, it was evident that people were getting knocked down in the stampede. Out of nowhere, scores of balloonishly overweight men in tight blue button-up shirts converged on all surrounding corners.

A new voice came over the PA: "Stay calm, folks. I'm Council Officer Gonzalez. Please help us." The chubby man had just mounted the stage. "There's a terrorist in the crowd detonating the bombs. We got three clearing stations. One on 7th Street, another on 8th Street, and the last is on 9th Street. Please get in one of the three lines for a quick ID check, and we'll try to find the bastards who just brutally killed your neighbors."

They're using the explosions to screen the crowd, Uli thought. He discreetly blended into the frantic rush of hippies streaming southwest. Pigger agents were corralling everyone into a line at the clearing station on 7th Street.

As Uli moved toward the rear of the line, he passed an older man holding a bag of groceries. He was the sole person walking against the crowd eastward. Uli followed slowly behind him until he spotted the man entering an apartment building on 7th Street within the confined zone. Uli caught the door just before it locked shut. He waited until the old man had climbed the first flight of steps, then slipped inside. Walking to the rear of the building, he found a door to the backyard. He climbed over the rear fence and was able to open another door to a run-down apartment building on 6th Street.

Once out on Avenue A and just south of the sealed perimeter, Uli looked over at the 7th Street checkpoint and saw the gangcops fingerprinting everyone. *That was close*, he thought. He had to get out of the open. Then he remembered the invitation from Fuck the Rainbow. Rubbing his hand through his mop-headed wig, he headed a few blocks southwest to the venue on lower Bowery.

A dirty white canopy announced *CoBs&GoBs* in black letters. Inside the dark alcove, a large guy on a stool pointed to a sign: *Quarter-Stamp*.

"I'm on the guest list," Uli said.

"Name?"

Uli realized he hadn't given the band a name and let out a frustrated sigh.

"Oh, wait," said the doorman, "this must be you."

Seeing the guest list upside down, Uli read, *Old hippie dude in army jacket and yellow pants*. He thanked the doorman and heard lite Muzak playing as he walked down the corridor to the rear of the venue where the stage was located. In addition to the scent of choke, he also inhaled a far more pleasant aroma—a hairy guy was operating a small concession stand selling steaming cobs of buttered corn, thus explaining the name of the venue.

When Uli reached the small dark auditorium at the end of the corridor, he realized that the Muzak he had been listening to was none other than the rebellious sounds of Fuck the Rainbow. He also saw why they had taken pains to put him on their guest list: the only other person in the place was some older lady who looked to be the mother of one of the band members.

The green-haired kid was the group's high-pitched vocalist and also played guitar. Orange Head was on drums and Blue Hair strummed a second guitar. A white-haired kid was playing bass. Uli noticed that the floor of the stage was covered with corncobs and figured that patrons used them to show their appreciation. The good news was that Fuck the Rainbow's gentle tunes were perfect for repose. Taking one of the empty booths in the back, Uli found himself lullabied back to a soothing sleep.

* * *

A sudden crashing of cymbals and drums pulled him back up. A loud new power had seized control of the littered stage.

"*Hey! Dude! Pull out of my bush . . .*" he heard shouted over the microphone. A group of lean hard bodies were shoving and spinning around on the darkened floor.

Following a deep yawn and good stretch, Uli rose and headed back toward the entrance, where he bought a warm corncob, well lubricated in a cup of butter. He salted it and asked the concessionaire for the time.

"Six o'clock."

Fuck the Rainbow had finished performing hours earlier. The new group of young men who had taken up the stage announced between tunes that they were playing covers of a different group called the Rolling Stones. Uli listened to two more songs before grasping that the band was probably bastardizing the lyrics.

"*I have a pussy and I want it to gro-o-ow out,*" the singer ranted. "*Pound it, bang it, slap it, slam it hard, hard as rocks, make my balls two big orbs in the sky . . .*"

Squinting through the darkness, Uli saw that all the boyish band members—just like everyone in the audience watching them—were actually young ladies. Evidently, the lyrics had been revised to suit the strange female subculture. The band's name, emblazoned on the biggest drum, was Girls Beat Boys.

Uli slipped out to the men's room. As soon as he locked the door of the smelly corner stall, he heard a couple enter.

"Someone spotted him in the park, so *blam!* Then the council came in, but . . ."

"Technically, I'm supposed to keep campaigning until the polls close. But what's the point, the whore's going to win anyway."

Uli recognized the voices immediately, but he didn't know from where.

"At least she's *our* whore now," the first voice spoke clearly. "Just pisses me off that Shub is getting his ass kicked even up in Queens. I mean, where's the loyalty?"

It was that horrible Pigger Deere Flare! It took a moment longer to place the second voice—Kennesy, the curly-haired deejay who ID'd him at Rikers.

"Come on," Flare said sensually, "I know where we can get a little R and R before getting back to PP."

Through the hinge space in the stall door, Uli watched the two women kissing. When one pulled back, Uli caught a glimmer of something shiny in the long bathroom mirror. A flush later and they were gone.

Uli decided to take a chance in his hippie disguise and follow the two women. He pulled on the cheap sunglasses he'd found during the windstorm and left. Outside CoBs&GoBs, he trailed them up Bowery.

From a block away, he saw the pair, arm in arm, enter a dilapidated building at the corner of 4th Street. A sign over the door said, *Mamasita's Blah Blah Theater.*

If anyone knew where the Piggers were holding Mallory, it would probably be Deere. Fearful of getting ambushed, he knew he had to play this carefully. He waited roughly ten minutes before another couple exited the establishment, then he slipped inside. A tall fold-out signboard listed three plays being performed that night as part of the Foul Festival.

An elderly ticket seller sitting in a closet behind a Dutch door said, "Welcome to the festival, how many?"

"Just one."

"Two of the plays began at five, but you really didn't miss much."

"How much for a ticket?"

"A sixty-fourth stamp." It was the smallest denomination Uli had heard of in Rescue City. He gave the man a sixteenth-stamp, told him to keep the change, then walked into the lobby.

Uli examined the titles of the three plays concurrently in progress. They were civic-mindedly enigmatic: *The Assassination of Councilman David James* by Jessica Exhausto, *Downzoned: A Battle of Building beyond Local Ordinance Limits* by Wilson Roberts, and *The Meteoric Rise and Mediocre Decline of A. Clayton Powell* by Chichi Chekovsky.

"Doesn't look like there's a comedy in the group," Uli said to the old man who had climbed out of the ticket booth and moved behind the narrow candy counter.

"They're the nexus of where Soviet proletarian social realism meets the French theater of the absurd," the man replied with a blank goose-eyed expression.

Uli noticed that this was the tag line written at the bottom of the sandwich board. "Why are they all local politics?"

"We only get grant money if we write something government-related."

Uli thanked him for the insight and entered the first theater. Far from a political thriller, *The Assassination of Councilman David James* revealed a politician taking a sad inventory of his political life. The only other person in the theater was a somnolent woman; Uli figured it was Ms. Exhausto, the playwright.

Next, *The Meteoric Rise and Mediocre Decline of A. Clayton Powell* was a one-man show. And only one man was watching.

Passing through the lobby to the adjacent theater, Uli came across a pair of double doors and pushed on them, only to find them locked.

"That theater's empty," the elderly ticket taker/candyman said. "The third play is thataway." He pointed to the last set of double doors at the end of the lobby.

"Thanks."

"I should warn you, this play is 646,212 pages of staged transcription with only one performance. It began three days ago."

"When does it end?"

"Two weeks from tomorrow, and the only intermission is in four days."

This would've been a good place to sleep last night, Uli thought. He entered the rear of the theater and counted six other heads scattered about in the darkness. Most of them had seats next to them filled with food, blankets, and other knickknacks.

"Article six, subparagraph two, distinctly prohibits the building of these brassy skyscrapers and you know it," stated one of the actors playing a councilperson, waving his hand imperiously in the air. "You, sir, are an upzoning menace!"

Uli glanced around and saw that there was someone next to a theatergoer in the back row who he had initially thought was alone. He found a comfortable seat near them and waited to see if the duet could be his targets.

"Developer John McLeod, you're a monster." An actor playing the real estate mogul's young apprentice was performing a monologue. "You fired me because I didn't ignore the landmark preservation laws of this fair city. Then you just went ahead and built your monstrosity, disregarding six civil ordinances! I'm fired? No sir, your ethical duty to the architectural integrity of this city is fired! No amount of shabbily slapped together men's shelters can pardon inorganic styles, no volume of recessed public spaces can compensate for a wildly seesawing skyline!"

Uli realized from the stylized dialogue that the play couldn't have been written just from transcripts.

One of the two theater patrons in the back row stood up and began applauding. Uli then discerned that his possible agents were actually a pair of seniors.

Heading out to the lobby for the last time, he found the ticket man fast asleep. Before leaving, he pressed his right ear against the locked double doors to the fourth theater and thought he heard faint amorous sounds. Peering to his far left, he spotted another narrow passage that looked like an entrance to the actors' dressing rooms. The snoring ticket seller had a large ring of keys hanging from one of the belt loops of his baggy pants. As Uli silently unclasped the key ring, he noticed a rusty steak knife under the box office desk and slipped it into his back pocket.

He quickly located a small key that fit the lock of the dressing room door. Opening it just a crack, he saw that the room was dimly lit and empty. A black velvet curtain separated the little room from the fourth stage. Uli entered and peeked under the heavy curtain into the small black box theater.

Upon a bare mattress on the dark stage, Uli made out two nude figures clinging to each other as though to life, feverishly kissing and fondling. It was definitely them. In the dressing room, he found a heavy drawstring and an empty wine bottle, probably from a cast party of some municipal melodrama past. The bottle looked just thick enough. With the steak knife he was able to cut roughly six feet of the thick string, which he wound up around his hand and slipped in his pocket. Sneaking back into the dark theater, Uli listened to the women in their ever-rising throes of lovemaking. He crept down as close as he could get without being detected and waited until he heard a particularly sharp gasp of ecstasy, then shattered the wine bottle across the back of one of their skulls. He jumped onto the sweaty body of the other woman, who turned out to be Deere.

"You cocksucker!" she shouted, as Uli spun her thin naked body facedown. Three fresh gashes, each one with four long clawlike scratches, ran down her upper back. Sitting on her lower back, he twisted her right arm up. Catching the other hand, he bent it behind her as well and bound her wrists together with the thick string.

The other woman, Kennesy, stirred when he flipped her away from the broken bottle onto her belly. On the right cheek of her skinny butt, Uli noticed a green tattoo of a hog—an insignia of her true Pigger loyalties. Uli lashed her wrists behind her back as well with the remaining string, but not before Deere struggled to her knees and started screaming. Uli kicked her back to the floor. Finding her flimsy T-shirt next to the mattress, he twisted it into a tight strip and used it as a gag, tying it firmly behind her head.

Glancing down, Uli gasped. A shrunken penis was bobbing between Deere's legs—she was a transvestite, just like Dianne Colder!

He grabbed them both by their lashed wrists and yanked them to their feet. He pushed the naked and cursing Piggers through the black velvet curtains and into the changing room, where he flipped on the overhead light and shoved Kennesy facedown on the floor. A small trickle of blood was seeping down the back of her neck from the broken bottle. Still in a daze, she just lay there.

He shoved Deere backward into an old armchair in the corner and removed her gag. "Who cut your back?"

"A nasty little whore."

"Okay," he pressed on, "it's very simple: you're going to tell me where Mallory is."

"Fuck you!"

Although he didn't have the live electrical cord that she and Underwood had used on him, he did have the old steak knife. "Let's say I cut out your girlfriend's eye, would that change anything?"

"You don't have the balls!"

"After you electrocuted them, I feel them every waking moment."

"Slice her open, see if I care."

"How about I pop out *your* eye?" Uli put the tip of the rusty knife to the corner of her eye.

"You'll do it anyway," Deere said—she was clearly one tough little prick.

Uli took her shirt and regagged her. Despite her kicking and twisting, he was able to flop her over and bind her ankles together.

Grabbing Kennesy, Uli brought her back into the auditorium where she couldn't see her beloved. He pushed her onto the mattress and tied her ankles together so she couldn't run. By the time he returned to the dressing room, Deere was struggling to get the thick curtain string off from around her skinny ankles. Uli tossed her on her spindly back and sat on her.

"Wha are you doin?" she mumbled through the cloth.

"One last time, where's Mallory?"

"Fug you."

Taking out the steak knife again and exhaling deeply, Uli thought of Oric's cruel death and jabbed the tip of the blade into the young sadist's face, then made a quick sharp incision down her right cheek.

"Top it! Oh gog!" Deere screamed and started gagging. When Uli pulled the shirt from her mouth, she howled out in pain.

"WHERE THE FUCK IS MALLORY?" Uli held the knife back up to Deere's eye.

"Leave him alone!" he heard Kennesy shouting from the next room.

"Torturing people is illegal," Deere said, controlling her pain. Blood rushed down her face and neck.

"Not according to Underwood."

"You're outside your jurisdiction. You're answerable to a greater authority!"

"Who do you think I am?" Uli demanded.

"Siftwelt said you were some big FBI hotshot."

"Where's Mallory?" He returned to his immediate concern.

"Dead, fucker."

Uli cracked her across the mouth, causing her to howl.

"I'll kill you!" Kennesy screamed from the next room.

Deere groaned out to her lover, "Don't tell him shit!"

When Uli clasped his hand over Deere's mouth, the cruel trans-vestite bit him. Dropping his weight firmly on Deere's skinny chest and tightly clamping her mouth and nose, Uli waited as his captive desperately struggled before finally passing out. Then Uli artistically smeared some of her blood around her eyes so that they appeared to have been cut out of their sockets. He returned to the theater, where Kennesy lay struggling.

"What did you do to her?"

"Come see for yourself." He undid the knots around Kennesy's ankles and led her back into the changing room.

"What the fuck did you do?"

"If he would just have told me where Mallory is," Uli responded, "he would've saved his sight."

"Is he dead?" Kennesy asked trembling, staring at her lover.

"No, and I'll prove it."

Uli pulled out his bloody steak knife. When he pressed it delicately into Deere's exposed groin, Kennesy shouted, "Stop! I'll tell you!"

"Where is Mallory?"

"I don't fucking know!"

Uli put his knife to Deere's throat.

"Just hear me out!" Kennesy cried. "Word has it a local Pigger gang is holding her."

"Where?"

"Some drug den up on 4th Street and C. They grabbed her from St. Vinny's."

"Why wouldn't they take her back to Queens or the Bronx?"

"The Crappers closed all roads off the island."

Uli remembered getting frisked on the bridge, and the roadblocks checking all cars. "Did they kill her?"

"No."

"What are they going to do with her?"

"I don't know. She's part of some elaborate new plan."

As if arising from death, Deere suddenly sprang up with her hands free and snagged the knife away from Uli, then brought the blade tip down, catching the top of Uli's collarbone. When Uli jumped away, Deere leaned forward and, with a sharp yank, cut the cord restraining Kennesy's wrists. Apparently Deere had only pretended to be uncon-scious and had wiggled her narrow wrists loose from their bind.

Uli dashed into the empty theater as Deere pulled on her panties. Uli located a small broom behind the door and stressed the wooden stick over his knee until part of the grain splintered out. Then he snapped it so that the end came to a sharp angle. He sprinted back into the changing room to see Deere still sawing the ropes around her ankles.

"Watch it!" yelled Kennesy.

Deere threw the steak knife across the room, missing Uli's head by inches.

Uli bolted forward and thrust his spear up into Deere's bony neck, shoving it right through her jugular. The tip of the broomstick came out behind Deere's throat, sending her choking with blood bubbling out. Kennesy threw herself across the room and grabbed the steak knife. When she swung it around at him, Uli blocked her elbow, shooting the long blade squarely into her sternum. The Pigger agent fell forward to the ground, thrashing back and forth.

"I assure you," Uli said to her, "your death is far more compassionate than what you put poor Oric through."

As the two Pigger agents lay dying, Uli inspected his small laceration. Though sliced, the skin over his clavicle was barely bleeding.

He passed through the lobby and up to the aged ticket seller, who was still snoring. He quietly clipped the ring of keys back on the belt loop of the old fellow's pants and left the theater.

The wind had started kicking up again. According to Kennesy, Mallory might be in some Pigger safe house on Avenue C. True to the socioeconomic trends of old New York, the farther east Uli walked, the more run-down the buildings became. Through the wind and sand, Uli could hear a dull throbbing beat down Avenue C. He followed the percussion to one of the few buildings that wasn't sealed up with cinder blocks, a dilapidated ash-colored brownstone.

Inside, a pack of people were moving haphazardly to a pulsing beat. A thick wave of choke smoke obscured the rear of the place. Semiclad bodies flopped and slinked. Most everyone appeared intoxicated. Ancient Middle Eastern music was blaring through massive amplifiers. Croak, choke, homemade liquor, and things he'd never heard of were being peddled.

With the remote possibility that Mallory was being held somewhere on the premises, Uli roamed around discreetly. He found that most of the upper floors were uninhabitable and there was no basement. After twenty minutes of careful searching, he was convinced that she was not in the building. He decided to lay low and try to spot more Pigger agents to mine for information. But judging by their flamboyant dress and convivial behavior, Uli sensed that many of the wild-haired youths were libertine leftovers from the Foul Festival.

About thirty minutes later, Uli observed a strange white-wigged man in a black turtleneck and his memory released another bit of hostaged information: "You're Andy Warhol!"

"I'm afraid you're mistaken," said the man's companion. "This is the artist Danny Varholski."

"And who are you?"

"His dealer." The oddball artist didn't move a muscle or utter a sound. "But there is an actual Warhol Superstar here—Valerie Solanas is passed out on the couch."

The dealer and his artist promptly exited.

"Hey! You!" a large Afro-haired man shouted at Uli. "You're that asshole who threw up on Allen Ginsberg yesterday."

"It was an accident," Uli answered, "and if *he* could forgive me, maybe you should try."

The man gave Uli a disgusted look and walked away.

Finding a solitary spot on an old couch, Uli sat down, exhausted, to collect his thoughts. In a moment, he closed his eyes. Despite the droning music, the filthy stench of the sofa, and his incomplete mission to find Mallory, his mind clicked off and he passed out almost immediately.

19

"**H**ey Scarface! He's here!" Uli heard. Opening his eyes, something hard rubbed against his face. A hiking boot was pressing gently across his nose and cheek. Three large, scary men were standing over him, all wearing turquoise shirts and green do-rags around their heads. One of them, who had a deep and jagged scar running across his face, was rustling through the pockets of Uli's army jacket. His head felt cold and he realized that his wig had popped off.

"You fellows with the Verdant League?" Uli asked, hopeful of their green gang colors.

"This is what they call a disguise," said one.

"It's also ironic," added the scarred man. "We're looking all over town for you, and we find you hiding out here."

"I'm afraid you've mistaken me for someone else," Uli said tiredly. The eponymous leader's scar looked almost like a lightning bolt starting at the right side of his forehead and jaggedly cutting past his right eye, ending in the middle of his chin.

"Special Agent Uli," said the man on his left.

"You've mistaken me for—"

The disfigured man crushed down on Uli's kneecap. He screamed in pain.

"That ain't cool, man," said a hippie lounging nearby, whom everyone ignored.

Uli swung his leg back, upending the scar-faced leader. One of the other thugs pulled out a large knife that looked like an artifact from the Bronze Age and placed it against Uli's throat.

"Don't!" Scarface yelled, grabbing the blade away. "They need him for something with Mallory."

"Was she elected?"

"Oh yeah."

When Uli tried to get to his feet, Scarface knocked him back down and a second man kicked him in the face.

"ASSHOLE!" the leader yelled at his comrade, shoving him away. Then he inspected Uli's scalp. "If you've bruised him so they can't use him, I swear I'll give them *you*."

Uli was dizzy and blood was coming out of his mouth and nose. He felt himself being flipped over onto his belly and his arms being yanked back painfully. A pair of plastic zip ties were snapped on his wrists. He heard the familiar sound of the tightening loop as it zipped along the hard plastic catch. A few minutes later he was pulled to his feet and shoved out the door of the run-down brownstone. They marched him westward down 4th Street. Despite his aches and pains, what bothered him most was the searing morning sunlight. Two men walked in front and Scarface followed as they moved wordlessly down the street.

When the group crossed Avenue A, Uli glanced around for some-one who might be of help. After all, this was a Crapper borough. A lot of the locals were out shoveling sand from yesterday's storm.

Spotting a council sand inspector, Uli momentarily hoped the man might intervene, but all he did was compensate the collectors load-ing the heavy cloth bags into the back of an official gray dump truck. Everyone else who noticed Uli being led, cuffed, through the streets politely ignored him.

As they crossed an unswept intersection, a car turned the corner and skidded on the layer of sand, slamming right into the two goons who were leading Uli. They flew up over the hood and onto the pave-ment. The car screeched to a halt twenty feet ahead. Uli was about to dash off when he felt the leader's large hand clamp onto the back of his neck.

"Oh fuck!" screamed the female motorist, visibly shaken. The two gangcops rolled in pain on the ground behind her.

"You stupid fucking bitch!" shouted Scarface, who now held Uli tightly by his cuffed arms.

"My God, what did I do?" The woman stepped out of her dented car to see if she could assist the two injured men.

"Get back in your fucking car!" the asshole leader shouted.

"Come on," the woman said to Uli, ignoring the command. "Help me put them in the backseat. We can get them to the Beth Israel Clinic."

"You stupid cunt!" Scarface yelled.

She tried lifting the more injured of the two, until the leader pulled out his own prehistoric knife.

"Watch it!" Uli tried to warn her as the man raced over.

Without missing a beat, the woman swung around, pulled out a small pistol, and pumped a single bullet into the man's broad chest. He dropped the knife and fell backward into a seated position.

"Fucking bitch!" Scarface looked down at his chest.

"Uli!" she shrieked.

Inspecting her closely, Uli realized it was the blond man who'd protected him from the angry mob at Green-wood Cemetery . . . but he was now a raven-haired woman.

"Let's get the heck out of here! Forget about these Piggers," she urged, leading him to her car.

"Wait a second! I think he knows where Mallory is," Uli said.

People were collecting on the curb now, staring benignly at the man with blood soaking the front of his shirt. His two large assistants were still rolling in agony.

"You sure?" she asked, and picking up the large knife that Scarface had dropped, she cut the plastic bands off of Uli's wrists.

"Yes, come on!"

They each lifted under an armpit and dragged the semiconscious leader into the backseat of the woman's car. Uli got in next to Scarface and compressed his chest wound as the woman sped off north.

"I don't want to be rude, but when I met you before—"

"I was undercover as a man," she replied.

"How do I know you?"

"I'm your sister Karen. You're Uli Sarkisian. Remember?" She peered at him intensely in the rearview mirror.

As they talked, both trying to get on the same page, Uli dropped the rag he was holding against Scarface's chest. A small fountain of blood shot out. He grabbed it back and continued compressing.

"How the hell did you get in here?" she asked.

"I don't know. I found myself stumbling along a street in Queens without any clue of who I was or why I was here, but then I saw your face at that funeral in Brooklyn . . ."

"I was working undercover."

"Maybe I came to rescue you."

"Uli, I just rescued *you*. I'm an officer with the council cops."

"What a coincidence!"

"It's no coincidence," she said. "About a week ago, I had this dream about some white-haired guy giving me instructions to kill Dropt. It must have been Newt Underwood. I thought I was hallucinating. Then I saw dogs racing at me and I knew I was connecting with someone, but I didn't know it was you."

"*You* were the one who told me to run!" he exclaimed, remembering the mysterious voice in his head. "Why didn't you meet me at Rock & Filler Center?"

"Oh, believe me, I tried. There were tons of Piggers in that funeral crowd. One of them heard what I shouted to you and I got delayed. I have an office at 30 Rock & Filler. I've been tracking you ever since. I sensed you hanging unconscious in some barn and tried to wake you up. Then I thought the DT were holding you in the Bronx. I felt this intense burning pain here and here." She pointed to her chest and lower region.

"I was tortured at Rikers."

"Here on the reservation, it's not unusual for siblings, especially twins, to have a psychic connection," she explained as they sped uptown.

"Why did that preacher scream at me in Brooklyn?"

"You tried putting him and his brother away ten years ago."

"I did?"

"Yeah, and when it was discovered that you had set them up, a jury acquitted them. But after the Manhattan bombing, they got detained here."

Uli wondered what kind of a person he really was. How could he send anyone into this hellhole?

Karen slammed on the brakes in front of Beth Israel Clinic on 16th Street. Uli helped her as she pulled the severely wounded man out of the backseat. His shirt and pants were soaked in blood. Together they dragged him through the double doors of the emergency room.

The putrid stench hit Uli immediately as he entered the lobby. Just as Marsha Johnson had said, the conditions of the hospital looked completely medieval. The unwashed mix of dried blood and dirt covering the floor was a perfect breeding ground for endless bacteria. Off to one side, near the receptionist's window, Uli noticed a blood-smudged spool of tickets that patients were supposed to grab upon entering. The rows of benches were packed with the sick and injured. Others were lying on the floor, bleeding from assorted wounds and orifices. Some must have been dead.

Ignoring everyone, Karen pulled out a gold badge and explained to the nurse on duty that her patient was top priority.

Within minutes, a man who Uli figured was one of the few real doctors on the reservation came down to the reception area and began treating Scarface's chest wound. The bullet had punctured his lung and was lodged in his right atrium. With a Crapper gangcop guarding the victim, Karen used the phone at a nurses' station.

"We have a very tiny window of opportunity here!" Uli heard her shout. "Once the Piggers realize he's in our custody, they're going to either move Mallory or kill her!"

As she continued talking, Uli spotted a bloodstained newspaper on the lobby floor. The headlines of the daily screamed, "Assassin Assassinated!" To his surprise, there was a photo of his missing coworker, Patricia Itt. According to the article, she had shot and killed Daniel Ellsberg while he was being led out of the Astoria police headquarters.

The doctor stuck an IV drip into the patient's arm, while an aide strapped a mask over his scarred face.

Five minutes later, the Pigger was carried into a small operating room upstairs. A team of Crapper gangcops arrived and further secured the area. Soon, four strange men rushed into the room, pulling on rubber gloves and surgical masks. There was something about them, in their dress and demeanor, quite unlike all others in Rescue City. Two of them were evidently nurses. One took surgical tools from a large plastic box and laid them out on a linen-covered tray. The other injected Scarface with painkillers, attached him to three portable monitors, and jerked his head back to slip a breathing tube down his throat.

"No," the apparent head of this medical group stopped Uli, "you can't interrogate someone with a tube down his throat."

Without even cutting the patient's hair, the doctor proceeded to run a small bone saw along the crown of his skull. Uli was about to mention that the bullet was in his chest, not his head, when he realized they weren't trying to save the man.

"I didn't know you had neurosurgeons here," whispered Uli.

"We don't," Karen replied. "Technically they're scientists: cleavings, incisions, amputations."

Uli grasped that her words formed the acronym *CIA*. "Where'd you find them?"

"They periodically send these 'experiment memos' to Pigger and Crapper headquarters. A couple months ago they put out a surgical memo to both gangs that in exchange for testing their latest procedure, they were willing to extract vital information from any hostile witness who is going to die anyway."

"I guess that's why they're not worried about keeping sterile."

One of the scientists opened what looked like a small wooden cigar box. Inside was an instrument that resembled a stainless steel yarmulke with dozens of long, thin needles pointing downward. Many intricate wires were shooting out of the top end. The scientist secured them into the back of a small black control panel. The steel points were delicately inserted into the ruffled contours of the Pigger's exposed gray matter.

"Revive the subject," said the lead scientist to the one controlling the anesthesia and oxygen levels. Within moments, the patient started coming to.

"You can question him now," the leader said, as if to do so himself would be somehow unethical.

"Where is Mallory? . . . Where is Mallory?" Karen inquired softly.

"Be more aggressive," the scientist coached.

"Where the hell is Mallory!"

"Fuck you!" the guinea pig spat back with his eyes still shut tight. "I— Fuck you— She—"

Another scientist standing behind the control panel read a display of vital statistics as he flipped switches and turned dials.

"You're not causing him more pain, are you?" Uli asked.

The scientist shook his head no.

Uli watched as another scientist monitored the physical reactions on the dying subject's gray semiconscious face. The needles were clearly having some kind of effect on the man's motor neurons, as his arms and legs involuntarily shuddered and twitched.

"Where is Mallory?"

"No fucking way . . . I . . . gonna tell you shit—"

One of the other scientists flipped a switch that seemed to take things up a notch. Scarface's eyelids started fluttering.

"Where is she!"

"No, I'm—" Scarface cringed, shutting his eyes again. "Stinking-fucking-Island! No!"

"Where?"

"No way! The dumps! No fucking . . . to the dumps. No fucking way . . . The fucking dumps!"

"What dumps?" Karen asked, as a technician fine-tuned the control panel.

"Stinking-fucking-Island!"

"The city dump?" she asked.

"His vitals are dropping," the lead scientist called out. Within a matter of seconds, all the portable instruments beeped and then flatlined.

". . . And he's gone," one of the other scientists said.

As the scientists congratulated each other on their success and started packing things up, Karen pulled Uli out of the room. In the hallway, a dozen Crapper gangcops were milling around.

"What'd you find?" one asked.

"He died before we could get anything."

They all looked dejected.

"Let's go," Karen whispered to Uli.

"Shouldn't we ask those gangcops to help us?" he said as they started to leave.

"No, we have a serious mole infestation. We still have a small chance of getting out there before they move her."

She made a quick phone call and then they jumped in her car and headed south. Moving down Bowery, Karen had the dispatcher put her through to her second-in-command—a Sergeant Schuman in Midtown. After asking half a dozen questions about the manpower of the present shift, she instructed him to assemble an initial crew of eighteen gangcops, plus herself and Uli, divided into five squads. Each four-person group would be assigned to new vehicles with bulletproof armor. Karen verbally compiled a list of supplies that included guns, bullets, walkie-talkies, spears, arrows, machetes, a hundred feet of rope, fifteen sandwiches, five gallons of water, cotton swabs, masking tape, and a box of nose pins.

"We're also going to need a medic, some new clothes for Mallory, and some basic medical supplies in case she's injured."

"Sergeant Jack is just going off duty with his squad," Sergeant Schuman informed her through the car's speakerphone.

"Put him on."

Within a minute, five more cars were added, doubling the armada to ten. They were instructed to meet Karen and Uli at the Manhattan side of the Staten Island Ferry Bridge as soon as possible.

Roughly half an hour later, the line of ten squad cars arrived. Karen parked her own car and they got in the front vehicle, leading the convoy.

Uli could feel the car sinking and rising as they drove over the wobbly bridge. The awful smell hit them like a bucket of cold water. Uli, Karen, their driver, and the two other gangcops with them immediately slipped on their nose pins.

"This stink was the price for establishing order here," Karen said, peering over the wastewater lapping against the sandbags of Manhattan. "The entire place used to be so dangerous you couldn't go three blocks in any direction without having some gang attack you."

"I heard that the guy who saved the place was some Indian mystic," Uli said.

"That's a load of shit," Karen replied. "Jackie Wilson started out as a ruthless ganglord. He was the top lieutenant in a small gang in Hell's Kitchen. When his boss got killed, Jackie took the gang into the desert. Actually, they were hardly a gang—thirteen warriors. They spent six weeks in the desert circling the city so that they wouldn't be caught by other gangs. Then they invaded the area that later became JFK Airport, which at the time was really just a big empty lot. There was nothing out there. Everyone thought he was crazy when he spent six months securing it like a goddamned fortress.

"Late one night, after he finally locked it up tight, he went into Brooklyn and hijacked a bunch of trucks. He filled them with as many logs and rocks and bags of concrete as they could carry and dumped everything on the big drain in Staten Island—trucks and all. That's where we're heading now. Then he blasted the retaining walls along lower Staten Island that held the sewage water back, immediately flooding the borough. Within a week, the airfield there, which was the only functioning airfield in Rescue City at the time, was under five feet of sewage. Feedmore's drones, which replaced piloted planes when the army pulled out, began landing at JFK—just as Wilson knew they would. Suddenly *he* was in charge of all the food and supplies for the entire city. Some gangs tried invading, but he was ready for them. He had his hand around the throat of this place. To his credit, he was fair, he treated everyone equal. People basically liked him. But if you wanted supplies, you had to do things his way."

"Who created the political parties?"

"After taking charge, Wilson ordered the three largest gangs at the time to become political parties and build a government. They ended up organizing into two parties. Wilson unified the city by establishing laws and elections. He became the first official mayor here."

"Why didn't he fix the drain after taking control?" Uli asked, looking out over the putrid waters of Staten Island.

"Oh, he tried. He had a hole dug into the pipe and spent a year or so employing an army of people to try to pull out all the debris and rebuild the retaining walls, attempting to make things like they were before. They erected this beautiful cofferdam to divert the water around the blocked sewage tube while trying to unplug it. But between construction mishaps and strange diseases, a lot of people died, and they were never able to reconnect with the original tube."

After passing rows of sunken and uninhabitable houses, the pavement below them narrowed into a particularly pitted stretch of road.

Uli saw large gashes in the blacktop and the twisted remains of giant rusty vehicles.

"Those were the personnel carriers from when the army was still here bringing in supplies," Karen explained. "People started attacking them, blowing them up en route from the airport."

"Where did they get the explosives?"

"Some old artillery depots had been left behind. Though no one will admit it, a lot of the ammonium nitrate was made right here."

"Why were people attacking them?"

"Everything started to go wrong. Electrical blackouts, food shortages. People didn't like their housing assignments. Then, when the government discovered that some terrorists had been inadvertently swept here, they turned off phone service. For the first few months we could even make calls back to Old Town. But after months of residents and soldiers getting killed, the army packed up and left one night."

"Was this when that reproductive disease struck?"

"The EGGS epidemic? No," Karen said. "That happened as soon as we got here."

When the road forked off in several directions, the convoy stayed to the east with the water to their immediate left. During one long descent, the bilious brown liquid seemed to have risen, completely washing out the torn and twisted road. At the point where the flooding was at its widest and shallowest, they were able to carefully drive across. With windows up, the entourage of cars slushed through dark waves of toxic water that came up to the doors, almost flooding the engines. Then they sped along the rising edge of the lumpy brown water until they came to a fork of five roads. Unsure of where he was going, the driver stopped.

"That way," directed one of the two gangcops in the backseat, pointing to the narrowest path.

"What the hell's over there?" the driver asked.

The gangcop had worked for the council's Department of Sanitation and explained that this was the way to the city dump.

"You're sure?" Karen said.

"I drove down here every day for five years," the cop replied.

The caravan soon came to what looked like an endless sprawl of smoldering garbage dunes. It was here that most of the nonbiodegradable trash from the city was deposited. Along a wide, damp field of filth, a number of tire fires sent up ribbons of thick black smoke. Robust little animals that Uli didn't recognize darted around.

That morning's squad of garbage trucks was parked off to the side with teams of sanitation workers still unloading them. Two small tractors shoveled the trash about. Karen and two of the gangcops stopped and rounded up a dozen or so workers. Swarms of black flies buzzed everywhere.

"Have you seen anyone out of the ordinary around here in the past day?" she asked them, as gangcops from other vehicles scoured the area for any signs of their missing leader.

"Two cars I didn't recognize sped down this road not ten minutes ago," said an older supervisor. Others confirmed this.

"Is there anything down there?" Karen asked.

"A couple of old abandoned buildings."

A stray dog began barking at a large rattlesnake slithering away from a nearby garbage pile.

In another moment they were all back in the cars heading down the barely identifiable path. A few more dogs appeared from nowhere and started barking at the convoy. The vehicles followed the road downhill. Several minutes beyond was a small, neglected cemetery with broken wooden crosses and a few toppled headstones.

As the cars rose up a steep hill, they came across a pair of old wooden buildings sagging sideways. They looked like they had been erected long before Rescue City was built. Five cars came to a halt in front of the smaller structure, while the other five pulled up to the larger one.

A pair of gangcops kicked in the door of the first building. A moment later, Uli heard someone shout, "Shit!"

He followed Karen inside. A lukewarm glass of tea and the thick aroma of choke indicated that it had only just been evacuated.

Suddenly, a burst of gunfire erupted from the second building. Karen and Uli exited the smaller structure to find that a gangcop had been shot through the head as he was trying to climb into a second-story window. The gunman had raced downstairs quickly enough to shoot a second cop, then retreated back upstairs.

"This guy's alone, he doesn't have Mallory!" Karen shouted to some of the others. "Come on!" Sprinting back to the car, she got behind the steering wheel herself. As others stayed behind to shoot it out with the lone gunman barricaded in the top floor, Uli and two others jumped in with her. Karen sped about a quarter mile before the path slumped down into a small depression where the dirt turned into soft sand, marking the beginning of the true desert.

Uli stared out over the dunes to their left and thought he saw a small cloud of sand. "What's that?"

Karen swerved the car up over the first dune and they immediately saw it. An older-model solicar was stuck in the desert about five hundred feet out. Its wheels spun uselessly, sending up a thick geyser of sand. Uli could make out two men trying to push its rear bumper as a third steered. But glancing back, he realized that besides Karen and the two gangcops, they were alone.

"We're not going to have a big element of surprise," Karen said, checking the bullets in her pistol. She drove halfway toward the vehicle before their own car got stuck in the sand. Karen threw open her door and ran ahead until the taller of the two men pushing the vehicle turned and spotted them. He slipped back into the car, while the other man pulled out a pistol and started blasting. The two gangcops with Uli and Karen immediately returned fire, hitting the man repeatedly.

Within seconds, one of the two remaining Piggers pulled a dazed but conscious Mallory out of the backseat and jammed a gun to the side of her head, which had been shaved bald. "Relax!" he screamed.

"Just back the fuck up!" yelled the other Pigger as he climbed out of the driver's seat holding a bottle. With wild eyes, a scraggly beard, and sweat-drenched flesh, he appeared to be some kind of addict.

"We can talk this out!" Karen called back to them.

The bearded man poured his bottle of clear liquid over Mallory and held open a lighter. "Back up or she goes up like a dry Christmas tree!"

"Can we just—"

"Back your fucking ass up!"

In one swift motion, Karen pulled out her pistol and fired a shot, hitting the man directly in his neck.

"Kill her!" the bearded man coughed out to the thin Pigger holding the gun.

"Do it and you're dead!" Karen warned, seeing that the young man was trembling.

The wounded Pigger struck his lighter and dropped it onto Mallory, whose dress erupted in flames. As fire spread across her body, Mallory rolled down the sand dune, immediately extinguishing the flames.

"Shit!" cried the thin gunman.

The bearded man crawled over and grabbed the gun out of the other man's hands and shot twice at Mallory. Before he could fire a third bullet, Karen shot him four more times, dropping him for good. The thin man grabbed the gun and put it firmly against Mallory's head.

"Back up!" he yelled shakily, then reached down and pulled Mallory up, smoke still streaming from her. Only now did Uli notice her exposed right arm, or what was left of it: everything below the elbow was gone.

"Look," Karen reasoned, "I know you don't want to kill anyone. You're young, and you have a choice. You can spend the rest of your days in unbelievable agony or you can have a privileged life."

"That's far enough!" the man spat back at Karen, who was inching closer.

"Fine." She stopped and held up her hands. "I can help you."

"No you can't!" shouted the kidnapper, holding one arm over Mallory's neck. His other hand held the gun to her skull. "I let her go, they're going to torture the shit out of me and you know it!"

"We can get you out of here!"

"No way!"

"I got Mnemosyne!" Karen barked.

"Bullshit!"

"If I show it to you, and promise you that we'll have you out of here before this day is done, will you release Mallory?"

He stared at her furiously.

"It's in a bag in my glove compartment," Karen said to the two Crapper gangcops, who jogged back to the car.

The other vehicles in their convoy were finally speeding over toward them. As one of the gangcops raced back to Karen with the bag from her glove compartment, the second went to hold off the rest of the team so as not to exacerbate the situation.

Karen removed a shattered plastic box from the bag. To Uli's surprise, he recognized it as one of the items he had found in Dianne Colder's hotel room.

"Where's the oxygen?" the kidnapper demanded.

"What's going on?" Uli asked.

"If I let her go," the kidnapper said, "you'll—"

"We'll take you to the hole in the pipe and slip you down there right now."

"And I'll—"

"You'll be a free man."

"And how do I know you won't kill me?"

Karen moved as close to the man as she could before he started flinching. "I'm in charge of all this," she said. "You just have to trust me."

He put his gun down and let Mallory walk away. Karen held out her hand and he gave her his pistol. Then together they walked back toward the rest of the group. Mallory hugged Karen with her one arm.

"You better hurry up, 'cause there are two other gangs around here somewhere," the Pigger kidnapper said.

"Where exactly?" Karen asked.

"They were going to meet us on the other side of the dunes, so they're probably looking for us now."

Karen signaled everyone back to the cars. After frisking the Pigger to make sure he wasn't hiding another gun or a knife, she had him sit in the second car of the convoy and kept Mallory in her own car, which was now sixth in the line. Sergeant Schuman, whose vehicle had been the last to pull up, said they had spotted a group of cars behind them as they entered the depression that Karen had discovered.

"We better get the hell out of here *now!*" Karen announced.

The convoy turned around and started driving back in the direction of Manhattan. Getting Mallory—the new mayor—back to safety was the first order of business.

"What did they do to you?" Uli asked the bald Mallory.

"They were going to do some kind of brain surgery on me," she said groggily. "Try to turn me into a zombie."

"How do you know?" Karen asked.

"I woke up in some operating room and found that they had cut off all my hair. They were about to operate, but then they discovered they didn't have the right tools or equipment." Mallory bent forward, revealing some strange markings on her scalp. "They had those fucking CIA guys come and inspect me."

Suddenly, renewed gunfire erupted in front of them.

"*Everyone's okay,*" a voice informed over the radio, "*but there's a gang up ahead, so we're going back down to the bottom of the hill.*"

All vehicles switched direction again and returned to the sandy depression. The front car had a new line of bullet holes running from its hood to its right fender.

"We were lucky," said the lead driver. "What could've been an effective ambush was ruined when we almost crashed into them. Three cars. They got out and started shooting. We were able to turn around quickly."

"How many men did you see?" Karen asked.

"Maybe twelve or so."

"If we continue up the other road," the former sanitation worker chimed in, "there used to be a route to the drain, but it was more of a footpath."

"I was just at the Verdant League headquarters, so I might be able to remember the way there," Uli said.

"That sounds like our best bet," Karen said.

No sooner had the new lead car proceeded twenty feet up the far hill than a volley of gunfire shattered the windshields of the first two vehicles. The driver in the second car was immediately killed. The gangcop riding shotgun managed to grab the wheel, throw the car in reverse, and steer it backward down to the bottom of the dusty depression.

"We're boxed in," the driver called out to Karen through his window.

When one of the cars tried bypassing the ambushers by driving off the road, the tires quickly sank into the soft sand, spinning pointlessly. They simply couldn't circumnavigate the two blocked roadways.

Multiple attempts to call for additional help failed since their cheap radios couldn't transmit beyond two miles. The terrain in the area was barren, without so much as a bush or tree, and Sergeant Schuman pointed out that if they tried storming up the hill, they would be picked off before they made it anywhere near the summit.

"There seems to be less fire power from the south," the sergeant observed. "Let's try to bust out that way."

One veteran gangcop suggested sending two of the armored cars up the hill side by side. When they approached the Piggers, the cops could bail out and try to secure a forward position amid a cluster of rocks at the top. From there they could provide cover for subsequent teams joining them.

"The longer we wait, the more tired we'll get," Karen responded. "Unless anyone has any better ideas, let's get a move on."

The sergeant asked for volunteers. Eight men boarded two armored cars; each one was given a handgun and a dozen bullets. As the two vehicles climbed up the slope toward the southern pass, heavy gunfire from both sides of the road burst through the reinforced windshields. The car on the left drew more fire, and when the driver was killed, the shotgun gangcop steered the wheel, trying to at least provide protection for the car on the right. From the backseat of the left vehicle, the two gangcops shot back until they too were picked off.

When both vehicles got within thirty feet of the enemy line, Molotov cocktails were tossed onto their hoods. Fiery gasoline spread through the broken windshields and into the cars. The tires of the car on the right were shot out, and when the driver took a hit, the three remaining cops bailed out. They rolled for cover, under a hail of bullets.

Meanwhile, the shotgun driver of the car on the left—the only surviving passenger—managed to keep his burning vehicle straight and slammed into the rock formation fifty feet above the other vehicle. It looked like a solid position for cover.

A third car zoomed up the hill, driven by the former sanitation worker. The vehicle drew fire, allowing the surviving cop in the first car to get a better position. All watched as he was able to shoot two Piggers, whose bodies came rolling part of the way down the hill. The other Piggers seemed to pull back, and for an instant there was a wave of optimism among those below.

Before more cars could join in the attack, a flurry of gunfire erupted behind them. Eight Pigger gangcops were racing down another hill into the sandy depression with guns blazing. Three Crappers were killed and two more were wounded before a defensive line was formed to repel the attack.

The beleaguered first group of Piggers seized the opportunity by attacking and shooting the sole cop perched at the top of the rocks. Then they lobbed down more Molotov cocktails, creating a blinding wall of flame around the second Crapper position below. Three Pigger gunmen rushed forward and shot freely into the group.

One Crapper gangcop managed to race through the flames, but he was immediately beaten, doused with gasoline, and set on fire. A marksman from below who tried shooting his burning comrade to put him out of his misery was ordered to cease. At that range it was a waste of valuable bullets.

"Shub himself has to be behind this," deduced a Crapper gangcop. The amount of bullets being fired at them was simply too costly for it to be a splinter gang.

"What now?" asked another.

"Wait until dark," suggested a senior guard from Mallory's security staff. "Then half of us can hold out here while the mayor and the other group head into the desert. They can loop around and hopefully reach Brooklyn by tomorrow afternoon."

"These fuckers aren't stupid," Karen said. "And there's no place to hide. We go into the desert, and even at night they'll pursue us. Only we'll be half as strong and have no cover at all. We're either going to break out or die trying."

At four o'clock Karen instructed Sergeant Schuman to move the vehicles to an isolated clearing to avoid sabotage. Everyone was divided into two groups to guard the perimeter. The sergeant ordered two trenches to be dug in case of a night attack coming from either direction.

20

Just before five p.m., while most of the entourage was still making preparations, scooping out packed sand with their bare hands, a barrage of gunfire sounded on the northern peak before them. Screams and cries could be heard over the hill.

"This is it!" one of the Crapper gangcops yelled.

All the men jumped into the unfinished trenches.

"They're coming!"

"But it doesn't make sense," Uli said to the gangcop next to him, pointing out the long rays of the setting sun over the surrounding hills. "Why would they give up their advantage and attack us in daylight?"

Everyone waited, but no Piggers came. More yells and gunshots were heard, but nothing was visible beyond the sandy bluffs.

"They're screwing with our heads," one gangcop hypothesized.

"No, bullets are way too expensive to use as distractions," an older cop replied.

A few minutes later, another exchange of gunshots and cries echoed in their little valley. This time, however, the sounds were coming from the road back to the city, behind them.

"What the fuck is going on?" a terrified gangcop shouted.

In the distance, two fat Piggers in broad-rimmed hats came dashing madly down the hill, holding their arms in the air in apparent surrender. Uli watched as some naked man jumped up behind them and stretched out a long bow. An arrow tip popped out through the front of one of the Piggers' chests along with a widening circle of blood. Another man wearing little more than a loincloth sprinted down, knocking the second Pigger to the ground. Unsure of whether or not it was some strange trap, the Crapper gangcops held their ground and witnessed as the nearly naked man pulled out a knife and slit the Pigger's fat throat, then calmly proceeded to scalp him.

"Holy crap," Uli said, realizing what was up, "those are Tim Leary's people!"

A dozen more Piggers, pursued by a horde of more scantily clad men, came into sight and quickly met the same fate.

From both the north and south sides of the road, roughly thirty men—members of the acidhead tribe bivouacked behind the Staten Island terminal—strolled down the hill toward Mallory as her guards cheered them on. Uli looked for Bea, but there was no sign of her. In a moment, Adolphus Rafique himself appeared at the rear of the pack.

"Welcome to Greater Staten Island," he called out to Mallory. "I heard you died."

"If you came here an hour or so later, that probably would've been the case," she grinned. "How many Piggers were up there?"

"About twenty or so. Five of them had rifles. Unfortunately, none of the ones on our side survived," Rafique said, then called out to the head of his second force coming down the far hill: "How many on your end?"

"Fifteen," the white-faced chieftain answered. It was Tim Leary, the former Harvard professor. He was wearing a white-and-green football helmet—the colors of the New York Jets. "Lucky we brought our bows and arrows. Most of those damn bullets that the lobbyist gave you were duds."

"I'll be glad to reimburse whatever bullets this cost you," Mallory offered.

"Call it Staten Island courtesy," Adolphus Rafique said with a smile. "It's our city too—and you've just won. Congratulations."

"It's been a long time since we were screaming at each other in city council meetings," she reminisced.

"What are you doing down here anyway?"

"They kidnapped me from St. Vinny's after I got pulled from the bombed headquarters."

Turning around, Uli spotted Bea emerging behind the commotion. When she smiled at him, he instantly recognized the tableau from the vision he'd had in the basement of Rikers Island. In that dream, she'd had her skull blown open. Now, he tackled her instinctively, to prevent the premonition from becoming reality. A bullet screamed over their heads and slammed into Rafique's chest.

Another round of shots killed the surviving Pigger kidnapper in the backseat of one of the parked vehicles. One gangcop dashed forward to protect Mallory, the mayor-elect, but he fell backward when another bullet blasted into his face. Bea shoved Uli off of her, grabbed Mallory by the elbow, and swung her behind the nearest car. Half a dozen Crapper gangcops and VL tribe members ran up the hill looking for the shooter. A freshly fired pistol was found, but other than a badger scurrying away, there was nothing else around.

"I was supposed to be guarding him!" Bea screamed, racing over to the fallen VL head.

Mallory stayed by Rafique's side as Leary and his tribe attempted to save him.

Karen offered to drive Rafique back to VL headquarters.

"He's not going to last that long," Leary's second-in-command replied.

An old tribe member, who appeared to be a medicine man, pointed out that the bleeding wasn't too severe. "The bad news is it looks as if the bullet shattered his neck."

Upon hearing this, Karen stepped aside to talk to one of Rafique's lieutenants.

"Is there something I can do?" Mallory asked.

"More than anything," Leary said, "he wanted you to see the blocked sewer. Fixing it was his greatest wish."

"How far is it to the sewer?"

"Not too much farther. I'll take you," Leary volunteered.

Karen drew close to them and interjected, "Hell no! It's way too dangerous."

"No, I'm never coming back here again," Mallory said. "Let's do this now."

Uli was off to the side waiting for Bea, who was standing over Rafique's unconscious body.

"Hey, this is your big chance if you still want out," Mallory called over to Uli. "Come on, let's get moving!"

"What?"

"We made a deal, remember? You get out of here in exchange for speaking to Rafique."

"What deal?" asked Bea upon overhearing the exchange. "You were supposed to help *us*! It's part of the vision and—"

"Can you give me a moment?" Uli said to Mallory. Turning to Bea, he explained, "You asked me to trust my instincts. Well, they tell me that I can't do any more here than what I've already done."

"Why did you push me out of the way?" she asked accusingly.

"I saw that you were going to get your brains blown out. I didn't know the bullet would hit Rafique." He gave her an awkward hug, then climbed into the backseat of Mallory's car next to Karen.

While the rest of the Burnt Men stayed with Rafique, Leary squeezed into the front seat of Mallory's car and the remaining members of the convoy departed up the hill and out of the sandy depression, heading south.

Leary navigated the circuitous twists and turns through the barren landscape. The terrain eventually rose slightly and then sloped forward, becoming more marshlike.

"So what exactly is this way out?" Uli asked Mallory in the silence of the car.

"That hypodermic needle you found in Colder's room is something called Mnemosyne," she said. "They call it the escape drug. It's one of the experimental CIA pharmaceuticals. The theory is that you inject yourself and then drop into the hole of the sewer pipe."

"No one has ever confirmed that it works," Leary spoke up.

"That's true, but about eight years ago one of our people found some Mnemosyne and our doctor was able to test it on someone. Supposedly their heart stopped and they didn't breathe for a full hour before coming to."

"The sewer pipe out of here must take longer than an hour, right?" Uli asked.

"It's a gamble," Mallory said, slightly perturbed. "We don't know the dosage or potency."

"Why does anyone even believe they can escape?"

"As a reward for certain acts, Shub has allegedly dispensed it to loyal friends to get out of here," Karen said.

"How many people has he given it to?"

"We don't know exactly."

"How about the toxicity level of the sewer water—wouldn't that alone kill anyone who enters it?"

"I remember a study that was done when my husband was mayor," said Mallory. "They discovered that the water that made it all the way to the pipe had already been considerably filtered through the rocks. It was much cleaner than the black sludge in the harbor."

"You don't have to go if you don't want to," Karen said softly to her brother. "It's your choice."

"It's the wrong choice, but he's going anyway," Leary said.

"How do you know?" Uli asked.

"Because that explains why I was told to bring this," Leary answered, removing his football helmet. Another divine gift from the prescient Wovoka, the alleged god and first mystical resident of Rescue City. When Uli failed to respond, Leary added, "If this is your choice, then this is your destiny."

After five more minutes of navigation, they came to a place where the brown waters expanded vastly before them, turning the western desert into a huge dung-filled swamp.

Leary suggested they park the vehicles, as the wheels were beginning to get stuck in the wet sand. Pointing to a large basin of still water, he said, "This is the northern rim of the sewer drains. We can walk to the hole from here."

The convoy parked along the swamp's edge and everyone got out. Four of the older cops agreed to stay with the vehicles and the others grabbed some food to eat as they walked.

"If he really is going down the hundreds of miles of piping," said Sergeant Schuman, "there are a few things I think you should consider."

"Like what?" Karen asked.

"Well, it might not offer much protection, but I have a sleeping bag in my trunk and a can of grease for the car."

"Good thinking," Karen affirmed. "The Mnemosyne might keep you from drowning, but the trip is long and that water must still be pretty corrosive."

Uli thanked Schuman, collecting the sleeping bag and can of grease from him. One of the other gangcops grabbed some of the rope they had packed. Karen took the small oxygen tank from the trunk of her car, and the group proceeded with Leary on their hunt for the elusive hole that Jackie Wilson had dug into the earth years before when trying to repair the damage he had done to the drain.

The group silently hiked fifteen minutes uphill through a smelly, soggy stretch filled with strange-looking cattails and other leafy foliage able to survive in the toxic desert marsh.

"So how did Rafique know we were in trouble?" Karen asked Leary.

"I told him."

"How'd *you* know?"

"Wovoka told us."

"Too bad he didn't mention that Rafique was going to be murdered," Uli said solemnly.

"Actually, I told him there was a good chance it would happen."

"How'd you know that?" Uli asked.

"Because Wovoka reminded us that everything is paid for with sacrifice."

"*Who?*" Mallory asked severely.

"Mayor Wilson," Leary clarified.

"The Jack Wilson I briefly knew eight years ago wouldn't piss on you if you were on fire," Mallory replied.

Leary didn't say anything, he simply looked off into the distance.

Although Uli had briefly trekked just west of here with Bea very recently, this landscape over the hole looked vastly different. He felt as though they had walked back in time to the Mesozoic era. In the primordial sludge, Karen pointed out percolating bubbles of carbonic acid produced by decomposing bodies. Broken rib cages, like driftwood, were caught up against mossy rocks and had fused into a vast, disintegrating organic mass.

"Were you really going to give my Mnemosyne ticket to Mallory's kidnapper?" Uli asked his sister.

"Sorry," she said, "but the guy could've killed Mallory. And she is our mayor-elect. That means a new era for the next four years. I just couldn't betray him after that."

"For the record," Mallory said, "I'm hoping that you'll try to win our freedom on the outside and come back here to tell us if there's any way out of this godforsaken place."

"Of course I will," Uli said. "And by the way, I worked with that woman who was arrested for killing Ellsberg. Her name is Patricia Itt and she's mentally incapable of pulling off that crime."

"I'll look into it," Mallory replied with exhaustion.

As Leary led them along, Uli could see through the tall weeds across the river to a pulverized and crumbling wall that was overgrown with strange vegetation.

"There!" Leary called out. "That's the monument that brought us from the brink of anarchy to this miserable joke of a democracy." It was the site where Jackie Wilson had dynamited the vast wall and dikes that held back the river.

As Leary brought the group around the reservoir of fetid waters, Uli glanced back at a cluster of low-level buildings emerging behind the sandy foreground. Though from this vantage it resembled a Middle Eastern city from ancient times, it was just southwestern Brooklyn, Nevada.

Leary led them onward to higher ground. Three menacing dogs appeared and started barking and growling at them. Leary shot one of them dead with an arrow and the other two dashed away. Ten minutes uphill, beyond the basin and the massive sealed grate, they came to a group of rising rocks.

After a sweaty duration of carefully footing and clawing up the rocks, the group came to the clump of large, jagged boulders that Uli had seen at a distance with Bea. It wasn't until he felt the cool wind rise in the midst of the hot desert that Uli realized they were close. One of the only indications that other human beings had ever been there was faded spray paint on a large boulder that read, *The Hol'-in-da Tunle*—another dumb play on a New York landmark. Between the rocks, a narrow crevice yielded a steady cool breeze.

The circular crack in the earth didn't look much more than three feet in diameter. Someone had crawled down and carefully chiseled through the thick rock, leaving a serrated hole. Staring into the bottomless abyss, Uli could hear a faint gurgling. Some water was apparently still escaping into the great drain.

Uli unrolled the sleeping bag.

"You should cover your entire body in grease," his sister instructed.

As Uli stripped down, it was clear that his eagerness to escape eclipsed all modesty. Naked, he opened the small bucket of grease and proceeded to rub gobs of it over his face, neck, chest, arms, legs, and backside. When he smoothed the gel over his seared groin, he felt a degree of relief.

One of the gangcops knotted the ends of two ropes around the top flaps of the sleeping bag and rubbed grease along the outer side of it so it wouldn't get stuck during the rocky insertion.

Karen reminded Uli that he had a small oxygen tank with roughly ten minutes of air. Once he awoke from his chemical slumber, he would have to turn the dial, put the tube in his mouth, and breathe, exhaling through his nose. With masking tape, Karen secured the tank around his back. Uli could see the word *Charon* printed on it—presumably a brand name.

"Listen, if you start hallucinating when you wake up," Leary said softly to Uli, "there are two syringes between the cushions of this helmet. Inject them into one of your veins if you want to have *any* chance of surviving."

"I'll consider it," Uli said.

Leary started moving around in a tight jerky hop, chanting. Uli realized the odd man was performing one of his Ghost Dances.

"This is it," Mallory said, as she took out the Mnemosyne-filled syringe and struggled to straighten the bent needle.

Uli gave his sister a final hug. "Sorry for putting you and whoever else into this hellhole. Once I'm free, I really will try to get all of you out." He embraced Mallory as well.

Uli held up his bare forearm, squeezed out a vein, and let Karen inject him. As he climbed into the sleeping bag and lay down, he immediately felt woozy. It was a strangely peaceful sensation as his breathing grew shallow. After a lifetime largely unremembered and a frantic week of chaos in Rescue City, the tranquility was truly glorious.

"I haven't seen my big brother in ten years," Karen said with tears in her eyes. "And now he's gone again."

One of the gangcops pressed his finger to Uli's jugular and said, "I don't feel a pulse."

"Either you're dead or it's working," Mallory muttered serenely.

Uli wanted to tell her he was fine, but he couldn't so much as bat an eyelash. It was over. Although he didn't feel panicky, it was very strange not being able to breathe. He could still feel his sister preparing him—taping his nose, ears, and lips with grease-covered swabs of cotton. He tried to lift his arms to help her as she fit a pair of goggles tightly over his eyes, but in another moment he couldn't feel much of anything at all. Karen slipped the oxygen tube near his mouth and Leary's New York Jets football helmet over his head, fastening the chin guard to secure it.

Uli heard a muffled voice say, *"Okay, he's ready."* Darkness spread inside of him as several gangcops lifted the bag upright. They loosely tied the top of the bag with the rope, then lowered Uli down through the rocky fissure and deep into the windy chasm. A few times he got stuck sideways and they had to relift and relower him. He never actually felt water, simply a dark rushing force that bent his body sideways.

When the rope was cut, he felt like a kite blown high in the air. The current swirled him around and he was utterly joyous. Experiencing a strange sensation without breath or light, he found himself focusing on a pigeon, then on his sister's face. His body seemed to be shaping the direction it was moving, with the pipes forming around it. He was the force around himself.

From this unbelievable velocity, a single fugitive memory broke loose, and from it, backward through vast convolutions of reasoning, an awesome deduction occurred:

She hates you! Your sister despises you! Karen tried to kill you! She blew up the truck in Midtown! Was I sent here to arrest her? But she's my sister! What would the charges be? And now, you dumb fuck, she did it. She dropped you down a sewer pipe!

I'm going to drown! But the drug was still working; he wasn't breathing, and couldn't move; and yet he was still conscious, remembering without distraction for the first time. Trapped inside this wet, submerged bag swirling downward. The cliché of remembering one's life when about to die seemed to be true, but since he didn't know his life, he wasn't sure, he had alien recollectio███████████: Times Square, Union Square, Madison Square, a strangely partitioned city . . . crisscrossed with hurricane fencing . . . ███████Hanoi, Moscow, Havana, Beijing, who was behind the bombing? That was ten years ago. How was he responsi███████ This was his generation's Kennedy assassination; everyone had theories, but no one knew for sure. He must be an FBI agent 'cause who else on the verge of death would be thinking about an unsolved bomb attack? This must've been a mission within a mission. Was he sent on a hit? He kept thinking it was an extraction, but who? And where was his support? Had everyone here gone rogue? Why would they have allowed him to drown down a drain? *Our father, who art in heaven,* he began to pray, but███████—*Catch the Q28 to Fulton Street, change to the B17 and take it to the East Village in Manhattan. Wait outside Cooper Union until Dropt arrives. Shoot him once in the head*███████strange image seemed to rise: a large old-fashioned-looking box that you could stick your foot in. Under these thoughts (memories?) seemed to be other memories (fantasies?)██████the two tall brothers who couldn't get along? *Robert, where is your brother Paul? What the hell is a fluoroscope machine?* ██████

BOOK TWO

THE
SACRIFICIAL CIRCUMCISION
OF
THE BRONX

BOOK TWO

THE
SACRIFICIAL
CIRCUMCISION
OF
THE BRONX

For Jennifer Belle

I will make a distinction between my people and your people. This sign will occur tomorrow.

—The Book of Exodus

1

██████elderly Coney Island███████████████ther██████Who am█
██

Paul had a tall skinny younger brother and a short shy sister. His mother Bella was an overbearing bull of a woman who despite everything always meant well. His father, meek and weak, was an utterly henpecked man. Robert, his brother, jumped when Mama spoke; since Paul was the oldest, the mantle therefore fell upon him to stand up to the czarina Bella Cohen.

The first girl Paul ever loved was a stunning Jamaican named Maria who was about ten years older than him and always had a cigarette burning. Bella had seen how hardworking and honest Maria was at Madison House, the do-good organization she supported, and hired her as a domestic. Young Paul couldn't take his eyes off of Maria's unbelievable curves. He was raised in turn-of-the-century affluence, with money from both sides of his family swirling around him. His childhood was spent mostly up in New Haven, Connecticut, where the servants called him *Mr. Paul* and his younger brother *Mr. Robert*. He'd tell them to just call him Paul, but his brother was always Mr. Robert.

When Paul hit preadolescence, the flood of cash rushed the entire family through some subterranean pipeline, flushing them out into a plush new brownstone on 46th Street just off of Fifth Avenue. As he and his younger brother reached college age, their mother wanted them to go to Yale, their hometown university. Mr. Robert was glad to comply, but Paul found the old school stodgy and was looking for a more liberal education. Woodrow Wilson, the progressive, opinionated president of Princeton, had just announced that he was running for governor of New Jersey. This excited Paul to such a degree that the young man selected Princeton as his first choice.

When he got his letter of acceptance six weeks later, he tore open the envelope right at the dinner table and made the announcement. Though his father Emanuel seemed happy, Bella silently nodded her big head in dismay. By making a major decision for himself, Paul hoped to teach his younger brother that he didn't have to be such a little mama's boy. His father opened an expensive bottle of cabernet and made a toast. His mother just sat there. To further irritate her, Paul guzzled down several glasses of the wine as though it were water.

While the others at the table talked, Paul's head began spinning from the wine and he had a strange daydream that he lay suspended, just floating in darkness. When he closed his eyes he felt as though he were submerged, bouncing along the sides of some kind of giant underwater conduit.

"Paul, what do you think?" asked his dad.

"I'm sorry, I wasn't listening."

Emanuel suggested that he consider a career in banking or finance. Light-headed, Paul pretended to listen as the alcohol just floated him along.

2

While attending Princeton, Paul Moses had lofty ambitions of being either a scholar or a statesman. At first he hung out with young gentlemen who dressed in herringbone tweeds and fussed over sybaritic subtleties, such as unusual pipe tobacco and exotic teas. Before long, however, Paul decided that it was all just a competition of vanity that gave rise to legions of nancy boys and self-involved powder puffs. Soon, he dismissed all the northeastern elite schools as nothing more than an extension of European royalty, American aristocracy at its most pretentious.

During school breaks, nonetheless, he displayed his newly acquired sensibilities to his brother and sister, reciting French symbolist poetry and discussing the latest advances in European art. Although Paul's father was proud to witness his son's growing sophistication, Bella rolled her eyes. Paul further enjoyed irking his mother by taking an active interest in the Zionist movement. Gradually, as he read more and more about how fellow Jews were being mistreated around the world, he became firm in the opinion that only when their people had the security of their own homeland would the persecution end.

"None of this would happen if they simply blended into the countries they're living in," Bella would say.

"But *we* are Jews," Paul would shoot back. "Do other groups have to deny who they are?"

The Jewish settlements in Palestine occupying unpopulated lots in the desert gave hope toward a permanent homeland for all Jews. Paul's other liberal sentiments were rooted more firmly in the plight of the workingman, particularly as championed by Eugene Victor Debs and the Socialist Party of America. It was primarily for this reason that he joined the Democratic Reform Club, a leftist organization at the college. In a fit of zeal he soon accepted the nomination and ultimately the office of its presidency. Although the position didn't offer many privileges, he did meet more girls.

What captivated him most about Millicent Sanchez-Rothschild was her strong, defiant face and cascades of shiny, thick black hair. He was delightfully surprised when he heard her explaining to another student why Oliver Wendell Holmes was the greatest juror who ever sat on the high court.

Millicent had just arrived from the University of Pennsylvania to hear a lecture that his club had organized. William Jennings Bryan, the Democratic presidential candidate of 1900, was giving a talk on how the Supreme Court was stonewalling labor reform.

After spending the majority of the evening talking with Millie, Paul asked her on a date.

"If you want to make the trip down to Philly, I'm all yours," she replied.

He took the first train the following week. In Philadelphia, they spent the afternoon just chatting. Or rather, she talked and he listened. She was from a wealthy Sephardic Jewish family that had settled in Mexico City. Despite the fact that her parents were rich conservatives, she was very progressive in her views. Rights of the workingman, socialism, the suffrage movement—they were in agreement about nearly everything.

Though Millie had many suitors, Paul continued seeing her throughout the semester, taking the train from Princeton on weekends and holidays.

Over the next few months, she shared various aspects of Mexico— its history, its conquest by Cortés, the destruction of the native culture by the Catholic Church. "The Mayans produced vast libraries that Bishop Diego de Landa ordered his priests to collect and burn in huge bonfires," she explained, "though a few books survived as the Maya codices, preserving some record of their heritage."

Millie's family, which made its fortune in mining, had benefited greatly under the repeated presidential terms of Porfirio Díaz. Yet she was part of a consortium of young Latin compatriots studying in the United States who despised "El Presidente."

Aside from her own desire for social justice, her beloved cousin Pedro Martinez—her rebel mentor—was a prominent member of an anti-Díaz group. Following a national convention of various liberal clubs in 1901 and 1902, the Díaz regime arrested a group of their leaders—including her cousin—and suppressed their publications. When Pedro was finally released, he migrated to the United States along with other radicals and they unified as the Mexican Liberal Party. They called for, among other things, guarantees of civil liberties, universal public education, land reform, and a one-term limit for all future Mexican presidents.

"How many times has Porfirio been elected?" Paul asked on one of his visits.

"Six, but last year he promised to retire at the end of this term, so we're all waiting anxiously."

Paul felt a strange jolt through his body and his knees buckled.

"You okay?" Millicent asked, taking his arm.

"I just feel a little light-headed," he said, and when he closed his eyes and let her lead him, he felt once again as if he were submerged in warm liquid.

"Paul, what's the matter?" Millie demanded, brushing his arm nervously.

"I'm sorry. I think I have a touch of the flu."

3

During spring break, Millicent joined Paul on a trip home to meet his family in New York. They arrived late in the afternoon and Millie found herself seated with Paul's parents and siblings for a wonderful dinner. His sister Edna brought up a recent strike that had been in the news. Millie commented how the American government was behaving like a Pinkerton private security force for various robber barons. Bella politely responded that things might be changing, as indicated by the fact that Teddy Roosevelt had been the first president to stand up to big business, ordering them to negotiate with labor unions during a major strike several years earlier.

"But he didn't go far enough."

"What was it like growing up in Mexico?" Edna asked, trying to steer her away from controversy.

"*Very* traditional," Millie replied tiredly.

Bella stared out the window tolerating Paul's precious coquette. As coffee and dessert were served, Edna asked a casual question about the suffrage movement and whether Millie thought a constitutional amendment giving women the right to vote could actually get passed. It compelled Paul's date to launch into one of her signature arguments for women's rights.

"Tell me, dear," Bella finally said, "what exactly is it your parents do?"

"My father is the head of a mining company down in Mexico."

"And do you think he exploits any workers there?"

"My own guilt doesn't excuse anyone else's," Millie replied.

"Young lady, I don't know who taught you the fine art of hypocrisy, but—"

"It's my life mission to give restitution. What's yours?"

"You can't talk to my mother like that!" Mr. Robert interjected, rising to his feet.

Paul had to bite his lip to keep himself from laughing. After an awkward silence, Emanuel made a comment about the weather.

When Millie left early the next day for the train back to Philly, Paul's mother called him into her study and explained that she didn't want him seeing "Señorita Obnoxchez" ever again.

"I love her," he said simply.

"How can any man love such a sanctimonious and vain woman?"

"I can ask the same of Dad," he snorted back.

"Paul, I made an effort to be nice to her and only got scorn in return."

As Paul stormed out of the room, he bumped right into the maid, Maria, nearly knocking her down.

"Pardon me," he said, but the words sounded strange, like they were muffled behind some invisible wall. Hard as he tried to reach out, he couldn't.

"Paul, are you okay?" Her face seemed to ripple as she spoke.

"I'll be fine," he muttered.

4

Though his younger sister Edna liked Millicent, neither his mother nor brother had anything nice to say about her. When Paul visited home toward the end of the summer, Mr. Robert inquired whether he was still seeing "that opinionated young lady."

"Sure I am, and I plan to see her as much as I can."

"You're certain you're not just using her to anger Mom?"

"Mom is such a stick in the mud. *Everything* angers her."

"I know she can be pretty bullheaded, but she is our mother."

"We're her children, not her whipping boys."

Mr. Robert nodded silently.

That fall, to their mother's great joy, Mr. Robert began attending Yale, joining the class of 1909. Soon the two brothers fell out of touch.

One day the following spring, Paul, as president of the Democratic Reform Club, was invited to a tea hosted by the dean of student affairs. There he was introduced to the tall, dapper Woodrow Wilson, who was now serving as governor of New Jersey. He had come earlier that day to meet the constituents of Princeton, where he had formerly presided. Paul and a few lucky others had the opportunity to chat with the bespectacled politician for nearly twenty uninterrupted minutes.

"Regarding workers," Paul asked, "what exactly would you do to alleviate their hardships if you became president?"

"Well, I'm not running for president, but if I was, I'd probably draw up a bill of rights for the workingman."

When Paul called to tell his sister that he had met his hero Wilson—who incidentally supported the idea of a Jewish nation—she interrupted to say that Robert, who had joined the Yale swimming team, was in the middle of a huge imbroglio with the man in charge of the university's sports funding.

"What happened?"

"He tried to get more money for the swimming team and ended up resigning."

"Good for him," Paul said, happy to hear that his brother was finally standing up for himself. He wanted to congratulate Robert for confronting the administration, but still felt uncomfortable about how they had left things regarding Millie and Mom.

On the morning of the summer solstice, Millie called him in tears. She'd just heard that President Díaz had formally declared that he was running for a seventh term—he had lied!

"Well, I'm sure he'll be defeated," Paul said, not knowing how else to respond.

"No, he won't," she responded. "People are afraid to run against him." Millie told him that Francisco Madero, a prominent member of a respected Mexican family, had announced that he was going to oppose Díaz in the election, but Díaz had Madero thrown in jail, effectively destroying the hopes for a democratic nation that so many had spent years patiently waiting for.

Over the next month, her like-minded compatriots at different universities joined together and formed an emergency organization, Latin American Students and Teachers Still Concerned about Mexico— LAST SCaM.

Now, every time Paul visited Millie in Philadelphia, she talked obsessively about how Díaz was taking some new and diabolical action to destroy Mexican civil liberties, such as abolishing freedom of the press, then undoing all the land reforms that had been put in place before him. American slaves and Russian serfs had been set free, yet Mexican peasants were still captive.

Paul spent much of the summer helping Millie, who along with her committee launched a letter-writing campaign to raise money for the cause of those oppressed in Mexico. When she heard that Francisco Madero had escaped his captors, she called Paul and declared, "You know what this means? Porfirio's days are numbered!"

"Well, there's still the small matter of getting him out of office."

"Porfirio has everything but the people. And the people *are* everything!" she countered. Even Paul found this a little hokey, but he didn't want to discourage her optimism.

Late one afternoon in early September, a week after he had started a new semester at Princeton, Paul got called to the pay phone in the noisy hallway. Pressing the earpiece against his temple, he heard Millie shouting, "It's about to commence! People are racing down to Mexico. The revolution's starting!"

"That's great!"

"I'm heading down there too. I'm going with four other women and six men from the committee."

"Sweetheart, you don't want to get killed. Why don't you think this over some more?"

"They can't kill all of us. Mexico is about to go into the fight of its life!" she shouted. "These blackguards are trying to steal the country from my people. There's no way I'm just going to sit here quietly while this is happening. I'm leaving tonight!"

He told her that she couldn't go without seeing him one last time.

"We're all boarding a train at 9:35 this evening," she said. "If you want to come, you better head over here now."

The train from Princeton to Philly left six minutes past every hour and took roughly ninety minutes. He barely made the next train.

He arrived in Philadelphia at eight p.m., dashed several blocks to the University of Pennsylvania, and headed across the sprawling campus. Men were not allowed up inside the women's dorm, so, trying to catch his breath, he called from the reception desk downstairs. When Millie came down, she led him into a dark alcove; once alone, she threw her arms around him and gave him a passionate kiss.

"Please don't do this," he pleaded.

"I don't expect you to understand," she whispered. "But this is my own . . . escape." It was as though she were drunk with the possibility of a new life awaiting her.

"Whatever does that mean?"

"It means when I'm visiting you at Princeton or even when I'm here on campus, everyone looks at me as this proud, smart, annoying girl, but that's only because I've done such a great job hiding my true self behind this pale face."

"What does that have to do with you now?"

"I was raised in Mexico City. I didn't know a word of English until I was six. Heck, my mother's father fought against the gringos when this country stole the northern half of our land more than fifty years ago."

"Look, fifty years ago my family were Jews living in Prussia," Paul replied.

"All I'm saying is that I'm stuck outside my country, trapped in a petticoat and a social stratum. Your mother was right when she said I was living on my father's blood money. And this is my chance to make amends."

She's going to get herself killed, Paul thought, and kissed her hard on the lips.

"Unacceptable! Unacceptable!" one of the university matrons shouted over to them, clapping her hands loudly.

"I still have to pack my bags," Millie said. She kissed him again and dashed back upstairs.

Paul paced tensely in the reception area. Some from Millie's committee had already come down with their steamer trunks and suitcases. A taxi sedan had arrived and was waiting out front. Once they all squeezed in with their luggage, there was no room left, so Paul stood on the running board, hanging on the side. Despite the wind as they drove, he kept shouting to Millie through the window, "Please reconsider! This is a dangerous idea!"

They finally arrived at the huge marble-columned station where redcaps with large wooden hand trucks grabbed their trunks and heavy leather bags. They met up with others who had come from various points nearby. After exchanging greetings, they all headed to the gated ticket windows. Paul waited until he was alone with Millie, then dropped to one knee and said, "Marry me!"

"What?!"

"Be my wife!"

The surprise in her eyes melted to a slightly amused sadness. "I'll do it if you come with me."

"That would defeat the whole point."

"Which is to keep me here."

"To keep you *safe*. Is there something wrong with that?"

"No, but I do love you, Paul," she said. "And one of the reasons I love you is because I know that if we were in Mexico City and you heard that America had been taken over by a tyrant, you'd come back up here to oppose him."

Not if I were a woman, he thought.

One of the fellows on the LAST SCaM committee, a skinny young man named Alejandro Torres, handed Millie a train ticket and the group walked over to their track. The first leg of the trip was an express train which would take them as far as St. Louis. Paul walked alongside Millie and a redcap valet to the door of the train.

"I'll write you at every opportunity," she said.

Paul boarded the locomotive with her. The entire committee had bought sleeping berths in first class.

"Where can I write to you?" he asked nervously.

She proceeded to scribble down her family address in Mexico City, as well as the addresses of three friends living in the countryside. "I'll write you as soon as I get down there, but if you don't hear from me, one of these people should know where I am."

"A person's life is defined by the caution of their choices," he said in an effort to sound authoritative. "This could be the worst decision you will *ever* make."

"Despite what you might think, I'm not trying to be a hero and I have no desire to die, but I love my country and I have to do this."

He remained with her on the train until the conductor called out, "All aboard!"

She walked with him to the Dutch door at the end of the car and watched as he stepped down onto the sunken platform. The conductor lifted the wooden step and jumped on board. As the train started pulling out of the station, Millicent waved.

Paul stood alone on the platform until the locomotive slowly vanished into the night.

5

Paul took the next train back to Princeton and returned to his dorm room just past two that morning. Unable to sleep, he skipped his French and Spanish classes and remained listlessly in bed. As he eventually began his daily routines, he once again felt strangely captive. It was as if he were sealed in some kind of long, narrow tunnel, wanting to get through it quickly and out the other side. Without her, all alone, he felt as though he were drowning.

Roughly a week later, he got the first postcard from Millicent, sent from St. Louis. She explained that they were about to board a second train that would take them to Galveston, Texas. She had to be in Mexico by now, he thought. A second postcard came two days later from Texas saying they were about to cross the Rio Grande.

Two and a half weeks later, a letter arrived detailing how it was too dangerous to go to Mexico City, so they were instead heading west to Baja. Apparently, several revolutionary organizations had formed their own governments in the area and Millie's group felt it could have the greatest impact there.

October went by without a single postcard. The Mexican postal service wasn't very efficient, and Paul figured that the political turmoil must have further delayed the delivery of foreign correspondence. Hard as he tried to invest himself in schoolwork, he found himself suffering from repeated attacks of vertigo. He would usually just lie in bed trying not to imagine the worst: short, fat, oily soldiers with large, dirty sombreros taking turns violating Millie as she spat out blood and noble slogans.

The only ideas distracting him came from *The Physical Sciences*, the primary text for his Introduction to Physics class that he was taking to fulfill his science requirements. Reading the principles of physics from Galileo and Newton, he found himself mesmerized as if he were engrossed in a mystery novel.

Finally, on November 3, he received another post from Millicent. The letter had been given to a friend who was heading into Texas. It began: *My beloved Pablo, I'm assuming you didn't get any of my most recent letters as I haven't received any from you* . . . It went on to explain that her committee had broken up. Two men had joined Pancho Villa's contingent in Chihuahua; four others had joined Señor Zapata in the south; but she and one other were still in Baja in a commune run by the Mexican revolutionary Ricardo Flores Magón. Despite these different factions, Madero was still generally regarded as the new hope for Mexico.

> *You'll be happy to hear that Señor Flores is a pacifist. He doesn't even have a military attachment. He's simply trying to lead by example. The other day a cavalry of federal soldiers galloped through, almost daring us to provoke them. We've been wearing clothes we bought here, trying to blend in with the locals, but we spend our days heading down the peninsula trying to familiarize the peasants with the issues of the impending revolution* . . .

The letter had been sent more than a week after it had been written from a town in Sonora, Mexico, called Córdova. As November progressed, stories about the brewing troubles in Mexico began appearing in the *New York Times*.

Bella called to invite Paul up to New York for Thanksgiving, saying she missed her oldest boy and wanted to hear how he was doing. He ended the short conversation without uttering a single word about Millie, knowing that nothing would bring his mother greater pleasure than hearing of the girl's reckless voyage.

Opening the *New York Times* on November 20, Paul saw the headline: "TROUBLES IN MEXICO; CALL TO ARMS." While still a fugitive from the law, Madero had announced from Texas that it was time for the people of Mexico to revolt against the tyrant who was holding their country hostage. Paul feared this would end with widespread bloodshed.

During the early train ride two days later for Thanksgiving, Paul felt on edge. When he finally arrived in New York City, he briskly walked the fifteen or so blocks from Penn Station to the family brownstone on 46th Street, near Fifth Avenue.

Upon greeting the maid Maria, he learned that his mother had been in a foul mood all day. Paul took a stiff belt of Scotch and listened as Bella bossed the help around. He couldn't stop wondering if the federales garrisoned in the small Mexican village of Córdova had noticed the young students arriving from abroad.

He retreated into the study and located some paper and a fountain pen. He started writing Millie a passionate letter about his constant fears and boundless love for her. Before he got very far, however, he was interrupted by joyous shrieks. Mr. Robert had just arrived home from Yale. Their mother squealed in delight, and showered her youngest son with kisses. Paul could hear Robert giggling boyishly in response. Though Bella had been told the story numerous times, she made Robert once again relay the heroic events in which, despite his having to resign, he raised an unprecedented amount of money for the Yale swimming team.

When Paul's sister Edna arrived, Bella's mood shifted. She started bellowing about how her favorite charity, the Madison House in Lower Manhattan, was misusing her funds.

"You should've donated the money to Lillian Wald instead," Edna said.

"Paul, come on down and say hi to your brother," Bella called out, ignoring her daughter's comment. Paul quit trying to write and joined them.

When their father showed up late, Bella berated him for making them all wait while the dinner grew cold. Emanuel didn't sound contrite enough, so his wife went on about how he was a lazy ne'er-do-well, spending his days just lying about the house.

"You were the one who forced him to retire," Paul muttered softly to himself.

Robert sat with a frozen smile on his face, waiting for his mother's tantrum to pass.

Bella looked angrily around the room and, seeing Paul glaring at her, she said, "Please tell me you broke up with that mustached shiksa."

Robert snickered.

"First of all, she's Jewish. Secondly, save your rancor for those who are afraid to defend themselves."

"Hey, Princeton boy," she replied, "don't forget who pays for you to learn how to recite French poetry!"

"Well, you can keep your damned tuition," he lashed back. "'Cause I'm done with that . . . that finishing school for robber barons!"

"I'll believe that when I see it!"

As Paul furiously headed for the front door, he heard Robert saying to his mother, "Let him just simmer down."

True to his word, when Paul got back to Princeton, he waited until Monday, then went to see the dean of student affairs and applied for a multisemester leave of absence that wouldn't affect his grades. Next he returned to his dorm room and packed his bags. He was about to call Bella, but instead called Robert. The phone rang until someone in the hallway of his brother's dormitory answered and said Robert wasn't around.

Paul kept calling over the next four hours until he finally got ahold of Robert. As soon as his brother said hello, Paul explained that he had just withdrawn from classes.

"Please say you're joshing."

"Absolutely not."

"Mother was just having some fun, but this is downright spiteful."

"I didn't do it out of spite."

"The semester's almost over, and then you only have one more year to go!"

"Robert, I have no choice. Millicent's down in Mexico and I'm sure she's in distress."

"Oh my," Robert said. "So what are you hoping to do, go down and rescue her?"

"I suppose." It sounded melodramatic even to Paul.

"But you're not seriously planning on fighting the government of Mexico, are you?"

"No, of course not, I just want to protect Millie."

"Paul, you're handsome, rich, and young. You don't have to get yourself shot in another country to save some wetback mistress. Hell, you can sleep with Maria—I know you fancy her."

"Damn you, Robert!"

"I'm sorry, Paul, but this is just crazy."

"Look, it's one of those things that if I don't do, I'll spend the rest of my life regretting."

"And how about if you get yourself killed? Do you have any idea how angry Mom would be if that happened?"

Paul smiled, but then realized that Robert was serious. Robert wasn't afraid of his older brother's death, only concerned about upsetting their mother. Paul replied that he simply had no choice.

"So you're really going through with it?"

"I am, and I hope you'll learn from this."

"What exactly am I supposed to learn, Paul?"

"That you shouldn't be afraid to fight for something you believe in."

Paul heard a sound that could've been a snort or a chuckle. He wasn't sure if Robert was indignant or amused.

"Good luck," Robert finally remarked.

Paul hung up the earpiece on the cradle of the candlestick phone. Trying to stand, he found that his left leg and right arm had fallen asleep—he must've pinched a nerve. After several minutes of nervously shaking his body, his circulation returned to normal.

He gave away many of his possessions and put the rest in storage, then packed a single rucksack of necessities. He headed straight to the train station and mapped out as direct a route as he could to the tiny Mexican village of Córdova. The trip was six days of continuous travel with four connecting trains. The food was awful, but Paul enjoyed watching as the passengers, climate, and landscapes slowly changed while they moved southwest. He also became friendly with most of the Negro Pullman workers on the trains. It was the first time he had traveled out west. The wide-open ranges and the soaring mountains stretched his imagination, but the endless rolling desert filled him with an inexplicable déjà vu.

As Paul's train eventually approached the Mexican border, he changed into a new suit to extinguish any suspicion that he was aligned with the revolutionaries. He didn't have a passport, but when the two federal soldiers marched slowly down the aisle, Paul handed over his Princeton University ID. One of them looked it over and handed it back to him.

The train stopped three more times, and each time a different pair of menacing soldiers walked down the aisles of the train, carefully checking the identity of foreigners and asking what business they had in Mexico.

"Just vacationing," he always replied with a tight smile.

When Paul eventually descended from his final train in Sonora, Mexico, he felt a painful crick in his neck; it seemed as if an invisible force was pinning his head in place. He assumed it had something to do with the pinched nerve he had suffered several days earlier, so he simply trudged along in discomfort.

6

Following a full day of travel on a mule-drawn carriage, Paul finally arrived at the small village of Córdova. Millicent's last mailing address turned out to be a home full of peasants.

"Are any students from America staying here?" he asked one of the men in his passable Spanish.

Paul was directed to Alejandro Torres, one of the original committee members, who said that Millie was running the canteen attached to a small brigade roughly fifty miles to the east. It was headed by Colonel Cesar Octavio-Noriega.

Paul was able to catch a ride there the next day. As rebel soldiers stopped the wagon upon his arrival, Millie came racing up with her arms spread wide.

"Paul!"

He kissed her hard on the mouth and squeezed her tightly.

That night, over soggy corn-flour burritos with rice and beans that tasted like they had been refried one too many times, she filled him in: Things had not been going well. When Madero escaped his captors and made his formal call to arms, he expected to find a trained army of sympathizers waiting to assist him when he crossed the Rio Grande. A small crowd was gathered there, but the ragtag group hardly constituted an army. Madero was forced to retreat back up to Texas. In Mexico, there were some minor skirmishes, but the expected uprising fizzled. Nonetheless, word spread and various insurgent leaders started joining together. Peasants began to grasp the significance of the fight and joined the insurrection. In the state of Chihuahua, Madero supporter Pascual Orozco took over the town of Guerrero. At the end of November, Pancho Villa captured San Andrés. Back in Sonora, another revolutionary, José María Maytorena, organized a series of small bands which soon infested the north. From the southern state of Morelos, the great Emiliano Zapata sent a delegate to Madero to discuss cooperation in fighting the Díaz regime.

"I can't believe you came all the way down here," Millie said excitedly to Paul.

"Believe me, I didn't want to," he replied, putting his bag down.

With a wide smile and a beautiful tan, Millie looked like someone else. She led him around the camp proudly, showing him off to her various friends and colleagues.

"Who is this?" Colonel Octavio-Noriega asked suspiciously. He was a short man with a bushy white mustache.

"My fiancé," Millie replied.

"Good, then he'll stay in your tent."

That night, Paul and Millie made love for the very first time. Over the following weeks, as the band rode east and then south, Millicent introduced him to a variety of zealous young comrades, many of whom had come from abroad to help with this struggle. All seemed to believe that a worldwide revolution was imminent. Paul sat quietly at night around the campfires.

"Civilization comes to the point," one Italian volunteer named Carlo struggled to say one evening, "where iz no longer need for the leaders who divide and exploit the workman."

Listening to them, Paul found a renewed faith in the American system of government. To Millie's displeasure, he told her that he had decided to stay out of all combat in Mexico. His sole task would be protecting her.

"Can't you see how bad it is here?" she appealed.

He replied that he did, but that he just didn't think these people were ready; the poor seemed to accept their fate and the rich clearly felt entitled to theirs. His noninvolvement soon became an ongoing argument between the two of them.

It all changed by accident one day, when a young Russian anarchist who was an expert sapper arrived under orders from Pancho Villa. Vladimir Ustinov, who wasn't much older than Paul, had ample experience with bombs from his time in czarist Russia. He had been sent out to teach various militias—some of which were filled with foreign fighters—how to construct homemade bombs to be used against the local garrisons.

In the turbulent state of Chihuahua, none of the peasant fighters spoke anything besides Spanish. Other than Russian, Vladimir only knew French. It often took him three hours to give a twenty-minute lesson, but that day he was pressed for time. Getting a full demonstration with all the equipment, Paul, who had studied French at Princeton, spent an hour learning from the Russian before the man had to gallop off to his next mission.

"So should I teach your soldiers?" Paul asked the colonel after the Russian departed.

"Teach them what?"

"What Señor Ustinov taught me—how to use the explosives."

"You're our official sapper," the commander said to him in Spanish. "Just instruct them as you need."

"But I'm not a volunteer," Paul explained. "I'm just here to protect my fiancée."

"Congratulations, you've officially been conscripted," the commander replied.

"Look, I'll teach your men what Vladimir taught me, but I refuse to kill people in a war that I don't believe in."

The commander pulled an old pistol from his cracked leather holster and pointed it at Paul's forehead. The young American stared angrily at the older man, refusing to believe that the bastard would pull the trigger.

"I'll teach and oversee your men, but I simply can't kill anyone. If you really are going to execute me, so be it."

The commander put the gun down and told him to wait outside the tent. Five minutes later, the man sent for Millicent, who he greatly respected. The two spoke alone for several minutes, then Paul was summoned.

"Okay, I've agreed to your terms. You can instruct Millie here."

"Millie?"

"Yes, she'll be your hands. Your first mission is tonight."

"I'm not going on any mission."

"Fine, then she'll do it alone. Instruct her as best you can. She's going out in a few hours."

"What's the mission?"

"There's a supply train passing two hours from here. She's going out with a detachment of the European volunteers to blow up the tracks."

"Millie can't do it."

Before Paul could opine that most of the European volunteers were criminals who'd sooner rape her than follow her, Millie spoke up: "I've done missions before."

Paul finally relented and agreed to be the militia's official sapper instead of Millie. His unofficial second-in-command, Carlo Valdinoci, was a quick study, with a keen sense of humor and a profound commitment to the cause.

Along with a dozen men, most of them Italian volunteers, Paul

rode out on horseback. Across the landscape, he could see a large regiment of federal soldiers patrolling both sides of the tracks. He had
his men tie up their horses at a safe distance, then waited until night.
He brought three men with him, proceeding forward on foot. They
were almost caught when a passing patrol found their tracks in the
moonlight, but they cautiously advanced from tree to tree and rock to
rock and reached the target undetected. Paul and Carlo hastily taped
a bundle of seven dynamite sticks to the side of one track, while the
others kept watch. Paul lit a slow-burning fuse and they ran like hell.

* * *

Over the next three years, his little group, known as the Italian brigade, carried out twelve more missions. Complicating matters was the
fact that they began running out of supplies. One sweltering afternoon
in February 1910, however, Vladimir Ustinov returned with several
large spools of wires and a plunger detonator. Due to the surge of
federal troops there, he had been sent back into the region and was
supposed to stay there for a couple of months.

After giving Paul instructions on how to attach the fuses, he explained that with the plunger they could dramatically increase the
amount of federales killed. Paul nodded, not revealing that he really
didn't want to be responsible for any casualties.

That night, passing a bottle of tequila over the large bonfire, the two men chatted. Vladimir explained in French how the food and liquor were killing him here—constant diarrhea—but he greatly enjoyed the work.

"Since the bloody attack in St. Petersburg by the czar's army on unarmed citizens a few years ago, Russia is much like Mexico these days," Vladimir explained. "Right on the verge."

"Then why are you here instead of Mother Russia?"

"Waiting for the right moment," Vladimir answered. "Everything has that moment when you can tip it over with a feather. One day soon America will have its own moment."

"I can understand your feeling that way about Russia, but in America we have an elected government."

"The United States has the same vast disparity between the rich and poor that every other country has, and its elections are rigged all the time. America just needs a single major event to topple the old apparatchiki."

"I met Woodrow Wilson and he's a good man. If anyone can fix things, he will."

"He might make some small differences, but he can't change the many social inequities that divide your country."

Paul wasn't interested in arguing, but Vladimir and the other young radicals in his brigade could talk about little else. Over the ensuing weeks, every time they met, the Russian youth would ask him if he was ready to help start the new American revolution. And every time, Paul would answer that America's major problems would be settled by Woodrow Wilson.

Soon it became a running joke. If the weather was bad or the federales had repelled an attack, Vladimir would say to Paul in broken Spanish, "Don't worry, your Wilson will fix."

"We kill Czar Alexander, we kill your McKinley, and we can kill Wilson when iz time," Carlo declared.

Paul sighed and wondered how he'd gotten himself mixed up with all these nuts.

He was able to send a letter home from the small town they were using as a central hub. Six weeks later, Edna wrote him back and told him that when their mother had heard what he was doing, she threw such a fit that their father had to call a doctor to settle her down. Since then, his name had not so much as been mentioned. Robert was doing graduate work and had a new girlfriend named Mary. Paul's favorite maid, Maria, had also met someone and was falling deeply in love.

7

Several months later, Paul received a tightly scripted postcard from his sister informing him that poor Maria had fallen on hard times. She had married that fellow, some Italian-Jewish guy from Rome. He had worked and saved and managed to buy an old house at a good price in a section of the Bronx called East Tremont. No sooner had she moved in with him than he got her pregnant. Then the guy just vanished into thin air. One of his friends claimed he had returned to Italy; allegedly he was connected with the Mafia.

Please give her five hundred dollars from me, and tell her to take it easy until she has the kid, Paul wrote back.

One day, while they were planning a complicated two-site detonation, Vladimir explained that Paul would need a watch in order to coordinate the second explosion. When Paul said that his wristwatch broke long ago, Vladimir gave him his own pocket watch, a beautiful gold piece with a miniature image of a handsome older gentleman glazed on the inside.

"Is this your father?" Paul asked, staring at the resemblance.

"It's the father of a Russian industrialist I executed, which is why I had to flee the country," Vladimir replied. "But he looks like my father, so I'm very much attached to it. And it keeps perfect time. You'll give it back to me the next time I see you."

Vladimir had to depart quickly to aid with another vital operation farther south. Several days after Paul completed his mission, he heard that the young Russian had been caught by the federales and was summarily executed.

Paul then discovered that over two hundred federal soldiers had been killed during his two-site detonation; he was horrified. While the others in the Italian brigade celebrated, he went to his tent and began packing.

"What are you doing?" Millie asked, entering quietly.

"This has gone on long enough!" he yelled. "Over two hundred men are dead because of me, and I never even *joined* this cause!"

"You in it now!" called Carlo drunkenly from outside the tent.

"Paul, we're winning. It's just a matter of time now."

"You manipulated me into this. And it's over. To hell with you, I'm going home."

"Octavio's outside," she whispered. "If you leave now, he'll have you shot."

"You tricked me into this and now look! You've made me into a damn murderer."

"Paul, don't ever say that. You came down here on your own. You knew my loyalties from the start. I never lied to you. Listen to me," she appealed softly. "You've given me everything I want. In return we'll get married and we'll have a family and a nice place near the city. We'll be very happy together."

He nodded his head and left the tent, but he eventually calmed down and stoically remained.

Under the two charismatic generals Zapata and Villa, the tide was clearly turning. Díaz had begun appealing publicly for peace, but Madero flatly rejected his efforts. To try to win back popular support, the tyrant attempted to reinstate land reforms. He even went so far as to dismiss most of his conservative cabinet, but it was to no avail.

Over a quick period of time, places that were Díaz strongholds like Veracruz, Chiapas, and Yucatán began seeing heavy insurgency. By the spring of 1911, the rebels had seized over twenty major cities.

Finally, when the revolutionaries encircled Ciudad Juárez, Díaz resigned. Within days, Madero was sworn in as the new president. Victory celebrations blanketed Mexico. The revolution was over.

"It's time to go home," Paul said to Millie upon hearing the latest news.

She nodded in agreement. But the very next day, the new president, who was expressing reluctance to enact some of the key reforms of the revolution, was assassinated. Several revolutionary leaders boldly declared themselves the rightful heir to power. Colonel Octavio-Noriega held his brigade together, waiting to see what compromise might be reached, but by the week's end it was clear that a new struggle for power had begun.

"They just need us a bit longer," Millie informed Paul.

"This isn't fair," he said through clenched teeth. "I came here to protect you and now a big chunk of my life is gone!"

A week after the assassination, Colonel Octavio-Noriega led Paul into his tent late one night and told him that the American was an indispensable part of his command.

"Carlo knows everything I do about explosives," Paul replied tiredly.

"It would have a detrimental effect on morale if I were to just discharge you," Octavio-Noriega said. Then, in a low voice, he added, "However, if you and Millie were to take a mule and leave some night and vanish forever, there would be little I could do."

The next morning, Paul hugged Millie tightly to his chest and whispered into her ear, "We're leaving tonight."

"We'll be shot."

"He's letting us go."

"But the fighting isn't over."

Paul explained that he had been given an unofficial discharge.

"But that wasn't our agreement." She turned away from him.

"You said that when we could leave without getting killed, you'd go with me," he replied sternly. "You promised!"

She didn't say a word to him the rest of the day, refusing to even make eye contact.

Early that evening, after packing a handful of essentials, Paul went out for a final meal with his comrades.

When he returned to his tent, he found that Millie hadn't packed her trunk. She was lying facedown on her cot, weeping uncontrollably.

"What's the matter?"

"I love you dearly, Paul. Truly, I do. And I know the sacrifice you made coming down here and helping me in this struggle. And if it's worth anything, these people love you and need you. So, if you want, we can marry and live here. We can even have children and—"

"You agreed to come back north!"

"I'm really sorry. I just can't abandon my country," she said, embracing him.

"You betrayed me to get me to kill people for you!"

"Paul, I love you. I swear it!" She wept aloud as he stormed out.

Taking one of the regiment's old burros, he rode and walked nonstop through the night and all the next day. Arriving at the nearest train station, he bought a ticket west that would take him to another train north. Caked in dirt and sweat, utterly exhausted, he had an odd succession of thoughts. *Did you abandon your post? Did you abandon a people in crisis, a people in need of you? Did you abandon a situation that you were culpable in creating?* He sensed that the thoughts were somehow not entirely related to Millie and Mexico, and that they were coming from somewhere else altogether.

On the third night of his slow train ride across the dry landscape, he found himself hot and unable to sleep. He frequented the vestibule at the end of the car where he'd open the top half of one of the double windows, allowing in a cool breeze. As he thought of all the bloodshed he had seen during his time in Mexico, tears came to his eyes.

"You okay, son?" he heard. An older fellow with a bushy mustache and only one arm was leaning against the opposite wall, puffing a corncob pipe.

"Yeah," Paul replied, wiping away his tears. "I'm just glad to get away from all the fighting below the Rio Grande." He didn't have any more to say.

"Son, I'm seventy-seven," the fellow said with a Southern twang. "Fifty years or so yonder, when I was about your age, I was a soldier for the Confederacy, and I don't mind telling you that this entire area we're passing through, and all the young men in it, well . . . you're passing through the land of the dead. You just couldn't imagine ever recovering from so much loss, and yet you do."

Paul responded politely and excused himself.

After four more squalid days without even enough money to eat for the final stretch, Paul arrived in New York's Pennsylvania Station. With a bundle of filthy and torn belongings under his arm, he walked up to his parents' home on 46th Street. When he rang the bell at eleven o'clock, Maria answered and let out a shriek upon seeing the bearded, wild-eyed scion of the Moses family.

Bella appeared at the door and immediately started yelling: "Didn't I warn you! Did I not say that a woman like that is only out for herself? Did I tell you that or not? Answer me!"

"You told me."

"And did you listen?"

"No, I didn't listen."

"And what happened? So much time wasted—for what?! You might as well have been in prison. Not to mention the fact that you could've very easily gotten yourself killed."

"I'm sorry." He wasn't about to share the risks he had taken and the murders he had committed.

"What sense is any of this? A Jewish boy getting himself killed fighting for . . . for what? Tar babies and jungle heathens? Why?"

Suddenly, Paul collapsed. Maria and Bella helped him into the bathroom, then washed him, fed him, and put him to bed.

The next afternoon, after having slept for more than sixteen hours, Paul came downstairs for a big brunch of matzo ball soup, whitefish salad, fresh bagels, and orange juice. Bella sat with him as he ate.

"What do you want to do now?"

"Just finish my degree," he said quietly.

His grades, his extracurricular activities, his attendance and conduct had all been excellent—it was summer, and with a little luck (and his family's connections), he could get back into school in time for the fall semester.

Inspired by Edison's many recent breakthroughs in electricity, Paul believed that technology could somehow level society's playing field and help foster true justice. He had learned that only a tiny percentage of the population in Mexico was literate, and he couldn't help thinking that if all the little villages had access to electricity, groups would be better able to assemble and share ideas. Individuals would be more compelled to learn how to read, and education made people more politically alert.

That night, in the sumptuous luxury of his parents' house, as he was drifting off to sleep, he felt once again as though he were drowning.

Bolting up, he turned to flip on his bedside lamp, only to realize he was naked and floating in warm black water, gasping for air. Like an eggshell cracking open . . . ██████████████████████ *Walk to Sutphin . . . Catch the Q28 to Fulton . . . Change to the B17 . . . Shoot Dropt!*

Uli had returned. It was as if Paul Moses had hijacked his identity and dragged him through his life, like down a sewage pipe, so utterly, that until that moment he'd thought he was Paul—whoever the fuck Paul was . . .

Desperately clawing at some kind of thick fabric wrapped tightly around him. A helmet chin-strapped to his head.

Feeling about, he found a small hose secured near his mouth. He sucked on it, hoping to draw oxygen . . . then remembered. Clenching his diaphragm to keep from choking, he nervously fingered the hose into a tiny tank attached to his naked back. He turned the little knob on top and a jolt of oxygen shot down his throat like a snake. Awkwardly, he gulped down several deep breaths, then turned the knob off to conserve his air supply. *Where the hell am I? And how do I get out?* He closed his eyes and tried not to panic. Strangely, the Mnemosyne, the drug he had been injected with to keep him alive in the black water, was still working. His eyes still shut, he took it all in, almost like a song playing constantly in the background, the life of someone named Paul, years ago. He was simply unable to stop the images rushing through his head.

8

Paul spent the new school term studying physics and electronics and began his thesis on Maxwell's unified theory of electromagnetism.

Each day in class, his thoughts returned obsessively to poor Millie and the hardships she must be suffering. He'd start scribbling letters to her, filling them with his testaments of love and regret, but invariably he'd tear them up, recalling what he regarded as her betrayal. He tried desperately to reroute all his grief and heartbreak into studying electrical engineering.

Several months after returning to Princeton, Paul opened the paper one morning to find an article about the bombing of a courthouse in Lower Manhattan, allegedly conducted by anarchists. Other bombings followed. He began to fear that Carlo and his band of Italian revolutionaries were responsible; this was not too far-fetched, as they had claimed to have agents in America. Over the ensuing months, courthouses, churches, police stations, and even the homes of politicians came under attack. Paul considered placing an anonymous call to the police department, but he wasn't sure what he'd say. He only had a few names, and he didn't know any locations or plans. Ultimately, he feared that his own identity would be revealed and he'd come under suspicion, so he kept silent and hoped the attacks would cease.

While Paul was down in Mexico, his brother had married his girlfriend and through hard work had already completed a graduate program at Oxford University. Using his mother's connections, he had gained admission to the prestigious new Training School for Public Service, the first of its kind. Young Robert Moses was promised a job with the Bureau of Municipal Research—the organization that had founded the school.

Bella was impressed with Paul's determination to catch up. When he finally graduated from Princeton in June 1912, his mother said she wanted to help him build some financial security so he could begin thinking about a family. "Opportunity is where you find it," she told him, "and except for Edison, I've never heard of anyone getting rich in electricity."

She invited him home for a big dinner to be thrown in his honor. Naturally, Mr. Robert was too busy to come. When Paul arrived early at the Midtown manor several days later, he followed Maria into the kitchen, still disgusted by the latest news he had read on the train to the city. The families of the victims in the recent Triangle Shirtwaist Factory fire, after having filed a civil lawsuit against the owners, had been awarded the insulting settlement of seventy-five dollars for each of the 146 victims, mostly young girls, who had been burned or fallen to their deaths.

Maria interrupted Paul's train of thought, mentioning that his mother had arranged a surprise for him that he wasn't going to like.

"Who's this princess?" Paul asked, spotting a pretty little girl peeking out at him from behind a curtain.

"Lucretia, come here and say hi to Paul."

Paul curtsied, asking, "Are you the duchess of Ferrara?"

"Who?" Maria asked.

"Lucrezia Borgia, duchess of Ferrara," Paul replied. "She had a ring with a secret compartment in it, through which she could easily poison her unsuspecting adversaries."

The toddler looked confused. "No," she said.

At that moment, Bella shouted out Paul's name from the living room, so he said goodbye to Maria and her young daughter. They were served drinks and sat talking for half an hour until Paul's father and sister arrived, then they all moved into the dining room.

Maria had prepared a fabulous red snapper dish. When they were finished with dinner, Bella announced that with Emanuel's help she had arranged for Paul to get a great job where he could make excellent use of his mathematical skills.

"It's in banking," his father quietly added.

"Kuhn & Loeb," Bella elaborated. "David Loeb himself secured you the position. You start in two weeks."

Paul sighed.

"It's a very prestigious firm," Emanuel said.

It was obvious to Paul that Bella had put tremendous effort into orchestrating this. Usually his father didn't make a peep. "Mom, I'm grateful for the offer, but I'm just not a banker. I want to—"

"Paul, you're still young. Why don't you just give this a chance?" Bella pushed. Paul smiled, not wanting to make a scene. "Just try it for six months and—"

"I told you repeatedly that I want to work in the public sector and I want to be an electrical engineer."

"Well, that's admirable, son, but . . ." his father began.

"What the hell do you know?" Bella burst out. "You're a damn kid who just got home from Mexico. We paid a truckload of money for your college degree."

"I don't even like bankers! You just don't listen!"

"Paul, please," his father said.

"Robert was right," Bella said. "I've turned you into a snot-nosed brat. You won't even try this before turning it down."

Paul rose, grabbed his coat, and hurried out as his mother continued yelling about his wasted time south of the border with Señorita Obnoxchez.

Paul awoke that night with the blanket pulled over his head, and he was once again unable to feel his arms or legs. He could feel an air pocket forming along the top of the blanket, but then he realized it wasn't actually a blanket. He was having a nightmare about being trapped in a bag filled with water.

But it wasn't a dream—and he wasn't Paul. He shook his limbs until sensation started to return.

I got to find some way out of here before I drown.

Reaching around, he twisted the knob on the top of the oxygen tank and took another injection of air.

Focusing on regaining his calm, Uli remembered that he had been inserted into the sleeping bag for protection. A piece of thin rope loosely sealed the top of it. With minimal struggle, he was able to snap the rope and pull the bag over him. It was immediately sucked away and he found that he was entangled in a series of crisscrossing lines of some kind. A faint ray of light from above allowed him to see that he was snared in a network of loose cables, like a big fishing net. He was still in the large sewer pipe he had been swept down. His helmeted head was being pushed into a pile of boulders that seemed to be holding down the base of the netting, preventing him from continuing onward. He remembered having read that the average person needed a breath every three or so minutes, but it felt like it had been at least five since his last one: the chemical injected into his system seemed to have lingering effects. He took another gulp of air, then realized he had to break through these ropes to have any chance of staying alive.

9

Uli wondered if the current of water pushing him against the net was powering some massive generator. He remembered Nikola Tesla's famous hydroelectric generators at the Adams Power Station, powered by the mighty waters of the great Niagara Falls. Their boundless megawatts of electricity were channeled down high-tension wires, bringing fifty thousand volts across New York State to the city.

Apprenticing as a field engineer with the Consolidated Edison Company of New York, Paul had personally inspected a great deal of the system. He had joined the ranks of the linemen in jumpsuits and had climbed up the poles and seen thousands of miles of power lines racked side by side. He had also descended into the many semi-flooded manholes, checking the countless transformers where voltage was stepped down to 220 and routed into households throughout the five boroughs.

Just a quick glance at the sprawling electrical grids that supplied the various communities of the perpetually expanding city—it was evident that a dramatic power shortage was looming. The mouths of ever more babes were suckling at the same fixed row of nipples. Multiple feeders rerouted electricity farther and farther away. It made Paul realize they didn't simply need more generators in New York; new ways of moving the turbines were also required.

Uli tried to hold onto the thoughts, but marinating there in the giant pipe, he now recalled the submarine that fired torpedoes into the luxury liner *Lusitania*. Over a hundred Americans had been killed.

Woodrow Wilson demanded that Germany cease its attacks on passenger ships. They complied. Still, domestic pressure increased and blowhards like Teddy Roosevelt denounced Wilson as a coward.

In April of 1917, the United States finally joined the war. After hearing Wilson's speech about making the world "safe for democracy," Paul, who had been working as an engineer for a few years but still hadn't risen to the upper echelons of Con Ed, decided to quit his job and follow his president's call.

He telephoned Robert and said, "Now it's *our* country at war, not Mexico. I'm enlisting. Will you join me?"

"Does Mom know you're doing this?" Robert asked.

"Not yet."

"Tell you what," Robert said. "If she gives you her blessing, I'll seriously consider joining you."

Paul replied that he would take his brother up on that.

The next day, when Paul visited his mother to tell her that he was intent on joining the army, she screamed, "What, did you meet another girl? Whenever you get aroused, you want to go invade some country! Who's the woman this time?"

"Lady Liberty," he quipped.

Bella argued that he had already gone through one war, which was more than enough.

"I'm still of draft age."

"No one's going to draft you. I'll see to that." Then, taking a breath, she calmly informed him that if he joined the army, he should never contact her again.

Paul hugged Bella, who didn't budge, and then left the house.

Later that week, when he told the recruitment officer that he was an engineer well versed in electrical circuitry, the man's eyes lit up. He said he had been waiting months for someone with half of Paul's qualifications. Paul had been partly hoping to get sent to boot camp and fight overseas. Instead, he was immediately commissioned as a first lieutenant and sent to some vague assignment in Washington, DC. There, he found himself working at a desk in the Weapons Malfunctions Report Unit—the WMRU—reviewing incidents of battlefield equipment breakdown. Initially it was only about half a dozen incident reports per week. Machine guns jamming. Grenades failing to explode. Trucks and jeeps malfunctioning in the heat of combat. Soon after starting, Paul explained to his commander, Colonel Gibbons, that he had no experience in weaponry, and asked to be transferred out.

"I'm drastically undermanned as it is. Reynolds doesn't even know how to hold a damn gun, much less assemble one. And Lindquist is a bloody pacifist. But you've all got great minds and you're quick learners. Transfer denied."

Paul's job was to assess if a weapon had failed for a unique reason or if there was a manufacturing flaw. A key focus was identifying makes or models that required modifications or recalls.

As America's involvement in the war heated up, reports started pouring in. Paul was promoted to captain and put in charge of all field artillery reports. Soon, however, the work fell into routine drudgery and he began daydreaming about the great struggle happening a quarter of the way around the world. Reviewing reports of the carnage, he found himself recalling his days in Mexico. There was little romance in planting sticks of dynamite and running like mad. Though he had seen dead bodies—and was even shot at once—he had never witnessed combat on the front lines. Most of the men in the militia barely had guns, let alone uniforms.

His mother never wrote, but he did receive letters from Edna once a week, and on occasion Maria would drop him a postcard updating him on life back home. Several times she enclosed pictures that her daughter Lucretia had drawn at school. And it was through Maria that he learned that Mr. Robert had finally gotten his first big break, an appointment in the Municipal Civil Service Commission under the "boy mayor," John Purroy Mitchel.

10

As Uli wrestled with the various squares of netting and tried to pull his way out, he thought, *A tank could tear right through this like wet toilet paper.* With its steel caterpillar wheels, it could roll right over mines and through waves of enemy fire. The common belief was that a good tank could quickly end the war.

America needed to develop the basic models for a big tank and a small one. This required a complex compromise between British and French designs, as well as the work of over seventy subcontractors and five different manufacturing plants for final assembly.

The entire process was taking so long that no one thought any of the tanks would actually see action during the war. Before the first American tank even rolled off the assembly line, the Germans managed to seize one from the British; with their own modifications, the

Germans started assembling their own battalion. Soon, the few American tanks in action began breaking down and Paul found himself sifting through stacks of incident reports late into his nights.

A recurrent malfunction quickly became apparent during a spring offensive. The men inside the smaller tanks were getting killed when mines exploded right through their floors. In the space of three weeks, eighteen tanks had been destroyed in the same way, killing more than thirty doughboys. Paul immediately requested to see the blueprints of these particular tanks.

The outer metal skin of the tanks was supposed to be five-eighths of an inch thick, yet the actual thickness varied in four different reports, and two of the torn hulls measured as thin as a quarter of an inch.

Paul contacted the military attaché at the Byrd & Hale assembly plant in Cleveland, Ohio, and asked for confirmation of how thick the hulls of their tanks were. He was told they'd need three days to research that information.

The next day he got a phone call from one Samuel P. Bush, who introduced himself as a government contractor.

"How can I help you, Mr. Bush?" Paul asked.

"I'm chief of ordnance, specifically small-arms munitions."

"You probably want Captain Reynolds. He's the case officer who handles small-arms malfunction reports."

"No, I want to speak with *you*."

"About what?"

"I just thought maybe I could stop by and we could talk."

"Fine."

At five o'clock, just before Paul was about to leave for the day, a swollen-looking man with a thick bushy mustache and a bowler showed up and introduced himself as Samuel.

"So you're a Yale man?" he asked.

"No, Princeton. How about you?"

"Stevens Institute, but both my father and son went to Yale."

"Were you hoping to raise some money for the alumni? 'Cause I can give you my brother's phone number, he went there."

"No," the older man chuckled. Looking around the stuffy basement, he said, "Listen, I'm starving. Would you care to join me for a bite? I know a place near here that has great chops—Dutch's."

Paul said what the heck, he was about to leave anyway. As the government contractor led him outside to his car, he explained that he was there because of the phone call Paul had made to the Byrd & Hale assembly plant.

"Oh, yeah, about the thickness of the hull of their two-man tanks. Did they contact you?"

"Not officially, no. It's just that I work with them a lot, and Shane Richards asked me what was up."

By the casual, unassuming way Bush drove as he talked, Paul's first instinct was that the man was there on behalf of some higher-ups in the War Department who were launching their own probe. When they entered the restaurant, the maître d' immediately recognized Mr. Bush and showed him to his "usual table."

In another moment, a fine bottle of French wine was uncorked and poured. Bush ordered two plates of filet mignon—both medium rare—then offered Paul an expensive Cuban cigar. Paul politely refused. That was when he first considered that the man might be representing corporate interests. Almost as soon as he thought this, Bush said, "The reason I'm here is because a group of us got heavily involved in America's new tank project and, well, we think of it as our own baby."

"Success has many fathers, and failure is an orphan," Paul replied.

"Exactly, but success doesn't come as quickly as we'd like. We're trying to get this thing on its wobbly little feet without any problems, and at this stage, if any little thing comes up, it can have a big effect on the war effort."

"Doesn't it help the baby if we heal it when it's sick?"

"We already know the hull is too thin. We've doubled the size of it, but we're trying to keep it a little on the hush-hush."

"I read that the thickness was supposed to be five-eighths of an inch, but some were measured at a quarter-inch, and if you multiply that discrepancy by the four thousand tanks which the government commissioned, that's a whole lot of clams saved."

"The tank in question, as you know, was put together from several different blueprints from French and English designs. So where exactly would you lay the blame?"

"Which company manufactured the hull of the tanks that blew in and killed over thirty young American soldiers?" Paul asked coolly.

Bush smiled and just stared at him as though he were a child. In the course of the next twenty minutes, as the subcontractor rattled off statistics to put the facts in a context that made them seem trivial, Paul's food was taken away uneaten. Bush ordered a Baked Alaska and brandy, and then more brandy. Other patrons stopped by, shook Bush's hand, and left.

"You know, these tanks were finished way ahead of deadline. No one even thought they'd make it out onto the battlefield in time. Do you know how many infantry soldiers they have saved?"

"They're death machines for the two men inside."

"And we've already taken measures out on the field to have the tanks reinforced with one-inch plates riveted to their undercarriage."

"Then that should be made public too."

"Maybe it will soothe your mind, Captain Moses, to know that all this has already been brought to the attention of everyone from the attorney general to the inspector general's office."

"Then why are you taking me out for dinner?"

"Because, frankly, there is enough stuff here to start a congressional investigation, though that in itself doesn't worry me. There are plenty of parties who can shoot smoke in all directions. What saddens me, and the reason I'm here spending my own dime and time, is the fact that this investigation could hurt our nation's new tank project." Some suited older man came over and gave Bush's hand a shake. Bush shook back without even pausing. "And I think a delay would put America at a strategic disadvantage that could affect us for the next fifty years."

"You're very popular," Paul said, referring to all the handshakes.

"That's how deals get made."

At this, Paul stood up. "If you can prove to me that these mistakes have been corrected, and if I don't see any more reports of this type, I'll consider sitting on it."

Bush said that he'd send Paul documents detailing all the changes underway as well as the new procedures they were using to reinforce the steel. "By the way, I'm very impressed by your credentials," he added. "I don't know if you'd be interested, but I can make great use of someone with your qualifications."

"I'm not a weapons inspector," Paul said. "I sort of got sent here by mistake."

"I know. You're an electrical engineer. I happen to sit on the board of several companies looking toward electrical expansions. They could make good use of your talent, sir."

Though he was indeed greatly interested, Paul feared that this was a veiled bribe and said that he was already committed to working at Con Ed once the war was over.

"Well, let me ask you this: would you consider doing some free-lance work for me?"

"What kind of freelance work?"

"I'll send you diagrams and you tell me in layman's terms how they work."

Paul said he'd be glad to try to help the contractor.

Three days later, Paul received a package with Bush's return address. Inside was abundant documentation from Byrd & Hale proving that the floors of tanks were being more heavily reinforced, along with a diagram of a simple artillery gun and a self-addressed envelope. The artillery piece in the diagram wasn't new, and after researching some data in various manuals, Paul wrote a letter describing the range of shells it fired and mailed it to Bush. A week later, he received a sealed envelope with three crisp hundred-dollar bills and a folded piece of paper that said, *Consultant Fee*. After wondering what to do, Paul simply put the money in the bottom drawer of his desk.

Over the course of the next six months, he received a new design of some weapon every four weeks. Most of them were simple artillery pieces, weapons that anyone could research during an afternoon in a military library. Each time Paul wrote a report and sent it to Bush, he'd get an envelope with three hundred dollars. Initially Paul found it amusing, never spending the fee. Before long, however, he started feeling a little insulted. Was this something that Bush hoped to extort him with? On the other hand, the incident reports regarding the hull of the new American tanks had abruptly stopped. The problem appeared to be corrected.

That December, Paul received an embossed invitation to an upcoming Christmas party at the Eldridge, a swank hotel in Washington. It turned out that two other officers in the WMRU had also gotten invites and were planning to share a cab to the hotel.

"Do you guys all know this Bush fellow?" Paul asked during the ride to the party a week later. They didn't. As Paul listened to them, it turned out each had been approached by someone in the War Department who introduced them to "how things get done here."

"I was told I had sent the wrong report out," said Captain Reynolds. Paul wondered if they, too, had been overpaid for minor consultations, though he sensed that the two guys didn't really want to discuss it. But thinking about it, he had never heard either man complain about money, unlike most others he served with.

When they arrived, at least a thousand men, most in uniforms, were crowded together in the grand ballroom of the Eldridge. Next to a forty-foot Christmas tree, an eight-piece band was playing "Auld Lang Syne." A large banner hanging from the ceiling read, *Merry Christmas—The Last Year of the War Thanks to You, Our Heroes in Uniform!*

Paul realized that the three of them from the WMRU were vastly outranked. Generals and admirals from all branches of the armed services flanked the four bars. Waiters served hors d'oeuvres.

"No girls here," said Reynolds to Paul and Lindquist, holding a roasted chicken leg in one hand and a gin and tonic in the other. "After I fill my gullet, I'm skedaddling."

Paul made no objection. He simply drank soda water and walked around looking at the other revelers. After thirty minutes or so, he heard someone shout, "Peter!"

Turning around, he spotted a tuxedoed Samuel Bush wearing a newspaper folded into a commodore's hat. The contractor squeezed out from a group of generals. Paul assumed he was addressing someone else until Bush grabbed his arm.

"Pete, how are you doing, pal?" Bush slurred.

"Fine."

"You did a great job with that last report—did you get my little honorarium?"

"I'm glad you mentioned that," Paul said. He reached into his pocket and handed Bush the seven envelopes of cash he had received thus far. "We both work for the same government, so I really don't think you should have to pay me."

"Oh, don't worry about it," Samuel Bush replied with a big drunken smile. "Buy yourself a nice Christmas gift."

"I'm Jewish, we don't celebrate Christmas."

"Suit yourself." Bush tucked the envelopes into his breast pocket. "You know I like you, Peter, you're honest and straightforward."

"Thanks."

"But let me ask you something. What exactly does an electrical engineer do?"

"Well, instead of wiring machines, for example, we can assess how much electricity is needed in a region, and we can map it out. In effect, we can wire an entire landscape."

"Why would anyone want to do that?"

"Areas with comprehensive power coverage display vast improvement in all major quality-of-life indexes, impacting everything from the economy to education and even crime rates. Numerous studies and reports have shown that—"

"Can you explain to a group of politicians why they might need things like new power plants or additional power sources?" Bush suddenly seemed to have sobered up.

"I suppose I can," Paul answered with a smile.

"And diagrams and all that technical stuff—you can make heads and tails of it all?"

"I suppose so. Why?"

"This war is going to end soon and I need someone with your skills." Bush didn't seem to remember that he had already offered Paul a job.

"It sounds like a great opportunity for someone, but I'm looking to *do* electrical engineering, not just pitch it."

"Well, if you were to take the job, I'd do everything in my power to see that you'd actually carry out some of the work. How does that sound?"

"I'm looking for something a little more civic-minded—I really want to work for city government. But I can recommend a dozen sharp engineers to you."

"No," Sam Bush said, "I want *you*."

"Why me?"

"You're an honest man and people sense that."

"How many people did you give the envelope test to?" Paul asked.

Bush smiled. "The job pays better than anything you're going to get in the public sector."

"Tell you what," Paul said. "Let me think about it."

Bush gave him a new business card and they parted ways.

Take the damn job! Uli thought, then pinched himself through to the moment. The upper part of his body had squeezed out of the underwater netting, but the oxygen tank strapped to his back had gotten stuck in the ropes. When he turned to free it, the tank snapped loose and shot forth into the dark pipe. He needed to breathe. There was only one way to go—up. Fighting against the water pressure pushing him forward, he hauled himself up toward the circle of light.

11

An oval of dull light overhead was like a message coming closer: *Your friend Carl from Mexico called to say he is in Washington but can't be reached anywhere by phone. He promised he would call back at the end of the day.* It was a note from the switchboard operator.

How the hell could he have tracked me down here? Paul wondered. He realized that his old comrade from Mexico must have passed through New York. Without even registering that he hadn't spoken to his mother in months, Paul immediately called her.

"Did you get a phone call from someone named Carlo?" he asked tensely.

"Paul? Is that you?"

"Yes, Mom. I'm sorry for being abrupt but—"

"You run off, join the army, then you call me one day hollering?"

"I'm sorry, Mom, I'm just a little tense."

"Since you left, I haven't had a full night of sleep. Every day I'm reading about young boys being sent to slaughter."

"The only way I'm going to die is if I get bored to death." He knew his sister had already told her, but to regain some goodwill he explained that he had a comfortable desk job in Washington.

"Well, I know I usually only say this about your brother, but to be honest, son, I'm proud of you."

"I haven't done anything to be proud of."

"People say Jews aren't fighters, but it makes me proud to say my son joined and he's an officer in the United States Army."

"Thanks, Mom. But listen, I need to know, did someone named Carlo Valdinoci call you?"

"I don't remember the name, but someone did call and say he knew you through Princeton." It sounded clever, like something Carlo would do.

"What did you tell him?"

"I think your father said you were stationed in Washington and told him how to get ahold of you. Why?"

"No reason," Paul said, sighing. "I was just surprised to hear from him is all."

"You're a bright boy. Is it any wonder people would want to be friends with you?"

"No, Mom."

"I'm not ashamed to say that this sharp brain of yours is what has probably spared you from being killed like so many others in France."

"Truth of the matter is that I wish I was over there."

Bella abruptly changed the subject and went on to say that his father and sister were both doing well.

"How's our dear Mr. Robert?" he asked.

"He's gambling his future on something that could make him quite electable."

"What's that?"

Over the past thirty years, she explained, when a local political leader delivered a precinct to some Tammany Hall boss, his idiot nephew or illegitimate son would get hired in return as an elevator operator or some other post. The city's payroll had become swollen with countless half-wits and useless employees.

Now, under the new mayor, Robert had dreamed up a complex scheme to grade the massive army of civil servants who had been haphazardly brought on over the years. This was becoming a key feature of Mayor John Purroy Mitchel's attempt to reform city government and save millions of dollars. The scheme, Bella continued, was called Standardization. It would take years to implement, but first Robert had to campaign for it to pass. "Your brother could run for mayor himself if he pulls this off."

At that very moment, Paul decided to accept Samuel Bush's offer. After all, it might similarly kick-start his fledgling engineering career.

Paul waited by his desk until five that afternoon. Sure enough, his phone rang just as he was about to leave.

"Capitán Pablo!" he heard Carlo's distinct accent. "How are you doing?"

"Good," he said curtly.

"You know, that address you gave me wasn't where you live."

"Carlo, you and I really don't share the same politics."

"This saddens me greatly," the Italian replied. "Someone with your skills fighting to help the peasant class would make a big difference in the struggle."

"I am committed to helping the poor, but I don't believe in violence. I don't approve of all the bombings I've been reading about. And I think our system of government can repair itself."

"Allow me to explain that mankind is in the fight for its life between the greed of the very rich and the rest of us. If we lose that fight, we will all be at the mercy of the rich forever." Carlo sounded far more articulate than the playful youth Paul remembered from Mexico.

"I disagree. But you don't have to worry about me going to the authorities, I simply ask to be left alone."

"Viva la revolución," Carlo declared, and hung up. Paul hoped this was the last he'd hear from the guy.

On a positive note, the call to his mother seemed to have reestablished their relations. She began teasing him with the title *Captain Paul*. She also gave him constant updates about his younger brother. Robert was attending dozens of municipal hearings, pitching the beauty and equity of his great Standardization Plan. "*It values competence over seniority, meritocracy over cronyism . . .*" Bella loved mimicking her youngest son.

Soon after Paul's phone enounter with Carlo, Samuel Bush requested a meeting with him in one of the Senate office buildings. When Paul arrived, he found the contractor huddled with a small group of men outside a Senate Armed Services hearing.

Instead of saying hello, Paul simply approached the contractor and asked, "Who exactly will I be explaining these engineering plans to?"

"These fellas right here," Bush said, pointing toward the hearing room. "You might be doing some public relations work with them as well."

"And if I take the job, you'll eventually get me signed on as the electrical engineer on some of these projects?"

"I'll try my damnedest."

Paul's stint in the army was almost over, as was the war. With no other immediate prospects, he accepted the offer. His formal title would be lobbyist/consultant for Byrd & Hale.

His first task was assisting Bush in trying to persuade a congressional delegation from depressed areas of the country to promote legislation that would develop electrical systems in their districts. A big region that the subcontractor had targeted for development was down in the Appalachian Mountains of North Carolina.

Several times, drawing on Paul's credentials as a former weapons incident report writer, Bush asked him to give testimony in congressional hearings to encourage further funding for tank development and more sophisticated armaments.

While spending time with Bush, and seeing up close how lobbyists could legally bribe politicians, Paul found himself quickly growing disgusted with his job. Much of his challenge here was to find ways that the congressmen could pitch these pork-barrel projects so that their constituents didn't think they were driven by private interests. But Bush was right: Paul's intelligence and sense of social purpose immediately appealed to people. Reporters used lines lifted directly from his press releases in articles and editorials. Politicians often supported endeavors that he pushed. Each time he talked about quitting, Bush assured him that if he stuck it out for just a few years, he could surely set Paul up with an ideal civil-engineering project right here in Washington, DC.

The sudden reek of shit woke Uli just as he broke into the oval of dull light. Gasping for air, he climbed up the rigging of ropes along a three-foot ledge leading toward a dark, open expanse. He could hear a strange mix of weeping and chanting.

Exhausted, he pulled himself onto the stone floor in a giant unlit chamber. It looked like a large train terminal, like Grand Central Station. In the faint flickering of dozens of little fires, he could make out a vast group of people encamped on the wide floor; most appeared to be seminaked.

"Casey? Is that you, son?" said a soft female voice from nearby.

"No," Uli mumbled, as he lay back exhausted and dripping on the floor. Popping off his helmet, he peered up at the large vaulted ceiling. Slowly catching his breath, he heard a periodic *boom . . . boom . . . boom . . .*

"Casey, what's the matter?" the voice asked. "You okay?"

12

. . . Uli thought he was actually hearing the far-off blasts. A series of bomb attacks throughout the US in 1917 had been orchestrated by anarchists following in the footsteps of Luigi Galleani. Russia had just revolted and these radicals believed that America, too, was on the brink. He remembered Vladimir Ustinov's declaration that the US just needed a little push to set it off.

Legislation passed quickly in Congress, allowing for a stiff crackdown on these radical saboteurs who were terrorizing everyone. A series of anti-immigration and anti-anarchist laws followed.

By June 2, 1919, when a bomb detonated prematurely and damaged the home of the newly appointed attorney general, Mitchell Palmer (and killed the bomber), all of America was horrified. Eight days later, sitting in his office at Byrd & Hale, Paul read that the identity of the bomber had been revealed as none other than Carlo Valdinoci—his second-in-command in Mexico.

Coming home from work one night a couple of weeks later, Paul felt his stomach churn when he saw that a memo from the Department of Justice had been slipped under his door. The letter requesting that he pay a visit tomorrow afternoon was signed *John Hoover*.

Paul took a taxi the next day to the Justice Department, a drafty old nineteenth-century building. Inside the lobby, he located Hoover's name on the building's directory. Marching up into the office, Paul passed a middle-aged secretary and stepped up to a handsome young page to ask if he knew where he could find John Hoover.

"I'm Hoover," the kid said.

"You're the person who left me this note?" Paul asked, arching his eyebrows in annoyance. Hoover rose silently and led him into his office and closed the door.

"Did you know one Carlo Valdinoci?" Hoover began.

"You mean the fellow who bombed the attorney general's home?"

"I'm not going to pussyfoot around, Moses. I know you served honorably here. I know you work for Byrd & Hale. And I know you fought in Mexico alongside this wop. I'm not after you. We got the entire anarchist mailing list. We know who's who and what's what. Now, I don't care if you fought against Porfirio Díaz, but I want some names and I want them now."

"I have to speak to my attorney first," Paul replied, feeling only resentment toward this oily kid.

"Mr. Moses. Either cooperate with us right here and now or, so help me God, the Department of Justice will be the worst enemy you've ever had."

After a long pause, Paul exhaled and said, "I didn't catch most of their last names. They were Italians. But I never even joined their fight."

Hoover took a legal pad and a fountain pen from his top desk drawer. "I'd like a complete timetable of when you arrived there. What missions you were on right up until you left. Then I want a list of first names or monikers of your confederates and basic descriptions of what they looked like and what they did."

Paul sighed and asked if he could have a few weeks to provide this information.

"I want it right now or you're under arrest. And if I feel that I'm getting anything other than the absolute truth, I'm going to press charges against you, and I guarantee I'll make them stick."

"I did nothing wrong."

"The attorney general of this great republic was attacked a few weeks ago at his home. We are in the grips of terrible times, Mr. Moses."

"I'm truly sorry about that, but—"

"Foreign agents have brought a war onto our shores and some of these bastards worked with you. I'm willing to overlook the possibility that you might very well be one of these sons of bitches, and I'll give you the benefit of the doubt that you are no longer in cahoots with them—*if* you do everything you can right this moment to help us find them." Hoover stared at him intensely.

Paul let out another audible sigh. Reaching across the table, he took the pen and paper and slid them in front of himself. Only when Hoover rose did Paul realize that another, larger man was standing behind him. Over the next four hours, Paul drew up an approximate timetable of missions, along with lists of places where they occurred and others he had worked with, deliberately lying about the names of those who he knew were harmless. By the time Hoover's assistant brought him a dry ham-and-cheese sandwich for dinner, Paul had come up with fourteen names, mainly Italian and Spanish, and one Russian—the late Vladimir Ustinov. By ten o'clock that night, hours after Hoover had left, he was allowed to leave provided he return first thing the next morning.

Paul came back at nine a.m. and sat across from young Hoover, who reviewed all the facts and figures he had written on the legal pad pages.

"Right now," Hoover said, "I really have only one question."

"What's that?"

"What the hell prompted a young man, someone who was an A student at Princeton, who comes from a position of wealth and privilege, to toss it all aside and go to Mexico to fight in some pointless wetback war?"

"Well, to be honest with you," Paul replied awkwardly, "I was in love with a girl and she brought me into it."

"I sensed that might be the answer," Hoover said with a smile. "The only woman you can ever trust is your own mother."

Paul smiled back, just wanting out.

"All right, here's the deal. A contingent of these foreigners who you broke bread with got munitions training south of the border and now they're using it up here. If everything you told us checks out, no charges will be filed against you." Looking Paul in the eye, Hoover pulled his seat forward and added, "But frankly, I'd like you to leave this city."

"I live and work here."

"Look, you've come here with a group of terrorists."

"I have no connection with any of them!"

"That might be the case, but we're planning on rounding them all up and tossing them out of the country. You were born here so we can't do that to you. But I'll sleep a lot easier just knowing that you aren't around."

"I work for a major corporation."

"Tell you what," Hoover said almost sympathetically. "I'll give you two weeks, so you can turn in your notice today."

"I've been absolutely honest and direct with you and I don't think this is fair."

"Mr. Moses, if I didn't think you were honest and if you didn't serve honorably in the military and attend Princeton, I guarantee I'd have you in jail serving at least three to five years."

"For what?"

"For my peace of mind."

As Paul left the old building and tried to hail a cab back home, he thought maybe this was all for the best. He was getting sick of Washington and he missed New York. Upon arriving home, he promptly contacted Bush and delicately explained that it was time for him to head back to New York. He was giving his two weeks' notice.

"Paul, you're throwing away a very promising, lucrative career here."

"It's not a money issue."

"You want to do design work, I promise I can—"

"It's not that, it's just that I've always wanted to work in the public sector in New York."

"Look, I don't want to make promises I can't keep, but we've donated a lot of money to the Harding campaign. I might be able to arrange a nice administrative appointment."

"I've decided I want my old job back," Paul lied, and thanked Bush for all he had done.

He had been using his spare time in Washington, as well as the data he had access to, working on a paper that examined New York City's power system losses and transformer tap settings. The gist of the study was that the metropolis could acquire electricity more efficiently by installing hydroelectric generators along the St. Lawrence River. When he showed his plans to an old colleague who had become an executive at Con Edison in New York City, he was quickly offered a job as a property assessor.

Meanwhile, Mayor Mitchel had abandoned young Robert Moses and his notorious Standardization Plan in an effort to regain some popularity. But it had made little difference, and in 1918 Mitchel lost his reelection bid to John Francis Hylan, "Red Mike." Bella said she had never seen her youngest son so crestfallen as he had become since losing his job. In addition, Robert had been stigmatized in the press as a privileged rich kid, an enemy of the workingman.

Bella told Paul how his brother had been contacting everyone he knew and was going out on every job interview he could get. It was ironic then, almost as if their fates were inversely related, that Paul got accepted into a prestigious new executive program at Con Edison— just the break he had been waiting for. He was now in line to move up the ranks and make some real policy decisions.

Seeing these developments as an opportunity to bridge a gap that had widened between them over the years, Paul decided to pay an unannounced visit to his brother. When he arrived, Robert's wife Mary invited him in, but told him that her husband was out looking for work. Robert called him back that night and explained apologetically that it was a bad time for him to see people.

Walk to Sutphin . . . Catch the Q28 to Fulton . . . Change to the B17 . . . ▮▮▮▮▮▮▮▮▮▮▮▮▮▮▮▮ *Shoot Dropl!* These words seemed at the core of Uli's identity. He returned to his last waking moment when his fucking sister had tried to kill him. She let him believe this was a legitimate way out . . . and it obviously wasn't . . . *She's the Robert Moses to my Paul. If I survive this, I'm gonna strangle her with my bare hands!* . . . Uli found that if he concentrated hard on something painful, he could remain in the moment. He pinched himself and counted at least thirty small fires illuminating the wide underground encampment. He was desperately trying to cling to external rungs in the here and now. A group of emaciated and bedraggled people were kneeling by a wall under what appeared to be a series of large, sealed sluice gates. Uli realized that this vast space was probably some kind of dried-out, obsolete catch basin. It appeared that water had once drained down this basin into the sewer pipe he had just climbed out of. Clusters of groaning people huddled around the huge, flat cement bottom of this empty reservoir. The walls of it sloped upward at about a forty-five-degree angle. All appeared filthy, most of the men in rags and loincloths and sporting beards of varying lengths. Several had no clothes on whatsoever, which made Uli feel less self-conscious about his own nudity.

"Are you sure you're not Casey?" asked the middle-aged woman with short auburn hair.

"No, I'm pretty sure I'm Uli . . . though I might be Paul."

"You didn't see my son? We were together and—"

"I didn't see anything other than that damn net down there. It blocked my escape."

"There's no escape," some longbeard called out. "People were drowning before we put up the net."

"How do you know?"

"Some guy told me."

"Who?"

"The black dude we elected leader. He was the one who set up the netting to try to rescue those who were flowing through."

"Where is he?" Uli asked, glancing around.

"Who?"

"The leader!"

"Oh, Plato vanished into the Mkultra years ago," the bearded man replied, and then, as if to emulate the leader, he wandered off.

13

The large chamber looked to Uli like some kind of vast primordial internment center. He remembered the roundups and deportations in 1920, including all the suspected anarchists that Attorney General Palmer and his boy, J. Edgar Hoover, had tracked down. A ship full of suspects had pulled away from Manhattan, deporting all the Red troublemakers back to Russia.

Just thinking of Hoover's lumpy old face, Uli felt a mix of loyalty, friendship, and despair—he wasn't sure if this was coming from himself or Paul. Uli vividly remembered him at the height of his power in the 1960s: Hoover, the stodgy authoritarian, shouting commandments down from high. *He saved your ass!* Uli heard. He thought Paul was talking to him, but then realized it was he talking to himself. *Hoover saved me? How* ████████████████████ In another moment, as Paul's memories came back into focus, he saw a different Hoover, slim and dapper, an ambitious young man who had secured his post in the Department of Justice through his mother's cousin. He could just as easily have served in the Department of the Interior, like his father had, or worked in any other sector of government bureaucracy, like some of his Washington relatives.

That August, Bella invited all three kids home for a family dinner. As soon as Paul showed up, she told him how Robert had recently traveled all the way to Cleveland for a minor bureaucratic interview, only to get rejected again.

When Robert and Mary arrived with their two baby girls, Edna and their parents greeted them at the door. Emanuel shook hands with his youngest son and tried to utter some encouraging words, while Mary complained to Bella and Edna about how their apartment on the Upper West Side was getting too tight with the birth of their second daughter.

"Well, you've just got to find a bigger place," Bella said with a wide smile.

"Robert!" Paul called out, coming down the stairs. "It's impossible to get ahold of you, brother."

As Paul approached his sibling, Robert replied, "You dumb son of a bitch, you've ruined my life!"

"Robert!" their father snapped.

"You can't talk to Paul that way!" Edna added.

"What the hell's the matter with you?" Paul asked.

"When Mayor Hylan took office, some little creep approached me and said that if I ever poked my big kike nose in City Hall again, he'd make sure the papers got wind of my Bolshevik brother."

"What?" Edna cried out. "Who said such a thing?"

"Evans, a Tammany Hall boy who they hired to get rid of me because of my reforms. He got the information from some muckety-muck in Washington. Why don't you tell them yourself, Paul: what was the real reason you quit your big Washington job?"

"What are you saying?" Bella asked.

"I'm saying that your oldest son became best friends with every bomb-throwing commie in North America."

"They weren't my friends. I told the government everything I knew about them."

"It was that damn Mexican girl."

"Watch it!" Paul warned.

"If you want to rub Mom's face in crap all her life, that's your prerogative—"

"Robert, that's an awful thing to say!" Bella interrupted.

"—but I'm not as forgiving as she is!"

"My relationship with Mom is none of your business!" Paul fired back.

"You gave your boy a Princeton education and in return he's become an enemy of this country."

"Just stop it!" Bella gasped.

"When are you going to get it?" Robert asked. "He hates us!"

"Shut up, Robert, I'm not saying it again!"

"She and Dad worked so hard to get you that interview at Kuhn & Loeb. Everyone knew about it."

"That's enough, Robert," Emanuel said.

"You thoroughly embarrassed her," Robert jabbed.

"I appreciated what you did," Paul said, turning to Bella. "I just didn't want to be a banker, Mom!"

"Instead, you became a goddamn lobbyist for an arms manufacturer," Robert said.

"Byrd & Hale owns a number of companies, one of which is munitions. They promised that if I did lobbying work, they'd reward me with an electrical engineering job," Paul explained to Bella.

"And you couldn't even do that, could you? Your past caught up with you and you had to quit," Robert continued. "Well, you ruined your career and now you've hurt mine too!"

"Look, Robert, I'm truly sorry," Paul said. "Yes, I knew some unsavory types down in Mexico, but I had no involvement with any of this stuff."

"I don't reward people for screwing up my life. I punish them!"

"I never meant to embarrass you."

"I think you should apologize to Paul," Bella said.

"I've spent my life carefully avoiding situations like this," Robert said, "and when I find out that my family has to pay the price because my brother wants to get in the sack with some hot little tamale—"

Paul slapped Robert, who nearly fell to the ground, remaining bent to one side for several seconds.

"Oh God!" Mary screamed. Her little girls shrieked. Even Edna covered her mouth.

"That's enough!" Emanuel shouted, stepping forward between his two taller, broader sons. But he didn't need to—neither brother was going any further. Uli knew that something irrevocable had just occurred between them.

When Paul grabbed his coat, only Maria, standing in the foyer, tried to stop him. He hurried out of the old brownstone, slamming the door behind him.

On his way home, Paul angrily assessed the full magnitude of his fight with Robert. For the first time, Paul had actually seemed to be in a superior position, and his brother must have decided that this calculated act would turn their mother's opinion around. Instead of being a failure due to his unpopular Standardization Plan, Robert was a victim of his brother's cavalier behavior. And Paul—who was finally doing well—was the clear cause of Robert's recent bad luck.

Further proof that this was a premeditated act, Paul noted, was the fact that he had repeatedly tried to meet with Robert in recent weeks to offer his support. Now it was clear that Robert had just been biding his time—all for this ambush. Some peon had probably revealed his meeting with that snot-nosed Hoover kid in Washington. Instead of approaching Paul and conveying his anger and frustration, Robert was using it as capital, exploiting this embarrassing development for all to see.

By the next morning, though, Paul decided he was being unfair, even paranoid. There's no way his younger brother could be this strategic or diabolical. He simply lacked the guile. Paul began to feel guilty for even thinking such a thing.

Over the ensuing days, the more he thought about it, the worse he felt about what had happened with Robert. His brother was a young father of two, and just when he thought he had reached some station of security—a plum assignment from Mayor Mitchel—it was pulled away in the most humiliating fashion. All the rage and frustration of being dismissed by the boy mayor and then being snubbed by Hylan and Tammany Hall and so many others—Paul could hardly blame Robert for losing his temper.

About a month later, Paul received a call from Bella with exciting news. Due to the blessed intervention of some politico's wife, Robert had just had an encouraging meeting with the newly elected governor, Al Smith. Great things were on the horizon. A week later, she called Paul again to announce that Robert had been appointed Smith's chief of staff. He was placed on a commission addressing the reorganization of the state government, something very much akin to what he had been feverishly trying to do for the city of New York.

Paul decided to call Robert at home, hoping to congratulate him. Mary picked up to say that Robert was still at the office. Paul told her that he was truly sorry for their spat, and that he wanted to apologize for his behavior.

That weekend, when Robert still hadn't called, Paul tried again. This time, Mary said that Robert had gotten his message but was too busy to call back. "He told me to say thanks. When things calm down, he'll call you."

Paul asked for his brother's work number, but Mary just giggled nervously and said that even she didn't know it yet. It was clear that despite Robert's reversal of misfortune, he was not yet ready to forgive Paul.

In mid-September, just as Paul was getting up the nerve to pay another unannounced visit to Robert at his New York City office, the unthinkable occurred: a horse-drawn wagon approached a lunchtime crowd at 23 Wall Street and detonated a hundred pounds of explosives along with five hundred pounds of cast-iron slugs, leaving scores maimed and dying. Thirty-eight people were killed and over four hundred were wounded. A note found nearby said, *Free the political prisoners or it will be sure death for all of you!*

Once again, a pair of officers from the Department of Justice paid Paul a visit, this time at his Con Ed office on 14th Street. They deliberately embarrassed him by pulling him out of an important committee meeting.

"We find it mighty strange that Hoover tossed you out of Washington and the bombings stop there," said one of the investigators. "Then you come up here and they follow you."

"I swear, I don't know a thing about it," Paul replied nervously. Things were going well at Con Ed and he feared that the investigators were now going to ask him to leave New York.

"You don't remember anything else from Mexico, do you?"

"Absolutely not. I told Hoover everything," he assured them.

Paul did not lose his job, and after six months at Con Ed, he became a chief consultant and had earned enough respect to finally be put in charge of his pet project, a large feasibility study on the energy generated by a dam on the St. Lawrence River.

No electricity down here, Uli thought as he roamed naked along the wide floor. Small votive candles lined rows of crooked walkways. Most people sat or lay upon clumps of papers. Office items appeared to have been modified into primitive tools: staplers were hammers; trash cans served as toilets; an old Underwood typewriter, caked with what appeared to be blood, may have been used as a weapon.

Uli heard occasional groans set against a constant chorus of weeping, and as he walked onward, they morphed into a kind of forceful chant. Uli spotted a group of the worshippers kneeling in lines, all facing the rear wall where the sluice gates were. One man stood in front, leading the group like a minister. The guy was holding what appeared to be homemade rosaries.

"How many people are there down here?" Uli asked the lost mother, who was moving along with him.

"I don't know. A bunch went into there." She pointed to a hole in the wall.

"What is this place?"

"They call it Streptococci River 'cause it's supposedly infectious. Everyone drinks the refiltered water."

"Where the hell did they get a water filter?"

She shrugged.

Someone must know that all these people are trapped, Uli thought. Then, making out the hole crudely cut into the wall, he said, "There's a way out! Why doesn't everyone leave?"

"Whenever people wander into the Mkultra they vanish, so the leader told us to wait until he finds a way out."

"Who is the leader?"

"A great memory man," some old beard passing nearby piped up.

"This is my boy Casey."

"I'm afraid not," Uli reminded her.

She suddenly turned angry. "What the hell did you do with my boy?"

"He escaped," Uli lied. "He made it all the way through the pipe."

"Thank God!" She put her hand over her heart.

Uli sat down. It was getting harder for him to focus. Paul Moses's life was pushing back through.

14

Paul excelled in the Con Ed executive training program, but he worked almost constantly. His mother invited him to various society functions, hoping he would meet a future wife. It was at one of these parties that he was introduced to a sexy divorcée named Teresa. She'd had two kids with her husband before leaving him for chasing every skirt that crossed his path. After five dry martinis, Paul confessed that while he had been with a number of women, few seemed to truly enjoy sex.

"Then I guess I'd be your first," she boldly stated, downing her drink.

Uli found himself thirsting for water, so he took a sip from a rusty old water pump, but spat it right back out. The dark liquid tasted like shit.

"You better learn to like it if you have any hope of surviving down here," said the lost mother.

He found an empty cardboard mat and lay down.

Paul was surprised that his brother was actually learning to play the game of politics and had succeeded in pushing through his massive overhaul of the state government. This involved an extensive consolidation of ragtag agencies and slapdash departments into a handful of more efficient ones. The money saved in eliminating redundancy alone was considerable. The restructuring earned Governor Smith such positive press that editorials began suggesting he'd make a good president. He rewarded Robert by elevating him to New York's secretary of state.

"This puts my boychick in line to run for governor himself," Bella speculated, adding that this was exactly what Robert wanted.

Through the aggressive campaigning of both parents at dinner one evening, Robert finally forgave Paul with a firm handshake. Relations, though never warm, became cordial. Neither brought up the anarchist charge nor the slap ever again.

For his part, Paul began overseeing other feasibility studies for Con Ed throughout the northeast. One day, a dear friend from his time in the army, Colonel Stuart Greene, who was now head of the Department of Public Works in Al Smith's administration, called to say that Paul would be perfect for a top engineering post in his office.

"Oh my God," Paul said to Teresa, who he was now dating, "it's exactly what I've been waiting for!"

He thought about calling Robert to see if he could put in a good word, but Greene said that it wasn't necessary—the appointment probably wouldn't require the governor's approval.

Paul shared the good news with his parents instead. The appointment would earn him the recognition he had always wanted. And since there weren't a lot of qualified men in electrical engineering willing to work at a government rate, he was sure it would lead to some prestigious appointment. The colonel had told him that the only drawback was that he'd have to commute regularly up to Albany.

Two days later, however, Greene called to say that the appointment had fallen through. There was no explanation as to why.

"Where exactly does that go?" Uli asked as they passed the only hole in the chamber.

"Leads to a fallout shelter," the mother said. "They found gas masks and old body-protection suits and stuff like that." She pointed to the black hose tracking up from the sewer pipe into a corner where five large metal oil drums periodically spat out recycled water into a giant wooden barrel.

"And what does everyone eat?"

"Crates and crates of C-rations."

"How long before the food runs out?"

The woman shrugged.

"If this is a shelter, there must be an exit somewhere."

"They're all sealed."

Casey's mom brought Uli over to her corner, where a bunch of dirty, crumpled papers were scattered on the ground. He collected some into a small pile and lay back down. The place was a massive echo chamber, and above the nonstop prayer-a-thon in the back he heard low moans that sounded distinctly sexual.

15

Teresa's father steered Paul toward a promising investment: a popular swimming club called Llanerch in Upper Darby, Pennsylvania, near Philadelphia. Its central location appealed to the affluent locals. The previous owner had died and the family needed to unload it quickly to avoid what was shaping into a major probate battle.

Paul's father, a savvy businessman, looked over the books and was duly impressed. It was a solid investment with a steadily growing membership.

"The secret is," Emanuel imparted, "if it's not broken, don't fix it. This place will keep earning you a profit as long as you don't push it."

"It looks a bit run-down," Paul said. "Maybe it could use a paint job."

His father gave him a check to cover the cost of the down payment. Two weeks later, before Paul could even bring his dad up for a weekend, Emanuel Moses suddenly died of a heart attack. Paul soon learned that he had left every cent of his fortune to Bella.

* * *

Finding a long strand of wire on the ground, Uli tied it around his arm so that a constant yet minor pain would keep him at least semiconscious. He figured that whatever was causing the visions of Paul Moses must also be afflicting all these other people. He remembered his sister Karen injecting him with the strange drug to keep him alive in the sewer pipe. He also remembered that crazy pseudo-Indian hippie Tim Leary inserting two additional hypodermic needles for him in the cushions of the helmet he had discarded earlier.

Uli heard a thumping sound and feared another intrusion from Paul's world. Peering up into the hole in the wall, he glimpsed a scrawny man with bony knees using a rope to carefully lower an overloaded hand truck down the forty-five-degree incline. Once safely level, the man wheeled over to the barrel of filtered water where a dozen empty trash baskets were stacked inside each other. A group of men came forward, each one taking an empty basket. Bony Knees passed out boxes of C-rations, which turned out to be nothing more than crackers. Each of the men crushed the crackers in their garbage can, then filled it with the awful water. They stirred their buckets until the crackers became a thick paste. People from different parts of the dark shelter began shuffling forward like zombies, holding out metal cups. Each person moved into one of twelve lines as the men ladled out gruel from their garbage cans.

"Suppertime!" Casey's mother announced, handing him a filthy cup. Uli got in line with the woman, who was once again entering her joyous cycle of believing Uli was her son.

Uli was famished and gulped the muck down. He hadn't eaten since escaping from Rescue City—that bizarre replica of New York concocted as a refugee center, which now essentially served as a giant prison in the middle of the Nevada desert. When he rose to get in line for a second cup, he spotted a tall brawny man wearing his New York Jets helmet.

"Mind if I see your headgear for a moment?" Uli asked nervously.

"Mine," the guy replied, his face covered with muck. Quickly and gently, Uli slipped the helmet off the man's skull. From between the insulating cushions in the top of the apparatus, Uli removed the two syringes that Leary had taped there. The large man's hand slowly rose, so Uli carefully fixed the helmet back on the guy's head. Uli then went over to one of the bonfires and located a dark vein in his right arm. He injected himself with both syringes, then tossed the needles into the open sewer hole. Near the barrel of filtered water, Uli found a bag that had been made from an old shirt. He slung it over his shoulder and discreetly slipped an unopened box of C-rations into it.

"Is there any way to get some clothes?" Uli asked Casey's mom.

"Shub had no right!" she said. Her thoughts had shifted to the former mayor of Rescue City.

"Look what he did to us," another lost soul roaming nearby joined in.

"By any chance, is anyone else thinking about someone named Paul Moses?" Uli called out into the large empty room.

"Moses, Charlton Heston," someone free-associated.

"Best clothes are on the dead," said some shorter beard, responding to Uli's first question. "But you have to get them before they start rotting."

"Where would be a good place to find some?"

"In the Mkultra—it's loaded with dead bodies. Just don't go too far or you'll never find your way out."

Coming across some shredded cardboard and frayed twine scattered among the litter, Uli fashioned himself a pair of basic foot protectors. It was difficult to walk more than ten feet without stepping on hardened human excrement.

"Does anyone know what's in there?" Uli asked, pointing toward the hole in the wall.

"The first floor of the Mkultra is called the Lethe; it's made up of secretarial pools," the short man replied.

"What the hell is the Mkultra?"

"Subdivisions and sections of a government installation. Our leader learned those names from documents he found. He's in there looking for a way out."

"He's probably lost or dead by now," someone else lamented.

"Anyone know what this guy looks like?" Uli asked.

"Black—he's black all over," a voice replied.

"Anything else?"

All were silent.

"Does anyone remember his name?"

"Blaster!" someone shouted out.

"No, not Blaster—Bomber, 'cause he bombed that hole!" someone else said, pointing to the jagged hole that led to the Mkultra. "And he had caring people with him."

"Caring people?" Uli asked. "You mean like a family?"

"Yeah, a wife and a kid, I think."

"Fucking Shub ruined all our lives!" someone moaned.

"Can anyone tell me who this Bomber leader is, or where I can find him?" Uli was becoming increasingly exasperated with the filthy, mentally impaired congress around him.

"Who's this new voice inquiring about the leader?" A long-bearded man shuffled up to Uli. In the dull glow of a distant fire, Uli could see that in place of eyes were dark empty sockets.

"Here," Uli replied.

The blind man delicately touched Uil's chin to confirm that he didn't have a long beard. "I remember the leader. He had some strange name like Play Dough. I never saw him, obviously, but I heard he was slim and black. He had a young wife and they had a child here."

"The EGGS epidemic from Rescue City doesn't affect people here?"

"I suppose not. People can still reproduce, but I heard the kid was born with a horrible birth defect—I'd be amazed if he was still alive."

"Why was he elected leader?"

"Aside from his memory and his great positive attitude, he was the only one who could read and make sense of all these forms."

"What forms?"

"If you go in there, you'll see them. There are documents scattered all over the place. Play Dough the Bomber seemed to believe the forms came from different departments and through them he could piece things together. He thought these may have been recently evacuated offices."

"How long after people arrive here do they start to lose their memory?" Uli asked.

"Who knows? This disease affects some people faster than others. I also know that here in the Streptococci River we look out for each other. This is your best bet for surviving until he rescues us."

"Suppose he doesn't?" Uli said. Then, in a loud voice, he called out, "If anyone has any advice on the best way out of here, I'd love to hear it."

"Across to the Sticks!" someone shouted back.

"What's that?"

"Some place filled with caves where people are trying to dig their way out," said the blind man.

"Where is it?"

"It's called the Sticks 'cause it's out in the sticks."

"But *where* exactly is it?"

The man smiled and shrugged. "Never been there, but I heard it has several levels. And some levels are more dangerous than others."

"Dangerous how?"

"I heard there are warring gangs and ferocious animals in there."

"What kind of animals?"

"I don't know."

"Are there any sources for food or water?" Uli asked.

"There are several caches for food," the blind man explained, "but we don't know where they are. And there are the drips, places leaking with water. People usually put containers down to collect it."

"And if you find a way out," someone else called out, "please don't forget about us."

Uli said he wouldn't and thanked them.

Climbing up along the slanting side of the huge basin, Uli reached the jagged hole roughly three feet in diameter. Up close, it looked like someone had roughly bored through the concrete. After crawling twenty feet in total blackness, scratching his back and belly in the process, he arrived at another large room. A tall, powerful man extended his hand and helped Uli inside, letting him pass. The bony-kneed guy and several others were standing about idly. As Uli walked past, he came upon dozens of stacks of empty wooden crates. He realized this must be the rations depot.

After heading through the back of the depot into a dank corridor, he found himself completely alone. He followed a distant, unsteady light out to an even larger space with a vast oak floor—presumably the Mkultra. Inside, he quickly discovered that the only sources of light were the flickering tips of several distant fluorescent tubes. Moving slowly through the silent darkness, Uli found his focus dissipating.

16

In the spring of 1928, Paul's mother fell ill and no one could figure out what was wrong with her. Paul told her maid Maria that he suspected it was just Bella's relentless desire for attention.

But the woman became even sicker and increasingly cantankerous.

Paul had started splitting his time between Pennsylvania and New York, consulting for Con Ed on a part-time basis so he could work on Llanerch. He came up one weekend to visit his mother. He tried to be patient, but she began mentioning "that bitch Millie" and his "wasted time in Mexico," and when he refused to react, she called him "another one of those goddamned bomb throwers who should've been shipped off to Russia."

"She's just feeling angry and threatened," Maria told him, but he knew that she was genuinely disappointed in him. And she would continue badgering over subsequent visits.

Hard as he tried to resist, he was eventually drawn in, at one point declaring that Millie was more compassionate than she'd ever be, and fighting in Mexico against oligarchs like her was the noblest thing he had ever done. When Robert saw what was happening on a mutual visit, he started taking his mother's side.

"Why do you always have to fight with her?" Robert yelled at him.

"This is between us," Paul shot back. "Don't butt in."

Robert, who had just lost his coveted position as secretary of state when Franklin Roosevelt was elected governor of New York, refused to be swept aside. "I know she can be annoying, but she's sick. Can't you just be decent for once, goddamnit?"

"It's not a matter of decency. This has always been our way of communicating."

"Oh, spare me the bullshit!"

"It's not bullshit. I'm telling you, she does this to stir our feelings."

But Robert would hear none of it.

Soon, Bella grew too weak to remain at home and was transferred to a private room at Mount Sinai Hospital. Paul escorted her there, along with Maria and her teenage daughter Lucretia. Initially the visit went nicely, but before long Bella made an obnoxious comment about the girl not being dressed appropriately for a hospital.

"Mom, don't worry about her dress not being expensive enough. This isn't a social."

"If it were up to you, we'd all be in rags," Bella accused feverishly. Her face was ashen.

"Not everyone inherited a fortune."

"You don't need a million dollars to dress well!" she rasped, and started coughing.

Maria waved for Paul to calm down. While Lucretia sat with Bella, Maria took Paul outside and said, "Go have a cigarette and cool down."

"She's so annoying!"

"She's dying, Paul. There's no need to fight anymore."

The next shift of nurses arrived and helped Bella use the bathroom. As they prepared to give her a sponge bath, Lucretia, Maria, and Paul said good night and headed out. When Paul realized the maid and her daughter were walking to the subway, he offered them a lift.

"We're all the way up in the Bronx," Maria said.

"I don't mind. In fact, I insist," he replied. So the three got into his car and drove up to East Tremont in the Bronx. Once there, Paul commented on how nice the houses were. He had imagined them living in more of a shack.

"The place is great, but it needs work."

"What kind of work?" Paul asked.

"That's the thing, I don't really know."

Paul, who had accumulated a wealth of knowledge about construction during his engineering career, offered to take a quick look.

Maria and Lucretia made dinner for him as he changed into dungarees and an old shirt that he dug out of the trunk of his car and crawled under the house. Next he went up to the attic, inspecting the load-bearing walls and integrity of the building.

"Well, the good news is, you have a nice old place that looks fairly sound," he explained half an hour later. "The bad news is that it can use a lot of little repairs." When Maria gave him a look of concern, Paul said, "Maybe I can come by and help."

"No, Paul, you've been kind enough."

"You've helped me so much with my mother and I'd really like to repay the favor."

Maria thanked him politely and he left.

Over the next few months, whenever Paul would bump into Maria at the hospital, she had a calming effect on him. When Bella would make a nasty remark, Maria would step in before things could escalate, giving him a chance to cool off. By the end of 1929, just after the stock market crash, Paul's relationship with his mother had improved to such a state that Bella began consulting him about her business affairs.

Uli knew this would be the beginning of the end for Paul. The Depression of the 1930s was just waiting for him. He wished he could find some way to impart this information—*Dump all your stocks and make peace with your dying mother!*—but it was as if he were picking up a radio transmission from fifty years before; all of this was so long ago.

Just like he had been told by the short beard, the first floor of the Mkultra—the Lethe—seemed to be made up of nothing more than large rows of desks extending on and on into the darkness, secretarial pools occasionally interrupted by waiting areas or conference rooms. As Uli traveled farther outward, he encountered large executive suites lining the edges of the massive floor. Warped and buckled parquet wood covered everything. He didn't see any staircases, but from time to time he'd come across gaping holes smashed through the ceiling into an upper floor. He'd shout up, but hear nothing back. When he found something that resembled a rope dangling out of one hole, he grabbed it and started climbing. Before he could make it very far, however, he heard a frantic whispering above him. Fearing an ambush, he slipped back down and stayed on the Lethe level.

Uli periodically called out "Play Dough!" in hopes of finding this mysterious leader. As his ears adjusted, he began hearing a variety of little clicking and scuttling noises. Some of the sounds were from the leaks, as people had strategically positioned trash baskets to catch the drips. But it wasn't until he saw the first rat with its bright white hair and beady pink eyes that he realized what accounted for the constant scampering he was hearing. Soon, he started spotting them all over—the Lethe was infested.

After an hour or so he saw his first human, a form moving about in the distance. Uli watched as the dark figure picked up one of the many drip-catching buckets and drank from it.

"Play Dough?" he called.

When the figure dashed behind a pillar, Uli remembered that he was in a hostile environment. He kept trying to imagine why the hell the government would create a vast subterranean office space. It was odd that he found no sign of living quarters. He wondered if maybe they were somewhere under the outskirts of a large city—possibly Reno or Vegas—where all these employees would have returned home at night.

If there was some pattern to the vast layout of the Lethe, Uli didn't recognize it. Occasionally a barricade of desks and chairs forced him to create new paths. Several lines of phosphorescent paint ran along the floor in different directions. Uli followed one until it dead-ended at a wall. At another point, he thought he felt a breeze. Looking up, he glimpsed a hole in the ceiling with large metal rods and rebar bent downward as though a small meteor had crashed through. He decided to investigate. Pushing a desk below it, he was able to jump up and catch one of the rods. He pulled himself up through the hole to a cracked wooden floor, where he had to carefully avoid getting splinters.

On this new level he found a series of laboratory counters. Broken glass littering the ground worried him since the old cardboard over his feet was not very thick. Inspecting the shards, he discovered they were shattered test tubes and beakers. *They must've done animal testing here*, he thought, noticing open cages of varying sizes scattered throughout. He wondered if there had been any germ-warfare testing, and if any pathogens were still airborne.

17

Uli covered his ears; for the first time, instead of resisting, he tried to engage the Paul visions. They were the only distraction as he walked, the only place to hide from everything around him. He remembered Paul constructing a large empty space like the one before him. It was a dance hall at his country club, Llanerch. And if people were coming for romantic evenings, Paul thought, they should have a cocktail bar. "Go the whole way," his girlfriend Teresa advised, encouraging him to add a restaurant, a nice place where a fellow could drop a chunk of change on his gal. But while visiting one weekend and seeing so many blue-collar joes eating sandwiches in their cars, Paul decided to add a diner. Then he figured a bowling alley would really tie the knot. He got in touch with a contractor, showed him the plans, and the construction soon began.

At the end of the year, though, Paul was drained. Despite the fact that the swimming club had had a profitable summer and he was drawing a good paycheck from Con Ed, he still couldn't cover the expansion. For the first time, due to the Depression, the income that had been consistently coming in since he bought the place started slackening. With bill collectors knocking, he broke down and asked his mother for an "advance" on his inheritance.

"Your brother just asked me for a twenty-thousand-dollar loan to build some goddamn public highway to his Jones Beach project, and now you want my money to add more water to your swimming pool?"

"Mom, the taxes from the people of New York should be paying for their highways. I'm building a family business that will soon be the most successful club in eastern Pennsylvania. Hell, I think it can attract people from as far away as here in the city."

Lying in her hospital bed, Bella took a deep breath and rolled her eyes. "Are you a moron? Who the hell is going to drag their family three hours out to Pennsylvania to a swimming pool, when your brother has given them an oceanfront resort for free?"

"For your sake, I hope there's no hell, 'cause you aren't long for this world!" Paul snapped, and stormed out.

A few days later, when he finally got up the strength to reconcile with his mother once again, she refused to take his calls. Over the course of the next two weeks, he'd listen to her phone just ring and ring. He didn't understand why she was so angry. They had always fought and frequently exchanged nasty remarks, but all was forgotten the next day. Why was this time any different? He couldn't even remember what he had said to her. It didn't matter; he needed to stay out in Pennsylvania and do everything he could to try to bring Llanerch up to speed as quickly as possible.

He called Edna to seek her advice.

"You should just go down and visit her. She's not doing well."

"I'll try," Paul said. Then, as an afterthought, he asked how Robert was faring.

"All last week, Robert kept talking about running for mayor on the reform ticket."

"Mayor?"

"Yeah, but the plan quickly fell through when he realized he couldn't get the support."

"I wish I had problems like that," Paul said.

"He just endorsed the new reform candidate."

"Who is it?"

"Some little Italian guy, a congressman from Harlem. If the guy gets elected, Robert's hoping to be appointed to his cabinet."

"Maybe he'll be the next chief of police," Paul kidded.

"No, he's secured appointments on several commissions, so he can't work full-time."

"I guess there's not much left after being secretary of state." Paul was glad that his bastard brother had been taken down a couple notches.

One Friday in Llanerch, after getting news that a businessman was interested in meeting with him on Monday to possibly buy a percentage of the club, Paul felt so exhilarated that he drove straight into New York to tell his mom the good news. Upon entering her room, he was surprised by what he saw. Nearly yellow from kidney failure, she looked awful. Flesh was just hanging off of her, and she was trembling with sweat. He gently woke her, but she was dosed with painkillers. Her eyes fluttering, she smiled a bit and muttered, "Hi, Paul."

"Hi, Mom." He tried to keep from crying.

She closed her eyes and resumed sleeping. The large woman he had known all his life—opinionated, strong-willed, and intrusive—had shrunk down to this dying little old lady. He sat next to her bed for three hours, until the nurse came by to help her with a bedpan.

"I'll come back first thing on Tuesday," he vowed, and gave her a kiss on her sweaty forehead. That afternoon he drove back to Llanerch through a rainstorm to oversee an important shipment and meet with a local banker.

On Monday morning he received a phone call from Edna at his Pennsylvania office. Their mother had just passed away in her sleep. "Why the hell didn't you stay with her?"

"My business is on the verge of going under. I had a crucial meeting with a potential investor this morning."

"We were all here except for you. Even Robert canceled his appointment with Governor Roosevelt."

A week later, gathered with his brother and sister in the office of their family lawyer, Paul listened as the will was read. He expected to hear that her estate, including what their father had left, would be divided evenly between the three children. Instead, the lawyer announced that it would essentially be split between Robert and Edna. Paul had been left the interest from a principal of one hundred thousand dollars—he had been cut from the will!

Upon hearing this, Paul looked over at his siblings, believing they would share in the indignity of it all, but neither of them returned his gaze. As the full magnitude of his mother's cruelty hit him, he felt as if his fate were sealed. Despite their many fights, he had always believed she loved him. He knew he had never stopped loving her.

"I can't believe this," Paul said, and asked the attorney if he could look at the will. Doing so, he immediately realized that the document had been rewritten in just the last few weeks. It was brand new, not the one he had seen when she first became ill.

"Paul, we talked with Mom . . ." his sister began.

"Edna, please let me handle this," Robert said. "Paul, this isn't about any of us. This is Mom's will, both literally and legally, and we plan to honor it."

"I can't believe she'd do this to me."

"What are you saying, Paul? That *we* did it?" Robert said.

"I'm saying that this is insane. And I can't believe that you two—"

"Goddamnit, Paul, I spent years—*years*—telling you not to fight with her! I begged you—"

"No one is going to tell me how to live my life!" Paul shot back.

"Oh, give it a break," his brother said. "No one's ever told you what to do with your goddamn life and you know it! This is about you constantly riling Mom."

"When I get attacked, I respond!"

"And this is what you get for it."

"This is unfair. Some of that money belonged to Dad and—"

"Paul, she didn't cut you out," Edna joined in, "she simply didn't give you an even share."

"I can't believe you two are going through with this."

"This is her last will and testament and, like it or not, we've agreed to stand by it," Robert said.

Even Uli hadn't expected Paul to be cut out of his mother's will—and though the two brothers weren't close, he never suspected a double cross. Uli's thoughts were accompanied by the persistent scuttling and squeaking of rats.

Large laboratory counters, chairs, and tables had been pulled apart and rearranged to section off areas of the vast wooden floor. It appeared almost as if organized battles had taken place here—but where would the bodies have gone?

At one point he spotted the faint flickering of a small bonfire. Uli cautiously approached a small group huddled before the flame. As he got within fifty feet, however, they noticed him and scattered.

"I just want to talk!" he shouted, to no avail.

Soon, he began spotting corpses. He inspected each one he came across, but the state of decomposition always made scavenging impossible. While carefully making his way beneath a massive obstacle course of broken desks, Uli reflected that the entire space felt like some giant skyscraper that had collapsed into just a few levels, spilling every which way. The only possible reason that he could imagine for building such a giant underground office space in the middle of nowhere would be for safety in the event of a nuclear strike.

Whenever he passed an upright desk, he scrounged through its drawers for supplies. In one drawer, to his delight, he found a small working flashlight. In another were two Mercury dimes. Besides these items, he found little else.

Proceeding through the darkness, he began hearing distant screams. He cautiously followed the cries for about five minutes until he saw what appeared to be a pool of light in the distance. Next to it, an older man was lying on his back. Flipping on the little flashlight, he saw that blood was running from the fellow's neck into a puddle of phosphorescent paint that had spilled from a bucket. The man had apparently been attacked while painting the lines that Uli noticed earlier. A small incision ran across the guy's neck, though he was still breathing.

"What were you painting?"

"Lines for Plato."

"Why? Where to?"

The man winced in pain.

When Uli confirmed that there was nothing he could do, he asked, "Who did this?"

"Fucking miner," the man sputtered. "Stole the vest Plato gave me. Had a stripe on it . . ."

Uli remembered the blind guy telling him about the diggers in the Sticks. "Where'd he go?"

The man pointed with his eyes toward his feet. A moment later he stopped breathing. Uli delicately undressed him—his ragged yellow tennis shoes, torn pants, and blood-soaked shirt, all probably recycled from earlier victims. He left the unfortunate man in his underwear. None of the clothes fit Uli but at least they stayed on.

He headed in the indicated direction for about twenty minutes until, much to his surprise, he saw it: a small stripe bobbing in the darkness. It was the murderous miner wearing the stolen vest, walking about five hundred feet ahead of him. For thirty minutes or so, Uli followed at a generous distance—down holes, across vast spaces, and through other ruptures in the ceilings and wood floors—until the killer sensed he was being pursued, took off the vest, and vanished.

18

The notion of dying in this hellhole, with all the rotting corpses around him, terrified Uli. Even Paul had friends. Yet other than Teresa and her kids, the only people who consoled him at his mother's funeral were Maria and her beautiful daughter Lucretia. Apparently, everyone believed he had neglected his mother during her final days. Robert and Edna stood near her coffin.

As the oldest, Paul spoke first. He eulogized his mother respectfully, explaining that despite the endless spats between them, their love had only increased over the years. Robert then spoke eloquently about her zealous philanthropy and eternal wisdom. Edna said that Bella had been both her mother and her best friend. They made their moody parent sound like a regular Florence Nightingale. Afterward, none of Paul's aunts, cousins, or close family friends seemed to even notice him unless he approached them directly.

Two weeks later, the family lawyer verified that Paul had been left with whatever interest could be generated from a hundred-thousand-dollar trust. Furthermore, that trust was to be administered by Robert and Wilfred Openhym, a cousin. The final humiliation was a clause stating that if Paul ever contested the will, he'd forfeit every cent. This had all the fingerprints of his dear brother.

Around this time, Paul started noticing Robert's name in the paper again. He had just been appointed as the first parks commissioner of New York City. Small articles began appearing, announcing ribbon-cutting ceremonies at small parks throughout the five boroughs. Soon the son of bitch seemed to be pulling playgrounds and swimming pools out of thin air. "Vest-pocket parks," they were called, unused city property that Robert snatched up and converted into recreation space. Then it was announced that after years of neglect, Central Park was being extensively renovated. A new restaurant, Tavern on the Green, was being built in a former sheepfold near the Great Lawn, which was being resodded and seeded.

Paul called Robert at his office one day, and when the secretary asked his name, Paul facetiously explained that he was a reporter intending to write a puff piece on how Robert Moses tamed Central Park. He was surprised when the call actually went through. As soon as Robert picked up, Paul said that he was sorry about the way things had turned out between them and that he had made peace with their mother's will.

"All I hope," Paul said, "is that maybe we can bury the hatchet and be brothers again."

Robert listened patiently. When Paul asked if he could secure a short loan for his business, Robert said that with his own mounting expenses, he simply couldn't afford it. Paul had already asked Edna and she, too, had claimed that her money was tied up and that she couldn't help him. The Depression was taking a toll on everyone.

Meanwhile, membership at Llanerch was continuing to slow down, so Paul began working around the clock at Con Ed to try to keep up with his growing debts.

19

Uli felt a strange sense of calm when he thought about Paul's relationship with Teresa. They worked really well together. And he took an immediate liking to her two kids. When she learned that he was planning to move out of his place to save money and was going to start sleeping in his Con Ed office, she insisted he move in with her.

One afternoon she popped in for an unannounced visit at his office and discovered that he hadn't come in at all that day. Teresa had divorced her first husband for cheating on her; for this reason, she'd been discreetly checking on Paul every once in a while. Usually he was at work, but occasionally he would simply vanish. When he'd come home, he always seemed quiet, even contrite.

She started suspecting the worst and hired a private investigator. After a month, she learned from her gumshoe that Paul had attended ribbon cuttings for five new city parks. The PI further reported that Paul would always stay in the back of the crowd and remain long after everyone else had left, inspecting his brother's latest projects.

One night over dinner, she delicately confessed what she had done and apologized for it. He didn't say a word.

"Paul, you have to push your brother out of your head. The feeling of betrayal will eat you alive. I know 'cause I went through this with Mike."

"Envy, jealousy . . . that's only a small part of it. When I see Robert and all he's doing with his life . . . well, it's the life I expected to live. His very existence is a monument of my failure."

Driven by Paul's growing despair, Uli became even more intent on making his own mission a success and finding some way out. As he moved in the direction where he had last seen the murderous miner, piles of stones started appearing in wooden boxes, which turned out to be desk drawers. They covered the ground, though there was not a soul in sight. He kept walking through the darkness until he eventually came to a corner doorway that opened to a long, narrow corridor.

Inside the passageway, a massive hole had been cut right into the cement wall and the hard stone behind it. A stale aroma of concrete dust and decay vented out. The hole forked off into three different directions; with his flashlight he could see that two of them were dead ends. Following the third channel and passing by several dark caves, he could hear faint snoring and movement. Peering into one of the caves, he realized he was in the presence of sleeping bodies—this was some kind of dank, narrow bunk room. Uli tiptoed away, fearful of waking them.

He eventually counted six tunnels that went varying distances into the earth. The opening of one foul-smelling cave in a particularly remote section of the tunnel system was covered by old sacks hanging from the low ceiling. Pushing through and flicking on his flashlight, Uli could make out dozens of shriveled feet; bodies were piled sideways like cords of wood.

As he ventured forward, he heard more moans and a constant shuffling of feet. The tunnel pitched downhill at a sharp angle for about a hundred feet, then opened into a larger area that seemed to be another supply depot. In fact, it turned out to be a treasure trove of stock. Stacks and stacks of wooden boxes, presumably food, and green metal barrels marked FRESH WATER were piled to the ceiling.

To Uli's horror, he discovered that what he had been hearing was a chain gang, a paddle wheel of filthy men and women—not particularly old, all nearly naked—shackled together at their wrists and ankles. Their lower quarters were spattered in dirt and excrement. They were passing each other wooden boxes and desk drawers loaded with stones and dirt. Uli watched them dump the contents of their boxes into a large pile in the depot area, then one by one loop back down into the same broad tunnel they had just exited—a human conveyor belt.

Strangely, though, there seemed to be no guards monitoring the activity. After twenty minutes, Uli stepped boldly into view. "Excuse me!" he said to one and all.

Some looked up as they passed, but no one said a word. They just continued dumping rocks and shuffling back into the service tunnel.

"Who's in charge here?"

None replied.

"Are you being held against your will?"

Nothing.

Drawing closer, Uli realized two things: First, the workers weren't really chained; they were merely tied loosely together with frayed rope. Second, they were all exhibiting some type of dementia. Uli shoved past them down a short tunnel in search of guards, or at least supervisors. Soon he arrived at a large dome-shaped room, where the tragic chain gang picked up boxes and then turned around. Not a single monitor or guard was anywhere in sight. As best as Uli could tell, each drone was simply following the lead of the person in front of him or her.

Uli squeezed past them back up to the supply depot.

Ignoring the human conveyor belt, he headed over to the mountain of stock. Unmarked wooden crates filled the place, much like those he had seen at the depot near the catch basin.

Moving along the far wall of the room, Uli started looking through them. Most were filled with C-ration crackers straight from World War II. There were enough survival rations here to feed a small army.

A moment later, he tripped over a small pile of dirty metal rods—digging tools. A large case of candles and a small box of matchsticks were sitting on one of the crates. Uli pocketed some matches, then lit a single candle and rummaged through the stock for food. Aside from the ubiquitous crackers, there were boxes of aspirin, lime juice, and NoDoz. After chomping down two tins of crackers, he popped open one of the barrels of fresh water. It tasted heavenly. As he chugged, a bedraggled young woman broke out of the line and grabbed his arm.

"Benny!" she groaned.

Jumping back in shock, Uli could immediately see that the poor woman was suffering from severe dementia. The rope attaching her to the chain gang had snapped. Gently pulling her off, he looked in her eyes and said, "I'm not Benny."

"Where is he?"

"Waiting for you," Uli answered, deciding that deception was kinder than the truth. He pointed her back toward the others and she slowly stumbled away. Uli returned to his crates.

A sudden loud crash was followed by low moans coming from a small utility closet. The poor woman was on the ground—apparently she had wandered inside the closet and climbed up on something which then collapsed. After Uli helped her out and directed her back down the service tunnel from where she had come, he checked out the closet. Turning on his flashlight again, he saw that a large rectangular fuse box had been dislodged and was hanging by a bunch of old cables. The wall next to the utility closet had a stack of crates leaning against it. Moving them carefully forward, Uli discovered that the utility closet serviced an old freight elevator. When he located a thin pipe and pried open its door, he found that the elevator shaft was packed solid with concrete, utterly impassable.

20

If Paul's mother had left him a hundred-thousand-dollar principal ten years earlier, Uli thought, it would've been a great help, but since it was the beginning of America's greatest depression, there just weren't a lot of good investments. And since Robert, of all people, had been assigned as the executor of his trust, Paul knew it would forever doom their relationship to one of suspicion and antagonism.

Robert deemed that the best investment he could find for his older brother was in purchasing a large, undervalued loft at 168 Bowery and letting the business that occupied the space pay out a monthly rent that more than covered the mortgage. This investment would be far safer than the stock market and would yield a larger return than any bank or bond. The problem was, the clothing company that occupied the loft was doing no better than the rest of the country. They had cut their staff down to a skeleton crew, and though they weren't going out of business, they were hanging on by just a thread. After the first two years, they were barely able to make their rent. Paul was only seeing a fraction of the money that he expected. When he finally demanded to inspect a financial report of his principal, he was horrified to see that both his brother and cousin—as well as a collection agent—were drawing income from his minuscule profit. Paul convinced Teresa to borrow ten thousand dollars from her father to help pay off his creditors.

By 1933 the Depression was in full swing, and to Paul's great dismay, Con Ed terminated his position. But the summer was a scorcher that year, and since he had already closed all the club's side businesses, greatly reducing overhead, the pool actually started earning money again.

One morning in February 1934, Paul opened the *New York Times* to read that Robert was running on the Republican ticket for governor of New York State. He closed the paper and shoved it into the garbage can without mentioning a word of it to Teresa. Upon learning the news later that day, she said that perhaps he should contact his sister. But he still felt betrayed by her because of the disinheritance.

"She has always liked you, Paul," Teresa argued. "Give her a chance."

When he finally got up the strength to call Edna and ask about Robert's run for public office, she said, "I learned about it in the newspapers just like you."

Exasperated, Paul told Teresa that he didn't want to hear anything more about Robert. Nonetheless, it was impossible to avoid his brother's progress. Robert's office published an aggressive campaign schedule to challenge the incumbent, Governor Herbert Lehman, who was trailing in the polls.

"If that son of a bitch gets elected," Paul vented, "I'm moving to Pennsylvania!"

"Now just calm down," Teresa reasoned.

"Don't ever tell me to calm down!"

Over the next few days, she found him increasingly difficult to deal with. In the mornings he stopped getting dressed; he just sat around in his T-shirt and boxers staring out the window.

After a lot of thought, Paul decided that this was his lot in life. His younger brother was destined to be successful and he was doomed to live in his shadow. *The sooner I simply accept I'm a failure, the easier life will be.*

"I don't think that's true at all," Teresa said when he shared his pessimistic outlook. "I just think he's having his time in the sun. Think about it: you launched a great business smack in the middle of a terrible depression. Any other time and you'd have been right up there with Rockefeller. Just wait, you'll have your day."

Feeling as though Teresa was his only rock to stand on, he finally proposed marriage and she accepted. Not wanting to get another awkward rejection from Robert's wife, Paul didn't bother to invite his brother, though Edna came to the ceremony.

With a family to support now, Paul contacted everyone he knew, trying to reignite his electrical engineering career, but there were only a handful of places hiring someone with his broad expertise. That April, out of the blue, he got an invitation to have lunch with a mysterious Mr. Paul Windels. It turned out that Windels was a close personal friend of Mayor Fiorello La Guardia.

The "Little Flower" had a serious problem and had asked Windels to help him find the right man to fix it. He suspected that Con Edison was vastly overcharging New York City on its monthly electricity bill. Finding a properly qualified person who could prove such a thing would be a challenge in such a small, tightly networked profession. Despite this, Windels had been referred by no less than four different people to Paul Moses. All seemed to agree that he had the perfect combination of faith in the public trust and bottomless knowledge of such particulars.

"So he's looking for a consultant?" Paul asked Windels.

"Actually, he's looking to appoint someone as commissioner of water supply, gas, and electricity, but of course it doesn't pay much considering the vast amount of work the post requires."

It was the break Paul had been waiting for. He told Windels that he was very interested in the job regardless of the salary. "You probably already know this," Paul added, "but my brother Robert, who is currently running for governor, is the city's parks commissioner."

"Well, I don't see how that will make a difference one way or the other," Windels replied.

"We're not on the best of terms, which doesn't bode well for me if he becomes the next governor."

"Actually, that might not be true," Windels speculated. "If he does become the next governor, and polls are giving him the edge, he'll have to resign his city post anyway."

That evening over dinner, Paul shared the good news with Teresa. "The job doesn't exactly come with a big paycheck, but it should make me highly employable for future work."

Over the next two weeks, Paul was on pins and needles about the appointment. Several times, he had the urge to break down and call his younger brother to see if he could convince him to put in a good word, but he resisted.

One morning, however, Windels called to say that La Guardia had unfortunately chosen someone else.

"Who?"

"Joe Pinelli?"

"Who the hell . . . ?" Paul had never even heard of the man.

"Welcome to the world of politics. Pinelli is an ignoramus, he's payback to some political boss in the Bronx. I think the mayor mentioned to some bigwig at Con Ed that he was about to hire you. They knew you'd crack down, so they agreed to roll back their rates, provided you weren't hired."

"This is unbelievable."

"Well, it's between us, because I honestly don't really know everything that happened. All I know is that La Guardia picked Pinelli and Con Ed agreed to renegotiate their bill. But listen, if it's of any consolation, I can throw some consulting work your way."

Paul felt cheated again, but he was too broke to turn down anything. Furthermore, he believed Windels had really tried to help him; he sensed his brother was somehow behind it all once again.

Paul did extensive contracting work for the city at a cheap rate, though it came to an abrupt end a few months later when Windels was dismissed.

Despite Paul's attempts to turn his leisure club into a year-round social mecca for suburban Philly, a more modestly priced club opened nearby. With bankruptcy looming, he kept thinking about how he had ignored his father's advice. *I had a moneymaker and ruined it.*

During one particularly masochistic moment, Paul got in his car and drove to the first day of the expansion of Orchard Beach up in the Bronx. He watched as his younger brother was chauffeured in a huge Packard to the VIP viewing stand. La Guardia introduced Robert as the man who had single-handedly conceived of and found funds for this wonderful gift to the people of New York City: "This is his very first outing as a candidate, so please give a warm welcome to the next governor of the state of New York, Robert Moses!"

As Robert appeared on the rostrum, and applause died down, Paul began to feel nauseous.

"Hello, ladies and gentleman," Robert began. "As you all know, I'm running for governor of this great state with your interest at heart. As you might remember, I tirelessly worked as secretary of state under the great Al Smith . . . and before him I worked under Mayor Mitchel, where I . . . I tried to devise a method of standardization to help eliminate bureaucracy . . . Well, that didn't go too well . . . but, see, that wasn't entirely my fault. What happened was . . . well . . . it's just too difficult to explain here and now . . . but if you look at the record, you'll see that I was stonewalled time and again . . . It's too difficult to explain, but let me assure you that this will not happen again if I am governor of this fair state. No sir."

Paul watched as his brother paused and stared blankly over the bewildered crowd.

"All I'll add is that if you vote for me, you'll greatly improve your own lot. Thank you!" Sweating profusely right through his shirt and cotton suit, Robert Moses stepped off the stage.

Paul found himself deeply moved by his brother's awkward naivete and began clapping, leading others to join in.

After the ceremony broke up, Robert hurried to his car, but Paul didn't try to approach him. At that moment, he knew there was no way in the world that Robert was going to win this election; in fact, he would never get elected to *any* public office. His brother was clearly and painfully devoid of anything resembling charm, guile, let alone wit.

Ecstatic when he got home that night, Paul relayed his brother's public humiliation to his wife, who was only happy that he was happy. The next day, Paul called the Moses for Governor campaign headquarters and requested Robert's entire schedule of public events. As time allowed, Paul would pop in at various appearances, and though his brother had shaken off his initial stage fright, he wasn't really improving his delivery. If he was bored or acting arrogant, the crowd had to just deal with it.

One day when Paul felt particularly depressed, he saw that Robert was giving a speech up in Nyack. He drove all the way there, only to discover that it was a press conference. He put on sunglasses and was able to slip in, though he stayed in the back of the room.

"Mr. Moses," one reporter asked, "aren't you concerned that your public works projects will take vital funds from welfare programs for the people of this state?"

"Please don't bother me with moronic questions like that," Robert replied. "The projects will help the people get work, period."

"But Mr. Moses, Governor Lehman said—"

"He's even less informed than you are, if that's possible," Robert grumbled back.

The man wasn't merely a bad candidate, he was clearly resentful of the entire campaign process. Comments like "You won't understand" and "Leave it to the experts" punctuated his extemporaneous remarks. Over the ensuing months, the polls gradually reflected his caustic personality. It was about six months into his run that Paul caught an article about Robert's slipping numbers. He had officially fallen behind the formerly unpopular incumbent. The election had been his to lose and now he was losing it.

The next time Paul saw Robert was at a synagogue in Great Neck. At the end of a wooden speech about how he would improve the economy, the candidate offered to take questions. Someone asked about his faith. Exactly how devout was he?

"I'm not really Jewish," Robert responded to the packed synagogue.

"But your name is Moses," the rabbi pointed out, allowing Robert a chance to explain more fully.

"I didn't pick it," he snapped back. After some additional perfunctory remarks, he thanked the stunned crowd, told them to remember to vote, and left the temple.

The margin by which his brother lost the election made Paul feel warm all over. Yet soon after this triumph, Llanerch got a tax bill for ten thousand dollars and Paul found he had no money to pay it. The end was near. The bank immediately initiated foreclosure proceedings on his pool club.

"I worked so hard and came so close," he complained over the dinner table. "I mean, it's a solid investment if I can just weather this damn depression. Now I'm going to lose everything."

Teresa got on the phone and within a week her father and aunt had ponied up yet more loans.

Someone must've dug all these rocks out of the earth, Uli realized, snapping away from Paul. He left the storage depot and pushed past the chain of laborers, heading back down into the dim dome-shaped room. He gazed up and for the first time noticed the large uneven tower of modified wooden desks. It resembled some kind of primitive ceremonial structure. Hanging from the top was a rotting corpse. Uli examined the body with his flashlight and realized it had undergone some kind of outlandish transfiguration. The feet were violently twisted backward. Worse, though, was the missing head, replaced with a long-snouted skull.

A dull clinking of hammers drew Uli away from the corpse and over to a large crack in the wall at a corner of the chamber. On hands and knees he descended into the burrow, where he followed a small tunnel maybe three feet in diameter shooting upward and a larger corridor that corkscrewed downward. Other smaller excavations began spiraling off from the corridor and soon he feared that he was getting lost. He flicked on his flashlight and noticed wires above him held together along a single small wooden bridge like a violin. Tinkering sounds surrounded him. People were digging. Moving along this main artery, he realized the wires along the top led into the various side tunnels. Suddenly, a box of rocks crashed out of one. Crawling down the tunnel roughly fifty feet, Uli came upon the bottom half of a sweaty, half-naked man digging furiously into the earth. He wore something black wrapped like a turban around his face and head; Uli assumed it was an improvised air filter.

"Hello!" Uli called out.

"Fuck off!" the digger shouted behind him. Uli withdrew to the outer corridor, where he fingered another wire leading to the next dark cave. This time he encountered another seminude turban-headed digger. Again, when Uli greeted the man, he was instructed to fuck off.

He continued examining the ten or so guide wires fastened to the low ceiling above him. Each hole was little more than two feet in diameter. As he crawled farther down, he heard the tinkering of yet another person.

"Who's in charge?" Uli called out.

"Fuck off!" the crazed miner responded, as though following the same script.

Eventually, Uli turned around and crawled back up the circular passage. Emerging in the domed room, and finally able to stand up again, he wiped dust off himself and followed the line of drone workers up the service tunnel toward the storage depot. After a few minutes he discovered they were now being led by someone. He sped up along the side of the tunnel. A middle-aged lady was directing the passive chain gang into the upper caves.

"Hello!"

"What?" the lady screamed, almost jumping off her feet.

"I didn't mean to startle you."

"Fuck off!" she shouted, lifting her hands defensively.

"Why is everyone so angry here?"

"We've all been trapped in this dungeon for years. What d'you expect?"

"Who's in charge?"

"Did you see the diggers in the Convolution?"

"If you mean those little caves with the nasty bastards, yes." Nodding behind the chain gang, Uli added, "I also see these poor bastards carrying rocks out of the tunnels."

"That's called occupational therapy, asshole! They're senile. I found them starving to death, and I rescued them."

Uli didn't respond. Turning them into unsupervised laborers wasn't exactly a rescue or therapy.

A few moments elapsed before the woman said, "Sorry if I'm a bit rude, it's just the best way to deal with most of these guys. This place makes everyone very agitated. I can see by your stubble that you're new here." She resumed leading her group upward.

"Yeah, I was just pulled from the sewer."

"Shit, someone told me they sealed up the sewage hole. Of course somebody else probably tore it open again."

"How long have you all been down here?"

"The longest have been here since Wilson dug that fucking hole in the sewer—nearly ten years," she said. "He was trying to fix the blockage he created and ended up opening this door to hell."

"The entrance to this hell was dug with good intentions," he quipped.

"So is Shub still mayor?" she asked.

"Mallory just beat him in the election."

"The former mayor's wife?"

"Yeah. Did you know her?"

"She was one of the Garlic Heads who they brought in to try to help organize the place. I heard that she had some kind of work to keep the election honest."

Mallory had said she'd been recently appointed to that post. How would this woman know that if she had been down here all this time?

"Whenever I find newbies, I always ask them about the place," she explained, as if sensing his doubts. "I try to keep track of the latest developments there." She continued leading the group up through the storage area and into a new labyrinth of tunnels. "They realize that if they all cling together, they can help each other survive. But they have no real hope of ever escaping."

"That must be why they pray."

"All the guys who've made it up here work nonstop. To their credit, they're still trying to get out, but none of them get along so they don't work together." She paused. "They're each intent on finding their own way out."

Uli extended his hand and introduced himself. The woman said her name was Root Ginseng.

"Hell of a name."

"I was born Persephone, a bad name for this illiterate age. When I was growing up, most people who read it pronounced it as *Percy-phone*. When I moved to San Francisco, I worked in a health food store and people jokingly called me *Root* and it stuck."

"Nice to meet you, Root . . . Hey, what is that central room anyway? And what the hell is that thing in the middle of it?" Uli asked, referring to the tower of stacked wooden desks.

"We thought this was the bottom of an old missile silo."

"If that's the case, wouldn't there be a launch opening directly above it?"

"That's why we built the tower and dug up into it, but it turned out to be a dud."

"How'd you manage to get all these guys to work on it?"

"Sandy and I somehow convinced most of them to put aside their differences and collect desks to build that tower up to the ceiling." This accounted for the absence of desks right near the Sticks. "But soon they were all fighting again."

"Fighting over what?"

"You name it. *That's my chisel. You drank my water. This is my area to dig. Quit breathing so loud.* Constant trouble."

"No truce lasts forever," Uli said as he walked beside her.

"They got about fifteen feet into the rock before they started shoving each other for elbow and leg space." She paused again. "I'll never forget hearing that awful scream as the first man fell to his death. Then a few days went by, and another man was pushed. Soon we realized they weren't just fighting, they were actually sacrificing people up there. When there was only about eight left from the original group, they gave up and went back to lateral drilling . . . You'll excuse me for asking, but who exactly are you?"

"I own a pool club in Pennsylvania and—" He caught himself. "Actually, I just crawled out of the sewer and I'm looking for a way out of this hellhole . . ."

Root reached her new destination and said it was time to take care of the babies.

"You have babies?!" Uli asked as he followed along.

"That's just what I call them 'cause they're as helpless as infants."

She headed into an abandoned cave and lit some candles. Uli saw right away that it was covered with dirt and human excrement. Root grabbed a shovel and scooped out the waste as though the place were a giant litter box. Then she laid down some new dirt and a chemical that seemed to mask the odor and spread out some pieces of cardboard— *voilà*, it was transformed into a giant bunk room.

Root moved into another dimly lit cave where others were standing around waiting. Following her lead, Uli grabbed a bucket and the two washed the group down, then dried them with pieces of old cloth. Next they led the men into yet another cave, where they handed out crackers and cups of water. After the meal, Root escorted another group into another cave where she had them sit on a long bench with holes in the seats—a makeshift row of toilets.

21

Paul imagined that his brother would someday retire up in Albany as a minor government functionary, a body second from the left in the third row of various group photos with central politicians in the front and center. When the first few expressway projects were announced, Paul made a joke about Robert wearing a T-shirt while digging ditches and shoveling blacktop out in Long Island. The highways cutting across so much private property—little farms and homes—immediately reminded Paul of the bad press Robert had drawn trying to enact his controversial Standardization Plan under Mayor Mitchel nearly twenty years before.

When Paul read that his brother had declined both city and state salaries and was living off his stolen inheritance, he concluded that this was one of the great secrets to his success. Though Paul couldn't contest the will without jeopardizing his little nest egg, he figured there had to be something he could do to turn his meager trust into more cash. He decided to call the clothing company renting his loft at 168 Bowery and see if he could sell them a long-term lease for a lump sum.

"Tell you what," said Mel Green, one of the proprietors, "would you take forty thousand dollars for the thirty-year lease?"

"Let me think about it," Paul said, but he immediately knew that this would be more than acceptable. He also knew that he wouldn't be able to reach Robert by phone, so he typed up the proposal and mailed it to him. A few weeks later, he got a letter back from his cousin Willy:

Dear Paul:

Robert and I have carefully considered your request and have decided that this really isn't a wise offer. We understand you've been shortchanged by these people in their monthly payments, but they still owe us all that money, and the depression should be over soon. Bowery Wardrobe promises to pay all back rent with interest as stipulated in the original agreement. Hold tight and I guarantee you'll get all the money that is owed to you. My best to Teresa and the kids.

Sincerely,
Your cousin,
Wilfred Openhym

After a terse follow-up phone conversation with his cousin, Paul hired a lawyer and brought a suit against Willy and Robert, stating that they were deliberately mismanaging his trust in order to bleed it for their own benefit.

Willy, in turn, showed up with his own lawyer at a subsequent arbitration meeting; he stated that Mr. Robert Moses was unable to attend due to government commitments. After reading the briefs and listening to arguments on both sides, the judge found Paul's complaint about mismanagement to be groundless. On the other hand, he ruled that it was unfair for Willy and Robert to extract income when the primary beneficiary wasn't earning his due. So he ruled that until Paul got his full back payments, they were not permitted to withdraw another cent. Although he wasn't able to accept Bowery Wardrobe's offer, Paul still felt he had won a small victory by depriving Robert of his money.

Meanwhile, Robert's professional life took a turn for the better with his greatest achievement to date—connecting Manhattan, Queens, and the Bronx with just one bridge. The throne for this accomplishment was the newly created Triborough Bridge Authority, of which Robert would be king. The endless stream of revenue from tolls would be used solely at Robert Moses's discretion.

"How can this be legal?" Paul shouted while reading the details in the *New York Times* at the counter of a coffee shop on Third Avenue and 52nd Street.

"Hey, buddy, you're scaring my customers," said the owner.

Paul ripped the newspaper in half, slapped a dime on the counter, and stomped out.

"I met him a couple times," Root said to Uli as he helped her bring some of the tired workers into a cave.

"You met Paul Moses?"

"No, Plato, the guy who got elected leader. The one thing I fault him on was his family. I think he left them 'cause his boy was handicapped. I told the kid he could have access to C-rations if he ever needed any."

"As far as I can tell," Uli said, "you've done a lot more than this leader in terms of finding a way out of here."

"Yeah, if overseeing a bunch of dead-end tunnels ever helps anyone. Hell, most of them are pointed downward or run parallel to each other."

"Why do you all even bother? The only way out of here is obviously up."

"Long ago, Plato told everyone that there were stairwells at the lowest levels of this place."

"Can't the diggers come up with a plan so at least they each dig in a different direction?"

"A man after my own heart!" she chirped, smiling. "I have to confess, it's exciting to be able to talk about this with someone sane."

She led Uli off to a small cave that she had converted into a private office. She carefully lit several candles, revealing a strange model built out of little sticks and blocks that resembled a spiraling tree lying on its side with eleven branches. The largest branch was the central corridor of the Convolution.

"These tunnels move in different directions," Root explained, pointing to several branches, "but most of them are loosely parallel."

Over a dinner of canned prunes and a square tin of Spam that she had been saving for a special occasion, Root told Uli how she had first climbed out of the sewer with a group of others about five years before. All were immediately warned against going into the Mkultra. They were told it was pure savagery. Over the first couple of years, she watched as her compatriots fell victim to the memory disease that ravaged the place. One day, though, she noticed that the ropes rising from the sewer were twisting wildly. A large man climbed up. His name was Herman, and after being warned against leaving the catch basin, he declared that he would get out of this place or die trying. She asked if she could join him and he consented.

They started off by climbing three levels through the vast abandoned installation. They cooked white rats and drank from the buckets of runoff water as they fought back roving gangs, psychopaths, and a host of other lost souls. Together, they hatched the plan to turn a group of mentally damaged men into miners.

"What happened to Herman?"

"He instructed me that when the day came that he couldn't remember his own name, I should kill him."

"Any idea why you were never affected?"

She shook her head.

"You didn't take any kind of medicine?"

Again, she shook her head.

"And you've been alone with the diggers ever since?"

"Actually, there was another woman already here when we arrived."

"Who?"

"She was suffering from partial memory loss and couldn't remember her name, so I just called her Sandy Corners, since she used to sleep in the sandy corner of the storage depot downstairs. She wasn't as far gone as the others."

"What became of her?"

"If you were in the silo, you probably saw her hanging there."

"I hope you're not referring to that mutilated body."

"Yeah, but the miners actually liked her. They decided that she would be a great offering to the gods, so they strung her up there."

"They liked her so much they killed her?"

"She was pretty out of it by then. It was more like a mercy killing."

"God," Uli murmured, "human sacrifice."

"The more dire a situation, the greater the need for some divine intervention. This is probably how all religions get started."

"What did they do with her head?"

"Lopped it off and replaced it with that dog skull."

"Where did they get the dog?"

"The Mkultra was originally a big laboratory, and scientists used all sorts of animals for experimentation."

"But why did they cut off the poor woman's head?"

"One of the miners, a chubby Italian guy, came up with the idea from some weird Aztec calendar he had found on his way through the Mkultra. Sandy's body represents the death guide Xolotl: head of a dog, body of a human. And we're all in some place called the Mictlan."

Uli was genuinely impressed by this woman. Working alone for several years now, she had somehow managed to control all these crazed human mole rats. In doing so, she had become the closest thing to a central force that this subterranean termite hill had. Inspecting the three-dimensional model of the tunnels, Uli asked, "Would the most efficient number of tunnels be—"

"Six, each going in a different direction." Pointing to her mock-up, she added, "These tunnels would maximize our chances of getting out of here."

"Why don't you tell the miners?"

"Oh, I tried—awhile back. I begged them! But all they say is, *Fuck off*. Most of them are pretty blind. Hell, half the time they're just trying to find their own tunnels."

"What do you mean?"

"After working for hours, they crawl out and sleep in the storage depot or Lord knows where. When they return, those wires along the top of the caves help direct them back to their own tunnels."

"Why don't we just redirect the wires so that they go into the six tunnels you identified?"

"The real problem is scheduling them so they don't overlap," Root said. "If one finds another in his tunnel, it's over."

Uli started checking through his ratty pants. "I thought I had a watch, but . . ." But he was thinking of the pocket watch Vladimir had given Paul in Mexico.

"Why do you need a watch?"

"With it, we could track everyone's work and sleep patterns."

"Not a bad idea," she affirmed.

The two headed up into the Mkultra, venturing far out to the furnished part of the Lethe. Searching through several hundred desk drawers, they found stacks of old Mkultra documents and boxes of No. 2 pencils which they could use to track the diggers. Root came upon an old windup alarm clock.

"What time shall we make it?"

Uli said he greatly missed the bright rays of early morning sunlight, so they set it for seven. Since there was no indication of a.m. or p.m., it was something they'd have to monitor carefully. The next stage was simply drawing up a list of names, or at least some way to assign the tunnels to different miners. Root said that so many of them had died or vanished—only to be replaced by others—that the diggers' identities had been reduced to types: there was a short Italian guy, a black guy who seemed to mimic the Italian, and a bunch of old white men.

Over the next few days, Uli and Root took turns waiting in the large silo, jotting down the times of the miners' comings and goings, as well as their sleeping habits.

It was much trickier than Uli had expected. Some of the miners would sleep erratically, while others rested at steady four- or six-hour intervals. While waiting for them to appear, Uli would close his eyes and let Paul's life pour through his brain . . .

22

By 1940, Teresa's father and aunt began asking Paul to pay back his loans. Out of work for several years, Paul was unable to comply.

He was growing increasingly obsessed with his brother's achievements: along with the Queens Midtown Tunnel, the vast Belt System—which included the Cross Island, Gowanus, Whitestone, Laurelton, and Southern Parkways—was also designed under Robert's stewardship throughout the early forties. Paul visited the various construction sites, watching the huge earthmoving machines alter the city's landscape. Rather than slowing anything down, the war seemed to be accelerating his brother's victories.

When Paul's wife said she'd finally had enough and didn't want to hear about Robert anymore, Paul tried to keep it to himself. One morning, though, she woke up to his shouts. When she asked what was up, Paul yelled that Robert had demolished the New York Aquarium in Battery Park as an act of revenge against those who had protested his Battery Bridge project.

"I want you to stop this!" she demanded.

"Stop what? *He* did it!"

"Did what?"

"He had the fish dumped into New York Harbor." Paul wept as though Robert had drowned his own children.

That was it for Teresa. She told him she was frightened of him. "I don't want you back in the house until you see a psychiatrist."

He reluctantly agreed. He knew there was something wrong with him. After a dozen phone calls, Teresa located Dr. Hiram Moshbeck, a distinguished man with a thick crop of wild gray hair.

On the doctor's soft leather sofa, Paul felt great pleasure in telling the older man how he once loved his brother. Though Robert was only a year younger, Paul had felt a strong urge to protect him against their overbearing mother. Even when his little brother would fight against him, he knew Robert was only trying to be a good kid.

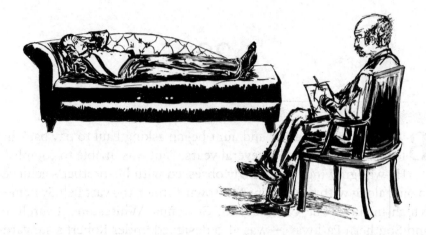

"He couldn't see it, but instead of rebelling against her, he rebelled against *me*," Paul deduced. The psychiatrist let him go on, and Paul explained how the real problem began when Robert stole his birthright.

"What exactly did he do?"

"He conned my mom into cutting me out of her will."

"Did you hate her for doing that?"

"No, I don't think she would've done it if she was in her right mind. I mean, we fought a lot, but we always made up. I never doubted Bella's love for an instant."

"And what was *his* relationship with your mother like?"

"He did everything she said." Paul then relayed the entire history of Millie, who he had loved and followed down to Mexico, and how much his mother had hated the woman.

"It sounds like your mother punished you and rewarded your younger brother because he listened to her and you didn't."

"That's all behind us now," Paul said.

"Your wife says you're obsessed with your younger brother."

"You must've read about Robert Moses in the news?"

"Sure."

"He's also prevented me from getting jobs. Jobs in the government."

"What about moving to another city?"

"I'm not going to be pushed from my home."

"Okay, then *you* have to push *him* out of your thoughts, don't you?"

"Just look at all he's done! He's behind all the highways, he's building bridges, parks, pools. It doesn't end!"

"So what? Why can't you just live your life and let him live his?"

"The man is a power-hungry megalomaniac and he should be stopped!"

"Then he will be," the doctor replied in a calm voice. "But how does that concern you?"

"He controls everything! You think I'm crazy? Just go look at all his accomplishments. He's behind *everything*."

The doctor sighed and asked Robert if he would repeat a simple statement.

"What kind of statement?"

"A declaration of independence."

"Sure," said Paul, mostly to appease the doctor.

"*Robert Moses did not pay for these pools, parks, highways, and bridges . . .*" the doctor began.

After a moment, Paul sighed and repeated the words.

"*He did not design, nor build, nor does he own these pools, parks, highways, and bridges,*" the shrink said.

Paul felt idiotic as he recited the phrase.

"*He is just one of a list of bureaucrats who is affiliated with the construction . . .*"

As Paul echoed the doctor, he told himself, *This will make Teresa happy.*

"*And if he were not alive, these highways and bridges and pools and parks would be built anyway . . .*"

Paul slowly repeated the doctor's declaration.

"*. . . by mayors, borough presidents, governors, with people's tax money and Board of Estimate votes, and by the countless people they hire. Robert Moses is merely one of many, many names. And, most importantly, he does not control my joy or pain. Paul Moses is master of Paul Moses.*"

When Paul finished the ridiculous recitation, the first session was officially over. The psychiatrist scheduled a second appointment, but Paul never showed up. When his wife asked why he hadn't gone, he said he didn't need it. The doctor had put things in perspective and he was feeling much better.

Teresa woke up one night soon after to hear her husband quietly weeping into his pillow. The next day, she found him making strange expressions at the breakfast table. She realized he was desperately trying to restrain his rage while reading the newspaper. Later in the week, while chatting with her kids, she heard a sharp yelp coming from the bathroom. Paul stepped out with a strange smile on his face. The following morning, Teresa delicately told Paul that she and the kids had become uncomfortable in his presence. She asked him to move out—she wanted a divorce.

* * *

During his first week with the alarm clock, Uli was able to keep track of both the habits of the miners and the tedious passing of his own long days. On the back of an old document recovered from the Mkultra enigmatically entitled "Project Artichoke," he and Root kept careful records, each taking turns sleeping so one of them was always awake. During that time, Uli told Root about his own amnesia, explaining that it predated his arrival in this place. This compelled him to remember how cautious Karen had seemed about his taking the sewer plunge. Was it Mallory who said that many others had taken this route out? Ultimately, however, it was his own arrogance that had prompted him to go, and now he had to deal with the consquences.

One day he asked Root how she had ended up down here.

"The same way as everyone else—trying to escape from Rescue City, Nevada."

"So you were living in the real New York City when it was attacked?"

"Oh, no. I came with the second wave, in '72, when they started calling antiwar activists terrorists. I was one of the Diggers."

"Diggers? You mean like these guys?"

"No, the Diggers were a group in San Francisco in the late sixties who helped young hippie arrivals. They were started by a guy named Emmett Grogan who's still in Rescue City."

"Were they anarchists?"

"Most were. When I joined there were half a million US troops in Vietnam—the My Lai massacre occurred a few months later. Then Bobby Kennedy and King were assassinated. A bunch of us went to the Democratic National Convention in Chicago where we all got beaten with billy clubs and arrested, so we—"

"I remember," Uli interrupted, wanting Root to continue with her story instead of giving him a history lesson.

"We eventually wound up on the attorney general's hit list and found ourselves detained in Rescue City. Emmett and some of us soon got tired of all the bad smells and hippie crap in Staten Island and decided to go up to Queens instead. This was just as the Piggers were taking over the Bronx and Queens and the Crappers were claiming Manhattan and Brooklyn. We refused to participate in all the partisan violence or declare allegiance to either gang, so a group of Piggers approached us and said we had to leave their borough."

"What happened?"

"We barricaded ourselves in a city park and decided we weren't going without a fight. To avoid a conflict that might've brought in the Crappers, the Piggers told us that if we moved down to Brooklyn and vanished for six months, they'd meet us near the drain hole in Staten Island and give us the escape drug."

"Why'd you trust them?"

"Emmett had defected and joined the Pigger Party by then, but we were dumb and desperate, like everyone else down here."

As Uli and Root talked, several of the miners left their tunnels while others came and resumed work. Root noted their movements.

Uli didn't know if it was just empathy stirred by Paul's painful yearning for Teresa after she filed for divorce, but he found himself quietly attracted to Root, a tough, smart survivor alone in this world of wackos.

23

Several weeks after Teresa asked him to leave, Paul dusted off his electrical engineering degree and his honorable discharge from the army and got himself a wartime posting. He was appointed superintendent of construction at the US Navy base in Bayonne, New Jersey. He was glad to finally have a steady job and paycheck, but it was too late to save his dying pool business, much less his marriage. Despite the impending divorce, he was still intent on paying back his loans to Teresa's family. The loss of his business and family left Paul, who was already in his fifties, constantly tired and listless. He put all his possessions in a storage facility and slept on a squeaky metal cot in his Jersey office.

Over time, Paul began to enjoy his time alone in New Jersey. He threw himself full force at his work as though he were fighting the war all by himself. He had never felt so utilized. He mailed a portion of each paycheck to Teresa as if he were buying back his hocked self-esteem.

One morning in late 1944, Paul woke in his cramped office and discovered an envelope from his ex-wife sitting in his mailbox. Inside, he found his latest check, uncashed. A simple typewritten note said, PAID IN FULL, *good luck in life*, Teresa. His debt was finally over. He called to tell her that he wanted to help with her kids' tuition, but the maid said that Teresa no longer wished to hear from him.

After the war came to an end, while everyone else celebrated, Paul wondered what lay ahead for him. He offered to stay on as an employee at the navy base.

"Paul, we don't really need any electrical engineers," said his boss. "But hell, I'm sure your brother can get you more work than you know what to do with."

Paul sent out his résumé to a few select places for jobs that truly interested him, but with the war over, an army of young men was coming back looking for employment. Fortunately, the Depression was over too, so Paul started once again seeing some income from his inheritance.

After he moved out of his New Jersey office, he rented a room in a cheap Times Square hotel—the Longacre—intending to live there only temporarily while looking for a new home.

As he'd return to his hotel room at night, however, the emptiness of his life began to suffocate him. Joining some other guys he had befriended in the area, he took to spending his days in the balmy spring of 1947 hanging out in Bryant Park. Most of them were veterans from the First World War and conversation was always lively. One older fellow who had also fought in the Spanish-American War showed him tips for living on the cheap, like taking him to soup kitchens. Paul didn't mind joining the ranks of nameless men eating side by side in basement benches. In a way, he felt he deserved it for failing so miserably. His greatest fear was being spotted by any of his former friends, so he made a habit of hunching over, shaving sporadically, pulling his fedora over his face, and never making eye contact with passersby.

One morning, while walking up Fifth Avenue, he spotted Teresa heading uptown on the other side of the street. She was wearing high heels, a beautiful dress, and a tiny black hat, holding a clutch purse. She looked like a million bucks; oddly, it occurred to Paul that he didn't look half-bad either. He had just gotten a haircut and happened to be wearing a nice shirt with his best suit. He experienced heart palpitations as he crossed the avenue and slowly approached her from behind. He was about to tap her on the shoulder when he caught a profile of her beautiful pixie face. She looked happy, an emotion he had rarely seen during their final years together. Knowing that his presence could only depress her, he stopped in his tracks and let her go.

Paul spent his days wandering around Times Square, which suited him given the state of his life. At the main branch of the New York Public Library—the best in the world—he became well acquainted with a small community of lost scholars and drunken intellectuals whom time had forgotten. He found that he could effortlessly sneak into movies and the second halves of Broadway plays during intermission. From St. Clement Church on the West Side and St. Agnes on East 43rd Street, he would collect used clothing and free food. Every morning he'd get copies of the *New York Times*, the *Herald Tribune*, the *Wall Street Journal*, and the *Sun* to check for his brother's name over scalding cups of black coffee.

One afternoon that summer, Paul was hanging out in the Horn & Hardart Automat across from Grand Central Station and skimming the *Daily News*. He was about to pour a cup of coffee from the coin-operated spigot when he heard a shrill female voice shout his name.

Before he could slink away, a beautiful dark-skinned woman was standing before him: "Paul Moses! How are you?"

"Fine," he said quietly, not revealing that he had no clue who she was.

"Paul! It's me—Lucretia."

He wondered if she had worked at Con Ed when he was there, or perhaps he had met her at the library.

"Maria's daughter!" she finally added.

"Oh my God!" It was the daughter of his mother's maid. He hadn't seen her in years. When she hugged him, it felt so strange being touched by another person—something he hadn't experienced in so long.

"How are you?" she asked.

She looked to be in her late twenties, but had to be in her thirties.

"Just fine. How's your mom?"

"She passed away."

"No!" Paul couldn't believe it; she was less than ten years older than he.

"She got lung cancer two years ago and died shortly after."

Paul wanted to give his condolences, but he couldn't even speak. Tears came to his eyes, and for the first time, he felt distinctly old. Poor Maria was the very first woman he'd ever had a crush on. And she had always been so fond of him.

"She tried finding you but you weren't listed," Lucretia said.

"The phone was in my wife's name," he muttered without looking up.

"What are you doing here anyway?"

"Waiting for a friend," he answered, instead of telling her that the St. Clement soup kitchen didn't begin serving until six.

"Are you still working at Con Ed?"

"No, but I consult for them from time to time. How about you?"

"I'm an accountant," she said. "I have about a dozen clients, all in the Bronx."

"Oh, that's right, your mother lived up there."

"Yeah, she left me the place. Hey, you have to come up for dinner."

"I'm not very good company these days."

"You have to! No one has ever made me laugh like you."

"Where in the Bronx is the house?"

"East Tremont. Don't you remember it?"

"Things have been a little frantic for me lately," he said. "But what's your address?"

As she scribbled it down along with her phone number, he thought he would just throw it away after she left, but then she asked, "How's Saturday at seven p.m.?"

"I don't know, I . . ."

"Promise me you'll be there."

"The Bronx is up north, right?" he kidded, knowing when he was licked.

At the bottom of a box of rations, Root found a tiny kid's compass that looked like it had come from a Cracker Jack box. They were now able to determine north, south, east, and west. Numbering all the tunnels in Root's three-dimensional model, they figured out the most practical caves to focus on. The trick now was to fool the men into digging in the selected caves around the clock.

After having monitored the sleeping habits of the miners—some snoozing like clockwork, others capricious and unpredictable—Uli and Root were ready to turn them into a coordinated digging machine. At one point while the two passed through the silo, Uli glanced at his companion and saw tears in her eyes as she watched her old friend hanging from the desk tower.

"There are corpses all over the place," Uli soothed. "Do you think they'd notice if we put another body up there instead?"

"I know where we can find a headless corpse," she replied after a moment.

"Let's try it."

The two hiked up to the funereal cave. Clamping their mouths and noses, they lit a torch and Root led him to the decapitated remains. The body was long deceased, so it didn't smell too bad. They delicately carried it back into the silo, careful that it didn't crumble, then Uli scaled the tower of desks and cut down Sandy's dessicated body. With a rope, he hoisted up the new corpse and strapped it in below the dog's skull. Just to be on the safe side, he wrenched the feet backward like Sandy's had been. Together they carried poor Sandy's headless body back up into one of the empty caves and interred her. Root gave Uli a grateful kiss on the cheek. For the first time since he had been consigned to hell, he actually felt good, and so did Paul . . .

24

. . . in fact, he spent a whole buck on a haircut and shave, complete with the cloud of talcum powder and a spritz of cheap cologne. He bought a new button-down Arrow shirt and picked out his least threadbare suit, which he went over with a lint brush. Then, at Grand Central, Paul gave the colored guy two bits for a spit shine. He bought a bouquet of flowers along with a box of Whitman's chocolates. Hopping on the IRT 6 train, he rode all the way up to the Bronx for dinner with his mother's maid's daughter. The closer he got to her house, however, the more angry he became with himself. Why the hell was he having dinner with some kid—a skinny, shy schoolgirl who would giggle and blush a lot—who he barely remembered? Maria never would've permitted this. He should've simply said no when she gave her invitation.

Forty-five minutes later, he finally arrived at 174th Street. From what he remembered, East Tremont was the Bronx's equivalent of the Lower East Side—working-class Italians who couldn't find anything on Arthur Avenue and Jews who couldn't afford the Grand Concourse. As he schlepped along, he tried to dream up subjects to talk about with this young woman. Should he tell her about his failed marriage? Or perhaps his failed career? He could describe his rootless life of reading newspapers and living off charity. Or he could talk about what everyone else talked about—Robert's tremendous and continuous success.

After crossing through a corner of beautiful Crotona Park—another of his brother's renovations—he searched for her address. He was delighted when he arrived at the elegant old house with a worn wraparound porch that he had last seen almost twenty years earlier.

As he knocked on Lucretia's door, a small dog started barking. A moment later, when she opened the door, his heart stopped. With her hair bundled up, wearing a beautiful dress, the young woman was truly ravishing. A tiny Yorkie barked incessantly as he stepped inside her spacious house. She put the animal in the yard and quickly made Paul a gin and tonic—his favorite drink from twenty years before.

"I once came up around here with my ex-wife to attend her cousin's wedding in Pelham Park."

"Oh, the rich part of town."

"So what's *this* part?" he kidded.

"The farther south and east you go, the worse things get," she said as she served him a Waldorf salad. "This is the middle, where the rich meet the poor. But at the rate things are going, I think in the next ten, twenty years even the South Bronx will improve."

Instead of revealing the miserable truth of his life, Paul served an appetizing lie: The pool club had been a modest success. He had sold it after ten years. He and his brother were still friendly, but not quite friends. Though his marriage had failed, he was still close to Teresa and the kids.

Soon dinner was ready, a terrific grilled fish-and-mango platter. He had to cover his mouth as he ate, because they spent the entire time talking without a single awkward pause. She asked many questions, about his mother, about growing up wealthy, about his time in revolutionary Mexico—things he no longer mentioned to anybody.

"When I was a kid," he confessed after dinner, "I had such a crush on your mother."

"Well, that's a coincidence," she countered, staring softly into his eyes, "because I've always been head over heels about you."

He coughed as she giggled.

* * *

The first miner to exit his tunnel was the short balding Italian from cave 14 who was working on one of the slower eastern routes. They refixed his guide wire so that it trailed into the more efficient tunnel 15, just a short turn away. Root pointed out that the closer they kept the diggers to their original tunnels, the less likely the men were to doubt themselves or cause a fuss.

Something else occurred to Uli and he hastily squirmed on his belly down cave 14. Sure enough, the Italian had left some things behind—a small crucifix, several cutting tools, and two empty jugs, one for urine and the other for water. Rolled in a corner was the stolen vest with the bright stripe. Uli then climbed down tunnel 15 and found that six boxes of shattered stones had been shoved in there—a detail that would've blown their scheme. Uli cleared it all out and placed the miner's possessions at the very end. Then, to disorient him further, Uli and Root piled large stones in front of his former tunnel.

The next tunneler to break for sleep was the Italian's buddy, the black guy, another eastward tunneler. Again Uli slithered in to grab his personal effects, while Root altered his wires to one of the targeted upward caves. Root was a little worried because the rock he would be cutting into was much harder than that of his former tunnel, but she agreed that it was a risk worth taking. The third tunneler already inhabited one of the selected caves, so they left him alone. Soon, all tunnelers had been rerouted to new caves except for one digger in a southwestern tunnel. Root suspected that the poor man's brain had turned to mush, as he seemed to sleep, eat, and crap around the clock in his dusty hole.

Before long, Root slipped back in her chair and nodded off. Uli let her sleep, but he noticed that a stick of gum had slipped out of her pocket. He hadn't seen any gum in the stock area, and he didn't ever remember her chewing it, so he assumed she was secretly hoarding it. When she awoke later, he didn't mention it.

"Want to take a nap?" she offered once she was up and about.

Though exhausted, he declined, knowing he would be too anxious to sleep until he was sure all the miners had returned and this phase of the plan was working somewhat smoothly. The miners would reach up in the blackness and finger their particular strings, almost like harpists, to guide them into their caves.

25

Not only was the food that night the best he had eaten in years, but Maria's beautiful young daughter felt like the antidote to a painful venom that had poisoned his heart and soul. It was the first time he could recall the weight of so many failures lifting from his shoulders. As he rode the IRT back down to grungy Midtown, he felt like a child again. It felt like fifty unsuccessful years were being miraculously rewritten. But as soon as he arrived back at his little room at the Longacre—his minimum-security prison cell—his life suddenly seemed all the more painful.

When Lucretia rang him a few days later, it was the first call he had received from outside the hotel.

"I really enjoyed our dinner together," she said.

"Me too."

"Well, why don't you get back up here and we'll have supper again tonight?"

Induced by his guilty conscience, he replied, "I just got a big job so I won't have any time for the next few weeks, maybe a month."

"Well, you can't be busy forever."

"I'll call when things slow down."

Three weeks later she called again. With tremendous difficulty, he said he was still busy. Hanging up the phone, he felt his heart break. He spent the week walking around in a haze. When she called once more a week later, it felt like hope and possibility were on the phone.

Instead of flatly turning her down this time, they talked late into the night. Finally he asked, "Do you believe some people are cursed?"

"No, just dumb."

The comment stuck like an ice pick, and Paul decided it was time to come clean. He didn't want to do it on the phone since it was apparent she was not easily put off. He finally consented to a second dinner.

It had been muggy and overcast all day, and rain just started falling as Paul stepped off the train. He walked six blocks with a newspaper folded over his head. When he arrived, he was winded and soaked. This time he made no effort to disguise his true self: His wet shirt was yellowed with sweat. He was unshaven. His threadbare suit was too loose on him and filled with holes, and his shoes were worn in the soles. She handed him a towel to dry off as he took a seat in the living room. Toto, her Yorkie, sat in her lap.

He wasted no time: "I lied to you before and, frankly, I want to set the record straight."

"Why would you lie about anything?"

"Because I was embarrassed."

"What can you possibly be embarrassed about?"

"Everything: I don't have a job. My pool business went belly-up. My marriage fell apart. And I'm basically broke."

Lucretia rose from her couch and moved to sit next to him. She wrapped her fingers around his and said, "The you that I liked was the oldest scion of a prosperous family who treated my mother and me like queens."

"Maybe that's why I lost everything," he said with a beleaguered smile.

"I didn't know you *had* everything."

"I don't have a job. I don't have a family. I don't even have a life."

"All you have, all any of us have, is ourselves," Lucretia said, "and I think you're a good person."

"You're not going to quote the Bible, are you?"

"Why, do you need religion to be good?"

"Whatever I am, I'm worthless."

"If you're a good person, you're not worthless."

Paul chuckled in frustration. "I don't think I'm getting through."

"You're sitting here telling me you're worthless, and I do believe what you say about not having any money, but most of all I'm wondering why you're trying to get me to think poorly of you."

"Because I'm bad luck. Everyone who comes into contact with me lives to regret it."

"You could've told me all this on the phone," she said. "I think you've come all the way up here because you like me. And I know I like you. I was never after your money, so it doesn't matter if you don't have it. I still like what I liked about you all those years ago."

He found it difficult to make eye contact. Outside, the rain was still coming down. In a moment, thunder filled the darkened sky. As Lucretia moved through the house closing windows, Paul thought about her situation: with her mother's demise, she was all alone. The interest she was showing in him was nothing more than an infatuation, a search for a father she never knew. In him, she found a man her mother had once looked on trustfully and approvingly. If Maria were here now, he thought, she would want him to be fatherly toward her only daughter.

"So, are you seeing anybody?" Paul asked Lucretia paternally.

"Yeah, you," she said with a smile.

"Look, I'm divorced and old, and I know it's a difficult process, but you have to stick with it and keep looking."

"Paul, I have just one question: do you find me attractive?"

"You're very attractive, but you're too young for me."

"Are you dating anyone else right now?"

"I'm virtually a pauper living in a Times Square hotel, so the answer is no."

"If you don't want to date me, that's fine," she said. "But if you think you're standing in the way of some Prince Charming, or that I'd be dating someone much younger than you, you're very much mistaken." She rose and headed into the kitchen with her Yorkie at her heels.

Paul assumed she was preparing to serve dinner. Instead, she returned with a dozen pots and pans, all piled inside one another. Paul just sat there while she walked around the house placing the cookware under various leaks that were starting to sprinkle down.

"Why don't you hire a roofer?" he asked.

"I've been saving up. But my first money is going toward the plumbing and electricity."

Paul asked Lucretia to give him a quick tour of the place, during which he recalled his own inspection two decades earlier. Very little had been repaired; small problems had become big ones.

"Have you ever considered selling this house?"

"I could never sell it," she said emphatically.

"Lucretia, you live alone. Why do you need all this space?"

"Because someday I plan to have a family and this will be our home."

"How much money have you saved so far?"

"Just a little over fifty bucks." She grinned. "Not enough to do anything yet."

"Actually, fifty bucks should be enough to fix your roof."

"I had it estimated at seventy-five dollars."

"We can do it together," he said. "I'll show you how."

"I couldn't ask you to do that."

"You don't have to. I wanted to help out when I first came here with your mother, but I was too busy. Now I only got time."

"You really want to fix my roof?" she asked with a big smile.

"This is our last date together," he said as he grabbed his jacket. "I'll be back early tomorrow to start work."

The rain began to taper. Lucretia watched as Paul walked out and up the block.

The next morning when he didn't show, she wondered if he had simply decided to vanish. At noon, though, he arrived in a Checker cab and started unloading things on her front porch. She dashed out to help him. Ten rolls of tar paper, two buckets of tar, a linoleum cutter, a five-pound bag of nails, and two hammers—he had made the purchases at Jack's, a local hardware shop on East Tremont Avenue. For the next eight hours, Paul rolled and cut the tar paper, nailing it down and then tarring the seams.

The following day he resumed his work. He was surprised by how many people passing in the street waved up at him, or called out something like, "Glad to see Lucretia's finally getting her roof fixed!" Apparently she was very connected to her community.

He left his tar-smudged clothes on the porch along with his old shoes. Not wanting to track dirt inside, he sat in the living room in his boxers and T-shirt. Lucretia made a wonderful codfish stew for dinner, which he hungrily forked down.

"I should be finished later this week," he said tiredly.

"Then you're spending the night."

"No way."

"Look, I accept that we're not going to be romantically involved, but it's ridiculous for you to go all the way downtown and then have to wake up and come all the way back up here. Especially when I have two empty bedrooms upstairs."

It took the remainder of his strength just to climb back upstairs after dinner and flop into bed. The next morning, she brought him a cup of coffee and a buttered bialy. He took a bite, slurped down the coffee, and went back out to the porch to put his work clothes on and climb out onto the roof.

He kept at this for the next three days. In the evenings they'd listen to the radio, chat, or read the papers. She'd often sit at her desk with a manual adding machine and do her accounting work, punching in numbers from a stack of ledger sheets. When he told her he knew where to find an affordable electric counter, she said she had one in the basement but it kept shorting out fuses.

After he was done with the roof, Paul checked out her electrical system. The cables were coated with a frayed fabric and connected to a haphazard array of circuit boxes with wooden backs. The place barely had enough amps to keep the lights on. Paul went to the local library to brush up on some fine points of household electricity, then proceeded to unscrew all the old fuses and pull the ancient wires from the walls. He took two days carefully upgrading her whole system with a centralized fuse box.

"You can make whatever repairs you want," she said, "but I refuse to let you pay for the parts."

He agreed to give her the receipts, but would only do so when he couldn't afford to cover them himself. Soon he finished the electrical work and plastered some of the walls. The following day, a neighbor stopped by—Ellis Dansberg, a licensed plumber. Paul asked him a dozen questions about fixing the leaky and rusted pipes.

"You wanna make sure you turn off the water to the branch you're cutting," Ellis explained in a loud, unmodulated voice. "You can use a hacksaw, but be careful not to leave burrs. I'd dry fit and solder as much of the extension on the ground as possible . . ."

Paul found plumbing more difficult than electrical work and was careful to only take on smaller repairs, making detailed notes as the man spoke.

He soon realized that it had been nearly two weeks since he had been back to his hotel room, and he was already in arrears. He called to learn that his scant possessions—mainly an archive of clippings about Robert—had been tossed out of the hovel.

The two of them began developing a comfortable routine: Lucretia would come home after work at five thirty and praise Paul's latest renovations. Then she'd prepare a meal for both of them, trying to make him feel at ease. Usually around nine o'clock, exhausted, Paul would silently head up to his room, shower, brush his teeth, and go to bed. Lucretia never tried to stop him, just wished him good night.

"It's my dream to someday hear the banter of children, even grandchildren, in this house," Lucretia said to Paul one morning as she held a pipe for him in the kitchen. He was soldering it to another piece.

"And someday, when you find Mr. Right, you will."

He spent the following week tapping the walls for rotten laths, ripping them out, loading the chunks of broken plaster into boxes, and piling them into dumpsters around the neighborhood at dusk. He mixed new plaster and started repairing the walls. Once through with that phase, he asked Lucretia what colors she wanted for the ceiling, walls, and baseboards.

"Let's go to Jack's together," she suggested.

They headed there and selected four different paints, along with rollers, brushes, drop cloths, and turpentine. This time, Lucretia put on her old shirt and overalls and joined him in the ambitious paint job, a base and two topcoats.

When they finished the living room, it looked so wonderfully different that she began inviting a stream of neighbors to come visit. They hadn't even begun painting upstairs. Lucretia's old friend Lori Mayer, who lived with her husband Bill in the house directly behind hers, came across the backyard and inspected the gorgeous remodeling. Another of her dear friends, May Kearne, and her husband Jimmy, both teachers at the local high school, thought the place looked positively dreamy.

26

Paul's marathon renovation job inspired Uli in his work with Root. The man's repressed feelings for Lucretia catalyzed Uli's growing attraction to his new friend.

One day, when Paul found some wilted flowers on the porch, he asked what was up. Lucretia casually answered, "Oh, it's just Leon."

"Who's Leon?"

"Leon Timmons Skacrowski." She explained that the man's mom and Maria had been the only two Jamaicans living in the area thirty years before; both had married half-Jewish men, so he and Lucretia had become childhood friends and then teenage sweethearts.

Leon's father had died about ten years before, leaving him an old scrap-metal yard on the south side of Crotona Park in Morrisania, commonly referred to by East Tremonters as the "slum."

"You should go to a game with him," Lucretia said. "He loves baseball."

"That's the one thing the Bronx has over anywhere else—the Yankees."

"When the Dodgers signed Jackie Robinson, Leon switched allegiances."

"The *Brooklyn* Dodgers?" Paul replied. "Last time I went to Ebbets Field, I fell through one of the damn seats."

"Leon will be happy to show you all the new ones."

For the next five days all went well. The laborers were moving an impressive amount of rubble. One of the diggers even commented to Root, "We'll break out soon, no thanks to you."

"That one doesn't like you much," Uli observed.

"He's really paranoid," Root said. "He keeps telling the others I'm some kind of CIA agent."

At one point Uli thought that a fat young miner ending his shift looked strangely familiar. He then realized that one of the guide wires had snapped loose. Before he could try to reattach it, the black miner and the young bespectacled man converged simultaneously at the mouth of the same tunnel. Uli heard a quick squabble break out, then saw the young man crawl out to the large silo and say, "Something screwy's going on here."

"What are you talking about?" Root asked.

"For starters, someone changed the path of my wire and I don't know where my things are!"

When Uli approached, the younger miner seized a rod from the ground as if he were being attacked.

"Just relax," Root intervened. Turning to the man, she spoke quietly: "Look, *we* redirected the wires, but we did it for a reason."

"What reason?"

"You seem fairly lucid, so I'm trusting you with this. I have a diagram I can show you."

"What diagram?"

"There are six tunnels going in six different directions that offer the best chance of getting out of here. Do you understand?"

Uli was now able to see the fat young miner up close. Suddenly identifying him, Uli lurched over and shoved him to the ground. When the man opened his mouth and revealed a missing front tooth, Uli was certain. "You're that little prick who grabbed me and Oric!" he snapped, then turned to Root. "He killed my friend Oric outside Cooper Union in Rescue City!"

"I didn't kill anyone!"

"That's Manny," Root said. "He just arrived two weeks ago."

Uli put his knees on the fat boy's arms so he couldn't budge.

"Hold it!" Root shrieked.

"He's a Crapper killer!"

"I only did it for the escape drug," the kid protested. "I just helped with your abduction, then I went down the sewer."

"You didn't expect to meet up with one of your victims, did you?" Remembering poor Oric dying in his arms, Uli immediately began strangling the kid.

"Wait a sec!" Root pulled Uli off. "We're here now and we need people on our side."

"This prick is a mercenary—he'd sell anyone out for a dime."

"That's not true!" Manny said, panting. "I only went after you because of who you are."

"Who is he?" Root asked, as she tried to pull Uli off.

"Former FBI," Manny said, gasping for breath.

"You're FBI?"

"You're nuts!" Uli shot back at Manny.

"He worked for COINTELPRO in the sixties."

"I suppose the Piggers told you that," Uli said.

"No, I recognized you from your photo. So did others who were content to just let it go—but I said no." Peering sharply at Uli, he said, "This asshole did everything from planting false evidence to illegal wiretappings."

A strange sinking feeling came over Uli, leading him to believe that the kid might be telling the truth. He tried to remember anything relevant. Then he said what he remembered most clearly: "My name is Paul Moses."

"That's a total lie," Manny responded.

"I was born in New Haven, my siblings were Robert and Edna, my parents were Bella and Emanuel, and I attended Princeton and fought in the Mexican Revolution."

"You fought *where*?" Root asked.

"The Mexican Revolution was something like seventy years ago!" Manny countered. "You'd have to be a century old."

"Then it was a different Mexican Revolution, 'cause I clearly remember being there!" Uli shouted back.

"Look, we're all buried alive, living like rats in some massive underground crypt. We could die here," Root reasoned. "Our only chance of getting out of here is by working together."

Manny said that under the circumstances he was willing to accept a temporary truce. Uli didn't respond—he was still wondering if what the boy had said was really true. Either way, it didn't matter; Root was right: they were all stuck down here and they needed the kid's help.

They decided to alter their plan accordingly. Manny quit digging and began helping Root control the miners. Meanwhile, Uli stayed alone at the top end of the Sticks to feed and tend to the laborers. Though all seemed to be going well over the next few days, Uli felt a growing anxiety that it was just a matter of time before one of the other miners discovered they were all being duped.

27

Paul came downstairs around dinnertime one September evening to find Lucretia sitting with her childhood friend Leon Skacrowski over a cup of coffee. The shaggy-haired half-Jamaican young man was rocking back and forth slightly as Lucretia chatted about old times. She introduced them.

"Sorry, I didn't know you had a visitor," Paul said.

"Actually, we're about to go see a movie," Lucretia said.

"A movie?"

"Yeah, and if we don't leave now we're going to miss the beginning," Leon added.

Lucretia grabbed her jacket. "Would you mind watching Toto?" she asked Paul.

He said that was fine.

This day marked the beginning of Lucretia's renewed romance with Leon. She seemed to be saying to Paul: *If you don't take me, this slow-witted man will.* One morning several days later, when Paul came downstairs and found Leon sitting at the kitchen table reading the sports pages, he realized that she had done the unthinkable—Leon had spent the night.

"I tell you," the young man said with pride, "now that the Dodgers have grabbed the pennant, there's nothing stopping them." After finishing his fourth heaping bowl of cornflakes, Leon thanked Lucretia for the wonderful night and left.

Paul exited the room in dismay. His renovation of Lucretia's house was nearly complete, so he had begun working on her overgrown garden in the back and along the sides of the building. He had already cut down three dead trees and spent the day uprooting half a dozen thornbushes to lay down a flower bed. Late that afternoon, Paul stormed into the kitchen, sweaty with cuts and scabs, and shouted, "Is this your way of getting back at me? If so, that's fine, but you're only hurting yourself!"

"What are you talking about?"

"Sleeping with that moron is what I'm talking about!"

"What business is—"

"You and I both know that you could date a thousand guys smarter and more handsome."

"I've known Leon all my life. He's a trustworthy man." Lucretia stared blankly at the far wall.

"I'll tell you what I think. I think you're dating a big dumb man just to spite me."

"And how about you?" she cried out with uncharacteristic fervor. "Why don't you admit why you're still here?"

"Twenty years ago I promised your mother I'd do some repairs and—"

"You finished weeks ago!"

Paul slumped down next to her and looked at the ground. "For me, the definition of love is . . . the supreme generosity of spirit beyond all selfish desires."

"So what are you saying?"

"I'm saying a person who feels truly worthless has no right to love someone else. I mean, the most loving thing I can do is leave here now and never look back."

Lucretia rose and gently wrapped her arms around Paul. Leaning forward, he delicately kissed her on the lips.

Uli could almost hear the quickening of Lucretia's soft breaths as he washed and fed the laborers. It took him a moment to realize that there were faint screams coming from the direction of the distant silo. Then he heard feet racing by his cave. He hoped that one of the miners had actually broken through into a new shaft and scurried toward the silo. When he reached the high-ceilinged room he discovered five miners surrounding Manny, who was bleeding profusely and backing toward a dark corner. Before Uli could intervene, the Italian miner came up from behind and cracked the kid across the skull. Others appeared and started beating him viciously. Root was nowhere to be seen. Uli ran back up to the storage area to look for her. Almost immediately, two other miners rushed in from the Mkultra.

"They got the kid!" Uli shouted, pretending to be among them. He recognized one of the miners joining the mob, whom he and Root had labeled "Dave," and followed him back into the silo.

"What happened?" Uli asked him.

"We found out that this bastard and that bitch were screwing with us."

"How?"

"From that," Dave replied, pointing up.

Uli glanced nervously at the corpse hanging from the wooden tower.

"I knew one of them had cut down Xolotl's body and replaced it with some other body," Dave said. "So I told everyone to be on the lookout and we discovered they were switching wires on us."

"Why would they do that?" Uli asked.

"The same reason she killed the other woman," said another miner who was listening in. "She's CIA! She's deliberately trying to make us waste our time here."

"Where is the bitch anyhow?" Dave asked.

"One of the guys grabbed her, but she hit him with pepper spray and ran away," the second miner said. "He got a solid punch off. Broke her fucking nose. We raced after her, but she disappeared in the offices."

Uli looked over to Manny Lewis's bloody body, which had been unceremoniously dumped in a corner.

"There's another guy too," the Italian said, his vest smeared with blood.

"Yeah, I remember a third guy," Uli heard someone else chime in. Eventually the miners simmered down and began milling around. Several crawled back down into the Convolution toward their caves.

28

Four months after their encounter across from Grand Central Station, Paul Moses finally broke down, bent a knee, and asked for Lucretia's hand in marriage. She wondered to herself how much longer it would take to get him to start producing children and money.

The first goal was easy. He initiated sex as soon as she woke up every morning and at night before bed—pregnancy was inevitable. Work, however, he rarely mentioned.

One Sunday after breakfast, as Paul flipped through the *New York Times*, Lucretia picked up a section of the paper he had tossed aside. It was the employment listings.

"You're an engineer, right?"

"An electrical engineer," he said, engrossed in an article about the creation of a Jewish state in Palestine.

"Let's see . . . where is that?" She carefully surveyed the various job headings.

"I've spent the past twenty years trying to secure something," he muttered absently. "Robert has built a blockade around me."

"Robert, your brother?"

Paul had worked hard not to repeat the same mistake he'd made with Teresa. He had been trying to avoid even mentioning Robert.

"How exactly has he blockaded you?"

"He kept me from getting a state position in Water Supply, Gas, and Electricity, and I'm pretty sure he blocked me from getting a city commissionership as well."

"Have you talked to him directly about this?"

"I tried," Paul said, then put his newspaper down. "He stole my inheritance right out from under me."

Lucretia sat perplexed, wondering what to say or do. She knew that Paul no longer had access to the vast wealth that once made him master and her mother servant, but his chronic unemployment was going to complicate things considerably. Even Leon, who she thought of as little more than a glorified garbage collector, had a job.

* * *

Several days passed and Root was still missing. Although the miners slowly figured this out and returned to their redundant tunnels, Uli was reluctant to lead the zombie-eyed laborers out of their caves to clean out the latest accumulation of rocks. That had been Root's job, and he feared mimicking her movements too closely. With their daily routines interrupted, the laborers were growing increasingly anxious. Uli tried looking after them, but feeding, watering, and cleaning that many was difficult, not to mention dangerous. The more energetic ones started wandering around aimlessly, and a few actually strayed back into the Mkultra.

After a week, a couple of the sickliest workers died. Then one morning Uli entered the silo to see a fresh chubby body dangling from the heights of the desk tower. It wasn't until Uli found the large head, which had been cleanly circumcised and tossed in a corner, that he confirmed it was Manny. They had violently twisted his feet backward— he was the latest offering to their bullshit death guide.

29

When Paul entered the kitchen, Lucretia and her friend May went silent.

"Paul," May began after a moment, "I was just telling Lucretia that you'd make a great high school teacher."

"Why in the world would you say that?" he asked, thinking she might be kidding him.

"'Cause you're smart and patient. You're a natural teacher."

"What are the qualifications to teach in this city?" he asked.

"Just a bachelor's degree, and then you have to take some courses to get your license. But you can do substitute teaching until you get one."

Paul could see his beautiful fiancée watching him apprehensively. In that instant he grasped that he had walked into an ambush: Lucretia had been dropping continuous hints about him getting a job; now she had enlisted a neighbor. All he could do was smile.

"That doesn't sound half-bad," he relented. "What's the pay and benefits?"

"Salary starts at thirteen thousand a year. There's health insurance and a pension plan, and they're always looking for people."

"So where do I sign up?"

Lucretia's face lit up.

"In Brooklyn Heights at 110 Livingston Street. Once you finish the certification, they put you on an availability list. But don't take any jobs—Jimmy will hire you right here in East Tremont so you can be within walking distance of your house. Plus, you get summers and holidays off."

Paul poured himself a glass of cold water and took a long sip. In a strange way, this simple plan could be the bedrock of a much greater goal: instead of recapturing a success he never really had and trying to shove it in his brother's face, he could focus on the more tangible targets of supporting his young wife and their offspring to come.

30

Memories of Paul were the only bright spot in Uli's life now. The only oddity was that he was always Paul. He imagined he was sitting in the back row of a small, sweet wedding ceremony at the local Temple Emanuel. Afterward they held a buffet-style reception at El Sombrero, a Mexican restaurant on East Tremont Avenue. One by one, over the course of the evening, the entire neighborhood seemed to stop by to congratulate the lucky bride and groom. They left wrapped wedding gifts or envelopes of cash, which were greatly appreciated. No one from Paul's side of the family showed up—nor had they been notified.

In July 1948, at the age of sixty, Paul finished his eight required courses at Hunter College while teaching several classes.

The day he received his teaching license from Albany was also the last day for that season's registration at the local high school. Lucretia called May Kearne because Paul was too embarrassed to contact her directly. Jimmy Kearne was head of the science department and juggled some assignments to free a schedule of classes for Paul.

Donning a crisp white shirt and a thin black tie for his first day of school, Paul stopped in the kitchen for coffee and swallowed his sense of dread over babysitting a bunch of working-class brats. He loved Lucretia and didn't want to disappoint her.

Paul arrived early to the school's science department and Jimmy gave him a curriculum, the various chemistry textbooks to hand out, his homeroom assignment, and a class schedule. "It's all about advance preparation. Make sure you have a box of chalk, an eraser, and if you need to go to the bathroom, do it on the breaks. Also, you've got to be on top of all the paperwork or it'll drown you: grading papers, producing lesson plans, homework—all have to be done regularly. It's not like college, don't let the kids teach *you*. Other than that, don't take no guff from no one, but be fair and you'll do fine."

Only one other brand-new teacher reported for work that day, a smart-alecky war veteran who was less than half Paul's age.

The task of teaching matched Paul's skills surprisingly well. The authority of his age worked greatly to his advantage. Within a matter of months, the gratitude in the community was visible. People in the street frequently greeted him with a cheerful "Hey, Mr. Moses!"

Lucretia saw it clearly. His hollow form seemed to fill out. His bitterness diminished. Even Paul's stooped posture seemed to rectify itself as he took pride in his work.

At the end of the semester, Jimmy Kearne wrote in his teacher's evaluation: *Paul Moses is a gifted teacher, subtly correcting students almost unconsciously. Fluent not just in the sciences and humanities, but in language skills as well. Relaxed, focused, firm, yet gentle, he is able to use his sense of humor as a motivational tool . . .*

At dinner one evening in January 1949, Lucretia announced that she was pregnant.

"Oh my God!" Paul exclaimed, then hugged her, gave her a long kiss, and said, "I just had the thought that in 2010 the baby you're carrying will be the age I am now."

Beatrice Moses was born on September 3, 1949. Lucretia wanted her baptized, and her old friend Lori who lived in the house behind theirs agreed to be godmother.

Paul had never thought he'd have a child, but as soon as he held the bundle that was his new daughter, he felt a swooning joy that seemed to instantly pardon his many failures. He loved Lucretia and Bea more than he had ever loved anyone in his life.

After a close call, Uli admitted to himself that it was just a matter of time before one of the miners deduced that he was part of Root's team. They'd kill him immediately.

He had finally lost faith that any of them would find a way to some miracle staircase out of there. The key reason he remained was the faint hope that Root might return.

To protect himself, Uli started assembling supplies. He had already found a small hand truck, rope, even a box of medicine. Stashing the supplies behind the mountain of stock in the storage depot, he glanced at the narrow metal door near the sealed freight elevator. With his flashlight, Uli could make out the small rectangular hole he had noticed before in the rear wall. Old cables dangling from the gap were attached to the large fuse box that had collapsed to the ground.

Through the rectangle, Uli could see about five feet up the black hole. Then he felt a cool, soft breeze. He quickly located one of the discarded metal rods that the diggers had sharpened to carve their tunnels. Using a large monkey wrench as a hammer, he began chipping down the sides of the small rectangular hole so he could look farther inside. The stone was difficult to break; after three hours, he was barely able to fit his forehead through the small slot.

31

Inasmuch as the price of comfort is the quick passage of time, the next three years of Paul's life seemed to finally be moving happily along. Doing his utmost to raise little Bea well, he would get up with her early in the morning and look after her until he had to head off to work. Lucretia would take Bea during the days. Frequently she'd cut across the backyard and drop Bea off with Lori, whose daughter Charity was only two months older. The two would play nonstop. When Paul came home in the afternoons, he could hardly wait to hold and kiss his little girl. He'd watch her while Lucretia went out on afternoon business appointments. She'd usually come home around six or seven, then they'd have dinner together.

Though Paul realized he would have no grand impact on civilization, life really couldn't be any better.

Some habits were a little difficult to break. Paul couldn't stop scanning the newspapers to keep track of his fascist brother. One project in particular caught his attention, like a tiny blip on his radar: the Cross Bronx Expressway, which had broken ground at one end of the borough and was slowly moving across it. He figured it would probably pass near them, along the northern edge of Crotona Park.

Little Bea was growing fast, and by her second birthday she was walking and talking more than all the other children in the playground. She was speaking in full sentences, grasping fairly abstract concepts for her age. Even her sense of compassion—reflected in her treatment of little Toto—was exceptional. By Bea's third birthday, Paul told his wife that he wanted to get her IQ tested, believing that she might very well be a genius.

"Maybe it'd be a good time for Bea to have a little brother," Lucretia replied.

Paul nodded silently, wondering how all of this would end up.

In the middle of his excavation of the hole, Uli heard loud scuttling. He figured the rats had finally gotten across the great divide and into the storage depot. He pushed a large crate aside and was startled to discover the upper half of an older child who was holding a long dagger in his right palm; his lower half, however, seemed to be planted right into the earth.

"There's no need for that," he told the juvenile. "Put the knife down."

"Where's Root?"

"She was chased off," Uli said. Then it struck him: *This must be the missing leader's handicapped son.* "Is your father Plato?"

"Yeah, he was the leader."

"Where is he?"

"He disappeared awhile ago."

"I heard he was very smart."

"He used to collect papers and read all the time—*read, read, read.* Used to say stuff over and over."

"What kind of stuff?"

"Used to talk about the projects."

"What projects?"

"Don't know. A bunch."

"Do you remember any?"

"All began with M-K. Artichoke, Leviticus—a lot about M-K Leviticus."

"What's M-K Leviticus?"

"Don't know. He used to say we're all in Langley. *Langley, Langley, Langley.*"

"Langley, Virginia?"

"Don't know."

"What happened to him?"

"He would go farther and farther down in the Mkultra."

"Why?"

"First he found all this paint you could see in the dark."

Uli remembered the glowing lines leading nowhere. "Then what?"

"He was looking for some kind of chemical, either flammable or nonflammable, I can't remember. Then one day he just didn't come back." Changing the subject, the kid said, "The lady told me I can always get supplies here. We're low."

"Sure, help yourself, just be careful of the miners."

"Do you know anything about helping sick people? 'Cause my ma and brother, they're sick people." The kid set down the short sword. Using his hands, he pulled himself forward into the light, where Uli finally got a chance to look him over. In place of legs was some kind of scorpion-like tail that curled under and peaked out of his long dirty shirt.

"Exactly how sick is your family?"

"They're both really hot, and my brother won't stop pooping. He's covered with red spots." It sounded like chicken pox. All things considered, it was astounding that anyone could be born, much less stay alive, down here.

"They both have fevers?"

"Don't know. Can you come take a look at them?"

"I'm no doctor, but I have some medicine I can give you."

Uli led him to the utility closet, where he had a pile of boxes filled with tins of pills. Some were identified as vitamins. Others were antibiotics, but didn't state dosage.

When Uli lit a candle, the kid saw the narrow rectangle that once held the fuse box and asked what it led to.

"I don't know. I'm too big to climb in, but I've been shaving down the sides."

"Want me to try?" It hadn't even occured to Uli to ask.

"That'd be great."

"I'll do it if you come and look at my sick family."

"I wouldn't know what to do. Like I said, I'm not a doctor."

"Please. I need help."

Uli realized that the child, with his congenitally malformed body, might be his only ticket out of this place—he couldn't refuse the kid's request. "You have my word that if you climb in there and tell me what you see, I'll examine your family."

The kid stared at Uli for a moment, then said, "All right, but could I rest first? I haven't eaten in a while and I've walked a long ways."

Uli gave him some crackers and water, led him to a small square of cardboard, and let him sleep.

32

At 1:38 on the afternoon of December 4, 1952, ten minutes before fifth period ended, some kid knocked on Paul Moses's classroom door with a note saying that he should call home as soon as possible. His first panicked thought was that something had happened to Beatrice. Why else would he get this message in the middle of the school day? He asked Sal Berg in the adjacent class to keep an eye on his students and dashed off. When he reached Lucretia on the phone, she told him that she had just received some kind of legal notice stating that all the residents on their block had to move.

"Can this wait until I get home?" he asked patiently, imagining it was a mistake.

"I suppose," she replied, though she sounded frazzled.

When he arrived home two hours later, he found that a number of neighbors had collected in the street, chatting with each other. Lucretia quickly showed him the notice that had been taped to their door.

It stated that they were in the path of the new Cross Bronx Expressway. The proposed roadway cut a swath between 176th Street and Fairmont Place, plowing through seven blocks of residential housing. Immediately he envisioned it: a man-made fault line opening from east to west—225 feet of concrete roadway coming right at them, tearing the earth in two.

According to the letter, all residents on the street, for blocks in both directions, had nine months to vacate their premises and find new accommodations.

"Hey, Paul!" he heard. His neighbor Robert Ward was crossing the street, holding up a road map. "Check out this freakin highway! It looks like the Bronx is getting circumcised."

"We're supposed to sacrifice our homes so that commuters from New Jersey and Long Island can get to work faster?" Paul responded.

"Paul!" he heard another voice shout over to him. "Your last name's Moses. You're not related to this clown, are you?" It was Howard Joel from half a block down. He came over with another copy of the same letter. Glancing at the bottom of the notice for the first time, Paul saw that it was signed: *Robert Moses, City Construction Coordinator.*

"No relation," Paul replied swiftly.

"Too bad," Joel said.

Lucretia peered down nervously. She'd never had any reason to lie to her neighbors and friends before. Paul excused himself and went into their house, then dashed to the upstairs bathroom and locked the door.

I knew it! he thought furiously. *That cocksucker has tracked me down and now he's coming after my family! I should've killed him when I had the chance!* He muttered aloud, "Teresa and that shrink said I was nuts! Well, *he's* coming after *me!* Now who's paranoid?"

When he heard Lucretia knocking around nervously in the bedroom, he splashed cold water on his face, took a deep breath, flushed the toilet, and came out to comfort her.

Over the next hour or so, as more neighbors gathered along the sidewalk, they started pooling their resources. One fellow across the street had a cousin in the mayor's office; he worked for the Department of Transportation. Another woman's brother was a lawyer, but he lived in Des Moines.

"We should organize right away," Paul announced for all to hear. After watching so many other neighborhoods being ripped in half by his brother's highways, he realized immediately what they should do to prevent this.

"What's the point?" one of the more knowledgeable neighbors said. "No one's ever been able to reverse eminent domain law."

"Politicians are motivated by public opinion. But we have to work quickly. We've got to make as big a stink as we can."

"What are we going to say?" Miss Rice asked. "That the city can't have a freeway 'cause we like our homes?"

"We have to tell people that if this can happen to us, it can happen to *anyone* in this city," Paul replied. "And we have to show them an alternative route for the expressway that displaces fewer families."

"What do you mean, like a tunnel?"

"No," Robert Ward speculated, "they can just as easily run the highway north of the park."

Although their street was filled with single-family homes, the next block over had a number of large apartment buildings. Paul pointed out that they must've gotten notices too. "We should go over there and start organizing people," he said.

Ward, Stein, Rice, and some of the others agreed to head over on Saturday to garner support. Within a matter of days, three hundred people had joined an ad hoc neighborhood organization calling itself MCBE—Move the Cross Bronx Expressway. They agreed to meet on a weekly basis in the multipurpose room at the YMHA.

Two weeks later, everyone got a second letter stating that the Tenant Relocation Bureau was going to help everyone find new accommodations; indeed, they had already helped those in the "Section One" portion of the planned roadway.

Though he fervently wished to take a leading role in the committee, Paul remained in the background, fearful that he would be revealed as Robert Moses's brother.

He met up with three neighbors the following Saturday to check on the progress that had been made thus far on the first part of the expressway. As they drove westward toward Section One, they could hear jackhammers and see clouds of dust rising in the air. Just before they spotted the hills of rubble and the earth-moving machines, they came upon rows of barren tenements and empty single-family homes. They parked in front of a condemned apartment building. Broken furniture and garbage, including long shards from a shattered mirror that once lined the hallway, covered the floor of the defunct lobby. The stink of human excrement filled the large room. Several of the men stepped inside.

"Hey, get out of there!" yelled Karen Farkis, one of the older members of the committee, pinching her nose. "You're gonna get mugged."

As they exited the wrecked building, they passed a hard-worn blonde in her twenties pushing a stroller inside. Two toddlers followed slowly.

"Where are you're going, young lady?" Mrs. Farkis asked, fearful for the petite woman's safety.

"Mind yer damn business!"

"Pardon?"

"Who the hells are ya anyways?" said the young woman with a thick local accent.

"Allow me to introduce us," Mrs. Farkis replied. "We're from East Tremont. We all live in houses that are in the path of the Cross Bronx and we wanted to find out how the planners dealt with homeowners further down the line."

"Oh, you're in for a real treat, sis," the blonde said, chuckling snidely.

"Were you evicted?" Paul asked.

"More like evicted to here. We were kicked out about six months ago from our home farther east of here, but the Relocation Bureau couldn't find us no place so they stuck us in this dump. The owners had already gotten kicked out of here."

"They're actually letting you live here?" Paul asked in dismay.

"Not for nothin. We got to pay rent. And we got to be able to leave within seventy-two hours."

"You're actually paying rent?" gasped another East Tremonter, Pauline Kennedy.

"Oh yeah, we're paying more than we were in our old apartment. In fact, there's another family living up—"

"You mean the city evicted the original residents from this building and now they're housing other evictees here?" Paul couldn't believe what he was hearing.

"Yeah, there are about a hundred families who were moved here. Hell, some of them have been moved two or three times. They just kick them like old cans up the eviction route," the young mother explained, then barked at her two children who were playing among shiny shards of broken glass.

"Have you at least asked to get into one of the new public houses the city is building?" Paul asked.

"We were told to get in line. There's a six-year waiting list."

"What kind of apartments did the Relocation Bureau offer you?" asked Bill Lawrence from the committee.

The woman let out a sharp breath in order to keep from crying and said, "You wouldn't put a dog in those places. I ain't foolin. And you can see my family is living in this hellhole. I mean, I've come down in the morning with my kids and found a bum takin a shit in the corner, so believe me, we'd take damn near anything."

"It's criminal!"

"Of all the families they evicted," she went on, "I don't know a single one that got housed permanently through that bullshit Reeviction Bureau. They just want to get you the hell out."

The group was aghast. The fact that a government agency in a democratic country could treat its citizens this way was unthinkable.

Paul took five dollars from his wallet. Others pitched in, and without saying a word, they offered the money to the young mother, who quickly snatched it and moved along. They walked around the vicinity and spotted at least a dozen other empty apartment buildings. Windows had been broken, doors were hanging off their hinges, piping had been vandalized, yet people were still living in some of the apartments. As the group drove back to East Tremont, terrified of what lay ahead, not one of them spoke.

Soon, another flurry of mimeographed letters arrived offering all owners and renters the generous incentive of two hundred dollars if they moved within the next six months. The letter reminded everyone that they would all be evicted anyway, so resisting it would only cost them unnecessary legal expenses.

The committee countered with flyers posted on street corners:

> *We Have to Hang Together*
> *or We'll Hang Alone.*
> *Don't Move an Inch,*
> *MCBE's Fighting for Your Home!*

Yet within a month, as word spread about how the city had treated the people of Section One, a third of all residents along the projected route had grabbed the offer and moved out.

"The wires are dead," Uli said to the scorpion-spined boy, referring to the electrical cables dangling precariously from the chiseled-out rectangular hole, still connected to the fallen fuse box. "You don't need to worry about getting shocked."

Uli hoisted the kid's body into the chiseled rectangular space. The boy was able slip his head inside, but his shoulders were slightly too broad. After pushing painfully for a minute, the kid climbed down.

"I got an idea," Uli said. He went out to the stock area and located a small can of machine grease. "Take off your clothes and rub this on."

The kid removed his filthy button-down shirt that hung over his midsection like a dress. Uli was distressed to see the severity of his disabililty as the kid slathered his shoulders and midsection with grease. It was as if his spine had traveled down his back like a third leg. But instead of a foot, it curled into a tail.

With Uli's help, the boy slowly worked himself into the stone opening. It was almost like watching a small animal trying to free itself from some trap. Then, suddenly, the kid's tail vanished completely.

"You okay?" Uli yelled into the rectangular window of darkness.

"Yeah!" the kid called back.

"Want my flashlight so you can see what's up there?"

"Yeah." A little hand reached out of the hole and Uli passed it to him.

When the kid flipped on the flashlight, Uli asked, "What do you see?"

"It goes straight up, then turns right, then . . ." The kid's voice grew muffled as he moved farther inside. The faint glow disappeared.

"Is it wide enough for me to climb through if I can get in there?" Uli called out.

"Don't think so," he heard back.

"Does the tunnel continue?"

"It goes over there." The kid was obviously pointing at something.

"Can you climb *up* the tunnel?"

"I need something to hold onto. There are two thingies with holes in them."

"How high up can you see before it gets dark?"

"Can't tell."

"Well, what *can* you see?"

"Don't know." The kid's voice was clearer now.

"Can you see past my height?"

"Oh yeah, about three or four times your height. That's when it gets black and kinda narrow." If the boy's sense of scale was at all accurate, that distance was already higher than all the tunnels in the Convolution.

"All right, come on back out here." When Uli helped the youth out of the hole, he asked, "How narrow does it get?"

"Don't know. I saw two lines of holes running up the back of something big."

"The elevator shaft?"

"I guess, but I don't know how I can climb up and hold the flashlight at the same time."

"How far apart are the holes?"

"Don't know, maybe . . ." The kid stretched his hands about two feet apart.

"And you can push your back against the wall?"

"Yeah."

"How big are the holes?"

"About . . ." The kid curled his fingers to roughly an inch in radius.

Uli collected a bucket of water and a bar of brown soap and let him scrub off all the grease. The boy started talking about his family again—he wanted to get resupplied and take Uli to look at his brother and mom, as promised.

All Uli could think about was the possibility of escaping from this underground tomb.

33

During the following weeks, Paul watched his neighbors walking around like zombies, their eyes downcast, their postures hunched. Some complained about being unable to sleep or eat. The elderly who hadn't yet abandoned their apartments stared sadly out their windows as though on a sinking ship. Those still motivated to put up a fight converted MCBE into the East Tremont Neighborhood Association. The elected head of ETNA, Lillian Edelstein, lived in one of the nicer buildings on the street with her sister's family and their mother. During one of their early meetings at the YMHA, they came up with a plan to enlist local politicians in their cause. Within a week, Assemblyman Jacob Gilbert and Congressman Isidore Dollinger had vowed to help them.

Bronx Borough President James J. Lyons was the linchpin. He had a seat on the Board of Estimate, which needed to sign off on the project before Robert Moses could get final approval for the full stretch of his precious highway. Unfortunately, Lyons seemed to constantly be elsewhere. His secretary suggested that they confer with the Bronx commissioner of public works, Arthur V. Sheridan, who supposedly had much more clout. Sheridan, in turn, sent them to someone else, who referred them to Edward J. Flanagan, who ushered the little group into his office.

Flanagan launched right in: "I've been following your situation very closely." Pointing to a wall map of the Bronx, he indicated the proposed route. "I don't understand why they don't just run the expressway along Crotona Park North."

"Brilliant idea!" Lillian Edelstein replied, not mentioning that they were already lobbying for this alternative.

"It looks even shorter and more direct," added Ralph Lassiter, another ETNA member.

"We need an engineer to make an assessment and demonstrate that this route would be more efficient and cost-effective than the planned one," Flanagan concluded.

Paul went home that night feeling like they actually had a chance of winning this. The next day in class, he got another message asking him to please call home during his next break. When he did so, Lucretia answered the phone in hysterics. He couldn't tell if she was laughing or crying.

"What happened?" he shouted.

"We're staying! We're NOT moving!"

"We won?" he asked.

"No," she choked out, breathing deeply to regain control, "we got . . . a letter stating . . . that we're . . . we were . . . *miscondemned*."

"What does that mean?"

"Due to a reappraisal, several houses on our block are going to be spared!"

"Which ones?"

"Abraham Hoff's home, and Lori and Bill's."

"How about all the others?"

"I think they're still getting evicted . . . but we're spared."

"That's great," he muttered, looking nervously around, "but . . ."

"Do you think your brother—"

"No way," he cut her off. "But I think we should keep this under wraps for a while."

Lucretia agreed.

Paul felt relief at first. Then, when the next period ended, he felt a gnawing guilt as he watched his students leaving his class, some of their families still facing eviction. Throughout the rest of the day he found it difficult to focus. He resolved that no matter what, he would remain in the fight with the rest of his neighbors.

Several days later, though, at the next ETNA meeting, May Kearne approached Paul and said, "We heard that your place is being spared."

"Yeah," he replied, embarrassed, "but I'm still with you guys."

"It might be better if you weren't," she said tersely.

"Huh?"

"Paul, we all know Robert Moses is your brother. Since you were being evicted, we didn't mind, but suddenly your house is being spared. Come on, we're not stupid."

"I haven't spoken to my brother in years! He doesn't even know I'm in the Bronx."

"Lucretia's a dear friend, and we're all grateful for your help so far, but there are people here who think you're spying for him, so it really would be safer for you guys if you just stopped coming to the meetings."

Paul felt like a quisling as she walked away. It occurred to him that Robert could have found out he was living here and given him and Lucretia this reprieve only to alienate him from the community. Lucretia was a proud member of the neighborhood and would feel profound shame for the situation he was putting her in. Although he didn't think she'd leave him, as Teresa had, he feared that this would drive a wedge between them. He therefore decided to keep quiet on the fact that he'd been asked to leave ETNA. That night, when Lucretia inquired about the meeting, he simply said it had gone well and didn't offer another word about it.

The following week, during the time when he'd usually attend the ETNA meeting, Paul took a walk around Bronx Park. The week after that, he checked out the Jewish section of Grand Concourse and the Italian part of Arthur Avenue. Subsequently, he headed south through the Negro areas of Morrisania.

As he returned home one night, he passed by a sign that read, *Skacrowski's Scrapyard*. A pack of dogs behind a hurricane fence barked ferociously at him until a heavyset man operating a large machine looked over.

"Hey, Paul!" he heard. It was his wife's one-night lover, Leon.

"Howdy," Paul greeted, walking quickly by.

"My mom told me that you guys were spared from the wrecking ball."

"More or less," Paul responded, stopping in his tracks. Abandoning discretion, he said: "Lucetia doesn't know this yet, but I was asked to quit ETNA because they think my brother was behind our exemption."

"You should tell her," Leon said.

"I know, I just feel awful."

"You did nothing wrong."

"I know. But this is what happens when your brother is the devil."

Leon's mother was away, so he invited Paul inside for a beer. They ended up chatting for three hours. Paul found himself ranting about how much he hated his power-hungry brother.

"What can you do?" Leon asked, opening another beer.

"Give him what we used to call a Mexican send-off," Paul said.

"What's that?"

"Five sticks of dynamite wired to the ignition of his Packard."

Leon laughed. "Sounds like a plan."

"He's more powerful than the mayor or the governor because he can't be voted out. He single-handedly makes million-dollar decisions that take money from education and social services, not to mention buses and trains. And no one can stop him!"

"Maybe you *should* kill him," Leon said somewhat earnestly.

Paul laughed. "I've been saying this for the last twenty years and finally I've found someone who agrees with me."

"Listen," Leon said, "if you want to work off your anger without risking the electric chair, you should come out to Ebbets Field with me. I got two tickets to the game this week and things are just beginning to heat up."

"Sorry, but I'm a dyed-in-the-wool Yankees fan."

"Yankees, spankies. Have you ever seen Pee Wee Reese or Jackie Robinson at bat?"

"Too bad the Giants keep kicking their asses . . ."

"Hey, with Gil Hodges in the infield, Duke Snider out in center, Roy Campanella behind the plate, and Don Newcombe on the pitcher's mound—"

"They still can't beat the Yankees."

"Give them time, they're gonna get there. They've won the pennant four times since '41."

"Yeah, but they were beaten by the Yankees each time."

"Wait till next year," Leon said. "Just wait."

As Paul walked home, he felt calm. Just a few beers and a little ventilation and he was so much stronger. When Lucretia asked about the meeting, he sat her down and said he had something important to share, then relayed his conversation with May Kearne.

"Screw them," Lucretia said, causing Paul to burst out laughing.

He returned to Leon's place a few days later with a cold six-pack of beer. Once again, the two talked into the night. Paul went on about why his brother deserved to die, and Leon went on about the Brooklyn Dodgers.

After the scorpion boy had scrubbed the grease off, Uli gave him some Spam and crackers and had him draw a diagram of the fuse-box tunnel. As best as Uli could speculate, thousands of pounds of concrete had been poured down the elevator shaft, but had apparently solidified before it could ooze around the back of the tracking, thus creating this narrow passage that went straight up.

"Did you see any light coming from above?"

"No, why?"

"It might go all the way up to the surface."

The kid looked perplexed. After a while, he rolled onto his back and dozed off. When he woke again, roughly two hours later, Uli was waiting with some gear he had assembled.

"I was thinking . . ." Uli began, holding up an old construction helmet, a small lantern—his flashlight was almost dead—and some wire. "If I can attach this lantern to this helmet and we can strap it around your chin, you can use these to climb up that tracking . . ." He indicated two large hooks with wooden handles.

"You said you were going to come and look at my sickers first."

"Well, that's true, but you just told me the entrance is narrow, didn't you?"

"Yes, but . . . you said you'd help my sickers first!"

"Fine," Uli replied, surprised by the kid's stubbornness. "Let's get going."

34

Over the ensuing weeks, Paul watched in anguish as the ETNA members fought desperately to save their homes. Neighbors in the group continued saying hi to Paul and Lucretia, but they rarely mentioned any progress in their efforts.

When Paul would see them handing out flyers on East Tremont, he had the urge to remind them that the only real power was money. He knew that if just one of them sacrificed their single-family home and sold it for ten grand, a donation like that to Lyons's reelection fund might make all the difference.

"Paying Murder Inc. five grand to make your brother disappear could also make a difference," Leon suggested.

One day upon opening the *New York Post*, Paul found ETNA's entire proposal laid out over a couple of pages. An unnamed engineer had performed a feasibility study demonstrating that by swinging the highway two blocks south, 159 buildings housing more than 1,500 apartments could be saved. It would also save the city millions of dollars. The next day's paper quoted Bronx Borough President James Lyons as stating that the proposal seemed worthy of consideration. Robert Moses countered by telling the press that the only reason Lyons was sticking his nose into this was because it was an election year.

A six-member Board of Estimate meeting scheduled for the end of April was going to cast the first of a series of votes on the highway. At that meeting, which would probably be presided over by the mayor, Lyons had a key vote.

"It's a shame we have this stooge Impellitteri in City Hall instead of La Guardia," Paul remarked to Lucretia.

"He probably steals money just like his predecessor," she said. Three years ago, the O'Dwyer police corruption scandal had been smeared over the papers and had compelled the former mayor to resign in disgrace.

"At least La Guardia would have told Robert to move the frigging route. I'm just hoping Lyons has a backbone."

As the Board of Estimate meeting approached, Paul, who had excellent attendance at school, took one of his sick days. He watched as roughly two hundred people, mainly housewives, lined into four chartered buses on East Tremont Avenue and headed down to City Hall. In deference to the general distrust that many of them had toward him, he walked east and caught the Third Avenue El. At City Hall, he stayed in the back of the large hearing room while the wives filed in and sat in the front rows.

Five minutes after the board members, including James Lyons, entered the chamber, Robert Moses arrived, leading the mayor. Robert pointed to the chair next to his own as though Impellitteri were one of his flunkies. Soon the room was packed. Scattered throughout were members of the press.

Mayor Impellitteri introduced himself and, rapping a small gavel, called for order. "We will be hearing from everyone regarding Section Two of the Cross Bronx Expressway through East Tremont, and we'll discuss an alternate route proposed by the East Tremont Neighborhood Association, then we will put the matter to a preliminary vote. Everyone testifying will get one minute to talk."

The housewives of East Tremont got to speak first. One by one, in an order orchestrated by Lillian Edelstein, they rose to the mic. Each stated how long she had lived happily in their little Bronx community. They explained how the construction of the expressway would force them to move, tearing apart not just their lives, but the whole community. As they testified, Paul noticed the members of the board growing slowly disinterested. Some scribbled notes. Others whispered to their aides. One was clearly reading a newspaper. He watched as his brother chatted softly with the mayor; at one point the two men actually chuckled as if sharing a dirty joke. When a housewife went beyond her one minute, a court clerk would drop his little hammer and mumble, "Time."

After roughly forty-five minutes, Lillian Edelstein gave a summary statement: "Mr. Mayor, Borough President Lyons, Construction Consultant Moses, and members of this esteemed board, there is simply no need for any of this grief since we have an alternate route that will save the taxpayers millions of dollars." To the mayor, she politely presented a coil of large pages, the formal blueprints that had been carefully drawn by a sympathetic engineer. Without removing the rubber band, the mayor handed them off to some assistant.

"Mr. Moses," the mayor said next, "would you care to respond before this board votes?"

Robert Moses stood before the mic, smiled pleasantly to all, then spoke: "We put a great deal of thought and effort into the planning of this expressway, weighing the interests of both this neighborhood and the city as a whole. My team of engineers selected the best possible route. They didn't do this for the concerns of a few, but rather for *all* New Yorkers, present and future. Let me add that I take no pleasure in asking anyone to move and that we are all grateful for your sacrifice."

The more vocal members of ETNA started booing, followed by others. The mayor's gavel repeatedly hit the table as he called, "Order! Order!"

"We were told that we would be given a fair hearing!" Lillian Edelstein shouted.

"And so you shall. Mr. Moses's opinion is not entirely the opinion of this board," the mayor said. He then mumbled something to a skinny bald man, who turned out to be a city engineer. He took the ETNA blueprints to a nearby table and inspected them closely.

All eyes were on the engineer five minutes later when he walked over and started whispering something to Borough President Lyons. An exchange between the two lasted a few minutes before Robert tiredly rose to his feet and walked over to Lyons's seat. He bent down and whispered something in the politician's ear that couldn't have been more than a word or two, then returned to his seat.

Several more minutes passed before Lyons leaned forward and muttered into the mic, "In light of what I've just heard, I'm going to have to support Mr. Moses's route."

"You've betrayed us!" Lillian Edelstein called out. The housewives began frantically talking back and forth.

"There will be silence in the chamber!" the mayor spoke up.

"Traitor!" someone yelled.

"I said you'd get your day in court, and this is it!" Lyons shouted at Edelstein. "There are many factors that—"

"Betrayal!" she shot back.

"You owe Mr. Lyons an apology," Impellitteri stated.

Robert started snickering at the women.

After more shouts of recrimination, the mayor tapped his gavel and a group of court officers entered. The room soon slipped into silence.

"We will now put this matter to a vote," Impellitteri said. "All in favor of the proposed route, please raise your hand." Three arms rose. "All opposed." The other three hands went up. It was a deadlock—the resolution would have to go to a larger vote in several weeks. But everyone knew that this had been the only real chance to stop the expressway.

Robert Moses, the mayor, Lyons, and other members of the board quickly exited through a side door as the housewives of East Tremont glared and booed at them.

"Your brother beat us! Happy, smart guy?" one of the East Tremont women snapped at Paul, who was sitting solemnly in the back.

He looked down.

"What do you mean *brother?*" another housewife asked. "He's my boy's teacher."

"Gilda told me: Paul is Robert Moses's *older* brother."

"Mr. Moses, is this true?"

As Paul rose silently and tried to exit the packed meeting hall, he heard others shouting:

"Yer whole family should drop dead!"

"Stay outta da Bronx, you bastid!"

"Give him a break, he lives in East Tremont too!" someone called out in his defense.

"Yeah, and they spared his house," another responded. "Big surprise!"

When Paul finally got out of City Hall and pushed through the crowd out front, he was filled with rage. He walked aimlessly for a while, his heart pounding in his chest. After half an hour he looked up to find himself standing in front of the loft on lower Bowery, number 168, the principal of which still technically belonged to him. He started beating on the stone walls of the old building until his knuckles bled.

Uli followed the legless scorpion kid as he gracefully angled up the long corridor and out through the barren zone that led to the Mkultra. Twenty-five minutes later, they reached the first groups of desks that the kid seemed to move right through while Uli stumbled around them. When they came to a spot with a small crack in the ceiling, the kid scurried up along a huge wooden pillar. Uli was unable to squeeze through, so the two had to walk another twenty minutes to a larger hole. Uli began wondering if the boy's body was defective at all, or if it had merely adapted to this perverse new landscape.

After traveling a distance on this upper level, they slipped back down to a lower floor, then after yet another stretch, the kid led him back up a level once more. Eventually, Uli lost track of where they were.

"Can't we just stay on a single story?" he finally asked, tired of climbing.

"Some floors are blocked and some sections are real dangerous."

"How are they dangerous?"

"They either do things to your middles or they're the people who don't like eating the rats or rations no more."

At some point, Uli commented on the absence of rodents.

"They don't come over this way, but you're lucky."

"Why's that?"

"'Cause when things first started out, there were a bunch of other animals a lot more dangerous—monkeys and cats and other stuff—but people killed them all off."

Uli noticed occasional spaces on walls where signs had evidently been removed. Along the wooden floors, he also observed more freshly painted phosphorescent lines leading into the distance, where he could make out far-off figures who seemed to be following them. Uli briefly considered that the futile circles the captives were traversing at least distracted them from their impending starvation. Though he spotted a few rotting corpses as he and the scorpion boy continued along, the roaming zombies soon became sparse and then nonexistent. Soon, too, the desks stopped. Then even partition walls disappeared so that there was only open space and concrete pillars. Swinging forward with his hands, the boy never seemed to tire.

At a leaky hole in the ceiling next to a steel column, the kid climbed through to yet another upper floor. Five minutes later, when Uli finally flopped up onto the next level, completely winded, he immediately smelled the harsh aromas of fire and death.

He followed the kid for another twenty minutes until he began tripping over something hard and crunchy on the floor. He flicked on his dimming flashlight and saw that this area, which looked like it had once been a massive filing room, was covered with carbonized bones and burned body parts. They were spread between rows and rows of empty filing cabinets stretching for dozens of yards at three-foot intervals. Reaching down, Uli realized that fueling this improvised crematorium were the contents of the filing cabinets. *Where does the smoke go? And for that matter, where does the oxygen down here come from?* There had to be circulation vents somewhere, but Uli hadn't seen a single one.

They climbed across a stretch of filing cabinets lined closer together until they reached a long wall marking the end of the floor. The kid seemed to know the entire place inside out. Arriving at a spot that appeared completely random to Uli, the boy slipped up the side of the wall and squeezed past a panel of wood in the ceiling. Uli pulled a burned-out filing cabinet over and used it as a stool to climb through the ceiling and into an abandoned tunnel that might have once been an air vent.

The kid struck a match and lit a candle, revealing that his father had created a secret nook here for his sad family. A middle-aged woman, deathly pale and feverishly thin, was staring past Uli, sitting in her own waste.

"Hello," Uli said, to no response. Something was moving under her filthy shirt. To his astonishment, he saw a small baby's head wiggling out—it was suckling on her flaccid breast.

"That's my brother," the scorpion boy said. "I call him Baby."

"I don't understand," Uli thought aloud. "The entire Rescue City is suffering from some kind of infertility plague—but here in this sealed dungeon babies are being born?"

Instead of responding, the scorpion kid reached into his mother's shirt and pulled his brother out. Uli was horrified to see that the body seemed to be little more than a long tail resembling a pink tadpole, but with little flapper arms. It couldn't be more than a few months old.

Over the course of the next hour, Uli helped the scorpion kid clean them both off as best they could and wash down the floor of the little nook.

The baby indeed felt feverish. Uli inspected the red dots along his tubular body but was confident it was only a rash, not chicken pox.

"What should we do?" the scorpion kid asked.

"Let's get them back to the storage depot. The water and air are better. They'll recover more quickly."

Uli carried the skinny salamander baby while the kid put a rope around his mother's wrist and tied the other end to his own. Slowly they made their way back into the Sticks. Because it was no longer possible to move up and down through the various levels, they chanced it and stayed mostly on the Lethe level, moving cautiously around the many desks and occasional decomposed bodies.

When they reached an area with desks piled so haphazardly that it became difficult to traverse, the kid asked Uli for help moving his mother.

"Maybe I can give you a hand," they both heard.

The dark outline of a man approached and lifted the mother in the air, so that Uli was able to grab her arms and together they moved her over the desks.

"Now, maybe you can help *me*," the man said. He was fully dressed in clean clothes. His shaved head and handsome face were covered with light stubble—a new arrival.

"How?" Uli asked, holding his ground, ready for a fight.

"When you passed through here earlier, I thought I heard the kid say you guys know a way out."

"What we found is little more than a hunch."

"A hunch is more than I got." The man had a rigid charm. As Uli conversed with him, the boy and his family lagged slowly behind. "You have a clarity of mind that's rare down here," the guy said to Uli, attempting to make small talk. "May I ask what you were in your life?"

"I was never affiliated with either gang in Rescue City, if that's what you mean." He wanted the man to go away, but since he looked fairly strong and wasn't being violent, Uli figured he'd let him ramble on until he just grew tired and left.

"Me neither."

"You seem like a nice guy," Uli said, "but I've learned not to trust anyone down here, and I'd advise the same of you."

"Where are my manners?" the guy said, extending his hand. "I'm Tim Mack."

"Paul," Uli responded, and shook the man's hand.

"By the look of your beard, it appears you haven't been here very long either," Tim said.

"Actually, I've been here for a while. I just cut it every few weeks," Uli said, not wanting to reveal anything about himself.

"Are you worried about this mental degeneration that seems to have afflicted everyone else?"

"It seems to miss some of us, thank God," Uli said. Glancing around, he realized he was now alone with the nutcase. "Hey, kid!" he shouted, but there was no response.

Dashing back into the darkness with Tim following close behind, Uli discovered that the kid and his family were nowhere in sight. Without the scorpion boy, there was no chance of escaping.

"You!" Uli knocked the bristly man to the ground and jumped on him. "Where are they?"

"What are you talking about?"

"You distracted me while someone grabbed them!"

"I swear to God I didn't."

Leaping to his feet, Uli left the man on the ground and rushed farther back in the direction from which they had come. After searching through the twinkling darkness, he eventually found the mother's tattered shirt on the ground. His flashlight illuminated distinct tracks from what appeared to be at least four people. They were clearly dragging something. Unswept by wind and not muddled by other creatures, the tracks were easy to follow over the filthy wooden floor. At one point they vanished, and Uli looked up to find a hole in the ceiling. He was able to climb up to the next level where the tracks resumed. He followed them until he heard sounds in the distance. As he closed in, he saw that there were five large men—a small hunting party. One oaf was half dragging, half leading the naked mother behind them. Over another man's shoulder was the salamander baby, who was making slight barking sounds, seemingly in pain.

"I'm hungry now!" said the man holding the mother's rope.

"We got to cook them first," said a short, obese, troll-like man, who appeared to head the expedition.

As Uli drew closer, he could see the scorpion kid hog-tied upside down and strapped to the troll's back. He seemed to be unconscious.

Noticing a four-foot section of pipe sticking out from the ceiling, Uli quietly nudged a desk over, stepped up on it, and yanked the pipe loose. He shadowed them for another ten minutes until they came to a large rupture in the floor. Uli decided this was his best chance. The three biggest men went down first, then the mother and kids were lowered into the hole by the two other hunters. Uli raced forward and walloped one across the head, cracking his skull.

"They got Slammer!" shouted the second man before Uli attacked him viciously with the pipe.

The three large men on the lower level grabbed their fresh meat and hustled off. Uli waited about twenty minutes before jumping through the hole and down to the next level. He glimpsed a bonfire across the vast room—this was their camp. He watched as the three remaining captors, apparently believing the attack was coming from a larger group, began scurrying through the darkness. Uli sprinted after them and slammed his pipe over the lead troll's skull, but then the other two seemed to realize that Uli was all alone. One man knocked him down. Bigger and stronger than Uli, they started punching him. A few other tribe members lumbered over from the bonfire and joined in the fight. They began kicking him from all directions. One man grabbed his arm and twisted it behind his back.

"I want his other arm!" one of them bellowed.

Suddenly, a gunshot rang out; then a second.

"Shit, I got hit!" one troll gasped.

The group immediately scattered, leaving Uli with the beleaguered family. Tim emerged from the darkness holding a pistol.

"How many more bullets do you have?" Uli asked, panting.

"Three, maybe. Why?"

"'Cause they'll probably come back."

Tim wanted to grab the little family and run, so Uli untied the unconscious scorpion kid and gently smacked him until he came to.

"We're lost and they're coming after us. Which way should we go?"

The kid glanced across the large floor and mumbled the quickest route back to the Sticks. After twenty minutes of running without any sign of being followed, they began to calm down.

"I'm sorry," the kid said to Uli. "They grabbed us from behind. I should've stayed with you."

"It worked out okay," Uli said. "We now have a new member of our little group."

They eventually reached the Sticks and headed through the tunnels into the storage facility. Behind the mountain of crates, hidden from clear view, they fashioned a relatively comfortable bedding area for the ill mother and her baby. Tim, who hadn't eaten since leaving the catch basin, chewed down a box of stale crackers. Uli bathed the salamander child in a tub of cool water to bring down his fever. Then he applied some topical creams for the rash and gave him both antibiotics and vitamins. He instructed the scorpion kid to keep giving his brother and mother water—they appeared severely dehydrated.

35

As Tim slept and the kid tended to his family, Uli returned to the utility closet carrying a hammer and chisel he had managed to find earlier. Digging into the hard stone, his mind drifted back to Paul and Lucretia. They tried to regain a semblance of a normal life, but their community was being torn apart piece by piece. Neighbors weeped openly in the streets. They heard other couples fighting in their apartments about where they would go after eviction.

Miss Dombrowski and the old folks stopped sitting out front on warm nights. The few neighbors who still spoke to Lucretia mentioned having trouble sleeping. It was as if the people in East Tremont were suffering the effects of a protracted battle that was bypassing the rest of the city.

On his way to work one day, Paul saw a sign taped to the Kearnes' door. In big red letters it announced, *If you do not vacate within 5 days, legal action will be taken.* When he looked through the windows, he realized the place was vacant. All their furniture was missing. The couple who had been so helpful in getting Paul his job had moved on without a word. Paul learned from a remaining neighbor that James Kearne had transferred to another school out in Jackson Heights, Queens. Lucretia burst into tears when she learned that May, her dear friend of many years, had left without even saying goodbye. The entire block, which used to be filled with families and children playing in the streets, was soon empty.

On January 1, 1954, New York City took title of the last scattered parcels of real estate in Section Two of the expressway. Despite this, some of the poorer and older families stubbornly hung on, squatting illegally in their former homes. Increasingly terrifying edicts from the city were taped to doors and lampposts. More threats of people losing their possessions or being thrown into the street followed. The elderly were the last to go. Many were foreigners—widows and widowers who had fled countries ruled by dictators, emperors, and a czar. They were just trying to wait out their remaining time. But one by one, before the city marshal arrived, they too seemed to just vanish.

Through one of her old friends, Lucretia learned about the plight of a family who had lived directly across the street all her life. The Orecklins had a disabled child and owned a nice single-family home that the father, Cecil, had fastidiously maintained over the years. They'd had their place appraised a few years earlier at twenty thousand dollars. Robert Moses's office offered them eleven thousand. When Cecil argued that they were dramatically undervaluing his property—something any outside land assessor could verify—he was told that this was a one-time offer, take it or leave it. Without any alternative, the Orecklins absorbed the loss and fell away.

While the little family recuperated, Uli tried to explain the Sticks to Tim, cautioning him about the insane miners below who had already killed one of his compatriots. Then he showed Tim the hole in the utility closet. Eager to get out, the stubble-headed man made it his personal mission to hammer through the dense stone walls, almost never leaving the little closet. After a few days, when the salamander baby's red dots started clearing up and the mother seemed to be improving as well, Uli softly asked the scorpion kid if he was ready for his climb.

"I don't want to leave them alone yet."

In preparation for the kid's ascent, Uli weaved a small body harness out of ropes, like a window washer's safety belt, that the boy could tie around his narrow waist and broad shoulders. To protect against a fall, he'd be able to hook the sides into the eyes of the metal track running up the elevator shaft. Uli also wired the lantern he had scavenged to the top of the helmet. He calculated that as long as the candles weren't tipped over, they'd each last roughly an hour while wax drained safely out the back.

Hunting through the storage depot, Uli located a bag for holding C-rations and three water bottles that could all be strapped to the kid's back. This would give him enough supplies for roughly two to three days. Uli also found several large balls of twine that he could tie to the youth in order to mark the height of his climb.

"I know you don't want to leave yet," Uli said, holding out the harness, "but I thought maybe we could do a bit of preparation."

None of it looked comfortable, but it all fit. The kid let out a deep sigh, clearly regretting ever having agreed to this. Uli knew he was going to have to convince the kid of the importance of the climb, but before Uli could start in on him, the boy said he really needed to be left alone with his family. Uli gave him the space, then resumed helping Tim chisel out the closet.

While they worked, Tim kept steering the conversation to his life in Rescue City. "The place has turned into open warfare; I figured I'd have a better chance of survival if I tried to get out. I just want to put it all behind me."

"Put *what* behind you?"

"First the bombing of Crapper headquarters, then the retaliation killings of a bunch of Pigger officials. And finally the brutal slaying of those two beautiful PP workers."

Uli remained silent and looked down at his feet.

"I know that a lot of people in Rescue City have done a lot of awful things, which is why they were sent there," Tim said, "but I was never a political type."

"Someone told me about the Crapper headquarters being blown up and a woman mayor getting elected," Uli said, playing dumb in an attempt to extract some details about the latest developments. "But I haven't heard much else."

"Things have gotten a lot worse."

"Worse how?"

"Somebody apparently blew up the sandbags holding the sewage back from Manhattan. The city's now flooded with shit."

Uli shook his head in despair. All hope that the place would become a more civilized society once the Crappers took over was gone.

36

In 1955, just as Leon had repeatedly vowed, it happened again: the Brooklyn Dodgers won the National League pennant. The Subway Series kicked off in Yankee Stadium and, just as most people had predicted, the Dodgers duly lost the first two games. Then, surprising everyone, they won the next three at Ebbets Field. They lost the next one in the Bronx—so it was an even three to three. It all came down to the tiebreaker, to be played on the Yankees' home field. Paul and Leon watched the game on a small RCA set. With each hit, Leon would jump in the air and his dogs would bark. But with each progressive inning, Paul kept thinking, *You're only setting yourself up for a big fall.* Soon, though, it was the bottom of the ninth and somehow the Dodgers were still in the lead. Despite his declared loyalty to the Yankees, Paul found himself rooting for their crosstown rival. When the game ended with a Brooklyn victory, both men jumped in the air and hugged like schoolboys, then they finished off all the remaining beer and passed out. Around one in the morning, Paul woke up, turned off the TV, and drunkenly walked the long stretch of empty blocks back home. The entire time, he kept asking himself aloud, "Dodgers won the World Series?" It sounded like a contradiction.

Uli lay down to rest, but before he could push Paul out of his head and fall asleep, he had an odd and mysterious vision: Leon was fucking Lucretia. Opening his eyes, he felt like he was seeing Paul's jealousy. He closed his eyes again, believing that since he had figured the dream out, it would be over. Yet almost immediately it came back even worse. Leon was violently raping her. For some reason she was immobilized. He was smacking her. Hitting her, strangling her. Her wrists were bound! Then Uli realized it wasn't Lucretia at all, nor was Leon the rapist.

Reawakened by this brutal tableau, his heart racing, Uli grasped that he was needed elsewhere. He had to get out of this dungeon as soon as possible. He roamed around the storage area looking for the scorpion kid, but eventually passed out sitting back against some sacks.

He came to when he heard rustling. The kid was back again looking for food. Uli delicately crept up behind him so he couldn't run.

"Look, I'm not forcing you to do anything you don't want to do," Uli began, startling the youth. "If you don't want to do this, you and your family can leave and I'll somehow figure it out myself. But if you help us and we escape, I promise that the first thing we'll do is get your mom and brother to a doctor. And I'll do everything I can to try to find your dad."

"So what exactly should I do once I'm up there?" the kid asked testily.

"I'm going to tie some twine to your waist. I want you to climb as far as you can up that shaft so I'll know how high it goes. And I want you to use the string to measure the narrowest parts."

"And then I'm done?"

"After you come out and we review what you saw, you're all done."

"Okay."

"But first I want you to train a little 'cause this is going to be tough."

"Train for what?"

"Climbing and lighting candles in total darkness and other stuff."

"How and where?"

"Well, I want you to practice using these big hooks, but the only thing to climb around here is the tower of desks in the silo. We have to be very quiet 'cause we don't want to alert any of the crazy miners."

When they went to the silo, Uli noticed fresh blood splattered around. Boxes had been knocked down and metal rods caked with blood suggested there had been a major struggle. After a brief search, Uli located two bodies: the guy he called Dave and an elderly miner appeared to have been strangled to death. There was no sign of any other miners in the vicinity.

Using the open area as a training zone, Uli instructed the boy on how to climb the desk tower.

"I don't need these," the kid responded. He set all the equipment aside and zipped right up the pile of desks. "How's this?"

"You've got to use that rope belt and clip into each new perforation as a safety precaution, in case you fall."

"What's a perfation?"

"The metal holes in the sides of the tracking."

"But there are no holes in these desks."

"Well, pretend there are."

The kid completed his first ascent up the tower while clipping the hooks from his belt onto any notch he could find. "I've been thinking," he said afterward. "I'd like something else."

"What?"

"I want my mom and brother."

"They're already here."

"I need them up in that hole with me."

"You mean in the utility closet?"

"Yeah. They're both small and they can fit in there. It has this long flat ledge inside where they can wait."

"But they're still sick. Why would you need them in there?"

"They'd be safe and I could watch them."

"I'll keep an eye on them for you."

"If you want me to do this, then they have to stay with me. We almost got killed when I took them out of our home."

Nodding his head, Uli reluctantly agreed. He just wanted this to be over with. He spent hours over the next few days drilling the kid on the fine points of climbing the elevator shaft.

"Since you'll have a candle attached to your head, you'll need to keep your head tilted back so you don't spill hot wax on yourself. But if you tilt it too far back, the candle could fall off."

"You sure all this needs to be done?" the kid asked, covered in sweat.

"The more prepared you are, the better your chances of surviving and escaping," Uli said for the third time that day.

After a final round of training, Uli deemed the kid modestly prepared for the challenge.

"Shouldn't I come down when I'm halfway done with the food and stuff?"

"No, 'cause that climb could go up a few thousand feet. It will be a lot easier to come down than it will be to get back up."

Tim would mysteriously vanish for long stretches of time. Uli had no idea where, nor did he care. So he waited until Tim went on one of his excursions before launching the kid on his great quest. The work of the newcomer had made a difference, as the kid didn't require any lubrication to enter this time. Uli lifted the mother and brother through, then passed along the various supplies.

"Listen," Uli warned up to the scorpion boy, "don't try anything heroic. If something looks scary, just get out. I'm not expecting you to rescue us. All you're doing is what we call reconnaissance. You're just checking out the landscape, then you'll come back here and we'll work out an escape plan together."

"Okay."

"And if need be, I can reach in and hand your mom and brother food and water. You don't have to come down for them, understand?"

"Thanks."

"Take care of yourself, pal," Uli said. Reaching into the tight space, he shook the nameless kid's hand and listened to him scamper up and away.

Over the ensuing hours, Uli watched the jerky ball of twine as if it were a clock and found himself feeling increasingly excited as it dwindled ever smaller. When the three hundred feet of twine was about to run out, Uli attached a second ball of twine to its end.

Uli wondered what he was going to do next. Even if the kid returned to say that he had climbed right up through a manhole to a sidewalk in Las Vegas, Uli knew he couldn't convince any of these homicidal miners or memory-challenged inmates to collaborate on an actual escape plan.

Two loud gunshots snapped Uli from his thoughts. He raced out of the closet to find a pair of miners beating Tim, who was desperately trying to fight back. The small-caliber bullets Tim had pumped into them had slowed the men down but apparently missed their vital organs. Uli jumped up and kicked one of the guys in the neck. The other dashed down into the service corridor with blood dripping from his chest.

"I can't believe it," Tim whimpered. Blood trickled from his ears; his skull was clearly fractured. "Fucker!"

Uli could see his gray matter on the ground behind his head. "I told you the miners are insane."

"Not them . . . *you!*" Tim seethed, grimacing. "*You* killed her . . . and I went through all this . . . just to . . . to get you and her . . ."

"What? Who?"

"Your sister . . . got *me.*"

"My sister?"

"Fucking hell! . . . I didn't mean to hit the bags . . . but they wouldn't give me the drug unless . . ."

Uli had no clue what he was talking about.

"There's the fucker!" Tim barked. A large miner wielding a rod suddenly came barreling out of one of the side caves. "Go get your sister, she's outside in the . . ."

Before the dying man could finish his insane rambling, Uli dashed into the Convolution. Crawling down into the ever-narrowing tunnel, he knocked into one of the steel digging rods, which he grabbed as a weapon.

He squirmed backward into a small tunnel that would only allow one man at a time. There he was able to hold the miners at bay.

"Just wait him out," one of the men said. Two hours later, as Uli began wondering how long this would last, a massive vibration rocked the whole area.

"Earthquake!"

"You pissed Xolotl off and now we're all fucked!" a miner shouted down at him. The rest of the miners slithered back up the tunnel before the aftershocks caused a cave-in.

Without thinking, Uli wiggled out of the cave and followed in the same direction, hurrying toward the utility closet. In the dimming candlelight, he spotted something billowing out of the little doorway. It wasn't until he actually touched it that he realized it was coarse hot sand, different from the rest of the dirt he had seen underground. He screamed for the little family to hang on as he frantically started digging the room out. He found a long, flat, wooden board and used it as a shovel, only to see more sand pouring down through the rectangular hole. An hour later, Uli admitted to himself that there was no chance the mother or salamander baby could still be alive.

It took a whole day of pushing the sand deeper into the storage area before it stopped cascading out of the little utility closet. When Uli was finally able to reach up into the rectangular hole, he felt around and managed to grab the mother's foot. He pulled her out first, and then her sad salamander baby. Both were dead, as he expected.

Soon, though, he located some better cutting tools and continued expanding the sides of the rectangular hole. Before long Uli was able to slide into the first chamber after slathering himself in grease. Immediately he realized that the kid had lied. Once he squeezed up past the narrow entrance, the shaft was much wider than he had been led to believe. He smiled. At his tender age, the kid had deliberately misled Uli so that he would have exclusive control of this possible escape route. That was why he had wanted his family in there. The bad news was that inside the corridor, sand was packed as tight as a brick. Uli tied a rag over his mouth and scraped sand down into the utility closet until it was full. Then he squirmed back out and hauled the fresh mounds of sand into the storage area.

After steering and pushing the sand down and out for another day, Uli crawled up through the corridor until he found the straight vertical shaft. Here, he discovered that the kid had lied yet again. There was clearly enough space for him to climb up. But Uli couldn't figure out what he was actually seeing. Staring up hundreds of yards of shaft, he made out what appeared to be a flickering ceiling of flame. It was as though he had dug all the way to the sun. *If I try climbing up there, I'll be burned to a crisp.* Observing the bluish fire for about twenty minutes, he considered abandoning this project and heading back to the catch basin.

As he mulled his options, he was startled by a distant voice yelling down to him. *"Help me, Uli!"* It sounded like his sister Karen.

Peering up the narrow chute, he wasn't able to discern anything through the curling flames. "How'd you get up there?" he called to the voice.

"Help me! I'm stuck!" Uli heard, and he knew he had to get up there as quickly as possible.

37

"The circumcision"—as his neighbor Robert Ward had called it— was a longitudinal line, a no-man's-land running several blocks wide across the middle of the Bronx. This barren stretch of the borough held the artifacts of a once thriving community. Everyone in East Tremont waited anxiously to see what kind of apocalypse would devastate the southern end of their beloved neighborhood. Weeks and months passed—nothing.

Living right on the boundary, Paul and Lucretia would hear windows being broken at night. People, probably kids, were rooting through the empty houses like vengeful ghosts. So far, not a single building had been demolished. When the remaining members of ETNA who hadn't been evicted sent a letter to Robert Moses's office asking if the abandoned area could be either guarded or fenced off, they were duly ignored.

One morning in December 1955, without any warning, a massive wrecking ball started slamming into the sides of one of the apartment buildings down the block. Soon a small cloud of dust covered the area. A gang of workmen besieged the place with all the annoyance of an occupying force. Jackhammers pounded constantly. For the next three months or so, the sound of demolition and the smell of brick and concrete dust filled the air. The work began at eight a.m. sharp and sometimes continued until seven at night. Squads of dump trucks and bulldozers carted off the piles of stones and rubbish. With them came the battalion of surly workmen holding red flags at major intersections. It was as if a wall had partitioned the neighborhood in two. They would block the pedestrian and vehicular traffic, sometimes for hours, not allowing people to cross different sections of the sprawling construction site.

Paul and others felt a strange relief as the last homes were leveled and the rubble was trucked away. But then the dynamiting began. It turned out that the expressway was to be sunken into the earth and the bedrock had to be made consistent. Residents of the area would hear periodic booms followed a few seconds later by a trembling of the earth. The mini quakes took their toll on building foundations, resulting in an appearance of fine cracks along everyone's walls and ceilings. Gradually those cracks grew bigger.

It was in this period that Paul and his wife first heard the little coughs coming from Bea's room upstairs. When Lucretia dashed in the first time, she found the child struggling to breathe. Lucretia and others in the area began sealing their windows and ventilation ducts at night, but a new skin of dust was always there at the end of every day.

After thirty years, even Abe Hoff moved, leaving the Moses family as the only people still living on their side of the block. One by one, many of the little stores along East Tremont Avenue—the social hub of the neighborhood—started going out of business.

Uli climbed back down out of the rectangular hole and headed into the Mkultra where he collected six metal wastepaper baskets. He stomped them flat, then molded them around his limbs, back, and head. He gathered as many bottles of water as he could find and shoved them up into the rectangular hole with the six crushed metal baskets. After carefully angling himself back up through the tight space, he tied the metal into a tight bundle and tethered it and the bottles to his belt loops.

It was a monstrous climb. Uli heaved himself roughly a foot at a time, resting every couple of hours. At one point, secured by ropes hooked to the metal track, he stopped altogether to take a long nap. When he awoke, he called out for Karen but got no reply.

Uli knew after some unmeasured length of time that he was getting close to the end because he began to feel the heat from the strange flames above him. In one small nook near the top of the shaft, he noticed a blackened indentation like a relief sculpted into the concrete wall. His stomach churned and bile rose to his throat. The crisp contours of a face above the jaw were all that was left of what Uli presumed to be the poor scorpion kid. In the bottom of his pocket, Uli found the two Mercury dimes he had snatched awhile ago from a desk drawer. He placed them in the tiny sockets where the eyes had once been—the only honor he could pay to the disabled youth.

After another half hour of climbing toward the ceiling of flames, one mystery was solved. A large pipe carrying propane, methane, or some other flammable gas that ran above this entire chamber—buried roughly ten feet below the desert floor—had exploded. Beyond the raging torch rising from the broken pipe, Uli could make out a sliver of blue sky—freedom.

It was a sunny day on the planet Earth. Uli wondered how the kid could have ruptured the thick pipe, but it only took a moment to realize that this wasn't what had happened. There must have been a gas leak. The candle affixed to the top of the kid's helmet must have touched off a dense pocket of gas, bursting an opening through the tons of sand sealing the top of the deep elevator shaft.

38

Crime rates in East Tremont exploded. People who used to leave their doors open found themselves getting burglarized. Those who would spend spring nights sleeping out front on their porches to catch the fresh air were awakened by muggers. Morrisania, near where Leon lived, went from being a modestly safe area to altogether treacherous. Though Leon was a hulking brute, his tiny mother seemed to be a lightning rod for criminals. Usually they just grabbed her purse and ran. She only kept a few bucks on her anyway. One afternoon, though, she had just withdrawn a hundred dollars from the bank and was walking along the street with her purse pressed to her chest. When some teenage punk tried to grab it, she held on with both hands. It became apparent that she wasn't letting go, so the mugger started slugging her. She finally released the purse when she fell, but the juvenile continued beating and kicking her. She made it to the hospital, but died two days later from internal hemorrhaging. For Leon—as Paul soon saw—his mother had been his primary companion.

Nice houses once worth a pretty penny were soon sitting empty in a buyer's market. Apartments that had attracted lines of potential tenants sat unoccupied as landlords lowered rents even further. Where Crotona Park had once been the southern border of a good neighborhood, the dividing line had now moved all the way up to East Tremont Avenue.

Paul felt there was a small dose of hysteria around the issue, but nonetheless took the precaution of installing bigger locks on their doors. Sure, the area had taken a hit and people had left in a panic, but he believed things were slowly stabilizing. A few of the old-timers, still committed to their faith that the neighborhood would be okay, were holding the line, believing that this acute depression would eventually reverse. It was just a matter of time. A silver lining to all this was that as a wave of new immigrants moved into the community, older neighbors who had once shunned the Moses family were now warming back up to them. People were again saying hi.

Over the dinner table during Easter 1956, Paul pointed out how, despite everything, they were really quite lucky. They had barely escaped losing their home, but after more than seven years of teaching Paul was now earning a good wage at a job he enjoyed. Lucretia, too, was getting more bookkeeping work than she could handle. Financially, things were actually going very well. As soon as Bea's elementary school let out for the summer, Paul decided they had to get out of the city before things got too hot and wild. Locking up the house, he drove Lucretia and Bea up to the Adirondacks for the month of July. He had just taken out hefty theft and fire insurance policies. Glimpsing the place through his rearview mirror, he half hoped it would be burned down when they returned.

That time in the country was just what the doctor ordered. Every moment was either relaxing or romantic. In early August Lucretia announced that she had failed the rabbit test again—she was pregnant. Their second child would be born in April.

Exhausted and covered in sweat, Uli prepared for his final ascent by pouring the last remaining bottle of water over his burning scalp. Moving slowly upward, he was able to pull himself onto a narrow ledge that seemed to mark the top of the sealed elevator shaft. The heat was becoming too intense to proceed.

Uli rested for several minutes, then strapped the heat-retardant body armor fashioned from the trash cans over his clothes. The massive blue flame was blasting away just ten feet above him. He had to somehow get around it to reach the earth's surface. He removed the flattened can from his head and used it to stab into the compressed wall, sending cascades of sand down the narrow shaft. As he progressed, he could feel his hair burning on his head. Taking occasional breaks to cover his scalp, he pressed on, shoveling a thick current of sand down below him for the next twenty minutes or so. Soon he had created a narrow upward rut along the side of the blasting spout of blue flame.

Retreating back down the shaft to where the heat abated, he rubbed his fingers over the blisters along his head, neck, and arms, and caught his breath. Using the last vestiges of his strength, he scampered like a sand crab up the narrow trench he had just created along the side of the giant fiery crater. Scooping the relatively cool sand around him for relief, his hand suddenly broke through into open space. He frantically hauled himself up and collapsed onto the desert floor.

Drenched in sweat, too tired and singed to even remove the body armor, he simply lay there panting under the burning sun. Smoke rose from his singed clothes. After a few minutes, he pulled the hot metal plates off his chest and arms and passed out.

39

In January, a week of unseasonably warm weather started melting the frozen crusts of snow. When Paul's teaching semester began, there was a sense of hope. Lucretia was in her sixth month of pregnancy and she somehow knew this one was going to be a boy. Though she didn't say anything, she wanted to name him Paul Junior.

Then one day in early February, Mr. Rafael, the new Negro head of the science department, popped his head into Paul's third-period classroom just as the kids were beginning a quiz. "Paul," he said, "I'll cover for you."

"Why? What's going on?" Paul stepped out into the hallway.

"It's your wife, Mr. Moses," a middle-aged police officer spoke up behind Rafael. "She's passed away."

"What?"

"We're not sure what happened," a second, younger cop said. "Someone found her on the ice, her skull was fractured."

"Lucretia's . . . ?" Paul couldn't even envision it. It was absolutely inconceivable. "Where is she? Where's Lucretia?"

"Come on," the first cop said, leading him outside. "We'll take you there."

They sped to the hospital. "One of the neighbors found her on the sidewalk in front of your house. She must've been lying out there awhile. He called an ambulance," the younger of the two cops explained over the siren. "Someone else said they saw some hooligan running away, but she still had her purse on her . . . Or else maybe she just slipped on the ice."

Paul wasn't listening anymore. Once they arrived at the hospital, a nervous young doctor said that they would need about thirty more minutes before their examination of the body was complete.

"What the hell happened?"

"We're not sure yet, but it looks like a subdural hematoma, a head injury due to her fall on the ice."

"Did she . . . just slip or was she . . . attacked?" Paul could barely speak.

"We're trying to ascertain that right now," the doctor said. "If she was hit we might find other marks or bruises, but she might've just fainted, which isn't uncommon for pregnant women."

"How about the baby?"

"I'm sorry, the fetus died with her."

Paul leaned against the clean white wall and slid to the floor. Over the course of the afternoon, Lori and several other neighbors came to visit him in the hospital, but Paul just stared off in shock.

"I'll get Bea from school," Lori offered. "She can stay with Bill and me until you're ready."

Consciousness is as tangible as any matter. It, too, must obey the laws of physics. With the velocity of decades behind it, Paul reasoned, *a life can't just come to an abrupt halt in space or time. Even if the conscious-generator fails, the psychic energy of Lucretia's being, the components and particles of her consciousness, have to be propelled forward in time, into the space we call the future . . .*

Soon a detective approached him.

"Where is she? Where is she?" Paul called out.

A sympathetic desk nurse got on the phone and rang the pathologist in the basement who said the exam was over and the grieving husband could come down and see his wife's body. The nurse directed Paul to the basement and he was brought into a viewing room. Lucretia was wheeled out on a gurney and he was left alone with her.

Only her face was visible. A sheet covered her nude, pregnant trunk. A black-and-red bruise the size of a walnut pushed out from the front of her skull. It seemed so unfair that this small broken part could end the rest of her. Paul pulled up a hard wooden chair and stretched forward, laying his head and arms over the top of her cold chest. The pathologist returned to the room ten minutes later to find Paul half sitting, half lying next to his wife.

"I'm so sorry for your loss," he said gently, "but I'm going off duty now."

"When can I see her again?"

"We'll surrender the body to whatever funeral home you want us to," the pathologist explained.

Paul nodded. He couldn't breathe. The man asked him something . . . He couldn't really . . . He shook his head no . . . The man led him . . . to the elevators . . . upstairs, instead of leaving . . . he stayed in the hospital waiting room . . . one floor above the morgue . . . near . . . his wife's body . . . for as long as he could . . . passing out in the chairs . . . then waking up . . . staying until . . . the next . . . day . . . Though he wanted to stop and stay in that one day with her . . . forever, the push-broom time kept shoving him forward.

The desk nurse told the hospital social worker that a friend of Paul's had left her number. The social worker called a Lori Mayer, who called Mr. Rafael at Paul's school and left a message that due to a personal tragedy he probably wouldn't be back for a while.

Lori and her husband then visited their old friend Stuart Fell at Fell's Funeral Parlor on East Tremont Avenue. They agreed to go see Paul together at the hospital and work out the arrangements. A few hours later, when they met him in the waiting area, he nodded silently as if he were in deep thought.

Lori asked the desk nurse if Paul could get some kind of help. Soon the hospital psychiatrist, a bearded man named Dr. Hugo, diagnosed Paul as suffering from acute grief. He gave Paul a tranquilizer and held him overnight.

The next afternoon, Paul seemed to be regaining connection. When he returned home, Lori brought Bea over. The little girl gave her daddy a kiss and told him that she'd heard that "Mommy is with God."

"I spoke to Detective Chalmers who's handling the case," Lori told Paul. "He said they've put up notices to see if anyone has spotted Toto."

"Oh, right," Paul replied absently. He hadn't even registered that her old Yorkie was missing.

When Lori left, Paul slumped into an armchair and watched as his little girl moved cheerfully around the house collecting dolls and other toys to play with. All he could think was that every item she touched had been bought by Lucretia. He couldn't accept that he wasn't going to see her again. *If I ever adjust to her loss, that would reveal the limit of my love for her. But her love for me was limitless, and I never once deserved any of it.*

When his brother had effectively erased him, making him a mere apparition around Midtown, she alone saw him floating inside Horn & Hardart in the summer of '47 and her love brought him back to the land of the living. Even when he had despised himself, she had rescued and revived him. She had become a kind of cast for his broken life, and now that she was gone he didn't even want to try to stand. Though he loved his little girl and knew his wife would have wanted him to take care of her, he simply couldn't focus.

Lori, when she dropped by around dinnertime to see how he was doing, found Bea eating from a bag of moldy bread.

"Would you like to come over for supper?"

Paul shook his head.

"What do you want?"

"Take her."

Lori said okay and brought Bea back home with her. The next day, Bill came by to tell him that Lucretia's body was now at the funeral parlor. The viewing would go on for the next two days. Solitude was all Paul desired, but he knew what Lucretia would have wanted. It took great effort to put on a suit and comb his hair. When he arrived and saw Lucretia in the coffin, he had to resist the urge to climb in and just lie with her, even be buried with her. He sat next to the box and stared downward as people filed along and gave their condolences. Everyone still in the neighborhood stopped by, signed the book, and paid their final respects.

Lori arrived with Bea, who was dressed very nicely, and pulled up a chair for the little girl to stand on. Looking down into the coffin, Bea whispered, "I love you, Mommy. Goodbye, Mommy. Goodbye."

The heat from the bright blue flame of the blasted pipeline—even at a healthy distance—was stinging Uli's burned face, pulling him awake. Half of him felt frozen, the other half fried. Calling out Lucretia's name repeatedly to no response, Uli finally corrected himself and called for

Karen, whom he had heard. Soon he admitted to himself that he must have hallucinated. Despite the cold desert night, the phenomenon of freedom compelled him to simply stare at the massive flame as though it carried the very mystery of life.

Poor Paul, Uli thought. The intense blue flame seemed to reflect the lonely man's burning anguish.

Eventually, Uli crawled away into the surrounding desert. Under the vast twinkling sky, it was almost as if he had remembered infinity with all its possibilities. Uli felt born again: the sandy breeze seizing his body reminded him that the planet was alive with both cruelty and tenderness. The fact that he was no longer trapped underground with physically and mentally impaired cannibals made him giddy.

The crescent moon offered little light. Around him in the darkness, all he could see other than the blue flame were the outlines of hills and large rocks. He was hungry and thirsty and knew he wouldn't last long. Yet, despite his exhaustion and pain, it would be better to walk now, at night, than under the great sledgehammer of tomorrow's relentless sun. He rose and staggered about a thousand feet before spotting a small trench into which he collapsed.

A few hours later he began hearing sounds. Several shapes were moving across the desert floor. He thought they were some kind of nocturnal creatures at first, but as the dark-blue sky lightened, he could see they were people. Three men passed far off to his left. They appeared to be wearing striped vests, and they also looked dirty and bewildered like those trapped below. The group was heading toward the large geyser of flame that roared forth from the ruptured pipe. The men seemed to be discussing something. Abruptly, two of them started pummeling the third, until the man collapsed to his knees. As the attackers moved away, Uli decided to wait several minutes before cautiously approaching the victim.

40

The motorcade made its way to Woodlawn Cemetery, where Lucretia's body was interred next to her mother's grave. Afterward, Paul and Bea were driven back to the house. A couple hours later, Lori stopped by and discovered them sitting quietly in the living room, both still in their funeral clothes. She fed Paul and took Bea back home with her.

Paul lingered around the house over the next few days, just sleeping and moving silently from room to room. On the afternoon of the third day, he heard a knock at the door. He answered to find Leon standing there awkwardly in torn overalls.

"Sorry I didn't make it to the funeral. After my mom's death, I just couldn't bear going through it all over again." Leon removed a fifth of whiskey from a brown paper bag.

Paul led him into the kitchen and set down two glasses.

"First my mom, now your wife."

"None of this would've happened if . . . ." Paul couldn't finish. He sucked down the burning liquor like cold water on a hot day.

Leon had barely finished his first glass by the time Paul had knocked back most of the bottle. When Leon realized that Paul had passed out and pissed his pants, he shook his friend awake and told him to clean up and get dressed.

"Why?"

"I need some company."

Leon drove Paul in his old pickup a few blocks south into Morrisania and parked in his driveway. His dogs barked nonstop as he helped Paul inside. His large home was filled with foil wrappers, empty bottles, soiled clothing, and old newspapers. Over the next week, Paul ate, drank, napped, and watched ball games on TV, all in the same tight armchair that had once belonged to Leon's mom.

Paul called Lori one afternoon and asked in a slightly drunken slur if he could speak to Bea.

"She's at school, Paul. It's two o'clock."

"I'm slowly getting back on my feet," he mumbled.

"No problem."

"Can you tell Bea I'll come get her tomorrow after school?"

"Sure, she'll love that." After a pause, Lori said, "Paul, I got a call from your boss at school, Mr. Rafael. He found someone to take over your classes, but he needs to know whether or not you'll be back next term."

"Great," Paul replied without really listening. Upon hanging up, he looked out the window and glimpsed the new railings of that goddamned freeway several blocks north.

"He's always taken everything from me," Paul murmured to Leon. "Now it's time to take back."

"You probably want to kill him more than ever now, but . . ." Leon trailed off.

"If you kill someone they don't feel pain. We have to let him feel—"

"It's over now. Maybe you should just live in peace."

"Fuck no! What that cocksucker did to this neighborhood . . . And those who stayed have been subject to years of tumult and harassment. There isn't a wall in my house that doesn't have cracks running through it. Not to mention that dust. Bea spent nights coughing herself raw. I mean, Lucretia would run tape along the doors and windows and we still couldn't keep out that goddamned dust and—"

Suddenly, shouts and screams erupted outside. Bottles were shattering, kids were fighting.

"This used to be a good street. Now we're in the middle of a fucking ghetto that's getting worse every day."

"Can you blame everything on one fucking highway?"

"THAT FUCKER TOOK EVERYTHING!!!" Paul shouted. Grabbing his overcoat, he stormed out the door.

He marched angrily up to Lucretia's home, but as soon as he got to the door, he felt it. Her presence was there waiting for him. *It's okay, Paul, pull yourself together, it'll be okay,* she whispered.

"It's not! We're fucked! *I'm* fucked!" he shouted into the emptiness. He stumbled back down the stairs and wound his way along the dark, chilly streets back to Leon's place. Once inside, he gulped water right out of the faucet until he gasped for air, then he kicked off his shoes and plunked down in Leon's mother's armchair, where he thought, *I'm taking it all—this whole fucking city—down with me!*

He awoke very late the next day and barely made it to Bea's school in time to pick her up. After buttoning her coat, Paul took his daughter's little hand and led her down East Tremont Avenue.

"Daddy, I'm hungry," she said.

Paul bought Bea her favorite meal: a slice of pepperoni pizza and, from a nearby diner, a side of creamed corn. Back at home, he gulped down a fifth of Scotch as she ate and they both watched television. Soon he passed out on the floor. When Lori woke him up at nine, she said that Bea had run across the backyard shouting, "Daddy's dead!"

"Well, obviously I'm not."

"Paul, little girls are very fragile."

"All right," he said softly, then went to the bathroom and shut the door.

"Should I bring her back home with me tonight?"

"No," he growled through the closed door, "not tonight."

Lori helped the little girl into her pajamas, made her brush her teeth and say her prayers, then put her to bed.

"Good night, Mommy," Bea whispered into empty space. Lori gave her a kiss on the cheek and sat next to her until she fell asleep.

Early the next day, Paul dressed his daughter and gave her a Hershey's chocolate bar. After dropping her off at school, he headed south to Leon's yard in Morrisania. His friend wasn't there, but Paul let himself in and rooted through his fridge, nibbling on a half-eaten turkey hero he found inside. He searched for a drink, but the house was dry.

Paul was awoken from a long nap by noises coming from the yard. Leon and some kid were feeding scrap metal into the big chopping and grinding machines.

"What exactly are you doing anyway?" he asked when Leon was done.

Leon gave him what he called his "twenty-five-cent tour." The yard, which appeared to be just a big pile of junk, was actually an organized arrangement of various types of metal. Down the center of the yard was a small metal-processing system with assorted machinery, including a hydraulic compactor, a small crane, and great shears for tearing up large pieces of scrap. Much of Leon's time was devoted to simply maintaining his outdated equipment.

Under the yawning desert sky, Uli approached the beaten and bloody man, who didn't look up once. "You okay?" he asked.

"My fall dey da, Play-o war me don rink and I egnor im." When the man looked up, Uli saw that his tongue was sticking out of his bleeding mouth.

"Where'd you come from?"

The man pointed at the ground and muttered something else. Uli didn't know if this poor fellow was mentally deficient or just suffering from a speech impediment.

"How'd you escape?"

"Play-o sho us."

"Where is he?"

"Doe know, roun ere." The man rose and started to walk off.

"Where are you going?"

"Back."

"Back where?"

"E-low, Mku-tra," the guy replied, pointing downward. "You com ew, or you ge kill."

"But we're out," Uli said. "We're free!"

"De uders righ."

"About what?"

"No un can cross da fleg-ethen. Das where de uders die."

"The what?"

"The fleg-ethen, the fleg-ethen." He pointed out across the sand.

"You mean the desert?"

The man shook his head no. "Don dree da wada."

"What water?"

"You see." The bloodied man moved off in the direction of his assailants, farther out into the endless desert. Uli followed at a distance as the sun continued to rise. Soon, he spotted the other two men several hundred yards ahead on their hands and knees. But a minute later, when Uli looked again, they were gone.

Upon reaching the area where the two assailants had vanished, the injured man kneeled down and began fumbling around in the sand. To Uli's surprise, the sad man pulled open what appeared to be a steel cellar door in the desert floor. Uli watched as he stepped right into the ground and vanished as well. Uli approached cautiously and found a rectangular door the same beige color as the sand. He pulled it upward and looked inside. Metal rungs lined the edge of a dark square chute; about twenty feet down, a massive fan was anchored beneath the grating of a floor. He considered climbing down to see exactly how and where this entrance connected to the rest of the subterranean chamber, but staring into the darkness below, he feared an ambush. He released the heavy door, which slammed, and looked around—dry emptiness.

His mouth felt as parched as the surrounding desert. He put a pebble on his tongue, something to form spit around, and started walking back in the direction of the blue flame, toward the gracefully contoured mountains in the distance.

41

A boxy skyline ran the length of the hurricane fence along the edge of Leon's scrapyard—stacks upon stacks of large wooden crates buried under the melting snow. Each crate was about three feet wide and five feet tall.

"Why don't we just scrap these?" Paul asked arbitrarily.

"We can't."

"Why, what are they?" Upon closer inspection, Paul saw that each had a small black screen and a large hole toward the bottom.

"Fluoroscope machines for shoe fitting. You put on a shoe and you can see it on the screen."

"Where'd you get them?"

"Some guy dumped them here because they got some kind of radioactive crap in them. I called the government to get rid of them, but they didn't do shit, so I'm just going to take them out some night and dump them in the river."

"They're radioactive?"

"Yeah, 'cause your bones turn up on the screen. You can see how well your foot fits in the shoe."

"Aren't you worried about getting contaminated by the radioactivity?"

"Nah, I spend hours listening to the radio and never reacted," Leon kidded.

The next day, Paul went back outside with his bifocals and a screwdriver set. He counted 103 shoe-fitting machines in all. On the back of one, he found a diagram that indicated precisely where in the box the radioactive material was stored—in a small lead cylinder—and it showed how to safely remove it without getting exposed. He remembered some things about radioactive elements from his college studies. He knew Marie Curie had died of leukemia due to radioactive exposure, as had her daughter. He had read that a professor at Yale, a physicist he once met, had died from radioactive poisoning while doing research for the government in New Mexico.

Early the next morning, after dropping Bea off at school, Paul traveled downtown to the main branch of the New York Public Library, where he turned a ten-dollar bill into a bag of nickels and proceeded to photocopy every document he could find dealing with radioactive material.

That evening, he and Leon split a six-pack and ate meatball Parmesan sandwiches while watching TV. Leon, however, wouldn't stop talking about the Dodgers.

"This is the Bronx," Paul said. "I mean, if you were from anywhere else in the country, I could understand your love of the Dodgers, but we can walk to Yankee Stadium from here."

"You know what? Yankee Stadium may be in the Bronx, but they should just dump it on Wall Street, 'cause that's where those pinstriped bastards belong. You go to a Dodgers game and you're rooting for working-class guys, Brooklyn boys, and that's all I'll say about that."

The junkman went out to his truck and came back with a fresh bottle of Scotch. He twisted the top off and poured two glasses.

Paul asked, "What would you say if I told you that the stuff in those old shoe gizmos is a distant cousin of what they dropped on Hiroshima?"

"So?"

"The radioactive material in each machine isn't powerful enough to really hurt anyone, but I know how we can make it so that no one ever drives down that fucking highway again."

"How?"

"We can dump the radioactive granules from those cylinders on it late one night, then inform the authorities anonymously. It'll be impossible to clean it up, and no one is going to drive over a radioactive highway. They'll be forced to bury the entire stretch under concrete."

Leon looked at him in silence for so long that Paul grew nervous. "What are you thinking?"

"That the next time a fucking community begs its leaders to move a highway a few blocks south, someone'll say, *Remember East Tremont*."

"There you go."

"On the other hand," Leon said, "judging by what happened to the Rosenbergs, you'll probably fry."

They kept drinking until Leon went to bed and Paul passed out in the armchair.

The next morning, Leon headed out to work in the yard as Paul sat in the kitchen over a cup of coffee and scribbled notes, considering his new project as though it were an engineering student's assignment. Gradually, though, he found himself focusing on Lucretia's death: it was the perfect murder *they* had gotten away with. He tried returning to his plan: what to do with the cylinders. A moment later, Lucretia's face came to mind again and he started weeping. He opened the near-empty bottle of Scotch, but put it down after a sip and again tried returning to the problem. Yet thinking of Lucretia—the delicate way her long fingers caressed his back and shoulders and ran through his hair, and the idea that no one would ever touch him again—led him to intense sadness, which eventually brought him to fury.

He tried wiring the voltage of her cruel death to the engine of his action. It was probably bad luck, but gradually he entertained the thought that there was some evil force behind all this, taking away the one thing he loved most. The theory of the evil force seemed to be strengthened when he considered how it had provided him with an idiosyncratic technical education. Now, as if to complete this puzzle, it had given him these very peculiar tools; specifically, it was the tossed-away vials of radioactive powder that led him to confirm that it was in fact an evil entity, because bad luck would've run out by now. *They've taken away what I loved most, so is it evil to do this, or am I doing this to the evil?* This pushed him onward until he passed by her old house, which he hadn't spent a night in for nearly a week. He stopped at the very spot where they had found Lucretia's body and thought, *Evil got away with it scot-free!*

He moved several blocks farther toward the Cross Bronx Expressway. Hearing the distant *whoosh*, he followed it a block and a half up to the giant trench that had cut his world in half. He came to see the chasm as where this cruel deity dwelled. Only now it had come alive. The ribbon cutting of the expressway had just happened three days earlier. Peering down and seeing cars passing in both directions filled him with paralyzing rage. For hours he simply stood and stared down at these large metal boxes speeding past, as if their very velocity had been fueled by the pain and suffering of himself and those he loved. When some portly fellow passed and glanced at him, Paul shouted, "What are you looking at?"

"Nothing, I—"

"They killed her!"

The man sped away before Paul could knock him on his fat ass.

He stood on the overpass staring downward, repeating, "You killed her! . . . You killed her! . . ."

When a dark-green squad car pulled up, one of the cops asked him if he was okay.

"You didn't care when they killed Lucretia and you wouldn't care if I jumped right into this fucking pit!" he babbled furiously.

"Calm down, pal."

An ambulance was called and Paul was carted off to the psychiatric ward at Bellevue Hospital, where he was diagnosed as suffering from acute paranoia with suicidal tendencies. Following several days of observation, the diagnosis was downgraded to clinical depression, yet still with suicidal tendencies. When the doctors finally learned that Paul's breakdown had been triggered by the recent loss of his wife, the diagnosis was further reduced to acute depression.

Two days after Paul's disappearance, Leon called the station house to file a missing person report. The police informed him that Paul Moses had been taken to Bellevue for a seventy-two-hour observation.

Paul, meanwhile, requested to stay at the hospital. He was given a steady dose of Thorazine and daily counseling with a rotund, pointy-bearded psychiatrist named Seth Greenwich, who quickly took a liking to him.

"I don't think I was ever happier," Paul said about his marriage. "I mean, I had really given up on life. My wife, my little girl, they brought me back from the edge. And what happens, she goes out and gets killed."

In a soft, almost dreamy voice, Greenwich asked, "Has the pain diminished at all?"

"If anything it's gotten worse," Paul said. "I keep asking myself why I'm still breathing and she's dead. I warned her that I was cursed. But I was selfish by ever marrying her. Now she's dead and I . . . I've lost all desires, I can't sleep, eat . . . I can't do anything. I just keep thinking that some asshole killed her." He made no mention of his brother.

"Paul, I checked the police records, and after a thorough investigation they classified it as an accident."

"It doesn't really matter. All that matters is she's gone. I can't stop thinking about it. I guess I've just gone crazy."

"You're not crazy, Paul." Greenwich reached over and touched his patient's arm. "I have a wife and she means the world to me. And if she were to die, I'd be sitting where you are now."

"Believe me, I want to get well. I want to clean all this out of my head and raise my daughter and enjoy what time I have left." Paul was almost seventy.

"Look, we've tried several different drugs and you say they're not working."

"They just blur the pain."

"There's only one thing left, but I'm not going to do it unless you really want it done."

"A lobotomy?"

"Of course not. Electroshock therapy. It basically neutralizes certain brain cells; supposedly it takes the edge off."

"Isn't it painful?"

"A little, but it's done over a period of time. Most patients who I've seen after electroshock are calmer."

"Will I have a different personality or anything?"

"Maybe a little memory loss, but that's it."

"Well, I'm *this* close to leaping in front of a subway, so let's do it," Paul said.

He was wheeled into electroshock twice a week, and eventually, after five weeks, he found himself thinking about nothing. Although his memory had indeed suffered a little, on the whole he was able to function better. When the treatments ended, he was finally released and set up with outpatient counseling.

Uli traced the footsteps of the impaired stranger across what seemed to be a dry riverbed. Noticing some dark birds circling ahead of him, he moved forward toward them. Several larger birds appeared to be picking at some dead animal in the distance. As he drew closer, he saw that they were digging into the fresh corpse of a coyote. He wondered if he should try to tear off a piece of the carcass or at least drink some of its blood. Even just a few drops of moisture in his mouth would be heavenly.

Approaching the dead animal, he thought he spotted a clear blue pool of water off to his left. He figured it was the water that the stranger had warned him not to drink. After just a few steps toward it, however, he saw the bodies. Two forms, both disheveled older men, lay still on the banks of the pond. Some kind of large bird, perhaps a vulture, was digging into one of their necks. A third body floated facedown in the water. This had to be what the speech-impaired man was talking about—the mysterious Phlegethon.

Uli stared at the water and realized it was completely still; it seemed to have neither source nor drain. He dipped his finger in the liquid and tasted a single drop. A burning sensation spread across his dry tongue, compelling him to spit out what little moisture had accumulated. The stranger with the speech impediment must have singed his tongue.

Uli sat in the shade of a huge rock several hundred feet from the toxic pond and thought, *At least I'll die under a beautiful sky.* Eventually he passed out.

He was awoken a little while later by a bird's screech and the sound of scrambling. He opened his eyes just in time to see a large, bearded black man in a loincloth. He had a high forehead, deep penetrating eyes, and glazed brown skin that made him resemble a bronze statue. Uli immediately sensed who he was. His body was marked by scar tissue and gashes that could only have been earned in battle. With a swift movement, the man lofted what appeared to be a burning trident into the pond. As soon as the spear hit the water, the fire expanded in every direction, turning it into a pool of flames.

"Holy shit!" Uli gasped. The large man then noticed him and dashed right up. With his last bit of energy, Uli caught the guy's arm and flipped him to the ground.

"Just as I thought—you're trained in self-defense," the prone black man observed. "Sorry for frightening you. Are you with the military or DOP?!"

"Neither," Uli replied, struggling to keep the guy pinned to the ground. "I mean, I don't really know."

"You're probably Justice. All the military were evac'd. Well, you're definitely the guy who blew up my family."

"You're Plato the leader?"

"That's what they call me here: Plato Bomber. They called me that 'cause everyone thought I blew up that hole from the basin into the Mkultra, but it was already there when I arrived. I just took credit to win their support."

Feeling no threat, Uli eased off him. "There was a leak in the gas pipe that exploded when your son got near it."

"He gave birth to the great blue feather then?" Plato's hippie-dippie way of talking reminded Uli of the Burnt Men in Rescue City.

"Yes, your son and I were trying to help each other escape. He had your wife and other son with him. They all died in the blast."

"They all died and you lived—good deal."

"I promise you it just turned out that way. We were working together."

"I know, I've already seen the proof." Plato glanced down in grief.

"What right have I to complain? I had a family, only to abandon them when I couldn't look at them anymore. My wife's brain was eaten away."

"Why did you choose to start a family in this hellhole?" Uli had to ask.

"Percy said she was infertile, along with everyone else. But what you're really asking about is love. I fell deeply in love with her in Rescue City but never had time to act upon it. She was actually with the army—she was a captain. When I came down here, she was assigned here too."

"Assigned?"

"*Consigned* to this hell, I mean, along with a couple others. When she came here, I thought we had a second chance at love. When she got pregnant, I thought we could raise him down here, just for a few years. There are large sealed-off corridors where they could live safely, away from the crazies. She said no way, so we requested transfers, but we waited so long that she had the kid, and he turned out to be severely deformed—what was the medical term, *sirenomelia* something? That's how she knew she got infected. And when our requests were finally granted, she refused to leave. And she kept venturing out of the safe corridors into the Mkultra."

"What about the second kid?" Uli asked, wondering why he'd repeat the same mistake twice.

"She was raped by one of those zombies. The second vegetable isn't mine."

"Your first son was no vegetable," Uli said. "For someone born in that shithole, he was smart as a whip, courageous, and he took great care of his mother and brother."

"It was just too painful to see him—to see any of them." Without another word, Plato turned on his heels and began ambling away.

Too exhausted to follow, Uli lay back down and quickly fell asleep. Roughly an hour later, the man returned, this time carrying a knapsack and a canteen of water.

"I tried to work with the others," Plato began. "Each member of my six-man team was supposed to go in a different direction to find a way out before returning to me. Instead, they ran off and drank from the lake of fire, where half of them died and the survivors scurried back down the hole like scared little mice—"

"Can you help me get back there?" Uli interrupted.

"Don't you want to get out of this place?"

"I'm starving and dehydrated and . . ."

Plato opened his knapsack and dumped its contents before Uli. There were two boxes of crackers, a tin of Spam, and a container of brown water that looked like it had come from the Mkultra. When Uli reached for the water, Plato caught his wrist and said, "We have to come to an agreement first."

"What agreement?"

"You want to escape and I need information."

"What information?"

"Information to find a way out for everyone else stuck down there."

"You already found a way out of the Mkultra."

"Yes, but to where? Death in the desert? I need to find a way out, and for that I need you."

"I don't know any way out," Uli said.

"You got out of there very quickly, so obviously you're pretty smart. Did you follow my lines to the stairwells?"

"What stairwells?"

"The ones behind the walls. The lady in the Sticks knows all about them," Plato said hesitantly.

"What do you know about her?"

"I know she's with them."

"How do you know?"

"'Cause I was with them. But I don't think you are. Though you might be and not even know it." He sounded slightly paranoid.

"With who exactly?"

"Maybe the NSA, maybe some other agency, maybe those Feed-more creeps, I don't know."

"What are you talking about?"

"Look," Plato said, pulling a large gun from the knapsack, "I'll help you, let you eat, drink, get some strength back, but then I'm going to inject you with a drug."

"Where did you find drugs?"

"Where do you think? They evacuated quickly and left everything behind. I didn't want to use it, but if experiment number 6,232 works, you'll save yourself and everyone else. And I haven't yet seen anyone die trying any of these drugs."

"What does it do?" Uli asked.

"It allegedly heightens intuition through memory hallucination."

"What were the other 6,231 experiments?"

"All I know after reading everything I could find down there is that this place was one big laboratory, and we're all the guinea pigs."

"What exactly is supposed to happen once I'm drugged?"

"Who knows, but it's all I got left. I've spent a month walking a two-day radius in every direction, trying to find the way out myself, and I've gotten nowhere. I can't do this alone anymore. So I'm making you an offer."

"With a gun in your hand?"

Plato passed the weapon to Uli. "That's part of the deal. I'll fix you up, inject you, then when you find it, shoot the gun in the air. It's a flare gun, so I'll be able to steer everyone else in the right direction."

"What is *it* that I'm supposed to find?"

"I'm not exactly sure, but I came across a document that described an emergency escape route somewhere through the desert. Maybe it's a phone or a dune buggy. You'll know it when you see it, and that's when you should shoot the gun."

"You think you can see a flare in this heat?"

"The flare stays in the air for around five minutes and has a twenty-mile visibility. I'll scan the sky every day just after sunset. That's when you shoot—just after the sun sets."

Seeing no other recourse, Uli agreed.

Plato removed a syringe from his bag and injected Uli's arm, then said, "Rest, eat, and drink before you start walking."

"Where are you going?" Uli asked as the guy began heading off once again.

"Back—I still have a million loose ends to tie up."

"Do you have any idea which way I should go first?"

"If I did, I wouldn't need you, would I? Just follow your intuition about anything weird." The tall black man marched off in the direction of the strange cellar door. Uli promptly fell back asleep.

He woke up several hours later starving and thirsty. He drank down half the container of black water and instantly felt a surge of energy. He chomped down some crackers and opened the Spam. The oily little tin tasted like filet mignon. It was already late in the afternoon, so he loaded the remaining water and crackers into a thin sack that Plato had left with him, slipped it over his shoulders, and took to his feet. Though the pond was still burning in spots before him, there was no sign of Plato. Whatever hallucinogens had been injected into his system, he didn't feel or see anything odd. Just empty space eternally unfolding and an occasional breeze bringing little relief.

He decided to walk through the night. As the moon began to rise, he sat down on a flat stone and had a few more crackers followed by a mouthful of water. Just as he was beginning to wonder if the shot in his arm was merely some kind of placebo, he spotted something racing madly across the desert. At first he thought it was a coyote, but even in the moonlight he could see that it was black, or shrouded in black. It was moving on four legs, but then it rose up to two. With a hood, or long black hair, a woman was running hard. She abruptly vanished over a hilltop. He checked in his bag and verified that he still had the flare gun. He took a deep breath and followed.

42

After seeing a board of education psychiatrist at 110 Livingston Street in Brooklyn, Paul successfully filed for retirement on a psychological discharge. He got less than a quarter of what his pension would have been, but he was able to secure additional Social Security disability payments.

"What'd they do to you at Bellevue?" Leon asked when he showed up at the scrapyard.

"Fried the pain out of my head," Paul said simply. He paused before adding, "Now I can truly focus on destroying that highway."

No longer working, his days were actually more hectic than before. Bea was back with him after having lived with the Mayers during his hospital stay. Between taking her to school in the morning and picking her up in the afternoon, he would visit the Midtown library and research various models of homemade bombs and improvised land mines.

One April morning, after taking his little girl to school, he sat and had a chat with Lori. "You were the person Lucretia picked as godmother for Bea," he began.

"Don't you think I know that?"

"I just want you to understand that this was a decision Lucretia made after a lot of thought. She really believed that if anyone was qualified for the job, it was you."

"It's a duty I've never forgotten."

"Do you know how old I am? I could drop dead at any moment."

"Any of us could."

"Well, I'm telling you this just to say that if, God forbid, something should happen to me, I want to rest assured that my little girl has a home with you."

"Paul, please, you're scaring me."

"The reason I'm telling you this is that I've made you the trustee of what little assets Lucretia and I have. That includes the house, which is paid for in full."

"I appreciate this, Paul, but I'm sure you'll live a good long life and once you get on your feet you'll be a great dad."

Paul thanked her and headed back to the scrapyard. Baseball season was kicking off the next day and Leon wanted Paul's help in selecting a new TV set.

Back in Rescue City, while dangling from the Goethals cliff and then leaving Staten Island, Uli had experienced bizarre visions. Now, seeing this figure dashing through the Nevada desert, he thought it might be the same woman. He had perceived bedraggled Armenian refugees being marched by soldiers from their villages to their likely deaths in the Syrian desert. He saw a young woman's husband disappear and her daughter being stolen from her. Eventually, the woman had been taken as a slave by one of the many marauding gangs. What the hell was she doing here in *this* hallucination?

Uli continued following the black-clad figure through the morning, but as the day wore on he slowed down a bit. She seemed to slow down with him. By noon, he was all out of water and most of his crackers were gone. Hot and dry, Uli swung one foot in front of the other feeling like his skull was going to crack open. At one point he spotted a plane overhead and wondered if it was a supply drone headed to Rescue City.

When the sun finally went down, he was utterly exhausted and had to stop, but she kept going. Uli made a mental note of which direction she was moving in and dozed off by a cluster of desert shrubs. It had to be about midnight when he awoke. The moonlight was strong enough for him to continue walking. *Tomorrow morning I'll find shelter and wait out the heat,* he decided as he pressed onward through the desert. He kept spotting her silhouette in the distance, yet the woman wasn't leaving any tracks in the sand. She had to be induced by the drug Plato had given him.

When the sun started rising the next morning, he told himself, *I must be at least five miles from where I started out. Shouldn't I have found some means of escape by now?* A grouping of rocks offered some shade from the growing heat several hours later, so Uli curled up for a siesta.

That afternoon, as the sun's rays began dissipating, Uli resumed walking toward the spot where he had last seen the woman. After half an hour, he hadn't detected a single trace of her and began to fear that the drug he had been injected with was wearing off. He briefly considered returning to the clump of rocks where he had initially spied her. Instead, he limped a few thousand feet farther before glancing down at what had to be a second hallucination. There appeared to be some kind of metal box, like a small telephone booth, planted on a circular concrete foundation. Moving forward, he discovered that he was looking at a gated enclosure around a pipe sprouting from the concrete. A sign on the side affixed to the base said, WARNING: *Water Station 27, US GOVERNMENT PROPERTY. Trespassing Strictly Prohibited!* ↑

Although there was a latch on the enclosure, there was no lock. Inside, Uli found a small hand-operated water pump. He immediately started working the metal handle. First it was just air, but then came a rumbling, and suddenly rusty water spat out. He dropped to his knees and stuck his sweaty head under the rush of water. He laughed aloud and drank as much as he could, then he just lay there as the increasingly cool water gushed over his burning head and sweaty body.

43

Over the next few months, Lori continued to help Paul look after Bea. At the end of each night, after putting his little girl to bed, Paul pulled out a bottle, thought of Lucretia, and quietly drank himself into a stupor. Lori sat him down one day and told him that he really needed a maid. The old house was filthy.

"Can't afford it," he replied flatly.

She shook her head in dismay.

Paul kept hoping that with time their lives would stabilize, but things only seemed to get harder. When Bea's homework assignments started getting more demanding, he found himself thoroughly overwhelmed and Lori began taking the girl four nights a week. In an effort to avoid his neighbor's constant supervision, Paul would bring Bea down to Leon's house, park her in front of the ball game, and proceed to get hammered with his buddy. Frequently, they'd all pass out in front of the TV. On most Monday mornings Bea would wake him up late. Paul would grab the keys to Leon's pickup and hit the gas. Without even stopping at home for a new change of clothes, he'd deposit her directly in front of the school. Soon he started receiving letters from Bea's teachers about her shabby dress, her poor performance in class, and her frequent arguments with other children. When he could put it off no longer, he visited the principal, introduced himself as a retired schoolteacher, and explained the tragedy of his wife's death. He said he was still going through a rocky period of adjustment, but promised that things were slowly improving.

Eventually, someone filed a complaint with the Society for the Prevention of Cruelty to Children. An attractive young woman, Honora Agnes Burke, was assigned to Bea's case. The social worker routinely visited the house to inspect the living situation. She'd open the fridge and find that vital foods and other requisite household items were missing, then she'd notice the garbage piled up around the house. A thick layer of dust covered everything. Paul would apologize and make some lame comment about missing a shopping day, and she'd just scribble notes into her small spiral pad.

"It's not me you should apologize to," Mrs. Burke snapped at him one afternoon. "I have milk and eggs and bread in my fridge, and my house is spotless. It's your little girl who suffers."

One cold night that spring, Paul fell asleep with an electric heater running. He woke up to the smell of smoke—a stack of old *New York Times* had caught on fire. He quickly put it out and first thing the next morning went across the yard to see Lori.

"What's the matter?" she asked, seeing the misery on his face.

"It takes every bit of effort I have just to keep from killing myself."

"Please don't say that."

"Whatever I was, Lucretia made me. It's as simple as that. I didn't want marriage and certainly not children. It all came from her. You saw it. I wouldn't have even become a teacher . . . Anyway, last night I almost burned the house down." He couldn't look up. "That goddamned social worker is coming by all the time and it's just a matter of time before she starts trying to take custody of Bea. I can't put her through that."

"Paul, I have a husband and a little girl myself," Lori said. "I can't do any more."

"Bea loves you like a mother and Charity like her own sister." He took a deep breath. "I want you to adopt her and give her a real family."

Tears came to Lori's eyes.

"By doing this," he continued, "at least I'll still be able to see her and be a presence in her life."

The next day, after Paul dropped Bea off at school, Bill and Lori came to the house and explained that much to their regret, they had to decline his request.

"Bea loves you guys and I thought you felt the same way."

"Of course we do," Bill said. "Hell, we even *want* more children. We just don't have the space. Our place is really just a living room and bathroom. Charity's room is tiny."

"How about this," Paul countered. "You guys move in here. This place is over twice the size of yours, and I fixed it all up a few years back. You can check the plumbing, electricity, and paint job—I did it all myself."

"This house was Lucretia's pride and joy."

"And her daughter will still be living here."

They thought about it for two more days before they consented. Two weeks later, Paul located a lawyer who would charge a reasonable fee to do all the paperwork. Before the month was over, Paul had thrown out all of Lucretia's clothes and knickknacks that he knew they wouldn't want. He had already brought most of his own things over to Leon's home.

The Mayers moved into Lucretia's house soon after Paul had vacated. They kept possession of their own house and decided to try to rent it out if they could find some nice tenants.

Keeping busy to avoid the inevitable anguish of giving up his daughter, Paul carefully read and reread the diagram on one of the fluoroscope boxes. Apparently, each time the button on the box was pushed, a coiled spring flipped open the small lead cylinder holding the radioactive pitchblende and an X-ray of a foot in the shoe appeared on the screen. With much sweat and concentration, Paul was able to extract the cylinder from the bottom of one of the old machines. It looked like a small brass pipe with a panel on the side.

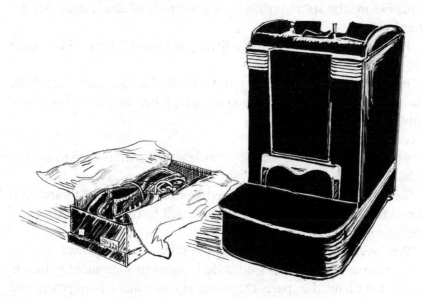

He was delicately removing the cylinder from a second machine one Saturday when Leon walked up to him in the scrapyard and said he was worried. He had just read a frightening newspaper article: Brooklyn Dodgers owner Walter O'Malley was seriously looking to move the team to the West Coast. Pacing around the yard as he spoke, Leon noticed Paul holding the cylinder and asked, "Is that the radioactive stuff?"

"Yep, and until I figure out how to assemble a bomb, I need some sort of lead-enforced chamber to safely store it in."

"Hey, I know where we can get a small lead-lined vault."

"That'd be a great start," Paul said.

The next day, Leon visited a scrap iron yard where he knew the owner had a collection of old broken safes. The strongbox he remembered seeing was roughly three feet tall and three feet deep, with three inches of lead and steel insulating it. Leon traded his friend twice the safe's weight in copper piping for it. Then he and Paul hauled it back to his yard and dropped it to the earth right near the fluoroscope boxes.

"Let me ask you an unusual question," Leon said to Paul. "Is there any way we can detonate this stuff that might somehow further our cause *and* help keep the Dodgers in Brooklyn?"

Paul chuckled, but then realized his pal was serious. Though he said nothing, the question compelled him for the first time to consider the idea of establishing multiple targets instead of just the expressway.

"No one should have to die for baseball," Paul replied calmly.

Browsing through the listings pages of several newspapers, Paul was able to find a lead smock formerly used by a dental technician. He also picked up an old army surplus Geiger counter, but it broke after just a few days. Over the ensuing weeks, a routine formed: Paul would remove one cylinder a day. He made it a point to be done by two in the afternoon—in time to shave, shower, and dress so he could meet Lori outside of Bea's school and walk them home. Sometimes he'd stay at the Mayers' for dinner before heading back to Leon's place for the night.

One evening, Leon showed Paul a column about Walter O'Malley's obsession with building a new stadium. The guy wanted to plant one right on the corner of Atlantic and Flatbush over the Long Island Rail Road yards in Brooklyn. The plan was being blocked by Robert Moses, who argued that the development would create "a China Wall of traffic" in Downtown Brooklyn.

"Your brother won't let the Dodgers leave New York City, will he?"

"Even Mr. Robert's not that stupid."

"'Cause I got to tell you: if he did, I really would consider killing him myself, and I ain't fooling."

Soon they read that Paul's brother had offered O'Malley use of a new stadium he was building out in Flushing, Queens. With that, even Paul felt some sense of relief.

* * *

Uli finished off the last of the crackers as the sun dipped out of view, then lifted the gun and pulled the trigger. The flare must have shot over a thousand feet in the air before it blasted open. This strange concrete buoy in this sea of sand had to be part of some kind of escape route. By blasting the flare into the sky, Uli had now fulfilled his bargain with the crazy black guy who had gotten him here.

That night, as he milled around trying to figure out his next move, choppy segments of Paul's memories cut through. He saw Lori repeatedly yelling at the old man for various reasons, all pertaining to Bea. The two were getting into frequent fights about parenting the girl: He didn't like the clothes she was wearing. Lori didn't want Paul feeding her crappy diner food and taking her out late at night. He accused her of monitoring Bea more closely than her own daughter. Lori said he was paranoid, and finally that she was sick of all the fights.

During the next day in the sun, as Uli imagined Lori and Paul struggling with each other, he simultaneously searched for the woman in black, but his hallucinations seemed to have dissipated. He eventually closed his eyes and rested.

"What we're trying to say, Paul, is we've had it," Lori snapped. "You win. Just take her and leave us alone."

Though Paul didn't speak, Uli knew the old guy had concluded that he needed to quietly back out of his daughter's life. Otherwise, there was no chance of her being raised by this decent family.

Suffering from severe hunger pains, Uli filled the container that Plato had given him with water and set out due west. A shiny half-moon amid a million little stars allowed him some visibility to keep an eye out for potential food sources. The night grew steadily colder. Then he thought he saw her again, a female apparition, walking across the desert floor in the opposite direction. He tiredly switched course and followed.

Rising sharply up to a small plateau of rocks, Uli spotted about a dozen large lizards enjoying the residual heat from the day past. They were each about three feet long from tail to snout. He found a flat rock and quietly tiptoed up and managed to slam three of them dead before the others disappeared. He slipped their hard little bodies under the rope he was using as a belt. He could still see the dark figure of the woman standing in the distance. As he quietly approached, she looked different—she was short, with precise features and an inviting smile. He walked stiffly toward her until she seemed to transform into the outline of a rock.

He pressed on for a couple more hours before he started shivering. Fortunately, he came upon a dried-out tree, so he snapped off some of the smaller branches, peeled strips of dried bark, and rolled them into a tight bundle. Using matches he still had with him from the underground storage depot, he lit a fire at the base of the tree. After a few minutes, the trunk was up in flames. He flopped the dead lizards on the fire and warmed himself while they cooked. Soon their skins were black and bubbling. When they cooled down, he ripped the short little limbs from one of them and chewed slowly. They were rubbery as hell, but they tasted good. He intended to save the other two cooked reptiles for later, but after many weeks of C-rations, the gamy, salty meat was just too tempting and he gobbled it all down. He spent the remainder of the night and most of the following day in a cool little rock hollow resting up for more hiking. Without even thinking, he drank through nearly half the container of water.

44

A t the main branch of the library on 42nd Street, Paul began reviewing published dissertations and scholarly articles to try to figure out how to turn a hundred-plus cylinders of radioactive material into a bomb. All bombs required a shell, an explosive element, and a detonator, but instead of shrapnel, the most deadly part of Paul's creation would be the pitchblende itself. The lead safe that Leon had gotten for him could serve as a bombshell. The real trick was finding enough dynamite to blow it open along with the lead cylinders inside. It all came down to cash. When Paul mentioned this to Leon, his friend asked how much was required.

"Maybe a thousand dollars for a box of dynamite."

Leon told him they could earn it scrapping.

That summer, the two men worked hard at cutting, grinding, and compressing ferrous and nonferrous metals from Leon's yard, then hauling them down to a blast furnace.

"You know," Leon said tensely, seeing the yard clearer than he ever remembered it, "I wish to hell your brother would cut the crap and allow O'Malley to build that fucking stadium in Brooklyn."

"I wish my brother would die painfully."

"I mean, think about it, the Brooklyn Dodgers should be in Brooklyn, not Queens. Am I right?"

"Sure, but hell, O'Malley's not being particularly flexible on location."

In the hot days of August, Paul woke up one afternoon with a hangover and realized that Leon, who was usually an early riser, was still in bed. His buddy had been nauseous for several days in a row.

"You should lay off the sauce for a while," Paul suggested that evening, after working the entire day on his own.

"I don't think that's it," Leon said, struggling to get out of bed. In addition to his increasingly pale complexion, Leon was suddenly losing his hair. When Paul went to the bathroom, he saw that the sink was splattered with blood. Leon said it was nothing—his gums were bleeding, big deal. It was obviously more than that, and Paul convinced him to go to the hospital. Leon was immediately diagnosed with late-stage leukemia.

"I was healthy as an ox till a few weeks ago," Leon said, barely able to breathe.

"It's very odd, leukemia coming on so quickly," the doctor said. "Do you know if any other members of your family had it?"

"No," Leon said tiredly.

"You must've been exposed to something that brought it on." The doctor prescribed Leon a full menu of painkillers and antibiotics. Because he didn't have much money and didn't want to die in the charity ward, Leon asked Paul to help him back to his yard.

Paul cared for him attentively, never voicing his fear that the crap in those shoe-fitting machines was somehow responsible. The following month consisted of nonstop nosebleeds, diarrhea, bedsores, and significant weight loss since nothing stayed in or down.

"I think that this might've been my own fault," Leon finally confessed.

"What do you mean?"

"I think this is what happens when you get radioactivated. Shit," he mumbled, coughing, "I knew I shouldn't have . . ."

"Shouldn't have what?"

"One day while you were down at the library, I took one of those things from the safe."

"One of the cylinders?"

"Yeah."

"What did you do with it?"

"Nothing, really. I mean, first I drove out to Queens . . ."

"Where?"

"Flushing."

"Why?"

"So the Dodgers would have to stay in Brooklyn."

"Holy shit! Where's the cylinder? Leon, you didn't empty it, did you?"

"No. I opened it and poured a little onto some newspaper."

"It just poured out?"

"Just like dark sand. I poured most of it back in but spilled some behind the old crane when I got back here."

Paul knew where he was talking about in the far corner of the yard. "How'd you get it open?"

"The little side panel slides open with your finger. It's held shut by a spring."

"Where is it now?"

"I put the cylinder back in the safe—but I never even touched the stuff!"

Paul said not to worry. Leon apologized.

Later, Paul took the old Geiger counter apart and carefully checked its bottom board lined with test tubes. When he prodded one of the old wires, the needle of the counter started bouncing. He managed to get the thing working again, so he put on the lead smock and walked around the scrapyard, where everything seemed fine. Checking inside Leon's truck, however, the dial flipped all the way to the red side and stayed there. Paul then went to the lead safe and opened it up. Again the Geiger counter's dial swung into the red. He closed the heavy door.

Paul carefully hosed down the interior of the truck, then tossed his clothes into the garbage bag and took a long shower. He got dressed, made some chicken soup for Leon's lunch, and helped him to the bathroom and then back to bed.

"I have something to tell you," Leon said later that afternoon in a hoarse whisper. "I put the house and yard in your name."

"Why?" Paul asked.

"I don't have any other relatives, so I thought you'd be best."

"But I'm an old man," Paul replied.

"You still need that box of dynamite, right?"

"Oh God."

"We didn't start this battle," Leon rasped.

"I guess not."

"They can't just tear a community in two . . . and expect to get away with it."

"That's true."

Leon looked strangely content.

When they heard the news on TV that the Dodgers were indeed leaving Brooklyn at the end of the year, neither man said a word. On September 24, 1957, Paul and Leon watched as the Dodgers played their final game in Brooklyn against the Pittsburgh Pirates. They won 2-0.

A few nights later, Leon said he had something to tell Paul.

"I'm listening."

"Remember that first time . . ." Leon was having difficulty breathing and could barely keep his eyes open. "Remember that morning when you came into the kitchen at Lucretia's . . . and you saw me sitting there eating breakfast?"

"Yeah." Paul remembered feeling his heart break, assuming she had slept with him.

"I just want you to know . . . we didn't . . . we didn't do nothing."

"What do you mean?"

Leon smiled softly and said, "It was her idea, and I probably shouldn't tell you, but she . . . she was trying to . . . to make you jealous. She called and asked me . . . to come by early and tiptoe in . . ." Leon chuckled. "Hell, we waited an hour before you . . . before you entered the kitchen."

"What are you saying?"

"She loved you and you wouldn't . . ."

"But you were her boyfriend, weren't you?"

"Never really been a ladies' man," Leon said softly. "Anyway, I guess Lucretia's plan worked."

"And all this time I thought—" Paul broke out laughing, as did Leon. Paul spent the rest of the night reveling in how clever—if not conniving—Lucretia had been. She had always seemed so naive.

Leon died six days later. When Paul found the empty bottle of sleeping pills under the bed, he wasn't wholly surprised. He called the police and had the body taken away, then arranged a funeral. Among others, Lori, Bill, Charity, and little Bea came. He hadn't seen his daughter in nearly a month, so she rushed up to him as soon as she arrived. He lifted her in the air and kissed her face all over.

Seeing his daughter in a pink outfit that matched Charity's dress, he knew that Lucretia would never have bought something so gaudy. That thought brought on a flood of memories, and sitting across from Leon's open casket, Paul started weeping softly for his wife.

Two days later, he borrowed Leon's pickup truck to purchase a bunch of supplies, then returned to the scrapyard. With a jackhammer, he tore a small square opening through the pavement at the outer edge of the property. The next morning he dug a hole six feet into the earth.

Using two-by-fours, Paul slowly hammered together a frame. That week, he mixed and poured several bags of concrete, fashioning a small container in the earth. When it dried, Paul carefully lowered the lead safe with the 103 cylinders down into the shaft. He topped it off with an additional bag of concrete, then covered the shell with dirt.

He didn't want to ever think about building a bomb again. His friend had died because of it—he didn't want to kill himself and Lord knows how many others just to get back at his brother. Most importantly, though, he certainly didn't want his little girl to become known as the daughter of one of the most evil men New York City had ever produced. All plans to build a bomb were officially off.

Soon afterward, he sold the pickup truck. Next, he took the title to the property to the Mark Lukachevski Real Estate Agency on East Tremont and put the scrapyard and house on the market.

"How much do you think you can get for it?" he asked Lukachevski, a man he had come to know in the neighborhood over the years.

"To be frank, at this point you'd have a difficult time even giving it away," the man replied earnestly.

Paul packed his few things at Leon's house and moved back down to the old Times Square dive where he had lived when he first reunited with Lucretia years ago. He stared out at the old familiar view, with crowds of people, *Long Day's Journey into Night* playing across the street. That seemed to be an apt description of his final years in the Bronx.

Uli felt relieved that Paul had abandoned his suicidal plan to attack the city. He had come to assume that this bombing scheme was the very reason he was having these memories in the first place, so he wondered anew how he was linked with Paul Moses.

He crawled out of his cool nook and scanned the horizon for any sign of his hallucinatory siren beckoning him—but nothing. As usual, she was being coy.

While he marched forward across the barren landscape, a symbol kept popping into his head:

$$\uparrow$$

He had seen it on the sign of Water Station 27. He figured it must be pointing to the next station. But then he froze. *They're probably all in a direct line!* Uli had been too distracted by Paul's grief and the female guide to recognize the clue. He had to go back. Only from Water Station 27 could he hope to find 28.

45

Sitting on a wheeled cart at the library, Paul noticed a bound collection of back issues of the *University of Pennsylvania Alumni Quarterly*. While perusing through several recent editions, he spotted an item from three years back. Under the heading *Class of 1908*, it read, *We've established a fund to assist one of our dear colleagues who is in special need. Millicent Sanchez-Rothschild worked tirelessly on behalf of the poor in Mexico and now needs our help. Please donate to . . .*

There was a name listed that he didn't recognize, *Irena Martinez-Smith*, along with an address on the Upper East Side. At first he was going to write a letter. But since it was a nice day and the woman lived only a mile or so from the library, he headed up to her apartment on 69th Street and First Avenue. He stopped at a diner along the way to comb his hair and straighten out his ruffled suit in the bathroom. Then he located the building and rang the bell. A handsome young man answered.

"I'm looking for a Mrs. Martinez-Smith," Paul said.

"What about, may I ask?"

"I saw that she posted a notice for funds for a Millicent Rothschild—"

"Mom!" the man shouted upstairs. He quickly vanished and an older woman came to the door.

"Can I help you?"

"I used to be good friends with Millie years ago, and I saw your notice. Since I live nearby," he lied, "I thought I'd just knock on your door and ask how she was doing."

"You knew Millie in Mexico?"

"No, here. I went to Princeton, though I ended up going down to Mexico with her. That was about fifty years ago."

"What's your name?"

"Paul Moses."

"Yes, Pablo, I remember her writing about you." She invited him inside, offered him a cup of tea and scones, then told him, "Millie was disinherited by her family."

"You're kidding."

"They completely turned their backs on her when she went down there to join the revolution. She was fighting against people her own father had put in power."

"I remember. Is she okay?"

"She came back from Mexico a number of years ago. She had problems there. She got arrested in the thirties and spent a number of years in jail, where she lost her eyesight."

"She's blind?" Paul felt numb at hearing this.

"Yes. After a while she was finally getting along, but then she had to move . . ."

"Where is she?" Paul was trying to hold back tears.

"She just got a new place, but it's all the way down in the Battery. On Broad Street."

"Is there a phone number?" Paul asked eagerly. "Can I call her?"

"She doesn't have a phone yet. That's one of the reasons I'm trying to raise money for her. She was so popular and beautiful back then. There were so many suitors chasing after her. I remember one of the Rockefellers was gaga over her. He was good-looking too. Would've given her the world, all she had to do was take it."

"I know," he said, almost ashamed to be among that group.

"Did you know she scored number one in her sophomore class?"

"I didn't know that." At least if he did, he had forgotten.

"Smart, attractive, she could've really been something," the woman said sadly.

Paul knew that she meant Millie could've been married to a powerful man, because he also knew that Millie couldn't have lived her life any other way than she had—fighting for the poor.

Millie now resided at 98 Broad Street. He thanked the woman for her time, then walked over to Lexington Avenue and caught the 5 train down to the last stop in Manhattan. Forty-five minutes later he was walking around the Battery looking for her address.

When he finally found her building, which had no downstairs doorbell, it was already five o'clock. It was located behind Fraunces Tavern, one of New York's oldest pubs. The ancient warehouse looked like it had been built back when the English ruled. Staring up, he wondered how he could get inside. He considered yelling out her name, but if she was on the top floor he didn't want to make her come all the way downstairs, particularly if she was blind. Wall Street workers were just leaving their offices. Paul waited as the rush hour crowds passed by, hoping someone might enter the old building. After an hour or so, he approached the chipped and warped door. When he pushed it, it rattled. With a sharp thrust of his shoulder, the door popped open.

Paul slowly climbed the long, steep, splintery wooden steps. Halfway up the exhausting ascent, he began remembering the last time he had seen her. He had left her in anger in revolutionary Mexico and was returning to New York to take his rightful place as the prodigal son of a privileged New York family. Now, other than the fact that he was still alive, he had nothing to offer her.

When he knocked on the door, he could hear someone rummaging around inside.

"Who is it?" a rusty female voice called out.

"Millie, it's me!"

"Who?"

"It's Paul, Paul Moses."

"*Oh my God!*" He heard her fumbling with the locks and the door swung open. Besides her dark glasses, she hardly looked older, just more dramatic.

"Millie, I can't believe it."

"Paul!" She reached out and grasped him. He hugged her so hard he realized he was hurting her, but she didn't utter a peep.

"I'm so glad you're still alive," he said cheerfully.

"It took me years to understand that I took you for granted!" she said, tears streaming down her face.

"I can't believe you're in New York."

Her hand grazed along his face to feel his expression. As he smiled, her fingers danced along his lips and cheeks until he kissed them.

"Do you know how many times I prayed that I had left with you all those years ago?" she said, hugging him again. "Almost every day since you left."

She brought him inside and made some tea. In the fifteen years after he left Mexico, various revolutionary governments had abused the sacred trust of the country's people and were quickly replaced. She had attempted to keep a foothold, working with different regimes who supposedly shared common goals.

"Tens of thousands died during those years of infighting," she explained. "At some point you realize that you're no better than those you're fighting against."

Eventually, a coalition government was established. She thought the worst was over and was soon appointed to the government as one of the three deputy ministers of education. Everything seemed to have stabilized for a short while. In 1932, however, one of the more ruthless generals who she had briefly collaborated with was brought to trial.

"It's ironic—we all celebrated when we heard the son of a bitch was arrested."

But in an effort to gain his own freedom, the general had implicated Millie and three others. He was ultimately executed, but she was indicted as a coconspirator in a complicated debacle that had led to the slow death of thirty orphans. Millie ended up spending five years in a women's prison outside of Mexico City. It was there that she started going blind, developing something called macular degeneration, which went untreated. She was also under constant attack as a convicted child killer, and after one of the many prison riots, she was brutally beaten and sexually assaulted by several guards. When she was released in 1938, she was so sick she was unable to walk.

She discovered that many of the other oligarchs who she had worked so hard to rid from the country had resumed their former places in the government. Without alternatives, she attempted to get in touch with her mother and brothers, but none of them responded. She was dead to her family.

"Despite all the pain and the thousands who lost their lives—so little had changed. All that work and sacrifice was for nothing."

She detailed how she ended up falling on the mercy of the church, an institution she had spent her entire life hating. They helped rehabilitate her, teaching her how to walk again with a cane. She learned how to read braille. They even hired her to work around the church. When she found someone who would write for her, she sent letters to old friends, members of the committee she had been a part of years earlier, to addresses she only vaguely remembered. Most of the letters came back stamped *Address Unknown*. Finally, though, a merciful letter arrived from her old girlfriend Irena Martinez. Her husband, Paul Smith, was a successful Wall Street broker. Millie requested assistance in getting to New York, promising she'd reimburse the cost of the ticket. Irena immediately wired her money and Millie arrived in the city just after the war, in 1946.

Irena helped her get a job through the American Foundation for the Blind giving private Spanish lessons to high school and college students. Irena also helped situate Millie in a comfortable rent-controlled apartment on the Upper West Side just off of Central Park.

"I looked for you as best as I could, but your family home in Midtown was gone. I tried tracking you down through Princeton, but after you quit working at Con Ed, they didn't know anything."

"Irena said you just moved here."

"Oh yeah, my old place was . . . well, unless you spent years in a dark jail you probably can't appreciate this." She smiled. "I was able to sit in the backyard most days and just be happy feeling the sun on my face." She had almost gotten her life back together when she was forced to move. The entire block of buildings was being evicted due to the new slum-clearance program. "They were turning the place into a housing project called Manhattantown."

"Awful," Paul said, neglecting to add that his own brother Robert was now the head of the slum-clearance program.

"Not necessarily. They promised to give us priority housing when they're finished constructing it, so hopefully in the next few years I'll get a new apartment and other needy families will have affordable housing too."

"How'd you find *this* dive?" The sound of foghorns was constant.

"Irena's son is a friend of the owner."

"Any farther south and you'd be in the water."

"For some reason, most landlords are prejudiced against blind, impoverished seniors. This guy took me in and I'm very grateful."

"Well, the place looks big," Paul said, glancing around. The apartment was one large ramshackle room with a beautiful view of the Staten Island Ferry terminal.

"How about you?" she asked. "What became of you?"

Paul smiled. It was almost as if the two had died and were comparing their lives from heaven. He related everything that had happened—his disinheritance, the failing pool club near Philadelphia, his failing marriage with Teresa, and her kids. Just when he'd thought his life was over, he had found a fleeting joy with a young wife and a beautiful daughter, with a second child coming. But suddenly—probably due to a slip on the ice—it had all been taken away.

It was soon dark and Paul and Millie were both exhausted, so they moved to her single bed and fell asleep hugging each other tightly, just as they had fifty years earlier. Her place was so big and cheap that within a month he once again gave up his room at the Longacre and moved in with her.

Attempting to focus on his immediate surroundings, Uli desperately tried to find his way back to Water Station 27, but nothing looked familiar. Early the next morning, as he began feeling utterly confused, he spotted a dust cloud just past a small hill—a jeep!

He stumbled up the hill and along the nooks and contours of the rocky landscape, where he glimpsed a man's head behind a windshield moving toward him in the distance. With the rising sun at his back, Uli figured that the driver was probably blinded by the low rays.

"HEY!" he shouted out, and waved.

The vehicle paused almost a hundred feet in front of him, and Uli couldn't imagine how the driver wasn't hearing him. It didn't matter, in a moment the jeep would be right before him. But as the vehicle neared, it slowly turned around.

"Wait a second!" Uli yelled as it sped away. "Fuck!"

Instead of hunkering down in the shade somewhere as he usually did before the day heated up, Uli feverishly continued searching for the water station. By ten a.m., the burned skin along his back and arms started throbbing. Around noon, unable to keep moving, he collapsed.

He awoke in darkness to the sensation of something slithering on his neck. It was some kind of small snake. He wasn't sure if it was poisonous or not, it didn't matter. He grabbed it tightly and bit down with his incisors. Its sleek little body whipped and convulsed around his face.

Uli chewed as much of the rubbery snake as he could, spitting out pieces, trying to extract blood or oil or any other moisture for his dried-out mouth. He closed his eyes as insects buzzed along his ears and lips, pecking at the blood splattered everywhere. He curled into a ball, so cold now that he could see his own breath in the pale moonlight.

46

Now in his early seventies, Paul was finally living with Millie again. Though they were poor, they were very happy together. When weather permitted it, they'd stroll over the Brooklyn Bridge or buy a cheap bottle of red wine, a wheel of Brie, and apples, and take the "five-cent luxury liner" to Staten Island. The worst part of their days was the vertical trek back up the long, splintery stairs to their apartment. Millie didn't have a strong heart so he'd rest with her on the climb instead of speeding ahead. Each landing was like a small base encampment. On bad days, when she was cold and feeling arthritic, it would take up to twenty minutes to ascend to the apartment. Occasionally she had to abandon the climb, moving all the way back down the stairs to visit the bathroom at the Chock Full o'Nuts on Broadway before trying a second time.

When they finally closed the door behind them, Millie would often comment that in just another year or so, when the housing project was finished, she'd be able to move back to her old neighborhood across from Central Park.

"And the place will have a balcony where we can sit down," she speculated one day.

"And don't forget the elevator!" Paul said.

She smiled.

In early 1961, Paul read that stage one of Manhattantown was complete. The first group of houses was accepting applications. So the two of them headed uptown, stood in a long line, and filled out separate applications to the New York City Housing Authority for a two-bedroom apartment.

"Can I ask," Millie said timidly to a short Mediterranean clerk, "how long I will have to wait for my new apartment?"

"Well, we have a lot of applications to review."

Millie mentioned that she had been evicted from one of the buildings to make room for the new project.

"She was told she'd be getting priority," Paul chimed in.

"I see that," the clerk said, pointing to a checked box on one of her forms. "Are you a married couple?"

"Not technically."

"Do you have any children?"

"No."

Peering down at the form, the woman let out a loud sigh. "May I ask why you need a two-bedroom apartment?"

"We were hoping to live together," Paul replied.

"Well, for starters, it would improve your chances if you were married, but it would also help if you applied for a studio apartment."

"My old place extended from the front of the street to the back of the building. It was the equivalent of two bedrooms, and I had full use of the garden."

"Lady, we have thousands of applications from hardworking families."

"But she lived on the site previously and was promised priority housing," Paul insisted.

"I know, but many, many people were displaced by the slum-clearance work. We're trying to prioritize for the neediest."

"It wasn't a slum!" Millie shouted. "It was a nice house on a nice street! And the only reason I left was so that other families could have a home."

"I understand."

"Look, she lives in a fourth-floor walk-up that takes her twenty minutes to climb, and she has a bad heart!" Paul was starting to get agitated.

"There's no need to raise your voice," the clerk responded.

"Paul, let me handle it," Millie said. He sighed and stepped aside. "When I received my notice to vacate, I also received this letter." She removed a folded piece of paper from her purse and recited from memory: *"We at NYCHA promise to rehouse you once new facilities are built on this site."*

"Look, I don't decide policy or choose the order in which people get their apartments. All I'm trying to give you is a reasonable expectation based on the information I've been given."

"Can I get the name and phone number of your supervisor?" Millie asked. The clerk handed her a mimeographed slip—apparently this was a common request.

Over the ensuing weeks, Millie left phone messages and sent a steady stream of letters to various NYCHA offices requesting an apartment assignment, to no avail.

In this period, Paul would sometimes head up to East Tremont and discreetly watch Bea leaving middle school. She had grown from a little girl to a tall, beautiful tween. She looked happy, joking and kidding around with others. *Lucretia would be so happy if she could see this,* he thought. Afterward, he'd walk by the scrapyard.

For the first six months after Leon died, Paul had dropped by and fed the dogs twice a week, but had felt too depressed to sleep there. When he saw on one visit that several of the dogs had been injured, he'd figured that kids from the neighborhood were throwing rocks at them. They had also been growing increasingly high-strung at being left alone. He'd brought the two most injured dogs to the vet, but the bills were more than he could afford, so he had them put down. Paul had taped up signs offering the other dogs up for adoption, but there were no takers. The animals were just too old and surly. Finally, he'd given in and put them all on leashes and walked the entire pack to the ASPCA. When the dogs were gone, kids started climbing over the fence, vandalizing the old yard. Before Paul could sell off the larger scrapping machines, the kids had broken them. After a while, he ceased paying taxes; gradually, more and more time elapsed between visits.

When Uli awoke a short time later he felt a bit stronger—perhaps it was the protein from the snake. He devised a game with himself, seeing how far he could walk with his eyes closed before either feeling like he'd collapse or walking into a rock. About an hour or so later, maybe a mile from where he had begun, he saw the outline of a large mesa off to his right and thought it might provide protection from the sun. But then he quickly decided he could still squeeze in another few hours of hiking before dawn; plus, he somehow sensed the water station was nearby, just behind the next boulder or rise.

When dawn arrived, the landscape was particularly barren. He spotted occasional cacti but none of them cast a large enough shadow to offer relief from the sizzling heat. As he increased his pace searching for cover, he could feel a slight prickling around his face and neck. Tiny insects were still tapping against him. Tiredly, he just kept dropping one foot in front of the other. He found himself counting out ten more steps, then five more, four more . . . The temperature rose steadily, and just after noon, as he staggered forward staring at the ground, he noticed something very odd. He dropped to his knees on the burning sand. A massive spider had spread some kind of long, narrow webbing on the scorched earth. When he reached down to touch it, he saw that it was too big to have been made by an insect. Someone had delicately etched a complex pattern in the sand, a series of small wavy lines. It took him several minutes in his dehydrated state, but he finally realized he was looking at tire tracks.

47

On November 3, 1962, Paul opened the *New York Times* and read that a group of housewives had effectively stopped Robert Moses from bulldozing a small playground in Central Park to turn it into a parking lot for officials. Unlike in East Tremont, this group had top-notch legal representation and their plight was plastered all over the city newspapers. Cover photos showed lines of young mothers pushing their baby carriages in unity, blocking massive earth-moving machines. Soon after that, Robert's plans for an expressway running through Lower Manhattan were brought to a halt. After so many years, his tyrannical hand had finally been stopped. His brother was finally being revealed as the fascist prick he truly was.

Paul's sense of triumph was short-lived, however, as he soon read that the fucker had retaliated against the organized mothers and the rest of New York by going after Pennsylvania Station. With its expansive skylights allowing natural light to bathe its vast Beaux-Arts interior, the station had supposedly been modeled on Rome's ancient Baths of Caracalla. That granite-and-travertine terminal, designed by McKim, Mead & White and completed just fifty-two years earlier, was in Robert's path of destruction. He was going to rip it down and replace it with a tightly compressed, hyperefficient conglomeration of shopping center, office building, sports stadium, and railroad terminal.

Sitting with Millie in Washington Square Park one afternoon, Paul read an editorial in the *New York Times* to her: "*Any city gets what it admires, will pay for, and, ultimately, deserves . . . We want and deserve tin-can architecture in a tin-horn culture. And we will probably be judged not by the monuments we build but by those we have destroyed . . .*"

"I used to wonder why old people were such curmudgeons," Millie said. "Now I know it's 'cause it takes a whole lifetime to see that it's all just getting worse."

"With populations exploding, pollution everywhere, and now the Bomb," Paul said, "I give mankind a couple hundred years, tops."

During their walks through Greenwich Village, Paul would try to paint a verbal picture for her of the things he saw. More and more frequently, he found himself describing an epidemic of flaky kids born in the forties with long stringy hair and bushy mustaches. Paul read about them as well: rock-and-roll music was their anthem; sex and drugs were their pastimes. Though they were lazy, he grew to admire their disdain toward authority. They were organizing against the war in Southeast Asia.

Paul read one article to Millie about their new breed of civil disobedience.

"Good for them," she said.

"I don't entirely agree with them," Paul replied. "I mean, the people of Indochina deserve the same breaks the rest of us get. If American GIs have to teach them that—"

"Where do you think these GIs come from? Some warehouse in Washington? Are *you* willing to die to free French Indochina?"

"Calm down," he said.

"Don't tell me to calm down. I saw thousands of good men and women die in Mexico—for what?"

"The only thing I'd be willing to die for is getting us one of those goddamned project apartments you got cheated out of in Manhattantown."

One afternoon in early December, Paul went up to the Bronx to pay a visual visit to his daughter. He saw her leave school late and then eat a slice of pizza with some cute young boy. When he arrived back home just after six, he opened the door to the lobby, climbed the long stairs up, and found a note on the door:

Your wife Nelly had a heart attack and is in St. Vincent's Hospital. Please call her there. —Chuck Womack (ambulance driver)

Paul dashed down the steps and caught a cab up to St. Vincent's, only to discover that Millie had passed away.

The following day, the super's son dropped by to say he was sorry about Millie's death.

"Thanks."

"We were just wondering if you'll be moving out."

"No, I'll be staying awhile."

"The rent is the same," the super's son said. Finding a new tenant to live in this barren section of town wouldn't be easy.

"Who discovered Millie?" Paul asked.

"I did, I called the cops."

"Was she unconscious?"

"No. She just called down the stairs that she couldn't catch her breath."

"So she didn't fall?" he asked, feeling some relief.

"Oh no, she was okay. I came up and found her sitting right there." He pointed just a few steps below the top landing. "She almost made it."

The kid said he had to take out the garbage and excused himself. Paul walked over to the step Millie had reached and sat down, gliding his fingers along the splintered wood.

Not wanting to die alone in the desert, Uli searched around for her—the raven-haired hallucination who might've been the young Armenian widow, or possibly, inexplicably, a Native American squaw. All he could see was a single barrel cactus near a distant mesa.

He stumbled forward about a hundred feet until the ground shifted and he fell to his knees. The earth was black and hard, like smooth igneous rock. Seeing the clean white lines running up the center, he realized he was on a highway. Suddenly, he was hit by a tremendous rush of wind—a car soared right by him without even slowing down.

48

For the next five years, as soon as Paul opened his eyes every morning, all he wanted to do was join Millie in death. The cobblestones below his window seemed to beckon him. *Just open the window and jump.* Still, a survival instinct compelled him to pull on his clothes and hurry out of the old building. He knew that only when he got outside would he be safe. He was simply too self-conscious to kill himself in public.

At a nearby coffee shop, he'd get a cup and flip through the day's *New York Times*. After all these years, the mayor had finally managed to push Robert out of his sacred spot as parks commissioner—but not before the old prick had managed to hijack the new World's Fair and turn it into a major debacle. The only real control Robert still exercised over the city emanated from his sacred Triborough Bridge Authority. The new mayor, John V. Lindsay, resented Robert almost as much as Paul did, yet despite his plea to the New York State Assembly, he couldn't pry the man loose. But it was just a matter of time.

Paul now believed that the only thing keeping him alive was some kind of extraordinary drive to see his younger brother banished completely from public life.

While sitting in the coffee shop one morning in early 1968, he spotted something on page nineteen of the *New York Times*. It was a small, grainy black-and-white photo of a group of diplomats leaving a meeting at the White House. Staring at one of the figures in the photograph, just three-quarters of the man's face, he realized it was his old friend Vladimir Ustinov, who had taught him to build bombs sixty years earlier in Mexico. The caption read, *Attaché to the Russian Embassy.*

"And I thought you were dead, comrade!" he muttered aloud. *I still have your pocket watch somewhere.*

"Refill?" asked the counterman, hearing him saying something.

Paul smiled and shook his head no.

When he returned home, he located a picture of Millie and then one of Lucretia—it was the first time he had looked at his wife's image in several years. He pondered a casual conversation he'd had half a century ago with Vladimir that could possibly become a genuine plan.

The more he thought about how to inflict maximum harm with the 103 cylinders of pitchblende, the further away the idea got from him. What was initially intended as an extreme act of civil disobedience evolved into a question: *Do I actually have the power to make Manhattan uninhabitable, and is this the best way to achieve my goals?* The crimes his brother had inflicted upon him—a career lost, a birthright stolen, loved ones who had died or shunned him—gradually eclipsed his concerns for the people of New York.

Like a nervous tic, his hesitation kept twitching through him over the next couple of days and nights. He began regarding it with a kind of intellectual curiosity: could he actually create a powerful bomb by simply wiring the contents of an abandoned X-ray machine to a triggering mechanism? He almost believed that merely thinking about the process would purge him of the desire. Soon, though, this was all that kept him awake.

Within a few days he became giddy and restless from the notion that *he alone*—an insignificant elderly man, a dismal failure, forgotten by others and nearing the end of his life—could bring down the greatest city in the modern world. By the time Paul finally decided to go through with the project, it had morphed into an intensely personal mission. While he felt that he had perversely squandered his own talents—being born of privilege only served to accentuate the catastrophe of his adult life—this act of political violence might very well be the closest to greatness he would ever come. Paul's thirst for importance in his twilight years rekindled a sense of power that he hadn't felt since his youth, when he still had a bright future before him, a reason to live.

Paul selected his dirtiest, baggiest clothes, then gathered as much money as he could find in the apartment, grabbed a threadbare fedora, and slipped Vladimir's old watch into his pocket. He got on a one thirty train and slept most of the way down to Washington, DC.

As he shuffled through Union Station, somebody offered him a dime. He thanked the man and went to a nearby liquor store to buy a pack of Salems and five small bottles of cheap Scotch. Once he had located the address of the Russian embassy in the phone book, he headed over in a cab. Paul scouted out doorways within a one-block radius where he could keep an eye on the large gray building. In one entrance, he found a wooden milk crate. He unscrewed the first bottle of liquor and slowly sipped from it to brace against the chill, then sat back and soon passed out.

It was dark when somebody shook him awake and told him to move it. He stumbled a few blocks and fell asleep in another vestibule.

The next morning, Paul grabbed a sandwich and smoked some cigarettes, trying not to cough. Again he slept in one of the nearby doorways. Later that afternoon he opened his second bottle of liquor. In yet another spot near the embassy, he drank himself into a slow stupor. The only conscious act he maintained was vigilantly monitoring the embassy door, watching a slow stream of people young and old as they came and went. If the US government had the place under surveillance—and he assumed they did—they were doing a superb job; he didn't see a soul.

He was awoken again a little later, this time by a cop who asked for ID. When he grunted that he didn't have any, the cop cracked his long wooden club on the pavement and told Paul to get moving. He staggered away and soon met up with a small group of winos who bummed cigarettes off of him and gave him directions to the local soup kitchen. He returned the next day, this time a block and a half from the embassy; once again, he proceeded to get plastered.

This went on for the next seven long days, until a random selec-tion of locals came to recognize him. The merciful passersby offered him handouts—cash, food, clothes—but most ignored him if they didn't act disgusted as they passed. Even some of the local beat cops started getting familiar with the harmless old bum who had inexplica-bly made the relatively nice area of Embassy Row his own. Every now and then, Paul would beg from passersby. Sometimes he'd catch cars stopped at a light and jump out to wipe down their windshields with balled-up newspapers. Most drivers honked or flipped on their wind-shield wipers, but some tossed him coins. Despite repeated threats from cops, it simply wasn't worth the paperwork to arrest him.

All the while, Paul kept his eye on the old embassy building, and though he couldn't keep track of every car, he soon identified the one he was looking for.

On the tenth day of living like a beggar in this posh DC neighbor-hood, he decided it was time to make his move. He had his target, a 1963 Mercedes-Benz that exited the embassy most nights between eight and nine. On a small piece of paper in tiny script, Paul wrote:

No one has seen me. Almost 60 years ago you asked if I was ready to tip the country to revolution. I now am, and I have radioactive cylinders, but no explosives or detonators, which I need if you are still offering help. You can find me in the area. —Pablo (your old sapper buddy from Mexico—Viva la Revolucion!)

Paul clamped the small note in the front plate of Vladimir's old pocket watch. Then he waited until eight, eight fifteen, eight thirty, nine, nine thirty. The dark-blue sedan finally exited the compound and stopped in front of him at the corner light. Paul moved forward and quickly started wiping down the windshield. When he held out his hand, the driver simply stared straight ahead. Paul stepped back and walked around the corner. When the light changed, the car turned tightly left as it had every night, whereupon Paul dove onto the hood and rolled off to the pavement.

"*Blyat!*" the driver cried out, screeching to a halt and jumping out of the car. "What the fuck?"

Paul leaped to his feet, pushed past the driver, and leaned into his open door. Two older men were sitting in the backseat, speaking in Russian.

"Vladimir?" Paul asked.

"*Da*," said an aged voice in the darkness.

Just before the driver could grab him, Paul tossed Vladimir the old pocket watch with the note tucked inside. Paul was shoved to the ground.

"What the fuck's your problem?" the driver/bodyguard shouted, then got back inside the Benz and sped off.

Paul slowly picked himself up and limped away.

The next day, instead of buying more liquor, Paul poured cups of hot tea into one of the empty Scotch bottles and sipped it patiently. The one thing he feared most was the cold weather—that alone would force him to leave.

Hope was nearly extinguished by the week's end, but since all that remained was death, Paul lingered in the area. Over the weekend, he broke down and rented a room in a boarding house. Each afternoon he'd walk back to the Russian embassy.

On a chilly afternoon during his fifteenth day in Washington, DC, while resting on a nearby park bench, Paul awoke to the sound of footsteps; a large man with sunglasses and an upturned jacket collar marched right at him in such a menacing way that Paul was sure he was going to get hit. Instead, the man dropped a tightly coiled dollar bill on the ground before Paul without even looking at him. Paul put his foot over the dollar and quickly snatched it.

It wasn't until later, while in the bright light of his little room, that he noticed a phone number. Along the margins of the bill, in a faint pencil, he read:

> *Don't mention any names, only that you want the merchandise, and negotiate for it. Don't contact me again!*

Paul walked cautiously toward Connecticut Avenue, making sure that he wasn't being followed. After ten minutes he was able to hail a taxi cab to take him to Union Station. He waited thirty minutes for the next train, arriving back to New York around one in the morning. He took the subway downtown to Millie's old apartment.

For the first time in a long while, he wanted to live. He knew he had to complete this last, greatest task before he could join those he loved and become part of the past.

Though it was nearly two a.m., he called the number scribbled on the edge of the crinkled dollar.

"Yeah?" said a young male voice.

"I was told you had explosives and a detonator," Paul said bluntly.

The voice laughed. "Let me save us both some time, Mr. G-man . . . The only merchandise of that sort I have is around 150 microspring release switches. But we don't know what the hell to do with them."

"What are they?" Paul was bewildered.

"A thousand bucks a pop is what."

"Are they detonator caps?"

"Nothing on them is explosive. Hell, I don't even think they're illegal."

"They work on a timer?"

"Nope, they're an Italian make, triggered by a tiny radiation detector."

"I don't understand. How can a radiation detector trigger a release spring?"

"Beats me. I think they were produced to fit into something else, but for the life of us, we don't know what."

"Can I see one?"

"Sure, for a thousand bucks."

"How about two hundred?"

"Eight. And that's the bottom-barrel price."

"Look, I just want to see if I can use it. If I can, I'll buy more."

"Eight hundred for one detonator. One hundred and fifty of them for ten grand. It's a wonderful deal."

"How about eight hundred for one, and 102 additional detonators for five thousand?" Paul countered.

"A thousand for one and six thousand dollars for the rest."

"Okay," Paul responded, with nothing else to lose. "I'll test one out and if it works I'll buy the rest."

The youthful voice told him to put a thousand dollars in small bills in a white paper bag and drop it in the public garbage can on the southeast corner of Washington Square Park at eight the following night, then continue east along 4th Street to a pay phone on Broadway, where he would be told where to find the detonator.

"How can you guarantee you won't steal my money?"

"Just do it or don't!" The phone line went dead.

Late the following afternoon Paul withdrew the money from his meager savings account, turned it into ten- and twenty-dollar bills, and stuffed it in a white bag. Then he went down to Greenwich Village and passed some time perusing books at the 8th Street Bookshop. At seven forty-five, he walked down to the park to see if he could spot anyone around. Nobody looked conspicuous. At eight, he dropped the cash in the can and moved on to Broadway as instructed. In his excitement, he virtually ran the whole way, and when he got there the phone was ringing.

"The detonator is in a white bag in the garbage can directly to your left." *Click.*

A small white bag was indeed sitting on top of the garbage. Paul rushed to Leon's scrapyard. There, he studied the device carefully. It was surprisingly small, about the size of a Zippo lighter. When the tiny screened tip, which he assumed was the radiation detector, was placed near the spot where Leon had spilled the pitchblende behind the crane, a small metallic armature popped out about an inch—and that was it! The guy on the phone had been right about one thing. The little metal tracks on the side of the mechanism suggested that the component was made to clip on to something bigger—but what? Since the mechanism lacked any detonator, he wondered how the hell he could utilize it.

What he had was a lead-lined safe buried outside which held 103 cylinders containing a low-level radioactive powder. Now he had this small radiation-triggered switch. *How can I rig this small device so it will release the pitchblende powder in the cylinders that they came in, so that I won't need to transfer the radioactive material?* He pondered this on his trip home.

It wasn't until he was sitting at the counter of the Broadway Chock Full o'Nuts the next morning that it dawned on him: *If I were to release one cylinder of the pitchblende, would it be radioactive enough to trigger a second detonator a block or so away?*

Trudging up the long splintery flights to Millie's—now his—apartment down in the Battery, he thought, *Maybe the spring in the detonator is strong enough to pull open the little panel of the cylinder.* Leon had said he could open it with his finger. Slowly, other thoughts started coming together: Instead of a single centralized contamination bomb, if they were spaced close enough to each other, one click might be able to start a chain reaction. If the pitchblende was all concentrated around Wall Street, it would be relatively easy to quarantine that zone.

He had enough to cover much of Manhattan. But he couldn't just leave them around; kids would grab them. They needed to be elevated *above* the street. Perhaps they could be positioned on the first-floor windows of key buildings. But wouldn't people see the cylinders and notify the police? Also, how the hell could he get access to the windows?

He considered these questions as he exited the Delancey Street subway stop. While looking upward for possible places to install the cylinders, something caught his eye: an old pair of sneakers dangling from a traffic light. He walked down Orchard to Broome and saw it again—someone had thrown another pair of sneakers up around the pole of a traffic light. He turned left and headed back toward Essex, where he found a third pair of sneakers suspended from their laces.

"Sneakers!" Paul shouted.

One small fuck-up! Uli cursed himself, thinking that a single lapse of observation and deduction would cause his inevitable death. His head throbbed in the heat and he realized he just couldn't get up again, much less walk. Closing his eyes, he could see Paul testing his hypothesis. He placed the trigger mechanism in a tree a block away from the spilled pitchblende. Nothing happened. When Paul returned the next day, he found that it clicked open.

Uli started chuckling at the thought of waking and nearly drowning in a giant sewer, only to find himself here, staring up at a massive burning sun, cooking to death on some goddamn interstate in Nevada.

Feeling the hot pavement tremble under him, he realized another car was coming. Somehow mustering a burst of energy, he rolled across the center of the two-lane highway. He heard the vehicle screech, then he clearly envisioned this older bald man named Paul Moses. But only a teenager jumped out of the car.

"I almost hit you, dude!"

"I know him!" Uli shouted to the kid. "I met Paul Moses somewhere."

"Dude, you look burned to a crisp!"

"I met him somewhere!"

"You need help, man. Want me to take you to the hospital?"

"I met him, but . . . I don't know where."

"Come on, try to stand up." The teenager hauled him into the front seat of his VW Bug, then gave him the remainder of his Coke, which Uli drank slowly. "Hold tight, I'll have you back in the city before long."

As the dry wind blasted Uli's face and "Take It to the Limit" by the Eagles blared on the radio, he tried to remember where and when he had seen this strange, bitter old man.

49

Paul had never climbed the steps up to the apartment so quickly. As soon as he got inside, he placed the switch in the toe of one of his large shoes. It was a snug fit—perfect housing for a small bomb. Several major questions loomed: Could the radioactive cylinders also fit in a sneaker? Could the detonator switch be rigged in the toe of a sneaker so that it would pull open the small spring-locked side panel?

It was time to build a prototype.

The next day he caught the subway up to Leon's old scrapyard in Morrisania that had been abandoned to the City of New York along with so many other buildings in the area. After being burgled by the neighborhood kids and set on fire and finally abandoned again, the yard was swarming with rats. Lugging an old winch, complete with chains, a heavy-duty shovel, a metal milk crate, and a hand truck, Paul was able to push it all through a jagged gap in the old hurricane fence. He slowly dug a hole at the edge of the property. When rats grew curious and came close, Paul would stomp the ground and they'd scamper off. After digging three feet, he struck something solid and knew it was the shell of concrete he had laid down years earlier. He used the end of his shovel as a pile driver to crack through the thin layer of concrete that sealed the small vault below. Soon he had chipped enough concrete away to run chains around it. Then, attaching the chains to the winch and the winch to one of the steel poles supporting the fence, he carefully cranked the safe out of the hole. The safe's broken door slowly opened with a loud creak.

Late that night, as rats scurried around the old yard, Paul remembered all the good times he'd had up in the Bronx when Bea was first born and he and Lucretia were deeply in love. He also remembered all the nights spent knocking back beers with Leon while watching the Brooklyn Dodgers. Around four thirty in the morning, he loaded all 103 sealed lead cylinders of pitchblende into a blanket-lined metal milk crate. He abandoned the tools and shovel in the yard and wheeled the loaded hand truck over to the elevated 5 train, where he slowly hauled it up each of the station's countless steps, lifting with his waist, until, bathed in sweat, he had made it to the top. The train arrived forty-five minutes later. The lonely ride downtown took almost an hour. He got out at City Hall and paid some kid a buck to help him carry the hand truck up to street level. He then wheeled it over to his apartment on Broad Street and spent the morning carrying ten cylinders at a time up the long flights of stairs.

The following day, after recovering from this extraordinary effort, Paul went out and purchased a soldering iron. Carefully, he welded a tiny wire to the spring panel of the sample cylinder, so that when the radiation switch clicked open the pitchblende would be exposed to the unsuspecting world. Paul then removed the laces from a large pair of ratty old Converse sneakers he had found in a trash can and was able to slip the cylinder inside and secure the detonator switch to one of the worn soles. When he was done, he laced the sneaker back up— it looked just like any other shoe. Using tweezers and a small knife, he cut along one side of the sneaker so that, if angled downward, all the pitchblende would be able to spill out onto the ground. He also carefully packed cloth in the sneaker to insulate the cylinder. That way, if the laces ever broke and a cylinder fell from a traffic pole, the slot wouldn't accidentally pop open when it hit the ground.

On the night of March 15, 1968, Paul finished his first prototype. Other than the detonator switch, for which he'd spent a thousand dollars, the rest of the shoe bomb had cost him less than fifteen dollars. In the future, though, he'd also have to pay for sneakers since he was unlikely to find many discarded pairs.

Since first moving in with Millie, Paul had been saving as much money as possible, buying cheap food in Chinatown and used clothing from thrift shops. All the while, he still received a steady trickle of income from the little his mother had left him, the disability checks from Social Security, and a tidy sum from the board of ed for his early discharge. Despite all this, however, he had only managed to save a little over five thousand dollars.

It had been weeks since he had called the number Vladimir had written on the side of the dollar bill. The line was busy this time. When he tried it again an hour later, it was still busy. He continued calling it frequently for the next few days. Eventually, someone picked up, but they didn't say a word.

"Hello?" Paul finally spoke.

"Harry?" said a female voice.

"No, I spoke to some guy a few weeks ago. He sold me a gizmo that could be used as a detonator."

"Oh, yeah, sorry. No refunds."

"I want to buy the other ones."

"Really?"

"Yeah."

"Twenty thousand bucks."

"We already agreed on four thousand," Paul lied.

"That guy's not with us anymore. You want the rest, they'll cost you twenty thousand smackers."

"I only have nine," said Paul, pulling the figure from thin air.

"Fuck it. Nine grand then. You know how we want our bills—small and old."

"I'll make them small for you, but it's going to be too much to stuff in a paper bag this time."

"And the numbers on the bills can't be sequential. Just drop off the cash at midnight in the same place you did last time."

"Midnight when?" Paul asked.

"Tonight."

"I won't be in town for at least three days," Paul lied again.

"In exactly one week then," the woman said, and hung up.

Paul immediately emptied his bank account and had the money converted into old five- and ten-dollar bills. He spent the next two days cutting up scrap paper into strips the dimension of dollar bills, wrinkling them, straightening them out again, and bundling them together with real bills on top and bottom to make the full amount look like nine thousand dollars.

At midnight on the designated day, Paul dropped a black plastic garbage bag with about four thousand fattened-up dollars into an empty garbage can at the corner of Washington Square East and 4th Street, then dashed like a madman to the corner of Broadway. This time the phone was not ringing. He dug through the same wire-mesh trash can where he had found the original detonator, but it only held garbage.

Shit, he thought, *they're counting the cash*. After five minutes of waiting, he knew they were on to him. He had taken three steps back toward the park when he heard the phone ringing.

He picked up the receiver and heard, "They're in a garbage bag on the other corner."

"Huh?"

"The southeast corner; the detonators are there."

"Where? What are you saying?"

"Look at the fucking kitty-corner!"

"Okay, I'm looking."

"See the garbage bags?"

"Yeah."

"They're in one of those bags."

Paul hurried across the intersection to a large pile of garbage. He patted along the sides of the bags, discovering that one seemed to contain a group of hard cubic items. He tore the bag open and there they all were, everything he needed.

Ambling down Broadway back to his apartment, all he could think was, *Damn, I probably could've stiffed them the full amount.*

As the VW sped across the barren landscape, Uli kept one eye open, once again searching for the shape-shifting woman who had led him across the arid sea of desolation. He knew she wasn't real, yet he feared she was somehow trapped, doomed to wander this desert forever. Eventually, he spotted a distant clump of buildings looming ahead of them—the sinful City of Las Vegas.

50

If the people who sold Paul the detonator switches wanted revenge for being shortchanged, he never knew it. Over the next couple years Paul would work on the project in fits and starts. After extensive bargain hunting, he found that the best and cheapest sneakers to suit his needs were a crappy Hong Kong brand that would probably fall apart after walking a single block. He purchased 101 pairs, all in size fourteen, at the bulk rate of $150. A month went by before he also picked up several two-pound cones of heavy-duty string. He cut it into four-foot pieces and looped them through the pairs of sneakers so that the laces were extra long for throwing. When lacing the shoes, he poked holes on the far right and left sides of the canvas so that they would hang at an angle that allowed for maximum dispersal of the pitchblende when the side panel clicked open.

Paul decided to keep two cylinders to use as triggers for the entire intricate bomb network. It took nearly two months of painstaking work to match 101 pairs of sneakers with the remaining cylinders and then solder the small wires to the spring switches of 101 detonators. Another month went into painting a bright white stripe along each of the little spring-shut panels. With careful positioning of the cylinder in the shoe, he would be able to spot this white stripe from thirty feet below. Since no explosives would be used, this visual aid would be the only way to detect if the sneaker bomb had been detonated.

Finally, he spent half a year carefully deciding where to place his little bombs. Once he tossed the sneakers up, there would be no getting them back. He guessed that they couldn't be spread more than two blocks apart, otherwise the level of radioactivity might be too low to trigger the next bomb.

Taping a street map of Manhattan to his wall, Paul used red thumbtacks to designate key targets—major intersections and important buildings—and white tacks for bombs bridging between them. He identified major business, political, and cultural institutions: City Hall, the New York Stock Exchange, New York University, Madison

Square Garden, Rockefeller Center, the Museum of Modern Art, Lincoln Center, the Empire State Building, and so on. Over the ensuing weeks, he modified his tack diagrams repeatedly.

After finishing his map, at the age of eighty-one, Paul slowly walked the route, pausing at the 101 intersections, searching out the supporting rods he might toss the sneakers over.

In the early morning hours of March 20, 1969, the first day of spring, Paul launched his little municipal odyssey. On day one, he was only able to sling three pairs up before heading home exhausted. The next night, he took cabs instead of walking and was able to sling sneakers around five more targets. At first he'd average about five tosses before the long sneaker laces caught the overhead bars and swung above the traffic lights. Only one sneaker contained the toxic cylinder; the second was just a counterweight. Gradually his throwing improved. But the task was always challenging: he had to do it in the time that it took for the traffic light to change. When he'd miss his mark, he would try to catch the falling sneakers. If he didn't catch them, his heart would freeze as he'd watch them hit the pavement. Each time he'd check, and he was always grateful the cylinder hadn't popped open.

And if all this wasn't pressure enough, he'd usually have a couple of sleepy drivers staring at him. Three times, after swinging the sneakers around the overhead poles, he glanced over to see a cop car at the light. The officers usually looked bewildered; one even smiled. Not once did they say anything, nor to his knowledge did anyone call in a complaint. In an empty city that was barely able to keep up with serious crimes, a crazy old bum walking alone in the middle of the night, tossing sneakers around traffic lights—a common practice among teenagers—simply did not arouse any serious concern.

Weather permitting, this became his daily activity. Hitting different sections of nocturnal Manhattan, Paul wanted a pair of sneakers dangling as close as he could manage to nearly every major target. He positioned three pairs around his brother's shiny new Madison Square Garden. Conversely, he deliberately circumvented Grand Central Station and—despite the fact that his brother had had a hand in it—the United Nations. He also wanted to hit Columbia University— that bastion of privilege—but he didn't have the bombing capability to stretch that far uptown.

At five thirty on the morning of August 3, 1969, seven months into Richard M. Nixon's presidency, Paul Moses hurled the last of his 101 bombs.

When he got home that night, imagining that both Millie and Lucretia were forever by his side, he tiredly announced, "Well, ladies, I've avenged you both, along with countless others that he screwed over."

Paul had two remaining cylinders at the house that he'd use to trigger all the others. It was simply a matter of opening the side panels and dumping the pitchblende out his window—then it was over. He didn't know how quickly the dust would travel, or how sensitive the sensors would turn out to be, but he felt confident that he had done everything he could to honor the lives of all those nameless citizens whose well-being had been destroyed by his brother and the heartless city that empowered him.

Paul spent the next several days constructing a small wooden frame to hold the two cylinders outside his apartment window. He soldered little wires to their panel doors and twined them together to attach to a single lever. Somehow, creating a formal trigger mechanism to set off the devices made this unthinkable task a little easier.

He established his own private D-Day as Labor Day 1969, but the day came and went. So he established a new D-Day, Halloween. At that point, some of the sneakers had been hanging for as long as seven months, so he used the intervening time to check around the city and make sure they were still in place. He was pleasantly surprised to find all bombs were where they should be, so he anxiously awaited the day on which he would give the city the greatest trick or treat in history. But taking the lever in hand when October 31 arrived, hard as he tried to detonate the cylinder trigger, he just couldn't do it. Thanksgiving would be better: no children would be out on the streets; people would be away for the holidays. Again he held the switch, but he still couldn't pull it. Christmas and New Year's both came and went.

It was 1970. *How much longer will I be alive?*

Despite a lifetime of pain and failure, Paul was being inadvertently forced to consider the true ramifications of what he had engineered. Although he planned to notify the authorities once the first bomb was detonated—in order to avoid human injuries—the poor would inevitably be impacted much worse than the rich.

Furthermore, newspaper reports indicated that his brother's ties to power were being slowly clipped away. Rockefeller was finally forcing Robert out of his Triborough Bridge Authority spiderweb, which was being absorbed into the MTA.

It wasn't until the second week of 1970 that Paul figured out what he had to do: go back across the city at night and carefully cut down all the sneakers.

With a sigh of relief, he clipped the wires to each of the two trigger cylinders, but left them hanging out of his window until he could find a suitable place to dispose of them. It then took several days to design and construct a twenty-foot pole made from three segments of light aluminum piping. He bought a flag holder's belt that came with a leather pouch to fit the pole into. On the other end he installed a large pair of spring-coiled scissors with a piece of thick string that dangled down to the bottom. He would first try to hook the sneakers to remove them, and if that didn't work, he'd pull the string and shear the laces, allowing the shoes to drop harmlessly into a heavily upholstered cardboard box that he'd place directly below. If this approach worked, the entire operation would take about ten minutes—multiplied by 101 pairs of sneakers. He planned to do it between two and four in the morning to minimize human contact. He even swiped an orange cone from a construction site, which he would use to block street lanes as he worked. He also bought a red vest to look modestly official.

The first night, though something felt off, he headed out. He waited until three in the morning, carefully screwing his three aluminum pipes together, running the string from the shears to the bottom, then heaved the contraption up. No cars were in sight in either direction so he walked into the intersection directly below what he thought of as Sneakers #1. He struggled to hook the rod under the long lacing. It was much heavier and more unwieldy than he had anticipated.

Just as he finally caught the lace, a fist from out of nowhere slammed into his face, knocking him and the pole to the ground.

When Paul came to moments later, a squat, middle-aged man was standing over him. Paul squinted and momentarily thought that he looked familiar, but quickly turned his attention to the fact that the guy had dismantled the pole and had already snapped two of the three pipes in half. The stranger began whacking the scissored end of the top pipe against the ground until it broke as well.

Run! Paul thought as he pulled himself up to his feet, only to be pushed forward, landing hard on the broken pavement. Jumping upon Paul's back, the man shoved a small photograph in front of his face.

"Recognize her?" The man's voice was shrill and unsteady.

It was a school photo of his daughter Bea. He hadn't had any direct contact with her for years and hadn't even seen her since he'd begun his sneaker odyssey.

"We know where she lives, and if you try doing anything to a single one of those fucking sneakers, if you even *think* about calling the police, I will fuck her while strangling her with my own bare hands."

Paul didn't make a sound.

"Think I'm kidding?"

"No," Paul said.

The man lifted him to his feet and spun him around so they were face-to-face.

"I can stomp you to death right this moment and make it look like one of the five unsolved murders that occur every week in New York. Or . . . I can let you crawl back up to your shithole on the top floor of 98 Broad Street and you can live out the few days you have left in peace."

"Look, those sneakers have radioactive matter in them," Paul appealed. "They have to be cut down or this city—"

"The sneakers are *ours*. You have nothing to worry about. We're not going to let anything happen to them."

"Why don't you just let me take them down?"

"We'll do it when we're ready."

"Who are you?" Paul asked, squinting his eyes again.

The squat man shoved Paul back to the ground and kicked him hard in the side. "Quit looking at me. Just go home and count your blessings."

Paul slowly rose to his feet. Without turning around, he limped painfully down the block and back up to his apartment. He cleaned his bloodied knees, put some ice on his bruised face, and wondered what to do. He had created an elegantly simple system of bombs that someone else had stumbled upon and was protecting. Who? Why? In his ninth decade, arthritis racked his knees and bent his fingers. When he wasn't tired, he was encased in pain. Worse, he was steadily losing his focus. His mind was wandering more freely each day. He pondered calling the police, notifying them of the dire situation, and then killing himself, hoping that since he'd be dead, *they* might leave his daughter alone. But there were no guarantees and he wouldn't put Bea in jeopardy.

"Being of sound mind and body, do you consent to continue your mission and—"

"I do ███████████████████████

"You're not going to remember this, which is why we're taping it, but I just want you to know for the record that none of this was planned. New York, the Mkultra—it was all an accident. But I don't need to tell you that, do I?"

When the patches were briefly removed from his eyes, Uli glimpsed a woman with two black eyes. Root Ginseng?

51

One afternoon in March, while sitting at the Midtown library studying microfilm detailing some of the complex legislation his brother had written under Governor Al Smith, Paul glanced over at a young fellow reading the *Daily News*. The headline proclaimed, "Bomb Factory Blows Up."

Paul panicked, nearly pissing his pants. He feared the headline referred to his unaborted endeavor. *But wait, nothing could have actually blown up. I didn't use any explosives.* He politely asked the man if he could scan the story.

"Why don't you buy your own paper, bub?"

"Here's a quarter, pal, just let me read the cover story, please."

The guy thrust the paper at him angrily. Paul quickly read the article. A bomb had gone off in the basement of some rich family's brownstone in Greenwich Village. On 11th Street, a bunch of hippies had been seen running from the blast. Relieved, Paul handed the paper back and tried returning to the old legislation he was researching, but felt too jittery. He soon left the library, and while walking along 42nd he spotted a pair of sneakers just where he had tossed them. He could still see the bright white stripe along the inside of one shoe, indicating that the little panel was still closed shut. All was still secure. He wondered how long the laces would hold before they'd fall on their own volition.

He calmly took the RR train down to Whitehall Station. At the top of the stairs, he paused and looked over at Sneakers #1, the pair closest to his house. A steady wind was gently swaying the shoes in a slow circle. He stood staring intently for a minute but couldn't quite confirm that the little white stripe was intact. He blamed his poor eyesight and ambled home, proceeding up the four flights that seemed to have gotten longer with each year. When he reached the top landing, he noticed that his door was slightly ajar. Entering, he discovered that the wooden frame was splintered.

Someone must've kicked the door in. He had a roll of ten-dollar bills in the top shelf of his cabinet. He immediately checked and found that the cash was still there. After several more minutes of searching through the apartment, he happened to glance over to the window where he had snipped the trigger wires. Someone had manually pulled the cut wires back, releasing the pitchblende. The shock of it hit him in the gut. Someone had activated the bombs!

He grabbed the phone and called the police.

"First Precinct," answered a desk sergeant.

"I'm calling to report that you had better remove all sneakers hanging from intersections throughout Manhattan or—"

The sergeant hung up on him.

Paul dialed again, but before anyone answered, he remembered the suffering Leon had undergone after being exposed to the granules.

"I gotta get the hell out of here!" Paul said aloud, feeling a strong wave of panic. He started tossing clothes, cash, ID, and a few other items into a shopping bag. Seven minutes later he was downstairs. Fortunately, the wind was blowing from the east that day. Paul realized it would be safest to head up Water Street. He made his way circuitously over to the Brooklyn Bridge and hurried out onto the walkway over the East River. Twenty extremely anxious minutes later, moving as fast as he possibly could, he reached Cadman Plaza in Brooklyn Heights.

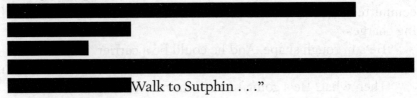

Walk to Sutphin . . .”

"He's saying it again."

"Like a broken record. What the fuck are we supposed to do with him? Maybe we should dump him onto Sutphin Boulevard?"

Chuckles.

"Give him some credit. He's the only one who made it out of that shithole alive."

Uli vaguely recognized one of the voices but couldn't put a name to it. His eyes were covered and he could feel that much of his skin was bandaged. He kept up his steady breathing so they wouldn't know he had woken up.

"I'm sure others made it out."

"He's the first we know about."

"It's a shame we caught him. Are you going to flush him back down the drain?"

"No, fucking Wilson is running wild down there. He should've been rotated out after his initial mission. And this guy never should've been sent in. Should've been disqualified as a conflict of interest due to his sister."

"Please! Don't even bring Karen up. I still feel crappy about that."

Me too, Uli thought.

"At least he's resourceful."

"Very! First he gets brained by Underwood and Chain, and then he somehow manages to kill them."

"I can't believe he didn't get killed by Patel under the bridge."

"He actually did us a big favor by getting rid of Underpants and Dickhead. Those two were a menace. I mean, you don't take an active agent and guinea-pig him! What's wrong with them?"

"So what are we going to do with him now?"

"I don't know. I can't let him go. But I don't want him to stay."

"You *can* kill him. I mean, everyone will think one of Underpants's men did it. And you don't have to worry about his sister anymore."

"The whole reason I sent Karen down there was that I figured at least the two would be together."

"So what now?" This voice was sounding exasperated.

"Eventually everything we do here will come out before some sub-committee hearing, and when it does, I don't want to find myself facing charges."

"He's in rough shape. And he could be a carrier."

"We can hold him in the tube for a while just to quarantine him."

"Then what? He's going to need more than a couple weeks."

"I know where we can put him—up in Pelham. Erica owes me big time, I'll have her sit on him."

"She'll kill him in the name of Jesus. Or he'll kill her."

"I should only be so lucky." The voice paused. "What I'll do is notify Marsha Johnson from PP—she knew him and she's friends with Erica. She won't kill him if someone else can rat her out. And Erica wouldn't dare touch Marsha."

"Are you going to interrogate him first?"

"What for?"

"He keeps babbling about someone named Paul."

"I know everything I need to know about that old prick."

Uli opened his eyes, gasping for breath. He was in a bed surrounded by strangers. Every part of his body was either numb or in pain. Two IVs were dripping into his arms and he had bandages wrapped around his limbs and face.

"Where am I?" He tried but was unable to rise.

"In the Bronx. My name is Erica Rudolph."

He was able to nudge aside the gauze covering one eye and saw Marsha Johnson, his old supervisor from Pure-ile Plurality, the community service organization with ties to the Pigger gang. "Bronx, New York City?" he asked hopefully.

"Bronx, Nevada," answered Erica, who looked a bit like an actress Uli somehow remembered, Donna Reed.

"I remember seeing Vegas," he said sluggishly. "How did I get here?"

"An angel brought you to our door," Erica said.

"Third-degree sunburns cover more than 70 percent of your skin. It's clear you got stuck in the desert." Marsha seemed more helpful than this other woman. She explained that he had been in a coma for at least a week. He was recuperating in a small room that resembled an attic.

"Where are the two guys?" Uli asked, glancing around.

"In addition to your burns," Erica ignored his question, "you have dysentery and you're severely malnourished."

"I just can't believe that after all I've been through, I'm back here."

"Where did you go?" Marsha asked earnestly.

"Do you know that hole in the sewer pipe down in Staten Island?"

"Yeah, you're supposed to take some ridiculous drug and—"

"I went down it."

"No doubt to evade the police," Erica said. "A news report says that you were last seen in handcuffs in a car with Officer Chain and Commissioner Underwood. It says you somehow got free and killed both of them."

"Does that sound likely?"

"Poor Patricia Itt had her right arm severed as punishment for the killing of Daniel Ellsberg," Marsha said softly. "I know she was innocent."

"What year is it?" Uli asked.

"1981." After a pause Marsha said, "What was it like down there?"

"Give me a break. I know why you're here." He was growing belligerent.

"Why?"

"Standard interrogation technique—good cop, bad cop."

"I'm not trying to interrogate you," Marsha gently protested. "I'm trying to help you."

"Where are the other guys?" he asked.

"What guys?"

"I heard two other guys talking."

"You were hallucinating," Erica replied impatiently. Taking a syringe, she seemed to inject something into his IV tube.

"You're the only Pigger I ever liked," he said to Marsha as he began to slip away, "so they obviously brought you in as the . . ."

"Not everything is as it appears," she whispered. "Just try to sleep."

Something—someone—was pushing back into his head, and he knew it could only be one person. He closed his eyes and saw Paul running down Court Street in Brooklyn until he reached a subway stop. Paul was heading for the RR train to God knows where. Racing down into the subway station, his stiff legs got jumbled and he found his large brittle frame collapsing, rolling head over heels down the steep stone steps. He felt his ribs crack as he hit the bottom landing.

"You okay, mister?" some high school kid asked, staring down at him.

Within five minutes, a transit cop arrived. Blood was dripping out of Paul's mouth and nose, and pain was shooting through his arms and ribs. Twenty minutes later, to his horror, an ambulance was rushing him back to a hospital in Manhattan.

An intern looked him over, gave him some pills, a shot, took an X-ray, and then wheeled him into a charity ward with three other men. He had two broken ribs, a broken arm, and a slight concussion. The good news was that neither of his legs were injured, meaning he'd be able to check out of the hospital sooner. Since he was a veteran and had no money, and desperately wanted to get the hell away from radioactive Manhattan, he was informed that he could get outpatient treatment at the VA hospital in the Bronx.

After nearly a week, shaky and alone, Paul checked out and took a cab up to the VA hospital, where they found a bed for him to complete his inpatient recovery. Over the following days, all he could feel was an intensifying guilt: *How could I have been seduced into constructing such an awful thing? What the fuck was I thinking?* He sweat through the night, begging the nurses for painkillers, sleeping pills, anything to knock him out.

One morning, he opened his eyes from a muddy, stale sleep and sitting in front of him was his brother Robert Moses.

"Hi, Paul."

Although he was just a little younger than Paul, Robert could still have passed for late-middle-aged. He was grinning pleasantly, as though it were before Paul had ever gone to Mexico, as though half a century hadn't passed and there hadn't been a million little cuts and stabs that had turned his world into a living hell.

"For starters, this is for you," Robert said, holding up two wrapped parcels. "This is a tape recording of the opening ceremonies of the Robert Moses Niagara Power Plant on the St. Lawrence River. I remember decades back when you wrote that study for Con Ed. Remember, you were dying to build the turbos there? And this other gift is a biography of me."

Paul was so overwhelmed he couldn't even speak.

"One of the nurses here is a cousin of one of my drivers," Robert explained. "He told me that you took a bad spill and were laid up, so I said, *Tell Rockefeller he'll have to wait! I'm going right over to see my brother Paul—*"

"You fucking cocksucker!" Paul finally erupted. "You awful fucking Hitler cocksucker!!!" With his good arm, he grabbed the hardcover book and hurled it right into Robert's face.

"What the hell . . . ?" yelped Robert, grabbing his nose. Blood came trickling down.

"Because of you, it's all fucking ruined!" Paul shouted as Robert rushed out of the room. "This whole city has been destroyed, all dead because of you, you dirty motherfucker!!!"

The hospital room began to fade. Uli envisioned Paul struggling for months with his arm in a filthy cast, unable to get a good night's sleep due to the broken ribs . . . When he got out of the hospital he moved into a hotel in Brooklyn and waited. Only when the full extent of the radiation clusters was slowly realized that summer was Manhattan declared a disaster zone. Come fall, all residents in the southern half of the borough were forcibly evacuated. Uli could see Paul in a slow-moving line with many other seniors, applying for temporary housing until the Manhattan contamination was cleaned up. Months later, when the borough was almost entirely shut down, the old man was wheeled up a ramp out at JFK Airport, onto a plane with others who had been accepted into the Rescue City program in Nevada.

Uli's final image, the last scene in this unwelcome biopic, was Paul Moses, an ancient stick of a man, sitting on a bench in Coney Island, Nevada. Uli saw himself and remembered a previous chapter in his own life, when he was a short-term inductee to the community service group Pure-ile Plurality. He happened to plunk down on the same bench next to Paul, and the older man tried to tell him his life story. Uli soon fell asleep, inadvertently leaning up against the old man. Resting head to head, something had happened. It was as though the nerve endings from the older man's shiny, hairless scalp had fused with Uli's short, bristly hair: memories shot into his skull, to slowly gestate and ultimately unravel during his comatose state in the sewer.

Eventually Paul Moses was gone. Uli fell back into a deep, chemically induced sleep as his body slowly healed, another sad captive in the Bronx.

BOOK THREE

THE
TERRIBLE
BEAUTY
OF
BROOKLYN

For Coree Spencer

For all these things were done by the people who lived
in the land before you, and the land became defiled.
—The Book of Leviticus

1

A massive black wave burst over the wall of sandbags along the Battery, flooding up Broadway. Manhattan was a giant sinking ship. The stern slumped forward, slipping down into dark turbulent seas. The wave roared up Water Street, as well as Pearl and Broad. People and cars were being tossed and swept uptown. For an instant he saw someone he knew swirling around in a whirlpool. He realized it was his sister. She reached up and shouted, "Uli, help!"

"Karen!" he screamed as she struggled to keep her mouth above the lumpy putrefaction. He jerked up to grab her and awoke.

He heard some soft voice whispering a chant and saw an angular woman praying over him. He was in a strange bed, his arms and legs tightly bandaged. Exhausted, he struggled to sit up.

"The sandbags along the southern end of Manhattan," he said. "They're gone!"

The middle-aged Donna Reed stopped praying, surprised to see him awake. "Yeah, that's old news. You missed all the fun."

As Uli began to get his bearings, she assured him that all was fine, and reached up above him, playing with something.

"How did you find me?" Uli asked. "Where's Marsha?!"

"Never you mind."

Uli realized she was toggling a switch on a tube which was connected to an IV bottle hanging above him. Before he could react, he went under.

2

One day in early November 1980, Paul Moses was sitting on his usual bench on the Coney Island boardwalk when he noticed a middle-aged man with rugged good looks who seemed somehow familiar. A Jehovah's Witness, perhaps. Paul offered some of his rugelach, but the man declined.

A little later in the day, the same man plunked down next to him on the bench. "Do I know you, sir?" Paul asked.

"We both fell asleep here yesterday," the man replied courteously.

"Oh, yes!" Paul said, then muttered oddly, "You're the parasite who crawled into my ear, and now I can't get you out of my brain."

At ninety-three years old, Paul's short-term memory wasn't great, but the years had earned him some privileges. "At my age," he said, "everybody is just five things."

"What five things?" the tired man asked.

"Five fingers on the hand. Five appendages on the body. Five books of the Torah. Five boroughs of this city—"

"So what five things are you?" the man interrupted.

"I used to be a father, a son, a husband, a brother, and an uncle."

"Aren't you still?"

"Now I'm a terrorist, a traitor, a coward, a monster, and a fraud."

"Pretty hard on yourself, aren't you?"

Paul explained that his younger brother was none other than the great city planner Robert Moses. Mr. Robert—as he called him—had robbed everything from him: he took Paul's birthright, withdrew all loyalties, denied all affections, and forsook all obligations. But that really came after.

"After what?"

Paul said that he had launched a sizable business enterprise in the years preceding the Great Depression, but it all came to nothing. Just before his beautiful socialite wife left him, all promises of a successful life had become null and void. For almost two years just after World War II he was simply floating without drowning. Then, inexplicably, a dark angel from his deep past appeared out of a brass coffee spout. Her name was Lucretia, and she swooped down and rescued him at the Horn & Hardart Automat on 42nd Street. She pulled him to her bosom and carried him on her angelic wings up to the East Tremont section of the Bronx. There she gave him tireless loyalty, sweet succor, and ironclad devotion. It was a love so extraordinary that even years after she was gone he still found it mind-boggling.

They married and had an adorable little girl, Beatrice. For a while, everything was golden bliss. All the pulverized pieces of his porcelain life had miraculously fused back together. Then, just as he was beginning to feel strong and hopeful, everything shattered yet again. His shiny young wife was found dead, crumpled on the frozen streets of the Bronx.

"What happened then?"

"What you might imagine: I became an alcoholic, got institutionalized. But the worst was yet to come. I lost my perfect daughter, Bea. My greatest curse has always been the fact that I'm a coward. After my wife died, I should've joined her. I should've just killed myself. Instead, after coming through that dark tunnel, I became someone else—I became a seeker of revenge." Before the stranger could comment, Paul added, "See, I was the one who dropped the radioactive fallout all over Manhattan and made it uninhabitable." At that moment, he recalled that he wasn't in New York City at all, but in the middle of an allegedly temporary government facility in the Nevada desert. "We're all stuck here because of me," he said sadly.

Paul paused to see how the stranger would react, but all he could hear was his own deep and steady breathing. Looking over he found that the man was gone. He was alone. Paul realized he must've simply imagined their dialogue.

He struggled to his feet and shuffled back to the Coney Island Old Age Home. His brain felt like a dirty sponge that had just been squeezed out. He returned to his small gray room and lay in bed in the darkness. In a sketchy underwater kind of way, he saw his entire life flow by.

Two mornings later, in the freezing predawn hours of Election Day, a strange, almost soothing odor slowly intensified until he realized it wasn't a metaphor for his diminished mental state but actual smoke. He switched on a lamp, sat up on the edge of his bed, pulled on his old flip-flops, grabbed his cane, and swung himself forward, balancing rickety hips on knobby knees and shaky ankles on bony feet. Halfway down the stairs, he started coughing as the smoke thickened.

One of the red-hot embers from the fireplace had popped onto the threadbare carpet, setting it on fire.

Instead of trying to yell with his reedy little voice, Paul flipped on the high-fidelity system in the corner. It was tuned to the one twenty-four-hour radio station in Rescue City. He turned the volume knob all the way up and the Rolling Stones' "Brown Sugar" shook the rafters. When the other old folks gradually awoke they could smell the smoke, which was now visible as well. Hurrying into the large kitchen, Paul located the garden hose which was kept under the sink. After spending five minutes desperately matching up the metal threads of the nozzle to the inner brass threads of the hose, he pulled the other end as far as he could into the living room and found that the flames had metastasized. They had burned through the old plaster lathe and were spreading inside the building.

Fortunately, to the blare of the music, the seniors were climbing out of bed, pulling on their slippers and robes, and creakily filing down the rear staircase which was still smoke-free. Aaron Nelson, a hero of World War I, was stuck in his wheelchair on the second floor, as was Miss Anita Fletcher, who was attached by a tube to a large respirator the size of a small air conditioner. Paul kept water on the flames on the ground floor, preventing them from invading the eastern side of the old building. Meanwhile, Bob Silva, the drink-sneaking night attendant, finally woke up, painfully hungover. Paul directed him to help the others carry Anita and Aaron down the steps.

Within ten minutes, all sixty-three residents of the Coney Island nursing home were safely out front, nervously clutching whatever small keepsakes and medications they could grab on their way out, watching their building go up in flames.

"What the hell happened?" Lieutenant Al Bud of the Coney Island gangcops asked Paul, who, he had learned, was the first person aware of the tragedy.

"I heard this glass shatter and went downstairs."

"Shattered glass?"

"Huh?"

"You *heard* shattered glass?"

"Yeah, glass shattering. I think someone threw something through the window, 'cause when I got down there, I saw the flames in the middle of the floor and the window in front of the house was broken."

"One of them Pig bastards must've thrown in a Molotov cocktail," a fire inspector said. He was referring to the rival faction, the We the People Party—or the Piggers, as everyone called them—who controlled most of the northern half of Rescue City. Brooklyn and Manhattan were run by the All Are Created Equal Party, commonly called the Crappers.

"You sure it wasn't just a spark from the fireplace?" asked another Crapper officer. The night attendant, Bob Silva, who was standing nearby, tried to appear sober. Among his nightly duties was making sure that the fireplace had been thoroughly extinguished after all had gone to bed.

"I'm telling you, the window was broken when I came downstairs and I didn't see any embers in the fireplace," Paul said. He had mixed feelings about not telling the truth and turning in the good-for-nothing drunk who had almost gotten them all scorched to death. But just last week, the Crapper headquarters had been blown up and both sides were now back on their age-old warpath. Paul knew that the elderly here, who were already Rescue City's lowest priority, would only get better treatment if he pitched them as a casualty in the latest political strife.

When the drunken scalawags in the neighborhood, who doubled as both firefighters and cops—gangcops, they called them—had finally put out the flames, there was little left to salvage. By then the sun had risen like a blood blister in the eastern sky. Below it, the polluted canal served as a comical substitute for the Atlantic Ocean in this particular Coney Island. Paul stared out over the copper patches of desert scrub—algae weeds and occasional strange cacti that he imagined might resemble the ocean floor, were it drained of all water. *Nevada* meant *snow-covered* in Spanish, but the state was actually one of the driest in the country.

When he took a deep breath and tried to relax, the only clear image that came to mind was the shiny brass head of some grinning gargoyle. It was the spigot that pissed brown at the old Horn & Hardart on 42nd Street—coffee! That was where he had first seen the most beautiful girl in the whole wide world, also coffee-brown in color: his soon-to-be wife. She had stood before him, moist with embarrassment. Only in retrospect did he know why she was embarrassed: she had been fully conceived with only one profound flaw, and that was her inexplicable, unearned love for him.

The way a single grain of sand can create a pearl, some sexy image of his younger, powerful self had gotten into her head when she was just a little girl. Over the years, she had covered that notion with layers and layers of romantic fantasies, until she saw him again decades later, ragged and wrinkled in the Automat. By that time he was little more than a bum, a prematurely old, unemployed never-was, while she was a beautiful Mediterranean-Jamaican hybrid that could only be produced in the great immigrant cauldron of New York City. Men gasped when she walked by. Women pretended not to look.

A sudden noise and he was back in the moment, a shriveled nobody stuck in the desert with hundreds of thousands of others in this government-manufactured ghetto, beyond walking distance from any other town or settlement—NIMBY, Nevada.

Lord knows, he thought, staring across the wide expanse around him, *enough people have died trying to break out of here.*

3

In November 1980, Mallory was elected mayor of Rescue City. The following January, Paul's daughter, Bea Moses-Mayer, woke up in the southernmost neighborhood in Staten Island, Nevada—Tottenville. She did what she had done every morning since the assassination: chewed a piece of habanero to wake herself up, wiped the tears from her eyes, and headed over to New Dope. She got in the long, wavy line for her free cup of croak—heavily cut methadone—and then lit up a pipeful of choke—the high-grade, homegrown Hoboken grass. Numbly, she found somewhere to zone out and mindlessly passed into the ether until early evening.

Two months earlier, before his attempted escape, Uli had tackled Bea on the sandy gulch just beyond Staten Island, saving her life. But this had allowed some Pigger assassin to shoot the Staten Island borough president, Adolphus Rafique, rendering him a brain-dead vegetable and leaving Bea in a permanent state of guilt and despair. She had been one of the bodyguards in charge of the borough president. She knew Uli liked her so she tried to forgive him, but he was gone, so she didn't have to test her forgiveness. Lately she found herself wondering if he had actually made it back. He had taken what was allegedly the only way out, escaping down the hole in the giant drain pipe. *He's either dead or free now,* she thought, sucking down her pot. She wished she had the courage to follow him. Either destination would be better than where she was now.

Despite the fact that she was often stoned these days, she was technically still employed by the Verdant League. When she was summoned to her old supervisor's office in the Department of VL Security and handed an envelope, she fully expected, and was almost looking forward to, a dishonorable discharge. To her chagrin, she saw that it was a new assignment—a low-rung job which she normally would've refused. But she knew if she did that she'd lose her free "medication" and would be tossed out of her tiny apartment in the terminal building. The Burnt Men tribe—her former residence—had already reassigned her tent to a new "warrior."

Worse, still, was that her pet cougar, which she'd raised as a kitten, had turned up dead in the reeds beyond the Bay of Death, officially cementing her loneliness.

The new assignment meant she had to ride shotgun with Abe Levitol, the director of New Dope, while he was getting new dope—that was her pun. She and Abe had to personally pick up the vials of methadone from the JFK airfield. Though it was an incredibly hazardous job, after getting repeatedly ripped off by his own employees, the director no longer trusted anyone to do it but himself. It was a simple enough task, so Bea took it. Once a week, she got up at four a.m., met Abe, and together they took the long drive out beyond Howard Beach, Queens. There they submitted a stack of forms and chatted with Emmet Grogan, the director of the Lotus methadone clinic in Little Neck, Queens. Upon retrieving their small weekly allotment for the clinic they would drive back through the abandoned buffer zone of southeastern Queens and northern Brooklyn, over the Zano, and back down to Abe's drug clinic in central Staten Island.

The first two times they did it without incident. In fact, Bea began dozing while Abe drove. By the third time, she was officially bored. The pickup was easy enough, but just before turning into East New York in Brooklyn, a car stalled ahead of them. A massive log suddenly swung out of an abandoned building and slammed into the side of their car. When Bea groggily came to, she and the little solicar were flipped upside down. Fortunately, rescuers had already arrived. She wearily reached into her pocket, found a piece of habanero, and chewed it to revive herself. Only then did she see that they weren't rescuers at all: three human cockroaches scampered around the car collecting all the loose methadone vials that were scattered on the overturned ceiling of the old vehicle. They were being hijacked. She heard gagging, and looked over at Abe. For an instant she thought he had swallowed his tongue in the accident, but then realized one of the hijackers had hastily slit his throat.

Without pausing, Bea reached down to her own knife which was strapped to her ankle. When one of the scavengers came close, she stabbed him in the spleen. Hearing him scream, guy number two, a large beefy fellow, raced around the vehicle to attack Bea, who was still pinned upside down in her seat. She spat the chewed-up hot pepper into her left hand and managed to smear the burning paste into the man's eyes. He screamed in agony. With knife in hand, she scrambled out of the car, only to be cracked over the head by a broomstick. She went down and popped back up, sticking guy number one again, this time hard in the chest. He backed away, cursing, and limped toward a machete he had left on the ground. Fearful that the third motherfucker would join in, she jumped onto Spleen Wound and punched her knife into his heart. Looking around, she saw that the third hijacker had crawled out of the vehicle, seen what had happened, and taken off north.

By this time, the creep she had blinded had also gotten clear of the car and was jerkily dashing up the block with his hands extended outward. Looking at her upside-down vehicle and her dead boss, she yelled, "Fuck!"

East of Bushwick and north of East New York, she was miles from nowhere in the most perilous part of Queens. She knew what she had to do, but couldn't do it alone.

If he hadn't been screaming madly as he tried to run, she probably would've lost track of the habanero-blinded creep. Following behind for a while, she watched him stumble tiredly before moving up alongside him. "Ready to die, asshole?"

"Kill me and I guarantee you're dead," replied the hulking brute as she put her blade to his throat.

"Wanna bet?"

"Not by me. Joe Gallo will get you," he panted.

"You work for Gallo?"

"Yes, ma'am. If you kill me, he'll come after you. I swear it."

"Where's your other pal?" she asked.

"Dario's a coward. He's probably up in Reno by now."

"What's your name?"

"Lorenzo Pistachio."

"Tell you what, nutcase, I'll give you a chance to live, but if you fuck with me again—that's it."

"Yes, thank you, yes," he babbled.

"Put your hands in front of you," she commanded.

Bea took off her belt and strapped his crossed wrists tightly together. Then, without touching him, she directed him to walk back toward the car. To her surprise, the other hijacker was still releasing a death rattle near her overturned vehicle. Then she realized it wasn't him at all, but the poor director. Miraculously, Abe Levitol was still alive, though he had lost a lot of blood. She instructed her blind prisoner to lie on his back as she checked out Abe's injury. Although his throat was slashed and he was covered in blood, it appeared that the knife had only nicked his jugular.

"It's okay, Abe," she said. "I got you."

Bea helped him out of the vehicle, and used a torn-off piece of the dead man's shirt as a compression bandage. The left side of the vehicle was smashed in and its right rear tire was flat, but the engine was still humming, the wheels spinning in empty space. She turned off the ignition and helped the blind giant back on his feet, then escorted him to one side of her solicar and directed him to put his bound hands onto its chassis.

"On the count of three we're going to push with all our might, understand?"

"Yes ma'am."

Bea counted and together they flipped the small car back on its wheels. Then she instructed her muscular prisoner to lie flat on his back again. Removing the one spare from the trunk, she changed the tire and helped the blood-soaked director into the backseat, where he duly passed out. She spent about five minutes retrieving as many of the uncracked methadone vials as she could from the ground and from the pockets of both the dead and blinded hijackers. Once done, she led the blind man away from the car, over to the far corner of the intersection, where she undid her belt from his wrists.

"What are you doing?" he asked.

Bea hurried back and started driving. The solicar moved more slowly than before, but it was still better than walking.

"Please don't leave me here!" the blind man bellowed, following the sound of her engine. "The dogs will get me!"

"The dogs were all killed!" she shouted. "Rinse your eyes, you'll be fine!"

But as she drove up the block, she spotted a pack of canines charging in his direction. In another moment they were upon him. In her rearview, she watched as he blindly whacked at them like a giant bear overwhelmed by wolves. Working as a pack, they tore at his clothes and limbs. Unable to deal with the idea of a man being eaten alive, she turned around and drove into the fray, scattering the beasts.

"Do as I say or I'll let the dogs have you!" she yelled out.

"I swear! I fucking swear!" he responded, now shedding blood. Bea belted his wrists together again, this time behind his back, and shoved him into the passenger seat where he leaned forward onto the dashboard.

It took them nearly thirty minutes before the damaged solicar sputtered into the parking lot of Kings County Clinic. Bea carried a nearly unconscious Abe inside, followed timidly by Pistachio. She released his wrists, and both men were given numbers and told to wait in the reception area. After an hour of holding the bloody rag against his neck wound, Bea realized Abe was going to die very soon unless he received immediate medical attention. She got the blind man to hold the compress on the director's neck wound as she cornered the head nurse in a corridor and bribed her with thirty-two stamps—all the cash the three of them had—to get her boss to the top of the treatment list. It was another fifteen minutes before Abe was brought into surgery. With only a thready pulse, he went under the knife.

"I'm obliged for yer not killing me," said the hijacker, after having his eyes washed out and limbs patched up. Instead of seeking revenge, he simply limped away.

Two hours later, stitched and bandaged, Abe Levitol was dumped in a post-op bed and given a transfusion. By early evening, another shifty nurse evicted him in favor of a patient who provided a larger bribe. The orderlies were about to unload his unconscious body back into one of the chairs in the waiting room when Bea awoke. She instructed them to wheel him out to her badly dented solicar.

As she backed her vehicle out of the lot, Bea realized her battery was low. It had not been recharged, and with the sun down, the car now only ran on stored electricity.

Bea slowly drove west into the black night, through the endless manifold of unlit Brooklyn streets, slowly making her way over the short red arches of the Zano Bridge. The car moved sluggishly, its gears grinding, as they barely made it across the rapid streams of shitty sewage and around the lunar crater–sized potholes of Staten Island. They finally rolled into the service entrance of the New Dope clinic nearly eighteen hours after they'd left. With a collective expression of shock, the clinic staff saw their unconscious leader slumped forward in the front seat, his neck bundled up with bloody gauze like a crimson turtleneck.

"Oh fuck!" the head nurse screamed, and grabbed a gurney. She ordered all available staff outside, where they lifted poor Director Levitol out of the banged-up, blood-splattered car, and wheeled him inside to a treatment room. He was immediately put on an IV and given attention. Bea, who was bruised and covered in other people's dried blood, grabbed the majority of the methadone vials and lumbered into the building.

"What the hell happened?" asked the deputy director.

Bea explained that they had been attacked. As the staff pelted her with questions, she realized she desperately needed her own cup of methadone. After knocking it back, she answered some preliminary questions and then passed out. When she awoke ten hours later, she gave VL Police Chief Loveworks a detailed account of the entire event for the record.

When she was done, Loveworks finished his tea, put down his pencil, and said, "Far out."

4

If Dr. Frankenstein, Walt Disney, and cocksucking Mr. Robert were given a multimillion-dollar budget and a tight deadline to concoct a new, slapdash, mock Big Apple amusement park, this place—Rescue City—would be their monster, Paul thought. That wasn't fair. For all its shortcomings, this really was a superhuman task. To come up with all the thousands of types of buildings, garages, sheds, driveways, bridges, tunnels, and water faucets, arrange them by streets, avenues, and culs-de-sac, complete with sewage and electrical systems, lined with sidewalks, traffic and streetlights—it was a construction project that, in its own uniquely bureaucratic American way, was a spread-out, every-man-is-a-king version of the great pyramids.

Nevada had been the atomic bomb testing site since the fifties. Cardboard cookie-cutter communities had been hastily erected and quickly blown away—all except this one. Supposedly this was once a military-situation city, built for maneuvers and bombing practice, but even that seemed unlikely. These weren't tents or trailers, and certainly not concentration camps. They were grand structures—the Vampire Stake Building, the Brooklyn Bridge, the Staten Island terminal building, and so on—that afforded a modicum of dignity, a passing semblance, even at times a modest extravagance. As an engineer, a student of logic and utility, Paul appreciated all of this.

The one thing he feared the most was that this whole rescue sham, this very place, had inadvertently stumbled upon something new. It was all a convenient trap designed to isolate the poorest, neediest strata of a financially distressed city and chop it off. Others mentioned this as well. But of all the people living here who believed that it was due to some complex conspiracy, only Paul knew that no covert government plan was responsible for the New York bombing—and the mass transplanting that had followed. He knew this because he, and he alone, had caused it.

If the government had intended to exploit the tragedy by turning this place into a permanent internment camp for New York's dispossessed, they had made a complete mess of it. Initially, when the military ran it, nothing functioned. Everything was buried in bureaucracy. Not even the river worked. Protests began within two weeks of arrival, and though they grew more organized, they also grew more violent.

The last straw came about two months later: the EGGS epidemic infected pregnant women; miscarriages occurred before anyone reached the first trimester. After that everyone went berserk.

"THIS IS PRE-MATORIUM!" screamed one local newspaper headline. "Zero Population Growth."

"WE'LL TAKE OUR CHANCES WITH THE RADIATION!" another headline declared.

Overnight the citizens wanted out, but none were permitted onto the steady stream of supply planes leaving the city, so they started killing the soldiers. Rather than engaging in open warfare, a year after Rescue City was founded, the army simply pulled out. Local gangs and governing bodies arose from each of the neighborhoods, and for a while there was constant fighting. Corpses left on the streets were soon commonplace. Assassination, murder, and torture were part of the new political process.

During the worst of the warfare, Paul Moses stayed in his assigned neighborhood in the Bronx, and though he saw violence and occasionally suffered from food shortages, he survived this tricky time of unrest and deprivation.

About eight months after the army left, amid such bloody infighting, one man finally rose above the fray. Jackie Wilson and his small yet fierce gang from Hell's Kitchen quickly got a stranglehold on the city's supplies and were able to consolidate the many warring tribes into two cohesive political parties: the We the People Party (the Piggers), who occupied Queens and the Bronx, and the All Are Created Equal Party (the Crappers), in Brooklyn and Manhattan. No one wanted Staten Island, so anarchists who weren't interested in engaging in the fight moved there.

As peace and order were restored and people were able to travel again, Paul found himself spending more and more time in Lower Manhattan, where he discovered like-minded artistic people. He also reunited with a group of friends from Old Town, who were now scattered throughout Greenwich Village, Nevada.

As Paul approached his tenth decade in the unseasonably warm summer of 1975, he packed a few of his most precious belongings and took to sleeping on the park benches in Lower Manhattan. By fall, even though his mind was still active, his body was crippled with aches and pains.

In an effort to outdo the Piggers' quality of life, the rival Crappers had set up four nursing homes—one in Manhattan and three in Brooklyn.

"They're more like art colonies than homes," said Paul's friend Rodger, who also hung out in the Village. "They feed you and give you basic medical care—I hear you can even get laid."

"I'm nearly ninety."

"Tell me you still don't jerk off," Rodger teased.

"I do, but it takes me all day."

At Rodg's suggestion, Paul looked into the Crapper nursing home program. He quickly discovered that all four of the new houses were already filled to capacity. He was wait-listed, but not for long. By the following month, someone had died in the Coney Island home and they had an available bed. After a short interview where he demonstrated basic competency and self-sufficiency, he was accepted.

That was five years ago. Now, as Paul watched the smoldering building being hosed down, he was out in the cold again. He wondered what had become of his buddy Rodg. Lately, old friends seemed to go to their deaths in groups, as if they were heading to some great party that he wasn't invited to.

Over the next week, sixty-two former occupants of the Coney Island Old Age Home were crowded into the three remaining senior care facilities, and one was placed elsewhere. No one had told any of the orphaned residents about the brand-new home up north. But because Paul was credited as the hero of the firebombing—alerting everyone and trying to water down the fire himself—he alone was offered a room in the facility located in a rather isolated section of Greenpoint, Brooklyn, an area that had seen more than its share of fighting in previous years.

Paul was assigned a corner room on the top floor, from which he could see Newtown Creek at the border of Queens. On his first day there, after he had made the acquaintance of his fellow residents, most of whom he deemed as either droolers or bed wetters, he noticed one who stopped him in his shuffling tracks. Her name was Lucille, and she bore a loose resemblance to what he imagined his beloved wife Lucretia would have looked like if she had never passed away. In fact, he had to force himself to look away as tears welled up in his eyes.

After unpacking his few items, chewing down a tuna fish sandwich with his eight remaining teeth, and taking a shallow nap, Paul grabbed his cane and went for his afternoon constitutional.

"The only thing you have to be careful of," Barry Englander, the center's director, had warned, "are wild dogs. The farther east you go, the more you'll see. They live in all the empty buildings here."

Paul walked around the neighborhood, and when he saw a pack of dogs or other strays, he would clap his hands together and they'd run off. He spotted a few of the old-time diehards who had evidently refused to move when the area became a war zone. Otherwise he seemed to have the streets to himself. Despite all the combat over the years, there was still an abundance of surprisingly solid and empty housing stock.

Almost immediately after Paul's arrival in Greenpoint, one of Mallory's first official acts as the newly elected Crapper mayor was to sit down with the ranking Pigger official, Borough President John Cross Plains of Queens, and extend an olive branch. "If you're willing to pull your gang out of Brooklyn and Manhattan, I'll get the Crappers out of Queens, and we can try to stop with these ridiculous back-and-forth invasions and elections."

It was clear that after years of battling, people on both sides were fed up. The Crappers ended their short-lived occupation of Howard Beach. In return, Pigger patrols immediately withdrew from Greenpoint and their Manhattan outpost of Inwood. Mallory gave a moving speech about reconciliation, which the two Pigger borough presidents publicly applauded, thus signaling a new era of peace, generally referred to as Pax Rescue City.

Overnight, all the alleged terrorist groups who acted on behalf of the two main parties ceased their car bombings and assassinations. The red and blue flags, and matching shirts and guards, all but vanished along the borders. Additionally, the Piggers and Crappers ended their monthly community elections. The charade of local politics was over. The north would be forever Pigger and the south would be forever Crapper.

However, a silent competition soon began: each of the two governments was intent on demonstrating that they could create a better, more civilized place to live. Yet the only program the Queens Piggers were able to effectively fund in order to establish an edge over their southern rivals was the dog-catching unit, which was really just an open hunting season on strays. Afterward, they sold the fresh carcasses to food vendors in the Bronx.

Brooklyn followed suit by hunting down its strays as well. But they also rounded up the exotic animals that had once made Rescue City a giant petting zoo. The north did likewise, and both groups sent all the animals to be slaughtered for food.

After the great hunt, many areas of the city seemed eerily empty. The first to notice that there was nothing to fear were the Verdant League truck drivers who picked up supplies every morning at the JFK airfield and drove through southern Queens and northern Brooklyn hoping to avoid unscheduled tolls and hijackings.

For these men, particularly those who hadn't had their sinuses cauterized to deal with the paralyzing stink from the blocked sanitation drain in Staten Island, this newly safe zone of northern Brooklyn and southern Queens was a refreshing break; a risk well worth taking.

Within weeks, many of the VL truckers had packed up their families and headed over to squat in one of the rows of abandoned homes. As soon as they started moving in, rumors circulated about this new haven. Friends and neighbors quickly followed suit. In rented solicars, on bikes, even by foot, almost the entire hippie-dippie community of central Staten Island, not as extreme as the Burnt Men, tired of the constant reek of shit and living so far from the action, started to migrate. People streamed over the Zano Bridge to the newly discovered community pressed up against the canal dividing these two formerly warring boroughs.

When the steady stream of arriving settlers would cross through Greenpoint and pass old Paul Moses, he'd smile and wave. Sometimes they'd ask him for directions through the unusual network of streets; he loved giving them, even though he didn't have a clue how to navigate the area. He soon took it upon himself to be the official greeter of Greenpoint. Before long, all the unscathed homes had filled up. Nearly twice as many other houses, which had either been burned out or had fallen apart due to years of neglect, were also grabbed and cobbled together.

The burgeoning little community had more than its share of eccentric and quirky members: pagan practitioners, poets of nature, out-of-shape nudists, musicians of self-styled instruments—all joined in the theater of these formerly empty streets. Because many of the new residents were young, hip refugees from Rafique's anarchist borough—along with the fact that they now had easier access to a wider assortment of the Brooklyn dealers who handled the sale of the cheap yet potent Hoboken crop—most of them were choke smokers.

The downside to living up there was the fact that Greenpoint wasn't really policed. At night, thugs from both sides of the borders began to prey on the unsuspecting arrivals, snatching whatever they could. When one middle-aged father fought back to defend his old solicar, he was viciously stabbed to death. Within a week the new settlers had organized several small block patrols. After one would-be burglar was publicly hung in northern Bushwick—his mutilated corpse left dangling from an old lamppost—crime fell to a trickle.

5

About a month after the start of the area's little renaissance, on an unusually warm December night, Paul was snoozing on the front porch of the Greenpoint nursing home when he was awakened by a single low thud that sent a rumble through the earth. He wondered if it was a small earthquake but quickly fell back asleep. Early that morning he was reawakened by a sharp cry. Sitting up slowly, he heard the night-shift supervisor yell out, "No!"

Some of the seniors were nervously standing around whispering.

"What the heck happened?" Paul asked Lucille, the beautiful woman who reminded him of his dead wife.

"Last night someone blew up the sandbags around Manhattan. A bunch of people are dead."

"What sandbags?"

"Haven't you seen Lower Manhattan?"

"I used to live down there," Paul said, confusing Rescue City's Manhattan with the original island where he had previously lived.

"The canal doesn't drain right, so the water was rising way up over the original retaining walls," explained another resident, Sophie Miller. "For years they've been stacking sandbags along the Battery to keep it from flooding into Manhattan. Last night, someone blew up those sandbags."

"Holy cow!" Paul envisioned a watery Manhattan island.

"Weren't they having that hippie festival down there?" someone asked.

"Yeah, it was packed," the night attendant said, red-eyed. It was the tenth annual Antiwar Convention.

"Well, I hope they got out okay."

"Nope, they didn't even see it coming. Lower Manhattan is currently under three to five feet of water."

"Oh God, all those people!" Paul remembered now that the canal water was so toxic that just swimming in it was tantamount to a death sentence. "Why did I ever put those fucking sneakers up?" he uttered aloud.

"What sneakers?" Lucille asked, but he just shook his head and looked down sadly. "Are you okay?"

"As well as anyone can be here," Paul replied.

"I know what you mean," she said, lighting a cigarette.

"What were you in your past life?" he asked.

"School teacher."

"Me too!"

"Where?"

"East Tremont," Paul said.

"Oh, I think I know that school."

They chatted for a while about the intrigues of teaching, then the conversation shifted to their former spouses. Lucille had been married once, back in 1939. Her husband was killed a few years later during the war. Paul recounted his own two marriages: his first divorce and the tragic death of his beautiful second wife.

"Were you in the war?"

"I was a construction supervisor for the last one, but I volunteered for the first one. They gave me a desk job in Washington."

"A desk job—lucky you. When Carl got drafted they sent him right to boot camp and then out to the South Pacific. Since colored troops usually didn't get a chance to fight, he thought he'd be okay, but he was on a frigate that got torpedoed his first day. They should've just shot him in New York and saved all the trouble of training and transporting him halfway around the world." It might have happened more than three decades ago, but her pain was as raw as if it had happened yesterday.

Paul was immediately drawn back to his own tragedy. "They are taken from us for no reason," he bemoaned. "For nothing."

"And we're left to spend the rest of our lives wondering why. Did we do something wrong?" she asked.

"Don't ever think that," he said without hesitation, although it was the very question that had plagued him since arriving in Rescue City. He wondered if it were possible that God was punishing him for what he had done *after* Lucretia had died.

Now, with the blasting of the sandbags and the flooding of Manhattan, so many of the city's luminaries had been extinguished in a single night, including both Allen Ginsberg and Abbie Hoffman. Mayor Mallory called for a week of mourning and held a giant five-borough funeral procession from the Bronx, through Queens, over to Manhattan, into Brooklyn, and then across the Zano Bridge; the deceased would be interred in the city's official graveyard out by the Staten Island dump. Many people lined the path to pay their final respects. Paul, Lucille, and other members of the senior home caught a bus over and watched the seven-car procession pass down Jackie Wilson Way.

Afterward, Lucille and Paul volunteered, along with many others, to help repair the retaining wall. They were deemed too old to shovel sand into canvas bags, and even less fit to join others in passing the bags from hand to hand. One supervisor politely said that if they were interested, they could bring water to the workers, which they did.

"It's uncanny," Paul overheard the Greenpoint nursing home supervisor say that night during a quiet communal dinner. "The same thing happened in the real Manhattan a decade ago."

"Back there it was a cloud of radioactive dust that covered the borough," Paul clarified, "and there were no known casualties."

"It's liquid shit here," Lucille added, "and they're fearing that hundreds will die."

"Maybe they'll fly us back to the old Manhattan while they're cleaning this place up," Sophie Miller suggested, making everyone chuckle.

In the weeks that followed, the four city "hospitals," which were more like large clinics, reported big jumps in the number of cases of infectious diseases. Those who had survived the actual flood went home and showered, only to fall sick days later due to the highly toxic wastewater.

6

Something was hardening, digging deep into his throat. Uli Sarkisian awoke realizing it was not a dream, but a pair of thumbs. Someone was on top of him, strangling him. Heavily sedated, Uli reached up and shoved the heels of his palms into the face of the person throttling him.

"You fucking killed her, didn't you? *Didn't you?!*"

Uli jabbed his thumb into the man's right eye socket, knocking him off the bed and onto the floor. He tried to sit up but could barely move. A moment later the madman was back on top of him. Uli was barely able to grab his hairy wrists when the door flew open and the middle-aged schoolmarm grabbed the strangler and yanked him off.

"He killed her! He's the son of a bitch—"

"He's the only chance we have of surviving the flood!" the school-marm interrupted. The quarreling subsided as they pulled away, and Uli slipped back into sleep.

He didn't know how much time had elapsed when he woke up a second time. Feeling chilly, he pulled the sheet over himself.

He remembered that the woman had introduced herself earlier as Erica Rudolph. Now she was standing over him, adjusting the plastic toggle switch of his IV, muttering again what turned out to be a prayer.

"Why? Who strangled me?" he asked groggily.

"No one, you had a bad dream."

Before he could protest that his throat was sore, he drifted back into a chemically induced sleep.

7

During the week after the flood, First, Second, and Third Avenues north of 14th Street resembled a traffic jam of shacks and hastily erected tents; one shabbily built habitat leaning against the next. When word got out that people from Staten Island were settling in the previously abandoned Greenpoint-Williamsburg area, the refugees of Lower Manhattan, who were by and large among the most liberal residents of Rescue City, also began streaming over the Brooklyn Bridge. The newly elected mayor and her many minions had hoped these displaced people would settle in the empty southeastern districts of Brooklyn—ideally around Flatlands—but they ventured northeast instead. The border areas that the Verdant League emigrants had just moved into had immediately become prime real estate. Since northern Greenpoint was already largely occupied, the waterlogged survivors pushed along the empty corridor across eastern Williamsburg.

The newly settled area was a narrow and neglected corridor only five or six streets wide. Along that isthmus of fallow land were rows of abandoned homes with crumbling facades and interiors in various states of disrepair. Within a matter of weeks, as the flood of Manhattanites left their ramshackle shelters, these old houses were quickly snapped up and gradually renovated. Soon, a second wave of cars and bikes began to swirl into the formerly abandoned northern Bushwick, filling up one house after the next.

Once Bushwick was completely populated, desiccated houses along the northern end of East New York were all that were available, but that's where it ended. The southern sections of all three neighborhoods had long been occupied by Crappers.

Initially the mayor's office perceived this new exodus as a good thing: it fortified the northern Crapper borders with former Manhattan constituents.

"The problem," said Gaspar Stenson, the gangcop captain who was technically in charge of security in the area, "is that these new settlers don't seem to recognize that they're a part of Brooklyn."

"Maybe we should step up patrols," Mayor Mallory suggested.

"Actually, just the opposite," responded Hector Gonzalez, the recently appointed deputy attorney general in charge of the council cops. "We put cops in there, they'll look like an occupying army. We should pull back and let Queens do the job for us."

"Queens?"

"Yeah, the gangs along the southern edge are renegades. They used to invade that area all the time. And once the Piggers start rampaging and bullying the locals, these new settlers will beg for our protection. The best thing we can do is just be nice to these people."

That became their tentative strategy.

During the following week, in January, the settlers who were trying to renovate their new homes discovered a pleasant surprise. On key corners throughout the northern end of the three splintered districts, someone had left building supplies. No one knew who left them, but many theorized it had to be the Crapper city government. Bags of nails, stacks of planks and two-by-fours, crates of hammers, hand-saws, and screwdrivers were loosely distributed around. When this was brought to Captain Stenson's attention, he in turn brought it to the mayor's new task force dedicated to these settlements. All were equally dumbfounded.

"So far, the Piggers haven't harassed them, and even more people are pouring in because of all these building supplies," the mayor said, exasperated.

"We can still wait them out," Hector Gonzalez said. "Once Lower Manhattan is drained and cleaned up, everyone will return to their former homes anyway."

An idyllic quality possessed the area, and the notion of living without gang violence and bullying in a place that didn't reek of shit made the place a low-budget Shangri-la. Throughout Rescue City this new strip suddenly became the most fashionable cluster of neighbor-hoods. Even after the very last run-down, half-burned-out East New York building was occupied by twice the number it was intended for, the stream of people continued. Believing there had to be more homes out there, beyond the reach of the two gangs, the latest immigrants ventured out past the cracked cement, massive potholes, dilapidated warehouses, and imitation industrial parks of northwestern East New York. Soon, heading east on Bushwick Avenue, they reached Rockaway

Boulevard—a wide four-lane road over which supplies were brought from the JFK airfield. The explorers didn't notice or care that they had inadvertently entered the southeastern corner of Queens, an area rife with dog packs, thugs, and hijackers.

These pilgrims drove outward, beyond the wide, sandy field once known as the Aqueduct Dog Track, searching for some forgotten, paint-peeled El Dorado. Instead, they passed semiabandoned warehouses, guarded by Pigger gangcops, lining the north end of the roadway, while rolling sand dunes buffered the south.

After a while, though, another road turned sharply south off of Rockaway Boulevard into the first distribution centers of the airfield. Yet the cars ventured desperately forward, and the most determined found the turnoff that went toward the distant mountains to the east. Eventually it looped around the airfield fence to the dilapidated ghost community of the Rockaways just along the edge of Jamaica Bay. This final neighborhood consisted of several side-by-side streets that looked like four strips of bacon. Each one was packed with narrow wooden bungalows that reached down around the far side of the Jamaica basin—all occupied.

Out there, where the last road hit the final sandy culs-de-sac, those searching for their Rescue City version of the American dream finally turned around and headed back empty-handed.

It was two young adventurers who made the next big breakthrough. Former members of the Burnt Men tribe, these back-to-nature guys from the southern tip of Staten Island were stranded when their old solicar broke down at the barren turn, just as the road curved toward the Rockaways. Since they still had a knapsack full of food and water, and there was no hope of reviving their vehicle, they opted to hike straight into the desert. From there they decided that if they couldn't find a home, at least they'd have an adventure. They hoped to trek all the way south around Brooklyn, along the outside of the canal, and back to Staten Island. After walking roughly forty-five minutes into the desert, they later reported seeing something rocky rising from the dunes. They found a giant maze of thickly stacked stones carved from a granite plateau, some kind of ancient ruin. Because it was so rocky, they jokingly called it Rockville Centre—alluding to Rockville Centre, Long Island.

Around the same time, another stolid explorer noticed a small break in the landscape bordering Rockaway Boulevard. Rummaging around, he discovered a buried street sign. Since he had brought an old map of Rescue City, he realized that the narrow sandy inlet just beyond the Aqueduct Dog Track was Hawtree Pass. It was a forgotten road buried behind the rows of tall, windswept dunes, under years of sand. He and his crew followed this narrow path to a small community of empty houses tucked next to the airfield. When they checked the map, they realized it was officially titled South Ozone Park—or SOP, as it was quickly nicknamed. Since the area was wedged between the airport and the desert, no one had ever even settled there. Though it was only four streets wide by four blocks long, they found that the place was filled with small bungalows that had never been lived in: sinks and toilets were still wrapped in decomposing cellophane. The paint had chipped and in most of the homes the windows were broken. Birds and lizards had flown and slithered inside, building large, multigenerational nests all over.

Once word of the new neighborhood spread, a mini land rush whistled in. Windows were hastily repaired; rotten exteriors were stripped, primed, and given a fresh coat of paint. Unlike the other three newly inhabited districts, this one had only one way in and no through traffic. The only problem was that this splinter community was technically situated in Queens.

At first, the Piggers didn't particularly mind the settlers taking over this place that they had forgotten. But a quiet concern grew when they realized that the roadway to SOP cut off the newly restored Howard Beach from the rest of Queens.

The political machine in Kew Gardens considered sending a detachment of Pigger gangcops down to either enlist or evict those in South Ozone Park. But, since the sandbag blast in the Battery was perceived by many as a covert Pigger attack, and the Crappers flowing in were refugees of that attack, the borough president of Queens, John Cross Plains, chose to give the matter a little time to work itself out.

"The last thing we need is Mallory sending in her gangcops to protect her constituents," he pointed out to his team. "We just ended the border war."

Two things had been quickly determined: first, a secret fanatical group called Domination Theocracy was very likely behind the sandbag attack in Manhattan; and second, they were operating somewhere in the northern boroughs. Vowing that any injury done to Manhattan was an injury to all of Rescue City, Borough President Plains promised full cooperation with the allegedly nonpartisan investigative force run by the council police.

The spirit of cooperation abruptly ended exactly seven days later. This was triggered by an overly aggressive real estate developer from Jamaica, Queens, who started purchasing all the infected lots of Manhattan property he could get his small, itchy hands on. In a matter of days, the developer had snapped up the equivalent of five square blocks of the flooded zone. It was Deputy Attorney General Hector Gonzalez who realized that this wasn't so much an economic venture as a political one, paving the way to turn Lower Manhattan into a new Pigger community; editorials echoed his concerns. Mayor Mallory was compelled to make a bold move—she suspended all real estate transactions in the area until everything was "back to normal," and immediately voided all that had been recently made.

The borough presidents from the Bronx and Queens gave a joint news conference stating that the mayor's decision was clearly a hostile act toward half of her constituency. John Cross Plains of Queens used the opportunity to point out that when Crapper refugees moved into South Ozone Park, he hadn't forced them to change their gang affiliations, nor had he evicted them.

The very next day, the most popular paper in Rescue City, the *Daily Posted New York Times*—which usually had Crapper leanings—reported that since being elected mayor, Mallory had allowed her deputy attorney general to fire all seven Pigger supervisors who used to be in charge of security at JFK. Now the airfield was operated almost exclusively by Crapper gangcops.

The two Piggers borough presidents were indignant, stating that the new mayor clearly had a partisan bias and agenda, and they demanded her immediate resignation.

The mayor responded that, with regard to the Manhattan land sales, she had only frozen them temporarily until after the area had been cleaned up—when their lost value would be fully restored. Mallory also said that she had done no more than her Pigger predecessor, Mayor Shub, had done, or, for that matter, any other politician. Shub, though, had done it subtly, over the course of many years.

8

After a few days of frosty silence, a news conference was called in the Yankee Stadium Civil Headquarters, where the Queens borough president spoke while the Bronx borough president looked on. Plains announced that the Pigger boroughs were being treated less fairly than the Crapper ones. Therefore, they were seceding from Rescue City and forming their own municipality—Rescue City North. He further explained that earlier that day, in a closed session, the councilpeople of the Bronx and Queens had held a special election, and they had elected him, a distinguished hero of the Korean War, as the first mayor of Rescue City North.

"This is not intended as a provocative or hostile act—we're not pulling out of this union. But we do share common sensibilities and interests with the Bronx that we simply don't share with Brooklyn and Manhattan."

Plains appointed an attorney general to handle matters of justice in the "northern" boroughs, then went on to state that he earnestly hoped the two cities could live in peaceful cooperation. "Our city council members will continue to attend weekly meetings, and if allowed, we will be glad to cooperate in all nonsecurity matters, such as Mayor Mallory's new wildlife roundup program. Matters that can be locally run, such as sand removal, will be done by us."

He went on to say that he recognized Mallory's right to administrate the airfield stock and council police force, but he hoped that these matters could be peacefully comanaged.

"Let me conclude by saying that this is not a first-stage effort to take power or grab additional property. The key reason we've done this is to actually build a solution and maintain peace and prosperity between our two groups."

Immediately, Mayor Mallory hurried to the sole Rescue City TV station and responded that she had been elected mayor by the entire city, and that this action on behalf of the Piggers was clearly illegal. Furthermore, the limited stock that was provided by the Feedmore

Corporation simply couldn't support two separate cities. "Only by consolidating our resources," she concluded, "can we hope to provide a decent quality of life for all the citizens here."

But everyone knew this was untrue. Shortly afterward, Mallory finally realized that since the city would be cleaved in two, she could demonstrate her strength by appointing a new attorney general for Rescue City South. Before she could even consider appointing Karen Sarkisian, the new head of the council cops disappeared without a trace while on the job. So the mayor assigned the post to the next best choice, Karen's hardworking second-in-command, Chuck Schuman.

Paul Moses soon noticed the resumption of gangcops patrolling the Greenpoint-Williamsburg borders. For the time being, no one cared about the new settlers; both sides were still too busy keeping an eye on each other. These patrols extended the entire length of the communities right up to the airfield.

In an effort to win the hearts and minds of the border residents, squads of friendly young men with shaggy hair, who seemed to be census enumerators, soon appeared in place of the gangcop patrols. Paul saw them going door-to-door with voter registration forms on clipboards, politely badgering people to sign a statement declaring their loyalty to the Crapper Party.

Although some signed, skepticism spread quickly in the splinter communities, so that many of the transplanted Manhattanites responded that they needed to think about it and refused to put their names down. Graffiti started appearing that said: *Autonomy = Power!*

Early the following week, flyers were mysteriously slipped under everyone's doors like takeout menus. Paul read one to Lucille and his fellow seniors in Greenpoint over dinner that night:

DECLARATION OF INDEPENDENCE
FOR THE PROPOSED CITY OF QUIRKLYN

1. If the Piggers can pull out of Rescue City, why shouldn't we be allowed to do the same?

2. The four community districts that loosely fall around the north end of Brooklyn—a) Greenpoint–East Williamsburg (or Green-Burg), b) Northern Bushwick, c) Northern East New York, and the rediscovered community of d) South Ozone Park (or SOP)—were only recently

resettled. These areas had been either neglected or ravaged during years of gang warfare and were later abandoned by both groups.

3. Since we are in neither Queens nor Brooklyn—and most of us are quirky people from other boroughs—is this not Quirklyn?

4. We already have block associations, which essentially offer a participatory police force (and other city services).

5. Civic history shows that 99 percent of all gang invasions involve a single neighborhood's gang force. Therefore, if our four communities pull together, we should be able to repel attacks from both the bordering Pigger and Crapper gangs.

6. If you enjoy living in an autonomous zone, and believe in our rights for sovereignty from the two groups that have ravished this city thus far, when the Pigger/Crapper officials come to your door and ask you to fill out a voter registration, reply, "No sir, for I am quirky and this is Quirklyn!"

Because the Greenpoint nursing home was organized and supported by the Crapper Party, someone from Attorney General Schuman's office soon arrived—a smart-looking fellow in a blue blazer who, Paul muttered, looked like a yacht skipper. Just after dinner, the skipper rose, went to the head of the table, and said, "My name is J.J. Weltblack, I've been the administrator up here for some time, and folks, we could really use your help."

"Wasn't this place a We the People district until recently?" some coot called out.

"That was just politics. It's always been Brooklyn, but now we got this new group, this new crew of choke-smoking kids—Potland, I call it."

"Did he say Poland?" a hearing-impaired elderly woman asked.

"No, *Pot-land*, like the marijuana drug."

"What exactly are you asking of us?" Lucille pressed.

"We don't know what they want, so we're just trying to keep an eye on them. And seeing how many of you have some time on your hands, we were wondering if you could help us out, and in return we might be able to help you all."

The young skipper unraveled a large tube of white paper and held it up. It turned out to be a rolled-up map of all the streets and build-ings in Greenpoint.

"What we're hoping is to find out who lives here now. Each street in the area, along with each building, has been diagrammed here. If any of you know who lives in these buildings, we're hoping you can just write their name on the house where they live." He pointed to a bunch of empty boxes on the large map. "We're not asking for any intrigues or heroics. We'd just like to know who's who."

With the night attendant Alvin Steward's help, the skipper then went out to his car and carried in a brand-new twenty-seven-inch color TV set, which they put in the community room. Silently, Alvin disconnected the older, smaller black-and-white set, and rewired the videotape machine into the new one and flipped it on. An old epi-sode of *Ben Casey* came on, which was black-and-white anyway, but it was the thought that counted. All applauded Weltblack as he thanked them and left.

"I know the vertical hold didn't work, but I prefer the old set," Paul said loud and clear. "Because I, for one, don't snitch on my neighbors."

"Just hold on there, fella," said a silver-haired fox named Melvin, but he instantly forgot his follow-up thought.

"Who's the neighbors and who's the snitch?" Jacob Gingold spoke for him. "This has been a Crapper neighborhood since Jackie Wil-son first established the parties. All they're trying to do is hold onto what's theirs."

"I'm too old to get into other people's spats," muttered a dark-haired geriatric.

"And I've already spent too much of my life regretting wrong deci-sions I made," Paul said. "I can't go through that again."

"By a show of hands, I think we should see who's for and who's against this snitching business," Lucille declared.

"This isn't about politics," Melvin retorted. "They send a food truck up here once a week."

"He's right!" shouted another old-timer. "Those twenty-pound turkeys on Thanksgiving and Christmas don't just fall out of the sky. We vote this down, and there's no more food."

The majority of the residents were clearly in agreement with Mel-vin's food-truck argument. Paul rose to his feet and, imagining his dear departed wife looking down on him, along with his highly ethical companion Milly, he said: "No one starves here. The place is buried under a mountain of crappy food. We can go to the airfield and get our own boxes of frozen and canned foods. What we can't get is our integrity, and I want to die knowing that I didn't sell out."

"I'm with Paul on this one!" Lucille shouted. "I'd rather starve with a clean soul than grow fat doing someone's else's dirty work."

The matter immediately went to a vote. Everyone except Paul and Lucille elected to undertake the Crapper request.

"Shame on you!" Paul yelled at them.

"You two are hypocrites," Melvin said. "You've been living on their dime all these years and they've asked for nothing but this in return."

"You're right!" Paul said emphatically, rising to his feet. "I'm leaving!"

"Me too," announced Lucille.

"Guys," said Alvin Steward, "let's not go crazy here! No one has to do anything they don't want."

"Sorry, but we'd rather live in the gutter than with Benedict Arnolds and backstabbers!" Lucille countered.

Paul and Lucille teamed up and began discussing their options. Lucille had heard about a place in East New York that was specifically looking for seniors. It was a ground-floor apartment that had just been renovated. So two mornings later they caught the hourly minibus that Quirklyn had just established, and headed east for an interview.

9

The image of Karen swirling in the center of a giant whirlpool was on replay in Uli's head. He kept trying to reach his sister, but only their fingertips could touch. The water kept churning her around and around, yet she was fighting and wouldn't go down. She was stuck there, and he was stuck watching her.

"I'm sorry for getting you into this mess, please forgive me . . . Goodbye, Karen, goodbye," he said tearfully, and using all his strength to lean forward, he was able to gently kiss her on her softly weeping mouth.

A giant fly had landed on the side of Uli's face and began sucking the moisture right out from his chapped lips. When he swatted at it, he accidentally yanked the IV needle out of his forearm. He slept a bit more, still weeping in his dream, but soon he felt himself sweating and began to stir.

The medication had dripped down his arm, wetting the dirty linen around his elbow. He awoke and, quickly realizing what had happened, was able to turn the toggle switch off. Then he reinserted the needle into his arm to dispel any suspicion. Over the next few hours, he felt the fog in his head from the sedative lift, and he started moving his arms and legs as much as he could to get his strength back.

Every half hour or so the door to his room would open, and the guard—the man who had tried to strangle him—would peek in. Uli always pretended to be dozing. After the guard left, Uli knew he'd have a bit of time to himself. Quietly he struggled to his feet and practiced walking around after being supine for so long. Then he crawled back to bed until the next inspection. He searched for a weapon—nothing in the room was useful. He couldn't find any clothes other than the dirty T-shirt and the stained boxers that he had on.

The next time the guard entered, he stayed in the room for a while, making sure the IV was attached to Uli's arm, but he neglected to check the little toggle switch. He listened to Uli's slow, steady breathing. When he finally left, Uli delicately moved the large cabinet blocking the one small window—his sole avenue for escape.

He knew that they would replace the sedative drip every few

hours, so he didn't have long before he'd be discovered. He opened the window and was just able to squeeze out onto the roof of the adjacent carport. Uli could see the distant sewage canal known as the Harlem River and was pretty sure he was somewhere in the South Bronx.

He looked for a possible route to the Crapper sanctuary of Manhattan. The roof had an old wooden trellis coming up the side that would undoubtedly collapse under his weight. A rusty solicar was parked below him in the driveway—its hood might absorb the impact, but the sound of his landing would likely alarm the guard. There was a clump of leafless trees in the neighbor's yard twelve feet away. If he didn't get impaled on the branches they might cushion his fall. Then, if he wasn't injured, he could head southward.

Uli was squeezing back through the small window when he noticed a vehicle turning the corner. It was a Pigger squad car slowly cruising to a halt just half a block away. If he could just get to the cop, he wouldn't have to run or hide. He'd be home free. As the officer got out of his vehicle, Uli heard a voice coming down the hall. He slammed his body into the opening door, battering it against the guard's head. When the man fell to the floor just inside the room, Uli kicked him in the skull until he was out cold.

"Lyle!" Someone downstairs had heard the racket.

"Yeah?" Uli mumbled in response. Slow footsteps were approaching. Uli grabbed the blanket off the bed, shoved it out the window onto the garage roof, and then went through himself. The gangcop down the block had retrieved something from a house across the street and was returning to his squad car. Uli tossed the filthy blanket over the neighbor's tree and, taking a running start, he jumped, snapping all the pointy branches before landing on his hip. Rising slowly with scratches on his arm and the beginnings of a bruise on his forehead, he heard a gasp. Erica Rudolph was staring out the window in horror.

"Officer! Help!" Uli shouted. As he staggered over to the cop, he realized that the flow of sedatives in his system had taken a greater toll than he first thought.

The gangcop turned and nervously looked at Uli zigzagging and limping toward him.

"I'm so sorry," Erica said, opening the front door of her house. "My brother is nothing but a godforsaken drunk!"

Turning, Uli peered at her, lovely as ever with her tense homemaker smile. The previously unconscious Lyle followed. Erica headed over to the cop as Lyle ran up and grabbed Uli by his shirt collar.

"Officer! She's holding me hostage!" Uli yelled, struggling with his captor.

"Let's get you back in bed," Lyle said, a beanie hiding the bloody head wound that Uli had just inflicted on him.

"Officer, these people are trying . . . they're . . . they're . . ." Uli had difficulty speaking, the residual opiates still slurring his thoughts.

"You are fucking dead!" Lyle muttered, too low for the cop to hear, as he finally secured Uli's arms behind his back and shoved him toward the house.

"My word, he can just chug Scotch down like its Dr Pepper." Erica was talking in a singsong tone.

Using all his concentration, Uli kicked back his heel, cracking hard into Lyle's shin. By shoving his body backward, he knocked Lyle on his ass. Too shaky to run, Uli grabbed an old rake that was leaning against the carport and, mustering up the last of his strength, hurled it like a harpoon right through the windshield of the police cruiser.

"What the fuck did you just do?" snapped a second cop, coming out of the passenger side.

"Officer, I'm glad to pay for whatever that glass might cost," Erica said as Lyle knocked Uli down and locked him in a painful quarter nelson.

The second cop rushed over to them on the ground. Before the officer could reprimand him, Uli smashed the heel of his free hand into the man's knee.

Both gangcops immediately jumped on Uli. Within moments, he was facedown and handcuffed. Lyle stood alongside, smiling.

"Officer, please! My brother's not right in the head!" Erica appealed. Finally, the first cop pulled Uli to his feet, but before he could toss him into the backseat of the squad car, Erica grabbed his waist and, feigning tears, refused to let her "brother" go.

"Release the goddamned prisoner, ma'am," the second cop demanded.

She held onto Uli for dear life. "My mother will just die if I—"

"Ma'am, release him or I'm going to arrest you, and that'll mean a nice, thick back scar."

"Can't you just clip his fingers off now?" she asked, as though she were talking about his fingernails.

"We don't do shit like that no more."

"Hostage, I'm an officer," Uli slurred as blood trickled from his own nose and lips.

Erica clung to his aching body as if it were a life buoy. "Look, I have some things in the house, perhaps there's some way I can compensate you for your pain," she said, trying her best to be seductive.

The second cop reached for a plastic zip tie, yanked her off Uli, and secured the backs of her slender wrists together. "Lady, you just earned yourself a scar."

Lyle could only watch as Uli and Erica were placed in the back of the car and driven away.

The two were taken to the local precinct, where their bodies were checked for priors—scars or amputated parts.

After a few hours of incarceration, the sedatives wore off enough for Uli to walk and talk more clearly. He was issued khakis, a T-shirt, and a small pair of flip-flops. He tried to explain that the woman who he'd been arrested with had held him hostage, but the guards didn't care. They just wanted to know his name, which he had thus far not provided.

Fearful that there might be a warrant out on him for killing Newton Underwood and company, Uli invented the name Huey Baxter. He figured he'd be able to talk to someone once he was transferred to Brooklyn, but he was quickly informed that the Pigger boroughs had just broken away and formed their own city.

Eventually, Uli was cuffed with a dozen other men and driven down a long narrow street, Crotona Boulevard, with a brick wall at the far end. The van turned into a courtyard, and the doors were only opened once the large wooden gate behind it was sealed. They entered an old building with an outdated sign that read, *Visitors Center*. Inside, he was shoved into a small room with a desk where he was checked by two guards for contraband. His fingerprints were taken. If they had his prints on file from earlier, they didn't turn up. He was marched into a holding cell, and an hour later the entire group of prisoners was taken into another room and pushed to their knees.

Uli looked up to see the fleshy face of an immense woman with sagging jowls, multiple chins, and a small eye patch that was deeply sunk into her ocular cavity. She was chewing on some kind of bone.

"Don't look up if you don't want pain," one of the guards warned.

"I'm Captain Polly Femus," the woman said. "This is my camp, and while you're here you'll do as you're told—or else."

After this ominous declaration, the prisoners were hustled out of the building into another courtyard.

Uli walked down a barred ramp into a spacious open-air prison yard. If it weren't for the muddy, wet ground, it wouldn't have been so bad. Almost immediately he was approached by half of a two-man team: an armless inmate named Bert, who used one leg to propel a large, red Radio Flyer wagon around. Bert introduced his partner Troy, who was lying on him and had one arm but no legs. Uli asked what the musky aroma in the air was.

"This used to be an elephant pen," Bert replied.

"You're kidding."

"All these cells around here were originally animal cages in the Nevada Bronx Zoo," Bert explained. Over the past couple of months, the few remaining animals that hadn't been set free years ago were killed for meat. Since the Piggers could no longer utilize the Brooklyn penal system, Mayor John Cross Plains of Rescue City North expanded the zoo into a proper prison; before it had mainly housed select criminals. "All the women are locked up over there." He pointed to a nearby wall. "That's the old cat house. Funny, huh?"

The two men had been partnered up in Rescue City's "Two Halves

Make a Whole" program, which aimed to help amputees function together. Though now, when one of them was jailed, the other was forced to go along. Bert was clearly the brains of the operation.

As the hours passed, Bert gave Uli an account of his thoughtless crimes and the amputation penalties for each. One by one, he had lost all the fingers on his right hand, for minor crimes ("Shoplifting and the like"). Then, they took three fingers on his left hand for assault ("I punched out a Staten Island anarchist for badmouthing the Vietnam War"). Next, he lost his already fingerless right arm for participating in a violent robbery. Soon after, he lost one leg and his other arm.

"What are you in for now?" Uli asked.

"We was framed," said Troy.

"I was asleep when it happened," Bert added.

"The cop said we was part of some Crapper conspiracy to disrupt the Pigger autonomy movement. I think they just rounded up the usual suspects, and we got caught in the net."

"It's not uncommon. Troy and a bunch of other innocent people lost a paw when the Crappers blew up the Stamp Treasury in Queens about five years back."

Uli hadn't heard about that one.

"I think it was 'cause we joined that protest against the killing of the feral dogs," Bert continued. "We're deathly afraid of wild dogs, but they kept the snake and rodent population in check and that's even worse for us. Anyway, they got my left leg for kicking a cop, which was pretty fucking extreme."

"You got a bad surlawyer!"

Uli panicked when he heard this, considering he had just punched a cop in the knee. "So what did you do?" he asked.

"Nothing! I swear it," Bert said. "I'm just praying they only take my last two toes. That'll make it tough to move around, but I think I'll still be able to hop."

"If they take the foot," Troy said, "we'll both have to get different partners."

"Think positive thoughts," Bert soothed.

"I miss this finger the most." Troy held up the stub of his left index finger. "That was the last finger I needed to . . . self-satisfy."

Troy had to use the bathroom so Bert shoved their cart off to a discreet corner where the bucket was located. Since Uli had come in last, he was unable to get anywhere near the sunny mound in the front—the driest spot in the yard. He located a moist yet quiet area against the rusty bars where he was able to rest his bruised and aching body.

After a couple of hours of dozing, Uli awoke to the stampede of feet. A box of sandwiches had just been tossed in and most of the prisoners were running for them.

Since miraculously surviving the desert, Uli had been almost exclusively sustained by an IV tube, so he was hungry for some solids. Scrambling in the mud, he was able to fish out a sandwich. It was wrapped in cellophane to keep it dry, but it was stiff as cardboard. Without taking a bite, he handed it off to Troy, who shared it with Bert.

10

Although some of the older residents in the four districts protested the independence of Quirklyn, no immediate action was taken. The majority of settlers tacitly supported the idea of independence. Block watch groups became the organizing forces for its rudimentary police, sanitation, and fire departments.

A few days after the Quirklyn flyer was distributed—and on the heels of the Pigger declaration of independence as well—the new head of the council cops, Hector Gonzalez, advised the mayor that they had to invade at once. They needed to reclaim not only the splinter Quirklyn neighborhoods, but the northern Pigger boroughs of Queens and the Bronx too: Rescue City had to be firmly reunited, and all confederates had to be rounded up and put on trial.

Mayor Mallory agreed, but she also knew she simply didn't have the support. She wasn't sure the thirty gangcop precincts of Brooklyn and Manhattan would obey if she asked them to rally their scant forces and invade the "north." The two sides were almost evenly split in population and supplies, and a protracted civil war could just as easily lead to the fall of Rescue City South. And, ultimately, this wasn't 1861—the secession was in some ways just a big ugly gesture.

But giving up the border neighborhoods was an entirely different matter—primarily because it was a battle Mallory was sure she could win, and it would send a clear message north to cut it with the shenanigans. Along with Gonzalez, the mayor called together the community leaders of various north Brooklyn communities: the city council members from Greenpoint, Williamsburg, Bushwick, and East New York, along with representatives from Bed-Stuy, Park Slope, Canarsie, and Flatlands. Mallory was hoping to create a coalition of their gangcop forces into a coordinated attack against the slender reed of Quirklyn.

It wasn't until she talked to some of the seasoned gangcop veterans that she learned that this was actually a lot more complex than she had envisioned. During Mayor Shub's reign, gang invasions against the

Piggers had usually involved a single robust precinct working against a weaker adjacent neighborhood across the border. Getting soldiers, who were usually overweight bullies, and random mercenaries to drive ten minutes away to a weaker area where they could beat up the locals and walk away with whatever spoils they could carry—that was one thing. Mobilizing a small army to simultaneously attack four zealous and unified neighborhoods was an entirely different matter and, since the desert metropolis didn't recieve new ammo anymore, warfare had regressed back to the dark ages. During the early years, before the first mayor, Jackie Wilson, had unified the place, large-scale gang battles mostly involved archers, lancers, and spear throwers. But as the conflicts wound down and boundaries were drawn, neither the weapons nor skills were required.

Another big problem was that many of the Crapper communities actually liked their new neighbors to the north. They weren't really invaders, more like glorified squatters; they had moved into abandoned buildings that no one really wanted. In fact, most were former Crappers who hadn't exactly renounced their allegiances. Additionally, the Piggers would have to invade this new strip in order to get into Crapper territory. So Quirklyn was actually a free line of defense.

Mallory briefly considered bribing various gangcop captains with new solicars in order to put together a fighting force. Ironically, it was Hector Gonzalez who convinced her that this was unnecessary. He had just received an unconfirmed report that the Piggers were dramatically increasing their gangcop presence in Ozone Park. He feared it could be their attempt to take over the JFK landing fields.

"If we go in and quash this Quirklyn thing," he reasoned, "the airfield will be completely surrounded by the Independent City of Pigs, turning our small security staff there into hostages. This new community is not looking for a fight. If we informally tell them we'll leave them alone, let them get food and basic supplies—as long as we get an easement around Rockaway Boulevard to JFK, they could serve as a barrier to the Piggers."

"I can't just give away our northern territories," Mallory replied.

"You won't need to. The Piggers like the fact that this new group is squatting on our northern borders, but the hippies have also taken over SOP, which cuts off Howard Beach and the Rockaways. Believe me, Kew Gardens does not like that. Eventually they'll invade."

"How will that help us?"

"It'll be a great diversion for the scant force of Quirklyn fighters,"

Gonzalez said. "At that point, retaking the Brooklyn districts will be a piece of cake, and I'll be able to do it with just the council police. Also, if you wait until the Piggers invade first, they'll look like the bullies. You'll look like you went in to limit the damage."

"Do you think your men can do it alone?"

"Hopefully. But you go to war with the army you have," Gonzalez said ominously.

After covertly accepting this plan, Mallory extended Quirklyn an unofficial olive branch through indirect channels.

11

Following his violent attack, it was a full two weeks before Abe Levitol, the director of the New Dope methadone clinic, was able to sit up on his own. His next official act was to send Tottenville a full report of Bea's selfless heroism. He detailed how she had single-handedly overpowered three violent hijackers, even going so far as coaxing the largest of them to help put their badly damaged vehicle back on its wheels.

When Bea was asked to come out to the VL headquarters to collect a medal for bravery, she balked. "When did they even start giving out medals?"

"This is an order," her supervisor, Police Chief Loveworks, replied sternly over the phone.

Bea arrived late the next day, but instead of being led to the head of security, or the Staten Island police trailers out back, she was escorted up to the office of her old friend Timothy Leary. There she learned that when Borough President Adolphus Rafique had been shot, Leary had secretly been asked to help run the show, in effect making him deputy borough president.

"You know," he said tenderly, "if you're still blaming yourself for what happened to Adolphus, you shouldn't."

"Ever feel like you don't even deserve to be alive?" she said.

He poured her a thimble-sized glass of bad Scotch. "The older I get, the more I feel that nobody deserves to be alive."

She nodded her head dismally as she knocked back her drink. "I was ordered to pick up some medal."

"We don't got no stinking medals here," he kidded. "I remembered that you were pretty good at self-defense and everyone here who read that report figured you were a regular supergirl."

"Karate, knife throwing, staff and spike training—none of it can compete with a single bullet," she said.

"They're cooking a string bean soufflé tonight. Why don't we get an early dinner and catch up, then you can spend the night upstairs in a nice room with clean sheets."

"I don't know if I'm up for it."

"You better be," Leary responded. "I have a top secret mission for you, and the only person who can tell you what it is has gone to bed for the night. He gets up at seven a.m. You'll meet him tomorrow."

12

Uli had been arrested on a Monday. Bert told him the way things worked: his case would be "pleabagged" by a pair of surrogate lawyers assigned by the Piggers' attorney general out in their new criminal justice building in Kew Gardens. "Without you being present, one speaks in your defense while the other argues against you."

"Based on what?" Uli erupted. "Where are the witnesses? Where's the evidence? There's no fucking trial!"

"Presumably, it's all in the gangcop's report," Troy said.

"But I punched the guy in the knee, he hates me!"

Bert looked grimly up at Troy. After a moment, he resumed the timetable of justice: "The lawyers will decide a sentence for you sometime between Wednesday and Friday. Over the weekend you—and everyone arrested the same day as you—will be read their sentences. Amputations will probably begin next Monday at around seven."

"Suppose I want to appeal."

"Get a banana," Bert said without a grin. The joke was as old as it was bad.

"So they cut off my fingers or something and I get out a few days later?" Uli asked.

"After our amputations," Troy said, "inmates are deemed to be patients and are usually held in the infirmary in a postoperative haze for another two days, then they're finally released—minus whatever part of them has been taken as a penalty."

"Oh God!"

Bert slowly pushed their wagon away to give Uli some space to adjust. He still didn't entirely give up hope that there was some higher authority who he could appeal to. He had a simple and reasonable explanation for what had happened if he could just tell someone.

That night, a convict who had been arrested a week earlier was yanked out of the pen for amputation. Uli quickly snatched the man's abandoned wooden crate and leaned it up against the bars in the muddy part of the cage where at least he could be dry and alone.

There, he wrapped his bare arms around his folded legs and tried not to fall over. This was going to be his new home for the next few days.

13

When Tim Leary greeted Bea at his office door early in the morning, he had no idea that she had been up all night. Before he could ask her how she had slept, she vomited in his wastepaper basket.

"You okay?" he asked, passing her a sheet of paper that said, *THE VL WEAPONS DRIVE.* She wiped her chin with it.

"This is the first morning in the past two weeks I haven't had a hit of choke or a cup of croak."

"Are you an addict?"

"Not really, just depressed and bored as hell."

"Let's remedy that," Leary said as he picked up his basket and led her out of his office.

"Where are we going? What's this mission?"

"Shush, it's a secret!" Leary placed the basket in front of the janitor's closet, and they headed up the stairs.

When they reached the top-floor landing, a security guard frisked them both. He then opened the thick steel door to the "throne room." Inside the large air-conditioned room, a conference was in session. Bea was shocked to see Adolphus Rafique lying in a customized bed, positioned nearly upright to minimize bedsores.

"Surprise!" Leary said. "He's not brain-dead."

"Holy shit!" Bea experienced a swirl of feelings due to the tremendous guilt she had been carrying about the VL leader's assassination.

"Good to see you too, Bea."

Nearly a dozen men were gathered, all young with long, uncombed hair. One of them looked identical to the older guy except half his age. They all sat around Rafique, and Leary led Bea to one of the two empty chairs across from him. Some kind of large inflatable belt buckled around the man's lower abdomen inhaled and exhaled for him.

"Leary . . . you're late . . . as usual." Rafique spoke to the mechanical pace of the pneumonic belt pushing his diaphragm.

"I should mention that I didn't tell Bea a thing," Leary replied.

"Welcome to Operation . . . Terrible Beauty, but we . . . don't call it that . . . anymore . . . You're aware of . . . this new strip . . . of land being settled between . . . Brooklyn and Queens?"

"Quirklyn," Bea said, still in disbelief that he was alive.

"Since the area is located . . . right between the two fascist boroughs . . . it is an ideal place where . . . members of both gangs . . . could defect. The hope is . . . that eventually . . . this new place will . . . gain independence . . . and, as others from . . . the two gangs . . . become increasingly disenchanted, they'll join in until . . . the revolution spreads . . . north and south. But some problems have . . . come up that could . . . kill it right off." Rafique gestured to a nearby aide, who quickly adjusted the dial on the respirator, allowing him to speak more fluidly.

"Aren't you concerned that the Piggers or Crappers are going to eventually just roll in and take the area over?" Bea asked.

"That's why we got these guys." Rafique pointed to the young men around him. "David Wojo, Jean-Michel Gaillard, and Keith Bowers will be head of security for Greenpoint-Williamsburg, Bushwick, and East New York, respectively." One tall, one short, and one robust African American kid each smiled and shook Bea's hand. "Antonio will be the head of security in South Ozone Park," Rafique added, "and Jack Healy is head of defense for the entire strip."

"Jack Healy?!"

"He's not here," Leary said. "Do you know him?"

"I know *of* him," she replied. Healy had a reputation of being Rescue City's premiere survivalist. When the VL had first taken over the toxic swamp of Staten Island, Healy was the one who created their weapons program. At the southern end of the borough, he was the man behind Project FF—a secret garden where the VL was able to convert human waste into viable explosives to use against the Piggers and Crappers. "So where exactly is Healy?"

"You'll meet him later," Rafique said. "The only person you need to know now—in fact your immediate superior here—is the Brain." A tall, bespectacled man stepped forward. His shirt was open to the waist, displaying a hairy chest, and when he smiled he revealed a gap in his front teeth.

"We all read the r-report of your h-h-heroics," the Brain said, shaking her hand.

"You must be smart if everyone calls you the Brain."

"Actually, my name is Joe Brainard, but since it starts w-with the word *Brain*, everyone teases me."

"The Brain's our chief campaign strategist," Leary said.

"Campaign strategist? Is there an election?"

"In last week's issue of the *Daily Posted New York Times*," Rafique cut in, "Mayor Mallory said that the last time Greenpoint-Williamsburg, Bushwick, and East New York had city council representatives they were elected by a Crapper majority, and until there are new election results that zone will still be considered Crapper."

"The thing is," Leary pointed out, "those elections were held when those areas were almost empty, so the new residents aren't being represented."

"The good news," the Brain added, "is that the Piggers have promised not to use force."

"Plains, the new mayor of Rescue City North, read Mallory's remark and decided to use it as a basis to repatriate his lost district of South Ozone Park," Leary said. "They filed papers for a formal election in their district in six weeks."

"Upon hearing that, the Crappers also filed papers for a formal election in *their* three lost districts," the Brain said.

"What do the residents of Quirklyn say to that?"

"They refuse to acknowledge the political system."

"And that's where you come in." Rafique turned to Bea.

"If the gangs win this election, it'll be the end of Quirklyn," Leary inserted. "We need a highly identifiable group that can run against these gang candidates."

"Highly identifiable?" Bea asked.

"Right, what does that even mean?" The Brain smiled.

Leary continued: "After brainstorming for the past week, we came up with a long list of possible individuals and—"

"The real problem is that among the only high-profile characters who came here were the antiwar people who the government d-detained over the years," Joe interrupted, "and many of them have developed affiliations with the Crappers."

"Only one particular group stood out," Leary said.

Bea rubbed the goose pimples on her arms. The air-conditioning was set high.

"Ever hear of the Andy Warhol Superstars?" Rafique asked.

A tiny lightbulb lit up in the back of Bea's head, and she remembered back when Rescue City was first settled. Some low-budget impresario, who went by the name Graham Cracker, found a clever way to launch his new Bowery club, CoBs&GoBs. He hired some of Andy Warhol's former actors who had been shipped to the desert during the initial exodus. For a number of years they'd emcee local bands and work the mic on vaudeville drag nights. They had funny names, were always high, and made a lot of dirty jokes. Occasionally they would introduce one of Warhol's films, which were usually projected against the rear walls as amateur bands performed. Since celebrities in Rescue City were scarce, people took notice of them. For years, a sign out in front of CoBs said, *Featuring Andy's Super Stars.* Someone eventually crossed out the word *Super* and scrawled *Stupid* over it.

"Whatever became of them?" Bea asked.

Leary and Rafique started laughing, and the other men soon joined in.

"What's so funny?"

"Your mission," the Brain said, "is to locate four of these formerly drug-addicted eccentrics."

"Why?"

"Ever heard of the term *slating*?"

"No."

"It means getting someone on the slate, to run for political office."

"Okay."

"We want you to locate these people and get them slated for the upcoming special election, representing the new city of Quirklyn."

"And time is of the essence," said Rafique from his hospital bed. "They have to be found and convinced to join our cause as soon as possible, so they can run in six weeks."

"We know for a fact that the Piggers have already picked their candidate for South Ozone Park. And I'm sure the Crappers will make their announcements by tomorrow."

"So you want the Superstars to run as VL candidates?" Bea asked, somewhat bewildered.

"Not VL. In fact, this will only work if Quirklyn presents itself as a homegrown alternative," Leary explained. "We're trying to offer it as an independent city."

"Have you ever seen any of Andy Warhol's movies?" the Brain interjected. His jerky movements made Bea wonder if he was speeding on amphetamines.

"Just a few minutes of them before I got bored. Edie, and that woman who shot him . . ."

"We were all very impressed by what you did for Abe Levitol at New Dope, and we were hoping you could take on this mission for us," Rafique said. "As you probably know, we're struggling to bring democracy back to this forgotten corner of the desert, because, like it or not, we're still in America."

Bea asked exactly what she was authorized to give these candidates in exchange for their political services.

The Brain, Leary, and Rafique exchanged glances.

Finally Rafique said, "Whatever it takes, just make sure the check is postdated until *after* the election."

Leary grinned while Joe Brainard looked tensely at the floor. Bea considered this for a few more moments and then said she would give it her best.

"Good," Leary said. "Why don't I bring you back to my office and we can discuss details."

Rafique thanked her and the young men of the Quirklyn militia team resumed their meeting.

"I can't believe he's alive," Bea said once she and Leary were outside the room.

"He never died."

"I thought he was a vegetable."

"After so many assassination attempts, he won't survive another—his best chance of survival is us keeping his existence a secret for as long as possible."

"Who's the four-eyed stutterer?"

"Back in Old Town, Joe Brainard was some kind of artist, and I think he dabbled in poetry."

"I've heard a lot of great things about Healy, but the few times I've seen him he barely spoke."

"He hangs with those young men. Maybe he's a queer—don't know, don't care. Healy picked them."

"Why does he get to pick the Quirklyn militia?"

"Healy's a decorated Vietnam War veteran, although he never mentions it. When he returned, he tossed his medals away and became a pacifist."

"So his team . . . ?"

"Jean-Michel Gaillard, Keith Bowers, and Wojo have all worked in Staten Island for Roger Loveworks with the VL police."

"I've seen them around. I think I recognize that Jean-Michel guy from the dope clinic."

"They really don't have the background for this. In fact, they're all artists of some kind." Leary unlocked his office door and continued:

"Which brings us to your job, Andy Warhol's protégés. The biggest problem is that we don't even know who is here."

Leary lifted a folder off his desk and handed Bea photos of all of the Superstars: "Edie Sedgwick, the prettiest, Paul America, Holly Woodlawn, Ultra Violet . . ." The names and photos went on for a while. "A good place to start looking would be at your old job, that meth clinic. That's one of the reasons we hired you." He handed her the complete file of poor images. "They all supposedly did a lot of drugs."

"Most of the methadone patients use pseudonyms," Bea said, "and I'm not a private investigator."

Leary explained that he had called Rescue City's three methadone clinics this morning—the Lotus up in Little Neck, Queens, the Meth Is Real Clinic in the East Village in Mahattan, and the New Dope. "I told them not to serve anyone until you give them the go-ahead. So they should all be there waiting for you." It was only nine o'clock. He handed her a set of rusty keys. "You can pick up a solicar from the Verdant League garage."

Bea went outside and got her assigned vehicle. It took her twenty minutes to drive up to New Dope. She parked a few blocks away and, messing up her hair, joined a crowd of about two dozen bedraggled methadone addicts. Those who hadn't passed out were wondering why the clinic wasn't open yet. The few habitués who Bea had come to know since she began using had no idea that she once worked there. She walked over to Loin, a tall, old white guy with a springy Jewfro. He was one of the most popular of the regulars, so she asked if he knew anyone who had ever worked with Andy Warhol.

"Yeah, Flightbag," he replied.

"Over there." Someone else pointed to a guy who looked to be in his forties, maybe fifties, who had passed out on a nearby stoop. His head was propped up on a TWA flight bag. Bea went over to him, flipping through the stack of bad photos that Leary had given her; she held one of them up to Flightbag's unconscious face. She could see the resemblance, but the rest of his body was dramatically different: from the thick creases on his yellowed face, saggy love handles, and ample saddlebags along his thighs and hips, he had undergone some nightmarish transformations.

Bea shook the man's shoulder. When he didn't awaken, she shook harder until he started to stir. Finally, putting up a surrendering hand, he sat up.

"Did you ever star in any Andy Warhol films?"

"I don't do autographs," said the transmogrified man. He ran his fingers through his greasy, prematurely gray hair. White crusts of bile ringed the corners of his mouth, which was missing teeth. He pulled a crumpled, half-smoked roach from behind his ear, straightened it, clipped it in his lips, then lit up and took a deep drag.

"Are you Ondine?" she asked.

"Open for bizwiz."

"May I ask what you got in the flight bag?" she asked, seeing that it was unzipped and filled with pages.

"Transcripts for my next book," he said. "Andy published my first one, *a*. Now I'm working on *b*."

"So you were in Mr. Warhol's films?"

"Why, is CoBs&GoBs having another 'Blast from the Past' night?"

"You know about this new strip of land sandwiched between Queens and Brooklyn?"

"I've spent years of my life sandwiched between queens and broke men," he kidded. "So what the fuck?"

Realizing she wasn't effectively communicating with him, Bea squatted closer, and in a slow, clear voice she said, "A group of us want you and three other Andy Warhol actors to run for city council."

"Course you do," he replied calmly. "Which three?"

Bea took out the folder of pictures and flipped through them, reading the most interesting names: "Edie Sedgwick, Paul America, and Ultra Violet."

"What do I get for helping you?" Ondine asked.

"What do you want?"

"The last nine years of my life back, and to get off this fucking desert island."

"If only," Bea countered.

"How about that escape drug?"

"We don't have any and I don't think it's real."

"The wine here is undrinkable. This isn't a fun place to speed, and there's no heroin, so that leaves us with this awful methadone—I want an endless supply! Without ever waiting in any fucking line."

"*If* I can get that for you," she replied, "it won't be until after the election is over."

"Oh!" He didn't seem to hear her. "I also want a complete set of Maria Callas records."

"I don't know that we can get Maria Callas out here."

"Well then, I better tell you the bad news. None of those people you just mentioned made it to this forbidden city: Paul America, Edie, Viva, Ultra, Holly, Taylor, Brigid . . . They all blew out of town the moment the news of the radiation bomb hit. Their sugar daddies and sweet mommies got them plane tickets to their posh country homes."

"But I remember a group of Warhol Superstars performing in the Village," Bea muttered.

"Yeah, there was a group who came here. Some of them were killed during the gang wars. Poor Billy Name was hit by a car."

"We need at least four Superstars to make this plan work."

"Jackie used to come down and get turned on, till she found out we were all stuck here for good. Then she went all Bette Davis as Baby Jane. Candy Darling still performs. She's the fatter half of a two-blonde act and they're inseperable. Every time I see her she's put on another hundred pounds. Oh! Then there's Six-Shooter Solanas. She used to be fun but then she went mad as a fucking hatter. Last I heard, they were all eating out of garbage cans in the Village. Now that it's underwater like Atlantis . . . no clue."

Bea held up her crappy reproductions that either blacked out or whited out most of the Superstars' features. "Which ones are they?"

Ondine couldn't make heads or tails of the low-quality photocopies. "Actually, I managed to save a few of Andy's films on one-inch videotape. I salvaged them from the Bleecker Street Cinema when the sandbags blew up and the Village flooded, but I don't have a tape player."

"I have access to one," Bea said.

"The rental price is a few stamps, and return them when you're done. They're all I have to show for my sped-up youth."

"Let's go."

"I ain't leaving until I've scored." Ondine glared at the closed doors. "For some reason these fuckers are opening late today."

Bea told him that if he wanted to get his fix, he should follow her. Although Ondine was skeptical, anything was worth a shot. The two walked around to the service entrance in the back where Bea got the security guard to let them in.

"Finally! I was instructed not to open until you arrived," one of the administrators said tersely when she saw Bea enter.

"Just service us, and we'll be gone." Ondine looked at Bea with a twinkle in his eyes. The price of his devotion was being able to cut to the front of the line at a methadone clinic.

The supervisor led them both into a treatment room and was

about to pour out two cups of croak, but at the last minute Bea declined, realizing that she needed to be sober today if she was going to get anything done.

After Ondine downed his dose, the man checked his mouth to make sure he wasn't holding it to resell later—a common practice on the black market.

Bea drove Ondine to his boarding house in the St. George section of Staten Island. As they approached, they each took out nose clips and sealed their sinuses from the awful smell of sewage. The water stunk acutely that day. Ondine had Bea pull over in front of a solitary wooden structure with dozens of laundry lines flapping from the rooftop all the way to the ground, making the place resemble an old clipper ship that had run aground.

A peeling sign above the door said, *Shell Sea Hotel*. Ondine led her up a creaky circular staircase to his tiny room on the top floor, where, amid old papers and crammed boxes, he unearthed four videotape reels that were stashed under his bed. He explained which of the Superstars were in each film. "I wish I had found *Chelsea Girls*. That film is my *Citizen Kane*."

Bea put the reels in a box and started to leave.

"When exactly should I expect to hear from you?" he asked, sitting on the edge of the filthy bed.

"Soon."

"So what exactly will this running-for-office thing entail?"

"Don't worry, we'll go over it like a film role. Your director will tell you everything."

"When?"

"Once I find the others. Then I'll come back for you."

Ondine gave her the number to the pay phone on the first floor. "Let it ring a long time and then wait even longer for me to come down the stairs," he explained. "It's still a lot quicker than driving out here."

Bea tiredly went downstairs holding the box of videos, heading back to the car.

14

"Basher: a right hand. Deitz: a right eye. Gilbert: a left foot . . ." The barbaric list of inmates and body parts they were sentenced to lose went on. The Bronx Zoo sergeant was reading from the names of men who'd been arrested two days before Uli had arrived, and they were only now hearing their grim penalties.

Throughout the rest of the day, Uli heard large men weeping like babies. Bert and Troy still hadn't been sentenced, but they were clearly scared. Uli noticed an odd Mediterranean man outside the bars, parleying with the condemned. It took him awhile to realize that the guy made a morbid livelihood out of photographing the prisoners flexing whatever limb they were about to forfeit.

Three men—all one-armed—were repeat murderers, and therefore each would lose a leg. They seemed bored as their photos were snapped. Two others were first-time murderers, both slated to lose arms. At one point the man with the bulky Polaroid camera asked Uli what he was in for. Uli explained he had struck a gangcop.

"You didn't!"

"But I had a good reason."

"I wouldn't worry," the man said dismissively. "You'll probably walk with only a couple digits or so. Worst case, you'll lose three fingers, but they'll spare your pinkie and thumb."

"I was hoping to find someone to explain—"

"Hope will kill you here." Holding up his clunky camera, the man asked, "Want a photo?"

"Of what?"

"Hold out your hands like you're about to play the piano. That's the standard pose for finger amputees."

Uli leaned close to the rusty bars. "I'll give you all my stamps if you do me just one small favor."

"Careful now, I report breakouts."

"Just call the head of Mayor Mallory's security detail."

"What's the number?"

"Call information, ask for the mayor's office, and have them put you through to Karen Sarkisian."

"Isn't she a captain?"

"Yes. Tell her, or someone at her office, that her brother Uli is being held in Pigger detention and is about to get his arms amputated."

"That sounds like two or three phone calls."

"I'm begging you!"

"I'm about to go on break, so I'll make a couple of speculative calls, but it's a stamp a call, and I want the payment first."

"Look, I'm locked in here. I'm not going anywhere. You're out there, I might never see you again."

"All right, mister. If you really are Captain Sarkisian's brother, I'll make your calls, but if you don't pay up, I'll tell you right now—you gonna lose more than a few digits."

"Fine."

15

When Bea arrived back at the terminal building, she carried the box of Ondine's tapes right into the audiovisual room on the second floor and then called up to the VL library and inquired about their Maria Callas collection.

"The opera diva?" the archivist asked.

"Yes."

He said he'd get back to her.

Bea had to wait a few minutes before getting access to one of the three video machines. By putting in a call to Timothy Leary upstairs, she was also able to secure a Polaroid camera. Eager to see exactly how charismatic these bizarre Superstars were, she looped the reel of the shortest of the videos into the large desk console. It was just a camera pointed at the Empire State Building, and after watching for about ten minutes Bea sensed it was all some kind of practical joke. She put in the second film, entitled *I, a Man*, which Ondine had explained was the only one with failed-assassin Valerie Solanas.

Having lost all her patience on the first film, Bea turned the fast-forward dial on the machine until she saw Valerie Solanas, then hit play. She watched as Solanas had some antagonistic dialogue with another actor, who seemed to have no idea what she was talking about. The scene ended with Solanas exiting, saying she had "to beat my meat." Though the episode made little sense, Bea appreciated Solanas's gender disdain. While rewinding and reviewing the short scene, she pushed pause and took several close-up Polaroids of the female Superstar. She didn't know much about Solanas, but there was something clearly lost about her.

Flesh, the third film, was about a hustler played by a handsome young actor named Joe Dallesandro. Bea couldn't imagine anyone enduring these films without the fast-forward button. When she came to various characters, she'd watch and compare them with her photocopies of the Superstars to see if she'd found the targets of her search. Finally, she located two of the figures whom Ondine had said were still alive in Rescue City: Candy Darling and Jackie Curtis. They had a small but amusing two-hander that was little more than back-and-forth banter. Again, Bea rewound the scene and snapped some pictures of them.

Roughly forty-five minutes later, Bea spooled in the last video— *Women in Revolt*. Ironically, the women in revolt were all men in drag. The story line followed three women who decide to give up men, abandon their careers, and become lesbians. They politicize into a group called PIG, Politically Involved Girls, which Bea saw as a wink to Valerie Solanas's SCUM—Society for Cutting Up Men. Like the other Warhol videos, the scenes were poorly acted. They all seemed improvised with no signs of rehearsal. In fact, it was hard to believe they had even gone through a second take. The sound quality, lighting— really, everything about the films—were unapologetically amateur. Bea could only wonder what had possessed Warhol to produce such unabashedly rank messes. Further, she questioned how these strange people could be denatured into credible politicians.

"Please tell me you l-located our Quirklyn ticket," Joe Brainard said, nervously entering the AV room. He looked a bit more solid than when she'd last seen him.

"I only found one Superstar. Some fruit named Ondine at New Dope." She paused awkwardly, because she sensed an effeminate quality in the Brain and didn't want to accidentally offend him.

"You sure it's Ondine?"

"He looked like he might drop dead at any moment, but it was definitely him. And he confirmed that he has seen some of the others."

"Which ones?"

"Solanas, the woman who shot Warhol, and two transvestites."

"Who?"

"Jackie Curtis and Candy Darling."

The Brain wrote down the names.

"He rented me these videotapes starring those who are still here." Bea showed him the Polaroids she had just taken.

"Oh good, let me see if there's time to put these on the campaign posters."

"But we don't even know if they're still alive!"

"H-h-hurry up," the Brain said. "I'll delay as long as I can."

He checked his Timex, then glanced at a jug of water and some Dixie cups on a nearby desk. He calmly took a container from his pocket and fished out several different types of colorful capsules.

"So, Tim Leary told me you were some kind of artist," Bea said, making small talk as she continued scanning footage. "How did you become a campaign manager here?"

Joe laughed and said: "Extortion."

Only the sound of the machine filled the room.

"It's just a long story," he added, alternating between pills and gulps of water.

"I'd love to hear it."

"I suppose it begins with Rafique. As soon as Mallory was elected, he saw the new peace between the Piggers and Crappers and figured there must be some way to exploit it. When his constituents first started abandoning Staten Island and heading over to Quirklyn, he thought this might be a good thing. He secretly had his men put building supplies out for the people to fix up the old houses."

"So *you* suggested running a new political party?"

"As a practical joke, I wrote out a six-point memo. At the heading I scribbled, *Declaration of Independence,* and I stapled a note to it that read, *What would happen if one night we slipped this under the Quirklyn doors?*"

"Like yelling *fire* in a crowded theater," she remarked.

"Frankly, I never intended for that memo to leave the room." Joe took the last pill and swallowed the rest of his water. "Someone wrote it in a memo. I don't even know how it got to Rafique, but he found it, and that night he made several thousand copies and employed about a hundred people to quietly put it under everyone's doors in the new districts."

"You're kidding!"

"No, and it probably would've ended right there, but Mallory got wind of it, and then the Piggers called for an election. I think he was hoping to motivate the Quirklyners to start their own political campaign, but . . ." Joe let out a sudden explosion of coughs and wiped the sweat from his brow.

"You okay?"

"I think I caught the Staten Island Fever."

"What's that?"

"They think it might be some kind of male version of the EGGS epidemic. The good news is it's manageable, but the bad news is there isn't enough medicine to treat everyone who has it."

"You're kidding!"

"And that's how, and why, I became the campaign manager for the breakaway republic of Quirklyn," the Brain said, almost jovially. Suddenly, checking his watch again, he announced that he was late for an appointment and dashed off.

It was only two p.m., and although Bea knew that finding these Warhol hopefuls was imperative, she didn't have a clue of how to proceed. That was when she remembered old Blue Cheese Face, as she thought of him—the man had a knack for finding people.

The phone rang. It was the library archivist informing Bea that she had found some tape recordings and vinyl records of Maria Callas performing the works of Verdi, Puccini, Bellini, and Cherubini. They even had one scratched-up shellac record that played on 78 rpm.

Bea drove up Hyman Boulevard. When approaching the Zano Bridge, she was surprised to see that the complex framework of skyscraper panels that had loomed over the area was entirely missing. Then she remembered that the new mayor had deemed them patronizing to the populace as well as a serious hazard during the windstorms. Over the years, several panels had fallen out—one of Mallory's first orders was that they be demolished. Bea wondered if the Mexican gang that lived under the bridge had undertaken the task themselves, as they were highly territorial. Even the gangcops didn't mess with them.

In another moment, she was heading over the Zano and into Brooklyn. She knew Blue Cheese Face lived somewhere in Sheepshead Bay and was some big muckety-muck with either the Pigger or Crapper government.

When Bea's mother mysteriously died twenty or so years earlier, this cop had been assigned to her case. After it went cold, her father had cracked, and her old neighbors, the Mayer family, had begrudgingly adopted her.

Over the years, the officer would stop by periodically to see how she was doing. As a child, she had noticed the similarity between his hard, scarred face and a wedge of blue cheese.

At eighteen, she moved out of the Mayers' place in the East Tremont section of the real Bronx and lived in a commune of hippies in a storefront apartment in East Greenwich Village. She had also dated a boy who worked at the Peace Eye Bookstore on Avenue A.

When New York got hit by the radiation bomb in 1970, she remembered, the evacuation signs went up overnight, giving Lower Manhattan residents a thirty-day notice. Most packed right up and left the city. On her area's "move or be moved" date in the summer, the

National Guard went from door to door, kicking them in if no one opened up. The few who refused to leave were forcibly removed. If they didn't require being taken away in cuffs, they were allowed to file onto one of two city buses: one for men, the other for women. Bea had boarded the female bus and heard the sounds of old ladies in the rear weeping. Everyone was evacuated out to Queens, where they had to dispose of their clothes, take group showers, and scrub themselves under supervision. Only then were they issued new clothes and assigned temporary lodging.

"We should've headed out west when we had the chance," said Tamborine, a hippie girl who had lived in her commune. A group who lived upstairs had taken their VW bus and headed over the George Washington Bridge two months before, when news of the attack first broke in the papers.

For months Bea lived in an outdoor encampment in Flushing Meadows–Corona Park. In the autumn of 1970, she was transferred, along with thousands of other Manhattan refugees, to a massive partitioned hangar at LaGuardia Airport. That winter, the federally sponsored Rescue City Project was announced.

She rushed to apply—at the time it seemed like a godsend. Joyful notions of a yearlong Woodstock festival filled her head. All the applicants had to be personally interviewed by a government agent. The key thing they looked for was whether someone had anywhere else to go, because space in the new facility was limited. During her interview, when asked why she couldn't move back in with her family, instead of mentioning the Mayers, who had adopted her, she explained that her mother had died years earlier in the Bronx and her father had vanished.

In February 1971, Bea was told she had been accepted. It was like a wonderful, belated Christmas gift—her own apartment in a cool new city, where she didn't have to worry about work or food. She could just have fun and find herself. A month later, she was bused out to JFK, where her acceptance letter served as an airline ticket. As she flew away from New York, her only fear was that it would all end too soon. Someone told her that tens of thousands of New Yorkers had arrived so far.

After the five-hour flight, as she was getting off the plane in the original airstrip in south Staten Island, Nevada, she saw a middle-aged man who looked familiar.

"Hey! Don't I know you?"

He looked bewildered. It was old Blue Cheese Face. She realized that under his floppy black fedora was a big, bloody bandage.

"You're Detective Lewis!" He looked paunchier than she remembered. "You worked up in East Tremont. You were trying to find my mother's killer."

"Your mother's . . ." He was confused.

"Are you okay?"

"You had a father, didn't you?" he asked vaguely.

"Yeah, Paul Moses."

"There were sneakers dangling from traffic lights, and . . . and . . ." He was clearly discombobulated. She pulled a snapshot out of her wallet.

Tears came to the man's tired eyes as he inspected the photograph of her father. "I didn't mean to hurt you."

"Not at all, you were a good cop," she assured him. She could smell the alcohol on his breath.

"Thanks. They told me that, but I didn't believe them."

When she asked him what he was doing in Rescue City, Detective Scouter Lewis shrugged. He knew his name but little else. He explained that he was no longer on the force. He had been in a bad car accident and suffered a head injury, but because drunk driving was suspected he wasn't eligible for disability; therefore he was stuck.

He concluded by adding that a lot of ex-cons had been sent to Rescue City as well, so he didn't want her telling anyone that he was a former cop.

A few years later, Bea bumped into him again in Coney Island, where he seemed much healthier and sharper. He was also quite curious as to what she was doing in Coney Island, and she told him she was going to the amusement park.

"You don't live anywhere around here, do you?"

She explained that she was part of the Burnt Men tribe in Staten Island.

During their conversation, he described his small house on the little bend in the narrow canal that everyone referred to as Sheepshead Bay. "If you ever need any help, don't hesitate to come by," he said.

16

When Bea finally reached the former policeman's neighborhood, she parked and found the local Crapper political headquarters that tripled as a stamp store and a precinct. She asked the group inside if anyone knew a man named Scouter Lewis who lived somewhere along the canal.

An emaciated old woman did—his house was the last one in a row of houses right on the waterway. "You can't miss it. All the other buildings on the street have collapsed into the water," she said.

Bea drove the few blocks to the last street before the canal. She parked, and as she headed up the little walkway to the only structure still standing, she heard a dog barking. The sound intensified as she knocked on the door.

When Scouter opened up, he saw her and flinched as though she were going to attack him. Behind him a small dog continued barking.

"Officer Scouter, are you okay?"

"Course," he replied. "It's good to see you." He turned to the little lapdog behind him. "Cirrus, quiet!"

"Cute dog," Bea said as she entered.

"His previous owner was killed, so he's having a tough time adjusting." He led her into his living room.

"The reason I'm here is that you once offered to help me, and I could sure use that help now."

"Sure. You're . . ."

"Bea Moses."

"I remember," he said, "but to be honest with you, someone at the Crapper headquarters found out I used to be a cop and asked me to help them, so I don't have a lot of time right now."

"You're with the Crappers?"

"Since the northern boroughs broke off and the new mayor appointed an attorney general, the Crappers have started this big crusade to improve their criminal justice system. Anyway—"

"I'm trying to find some people and I haven't a clue how to begin," Bea broke in.

He sighed, offered her a soft drink, then had her sit at a desk while he grabbed a legal pad and a stubby pencil. "Tell me everything you know about them," he said, sitting down.

Bea detected the smell of liquor on his breath. She told him everything she had dug up on the three living subjects of her Warhol search, and that they were all entertainers who suffered from chemical dependencies. She also showed him copies of the Polaroids.

"Pill-popping swishes then?" Lewis asked without a hint of judgment.

"Actually, they're drag queens."

"Have you checked out New Dope?" he asked, inspecting the photocopies.

"It was my first and only stop," she said.

"I'm too old and weak to go running around. Anything I'm going to do will be by phone. Come back tomorrow. You'll have to do all the legwork yourself."

She thanked him and rose, collecting her stuff.

"Can I call you?" she asked, as he walked her out the door and down the driveway. "Save myself the long drive out here?"

"You can try. For some reason, my phone rarely gets incoming calls. That's the way this roach motel is—everything comes in, nothing goes out."

Since the three Warholers were regarded briefly as minor celebrities, it only took about a half hour of calls before the former detective located the owner of one of the drag clubs—the Period Club—which had been in the East Village before it was flooded. Although the man knew the Warholers, he hadn't heard from any of them in a while. He told Lewis that Candy Darling was still doing her two-person act somewhere in Brooklyn.

"Not sure where, but I think I have the number of Candy's husband— he worked for me as a plumber."

"You mean *his* wife, don't you?" Scouter asked.

"A little advice: don't mess with the pronouns," the club owner said sternly, then gave him the phone number of Buck Joey, Candy's common-law husband.

"What if I don't know their pronouns?" Scouter asked.

"Call them *she*."

The fate of fellow Andy Warhol Superstar Jackie Curtis was an entirely different story. Lewis located someone named Oscar Wilder, one of the few Superstar sycophants who had fanatically kept track of Jackie Curtis in Rescue City. Lewis told Wilder he'd give him two food stamps if he could impart Curtis's whereabouts. Though Wilder couldn't provide the answer, he seemed to know everything else about her: Curtis had become increasingly claustrophobic over the years. She was having panic attacks about being stuck in the Nevada desert, so she used methadone to soothe her "spells."

"She's a croak addict?"

"She got off of it, and became intent on leaving." Wilder explained that in 1975, Curtis joined a secret group consisting of a dozen people who were working on a plan to escape from Rescue City. They systematically embarked on a series of two-day hikes in all four directions of the compass. They would've gone farther, but that was as long as they could last on the canteens of water they could carry. The hopeful escapees searched for water sources and possible clues about the nearest path back to civilization. Finally, in 1977, pooling what they'd learned, they decided that the southern route, with a natural spring two days out, showed the most promise. They brought ten large dogs and assembled as much food and water as the canines could carry—enough for about five days.

"What happened?"

"Roughly two weeks later, sunburned, dehydrated, and exhausted, Jackie and one of the other explorers turned up at the Lotus methadone clinic up in Little Neck, Queens."

"Then what?" Lewis asked.

"All she said was she'll never eat dog again."

"How can I get ahold of her?"

"You know who might know? The Warhol Warthog. He looks and acts like a short, fat Andy Warhol, and he runs a gallery somewhere in Brooklyn. I recently saw a fake photo of Jackie, dead, hanging from a noose in there."

"What's the name of the place?"

"Some clever wordplay on Warhol's space; something like Art-C. No, Factor-E. That's it!"

"Thanks."

"So when am I going to see my two stamps?" Wilder asked.

Lewis hung up on him, and looked up the number for the gallery. A squeaky voice answered.

"Do you happen to represent any of the artists who worked with Andy Warhol back in old New York?" the detective asked.

"Well, there is a stimulating new artist who many believe has surpassed the master."

"Would you know the whereabouts of any of Mr. Warhol's former cohorts?"

"Yes, but everything comes with a certain price, dear sir."

"How much?" Lewis asked.

"I'm not a snitch, but if you were to purchase one of Mr. Varholski's works . . ."

"What's the cheapest one?"

"*Unpainted Canvas Number 23* is still un-red-dotted and listed at a mere twenty stamps."

"All I have is ten stamps and I'll need the address of Mr. Candy and Jack Curts."

"Jackie Curtis," the owner corrected, "and hers is the only address I have."

"Fine, what is it?" Scouter asked, hoping to con a second fool out of information for free.

"Once ten stamps have been deposited at my Park Slope gallery location, you'll get it."

17

Late the next morning, Bea called Blue Cheese Face's place and was delighted when, after a dozen rings, the old detective groggily answered.

"Want me to call back?"

"No, I should've been up hours ago. I got some leads on those assholes—I mean Warhols," he possibly kidded. "You should be able to find them yourself."

He gave her Buck Joey's phone number and the address of the Warhol Warthog. Lewis instructed her to bring ten food stamps to the Factor-E Gallery to get Curtis's current address.

"Oh, listen," he added, "there is one piece of sage advice if you want to be taken seriously with this crowd. Call them all *she* unless they tell you otherwise."

"Will do. Any luck with Valerie Solanas?" Bea asked.

"I still have a few feelers out," Lewis replied. "Call me tomorrow and we'll see."

Bea thanked him.

First Bea called up Buck Joey. When a male voice answered, she asked for Candy Darling.

"Gosh nabbit," the man said with a distinct Western twang, "now why'd you have to go and bring her up?"

"I just need to speak to her for a minute," Bea replied, not knowing else to say.

"She ain't here. Last I heard she was breaking hearts with Cookie Mueller at the Dreamy Steamy, that bathhouse over in Vinegar Hill. If you see her, will you pass along a message? Tell her to just come home. I don't want nothing but her pretty face."

Bea assured him that she'd pass the message along. She packed up a few items she might need, including her bowie knife, and hopped in her car.

* * *

The tiny, tucked-away community of Vinegar Hill, Brooklyn, was a couple blocks of mainly older, run-down houses and shacks. Bea had heard that this was a small gay community, but it appeared to have ballooned in size since Lower Manhattan flooded. The few streets were filled with bushy-mustached men who showed a predilection for black leather vests.

"Would you know a place called the Dreamy Steamy?" she asked one fellow, who resembled a beanpole in cowboy boots.

"Yeah, but you don't want to go there unless you got a penis—and a thick one at that."

"I'm looking for Candy Darling," Bea said.

"Oh, Fatty and Skinny. She's right at the bar, you don't need to get toweled up for that." He pointed to a large brick building down the block.

The buckled wooden floor was crowded with folding chairs and small circular tables. The deep voice of Nico singing "I'll Be Your Mirror" blared through hanging speakers. In the front was a long wooden counter, and at the rear was a short dark stage.

"Miss Darling?" Bea asked the topless bartender, a man with rippling, hairless pectorals and nipples capped with pasties. He gestured to a side door behind the stage. Bea opened it, and followed the faint scent of eau de toilette to a small dressing room. Giant, interlocking Chinese fans were the only things hanging on the otherwise stark, paint-starved wall. Sitting up in an old love seat was an extra-large helping of Candy Darling, with a big towel wrapped around her head. She looked much wider than in the videotape.

A scratched-up Queen Anne vanity possessed every available cosmetic Rescue City had to offer. In front of the bright lamp Candy held a magnifying mirror in one hand and a long-handled tweezer in the other. "Is that my prune-tini?" she asked.

"Actually, I'm here to make you a rather unusual business proposal," Bea said.

"I'm part of a team, like Fred and Ginger. And my partner Cookie handles all offers, but I'll be glad to listen."

Bea considered an enticing way to describe the political campaign. "It's a portable talent contest," she began, "in which you'll be doing a series of improvisations at a wide variety of venues—"

"We don't do contests."

"You'll be paid either way."

"And we'd be taking our act on the road?" Candy sounded excited.

"You'd be getting your name way out there."

"We're a triple threat, you know. Singing, dancing, and vaudeville."

"Perfect." Elections were indeed kind of vaudevillian. "The thing is, we'll write the jokes for you."

"Who's we?" Candy asked.

"Our organization. See, here's the thing—it's not so much entertainment as a political campaign."

Candy stopped looking at herself in the mirror and glanced up at Bea. "You've mistaken Carmen Miranda for Carmine DeSapio. We don't go in for all this gang-violence shit. We're both avowed pacifists."

"Neither do we! That's why we're starting this campaign. It's for a new party that's running *against* the gangs."

"What party is that?"

"It's in that neighborhood up for grabs between Brooklyn and Queens—Quirklyn."

"Cookie and I don't do politics. Violence is bad for our complexion."

"Look, they've declared themselves independent and the two other gangs have agreed to a civil election."

"Even if I said yes, Cookie would never agree to it."

"Just you would be running, along with some of your old Andy Warhol Superstar troupe."

"But . . . but I . . . I don't want to be a politician!" Candy cried out.

"You won't have to be. Just get elected, and we'll take it from there."

The door opened and a second blonde, who looked like a slimmer version of Candy, entered the room.

"We'll be glad to pay you a lot of money," Bea said for both to hear. "Enough to retire on."

"We'll do it," Cookie Mueller jumped in, without even knowing what Bea was offering.

"She wants us to run for office," Candy explained.

"It'll just be a month of work, then you can vanish," Bea said.

"Exactly how much will we get for this month?" Cookie asked.

Bea knew she had to hit them with an overwhelming offer or they'd simply decline. "A thousand stamps," she said, even though she knew she didn't have the authority to make such an extravagant offer.

"A thousand food stamps?!"

"Well, she ain't selling *postage* stamps," Candy muttered.

Cookie looked at Candy with a big smile and softly nodded.

"Looks like I'll be a Candy-date for a while," the Superstar punned.

"Candidates customarily run alone," Bea coaxed, "so we really want you to do this solo."

"No amount of money—no amount of *anything*—can get me to perform without my Cookie," she said dramatically. "That woman is the extra-virgin olive oil to my Vinegar Hill! I just don't have the strength to go on a stage without her."

"How about this," Bea countered. "You can campaign together, but only *you* get billing. Cookie's name isn't appearing on anything."

"That's fine," Cookie said, "as long as we get the thousand stamps."

"Plus an endless supply of Wilkinson Sword razor blades and skin lotion," Candy tossed in. "This place is just hell on my creamy whiteness."

"Done."

"So what other Superstars did you have in mind?"

"We got Ondine and Jackie Curtis," Bea lied. "But we need one more."

"What are you paying them?"

"I'm not at liberty to say, but I promise that you're getting the most—by far."

"Who's your fourth candidate?" Cookie asked.

"We're still looking for Valerie Solanas."

"I always avoided her, even before she shot Andy," Candy said.

"Well, you'll be running in different districts, so you won't have to see her much."

"You know, when you first walked in, I thought . . . well, aside from the fact that you're about a foot taller and three shades darker, you really do look like Violent Val."

"Oh," Bea suddenly remembered, "do you know someone named Bucky Joe?"

"Yeah, he's the reason you should never sleep with your stalker. Why?"

"Never mind." Bea asked for Candy's phone number and told her that she'd call in a few days when they put together the rest of the political ticket.

She drove southeast to Park Slope and stopped near the address listed for the Factor-E Gallery. Down a short flight of stairs, she looked through a large plate glass window painted black. As Bea approached, she was able to peek inside through a large scratch in the paint. No art adorned the plain white walls. A short bald man in a purple velvet jacket was staring at himself adoringly in a small heart-shaped wall mirror. When she knocked, he opened a cupboard door where a life-size bust of Abe Lincoln was wearing a thick white wig and dark sunglasses. The little man put the glasses and shaggy wig on, checked himself again in the mirror, then unlocked the door.

"Are you the dealer here?" Bea asked.

"I am the artist Danny Varholski, who also happens to be a dealer." The small man spoke with a slow, luxurious, and ever-so-condescending tone.

"A friend of mine spoke to you yesterday and you told him you could provide the location of Jackie Curtis in exchange for ten stamps."

"Someone spoke to me about buying *Unpainted Canvas Number 23*, and I mentioned that I might have access to her whereabouts." Varholski kept her at the door.

"Well, how about I buy the canvas, and you tell me where she is."

"I said I *might* have access to her location," he said, biting each word. "But I need to have a piece of the action."

"What action?"

"Oh please," Varholski chuckled. "When one person calls there might be a sale, but when two people are sniffing about, there's action."

"Look, do you want the stamps or not?"

"Until I know exactly what's going on—"

"Nothing's going on."

"—and who's getting what—"

"No one's getting anything!"

"—until I feel that I get the 15 percent entitled to me, I'm afraid Jackie Curtis's address will remain a mystery."

Bea felt like she was stuck in one of the more pointless scenes of the Warhol movies that she had just watched in Staten Island. Without wasting another word, she pushed her way inside.

"Just where do you think you're going?" Varholski yelled, trying to block her.

Bea shoved the diminutive dealer into a chair in the center of the room and knocked it backward onto the floor.

"Saints alive!"

When the little man tried to scamper to his feet, Bea stepped on his right hand.

"That's my fondue hand!" Varholski squealed.

As he started rising, Bea kicked him back to the ground.

"Okay! I'll tell you anything you want!"

"Where is Jackie Curtis?"

"I need my . . ."

Bea got off the dealer's hand.

Varholski slipped an index card with neatly printed information out of his velvet jacket pocket. Bea took the ten stamps from her own pocket and dropped them onto the floor.

"Hold on, you purchased some un-art!" the dealer yelled as she walked out.

18

Just after sunrise, the sergeant and his men stood outside Uli's elephant pen with a clipboard. "Okay, stumpies, good news: the price you'll be paying to society has been decided!"

A group of about twenty prisoners who, like Uli, had been arrested on Monday listened nervously.

The man looked at his list and began reading: "Sam Bayato, a left eye."

"No!"

"Rick DeNada, a right hand."

"But I didn't do nada," DeNada responded.

"Harold Genghis," the sergeant resumed, "testes."

"But she asked for it!"

"Bill Hayes, a left pinkie toe."

"They said I'd just get a back scar," Hayes muttered.

"Bertram Haywood, a right leg."

"It's all I got left!" Bert called from his wagon.

"Hugo Haxter, a left hand. Troy Jenkins, a back scar."

"For what?" Troy echoed his partner.

"Nevada Brooklyn, right arm."

"T'aint fair, I tells ya."

"Ron O'Hara, testes. Shome Pinza, a right arm."

"I'll cut off *your* right arm!"

As the sergeant continued rattling off the names and parts to be amputated, Uli failed to hear his. When the man concluded his litany, Uli thought that the jailhouse photographer must have notified his sister and the Crappers had indeed intervened. But a half hour later when another inmate, Nevada Brooklyn, checked whether his own sentence was correct, the sergeant went down the list and realized an error had indeed been made. Brooklyn was sentenced to lose a leg, not an arm.

"Excuse me, officer," Uli called out nervously, "you didn't say my name!"

"What's your name, asshole?"

Uli gave the name he had made up: "Huey Baxter."

"Hugo Haxter, a left hand," the guard replied calmly.

"But I was just supposed to lose a finger or two!" Uli exclaimed.

The sergeant shouted out the name of the first prisoner to be rehabilitated: "Sam Bayato! Let's set you free!" When no one stepped forward, he opened the cell door and his gang of cronies rushed inside, grabbing an elderly man who was weeping and clinging to the bars.

Uli and the others watched as Bayato struggled pointlessly with the guards. Three other men stood around with clubs, waiting for anyone else in the elephant cage to make trouble—none did.

The notion that they were going to pluck Bayato's eye out of his head seemed inconceivable. It made Uli feel that his left hand was a small price to pay. A large guard finally pinned Bayato in the hot sticky mud, cuffed him, and dragged him out. The remaining prisoners watched as they dragged him across the square to the former visitors center that had been converted into a punitive surgical theater.

Approaching the spot where they had grabbed the inmate, Uli could see that in his despair he had dug out some of the mud and dirt along the base of the bars. The ancient concrete that had been exposed in the process was fractured and dried out. Uli sensed that it would take little work to knock out at least one of the bars.

He spotted poor Bert, who was staring off in terror of losing his last limb. Troy, by contrast, seemed relaxed; a scar on his back was nothing. Uli softly asked him what the operations were like.

"You don't feel a thing," Troy replied. "It's *after* the surgery that the pain comes."

"Why after?"

"These people aren't even doctors. Most of them were X-ray technicians or ambulance drivers. What do they know about amputation? Your nerves are never the same. You constantly suffer these phantom pains. If I had to do it over again, I'd take a shot at escaping before they cut me."

"What kind of shot?"

"There." Troy's eyes flashed upward. The thick bars of the elephant cage were about eight feet tall, ending at a gap just wide enough to squeeze through.

19

It was only midafternoon when Bea left Factor-E Gallery, so she drove north to upper Greenpoint. First she located the residence that Joe Brainard had told her about, where the unselected Greenpoint-East Williamsburg candidate would dwell. It turned out to be an unlocked storefront with a sign that read, *QUIRKLYN PARTY HEADQUARTERS*. A dozen handwritten notes had been shoved under the door. Bea snatched one up and read aloud: "*You're dead, assholes!*" A variety of other notes shared this sentiment, until she found one that read: *I'm with you guys!* One typed letter that was neatly folded into an envelope turned out to be from the Crapper Political Action Committee. It read:

> *To Whom It May Concern:*
>
> *We propose a series of three debates over the next four weeks that will allow the temporarily resettled constituents of Greenpoint-Williamsburg (minor), Bushwick (minor), and East New York (minor) an opportunity to assess the pros and cons of what each party has to offer. Please contact us at your earliest convenience to sort out the details.*
>
> *Mallory*
> *The Office of Mayor of Rescue City*
> *218-938*

Bea crumpled the letter into a ball and tossed it aside. Without a doubt, she knew that her candidates—provided she even located them all—would not be up for a debate. Walking through the little storefront, she realized there was a large residence in the back with a well-stocked kitchen. As usual, the food consisted of boxed and canned brand names she had never heard of, like Yum-m-my Inc. and Stirpize Foods. She took a box of crackers and a tin of sardines. Unfortunately, there was no liquor. On the living room table, though, someone had left a bag of nicely rolled joints, which she duly pocketed.

Twenty minutes later Bea was driving around the area searching for the address that the Warhol Warthog had given her for Jackie Curtis. Bea saw that every corner in northern Greenpoint and eastern Williamsburg had big blue cardboard signs announcing the Crapper campaigns in the three districts: Ivan Biggs was running in Greenpoint-Williamsburg, Sandy Stewart Faustus in Bushwick, and Geoff Killing in East New York. Long banners were stretched across some of the busier streets. There were also some handwritten purple signs with the ominous phrase VOTE QUIRKLYN.

Bea passed through an area that consisted of identical tract housing divided by hurricane fences. She could see why the flooded evacuees would prefer moving here over southern Brooklyn with its tight geometric barracks, which had been designed for troops, not families.

At one point, she crossed through Quirklyn into Maspeth, Queens, and though no residents were visible, she was impressed by the clean, well-kept streets and nicely painted buildings. She realized that although this area was uninhabited, the Piggers had the good sense to maintain it to give the illusion that the houses were still being occupied to discourage any squatting.

She drove back south, and soon located Jackie Curtis's address. An older woman in a thick wool turtleneck answered the door.

"Is Jackie Curtis here?" Bea asked.

"What's your business?"

"Just friends."

"You're not delivering any money to him, are you? 'Cause he owes me rent, and I won't let him leave until he pays it."

"No money. Is he here?" Bea wondered if the renter was holding Curtis hostage in the backyard.

"No. Go three blocks down and one over to McBarren Park. He wastes his days there."

Bea thanked the woman, got back into her solicar, and followed the directions until she arrived at the park's edge. Driving all the way around it, she saw that a dozen or so shady characters had commandeered the seesaws and were sitting at the base of the slide of the small playground, either smoking choke or drinking beers. Since the reproductive epidemic had hit within the first months, the only children in Rescue City were ones born in Old Town, now mostly in their teens, so playgrounds had often become havens for the ne'er-do-wells.

As Bea came within a few feet of the loafers, a high nasal voice shouted, "We're not leaving, so don't fucking ask us again!"

"Jackie Curtis?" she inquired.

One of the denizens pointed over to the swings where a tall gaunt figure was suspended on the farthest one. Bea thought she was a forlorn senior citizen, but then, walking around to the front, she saw the faintest resemblance to the underexposed photocopy Leary had given her.

"Are you the Andy Warhol Superstar Jackie Curtis?"

"That's me," she replied without even looking up.

"My name's Bea Moses." She noticed that two fingers on Curtis's right hand as well as her thumb on the other hand were missing. "I have an offer for you."

"Does your offer involve getting me the hell out of this shithole?"

"No, but it can involve a comfortable amount of stamps," Bea replied.

The former performer had sunken cheeks and deep rings under her eyes. "Unless you can get me out of here, there's nothing else I want."

"No one has ever confirmed that the escape drug really works," Bea pointed out.

"I'd rather be dead than be stuck here a moment longer."

"If you really feel that way, why haven't you just . . . . ended it?"

"Because the possibility of freedom still exists. And I'm a fucking coward."

"Even here, freedom is relative. And the two gangs that run this place take what little freedom we do have away from us."

"I'm famished," Jackie suddenly announced. "I keep forgetting to eat."

"I got some snacks in my car," Bea said with a smile. "Saltines and sardines."

When Jackie got up, Bea realized she was around six feet tall with zero body fat. The poor woman looked like she was starving herself to death.

"So you live up here in Quirklyn now?" Bea asked as she opened the car door.

"I lost my Manhattan residence in that fucking flood bombing, so yeah, I'm stuck here now. That's part of the joke—we're stuck in this open-air prison and still have to pay rent."

"You know that famous quote from Sartre while he was living in Paris after it had been conquered by the Nazis: *Never were we freer than under the German Occupation.*"

"The first thing I'm gonna do when I get out of here is go to France and punch him in his big frog face," Jackie replied, getting in Bea's car. "'Cause that is such bullshit!"

"I get your point, I do, but frankly, it gets a lot worse. The fact that we can walk around through these awful streets," Bea popped open her glove compartment, "or enjoy the sunset, feel the breeze on our faces, it all makes a world of difference." She took out a box of crackers and a tin of sardines and opened them on the dashboard.

"I had a fucking destiny, goddamnit!" Jackie cried, punching the dashboard.

"I understand, I really do. Hell, I don't want to be here any more than you. I'm just trying to not let them take away more of my freedom than they already have."

"So what do you want?"

"There is a small group of us living here who love your work."

"So you're a fan club or something?" Jackie picked up a mustard packet, tore it open, and squeezed it onto the sardines.

"Not quite. We actually want you to run for one of the city council seats that are coming up."

Jackie was preoccupied with balancing a small sardine on a cracker, but before biting it she asked, "What the fuck are you talking about?"

"You probably heard that these four districts are filled with like-minded people who have stated that they aren't Piggers or Crappers. They're trying to resist this bullshit that we live with and they—we—are hoping you'll run for one of the seats."

"Oh God, you're not talking about that Declaration of Independence nonsense, are you?"

"You said it yourself, Jackie, it's about freedom! We want to help make this tiny area special and keep it as a separate municipality."

"You want to keep the four new districts together." Jackie chomped down on the tip of a cracker.

"Exactly."

"So you'll need a cohesive group of candidates to run as a single party through all four districts," Jackie continued, not missing a beat. "Who are your other three?"

"Well, we realized that though only a few people know you individually, a lot of the hip, young downtown types who moved here know about the Andy Warhol Superstars. So we're hoping we can get four of you together."

"I should've figured. Fucking Warhol! Another lifetime ago—and I'd really rather not go back there."

"You have a solid following here and name recognition."

"And what happens if we do get elected? Ever think of that?"

"We're sure you will get elected. That's what we want."

"We wouldn't even agree on what color toilet paper to use . . ."

"It doesn't really matter, none of you would get seated at any city council meeting. They don't even seat the VL and they've run Staten Island for years."

"So, what's the point?"

"Look, we'll try and see where things go, and even if we don't win, it's called *pushing back*. We can't just just roll over to whatever bully shows up with a baseball bat."

"Who else is on board?" Jackie asked.

"Ondine and Candy Darling."

"It'll be nice to see Candy again. I'm surprised that swarthy wop is still alive. Who's the fourth member?"

"We haven't chosen a fourth yet, but it looks like it might be Valerie Solanas."

Jackie smiled. "I knew you were going to say that. Anyone ever tell you that you look a little like her? I was kinda hoping you had come to shoot me."

"You're the second person to tell me that today," Bea said. "You don't know if any other Superstars are here, do you?"

"I ran into Eric Emerson in Cobble Hill once, but I think he was killed in one of those gang battles." Jackie held another mustard-covered sardine a moment before whispering, "Though he left me standing at the altar, I forgave him, and now that beautiful angel has returned to heaven."

"What would it take to get you to help us?"

"Get me that escape drug and I'm on board."

"All right," Bea said after a short pause. "I'm a little concerned about one thing, though. Back then you were supposedly so . . . trans . . . trans . . . formative."

"I now think of myself as a trans-existentialist, hovering between life and death."

"Yeah, but we need people to recognize the old you."

"I'll wear whatever costume you want, but frankly, I'm just not the sassy little queen I once was. I feel as though I had my life stolen from me. Like a ghost, just here to haunt myself."

Bea felt badly for her. "We would have speeches for you to deliver, Jackie."

"The less I have to do, the better."

Bea asked her to keep a lid on this whole endeavor until they were ready. She added that they should be able to locate Valerie Solanas in the next day or so.

"Who's behind this?"

"I'm part of a larger group. It's best we remain anonymous."

"Great," Jackie said tiredly.

"Can I come by and pick you up sometime tomorrow morning? Say around eleven?"

"See you then," Jackie said, and continued nibbling on her sardine à la mustard in the front seat of Bea's car.

20

It was dark by the time Bea returned to her Williamsburg "head-quarters." She called Candy Darling and asked if she could come alone to the first official Quirklyn meeting in Williamsburg—Cookie Mueller could join her once all the initial arrangements had been ironed out and everyone was comfortable together.

"When do I announce my candidacy, Madam President?" Candy asked in her best Marilyn Monroe voice.

"You all will this Saturday," Bea said.

"As long as we are on that stage together, all is well."

Bea reassured her and gave her the address in Greenpoint–East Williamsburg, or Green-Burg, as everyone had started calling it.

Next, she called the pay phone in Ondine's boarding house in Staten Island. As she had been warned, the phone rang for five minutes before someone finally answered. Then she waited another ten minutes for Ondine to climb down the stairs and pick up.

"Can you come to our first Quirklyn meeting tomorrow at noon?"

"Sure, just pick me up in front of my place at eleven."

"Can't you take the bus?" Bea asked.

"Please don't ask me to do that. I don't even know the bus lines and you have to transfer for each borough and—"

"Fine. I'll drive down and pick you up." Bea was too tired to argue.

She sat down, began to fall asleep, but soon woke up due to hunger. She had just placed a can of ravioli on the hot plate when Joe Brainard called and asked about the status of the mission.

"Three down, one to go," Bea replied.

"Who do you have so far?"

"Ondine, Jackie Curtis, and Candy Darling. I'm still having problems finding a fourth," she said, realizing the hot plate didn't work.

"I was hoping we'd get Edie Sedgwick."

"The only other stupid star who made it out here and is still supposedly alive is Valerie Solanas," Bea informed him, as she began forking down the cold pasta.

"Didn't she kill Warhol?"

"She only shot him. Listen, I told all three to meet me here tomorrow at noon."

"Great," Joe said. "I'll take it from there."

To celebrate the near completion of this freaky mission, Bea also ate a small can of diced pineapple for dessert, then went to bed.

21

It wasn't until the sixth condemned convict of the day was dragged out of the elephant pen to be amputated that the photographer finally showed up and told Uli the awful news: his sister Karen Sarkisian had been killed. The new attorney general of Rescue City South was now Schuman, whom Uli remembered as Karen's assistant.

Before he could even start grieving over his sister's death, and before the sleazy photographer could request his payment, Uli said, "All right, for the same price, call Schuman's office and explain that Uli Sarkisian is about to get his fucking arms amputated."

"First, pay me," the photographer replied.

"Like I said before, if I pay you there's no reason for you to do it."

"Okay, show me that you have the stamps and I'll do it."

After a long pause, Uli asked, "How much would you charge me for *not* showing you the money?"

"Oh man, I'm going to get screwed on this one."

Uli was stripped down to his boxer shorts and dirty T-shirt. He held up his hand and said, "If I don't pay you, you can have my right hand."

"What can I do with a right hand?" the photographer said, then paused before adding, "Gallo says everyone's worth something."

"Who's Gallo?"

"What do you do for a living?"

"I used to be an FBI agent," Uli said.

"Seriously?"

"So I'm told."

"Shit, I should kill you for that alone. Okay, if I call this individual for you, would you be willing to sign a statement that says you will be in our debt?"

"Whose debt? And for what exactly?" Uli asked.

"You're FBI."

"I'm not exactly affiliated with them any longer."

"I understand, but with your skills, you can probably do a hit," the guy said simply. "Relax, in this place that doesn't mean much. People get away with murder every day, and they're not even ex-G-men."

"You mean an assassination?"

"No, Mr. Gallo doesn't dirty his hands with politics. It'll probably be something tasteful—Mr. Gallo is a very classy guy."

"Then why did you say a *hit?*"

"You asked me something, and that was the worst thing that popped into my head. If I call this person, and relay this message, will you agree to do Mr. Gallo any favor whatsoever?"

The sergeant came out of the visitors center to announce the next name on the list of condemned men. Uli held his breath in fear.

"Bertram Haywood!"

Instantly, the poor man used his one good leg to propel the wagon containing him and his legless partner through the wet mud to the farthest edge of the outdoor pen. The gang of guards opened the gate door, snarling and snapping as they raced over. Troy held on to the cell bars, but one of the men grabbed Bert's remaining leg and tugged him off the cart and across the courtyard.

"No man deserves to be treated like this!" Troy shouted.

"Not my leg, please!" Bert screamed. "It's all I got. Please! I didn't do nothing!"

"All right, I'll do anything!" Uli said to the photographer in desperation. "Just move it."

"I want you to understand, Mr. Gallo ain't Crapper or Pigger. He don't care who you are, or who you know. If you don't pay him back— he'll get you."

"Fine."

"Smile," the guy said, snapping a Polaroid of Uli. Without waiting for it to dry, he took out a thick marker and wrote three letters on the back of the picture: IOU. "Sign at the bottom, then tell me exactly who to call and what to say, because you're paying for my services, not the results, *capisce?*"

"When do I have to pay back this favor?" Uli asked as he signed.

"When we find you."

Uli instructed the photographer to call the new attorney general Schuman and Mallory's office and explain that he was being held in Pigger lockup in the Bronx Zoo, and could they please come in the next few hours or he would have his arms amputated.

"Double arm amputation is extremely rare," the man replied. "May I suggest that I say just one arm?"

"Whatever works."

"If I can get through to either of those people, and if they actually care that you're stuck in here, they're going to ask me for some proof. They don't know me, so I could be setting them up for an ambush."

Uli realized he had a point, so he thought about what detail he could offer to prove his identity. "For Schuman, tell him, *Thanks again for the sleeping bag and can of grease from the trunk of your car.* If you get ahold of Mayor Mallory, say that I greatly enjoyed our sandy night at the Bedmill Hotel in Bensonhurst."

"You know she's still married to Mayor Willy, her paralyzed husband. You sure you want to say that?"

"It's the only private detail that we shared," Uli replied.

The man jotted down some notes and told Uli he'd see him soon, hopefully.

Uli watched the photographer calmly walk back toward the visitors center.

22

J oe Brainard tried to sleep, but he couldn't get it out of his head that Rafique had lied to him. Or maybe he just didn't know, or maybe someone had lied to Rafique. Regardless, the sickness he had wasn't just some kind of ground or water virus. Was it a bacteria, or a parasite? Was it possible that there was a single hydra-headed ailment, the symptoms of which could evolve over time? Joe had spent nights dwelling on his affliction, trying to divide the paranoia from the reality. Lately, perhaps due to this obsessing, his memory had been lapsing. Something awful was definitely going around. And he didn't believe, as some suspected, that it was the male strain of the government-engineered EGGS epidemic that kept women from reproducing.

Prior to beginning his regimen of the six different types of pills that he took three times a day, Joe Brainard would wake up each morning in a pool of sweat.

During the past few weeks, when he realized he wasn't dying, or at least not soon, he found his thoughts spinning back to Tulsa, Oklahoma, only three states east of Nevada. He had grown up with so many other adventurous young men, poets, intent on leaving their artistic marks on a limitless world that was only getting bigger and better.

When he wasn't depressed by his current condition, Joe Brainard found himself amused by the absurd string of unlikely events that had plucked him from being a graphic artist and poet in the eastern edge of Greenwich Village, and transformed him into a campaign manager in this scaled-down, washed-out facsimile of New York City.

He picked up his notebook and made a new addition to his latest work:

I wonder—when the very last of us, the youngest, is on his death bed in 2068, will one of those constant drone planes finally land with a single living pilot on board? And will that pilot come to that survivor's bedside and inform him that New York City is finally cleansed, ready to be repopulated? I wonder.

Suddenly his phone rang.

It was Bea, who sounded frantic. She said she had woken up late. Was there any chance of him collecting Candy Darling and Jackie Curtis and driving them to the Green-Burg headquarters for the big noon meeting? She was going to have to spend the entire morning trying to locate Valerie Solanas.

"Okay."

"Oh, also, could you pick up Ondine en route from Staten Island?"

"Where exactly is he?"

"At the Shell Sea Hotel on the St. George landing." She gave him the address and the number to the public phone in the hallway. Just to be on the safe side, she warned him not to let Ondine talk him into detouring to New Dope for a fix—they needed him to be sharp.

Joe said he'd do what he could. He couldn't tell her that he felt so weak this morning that he didn't even know how he was going to get out of bed. Dragging himself up, he took his first cocktail of pills, and because today was special, he slipped in an amphetamine. Within minutes he started dressing.

Bea knew the single linchpin to the success of the day would be Valerie Solanas. Without her, they were all screwed. She had tried calling Scouter Lewis repeatedly the night before and that morning, but the phone just kept ringing.

"Pick up, pick up, pick up," she muttered as it rang. By nine a.m., she realized that she was all out of time. She dashed to her car and began the long drive to southern Brooklyn. The entire time, she prayed that Lewis had located the final member of the Warhol quartet. And even if he had, she still had to actually find Valerie and persuade her to join the wacky campaign.

When Bea finally arrived in Sheepshead Bay, Lewis's door was ajar. The annoying dog was barking his little head off, but the old detective didn't answer when she called out his name. As she entered, she could see him sitting with his back to her, his feet up on the desk. He was staring so intensely at his worn sneakers that it looked as if his retinas were going to detach.

"Maybe it's time to get a new pair," she joked.

"I found your friend," he said softly. Clearly he was already a little drunk. "She's sitting right there."

"Where?"

"Brown paper bag on my desk."

Instantly, Bea felt her hopes collapse. Lifting the large bag from the crowded desk, half expecting to feel the weight of an urn full of ashes, she emptied the contents onto an empty chair: a black Mao Tse-tung hat, a small dark-blue peacoat, and a stapled stack of pages entitled *SCUM Manifesto*, as well as some loose sheets of a manuscript with the word *Unlubricated* on the top page. There were also a couple of snapshots. In one photo Valerie stood awkwardly in front of Max's Kansas City nightclub in Old Town. The second photo was of a more gaunt, run-down version of the woman standing in front of Max's Nevada City—the recreated club across from Onion Square Park. Bea realized that she really did resemble a younger, darker, happier version of Solanas.

"That was all there was in her rooming house, according to her landlady," Lewis said. "She was going to toss it, but I figured you might be interested."

"What happened?"

"What always happens: she died."

"When?" Bea looked closely at the second photo. Strangely, she had found herself being drawn to this oddball.

"Oh, you're going to love this—two days ago."

"What!" Bea gasped.

"She was still alive when you came here and asked me to find her," Lewis said.

Bea's brain started calculating. "Someone must've found out what I was trying to do . . . and killed her!" She immediately began wondering if she could actually trust this man.

"No way," he said. "She was hit by the floodwater, like everyone else. She got pulled out, but came down with typhoid, which turned quickly into pneumonia. She died at St. Vinny's."

By the look in his eyes, Bea could see that Lewis was truly saddened as well. The man was a jagged mix of brutal and humane.

"I don't mean to be rude," he said, petting his lapdog, "but I've got someone else coming by and I have to get ready."

Bea put Valerie's scant possessions back in the bag, thanked the man for his help, and departed. She didn't know what she would do with Solanas's things, but since it was all that remained of the woman, she couldn't just trash it.

Returning to her car, Bea flipped through the *Manifesto* and found herself first amused, then hypnotized by its fierceness. The work had been reduced to a terse, angrily worded argument calling for the destruction of the male sex. *She confused male weakness with human weakness,* Bea thought. If Solanas knew that women were no better, the work would've been an argument for the annihilation of mankind itself. Faintly penciled throughout the margins, Bea noticed the recurrent phrase *ha ha!* For an instant she wondered if the manifesto was intended as a big practical joke.

Catching her own reflection in the rearview mirror, another prank crossed her mind. Taking a brush from her bag, Bea swept her hair back and tried to imitate Valerie's indifferent facial expression. Comparing herself with the second photo in the shopping bag, she thought the only thing that was off was her complexion—if Solanas sported a constant tan, as she might in this desert environment, they could pass for sisters.

Bea suddenly wondered if she could actually get away with it. Then she remembered what Jackie had said—that she was a head taller than Solanas. But this was another detail that only those who knew her would detect. Due to her troubled personality, Solanas was never very popular, so it wasn't as if there would be throngs of good friends who might notice all the little discrepancies.

When Bea arrived back at the Green-Burg headquarters it was only eleven thirty. She found Joe Brainard waiting in front, a collection of chain-smoked butts on the ground in front of him. Although it was warm outside, he was wearing a wool sweater. Like before, the shirt was unbuttoned and she could see his thick black chest hair curling out. He hadn't yet spotted her, so Bea pulled on Valerie's peacoat and cap, got out of the car, and walked over to him, not making eye contact.

"Is this where Bea Mayer lives?" she mumbled.

"Are you . . ." Brainard trailed off. Bea knew he had just seen Solanas in the recovered Warhol footage of *I, a Man*. ". . . Ms. Solanas?"

She saw that the Brain was sweaty and trembling. He looked pale. "Are you okay, Joe?"

"I just got a touch of something. I'm fine," he said, then chuckled. "You really fooled me."

"Where's Ondine?" she asked.

"Passed out in the backseat of my car."

She opened the door to the headquarters and led him inside.

"So where's Solanas? What's with the costume?" Brainard asked.

"Actually, it's probably the only chance we have of pulling this thing off."

"What do you mean?"

"Valerie Solanas is dead."

"Please tell me you're lying."

Bea pursed her lips; his twisted in response.

"She survived the flood, but died of an infection."

"Shit!" He took a long draw from his cigarette.

"I've thought about it," Bea said, "and it's either me or no one."

"There must be another Superstar somewhere."

"Unless we can get back to New York and kidnap one, I'm it. All of the others are dead, and we got less than six weeks before the election."

Joe sighed.

"Do you think people will realize I'm not her?"

"You look like her, enough to fool me. But what happens if someone who knew her well shows up while you're campaigning?"

"She was supposedly a recluse to the end. People seemed to prefer the *idea* of her to the actual her."

"That's probably true of all of them," Brainard said.

"It's probably true of every politician, so it's just a risk we'll have to take. It might actually be better this way," Bea opined. "I can make her charming and help handle the group while being a part of it. And if I do get caught, no one's going to lynch me, I'll just step down."

"If you get caught, you'll *all* probably have to step down."

"Did Rafique have a plan B?" Bea asked.

The Brain shook his head no.

"So if I don't do it, it ends right now." Then she asked, "Where are the others?"

"Candy asked if she could come at noon and Jackie's landlady said she wouldn't be back for at least another hour."

"I can pick her up if you're not feeling well," Bea said. "What's the plan?"

"For starters, I was going to ask them all to spend the next day or so here to just get used to each other again."

"So I'll have to sleep here with them? Is that even safe?"

"They're three gay men, and you're a violent dyke. If there's a menace here, you're it. You're all running as this Warhol group. We want people to see an esprit de corps."

"Were you going to come and meet them?"

"I'm the campaign manager, but frankly," Joe let out another sigh,

"I'm not doing too well. If you can stay with them and take care of daily operations, I'd be able to conserve my strength and focus on bigger items that still need to be done."

Bea was nervous that she had just gotten in way over her head. "Okay . . ."

"You go get Jackie," the Brain said, looking at his wristwatch, "hopefully Candy will arrive soon, and then we'll get started."

"But after Saturday, when we've announced our candidacy," she clarified, "then we each stay in our own homes, right?"

"Absolutely. Everyone has to maintain a residence in the district they're running in." Brainard crushed his cigarette and started walking to his car.

"You know what would really help?" Bea said. "A couple of boxes of wine. Just enough to get them buzzed."

"Good idea. I'll pick some up."

Bea sped the few blocks to Jackie's rented room. She parked out front, raced up the walkway, and rapped on the door.

When the landlady saw her, she instantly started screaming, "That deadbeat faggot snuck out with his bags fifteen minutes ago, and he owed me two weeks of back rent!"

Bea hurried back to her car and drove over to the nearby playground. From behind the wheel, she saw Jackie sitting—a tall, lone figure on the last of the empty rows of swings, staring off into the stillness, her duffel bag at her feet. Bea went over and said hello. Jackie nodded silently. Bea picked up her bag and quietly led her to the car.

23

By the time Bea got Jackie Curtis to headquarters, the Brain had visited the local stamp shop in Crapper-occupied Williamsburg, where he had picked up two gallon-sized boxes of white wine. He drove back to Green-Burg, then shook Ondine awake from the back-seat and led him into the storefront.

"What is this headquarters shit?" Ondine asked, puzzled by the sign on the window.

"In a couple of days you'll each be living in the Quirklyn headquarters in your own districts."

"Oh, that's right, we're doing some kind of election scam."

Bea wasn't sure how long it had been since the Warholers had last seen each other, or how close they once were, but when Jackie Curtis spotted Ondine she simply nodded. Slightly intoxicated, Ondine nod-ded back and checked his pockets for a cigarette. It was almost noon.

"Guys," Bea said, "we're gonna wait until Candy Darling gets here before we start going over the job."

As the two Warholers chugged down small cups of fruity white wine, Joe Brainard came in and explained that he was one of the main Quirklyn organizers.

"What the fuck is this Quirklyn group going to do anyways?" On-dine asked.

The Brain looked to Bea, who smiled and said, "A small group of influential people who live here have decided that they've had enough of these gangs bullying us."

"Where'd you get all the stamps and resources?" Jackie asked.

"Well—" the Brain began, but before he could start weaving some intricate lie, there were three delicate raps on the door and it swung open.

Candy Darling, who had gained considerable weight since leaving Old Town, entered light as a feather in heels. She carried a huge suitcase in one hand and a half dozen wig cases strung together in the other.

The Superstars rose and they all hugged. Bea sensed they were all embarrassed by different shortcomings: Jackie by her depression, as evidenced by her emaciated and skeletal state; Ondine by his bloated yellow face, indicative of years on the Feedmore-sponsored methadone program; and, of course, Candy Darling, who was now obese.

"I meant to ask," Jackie said after an awkward silence, "what's to keep the two gangs from just invading this area and throwing us all out?"

"All sides are vowing to keep the peace—Pax Rescue City," Bea said.

"What'll keep them from manipulating the results?" Candy asked, checking out her lipstick in her compact mirror.

"Since the Crappers broke away and are also involved in the 'Quirklyn crisis,'" Joe Brainard answered, "the Election Commission in Kew Gardens has agreed to install a three-man panel in each district to oversee the results as they come in."

"Won't people wonder how we came together and decided to run as a group?" Jackie asked.

"I'm sure they will, and I'm even more certain the two gangs will, so I'm gonna tell you—the VL is behind this. That is a secret, and if you tell anyone it'll ruin our chances of getting elected. But since I think you would've found out anyway, I'm expecting each of you to keep it confidential."

"What'll we tell people—that we just met on the street and decided to run?"

"Sure, why not? You were all associates from Old Town, and you were residents of the Village, which was just flooded. Documentation has already been created establishing residency in the four new districts you'll be representing: Candy Darling, you're living in this apartment in Green-Burg, Jackie Curtis is living in Bushwick, and Ondine is headquartered in East New York."

"I hope we have working phones," Ondine said.

"And well-stocked fridges," added Candy.

"This weekend in McBarren Park during your coming-out party, when you declare your candidacies, you'll meet your drivers who will then take you to your new homes."

"Will my driver do whatever I tell him?" Candy joked, showing a glimmer of her former self.

"The first day we learned that the Piggers formally filed for a campaign," the Brain resumed his orientation, reading from a notebook, "we began an information campaign to unify the region and get the locals to think of themselves as independent. We tied up purple ribbons and put up VOTE QUIRKLYN posters."

Candy produced a poster she had ripped down from a nearby lamppost. "Tell me this ain't us."

The poster was a simple graphic with Ernie Bushmiller's 1930s cartoon character Nancy and a thought bubble that read:

WHEN? SATURDAY AT NOON!
WHERE? MCBARREN PARK, GREENPOINT!!
WHAT? PEACE RALLY & COMING OUT PARTY
FOR THE QUIRKLYN PARTY CANDIDACY
FOR CITY COUNCIL!!!
WHO? YOU GUESSED IT!!!!
YOUR OLD FRIENDS—
THE ANDY WARHOL SUPERSTARS!!!!!!
COME BY, SAY HI! MUSIC, FOOD, 4-FREE!
FUN IN THE SUN! YUM!

"Do you like it?" the Brain asked with his sweet gap-toothed smile.

"For starters," Jackie said, "our names and pictures aren't even on it."

"Glad you reminded me," the Brain replied, clearly a bit nervous. "I got some Polaroids, but they weren't so good, so . . ." He pulled a thirty-five-millimeter camera out of his knapsack and clipped on a flash. "I'd actually love to take everyone's ph-photos now for publicity materials."

Bea asked Jackie if she had any of her former camp wardrobe. Jackie opened her duffel bag and took out an ancient and faded white wig that looked like a mop. Candy quickly grabbed a long, frizzy-haired wig from her own stash and offered it to Jackie.

"My color was more platinum than gold, but I guess it'll do," Jackie conceded.

Ondine agreed to pose first since he never went in drag. Because the film was in black-and-white, Joe didn't worry about his yellow complexion, though he did focus from a downward angle to hide Ondine's double chins, and had him suck in his cheeks.

"Nothing personal," Ondine sighed, "but only Jack Smith could make me beautiful on film now."

"Was he a Superstar?" Bea asked.

"He'll always be one to me," Candy replied.

They all sighed, remembering how the once great film director had blown himself up at the Food Stamp Office when the Piggers first turned the city into a free-market economy years earlier.

Bea watched as Jackie slipped on Candy's wig and awkwardly applied her makeup. She seemed to have forgotten how she used to look, so Candy patiently helped her.

Meanwhile, Brainard shot a dozen photos of Ondine, doing his best to make him look like his former self. After fifteen minutes, the photographer was ready for his next subject—Candy. Jackie posed last. By the time the Brain was done with the photographs, a lot of wine had been consumed and everyone had calmed down.

"Oh, we still haven't taken photos of Valerie Solanas," Brainard said to Bea. The other Warholers immediately grew silent.

"Where is she?" Candy finally asked.

"In the car, I'll get her," said Bea, rising slowly.

"Christ, I hope she didn't bring her pistol," said Ondine.

"Both the Piggers and Crappers will be running on the platform of 'This is *our* land,'" Brainard said, taking advantage of the nervous silence. "What we want to emphasize is that Quirklyn was abandoned by them, and we're the new *us*—an us without any violent ties, an us not connected to all the brutality. The two gangs have a proprietary attitude and are casting us as outsiders, but they're also vowing to keep things peaceful."

"Cookie and I are avowed Buddhists, so . . ."

"We are not putting anyone in jeopardy. You don't have to worry."

The door opened and Bea, in the dark-blue peacoat and Mao cap, gave her best Valerie Solanas expression behind black sunglasses.

After five awkward seconds, Ondine burst out laughing, the others joining in. "Oh shit! Look at the hottest little drag king in Nevada!"

Bea explained that she was going to be running in the election as Valerie Solanas.

"Tell me you're kidding," Jackie said, smiling for the first time.

"We need four Warholers, so it's me or no one."

"Nothing personal, lady, but you didn't fool me for a sec," Candy said. "Your hair's all wrong."

"Look," the Brain said, "you are three of the only people who were a part of the whole Factory thing. Unless she was a member of a book club or sewing circle somewhere, only you will be able to tell that Bea isn't Valerie. So if we're going to pull this off, you've all got to stay together. From now on, we'll only call Bea Valerie. No slipups."

"What happens when Crazy Daisy shows up with a six-shooter, like she did with poor Andy?" Ondine asked.

"She just passed away," Bea broke the news.

"Good riddance," Candy muttered.

Ondine started making jokes and pretending to shoot everyone. Joe Brainard let out an exasperated sigh. Bea was about to give a hostile response, but Brainard shook his head.

"By the by, I can help you shape that knot of seaweed on your head into Valerie's unimaginative hairdo," Candy said, fishing a pair of shears out of her suitcase.

Bea took off her jacket and pulled a chair out to the backyard. Candy grabbed a comb and joined her. Though she said she didn't need to see it, Bea showed Candy the photo of Valerie to refresh her memory. After running the comb through her hair and straightening out the snags, Candy started clipping. It wasn't long before she'd made Bea look even more like Solanas. Afterward, Joe positioned Bea and took some photos of her as well.

"Maybe she should be holding a gun," Ondine said. "She was most famous for her assassination attempt."

"Yeah, but I think we want to downplay that," Bea replied, considering the liability of running an attempted murderess.

"Okay, ladies," the Brain said, "we put a lot of work into finding out what matters to the residents of Quirklyn, and we came up with four simple points: First, you're running on the concept that Quirklyn is a fiercely independent republic of artists and hip people, and you should emphasize that you yourselves are artists—"

"'Cause we damn well are!" Candy cut in, snapping her fingers and shaking her ample hips.

"Secondly, you're offering an alternative to the spectacular gang violence that has turned Rescue City into a homicidocracy."

"We'll *kill* with that," Jackie punned.

"Our third point is a little tricky because of today's announcement in the newspaper." The Brain held up the day's copy of the *Daily Posted New York Times*, displaying the headline "Trials Come to Rescue City!" "The Crappers are initiating a new trial system."

"Oh shit," mumbled Bea.

"Not quite," the Brain replied. "They're still continuing with the amputations, whereas we're proposing a prison, and that's a big difference, so our third point is, we believe in a fair criminal justice system that has yet to be developed."

"Who gives a shit about that?" Ondine asked.

"During Mallory's mayoral campaign, every poll showed that it was the primary objection people had to Shub's administration, on both sides," the Brain said, looking down at his notebook. "Almost everyone has a loved one who has lost an extremity for some minor infraction or trumped-up charge."

"Tell me about it," said Jackie, displaying her missing fingers.

"And that leads us to the last thing that people object to, which the Crappers aren't addressing: we believe in term limits—unless of course no one else within the district is running, which should grant you all a couple terms."

"In what sleazy gay bar's bathroom stalls do we give these talking points?" Ondine asked.

"This election is going to be run on a local grassroots level. The main thing will be staying in your district for the next month and trying to spend as much time outside as possible. Hobnob! Get to know your neighbors, blend in with them. Talk with them about anything, but when you can gracefully assert any of these four points, do so. A lot of your campaigning is going to be at close range and spontaneous. If you see a bunch of people gathering somewhere, join them. We'll do our best to find people congregating and throw you into the mix, but a lot of it must be your own initiative—opportunity campaigning. Your job is to mingle, introduce yourself, and explain what's happening."

"God! I hate talking to people, they're such morons!" Jackie grumbled.

"We're doing this for a whole month?" Ondine asked shakily.

"That's right—starting with your announcement this Saturday afternoon," Bea said.

"With all due respect, this isn't what Cookie and I signed on for," Candy complained.

"Who the fuck is Cookie?" Jackie asked.

"You told us it would be a series of performances," Candy said to Bea.

"Frankly, I just don't know if I have the . . . strength," Ondine lamented.

Bea tried to reassure them, but the Brain could see everyone's worried expressions. The social butterflies they once were had returned to their cocoons; the Brain figured it would take a little time to bring them out again. Bea opened a new box of wine, and the Brain nodded toward the door. It was time for him to go.

"I gotta tell you, I'd leave right now if we hadn't agreed on terms," Ondine said.

"Same here," Jackie added.

24

Retreating to the outer office, Joe Brainard explained that he had to return to Tottenville to make sure four cars and drivers/bodyguards were on their way to keep an eye on the new candidates. Before leaving, though, he asked Bea one question: "What exactly did you offer them in exchange for their participation?"

"Rafique said, *Whatever it takes*."

"So what did it take?"

She told Joe that she had offered Candy a thousand stamps. Joe stared at the western sky for what seemed like five minutes before he finally nodded. Then she said that Ondine had requested an unlimited supply of methadone.

"And Jackie?"

"She wants a syringe filled with the legendary Mnemosyne drug."

"That's easy enough—two packets of sugar and a teaspoon of water. 'Cause if anything, I think it's just poison."

Bea cringed at that, because she was hoping that Uli—the only person she knew who had been injected with it—was still alive somewhere. "Joe," she said softly, "I don't want to sound like I'm backing out, because I'm not, but do you really think this Superstar campaign is realistic?"

Peeking in at the group, the Brain watched as Candy Darling ate potato chips and yakked away at Ondine, who had nodded off. Jackie had a vacant expression as though she had just come out of electroshock.

"We have to try," he whispered.

"How do you motivate the unmotivated?" Bea asked.

"Later this afternoon, the Crappers are having their first rally in Bushwick—they're introducing their three candidates. I figure if we bring Ondine, Jackie, and Candy out there to show them what we're up against, it might outrage them toward action."

"What'll I do with them until then?"

"They're a bunch of prickly pears; step back and let them just get used to each other again." Fishing through his pocket, the Brain pulled out a brochure. "Also, if you could have them commit the four key points to memory and try to build anecdotes for them, that'll be useful—but today should be easy for them."

"When are you going to go over the big coming-out rally speeches with us?"

"That's one reason I need to leave now. I have a guy working on it who's excellent; I'm meeting with him first thing tomorrow morning," the Brain said, and headed out the door.

Bea returned inside to see that Ondine had woken up and was exchanging pills with Candy while Jackie silently looked on.

"So are we all ready for a great campaign?" Bea asked, clapping her hands together.

"Thirty days of hobnobbing with hobgoblins," Candy said dully. "Last time I made that much small talk was at an orgy with dwarfs."

"All of Andy's films were improv," Ondine said. "This will be theater."

"It's still insane," Jackie interjected. "My God, we're facing the kind of schedule that killed Judy Garland."

"Oh remember," Candy said sadly, "that was one of the last things we did in Old Town—remember Judy's funeral?"

"If I can dress as Valerie Solanas and do this," Bea finally said, "the rest of you can do your parts too. It's a little more than a month and you girls will be staying in nice apartments the whole time."

"What exactly are *you* getting out of this?" Jackie asked suspiciously.

"Nothing. Absolutely nothing," Bea replied honestly.

"You're sure this isn't part of a cult or something?" Ondine asked.

"We just think the Crappers and Piggers have run this place into the ground and it's gone far enough."

"What's going to happen after the election?" Jackie asked. "I mean, aren't people going to know we're all phonies if we just pack up and leave?"

"We'll worry about that when the time comes."

"We're thinking we might be able to stay on and help you guys," Ondine said.

"Stay on where?"

"In these nice headquarters you've set up for us," Candy said. The little group had evidently come up with their own scheme.

"It's not up to me," Bea said.

"You know we'd work a lot harder for your communist cause—"

"We're not communists."

"Well, whatever scam you guys are pulling, we'd be loyal to that," Candy said, looking around at her new apartment. "If we could live in these homes permanently."

"I've already negotiated very generous terms with each of you."

"That's too bad, because I'm tired of being homeless," Jackie joined in.

Bea was afraid of pushing too much bullshit. "Look, if you do a good job, I'll look into seeing if you can stay on, but any problems and it's over."

"Thank God! I'll kill myself if I have to spend another day in Stink Island. I swear, it's like having your nose stuck up some old man's hairy asshole," Ondine said.

Candy and Ondine were clearly elated by the prospect of a clean, well-stocked home—helped along by their recent ingestion of happy pills—but Jackie still looked glum.

"What's pinching your nips?" Candy asked.

"Being together with you guys," she responded. "It makes me think of the old days: singing, dancing, acting. I really felt like my career was going somewhere."

"Yeah, we had everything but money," Candy said.

"The old days weren't easy," Ondine pointed out. "I was always broke. Would it have killed Andy to let us stay at his place in Montauk during this whole mess? I mean, our lives are totally fucked here."

"We can change that!" Bea said. Like a cheerleader, she called out: "What are the four points that we Quirklyners stand for?"

"Keep your dick taped back, your hoses pulled high, walk tall, and don't smudge your lipstick?" Candy shot back.

"Ladies, you have got to learn this! Four simple rules set us apart from the two gangs, and if you don't know them, this just ain't gonna work. And if this don't work," she looked at Jackie, "you don't get your escape drug." To Candy, "You and Cookie don't get your stamps." And finally to Ondine, who was nodding off again, she yelled, "And you don't get your methadone!"

"And you don't get to go back to Kansas," Jackie muttered.

"That escape drug is bullshit," Ondine said with his eyelids half closed.

"How the fuck do you know?" Jackie snarled.

"He's right," Candy said. "You'd have better luck taping your ruby-red balls together, 'cause no drug is getting you outta here, sweetie."

"I've made my deal, and it's nonnegotiable," Jackie replied.

"Number one," Bea said, consulting the brochure, "we alone believe Quirklyn is an independent state of artists. Number two: we're not just trying to win city council seats, we're looking at this as an alternative to the two gangs that hold this place hostage. Number three: we believe there should be a fair criminal justice system, replacing amputation with incarceration. And lastly, we believe in term limits." Bea paused. "So what are the four points now?"

"*Doe, a deer, a female deer,*" Candy burst out singing, "*ray, a drop of golden sun. Me, a name I call myself, far, a long, long way to run . . .*"

"Goddamn it!" Bea yelled.

"Quirklyn's an indy-fucking-pendent republic for beauty queens," Candy started. "We're running to stop the gang bang we keep getting from both ends. We want to start a fair criminal justice system that doesn't cut off your foreskin just 'cause you need some eyeliner, and term limits to drive the pimps out!"

"Great," Bea said, trying to loosen up. "You should make it personal, customize it for yourself. How about it, Jackie?"

"I don't know. Start an artsy-fartsy art colony, end the two-gang thing, get justice and term limits," she said succinctly, and gulped down another glass of boxed wine.

Bea shook Ondine's shoulder and tried to rouse him to repeat the four points as well. He started slowly, but then forgot, so Candy stood up and acted it out like a game of charades.

"Don't you have to prepare too?" Jackie asked Bea.

"What do you mean?"

"Well, you're running too."

"So?"

"So you're a pussy-eating dyke named Valerie," Candy jumped in. "Let's see you do that."

"Was she actually a lesbian?" Bea asked.

"Well, unless I'm mistaken, that *Scummy Manifesto* meant she wanted to cut up men—that doesn't sound pro-hetero."

"Thank you," Ondine chimed in, "Jacqueline's right! There are going to be some people at this thing who probably knew her, and she was one scary fucking bomb thrower!"

"You have to remember two things," Jackie said, enjoying the fact that she had turned the tables on Bea. "First, you're as mad as a motherfucker, and secondly, you like snatch and can't lick enough of it."

"Relax," Bea replied.

"Say it, sister!" Candy exclaimed. "You're as hard as nails and soft as cotton candy."

"I'll work on seriously nurturing the dyke inside of me," Bea said, "if you guys just keep thinking about your own roles. You're politicians now, and you have to try to rise to the occasion."

"What scares me the most," Ondine said, "is the fact that we're each going to be all alone."

Candy looked down nervously, because she was going to be working with Cookie and wasn't sure if the others knew that.

"We're getting you all private drivers," Bea explained, trying to prop them up, "who are trained to serve and protect you."

"I need a cigarette," Candy said.

"I need methadone," Ondine said, "and I'll be needing a lot of it over the next four weeks."

"I need a mentholated cigarette," Jackie Curtis concluded.

Bea and Candy chatted as Jackie and Ondine passed out. Candy told her about what life had been like in downtown New York. Bea took the opportunity to ask questions about the person she was going to impersonate.

"What exactly happened between Valerie and Andy Warhol that led to the shooting?"

"Oh, Val had written a play that she wanted Andy to produce. Of course, she only made the one copy, and he lost it. So she'd call him and ask for it back, and he'd just say he was looking for it."

"And she finally broke down and shot him?"

"Well, I don't know if it was just the play," Candy said. "It might have been other things too."

"What other things?"

"After she shot him, she surrendered to a traffic cop and supposedly said something like, *He had too much control of my life.*"

"So she was paranoid."

"Not really," Ondine mumbled, waking from his stupor. "Everyone thought so at the time, but I knew exactly what she was talking about. Andy took all of us out of nowhere. And look at us, we're all pretty delusional to start with. Andy cast us in all these little films. I mean, who else would ever be interested in us? We're freaks. But then people started writing about us in magazines and putting our pictures in the papers." In another moment, Ondine fell back to sleep.

"So?" Bea wasn't sure what Candy was getting at.

"Hon, I've taken every drug in this world, and let me tell you:

celebrity is by far the most addictive. You get a little of it and you immediately want more. I used to think of Andy as our fame dealer, our celebrity pimp. The thing is, he really wasn't, but I think that's what happened to poor Valerie. She just thought, *Whatever I end up becoming, it's all up to Andy.*"

Bea continued to ask for details about Valerie Solanas's voice, phrasing, and physical behavior, how she carried herself and dressed, until around two thirty, when the phone rang. It was the Brain calling to remind Bea to take the Superstars to the Crapper rally beginning in half an hour on Bushwick Avenue. She woke Jackie and Ondine and told them she had a surprise.

"What kind of surprise?" Jackie asked.

"A big party," Bea said, and told them to hurry.

Twenty minutes later, the four of them were in the car and driving through ramshackle Williamsburg and into the narrow streets of upper Bushwick.

Crapper campaign posters were taped to lampposts and glued to the sides of run-down buildings:

Vote City Council Member Ivan Biggs for Greenpoint-Williamsburg

A Big Change Is Coming to Brooklyn—Trials

City Council Candidate Sandy Stewart Faustus for Bushwick

A fourth poster also announced the trials and introduced the candidate from East New York—Geoff Killing.

"Isn't there a fourth city council candidate?" Jackie asked.

"Yeah, Dennis Izzlowski," Bea said. "He's the Pigger candidate that I'm running against in South Ozone Park in Queens. You won't have to deal with him."

She drove her little car past a bulge of at least a hundred people gathering in the street and trying to squeeze into a large empty lot. She parked a few blocks away and her little quartet marched back to the lot, which was landscaped with small leafy trees still in their planter buckets, placed about in an attempt to transform the sad little space into an impromptu park. A portable steel stage had been hastily assembled, and someone was speaking from it. Bea and the three candidates moved through the crowd until they could see their adversaries seated on the stage—middle-aged men in boring gray suits. Since Candy and Jackie were in drag and Ondine just looked strange, they stood out in the tight crowd.

An older balding man was in the middle of a speech, although he was so relaxed and folksy that it sounded more like a chat: "I don't like being the bearer of bad news—too many people kill messengers, if you know what I mean." Laughs. "But since Rescue City was started, this stretch of land between the two boroughs has changed hands twenty-seven times. My God! Twenty-seven times! Our main concern as Crappers would be to post a strong garrison up here to serve and protect y'all. So when the Piggers swoop down for attack number twenty-eight, as I'm sure they inevitably will, we'll be ready for them. By the way, I don't blame this new group that's trying to start an independence movement—hell, I admire those kids. Only problem is that doing it here is kinda like trying to build a sandcastle on a stormy beach; there's a reason this area is empty."

"They're hustling fear," Bea muttered a little too loud.

"By the looks of your little group," some large middle-aged woman responded, "I'd say *you're* the one hustling fear, dear."

None of them responded. But the woman and her short, angry-looking husband were now focused on them. They kept listening to the speaker, who turned out to be the Crapper councilman from Bushwick South. One by one he introduced the Crapper candidates, Ivan Biggs was a chunky man with a square jaw who would be running against Candy Darling in Green-Burg; a skinny kid with prematurely gray hair named Sandy Faustus would be going up against Jackie Curtis in Bushwick; and a wide balding man with a walrus mustache, Geoff Killing, was running against Ondine in East New York.

All three of them said a few words about what their candidacy represented, yet each chose a unique way to give the same veiled message: *Vote for us, or the Piggers are going to get you.*

Bea noticed Ondine leaning forward, beginning to nod off. Candy was politely listening, and Jackie was just staring off into space.

"What the hell are you supposed to be anyways?" Bea heard. Candy was in the middle-aged woman's crosshairs.

"Please mind your own beeswax," Candy replied.

"You're not a woman, I know that, 'cause *I'm* a woman." She definitely didn't look like she was from from Quirklyn.

"I'm more a—"

"I'm just trying to figure out whether you're a Macy's Thanksgiving Day float or a hippo in a dress," the woman said loudly.

"She ain't ever gonna fuck your ugly husband, so you can stop worrying, bitch!" Jackie blurted out.

Everyone in the vicinity laughed, interrupting Geoff Killing's speech.

Bea decided it was time to go. As they walked back to the car, the husband ran up behind and shoved Candy. Bea grabbed her before she could fall down, and without missing a beat, Jackie stepped back with her long legs and kicked the guy in the balls.

"Faggots!" the wife shouted, grabbing her man. Jackie's eyes lit up, and Bea had to drag her away.

It wasn't until about ten minutes later, while they were driving back to the Green-Burg headquarters, that Jackie came to life. "He's totally right!" she suddenly declared. "We *are* faggots, and we should be loud and proud about it. Like we used to be!"

"Absolutely," Candy said, rolling her eyes.

At the headquarters, Bea opened a large tub of Beefaroni, which she spooned into a pot. The only spice she had was hot sauce, which she shook over it liberally. The three Superstars downed two more boxes of white wine, and by the time the food finally started bubbling, Jackie was sleeping in an armchair, Ondine was lying on the threadbare carpet on the living room floor, and Candy was snoring away in the queen-size bed. Bea put the food in the fridge, and opened up a cot in the outer reception area of the headquarters, where she fell asleep too.

25

It was like being in a never-ending game of Russian roulette. Everyone waited with bated breath for them to name the next condemned man. Once it was announced, there was a general sigh of relief for all but one. Then all the men in the pen would remain frozen and watch as the poor bastard raced to the back, clutching onto the rusty bars with all his might.

The guards had it down to a science: five of them would open the door and then lock it behind them. Two would stand around protecting the other three, then two would grab the guy by his waist or limb, while the senior guard pulled out a ball-peen hammer and whacked the fingers clinging to the bars until he let go. Then they'd cuff the unlucky prisoner and drag him out. Hearing one poor bastard screaming for help as he was pulled away, Uli was reminded that he would only have a few more hours at most before they came back for the next guy, possibly him.

He was all pins and needles when the jailhouse photographer still hadn't shown up to spring him. Every time he saw more than two guards leaving the visitors center, he would feel his heart going pitter-patter and he'd start hyperventilating, expecting to be grabbed next and have his hand lopped off.

Two more prisoners were pulled out of the pen for judicial amputation. As the day wore on, Uli decided that he would try to break out tonight. The tricky part was doing it in front of everyone else without getting caught. Casually, he took his wooden crate to the most remote part of the pen and pretended to fall asleep.

Although he wasn't in great shape, he still had all his limbs and digits intact. He waited until the sun had completely set and most were fast asleep before making his move.

Uli jumped up on his crate and was able to shimmy up the remaining few feet of the bars to the crossbeam at the top of the pen. As several of his still-awake fellow prisoners silently peered up at him, he swung his body sideways like a pendulum until he was able to pull up and perch at the topmost bar.

"Oh shit, it's Tarzan the Ape Man!" called out an inmate named Snyder.

A bulldog-faced man whom everyone called Churchill silenced him as Uli carefully wedged himself through the opening.

"It's breakout time," Snyder said loudly.

"Shut up or I'll kill ya!" a third convict rasped, then called up to Uli, "Hey, you're going to need this!"

Uli slipped down the bars about a foot, at which point he lost his grip and fell to the hard ground—he was free!

The raspy convict was shoving a discarded old coat through the bars. "Take it!"

"Why?" Uli asked.

"To clear the barbed wire at the top of the wall."

Uli silently grabbed it and raced across the yard. He was nearly at the old brick wall that encircled the zoo when a guard came out from the visitors center to do his rounds. Uli dove into the overgrown hedges and waited until the guard flashed his light around at the reclining prisoners.

Uli was grateful that the guard was too lazy to count the men, many of whom lay upon each other like a pack of dogs. When the guard returned inside, Uli realized the old wall was too high to climb, though there was a crooked tree surprisingly close to it. He hurried over and lifted himself up its lower branches. A second guard came outside. Instead of inspecting, this one only lit a cigarette.

When the guy was done, Uli climbed to the top branch, then swung over and jumped onto the brick wall, which was about twelve feet high. Just as Raspy had warned, he saw looping curls of old barbed wire fixed along the top of the wall. He carefully draped the tattered coat over the spool of sharp metal, and slowly angled over the wall. He dropped and hit the ground outside with a solid thud, then started running slowly and steadily, but there was nowhere to hide.

He made it about five blocks before a bright light shot on and he heard blaring sirens.

Simultaneously, several cars came zooming up behind him. The closest one screeched, colliding into him, and he was knocked out cold.

When Uli awoke, he found himself strapped onto a moist gurney. Polly Femus, the commandant of the zoo prison, was standing over him chewing on what looked like a large drumstick.

"What's going on?" Uli asked groggily.

"I'm getting a big helping of you soon," Femus said. "Your little stunt just earned you the next place on the chopping block."

"Huh?"

"For your little Houdini number, we're taking your whole arm," she said, grabbing it.

"But . . . I didn't even . . ." As he struggled with his restraints, a male nurse injected him with a syringe.

"When you awake," Uli heard, "your friends might call you Lefty, but to me you'll always be Tasty."

He drifted off to the sound of her cackling.

26

J oe Brainard woke everyone with a carton of cigarettes. First they
took turns using the bathroom, which was no small endeavor, then
they had their first cigarettes—all of the candidates smoked. Bea put
on a big pot of strong coffee. While sitting tiredly over their cups,

the Brain explained that sometime later today a theatrical consultant, Charles Ludlam, would be arriving to produce their little launch rally scheduled for tomorrow.

"How did last night go?" he asked. "Did you all go over your agendas?"

"Yeah, we know your fucking points," Ondine said tiredly.

"The four points are important," the Brain said, "but people have voted for the opposition purely on likability. We picked you guys 'cause you're genuine, colorful, honest personalities. In my opinion, the best New York has to offer. And the folks in these districts share those same sensibilities. I remember what sensations you were back in the old downtown scene."

"What are you saying?" Jackie asked.

"Just pick up the pace a bit. Be visible, friendly, introduce yourselves, shake hands, be charming."

"Yeah, small talk, we know," Candy sighed.

"Well, it's not just talk. Do a little homework. Become familiar with your little stretch of blocks and their own particular needs. How is sewage in your area? Is it flooding on this block or dark on that street? Go on your own fact-finding missions and see what needs repairs. Ask people what bothers them. Acquire *substance!*"

"I thought that was your job," Jackie said, holding her head.

"Yeah, we're just performers!" said Candy.

"We can use your help," the Brain said.

"What a coincidence," Candy said. "We can use *your* help—some assholes assaulted me yesterday."

Bea filled Brainard in on what had happened at the Crapper rally. He promised their bodyguards would arrive soon.

Because Ondine hadn't received his usual shot of methadone, he quickly nodded off. The Brain made a phone call and promised that someone from New Dope would bring a vial. Jackie said she was having pounding migraines, so Bea promised she'd pick up some aspirin.

Since none had eaten much last night, Bea opened, sliced, and fried up a tin of Spam that she found in the pantry. When it was seared, she covered it in imitation maple syrup, called it Vermont Canadian bacon, and served it on saltines. Ondine only ate half his plate, and Jackie didn't even touch her food, opting to simply smoke and drink coffee. Soon, Candy had finished off the last of the Spam.

"All right," the Brain said after they all were done, "I have an exercise."

"I don't believe in exercise," Candy said.

"Me neither," Jackie said. "I'm not killing myself, but hell if I'm doing anything that will lengthen my life even a day longer!"

"It's not that kind of exercise. Pair off into two groups, and each of you will take turns being the politician and the man on the street."

Candy and Bea paired up, while Jackie joined Ondine.

The Brain listened in as Jackie cleared her throat and said: "Hi, I'm Jackie Curtis and I'm running for city council on the Quirklyn ticket. I came here with the rest of you a little under ten years ago and have watched as the quality of life has steadily gotten worse—"

"Oh God! Why don't you just say the Pledge A-fucking-legiance," Ondine jumped in.

"He's right, your remarks should be short," the Brain said. "You want to trigger a dialogue, not scare anyone off."

"All right, I need a fucking minute," Jackie snapped. She covered her face, trying to get into character.

The Brain turned to Bea and Candy Darling.

"Hi, my name's Bea—"

"Bzzz," the Brain said, "wrong name!"

"Oops!" She covered her mouth. "I'm Valerie Solanas, I'm a resident of South Ozone Park and—"

"Don't speak like a politician. Speak normally. You're going to be doing this in South Ozone Park, so say, *I just moved here.*"

"How about, *I'm hoping to make the world a little better?*" Candy asked.

"For the first week or so keep it small and simple," the Brain replied.

"Let's see *you* do it," Candy said.

"Okay. Hi, my name is Joe, I live a few doors down. What's your name?" Everyone looked at him blankly.

"What the hell was that?" Jackie asked.

"That's called getting to know your neighbors. This is just about breaking the ice. Once you get to know them, you can work your way up to bigger topics. We'll provide brochures with facts and figures that you can hand out."

"Can we use props?" Candy asked.

"What kind of props?"

"*Would you like an upper to brighten your day?*" she practiced, smiling broadly as she held out an amphetamine.

"Instead of an upper," the Brain said, "why don't we start with a piece of candy, then you can say, *Hi, I'm Candy, would you like a piece of candy?*"

"I wish my name was shit so I could fling that at them," Jackie murmured.

Over the next few hours, the little group continued practicing the friendly banter and short exchanges. The Brain emphasized that constituents were frightened of sarcasm; they were also suspicious of intellect. Simple honesty was ideal. Candy and Bea were the best at it—they were able to talk as if they were smart children. Ondine, on the other hand, struggled with a mocking tone that had simply become a natural part of his personality. For Jackie, it was a constant battle holding back depressing or contemptuous remarks.

At one o'clock, Cookie Mueller showed up. Earlier that morning, Candy had told Brainard that since they'd be working together, it would be wise for her to join the training exercises.

A little before three there was another knock at the door. The Brain let in a small, bald, mostly unimpressive man with very expressive lips and eyebrows. Cookie and Candy were practicing in one corner, Ondine and Bea were working on pleasant solicitous exchanges in another corner. The bald stranger watched until Jackie interrupted the exercise with the comment, "Don't you wish they'd just die?"

"Allow me to introduce—" the Brain started.

"We all know Charles Ludlam," Jackie cut in. Ludlam had been the founder of the Ridiculous Theatrical Company in the Village, and had produced a string of camp hits that had been the rage of the downtown and gay nightlife scenes.

"He's agreed to help us."

"And I've got a vision for the show which will tease and enchant them into voting for you," Ludlam said with genuine excitement.

"Charlie," Brainard said softly, "we agreed that we're not doing any dance numbers."

"It'll all just be talking, but with a little beat. We'll have music in the background, and because you're all going to be in drag, I'm having the band play the Beatles' 'Get Back.' You'll talk in the foreground: short remarks with a fun beanbag bounce to them."

"We're going to be onstage?" Jackie asked.

Ludlam described the set they'd be using tomorrow. Next he showed each of them how he wanted them to come on and where they'd each stand.

"What the hell are we supposed to say?" Ondine asked.

The bald man opened a folder and handed out scripts with each of their names at the top. He asked them to pull up chairs, sit in a circle, and read their lines. Then he had them work on delivery and pacing for a while before they got the show on its feet.

"Cookie Mueller and I were hired as a two-person act," Candy said.

"I know, I've seen your show," Ludlam responded. "Look at the script, I've got you bouncing jokes off each other."

The pieces were short and punchy, informative yet written for a gentle comic effect. The more they went over their lines, the more the director revised the words and fine-tuned the details, gestures, and expressions, giving each of them a distinctive character and flavor.

"Isn't this supposed to be a political rally?" Jackie asked, clearly displeased.

"You still need it to be entertaining," Ludlam said. They ran through it several more times, making small changes.

By seven p.m., the forty-five-minute performance was starting to take shape—it had spunk. Soon, however, Jackie was falling asleep and the others were starting to drop lines. The Brain finally said they had done enough for the day.

"These scripts are less than a thousand words apiece, so I expect you to all be off-book by tomorrow morning," Ludlam said. He was covered in sweat. When Bea followed him and the Brain into the kitchen, she saw the two of them unscrewing the tops of various containers, lining up an assortment of pills. Whatever sickness the Brain had, Charles seemed to have it too. A few minutes later, medicated, the two campaign organizers came back to the living area.

"Have them go over it a few more times before the rally and they should be fine," Ludlam said before he left.

"It'd be great to eat out tonight," Candy suggested, sick of the heated canned food that Bea had been preparing.

The Brain agreed and pulled out some stamps. The group piled into his car and headed south, out of Quirklyn and over to Downtown Brooklyn where a cluster of not-awful restaurants were peppered around the grand outdoor clothing bazaar on Jay Street.

Tempted by the mountains of tacky clothes on sale, Cookie and Candy started digging through them looking for bargains. Jackie, who was broke, begged Joe for some stamps so she could purchase a campaign wardrobe, heels, and much-needed accessories. She was ready for her big return.

"No one's going to vote for a badly dressed candidate," she argued. The Brain agreed.

Twenty minutes later, Cookie returned with two over-the-top frizzy platinum wigs, three bright boas, five sequined minis in various electric colors, four red bras, a dozen pairs of pantyhose, and four of the tallest platforms Bea had ever seen. Candy had found three heavy-duty, extra-large corsets, and two girdles that required long lacing.

Among the crowd of shoppers, Ondine spotted one dude he recognized from Red Hook, and was able to score a bag of uppers that turned out to be downers. Discreetly, he offered some pills to Candy and Jackie. Both declined.

The best eatery on Jay Street, Angelika's Treehouse, was a "healthy food restaurant," a hybrid of canned foods combined with some of the local fare that had been grown in the greenhouses of northern Queens.

All except Jackie had the blue plate special—a reptile bourguignonne consisting of snake, turtle, and lizard parts. It had simmered so long in beef broth that, to everyone's satisfaction, it tasted like low-grade beef. Between the five of them they split six bottles of "wine drinks," although Joe barely had a glass and Bea had none at all.

When Bea drove them back into Green-Burg, the three candidates had passed out in the backseat by the time they arrived. As they pulled up at the house and the three Superstars began to stir, the Brain called their attention to someone sitting in a car a few doors up from their headquarters, holding a camera with a long lens, snapping photos of someone inside another house.

"It's not us he's after," Jackie said, relieved.

"He's probably trying to catch his cheating wife," Bea speculated tiredly.

"Or he's a Crapper agent who got bored waiting for us," the Brain said.

"How would photos be used against us?" Bea asked.

"None of our candidates except Candy have even been to their homes in the districts they'll be running in." Brainard seemed to panic at this thought. "Call me paranoid, but I don't want to take any chances. Why don't we drop everyone off at their registered homes tonight?"

"But we don't have our drivers/bodyguards yet," said Candy.

"You haven't even announced your candidacies yet," the Brain countered. "I'll make sure you get them by then."

"It's a long trek back if we're all supposed to be at McBarren Park by noon tomorrow," Jackie said from the backseat.

"I'll call now and make sure your drivers pick you up at your homes in the morning. You'll easily be in the park by eleven."

Brainard dug through his pockets and handed three sets of keys to Bea. Since she was now officially Valerie Solanas, she had to go the farthest east, to South Ozone Park—the name sounded like outer space. Seeing that the Brain was feverish and wrung out, Bea suggested he stay in Green-Burg for the night and go to bed. She could drop them all off at their new abodes. Shakily, he told her that he'd left a hand-drawn map in the glove compartment in case she got lost.

27

Since they were already in Green-Burg, at Candy's designated home, she, Cookie, and the Brain got out. Bea drove east about a mile to Jackie's assigned apartment in Bushwick. It was easy to find, as the words *Bushwick Quirklyn Headquarters* were stenciled on the storefront window.

Ondine, who had drunk the most wine, was still out cold in the backseat, so Bea got out of the car and helped Jackie carry her new wardrobe into the building. Just like in Green-Burg, they found letters both for and against the Quirklyn organization that had been shoved under the door. Bea picked up a letter from Mayor Mallory, inviting the candidates to a debate. She slipped the solicitation into her pocket as she followed Jackie to the living quarters. Bea was surprised to see a nice little garden in the back, filled with desert flowers.

Inspecting the three large rooms, Jackie smiled. "This is the nicest place I've lived since I've been here."

"It's nicer than anywhere I've *ever* lived," Bea said.

"Just look at these curtains!" Jackie gushed. "Now if only I could find the right man."

This levity was a promising sign that Jackie might finally be relaxing. Since her fridge was modestly stocked, Jackie poured them each a glass of apple cider. Bea told her to try to get a good night's sleep, then returned to her car.

Ondine was snoring loudly in the backseat. Bea popped open the glove compartment and found the map that the Brain had mentioned. She tried waking Ondine up, hoping to get him to help navigate to the East New York headquarters, but it was impossible. As they drove a few miles east, so many streetlights were out that Bea had to pause below a working one just to review the map. When she spotted rows of carbonized houses, evidence of past battles, Bea sensed she had arrived in East New York. This area had suffered more gang skirmishes over the years than any other neighborhood in Rescue City. She drove down Metropolitan Avenue along a high, terraced street that looked down over the rest of the Brooklyn community. Finally Bea located the cross street of Ondine's address.

After another fifteen minutes of going from door to door, checking addresses with a flashlight, Bea finally found the building. Then it took several desperate minutes of hard shaking, and checking his breathing, before the candidate finally woke up. Ondine surveyed the dark empty street and said he didn't feel safe staying here alone, but before Bea could reply, he stumbled out of the car and vomited his guts out. The only other car on the street was parked across from the tiny Quirklyn headquarters, compelling Bea to wonder if it was under surveillance. After several minutes, Ondine rose to his feet and Bea helped him into the building.

"Shit," she muttered. His place turned out to be on the fourth story of the rickety structure.

Ten minutes later, Bea finally got him up one flight of stairs and parked him on the landing of the second floor, winded and covered in sweat. She didn't think she could go any farther. She considered dragging him back down and bringing him out to her place in SOP. But before she could pull him back to his wobbly feet, she heard the front door open downstairs.

Soft footsteps were shuffling up toward them. Bea grabbed a large stone that doubled as a doorstop.

A thick, statuesque woman appeared. "Miss Solanas?" she asked.

"Yeah?" Bea said, still holding the stone.

"Joe Brainard told me to come here pronto. My name's Carol."

"Great. Help me, Carol." She dropped the stone.

Carol got in front of Ondine, tossed him over her shoulder, and carried him like a firefighter up the steps.

"I would prefer to be *your* driver," she said as they walked. "I loved your manifesto, but they assigned me to Ondine."

Once they got Ondine into his bed, Bea went through his pockets and found his stash of pills, which she duly flushed down the toilet.

"He's got a bit of a drug problem, so keep an eye on him tomorrow morning. We need him to be clean and sober for the rally at noon in McBarren Park."

"Joe told me."

Bea saw that the only clock in the place was set on an end table near the bed. She set it forward one hour and asked Carol not to tell him. Bea then said she'd see them both tomorrow.

Within ten minutes she was back in her solicar, driving east to

South Ozone Park. As Metropolitan Avenue descended at the eastern end of East New York, Bea realized that the terrace was a natural barrier that would make a Crapper invasion difficult. Just as the Brain had said, someone from the VL had intermittently wrapped stupid purple ribbons around lampposts and put up *Vote Quirklyn* signs.

Gradually traffic increased, and soon she was locked in a tight convoy of empty minibuses heading out to the airfield. When Metropolitan turned into Broadway and then became Pennsylvania Avenue, Bea began to hear the nonstop grinding of airplane engines in the darkness. As she reached Liberty Avenue, she could make out their lights in the distance as they took off and landed. Driving past an ancient blockade, she saw a faded sign that must've been erected for the new refugees that said, STAY OUT OF QUEENS!

Cracked concrete foundations filled with weeds were the only signs that civilization had ever existed here. Bea remembered others referring to it as "the dead zone," a barren stretch between distant communities. Continuing eastward, she drove straight toward the outline of some distant mountains until she spotted the sign: HOW-ARD BEACH, QUEENS. This was the problematic neighborhood that Quirklyn had technically severed from the rest of Queens.

Miraculously, in the darkness Bea made out a small hand-painted sign that read, SOP—*Hawtree Pass*. The road crossed from a broad, funnel-shaped area into a narrow corridor surrounded by steep dunes. She headed south between the sheer hills of loose sand, and after passing through a small maze, the landscape suddenly opened to a hidden community. Guided largely by the light of the moon, Bea drove her solicar between a series of small bungalows on her left and a huge sandy field on her right—the former Aqueduct Dog Track. The desert marked the eastern border of the community, and JFK Airport ran along the southern end. The sound of planes taking off and landing at steady intervals was deafening.

Driving along the four dark, narrow streets that comprised SOP, Bea could see why the initial residents bypassed the community, but also why the new settlers had come this far out. Probably due to the insane noise pollution, this enclave had been overlooked and therefore completely spared from the fights and fires that had ravaged most of the city. Hidden away behind the sands and airfield, the old bungalow community vaguely reminded Bea of the Rockaways in the real Queens.

Though she couldn't see any street signs or address numbers, she could still make out the sporadic purple ribbons. Checking the hand-drawn map in the moonlight, she then headed down the westernmost street. She looked over the sandy JFK airfield and could just see a pair of brown towers rising on the horizon. They had to be part of the strange philanthropic organization Pure-ile Plurality.

It wasn't until midnight that Bea found Valerie Solanas's newly renovated home. It was the second-to-last one on the final block, next to a large empty house that was still under construction.

Upon examining the various floors of her new abode, she was immediately reminded of her childhood home in East Tremont in the Bronx, a place she hadn't thought much about in years. Thankfully, she found that her telephone worked. Though it was late, she dialed the Green-Burg HQ. The Brain picked up after the first ring.

She told him she had dropped everyone off safely, then asked, "What is that big new building going up next door?"

"Oh, we bought that one too—it's the new South Ozone Park–Quirklyn militia," he said. "Jack Healy should be there if you need help."

"Are there soldiers?"

"Jack's there with his younger cousin Pat, and the other Vietnam vet you met at the first meeting—Antonio Lucas."

Bea started yawning so the Brain told her to go to sleep. Tomorrow was going to be a big day. She washed up in the bathroom, then stripped down and turned off the lights, but her sleep was delayed by the periodic roar of drone engines. After an hour or so, partially from exhaustion, but also by imagining that the intermittent roars were God himself snoring, she finally dozed off.

28

Three sharp knocks cut through the roar of airplane engines. It was a new day. As Bea rose, she figured it was her driver and feared that she was already late for the big rally. But looking at her wristwatch, she saw it was only nine a.m.

As a second volley of knocks sounded, she pulled on her pants and shirt and went to the door. Looking out one of the eight small, lace-curtained glass frames that covered her front door, she saw a well-scrubbed family of six standing out front.

"What's up?" she asked, squinting as she cracked the door open.

"May I inquire if the head of the house is home?" said a bald man.

"That would be me."

"Oh, no offense, it's just that most of the ladies here have a man, but I'm all for women's lib. Anyway, the name's Dennis Izzlowski." The man shoved a large hand at her. She shook it quickly. "This here is my tribe."

A woman with big blond hair and three postadolescent piglets snorted, "Hi!"

For an instant, Bea groggily feared that the man was trying to give away some of their litter.

"I'm running for city council on the Pigger ticket. I saw your car out front, and I just wanted to get to know you."

"Hi," Bea said politely.

"As you know, we're having an election in less than six weeks, and this being Queens, which happens to be the largest Pigger borough, you can understand how we're a little nervous about losing one of our most important districts."

"Sure," Bea said, "but I was sleeping. Can we talk about this later?"

"I've talked with all the other neighbors except you. Would you mind if I ask when you're available so I can come back and chat?"

"I should be around this afternoon, we can talk then," she lied. Before she could shut the door, he handed her a brand-new T-shirt.

Under a picture of his face was the phrase *We the People Are South Ozone Park!* "Thanks," she said.

"Would you mind if I asked your name?"

"Val," she said, staring at the shirt.

The smile froze on his face for a moment, then in an odd, disembodied tone he asked, "You're her, aren't you?"

"Pardon?"

He reached into his jacket pocket and took out a flyer. It said, MEET *&* GREET THE *QUIRKLYN PARTY CANDIDATES—Valerie Solanas Is Running for City Council in South Ozone Park.* "Is this you?"

She smiled. "Yep."

"You killed Andrew Warhol?"

"Actually, I only winged him."

"Well, I think it's only fair to warn you that if you try any monkey business with me, I will defend myself."

"Just don't try to control my life and we'll be fine," she replied, then shut the door. *We're fucked*, she thought. This guy, and his picture-perfect family, had met, memorized the names of, and probably licked the ass of this entire community.

Bea tried to go back to bed but she was too shaken by the encounter. This was going to be infinitely harder than she had thought. The Piggers looked far more determined than the Crappers—just the fact that he knew where she lived made her concerned about an assault of some kind. Rustling through the kitchen shelves, Bea found some stale coffee and a percolator in addition to powdered sugar and milk. She brewed a pot, then turned on the shower.

She was in the middle of washing her hair when she heard something over the rush of water. Before she could shut off the water to listen more closely, the bathroom light went out.

"Folks, an interloper has infiltrated our ranks!" she heard faintly over a megaphone. "In many a tight-knit community, when an unwanted outsider enters the clan, they are shunned. We too must show this outsider that she is not welcome among us!"

Bea wrapped her hair in a towel, pulled on clothes over her wet self, and went to the door. She could see the Piggers had wasted no time: a small flatbed truck had been parked directly across from her house, and Izzlowski was standing on it holding a megaphone, his Christmas-card family gone. Apparently they were only for enchantment, not intimidation. In their place were about a dozen "campaign workers"—scary, burly men who folded their hairy arms and stared as if just wanting a couple of minutes alone with Bea. One of them was climbing down from a nearby utility pole, explaining the sudden lack of electricity. The Piggers probably had the community's vote sealed up already, so they had obviously decided to bring the campaign right to her door. Because of the flatbed PA system, a significant crowd was out, gathering along the edges of the street to see what all the commotion was about. As Izzlowski kept ranting, more residents from the area came over.

"There she is, folks!" Izzlowski said to the crowd. "The executioner of one of America's finest artists. The woman who brutally butchered the great Andrew Warhol, who, if I'm not mistaken, was related to Norman Rockwell—a personal favorite to many of us. Guess what? Now she wants to represent you. That's right! She's one of Quirklyn's fellow travelers and now she's trying to hijack our little district."

Outequipped and outnumbered, Bea was about to retreat inside when the door to the adjacent house opened. A tall man with a crew cut emerged—Jack Healy, the head of Quirklyn defense should it ever become an independent republic. Two of his strange accomplices were standing around holding wooden bats. He smiled at Bea.

Emboldened by the thought that she wasn't alone, she shouted, "If I may reply—"

"No, you may not!" Izzlowski yelled back, and immediately put on a recording of "The Star-Spangled Banner."

A minute into the song, someone from Healy's building came out carrying a white square of plasterboard with writing in black marker. He held it up to the growing crowd: *A REAL AMERICAN WOULDN'T BE AFRAID TO LET OTHERS SPEAK!*

Izzlowski saw SOPers reading the sign and nodding. In a moment the volume went down.

"For starters," Bea spoke to the crowd, "Andy Warhol and I were close personal friends until I felt he had betrayed me. Shooting him was wrong, but he fully recovered. And I paid the price for my actions. He is alive and well, living in luxury somewhere beyond the desert, while we're all stuck here in Rescue City."

"Well, thank God for that, but we don't care," Izzlowski said through his megaphone. "We still want you out of our neighborhood."

"This isn't *your* neighborhood, Pigger puppet!" Bea responded, drawing chuckles from the crowd.

He seemed a bit rattled. "We're hurling insults already, are we?"

"Why don't you take your gang of bullies who turned off my electricity and go back to your homes up in Queens?"

"Do you hear this, folks? This criminal is telling us about *our* neighborhood. This is Queens, and Queens is Pigger!"

"Well, we didn't move to Queens, 'cause we're not Piggers!" Bea shot back, walking toward him. "And we're not in Brooklyn, 'cause we're not Crappers. But I'll tell you what, and who, we are . . ."

"Please do," he replied sarcastically.

"We're victims of your two gangs. No one wants to be here, but our homes were flooded with sewage water from a terrorist act caused by your gang wars."

Izzlowski was momentarily silenced, so Valerie stepped forward and addressed the crowd: "Folks, try to imagine what Rescue City might've been like if we didn't have Piggers or Crappers. Try to imagine your friends and loved ones who were brutally killed—they would still be alive today! Try to imagine all the buildings and communities that would still be standing, that we could live in, instead of having to listen to the drones overhead because this is the very last refuge available for people like us!"

One of Izzlowski's henchmen tried to interrupt: "You're in Queens now, lady—"

"Like all the rest of you folks," she went on, "I have settled in this abandoned home, but now we have to deal with these rude gorillas who climbed down *from* Queens to protect their abandoned turf." She pointed at the utility pole out front. "Why am I not surprised? Because that's their idea of democracy. Let's show these bullies what democracy really looks like! Let me use their aggressive provocation to announce that yes, I am Valerie Solanas—flawed, imperfect, ex-con, fellow New Yorker, and proud lesbian. I have never been and never will be a gang member, and I'm not afraid of these thugs. And yes, I am running for city council representative of this reclaimed area. In a little over a month, when you go into the privacy of your voting booth, think about this moment when they woke me up and tried to intimidate me. And if they do win, think about that moment in the future when they will turn off your electricity while you're taking a shower, and force you out of your house because you stood up for your rights!"

There was dead silence until one distant person started to applaud. A Pigger guard immediately hurried over and tried to stare down Bea's supporter, a tall, broad-shouldered man with a thick head of wavy black hair and a big wiry beard. Not the sort of person she expected.

Although a group of Pigger gangcops loosely circled around trying to intimidate him, he continued slapping his palms together as he moved forward. He was so far away, Bea wondered how he could even hear her, but he just kept applauding until those around him started up as well. Within two minutes, almost everyone was clapping with him.

"Turn her lights back on!" hollered the guy, chanting and clapping along. "TURN HER LIGHTS BACK ON!"

Izzlowski finally nodded over to a wiry man who scurried up the utility pole and rewired her place. Realizing they were only hurting their cause, the candidate quickly disbanded his group and drove away. Jack, the silent commander from next door, went back inside.

When Bea closed her door, she realized it was already eleven fifteen and her driver still hadn't arrived. She hastily fixed herself up and prepared to drive herself, when she heard a knock at the door. It was the thick-maned clapper.

"I'm Reggie, your driver." He smiled shyly as he entered. "I didn't want others to know that I was working for you. Also, I don't have a car, but Joe said . . ."

Bea grabbed Solanas's signature peacoat and black Chairman Mao cap, and shoved past him. They had to hurry if they were going to make it to McBarren Park by noon, so she drove. As they left SOP, Bea had to brake suddenly when a city minibus came barreling out of nowhere. She looked back in her rearview and glimpsed the bus speeding down a narrow road that led to the odd religious cult across from the former dog track.

29

Pure-ile Plurality, the philanthropic religious organization that allegedly serviced all of Rescue City, was located near the northern edge of Brooklyn in Howard Beach, Queens. The outreach workers living in the PP building complex were seriously conflicted. Initially, they were happy to see the flood-ravaged survivors, mainly liberals from Lower Manhattan, pouring into the formerly abandoned corridor that was technically Crapper territory. But then the refugees started bubbling out over the abandoned homes of East New York, and into the former ghost neighborhood of South Ozone Park. Still, PP members had hope. After they adjusted to the shock of seeing this empty community being settled, Rolland Siftwelt, head of the organization, preached tolerance—eventually these new residents would understand where they were. Like immigrants coming to a strange country and adopting the different culture, these people would adapt and establish themselves as the newest Pigger neighborhood. Still, these odd pilgrims seemed unusually left-wing, somewhat brash, and uncharacteristically bold in both dress and conduct.

Late at night, PP residents would look over the airfield and hear the sounds of music, tom-toms being beaten, trumpets blaring, and peals of laughter bursting the once-silent night. The newcomers stayed on their side of the abandoned Aqueduct Dog Track, and Pure-ile Plurality remained on its side. Then the Quirklyn autonomy fever blistered up out of nowhere. This infectious independence movement had started in the perverse shadow of Green-Burg, and now these furtive rebels claimed that the four districts should be unified into one. In an effort to drive them into the open, the Piggers had been forced to file for an election and run a new candidate. Out of nowhere, ribbons and posters started popping up all over the area, declaring that the election would be a mandate for the region's independence.

Fear struck the insular community of Pure-ile Plurity. If this new group managed to win and make that northern stretch of real estate independent, they would effectively sever Howard Beach—and the

Pure-ile Plurality organization—from the rest of Queens and Pigger rule.

Rolland Siftwelt pondered this growing problem carefully. Much of SOP's infrastructure, including electricity and water, went through Howard Beach, so first he contemplated unplugging them from the rest of the city's power grid. But he soon realized that this matter was beyond his scope, and the next question was whether he should personally appeal to the new mayor of Rescue City North, John Cross Plains, to involve the gangcops and drive the "squatters" out. The bigger problem was that his own organization was divided.

"Rescue City was initially a haven for those of us made homeless in the Manhattan dirty bombing. Now the new Manhattan is flooded! Would God forgive us if we refuse these poor people refuge?" asked one executive staffer, sharing the concerns of others.

On the day before the Quirklyners were to introduce their candidates, Siftwelt selected one of his most reliable supervisors, Marsha Johnson, to discreetly head over to their inaugural rally in Green-Burg and prepare a report. "What I really want to know is: are these people a potential threat to us?" he said to her. "Do they think we're old fogies? Will they eventually try to expand beyond the field and move into our offices? In short, should we be worried? Should we try to have this nipped in the bud? Or should I embrace them and make them allies now?"

On the bus ride over, as Marsha passed a variety of campaign posters of the Quirklyn candidates plastered on buildings, she realized that she knew them from Old Town. More accurately, she knew *of* them. They had all been part of Andy Warhol's crazy ensemble, which she should've realized immediately, as they were being pitched as the "Warhol Superstars." Though she had seen them around back then, she hadn't been close to any of them. And thankfully, she was pretty sure none of them knew her. The only Warhol Superstar she hadn't seen in person was Valerie Solanas.

Solanas had shot Warhol back in '68; after her trial, she had been tossed in the loony bin, where she remained during the turbulent summer of '69 and the big contamination of the city. She had also missed the mass transplant to Nevada. Of course it made sense that once Solanas was freed, they'd dump her here. Marsha let out a great sigh of relief that she had never revealed her wild years to anyone at PP; now in a position of great responsibility, she desperately wanted to keep it that way.

As the bus paused for a minute next to a campaign poster for Solanas, Marsha stared at the woman's image; it was hard to imagine her
as violent. She had a sad smile and sweet, tender eyes that immediately
made an impression on Marsha.

When she arrived at McBarren Park, she was impressed by the
crowds of young people who had come from all five boroughs, bringing a vibrant, youthful energy. A stage had been built on the far side of
a giant, dry outdoor pool, and a band was playing familiar rock tunes.

A big banner above the stage announced, *We're Tossing Our Wigs in the
Ring!* Another poster said, *This Is Our Coming Out Day*—code words for sexual deviation. Sitting down on a patch of sharp weeds near the empty
pool, Marsha watched as long-haired youths smoked Crapper-grown
marijuana, which was mysteriously being handed out to all. People
were picnicking, lounging, and throwing Frisbees.

She realized what had happened. The greatest attraction of joining
one of the two gangs had been protection from the opposing gang.
Now, due to Pax Rescue City, the fear had been lifted, and the gangs
offered nothing other than a painful reminder of the old, bloody days.

After half an hour the band stopped playing and people cheered as
antiwar activists got on the stage and held a moment of silence for all
the great leftists who had died in the Manhattan flooding. Then some
of the surviving activists issued statements against the war.

Marsha, a black woman who understood the very real communist
threat and the reason the US was fighting in the Far East, found these
men's comments annoying. They enjoyed America's freedoms while
simultaneously protesting its battle to protect those freedoms.

Finally, some guy with black-framed glasses and a gap between
his front teeth took the mic and thanked the crowd for coming; all
cheered. When the man raised his hands, people quieted down. "My
name is Joe Brainard. Folks, this is a historic day, and I don't think
I have to tell you why. Like many of you here, I am a member of the
Quirklyn Party, a party that in approximately one month will be as
broadly recognized as the other three parties." More cheering. "The
difference between us and them is that Quirklyn will truly be a political party, and not just a violent gang masquerading as one. We will
not assemble groups of thugs with chains, clubs, and machetes. We
will not employ car bombs, or force ourselves upon others. We will
not arbitrarily take the law into our own hands and chop off limbs
without a trial—or even *with* a trial! Our candidates will have two
terms in office, not be lifelong appointees. The four candidates who

will lead us into independence are people you know from the old days when they first gained their celebrity, and maybe even notoriety—I'm honored to introduce the Andy Warhol Superstars!"

A burst of applause, and the band started loudly playing "Get Back."

"It is my honor to introduce to you the great Candy Darling, who will be running right here in dear Green-Burg . . ."

Marsha watched a fat man in a blond wig wearing loose billowing women's clothes rise up from the back of the stage, curtsy just a bit, and sway to the Beatles song.

"The fabulous Jackie Curtis hopes to represent the fabulicious district of Bushwick . . ." A tall, skinny man with a long, bubbling wig appeared, waving and blowing kisses. "The delectable Ondine desires to give a voice to those of you who have come west from East New York . . ." Another strange-looking man walked slowly onstage, then stood perfectly still as though afraid of falling. "Last, but never least, the wonderful Valerie Solanas hopes to do her best for the rediscovered colony of Atlantis, also known as South Ozone Park!"

The woman Marsha had seen in the political posters smiled timidly and waved. The cheers for her were the loudest, and Marsha noticed the candidate named Curtis rolling his eyes with apparent jealousy.

"Each of these good people have risked their own lives stepping forward despite death threats, all in the name of freedom and tolerance, and they will now say a few words about what it is they have to offer." The gap-toothed man looked over his shoulder to make sure all was well, then said, "Madame Darling, the world welcomes you!"

Candy Darling and another blonde stepped up to the mic stand. Candy began: "Allow me to introduce the cookie who never crumbles, the always tasty Cookie Mueller!"

Cookie started their little vaudeville routine: "Welcome to our campy pain . . ."

"We'll be campy-paining together," Candy joined in, "and together we hope to communicate your dreams . . ."

"Not amputate your extremes . . ."

"We'll make this the land of the free . . ."

"So if you vote—"

"Not for her, but me," Candy cut in. "To represent you . . ."

"In Williamsburg-Greenpoint . . ."

"Or Green-Burg—a district that's brand new . . ."

"You won't have to shout, we'll listen fully . . ."

"Instead of terrify and bully!"

"Aren't they adorable, folks?" said Brainard as the duet stepped back into the line of slowly swaying candidates.

Trying to keep up the energy, Ondine dashed forward and duly stumbled, falling off the stage into the crowd below. Some of the Quirklyn security force was able to catch him and quickly roll him back up on the stage.

"First step's a fucking doozy!" he slurred, then giggled a moment. "Hi, ladies *in* germs. Hope no one has the EGGS, a disease that started when Jackie Wilson blew up the drain to bring the gangs to their knees. Just let that sink in a moment, 'cause I know many of you came here hoping to raise a family using these valuable years toward something productive. Instead of just a prison sentence. Everyone blames the government, but few seem to recall that this was created by gangs right here."

Marsha knew this was untrue: the EGGS condition had existed prior to the sewage crisis. She was sure Joe Brainard caught the mistake, but he applauded anyway. Cheers went up and lasted long enough for Ondine to start nodding off. Brainard prodded him awake, and he mumbled for about a minute into the mic but no one understood a word.

When he finally took a breath, Brainard snatched the mic from the stand, and said, "Need he say m-m-more, folks? Need he say more?"

Marsha watched as the next speaker, the tall, bony transvestite stepped forward. It was immediately evident that he was very uncomfortable.

"Howdy, one and all," he began before even reaching the mic. "I'm Jackie Curtis, hoping to represent you pussies in Bush-lick. When Andy Warhol first met us he told us he wanted to do films that would be new and original, and he asked us to star in them." Curtis paused. "Actually, that's a load of shit." He pulled off his frizzy wig. Turning to the band behind him that was still playing softly, he shouted, "Stop the music! I can't do this! I'm sorry."

The band stopped playing. Joe Brainard looked nervous.

"Look, those of you who remember what New York was like ten years ago, well, it . . . it was dirty and dangerous, but it was also a wild, liberating experience. This place has been the exact opposite—I literally feel my will being strangled away. And I look around me here today, and I see that I'm not alone. The best of us have drowned our sorrows in foods, or drugs, or booze. The worst of us have accumulated brute power and worthless food stamps. Hard as we try, we can't do a lot about being stuck here, and I personally have spent years trying to break out. But there are some things we *can* do to make our lives a little more livable. For starters, certain truly despicable people have managed to exploit our misfortunes for their own benefit. They're the ones who have made a career of dividing and conquering us. You want to know what this whole Quirklyn thing is about? It's about changing what little we can to make better lives for ourselves. To me, this election is us taking back our lives as much as we possibly can."

Instead of clapping, people seemed to be actually thinking about what he was saying. When the applause finally began, it came in cascades.

As the noise died down, the gap-toothed man said, "It is now with great joy that I present to you the final candidate of our great new party— Valerie Solanas, who will be running in South Ozone Park!"

"Hi, everyone," she said hesitantly. "I can't hope to top those wonderful heartfelt words from Jackie. She spoke for all of us with her pain and honesty. Still, some folks have asked me good questions, like what we hope to gain by creating a political group that is younger, smaller, and weaker than the other two. Well, aside from so many things that have been touched on, I just want to say that the amputation system used by the Piggers and Crappers is truly evil. There have been reports that the Crappers are in the process of implementing a brand-new trial system, where someone accused of a crime will have the chance to participate in their own defense. Much as I commend this effort, they still refuse to end the barbaric amputations. Just look around this crowd and you'll see too many missing limbs, and even among those who actually *are* guilty, these often aren't all the result of violent crimes. Some people just screw up and then have an arm, hand, or finger amputated. Would giving them a second chance have been so awful? I committed an awful crime; I shot a famous guy and I shouldn't have, but I got a second chance. And that's why I'm here now, trying to give you *all* another chance. And for the record, we're not talking about pardoning crimes here. I mean, we're in a fucking desert! It isn't that hard to figure out another way to incarcerate offenders. Neither gang will even consider this! So, we've decided to do this on our own. Become part of a movement that rejects violence as a tool, and selects justice as a system! We might not return to civilization, but we can bring civilization to us!"

Marsha turned to a goateed young man next to her who was applauding and asked, "Have you heard of her before?"

"Yeah, she's the one who shot Orwell!"

"The guy who wrote *Animal Farm*?" Marsha played ignorant.

"No, Warhol!" the young man corrected. "The artist who doesn't paint! She wrote that thing."

"What thing?"

The guy pointed to the rear of the crowd. Since the rally was now just the band playing, Marsha pushed her way through and looked over the large picnic table covered with cheaply photocopied and stapled books. Among the titles were cookbooks like *How to Turn Canned Rations into a Delightful Albanian Dinner*, political diatribes like *Pig in Crap & Crap in Pig*, and poetic rants like *Rescue City Complaints*.

"Do you have something by Valerie Solanas?" Marsha asked the woman running the table.

Unable to compete with the band, the woman silently pointed to a small booklet entitled *SCUM Manifesto*. Marsha vaguely remembered it. She paid a quarter-stamp and slipped it into her handbag.

Before the rally ended and the crowds mobbed the road, Marsha left. On the bus ride back east, she took the opportunity to read the manifesto, and almost immediately found that she couldn't put it down. Even before the bus arrived at PP, she had finished it and started reading the slim work a second time in greater detail. After years of living in PP, an organization run by men, she realized for the first time how she had subtly and unconsciously grown adjusted to their worldview.

When she walked into the Pure-ile Plurality complex, she slipped the small book into her purse as though it were pornography.

Around midnight, Marsha pulled on her camisole and slippers and began her long walk to the little pier that fingered out into Jamaica Bay. As the cool night air whistled up her slip, she heard faint laughter in the distance, noise from the new neighbors to the northeast, and froze. She saw a flicker of lights from where there had always been darkness. For the first time ever, she felt as though the sanctity of their little compound had been breached. She put her hands over her small breasts and crotch.

Marsha hastily returned to her room, locked her door, and nervously flipped on the lamp. Valerie Solanas's manifesto was at her bedside on top of her Bible. Hoping to wash away any sense of shame,

Marsha grabbed it as it was close at hand. Yet as she reread it, the words screamed things that she had thought in anger, but never had the courage to even whisper. Although it was a little extreme, at times even comical, the message was abundantly relevant. Upon the sins of male sexuality, Solanas had put forth a legitimate proposal: eliminate men and free the earth of their vile customs!

* * *

When Marsha was summoned to Rolland Siftwelt's office the next morning, she felt unusually tense.

"So how was it?" he asked firmly.

"Pardon?"

"The rally?"

She gave her report on the Quirklyn campaign launch and assured him beyond any doubt that this ragtag group in South Ozone Park was quite harmless, and a little diplomacy could turn them into potentially useful neighbors.

"Fair enough, I'm getting a little sick of the Piggers," he responded. "When these people hold their campaign out here, we'll head across the field and shake some hands."

Throughout the next few days, as she thought more about Valerie Solanas, particularly the one criminal act that seemed to define her, she wondered if Andy Warhol had abused her in some way. Instead of sucking all that pain down, Solanas had reacted. Not only did the woman buy a handgun and shoot the pig, but she also hammered out her wrought-iron philosophy, a declaration for all women. Maybe it was that level of commitment, or perhaps it was the fact that now she had the moxie to be a political David in this awful land of two warring Goliaths, but whatever it was, Marsha found Valerie Solanas courageous and liberating. *If only I had that kind of courage,* she thought.w

30

"See if these fit." A young man tossed a paper bag containing sweatpants, a sweatshirt, and a pair of hospital slippers on top of Uli's slowly awakening form.

"What's going on?" he asked groggily. He lifted his hand to see if it was still there.

"The name's Maury Hotchkiss. I'm the All Are Created Equal liaison officer to the Bronx, and you, sir, are the luckiest man in Rescue City."

"Huh?"

"I think I'm the first person who has ever rushed into a judicial amputation room and grabbed the scalpel out of a surgeon's hand."

"You know I almost broke out of here?" Uli's heart was thumping wildly.

"Yeah, that really pissed them off. They were just about to release you."

"They were in the process of chopping off that week's limbs!"

"Apparently they were waiting for the last prisoner before issuing you a pardon. They were afraid that seeing someone getting pardoned in the middle of the process might start a riot. You need to have a little faith."

Uli, who had already resigned himself to losing his hand, held it up and kissed it. "Thank you, Karen."

"Your sister vanished and is now presumed dead. You were supposedly gone too—where'd you even come from?"

As Uli pulled the sweats on over his filthy undergarments, he informed Hotchkiss that the woman who had held him hostage, Erica Rudolph, had been arrested.

"Yeah, we know. She was extradited to Rescue City South yesterday." Hotchkiss explained that she was a DT terrorist, then he led Uli out of the zoo complex and to his car.

Looking down the long, bare corridor of a street, Uli commented, "I might've actually escaped if there was anywhere to hide."

"Only a handful of people know this," Maury replied, "but somewhere in the back of the zoo there's supposedly a fish house that supposedly has some kind of tunnel."

"To where?"

"No clue. A lieutenant from the army who was in charge of utility and public works told me about it before they were evacuated six months after Rescue City was activated. Back then this place was still a zoo."

Ten minutes later, Hotchkiss drove Uli over the loop of the sewage canal referred to as the Harlem River that separated the Bronx from Manhattan, and south down Broadway to Midtown Manhattan.

"Weren't there large panels over there?" Uli asked, pointing east in the mid-50s.

"Yeah, the two simulated skylines. Up here and down in Staten Island. The mayor had them dismantled."

They arrived at Rock & Filler Center and were frisked and led into a freight elevator which took them to the executive suite, the second floor from the top, just below Mallory's new private residence.

"We figured that after what you've been through, you could use a little time. Shower, get a checkup, grab a bite, recharge; by then the mayor should be down to see you."

In the dormitory, Hotchkiss pointed out a nice clean bathroom complete with fresh towels, then told him that if he needed anything, he should just dial zero. Uli thanked him and Hotchkiss was gone.

Uli couldn't remember the last time he took a shower, so he stayed under the wonderful warm water until he heard a knock at the bathroom door. The on-duty nurse had arrived and wanted to give him a quick checkup. He dried quickly, and the older woman carefully inspected each of the wounds he had acquired while imprisoned in that subterranean hell.

"Where can I grab some chow?" he asked.

"They make good sandwiches here," the nurse said. She picked up the phone, dialed zero, handed it to Uli, then left.

They had various deli sandwiches—corned beef, brisket, and roast beef, all hot. "Roast beef on rye with mayo," he said.

Ten minutes later there was a knock on the door. He opened it, expecting a sandwich, but instead, a security detail rushed in and checked the entire room. Before he could ask about his sandwich, they swiftly exited.

A moment later, the mayor of Rescue City South, Mallory, entered with an entourage. "How the hell did you climb out of that sewer?" she asked without even a proper greeting.

Uli recalled the single amorous night they had spent together. She looked even more radiant than he remembered. "I don't know, but there are still hundreds trapped down there who desperately need to be rescued." Uli glimpsed her missing arm and felt grateful that he had both of his.

"Where exactly are they?"

"No clue," Uli said. "In the desert somewhere. I passed out in a car heading toward some city."

"How the fuck did Erica Rudolph wind up kidnapping you?"

"Again, no clue. I just woke up in a bed covered head to toe in bandages. I heard the Piggers seceded from Rescue City."

"True, we're now officially two separate cities, which might not be a bad thing, if the peace holds out. We don't have the manpower to bring them back, but really, where are they going to go? They've actually been pretty easy to work with since the partitioning."

"Maybe if Lincoln had let the South leave the Union," he said with a smirk, "America would've been a slimmer, smarter country."

"Did you know that in the ten years that people have been diving down into that hole in the sewer pipe, you're the only person who has ever come back?"

"That is the mouth of hell."

"So what happens down there?"

"You end up in a big net and then a giant underground rat maze. Seal that hole up before anyone else can slip down there; I still can't believe I got out alive."

"Shub sealed it a few years ago. Cemented it over. They busted it open. I'll order it sealed again, but I'm sure it'll be reopened. When people get desperate and need a way out, that's where they jump. Tell me what the area looked like where you got out."

"Just desert. I made it to some highway and passed out." Pausing a moment, he asked, "So where's Karen? I heard she was dead."

"That's the story we put out, but we never got any confirmation. She has simply vanished."

"Where does one vanish here?"

"We're a penal colony surrounded by desert—who knows? It's still an ongoing investigation."

"Shit!"

"I knew your sister back in the old days," Mallory said.

"What old days?"

"We were both in this student organization. I'm only telling you this so you'll understand how close we were; I trusted her with things I wouldn't trust anyone else with. After you went down the drain, we began working out a peace treaty with the Piggers, and then Domination Theocracy blew up the sandbags protecting the Battery."

"How exactly did they do it?"

"According to anecdotal reports, they parked four trucks on the Staten Island Ferry Bridge above the dam and blew a fucking hole right through it. And they timed it during the POW conference, drowning all our major activists."

"Awful. Can that bridge even hold four trucks?"

"Yes indeed. And those who we managed to rescue came down with a whole host of infections. People are still dying from it."

"It's truly tragic."

"Have you heard anything about what's happening to our communities in northern Brooklyn?"

"Yeah, the contested areas with the new settlers. In the Bronx Zoo all we have is conversation to kill the time. I heard they also took over a Pigger neighborhood."

"A neighborhood the Piggers didn't even know existed."

"So what are you going to do?"

"Most of the new settlers are from the flooded parts of Lower Manhattan, so we've drained the borough and are doing our best to scrub it down as quickly as possible so we can return them to their homes."

"So the problem should work itself out," he said.

"Yes and no. The new group has been using their political campaign to put our criminal justice system on trial. Admittedly, I've always found it barbaric, so I'm using this opportunity to do a little reforming."

"After spending the past week in a former elephant pen waiting to have my hand amputated, I'm inclined to agree," Uli said.

"Unfortunately, we just don't have the resources to build a proper prison," Mallory continued, "but we can pay more attention to the law."

"What does that mean?"

"We've been developing the classic two-argument model with a sitting judge, something we've never had before."

"Who is the architect for your new legal system?"

"Do you remember Officer Chuck Schuman? He was your sister's assistant; now he's my newly appointed attorney general. In addition to bringing back classic trials, he's been struggling to restore the Bill of Rights here, but he's never done anything like this, and the switchblade tip of the legal system is my gangcops."

Uli sensed that Mallory was going to ask for his help in some matter so he just listened quietly.

"In hopes of presenting the Crappers as a kinder and gentler system, we're holding all prisoners until we've begun our trial program. But we have inmates piling up and we simply don't have trained personnel to do the work."

"You mean as prison guards?"

"I mean as lawyers. But we're improvising. In fact, we got all twelve former lawyers on our staff, most of whom were disbarred, to act as judges, and we're working fifteen hours a day to train and prep what we refer to as surrogate lawyers or *surlawyers*. But teaching them to build and argue a case, cramming two years of law school into four weeks, is a monumental task."

"Four weeks?"

"We need to start our trials on the day of the Quirklyn election. Did I fail to mention that there is a very real political component to all this? We have three candidates who are going to try to win those districts, and we need to demonstrate that our new criminal justice system is the most sophisticated. It'll be a key campaign point for our candidates running in Quirklyn, which leads us to why you're here. I need your help."

"To do what?"

"Legal protocols. The culture of the gangcops needs to be radically overhauled. They need to be brought in line."

"It sounds like you need some kind of police academy."

"Absolutely, along with a law school. But right now Schuman has asked to assemble the senior officer liaisons from the thirty or so gang precincts in Brooklyn and Manhattan, as they're the ones who are supposed to teach the protocols to their men."

"And who's teaching these senior officers?"

"You're a former FBI agent," Mallory finally disclosed. "That makes you the most qualified law enforcement officer here. I need you to teach them basic police techniques like gathering evidence and witnesses, get them to stop acting like a street gang, and help build relationships with their surlawyers."

"If you told me I used to be a milkman, I'd believe you," he confessed. "I still don't remember a thing of my training."

"From what I understand about amnesia, if you're a brain surgeon you might not be able to explain it, but if someone puts a scalpel in your hands, you should be able to operate."

"Would you really want me operating on your brain?"

"I'd rather have you do it than someone else who's unqualified, knowing that you did it a thousand times before."

"All right," Uli said, "are there files for all the criminals being held?"

"Yeah, but the surlawyers are currently using them. You'll have to sit tight."

"Tell you what. Let me use the spare time to look into the Manhattan sandbag bombing case."

"That's the one case that's cleanly closed. Erica Rudolph confessed."

"I need to know how I woke up in Rudolph's attic in the Bronx, and why she of all people is behind this bombing. The coincidence is too great."

"As long as you start working on the pending cases once they're available," Mallory said, rising to leave, "knock yourself out. You have an office waiting for you on the eighth floor of the Williamsburgh Savings Bank Building, where our criminal justice system is based. We've also included an apartment for you on the plaza and access to the car lot."

"Fine," he agreed. She had spared his arm. He had no choice.

Discreetly pointing to his wrist, one of Mallory's aides signaled to the mayor that she was late for an appointment. Someone gave Uli an envelope stuffed with food stamps, as an advance on his first paycheck, and a card with the address to his new apartment. The mayor wished him good luck.

With nothing else to do and with no possessions other than the clothes Hotchkiss had given him, Uli was ready to leave. Downstairs, he paid a cabbie a half-stamp to drive him to the Williamsburgh Savings Bank Building.

As the taxi crossed over the Brooklyn Bridge, the red clockface and green cap of the Williamsburgh Savings Bank Building stood out. To his right, Uli noticed the tip of Staten Island and immediately thought about Bea, the woman he had grown close to while down in Tottenville.

It couldn't have been a coincidence that she, of all people, was the sole daughter of Paul Moses. If the old man was still alive, Uli knew that after what had happened in the dungeon depths of the Mkultra—

when he had experienced Paul's life memory—fate had inexplicably appointed him the task of reuniting father with daughter.

"I don't mean to bother you," the driver spoke up, "but I saw you leave Rock & Filler Center. Are you part of this new criminal justice system?"

"Why?"

"My son and two of his friends are in lockup and have been sitting in jail for a while now. They say they're holding them for this new trial system. So I was just wondering when things were going to get started again."

Uli replied that hopefully the first trials would commence in just a few weeks.

"Since the Piggers broke away," the driver went on, "Mallory has said that without a proper trial, no more criminals are going to get stamped-and-amped"—slang for processed and amputated. "And that's great, but they're tossing them all in the Prospect Park Zoo till they get going."

Uli didn't have the heart to tell him that they weren't ending the amping—just the stampings, the hasty negotiations. He said that as a former detainee, he would rather spend an additional month in jail in exchange for a fair trial than lose an arm and get out quickly.

When the cab stopped in Downtown Brooklyn, Uli generously paid the driver a full stamp. He spent about half an hour purchasing a new wardrobe—an assortment of underclothes, pants, shirts, shoes, and a decent suit. As he got close to the Williamsburgh Justice Plaza, he stopped at Stamos's Stamps, a stamp bodega, and picked up some toiletries and food.

The Williamsburgh Justice Plaza was a building complex on a secured square, with a central building, the tallest in Rescue City. He first located his apartment on the plaza. The doorman downstairs had been notified of his arrival in advance and was given a description of the new deputy attorney general.

"The only place we really have available here is your sister's old apartment," the doorman said, helping him haul his bag of clothes up to the fifth floor. "We've put all her personal effects into the closet."

"Fine."

The man gave Uli his sister's house key, then left him in the scantily furnished two-bedroom apartment with a southern exposure, overlooking the plaza.

Since the phone in his apartment worked, the first thing Uli did was check the slim directory for all of Rescue City to try to find the phone number for Paul Moses—whose memories he had mysteriously lived through while underground. Amazingly, he found a listing. When Uli tried calling the number, he got the signal that meant it was disconnected. Next, he checked the Staten Island section for a number for Paul's lost daughter, Bea. Though the poorly photocopied stack of pages looked like they had been assembled in the past few years, there was no reference to either the Burnt Men or the Verdant League. Finally he looked up *Grogan*, as in Emmett Grogan, the man who was supposedly friends with Root Ginseng—the woman he had befriended in the Mkultra. Again, there was no listing.

Uli put away his new clothes, ate some canned spaghetti he found on a kitchen shelf, then tried to sleep but was unable. This was his first night in a long while that he wasn't imprisoned. Staring out the window at the dense constellation of lights around him, he truly appreciated his freedom. It was wonderful not being locked in an animal pen, held hostage by religious fanatics, or sealed in a subterranean dungeon.

31

Joe Brainard's "Get to Know Your Neighbors" strategy was generally easier than the Superstars had expected. It involved the candidates walking around their districts as much as possible. Candy and Cookie began taking their "Easter bonnet strolls" through Green-Burg twice a day. Their wardrobes were amusingly provocative. Whether they were skating Southern belles twirling parasols, or disco divas in pink miniskirts and high heels, they always attracted comments. Jackie snidely remarked that they should get paid less, as their ensembles were doing the work for them. All they had to do was pleasantly respond to people. Usually they'd make jokes about themselves, and from there they'd cleverly steer people into conversations about their plight and the moral imperatives of voting for the Quirklyn ticket.

Jackie in Bushwick and Ondine in East New York were having a bit more trouble. Learning from the Cookie-and-Candy model, the Brain replaced Jackie and Ondine's chauffeurs with people who were less bland bodyguards and more conversational catalysts. These intermediaries became the driving forces in getting them out of the house each morning and keeping them visible.

Believing that strangers would be more vulnerable to a single woman, Bea told Reggie, her driver, to keep a "visible distance" as she pandered through the grid of South Ozone Park homes where she made a passionate mission of turning strangers into friends. Many had seen or heard of her encounter with Izzlowski and were sympathetic. For those who didn't know about it, when she introduced herself as the Quirklyn candidate, the first question people would usually ask would be about the Warhol shooting—Valerie's greatest claim to fame.

"Were you trying to kill him or just scare him? How many times did you shoot him?" and on and on.

Bea felt like such a fraud, constantly having to explain and defend this other woman's actions. She would relay what Candy had told her about how Andy had become a false symbol of power for all of them. The shooting was clearly a momentary lapse in judgment that fortunately did not turn fatal. She soon learned, but would never mention, that she also shot an art critic named Mario Amaya, but only grazed him. She had been diagonosed a paranoid schizophrenic and served three years in a psychiatric facility before they felt she had regained her senses.

After their questions about the shooting, Bea would attempt to quickly segue into her new life as a politician.

"So what exactly is this Quirklyn thing all about?" people would eventually ask.

"I like to think of it as a friend-ocracy," she'd begin, then slowly she'd reveal the four points of their platform.

By the middle of the first week, the three candidates in the Crapper neighborhoods started getting heckled. It was Cookie and Candy who first reported this to Brainard.

"Let Biggs debate!" people had begun screaming at them. They were referring to the Crapper candidate, who had repeatedly invited his Quirklyn adversary to debate.

During the second week, Bea began to see Izzlowski also walking around SOP, making small talk with the locals. He had changed his clothes into something more casual, and jettisoned that Christmas-card family—apparently he had discovered that no one here gave a shit about family values. That Friday, in the middle of one of her morning meet and greets, Bea heard someone shouting her name. She turned to see the Pigger candidate waving at her with a friendly smile as he was crossing a street. She politely waved back.

The next day she got a visit from Brainard, who asked her if Izzlowski had requested a debate. When she said no, he explained that the Crappers were on a debating rampage; first they had started handing out posters, now they were slinging banners across key streets throughout all three of their districts.

"What exactly do they say?" Bea asked.

Joe gave her a brochure:

WE'VE REPEATEDLY CHALLENGED
THESE QUIRKLYNERS TO DEBATE—THEY'VE REFUSED!
WANT TO KNOW WHY?
ASK THEM WHO THE REAL POWER IS BEHIND THEM.
THIS IS WHY THEY WON'T DEBATE!
IF YOU WANT SOMEONE

WITH NOTHING TO HIDE, WHO IS BRINGING
YOU THE FINEST SYSTEM OF JUSTICE?
<u>VOTE CRAPPERS!</u>

"Why don't we just debate them?" Bea asked.

"Do you think this group is up for it?"

"Sure, especially if *not* debating is hurting us."

"We'll see," the Brain replied. They had less than four more weeks to go.

32

The new deputy attorney general of Rescue City South, Uli Sarkisian, was awakened the next morning by the ringing of his phone. It was Tatianna, the attorney general's secretary, who told him that at nine a.m. he was going to have his first meeting with the gangcop lieutenants from Brooklyn and Manhattan—liaisons for the new trial program. Attorney General Schuman was hoping to meet with Uli first, so could he please report to his office at eight a.m.

"Fine."

He showered, put on his new suit and tie, and walked around the Williamsburgh Justice Plaza. It was surrounded by concrete barriers blocking potential car bombs and manned by police checkpoints. Apparently the city council police and Rescue City South criminal justice system spared no precautions when it came to their own security.

At eight a.m., Uli entered the Williamsburgh Building. There, looking at the building directory, he discovered that floors two through five were being remodeled into courtrooms specifically for the trials program. Floors six and seven had been reinforced as holding pens for prisoners brought from Prospect Park, and the top three floors—eight, nine, and ten—were the administrative offices for gangcops and new surlawyers.

"Can I help you?" asked the security guard.

Uli gave his name and new title.

"Is there anyone here who can vouch for you?" the man asked.

Attorney General Schuman was the only person he could think of.

"You're going to have to wait until a guard comes down, 'cause I can't let you go upstairs without an escort."

"Can you call him?"

"We don't call the attorney general. He calls us."

"I'll vouch for him," Uli suddenly heard. A short, dark, balding man appeared behind him.

"Thanks," Uli said, wondering who this guy was.

The security guard gingerly frisked Uli and waved them through.

As they walked away from the security station, the man introduced himself. "Call me Hector. I'm head of the council cops."

He extended a small, delicate hand, which Uli shook as they stepped onto an elevator.

"I worked with your sister a few years ago when she was up in Harlem," Hector said. His voice was so high it was almost squeaky.

"Have we ever met?"

"I was at Cooper Union when the building was bombed. Believe it or not, I remember you working on the excavation. I also remember after that when you were wanted for killing some Piggers and pictures of you were plastered all over the place—I didn't think you'd last a day."

"Me neither, yet here I am now, working alongside you," Uli replied as the elevator shot up. "So what is it that council cops actually do?"

"Up until Mallory was elected, their primary function seemed to be hunting down alleged international terrorists who were swept up here." Hector grinned and added, "Your sister had my job before me."

"Is the Nevada desert a big terrorist haven?"

"In fairness, they did find about half a dozen confirmed members of various radical organizations, like SNCC and such. Most of them were working against the war in Vietnam."

"And the cops arrested them?"

"They couldn't. All of them either held elected posts or are specialists who can't be replaced, like doctors or lawyers." Hector chuckled. "But if you read the reports, the leads they pursued over the last ten years would make any spy thriller sound boring."

"How's that?"

"Fueled largely by insane newspaper claim, the council cops were looking for members of every major terrorist group, from the IRA and Baader-Meinhof to the Red Brigades."

"What are you investigating now?" Uli asked.

Hector stiffened. "Quirklyn."

"What's Quirklyn exactly?"

"A smattering of cracked streets along the top edge of Brooklyn, a swath of crumbling and burned-out buildings that were abandoned long ago."

"Maybe we should let it go then."

"When Pakistan broke away from India, everyone thought the problem was solved. But now they want more land and other parts of India are breaking away."

"If Pakistan and India weren't partitioned, civil war might've torn the entire place apart," Uli rebutted. "I think a better analogy is a limb with gangrene: amputate it and you save the rest of the body."

"A gangrenous limb doesn't keep assaulting the body. Breakaway countries are future enemies, waiting to spring. There's no resolution, just more dispute," Hector reasoned. "We should've fought against the Piggers when they declared their independence, and kept them in the city. Then this Quirklyn thing never would've happened."

"So who exactly are these Quirklynites?" Uli asked.

"In my opinion, this has all the hallmarks of Adolphus Rafique—an antigang provocateur extraordinaire—and if I can get any solid evidence of it, I'm going after him."

The elevator door opened on the tenth floor, and Hector led Uli past a pool of paralegals to Tatianna, the woman he had spoken to earlier that morning.

"That used to be Mayor Shub's old office," Hector said, pointing to Schuman's door. "Mallory prefers Rock & Filler Center."

The secretary ended a phone call and told Uli to go right in. He found the attorney general staring nervously at papers in a room filled with clothes and other personal effects. Chuck Schuman looked like he had aged a decade—probably due to to the sheer weight of endless responsibilities recently bestowed upon him.

Against the far wall was a chalkboard. In bold letters along the top it read:

THE BILL OF RITES *Progress Report*

1. *Freedom of religion, speech, the press, and the rights to assemble and petition—none care*
2. *Right to bear arms—the one big mistake they never shudda got*
3. *Housing of soldiers—irrelevant*
4. *Search and arrest warrants—pending*
5. *Rights in criminal cases—pending*
6. *Right to a fair trial—pending*
7. *Rights in a civil case—irrelevant*
8. *Bails, fines, and punishments—pending*
9. *Rights retained by the people—seem fine*
10. *Powers retained by the states and the people—not our problem, thank God!*

"I'm so sorry about Karen," Schuman said as he rushed over and warmly shook Uli's hand.

"What exactly happened to her?"

"I heard she was investigating DT, before the bomb attack. Then she just disappeared. We looked for any signs that she was abducted but found nothing."

"Did anyone go through her things?" Uli asked, since he was now living in her place.

"I've gone over everything myself," Schuman said, looking down. "If it wasn't for the fact that she rerouted the antiwar convention down to Lower Manhattan, she would've immediately been appointed attorney general, and I'm sure she would've been much better than me. I'm so glad that you, her brother, are here. The first guy who was assigned to train the gangcops is a complete waste of time. And we're going to start our first trials in just four weeks. That's probably not much time to train anyone."

"Who am I replacing?" Uli asked.

"Scouter Lewis—who is now officially your assistant. He kept missing days, so most of the lieutenants from the various precincts stopped coming in for the orientation."

"I don't suppose there are any textbooks on—"

"Nope."

"Why was he ever hired?"

"He was one of the only former New York City cops who made it here, although we can't exactly check anyone's résumé. When Mallory contacted me last night to say you were taking over, I had my secretary call everyone in to report for your new class."

"Just to be sure, what exactly am I training them for?"

"Didn't Mallory tell you?"

"I'm a little slow."

"How to make the gangcops work with the new surrogate lawyers."

"That's right," Uli replied tensely.

"If it's of any consolation, it's got to be easier than my job," Schuman said. "I've been living out of this office, working around the clock, overseeing a small staff of ridiculously unqualified people to give lessons to the small army of even more unqualified surlawyers to grow a fucking brain."

"Who exactly is your ridiculously unqualified staff?"

"I got a former assistant district attorney who was dismissed due to his drug habit, a former Legal Aid lawyer who might very possibly be psychotic, an immigration lawyer who from his observations is probably a pedophile, a traffic court judge with serious anger problems—all of whom were disbarred for obvious reasons—and a bunch of antiwar activists who . . ." Just reciting his staff exhausted Schuman, and he trailed off.

"Since there are no textbooks or syllabi," Uli asked, "do you have any advice on how or what I'm supposed to teach them?"

"Sure, best way to handle them is like interns at a hospital. Do rounds on various pending investigations. Give them basic, easy-to-follow instructions on how to gather evidence—things to use in court. Pinpoint where they're wrong and how things have to be done differently. You've got only a few weeks to give them a crash course on basic police procedures and techniques before the actual trials start. Keep in mind that everything you teach them in the afternoon, they are going to teach to their own men the following morning."

"And by actual trials, you mean . . . ?"

"The whole *Perry Mason* rigamarole. It's time to pay our Bill of Rights." Schuman tapped the chalkboard behind him, then pulled a sheet of paper from the top of his desk. "Aside from whatever procedures you might teach them, a lot of their new assignments are going to be following the new protocol."

"What exactly is that?"

Schuman handed the page to Uli. "We're still working on it, but this is the latest draft of what our surlawyers need from the gangcops in order to intelligently argue a case. I'll send you an updated version once it's complete."

Uli looked over the badly misspelled, heavily marked-up protocol list-in-progress: *Crime seen fotos, arest reports, witniss statments . . .*

"Oh shit!" Schuman exclaimed. "I just realized I won't be able to send you the crime files until we're done with them. Right now the surlawyers are going over them."

"Until you do, I'm sure I can find something to teach in terms of basic procedures," Uli said. "One other thing—before I made the awful mistake of going down the Staten Island sewer, I remember hearing about some mysterious team of scientists who used to perform these bizarre experimental surgeries . . ."

"That's another positive consequence of our treaty with the North. Since we're now at peace, both sides have agreed not to use the CIA brain cutters." Lowering his breath, he added, "With one exception."

"What's that?"

"There was this one enigmatic kid, very few people ever saw him. Hell, he might not have even been real. He was called Karove and he's supposed to have telepathic powers—someone said he was able to predict the outcome of close elections. Anyway, we're supposed to call in the brain cutters so they can engage the experiment if we find him."

Uli didn't say anything, but he knew that "Karove" was dead.

The attorney general told Uli that Tatianna would help him get settled in. She led him to a snug office with a cloth sofa, wooden desk, and his very own secretary, an old woman named Sheila.

"Was this Karen's office?"

"No, we're keeping that available as a memorial to her," Tatianna said solemnly.

Uli still had about twenty minutes before he had to report for his first class with the lieutenants, so Sheila brought him a short stack of administrative forms to fill out, along with a laminated photo ID.

"Also," she remembered before leaving, "some woman named Marsha Johnson from Pure-ile Plurality called for you earlier. She left a number, you want me to call her back?"

Marsha Johnson had been his supervisor when he worked at PP. He remembered how, when he first awoke as a hostage in the Bronx, she had appeared at his bedside. He had thought she'd help free him, but based on the way things turned out, it seemed she hadn't even tried.

"Call her immediately," he said angrily.

"I'll buzz you when she's on the phone."

"Also, send in my assistant, Scouter Lewis."

"He doesn't show till everyone leaves. And he's usually drunk." Sheila exited the room.

Uli filled out forms until the intercom buzzed; Marsha was on the phone.

"Why the hell didn't you tell the authorities where I was being held?" he roared at her.

"They said if I didn't do anything they'd eventually let you go unharmed."

"You know I can have you arrested for collusion!"

"I did no such thing, and you're free like they promised!"

"How the hell are you involved with them anyway?"

"Erica Allen Rudolph worked at PP during the first few years. I saw her literally give food from her plate and clothes off her back to the needy."

"She blew up the Manhattan sandbags! Over a thousand were killed and they're still dying."

"I didn't know that."

"She held me, sedated, in some attic in the Bronx. I only escaped by getting myself arrested and spending a week sitting in elephant dung in the fucking Bronx Zoo, waiting to have my hand chopped off!"

"Look, I just opened the papers and saw that you were appointed to the new justice department, which is why I called."

Through his office window, Uli peered out at the desert off to his south and east. Below him, Jackie Wilson Way, or Flatbush Avenue, the main artery of Brooklyn, was bumper to bumper with traffic.

"I made Erica promise that she wouldn't hurt you, and she didn't."

"When things calm down here," Uli said, "I'm coming up to Howard Beach and we're going to have a long face-to-face talk."

Sheila came to his door, tapping on her wristwatch. It was time for his first meeting. As Marsha continued apologizing for not being more courageous, Uli hung up. Sheila gave him the room number of the class and an attendance sheet for his thirty gangcop students including what precincts they were each from.

33

It was a large box of a room with a chalkboard in front. Uli stood before a group of about thirty large, older men who looked more pissed than bored.

"I'm the new deputy in town—Deputy Attorney General Sarkisian," he introduced himself softly. "I'm not good with names, so I'm just going to call out your district. Respond if you're from there." First he read off the Brooklyn contingent: "Greenpoint, East Williamsburg, Brooklyn Heights, Clinton Hill, Bed-Stuy–Bushwick, East New York, Red Hook–Carroll Gardens–Park Slope, Sunset Park–Windsor Terrace, Prospect–Crown Heights, Wingate–Bay Ridge, Bensonhurst, Borough Park–Ocean Parkway, Coney Island–Brighton Beach, Prospect Park South–Midwood, Gravesend–Sheepshead Bay, Brownsville, East Flatbush, Flatlands-Canarsie, and finally Cypress Hills." After each place he heard a grunt of some kind.

Uli then called out the Manhattan districts: "City Hall, LittleHo-Town, East Village, West Village, Gramercy Park, Chelsea, Midtown, Upper West, Upper East, Harlem, and Inwood." All representatives were present.

"What exactly will we be learning?" asked the gangcop lieutenant with muttonchops from Gramercy Park.

"Yeah, what the hell do we have to come out here for, anyway?" mumbled a Brooklyn gangcop.

"We had a system that was working fine!" another voice shouted.

"That bitch froze all our cases!" someone else called out.

"Yeah, why can't she just leave us alone and let us do our job?"

"If anyone wants to say something, be a man and state your name!" Uli stared them down like a bunch of schoolchildren.

"My name's Lieutenant Anthony LaCoste from East New York, and we all got prisoners coming out of our asses," a large redheaded gangcop with a bushy mustache barked. "We all want to know why we can't use the old-fashioned justice that we've been using."

"Two days ago, I was sitting in a Pigger prison cell in the BZ waiting to have my hand chopped off," Uli replied. "Do you know why?"

"Why?" LaCoste asked.

"'Cause I was kidnapped and held hostage by that fucking group who blew up the sandbags in the Battery, and the only way I could escape was by harmlessly whacking a gangcop in the knee. They arrested me and my captors, and instead of doing basic police work and realizing that there was a good fucking reason for what I did, they found me guilty and sentenced me to have my hand amputated!"

"That's the Piggers," LaCoste countered. "That ain't—"

"It's *all* of you! Gangcops act like gangcops, North and South. There's no accountability and it's out of control!" Uli snapped.

"We have a 100 percent conviction rate."

"Yeah, 'cause there's no opposition! You don't solve cases, you just close them."

"Bullshit!"

"Haven't you ever wondered why, despite all your convictions, your crime rate always stays the same?"

"That's not fair!" yelled redheaded LaCoste. "We check the work of our men, and when a case is weak, we reject it."

"Even if they are guilty, do you really think a person should lose a limb over a robbery? This system has turned this place into a colony of cripples and gimps," Uli pressed.

"Hey," LaCoste replied, "we got stuck in a city filled with lowlifes and and ex-cons!"

The entire room broke out laughing, as many of them were former criminals themselves. Uli now remembered that he had met LaCoste the first day when Chain hijacked his bus and hung the Carnivals.

"Be that as it may, our criminal justice department should be more than a stamp-and-amp butcher shop; it should have a series of checks and balances with impartial judges, be guided by a system of rules in order to carefully assess levels of guilt, punish accordingly, and give the innocent reasonable doubt."

"Fine, but what does that have to do with us?" someone called out.

"All this has to work together or we're no better than wolves at the top of the food chain." Someone else was about to interrupt, but Uli slammed his palm down on his desk and shouted, "From now on, you only talk when I ask a question! Understand?"

"Or what?" mumbled LaCoste.

Uli walked over and stood directly in front of the man, who looked away contritely.

"From here on, all criminals will be given legal counsel," Uli said. "And their lawyers will try to make you all look like liars, so let's all carefully consider . . ." He picked up a small piece of chalk and wrote: *HOW TO BUILD A CASE THAT CAN HOLD UP IN A COURT.* "Also keep in mind that . . ." he wrote as he spoke:

1. *Violence against criminals will be looked for, and not only can it serve to free the criminal, but* you *can be arrested because of it.*

"So don't do it and don't let your men do it! We'll also go through . . ." He wrote:

2. *Methods of legal interrogation: soft interrogation vs. hard interrogation.*
3. *Collect usable evidence with cameras and tape recorders.*

"It's no longer your word automatically winning out against theirs."

4. *Work with the assistant district attorney who will be arguing your case.*

"What do you do when you are sent to a crime?" he asked his class.

"Arrest the criminal, stupid!" someone replied, and everyone laughed.

"And how the hell do you know who that is?" Uli shot back. "'Cause some one-legged lowlife you just had a beer with told you?"

Silence. Uli wrote:

5. Investigate the crime scene and examine the corpse!

"Suppose you can't find him?" yelled out LaCoste.

Looking around at the class, Uli suddenly realized that no one was writing anything—in fact, they didn't even have pencils or paper.

"I'll tell you what you do," said the fat lieutenant from Windsor Terrace. "You grab all the usual suspects and beat the shit out of them until one of them talks."

Uli threw the piece of chalk at the board. "I was recently tortured, and I would've confessed to *anything* to get them to stop electrocuting my dick!" The room went silent once again. "If you're so stupid that you want to maim some poor son of a bitch who is now going to be your sworn enemy for life, while the guilty party is still out there—go right ahead."

"With all due respect, we haven't had any cases of revenge yet," said LaCoste.

"Anyone have any clue about who blew up the Manhattan sandbags?" Uli was tired of speaking in hypotheticals.

"That crazy fucking religious gang. They just caught the lead whore," said one of the older gangcops from the Inwood precinct.

"How do you know she did it?"

"She confessed."

"Okay, I did it," Uli replied. "Do you believe me?" No response. "What would motivate DT to blow up the fucking sandbags?"

"To reignite the conflict between the Piggers and Crappers," La-Coste responded. "And believe me, the Piggers are working on it much harder than we are."

"That's bullshit," said the gangcop from Cypress Hills. "The dead-end Piggers who worked for Shub were the ones behind the blast. You think it's just a coincidence that this happened when Mallory came to power?"

A passionate debate ensued; theories started flying around the room.

Uli used the interlude to step out of the classroom and find Schuman's secretary, Tatianna.

"How can I get transportation?" he asked.

"You need a car?" She reached for a form.

"I need a bus, or something to move my class."

"We have some prisoner vans available," Tatianna said. "But they only hold six men apiece."

"I got thirty men."

"Five vans should be enough, let me see what's up." She got on the phone, and soon handed Uli five sets of keys and told him to head to the car lot downstairs.

"Grab whatever you came with," Uli announced, returning to the classroom. "You're going to get a crash course in investigating a crime scene."

He ordered everyone into the tiny elevator and they went down in groups of five into the cramped lobby. In ten minutes, the convoy of five prisoner vans was headed through Downtown Brooklyn and over the slender reproduction of the Brooklyn Bridge. Uli rode with a gang-cop lieutenant named Felix from the City Hall precinct—the crime scene they were going to was in his jurisdiction. A half hour later they were streaming down Third Avenue toward the Battery.

For most of them it was their first time seeing Lower Manhattan since it had been drained of the sewage water. Teams of masked and gloved workers were spread all over with long wooden poles fastened to scrub brushes. The area was slowly being disinfected.

Uli got out of the lead van at the bottom of the island. The wall of obliterated sandbags was still being reconstructed, this time twice as thick. From there, all could see what was left of the Staten Island Ferry Bridge. It looked like a pier extending from Staten Island over the filthy harbor.

"Are the photographs at your precinct?" Uli asked Felix.

"What photographs?"

"Of the scene." He paused, then added, "After the crime occurred."

"None were taken, as far as I know."

"How about photos of the trucks?" Uli asked.

"What trucks?"

"The trucks that blew up the sandbags."

"There are none," the gangcop replied.

It took Uli a moment for this detail to sink in. No photos had been taken of one of the worst crimes committed in Rescue City since it was established.

"Well, where exactly are the trucks?"

"At the bottom of the harbor, I guess," said Felix.

"No one fished them out?"

"Hell no, trucks are heavy, and that harbor is dirtier than an un-flushed toilet."

"Isn't that an interesting coincidence?" Uli said to his class. "The crime was committed at a location where the evidence couldn't be retrieved. Well, we're gonna recover it."

Toward the western edge of the island, under a sign that read, *Bay-onne*, Uli spotted a large barge with what appeared to be a small crane. He learned that it had been left years ago by the military to scrape out the sediment that had built up along the bottom of the harbor. Clearly, it had long since broken down—parts of the harbor were so shallow that it looked as though you could nearly walk across.

"That's probably the reason the sewer got clogged," Uli speculated, referring to the buildup of human waste.

"It's also the reason we had to put sandbags around Manhattan," replied Felix, "but what can you do?"

Uli was able to locate a phone at one of the nearby guard stations. He called the attorney general's office and explained to Tatianna that he needed to fish something heavy out of the bottom of the polluted harbor. She said she had no clue how to do that. No city agency or authority was in charge of something like that.

"We'll just have to improvise," Uli said to his class.

"If you want us to work in these waters," cautioned a lieutenant from Sheepshead Bay, "we'll need protective gear or everyone will get the infection."

Another gangcop, a helpful fellow named Christopher Bleek from the West Village precinct, seemed to know all about the fetid harbor. He also knew the harbormaster, a sinecure for some politician's lazy nephew.

Within ninety minutes a fleet of small rowboats were at Uli's dis-posal for as long as he needed them. Bleek also had his precinct send a squad car packed with hooded raincoats, face masks, and rubber gloves. But it was Felix who managed to do the impossible: he found two trucks and had them cart over bundles of long, thick chains, along with an assortment of hooks and winches.

Two hours later, Uli asked Lieutenant Felix, "How the hell can we get that barge over here?"

"For starters, both the engine and that crane on top are rusted frozen," Felix explained. "It's more like a large raft. If it isn't stuck to the bottom, maybe we can pull it around."

34

"He called me a coward!" Bea said on the phone to the Brain. "Who did?" He was not feeling well that morning and had missed the framework of her hastily told story.

Bea told him that when she had walked into the only stamp store in South Ozone Park that morning, Izzlowski was already there campaigning. When she tried to greet her potential constituents, Izzlowski interrupted, claiming that she and her entire group were cowards because they refused to enter a public debate.

"And I know I can beat him! He's not that bright."

"You're forgetting several crucial details. First of all, you're not . . . *you know who*," the Brain said, in case the line was tapped. "And if he should present some irrefutable evidence regarding . . . *that*, it's curtains! That's it. And not just for you, but for Operation Terrible Beauty."

"If he can prove that I'm not . . . what difference will it make if he does it there or somewhere else?"

"It can be refuted elsewhere, but right there it'd be disastrous."

"Well, it's too late," she said. "I agreed to debate him."

"He tricked you!" Brainard said. "Think about it, this must've involved both gangs. Once the Crappers hear about this, they're going to say, *What about us? If she's willing to debate the Pigger candidate, why won't the others debate us?*"

"Joe, I'm sorry, but I'm a human being and I have my pride. I believe in this cause. We can win this debate."

What worried him the most wasn't the debate. It was the fact that she, the most controlled member on the ticket, had overridden his authority. In the next district over, Ondine was missing work one day after the next, staying home allegedly due to the flu, but probably because of withdrawal.

Jackie Curtis was another story. She made daily appearances in different parts of the neighborhood, but according to her driver, Tom Collins, on most days it would've been better if she hadn't. If she wasn't passing out on on stoops and benches, Jackie would curse at prospective voters, or rant about the insignificance of living in Rescue City. One day she staggered out in only nylons and a wig, and insisted on being chauffeured around the area. Collins dragged her back into the house before anyone could see her.

Jackie's only piece of good luck was that her Crapper opponent, Sandy Faustus, seemed to bathe in voter repellent. Though Faustus's message was solid, his tone was patronizing. His facial expressions alone exuded cocky privilege and sheer entitlement. During one particular public appearance, instead of talking about the issues, he actually instructed the crowd on how to vote for him by tapping the tiny switch then pulling the large lever—as if they were imbeciles.

Cookie and Candy were the dream team. They seemed perfectly designed for the youthful, happy-go-lucky Greenpoint-Williamsburg constituents. People would come out of their homes to chat with them and they felt better afterward.

If the election were held today, the Brain thought, they'd win hands down. Despite Izzlowski's retooled campaign, Valerie Solanas had also proven quite popular in SOP, and would probably also edge him out. Only Ondine in East New York would lose without question.

Something had to be done quickly, but the Brain had no clue what. When he consulted Charles Ludlam, the only thing the former theater director could think of was holding another political rally.

"Flightbag needs more flights!"

35

Paul Moses's girlfriend Lucille had recently received a call from an obnoxious friend informing her of a small, recently renovated apartment building in East New York.

"They're looking for either a gimp, a light-skinned spic, or some old farts to smush out their candy-ass rainbow image—no swishes, Chinks, or spades—so I thought of you."

Lucille, who had never considered her friend a bigot—just a hyperneurotic button pusher—thanked her for the heads-up.

An athletic young man named Elk, the head of the little East New York commune, interviewed the couple, who had just vacated their senior citizen home in disgust.

After hearing about their vast life experiences, Elk happily welcomed them into the house. They had a nice ground-floor apartment available immediately, but he warned them that loud music was played until late at night. Neither minded as they both had trouble hearing.

The first week came with some adjustments. Living without the help of the nursing home required a lot more work than Paul ever remembered—just tying his shoes took fifteen minutes—but he and Lucille were still fairly energetic for their ages. With food co-ops, various recycling stations, and even a nearby sexual crisis center—whatever that was for—East New York seemed more like a happy anthill than a Rescue City neighborhood.

Everyone in the commune was so nice. Watching the kids make fools of themselves with their earnest altruism was entertaining enough, and Paul also enjoyed the companionship. Kids were dumb enough that they actually liked to listen! He enjoyed getting up early and sitting out front to say goodbye to them as they marched off to work.

"What do you mean *work*?" Lucille asked upon hearing him say this. "This place is just one big welfare colony."

"Good point," Paul said. It gave him a topic to talk about, and the very next morning he asked one of them, "Where exactly do you work?"

"DDQ," the young man responded enigmatically, without stopping.

Lucille would spend her mornings cleaning up while Paul went out for his morning constitutional. After venturing several blocks along the northern end of Quirklyn, he would follow the trail of purple ribbons tied to the lampposts. When he started to grow tired, he'd sit down on some steps, lean back, and fall right asleep, then return home refreshed and with an appetite. With the memory lapses and constant drops in energy, being old was kind of trippy without the burden of having to score drugs. And no one bothered you because it was like being invisible. The only downside was the occasional realizations that he had wasted his once-promising life and abandoned his beautiful daughter.

Three weeks after the new political party had launched its candidates in McBarren Park, two things happened to Paul. First, he spotted his young landlord, Elk, walking to work late. Then, at that same moment, he noticed a cardboard sign announcing:

> Meet Your Local Quirklyn Representative, Ondine,
> & the Other Quirklyn Party Candidates:
> The Andy Warhol Superstars!!!!
> This Tuesday in Cypress Hills Cemetery Park, East New York.

Paul focused all his attention and tailed Elk until he reached an elevated, terraced street; it was the southern border of Quirklyn, Metropolitan Avenue. There he saw his boy landlord enter a large building. Inside he heard the muffled whir of circular saws and a cacophony of hammering. Paul remembered seeing another large building just like it, also being worked on by a youthful team, and guessed they were both administrative centers for the new area.

Later that same day, Lucille spotted more posters advertising the upcoming Quirklyn rally. Over dinner that night she suggested they attend.

"Why?"

"This is the reason we left the nursing home in the first place," she said. "Don't you want to see what we sacrificed everything for?"

"Sure, what the hell," he agreed.

The next day, while meandering eastward, Paul heard someone coming up behind him and turned to see Elk coming his way. Evidently he was heading back to the construction site.

"May I ask you something?" Paul began, trying to be coy. "Is DDQ a part of ETNA?"

"DDQ is the Defense Department of Quirklyn. We're erecting guardhouses in case the Crappers attack."

"So you do construction?"

"Yeah, but once the current project is complete, I'll be working for the Quirklyn militia."

As Paul walked with the young fellow, they talked about the political independence movement, and how Elk felt Quirklyn was the most exciting thing in his life. Paul mentioned that many people had felt the same way when Russia revolted, or when he was just a kid and Mexico had its revolution. Many had hoped that America would follow suit.

Soon they arrived at the big house. A human conveyor belt of young men and women was lined up outside, passing two-by-fours and other building materials out of a truck parked in front.

"Can I help?" Paul asked Elk, who was already joining in.

"Sure," he replied, handing Paul a bag of nails.

As Paul was about to walk inside, a short, thick, tan fellow who seemed to be security took the bag from Paul and blocked him.

"It's okay," Elk said, "he's cool. He and his wife are in my commune."

Paul had to go home anyway. He knew Lucille would be worried since she was expecting him back soon, so he thanked Elk and headed home.

The next day at eleven a.m., Paul and Lucille slowly hiked up to Cypress Hills Cemetery Park for the local Quirklyn rally.

Along with clouds of pot smoke, festivity was in the air. A band was playing on the large makeshift stage. A crowd was pouring in, but apparently the candidates were nowhere to be seen. Paul spotted Elk and some of his buddies from the commune lying on the patchy lawn, having fun in the sun.

"So we're going to see this Iodine fella?" Lucille asked him.

"Ondine," Elk corrected. "You might've already seen him. He's been wandering around the area lately."

"The last political rally I remember going to was in '34," Paul said. "My brother was running for governor of New York."

"Your brother was governor?"

"No, he lost, thank God, but—"

Suddenly, the band stopped playing as a fellow with black-framed glasses got up onstage. The man touched the mic to be certain it was working, then introduced himself as Joe, a member of the Quirklyn

Party, and thanked everyone for coming. "Without wasting any time, allow me to introduce the next city council representative from East New York—the great water nymph, Ondine!"

All cheered as a group of people shuffled up the steps behind the stage. The candidate wore dark sunglasses as he slowly walked up to the podium.

"Howdy, I'm Ondine, and I'm honored that you all came here to rally for me and my fellow candidates. I remember how when we first arrived and the military was in power, they tried to run things, and we all hated them—because they were obnoxious, and they all dressed alike. But then after a couple of them got killed, they pulled out, and I felt bad, 'cause it was nice seeing all those hot young guys, you know, and then, oh my God . . . instead of coming together, all the people here just disintegrated into a rude bunch of gangs and bullies. Remember? And you'd hear those awful screams at night, and gunfire and the dogs howling, and in the morning you'd see those half-eaten bodies everywhere—yuck! It was just disgusting. And scary! Well, guess what: now, for the first time, you can actually do something about it."

Everyone watched as the candidate's pants seemed to shimmer magically before their eyes. It took a moment before Paul realized that Ondine was literally losing control of his bladder.

Without a pause, Ondine just kept on talking: "You can vote for a party that believes in fairness—in representation, justice, and in power. Now, it's my honor to introduce you to my fellow candidates, who are artists like many of you!"

As a pair of women who looked like a fat and thin Marilyn Monroe stepped up, a campaign worker followed, quickly mopping up the puddle of pee.

"Hi, I'm Candy Darling of the Quirklyn Party, hoping to be elected by you Green-Burgians out here."

"And I'm Cookie Mueller, First Gentleman."

"If you vote for me, I'll protect you from Queens!" Candy said.

"Like you?" Cookie asked with a smile.

"Why don't you debate?!" someone yelled up at them, interrupting their little routine.

"Because name-calling isn't debating, and that's all they want to do, and it's stupid. But we know you're smart, so please vote for us in two weeks. Thanks!"

Applause went up and the two took seats behind Ondine, who

again stood up. "Now I'd like to introduce the candidate from Bushwick—the inimitable Jackie Curtis!"

A frizzy-haired blond woman walked up and quietly said: "I'd like to be known as the candidate who doesn't do anything. I won't spend your resources on what isn't in *your* interest, or suspend your rights for what isn't *your* security. Support me and I won't do nothing for you, or to you. Thank you." She tried to curtsy, fell down, got up, then sat down, causing everyone to laugh.

"Isn't she wonderful, folks?" Ondine was wearing a new pair of pants that were too tight for him. "It's finally my pleasure to introduce the man who shot Liberty Valance—Valerie Solanas!"

Paul and Lucille watched another candidate climb up the stairs.

"Actually, I'm the woman who shot Andy Warhol, but we worked it out. He got a million dollars for his soup can, and I won a one-way trip out here with you good folks . . ."

As Paul's tired eyes fixed and focused on Solanas, he found himself thinking about his little girl, whom he hadn't seen in almost twenty years. As the candidate spoke, something nagging inside of him rose to the surface. "That's her," he finally muttered. Lucille ignored him.

How can this be? He hadn't seen Bea in a very long time, yet despite the fact that she was wearing a peacoat and small black cap—the gestures, the voice, the way she carried herself—it was definitely her.

". . . Let's turn this election into our emancipation from the two gangs that have spent the past ten years killing and ravaging us."

Paul felt faint and started tipping over.

"Are you okay?" Lucille asked. "You look like you've seen a ghost."

"I must be hallucinating," he said. "Please take me home."

While the candidate who was pretending to be Valerie Solanas continued her speech, the two seniors slowly rose from the dirt, bade farewell to Elk and their younger compadres, and headed back to their apartment in the commune.

36

"I just don't think saying you're the candidate who *won't do anything* is helpful," Bea said to Jackie during a meeting at the East New York headquarters.

"What a sniveling self-righteous bitch you've become!" Jackie lashed out.

"Ladies, let's calm down," Candy said.

"And I thought your 'boobsie twins' act was atrocious!" Jackie fired back. "You two should both be on a diet!"

"Calm down, Jackie," the Brain said, returning from putting Ondine to bed.

"I thought it was very clever," Cookie retorted.

"Me too," said Bea.

"The only reason you're even here is 'cause Valerie is dead!" Jackie snapped.

"Too bad you can't demonstrate that clarity onstage," Bea replied.

"We wouldn't have to be so good on the stage if you didn't fall into that Pigger debate trap!" Jackie snarled.

"That's enough!" Brainard cried out. It had been two days since their East New York rally, and this meeting was supposed to be a review of the next public event.

"What are you talking about?" Cookie said.

"The Big Brain didn't tell you?" Jackie yelled. "The wicked dyke from South Ozone Park volunteered us for a three-day debate with the Pigger and Crapper candidates!"

"These people think we don't have any balls!" Bea said.

"Balls? You're hanging with the girls now, sweetheart," Jackie said. "And guess what? None of us want to run with you."

"That's not necessary," Brainard said. He felt too weak to tell everyone to go home.

"No. She asked for it and she's going to get it!" Jackie was unleashed. "Valerie was cuckoo-bananas, but at least she was the real deal!"

"Go fuck yourself."

"You're not even a pussy eater!" Jackie was so close that Bea could feel flecks of spit. "Now you're going to tell me *you* got balls?"

Bea decided that if Jackie came one inch closer, she would knock her on her bony ass.

Instead, Jackie grabbed Tom Collins by his tie and dragged him out to her car to head back to Bushwick. Candy quietly followed, and then Bea left for her own district.

Joe Brainard hadn't slept in a week and could barely get off the sofa. *When is it no longer worth it?* he wondered. *When are the pills, the nausea, and this insane mission to monitor these fruitloops just no longer worth the effort?*

He put a cold compress over his eyes and was trying to catch a little shut-eye when he heard it. A strange, tinny, mechanical voice was steadily growing closer. It took a moment to realize he wasn't imagining it. He used what little strength he had to sit up, remove the compress, and look outside. A solicar with a double-headed bullhorn was cruising up the street.

". . . *They won't grant you the same respect they grant the Piggers,*" an amplified voice blared. "*Think we're kidding? Go to South Ozone Park and watch the Quirklyn candidate, Valerie Solanas, debate the Pigger candidate, Dennis Izzlowski. We'll be there with a couple of questions as well. They think they can shut us out, folks. Don't worry—they got another thing coming . . . They won't grant you the same respect they grant the Piggers . . .*"

The message was on a loop. As the vehicle drove on and the noise faded, Brainard put the compress back over his face and closed his eyes.

37

Searching for solid evidence for the Manhattan bombing case, Uli ordered everyone to put on their protective gear, complete with nose pins, face masks, and galoshes, and divided them into fifteen pairs. Each pair climbed into a boat. One rowed while the other dragged a chain with a grappling hook from the rear. In parallel lines, the little fleet proceeded out from Manhattan toward Staten Island. They rowed nearly in unison, ten feet apart. Over the course of the next three days, all fifteen teams hooked onto various items—discarded crates, old refrigerators, bike frames. But no truck parts.

It wasn't until the fifth day that two boats snagged onto what seemed to be the same thing, and it wouldn't budge. Something big roughly two hundred feet out. Four other boats were able to get hooks onto it, but even in concert, they could neither hoist nor drag it to the sandbags.

Since the Bayonne barge with its crane was the closest heavy-duty float, Uli hooked a winch onto it. They were in the process of cranking the submerged object up onto the barge when they all heard distant shouts.

"Hey! What the hell?"

From the barge, Uli could see some older fat guy standing on the newly reinforced sandbag wall lining Manhattan, holding up a walkie-talkie, trying to get him to turn his on.

"Who the hell is that?" Uli asked Lieutenant LaCoste.

"That's the drunken asshole who was supposed to teach the class before you."

"Who told you assholes to leave the building?" Scouter Lewis shouted. Uli flipped on his walkie-talkie, and heard him squawk, "Get back here right now!"

"Scooter," Uli said, "how did you find out we were here?"

"My name is *Scouter*. Who the fuck is this?"

"Uli Sarkisian."

"Is that a name or did you sneeze into your walkie?" Lewis countered.

"It's the name of your boss. I guess no one told you that I arrived almost a week ago. I'm glad to see you finally showed up."

"Oh, you're Karen's brother." There was an awkward pause. "I heard they were appointing someone, but—"

"I'll take that as an apology."

"Mr. Sarkisian, I didn't mean to get nasty, but if you end up rupturing the new sandbags, you could flood Manhattan again."

"We're nowhere near the sandbags. In fact, *you* are. Now, I want you to go back to the Williamsburgh Building and wait for me there like a good little dog."

All the gangcops laughed as they saw the older man storm back to his car and drive off. Soon, they had to hang a second, then a third winch from the rusty crane in the center of the barge. Finally they got movement.

The item emerged from the dark waters, but it wasn't a truck at all. It was the wrecked shell of a car, and upon getting one of the lieutenants to take Polaroids of it, Uli pointed out that the bags of fertilizer in the backseat had never detonated.

"I guess only three vehicles blew up the sandbags," concluded the gangcop officer from Red Hook–Carroll Gardens–Park Slope.

Uli ordered the group to widen the grid and search for the other vehicles. It took another day before a rowboat team snagged a second bulky item from the filthy shallows. Since this one was relatively close to land, it was partly dragged, partly lifted along the wall of new sandbags. Just as it was being cranked up, one of the chains broke, and it tumbled back into the shitty waters. Since it was late, Uli instructed them to float a buoy over the wreck and pull it up the following day.

In the morning, the first four gangcops who arrived put on their protective gear and, using chains and hooks, were able to pull the vehicle back up and over the sandbags. Without even taking a close look, it was obvious that this bomb hadn't exploded either. The entire front of the car was bent upward like a sled. After hosing it down, Uli located the frayed torso and legs of a headless driver, along with more bags of unexploded fertilizer, and took another set of Polaroids.

"Considering that this car, loaded with explosives, was blown off the bridge by some larger explosion," noted the gangcop lieutenant from Prospect–Crown Heights, "it's amazing it didn't explode itself."

"That leaves only two more cars to carry the bomb that did all this destruction," the lieutenant from Harlem deduced.

"Is it possible that only two cars could have enough explosives to tear such a massive hole through fifteen feet of sandbags?" Uli said. "Maybe this was done with more than four vehicles."

"Even if dynamite was packed on the roof and hanging out of the trunk, I don't see how two cars could do all that," said the gangcop from Chelsea, who apparently had a lot of experience with car bombs.

"Keep looking," Uli replied.

38

The Crappers and Piggers were stepping up their "Warholers are cowards" campaigns, and the limited poll numbers showed that their message was getting through. Rafique was reluctant, but like Joe Brainard he finally agreed that if they had any hopes of winning the election, their crazy Quirklyn candidates had to debate.

"Can we do this all in one fell swoop?" Rafique asked.

"I don't think we should. If we're going to do it, we should go all the way," the Brain said. "Four debates, one in each district."

When Rafique rolled his eyes, the Brain proposed an idea: instead of one-on-one debates, they should hold a collective debate—within each of their time limits the entire ticket would have the chance to speak and reply to the others. "That'll allow the quicker, more sober candidates to help the slower, burned-out ones," he said, not naming Ondine and Jackie.

Rafique consented, and instructed the Brain to make this the one precondition to the debate. On Quirklyn stationery, the Brain sent a letter to both the Crappers and Piggers.

Within a matter of hours, both gangs agreed to this odd format, adding a few provisions of their own: each candidate had to provide an introduction prior to the group debate. The rest of the debate—six-minute intervals, three for each side—would follow. Four debates would be spaced out over the last ten days of the election; they would begin in five days.

The Brain counterproposed some minutia regarding the rules, but all quickly agreed. The most difficult detail was finding debate moderators; soon, four prominent citizens had been selected—one from each of the contested neighborhoods. They were basically glorified timekeepers, in charge of refereeing any fights but not permitted to editorialize or ask questions. After the opening comments, each side would have the right to ask the other side questions, or answer or ignore those directed at them. Again, these were mostly the Brain's ideas.

Further good news was that the Quirklyn candidates didn't have to do any work to publicize the event. The two gangs were so certain of their oratorical victories, they put posters everywhere from Green-Burg to SOP announcing the debates.

Rafique had several of the sharpest minds in Staten Island—mainly antiwar activists—come in to help prepare the candidates. All the Warholers were instructed to act "presidential"; queries that were clearly rude, too personal, or misleading should be ignored. When possible, opponents' questions should be rephrased to best suit the Quirklyn candidates' optimal responses.

Most of all, they were told not to lose their tempers, and each one was instructed to help keep the others calm. "If any one of you gets angry and lashes out," the Brain warned, though he was really just talking to Jackie, "you're all going to look like idiots. Keep in mind this isn't about winning a fight with anyone, it's about making an impression on impartial constituents."

Although they stuck to their guns on not diluting their Warhol personas, they were prepped on subtle ways to present a dignified image of power, regulate tone, and deal with stress.

Bea was appointed the unofficial captain of the little debate team. In the event of uncertainty, she had the right to decide who got to talk.

The first debate took place in Green-Burg, on the stage near the empty pool in McBarren Park, with at least four hundred attendees. For Candy's sake, the Brain let Cookie sit at the table with her, provided she didn't say anything. She was introduced as "an undomesticated running partner."

After winning the coin toss and being told he could go first, the Green-Burg Crapper candidate, Biggs, put a small box turtle on the table in front of him. He introduced the reptile, Mr. Turtle, as his "domestic running partner," to laughter. He then began wasting his introduction time, putting his ear next to the turtle's head and having a one-sided dialogue with it. This ended when he said, "That's very rude, Mr. Turtle, but I'll ask. Mr. Turtle was wondering if you fellas are a bunch of silly faggots."

"Our sexual proclivities are no one's business but our own," Bea replied before Jackie could say something profane. Though it was still within Biggs's time, the moderator didn't reprimand Bea.

"I myself am normal," Biggs continued. "And I think that normal people have the right to have another normal, healthy person represent them—"

"Really?" Jackie interrupted, "'cause Mr. Turtle was wondering when it's *his* turn to nail your shell."

The crowd burst out laughing.

"Order, order," the moderator called out, hitting a small gavel on his table. "I will ask the Quirklyn candidates to please hold their tongues until it is their turn to speak."

"Thank you," Biggs said. With the remainder of his time, he explained how the Crapper government was launching a new criminal justice process that would allow the accused to actively participate in their own defense. "It's a radical departure from the pleabag system and we're initiating the first actual trials on election day."

"Time!" called the moderator, striking his gavel once again.

"So already the impact of our campaign has yielded wonderful results," Cookie began. "Imagine how much more we'll do if we get elected!" Applause went up.

During the next four minutes, Candy politely read from a short statement the Brain had written about one key goal of the Quirklyn campaign: offering an alternative to the barbaric system of two-gang government that had held the people hostage for nearly a decade.

During the third interval, Geoff Killing asked who the organizers of Quirklyn really were. He pointed out that even though they had headquarters in each district, when he knocked on their doors no one ever answered. "They seem to have a bottomless budget, yet we haven't found a single person who has donated a stamp or grain of rice to their . . . cause!" He paused and addressed the Quirklyn candidates directly: "Either you people just sprang out of the ground one night, or some powerful organization that already exists—like the Domination Theocracy which blew up the sandbags, or Joe Gallo's little family, or maybe the goddamned CIA—put you clowns up to this."

"Please," Bea said, "just one look at us and you can tell that neither the CIA nor the mob, and certainly not Jesus, would come anywhere near us."

"And we sure as hell know who your pimp is," Jackie shot back. The audience laughed again and the moderator called for order.

"It took weeks of begging them to debate," Faustus countered. "And another week of literally campaigning against the fact that this . . . clown car *wouldn't* debate us, before these people finally came to this table so we could get the answers that you need."

"Time," said the Green-Burg moderator, looking at his watch, giving Killing five seconds to wrap it up.

"Allow me to introduce not just myself," Jackie said to her opponent, while unfolding a statement she had written on the back of an envelope, "but all those standing before you right now, who you are hoping will be your constituents—we are artists, performers, dancers, and poets. We are among the most creative people of New York's Greenwich Village. Much like monks and other holy folk, we've chosen to sacrifice material comforts for a vision that, ideally, makes the world a more beautiful, meaningful, and moral place."

"Bullshit!" Candidate Biggs shouted.

"Yeah," Faustus joined in, "artists can't afford headquarters and the resources that these people have!"

"Who's the real power behind you?" yelled Killing.

"The US Constitution, asshole!" shouted Ondine.

"Order, order!" the moderator called out.

The Crappers used their remaining intervals to offer more details on their new trial process, and to hurl the same question over and over: who was the real power behind the Quirklyn slate, and what were they hiding?

Jackie finally stood up and shouted to the sympathetic audience, "Who's behind us?"

"We are!" a bunch of people yelled back.

"Who's the power behind us?" Jackie repeated.

"WE ARE!" the crowd roared back.

Many applauded and that was the end of the first of the four debates. Though it wasn't quite a resounding victory, all agreed that the Quirklyners had edged out the gangs.

39

As the small fleet of rowboats trawled back and forth off the res-urrected banks of Manhattan, some of the lieutenants brought oxygen tanks along with their own masks. In the heat of the afternoon, the stink of the harbor was excruciating. It took another two days be-fore a boat finally located a third large object almost halfway to Staten Island. It was too far from Manhattan to drag back to shore, but the water there was fairly shallow.

One lieutenant, Walter Snell from Gravesend, Brooklyn, loaded buckets of clean water onto three boats until their edges were danger-ously low in the harbor. Dumping the clean water on the location, the silhouette of a third vehicle slowly appeared below them.

"Again, it's a car, not a truck," Snell said into his walkie.

One man snapped photos, while another lieutenant used a pole with a hook at the end to fish out some of the unexploded fertilizer bags from the backseat. This meant that only one car bomb had blown all the others away and flattened the wall of sandbags.

"That must've been one powerful fucking car bomb!" said LaCoste.

The group of lieutenants was about to resume the dredging of the bottom of the harbor for the final vehicle, but Uli ordered them to stop. "Based on the condition of the other cars, the primary car bomb was probably blown to pieces," he said. "The chance of snagging such small pieces is unlikely."

"There's no way one car could blast a hole through that dam," said the gangcop from Brooklyn Heights, echoing what they all were thinking.

Uli glanced up and saw a supply drone circling the sky overhead. He wondered aloud if there was any chance it hadn't been a car bomb at all, but a missile.

"That sounds insane," replied Snell. "Why the fuck would anyone fire a missile on us and make it look like a car bomb?"

"We found three vehicles with unexploded bombs in the back. How else could this happen?" the gangcop from Harlem asked.

"We need to find some witnesses," Uli said to Lieutenant Felix from the City Hall precinct, who had been a part of what they jokingly referred to as the "preliminary investigation."

"We had a dozen sentries on duty along the sandbags that night," Felix replied.

"Can we talk to them?"

"All but two are dead."

"Let's go find them."

The lieutenants returned to their vans, and Felix called his precinct and asked for the names and addresses of the two surviving sentries who had been on duty that night.

It turned out that one was in a coma; the second was a guy named Jon Freige. He was recuperating at his new home in Sheepshead Bay.

Uli led the convoy of five vans there—over the bridge, down Jackie Wilson Way, along the length of Brooklyn. When they arrived in Sheepshead Bay an hour later, Freige's wife directed the group of officers to her husband, who was bundled in blankets on a sundeck out back.

"What the hell?" He was startled by the stream of men pouring into his backyard.

"Don't be alarmed," said Lieutenant Felix.

"What the hell do you want?" With pale skin, a runny nose, and watery eyes, Jon Freige looked worse than they had imagined.

Uli stepped forward. "I was just wondering if you could tell me what happened on the night of the explosion."

"Oh." The convalescing sentry took a deep, raspy breath, then let it out slowly. "Well, I was actually about five hundred feet away, three sentry boxes over. You should ask Floyd . . ."

"Unfortunately, you are now the closest living sentry to the crime scene," Uli said.

"Oh no, Floyd died too?" Tears started rolling down the man's pasty face. "He was stationed to my east, next to Bernie's box. He was the sentry who was immediately under the bridge when the bomb went off." Overcome with emotion, the man fell silent.

"Jon, we got a long drive back, so . . ." prompted the officer from Prospect Park South–Midwood.

Uli raised a finger to quiet him. Before Freige could resume talking, his wife came out and asked if any of them wanted a beer.

"I'll have two," replied the gangcop from Borough Park–Ocean Parkway, unleashing others to chime in.

"No thanks, we're all fine," Uli said on behalf of his group. He returned to Freige, who was regaining some composure. "Please, tell us about that night."

"All I remember is sitting down on my stool, nothing unusual, just like any other night." The man lapsed back into silence, but Uli sat perfectly still and let the quiet hang in the air until he continued. "Okay, the truth is that I dozed off. I woke up when I heard the blast." Again he paused, perhaps in shame. But when no blame followed, he spoke again: "I glanced to my right, just as this black cloud tumbled toward me. It looked like some giant, rubbery, living thing. I used all my strength to jump up on it as it hit. Next thing I know, I'm twisting and somersaulting up Broadway, gasping for air. I can see and feel other things swirling around me—people, cars, you name it."

"Did you know the sandbags had been breached?" Uli asked softly.

Freige nodded yes. He was slumped forward, apparently exhausted by the memory.

"You don't remember hearing any planes, or seeing anything in the sky?" Uli moved closer to him, away from the others.

"No, nothing conspicuous."

"How exactly did you escape?"

"I remember rolling, falling down a hill until I whacked into something hard. It was the wall of a building on Wall Street. Reaching out, I grabbed onto a window ledge and was able to climb into the second-story window, just above the water level. I reached through the shattered glass—if I didn't have my jacket on I probably would've severed an artery—and pulled myself onto the floor of an apartment. The entire building was shaking as the water rushed through."

"Must've been awful," Uli said.

"I had all that shitty water in my mouth and nose, and I knew it was deadly. As a guard, I'd always been warned about the toxicity levels of the water—you know, occasionally it splashed over. Every night we were required to gargle and take long showers, which I always did. So when I got to that Wall Street apartment I found a liquor bottle, regurgitated, then repeatedly gargled and spat. Then I just took a bar of soap and scrubbed myself down as much as possible until the water pump stopped working. That's probably what saved me. I mean, I got sick like everyone else, but I'm sure I'd have been dead otherwise."

"How'd you get out of the apartment?"

"About an hour later, I heard footsteps, so I went up to the roof and found others who had swum up there just like me. I told everyone to try to clean the toxic water off, but no one ever listens. Anyway, it wasn't until the next night that we heard the whistles from the rescue boats. After the initial flooding, the water level went back down, but it still stank like hell. Some people got hungry, thirsty, or were feeling sick. They just climbed in and walked right through the flood. But I knew they were going die, 'cause that water might as well have been fire."

"When the sandbags blew, do you remember hearing one explosion or two?" Uli asked.

"Just the one," Freige said confidently. "One big boom."

"I know you were asleep, but did you see a flash? Maybe a green light?"

"I don't remember."

Uli thanked the sick guard, told him to get well, and then led his thirty pupils outside. He chided them: "If the reason he's the lone survivor is because he was working for a terrorist organization, wouldn't it be easy to quickly poison a crew of crucial lieutenants by slipping something into their beers?"

"But his wife isn't exactly a—"

"Even if she was the blessed fucking Virgin, always act professionally. If you want to drink or eat, do it on your own time with your own dime!"

"You kept asking him how he escaped—do you think he was involved in the explosion?" asked Felix.

"No, I don't," Uli replied, "but recovering a memory is like trying to find a needle in a haystack. You want them to return to the scene, review and linger on it. I've seen people visualize and recall details that they missed the first time. Frequently, you're looking for stuff that they themselves don't see."

"So what'd we get from this?" asked LaCoste.

"Did we get anything useful from this interview?" Uli addressed the whole group.

"No," muttered the lieutenant from Harlem.

"Why not?"

"He didn't give us anything to check out."

"That's right," Uli said. "We were looking to confirm a suspicion, but we got nothing to go on."

"So where does that leave us?" grumbled LaCoste.

"We need to find a new direction," Uli said. "So, who else might shed more light on this?"

"That fucking cunt," the Chelsea gangcop suggested.

"Give me a name, not a body part."

"Erica Rudolph," said LaCoste.

"Yes, we need to interview her," Uli said. "But not today. Today is done."

The group piled back into their vans and drove to the Williamsburgh Building. From there, they returned to their separate precincts.

When Uli entered his office, he discovered a smelly old man stretched out asleep on his couch. Uli kicked his foot, and realized it was the good-for-nothing Scouter Lewis who had yelled at him from the sandbagged shores of Manhattan.

Reeking of booze, Lewis sat up, got his bearings, and said, "Sorry if we got off to a bad start, but—"

"You're fired," Uli said.

"What!"

"I've been here almost two weeks and this is the first time I've even seen you in this office."

"Just hold on."

"You were supposed to teach these men professionalism, and you couldn't even get here on time—much less sober."

"That's not fair! I got forced into this job."

"And now I'm forcing you out."

"Give me one chance. I can prove to you how valuable I am."

Uli would've said no, but he had a strange feeling that he'd met this man before, in some deep, painful way, and he wanted to find out how. He decided to give the drunk another chance. "If you're not here by nine tomorrow, don't come at all."

40

The second debate occurred two days later, on Bushwick Avenue, and this time Crapper candidate Sandy Faustus spoke first: "In Rescue City, we were born in violence. A violence none of us asked for or wanted. Think about it: a violent act took away our homes and thrust us out here, and we're trying to do the best we can to be civilized. I didn't join the Crappers when they first formed. I waited until I saw my friends and family members butchered by other gangs. Until three houses that I lived in with my wife were burned down. Until we were nearly starving because the food was cut off. Then we had a choice—join them or die. Simple as that! The great German politician Otto Von Bismarck called it *realpolitik*. It means that power determines right, and if I wanted to survive I had to take a side. And every one of you, like it or not, had that same exact experience. I know this 'cause you are alive. Now, I could tell you why I thought the Crappers were the best choice, and I'm sure my new friend, Pigger candidate Dennis Izzlowski, who is now seated next to me, could tell you why he believed the Piggers were the superior side, but this isn't about us. This is about survival. What began as gangs turned into political institutions.

"This country was born in a revolution, and those revolutionaries became its founding fathers. The All Are Created Equal Party is committed to peace and justice, evident by the launch of the new trial system. Eventually, I think we will start a prison system and end amputations altogether. Frankly, who knows what the future holds? This new group, Quirklyn, is starting out with the best of intentions, I'll give them that. But there are tensions in this place, and when push comes to shove, all this sweet talk is just talk. No one joins a gang for its sweet talk or high-mindedness, you join it 'cause when head-breaking time comes, you want the biggest stick. That's what we're offering when you vote for the Crappers."

A healthy applause immediately erupted from the crowd. Faustus's argument was fair and sensible—the first one that hadn't tried to insult the opposition.

It was Jackie's district so she went next: "If you live in constant fear of which gang is stronger, I could see this man's argument holding water. But I've lived here for ten years, and maybe it's because I never got into politics or joined a gang, but I've never been hurt. The very reason the Quirklyn Party exists is 'cause we want more than just a reprieve from the fear that the two gangs have instilled. If they're both the parties of protection, I would argue that we're the party of little things, like the pursuit of happiness, fun, hope, and adventure, and the idea that we can do something more meaningful with our time here than swinging a bigger stick than the other guy. If you want those little things that make life worth living, then vote for us."

Bea was amazed by both Jackie's lucidity and civility.

This debate followed a slightly different format than the previous one. When it was the Crappers' turn to respond, Faustus rose again. He pulled out a diagram with a series of multicolored arrows and placed it on a small wooden tripod. It showed that the three contested Brooklyn districts had been occupied, attacked, and reoccupied by both the northern and southern gangs more than any other neighborhood in Rescue City. "This is precisely why this area was vacant—because those who weren't killed or wounded found the sheer turmoil of battle maddening. Folks, I admire Mr. Curtis's hopes and dreams, but do you really want to gamble your lives, and the lives of those you love, on those ideals?" Leaning into the mic, in a low voice, Faustus added, "Vote for us and we'll protect you. And you can handle your own happiness."

"That sounds like a threat to me!" Bea cut in.

"Hey," the tense moderator from Bushwick admonished, "wait your turn!"

"We just don't like—"

The moderator reached over and unplugged Bea's mic.

"Folks," Faustus rebutted, "we're not threatening anyone, I'm just presenting the facts. Keep in mind that if you get invaded, no man in a dress or argumentative lesbian is going to be much help!"

"Time," said the moderator, looking at his watch, then he plugged Bea's mic back in.

"Ladies and gentlemen," Bea started softly, "please keep in mind that when the mob extorts a business, they don't say we're going to attack you, beat you, kill your family, or burn you down. They say, *We're selling protection*. They say, *We want to protect you.*"

Several Crappers in the audience started booing her, but the sentiment didn't spread.

"This is a classic case of confusing the messenger with the message," Faustus said. "If you want to punish us for relaying an unpopular message, so be it, but keep in mind that these people sitting across from us—the Quirklyners—don't want this message to get out, simply because they can't defend this district should it come under attack."

Jackie stood up again. "When a bunch of drunken fatties push us out of here . . . that'll be the coldest day in hell."

The moderator told Jackie to quiet down, and a portion of the crowd cheered at her censure.

This debate seemed to be a draw; both sides got some decent shots in. Clearly, someone had sat down with the gang candidates and counseled them to tone down the nastiness.

Eavesdropping on several spectators, Joe Brainard learned that people were indeed worried about an invasion, though they didn't want this worry to govern their lives.

That evening, the Brain conceded that his strategy of having the stronger candidates cover for the weaker ones was proving ineffective, although it hadn't exactly backfired. Candy had spoken up for herself in Green-Burg, and Jackie had held her own against Faustus in Bushwick. The Brain wasn't concerned about Bea, but the next debate was in East New York, Ondine's district—their Achilles' heel.

Ondine's health, which had caused him to miss more campaign days than any of the others, seemed to be steadily declining. They all knew what the problem was—booze and drugs. Over the past two weeks, he had skipped almost seven days, staying in his bed, where his driver had to bring him food, clean up for him, and help him use the bathroom.

A few days before the East New York debate, the Brain paid Ondine a visit, ostensibly to help him prepare. One of Ondine's opera records was playing in the background; the Brain took the liberty of lowering the volume.

"Everyone knows you've got a serious drug problem. Hell, Bea found you at the methadone clinic, and we plan to honor your agreement with her once all this is behind us, but we just took several straw polls and found that you're our weakest link. We really have a chance of winning this, but we need all four districts—all or nothing. Your debate is coming up very soon, and that's our one big chance to turn your numbers around. So we're all begging you to stay clean and sober, just until after—"

"Hold on, I've been clean since we started this," Ondine cut in indignantly.

"Give me a break, you're missing almost every other day of campaigning."

Ondine pulled up his shirt, revealing large scabs that seemed to be forming under his skin. "My liver's never been too good, but in the last few weeks I think it's finally conked out . . . I sweat nonstop. I got the runs so bad I've been using newspaper as diapers, and my head is throbbing."

Joe apologized for jumping to conclusions. As he examined the man's back, he recognized the scalloped marks that were symptomatic of his own ailment. "I might have something for you."

"What are you, a doctor?"

"Something's been going around and I think you caught it."

"What is it?"

"Have you heard of the Staten Island Fever?"

"Oh shit, I think so."

"I've got some pills that have been working for me. They take effect pretty quickly, but this changes some things."

"Like what?"

"You can't drink. Or take any more methadone."

"You're not trying to get out of our deal, are you?"

"It's your call," the Brain said. "You can either get the treatment pills or the methadone, but not both. If you keep drinking and taking drugs, you're just going to waste the medication, and I don't have much of it. It's one or the other."

Ondine let out a sigh and nodded. He wanted the pills.

Brainard retrieved the various containers from his trunk, doling out half of his weekly supply. "Take one before each meal, one after a meal, and then this one in the morning, this one at night. And this one, but only after you take your first dump."

Ondine jotted down notes on the times, put the pills in various empty teacups, and thanked the Brain, promising sobriety—at least for the next week.

The Brain went over several talking points, since the Superstar was expected to do the opening oration. He also had Ondine read a prewritten statement, designed to undermine the Crapper fear tactic. The Brain made him read it aloud a couple of times while he held a stopwatch. It had to come in under the allotted minute.

"Everything is riding on this debate," Brainard said earnestly, then instructed him to get some rest. While Ondine napped, the Brain and Stew Jackson, the candidate's driver, searched for any stashes of drugs or alcohol. Not finding any, they went shopping and straightened out the place, then the Brain prepared some of the restorative homemade soup he made for himself. *It's the sick leading the sick,* he thought.

Despite Ondine's diarrhea and nausea, Brainard helped him through the next few days, writing and rewriting his introductory speech, while making sure he was keeping sober, resting, and preparing. On the last night, just as Ondine's fever broke and he was finally showing signs of recovery, the Superstar vowed that he would be on that platform the next day.

Twenty hours later, on the same collapsible stage provided by the Crappers in Bushwick, both groups were seated at their long tables in East New York. Charles Ludlam had helped a sweaty Ondine apply flesh-colored foundation and mascara, trying to make him look as healthy and sexy as Maybelline cosmetics would allow. To keep cool, Stew Jackson fanned him with a towel, but Brainard could see him trembling.

"Use the pain to keep you focused," Jackson said. Ondine nodded.

The crowd started to fill Cypress Hills Cemetery Park; it was clearly going to be the biggest turnout so far. A defrocked priest named Paddy O'Reily was the closest thing the area had to a prominent citizen. At four p.m., the agreed-upon time, the former cleric introduced himself and the candidates. "By a coin toss, the first speaker will be the Quirklyn candidate, Mr. Don Dean."

Ondine rose to his feet, leaned into the mic, ignored the name error, and began: "To date, the most persuasive argument my opponents have pushed has been fear. We, on the other hand, present four fundamentally new and different points. With our opponents, you're voting for the status quo, more of the same. With us, you're voting to move forward. Your vote might lack the support of fat, oily men with bloody baseball bats and rusty chains, but it is far from a hollow statement. Your vote sends a chilling message to them: *We want you and your brutal system gone.* There are times in history when revolution is in the air. All it requires is a slight push. You might not believe it, but all eyes of Rescue City are upon Quirklyn today. I am telling you, the direction that Quirklyn goes, all of Rescue City will eventually follow."

The applause exploded and lasted almost as long as the speech itself. The Brain bit his lip; the entire thing was a theatrical miracle:

hours of rehearsing, coaxing, nursing, and various pharmacueticals to make the otherwise insane, profane, and dying man look smart, cogent, and in control.

When the clapping finally tapered, the ex-priest rose and introduced Ondine's handsome adversary, Geoff Killing.

"My opponent is absolutely right about one thing!" Killing warned that if Quirklyn won this election, there would be a swift and brutal reprisal. The battle would be used as an example to show the more rebellious members of Rescue City that an uprising would not be tolerated. His Gothic descriptions of horrors from the attack that would follow seemed to have no end, compelling a few of the more timid listeners to leave.

Killing concluded by telling the crowd to look around at the homes and buildings, which many of them had just acquired. "Now close your eyes and imagine them all burned to the ground. Imagine nothing more than a carbon stain between two boroughs—that's what I'm trying to prevent."

"Fearmongering!" someone yelled out.

"Yes, I am fearmongering!" he shouted back. "And do I like this message? No, I don't. I don't particularly care for gangocracy, but this vote isn't going to change anything. You can vote against the message I bring you, but as sure as I'm standing here, it'll come true. If there is a silver lining to this dark cloud, it's the fact that these gangs are actually giving you a choice. Join us and stay in these nice homes, or we're out. I include myself because I live here too and I don't want to leave. Let's compromise with the uncompromising—that's my message of hope."

An explosion of applause followed, like a retaliatory volley to the prior speech.

The next four intervals of arguments were variations on the same key points. Though Killing's speech was effective, Ondine's opening statement won out—another razor-thin Quirklyn victory.

41

With less than a week to go before the elections, the Quirklyners in all four districts held a frail lead, compelling the Crappers, particularly Deputy Attorney General Hector Gonzalez, to curse ever proposing the verbal contest in the first place. The final debate would take place in SOP—the only Queens neighborhood involved in the election. The Piggers were letting their Crapper allies know that they were intent on doing whatever was necessary to win back their one imperiled district.

The past two weeks had begun to wear on Bea. She didn't so much mind being heckled by stray residents during her morning meet and greets, but since the debates had begun, all the Warholers found themselves constantly being followed by mysterious cars and strangers who seemed to always linger in the distance. Also, someone was periodically throwing firecrackers in front of Bea's house in the middle of the night, waking her up. This had finally ended when Jack Healy put up a roadblock in front of her cul-de-sac, so cars and bikes couldn't speed through.

When the day of the final debate in South Ozone Park arrived, Bea was relieved. It would be staged at the entrance to the little community, in the small field at the start of Hawtree Pass. Bea had selected a tough but fair old bird named Steven Wainwright to moderate. Izzlowski vetoed him, and counterproposed an unfamiliar SOP citizen, so Bea vetoed that. This went back and forth, until Bea nominated a rather mild-mannered, elderly man named Mortimer Minkers, and the Piggers eventually agreed.

Instead of the small collapsible stage that the Crappers had used, the Piggers built a huge, ostentatious wooden stage complete with a large canopy for lights, and two semispiral staircases down the sides. Despite the stage's broad size, the two tables were positioned relatively close together, with a small podium for the moderator inserted between them. It wasn't until the last moment that the Quirklyners discovered the biggest surprise: all of the Crapper candidates from the other districts had failed to show up. Dennis Izzlowski would be sitting at his table alone.

"I should've figured they'd pull a stunt like this," the Brain muttered.

"Who?" asked Bea.

"Both sides. The Piggers are distancing themselves from the Crappers—I'm sure they asked them not to come." Learning from the example set in the Bushwick debate, Brainard wondered if it might be better if Bea met her opponent solo. It would make her appear sympathetic if she fought her own battles—just like Izzlowski.

"Thank God." Jackie was relieved, hating the public scrutiny, and Ondine always preferred being off duty.

"Okay, one-on-one it is," the Brain decided.

Although the previous debate in East New York had been well attended, this one was completely mobbed. Many people throughout Rescue City who had missed the other debates, which had become the most talked-about events on the reservation, decided to catch this great finale. By early afternoon, people were pouring in from the southern end of Staten Island to the northern tip of the Bronx. At the last moment, Brainard changed his mind. Considering the volume of people that would be present, he decided it was an important opportunity for them to see the entire Quirklyn ticket, so he had Jackie, Candy, Cookie, and Ondine sit silently next to Bea.

Pigger technicians seemed to have anticipated the big outpouring, as additional speakers were hastily brought in. People would be able to hear echoes of the debate across the airfield. After the sound system was tested, Minkers, who spoke in a soft voice, seemed to ignore the notion of impartiality. Instead of noting that the Crapper candidates had failed to show up, he simply said, "Tonight is a magical evening, isn't it?" He briefly touched on the great significance of the event: "Whatever the outcome may be, this is the first noncombative three-party election we've ever had here, and I think we would be remiss if we failed to see that as a victory in itself." All cheered.

By the flip of a coin, Izzlowski got to speak first. He cleared his throat, tapped the mic, and ran his hands over his slick bald head. "Let me begin by telling you a little about me—the man who is running. Yes, I am a member of the We the People Party. But no, I am not what you might call a party man. This tiny council seat in this recently revitalized area of Queens is not exactly sought after; there was no primary among my fellow Pigger candidates. In fact, what I'm going to say to you tonight does not necessarily represent the views of my party or its affiliates." He sneered. "In fact, call me a thief, but when I hear good ideas, I take them. So, if elected, I'm going to offer some of the same goodies that my Quirklyn contender has put on the table. I have a first draft of some legislation for a new penal system, especially now that my Crapper colleagues have initiated a trial system. I will build on that and propose the creation of a prison, which I will ardently fight for during my time in office. Number two, though it's not legislated," he gestured to the sky, "I promise you here and now that I, Dennis Izzlowski, will step down after my second term, curtailing any temptation for power, and allowing another noble candidate to represent you in South Ozone Park. So let me recap: I am putting two of Quirklyn's best points right on the table alongside them. But I have more to offer—much more!"

Izzlowski put his hand along the side of his mouth as if he were relaying a secret. "Did you know that we Piggers have an excellent civil engineering department? We also have good public works resources just beyond those dunes. We can make this forgotten garden blossom. If you give us a chance, you will see the roads repaved—indeed, there should be more than a single dusty road in and out of SOP. Also, this place is pitch black at night. We'll put a working streetlight on every corner. We'll make sure there are not one, not two, but *three* bus routes in and out of here. We'll also bring in tools and other supplies to help you fix up your houses. In order to get to Manhattan, and all points south, everyone has to take this long, bumpy detour around the Aqueduct field and down through Howard Beach—which, by the way, is the Queens community to your south. If elected, I guarantee that a new road will be constructed and paved *through* Aqueduct, which will make your drive to the rest of the city infinitely shorter, safer, and more pleasant . . ."

Joe looked at his wristwatch and realized that the Pigger candidate had been talking far past his alloted time. "Hey!" he shouted over to Minkers, who was politely listening.

"Time's up," the moderator said into the mic.

Yet Izzlowski didn't stop: "We can argue about ideas and principles, but what my competition can't offer are any of those wonderful conveniences that will make this community as updated as any in this reservation."

"Your time's up!" Joe Brainard shouted.

Cheers went up. A small but loud group near the front of the stage kept applauding, and the claps were amplified by the speakers. Since Minkers made no attempt to silence anyone, this kept going for a while.

"Now it's Quirklyn candidate Valerie Solanas's turn to talk," the old man finally said.

Bea rose and waved to some people in the crowd. "Hi, I'm Valerie Solanas, and over the past few weeks it's been my pleasure to meet and chitchat with many of you—"

"Assassin!" someone shouted out near the front.

Bea ignored it. "Mr. Izzlowski has snatched some interesting plates from our table, but let's just consider—"

"Man hater!" another booming voice shouted.

"Let's have order," the soft-spoken moderator suggested.

"Miss Solanas," said Izzlowski in a calm but loud voice, "I think they're referring to your shooting of Mr. Warhol."

"Mr. Izzlowski," she countered, "we agreed to respect each other's time intervals."

He apologized.

"What Mr. Izzlowski is trying to do is—"

"Shoot you?" someone called out. A cluster of people laughed.

"I just think if you address their questions you'd silence your critics," the Pigger candidate said with a self-satisfied smirk.

"Mr. Minkers," Solanas chided, "your job is to keep order here!"

"Order, order," he said, simply staring at his stopwatch. The man had either been bribed or was simply defective.

"For starters," Bea continued, "the Piggers didn't forget about this region. South Ozone Park can easily be seen from the top floors of Pure-ile Plurality. They had ample opportunities to make repairs and renovations to it, even in the past few weeks, and they haven't lifted a shovel." Bea then offered an overview of the four pillars of the Quirk-lyn platform.

"Shoot her!"

"Time!" called out Minkers.

"The Piggers had a chance to show good faith here and they did nothing," Bea went on. "Now it's our turn!"

"Miss Solanas, I don't mind that you're talking during my time," Izzlowski said, "but when you say *our* turn, it makes me wonder, because many of the people who moved to this cozy new community are families. I'm not going to ask these fine folks if they want a homosexual representing them, but it seems they are repeatedly asking questions regarding your ghastly act of attempted murder—"

"You're not fit to lick her combat boots," Ondine called out.

"Don't you dare talk to me like that, you vulgar little faggot!" the Pigger shot back.

"What did you call him?" Jackie jumped up on her heels.

Brainard signaled frantically from the front row for her to sit back down.

"You're deviants, all of you. Having sex with whatever comes across your perverted path!"

"Let me tell you a little about us!" Candy fired back.

"Mister—I mean *miss*," Minkers said, "it's the Pigger candidate's turn to—"

"No, no, please, let the homosexuals speak," Izzlowski said magnanimously. "I'd like them to lisp their way out of this one."

"Valerie did what many of us wanted to do!" Candy said.

"You mean when she shot one of America's most prized artists, Mr. Warhol? You *all* wanted to do that? What are you, murderers?!"

"Time," said Minkers, looking at his watch. "Miss Solanas has the floor for the final five minutes."

"Just hold on here, I let her talk during my time," Izzlowski said.

"Tough titties, honey cup! Your dick is small, and your time is up!" Jackie rhymed.

"Shut up, you little pansy!"

Ondine blew Izzlowski a kiss and Jackie gave him a wink.

"In my day, you all would've been packed off to the Marines. Two tours in 'Nam, and either you'd come back a man or you wouldn't come back at all!"

"There's come on your back?" Candy called out.

"Until you pull that wig off and remove that dress, I'm not even—"

"You'd like to remove her dress, wouldn't you?" Ondine taunted.

"Then he could come on your back!" Jackie added with glee.

Bea sat silently as Izzlowski grew redder and redder.

"Oh, he already came on my back, darling," Candy smiled, "in the orgy room of the Dreamy Steamy Bathhouse!"

"I thought I recognized him!" Cookie threw in.

"It took awhile 'cause others were already on his back," Candy continued taunting.

"My wife and kids are here!" Izzlowski roared.

"Well, I sure as hell ain't going to come on *their* backs!" Candy finished.

Fitfully, the Pigger candidate rose from his table and crossed over to the Quirklyn side. As he approached, Candy pulled off one of her high-heeled shoes.

"Hold on!" Bea jumped up as Izzlowski took a swing at Candy. When he clipped Candy's arm, the Superstar let out an unbelievable shriek. Jackie, Cookie, and Ondine rushed at Izzlowski.

The crowd below them went crazy—shouting, laughing, and screaming—as Bea did her best to pull Izzlowski out from the melee. It wasn't until a group of Pigger security guards raced onstage that Jackie and the others stepped away from the opposition candidate.

The wires for the public-address system had been pulled out in the skirmish, but everyone saw Bea help Izzlowski to his feet and extend a conciliatory handshake, which he slapped away, cursing at her while pointing down to his family seated at the base of the platform. Bea calmly held her ground, trying to maintain civility, as he and his security staff marched off the stage.

Bea stood for a moment and waved, smiling to the crowd before her. Everyone started clapping. At that moment, despite Izzlowski's surprise strategy of co-opting the Quirklyn agenda and offering solid infrastructure repairs, the Brain sensed that Bea had at least fought him to a draw.

42

"Where are they holding Erica Allen Rudolph?" Uli asked his secretary Sheila at the beginning of his third week on the job.

"You mean that DT terrorist lady?"

"Yes."

"Maximum security downstairs."

"Would we need a pass or something to speak to her?"

"Who's we?"

"My students and I."

"You're kidding, right?"

"They have to learn the new way that things are done so they can teach their men."

"Well, if you want my opinion, I think your photo IDs are more than enough."

"Please call down to the jail and check, because if I have to come back with thirty angry gangcops, we'll both regret it."

Sheila picked up the phone and Uli returned to his office. Five minutes later, she called back to say that if they had their badges they'd be allowed access, but she also informed him that the only way to get to maximum security was through the slow, crowded elevator in the lobby.

It was not yet nine, so Uli went down to collect his men as they arrived. They checked their knives and other weapons, and, in six groups of five, boarded the only elevator that went to the incarceration floors.

Roughly half an hour later, they had all finally made it to the seventh floor, and were informed by a condescending sergeant that the prisoner was currently sick.

"Come back in a few days. She'll be fine by then."

"Do you know who I am?" Uli asked.

"The Easter Bunny?" the sergeant said, causing one of his fellow guards to snicker.

The gangcop from Flatlands-Canarsie, who happened to be the

largest in the group, reached down and yanked the sergeant's shirt, popping two of his buttons. "This is the deputy attorney general, sonny. You're going to do as he says or . . ."

Uli motioned for the gangcop to back off. "What's your name, sergeant?"

"Ronald Field," the man said nervously.

"Sergeant Field, I can call the attorney general and have you fired, and still see Miss Rudolph in five minutes, or you can keep your job and take us to her right now."

"I just didn't want you all to catch whatever she has. Mr. Deputy Attorney General—"

"Mr. Sarkisian will do."

"Mr. Sarkisian, why don't I have the prisoner cleaned up and brought to the conference room where you can all see her?"

"Maybe you didn't understand," said the grumpy gangcop from Flatlands-Canarsie. "We're here to see the prisoner *now*."

"I need to warn you that you'll have to walk through a narrow prison corridor. The inmates like to spit, throw feces, urine—"

"Whatever they throw, I'm sure we've all been hit with before," Uli replied.

The sergeant instructed one of his men to escort the group between two walls lined with cells containing both men and women. Several prisoners cursed as the group squeezed past. Most of them behaved themselves, particularly those who knew some of the cops, occasionally pleading with them to be released. The only advantage to the old criminal justice system was that the prisoners had not usually been held for much longer than a week or two. Some of these inmates had been waiting for nearly a month.

Rudolph had been thrown into the farthest, dingiest, filthiest cell on the floor. The woman, who had initially reminded Uli of the 1950s American sweetheart Donna Reed, was cowering behind an old mattress. The rest of the group remained outside the bars as Uli instructed the guard to open her cell.

Her eyes were closed and she was frantically praying. It took Uli a moment to realize that she was under the mattress because she was naked.

"Where are your clothes?" He was astonished.

"They took them." She was quivering, peeking out from behind her mattress, marked with cuts and bruises. "They keep attacking me. God saw everything and will judge!"

"Who did this?"

"The guards. They keep sexually assaulting me in ways I never thought p-possible!"

Taking off his own shirt, Uli offered it to the injured woman, who refused to make eye contact. He instructed the guard to bring a fresh prison jumpsuit at once.

"I tried to look after you when you were in my care," she chattered at him. "Please don't leave me alone with these monsters!"

"I won't," Uli assured her. When he offered his hand, she clenched it with both of hers. He could see dried blood on the cold floor and other bodily fluids smeared on the filthy mattress.

Now he knew why the sergeant didn't want them to see her. The rest of the gangcops watching from outside the bars didn't seem particularly outraged at her treatment.

Uli soon got her a pan of warm water, some towels, and a jumpsuit. "A lot of people were killed and injured by what you did in Manhattan," he said.

"If I knew those four trucks were going to blow up . . ." She trailed off and went quiet.

Calling the attorney general's office from Sergeant Field's desk, Uli saw to it that Rudolph was immediately transferred and given special protection by one of Schuman's own trusted captains from the Brooklyn Heights precinct. He also took down the names of three guards who she said had viciously violated her: Sergeant Ronald Field, Officer John Yost, and one Doug Flint.

"You're not going to really get them fired, are you?" asked the gangcop lieutenant from Prospect Park South–Midwood, as they waited for the elevator.

"Think of justice as a ship: a single leak can sink the whole institution," Uli said.

"The bitch got what was coming to her," the lieutenant from the Upper East Side muttered.

"If Erica Rudolph was a six-foot-six, 350-pound man and those guards raped him, I'd still disagree with it," Uli said. "But at least I'd think it was an even match. She's a small woman—any one of us could easily overpower her. That makes those guys bullies, pure and simple."

"She's also a fucking terrorist! She was behind the flooding of Manhattan and the death of hundreds of people!" yelled Lieutenant Felix, whose district had been completely submerged.

"You're not going to tell me that if we catch some terrorist who just committed mass murder, raping and torturing that person doesn't send a message to other terrorists," added another lieutenant.

"I think it's bad enough that we amputate instead of incarcerate, but at the very least, if we are going to torture our criminals, we should have the balls to make it a part of our sentencing guidelines. There is absolutely no deterrence if a person doesn't know whether or not they'll be treated fairly."

"Fine with me, man. Let it be part of the punishment. She already admitted her guilt."

"Really? Did any one of you hear anything unusual in the little that she said?"

"Yeah, she didn't know she could get her ass fucked," said a voice from the back. All the cops burst out laughing.

"Rudolph made an exculpating remark that any good investigator would've caught," Uli said.

"Excul-whating?"

"She mentioned four *trucks.*"

"Yeah, 'cause all the news reports mentioned four trucks."

"But she's the terrorist who pleaded guilty. She was supposedly the *mastermind* behind it, or at least knew about it, right?"

"So?"

"This is why we use this word *allegedly.* You were all with me on that barge—did any of us pull a single truck out of that toilet bowl?"

"Slip of the tongue," said one of the gangcops. "I'm sure her people did all the dirty work."

"Yeah, saying *truck* instead of *car* don't make her innocent," someone else chimed in.

"Having a sore ass can be very jarring," added a third lieutenant, provoking more laughter.

"This falls under the category of knowing your suspect," Uli explained. "Though I was unconscious during most of the time when I was held as her hostage, I was able to study her closely. The entire time, in addition to being fairly decent, she was quite articulate, very organized, and controlled. She worked well under pressure. Even when I was begging for that Pigger gangcop to help me, she was cleverly arguing that I was her drunken brother, and she almost got me back in captivity."

"So you're saying . . ."

"She didn't slip up by saying *trucks*, otherwise she would've corrected herself. I've seen her do that. She simply didn't know."

"It sounds like you're trying to get her off."

"I know for a fact that she held me—and me alone—hostage. For that reason I personally am content to let her die. But hell if I'm gonna let the real mass murderers get off!"

The elevator door finally popped open. It was already crowded with two guards and three prisoners, so only one other passenger could fit. Uli boarded and said, "See you all back at my office."

When Uli returned to his desk, the updated protocol list was sitting on it. Apparently it had just been completed by the attorney general. Unlike the earlier draft, this one was a cleanly written, itemized list of what every gangcop was expected to prepare before completing an arrest and turning the case over to the surlawyers.

"I guess you better make thirty copies," Uli said as Sheila came into his office.

"You want me to stick 'em in the files?"

"What files?"

"You know, the five boxes."

"What boxes?"

"The ones the attorney general sent down—I stuck them in the conference room. Files for each of the prisoners currently being held in Brooklyn and Manhattan, I think."

"You have the prisoners' files?"

"Yeah, they've been sitting near my desk for the past few days," she said. "I told you, didn't I?"

"No! I told the mayor I'd only investigate the sandbag bombing until . . ." Uli took a deep breath to regain his composure. "I've been waiting since day one for those files."

Instead of firing her for gross incompetence, which seemed to be the norm, he asked her to bring the boxes in.

"Some of them had stuff in them from what the surlawyers did."

"Just bring them all into my office at once!" Uli snapped.

By the time the thirty gangcops arrived back in Uli's office, the five boxes containing each criminal case in Rescue City South were piled on his desk. On top of them was a small stack of freshly photocopied protocol sheets.

It took another ten minutes for Uli to get empty boxes for each of the lieutenants. Finally the files, organized by district, were distributed to each lieutenant.

When the task was complete, Uli announced: "For starters, you are each responsible for your precinct's files. You lose them and you have to reinvestigate each case, or release the prisoner. I want you all to write your own names, the name of the arresting gangcop, and your precinct numbers on each file. Then I want you to start with the oldest cases. For the remainder of your time here, you'll be working alone on the protocol requirements for each case and I'll be checking your work."

"What about the sandbag investigation?" asked Lieutenant Felix.

"This takes priority." Uli picked up a protocol sheet and waved it in the air. "In accordance with this, you've all got a variety of forms to fill out. Pick up your lists and let's look at this together."

The men silently read along with Uli, who paraphrased aloud: "In addition to the arrest report, and a list of priors as gleaned in part from an amputation and scar inspection, every new file should include at least five pictures of the crime scene, interviews with all suspects, as well as interviews with witnesses—"

"Isn't this the surlawyer's job?" interrupted the lieutenant from the Upper East Side.

"It was no one's job, now it's yours. You investigate the crime and make the arrest. The surlaywer will go over it, tell you what's missing, and point out any weaknesses in the case."

"We can't do this alone," a lieutenant protested, "this is way too much!"

"You don't have to, the arresting cops do. Just study those forms, make copies for everyone, and tomorrow morning during your precinct's roll call, explain all these new points to your men. It should be pretty clear."

"This has got to be wrong," Felix mumbled, looking at the endless list of documentation required for an arrest. "Hell, most of my cops are flat-out unliterate."

"Then teach them to read and write, or you're going to have to do their work for them," Uli responded.

"Yeah, and we're never gonna have time to do any arresting!" called out Walter Snell from Gravesend–Sheepshead Bay.

"And suppose that in doing all this shit we accidentally end up finding that the prisoner ain't guilty!"

"That's the other guy's job, isn't it? The defense surlawyer?"

"Not anymore. It's all up to *us*," Uli concluded, "but I'm pretty sure your precincts will be getting a small secretarial staff to help you with this."

Except for two gangcops, Al Bud from Coney Island–Brighton Beach and Lou Stella from Wingate–Bay Ridge, everyone was told to take their files of active cases, go back to their precincts, and, starting with the oldest cases, have the arresting cops fill out the necessary paperwork. Then bring them in tomorrow.

"All the cops have already gone out today," said one lieutenant.

"Fine. Go to your roll call tomorrow morning, then be here by noon. When I call your names, I want to see some completed cases ready to send to trial," Uli clarified.

Everyone grabbed their boxes and filed out grumbling, except for the two gangcop lieutenants whom Uli had asked to remain; they stared nervously at him.

"What the hell did we do?" asked Stella.

"I have two special jobs, and you guys are nearest to the assignment locations. They're simple missing persons cases."

"You want us to make someone go missing?" asked Al Bud.

Ignoring his question, Uli turned to Stella. "Have you heard of the Burnt Men tribe?"

"Bunch of acidhead freaks at the bottom of the Staten Island sewer?"

"Go down there and locate a woman named Bea Moses-Mayer. They all know her. Tell her I have something urgent to tell her, but I need to see her face-to-face. Tell her you can drive her to me, but if she doesn't want to come, don't force her or threaten her. Be polite."

"Got it," Stella said, taking some notes.

Turning to the second gangcop, Uli said, "Your mission is a little trickier. Check out all the nursing homes in Coney Island."

"There was only one, and it burned down recently. I handled the case myself. We arrived too late to put it out."

"When was this?"

"The day of the mayoral election, I believe."

"Find out where its residents were sent to. I'm looking for one very tall, bald guy who has got to be in his nineties. His name is Paul Moses."

"I remember Moses! He was the guy who led everyone out of the building."

"Can you find out where he is now?"

"Will do."

It was time to introduce Paul Moses to his long-lost daughter.

* * *

Around ten the next morning, Uli's derelict number two man, Scouter Lewis, left a message with Sheila saying that he was ill and unable to come in to work.

By one p.m., when the last gangcop lieutenants finally arrived and took their seats, Uli asked them to stand up and present their finished cases. Since no one volunteered, Uli took out his roster sheet and had the Manhattan gangcops go first, in alphabetical order by precinct—the lieutenant from Chelsea was told to stand and deliver.

"I didn't really . . ."

"Tell me about your oldest case," Uli said.

"The perp's name is Benny Moonbeam," the gangcop read off. "He was arrested for burglarizing several apartments that were empty due to the flooding."

"You have photos, evidence, witness statements? What have you done?"

The officer had done nothing. There was no list of priors related to the perp's amputations and scars. No photos, no witness statements, no report by the arresting gangcop. He had nothing more than a file with the man's name and charges scrawled illegibly on it.

"I let you all off yesterday afternoon. What the hell did you do?"

"I looked for two of my suspects who are being held here to see if I could get a confession, and I couldn't even find them," the lieutenant said. "Then I tried to find the arresting officers, and they were out in the field somewhere. Just like I said."

"Why couldn't you find the suspects if they're being held here?"

"They sent the overflow from Prospect Park to the outdoor pen at Sheep Meadow."

Apparently, part of the dusty field in the center of Manhattan known as Central Park had also been ringed with a hurricane fence and converted into a temporary holding cell.

"What did *you* do?" Uli asked the next lieutenant.

"I distributed all my files and the protocol sheets to the arresting officers in my precinct and—"

"Yeah, this morning," Uli cut in. "What did you do last night?"

"With all due respect," said the old gangcop from Inwood, "how are our boys supposed to know who did what, who the witnesses are, and all this other stuff?"

"That's actually a good point. From now on they have to keep logbooks. And write everything down at the time of the arrests. There's got to be records of everything. As well as photos."

"We don't have a single camera in my entire precinct," said one of the men.

"If you need any equipment, see Tatianna," Uli said. "All right, I'm not going to ask how you wasted yesterday, but as of today, we're going to have a scavenger hunt. Everyone is going to take their three oldest cases, and either you'll go to your precinct and track down the arresting gangcops and have them do it, or you'll take photos and get all the forms filled out yourself. If by tomorrow I don't see some paperwork, I'm going to release your perps."

"What if we need help?"

"Throughout the day I'm going to stay in the lobby. You can drop in and give me updates and I'll check your progress."

As soon as they all left, Uli summoned the two gangcops he had given special assignments to. First he asked the one from Wingate-Bay Ridge to report.

"So, I go down to Staten Island to the Indian tribe down there. Okay, so they're all mum on this Bea lady, so I grabbed one of them hippie nitwits and smacked him around a little. He starts singing—said this Bea girl had gone to work at the VL headquarters, so I went into their police trailer and spoke to someone named Birdshit Sunflower or something like that, okay? They said she got depressed about Rafique getting shot up and all, 'cause she was like his bodyguard, so she went out alone in a canoe and paddled across the flooded airfield down to the Goethals. And a week or so later, someone found her empty canoe. They figured she fell into the swamp and drowned, so she's joined the great spirit of the mountain lion or some shit."

"How about you?" Uli asked the next lieutenant.

The gangcop from Coney Island-Brighton Beach, Al Bud, conveyed that he too had been unable to find his subject, Paul Moses. But he was still looking.

Uli sighed.

"I actually found out that it wasn't the Piggers who set the fire, but some drunken night attendant, and that's why Joe Gallo had him offed. So, I inadvertently closed an arson case."

"What about Paul Moses?"

"Due to his heroism he was transferred to a new senior center in Greenpoint run by the Crappers."

"Wait a sec," Uli said, vaguely recognizing the name. "Who is Joe Gallo again?"

"He's the number one mobster in Rescue City."

"I remember." The name had stayed with him from his time in the Bronx Zoo. "So you got nothing else on Moses?"

The lieutenant took out his notebook and read from it: "*When flood victims started moving into Greenpoint, DAG Hector Gonzalez sent his man up there to ask the seniors to be the eyes and ears for them. Moses and some lady friend got all riled up, made some comment about not naming names, and moved out.*"

"Where'd they go?"

"I don't know, I did all this by phone."

"Why didn't you go up there and look?"

"Well, it's a little difficult 'cause I get limited use of the precinct car. And ever since the Quirklyners have been contesting the area in this special election, our buses don't run through there any longer."

"So you simply stopped looking for your subject?"

"Hey! I'll finish the damn job. Just give me a few days for the work to die down and lend me a car."

43

As soon as he returned to his office, Uli got a call from the attorney general, who asked if he had received the latest protocol list. Uli said he had and that his men were working on readying cases for next week.

"Glad to hear it," said Schuman.

"I also wanted to ask if it would be possible to interrogate Erica Rudolph one more time."

"She already confessed. Frankly, we'd all like to get her sentenced and put this whole nightmare behind us."

"I understand that she's guilty," Uli didn't want to argue with him, "but I know there are others, and I'm pretty sure she knows a lot more than she's saying."

Schuman consented but explained that due to the abuse she had suffered while incarcerated, she was being secretly held at the Brooklyn Heights police precinct. Not even the gangcops in that precinct knew she was there. "When you arrive, don't give your name or her name, just ask for the captain. If they ask, give a fake name. I'll tell him you're coming."

Grabbing the Polaroids he had taken of the unexploded bags of fertilizer and the blasted cars in New York Harbor, Uli dashed out. At a nearby stamp shop he bought a religious item that he thought might be helpful. After a bit of waving, he was able to grab a livery car on Jackie Wilson Way, and arrived at the Brooklyn Heights precinct within twenty minutes. He told the desk sergeant he had an appointment with the captain.

"Who the fuck are ya?" the sergeant asked.

"Officer Aldo. He knows me," Uli said.

The potbellied captain soon arrived and promptly directed Uli to a corner office on the top floor where Rudolph was being held. "Best if you go alone," the man said out of the side of his mouth, then veered off.

After being inspected through a peephole and waiting for five minutes, Uli was finally let through a wooden door. One of the captain's own sons, also a gangcop, was watching the prisoner. Erica Allen Rudolph was sleeping on a small cot against the wall. The only bars in the room were over the narrow window. Uli told the guard that he needed to interrogate her, and if things got a little loud he shouldn't react.

"I've been with her for twenty-two hours nonstop, I need to take a break anyway," the gangcop said, and locked Uli inside the cell.

"Ma'am," Uli woke her gently.

Rudolph jumped up and moved quickly away from him.

"I thought this might give you some comfort." He handed her the cheap set of rosary beads, and she took them gently in both hands.

"I heard about the new justice system these people are setting up. Can I get justice for being raped?"

Uli ignored her request. "I need to ask you a couple of questions."

"Sure."

"First, I want to know why Marsha Johnson was present when I woke up in the Bronx. What does she have to do with all of this?"

"I'm afraid you're mistaken, she wasn't there."

"I saw her. Now if you're going to lie about the easy questions . . ."

"I've heard about some kind of torture device that the CIA has been using to pull thoughts right out of people's brains," Rudolph said tensely.

"They don't use it anymore." Uli sat down next to her. "Let's talk about the explosion."

"Four trucks drove over the Staten Island Ferry Bridge, blowing up the sandbags, causing a flood to spread over the southern end of Manhattan." She spoke very quickly and methodically.

"You're sure they were trucks?"

"Minibuses."

Uli took the Polaroids out of his pocket and placed them before her. "They were cars, just solicars."

"Okay," she said nervously, "four *cars* drove over the Staten Island Ferry Bridge, blowing up over the sandbags—"

Uli pointed to another photograph, interrupting her: "Do you know what that is?"

"No."

"That's an unexploded bag of fertilizer." He pointed to details in two other photos. "There's another, and there's a third. All undetonated bags of fertilizer."

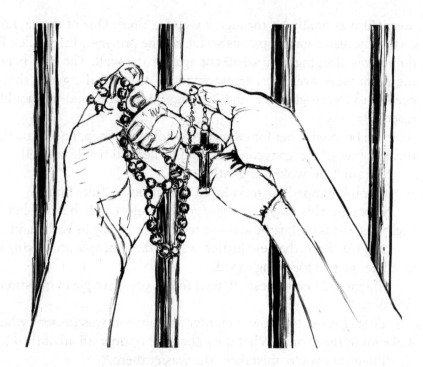

"What are you telling me?"

"I'm telling you that you obviously have no idea what went on with the sandbag explosion."

"He said they were going to use hijacked trucks, like they did at Cooper Union," she muttered to herself.

"Who said that?"

She pursed her lips silently.

"If you help me find the man who betrayed you, we might be able to catch him. It could spare your life, reduce your amputations."

"No one betrayed me!"

"Let's talk about something else," Uli said, growing frustrated. "The last thing I remember before waking up in your attic was being picked up by a car in the middle of the desert."

Rudolph looked down.

"How the hell is it that *you*, of all people, found me and were able to take me hostage?"

She sat silently.

"You must have connections outside of this place."

"If I did, don't you think I would've left here long ago?"

"Who the hell drove those cars that got blown up on the bridge?!" he shouted.

"I don't know." She sounded sincere.

"Who brought me to your organization?"

"I don't know."

"You said they repeatedly raped you at the Williamsburgh Building—"

"They did."

"—and despite the fact that you held me hostage, what did I do for you?"

She didn't respond.

"Did I protect you? Tell me, goddamnit!"

"I didn't see anyone," she finally said. "We just found you. I swear."

After sitting in silence just glaring at her, Uli rose and left when the gangcop guard returned.

When he returned to the Williamsburgh Savings Bank Building, he set up a small desk in the lobby and had his calls rerouted. Over the ensuing days, he remained there as lieutenants reported to him, sometimes bringing their sergeants and other arresting officers with them. Uli would scan the forms and look for weaknesses. Usually he'd just scribble an abbreviation on the file cover.

ALB meant *Where's the alibi?*

MTV meant *What's the motive?*

EVD meant *Where's the evidence?*

WIT meant *Who are the witnesses?* and so on.

Uli also added ideas of his own to the attorney general's protocols, such as:

All gangcops should be issued a cheap camera and take at least two long shots and three close-ups of salient details to the crime scenes. Do spot inspections of your men's logbooks to make sure they write the names and addresses of witnesses, so they can track them down later if needed.

As the revised checklist of forms and updated protocols were explained by the lieutenants at roll calls over the next few days, a visible anxiety bridging on panic flurried down the ranks. The larger, more brutish men, who in the past had been the alphas, now looked for more support from their bookish brethren. There was even talk of letting the illiterate gangcops go.

Uli informed Schuman that the new trial system required more time for the paperwork. In keeping with this, the attorney general ordered that three hours should be set aside each day to allow gangcops to tend to the new red tape.

More problematic were the suggestions of things to come. "If we have to put all this work into a single arrest to make sure they're on the up-and-up, it's going to mean fewer people getting arrested," one gangcop lieutenant pointed out to Schuman.

"Maybe so, but after so many years, I think we've thinned out the more violent from the herd. It's time for some fine-tuning. The mayor feels it's time to bring back some civility, and I agree."

Despite the requests from his liaison lieutenants for more investigative training and less red tape, Uli followed orders and stayed at his desk in the lobby from eight a.m. until six p.m., as the steady carousel of gangcops came in for guidance.

During his free time, Uli continued his own little investigations—he asked every gangcop he met if they had known his sister, and, among those who did, he inquired if they had any knowledge of her disappearance. The answer was a consistent no. If anyone knew anything, none were talking.

One morning, Lieutenant Al Bud stopped by to run a couple of unresolved cases by him.

After Uli finished checking the paperwork, Bud said, "If you still need help finding Paul Moses and you can get me a car, I have some time today."

Uli hurried upstairs to Schuman's secretary and filled out a statement of responsibility for a solicar. Tatianna gave him the keys to vehicle number 160, but when he returned downstairs he found two other lieutenants waiting with their stacks of cases and questions regarding the latest protocols.

Uli gave Bud the car keys. "Remember," he warned, "don't scare Paul, he's an old guy. In fact, just locate him and tell me where he is and I'll do all the talking."

"Gotcha."

As soon as Bud headed off, another gangcop showed Uli photos he had taken at one of the crime scenes—*after* it had been cleaned up. As Uli explained that the pictures were useless—they had to be taken immediately after the crime to be used as evidence—a huge blast from outside shattered the lobby windows of the Williamsburgh Building.

Uli ran out the door along with a crowd of others, over to the official car lot. Fire was shooting from the window of one of the solicars.

"Oh my God!" When Uli pushed through the parking lot, he could see Al Bud's body burning inside. He was clearly dead; his brain had been blown open like a giant pimple.

"I can't believe the Piggers are starting with the car bombs again," said one of the lieutenants.

"That's unlikely," Uli replied. The smell from the fire made him think it was plastic explosives, probably C-4. He vaguely remembered how in Vietnam soldiers would break it off from Claymore mines and eat it to fake sickness so they could get home early.

Uli now thought this must've been the explosive used at the Staten Island Ferry Bridge. What else could be powerful enough to pack into just one car and blow up a ton of sandbags? It also meant that whoever blew up the bridge had probably just tried to blow him up as well.

44

After the fire was put out and the body was moved to the morgue, two older overweight men approached Uli, who had returned to his little table in the lobby. One of them asked: "Why do you think they killed Bud?"

"I'm sorry, who are you?"

Captain Sal Bloom showed Uli his council cop ID and explained that Schuman had just put them in charge of the investigation.

"That was quick," Uli said.

"As a matter of fact, we're reviewing the Manhattan sandbag explosion as well," Captain Anatole Williams said. "So we've taken a special interest in powerful car explosions."

"I thought that investigation was closed," Uli said.

Bloom ignored his comment. "I heard you were a big FBI agent."

"CISPES," Uli inexplicably found himself muttering.

"Kiss kiss?" Williams said, smirking.

"Nothing," Uli said. Other than the name, he remembered nothing else about it.

"We're looking for possible suspects," said Bloom.

"I can't think of anyone who might do something like that—booby-trap a car to kill a lieutenant from Coney Island," Uli replied. "But something did cross my mind."

"What's that?" asked Williams.

"He looked a lot like me, and I was conducting my own investigation."

"Of the sandbag explosion, we heard."

Uli considered mentioning that he feared some undercover government intrusion, but he didn't want to sound paranoid. "Are there any recorded cases of C-4 being shipped here?" he asked Bloom.

"No, why?"

"I thought I smelled it at the explosion site."

Bloom showed no interest in Uli's analysis. Instead, he said they'd be in touch, and the two men returned upstairs to their offices.

"You okay, boss?" asked Scouter Lewis, his rarely seen rock-faced assistant. The large man stepped right through the shattered glass of the lobby window frame. "I heard someone took a shot at you."

"Actually, it was a car bomb," Uli said, "but I'm not sure I was the target. What the hell are you doing here? You've been fired."

"Uli, I know we got off to a bad start, and I'm sorry for that. I've had this awful cold, I caught it during the big influenza that hit after the flooding—"

"Let me ask you something," Uli cut in. "Do you know me from anywhere before here?"

"I don't think so. Why?"

"You look familiar as hell."

"With this ugly face, it's a wonder anyone would admit to knowing me," Lewis kidded. "Actually, I was friends with your sister when she first arrived here."

"You knew Karen?"

"Oh sure. She was my assistant in the Shub years, when Chain put me in charge."

"Do you know anything about her disappearance?"

"That's the big question—everyone wants to know. I wish I did."

"You were a cop in Old Town?"

"I'm told I was, but to be honest, I don't remember much about it. I suffered from a head injury when I arrived, like you. When I came here, I worked for Chain, and he put a lot of trust in me. I guess I would've been what you are, a deputy AG, but we didn't have nice titles back then. Look, if you can just give me another chance."

"You've got a serious drinking problem."

"You're right, but listen, I know a lot of people on both sides of the border. And I know you think someone is gunning for you."

"Who told you that?"

"Give me a little time and I'll find out who."

"Any help would be appreciated," Uli said perfunctorily.

"Have you gone up to Quirklyn?"

"Not yet."

"A lot of strange things are happening there. That's where I'd start." Perhaps charged with purpose, or perhaps simply due to his need for a drink, the stone-faced man silently left the same way he'd come—through the lobby window frame.

45

The awful thing about being a good investigator was that Uli knew he was his own best chance of finding whoever had tried to kill him—particularly since they'd probably try again, and get it right next time.

He stopped shaving when he began camping out in the Williamsburgh Building lobby for at least ten hours a day. After a week of feeling like a sitting target, he decided to change his look. He sneaked outside to Stamos's Stamps, where he bought some blond hair dye, a razor, a floral shirt, and dungarees; casual clothes he'd never normally wear. Back in his office bathroom, after a bit of creative shaving and styling, he had a bristled mustache and sandy-blond hair. With dark sunglasses, Uli looked like a surfer bum who refused to admit he was old. He visited Tatianna and asked her if anyone knew which car he would be taking before she had given him the keys.

"No, I just picked them randomly, why?" She paused. "You got yourself a new look, huh?"

He explained that his car had been blown up, but he couldn't figure out how someone was able to install the bomb so quickly. She informed him that he didn't need to worry about it again as Schuman had just ordered a fence constructed around the car lot, and around-the-clock security to prevent any future tampering.

"I need a new set of wheels," he said.

She had him fill out another car requisition form, then gave him the keys to solicar number 145.

The next day, Uli hastily made sure the undercarriage of car 145 was clear before putting the key in the door. Then he began the long and perilous drive east to Howard Beach. It was time to pay an impromptu visit to the person who knew he had been kidnapped and did nothing to help.

WELCOME TO QUEENS! NOW FUCK OFF!!! read an old graffitied sign as he neared Pure-ile Plurality. Behind the small planned community of sandblasted houses lining several crisscrossing streets, up against the large oval basin known as Jamaica Bay—the clean-water reservoir for the entire city—were a cluster of monolithic buildings and the abandoned pier that fingered out into the water. Presumably the structures had been situated there to store supplies from the air-field, but had been repurposed into something quite different.

Soon after the military pulled out and Rescue City burst into gang-land pandemonium, a strange cultlike group had taken over the un-used buildings. Some said Pure-ile Plurality had a strict but somewhat veiled religious agenda, and others claimed it was the humane face and propaganda wing for the Piggers.

Either way, nearly ten years later it was the largest philanthropic agency within the city, with tentacles reaching into four boroughs—Rafique refused them entrance into Staten Island. Marsha Johnson was the only female to sit on their eight-person executive council. Uli had briefly worked for PP, just prior to his escape attempt, and Marsha had been his supervisor. When he found himself being held hostage by Domination Theocracy, the fanatical terrorist gang, and saw her sitting across from him alongside his captors, Uli had been shocked. Now he wanted answers.

At the Pure-ile Plurality receptionist desk, he asked to see Miss Johnson.

"Who shall I say is asking for her?"

He gave a new pseudonym, Paul Hughes. Then, fearing Marsha might decline to see some unknown male, he added that it was an urgent matter regarding the late Deere Flare.

Ten minutes passed before the tall, tanned beauty came slowly down the main staircase. She immediately tensed up when she spot-ted him in the reception area.

"Uli, you look strange with that blond hair," she said once she was within speaking distance. "You're not here to arrest me, are you?"

"A quick chat."

"I have plans all afternoon, I'm supposed to hit the road."

"Well," he held up his car keys and smiled, "I'll drive and we can talk."

She led him out of the building before responding. "I was about to go on a long walk that way." She pointed to the sandy field behind PP. "I'm supposed to meet Rolland in an hour."

"Rolland Siftwelt, the head of this place?"

"Yeah, he wants to meet his new neighbors to the east," she said, evidently referring to the disputed zone of South Ozone Park. "There's a political rally there today."

"But the Piggers are running a candidate, aren't they?"

"True, though this new group might actually win. They moved into the area and made it livable. Why shouldn't they pick one of their own people?" Marsha didn't add that she had found herself strangely enchanted by the radical feminism of Valerie Solanas over the past couple of weeks.

Together they drove north, through the bottom edge of Ozone Park, Queens, which was empty of everything but sandy roads.

"The Quirklyners are having their final rally up there today," she explained. The road that led up to the airfield highway was filled with potholes, so they bounced along slowly.

"Their candidate is that oddball who shot Warhol?"

"Yeah."

"Never cared much for Warhol. Always was too cool for school."

"Look, I'm truly sorry about what happened," Marsha said.

"You shouldn't've told me that you would help."

"Erica promised me she wouldn't hurt you no matter what. And I was brought there against my will. You weren't the only one."

"She's responsible for the largest single mass murder that ever occurred here."

"I didn't know that at the time."

"And she's still not cooperating with us."

"Cooperating in doing what? You've rounded them all up."

"Things don't add up, and she's not talking."

"Do you want me to talk to her?"

"Do you know someone named Emmett Grogan?"

"No, but I spend most of my time either here in Howard Beach or doing outreach work in Brooklyn."

They soon reached Pennsylvania Avenue, and began to hear the occasional drone planes dropping off supplies for the city.

Marsha directed Uli onto what looked like a very large shoulder along the dunes, but as he drove it turned into a narrow pass called Hawtree. Steep dunes obscured both sides of the road at first and then opened into the small community of South Ozone Park. Along one side was a large field, the old Aqueduct Racetrack, but since there were no horses out here it had become a dog track. That ended when the civil strife began and the army withdrew; since then it had been reclaimed by nature. Looking across the empty field, Uli knew that when the

Piggers finally got tired of this Quirklyn democracy crap, that's where their assault would be coming from. It was the best staging area for their foot soldiers.

"What I can't figure out is why she wanted me to see you," Uli said, picking up their conversation about Rudolph.

"She didn't."

"But you told me—"

"I didn't tell you everything. I got an urgent message from Rolland to report to that address and wait for him. When I did, she arrived five minutes later with her thug dragging you inside. She said you were someone else, but I recognized you, so I told her that she was lying. I told her that you used to work for me. And it was obvious that you were in bad shape. I wanted to get you to a hospital, but she said you'd die there, which I thought was true. She actually had all these medical supplies. She was going to take care of you herself. I insisted on staying with you until you came to."

"Rolland sent you there?"

"I got a message that he did, but when I asked him about it, he had no clue."

"So who did it? And why?"

"All I could think was that whoever sent the message wanted me to see you with her," Marsha said. "My guess is they wanted to protect you. If Erica killed you, she'd also have to take me out, and if she did that, she'd have PP after her."

"It would've been nice if you had actually protected me," he said testily.

"She promised that she'd release you unhurt."

"You told me."

"Maybe you should be talking to Erica about all this."

"Believe me, I tried," he said, "but she ain't talking."

They silently drove down First Street, following small groups of people who were walking to the rally. Most had gotten off the Quirklyn minibus and were heading toward the music at the south end of the little community.

The roof of a van had been hastily converted into a platform. Banners, campaign posters, balloons, and, of course, the ubiquitous pot smoke filled the southernmost street that bordered the top of the JFK airfield. Marsha looked for Reverend Rolland Siftwelt, whom she knew was traveling with an entourage down from Kew Gardens where he had met with Mayor Plains, but apparently he was running late.

"God, everyone smokes dope here," Uli said, fanning away the ribbons of smoldering cannabis.

"*This* is what I'm talking about," Marsha replied disapprovingly. "When you elect a politician, you also get their vulgar lifestyle."

"The Crappers are the ones who grow all the choke," Uli said. "Whereas your great Piggers handle the sale of croak."

Most of the area's residents were emerging from their little bungalows. Uli was surprised to see a small community of families. Middle-aged couples who had brought their infants to Rescue City a decade earlier now had young teens and were anxious to protect them from the violence that defined the place.

"Everyone seems to think they discovered this neighborhood in the last couple months. Truth be told, we in PP saw this place years ago," Marsha grumbled as they waited for the rally to begin.

"Why didn't you tell anyone?"

"Siftwelt talked about turning it into a PP colony, but we never enlisted enough people. He also said that the buildings were overrun with carrion, snakes, all these desert creatures, and the only service road in here, Hawtree Pass, was basically sealed up by the dunes. Hell, I walked over the field once with some friends a few years back and most of the plumbing and electricity had been ripped out by scavengers."

"Apparently they were able to reinstall it pretty quickly."

Among the locals, various ugly men with bad haircuts and pregnant-looking bellies were scattered around. Uli knew they were Pigger gangcops, and learned that their candidate, Izzlowski, had just given his own rally earlier that morning.

Soon a small convoy of solicars pulled up and a bunch of curly-haired kids jumped out, puffing up their scrawny chests. They had to be the mysterious Quirklyn security unit, and they quickly spread themselves around the street.

"Marsha!" some guy shouted. It was another PP supervisor, who informed her that Rolland and his black-suited contingent had arrived. They were sitting in a van up the block, so Marsha went off to greet him.

The scrawny Quirklyn guards created a six-foot perimeter in front of the van/stage. A car pulled up, and a tall slim man with glasses got out and went into an adjacent house. Over the next ten minutes, recorded music played while Uli milled around the small crowd of SOPers. One of the skinny kids offered him a free bag of choke, which he declined, but he did take a cup of water.

A murmur rose from the crowd—apparently the candidate was finally exiting her house. In a moment she and her escort were up the ladder and standing on the roof of the van. Pushing through the growing group, Uli saw an attractive woman with curly black hair, wearing a Lenin cap and what looked like a Nehru jacket. Folks cheered and the music abruptly stopped.

"Good afternoon! My name is Valerie Solanas, and here we are in the homestretch. In just two days, your votes will decide whether you want a new political system in Rescue City, or whether the Piggers will take what they feel is theirs. Either way, I've had the honor of getting to know most of you, and I feel like I've made some real friends here who I will cherish forever. During the rather crazy debate we had the other day, Mr. Izzlowski offered some generous promises, I'll admit, but I also think it's important to look at the Piggers' track record. I did a little research and discovered that they've made similar promises in the South Bronx, as well as in Astoria, Queens: to build new roads and renovate homes. In fairness, there were no third-party candidates running in those places, so maybe that's why those promises went unkept."

"There's no difference between any of yous!" some heckler shouted.

"Wanna know the difference?" Solanas called back. "To them this is an election. For us it's a declaration of independence!" Everyone cheered. "To them this would be just another annexation of land, another marble in their bag of marbles. To us this is *all* there is and *all* there ever will be! To us this is *home!*" Wild hurrahs erupted. "To them you'd be their latest conquest. To me we're the last hope for a new future."

When the clapping died down, the woman stepped close to the end of the stage, right above Uli, and cleared her throat. "What I'd like to say now is beyond politics. I want to congratulate you regardless of how you vote. Call me corny, but even in this sandy, far-flung outpost, democracy is still the quality that gives us our identity as a people. And the fact that we can gather out here, in this forgotten place, and present ourselves for your selection, tells me that there is something in our very DNA as Americans that makes us better than most."

Thunderous applause followed. One of the only people not clapping was Uli, who couldn't stop staring at her. He could no longer dismiss the increasing suspicion that this wasn't Valerie Solanas at all, but Paul's daughter and his almost-lover: Bea Moses-Mayer.

"What's the matter?" asked Marsha, who had pushed through the crowd to return to his side. "You look distraught."

"Sorry," he said.

Solanas waved her arms in the air and climbed back down the ladder.

"Aren't there four of them?" Uli asked.

"Yeah, but believe me, the other three are a mess," the PP supervisor replied. "She's the only genuine article in the group."

Valerie Solanas suddenly stepped into the crowd, which parted before her. She waded through, slowly shaking hands. Uli was struck by what a natural politician she was, by her warm exchanges as she embraced those around her. Calmly and systematically, she lingered until she had greeted almost everyone.

Uli noticed Marsha bobbing up and down like a little girl and was amused by what appeared to be a minor infatuation with the candidate. "Ms. Solanas!" he called out as she came near—Marsha instantly shrunk away. "May I introduce my friend?"

The candidate turned and froze. Her eyes went wide and she seemed to forget how to breathe—clearly she was astonished to see him.

"Is that you? What are you doing here . . . alive?"

"Allow me to introduce Marsha Johnson," he boomed before she could say more. "She's a supervisor from Pure-ile Plurality, and an esteemed member of their executive council."

After an unusually long pause, Solanas broke her stare and said, "Oh, yes, I'm supposed to meet with Mr. Siftwelt shortly."

"Yes, he's waiting for you." Marsha was now smiling broadly, and she took the candidate's hand awkwardly. "I can't tell you how much I admire you, Ms. Solanas. I think that what you say makes complete and utter sense."

"Well, if you can relay to Mr. Siftwelt that I'll join him in a few minutes, I'd be so grateful," Solanas replied. Then she was swarmed by her geeky security staff and swept backstage into her house. Just as quickly, Marsha bade farewell to Uli and went off to join Siftwelt and his entourage up the block.

Considering how freely Bea had moved through the crowd, Uli was amazed that neither the Piggers nor the Crappers had sent in an assassin with a shiv to take her out. They wouldn't even need a car bomb.

* * *

One of the scrawny Quirklyn kids approached Uli and asked if Ms. Solanas could see him alone for a moment. Uli was escorted past the small barrier of bodyguards and campaign workers—no one even frisked him.

The kid led him into the candidate's home. As soon as Uli entered, the kid left and Bea startled him by immediately kissing him on the mouth. He could taste alcohol on her tongue.

"That mustache and blond hair make you look like a porno actor, and you look like you lost thirty pounds," she said.

"I lost the weight while in hell, and now someone's trying to kill me, so I'm using this disguise—"

When Bea kissed him again, he sensed that she wasn't just drunk, but high as well. She'd hid it well in the crowd.

"I had no idea you liked me this much," he said.

"I'm sorry, I guess it's because I'm posing as a lesbian."

"How does that make me more attractive?"

"Call me crazy, but I've always been turned on by doing anything I'm not supposed to do. And I'm definitely not supposed to do this." She kissed him once more and ran her hands down his back and along his thighs. He found himself growing aroused and instantly felt pain— the neurological injury incurred during his torture by the Piggers prior to his escape attempt had made stimulation turn into blinding agony, and he was forced to push her away.

"Last I saw you," she said, "you were on your way to be dropped down a sewer pipe."

"And last I saw you, you were Bea Moses-Mayer, who allegedly drowned herself in the Bay of Death."

"When assembling the Quirklyn slate, we came up one Andy Warhol Superstar short, and everyone said I looked enough like her to pass. That woman you were with, is she really a supervisor at PP?"

"Yeah, why?"

"They're very influential with the Piggers. A lot of Quirklyners feel like the only reason we haven't been assaulted is because PP likes us. I'm not exactly traditional, but I like that there's an established institution that appears to be backing us."

"If Ms. Johnson is any indication of their integrity . . . well, they're a strange brood."

"Why do you say that?"

"Let's just say, when someone stands naked and vulnerable before you, you kind of assume they'll help you if you're being held hostage."

"You have got to explain what you're talking about."

"Remember when I left Staten Island after we first met? I thought PP might be a good place to . . . infiltrate. I stumbled across this bizarre mating ritual." He lowered his voice. "Late at night, they go out into this abandoned warehouse on the pier on Jamaica Bay . . ." He pointed in the distance.

"I've seen it, it's not far from here," she said, smiling.

"Well, if that dock's a-rocking, don't go a-knocking."

"What exactly are you saying?"

"I'm saying that at night they all go out there and fuck like bunnies."

"Oh my God," Bea said, smiling wider.

"The weird thing is, they don't acknowledge it—in the light of day it's like nothing ever happened."

"So, did you have sex with her?"

"I wanted to, but no."

Solanas's reedy-voiced assistant called out for her.

"I should run," Bea said.

"Hold on." Uli grabbed her arm before she could dash. "Something happened to me when I was down there in the sewer, and it concerned you."

"What?"

Uli considered how to tell her about the impossible epic of her father's sad, painful life that had slowly unspooled in his head while down in the Mkultra. He knew how insane it would all sound. He also considered that this tricky political campaign would be over in two days, and revealing that her father was in Rescue City, still alive, might be severely distracting. "Give me a little time after the election," he said instead, "and I'll show you everything."

"Why don't you just give me the five-second version?"

"Believe me, you'll appreciate it more if I show you."

"Fine."

"Oh, something else I should probably tell you, in the interest of full disclosure," he said. "Technically, I'm working for the Crappers."

"Let me guess, you're an honorary sand sweeper in Park Slope?" she joked.

"Actually, I'm a deputy attorney general with an office in the Williamsburgh Building."

"What!"

"You probably heard of this trial program since it is a direct response to your campaign. I'm in charge of making the Crapper gang-cops more legally atuned for the upcoming trials."

"Wow! The Crapper candidates have been throwing this in our faces during their campaigns—the pilot trial programs!"

"Enlightenment has finally come to Rescue City."

"A shame Mallory couldn't have initiated it when she still controlled the whole city," Bea said. "Well, our justice system is still a ways off, but we're hoping to open our own prison in addition to trials. End this amputation crap once and for all."

"How exactly are you going to build a prison within this prison?" Uli asked.

"We already found one," she said softly. "Rockville Centre."

"What's that?"

"It's a very large, very old Native American dwelling with a lot of thick walls. It's about half an hour southeast of here, in the desert."

"Wow! What were you doing all the way out there?"

Bea paused a moment. She thought about telling him that Rafique had wanted to assess the feasibility of constructing a road south from Quirklyn, around Brooklyn, and across the desert to Staten Island—in effect annexing their newly created territory. But the terrain had been deemed too difficult to build on so it was canceled. "A picnic," she lied curtly. "So, what exactly does your trial system offer?"

"All the sexy stuff: witnesses, evidence . . . hell, we even got judges."

"I'll believe it when I see it."

"It's starting the same day as the election up here. If you win, I'll be glad to help you set up your own system."

"Doesn't your loyalty forbid helping the enemy?"

"I was unfairly held and almost had my hand amputated by the Piggers, so I'm loyal to the best vision of freedom and justice that this place can offer. Along those lines, if I were you, I'd get as many men together as I could and have them dig defensive trenches along that field." He pointed to the old Aqueduct Dog Track. "'Cause when the Piggers attack, they're coming from over there."

"Listen, I know this is treason, but if you come across anything that might help us while working in the Williamsburgh Building, feel free to call."

Before he could respond, the door swung open.

"Bea, come on, they're waiting!" Her tall, gap-toothed strategist was standing there covered in sweat.

"Take a breath mint and lose the Mao jacket," Uli interjected. "Siftwelt might ignore your lesbian preferences, but he hates drunks and commies."

Heeding his advice, Bea tossed her jacket on the sofa, grabbed a piece of mint gum, and walked Uli out the door. His parting comment was a whispered reminder to call when she turned straight again.

46

Since Marsha was nowhere in sight, Uli got back in his car and slowly drove through the retreating crowds on Hawtree Pass. As he exited the wide entrance before getting on Rockaway Boulevard, he saw a tight gathering at an old bus stop and hit the brakes. He put his car in reverse and pulled up alongside the oldest—and tallest—person in the group.

Uli leaned toward his passenger-side window, unrolled it, and shouted, "Mr. Paul Moses, is that really you?"

"Do I know you, sir?" Paul replied. Along with the rest of the crowd, an old woman who seemed to be his companion kept searching the barren highway for a bus.

"We haven't been formally introduced. My name is Uli Sarkisian. I'd be honored to drive you and your lady friend home, wherever that might be."

"Let's go," said the old woman without waiting for Paul's consent. She was about to keel over in the heat.

"So who are you?" Paul asked again.

"My name is Ulysses Sarkisian, call me Uli." They shook hands, and the woman, who introduced herself as Lucille, pulled up the seat and climbed in the back.

"You're not related to the Aardvarkians over in Bushwick, are you?"

"Aardvarkian?"

"He and his family run the Armenian diner near us."

"I don't know him."

"You should go and introduce yourself," Paul said. "It's a good restaurant and they like other Armenians."

"I hope you're not a taxi service," Lucille squawked, rolling down the window, "'cause we don't have stamps."

"Actually, I'm the one of deputy attorney generals of Rescue City South."

"In my day, no one would've ever trusted an Armenian with a handgun," Paul said with a wry smile.

"Well, I don't have one, so I guess things haven't changed much," Uli kidded back.

They drove for about ten minutes before Lucille nodded off and started snoring.

"You know, we met once, not very long ago. A couple times, actually."

"We did?"

"Yeah, on the Coney Island boardwalk," Uli said. "We both fell asleep on the same bench. I was working for PP at the time, trying to get people to join."

"I have no recollection."

"I assume you came to the Quirklyn rally to see your daughter."

"My *what*?"

"We both know that's not Valerie Solanas."

"Are you crazy!" Paul hissed, looking over to see that Lucille hadn't heard.

"Look, I was going to wait to do this until after the election, but you should do it right now, shouldn't you? I mean, I can turn around."

"Hold on, what the . . . who the hell . . . How do you know any of this?"

"You're going to think I'm nuts, but I experienced some kind of memory transference."

"A memory inference?"

"I don't know what else to call it, but I think I've . . . experienced your memories."

"What does that mean?"

"Images, voices, smells, tastes, information—all belonging to you; more or less chronologically formatted. Kind of like watching a movie."

"The Ghost of Christmas Past gave you a tour, huh?" Paul thought Uli was still kidding around.

"I know it sounds nuts, but this whole place is nothing but a big psychic laboratory."

"Exactly which memories of mine did you suffer?" Paul was grinning—he clearly didn't buy any of it.

"I'll just say, I know about the sneakers."

"What sneakers?"

"The sneakers that you put the pitchblende in."

Paul stared straight ahead for a few moments, then finally said, "So, what is this? . . . Am I under arrest?"

"You should be, but I'm not turning anyone in. Hell, there's no one here to turn you in *to*."

"The whole sneaker thing was a way to work out my own bitterness. For the life of me, I never thought I'd complete it. And when I did, I never thought they'd be detonated."

"I know, I saw you trying to take them down. There's a lot I'm still trying to understand."

"Who exactly are you?" Paul asked with a sudden urgency.

"That's part of the mystery," Uli said. "I don't really know. I found myself walking near here awhile ago. I've remembered some things, like that I was in the FBI."

Paul looked bewildered.

Uli continued: "I'm friends with your daughter, and I know she'd love to meet you, so why don't—"

"I'd rather die."

"Why?"

"I abandoned her when she needed me most." He was barely audible.

"She's still young, I'm sure she'd forgive you."

"I can't even forgive myself."

"Mr. Moses, you must be ninety-three or so."

"Give or take."

"The life expectancy in the US is roughly seventy-three; here it must be at least twenty years younger than that. If there is a god—something I'm less inclined to believe with each passing day—I'd say he's given you one great gift, and that's time."

"If I'm not cursed with it, no man is."

"Your pool club failed, your first marriage failed, your beloved wife Lucretia died—none of that can be altered. But reconciling with your daughter, that's something you can still fix."

Lucille snapped out of her deep sleep. "Make a right here."

Uli made the turn. "Remember that man? The one who stopped you and bent the retrieval poles you built?"

"God, you really did see everything . . ."

"Do you have any idea who he could be? He seemed familiar, but I didn't get a good look."

"Yes. It occurred me to a few years ago that I had seen him before. I think he was the fella who passed me information from Vladimir outside the Russian embassy."

"So you think Russians might be behind this?"

"What the heck are you two talking about?" Lucille broke in. "You sound like an 007 novel."

"Nothing," Uli said.

"It was a smart move. Vladimir sending someone to follow me, to make sure I used those detonators. I mean, think about it: the Soviets and the Americans have poured billions of dollars into developing weapons to blow each other up. And here, for almost nothing—no casualties, no costs, no way to trace it—they're able to hit the financial center of New York, of the whole country."

"The Russians wouldn't do something like this," Uli said. "The bombing didn't take out any significant military targets. It had zero kill power, it had absolutely no lasting strategic value, and they would have risked a lot more in being caught."

Lucille directed Uli to the commune where they lived. Uli helped Paul out and walked him to his door.

"You hungry?" Paul asked him.

"Yeah, but I don't want you guys to go through any trouble on my account."

"Oh, we won't," the elderly man assured him. "I was just going to say that you should head over to Aardvarkian's diner, it's only a few blocks away. If you tell him you're Armenian, maybe he won't spit in your *lahmajoun*."

Uli promised he'd come by and visit again. He wanted to convince Paul to reconcile with his daughter while there was still time, so he gave him his telephone number at the Williamsburgh Building. "When you're ready to see her, I'll be glad to drive you there myself and introduce you."

Paul didn't respond.

Uli bade them farewell and sped off west. When he got to Bushwick, he turned a corner to head south and immediately hit the brakes.

LITTLE ARMENIA—the sign read. It was the restaurant Paul had recommended. Though Uli didn't have any visions of murdered ancestors from his past at this particular moment, he knew he had to stop.

The eight tables were packed with locals enjoying the closest thing to Armenian food that could be found in Rescue City. A counter that ran along the back grill only had one seat left, next to the bathroom. On the far wall, a sign simply said:

BREAKFASTE—1/2 stamp
LUNCH—3/4 stamp
DINNER—1 stamp
(Tips graciously accepted)

Though it was a little pricey, the food looked great. Thick, juicy "lamb chops" were wonderfully grilled and served on a bed of pilaf with a heaping side of okra. Since all the imported food on the reservation usually came in cans and boxes, and Uli had never heard of lamb making it here, he wondered whether the meat was hog or dog. After twenty minutes of waiting patiently, he realized the downside of the restaurant was the slow table service. By their physical similarities, he guessed that the entire restaurant staff was related: the cook looked like the father, the waitress was the daughter, and the cashier was the teenage son. Everyone pitched in where they were needed.

Eventually, the daughter put a heaping plate of food in front of Uli.

"I didn't even order," Uli said.

"If you're sitting here during dinnertime, you must want dinner," she reasoned.

"I actually wanted lunch."

"It's the same meal but the price changes after three."

Uli realized he had missed the lunch discount by two minutes—even though he had been there for much longer. Now he knew why service had instantly picked up. Yet he was pleasantly compensated by the tasty food. It was a little better than the Burnt Men dishes, and infinitely superior to the awful fare of PP.

As the last of the lunch-hour crowd vanished, the wild-haired, wild-eyed cook paused before Uli and said in his native tongue, "Tell me you're not Armenian."

"I sure as hell hope not," Uli responded.

When the chef burst out in a belly laugh, Uli realized he had replied in fluent Armenian.

"Your name isn't really Aardvarkian, is it?"

"No, but it's pretty close," the man said. Painted on the far wall was a faint, half-finished fresco featuring a large map of Brooklyn and Queens. In the middle were the four tiny, crooked districts of Quirklyn, and in big letters over the region it said, *Little Armenia.*

"Your diner's not that big."

"I was more trying to make a statement about Armenia. Our country has always been wedged between great world powers."

"You mean communism and democracy?"

"And before that, the sultan and czar, and going back about five hundred years before Christ with Darius and his Persian Empire, and the great Scythian tribes to our north—so it makes sense that we're here now."

"How exactly did you wind up here?" Uli asked.

"Detained—I was an antiwar organizer in Berkeley. They let me bring my family with me, thank God, since this was really built for the New York refugees. As the two gangs endlessly battled and everyone moved out, we refused to leave. And now this little area calls itself Quirklyn and is trying to break free, and I like that—it gives me hope that maybe someday Armenia will do the same."

"Armenia." Just saying the word made Uli nervous.

"To me Armenia is a state of mind," the restaurateur went on, "a metaphor. The only vital place where true freedom can be found, a tiny space between two battling giants."

"It takes just one of those giants to knock us out," Uli said.

The man smiled. "My son's still a registered Pigger and my daughter's a registered Crapper. Just in case."

"Do you think any of these Warhol people really have a chance of getting elected?"

"Frankly, I don't know anyone around here who cares for homosexuals, drug addicts, or artsy types. But everyone despises these fucking gangs, and that enemies-of-my-enemies saying still holds true."

Neglecting to mention that he was a high-ranking official for the Crappers, Uli finished his plate, paid his stamp, and said goodbye with a handshake, which the man pushed aside to give him a bear hug.

Uli returned to his car and drove along Bushwick Avenue, the main east-west artery in Quirklyn. He found that many of the roads going north and south had recently been torn up. Apparently, the Quirklyn rebels weren't waiting for the election—they were proactively taking defensive measures against a possible invasion. Before long he noticed a car in his rearview mirror that appeared to be tailing him. But it had vanished by the time he was approaching Downtown Brooklyn.

47

During the final days, all the candidates made an aggressive drive for votes. Dennis Izzlowski was going door-to-door, offering food and favors to constituents, asking people if they had seen his victory over "the fag interlopers" at the rally. A few people commented that they had missed it, but had heard how untoward his behavior had been.

"Let's not give away our homes to commie queers," he urged. "Don't forget to vote!"

"You know," said one resident, "I plan on voting for you, because I think you guys can put in roads and fix streetlights—which are the things we really need here—but when Valerie Solanas knocks on my door and talks to me, she's never said anything nasty about you, and I greatly respect her for that."

"If I sound a little snippy," Izzlowski replied, "it's just 'cause I don't want these people around our children."

"Anywhere else in America folks might share that sentiment, but a lot of us around here were from Greenwich Village in Old Town, and I always thought they made for colorful neighbors. In any case, I never heard of anyone raping or recruiting, so I really don't mind."

Izzlowski smiled politely and left. If using antihomosexual rhetoric against openly queer candidates was hurting his campaign, it would be the first time in history that this was the case.

Throughout the other three districts, the Brain got a group of assistants from Staten Island to help the Quirklyn candidates with their final push. Ondine was only getting worse. The Brain procured him a wheelchair and more pills, and had his driver push him throughout East New York, shaking hands with anyone he could and making jokes about wheeling as opposed to running for office.

A week before the big vote, the Election Commission in Kew Gardens had sent out flyers establishing new polling centers in each of the districts. They explained that in order to vote, residents had to bring signed statements from at least two neighbors verifying that they lived where they claimed. The flyers promised that the legitimacy of all voters would be checked. Each polling station would have three assigned representatives to oversee and count the votes: one from the Piggers, one from the Crappers, and one from Quirklyn.

48

At ten a.m. on Monday morning—election day in Quirklyn—the fifteen gavels of fifteen judges tapped their fifteen desktops in separate courtrooms on four different floors of the Williamsburgh Building, bringing to order the first open trials.

An exhausted Uli, all thirty of his lieutenants, Schuman, and most of the tiny Crapper brain trust spent the entire time racing between the courtrooms, checking to make sure all was well on both sides of the aisle. They kept track of which gangcops and judges had gotten the gist of the new system, and who was falling behind. From time to time there was yelling and a crew of bailiffs would dash toward the courtroom to handle the disturbance.

By late afternoon, Uli finally found a moment to relax on one of the spectator benches in a large trial room. He tried not to fall asleep as he listened to the case: a huge, powerful man named Mother was accused of viciously slashing both his wife and her lover to death. Uli had made sure that the gangcop from Sheepshead Bay had done thorough detective work—supplying gruesome postmortem photos, identifying a number of witnesses who had seen repeated episodes of domestic violence as well as the accused man's drug abuse.

Uli grew steadily disheartened as he watched a bullshit artist of a defense lawyer named Unger skillfully outargue the assigned prosecutor, who had performed well on all the written tests but utterly lacked verbal skills.

"Shit," murmured the lieutenant from Clinton Hill. "This would've been an open-and-fucking-shut amputation in the old days."

The good news was that five of the other young ADAs had managed to push through weak cases with sheer eloquence, effectively trapping suspects on the stand in their own poorly spun web of lies.

The morning after the Quirklyn election—day two of the trials— everyone was eagerly waiting to hear the results when four sharp raps at Uli's office door brought him to his feet. His secretary pushed it open and shouted: "The two city council investigators who were assigned to your carjacking case, Sal Bloom and Anatole Williams, were just found stabbed to death!"

"Where?"

"Upstairs."

"In this building?"

"Yes! Just now!"

The council cop offices were just a floor above Uli's. Lieutenant La-Coste, whom he met in the hallway, joined him on the elevator. Together they walked over to the far side of the almost empty floor.

The bodies lay where they had fallen, right at the bases of their desks. A large pool of glistening blood made them look like two mountainous islands in a dark-red sea. Sal Bloom had a knife wound to the neck, and the other, Williams, who had died with his own knife in hand, was stabbed clean in the heart. Both bodies were still warm. The only possible witness, a secretary named Judy Miller, claimed she had just arrived. She was the one who had called downstairs.

Before Uli could search to see if the killer was still on the floor, the elevator doors opened again and three men stepped out: the first two were Attorney General Schuman and Deputy Attorney General Gonzalez.

"The secretary's lying," said Lieutenant LaCoste. "Give me an hour and I'll get the truth out of her."

Before Uli could reply that they didn't torture anymore, the third man from the elevator said, "I killed them." It was Scouter Lewis.

"You're under arrest, cocksucker!" barked Gonzalez.

"Don't touch me!" Lewis said, smacking the bald DAG across his loose face. "It was self-defense!"

"All right, stop it!" Schuman stepped between them. "Why didn't you call the authorities?"

"I just did! I went downstairs to report it to my superior." He pointed to Uli.

"No you didn't," Uli said.

"Ask your secretary, I just left a message for you." Lewis didn't have his usual aroma of booze.

"What happened?" asked Schuman.

"Deputy Attorney General Sarkisian gave me a special assignment. I was investigating these men."

"Where the hell did you get the authority to investigate my department?" Gonzalez yelled at Uli.

"I didn't authorize any such thing!" he fired back.

"Did I not offer to look into who blew up your car?" Lewis said. "And did you not say to let you know if I found anything?"

"Is this true?" Gonzalez pressed.

"You said you were going to investigate the car bombing, not the city council police!"

"Again, who the fuck are you to investigate my officers?" Gonzalez asked Lewis.

"When I learned that the same two officers who had made no headway on the Manhattan sandbag case were also making no headway on this attempted murder, I figured it was an obvious place to start. I followed them for the past few days—whenever they went out together, I was right on their asses."

"And what did you find?" the attorney general asked.

"At first, nothing. I was prepared to look elsewhere. Last night around midnight, I watched them perform several field interrogations, then they jumped in their car and drove like madmen for three hours every which way in Brooklyn. Sure enough I lost them, so I played a hunch and headed over to the Pigger gangcop headquarters in Kew Gardens."

"They were city council cops, you moron!" Gonzalez rasped. "They have jurisdiction in the northern boroughs—"

"I WAITED FOUR HOURS OUTSIDE THE PIGGER POLICE HEADQUARTERS ON ROOSEVELT BOULEVARD!" Lewis yelled over Gonzalez. "Then I followed them back here. As soon as I got off the elevator, I saw Officer Anatole stuff something into his desk. I asked if he'd mind if I took a look inside."

"Having backup is standard procedure in situations like this," Uli stated calmly.

"Look, I used to be an officer with the council cops. It was a calm, civilized conversation between two police officers who I've known for years, and if he'd said no, I would've thanked him and left. I didn't see any potential for violence. When he said, *Be my guest*, I opened the drawer and found this." Lewis held up a yellow pastry box with the words *Vanilla Cake* printed on it, but inside was a folded blueprint of the Williamsburgh Building.

"That proves nothing," Gonzalez said.

"Before I could thank them and leave, Bloom pulled out a knife and lunged at me."

"And what did you do?" Schuman asked.

"What was I supposed to do? I grabbed it, twisted his wrist, and shoved it into his fucking neck. Then, as the other asshole whipped out his blade, I grabbed his elbow and stuck the knife in his chest."

"Then what?"

"Then nothing. I was shaking like a leaf, so I went downstairs, told Sarkisian's secretary, lit a cigarette, saw you go into the elevator, and jumped in behind you." He spread out the blueprint on a table. "Now, if you look closely at this diagram you'll see that they marked off a space on the fifth floor, which is a high-security courtroom—"

"If charges aren't immediately filed against this cocksucker, my city council cops will kill him themselves!" Gonzalez broke in.

Schuman told him to calm down; at the very least, Lewis would be suspended.

"He's not going to be arrested?" Gonzalez asked incredulously.

"This will be investigated like any other murder," Schuman replied.

Uli offered to oversee the investigation himself. He had disliked and distrusted this lazy, drunken asshole from the start. His arrogant ignorance reeked of some kind of guilt. Now, without witnesses, Lewis had admitted to committing a violent double homicide and there was no evidence to prove otherwise. And as if the murders weren't bad enough, he claimed that he did it while investigating Uli's attempted murder, so both Gonzalez and Schuman were now suspicious of him as well.

Later that afternoon, while doing more spot inspections of the different trials, Schuman bumped into Uli outside a courtroom.

The attorney general was nodding his head solemnly, and Uli feared Schuman was going to dismiss him for the Scouter Lewis debacle. Instead, he confided his greatest concern: "Yesterday only thirteen open-and-shut cases were deliberated upon and brought to sentencing."

"That's a lot for one day."

"The problem is, there were twice as many new arrests just yesterday," Schuman said. "Nearly five hundred accused people are being held in every available incarceration space. Unless we seriously expedite things, this trial experiment just isn't going to work."

"I hear the gangcops have been putting convicts to work on public projects; maybe we can make it part of the sentencing."

"For the nonviolent offenders," Schuman agreed.

"Just plea-bargain directly with the prisoners."

"The mayor and I talked about that this morning. The whole point to the trial system is the trials! We were hoping to wait until after the Quirklyn election before going to plea bargains, but we'll have a riot on our hands if we don't speed things up."

"What about the Erica Rudolph trial?" Uli asked. "It's just for sentencing, isn't it?" Rudolph had repeatedly stated her guilt.

"Yeah, Thursday afternoon. Everyone'll be here."

An hour later, Uli was heading downstairs to check on another trial when he heard, "Hey, palsy," from behind him.

Among the rush of courtroom support staff, Uli spied the jailhouse photographer responsible for springing him from the Bronx Zoo. "You abandoned me!" he hissed.

"Abandoned you?" The photographer pointed at Uli's intact hand and said, "Looks to me like I came through."

"I thought you were going to come back and tell me all was well. I broke out of jail that night and almost got killed."

"It took me awhile to get ahold of someone who gave a shit about you. And now look, you're a big muckety-muck here." The man dug through his camera bag and held up the Polaroid he had taken of Uli in his filthy clothes, banged up in the elephant pen. On the back was written IOU. "There are three guys in your jail who are facing the scalpel. Free them and your debt's canceled."

"Are you kidding?"

"I am absolutely sincere. For the record, your debt isn't to me, it's to Joe Gallo."

Uli's heart was racing. "You saved me, and I'm only one person—I'll free one of them."

"This is what Mr. Gallo and I feel is fair."

"I will consider doing this on two conditions," Uli said. The man immediately looked pissed. "First, I don't ever want to see you again, and secondly, I want to meet this Gallo guy."

"I'll have to check with him and get back to you on that."

"Write down the names of the three prisoners and I'll see what I can do," Uli said.

The man handed him a matchbook with *Bill "Brass" Basolini*, *Rick "Pins" Forenzi*, and *Mark "Happy" Rizzo* neatly printed on the back.

After checking the progress in a few more courtrooms, Uli went up to the top floor of the building. In a large utility closet converted into a temporary records room, he pulled out their files. All three had been arrested for assault and battery. Reading the newly attached arrest reports—as well as the newly required victim complaints—Uli got the sense that these guys were either loan sharks or strong arms, which was a relief because he had already decided he wasn't going to let off any killers.

Although none of the defendants had been assigned surlawyers yet, the arresting gangcops had done most of their homework. Even so, missing from the files were a few key pieces of documentation. Uli removed the witness statements and the Polaroids of the bruises the thugs had inflicted. Since Schuman was putting everyone under a lot of pressure to keep up the pace, Uli knew that when the ADAs finally got around to opening these files, they'd be forced to release the men for insufficient preparation. At worst, Gallo's associates would have painless surgical scars on their already scarred backs.

49

SPECIAL ELECTION RESULTS

Greenpoint-Williamsburg

Crapper 949

Quirklyn 3,483

Candy Darling (QUIRKLYN) elected

Bushwick

Crapper 1,702

Quirklyn 1,723

Jackie Curtis (QUIRKLYN) elected

East New York

Crapper 1,223

Quirklyn 1,226

Ondine (QUIRKLYN) elected

South Ozone Park

Pigger 634

Quirklyn 1,261

Valerie Solanas (QUIRKLYN) elected

"AN UNCLEAN SWEEP!" the *Daily Posted New York Times* reported on the four-district victory for the new political party. Uli read the paper in Stamos's two days after the election, feeling happy for Bea, whose name now and forever would have to be Valerie.

Inasmuch as Uli knew that Dennis Izzlowski had been consistently nasty to Bea, he was relieved to see that she had genuinely trounced him. Although the Quirklyn candidates had won all four districts, in Bushwick and East New York, Ondine and Jackie had only won by razor-thin margins.

Despite the fact that the Piggers and Crappers had official observers who confirmed that there was no evidence of voter fraud, neither of the gangs formally accepted the results. And though everyone in the Willamsburgh Building was pissed about the defeat—particularly Gonzalez, who had been involved in trying to recapture the districts—Uli heard no talk about reprisals.

50

Throughout the day, bad champagne flowed and good choke was smoked in celebration of the four victories. It was Tuesday; the last votes had been tallied in the predawn hours.

Joe Brainard regarded the election as his greatest work of art. Even though he might not live to see what it would turn into, he had done everything he could to start the ball rolling.

Late that afternoon, as SOPers amassed in the street in front of Bea's house, residents started chanting: "Speech! Speech!"

Although drunk and high, Bea waddled outside with her body-guard-driver Reggie close behind.

"On this great day, we have achieved a . . . a . . ." Smiling tiredly, her mind went completely blank.

For the longest minute, everyone just stood and waited, until Reggie whispered to her, *A great victory for democracy. Thank you all for voting for me.* She repeated the final line twice.

As people applauded, Bea waved and staggered back into the house, which was packed—mainly with men who were in charge of security in SOP, and others who happened to be visiting them. Intent on wiping away all the anxiety of the past week, Bea grabbed yet another cocktail and lit up yet another joint. While sipping and toking away, she heard a voice directed toward her.

"Hi there. Even though I'm not supposed to come here, I just wanted to unofficially congratulate you on your victory."

Bea saw a tall, ravishing black woman standing before her. It was one of the executives from PP, Uli's strangely sensual friend, Marsha Johnson.

"Smoke?" Bea offered her the joint.

Marsha stammered some nervous nonsense about not being much of a smoker, but Bea held the joint to her lips so she took a puff. All the guys around them started applauding their candidate, causing Bea to blush. She grabbed the beautiful woman's hand and led her into the back where they wouldn't be on view.

The two smoked several more buds of Hoboken Gold, the top-grade Crapper choke. Then, totally stoned, they fell into a silent stupor. Bea closed her eyes and listened to the noise from the partygoers in her house. Beyond all the outside sounds she realized Marsha was talking to her.

". . . When I heard that someone who was famous for shooting an artist was running as a candidate here, I was a little suspicious, but then I read your manifesto. As a woman who can't have children, I put my energies into a meaningful career, but I constantly have to struggle for a place among men. And I have to struggle with their abuses all the time—I usually just pretend it's not happening, but . . ."

"What exactly are you saying?" Bea's attention was dissipating.

"I guess . . . I just have to confess that several times I myself have felt like cutting up men, and not just one of them, like you did, but all of them at once. Every last one of them." The tall woman started giggling. "Maybe something's wrong with me."

At that moment Bea leaned forward and kissed her, plunging her tongue through Marsha's tight, tense lips. First reluctant, struggling to relax, the PP supervisor finally relented.

Bea could feel the woman starting to loosen up, so she slipped her fingers over Marsha's shirt, rubbing her small breasts over the multiple layers of thick fabric. Marsha's eyes seemed to gloss over as she sank into a subconscious state, breathing steadily. Bea yanked the shirttail out of her tight waistband and slipped her hand up along Marsha's firm abdomen, straight up to the coarse restraints of her brassiere. As the other woman kept breathing deeply, Bea pulled at the straps and fine wires until the supervisor's top was exposed. She bit at Marsha's bottom lip and pinched her hardened nipple.

The PP supervisor's eyes popped open and she began awkwardly reciprocating, slipping her hands down Bea's back and into her pants, cupping her round ass cheeks. A moment later, Bea spun Marsha around onto a sofa and stealthily undid her belt. Her hands were in Marsha's pants, running her middle finger along the outreach worker's wet undergarments.

"We really shouldn't!" Marsha whispered, shutting her eyes tightly. But she was unable to resist. Bea stroked her gently and the PP supervisor faded into sensual waves of a whole new pleasure.

Suddenly the bedroom door was flung open.

"Oh shit!" Reggie exclaimed. Before he could back out, Joe Brainard,

Jackie Curtis, and about six other half-drunk celebrants tumbled inside the dark room, yelling, "We won!"

Marsha screamed, shoved Bea off of her, then pulled up her pants and yanked down her shirt. A few seconds later she was on her feet, bolting past the drunken revelers and out the door like a frightened deer.

"Wait!" Bea shouted as Marsha dashed into the night. Bea rushed outside and watched the woman's dark form flit across the sandy landscape, back toward the distant liver-colored towers of PP.

"Sorry," Reggie murmured as he came outside.

They stood there another minute as someone flipped on Bea's hi-fi system. Music blared. People from the neighborhood were still arriving; it was a district-wide victory celebration, and she was the one person everyone wanted to see. Bea sighed and took refuge in the soldiers' barracks that the Brain had had constructed next door, slamming the door shut behind her.

In the empty bedroom reserved for Jack Healy, Bea lay down. Judging by the full ashtray of cigarettes and the open notebook on the edge of the bed, she figured someone else had been staying there. Picking up the notebook, curious whom it belonged to, she read:

> Did New York City ever really exist? The older I get, the more I believe it was all just a phantasm. (This is kind of how I imagined purgatory to be.) This slim reed called a memory is all that connects me now. And the notion, the purpose, the great dream we all share is that someday we will eventually return to that place that was far from wonderful, but quite simply the closest we could get to livable.

Bea flipped through the pages of the journal. Most of it seemed to be shards of memories from someone's past, not really connected to anything. Random tableaux, each poignant in its own little way about life in Old Town, before the great evacuation. Having pierogi on Second Avenue with mustard instead of sour cream; feeding challah crumbs to diseased pigeons in front of St. Mark's Church-in-the-Bowery; a hot summer day in dilapidated Coney Island, walking along the filthy sand lined with Russian émigrés to Brighton Beach; shopping for socks at Mays in Union Square. The thought that she might never return to New York City brought tears to Bea's intoxicated eyes.

When she heard footsteps approaching, she put the book down exactly where she'd found it and got out of bed just as Joe Brainard entered.

"They're all looking for you—the guest of honor!"

"More like the guest of *horror*. All that fucking noise. I couldn't go back inside."

"Stay," he said, picking up the journal, "I was just grabbing a few of my things before returning to Staten Island."

"Returning?"

"Sure, my work here is done," he kidded. "Now just kick back and be corrupted."

"God," she sighed, still toasted, "you do something that demands so much of you, and you don't even know it. And then everything stops and you're still going a million miles a minute, and . . ."

He nodded slightly. "The secret is learning to calm down. I'm still working on that."

She smiled. "It's strange. The worst is over, right? But I have this awful feeling it's just beginning."

"It doesn't matter. Something beautiful happened here tonight. And without *you*, without all you did, there'd have been no chance to pull this off."

"I'm sure Rafique would've found someone else."

"You can look back at this moment at any time in your life and be proud of what you did here. You know that, don't you?" When she didn't respond, the Brain grabbed a few more possessions scattered around the bedroom, wished her good night, and headed out.

Bea lay back down and switched off the light, trying to sleep. But thoughts of Marsha Johnson kept her head spinning. The woman's odd combination of authority and innocence made her seem like a sexy novice nun, like a virginal superwoman. Even her long, lanky, muscular body was a kind of paradox. After an hour of sleeplessness, Bea pulled on her boots and went downstairs. She tiptoed past Reggie who, like a loyal dog, was asleep in the foyer. She exited out the back door. Over the intermittent roar of airplanes lifting and landing, which she had strangely come to find comforting, the party was still raging inside her home.

The one thing she found endlessly fascinating that was doubtlessly better here than in Old Town was the sky. In its awesome vastness she could feel either the complete absence or the total presence—depending on her mood—of what could only be called God.

Bea lumbered through the darkness, heading due west, enjoying the crisp night air. She picked up a stick before crossing through the empty Aqueduct field, looking and listening carefully for the snakes that sometimes slithered through. Halfway across, she could make out the faintest outlines of the old dog track, covered under years of wind-swept sand.

After twenty minutes of drunken ambling toward the distant buildings that made up the PP complex, she finally made out the soft glint of the Jamaica Bay reservoir behind it. She slowly and silently circumnavigated the dun-colored buildings, until she spotted what looked like a low warehouse that fingered out over the flat, still waters on the long pier. She just stood and stared at it. What Uli had told her sounded insane. How could an entire group of supposedly principled people silently conspire and participate in such a lie? How could they regularly perform intimate acts at night, and in the light of day pretend as if nothing had happened? Since it was essentially a patriarchal system, she figured the men got to pick the submissive women. Did they choose consistent lovers, or did they screw different people? And what of the women? If they didn't want to be with a particular man, could they turn him down?

In the darkness she spotted a lone figure, a portly man, leaving the building on the pier. A moment later she saw a skinny brunette walking out from the complex of buildings toward the water. Bea followed her. Through the haze of liquor still in her system, Bea watched as the woman reached the oddly dilapidated warehouse. She remained at a healthy distance as she watched the brunette climb in through a broken window. The thought that Marsha could be in there compelled Bea forward.

Although cinder blocks sealed the doors, one of the windows was half covered with a plywood board, so Bea pushed it to one side and entered the large hollow structure. The only light was from the moon, coming in through the upper windows, and soft sounds were audible above her. She carefully headed up the concrete steps, which immediately opened up to a larger room. As her eyes adjusted, she realized there had to be about thirty people scattered throughout.

Not surprisingly, men seemed to outnumber women by more than two to one. To their own slow, soft rhythm, people were shuffling around. Bundles of their clothing were piled where the floor met the wall. Bea immediately realized that most of the men were nude, while most of the women were partially clad, a hint of modesty; many kept their shoes on.

About half of the people were having sex, pressed up against the walls or windows. Most of the others were watching, some jerking off. Perhaps because she was still completely dressed, no one seemed to notice Bea. She watched as a few would fuck for a while, and then most guys who ejaculated would just pull on their pants, without even a wipe, and leave. Those who hadn't seeded moved to other lovers.

Instead of feeling turned on, Bea found something spiritless about the mass intimacy, even a bit ghoulish. Few uttered sounds—maybe an occasional moan or groan, but no one expressed any words—as though afraid to be revealed.

One extraordinarily large erection appeared to float by on the strength of its own turgidity. It carried a small man behind it to the farthest end of the darkness. That's when Bea noticed a narrow doorway in the corner that led to an even larger room in the rear that was at the top of the pier. She went inside. As this room was not bathed in moonlight, it was difficult to see faces. But to the left Bea could make out the gorgeous Amazonian torso that could only be *her*. She was facing the cinder-block wall with her arms, hands, and fingers extended as if pressed up against it by some unseen force. Two smaller stocky guys seemed to corner her. Slowly the large-framed woman bent her knees, allowing the more aggressive bull full access. He entered her, and then shoved her head down. Bea's heart began beating faster as she watched Marsha fellating the second man while the first copulated with her. She felt a surge of anger, wanting to grab a weapon and kill the bastards right where they stood.

The fucking was too angry to be called anything like love, or even intimacy. It seemed as if the entire place was mechanically raping itself. The second man's face opened as though he were letting out a scream, but no sound, no emotion, was emitted. Bea knew he had just squirted in her mouth. Just as quickly, he drifted off into the darkness.

Bea kept watching as Marsha pulled herself back up along the wall, where she finally paused, bracing herself as though she were about to be flogged. No sooner did she assume this position than some plump, bald bastard stepped forward. Bea strode over and firmly put her hand on his hairless, bosomy chest and pushed him back. Like a trained chimp accepting the correction, the chubby man docilely receded as a second, even chubbier man approached.

It was then that Bea stepped between them and delicately slipped her middle finger into Marsha, who was still facing the wall. Hearing her sigh softly, Bea inserted a second and then a third finger, rubbing them from side to side. Although she tried loosening her up, Marsha remainded extraordinarily narrow, moaning quietly to the beat of the knuckles pulsing inside her, pressing her face against the cool wall. As Marsha started approaching orgasm, she stepped to the side, pulling away from Bea.

Yanking her by her hair so she wouldn't budge, Bea whispered, "You took it for them, now you'll take it from me!"

Marsha gasped. At least a dozen other flagellates had accumulated at a respectful distance, observing the only lesbian encounter. But upon realizing her suitor was female, Marsha disconnected and stepped away.

Bea grabbed her by the wrist and, pushing through the spectators, led Marsha across the dark room until the supervisor pulled her hand free. Bea thought she was being rejected again, but Marsha was just grabbing her clothes and flip-flops. Together they headed downstairs, where the sight of Marsha's perfect face in the moonlight made Bea's heart skip a beat. Marsha pulled a little slip over her body, and a moment later the two were dashing across the abandoned dog track, back to South Ozone Park.

51

"**Y**ou must be one wildly important motherfucker," said LaCoste, the redheaded lieutenant, as Uli exited his vehicle in the city council parking lot. "A week ago they blew up your car, and now you got a whole new one. Aren't you afraid they're going to blow this one up too?"

"Supposedly the bombers have been caught and killed by my trusty assistant, Scouter," Uli replied tersely. "How's your prisoner situation?"

"Awful. They've taken me off legal protocols and put me on jail duty. Now I have to spend my days with all these fucking inmates."

"Yeah, I heard."

"The quality of this mercy is twice the time and three times the stampage. Bunch of pansy-ass shit, if you ask me."

"It'd seem very fair if you were one of the accused. So, do you guys put your prisoners on labor details?"

"Sure, so do the Piggers. Mainly on sand sweep-up. The captain wanted them on roadwork, but we can't get enough materials or equipment from the council. There just isn't that much for prisoners to do around here."

"I have a job for them," Uli said.

"Yeah, well, go to an employment agency. No one here needs food stamps."

"What *do* you need?"

"My precinct is always short on wheels," LaCoste said, clearly admiring Uli's mildly dented solicar.

"Yeah, but if Schuman discovers that I'm swapping his vehicles for favors . . ."

"They're going to be used for what they should be used for—police patrols."

"How many man-hours of work would this fine set of wheels get me?"

"Well, of the 150 men that we're holding, if you subtract the amputees, troublemakers, and loafers, you'd be lucky to come up with seventy-five that are at all useful. And if I can get you them for a single day, that'd be a minor miracle. What are you planning on doing—building a pyramid to yourself?"

Uli smiled, but didn't say a word.

"We could really use the car, but I need to know what you want those men for before I can even think of lending them out."

"How do you feel about the Piggers?" Uli glanced around.

"I lost two brothers and four of my best friends to them. But we're at peace now."

"Well, I'm not sure who we are."

LaCoste laughed. "Yeah, that's a great idea, let's march our prisoners into Queens and just take it all back."

"There's another gang on the block who hasn't declared peace with the Piggers yet."

"Please tell me you're not talking about those Quirklyn faggots who just stole our border districts."

"They also have a district in Queens."

"You mean South Ozone Park?"

"Do you know the Aqueduct track?" Uli asked.

"Yeah, I used to make bets there when I was a kid."

"I'm talking about the dog track here in Nevada."

"I used to make bets there too, when they ran dogs. But then Gallo ended it, said too many people were ripping him off."

"They need trenches dug and they don't have the manpower."

"Why?"

"Because you and I know that eventually the Piggers are going to attack them, and when they do, they'll probably come across from Howard Beach, which is their closest neighborhood."

"And how does that concern us?"

"You bus your prisoners out there one quiet morning. They spend the day digging ditches, leave just as quickly, and you get this fine new solicar." Uli whacked the hood. "Then, when they attack and a dozen Pigger bastards die in the fight, it's a win-win!"

"Piggers have surveillance teams all over there, just as we do. If one of them catches us digging trenches for the Quirklyners, it's the same as a declaration of war."

"Frankly, I don't think they give a shit, or else they would've done something immediately after the election."

"If I go out there and I see a single Pigger anywhere . . ."

"Fine. If you see anyone, you can withdraw your men."

"And I still get to keep the car, just for wasting my valuable time."

"Deal."

"You sweet on some little chicky up there, Deputy?" LaCoste asked.

"Those fuckers almost took my hand. I still have a score to settle," Uli growled.

"Well, one car buys you my consideration, but seventy-five men working for twelve hours is at least two cars."

"I don't have two solicars."

"They replaced the last one pretty quickly, maybe they'll give you a third."

"The last one was blown up, along with the lieutenant from Coney Island, right here," Uli reminded him.

"Tell you what: you can say you were doing some important police business in East New York and your car was stolen. I can corroborate, really ham it up in the report."

"Yeah, and when they see you driving two new cars around, I get arrested for stealing Crapper equipment."

"Actually, in our precinct we still have six solicars registered with Williamsburgh, and only four are operational. So once we file down the registration numbers, they'll be none the wiser."

"How about this—I'll give you this one, and later we'll dream up some nice dramatic stolen-car report for a second, but I want the job done first. *And*, if Schuman's secretary rejects the request for a second car, no hard feelings."

"Fair enough," LaCoste said, grabbing Uli's hand. "My precinct captain is scheduled to observe the trials on Monday. So at eight a.m., I'll check out the field. If it looks clear, I'll have the vans drop off all our usable prisoners, along with six guards, which will be just enough to get them out to South Ozone. You should supply at least ten of your own guards, water, shovels, and bathroom facilities. And lunch for seventy-five—they'll work a lot better."

"Fair enough."

"I need them back by the evening shift change, which is five p.m., so that's nine hours to get as much use out of them as you can."

Before entering the Williamsburgh Building, Uli detoured over to Stamos's Stamps where he paid a quarter-stamp to make a phone call to Bea. He listened tensely as the phone rang over and over.

During his lunch break a few hours later, he tried calling her again—no luck. When he left work at five p.m., he tried her for the third time, and after the tenth ring, she finally picked up.

"Don't say either of our names," he began. "This call is probably being bugged."

"You're not going to ask me if I'm naked, are you?" she giggled. She sounded strange.

"Remember when you asked if I would help you?"

"Is an attack imminent?" She was sobering up quickly.

"I mentioned a defensive trench."

"Yeah, but we simply don't have the manpower."

"Well, if you guys can provide food, supervision, and shovels, I got you seventy-five men who are ready to work a single nine-hour day. And a few guards, though we'll need maybe ten more."

"Sounds like a surprise Crapper attack."

"If you don't want to do it, that's fine, but I can guarantee it's legit, and with that kind of manpower you could have the entire trench done in one day. If you do want it, they're coming at a specified time and you have to be ready for them."

"When?"

"Do you remember when I last saw you?" Uli asked. "Think about it, but don't say it."

"Yeah."

"What day is two days after that? Think of it, but don't say it."

"Okay," she replied after making the calculations.

"They'll be there a week from then from eight until five. Use the next few days to try to plan as much as possible: make a couple hundred sandwiches, get water, and dig a latrine trench for a bathroom. When the guys arrive, try to get them all on the field to show them where to dig. And watch them—they're prisoners, they have to be supervised and returned safely."

"Can I think about this?"

"Unfortunately, I really need to know right now. Yes or no?"

Without the time to go up the chain of command, Bea simply said, "Let's do it," and hung up.

52

Earlier that morning—the morning after the victory celebration and the nighttime excursion across the field—Bea and the rest of SOP awoke to the sound of hammering.

Jack Healy, his cousin Patrick Healy, and Antonio Lucas, who were now the heads of security for the new independent city of Quirklyn, went outside to find that wooden posts with street signs were being erected on each street corner. After deeming it harmless, they returned to the garrison next door to Bea's house.

Without asking for permission, an artistic group of SOPers had carefully painted the names of eight New York writers and artists onto homemade street signs and placed them alphabetically on the street corners of their small community

The north-to-south avenues in SOP were named after male artists: The first was Kerouac—who had began his book *On the Road* in the actual Ozone Park in Queens. Ochs Avenue was next—named after the folk singer who had just committed suicide in Rescue City. O'Hara Avenue followed—in honor of the poet killed by an errant dune buggy back in Fire Island. Pollock Avenue was named after the abstract expressionist, because "the street runs both ways just like the bipolar artist," according to the sign painters.

The four east-to-west streets were named after female New York artists: Billie Holiday—the only black person and singer in the group—was the first street below Hawtree Pass. Edna St. Vincent Millay was below that one, Dorothy Parker was the third one down, and Edith Wharton was the southernmost road in SOP.

Still in bed, Bea glanced out a window at one of the signs outside. The fact that she now lived by the corner of Edith Wharton Street and Kerouac Avenue couldn't make her happier. Plus, Marsha Johnson was fast asleep in her arms; she couldn't stop staring at her. It felt as though she were tasting her with her eyes. If love had any one undeniable quality, it was insatiability—she simply couldn't get enough of this tall, powerful, gorgeous Amazon.

The PP supervisor had dashed off with her just last night. Bea thought perhaps she should wake her up so she could sneak back before anyone found her missing, but she just couldn't do it. The sensations in her heart and soul were so wonderfully constricting, like back when she was on methadone. It was difficult to even breathe. A single phrase kept strumming in her heart: *She's mine!*

When the supervisor finally squinted and began to stir, Bea held her tight and attempted to delicately kiss every inch of her face, like raindrops falling down, until sweet Marsha fell back asleep.

"I'm starving," Marsha muttered when she woke for good thirty minutes later.

Bea rose and toasted some homemade corn muffins and brewed some locally cultivated mint-leaf tea. But before they could eat anything, the two started kissing again. Soon dueling tongues and fingers, then candles and feathers, led to a whistle-stop of orgasms. The time between was full of holding and fondling.

When the phone eventually rang, it was ignored. When it rang a second time, Bea put a big throw pillow on top of it. While lying in bed with her new lover, she felt free from the whole nightmare of Quirklyn. The election was over, she was reaping her glory. It was as close as she had come to escaping from Rescue City.

Then Marsha spoke: "I can't believe I'm in love with Valerie Solanas."

Bea sat up, unable to make eye contact. *Shit, I ought to tell her.* But the idea of having to explain why she was pretending to be a dead feminist felt exhausting.

Marsha reached toward her, and another cycle of lovemaking instantly ensued. Around five p.m., when she finally began to feel guilty about all the heathen sex, Bea heard the muffled ring of her phone and she answered it.

It was Uli Sarkisian, whom she had been wanting just the other night. He was nobly offering the service of seventy-five men to dig the defensives trenches along her district. This was something that Joe Brainard had mentioned as well, but Rafique had been unable to think of a way to discreetly ship up the manpower without being discovered.

Although she was supposed to clear this type of thing with Staten Island first, the offer sounded generous, and she trusted Uli, so she agreed. After hanging up she started dialing the Brain, but heard Marsha heading into the kitchen. So she joined her instead, and they ate muffins with jam and sipped cold mint tea.

"So what was it like shooting Warhol?" Marsha asked.

"Bang-bang," Bea answered, feeling like more of a liar with each passing minute.

"Usually when they fix you," Marsha said, staring into her eyes, "they make you even more broken."

No sooner did the words leave her mouth than Bea leaned forward and kissed her. Slipping her hand down along Bea's shoulder and thigh, Marsha gently massaged her, and soon they were making love yet again. The phone rang several more times but Bea was too distracted to answer.

Early the next afternoon, the sound of pounding on the front door woke Bea up. Not wanting to disturb Marsha, she quietly wrapped a sheet around her shoulders and peeked out the window. It was her driver, Reggie, who told her that Joe Brainard had been trying to reach her yesterday and this morning, and to please call him back at once.

She assured him she would, but just crept back into bed. *How many times do most people really fall in love in their lifetime? Just a handful,* she thought. After making such a huge sacrifice for this Quirklyn ordeal, she felt entitled to a little self-indulgence.

When the Brain drove up two hours later, he angrily rushed past Reggie, who was seated on the front porch. Before he knocked, he looked through one of the small glass frames that lined the door. A tall, nude woman of a mocha color was strolling around, and it wasn't Bea. He decided to wait a moment, then gently knocked.

Bea answered the door in a robe. "Hi!" she said, cheerier than he had ever seen her. "What's up?"

"Didn't Reggie tell you that I've been attempting to reach you?" He was trying to not sound pissed off.

Her eyes were red. "Yeah, I'm sorry, after the election I was a little wiped out. What's up?"

"Nothing pressing, it's just worrisome when I can't reach you. Can I come in?"

"Of course. Actually, I've been meaning to call you; I got some good news." The place reeked of pot smoke.

The Brain sat on the couch as the bedroom door swung open and the formerly nude woman appeared, fully dressed. It only took a moment for him to recognize her as the executive supervisor from PP whom he had met with Rolland Siftwelt.

"I was just going for a walk," Marsha announced.

"We'll be done soon," Bea said, giving her a sensual kiss on the lips as though Brainard wasn't even there.

"I didn't know you were, um . . . with the ladies," he said, slightly embarrassed, as Marsha stepped out.

"It was kind of inspired by Valerie Solanas—an impoverished lesbian."

"She wasn't impoverished. Her family had money. And I don't think she was a lesbian. I met her once, and I saw her around a lot."

"Really," Bea said, "she wasn't a lesbian?!"

"I don't think so."

"Well, it doesn't matter. This is different. I feel so . . . I never felt . . . I want to marry her and have kids. Does that make any sense?"

"Our type can't marry." Brainard smiled sadly. "But the good news is, if we keep a low profile, we can usually live in peace."

Bea looked down. It was the first time the Brain had ever even suggested to her that he was gay. She changed the subject: "Do you think the Piggers are really going to invade SOP?"

"Well, there's no indication that they're planning an attack soon, but who knows. We got Jack and his group keeping an eye on things."

"If they do invade, do you think they'll be coming from across the Aqueduct field?"

"With the airfield to the south, and the rolling dunes to the north and east, I guess the dirt field is probably the easiest approach. So yes, but I don't think sleeping with a supervisor from Pure-ile Plurality is going to help." Though he said this with a smile, in truth he was a bit suspicious of the PP supervisor.

"Suppose I can get a large group of laborers, for one day, to dig defensive trenches out there." Bea nodded toward the old dog track.

"Are they coming in a large wooden horse? 'Cause I think I know how this will end."

"No, it's legit, I guarantee it."

The Brain immediately stepped outside and Bea followed. One of the security chiefs, Antonio Lucas, was standing in front of the barracks next door, smoking. The Brain asked to see Jack Healy; Lucas stubbed out his cigarette and went inside.

"Have these guys had any real police or military training?" Bea asked.

The Brain reminded her that Healy was one of the few people in

Rescue City who had actually served in Vietnam as a field officer. He had been wounded and decorated, but when he returned he joined Vietnam Veterans Against the War, and had tossed his medals into a crowd of protestors at one of the rallies, swearing never to fight again.

"Does that mean he's a pacifist?" Bea asked.

"He seems more reluctant about violence than the others, but I think when things start heating up, he'll find his motivation."

"What's up?" Healy was standing right behind them. Both wondered if he had heard what they were saying.

"Bea has access to seventy-five laborers who can dig a defensive trench along the Aqueduct field to prepare for a possible invasion."

"What laborers?"

"They're seventy-five Crapper prisoners," she explained. "I'm dear friends with one of the deputy attorney generals. He said we'll have to feed them, and he can only spare a few guards, so we'll need at least ten of our men, and we'll need to provide shovels."

"In the past, both sides have frequently given convicts the option of taking part in gang invasions as an alternative to amputation," Healy said. "How do you know they're not an attack force?"

"Maybe my friend is being duped, but I truly believe he wouldn't lie to me," Bea said.

"It hardly sounds like a risk worth taking," the Brain cautioned.

"If seventy-five men want to invade us," Jack said, "uninviting them won't make much difference—we can't fight off that many."

"Do you think digging a defensive trench along the length of the community would be helpful?" the Brain asked.

"Not really, since we don't have the manpower to fill it. What would be useful would be a huge moat up in Hawtree," Healy said with a smile. "It's pretty narrow, and it would block all vehicles from streaming down and invading us."

"How would people be able to drive in?" Bea asked.

"We can create a small parking lot for cars with a narrow bridge to pass over, then make a second parking lot on our side with bikes and vehicles for our people. It really shouldn't take that much work."

"Where the heck would we get the materials to build a bridge?" The Brain was humoring the handsome security chief.

"That huge wooden stage that the Piggers built is sitting there rotting in the sun. I bet we can recycle most of the wood from it."

"So I should tell my Crapper friend no?" Bea asked.

"No, let's do it. I'll start working on the specifications."

"I thought you said we don't have anything to fill a trench with," the Brain said.

"Punji sticks. They were sharp sticks we avoided in Vietnam. Usually bamboo and dipped in Charlie's shit. I stepped on one once—very painful, bad infection. The platoon had to take turns carrying me. This way the Piggers would be forced through Hawtree Pass, which would be much easier to defend."

"We'd have to provide ten guards, sandwiches, and toilets for the seventy-five men," Bea said. "And shovels."

"Shovels and food aren't a big deal," the Brain said. "I'm sure I can scrounge them up from the other districts."

"And I can borrow a dozen men from East New York and Bushwick for a day and make them into guards," Healy added. "The real problem is supplies. We need wood to make into spikes and thin boards, and then we need to cover the trenches in sand."

"That entire row of houses along the southeastern edge of Pollock Avenue is empty," Bea said. Brainard and Healy grinned at her use of the new street name.

"And most of those buildings are dilapidated," the Brain said.

Healy's men only had a few days to prepare—they had to start immediately if they were going to get tools and a van over to the six most run-down bungalows in SOP. They would have to strip the houses of the two-by-fours they needed to create the punji sticks.

Brainard bade them both farewell and headed west to start hunting down shovels and food for the laborers.

Healy was quickly able to borrow several men from the other districts to salvage materials from the old houses. He also carefully diagrammed the task, mapping out and staking a series of narrow intersecting trenches. The point was to defy predictability, so sometimes the trenches ran parallel, other times perpendicular. Healy decided that they didn't have to be more than a foot wide, but they had to run at least four feet deep, so when the attackers stepped on them, the thin boards concealing the trench would crack and their weight would drive them hard onto the sharpened spikes below.

Healy also wrote up an intensive work schedule. The laborers could spend the first part of the day digging the trenches. Then, in the afternoon, they'd wedge narrow four-foot spikes into them. For the last couple hours, the force would carefully cover the trenches with flat lauan boards—ready to collapse when stepped upon. Afterward, the boards would be concealed under sand, which the wind would provide within a couple of days.

53

The Erica Allen Rudolph sentencing was a major event in Rescue City. In addition to providing justice for so many who had been painfully killed, it was also a great opportunity for the Crappers to demonstrate their transparent trial system. Seating was first come, first served for all 108 chairs.

Not wanting to squeeze past the crowds in the hallways, Uli sat in his office reviewing the Sisyphean stack of criminal cases that, regardless of how hard he worked, seemed to grow taller each day. Suddenly his door whipped open and a middle-aged man in a new sharkskin suit with a shiny widow's peak took a seat before him as if he owned the place. Close on his heels were two well-dressed teenage boys.

"I was told you wanted to see me."

"Who are you?" Uli asked, rising to his feet.

"Gallo and sons." The man checked his watch. "And we're a little pressed for time."

Illegally freeing the three thugs must've pleased Gallo. Behind him in the hallway, perhaps too large to enter, stood a man who resembled a grizzly bear in a cheap black suit.

"So you're Mr. Gallo?" The guy looked too smart to be a ruthless gangster. And with his boys, he simply looked like a family man. "Do your sons want to wait outside?"

"They're my partners."

A memory unfroze in Uli's head. "You weren't once known as Crazy Joe, were you?"

"What can I do for you?" Gallo asked impatiently.

"I'm doing my own little investigation, and I was wondering if you could help."

"What exactly do you need from me?"

"Do you know any way to get C-4 explosives?"

"I don't even know what that is."

"In that case, do you think you can help me find someone who lives up north?"

"You're the deputy attorney general, why don't you use the council cops?"

"I don't trust them," Uli said.

"Force and prudence are the might of all that ever has been, or will be, in this world. Machiavelli said that about government."

"This government has neither force nor prudence," Uli responded. "Emmett Grogan is the man I'm looking for."

"I'll try to find him for you, but I want another of my men freed."

Uli agreed, provided the prisoner wasn't accused of murder.

After the mob boss left, Uli was on the phone trying to get permission to interrogate Erica Allen Rudolph one last time. Ironically, it was his fault he had lost the permission in the first place.

Over the past week, he had successfully convinced Schuman to change Rudolph's surlawyer so she would at least be competently defended, but the first thing the new lawyer did was exercise Rudolph's newfound right not to self-incriminate—he forbade her from talking to anyone. "She doesn't say a word until after the trial is over," the lawyer had said.

Just as Uli was about to head downstairs to watch the sentencing, his phone rang. All he could hear was deep breathing.

"Whoever you are," Uli threatened, "I'll find you."

"Hello?" squealed a frail voice on the other end.

"Yes, who the hell is this?"

"Paul Moses."

"Oh, sorry!" Uli chuckled, realizing that the old man must not have heard him answer. "How are you, sir?"

"I just saw a ghost," Paul said, "and it scared the bejesus out of me."

"What do you mean?"

"I can't . . . I don't want him to even see me . . . much less know I'm here. He'd kill me."

"Who? What are you saying?"

"I was in the lobby of your Williamsburgh Building, about to go upstairs, and I saw that son of a bitch—that bastard who's responsible for all this—striding right past me plain as day. I think he had someone with him. He walked right by, nearly knocked me down. The cocksucker didn't even see me."

"Who are you talking about?"

"Oh my God, you're with him, aren't you?"

"I'm with who?"

The line went dead. If Paul had just been in the lobby, there was only one pay phone in the vicinity. Uli jumped to his feet and dashed out of his office. Since the elevator was always at least a five-minute wait, he took the emergency stairs, jumping four steps at a time, shoving past people in the lobby. By the time he had crossed the Williamsburgh Justice Plaza and reached Stamos's Stamps, there was no sign of the nonagenarian. He ran toward the bus stop for the route that went nearest to Quirklyn, and from blocks away he could see the old man moving as fast as his rickety legs could carry him. Although he was tall, he looked thin as a reed, like he'd snap if someone tapped his waist.

"Paul!" he shouted.

The man either didn't hear or was ignoring him.

"I'm not going to hurt you, please," Uli said, catching up with him.

"I can't believe . . ." Paul was winded and sweaty. "I'm so dumb . . . I would've figured this out a few years ago . . . but my brain's just not turning like it . . . used to."

"Paul, if I was going to kill you, I would've done it when I first saw you."

"Maybe, and maybe not." Paul was trying to flag down a cab on Jackie Wilson Way.

"You have to trust me. This entire place can drive you insane with paranoia."

"Shit! I can't believe she wound up in this dump."

"Who?"

"My little Bumble Bea!" he yelled, and slapped the side of a corner building. "I gave the Mayers enough money to get her out of town; I gave them the damn house. I can't believe my own daughter is stuck . . . in this toilet bowl!" The man's withered face was crinkled up with tears.

"It's going to be okay, Paul. She's a good woman. You should be proud of her."

"I spent nearly a year trying to detonate those bombs, but I kept thinking of her, and I couldn't bring myself to . . . ruin her future. As God is my witness, I tried to take those damnable things down!"

"I know, I saw you try," Uli assured him. "Like I told you, I had these visions—memories, *your* memories—in my head. Memories of your life, from boyhood right up until you got sent here."

"If you really saw my memories then you should know what I

know," Paul said, still waving for a cab. "Hell, you should know why I'm distressed right now!"

"I don't see your memories anymore. They ended when you got on the plane to Nevada."

Paul shook his head in disbelief as a solicar taxi finally appeared on the horizon.

"Look, I saw you fall in love with Millie as a young man in college," Uli explained. "I saw your relationship with your first wife go sour as you became obsessed with your brother. I saw you lose your pool club in Pennsylvania during the Great Depression, and I saw Lucretia—"

"You saw her!"

"Yeah."

"Did you see what happened to her?" Paul asked desperately.

"What do you mean?"

"I mean, who the hell killed her?!"

"I only saw what you saw: the chairman of your high school science department notifying you and the police driving you to the hospital—"

"All right," Paul interrupted, "did you see how I was able to extract the radioactive material from the fluoroscope machines?"

"The pitchblende in Leon's scrapyard? Yeah, I saw that."

"And how I was able to make it into a weapon?"

"Through the sneakers."

"No, before that. Did you see how I set up a triggering mechanism?"

"You mean those little metal things that popped open when they detected radioactivity?"

"Good boy." The old man sounded almost happy. "And did you see where I got them?"

"No, I just saw you on the pay phone on 4th Street and Broadway in Greenwich Village."

"But didn't you see *who* I got the number from?"

"You mean in Washington?"

"Yes! Who gave me the information so I could get those detonator caps?"

The taxi finally screeched to a halt in front of Paul.

"You mean that old guy you fought with down in Mexico—Vladimir?"

"Did you actually *see* Vladimir give me the caps?" Paul was growing increasingly lucid.

"No! No, he never gave them to you." Uli knew he was being tested. "He just gave you a phone number—"

"You saw *him* give me the number?" The old man wasn't giving up anything; he was steering Uli toward something he had already witnessed—Paul wanted proof that he wasn't lying.

"Yeah, you approached Vladimir in his car, near the Russian embassy in Washington, DC, and he gave you a number to call."

"*He* gave me the number?"

"Yes, *he* gave you the number."

Paul made a discouraged face and popped open the solicar door, which meant that Uli must've answered incorrectly.

"You gave him back his old pocket watch," Uli added as Paul slowly pulled his long, skinny legs into the vehicle. "Years earlier, he told you to contact him when you were ready to start the revolution."

Slamming the car door closed, Paul didn't respond to Uli, instead directing the driver to step on it. Uli watched dejectedly as the taxi sped off, not knowing why Paul had been so upset.

As Uli slowly started walking back toward the Williamsburgh Savings Bank Building, he tried to recall those chilly days Paul had spent in Washington pretending to be homeless. The elderly man had been hoping to reconnect with an acquaintance whom he hadn't seen in over half a century. As he recalled the events, Uli suddenly realized that Paul was right: he never actually saw Vladimir again after that incident when he stopped his car.

"It was that other guy, the ugly one who gave you the dollar," Uli said aloud, as though Paul were still there. He felt like an idiot: they had spoken about that man when they met less than a week ago. Stopping, he closed his eyes and felt it—a freezing-cold day in Washington, DC. A man was coming toward him. The man's coat collar was pulled up over his hard face, hiding his mouth.

Uli now remembered that Paul had seen that same face more fully, three years later . . . in Manhattan, the night Paul had tried to remove the first pair of sneaker bombs with his long aluminum poles. He was the same cocksucker who tackled Paul and broke his bomb-disposal device.

"Holy shit!" Uli uttered, grasping why Paul was so terrified and distrustful. It was Scouter Lewis! The son of a bitch worked for the Russians, passing the phone number to Paul, and later it was Lewis who had prevented him from removing the sneaker bombs from the traffic lights!

Paul must've just spotted him entering the Williamsburgh Building. But Schuman had suspended Scouter after the murder of the two council cops. What was he doing here?

Uli raced back into the lobby, through the crowd of spectators who had come to see the Erica Allen Rudolph trial.

"Did you see Scouter Lewis come in here?" he asked the sergeant at the door, who was clearing people as they headed over to the elevator and then up to the courtroom.

"Who?"

"Scouter Lewis from the council cops!"

"Yeah," said a gangcop who was assisting the sergeant. "He went up about twenty minutes ago."

"The man was suspended pending an investigation! Why did you let him in?" Uli shouted.

"Mallory explicitly said that every citizen, even Piggers, could view the trial provided they allow themselves to be searched first," the gangcop replied. "He didn't even have a fingernail clipper on him."

Uli deduced that Lewis could only be here for one reason. Immediately, he asked the sergeant to call up and have him arrested.

"The man is a potential assassin," Uli told the sergeant after he got off the phone. "On my authority, instruct the bailiff to have Ms. Rudolph brought back to her cell until the threat is over."

The sergeant got back on the phone, but just held it to his ear for a while. Uli wondered why he wasn't passing along the orders.

"How many?" the sergeant finally asked, and his face paled. Then, turning to his assistants, he shouted, "Clear the lobby right now! We got victims coming down!"

One assistant pulled out a bullhorn and announced, "ATTENTION! ALL ARE ORDERED TO IMMEDIATELY VACATE THE PREMISES!"

"What's going on?" Uli asked. One security guard stopped any additional people from entering, and two others began physically blocking and directing the crowds.

The sergeant explained that an explosion had just occurred on the fifth floor. According to the guard up there, at least ten people had been killed, including the judge, both surlawyers, and four court officers.

Moments later, ten severely injured people wearing shredded and bloodied clothes were helped out of the smoky elevator. The next elevator held less-injured people, and soon they were ferrying the minor injuries down.

Uli noticed two men, including the large bodyguard, tending to a bloody and semiconscious Joe Gallo. Apparently, his key reason for coming to the building had not been to meet with Uli but to bring his kids to the sandbag-bombing sentencing.

It wasn't until all the wounded and the spectators had been brought down that the gurneys were wheeled up so that the deceased could finally be ferried out. Uli was surprised by the fact that neither Scouter Lewis nor Erica Allen Rudolph were among the living or the dead. Gallo's two teenage boys had been killed. Uli finally squeezed his way past the last of the evacuees and headed up to the fifth floor— he wanted to see the wreckage for himself. The smell of burned plastic immediately confirmed his suspicions: it wasn't a huge bomb, but effective at close range. Nobody seemed to have a clue how anyone could've gotten it past the security.

"What exactly happened?" Uli asked the bailiff, Feingold, who had been stationed at the door.

"A group of people entered, including one young fellow holding a box. I should have stopped him, I just knew something was off."

"A box?"

"Yeah, but there were a lot of bags and stuff, all checked or stopped downstairs."

"Then why did you think something was off?"

"He was muttering something to himself, over and over."

"What?"

"I didn't hear. Then, instead of taking a seat in the benches, he marched right up to the front of the room. The other bailiffs saw him right away, and several were rushing up toward him when he blew himself up."

"What blew up exactly?"

"The box, I guess. It looked like it was for a cake or something."

Uli recalled the yellow box Scouter Lewis had said he found in the dead council cop's desk. He also thought of what had happened to him when he first came to his senses in Rescue City—the apparent brain implants had caused him to repeat detailed instructions to assassinate a politician. Someone had tried to turn him into a living bomb, but he had snapped out of it before reaching his target. Uli wondered if the same thing might've happened here.

54

"What was your life like before?" Marsha asked, a frequent question in Rescue City for people who first met there.

Bea talked about living in the Lower East Side, working as a part-time cashier at the 8th Street Bookshop, and volunteering for a group that protested—and effectively stopped—the construction of the Lower Manhattan Expressway. "But . . . but . . ." Bea remembered that she had to preserve the Valerie Solanas lie, and she really knew nothing about the woman's life. She nervously covered her face with her hands and mumbled, "It was all such a blurry nightmare, I just prefer to forget it."

"Was it 'cause of Andy Warhol?" Marsha asked, running her fingers through Bea's short hair.

"Oh God, the man was just out of control."

"In what sense?"

"It was all very disturbing. I've just tried to block it out." Bea thought, *I have to tell her, I have to tell her the truth!*

"You can tell me anything, dear," Marsha said, gently rubbing Bea's back.

"Please don't ask me to relive it." Bea cringed, pretending that Warhol was the source of all her anguish.

55

Even though Uli was no longer part of the investigation, the attorney general relented and let him interrogate Erica Allen Rudolph one more time. Her surlawyer had been killed in the courtroom blast, and could no longer object.

Still, Rudolph didn't trust anyone, and she insisted that her new lawyer sit in on the interview. In her cell back in Brooklyn Heights, Uli noticed new cuts on the arms and face, but nothing serious.

"This courtroom attack today," he said, "along with the one at the sandbags and another outside the Williamsburgh Building—I believe they are all coming from outside the reservation, and I think you know it."

"I have my suspicions but I don't know anything for sure."

"What are your suspicions?" When she didn't reply, Uli added, "Four Crapper court officers, your lawyer, and the judge all died protecting you."

Rudolph chuckled.

"What's so fucking funny?"

"You're putting me on."

"I'm what?"

"My suspicions are *you!* You're not from here, you come and all this happens, and now you're interrogating me—that's what's funny!"

"How about the thousands who died when you blew up the sandbags, was that funny? Oh, I guess it's okay because you killed them for God."

"You just said some outsider interfered."

"Yes, but you still ordered the attack, which makes you equally guilty."

"That's why I'm pleading guilty."

"So you did order the attack?"

"I thought they were just going to bomb the Crapper whore, I didn't think they would blow up the sandbags. I wouldn't have been a part of that. But ignorance is no excuse. I take full responsibility."

"And by taking responsibility and pleading guilty, you're ending the investigation, thus preventing us from capturing the real murderers."

"That's not my doing. I'm only accountable for my own guilt."

"If you have enough of a conscience to know you're guilty, you should know that the real perpetrators need to pay for what they did." Uli paused. "Who were they?"

"A man approached us with a plan to get rid of the Crapper whore and said all he needed was a little help."

"What kind of help?"

"He said he had the vehicles and fertilizer, he even had a driver. He just needed three more bodies behind the wheel. His name was Tim."

From the recesses of his own brain, Uli recalled a name: "Tim Mack?"

"I don't know."

"A short, muscular man?"

"I never saw him, just spoke to him."

To show her that she wasn't the only source of information for him, Uli said: "I already confirmed that Marsha was there when I woke up."

"Good for you."

"What I still want to know is how the hell you found me."

"I told you—honestly, you found us."

"How?"

"A couple weeks after the bombing, Lyle opened the door and there you were. We thought you were some bum who had fallen asleep on our doorstep in the Bronx. We stepped over you, figured you'd eventually sober up and leave. About an hour later, the phone rang and some guy told us who you were."

"Was it Tim?"

"No, it was a different voice."

"What exactly did the caller say?"

"That the man lying in front of our house was payback for a job well done. Then he hung up. This was after the sandbag explosion, so we were a little paranoid. Finally, I went out and looked you over. That's when we realized you were in bad shape—malnourished, barely breathing. I also noticed severe burns along your back, neck, and legs, and you were seriously dehydrated."

"Then what?"

"Marsha showed up. She said that Rolland asked her to come. The three of us carried you inside."

"And then?"

"Marsha told us who you were, and I remembered that some guy named Huey was wanted by the Piggers awhile back for the murder of Newton Underwood. You matched the *Wanted* poster of him. We heard how Huey was also credited with rescuing Mallory after she had been kidnapped by the Piggers, and that's when we figured we'd try to use you as a bargaining chip if we ever got caught. We didn't expect you to escape first."

Without further questions, Uli thanked her and headed home to his sister's old apartment on the plaza.

Early the next morning, when Uli was walking to his office, some grizzled voice called out, "Hold up, pal."

He turned to see Gallo's enormous bodyguard waiting at the side of the Williamsburgh Building. Uli noticed a black armband over the upper right sleeve of the man's blue jacket.

"I hope Mr. Gallo's still with us."

"He is, but his boys weren't so lucky."

"I'm truly sorry."

"He wants to see you. Pronto."

"Why?"

"Information."

"Where is he?" Uli asked.

"Near. You got nothing to worry about, it's safe."

If the man wanted to kill him, Uli figured, he would've just done it, so he followed the guy off the vehicle-free plaza to a brand-new solicar parked in a guarded lot a block away. In silence, the two drove south through the endless rows of small look-alike streets of residential Brooklyn. As they got closer to Sunset Park, the churches were adorned with onion-topped domes and there were large statues of upset men inciting the masses—leftover Russian landmarks from when the area was a military training ground.

Speeding alongside a dark, empty field, Uli saw the outline of headstones and realized it was the Green-wood Cemetery, where he had been attacked on his second day in Rescue City. Ten minutes later they were heading over the Zano Bridge into Staten Island. Uli was about to complain that he didn't know this was going to be such a long trip, when the bodyguard peered into the rearview and made a screeching U-turn back toward the bridge. He was making sure he wasn't being tailed.

Twenty minutes later they parked in the narrow driveway of a small run-down building in Bay Ridge, Brooklyn. Two men in sweat suits with greased-back hair and gold chains sat outside puffing cigarettes. The woolly mammoth bodyguard had to turn sideways to fit through the doorway. In the entrance was a large crucifix with candles lit at the base. The place reeked of mothballs.

The man led Uli upstairs, past a large woman working in a steamy kitchen. In a dimly lit bedroom covered in dark drapes, the gang boss was lying unconscious, his body bandaged up like a mummy, IV tubes dangling from both arms. When the woman came in and checked Gallo's blood pressure and temperature, Uli realized she was his nurse.

"Please wait outside," she said to them as she prepared a hypodermic.

They went into a sitting room where an old photo album lay on a side table. The large man flipped on the TV, but when he fell back into a chair, he groaned in pain.

"You okay?"

"That fucking blast threw me across the room." He took off his jacket. There were spots of blood covering the front of the man's extra-extra-extra-large shirt. He pulled out a small metal tin of bandages and a tiny dark bottle of iodine, which he shook and put down. Yanking his thick black tie to one side, he unbuttoned his white shirt. Uli watched squeamishly as the man delicately removed a stained bandage over his sternum. There was a large, crusted bloodstain shaped like a giant clam right in the center of his chest.

Even Uli could see he desperately needed stitches—if not a skin graft. He tried to focus on other things as Gallo's crony cleaned and rebandaged his wound. Before he was done, the nurse came in and announced that the boss was ready for company.

The bodyguard quickly buttoned up, pulled his suit jacket back on, straightened his tie, and led Uli back into the bedroom. One blood-filled eye was peeking through layers of fresh gauze.

"On behalf of the mayor and attorney general, I'm so sorry for the loss of your sons."

"I was shipped here with everyone else ten years ago," Gallo whispered. The two strips of bandage over his face twitched back and forth as he continued: "In all that time, a lot of people came to despise me, but no one has ever so much as uttered an unkind word. Yesterday my boys were killed, and if I didn't have the resources to get top medical aid, I'da been dead as well."

"You weren't the target of the attack."

"This isn't about vengeance," Gallo said with difficulty. "But if in a few days this cocksucker's head isn't hanging from my lamppost with his balls in his teeth, then *my* head will be there, *capisce*?"

"Believe me, we're doing everything in our power to—"

"I heard you have a suspect."

"Actually, we have a couple."

"You asked me for someone's location." Gallo nodded to his goliath bodyguard, who gave Uli a card. "There's his number and address. Now, I think you have a suspect for me."

"Like I said, I have a couple," Uli responded.

"You have *one* name," Gallo corrected, looking at him severely with his single bloodied eye. Uli glanced nervously around the room. "Here's how it's going to work: you're going to tell me who he is, I'll call you and let you interrogate him as long as you need to, and then he's mine—understand?"

Uli knew Gallo was smart, powerful, and incredibly angry. He decided to level with the man. "Whoever did this used plastic explosives. That means they didn't come from the reservation, because you can't get that here. Even my suspect doesn't have that kind of power or abilities, but I think he must know who does, or who's behind it."

"And his name is . . ."

"It's probably the same person or people who hit the sandbags."

"I need a name!"

"I might have someone who would know who's behind this, but he's very intelligent and resourceful, so it'll take a lot of luck, interrogation, and footwork to get to the real culprits."

"So, you'll tell us this guy's name, and we'll help you find out who's behind it."

"An investigation is like working out a math problem—it's loaded with hypotheticals, all of which need to be proven; many times they lead to other places . . ." Uli noticed that the grizzly bear as well as two other large men were inching their way toward him.

"Unless the next two words out of your mouth are the name of the—"

"Scouter Lewis," Uli blurted out. It wasn't entirely out of fear. The man appeared to be in hiding anyway, and he was very cunning. Uli thought this might actually be his best chance of apprehending the man. Even if Lewis got whacked, between what he did to Paul Moses and the rest of New York City, he certainly deserved whatever awful fate befell him.

"We need a description," said one of the bodyguards.

Uli provided a brief description of Lewis. Gallo's bloody eye was blinking—he was beginning to nod off—but his sidekick took out a notepad and scribbled it all down.

"I hope you'll keep your word and allow me to interrogate him first," Uli said. "Otherwise you might be letting the guilty parties get away."

Gallo's eye stayed shut. His wrappings were no longer twitching, so the large bodyguard grabbed Uli's forearm, walked him back out to his car, and silently drove him back up to the Williamsburgh Building.

As Uli got out, he realized that even if Lewis knew the answer, he would probably never say a word. The man was tight as a clam.

56

The morning of the second Domination Theocracy sentencing trial in Brooklyn, a Monday, Joe Brainard awoke shivering in his bed, which was soaked through with sweat. He began to wonder if the pills were real or if he was just being given a placebo to help keep him working for the VL. He showered and slowly, tiredly made his way to his car. He had to pull over twice to doze before he could reach his destination.

Though he had initially refused to get involved in this exhaustive task—and then only agreed to do it because his life hung in the balance—the Brain had come to see the true importance of Quirklyn. It was nice to feel optimistic in a place where hopefulness had long since dried up. As he finally pulled into the last leg of his drive, reaching the narrow roadway between the dunes marking the entrance to South Ozone Park, he came to an abrupt halt.

There they were! Gangs of shirtless men whom Bea had somehow mustered out of thin air. They had been divided by Jack Healy's borrowed force into seven working groups. Each had been given shovels, and they were digging along the four-block stretch of packed sand marked off with a series of wooden stakes, connected by red ribbons going every which way: prospective trenches. Both confused and amused by the sight, the Brain U-turned and headed over to East New York to visit Councilperson Ondine.

Since taking the pills, Ondine's health seemed to be steadily improving.

"Where did you get this stuff?" He was amazed that he was getting his strength back.

"The black market."

"I've called everyone I know, and no one has heard of pills for this Satan Island Fever."

"Keep it to yourself if you want to keep getting them, okay?" the Brain said.

"But I have friends who are sick."

"Look, the truth is, whatever you got, I got it too! I'm splitting my prescription with you, and if I could, I'd split it with everyone. But since I've divided my script, I've been getting weaker."

Brainard soon left to check out the line of garrison houses built by Gordon Clark, the VL designer in charge of erecting defensive bulwarks along the southern edge of Quirklyn. Work seemed to be going steadily, so he continued to Bushwick on his survey of the breakaway districts.

Back in South Ozone Park that afternoon, Brainard learned that a bunch of the younger, more energetic SOP residents had grabbed shovels and joined in, digging the crisscrossing trenches along the western edge of the Aqueduct field. A dozen piles of dirt, dug up from the trenches, divided the old track.

Before starting his long drive back to Staten Island, the Brain gave one piece of advice to Jack Healy: "If the Piggers ever do attack from across the field, those mounds you created are going to provide protective barriers for them. You might want to flatten them out quickly."

"That's a great idea!"

Brainard assumed that Healy was being sarcastic, and left.

Healy called all four districts trying to get his hands on as many boxes of screws, washers, nails, and ball bearings as he could, explaining that he needed them for the new bridge project at Hawtree.

By early evening, his labor force had swelled so considerably that Healy had Antonio Lucas take a bunch of them over to Hawtree Pass. The entrance to SOP was shaped like a wide funnel along the airfield highway; Healy explained that he wanted a deep, long pit dug right at the base of that funnel where it narrowed into the dunes.

"How deep?"

"Deep! Twenty feet, but I want to put in wooden supports so the sand doesn't cave in. And I don't want anyone to be able to climb up it."

"But how are we going to get in and out?"

Healy explained the plan he had discussed with Valerie and Brainard—building the narrow bridge over this new moat, making SOP far more defensible.

If just one Pigger were stationed on the rooftop of the Pure-ile Plurality compound, they'd have a perfect view of the work being done to keep them away, but as of yet—fingers crossed—none had been spotted in the vicinity.

* * *

The next afternoon, the Brain drove back through Quirklyn to South Ozone Park, but he couldn't enter. The only entrance was cut off by a brand-new moat.

"All we need now are alligators."

It was at least twenty-five feet down by twenty feet across, with wooden structures on both sides holding back the dunes. Patrick Healy, one of the heads of security for SOP, explained to the Brain how to crawl around the hastily erected wooden ledge in order to get through. Once on the far side, he was offered a bike so he could pedal down to Bea's house.

After less than a block on the bike, the Brain screeched to a halt and gasped: the Pigger invasion had already begun! Instead of crossing the field, a dozen strange men, all wearing formal dark suits, were climbing down from the steep dunes that buffered the community from Rockaway Boulevard. The Brain watched as they tumbled, brushed themselves off, and stiffly marched down Billie Holiday Street. They pulled out their walkies and started combing through the area. In another moment, however, the Brain realized that they couldn't be soldiers.

He pedaled up alongside one of them, a short, bald black man, and asked what was up.

"Our supervisor vanished. She was last seen around here on the night of the election, so we thought maybe someone around here saw her."

"It would've been better if you went through our checkpoint," the Brain admonished.

"Well," the man chuckled, "in the event someone *has* abducted her, we figured we needed the element of surprise." He handed Brainard a flyer with Marsha Johnson's face; it listed her height as well as a phone number to call if she was sighted.

The Brain glanced around nervously to see if they had noticed the spike trenches that had been built the day before. He immediately saw something that enraged him: all the sand displaced from the digging, which should've been evenly scattered, was still in a dozen evenly spaced piles. Each mound rose roughly four feet high and offered solid defenses for possible attackers.

He didn't see Jack Healy, so he decided to try to speak to Bea first. When he resumed biking down to her house, he found Reggie on the front porch pacing back and forth.

"Is she home?"

"Oh yeah. They both are. Been at it all morning."

The Brain rapped loudly on her door and waited a couple of minutes until it opened a crack. "Valerie, we have to talk," he said.

When she opened the door, he stepped inside. Not seeing Marsha, he quietly asked, "How long has she been here?"

"What business is it of yours? Everyone voted for Valerie Solanas knowing full well I'm a lesbian."

He handed her the flyer.

"Oh shit," she murmured, reading it.

"There's a team of PP outreach workers putting these up in South Ozone Park right now."

"No!"

"Did she tell anyone she was leaving PP?"

"Not quite. Things were a little . . . abrupt."

"Bea, this community is fairly isolated. All signs indicate that unless those holy folks from across the field make a stink, the Piggers might actually leave us in peace." The Brain paused. "As far as I know, they didn't say a word about yesterday's work in the field. But this relationship is the kind of thing that could trigger PP into contacting the Piggers."

"I don't think you understand." She was clearly distressed. "We're in love!"

"Bea," he whispered, "we've got a frail victory here . . ."

"I know, but . . . suppose I tell her to go back and square things up with Pure-ile Plurality. Then she can come back here legitimately."

"I can't do that," Marsha said, stepping out of the back room. "Rolland would never let me leave."

"Look," the Brain began earnestly, "our number one priority here is to plant the seeds for an alternative society, a way to end the rule of these two gangs that run this place like a prison yard. We did the impossible, setting up this independent community and winning the elections. You can't lose that for all these people who voted for you."

Tears immediately came to Bea's eyes; sitting down, she had to bite her lip to keep from gasping. Marsha began to cry as well.

"I'll just have to resign," Bea sighed.

"You can't!" the Brain said. "You resign and the Piggers will step in immediately."

"So I'll name a successor."

"If you leave a week after getting elected, they will regard this whole contest as a sham—and rightly so. Then the Crappers will come in to reclaim their lost districts too, and it'll all fall apart."

"How about if I just remain in hiding?" Marsha said.

The Brain took a deep breath and wondered what the hell he was going to do.

57

The next day at work, Uli took out a map of Rescue City and located the address that Joe Gallo had given him. The man he was looking for lived in a community called Little Neck at the northern edge of Queens. He picked up his phone and dialed the number.

"Lotus. How can I direct your call?"

Uli asked for Mr. Grogan.

"May I ask what this is about?"

"I want to ask him about an old acquaintance."

A moment later, a new voice came on the line: "Emmett Grogan speaking."

"My name is Uli Sarkisian, I'm the deputy attorney general for Rescue City South."

"What's up?"

"May I ask what exactly your organization does?"

"We're the only methadone clinic in Queens and the Bronx, why? Did you arrest one of our patients?"

"Did you know Root Ginseng?"

"God!" he gasped. "It's been a long, long time since I heard that name."

"I . . ." Uli was reluctant for a moment. Finally he just said: "I saw her a few months ago."

"Is this a fucking joke?"

"I wish it were. Have you heard of Mnemosyne?"

"That's that bullshit escape drug, isn't it?"

"Didn't Root and your group try to get some?"

"Who exactly are you?"

"Look—I took that escape drug and found myself trapped in a large underground maze."

After a pregnant pause, Uli heard: "So how exactly did you get out?"

"It's a long story, but she was down there too."

"So why didn't you help her?"

"We got separated."

"And she told you to call me here?"

"She mentioned that she worked with you in San Francisco, with the Diggers."

"And now you want methadone?"

"I just wanted to confirm her story."

"You found her name somewhere, you know I'm in charge of the clinic, and you figured you could manipulate me—nice try." Grogan hung up the phone.

No sooner had Uli put the phone back in its cradle than it rang again. Thinking Grogan was calling him back, he immediately picked up.

"Where the fuck is my car?" screamed the voice on the other end.

"Who the hell is this?"

It was LaCoste, the lieutenant from East New York. Uli said he would get it to him soon and that there was no reason to get nasty.

"I just learned that instead of digging trenches, my seventy-five prisoners were put to work laying spikes and boards and then covering them up."

"I didn't know they were going to do that," Uli said, "but what difference does it make?"

"There's a big difference between defensive ditches and deadly booby traps, asshole!"

"Either way, they'll be used against Piggers, so screw you!" Uli shot back.

"Because of all this chaos from the fucking explosion, my captain came back to the precinct early, so I got caught! Now he says that if he doesn't see two shiny new police cars, pronto, he'll knock me back down to patrolman."

Uli assured LaCoste that he would uphold his end of the deal and drop off his current car. Once he filled out another requisition form he would get the second one over to LaCoste as well.

Sheila stepped into the office and interrupted Uli's call, letting him know that Attorney General Schuman was on the other line. Uli immediately took Schuman's call and discovered that Erica Allen Rudolph and her guard had just been found brutally stabbed to death.

"Was she still being held in Brooklyn Heights?"

"No, too many people knew about it," Schuman said. "Gonzalez moved her to an apartment in the West Village that had just been disinfected."

Since Uli believed that Scouter Lewis had tried to blow her up in an open court, it seemed safe to assume he was behind her death as well. *What was he trying to keep her from saying?* he wondered. Before Schuman hung up, Uli asked him if he knew where Joe Gallo lived in Brooklyn.

"I don't know where he lives. He usually hangs out at the Cicone Social Club."

"Where's that?"

"At the northern edge of Ozone Park, where Queens meets the desert. Why?"

Uli explained that he had a hunch.

Schuman advised him to go through Deputy Attorney General Gonzalez if he was planning to act against Gallo. Uli considered heading upstairs and asking one of the council cops if they could escort him to Ozone Park, but he feared that most of them were already on the mobster's payroll. Uli was having trouble trusting anyone right now and was worried about being attacked next, so he asked Sheila how he could get an official gun, which was permitted through his DAG posting.

Sheila went to Tatianna's desk and came back with a poorly mimeographed form—No. TE4-1860. The questions included:

> *Who might be shot by this gun?*
> *How many bullets will you need?*
> *Reasons for gun:*
> **Please note: slugs and shells must be dug out and returned.*

When Uli considered that Gallo could probably get ahold of this form, he tossed it. He couldn't leave a trail.

He took the elevator back down to the lobby, then headed to the first aid station on the fifth floor, where he could grab some painkillers, bandages, cotton swabs, sedatives, and antibiotics—without requiring any permission. He was ready to head north to stalk the human grizzly bear, Gallo's bodyguard, who was far more visible than his convalescing boss.

As he followed a secretary onto the elevator, two gangcops he recognized were clearly trying not to snicker. After the woman exited on the next floor, they burst into laughter.

"What's the joke?" Uli asked.

"Nothing about her," one of them assured.

"Before she got in," the other said, "we were just talking about the whole mess in Howard Beach."

"What mess in Howard Beach?" Uli asked.

"Just stupid stuff," said the first gangcop, with a warning look at the other to keep quiet. The elevator door opened again and the two exited.

Lieutenant LaCoste was inside a courtroom overseeing a tricky robbery trial when Uli tiptoed in and tapped him on the shoulder.

The large redheaded lieutenant gestured for him to step outside. Once they were in the hallway, he yelled, "You owe me a car, motherfucker!"

Uli shushed him; based on what he had heard in the elevator, he said, "You're only pissed 'cause we're invading them now."

"Who the fuck are you working for?" LaCoste asked suspiciously.

"The Piggers tortured the shit out of me at Rikers Island. I'll side with anyone who's against them."

"Look, I held up my end of the bargain."

"So the Piggers *are* invading?" Uli said.

"All I know is that PP is pissed as hell at them."

"Why?" He remembered how Rolland Siftwelt had come over to give the new district his blessing.

"Apparently, that dyke from SOP snuck into their hive and stole their queen bee."

"Who is this queen bee?" he asked, fearing it was somehow related to Bea.

"Some bigwig supervisor there; she's black."

An electric shock couldn't have zapped Uli any harder—he tried to imagine Bea having relations with Marsha Johnson, but the whole thing sounded preposterous. And if that wasn't bad enough, he remembered introducing the two women.

"Are we involved in this?"

"Word is, it was part of a deal Gonzalez had with the Piggers."

"What kind of a deal?"

"When they go in, we take advantage of their attack and reclaim our districts."

LaCoste had to return to the courtroom to keep an eye on one of his rookies, whose fragile case was coming up next on the docket. Uli dashed down the stairwell, out of the building, and into Stamos's Stamps, where he called Bea's number in SOP. Her phone just rang and rang and rang.

That was the limit of his charity for the republic of Quirklyn. Uli decided that he was all out of time too. If Gallo's boys had found Scouter Lewis, the drunk was probably dead by now, and if that was the case, Uli would've lost the only real clue he had to unraveling the mystery of this place.

He sped as fast as he could to the Cicone Social Club in Ozone Park. He had a strange feeling that he was being followed, but every time he looked into the rearview, no one was there.

58

Earlier that day, clutching a cane and a small leather satchel containing all his worldly possessions—the meager accumulation of nearly a century of life—Paul Moses followed Lucille off the Quirklyn bus at Hawtree Pass. A group of guards wouldn't let them enter unless they agreed to being frisked, so they did as instructed. Afterward, they were asked what their business was in SOP, and Paul explained that he wanted to meet the new city councilwoman.

Amused by the notion that this old man was looking for a radical feminist, the security guard led him across the just-completed wooden walkway over the twenty-foot trench. "You can try to see her," he said, "but she's very busy."

"I'll take my chances," he replied.

"If you want to wait here, we have a car that shuttles the disabled and old folks around SOP."

Paul said they'd prefer to walk.

The guard gave them directions to Valerie Solanas's house—four blocks down, at the bottom of the community. Lucille marched angrily ahead of him along Kerouac Avenue, passing the Aqueduct field on their right where Jack Healy and a handful of others were putting the finishing touches on their intricate network of deadly furrows.

Lucille suddenly turned and yelled, "I can't believe we're doing this! You're ninety-three and the temperature is probably the same! You could drop dead at any moment!"

"That's exactly *why* I have to do this now! Today!" He wiped off his sweaty brow.

"You don't even know where we're going!"

"I told you—to see my daughter!"

"You don't *have* a daughter!"

"Yes I do, her name is Bea Moses."

"But this woman's name is Valerie Serious or something."

"She's confused is all."

"No, *you're* confused. Do you know how insane this sounds?"

"Yes, but it's true!"

"Listen to reason, Paul," Lucille cried. "You're going to see a woman who has a team of security guards, and they're going to bonk you on the noggin when you try to tell them she's your daughter."

He ignored her, and just kept shuffling along until he needed a break. He sat on a curb, breathing heavily as Lucille stood over him, offering shade. Twenty minutes later, they finally reached the large home at the corner of Wharton and Kerouac. Nearly collapsing and drenched in sweat, Paul hobbled up to the official residence of Councilperson Valerie Solanas, and a towering guard stepped forward. Three others were sitting down nearby, playing cards.

"Can I help you, sir?"

"I'm here to see my daughter," Paul panted.

"Your daughter?"

"He's a little confused," Lucille said, limping up behind.

"I'm sorry, but your daughter's not here," the large man said gently.

"She's in that house and I mean to speak to her."

"Your daughter is not here, sir," said a more forceful bodyguard, putting down his cards.

"She sure is, and if you fetch her, you'll see for yourself."

"Okay, pal, it's nap time." The second guard began lightly pushing Paul back toward the street.

"Hey! I've been on this earth nearly a hundred years and I know my daughter!"

"Now take it easy, Paul," Lucille soothed.

"Sir, please leave the premises," said the first man.

Paul suddenly lurched forward and took a swing at the other, larger guard.

The first one stepped in just in time to catch Paul's bony fist as if it were a softball. He didn't want this confused elderly man to get himself injured by one of the young hotheads on the security force.

As Paul shouted and struggled against the man, the front door opened and Bea poked her head out. "What's the problem?" she asked.

"Some crazy old coot," the larger security guard said.

Bea watched from twelve feet away as her bodyguard Reggie yanked the fellow's arms behind his back. In a moment, his thin and trembling wrists were cuffed together.

"Easy there!" Paul yelped.

"Says he's your father," the second guard said with a smirk.

"Hold up!" Bea barked, and walked down the steps.

"Bea!" Paul said, staring at his daughter. "Bumblebee! It's me!"

"Her name is Valerie Serious," Lucille corrected him.

"Dad!" she shrieked, recognizing the old man whom she had last seen over twenty years ago. As one of the security guards clipped the plastic cuffs binding Paul's wrists, Bea hugged and kissed him.

Utterly baffled, everyone else gaped.

"Who the hell is Bea?" the larger guard muttered.

"My God!" Lucille said, equally bewildered.

Bea led her father and his girlfriend into her house. Fortunately, Marsha was taking a shower upstairs, away from all the action.

59

"What the hell are you doing in Rescue City?" Bea asked. She was having trouble controlling her emotions.

"After the bombing, I was brought here like everyone else," her father explained tiredly.

"I mean, where have you been for the last twenty years?"

"I'm sorry, sweetie, I just . . . I was such a wreck after your mother died. I drank every day, I was committed for a while. I lost it, and I couldn't put you through that."

"You used to come and visit me," she said softly, "then one day you just stopped. I thought I had done something wrong." Tears came to her eyes.

"I never stopped seeing you, I just couldn't . . . speak to you anymore." He felt his throat tense up. "I used to watch you leave school and walk home, I just felt too ashamed to approach you." He held her and she hugged back, and the two wept.

"God," she said, staring at all the lines on his face, "you've gotten so old!"

Both broke out laughing.

"Believe me, I tried to stop aging," Paul said. "Then I kept waiting to die, but it just wouldn't happen. I probably would've killed myself if it wasn't for you—hoping to see you, to be with you again." He paused, then asked, "So what's this Valerie Serious thing all about?"

"So-lan-as," she pronounced. Then she filled him in on how the Quirklyn Party was trying to end the tyranny of gang violence, and that she needed him to pretend he was an old friend, not her dad. He had to call her Valerie.

"Valerie," he tried it out. "It's a nice name. Sure, I'll play along." He told her that he and Lucille were living in East New York, but was afraid they might be too exhausted to make it all the way back home.

"You have to stay with me," she said. "I got a lot of room here."

No sooner did he agree than Bea realized that if she introduced him to Marsha, she might figure out that Bea wasn't Valerie Solanas at all. "Actually, there's a really nice place right next door, with a lot more privacy."

"Whatever's easiest," Paul said.

She called Jack Healy, but since he was out, she got Antonio Lucas instead. Bea asked if an old friend and his companion could stay in the guest room, assuming Joe Brainard wasn't there. Lucas said that was fine, the unit was empty.

As soon as they were situated, Paul and Lucille collapsed on the small bed and fell fast asleep.

60

Earlier that morning there had been a meeting with each of the men whom Rafique had assigned to protect the infant city of Quirklyn: David Wojo of Green-Burg, Jean-Michel Gaillard of Bushwick, Keith Bowers of East New York, and Jack Healy, who was standing in for South Ozone Park. They were sitting in Rafique's office at the top floor of the old terminal building when Joe Brainard arrived after a bad night.

"We got a big problem," the Brain said.

"We heard," Rafique replied tiredly. "Bea's gone dyke." News of her sexual transformation was the buzz at the VL.

"And I'm the last person to begrudge her that," the Brain said, "but yesterday, for the first time, we spotted Piggers around SOP." Knowing that Rafique would have a fit if he knew, he didn't mention the suited PP members who had been posting signs throughout the neighborhood regarding their missing supervisor.

"How many men did you see?" Gaillard asked.

"Three: two on the roof of PP, one on the dunes just north of SOP. I don't think anything's imminent, but . . . ."

"If it's all because of this PP woman," Bowers said, "maybe if she returns, the problem will go away."

"But she's not leaving and Bea won't throw her out," the Brain explained. "She's in love."

"What happens if we just go in, grab her, and toss her out ourselves?" Wojo asked.

"Bea will leave," the Brain said.

"She was supposed to help us with the election, and she did a great job," Rafique said. "So maybe it's time to let her go."

"The Piggers are still claiming that the election was a fraud, but the people in the neighborhood really like her. If she leaves now, Izzlowski and the Piggers will move in the very next day, I guarantee it."

"As best as I can see," Rafique said, "that just leaves us one choice: we have to abduct this Marsha person and make it look like PP took her back."

"And do what with her?" the Brain asked.

"Leave her in front of PP."

"But she's in love too. She'll just go back to Bea."

"At least they'll see that we're not holding her," Rafique said with a shrug.

"But if she comes back—"

"Joe! We have to do something," Bowers broke in. "Otherwise, we'll lose the whole enchilada."

"Can you get Bea out of the house?" Wojo asked.

"I guess I could have her meet me at the garrison next door," the Brain said. "The real problem is Reggie, Bea's bodyguard. He's very independent and very protective."

"Does he take any days off?"

"Actually," the Brain said, "he seems to always be there; he even sleeps on the porch."

"We'll just summon them both to Staten Island," Rafique suggested.

"On that day," Wojo said, "I'll go in with a couple guys. We'll grab Marsha, cuff her, and dump her in front of PP."

"They have a guard on duty in their lobby, don't they?" Rafique asked.

"Yeah, why?"

"I want Quirklyners to believe PP took her back. And PP should believe, beyond any doubt, that if she leaves them a second time, she does so of her own volition. So they can't blame us."

"And how do we do that?" the Brain asked.

"Have your abductors wear the PP monkey suits, hog-tie her, and dump her right in the fucking PP lobby."

"But once Marsha returns to South Ozone, she'll tell Bea."

"Maybe, but I suspect that this woman is ashamed of what she's doing," Rafique said.

"Why would you think that?"

"Because if she wasn't embarrassed, she wouldn't disappear like a teenager. She'd either discreetly have an affair, or she'd leave PP and accept the consequences like an adult."

"No one can be hurt," the Brain declared emphatically.

"I agree. If Bea or anyone else comes after you," Rafique stressed to Wojo, "just break off and run. And if they catch anyone, don't fight. There's no need for heroics or accidents. Joe will just explain that we had to do this to preserve the peace."

"She'll be so pissed," the Brain muttered.

"What choice do we have?" Wojo said. "Anyway, I'm sure it'll go smoothly."

"If that's it . . ." Rafique was eager to get on with his day.

"Actually, I have another problem." The Brain glared at Jack Healy, who just sat there silently. "I don't like embarrassing anyone, but in excavating the Aqueduct trenches, Jack created a series of mounds that'll be a fortress for the Piggers if they ever attack."

Healy smiled awkwardly. "He's right, damnit."

"I mentioned this awhile ago," the Brain said.

"I'll flatten the freaking mounds," Healy said, "but when am I going to get some men? Right now, it's me, Antonio, Patrick, and whoever happens to drive by. If the Piggers do attack, it'll be over before it begins."

"How many soldiers can your little garrison hold?" Rafique inquired.

"Forty. But we can put an unlimited number in the field and around the area. Any chance we can get some exploding sheets from the Fecal Farm?"

"Don't even bring that up," Rafique shot back. "We do that and they'll know it's us and attack before the day's out. But we have a good stockpile."

"We could also use some men in Green-Burg," Wojo added. "We don't have a field protecting us. They can hit at any time."

Rafique said they might as well start distributing their weapons and drilling the men immediately.

"What kind of arsenal do we have?" Gaillard said.

"What's our weapons count?" Rafique asked Timothy Leary, who had just walked in and was standing near the door.

The quiet man pulled out a notepad that had the tallies of homemade lances, knives, bows, and arrows that had been put together over the past several weeks in anticipation of the possible conflict. "As of last night, 256 spears, 3,008 arrows, 456 lances, 22 swords, 824 machetes . . ."

As Leary spoke, Brainard found himself visualizing wounds from the potential stabbings, slashings, and mutilations. He could imagine desperate young men on both sides, overpowered, shouting for help as they were pierced by these weapons. He rose to his feet, claiming he had to use the bathroom, then stepped outside to smoke a cigarette as Rafique, Leary, and the other members of the militia continued their discussion.

* * *

That night Joe Brainard wrote in his journal:

> *Is the quality of freedom that Quirklyn is offering really that much greater than what the other boroughs offer? I remember my mother saying that it's all fun and games until someone gets hurt.*

61

Uli arrived at the Cicone Social Club around eleven thirty. He parked at a discreet distance and waited outside for several hours until he spotted the grizzly thug—Gallo's protection.

Into the late afternoon, Uli followed the man as he did various chores—shopping for this, picking up that. Around five o'clock, Uli finally saw the bear drive up to a big building that looked like it had once been a bank, just a few blocks from the social club. An American flag and a small glass enclosure with a statue of the Blessed Virgin Mary were fixed on the front lawn; several parked cars were scattered around. Uli knew this had to be Gallo's main home.

He noticed a pair of bikes leaning on the side of the large house. A basketball hoop was set up in the driveway—reminders that the gangster's greatest connection with humanity, his two boys, was forever gone.

If anyone here has the power and resources to locate and seize Scouter Lewis, it's Joe Gallo, he thought. The only question was whether or not Gallo had already found the man. If Uli went in now, and Lewis wasn't being held there, he wouldn't have a second chance: Gallo would probably just torture and kill Lewis—wherever they had him—and dump the corpse in the desert. Uli needed some kind of confirmation that they had the guy. There were garbage cans sitting out in front of the house, so Uli waited until late; when it was pitch black out, he hurried up, opened a can, grabbed two bags of trash, then discreetly walked back to his car and drove off.

Several blocks away he examined his prize: discarded cans, empty liquor bottles, sandwich wrappers, a porn magazine produced in Rescue City, and a mountain of cigarette butts—all the usual debris that half a dozen transposed goombahs might produce in the course of a single day. Occasionally there were crusty bandages, and Uli figured the injured mob boss had been brought there to convalesce. Nothing suggested torture.

* * *

The next day after work, Uli tried calling Bea again; she finally picked up.

"I've been trying to get ahold of you!" he yelled.

"Hey, I've got a district to run!"

"Did you know that Pure-ile Plurality has asked the Piggers to invade South Ozone Park because they're claiming you're having a tryst with their supervisor?"

"Where'd you hear that?"

"Why do they think that?"

"Because it's true," she confessed.

After a moment of silence Uli said, "I didn't put my ass on the line so that you could explore your sexuality!"

She hung up on him.

Uli took a minute before calling her back. Surprisingly, she answered. Instead of being accusatory, he tried to be delicate. "You're not just jeopardizing your own district, you know. If the Piggers go into South Ozone Park, the Crappers will reclaim the districts in the west."

Bea let out a sigh and disclosed that things had grown even more complicated.

"*More* complicated?"

"After not seeing him for twenty years, my father just showed up at my door, out of the blue."

"Great, Paul finally came to your house!"

"How do you know his name?"

Uli ignored the question. "Did he tell you anything?"

"We talked a little, but we still have a lot to work out."

"You and Marsha are still young. Your father should be your priority right now. Can't you just take a break from your relationship until all this blows over?"

"If only love was convenient, life would be so much easier."

"He's got a lot to tell you and there's not much time," Uli said cryptically.

Bea knew that he was right; everyone was saying the same thing. In fact, almost every day since Marsha had arrived, she had been rehearsing in her mind how she would break the news that it was over. Each time she thought of it, she was filled with sadness.

"I've never felt this way before. She's the whole package." Bea could barely speak through her tears. "I'd rather cut off my own hand than lose her."

"I don't want to sound callous, but love comes and goes," Uli said.

"This is so much bigger and more important. You'll see that as you get older."

"Frankly, I wish I could just run off and live in the desert, I really do. But then Joe says the Piggers will grab the district if I'm not here, so I can't even leave."

It sounded to Uli like she was experiencing the very opposite of love.

After getting off the phone, Uli sped back to Gallo's manor. Through binoculars, he watched the doors and windows from a block away. Some time after the garbage cans were put out, Uli snatched a couple more bags, stuffed them in his car, and took off.

At home he sifted through them, and that's when he found it. In the bottom of the garbage bag was a large, bloody towel. Unless Gallo's wounds had suddenly ruptured, it had to be from someone else. Uli hoped it wasn't Lewis, as he doubted anyone could survive losing this much blood. Without immediate medical attention, the injured man wouldn't be long for this world.

It's tonight or never, Uli decided.

62

Two hours later, Uli was waiting around the corner, watching Gallo's home in his rearview mirror. He knew he had to make a move if there was any chance of getting Lewis alive, but it was crucial that he wait for the fewest possible thugs to be in the house before trying to capture the old drunk. Late that night, however, he saw an official city council police car pull up in front. Three officers whom he recognized from the Williamsburgh Building got out. One of them was holding a small wooden box with a handle on top. The other two opened the trunk and pulled out a body. When they put the bloodied victim on his feet, Uli saw that he was still alive. His hands were cuffed behind his back and a blindfold was wrapped tightly over his eyes. But it wasn't Scouter Lewis.

The three of them led the man into Gallo's house. Now Uli recognized the prisoner. He had a distinct handlebar mustache, and Uli remembered seeing him forcibly twirling strands of information right from Scarface's spaghettilike brain, revealing Mallory's whereabouts. So he must be one of those shady government agents who were somehow able to vanish like smoke.

The cops must've abducted the man, and now Uli knew why: they were holding Lewis inside and needed the other prisoner to extract information from him. Most likely they'd kill both in the process.

A minute later, the three council cops left the house and drove away.

Since Joe Gallo's residence was as close to suburban as Rescue City could get, Uli was easily able to walk around to a side window and peek inside. It was a large two-floor ranch-style building. He counted only two guys inside, including the injured grizzly bear. He could faintly hear orders being shouted from upstairs. Uli circled around to the backyard and spotted an open window leading into a dark, empty room lined with odd figurines in the window. Climbing through, he realized it had to be one of Gallo's dead boys' bedrooms. On a bookcase there was a large brass baseball trophy that would make a perfect bludgeon. Uli slipped it into his belt and crept toward the center of the house, where he heard a television set blaring. Above that was a series of low, intermittent thuds and groans—someone was being pummeled. He could also make out two male voices.

Uli heard heavy footsteps approaching and ducked under a long oak table just as the large bodyguard came stomping into the room. A door slammed shut to the left—the grizzly bear had gone into the bathroom. Pulling out the trophy, Uli snuck into the living room, where a second thug was facing away from him, watching the TV. There was no sign of either Lewis or the CIA head scalper. With all his might, Uli whacked the heavy marble base of the baseball trophy across the man's skull, causing the little brass batter to snap off. A toilet flushed simultaneously with a shout from upstairs.

Uli searched the thug's body for a gun, but could only find a long, dull-tipped dagger in his jacket pocket. He rolled the body up against the sofa, out of view from the doorway. Then, sidling up against the side of the living room door with the dagger out, he waited for the human bear to lumber back.

The clumsy footsteps grew steadily closer, but stopped abruptly. Uli saw that one of the unconscious man's feet was sticking out from behind the couch, and the bear had probably noticed, so Uli spun into the doorframe and whipped the dagger upward. The dull tip pierced the giant man's gelatinous neck but missed the jugular. The bear reached up and yanked the dagger out as if it were a splinter, then grabbed Uli by the throat. Uli was able to get off a punch and a kick in the balls but neither strike had any effect and the bodyguard started to crush his throat. Though Uli kept punching and kicking, he was unable to breathe. His vision broke into tiny dots; as he stared forward at the giant man's barrel chest, he dreamily remembered the clam-shaped wound. Using the last of his strength, Uli squeezed his hard, stubby fingers into a claw and shoved forward through the fabric of the bear's shirt.

"Aargh!" the man moaned, but didn't release.

The thick mesh of cloth and bandages folded inward under Uli's fingertips. Uli twisted his shoulder, shoving his whole hand two inches into the man's giant chest, through the narrow wound, scratching into his muscular throbbing heart. Finally, the bodyguard dropped Uli to the ground and clutched at his gaping chest. Uli's hand came out, making a popping sound. Unplugging Uli from his sternum was like pulling a large cork from a wine vat—the blood just flowed from the bear. Gasping for breath, Uli grabbed the dagger from the ground, then felt the giant man's hand clamp down on his back, ready to finish him off. Uli came up quickly and jammed the knife into the man's bloody sternum. Seizing it with both hands, he leaned onto the dagger with his full weight. Slowly, as the thug slid to the floor, he bellowed low.

Taking a deep breath, Uli saw that his own body was bathed in sweat and blood. He stood up for a moment and then fainted on top of the grizzly bear. He must've been out a few minutes before thuds and yelling from upstairs revived him. Staggering into the bathroom, he splashed his face, gulped some water, and caught his breath. Then he returned to the two bodies in the living room.

The bear's shirt was slick with a molasses-thick bloodstain and his huge trousers were drenched in piss. Uli riffled through the man's clothes until he found what he was looking for—his gigantic gun, which came out covered in some kind of talcum powder. Before Uli could inspect how many bullets were in the chamber, a shriek of agony from above pulled his attention away.

Uli dashed upstairs and peeked into a dark bedroom. He could make out Gallo, still lying in bed, out cold, an IV drip hanging overhead. His matronly nurse, the same one from Bay Ridge, was passed out, snoring loudly. She was propped up on her arm, which was leaning on a night table crowded with pills, swabs, a roll of gauze, and several hypodermic needles.

"I can't do it . . . I can't do it . . . I can't do it . . . I can't do it . . ." Uli could hear a voice muttering faintly.

He tiptoed out of the bedroom and down the long hallway lined with nicely framed action photos of Gallo's happy, well-dressed boys. The door at the end of the hall was open, and that was where the noise was coming from. As Uli approached, he saw newspaper pages evenly placed on the floor, as if someone had been painting. Furniture was pushed to one side and the curtains were pulled closed. In the middle of the room, two large men were standing over a single wooden chair. Scouter Lewis was sitting, wearing a tight blindfold. Uli was relieved to see that although he was bloody, he didn't look badly injured. A thick chain, a pair of garden shears, a scalpel, and a lead pipe were some of the implements of torture scattered haphazardly on the floor. Uli looked around for the man with the handlebar mustache and spotted him slumped in the corner; the poor bastard was drenched in blood and had clearly been tortured.

But how were they able to injure him so severely in such a short amount of time? It took Uli a moment to realize that he had made a mistake: the man in the corner wasn't the CIA agent, it was Lewis. The man in the blindfold they were preparing to torture was the CIA interrogator; they had simply clipped his mustache off.

Bound, maimed, and covered in blood, it was evident that they had tried to get Lewis to talk—about what, Uli didn't know. He deduced that only when that failed did Gallo call someone at the council cops, who had managed to ambush this scientist.

"Do it," one of the two thugs said, "or you're dead. It's that simple."

Much to Uli's surprise, the CIA memory extractor had obviously refused to use his sadistic technology on Lewis.

"I can't do it alone!" the scientist growled back. "I need the two other technicians!"

"I'll do it with you, asshole!" one of the thugs snapped.

"Look," the scientist yelled, "the man's too far gone! He might even be dead!"

The second torturer, who was sipping from a cup of coffee, threw the remainder on the lump in the corner. Uli saw Lewis move.

The second thug kicked Lewis. "Hey! Tell the man you're still alive!"

"Be . . ."

"Be what?" the interrogator responded.

"Tell her . . . I'm sorry," Lewis said.

"Who?"

"Bea . . . Mayer."

Uli wondered how the hell Lewis knew Bea.

"This is what's going to happen." They were talking to the memory man. "I'll cut you loose, and you're going to slice his head open and stick that thing on his brain, or—"

"Just kill him yourself."

"We're not killing anyone."

Uli watched the second thug, a tall, fat man, take a small blue canister out of a canvas tool bag, then light it—an acetylene torch. Calmly, the man stepped over and ran the tip of the flame along the bare back of the blindfolded CIA operative.

"ALL RIGHT, I'LL DO IT!" he screamed.

The thug removed the flame and the scientist slumped forward, panting in pain.

Uli realized that neither of the victims was going to survive much longer. Taking a deep breath, he sprinted inside and with all his might slammed the barrel of the massive stolen pistol across the back of the first torturer's skull, knocking him out cold. The other thug, still holding the torch, came at Uli, who pointed the gun directly into the man's face and pulled the trigger. There was a loud click. Uli clicked again—it wasn't working, so he dropped the gun. The man turned the dial, shooting the flame of his blowtorch forward. He waved it at Uli, backing him into a corner. At that moment the burned, blindfold-ed scientist rocked sideways, knocking into the gangster and causing him to drop his torch. As the man went to retrieve the burning can-ister, Uli jumped forward and punched him in the throat twice. The torch lay burning into the floor.

Though he was gagging, the guy was at least a hundred pounds heavier and a foot taller than Uli, and he was able to hit him squarely in the side of his head and send him staggering across the room. By the time Uli recovered, the thug had grabbed a bloody pipe and was coming at him. Uli swept his leg and the man fell into the wall behind him. Snatching up the garden shears from the floor, Uli stabbed one of the long blades right into the bastard's fat throat and held it there.

While the man spasmed to death, Uli realized there was now someone else in the room, staring at him from the doorway—Gallo's nurse. All the noise had pulled her from her sleep.

"Please don't hurt me." She was trembling.

Uli grabbed the acetylene torch, turned it off, and stomped out the fire that had spread onto the floorboards.

"What's going on?" the CIA scientist choked out. He was still blindfolded and lying on his side, tied to the fallen chair.

"Is Gallo awake?" Uli asked the nurse. Taking a piece of rope from the floor, he tied the unconscious thug's hands behind his back.

"No, he's sedated."

"Untie me!" the scientist demanded. Uli grabbed a knife and cut the ropes, then pulled off the man's blindfold.

"Bring me some painkillers and antibiotics," Uli said to the nurse, who was frozen in terror. "Move it!" He turned back to the scientist, who was cringing over his own wounds, and gestured toward Lewis. "Can you help him?"

"Thank you for saving my life," the scientist said, then limped over to Lewis and began a verbal audit of his wounds: "They gouged out one of his eyes, cut off six of his fingers as well as his ears and some of his lips; they burned the hair off his head and the skin off both arms. Why this man isn't dead—I don't know."

"What can you do for him?"

"Without a team of doctors—not much."

When Gallo's nurse returned with various medications and some needles, the burned scientist injected himself with some painkillers, and then used a separate needle to inject Lewis as well. Next, he gingerly applied ointments and other medicines to both himself and Lewis.

Uli picked up the bear's huge pistol and checked the chamber. He saw that a thick, chalky substance had blocked the hammer from striking the back of the bullet. Uli tasted a fingertip of it and realized it was mint. The bodyguard must've had a pocketful of after-dinner mints that, over time, had gotten crushed up and clogged his pistol. Bullets here were so valuable that guns were only used in extreme cases. The pistol had probably been hibernating in that pocket for months. Using a sliver of wood from a cracked floorboard, Uli cleaned out the chamber.

While the scientist and the nurse worked on Lewis, Uli did a tally of his own: two gangsters who likely hadn't seen his face were unconscious, and he had killed two others. The CIA doctor would probably slither quietly back to whatever stone he had been hiding under. That left only one witness who would be able to ID him to Gallo—this poor nurse.

"Can you two help me get him downstairs to my car?" Uli asked.

"If you take me with you," the scientist replied.

Uli agreed.

As the nurse turned to help lift the patient, Uli pointed the gun and fired. The woman was flung forward, splattering blood along the back of the scientist, who didn't so much as bat an eyelash. All he did was fetch the wooden box in the corner and look inside—it was the steel yarmulke that Uli had last seen in the Beth Israel Clinic. Once the crown of skull bone was removed, the device could be clipped over the brain in order to bypass the subject's willpower and have them answer all questions honestly.

"You saved my life," the scientist said to Uli, "and this man is dying. So if you want some kind of information from him, I can give it a try."

"The CIA can keep its Dr. Mengele experiments for itself. Let's try to save him."

Uli grabbed Lewis's upper torso, the scientist grabbed his ankles, and together they carried him downstairs.

"The CIA doesn't operate inside the US," the scientist said as they walked. "We're not with them."

"Then what is it you people are doing here?"

"Our mission dictates that we only deal with memory experiments. But we stumbled into psychic events along the way, so as of a few years ago we started doing those as well."

As they left the house, the sun was coming up. Uli knew that if he didn't get to work on time today, and couldn't produce a solid alibi, he'd never get away with any of this. Despite several tourniquets and compression bandages, Lewis was bleeding all over Uli's car. The scientist said that although no major arteries or veins were severed, if the man wasn't taken to an emergency room immediately, he'd bleed out. Uli also knew that hospitals would be the first place Gallo's men would look.

In the distance, he spotted a city bus. "That bus is heading toward Manhattan and I'm going the other way," Uli said. "I suggest you take it to wherever you're going."

"That's fine," the injured man replied, apparently just glad to be alive.

Uli sped ahead of the bus in order to catch it at its next stop, and gave the man a food stamp for fare. He wished him good luck.

"You saved my life, and I'm sorry about the way things went." The scientist looked strangely at Uli. "You should get out of here yourself before it's too late."

"How?"

"I don't have the authority, but Scouter Lewis does. He owes you for his life. Just tell him you want out."

The partially tortured and bloodied scientist boarded the Q21 as soon as its doors opened. Uli pulled a U-turn and raced off.

63

Spotting the dark towers of PP in the distance, Uli turned left and drove east until he reached Hawtree Pass, then came to a sliding halt. He was shocked to see that they had completely dug out the road, turning it into a small parking lot that ended at a deep trench. A narrow wooden bridge had been erected down the middle. Before he had time to turn around, six Quirklyn guards surrounded his vehicle, peering in at the bloody, unconscious man in the backseat.

"I need to bring this man to Councilwoman Solanas immediately," Uli said.

"What's this about?" asked the ranking sergeant.

"It's confidential, but she'll know. It's a matter of life and death."

"What are your names?"

Uli told him, and explained that the man next to him required immediate medical attention, which was obviously the truth. Uli and Lewis were both frisked for weapons, and the sergeant dashed into his guardhouse and called Ms. Solanas. Uli could hear him giving their names and descriptions, and then the sergeant ordered his men to carry Lewis over the wooden bridge to an awaiting solicar on the far side. Within five minutes they arrived at Solanas's door. The councilwoman was standing outside waiting for them.

"Where's your father?" Uli asked as he helped carry Lewis out of the car.

"Asleep," Bea said, nodding toward the garrison next door. "What the hell happened to poor Blue Cheese Face?"

"He was tortured."

After carrying the man into the guest bedroom, Uli asked, "Do you guys have a doctor or anyone with medical training?"

Bea called up her strategist, a man named Joe Brainard, who in turn contacted the VL in Staten Island, who after a few phone calls of their own informed him that they couldn't get anyone out there for at least a day. They would have to apply their own bandages, antibiotics, and painkillers.

* * *

After an hour, when Lewis finally came to, he moaned, "I need a doctor."

"We're working on it," Bea said sadly.

Lewis whispered a six-digit phone number in her ear and told her to call immediately. "Tell Rufus it's me, and say . . ." He thought a moment. "Say that Antlers is in South Ozone Park."

As one of her aides made the phone call, Bea pulled Uli aside. "Who did this?" she asked.

"First tell me how you know him," Uli countered.

"He was the detective investigating my mother's death a long time ago in Old Town."

"He told you that?"

"I remember him from back in the fifties in East Tremont. Why?"

"He's no goddamned detective."

"Who is he?"

"He was the one who prevented your father—" Uli froze. She probably didn't know that Paul was behind the New York bomb attack. So who the fuck was Scouter Lewis?

"He prevented my father from doing what?" Bea pressed.

"From being with you. It's a long story."

"I need to hear it."

"Ask him," Uli said, searching for a clock. "But if I don't get to work on time today . . . I'm dead!"

"What did Scouter do to my father?"

Uli understood the danger here. "All right, I'll tell you everything, provided you make sure your father doesn't discover that Scouter's here."

"Why?"

"'Cause he'll kill him. And if Scouter dies, I'm stuck here forever."

"If I'm going to risk my ass taking care of him," Bea said, "I need to know *something*."

"I think he was behind the Manhattan bombing, okay?"

"You mean the sandbag bombing?"

"No, I mean the *original* Manhattan contamination. The one that put us all out here in Nevada."

Bea went silent. Uli told her he'd be back as soon as he could to try to fill in some of the blanks. All she had to do was keep Lewis alive until then.

* * *

He made it to the Williamsburgh Savings Bank Building at nine thirty, a half hour late.

Upon arriving at his office, Uli left orders with Sheila that he was not to be disturbed. Locking his door and closing the blinds, he flopped down for a much-needed nap. He would've preferred to stay in SOP with Lewis and sleep there, but he knew that once Gallo's surviving men arrived for the day and saw all the carnage at the house, they'd get around to investigating Uli, among others.

Uli bolted awake when his office door flew open. The other deputy attorney general, Hector Gonzalez, stepped inside without being invited and squeezed down on the sofa next to him. Uli had been avoiding him the past week.

"Did you know that a small army of Crapper prisoners went to the old Aqueduct Dog Track and dug trenches for the enemy?" He was clearly pissed.

"What is it I can do for you, Hector?"

"I don't give a shit what those people do in Queens, but they're squatting in three of *my* districts and I don't like it."

"Why are you telling me this?" Uli yawned and rubbed his fingers through his greasy hair.

"Let me tell you a little bit about *me*. I used to be an idealist. Hell, when I first arrived here, I was in the Burnt Men tribe. No one knows that."

"Hard to imagine you in a teepee." Uli was amused that such a tight-ass was once a hippie.

"In fact, I think we know some of the same people from there."

"Like who?"

"Bea Mayer," Gonzalez said, studying Uli's face. "Would you believe me if I told you we were once like brother and sister?"

Uli didn't say a word or even breathe.

"Now, I would've turned the bitch in the first day she claimed to be Valerie Solanas, but she was in South Ozone Park, and the fact that they took over that Queens community was a big plus for us. It guarantees us access to the airfield."

"Again, Hector, why are you telling me this?"

"'Cause I know you fucked her." The DAG paused and watched for Uli's reaction. "So you must have loyalties there."

Instead of refuting this, Uli just smiled.

"You want to help an old lover, fine. But the Piggers find out that you used Crapper prisoners to dig their defenses and we're gonna pay. And that's where it falls in my lap. And one way or another, I'm gonna get my districts back!" Gonzalez then stormed out of his office.

At that moment Uli realized that the man was on Gallo's payroll. He had popped in unannounced to check on Uli. The fact that he had been sleeping was unfortunate, but at least he was in his office, so it created some doubt. Although Uli sensed that Gonzalez had probably been behind the abduction of the brain cutter, he wondered if he'd had a hand in grabbing Scouter Lewis as well. Regardless, the chubby DAG seemed sincerely tense. He was sitting on something big. Uli wondered if something was up in the breakaway city.

He went downstairs to the courtrooms in search of his favorite unwitting informant. It took fifteen minutes before he spotted Lieutenant LaCoste talking with several of his men. Uli followed him out of the building and onto the plaza, hanging back until the lieutenant separated from the group. Then he sped up, discreetly passed LaCoste, and pretended to be searching for something he had dropped on the pavement.

"Hold up, Deputy Dog! Where's my damn car?"

"Oh, I was going to come by tomorrow!"

"Fine, you have one day."

"Which would undoubtedly be the same day we're attacking Quirklyn," Uli said.

"Give me a fucking break," LaCoste chuckled.

"What?"

"You know, you're not even good at milking people for information. The last person I'd tell about the Quirklyn invasion would be the guy who helped set up their spiked trenches."

"Those trenches are supposed to be used against the Piggers, not us. Ever hear the concept *enemies of my enemies*?" Uli asked.

"They stole our districts!"

"I said this before and I'll say it again: those fucking Piggers electrocuted my balls. You want to see the scars?" He started unzipping his pants but LaCoste waved him off. "Want to know why I helped SOP? Because they're the only one's who are still fighting them."

"Fine! You want information? Give me your car right now and I'll be straight with you," LaCoste said.

"Okay, but if I think you're bullshitting me, I'm not filling out the report for the second car."

"Truth is, no gangcop I know was asked to participate in any action against Quirklyn, and I don't know nothing about no invasion. Now, the keys please?"

"But you *do* know something," Uli shot back. "I know you do."

"Okay," LaCoste sneered. "Little more than a rumor really, but I'll tell you—so that if you *don't* give me my car, I'll have a clear conscience about bashing your fucking skull in."

"Go ahead."

"I heard we've been developing some kind of secret weapon in Hoboken."

"Who's *we?*"

"Hector Gonzalez, probably."

"What kind of weapon?"

"Something involving the air."

"Like an airplane?"

"If someone in this place built an airplane, wouldn't they just escape?"

"*You* said air."

"Pal, you officially know what I know. Now where's my fucking car?"

"Wait a sec." Uli trotted over to the city council parking lot. He showed his ID to the guard on duty and got his assigned vehicle, then pulled up alongside the lieutenant. He stepped out and handed La-Coste the keys.

"It was nice doing business with you," the man said as he drove off.

Uli headed back up to the tenth floor, where after waiting twenty minutes for the attorney general's secretary to return, he duly explained that his car had just been stolen.

"Where?" Tatianna asked, clearly pissed.

"On Seventh Avenue in Park Slope," he lied.

She had him fill out a new requisition form, which took about five minutes. He contritely handed it back and waited for his new solicar key.

"You live here on the plaza, don't you, Deputy?" Tatianna said.

"Why?"

"Then you won't have far to walk. We have a one-car limit. Since you're a deputy attorney general, I gave you an extra car before, but that's it."

"My first car was blown up during an assassination attempt, not stolen."

"Sorry."

"I need a car to do my investigation! Otherwise I'll have to order a lieutenant to drive me, and that'll take both a car *and* a driver."

The executive secretary let out a deep sigh, warned him that this was his very last one, and handed him the key to solicar number 233. Uli assured her that he'd be more careful and left.

As he drove out to SOP, he wondered about this new secret weapon that LaCoste had mentioned. How the hell could he get out to the Hoboken fields to check it out? He knew that there were no bridges over the highly toxic Hudson leg of the canal; the place was strictly off-limits.

By the time he reached Rockaway Boulevard, he had confirmed that no one was tailing him. Soon after, he reached the Hawtree Pass turnoff. There he parked, cleared the security station, and once he was over the wooden bridge, he borrowed a rusty old bike to ride down to Solanas's house.

Minutes later he was being patted down by a guard just as Solanas's driver Reggie arrived.

"Has Scouter's doctor gotten here yet?" Uli asked him.

"Not yet. We've been doing the best we can, but the painkillers aren't working."

Reggie led Uli into Valerie's guest room where they found Lewis writhing in pain, trying to pull his bandages off.

"Why aren't I in Kings County?!" Lewis growled to Uli, recognizing his voice.

"'Cause Gallo's men would grab you within minutes. You killed his sons!"

"I *told* you guys that they were targeting that courtroom! Everyone ignored me! Hell, Schuman took my badge because I defended myself against those two corrupt cops who tried to kill you. And Gallo took my fucking eye!"

"You were spotted going into the Williamsburgh Building just before the bomb went off," Uli said.

"To try to stop those machete-wielding pricks. They're on the brink of burning the whole place down! That's why the sandbags were hit!"

"Who is?"

"Those imitation-wetback motherfuckers!"

Uli inspected Lewis's single eye and decided he was probably high. "For the record, you were never a cop."

"Yes I was, ask Bea!" Lewis yelled. "She told me—"

"She was a kid when she met you," Uli shot back. "She had no idea what was going on . . . Who the fuck *are* you!"

"Aren't I Scouter Lewis?" the man asked nervously. Uli realized that he truly might not have any memory of his life prior to Rescue City.

"You don't remember working in Washington, DC, at the Russian embassy?"

"Hell no! I hate commies!" Then he uncertainly added, "Unless they're working for us."

A handsome young Quirklyn soldier ushered in a man who looked like a showy cosmonaut.

"Where the fuck have you been, Rufus?" Lewis snapped. It was the same mysterious fixer Dianne Colder had requested when her neck was broken.

"I thought you had a safe spot," replied the middle-aged man with combed-back hair wearing a chrome-and-yellow jumpsuit. In one hand he held what appeared to be a tool chest, in the other was a leather medical bag. "Wow. Henrich told me they did a number on you, but I wasn't expecting this!" he said upon inspecting Lewis's wounds.

"I'm in fucking agony!"

Rufus opened his bag, took out a hypodermic, and injected Lewis with morphine until he was out cold. Pulling on gloves, he asked everyone to leave and to close the door behind them for sanitary purposes. Uli stood off to the side and watched as the man delicately removed the oozing bandages that Marsha and Bea had wrapped around Lewis's head and shoulders earlier. Uli had to leave when Rufus used a large syringe to flush out the man's blood-caked eye socket.

When he returned twenty minutes later, Rufus was in the middle of cleaning each knuckle socket. Then he carefully applied antibacterial ointments. As Lewis was being sutured and rebandaged, Uli realized he was muttering something.

When Rufus stepped out to use the bathroom, Uli quietly asked Lewis, "Why'd you blow the Manhattan sandbags?"

"Either the wetbacks or that Manhattan loverboy . . ."

"What loverboy?"

"That other nutjob, dear Deere."

"Deere Flare?"

"Yeah."

"Do you know anything about this secret weapon the Crappers are going to use against Quirklyn?" Uli probed.

"Huh?"

"The one in Hoboken—how can I get there?"

"Take the tunnel," Lewis mumbled.

"What tunnel?" Uli wondered if the injured man was talking about Rescue City or Old Town.

"Oh, but you have to go through the north, 'cause they bricked it up . . ."

"Bricked *what* up?"

"I'm so sorry, Karen. I really am, dear heart . . ." Lewis was growing increasingly incoherent.

"Where's Karen?"

"Not prepped, no air tank, but down the hatch, down the pipe—down down down the drain, poor Karen."

"Wait a second, Karen went down the drain?"

Without warning, another needle was injected into Lewis's arm and he slipped back into unconsciousness. Rufus had given his patient a powerful sedative.

"He needs sleep!"

"You only put him under to keep him from talking to me!" Uli snarled.

"You can ask him anything you want tomorrow when he wakes up," Rufus said, then left the room again.

Uli grabbed him in the foyer and shoved him against the wall. He patted him down for a weapon and any possible ID.

"Get the fuck off of me!" Rufus yelled.

"Who the fuck are you?"

"I'm a doctor, now let me go!"

"What kind of suit is that?"

"Whoever called gave me a code that meant Scouter had found a hot spot. I thought I was here to do a health inspection of this place."

"For who?"

"The EPA."

Uli released him. "The Environmental Protection Agency? How's Scouter involved in all this?"

"He's a liaison officer for outside agencies, as am I."

When they heard moaning, the doctor hastily returned to Lewis's room. "I'd better stay with him," he said.

Uli needed a breather, so he stepped outside.

The young Quirklyn soldier who had been assigned to Lewis followed him. "So what's this about a secret weapon in Hoboken?" He couldn't have been much older than twenty, and had obviously been eavesdropping on Uli's interrogation.

"Mind your own business." Uli was in a foul mood.

"It *is* my business. My name's Pat. I'm one of the security commanders for South Ozone Park."

"I'll take care of it."

"How about we do it together?" Pat said. "I can help you."

"Help me do *what*?"

"Whatever it is you're planning."

Uli sighed. "Well, unless you know some way we can fly across the sewage canal to Hoboken . . ."

"I know where we can get an inflatable raft in Greenpoint. We can take it to the Hudson bend and paddle across to the fields."

"Actually, that does sound like a plan. But it would be a better plan without you."

"You need backup."

"Look, son, I'm a deputy attorney general for All Are Created Crappier, and the Hoboken field is their territory. So, by coming with me, you'd actually be putting us both in jeopardy."

"Then we have to make sure we don't get caught," Pat said simply.

Uli was too tired to argue, so the two men took their bikes up to Hawtree Pass.

"Do you know how to drive?" Uli asked after they crossed the short bridge to his car. Pat said he did, so Uli let him take the wheel as he stretched out in the passenger seat and tried to get some shut-eye.

64

They reached the Green-Burg garrison roughly half an hour later. A tall, skinny kid named David Wojo led Pat and Uli inside. Apparently he was in charge of security there.

"We never took the raft out of the box, so you might want to test it first," Wojo said when they told him their plan. He also threw in two face masks and two flashlights, since it was getting late. "In case the water splashes up, you don't want to get it in your mouths."

As they packed the raft in the back of the car, Uli saw that it came with two little oars that looked like large tennis rackets. Uli thanked Wojo, and they drove off to hunt down the secret weapon in Hoboken.

Eventually the little car puttered over to the western edge of Manhattan, which was bordered by the Hudson bend, the large sanitation canal that snaked around Rescue City. The canal was only about two hundred feet across, but the toxic liquid had a fairly strong current. Fearing it might be difficult to navigate with the tennis-racket paddles, Uli instructed Pat to drive farther north on the West Side Roadway until they finally located a good place to launch up at Riverside Park.

It was dark out when Pat parked. Concerned that he could lose things on the mission and not wanting to leave them in the car, Uli buried his keys, stamps, and ID in the earth nearby. Then he helped Pat take the raft out of the trunk and unfold it. They spent the next twenty minutes taking turns on the foot pump until they started hearing air hiss out of a tiny hole. Fortuantely, it was still usable.

"Kid, I don't want to fight with you, but I'm going to say this one last time," Uli warned. "It would be a lot smarter if I went solo. I can talk my way out of a problem, but I might not be able to if you're with me."

"If you want the raft, you get me," Pat replied. And that was that.

Grabbing the flashlights and removing their shoes for fear of added punctures, the two men strapped their face masks on and gently placed the little float into the canal. Wordlessly they paddled, Pat in front and Uli in back, as the filthy waters carried them southward.

Uli could smell the liquid refuse much more pungently here than in Brooklyn. Along the shores of Manhattan, he saw the evenly spaced sewer pipes intermittently dripping waste into the fetid canal. They were able to navigate more rapidly than Uli had anticipated, and after only thirty minutes, the raft slowly edged up along the Hoboken shoreline. They searched for gangcops, but in the darkness could barely even see the conical orange sentry stations guarding the far side. Pat had great eyesight and noticed a fine line of strings along the shore—either electrified wires or sensors to detect anyone trying to infiltrate. Soon they floated past the last of the stations.

"We're too exposed here," Uli whispered. "Let's head back."

Disregarding him, Pat started frantically paddling toward Jersey. *Shit*, Uli thought, and he started paddling too. Then they heard a *thunk* and felt the little raft jerk to one side. Air was hissing out loudly now, and they could see a volley of arrows sailing overhead.

"Get down!" Uli yelled, and dropped forward.

Pat was trying to navigate, missing the initial volley, but Uli heard him moan and saw an arrow sticking through his arm. The kid didn't utter another sound. No sooner did Uli think, *At least it's not life-threatening*, than a second arrow struck Pat squarely in his lower back. Uli could see its head coming out through his flat abdomen. He grabbed Pat just in time to keep him from falling into the polluted water.

As the raft hissed out air, the current carried them downstream toward the Hoboken side. When the shriveling raft snagged against some rocks, Uli took hold of Pat and heaved him onto the damp, putrid sands of New Jersey, Nevada.

Although the militiaman was bleeding, the flow wasn't excessive. The arrows seemed to have missed all his major arteries. Uli was able to pull the first arrow through the younger man's arm. Pat said the second one didn't hurt too much. Uli took hold of his arm and they hobbled south toward Staten Island. After about five minutes of walking in the darkness, with Patrick steadily losing blood, Uli stumbled on a barrel cactus.

"Shit!" he yelled as the cactus needles pierced his shin. He fell, dropping the injured man to the ground. As he tried to stand, a boot kicked him in his ribs, knocking him down again.

"What the fuck?" Uli groaned.

Another foot stepped on his lower back and he felt a sharp object shoved into his neck. His wrists were yanked behind his back and cuffs were fastened tightly around them.

A second man began applying compresses to Pat, who had passed out. Uli heard one of them say into a walkie, "Yeah, we got 'em."

"Hold on," Uli said.

"Are you Piggers?"

"No," Uli replied. "We were just rafting when we went off course."

"What are your names?"

"I'm Huey, and this is my friend John."

A foot kicked him in the back of the head in response. Two Crapper gangcops carrying a stretcher came over and lifted Pat onto it.

"Where are you taking him?"

"He needs medical care or he'll die."

Uli watched as the young man was carried away. A moment later, Uli was painfully hoisted up to his feet and pushed forward into the darkness. After about twenty minutes of walking, one of the men said, "You know, you're the first assholes who made it all the way across. Usually we get them midstream. When they sink there's no trace."

Uli was marched up to a small outdoor animal cage that could only hold a single prisoner. "Look," he confessed as they opened the cage door, "I'm not who you think I am."

"You're exactly who you were this morning," said someone he couldn't see. His cuffs were clipped and he was locked inside. Hector Gonzalez appeared out of the darkness. "Though I'm not sure about your buddy."

"I just paid him to help me."

"You probably put some time into your cover story," Gonzalez said, "so it'd be rude of me not to listen. What the hell are you doing here, Deputy?"

"I heard the Piggers were going to attack," Uli said.

"That's not even good bullshit."

"I just wanted to see the place for myself."

"See what?" Gonzalez asked. When Uli didn't answer, the DAG looked at his watch and said, "Schuman and the mayor don't wake up until eight o'clock. If I force the truth out of you, it might piss them off, so while I work on your friend, you can try to come up with a better story. How's that?"

"He's been badly wounded," Uli said, hoping for some compassion.

"You have my word that I won't harm a hair on his head," Gonzalez said, and walked off.

The cage was too tight to lie down or sit up straight, so Uli half leaned, half squatted, and worried about poor Pat. When a swarm of mosquitoes started biting his ankles, he was unable to even swat them away.

As the sun came up hours later, Uli realized he was right at the southern end of the Crappers' vast choke field. Rows of tall, leafy cannabis plants rolled endlessly northward. To his rear was a defensive field of small cacti extending to the south and west; beautiful purple flowers with yellow stems bloomed from them, and Uli figured it was peyote.

Two new guards recuffed him while he was still in his cage, then opened the gate. Gonzalez was nowhere in sight as Uli was marched north up a steep slope. For an instant, over the distant fields, Uli glimpsed what appeared to be the top of a large balloon—if there was a secret weapon, that had to be it. When they reached the banks of the canal he was told to jump with his hands still cuffed onto a motorboat.

He was ferried across to Manhattan and loaded into a car, then driven to Midtown.

Uli was shoved into Mallory's office in Rock & Filler Center, where she, Schuman, Gonzalez, and the commissioner of marijuana production, Roche, were all sitting around a large table. Uli's plastic cuffs were finally clipped off.

"Deputy Gonzalez claims he trapped you in the fields of Hoboken," Mallory said without looking at him. "What the hell were you doing there, Uli?"

"Checking out the defenses," he replied.

"Uli, we're not fucking around," Schuman said. "We already found out that you were with Jack Healy, head of the Quirklyn defenses."

"His name is Pat," Uli said. "And they oppose the Piggers, not you guys."

"Are you working for Quirklyn?" Schuman asked.

"I don't care who you're working for. You betrayed us!" Mallory snapped.

"Why they are sniffing out Hoboken—*our* long-established territory—is what baffles me," Gonzalez said.

"What baffles me," Uli responded, "is that—" He was about to suggest that Gonzalez was on Gallo's payroll, but with no proof to substantiate it, he went silent.

"Were you considering an attack?" Gonzalez asked.

Uli knew that if he mentioned he was checking out the possibility of a secret weapon in Hoboken, they'd want to know his source.

"You're under arrest for high treason," Schuman said. "And the penalty is death."

"I suggest a summary execution," Gonzalez added.

"No. He and Karen saved my life—preventing the Piggers from stealing the mayoralty and this government—and he did an excellent job overhauling the gangcops. We owe him for that." Mallory finally looked Uli in the eye. "I'm giving you amnesty, but you're still stuck in Rescue City with the rest of us, and whether you go to Queens, Staten Island, or South Ozone Park, you won't get anywhere near the privilege or luxury we gave you."

"We need your badge, and the keys to your house, office, and car," Schuman said.

"I don't have them." Uli turned his pockets inside out.

"As part of your persona non grata status, we allow you to pass, but you have no rights here," Mallory continued. "You can be grabbed any time you're in our boroughs and arrested for trespassing if you spend the night here. Now, get the fuck out of my sight."

"May I ask where Pat is?"

"His name was Jack. He was extradited last night to Queens, where there was a warrant for his arrest," Gonzalez said. "Sadly, I learned he died of his wounds soon after arriving."

Guards escorted Uli out of the building.

After making sure he wasn't being followed, he walked all the way back up to Riverside Park, where he unearthed his wallet and keys. His car was right where he had parked it. He drove to the first stamp shop he could find and dialed Bea.

Before he could explain anything, she said that Jack Healy, head of Quirklyn defense, was concerned about his missing cousin, Patrick.

A male voice came on the line: "I'm Jack Healy, head of security here. I heard my cousin—"

"Damn," Uli mumbled.

"What?" Bea said, still on the line as well.

"Gonzalez thought the kid *was* Jack Healy."

"Where is he? Where'd you go?" Jack asked.

"I heard about some secret weapon in Hoboken and was going to check it out. I tried talking him out of it, but he insisted on coming."

"Put him on the phone," Jack said.

"As we were crossing the Hudson, he was struck by a couple arrows. He was wounded, but we were heading south until I tripped—"

"What are you saying?" Jack broke in.

"They caught us. He was supposedly extradited to Queens last night, where I was told he died. But it was really that fucker!"

"What fucker?"

"Hector Gonzalez, the deputy attorney general in charge of the city council police force."

Jack explained that he and Antonio Lucas had spent the day before trying to navigate a possible evacuation path over the north end of the Aqueduct field. During that time, he had left Patrick in charge of the garrison, assuming it would be a safe and easy assignment.

"I'm sorry," Uli said softly. "I told him coming would be a bad idea, but he said he could get a raft and I figured it'd be quick in, quick out."

"Fuck!" Jack shouted. "Only Patrick could turn a recon into a suicide mission." He abruptly disconnected.

"Uli," Bea said, "I have bad news. Last night . . . Scouter and that weird doctor vanished."

"Vanished?"

Suddenly, the line went dead.

Not having slept all night, feeling feverish and barely able to keep his eyes open, Uli walked back to where he had parked his solicar. Once there, he rolled up the windows, closed his eyes, and drifted to sleep.

65

It took Bea a second to realize that Uli hadn't hung up on her. The lights in her house had also gone out. Jack dashed off, and Reggie came rushing in to make sure she was okay.

"Where's Jack going?" Bea said.

"He's putting his men on alert," Reggie answered.

Rafique had dispatched forty men under Jack's command to the South Ozone Park garrison. For the past three days, the men had been divided into shifts and posted at key points around the community. The militiamen who wound up in this far-flung district regarded themselves as unlucky—not only had Jack been drilling them nonstop in weaponry, archery, lancing, and knife fighting, he was also the only one of the five Quirklyn security captains who wouldn't allow them to drink or smoke choke on or off duty. Sixty bows, five hundred arrows, two hundred spears, and a hundred lances had been provided to SOP from the Staten Island arsenal.

"Valerie," Reggie said, "Joe is dropping by. Healy said it might be a good idea for you to evacuate with him until this is over."

"I'm the elected representative of this district, I'm damn sure not going to abandon my people. Have Joe take my father and his girl-friend out."

Marsha entered the living room. "Did you call me?"

"No, why?"

"I thought I heard someone shouting my name."

They all listened in silence for a moment until they heard a strange, distant bellow, which slowly grew louder: "MAR-SHA!"

Peering out the window, Marsha, Bea, and Reggie spotted one, then another: two sweaty men running stiffly in their black suits like a pair of human beetles. Instead of trying to cross the dirt field and deadly trench, they were again dashing down from the steep, nearly impassable dunes and along the eastern edge of Kerouac Avenue. Two more appeared running up Edith Wharton Street, holding neck and chest wounds. They were repeatedly shouting, "MAR-SHA!"

A detachment from the Quirklyn militia, positioned along the south side of the trench, charged toward the invaders. One of the men turned out to be Jack Healy himself, holding a lance.

Marsha watched in horror as Healy, still furious about the loss of his cousin, stabbed one of the suited men viciously in the back.

"No! That's Pastor Nestor!" she shouted, running outside.

As the other man turned to help the first, a soldier drove a stake into his stomach. The impaled man ran about ten paces down the road before collapsing.

"THEY'RE PACIFISTS!" Marsha screamed.

"Marsha!" Bea yelled. "Wait!"

Pastor Nestor gasped, "There she is!"

"They raped you for years!" Bea shouted after her.

"No they didn't!"

Marsha kept yelling as Healy grappled with another suited man who had knocked down one of the SOP militiamen. Pulling out a large walkie-talkie, the stiff black suit shouted, "I see her on the corner of Wharton and Kerouac! Marsha, over here!"

Healy tackled the man just after he gave the location.

Moments later, Rolland Siftwelt himself appeared on Kerouac Avenue with his bodyguard and personal assistant on his heels. Bea grabbed Marsha around the waist, trying to restrain her as she shouted, "I'M COMING!"

One of the younger Quirklyn soldiers shot Siftwelt's bodyguard in the back with an arrow. Someone else wrestled the soldier to the ground before he could bow another arrow.

Siftwelt spotted Marsha on the front lawn, ran up, and tried pulling Bea off of her. Bea jumped on Siftwelt. It was Reggie who finally hurried over and helped Rolland, pulling Bea off him and allowing Marsha to break free.

"He's a fucking pervert!" Bea shouted to Marsha as Reggie held her back.

"And you're a shiftless fraud and a charlatan!" Siftwelt countered. Turning to Marsha he said, "This woman is not who she claims to be!"

"What do you mean?"

"She's an impostor!" he exclaimed. As he reached into his back pocket, another Quirklyn militiaman shot an arrow at Siftwelt but missed, hitting his personal assistant in the neck.

"My God, Jed! I'm so sorry, Jed!" Marsha yelled to the mortally wounded assistant.

"Cease fire!" Bea shouted to all around her.

Another PP bodyguard hurried over and helped Jed as blood squirted out of his neck.

Siftwelt shoved a small glossy photograph in Marsha's face. "This is what Jed died for—so that I could show you this! She's a false prophet! You've been seduced by Satan, sister!"

Bea glimpsed the small photo, which had been required for the Rescue City application a decade earlier. Below was a typed caption that read, *VALERIE SOLANAS*. Though similar in appearance, it clearly wasn't Bea.

"Oh my God!" Marsha was aghast. "Who *are* you?"

"I'm sorry." Bea started to approach her.

"Keep away!" Marsha yelled furiously.

Siftwelt began praying over Jed's dead body.

Healy explained to his men that this was not a Pigger invasion, but a poorly timed misunderstanding.

"My name is Bea Moses-Mayer," she came clean to Marsha. "I wanted to tell you from the start, but you seemed so enamored of Valerie Solanas—I was afraid of losing you."

Marsha smacked her lover across the face. "You're just another goddamned liar!"

"Men acting as women, and women acting as men." Rolland shook his head in shame. "We don't get to decide such things."

"I've been seduced," Marsha said softly with downcast eyes.

The philanthropists carried their dead and wounded over to one of the Quirklyn vehicles. From there, they were escorted back to Hawtree Pass. Three members of PP had been killed and two others were wounded. None of the South Ozone Park militia were injured.

It wasn't until an hour later that Joe Brainard arrived. When he learned that three members of PP were dead, he kicked a wall, though he didn't mention to Bea or anyone else that David Wojo had planned to kidnap and forcibly return Marsha to PP tomorrow—one day too late.

"This PP debacle," the Brain mumbled to himself. "We just signed our own death warrant."

66

Word went out that the security in South Ozone Park had repelled a fierce attack. At Joe Brainard's insistence, no one confirmed or denied this. He knew that Rafique would want to deal with this himself on a higher level. In the ensuing hours, those who had seen or heard about it carried distorted details of the news, and word quickly spread westward. Citizens of East New York, Bushwick, and Green-Burg heard that the tiny, far-flung community of SOP had effectively quashed a well-orchestrated assault by an elite team sent from Kew Gardens in Rescue City North. They were happy for their comrades to the east, and relieved because all had assumed the invasion would begin with the Crappers, since Quirklyn was mostly made up of reclaimed Brooklyn land. Because SOP had put down the attack, the hope was that this might discourage the Crappers from doing likewise in the other districts. Soon everyone in the three Brooklyn neighborhoods of Quirklyn began calling their friends in South Ozone Park, wanting to confirm what David Wojo had termed "the Spartans-in-SOPmopylae victory." This overloaded the phone lines.

"We need to be able to communicate!" Joe Brainard was frantic. Healy was able to turn off the phone service to the rest of Quirklyn, only allowing calls coming in from Staten Island.

It wasn't until an hour later that Rafique finally called. He said that despite repeated attempts to connect with Siftwelt through back channels to try to make reparations, no one was taking his calls. Rafique suggested that Valerie Solanas's office issue a statement of sincere regret about the unfortunate events. "They should add that they are conducting an investigation, and will put those responsible on trial." He concluded by ordering them to also mention in the release that they would be erecting a memorial for the PP members who were accidentally killed or injured in the mishap.

"A trial?" the Brain asked.

"Better we lose a couple men than the entire city," Rafique replied.

* * *

Shortly after Rafique's directive, as the sun was starting to set, one of the Quirklyn guards tried to call his friend at the Green-Burg garrison, but the line was dead. As he rose to inform Jack Healy, the electricity to the entire community suddenly went off. Without an emergency generator, all of South Ozone Park was soon dark.

"This is it!" someone yelled in the garrison. The men scrambled to take their assigned posts around the area.

"I want Gunther, Jonas, and one other to grab bikes right now," Healy commanded his men. "Each of you go to one of the three garrisons—Green-Burg, Bushwick, and East New York. Put them on alert and come back with a status report! Men and artillery!"

The three runners grabbed bikes and pedaled off with flashlights.

Torches were lit along all four borders of South Ozone Park. Soldiers and volunteers with lances and bows and arrows vigilantly monitored their four frontiers—the dunes to the north and east, the fence bordering the JFK airfield to the south, and the Aqueduct field to the west. Avoiding the spiked trenches, Antonio Lucas crept out over the Aqueduct field and stealthily reached the PP parking lot, where he confirmed by walkie that though there were people who looked like armed Piggers arriving, they were far from ready for an attack. By the time he returned an hour later, reports were coming in that some guards smelled smoke along Hawtree Pass.

"Shit," Healy muttered.

"What?" asked Lucas.

"The Crappers must have already begun their attack. At least they're not coordinating with the Piggers."

"How do you know?"

"We have at least four or five hours before the Piggers will be ready to hit us." He urgently needed reconaissance, but his bikers still hadn't returned, so he put Lucas in charge. "Don't do anything. Just sit tight till I get back."

Healy hopped on a bike and headed toward the Hawtree Pass bridge. When he arrived, his fears were confirmed. People were streaming in, all with the same report: the Crappers were in the process of trying to take back their districts.

Healy warned the sergeant and the men on bridge duty that the enemy might try to slip through with the refugees. "Check everyone coming through, pat them down, and if anyone looks in the least bit suspicious, have them held in the parking lot."

With that, he jumped back on his bike and began pedaling against the stream of refugees along Rockaway Boulevard. When he reached East New York, there was smoke in the air. Through the haze he spotted one of his bikers and flagged him down.

"Gunther, what'd you find?"

"They wiped out the Green-Burg garrison. They seem to be moving east in a clean sweep, herding everyone toward SOP."

"When you say wiped out—"

"The place was on fire when I got there. I saw some bodies, but I couldn't account for everyone, so some might've escaped. I'll go back if you want."

"No. You did your job, get back to Hawtree."

Gunther pedaled away and Healy pressed westward. Soon he spotted flames—a building was burning. A few blocks later, he saw a second fire. It was just enough to create a panic. The buildings were spread too far apart to join into a conflagration, and fortunately it wasn't windy at that moment.

At the East New York garrison headquarters Healy screeched to a halt. The front door was locked and flames were shooting out of the top of the building. By climbing over a fence he was able to enter through the rear. There he found the body of another one of his bike runners. The kid, whose name he couldn't even remember, had been shot in the back of the head. Down in the basement, Healy discovered the bodies of Keith Bowers, the garrison captain, and five of his men. They had zip-cuffed wrists and slit throats.

A minute later Healy heard a strange mechanical announcement growing closer. When he climbed out of the burning building and back over the fence, he saw Crapper patrol cars approaching on both sides of the street. From the bullhorn of one minibus, he heard: *"No one has anything to fear! Your homes in Manhattan have been scrubbed clean. Hot food and drinks await you in the relocation center. From there, we will drive you back to your former homes. This area has been officially declared a hazardous zone, so you must leave!"*

Healy continued against the flow of people westward, until he heard, "Halt right there!"

Three men holding pistols and wearing blue Crapper uniforms had just turned the corner up ahead.

Healy put his hands in the air, smiled nervously, and said, "I'm trying to find my family!"

"Where do you live?" one asked.

"A few blocks down, I just wanted to grab my belongings—"

"This area is off-limits. But the relocation center has just opened up. It's two blocks south, and they'll take care of you there. You have nothing to worry about."

"Am I a prisoner?"

"Absolutely not. Did you move here after the Manhattan flooding?"

"Not quite, I'm actually from Staten Island."

"No matter," said a second Crapper gangcop. "There's prime real estate available in Manhattan for cheap."

"Okay, so I just walk two blocks south and—"

"I'm going that way myself. I'll take you there."

The Crapper broke off from his group and walked Healy into what was formerly a parking lot.

"Hungry?" the man asked Healy, who nodded. The cop escorted him to the rear of a long line of people who were moving past folding tables with large platters piled high with sandwiches. Next were buckets filled with bottles of sweet orange-flavored water. The cop stood there for several minutes, watching Healy in line, then returned to his group.

Healy noticed trucks and police vans lined up to take the Quirklyners back down to Crapper territory. Gangcops were milling around on the perimeter, loosely keeping guard. Evidently they were trying to make their invasion look more like a rescue mission.

Healy grabbed a sandwich and wandered around until he found an opportunity to break away and fetch his bike where he had left it by the garrison headquarters. He avoided more waves of people by pushing his bike down back streets, where he was able to dodge the sparse cop patrols and then bike on to Bushwick.

After forty minutes of trying to pass undetected through the crowds and the occasionally burning streets of Bushwick, Healy heard megaphones and then saw hundreds of people crowded together. It had to be the Bushwick relocation center. There was a long line of refugees waiting for vans, presumably to be "repatriated" back to Manhattan.

Off to one side was a small infirmary area for some of the evacuees, maybe twenty-five in all, who had presumably been injured during the invasion. Among them he spotted Jonas, the third runner he had sent from SOP.

"Holy shit!" Jonas said, sitting up. "Did you bring anyone?"

"Just me. What happened?"

"I learned from one of the neighbors that they drove up—"

"Who?"

"The guy in charge of the assault force is a lieutenant named D'Angelo."

"What'd he do?" Healy asked.

"His team blew open the front door of the local garrison. Best as I could tell, they slaughtered everyone and set fire to the building. I heard someone on those speakers saying that they were liberating everyone and directing them here, but a lot of the Quirklyners just pushed through and headed east to SOP."

"When did you arrive?"

"Just after they attacked the garrison. There were a bunch of people out front. When I ran in, they hadn't set fire to the building yet. There was a group of Crapper gangcops still going through the place. A handful of them were trying to keep people from heading east, so I bypassed them and led a bunch of people from Green-Burg around the corner, but then the smoke really hit. Next thing I know, I wake up here."

"Where are the Warholers?" Healy asked.

"Who knows? Are the Piggers attacking SOP?"

"Not yet."

"We gotta get back—my wife and kid are waiting for me."

"First I need to know what's happening in Green-Burg."

"Everyone says they hit there first."

"Where are all the people?" Healy asked.

"Probably like here—in relocation centers or they're refugees heading east. I heard all the buildings were emptied."

"Have you seen this Gonzalez clown?"

"Oh yeah. He's driving around in a mobile command center, a van, but he doesn't get out of it. Lieutenant D'Angelo is the tip of his spear. He runs the militia."

"What does the van look like?"

"It's green, but he's heavily protected," Jonas warned.

"The Crappers seem to have barely enough men for this attack," Healy observed.

"Yeah, not enough to force everyone out. Which is probably why they're doing all this reach-out diplomacy."

"Well, be careful. They might only be roving gangs of Crappers, but they're well stocked with bullets."

"Why don't you come with me?" Jonas suggested. "We have a better chance together."

"I have to find Gonzalez," Healy replied, and sped off westward.

67

. . . The old man was being followed. He was tall, bald, standing out like a buoy in calm seas—what the hell was he up to? What could he do with that bag of useless fucking triggers? . . . Followed him right down Broadway, all those empty streets of the Financial District like empty shelves, right down to barren Whitehall . . . Watching from across the street. (But who was he? And who was doing the watching?) A dim bulb on the top floor of the old building was flipped on—the ancient man had finally climbed all those stairs; he was standing at the edge of life. What could an old man want with those doohickeys? Why was the FBI, or whoever they were, using THEM to hand off a bunch of useless triggers— ████████████*alk to Sutphin*█
████████████

"Blow job for a stamp?" Some decrepit creature wearing clothes that were far too tight tapped on the passenger-side window of Uli's vehicle.

"Fuck off," he replied automatically, still in the fuzz of his Mkultra memories. Though it made no sense to him, the details were vivid. Before he could consider it further, he smelled something odd. When he looked to his right, his jaw dropped.

Above the Midtown Manhattan skyline, a thick, impenetrable wall of black smoke was being slowly pushed westward by a strong wind. Either northern Brooklyn or southern Queens was turning to ashes before his very eyes!

Uli pulled up to the first open business—an old coffee shop on 14th Street—and went inside. He ordered a cup and asked the clerk what the hell was happening across the river.

"Crappers had enough. Burned the bums out. Good riddance, I say."

"Heard anything about South Ozone Park?"

"Some guy just came in and said he heard they're under attack. The Piggers must be doing what they do best. I wouldn't want to be there."

Uli dashed out, leaving his untouched coffee on the counter. He jumped into his solicar and headed over the bridge to Brooklyn, and then north, into the black wall of smoke. He turned on his lights, slowed way down, and rolled up his window tight. After close to an hour of crawling along, the traffic finally came to a complete halt.

Some Crapper gangcop wearing a gas mask appeared along the edge of the road and started speaking into a megaphone: "All traffic heading up to Queens is being rerouted into Manhattan. All traffic to the airfield is closed for the day. All vehicles must turn back. The area is under attack. Any vehicles in the area will be deemed hostile!"

Uli and most others turned their vehicles around. He drove south to the nearest Crapper police precinct. There, he showed his badge, which he had yet to turn in, and was able to slip his car into the precinct parking lot. The only spot available was between two pulverized vehicles that looked like they had been used as car bombs. Uli flashed his badge again and asked if he could borrow one of the precinct's many bicycles, which were kept on hand for local beat cops. They issued him a rusty but functional one with broad wheels. He pedaled back up to the congested roadway and toward Howard Beach. When he neared the PP complex forty-five minutes later, he found the route had become clogged with gangcop vehicles.

68

J ack Healy glided through the endless veil of smoke and growing darkness, his mouth now covered with a Crapper gas mask he'd found in the chaos. He passed stragglers from Green-Burg and spotted gangcops doing their house-by-house sweep eastward. Although occasional sirens and screams filled the air, the battle here was clearly over.

Just as Jonas had said, the Crappers had begun systematically setting Green-Burg aflame. The closer he got, the thicker the smoke. He pedaled toward a group of a dozen Crapper gangcops wearing gas masks, parked on bikes. One of the cops called out to him, "Hurry the fuck up! Gonzalez is already here!"

A large green van appeared down the street and stopped before the squad. The passenger-side window rolled down a crack—enough to let words out but no smoke in. Healy waited until those in command had gotten their assignments from who he assumed was Gonzalez. Finally, he got off his bike and approached.

"Deputy Attorney General Hector Gonzalez?" he asked.

"Who the fuck wants to know?" said the driver, a greasy-haired bastard with a thick mustache.

"Lieutenant D'Angelo told me he couldn't get ahold of Gonzalez by walkie, so he sent me to deliver a message," Healy said, his mask still pulled over his face.

"Everyone has a fucking walkie, why doesn't he just borrow another?"

"He's paranoid that the Quirklyners can listen in." The mustached man eyed him silently for a few moments, so Healy turned his bike around and said, "I'll tell him to borrow someone else's—"

"Just tell me the fucking message."

"He said it was for the DAG's ears only."

"I'm the DAG," said the driver.

"I'll tell him to borrow a walkie." Healy got back on his bike.

"Open the door!" Healy heard from the back of the van. "He can take us to D'Angelo."

The side door of the van slid open, revealing the chunky deputy attorney general sitting in a swivel chair that was fastened to the floor. He was eating potato chips and studying a large map—presumably plans for the different stages of the attack.

The greasy driver pointed at Healy. "Get in, son, you're coming with us."

"What about my bike?"

"Fuck your bike. Get a new one."

Healy released it, and stepped into the back of the van.

Immediately the mustache turned on the engine. Loud pop music played as he began speeding eastward.

"So what's D'Angelo's message?" the DAG asked, still looking at the map and some notes on a makeshift desk.

Healy clamped his large hand over Gonzalez's mouth while he shoved his bowie knife deep into his loose, paunchy abdomen, sawing upward as if he were gutting a fish. Gonzalez's thin, clawlike fingers squeezed Healy's forearm and he groaned in agony.

"You say something, boss?" the driver called out. A partition shielded him from a clean view of the backseat.

"Nope!" Healy called back. Then he whispered into Gonzalez's ear: "That kid you sacrificed to the Piggers yesterday—he was my cousin. So when you see him, tell him I sent you as a gift, understand?"

"So where the fuck am I going?" shouted the driver.

"I'll show you," Healy responded, releasing Gonzalez's limp and bleeding body and letting him drop to the floor of the van. "Oh wait! We're here!"

"There's nothing here." The driver slowed down and peered at the empty buildings around them.

"Stop now!" yelled Healy.

No sooner did the driver brake than Healy reached through the partition and plunged the blade into the man's throat, tearing open his jugular along with his esophagus.

"Oh God!" Gonzalez moaned. He had crawled to the rear of the van and was trying to get out the back door, but was unable to reach the latch.

"Nope, just me," Healy replied grimly. He glanced around and spotted a length of frayed rope peeking out from under the passenger seat, then wrapped a quick slipknot around Gonzalez's spasming legs.

"Hold on . . ." said the dying DAG.

"You want out?" Healy asked, kicking open the back door. Gonzalez's body tumbled out onto the street, except for his legs. "Now *you* hold on."

Healy moved to the front of the vehicle, yanked the gasping driver out, and slid into the driver's seat. Gonzalez desperately tried to undo the rope around his ankles. He had only managed to get one shoe off before Healy hit the gas and sped up an empty side street. He relished the brief shrieks of the man who had brutally killed his flesh and blood.

After about a mile back toward East New York, as traffic began thinning out, Healy came across what appeared to be a cluster of refugees carrying bundles of their belongings. He honked at them, planning to offer them a ride east, but they recognized the van and scrambled off the road in panic.

At the end of a coiled wire hung the hand mic for the CB radio. He knew from the contraption on the roof that there had to be some kind of loudspeaker, but he couldn't figure out how to work it. He pulled to the side of the road and cut the rope hanging out the back door, leaving the bloody pulp of the DAG's body against a curb.

Driving up Bushwick Avenue with his headlights off, Healy spotted another group of evacuees. Before he could try to help them, he noticed the lights of another vehicle idling in the distance and stopped again.

It was an advance team of gangcops racing through the empty buildings with canisters of fuel, generously splashing it on and around the structures. One of the cops saw his van and pointed it out to the two sergeants who seemed to be supervising the operation; one waved at him. He had to make a move, so he flicked on his headlights and drove slowly toward them. Approximately twenty feet away, he hit the gas and mowed down the two sergeants in front of their shocked men, who began shooting. Healy sped forward until he came to another ragtag group of evacuees. Among them, he could see David Wojo and some of his injured men from Green-Burg.

He flipped several switches on the dashboard and finally heard the static coming from the bullhorn on the roof, so he grabbed the mic and called out, "Wojo, relax! It's me, Healy! It's Jack Healy from South Ozone."

Wojo, who appeared to have suffered a shoulder wound, stared at the vehicle as Healy waved out the driver's-side window. Wojo ordered his group to stop.

Within minutes, Healy was shepherding the dozen or so bloody and aching Quirklyners down Broadway, using the megaphone to pick up others along the way until the van was packed. People were still streaming eastward.

When they reached Hawtree Pass he saw Jonas, whom he had left at the Bushwick relocation center. He was part of a small contingent of Quirklyners armed with lances, checking the refugees, making sure none of them were armed or possible Crapper agents.

"Are you game for a riskier job?"

"What's up?" asked Jonas.

Healy explained that he needed someone to drive the van back and forth down the main road to pick up as many of the stragglers as possible.

"I can do that."

"If you see any Piggers, speed off, 'cause they'll be out for blood."

The large number of refugees at the Hawtree bridge required that the guards climb into the ditch and add additional supports so it wouldn't collapse under the weight.

The streets of SOP now looked like a refugee camp. As Healy approached Bea's house, he found that she had organized volunteers to help bring out food and water for those arriving. When she saw him, he mouthed, *Joe,* and pointed to the compound next door, then held up five fingers—he wanted to have a meeting at his place in five minutes.

69

Joe Brainard was in the back of Bea's house helping gather food and serving the seniors, all of whom seemed to know her father. Bea came in and said that Healy needed them both, pronto, so Reggie took over and the two headed next door.

As they entered the large room downstairs, Healy was scribbling on a chalkboard, talking to Antonio Lucas. David Wojo, with torn clothes and bloody wounds, was sitting down, his eyes closed. Jean-Michel Gaillard was unaccounted for, leading all to believe he was dead.

"So, what'd you learn?" Brainard had heard that Healy had some some reconnaissance of the breakaway Crapper districts.

"They've gone. And although refugees are still coming in, it looks like they grabbed the Warholers," Healy said. "But based on what I know, I don't think the Piggers are going to attack anytime soon—"

"Why not?" Bea interrupted.

"For starters, they know we booby-trapped the field, and night attacks are tricky unless you have the right equipment." Healy turned to Wojo. "What do you think?"

"Even if the Piggers don't attack, the Crappers might hit tonight," Wojo said. "The latest refugees are saying that the gangcops in Bush-wick are hell-bent on revenge. They'll probably just come through Hawtree." He had a fresh bandage on his shoulder.

"Maybe, maybe not," Healy said, not sharing that he had taken out their leader. "As long as we can get the Quirklyners on Hawtree and Rockaway Boulevard across that footbridge, I think we're okay. They should offer us some added reinforcements."

"It's not unheard of for Piggers and Crappers to work together," the Brain pointed out.

"Hell, if they undertook a coordinated attack, they would've taken over by now. Their animosity is our greatest ally."

"The Piggers will probably strike at first light, and with over-whelming numbers," Antonio Lucas said. "The Pigger gangcops are better trained, less community based."

"So, in the morning we die." Brainard wasn't good at acting brave.

"The good news is we have a couple tricks up our sleeves that should draw it out, maybe even allow for some to escape in the confusion. The bad news is we're boxed in here without anywhere safe to flee to, and unlike the Crappers, who actually tried to turn the attack into a repatriation to repopulate Lower Manhattan, I don't think the Piggers have any intention of reconciling."

"We're fish in a barrel," said Wojo.

"Hold on here," said Brainard. "Why don't we talk terms? If we surrender right now, no one gets hurt."

"Best-case scenario? Everyone loses a hand," Healy said. "The top people—myself, Bea, you—at least an arm, maybe we're blinded. You all ready for that?"

"I'd rather die fighting than lose my hand," Lucas declared.

"If we don't have a choice, maybe going through life with one hand is better than death," said Wojo.

"Maybe we *do* have a choice," Bea said. "I know somewhere we might be able to retreat to."

"Do tell," the Brain said.

"The desert behind us."

"Behind us are a bunch of raw, nearly impassable dunes covered in cactus," Lucas said. "And Rockaway Boulevard is filled with angry Crappers."

"But to our south is the airfield," Bea said.

"With drone planes taking off and landing," Lucas said, "how the hell are we supposed to move a thousand people across it?"

"Along the northern edge."

"And take them—where?" Healy asked. "Into the desert to die?"

"The real question is, if we leave here and give the Piggers back their district, do you think they'll press their attack, risk greater casualties, and come after us?" Bea asked.

"The Crapper gangcops let everyone go as soon as we left the buildings," Wojo answered. "They only attacked those who fought back."

"It'll probably depend on what shape they're in," Lucas said. "Whether they still have the will to fight."

"If we can get most of these people out of here," Healy said, "I'm pretty sure I can hurt them enough so they won't press their attack. But where will we go?"

"Rockville Centre," Bea blurted out. All looked puzzled. "It's far enough into the desert that it can't be seen from the Rockaways—we can lay low till we regroup. And if they do attack, it's elevated with solid defenses."

"Rock & Filler Center?" Lucas said.

"No." Only Bea and a handful of others had seen it; she bounced out of her seat, grabbed a chunk of chalk, and drew a quick map on the board—South Ozone Park, JFK Airport, and the desert beyond. Just outside the city limits, she drew a big X. "*Rockville Centre* is the code for an old Native American settlement we stumbled across out here." She pointed to the barren landscape behind her. "It looks like a prehistoric fort or something. We were hoping to convert it into the new Quirklyn prison."

"Where exactly is it?"

"About three or four miles southeast of here, in the desert."

"So we're going to take a thousand exhausted people and skip quietly across the JFK airfield without being noticed?" said Wojo.

"It's not that far," Bea said. "And they all have legs."

"How long can a thousand people last in the desert?" Lucas asked.

"We have enough food and water for a full day," Bea replied. "We can hole up there for a night, just in case the Piggers do come after us, and everyone can get their strength up for the next day."

"Then what, return here when the Piggers go home?"

"If we can get a runner through right now to notify Rafique in Staten Island," Bea started to draw a new diagram, "he can get us some barrels of water to rehydrate the most desperate cases. Then we should be able to circle around southern Brooklyn to Staten Island."

"With a thousand people not in particularly great shape, that's at least a two-day walk," Wojo said.

"It won't be easy or pretty, but if we pull together, it'll still be a lot easier than going through life with one hand."

"If they see us evacuating, they'll attack immediately," Lucas said.

"It's already dark, and the wind is picking up," the Brain said. "If we burn down some of the houses in front of the Aqueduct field, there should be a lot of smoke—that'll be a pretty good cover." He was trying to stay positive.

"We have to be careful, even with the smoke," Healy said. "They've got spotters on the roof of PP, and they have telescopes. We have to get cracking, organize everyone into groups, and start moving them out right now."

* * *

Healy sent his runner Gunther out to Staten Island. His message was simple: bring as much water as they could to Rockville Centre. The Brain advised him that he would probably encounter the least resistance if he headed south through Brooklyn, though it would be a formidable trek.

The Brain and Bea focused on the civilian evacuation, while Healy and the surviving members of the Quirklyn militia tried to gather, train, and post their men. Since they were still confident that the attack would come from across the Aqueduct field, they took whatever new recruits they could and used them to reinforce the gaps along both the field and Hawtree Pass. Healy also had one of his men assemble noncombatants—mainly the elderly—who, with broom handles and whatever else looked like a weapon, could march in formation up and down Kerouac Avenue, giving the impression of a much larger force.

In the meantime, Bea and Brainard pulled together a group of fifty-two volunteers and divided them into four committees: Group Intake was responsible for enumerating and identifying everyone; Group Trailblazing had to create the route; Group Supplies would gather the stock for the trip; and lastly, Group Grouping would process the nearly thousand men, women, and youth, and divide them into ten groups of roughly a hundred people each. Brainard specified that each group should have about the same number of slow and fast people, so that they all basically traveled at the same rate. Once the groups were established, each one would be assigned an executive officer and four junior officers. Group Supplies was also responsible for distributing the stock and making sure everyone received and carried approximately the same amount. All were to be informed: "This has to last you for a couple days. So if you pig out, you'll go without."

Upon Healy's advice, Jonas was relieved of his van-shepherding job so he could take command of Group Trailblazing. A few weeks earlier he had ventured out with some of the others and reached Rockville Centre, the ancient Native American settlement on the edge of the desert. He wasn't entirely confident about its location, so Bea spent twenty minutes trying to draw a map before she finally threw up her hands and said, "It can't take more than a couple hours round trip. I'll take you there myself."

With bows, arrows, knives, flashlights, and a walkie, Jonas's team—including Bea—clipped the eight-foot chain-link fence and rolled it back to get onto the airfield. They scuttled along the trench of dirt between the hurricane fence and the tarmac runway. Fortunately, the trench was sunk about four feet into the earth, so if they stooped over they were only visible if someone looked through binoculars.

It took fifteen minutes for the group to work its way across the northern margin of the field, which spanned three runways, to the midpoint of the airstrip, where a single service road led to the hangars. This was where the supplies from the drones were divided by borough and eventually shipped out. It was also the most vulnerable point of attack, because there was a one-man guardhouse nearby, though it faced away from them. A council cop, a heavyweight, older man, was hunched forward on a stool; he was responsible for checking the vehicles and papers of anyone who entered the airstrip. Since it was dark and the air traffic was relatively heavy, the group didn't have to worry too much about being seen or heard. When the fourteen of them made it across the final four airstrips to the northeastern corner, they clipped another fence and exited the airfield. Here they crossed the tail end of Rockaway Boulevard, which marked the eastern border of Rescue City; this stretch was a fairly barren path at the edge of the airstrip that wound down to the Rockaways.

As they hurried across the path, a single solicar whizzed by. One of the scouts noticed it had slowed down as it passed where the fence had been cut, and he feared they might have been identified.

"Let's be hopeful, just this one time," Jonas said.

After thirty minutes of walking across the sandy dunes, they reached the beginning of the desert brush. In the windy darkness, hidden from view by piles of sand, Jonas turned on his flashlight. The group wandered east toward the distant mountains, where Jonas ordered them to fan out and explore the landscape. "Just make sure you can see your partners to the right and left."

Soon, at Bea's suggestion, they turned slightly north. The parched, monotonous scrubland revealed no settlements, so after a nervous half hour, Jonas ordered everyone to turn 180 degrees—southward. Finally, fearful that they'd lose sight of Rescue City and get completely lost in the desert night, Bea insisted that they turn back west.

"Do you remember any of this?" Jonas asked, trying to stay calm.

"Not really," Bea replied. "We might as well be at sea."

The scout at the northernmost edge of the group practically walked into a ledge of stones that seemed to rise from out of nowhere. Using the flashlight, they could make out a zigzagging skyline of uneven and eroding walls. Together they scaled the side of the twelve-foot plateau and called Antonio Lucas on the walkie, confirming that Rockville Centre was empty and well hidden—a natural barrier against a possible attack. Four men remained, guarding the perimeter, while Bea, Jonas, and the eight others returned, marking the shortest and clearest path back to the airfield.

By the time the Trailblazing scouts finally made it back to SOP, Group Grouping had organized the first cluster of evacuees—a hundred people were stationed behind Bea's house, where the fence was clipped. There, they were issued one-tenth of all the supplies and stood awaiting their marching orders. Lucas soon ordered the team to move out. Group Trailblazing explained that it would be best if they moved in twos across the sunken margin of the airfield; that way they could help each other if one fell. Trailblazing scouts would meet them at the interior road of the airstrip, where they'd be sent across carefully so as not to be seen by the guard on duty. Then a Trailblazer would make sure it was all clear both ways before waving them across Rockaway Boulevard.

"About a hundred feet into the desert there's a big ditch," one of the Trailblazers told the head of the group. "That's where the next scout will be waiting for you. He'll hold you until the last of your team arrives, then another scout will escort you out to Rockville Centre. Don't try to proceed without the scout or you'll get lost in the desert, understand?"

This was the plan for all ten groups.

70

As the Crapper gangcops continued burning down the splinter neighborhoods of Quirklyn, the noxious black smoke thickened. When the wind picked up, the smoke began drifting southeast and soon covered Howard Beach as well as the Aqueduct Dog Track. Through the haze, Uli saw what appeared to be a rally. Pigger gangcops, maybe two hundred in all, had been grouped into squads of ten and were being issued weapons: lances, knives, and bows and arrows. Select men were given loaded pistols.

Just as Uli had predicted, Pure-ile Plurality and its adjacent field had become the staging area for the invasion of South Ozone Park. *How could this get so out of hand?* he thought. He kept his head down so as not to be spotted. One bald, goateed gangcop, presumably a captain, was yelling to another man who looked like an administrator: "We need to use the Crapper victory! We can't wait another day!"

"Okay, Farrell, just calm down!"

Uli's concern for Bea was intensifying by the minute. He casually put his bike in the rack at the rear of the PP complex and walked through the area as if he still worked there. A group of older gangcop officers was standing near a table, grabbing Spam-and-Velveeta sandwiches and coffee that PP had set out for them. Uli grabbed a sandwich too, stood around, and ate it slowly.

"They crisscrossed the field with booby traps, and due to the smoke we have zero visibility," he heard one officer say to the bald hothead.

"Yeah, we got that under control."

The invaders knew all about the camouflaged spike trenches. Before long, Uli saw three large trucks arrive. Two were loaded with crates filled with small dogs who were barking nonstop, and the third was crammed with long planks of wood. The canines weren't exactly attack dogs, just small strays that had probably been rounded up throughout the Bronx and Queens. Each squad of Pigger gangcops was issued one dog with a very long leash. From the third truck, two men in each group took an eight-foot-long plank, presumably to plant over the booby-trapped field.

After eating, the squad leaders assembled around a table in the lobby of PP. At a distance, Uli could see the bald captain pointing to a hastily drawn map of the former racetrack and sharing his battle plan, indicating where each group was supposed to either diverge or converge as they crossed the sandy field for the assault.

When the meeting broke up, Uli assumed the attack would commence at once, but they kept waiting. A half hour turned into an hour, then two hours, then three. Uli finally snuck over to the empty sex pier, which gave him a decent view of the proceedings. Around three in the morning, something awful happened: the wind shifted north, sending the stream of black smoke over Queens and clearly revealing the Aqueduct field in the moonlight. Even from where Uli hid, he could make out the little boards covering the spiked trenches. *They're screwed!* he thought. The black smoke had been a key advantage that SOP had over their attackers.

Yet still the Piggers didn't advance.

Soon Uli saw what the Piggers had been waiting for. A new convoy of vehicles arrived: on the back of some old trailers were six odd, converted vehicles that resembled low-budget tanks. As he studied them from afar, he realized they were actually modified vans. Caterpillar tracks replaced the tires, and thick metal plates were welded to the windshields and sides, allowing for only a small hole to look through. A team of men with monkey wrenches hastily got to work, putting together what looked like a jungle gym on the roof of each vehicle. By the frantic pace, Uli knew they were trying to take advantage of the still-smoke-free view. But after several hours of clear skies, the wind shifted again, plunging SOP back into obscurity.

While Uli was pondering the exact purpose of the vans, he heard a shrill voice badgering the gangcops.

"They're sinners and should be expunged!" It was his old recruiting partner, Patricia Itt. Though she'd had her arm cruelly amputated, the injustice made her no smarter.

Suddenly two PP patrols entered the pier. Uli slipped behind a wall, then scurried into a small toolshed next to the empty warehouse. Although it had been unguarded a moment earlier, the place was now crawling with patrols.

71

As the third and fourth groups were being prepped for evacuation to the desert, Cookie Mueller, who had managed to get out of Green-Burg, marched up to Bea, who was standing just off Kerouac Avenue. "This is absolutely unacceptable," Cookie said.

"What happened to Candy?"

"All I know is that when I returned to our official residence, it was empty and everything was destroyed."

"I'm so sorry."

"Candy and I never agreed to anything like this. We were told we'd be kept safe. Now I have no idea if she's even alive!"

"We're trying to make the best of the situation."

Cookie explained that she now represented a group of fifty pacifists, mainly born-again Buddhists from Green-Burg, who had barely escaped in the night. After witnessing all the mayhem, they had made a collective decision.

"As much as I'd like to hear about it, I'm a little busy right now," Bea said. "Can this wait until after the attack?"

"That's just it! We don't want to be attacked!"

"Right now, the only objective is getting out of here alive."

"Yeah, but you're leading a thousand exhausted people out the back door when the front door is wide open."

"What does that mean?"

"We should just cross the field and surrender. They're letting us return to our old homes in the Village. What more could we even hope for?"

"That's the Crappers. These are the Piggers, and they're not nearly as forgiving."

"Do you really think they would kill all of us?"

"I don't know, but they haven't offered terms so we're not taking that chance."

"But you *are* taking a chance—by staying here marching morons with broomsticks back and forth when we're about to be attacked."

"Look, we're evacuating people right now. Why don't you go behind my house and I'll make sure you guys are next."

"I got a better idea," Cookie countered. "We'll be the first ones to try to peacefully surrender."

"I'm afraid that's not possible," Bea said.

"Unless this is no longer a democracy, we're exercising our right to leave."

"Look," Bea reasoned, "we're all exiting through the airfield right now, so—"

"I'M NOT GOING TO DIE IN THE GODDAMNED DESERT!" Cookie shouted, then started to march toward the old Aqueduct Dog Track, her group of pacifists following slowly behind.

"Want me to stop her?" Reggie asked. He had been promoted from bodyguard to interim sergeant and was posted at the corner of Kerouac and Wharton.

"No. If we don't protect the rights of the minority, then what are we fighting for?" Bea raced up to Cookie and said, "At least let me get one of the soldiers to show you how to get through the field safely, without falling into the spiked trenches."

Cookie consented, and Bea asked one of Reggie's men to lead them across.

"All I ask is that you don't tell the Piggers that we're escaping."

"We won't say a word, I promise."

In single file, Cookie and the rest were led out through the black clouds, past the zigzag of hidden trenches.

The evacuees who were waiting for their turn to travel across the JFK airfield watched as the pacifists moved westward. One of the more panicky men jumped to his feet and sprinted over to join them. Within ten minutes, what had started as fifty-two eclectic citizens of Green-Burg had turned into a group of more than three times that number.

"We urge you to stay with us!" Reggie yelled repeatedly through a megaphone, to little avail.

72

"Hey! I remember you!" One-armed Patricia Itt had appeared out of nowhere and was peeking into the toolshed where Uli was hiding.

"Hi, Itt," Uli replied casually.

"What in the blazes are you doing in there? I heard terrible things about you. I heard that you betrayed us!"

"That's crazy," he said.

"It ain't crazy. You're a spy and I'm turning you in!"

As though a silent siren had been sounded, gangcops were suddenly scrambling in the darkness, screaming and pointing across the field. "They're attacking us!"

Uli slipped out of the shed and started backing away.

"Hold on, traitor!" Itt grabbed him with her one hand.

"I'm a gangcop now," Uli told her. Before she could blather any further, he broke free and sprinted toward the smoky field.

Commanders were ordering the Pigger gangcops to take defensive positions against what appeared to be a surprise Quirklyn attack. After a few minutes, Cookie's group emerged in the distance through the clouds of smoke, waving white skirts with hastily painted doves, and with chicken feet scrawled on their foreheads and hands. When they got within earshot, the Piggers heard them singing, "Kum ba yah, my Lord . . ."

For an instant, the gangcops believed it was the beginning of a full-scale surrender. But the sentries on the roof of PP quickly dispelled this notion. A squad of cops immediately ran out and began shoving the pacifists to the ground, clubbing them liberally and frisking them for weapons.

Some of the pacifists toward the rear turned and began racing back to SOP. A contingent of Pigger soldiers who had been waiting along Jamaica Bay charged forward, cutting them off. Uli took advantage of this mass diversion and dashed back to PP's sex pier.

Jamaica Bay was the only place on the reservation where the water was somewhat clean, so Uli jumped right in. Aided by the moonlight, he moved along the shallow banks of the reservoir until he reached the southern edge of JFK and spotted several groups of men in the distance. Security at the airfield was more intense than Uli had thought. Upon closer inspection, he saw that they were actually stevedores unloading wooden palates off arriving planes.

Uli continued moving through the shallow water along the airfield, all the way to the third of the eight runways, and hoisted himself up onto the tarmac. If it were any other day, when the whole area wasn't smoldering under a noxious smoke screen, he would've been spotted immediately.

Uli caught his breath and wrung out his shirt, though his shoes and pants were completely soaked. He headed over between airstrips number four and five, where a drone had just touched down, and started jogging along the white line down the center.

He was about halfway along the runway when a huge military freight plane appeared in the sky, coming right at him. Uli plodded on through the plumes of black smoke. He was now able to make out the distant bungalows and little houses of SOP near the northwest corner of the airfield, as well as a grouping of about ten hangars where supplies were being forklifted.

Uli still wasn't sure whether he had been tortured or operated on when he first arrived, but whatever it was, he had a strange sense it had happened here.

As he moved toward the western edge of the runway, he felt like a wooden duck in a shooting gallery—fearful of the pilotless drones that roared out of the sky. The reservation had to import thousands of pounds of supplies each day to sustain all the people occupying it. Then he noticed something odd: a periodic pulsing across the northern edge of the airfield, heading eastward. It was like looking at blood streaming through a vein under a microscope.

Before he could sort out what was happening, a huge meteor sailed overhead and into one of the houses that lined the northern fence.

"Holy shit!" he blurted out. Then there was a second one. *It's not a meteor*, he realized, *it's a fucking missile!* Uli didn't think anyone here had that kind of technology. Another one blazed above the southern end of SOP and crashed into several houses.

Exhausted, Uli steadily walked the remaining thousand yards, bumping into a cluster of people who were zipping along the northern edge of the airstrip.

"Move aside!" he yelled to the panicked evacuees. Instead of struggling against the surge of people pouring through the narrow hole in the hurricane fence, he scaled the fence and found himself in Bea's backyard, which was packed with those nervously waiting to depart.

A bucket brigade was in the midst of putting out the fire from the last fireball when another one slammed into the houses on the northeastern end of Kerouac Street. In the short time since he had jumped into the waters of Jamaica Bay, the Piggers had officially begun their assault.

All in all, it was a fairly restrained chaos in SOP. While some were running around and screaming hysterically, others were valiantly stepping forward, calmly helping the injured or passing buckets of water to douse the flames.

Uli noticed a small group of people near the fence who appeared to be in charge. Bea was the only woman among them. As he approached, one of the Quirklyn guards stopped him.

"Valerie!" he yelled out.

"Uli! How'd you get in?" she called back, waving to the guard to allow him to approach.

"Where's your father?"

"I had him and his girlfriend brought down to Staten Island to keep them safe . . ."

As Bea spoke, Uli had his first clear view of the source of the fireballs: they were coming from the metal-plated vans with the caterpillar tracks. The ridiculous jungle gym contraptions that had been hurriedly rigged to the roofs were improvised catapults. That poor young man Patrick had been killed looking for the Crappers' secret weapon, but now it looked like it was the Piggers who'd had it all along.

Then Uli saw something that made no sense: a dozen huge mounds of sand, which had evidently been scooped out from the network of trenches, were evenly piled along the middle of the former dog track, offering protection for the oncoming attackers. Neatly grouped formations of advancing Pigger gangcops moved like chess pieces, taking their positions behind the mounds; the six improvised catapults were spread out with geometric precision between them. They began lobbing more fireballs along the entire length of SOP. All watched in horror as the large orbs broke apart on the streets and the little wooden bungalows that faced the old track.

Bea suddenly dashed away. Uli thought she was probably calling for reinforcements to extinguish the flames, but he quickly realized there was a new threat. At least five hundred evacuees who were still squeezed in the backyard behind Bea's house were in hysterics, swinging the hurricane fence back and forth in unison. If they succeeded in knocking it over, the narrow path across the top of the airstrip would be choked with panic-stricken bodies.

Bea ordered fifty of her soldiers, mainly archers who were already thinly spread along the southern end of the front line, down to the airfield. They angled in and shoved everyone back from the shaky fence.

As Uli headed up to the command post, he could see someone frantically shouting at the guy who seemed to be in charge—Jack Healy.

"I fucking warned you!" a gap-toothed man shouted. Uli had seen him before and realized he must be the strategist Bea had mentioned, Joe Brainard.

"Now?" one of Healy's men asked.

"Not yet," Healy replied, ignoring everyone and staring out at the field.

"We're fucked 'cause of you!" Joe Brainard rasped.

More Piggers were calmly marching forward from the direction of PP. The wind had shifted again and bright floodlights were making it very clear that once the gangcops reached their positions behind the mounds, they were going to begin an all-out assault.

For the next fifteen minutes, the thin line of archers shot wave after wave of arrows into the air. In exchange, the six catapults fired mercilessly into SOP, and the center of the community was now hopelessly engulfed in flames. As the last group of northern combatants marched out in broad formation, Uli was reminded of awkward nineteenth-century military regimentation. Soon the advance guard with dogs and boards began moving. They carefully marked the spiked trenches and covered them with planks, rendering them harmless.

"Okay, move them forward," Healy muttered into his walkie.

A long, clean line of older men and women with broomsticks and bows and arrows—fake soldiers—came out along Kerouac Avenue and slowly squatted down between the few real archers. There were less than a hundred of them, spread loosely along the eastern edge of the field—apparently, this was all that Quirklyn could muster. The Piggers pulled back tightly behind the sand barriers to dodge the new wave of poorly aimed arrows.

I'll climb back over the fence and move back down through the airfield to Jamacia Bay, Uli thought, planning his escape. Then he heard Healy yell into his walkie, "NOW!"

Simultaneously, the twelve equidistant mounds of sand exploded. Uli saw clouds of red as body parts blasted into the air.

"Holy shit!" Joe Brainard yelled. Other than the sound of a drone landing, only moans could be heard. No one could comprehend what had just happened. The dirt settled, and through the pockets of visibility Uli could see that where the mounds once stood there were only craters, and behind them the mangled bodies of several hundred Pigger gangcops. A few were crawling away with severe injuries. The motorized catapults were battered as well, their drivers trying to figure out what had just occurred.

"Now! Now! Now!" Healy shouted.

Antonio Lucas gave an order into his walkie and two dozen lean men dashed forward with spears, right up to the catapults. Two of the drivers saw the men coming and started rolling backward toward Howard Beach, but the slow vehicles were quickly overtaken. Although the machines could still lob fireballs, they were neither quick nor precise, and they needed the infantry to protect them. Shoving their lances through the various window slots, the SOP soldiers were able to quickly kill the drivers and overpower the remaining support crew.

Morale abruptly shifted. Other SOP volunteers joined the assault teams in the field, where they finished off some of the wounded Piggers, lancing them as they tried to retreat back to PP.

"What the fuck just happened?" asked one mystified SOP resident.

"The mounds were packed with barrels loaded with ammonium nitrate and ball bearings, wired to a single charge," answered Lucas.

"Where did you get the bombs?" Brainard asked. Rafique had not wanted any trace of VL explosives employed against the Piggers that might provoke a retaliation against Staten Island.

Healy didn't respond.

By the time the Battle of Aqueduct Dog Track was over, almost three-quarters of the evacuees had successfully exited. There were a little less than two hundred people to go.

A voice from a walkie from one of the SOP militiamen stationed out in the airfield sounded, *"Help! We fucking need help!"*

"What's going on?" Lucas responded.

"I don't know how to use this," some elderly female voice sounded, *"but that fat security guard in the airfield just saw us running across the road and he—"* The message abruptly ceased.

Bea ordered the guards to halt the evacuation.

Uli had a pretty good idea what the message was about. The passage through the fence was so crowded that he had to climb up over the chain link and race along the trench until he could see what was happening. One Trailblazer scout was on the ground, unconscious, and a giant Crapper guard was strangling the life out of a second one.

A few of the evacuees were still dashing by, too panicked to even help the poor men.

Uli jumped on the Crapper's back, locking his forearm over the guard's fat neck.

"You got me," the man choked out, "I give up."

Uli considered tying him up, but the giant man had just attacked two scouts.

"I was only doing my job," the guard said, still struggling for air.

"Okay," Uli relented, "you're now a prisoner of Quirklyn."

"You're the boss," the man replied.

But Uli knew he wasn't. This man was nearly twice his size; once he regained his strength, Uli would lose his momentary edge. So he took a deep breath, then yanked out the long bowie knife hanging from the guard's waist and jabbed it into his sinewy neck.

"Motherfucker!" the guard gurgled. When he flopped over, Uli realized with dismay that it was one of the lieutenants he had spent time training.

One of the other uninjured scouts finally came over. "What's up?"

"Keep them coming," Uli yelled angrily, referring to the evacuees.

The Quirklyner pulled out his walkie and gave instructions.

Uli noticed that no one was stationed in the JFK guardhouse. Grabbing the dead man's visored cap from the ground, Uli said to the scout: "I'll man the station until everyone's through. If you see my hand go up, hold them and wait for the coast to clear. And make sure to tell me when the last man's gone."

73

Jack Healy was instructing Antonio Lucas to see if their soldiers could turn the mobile catapults around and lob some fireballs back at PP when they heard the sounds of distant popping, like someone had set off a pack of firecrackers. Shouts came over the walkie: *"We're under assault! Bullets!"*

"Casualties?"

"At least a dozen, twice that number wounded, and there are still more pouring in all the way down the line. Over."

The Piggers had probably intended this new attack to be a supporting action, but with the surprise sand-mound explosions it was now the principle assault.

"Torch the bridge!" Healy shouted into his walkie as he jumped into a solicar and sped up the hill toward Hawtree.

"Already did, but they have ladders and there are too many of them. We have to fall back!"

Healy immediately ordered a large group of men and women up to Billie Holiday Street at Kerouac Avenue—the near side of Hawtree Pass.

The Piggers had dropped ladders into the trench and were taking turns vaulting across the divide. Second, smaller ladders were tossed up along the surrounding sand mounds.

As Healy reached Hawtree he could see fierce hand-to-hand combat taking place along Billie Holiday Street. Although the SOP reinforcements attempted to create a new line of defense, the Piggers were breaking through and running south, hoping to outflank them.

"Holy shit!" Joe Brainard heard. "They're all down here! Who's got the walkie?"

Peering outside the garrison headquarters, he could see that a bold pair of Piggers had made it across the booby-trapped field after the blast and reached the southern edge of SOP, the holding area for the final two groups of Quirklyners who were still slowly draining across the airfield. The Brain hurried out of the garrison.

"Farrell! They're exiting above JFK," yelled one of the Pigger soldiers into his walkie. "Come in. Over! . . . Fuck, the battery's dead!" he called to his buddy, tossing the walkie aside. "We have to tell them ourselves!"

They began heading back north toward Hawtree.

"Those guys are revealing our position!" Brainard yelled to a couple of archers who were managing the crowd, then raced ahead to keep them in sight.

The archers hurried over to Bea's front lawn and began shooting arrows at the fleeing Piggers. One of them drew his pistol and returned fire. The archers took cover, but a bullet struck Joe Brainard in his chest, knocking him to the ground.

"If they get back to their group, we're all dead," the Brain whispered.

As the Piggers dashed furiously uphill back to their lines, Reggie and a young militiaman from East New York named Elk caught up.

Elk tackled the slowest Pigger and was able to grab a stone and slam it into his skull. As the other Pigger stopped to help his comrade, Reggie plunged his knife into the man's sternum.

With the last of the SOP militia forced to run north to provide reinforcement, the remaining refugees finally knocked the wobbly fence down and poured out across the airfield.

Avoiding the pandemonium, Bea saw the flashes of gunshots up the hill. As she headed up, she slowly recognized his black-framed glasses in the firelight.

"Joe!" She raced up but immediately saw that it was hopeless.

"I had a great ride . . . Really, I did," he tried to console her. "I remember . . . so many funny things, I remember so many sad, wonderful things . . . Too bad there's no safe . . . lasting place . . . to leave all the wonderful memories."

74

Four blocks northeast of Bea's house, the last of the SOP militia had retreated to the dilapidated and uninhabited houses on Pollock Avenue that had been picked apart for spikes. Over the next forty-five minutes they moved south as the Piggers pressed their attack to Millay Street. In a cannibalized structure on Parker Street at the end of Pollock Avenue, wounded and weary men took refuge on the top floor. Healy and Lucas had them spread out and away from the windows to prepare for the final Pigger onslaught. For a while there was silence, then smoke and crackling sounds filled the air. Then flames broke through the back wall—the Pigger gangcops had doused the rear of the old house with kerosene.

"Everyone out!" Healy yelled. Most of his men made it out onto Pollock Avenue, but the Piggers flipped on large battery-operated floodlights and bullets started flying again.

"Don't kill them!" Healy heard as gunfire flashed around him.

"Just get them on the ground, boys!" shouted a bald officer with a goatee. "I got something special for them!"

Healy and David Wojo stared at the airfield fence in the distance. Suddenly, Wojo was hit in the back, falling forward and knocking Healy down as well. Looking over, Healy saw Lucas on the ground with bullet wounds in his back and right leg. Almost all of his remaining men were down as well.

"You killed at least two hundred of our best men!" the bald prick shouted. "Time to pay them back!"

Lucas lay perfectly still until a Pigger soldier walked by with a machete, looking for an easy victim. Before he could use it, Lucas plunged his dagger deep into the man's groin. When the unsuspecting Pigger screamed in agony, another Pigger put a bullet in Lucas's head.

As the wounded Pigger staggered away, his machete fell to the ground. Healy rose and took two steps toward it before he felt an unbelievably painful blow to his left calf that sent him back down. The bald bastard was standing over him, holding his own bloody machete.

"Let's see you run now." The Pigger had hacked off Healy's left foot.

Dragging himself along, staring through the convolution of shrubs and fence before him, something caught Healy's eye. In the light from the airfield, he could make out dozens of legs running past: the final group of Quirklyners were escaping. Healy heard the grunt of the Pigger captain yanking his machete up with both hands. A moment later, the commander of the Quirklyn defenses was decapitated.

75

As the final pair, an elderly couple, frantically clawed their way over the collapsed fence and into the packed dirt of the airfield trench, Bea realized that she was the last Quirklyner in South Ozone Park.

Most of the small houses were on fire. The corpses of Quirklyn fighters were scattered all around. She heard the shouts of the Piggers closing in, and raced to the far side of the fence. She grabbed the collapsed pole with chain-link fencing attached and lifted, angling it back into the posthole. It might buy them a little more time and take some of the Piggers longer to figure out where all the survivors had gone.

Bea kept low as she ran along the dark trench, repeatedly stumbling on articles of abandoned clothes and dropped belongings. To her left she could still hear shouts, cries, and occasional gunshots. Soon she passed the final house of SOP and moved parallel to the tall dunes. Bea came up behind a large, hairy man who was moving unsteadily in front of her. In the flickering of flames from the burning houses, she could see pots and pans strapped to his back like a pack mule. He stumbled across three bodies where the service road began, the cookware making a huge racket.

"Mr. Aardvarkian!" Uli called, spotting the man from where he was stationed in the small guardhouse. Uli saw only one other lone figure running behind the Armenian. The scout who was supposed to notify him when the last Quirklyners came through was gone. Uli picked up a pan that had spun loose. "Let me help."

The cook snatched the pan out of Uli's hand and snarled, "I don't need your help, snitch."

"What's your problem?" Uli asked as Bea loped up behind him.

"I figured out who you are!"

"Who I am?" Uli asked.

"You're that FBI prick who betrayed us," the restaurateur replied.

"Betrayed who?"

"You arrested Gourgen!" the man said in Armenian.

"Gorgon?" Uli replied. "The Greek mythological creature?"

"Yanikian!" he said in English. "You Turk collaborator!" Aardvarkian raced ahead.

The name was sharply familiar, but not identifiable. Before Uli could catch up and ask Aardvarkian what he meant, Bea grabbed his arm and told him it was time to go.

"What about the others?" Uli asked, failing to see Healy, Wojo, or any of the other Quirklyn militia.

Bea kept moving; Uli followed. Five minutes later, they climbed through the cut hole in the fence, which was lined with torn shreds of fabric from the hundreds who had rushed through before them.

Outside the airfield, Uli saw the bodies of three dead refugees that had been shoved aside to keep the pathway clear. They had died while trying to escape, possibly having been trampled. Uli, Bea, and Aardvarkian crossed Rockaway Boulevard and headed down the sandy slope on the other side. Even in the darkness it was easy to make out the hundreds of footprints trailing into the desert.

Uli let Bea and Aardvarkian hurry ahead, then took off his jacket and started wiping down the sandy path behind them as they made their way to the ancient settlement in the desert.

76

By seven the next morning, Gunther, the runner from Quirklyn, had reached the terminal. He reported that Quirklyn had fallen and relayed the evacuation plan for the survivors. Rafique immediately sent out three teams on motorized tricycles to shuttle barrels of water as far as they could toward the Rockville Centre settlement. As a courtesy, someone was assigned to let Paul Moses know that his daughter was okay.

Paul and Lucille had been put up in a small shack across from the terminal building.

Upon receiving the news at eight that morning, Paul rose to his feet, unable to sit still.

"There's little we can do here," said Lucille, who was reading a worn copy of *Valley of the Dolls*.

"I'm going for a short constitutional," Paul said, hoping to drain off his anxiety.

Lucille reminded him about the noxious smell, so he put on the standard nose clip and walked away from the hippie community and toxic swamp, thinking about what his poor daughter must be going through.

Before he could get very far, a car pulled over next to him, sending up a cloud of dust.

"Excuse me, sir, someone wants to see you," the driver said.

Thinking it might have something to do with Bea, Paul came toward the passenger-side door, but there were newspapers taped inside the window, blocking his view, so he opened the door.

In the moment it took for Paul's eyes to adjust to the darkness, he registered the scent of an expensive cologne, something he hadn't smelled in over a decade. Then he realized that sitting inside the car, in a fine gray suit with a white cotton button-up shirt and blue tie, complete with a gold tiepin, was none other than his brother—the great Robert Moses—wearing dark sunglasses.

"What the hell are you doing here?" Paul asked.

"I sent someone else to get you, but the guy vanished." Robert removed his sunglasses.

"What the hell?"

"This is a rescue mission, you ninny. Now get in! I'm here to bring you home."

"Like hell you are!" Paul slammed the door shut and started walking back toward the shack.

The aged bureaucrat reopened the door and hoisted himself out of the car. "Paul!" he called, slowly marching toward his older brother.

"Fuck off!"

"I came a long way to make peace with you."

"I don't want your peace." Paul continued walking away.

"Do you really want to die in this miserable stinkhole?"

"You think you can just steal my inheritance, screw up my life, and expect me to forget it?" Paul said, turning around.

"Hey! When this country was going through its worst depression, you spent thousands of dollars, far more than your share of the inheritance, on that boondoggle out in Pennsylvania!"

"You're a fucking thief!" Paul yelled, then smacked Robert with an open palm across his sweaty face, sending him reeling back.

"You son of a bitch!" Robert cried out, and staggered back toward his brother.

Although both men were in their nineties, Paul had just napped, so he was slightly more agile. He pulled back and issued a sharp up-

844 🌱 Arthur Nersesian

percut into Robert's jaw. Then he followed up with a solid shot to his brother's right eye and a third punch to his cheek.

"Shit!" muttered Robert. Finding a bit of blood coming from either his nose or lip, he furiously lunged forward, swinging his arms wildly.

Half amused to see his brother acting like an angry schoolboy, Paul shuffled backward. Robert began to stumble, landing right on his face. Once he was down, Paul was set to give the old asshole the thrashing of a lifetime. But as he backed up a step, an inch-high tree stump blocked the heel of his shoe. Paul Moses collapsed backward, cracking his skull against a large boulder that served as a marker for the bus stop. His body slumped up against it in a sitting postion.

Seconds later, Robert lurched forward onto his older brother's body. Still furious, he punched Paul twice in the face.

"You worthless son of a bitch!" Robert Moses shouted, slowly struggling back to his feet and catching his breath. "You're a goddamned ingrate! I'll give you a complete accounting: I tabulated every cent you withdrew from Mom's account, and subtracted it from your share of her estate. You got more than I did! MORE!" Still gasping for air, he sat down next to Paul, who hadn't budged. "You want to rot in this goddamn desert, be my guest! I'm done with you! But at least I tried, which is more than you ever did for me." He loosened his tie, unbuttoned his collar, and pulled a handkerchief from his pocket, dabbing at the blood on his face.

"Is he okay?" asked a nearly naked member of the Burnt Men who was passing by.

"Where the hell's my driver?" Robert barked.

"Dude looks . . . dead," said the hippie, staring into Paul's eyes.

Robert turned and saw that his brother's eyes were open, but his pupils were fixed. "Paul!"

"He's not breathing," said the hippie, putting a finger over Paul's nose and mouth.

"Paul!" Robert yelled again, shaking his older brother frantically.

Approaching to find the two brothers down, with a long-haired freak in a loincloth standing above them, the driver drew his pistol. When he saw the hippie pointing at the blood streaming from the back of the older man's skull, he holstered his weapon and grabbed Robert Moses's arm.

"Come on, Mr. Moses, we need to go!"

"My God, Paul!" Robert pushed his driver away.

"What'd you do, man?" asked the tribesman. "I saw you fighting!"

"Walk away *now!*" the driver ordered, pulling out his pistol again.

"Fuck that, man! This is Staten Island! I'm placing you both under citizen's arrest," said the fearless hippie.

"Mr. Moses," the driver said, backing up to the car, "I'm leaving—with or without you."

Robert remained in shock, staring at his dead brother lying before him. He saw through the wrinkles, back to the boy he had known so many decades earlier. "I've come two thousand miles to help you, Paul! To save you! And you do *this* in return!"

The driver got back in his car and sped off as five others in loincloths arrived on the scene.

"This old dude killed that old dude," explained the first tribesman.

"Bring him to Loveworks," one of the new arrivals said.

"I'm Robert Moses! This was an accident! This is my brother!"

The group of shaggy Burnt Men helped the protesting senior citizen to his wobbly feet and escorted him to the group of old windswept trailers beyond the terminal building that made up the VL police department.

77

. . . *In a sunlit apartment, not a nice one, it was just a run-down rent-controlled dive, he saw hands too tight and slender to be his own frantically sliding through shelves, searching through cabinet drawers, the figure running from room to room—Uli recognized the place—finally noticing the strange lever at the window, heading for the odd contraption that looked like the kind of switch they showed in prison movies where the warden electrocutes someone on death row. A soft, sad, delicate voice called out before he could get there, and suddenly everything changed.* "Uli!"

He was in a dark, dank cave. It was the abandoned government facility where he had escaped by crawling out of an elevator shaft and around an intense flame.

The tall black man who helped him, Plato, had just finished opening a wall panel that was a hidden door to a cast-iron stairwell. Uli could see the dim outline of stairs crisscrossing above him. Plato struck a match and dropped it on what had to be flammable liquid. Was it the same liquid he'd set aflame with his burning trident? Smoke rose through the vast underground chamber. Vents at the top of the stairway were whirring, sucking the smoke upward into a distant sunlit rectangle—the place was finally liberated! Freedom!

The flames were hampered by the fact that the walls were leaking water.

"FOLLOW THE GLOWING LINES ON THE FLOOR!" *Plato yelled as smoke slowly filled the enclosure. Bodies at rest rose and moved, shuffling along the fluorescent yellow-green paint along the floor that led everyone to one of four staircases.*

"EVERYONE OUT! Get out before you choke!" *shouted the tall man. He was moving quickly, waving a flashlight, directing the route.*

A door opened and Uli saw someone he barely recognized—a woman.

"Oh God! What have you done?" *she called to him.*

"It's finally happening!" *he called back.* "Get them moving!"

"Did you inform Richard? The basin dwellers?"

"Days ago. They trimmed their beards and are herding them out right now!" *he explained before the woman moved into some hidden enclosure. Uli could see inside. Lying on a cot he glimpsed his sister Karen, then heard,* "I NEED ALL YOUR ATTENTION!"

Again the scene seemed to change and he was back in the run-down apartment.

He watched as the slender, searching hands moved toward the electric-chair lever that was bolted near the old windowsill. The fingers wrapped nervously around the handle, paused a moment in uncertainty, then pulled the switch from one side to the other—nothing!

"*The good news is that there's no sign the Piggers are pursuing us . . .*"

Uli awoke, still hearing the voice which mutated to an exhausted Bea: "We're all heading south. We should have enough food and water to get us the eight to ten miles to the far side of the canal across from Brooklyn. There should be more water waiting for us there. Then we'll swing below the dumps, across to Staten Island."

She was laying out the rest of the escape plan to all the Quirklyn refugees, many of whom were weeping softly.

Uli closed his eyes again. He had been the last to arrive at the ruins of Rockville Centre. Before he could black out again, he heard the whimpering voice: *Help me, please! Help me, Uli!* Opening his eyes, hoping to extinguish the sound, he heard it even clearer: *Please! I can't breathe!*

"Where are you? What's the matter?" he softly asked the emptiness around him. Some of the other refugees looked over at him.

Smoke! I can't breathe, there's smoke everywhere!

Uli rose and looked back toward where they had just fled from. Black smoke was still rising from the direction of South Ozone Park.

We're trying to get out! It was his sister's voice.

"KAREN!" he shouted.

"Keep it down!" hissed one of the Quirklyn refugees.

Help me!

Frantically looking around in the light of day, Uli surveyed the remains of what had once been a small, walled Native American village.

Help me, Uli!

A teenage boy, who must've come to Rescue City as a baby, was staring into the cool morning desert to the northeast. Uli followed his gaze—what looked like a giant strand of black hair was rising over the horizon.

Taking a couple steps in that direction, Uli heard Karen plaintively whispering his name over and over.

As the mass of refugees was instructed to organize back into their assigned groups, Uli made his way over to Bea, who asked if he wanted to bring up the rear again.

"I'm not going with you," Uli replied.

"Where are you going?"

Uli pointed to the strand of smoke. "My sister's out there."

"That's got to be at least twenty miles away," she said. "A drone probably crashed."

"It's her."

Too tired to argue, Bea had someone get a large bottle of water for Uli, and she gave him some of her own rations—six dried-out cheese sandwiches. She had too many people to help to waste time trying to talk sense into him. "If you . . . make it back, you're welcome to join us down in Staten Island," she said.

"Thanks." Uli gave Bea a hug, and told her to try to stay out of view as they passed Brooklyn.

"All those Quirklyn people who were murdered, all my people . . . This is all my fault," she mumbled, red-eyed, peering off into the desert.

"That's bullshit! It was all just a matter of time; they were going to take it all back eventually. We all knew that. You've got all these people who need your strength now."

She nodded and started heading off. Her giant, wounded, bedraggled assembly was slowly on the move southward, outlining the bulbous borough of Brooklyn, Nevada.

When the last were eventually gone, Uli turned east, walking alone into the desert. Still hearing his sister muttering his name, he tiredly called out, "Hang on, Karen, I'm coming!"

BOOK FOUR

THE
POSTMORPHO-GENESIS
OF
MANHATTAN

For Kim Kowalski

And when you shall come to the mountains, view the land, of what sort it is, and the people that are the inhabitants thereof, whether they be strong or weak, few in number or many. The land itself, whether it be good or bad, what manner of cities, walled or without walls. The ground, fat or barren, woody or without trees. Be of good courage, and bring us of the fruits of the land.

—The Book of Numbers

1

10/27/80

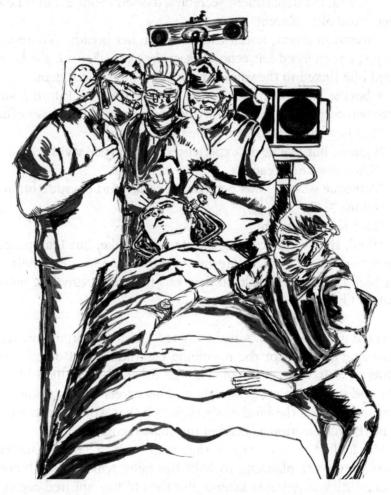

K aren Sarkisian was flung on her back like a giant rag doll, multiple hands pinning her down with her wrists and feet pulled apart. A bright white light was flipped on, blinding her. Her head was placed onto a hard block, a rubber strap across *her forehead holding her skull in place. She felt a pinch on her arm that could only be a syringe—she was being injected with something that made her limp but didn't numb any of the pain. Unable to scream, she felt her scalp being clipped. She heard roaring sounds in the background, which meant she was probably at the JFK airfield. Something wet swabbed her bare skull, and then she heard the high-pitched whirring of a surgical drill and a dull grinding noise, which went on just long enough for her to smell the faint odor of her own burning cranium. Then silence. It took a moment for Karen to realize that a long, slender pair of tweezers was pushing deep into her gray matter: something small and hard was being inserted into the soft folds of her brain.*

"HELP! HELP!" She bolted upright on the sofa.

Tatianna, the department secretary, dashed inside Scouter Lewis's office. "You okay, Karen?"

Covered in sweat, Karen tried to catch her breath. Whatever she had just experienced left echoes: *Shoot him once in the head*, she heard, a sound bite linked to the vague image of a white-haired man.

A bovine snort from across the room settled back into a steady snore and compelled her and Tatianna to quietly exit Lewis's office.

"You just had a daytime nightmare," Tat said.

"I guess, but I've never experienced anything so vivid."

"What was the dream?"

"Someone was . . . was performing some kind of crude brain surgery on me."

"Like that CIA team?"

"Well, they weren't using the steel yarmulke, but I suppose so," Karen said, peeking back into her boss's office. Scouter Lewis, who had been hitting the bottle all day, was facedown, drooling onto the blotter of his desk, snoring away.

Several days earlier, Lewis had assigned Karen the formidable task of overseeing security for the upcoming eighth annual Domestic POW Conference. It was an assignment she dreaded—a million little details, and if it went poorly it might end her career—but she knew if all went well, it was the kind of spotlight job that would put her in line for her boss's position as head of the council cops.

She looked over a map of the small park in Lower Manhattan where they were planning to hold the rally, which every hippie in Rescue City was going to attend. But the old free-spirited organizers had requested to hold the event just south of the buffer zone in a large, open area in Brooklyn referred to as Fort Greene Park. When Karen was offered the assignment, the first thing she did was try to explain to the hippies the hazards of the location. Despite the power share, gang violence along the border had been surging. They had adamantly refused to budge, so Karen had tried to enlist some of the celebrated antiwar organizers to help her. But both Abbie Hoffman and Tim Leary felt that the location near the border was crucial. In fact, Hoffman explained, "We originally all wanted to do it at McBarren Park, in the dead zone of Greenpoint–East Williamsburg, so that it would be a nonpartisan event."

"But the Piggers support the war," she had countered.

"That's the point!" Allen Ginsberg, the famous poet, argued. "We're opposing a war in Vietnam that we can't really protest, so at the very least we should try to win over some of these poor, misguided lamebrains here instead of just preaching to the choir."

Frustrated, Karen had gone into Lewis's office to appeal for his help in relocating the rally, but she had found him passed out at his desk. Since it was late and she was tired, she had taken the liberty of curling up on his sofa. That's where she had dozed off before being awakened by the awful brain-surgery nightmare.

A few more hours elapsed as she waited for her boss. Closing her eyes briefly, she saw a pack of rabid dogs rushing at her. *Run!* she imagined telling herself. Then Lewis staggered out of his office and into the bathroom. After some loud retching sounds and a thick cup of coffee, he was ready to talk.

As she began to explain her concerns, he took another gulp of coffee and said, "You know, Gonzalez thinks it's safe in Brooklyn, so maybe I should give *him* this assignment."

"Yeah, 'cause then Gallo can run all the franchises. Don't play with me, Lewis. You want this done right, put it in Manhattan."

Both of them knew Lieutenant Gonzalez was on Gallo's payroll.

As they sat there talking, she couldn't miss the irony of the situation: policing a rally that, years earlier, she would've been organizing. When she had been a leftist radical back in Old Town, those policing the rallies like Lewis were the enemy.

But Lewis didn't know about her past or care; the only question he'd ever asked her about herself was when he saw the *ian* at the end of her last name; he wondered if she was Armenian. She'd muttered "Yes" and he didn't follow up. As best as she could tell, few other Armenians had been shipped out to the Nevada desert after Manhattan got hit. It made sense: they were a hardworking people and had the resources to move without requiring government handouts.

A few years after Rescue City started, when the detainees continued pouring in, one wild-haired radical, a famed Berkeley antiwar activist, showed up with his entire family. He added a few letters to his last name to make it amusing—*Aardvarkian*. On the housing request form, question number twelve asked: *What unique service could you provide to our community?* Without consulting his family, Aardvarkian had written down his dream occupation: *I'd like to start an Armenian restaurant.*

He was offered a beautiful concrete storefront in the middle of nowhere that no one wanted. It was a building in Bushwick, designed to be a restaurant, but had the misfortune of being built in a neighborhood that had been abandoned after countless clashes along the Pigger-Crapper border. And yet, within a month he had it up and running, and due to its exquisite food, people from both sides of the border flocked to it. Upon learning of the only Armenian restaurant in town, called Little Armenia, Karen had visited soon after it opened and introduced herself as a member of the tribe.

"What's your last name?" Aardvarkian quizzed.

"Sarkisian," she replied.

He introduced her to his wife, children, and mother, who were all thrilled to meet a fellow countryman. They hugged, laughed, and chatted in the mother tongue. Just hearing the language she had learned while growing up made Karen homesick immediately. Although she liked all of the family members, she developed a special affinity for Dora, the matriarch and a survivor of the genocide, who instantly adopted Karen as if she were her own granddaughter. Karen would usually come over once a week and just hang out for the evening.

Like many eccentric older women, Dora would pancake rouge on her face, which Karen took as a sign of vanity. But after celebrating Armenian Orthodox Christmas in '75, she finally realized why the woman wore all the makeup. When Dora washed her face before going to sleep, Karen saw symmetrical scars looping both sides of her cheeks. During the genocide, the Kurds had sold Armenian girls to brothels, where they were branded by their pimps. Dora had worked there for two years before she found an opportunity to escape.

When Lewis finally gave Karen permission to move the rally out of Brooklyn, she celebrated by heading over to Little Armenia up in Bushwick. While serving her, Aardvarkian explained that his mother was not doing well. "She was diagnosed with early lung cancer a few years ago. She was treated, but now it looks like it's come back."

"Oh God."

"If you can find a minute, she's at St. Vincent's Hospital and she's asking for you."

"I'll stop by."

After lunch, Karen informed the rally organizers that their antiwar event would have to be moved to Lower Manhattan, and that was all there was to it. Then she went home, drew a bath, lowered herself into the soothing water, and fell asleep.

The loud ringing of the telephone perched on her toilet tank startled Karen awake. She almost dropped the handpiece into the tub as she answered it. Chuck Schuman, her assistant, was on the other end calling to report that Daniel Berrigan, one of the two Berrigan detainees, had just passed away the day before.

"Sorry to hear it," she said drowsily.

"You told me to keep you posted on any developments that might affect the rally, and I know he was a big antiwar guy, so I figured I should tell you. He's being buried down in Sunset Park tomorrow morning—a big funeral."

She thanked him, hung up, and closed her eyes. Still in that transient state between sleeping and waking, she could hear a strange static as though her brain were caught between two radio channels: *Catch the Q28 to Fulton Street, change to the B17, take it to the East Village . . .*

"What the fuck?" she wondered aloud. Someone else's words were running through her mind. All had heard about the heightened psychic sensitivity on the reservation—another CIA-generated phenomenon—and that allegedly certain siblings were able to telepathically link up with each other, but it had never happened to her. Still, the enigmatic chant kept running through her brain like a bad song.

She toweled off and went to bed. She pressed a pillow between her knees and thought of Fenwick. He was both a crappy lover and a bad sleeper, but he was the only person she had slept with in the past five years. When a friendly bomb he was trying to neutralize detonated, it had saved her the trouble of having to dump him.

Soon, she was back asleep . . . She felt an intimate sensation from deep in her loins—she was having sex. It took Karen a minute to realize that she was sleeping with another woman, or was dreaming that she was, which was bizarre as she'd never desired this before. What was even stranger was the gradual realization that *she* had a penis—or was it a banana?

Back in Old Town, if she had a weird dream she might try psychoanalyzing it, but Rescue City was different. This place was a giant laboratory. It was known that they put things in the food and water and strange chemical fumes constantly filled the air. Tatianna once likened it to living in New Jersey, multiplied by a million. Many believed that secret experiments were constantly being performed on the interned community, and it happened beyond the checks and balances of the press or anyone else.

In short, she knew something was up, so she didn't read too much into the dream. She figured that it was anxiety about the upcoming antiwar rally. She wondered if maybe the old lefties were going to pull something in response to her changing their venue. If so, they'd probably let it slip at the Berrigan funeral, so she decided she needed to check it out for herself.

Karen left her apartment the next morning, crossed the plaza, and headed to her office up on the top floor of the Williamsburgh Building, where she kept a variety of cheap disguises in the bottom drawer of her desk. After years in Rescue City, where it seemed like everyone came to know everyone else, she had to rely heavily on costumes if she wanted to do any basic surveillance work. She often used male disguises, and had recently purchased a blond male hairpiece and tacky suit.

Karen spent an hour in front of the mirror carefully applying makeup to transform her features, the entire time thinking, *I shouldn't have to do this crap anymore, I should just assign someone else.* But she couldn't trust anyone else with the job, so she practiced her male gestures and voice. After a while, when Tatianna arrived for work, a fully disguised Karen walked up and asked if she could direct her to Karen Sarkisian's office.

"Who are you? This is a restricted area!" Tatianna replied, and picked her phone to call security.

Karen burst out laughing.

"Oh my God!" Tatianna said, realizing what was going on.

Feeling confident in her costume, Karen left the office and drove south to Sunset Park. At the Green-wood Cemetery, she angled through the crowd of elderly grievers until she got to the beautiful handmade casket, which was standing open next to the rectangular hole that would be the grave. While most were buried out in Staten Island, this was the largest cemetery in Brooklyn.

She paid her respects to Berrigan's gray-suited corpse, briefly wondering from his suspiciously blue face if maybe he had been poisoned.

The older antiwar organizers had been dropping off at a faster rate than usual lately. Due to a lack of medical expertise, as well as no real forensic lab or trained staff, no one knew why. Karen discreetly checked cars parked around the cemetery for ones that might have been stolen and loaded with explosives, but none were close enough to the crowd to pose any real threat.

Finally, the surviving Berrigan brother stepped next to the closed coffin and slowly began his eulogy. Instead of listening, Karen kept scanning the crowd. A few suspicious characters stood here and there along the fringe. Soon, she realized someone was staring at her. She glanced over and recognized another council cop, Cedric Mays, also undercover, probably working his own case. When the tone of Berrigan's eulogy abruptly changed, Karen tuned in to the middle-aged priest: "From where I presently stand, I too can see the shame and pain that a single man can inflict upon an entire nation! And that man is . . . Uli!"

Karen was sure she had misheard him. Several people in the crowd appeared confused as well, shouting out questions to him. In response, Berrigan pointed a crooked finger toward a crowded minibus that had just pulled up in front of the gravesite. A few passengers inside were watching the service through open windows. As Karen tried to focus on their faces, one of the windows closed shut.

Next thing she knew, people started shouting and rushing across the lawn into the street. Karen pushed ahead to see who the oldsters were confronting. When she finally got close up, she was shocked to see that the mob was trying to pluck someone right out of the bus's window. The crowd parted and she finally got a view of their target. Of all the people in the world, they were attacking her very own brother, Uli, whom she had last seen a decade earlier back in Boston. She watched in shock as arms reached in, grabbing him by his shirt and torso. As he desperately fought to remain in the bus, people started punching inside the window. Instinctively, she dashed through the crowd of mostly seniors and knocked down a lady with an umbrella who was about to jab Uli in the face. Karen fought several of them off as Uli dangled out the bus's window.

"What the fuck are you doing here?" she asked her brother.

"I don't know!" he shouted back. "Who am I?"

Some old fart whacked him over the head. Karen knocked the guy on his ass and helped shove Uli back up through the window.

As the bus began to pull away, Karen noticed a large mustached man dashing toward her with a machete—one of the Zano Gang, as the council cops called them. She raced up to the bus, clipping her arm around the narrow metal window slot. Uli tried to pull her inside, but he was battered and disoriented.

"I can't hold on, my arm is slipping!"

"Who am I?" Uli asked again, but she didn't respond; she was using every iota of her strength just to hang on.

"Uli!" Karen finally yelled back. "Meet me at Rock & Filler Center!"

"I'll get off *now*!"

"No, just meet me at Rock & Filler Center at three!" she shouted, wanting him out of harm's way. Then she let go and fell back onto the road.

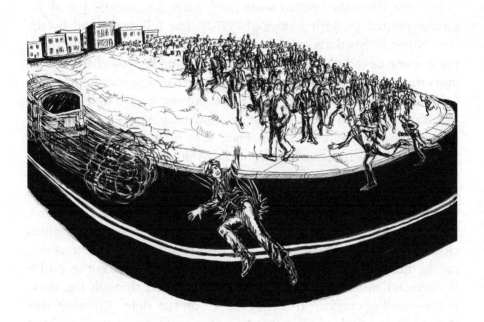

When Karen's bruised body finally came to a halt, she realized that she had just aided the enemy—Uli was FBI. *What the fuck is he doing here?* Suddenly she wondered if his presence had anything to do with all the weird dreams she'd been having. Karen shoved the blond wig and suit jacket into a trash can, adjusted the collar of her shirt to give it a more feminine slant, then ran her fingers through her hair and applied some lipstick. Soon, she found herself passing unnoticed by some of the mourners whom she had been battling ten minutes earlier.

She knew that Uli had worked with the COINTELPRO program, which was designed to infiltrate and bring down key left-wing groups from within—almost all of which were civil rights–based or in opposition of the Vietnam War. When Karen returned to her solicar, parked just a few blocks away from the cemetery in Sunset Park, she decided she had better head back to the Williamsburgh Savings Bank Building and try to figure this out. As she drove north along Third Avenue, she remembered that Uli had no clue who he was. He was clearly suffering from amnesia, and more than a few people here would relish the opportunity to exact revenge upon him.

Back in her office, Karen made some scheduled phone calls with antiwar activists, ate, and contemplated her brother's sudden appearance. Although she hadn't heard of anyone stepping off a drone in quite some time, she needed some intel. After the initial surge of detainees poured in during the early 1970s, few followed. And by the time Nixon finished his second term and left office, as far as she knew, not a single new detainee had followed, leading her to believe the rumors that Reagan was trying to end the internal deportation program.

Deere Flare was a slippery little shit, but she was so well informed that Karen believed she had to be on a federal payroll—or at the very least boning someone who was. Flare kept a pied-à-terre at a seedy flophouse a few blocks away from the Williamsburgh Building that she used when she was downtown.

About an hour later, Karen parked nearby and pushed her way through the bargain hunters who chronically cluttered Downtown Brooklyn. When she entered the lobby of Deere's dive, she walked closely behind an old couple so the desk clerk wouldn't call upstairs. As she hurried up the first flight of rickety steps, the entire building seemed to shake below her feet. She moved through the dark, funky-smelling corridor to the last door on the right. Knowing that the old lock was loose, she used her hip to shove it open without knocking.

A small white man with a small red pecker popped up like a slice of white bread in an overwound toaster. Deere pulled a pillow over herself and yelled, "We need a fucking moment here!"

Karen grinned as she stepped back outside, closing the door behind her. A moment later, the red-peckered slice of white stepped into the hall, still tucking in his shirt and pulling on an unlaced shoe.

"Sorry," Karen muttered, pushing past him.

"I know you didn't mean to," Deere said as she entered, "but you did me a favor. He was only making me sore."

Deere, who resembled a small, muscular Audrey Hepburn with a pronounced forehead, was sitting up in bed wearing a black bra that covered her shaved nipples. When Karen had first met Flare outside Columbia's Ferris Booth Hall years ago, she looked more like a chubby Sal

Mineo. The androgynous youth had decided she was a rebel, not just sexually but politically as well. Despite her small stature, she would square off against anybody if they so much as looked at her funny. It wasn't until she'd arrived in Rescue City that she'd finally had the confidence to make the transition. Since then, Deere had dropped her political ideals, started wearing sensible clothes, and sold herself to the highest bidder. Currently in her late twenties, she had acquired substantial power just by playing the two political parties against each other. She helped the Piggers when the Crappers didn't pay her ever-rising fee, and vice versa.

"A stalker is just a charmless lover," Deere said now, applying her lipstick. On a small table lay a REELECT SHUB! brochure, and Karen figured she had been at a rally.

"Didn't you just tell me, *This is the eighties, I'm down with the ladies?*"

During her latest libidinous revelation, Deere had discovered her appetite for young lesbians. "If you mean Kennesy, we got a date next week," she replied.

"That's the difference between men and women: women date."

"We're catching some boring play at the Foul Festival."

"Look, I need some help," Karen cut to the chase.

Upon inspecting herself in the mirror, Deere decided that she hated her skirt—which looked more like a kilt—and yanked it off, revealing her distended penis. "How do Scottish men hide their shillelaghs in these?"

"I was just down in Sunset Park at the Berrigan funeral," Karen continued, "and guess what happened?"

"A big bomb blew up a bunch of boring hippies?"

"I saw my brother."

"Your FBI-agent brother?" Deere asked as she tried on a pair of crushed-velvet bell-bottoms.

"So you haven't heard anything about him being here?"

"You see a phone? I've been busy screwing that twink."

"Well, you must've heard *something.*"

"The only rumor I heard was about some CIA-engineered seer who was either abducted or rescued, depending on your gang affiliation."

"Anything about new arrivals?"

"Newt Underpants is always looking for fresh assassins." By *fresh,* she meant they were always looking for people who couldn't be traced back to a Pigger gang. "If you want updated information, you should be speaking to blondie."

"God, I hate that cunt," Karen muttered.

"She's freaking out about the upcoming election, afraid that the Crappers are going to socialize the place, and the last thing she wants is Dropt getting elected mayor here."

"What's the big deal with this election? Shub is just going to steal it again."

"No, no," Deere said. "Not this one, this one's special. The campaign will be dirty as usual, but they're making damn sure that the count is clean—ask your friend Mallory, she's on the special commission."

"Why is that?"

"Apparently, while speaking before the General Assembly at the UN, Brezhnev referred to this place as *America's gulag*, and Ronnie Reagan got pissed," Deere explained, pulling on some blue panties. "Word is the Feedmore Corporation will start reducing our luxury items if we don't get our house in order." Everyone had heard that there was a team of independent auditors floating within the population, but no one knew for certain.

"Did Colder tell you this?"

"Colder doesn't tell anyone shit. I got this from the same place I get everything—the corner stall of the men's room in Kew Gardens."

"I thought you used the ladies' room."

"Only when there's no line."

Karen had actually heard the same thing from Mallory, who had told her how she'd gotten a prestigious appointment as one of Horace Shub's commissioners to inspect the voting machinery prior to the mayoral election—something that had never been done before.

"So what are you going to do about your brother?"

"Find out what he's doing here."

"I'm sure he's not here to arrest you. I mean, that would be so passé. But if he knows you're here, he might know about the rest of us."

"If anyone knew we were here," Karen responded, "we'd either be forcibly detained or we'd be killed."

"You're a police captain," Deere countered, "have someone arrest him. Clip off his fingers or toes, that'll calm him down, and then you have a civilized talk."

"You don't know my brother. He's very wily and resourceful. If he's coming to get me, he'll just keep coming."

"Not if you kill him first."

"Then they'll just send someone else," Karen said, glancing at her watch. Deere didn't know shit, but Colder might.

"Listen," Deere stopped her before she could run out, "do you think you could do me a favor and cut someone loose?"

"You know the way it works—squid pro quo."

"Fair enough, I'll find you some juicy squid."

Karen headed down to the lobby, where she paid a quarter-stamp to make a call to the Williamsburgh Building.

After the army pulled out, Jackie Wilson, the most powerful gangster in Rescue City, had worked to convert the gangs into a city government. There was also a brief purge of suspected covert agents, but Wilson ended it before it could become a witch hunt. The Crappers and Piggers took control; life grew more stable. Eventually, in an effort to be transparent, the company that had won the bid to stock Rescue City with food and supplies, the Feedmore Corporation, decided the reservation was stable enough to send in a single overt agent to represent their interests.

One day in November 1976, a slim, quiet blond man stepped off a drone supply plane and introduced himself to all upper-level officials, including Karen, as Don Colder, a Feedmore employee—then he duly vanished. People suspected he too had been executed. Shortly afterward, a fabulous blond woman stepped off another drone. She acted as though she had just won an Oscar for best actress, hugging and kissing bewildered government leaders as though they were adoring fans. When they asked who she was, she introduced herself as Dianne Colder, a former Washington lobbyist for Feedmore who had been reassigned to Rescue City.

"Someone named Don Colder, who looked a lot like you . . ."

"He was my shy brother," she'd say with a smirk.

Her job was to assess the usefulness of the Feedmore stock, as well as making sure that it was equitably distributed. Over time, adjustments were made and all were happy with the results—products that were dumped unused vanished from the drones, whereas other sought-after items came in larger volume. Soon she just focused on the "luxury items." When she discovered an entire shipment of portable black-and-white TVs being warehoused by a gang leader–turned–gangcop captain in the South Bronx, she brazenly confronted him.

"What the fuck are you going to do? Send in the military?" the captain replied in front of his men. "We'll send them back in body bags like we did before!"

She only smiled. Not another television set, portable or otherwise, was unloaded in Rescue City.

Karen had immediately sensed the woman's godlike power and, after deciding that little good would come from kidnapping her and trying to use her for leverage with Feedmore, she went the other way and asked Colder if she would like a bodyguard during her visits to Rescue City. The woman politely declined, saying she could take care of herself.

"If anything happens to you," Karen had said frankly, "I'm concerned that your supervisor is going to punish the rest of us."

"I'm here at my own risk."

"You're the only official from the outside who we have here—you have to understand that this makes you a natural target."

"Since you asked, this job was supposed to be undercover—but I don't play that way. Don't you worry your pretty little self about me."

Karen had her followed nonetheless, and asked for close tabs on her personal life. To her surprise, she discovered that instead of residing in one of the few safe areas of town, the lobbyist had taken a cramped room in one of the sleaziest hotels in the East Village, the Class-A Lady. It was Deere Flare who informed Karen that the Feedmore lobbyist liked the rough trade. The area was packed with sleazy bars. "Supposedly, she tells her tricks that she's the one holding them captive in the desert, then she lets them go crazy on her."

"Do me a favor," Karen said to the blonde. "If you come across another problem here, like a gangcop stealing TV sets, would you honor our chain of command and bring it to my attention? In addition to you staying out of harm's way, this is also my job."

Colder wouldn't say yes and she wouldn't say no.

Over the years, Colder would periodically vanish like the cigarette smoke she was constantly exhaling. She'd reappear just as quickly when the situation called for it.

One morning, Karen arrived at work to find her office filled with cigarette smoke. "You said if I had a complaint to come to you," she heard Colder's voice.

"What's the problem?"

The lobbyist explained that in the past month Gallo's boys had been grabbing all the luxury items as soon as they were unloaded at JFK. If this continued, Feedmore was going to stop shipping them in.

Karen spoke to one of Gallo's lieutenants, who said he couldn't control it, so she launched the organized crime unit within the council cops. Soon frustrated with the slow progress, she recalled how reasonable Gallo had been during the early days when the city government was still forming.

One afternoon, Karen waited a block and a half away from the Cicone Social Club until she saw his car pull up in her rearview. The giant bodyguard opened his door as she approached calling out, "Joe Gallo!"

The guard turned, holding his big pistol. Karen threw her hands in the air. Gallo recognized her and waved for the guard to holster his weapon.

"I'm here to give you some information, which you're welcome to disregard."

Gallo quietly listened.

"If more than 25 percent of the luxury items disappear from distribution centers, Feedmore is going to stop sending them."

Without a response, Gallo resumed walking into the social club. Karen returned to her car and drove off.

Within a week, 60 percent of all luxury items at JFK were making it to the distribution center—up from 30 percent.

Colder decided to thank Karen personally. She entered Karen's office soon thereafter and sat down next to her while she was working on some forms. "I wanted to thank you for dealing with the sticky fingers of this place," Colder said. "And I thought maybe I can show my appreciation with my own gentle fingers." She raked her fingernails along Karen's inner thigh.

"Thanks," Karen said, snapping her legs shut. "I'm a devout celibate."

"Shame," Colder said, rising.

The next day, Karen found an expensive pair of skis resting on her desk—even though there were no slopes anywhere near Rescue City. Karen returned the skis and told Colder that if she ever needed a favor, she'd ask for it.

It was now time to call in the favor. Using a pay phone in the filthy lobby of Deere's hotel, Karen called Tatianna—the stressed-out nerve center of the city's criminal justice system—and asked if she knew where to find the platinum lobbyist.

"I'm looking at the little dingbat right now. She walked in a minute ago, took some diet pills, and passed out on the sofa here."

"Don't wake her, I'm on my way," Karen said.

As she crossed through the crowded area, dodging solicars, beggars, and shoppers, she could see the last vestiges of a Shub reelection rally on Jay Street. The mayor himself, the little boob, had been there. While circumambulating the now-sparse crop of Shub zealots—with their posters, flyers, and merchandise—Karen heard talk of a bomb scare. It was a false alarm involving a chubster with a big pee stain on his pants. Five minutes later Karen was inside the Williamsburgh Building. After waiting forever for the crowded elevator, she reached the top floor where, just as Tat had said, she spotted the blond lobbyist with her black leather miniskirt curled up on the old sofa in the corner office, snoring away. Her red panties were peeking out.

When Karen walked past, Colder rose to pee.

"I understand my brother is in town," Karen said, ambushing her in the men's stall.

"Your parents must be so proud—two children in the black hole of Never-ada."

"Did I ever tell you about my brother?"

"Nope, and I don't care."

"He's an FBI agent."

"Well, I'm not." Colder's eyes were shut as she continued urinating.

"So there's no way you could help me locate him?"

"Wait a sec, an FBI agent? Wasn't one supposed to arrive yesterday?"

"I don't know."

"Holy shit! *He's* your brother?"

"*Who's* my brother?"

"That fucker just gave me the slip on the bus going to Manhattan."

"How?"

"He jumped out a window, but the information ends here unless you tell me something," Colder said abruptly.

"I don't know shit," Karen replied. "That's why I'm talking to you."

"Come on, you must've had some communication with him," Colder prodded.

As they exited the bathroom together, Karen noticed someone waving at her from down the hall. It was Cedric Mays, the undercover cop she had seen at the funeral. Colder noticed him too and waved back.

"Do you know Cedric? Maybe we can all work together here," Colder said, "like a task force."

Karen knew that once the lobbyist started digging, Mays would certainly reveal that he had seen her at the Berrigan funeral and tell her about the odd skirmish at the minibus. Therefore the information was officially declassified. "I just saw my brother about two hours ago down in Sunset Park," she revealed.

"Who was he with?" Colder asked, lighting up a cigarette.

"No one—he was hanging out the window of a minibus. If he was traveling with someone, I didn't see them. Is he in trouble?"

"All I know is that I was supposed to meet and greet him. What's he doing here?"

"Again, that's what I'm asking *you*."

"All I can tell you is that right now, he's officially gone rogue."

"Rogue?"

"Supposedly he's escorting someone."

"Who?"

Colder inspected her face in a pocket mirror. "You don't get that unless you give me something."

"I don't know anything, but if he's here, he's going to eventually make contact with me, and when he does I'll call you."

"Rumor has it that he's traveling with some guinea pig who's essentially an experiment in progress," Colder said.

"What's an experiment in progress?"

"He's supposedly the result of some twisted CIA project that Newt Underwood has been guarding."

"A project?"

"A seer, I think they call them." Colder popped down a pill. "I swear, NoDoz are as addictive as cashews."

"Uli is with a seer?" Karen asked incredulously.

Until this moment the existence of a seer, or rather talk of a CIA-engineered psychic who was able to see the outcome of local elections, had only been another Rescue City legend. Karen had once heard of the mission to find the man code-named *Karove*, but she hadn't believed it was real.

"If you want to know any more about that, you'll have to ask Underwood or Chain," Colder tried to redirect her.

"I'm asking *you*," Karen grabbed her arm, "and in case you forgot, you still owe me for shutting down Gallo's luxury-item theft ring."

"Fine. Roughly a month ago, somebody broke into a secret CIA facility in the Bronx and stole the guinea pig they were developing."

"Who stole him?" Karen asked.

"An eyewitness said the suspects were a middle-aged couple. But yesterday, I heard over a walkie that they were captured and hung by Chain in Borough Park, so now the fat man's with your brother."

"And this fat guy is supposed to be the psychic who everyone says doesn't exist?"

"Yeah. But apparently, whoever Karove is, he has a brother, and word is that this brother has been hot on his trail trying to get him back."

"A brother?"

"Yeah, just like you."

"What does this brother look like?"

"From what I hear he has long stringy hair and is balding—but at least it's not turning gray like yours." With that, she lay back down on the couch and closed her eyes.

If Karen informed Colder where her brother was supposed to meet her, the lobbyist might kill him. The problem was that Uli was likely sent here on a mission for Colder, and since she was pro-Pigger that would be a problem. On the other hand, she felt awful about ratting out her own brother. She desperately needed to know why he'd been sent here.

Karen left her office discreetly and crossed the guarded plaza to Stamos's Stamps, the main convenience store for the area. At the pay phone bank in the back, she waited for one of the three phones to become available. Despite her disdain toward fratricide, she couldn't chance it—it was time to call Akbar.

3

A number of years back, soon after she'd arrived in Rescue City, while reviewing a weekly stack of judicial amputations, one name popped out—a detainee from New York who had been an old acquaintance. Karen hit the form with the *Commutation* stamp and initialed it. When the detainee saw the form and figured out whom the initials belonged to, he put his past grievances aside and waited for her outside the Williamsburgh Building.

Akbar approached her cautiously as she was walking to her car. "I just wanted to thank you for my arm. Can I ask you a question? I've seen Mallory, but she's not the Mallory—"

"Are you truly grateful for still having your arm?" Karen interrupted.

"Yes."

"Then do me a much smaller favor and just forget she ever existed."

He nodded solemnly. "On a different note, I'm in a bit of a spot, as I still have some contractual obligations . . ." He explained that he accepted commodities in exchange for rubbing out small-time hoods.

Recognizing an opportunity to expedite justice, Karen worked out a mutually beneficial arrangement: he could continue his little assassination franchise, provided he cleared the hits with her first. In return he had to do the occasional job for her.

Up until now, she had never called in her payment.

"It's me," she said to Akbar on the phone in the back of Stamos's. "I have two targets traveling by bus to Rock & Filler Center. They'll be there at three o'clock—it's a priority mission."

"That doesn't leave me much time." It was two p.m. "Is there a photo?"

"No."

"What are the targets wearing?"

"Not sure—one is chubby, younger, and slow; the other is quick, handsome, and middle-aged."

"Any noticeable scars? Hair color?"

"Uli cultivates an inconspicuous look."

"You're not giving me anything to go on."

"He's always punctual. Oh!" She suddenly feared retribution from Colder. "His death can't look like an assassination."

"Well, with the time restrictions, all I can do is . . . you know, *gang violence*," he replied, using a known euphemism.

"That'll have to do then."

"Are they traveling by car?"

"They'll be in a bus," Karen said

"They're rerouting buses because of today's rally in Onion Square. Only tour buses will be going up to St. Patty's today."

"Oh," she remembered to add, "they might be pursued by a balding guy with long, fringed hair in a car."

"This definitely isn't going to be clean or pretty," Akbar said in lieu of goodbye.

Karen hung up. She tried to stay calm and pretend that this was any other day. Typically on weekday afternoons she would meet Mallory at her office in Cooper Union and they'd chat and have a quick cup of tea. When they'd first arrived in Rescue City nearly a decade ago, their weekly meetings—which had included Mallory's husband William Clayton, Deere, and others—were intended to coordinate efforts to radicalize the underprivileged populace. That had been the primary reason they had infiltrated the reservation in the first place. Over time, as members died or dropped out of their little political cell, they found their talks veering further off course. Now they simply chatted about their lives.

Today, however, they wouldn't have tea: Mallory was in Queens for her role as election commissioner; she had to turn in a form to Kew Gardens by three o'clock. Karen left Stamos's and walked to her Williamsburgh office. While reviewing documents on a peace rally happening in Onion Square, she received an unexpected call from Mallory, who had some free time before her deadline.

"You're not going to believe what's happened to me over the last two days!" Mallory said.

"Tell me."

"I made it all the way out to Rockaway to check on their machinery. Someone kills my guard and steals my car. I take the bus back, meet these crazy people, and we wind up getting hijacked by Chain. Who, fortunately, didn't recognize me."

"That *is* fortunate," Karen said. "Who are these crazy people?"

"This couple and a fat fella who they claimed was their kid. Oh, and this sexy disheveled guy who was wandering around JFK, claiming he had amnesia—"

"Can I ask you an odd question?"

"I guess."

"Do you have a scar on your right buttock?"

"Did you see me change or something?" Mallory laughed.

"So you do?"

"Yeah."

"Did you . . . ." Karen exhaled. "Were you intimate with the amnesia guy last night?"

"How the hell would you know that?"

"I know this is going to sound insane, but I think you had sex with my brother."

"Your brother? Wait a sec, didn't you once tell me your brother is in the FBI?"

"Yeah, but he's here now."

"What's his name?"

"Uli."

Mallory paused. "I don't think he even knows his name. Come to think of it, he does look like you. That's probably the reason I trusted him."

"Where did you meet him?" Karen asked.

"At the bus stop over on Sutphin Boulevard. He looked dazed."

"He's very sharp, so it's hard for me to believe he wasn't playing you."

"If that's the case, he's the best actor I ever met, 'cause something's definitely wrong with him. He doesn't seem to know who he is. But he was nice and good-looking so—"

"I think he's meant to be working with Dianne Colder, which means he's affiliated with Underwood and Chain."

"Oh shit!"

"Relax, I'm having them taken care of."

"Taken care of—how?"

Karen looked at her wristwatch—it was two thirty.

"Karen, what are you saying?"

"Do have any idea how many good people he's either arrested or killed? How many awful fascist causes he's protected? Hell, we might even be the reason he's here! He might be here to arrest us."

"But he's your brother and he has amnesia! And the FBI doesn't give a shit. They turned this place into a prison, so they got us already."

"They think *you're* dead," Karen replied impatiently. "The rest of us don't have that privilege. When his memory returns he'll remember seeing me."

"You're making a big mistake; he's not here for you. He saved my ass! I would've been dead without him."

"How?"

"Chain was about to use that ridiculous eye scanner on me and your brother jumped in."

"He played a big role in COINTELPRO, their specialty was infiltration. I think that's why he's here now."

"I hope you're wrong, 'cause I left him escorting a man who might be our answer to Karove. He said his name was Oric," Mallory explained. "He seems to be able to predict the outcome of elections."

"You met Karove?"

"Yeah, your brother's supposed to bring him to headquarters."

"According to Colder, he's not the answer to Karove. He *is* Karove. He's the reason we lost at least three council seats, and if he's killed, they're not going to be able to replace him."

It occurred to Karen that if Akbar killed Uli, he might also try to kill the Crappers' latest asset, but they'd probably lose him anyhow and at least the Piggers wouldn't have him.

Mallory needed to go, and Karen had to leave anyway. She still had to check out security at the small peace rally at Onion Square.

When she arrived ten minutes later, she was immediately pissed off. The square, which should've been cleared of cars, was lined with traffic and there was nothing she could do about that now. On a positive note, the little rally had already peaked so if anyone had planned to trigger a bomb, they would've probably done it by now. At the makeshift stage, a string of second- and third-tier activists were still waiting for their shot at the podium. Hordes of wavy-haired youths waved their fists and responded with synchronized slogans like, *"Our lives are horrible! Another world is possible!"*

At three, Karen returned to her car and drove up to Midtown. If Akbar had successfully done his dirty work, her poor brother and his seer sidekick were dead.

As she drove north on Park Avenue, she could hear sirens growing louder and began to see smoke billowing in the distance. When traffic came to a sharp halt she put her siren on and drove along the margin of the street, occasionally climbing onto the curb to get around stalled vehicles. On 50th Street, when she finally made it over to Fifth Avenue, it was pure mayhem: people were screaming, crying, and standing mutely in shock; others were lying on the ground bleeding. Twisted, smoking metal was scattered all around. Ambulances and cop cars had already poured in from all directions. Karen got out of her car and pushed through waves of dashing pedestrians. The injured and dying were already being rushed off to St. Vincent's Hospital, and a gangcop sergeant whom Karen recognized was directing traffic.

"What the fuck happened?"

"A large car bomb killed at least a dozen people. Most of them were on a tour bus."

She felt her knees go weak: this whole mess was on her. Only now did it cross her mind that this must've been what he was referring to when he said he'd have to make it look like gang violence. When she started to ask about the identity of the victims, the sergeant just nodded in dismay, pointing to a tarp on the sidewalk that covered a number of bundles. Lifting it up, she wasn't prepared for what she saw. It was mainly a series of charred, bloody lumps with bones sticking out of them like skewers—incinerated body parts. She tried to see if she could ID any parts that might belong to her brother, but her stomach started cramping up, so she dropped the tarp and breathed in and out slowly.

A van pulled up and morgue workers wearing waterproof gear and gloves started loading the parcels of meat and bones onto a gurney. Tears came to Karen's eyes as they hauled the gurney into the back of their van and headed off to the morgue in the basement of Beth Israel Clinic.

"The Karove experiment was a multimillion-dollar, multiyear experiment by Feedmore labs," Karen heard someone saying. "It's the kind of product that makes this place profitable." It was Dianne Colder, who had just arrived.

"Are you talking to me?" Karen asked.

"I find it odd that you were asking about Karove and your brother, then there was this car bomb and now you're crying."

"We have no ID of the dead," she replied.

"Don't worry, we'll get it, and if they're among the dead, I'm coming for *you*."

Still stunned by the carnage, Karen was unable to respond. Colder went back to her car and Karen walked the half block over to 30 Rock

& Filler Center. After clearing lobby security, she took the elevator up to her Manhattan office. Once inside, she locked the door and sat frozen in silence as she tried to come to terms with the heinous crime she had ordered.

Five minutes later her phone rang. It was Scouter Lewis, calling to confirm the news about the car bomb explosion. She told him it was true.

"You take the lead, I'm sending a team right over," he said, and hung up.

A moment later, her phone rang again. She answered and heard Akbar say, "Mission accomplished."

"Are you fucking insane?"

"I told you that with the time constraints—"

"I know what you told me, but you don't use a bazooka to swat a fly!"

"You gave me no description, you just told me they'd be at Rock & Filler Center at three, and that I could use gang violence. All they use nowadays are car bombs."

"All right, I got another job for you. This time I'll be very specific: a tall, skinny blonde named Dianne Colder who will probably be wearing a miniskirt."

"Two hits in one day?"

"She has a room at the Class-A Lady Hotel on 4th and First Avenue."

"You want me to hit this lady?"

"Make it look like a robbery."

"Suppose she's with others?"

"One other person can die, and it can't be a gangcop—otherwise, call it off." Karen paused a moment and again amended, "Colder was supposed to meet my brother. If you're able to get her alone, find out what her mission with him was, then kill her."

"How much leverage can I use on her?" He meant pain.

"Don't hold back."

Karen hung up the phone and lay down on her sofa, hoping to take a short nap, but the images of the bloodbath she'd caused haunted her. She pulled her shoes on and left the Rock & Filler office, driving over to the morgue at Beth Isreal to check out the eight men and women whose deaths she was responsible for. By flashing her shield, she was able to get one of the nurses to pull open the refrigerated shelves and roll out the body parts.

Karen inspected the heads and torsos, desperately trying to find her brother's remains, or at least those of the seer, but the parts were blasted beyond recognition.

When she went back out to the waiting area, she was mortified to find a growing mob of weeping family members. She learned that the head nurse had notified them that Karen Sarkisian, a captain from 30 Rock, was determining the identities of the dead, so she had to immediately apologize for this misunderstanding. As an act of contrition, she stayed till the early morning hours trying to console the inconsolable. Exhausted, she finally lay down and passed out on one of the bloodstained wooden benches that lined the rear of the emergency room.

4

S pinning, spiraling downward headfirst through the guilt of so many deaths, so many body parts, she felt a sharp, painful tug around her ankles—as though a rope had been tightened around her feet, cutting deeply into her flesh. She was hanging upside down from a roof beam, gently swaying like a side of beef. Her wrists and ankles were bound. She was inside a bare wooden structure that at first she thought was a dungeon, but brightness was coming through. She realized that she was in a barn! Nearby, someone else was also groaning, bound up—a fat guy was outside, *dangling over what seemed to be a large pen. A moment later, she glimpsed a herd of swollen animals, smaller than horses or cattle. There were pigs—no, hogs, no, wild razorbacks—grunting and rustling around below. They were snorting and lunging upward, snapping their large teeth above sharp tusks.*

Through the sound of snoring, she realized she must be asleep, but she wasn't herself. She was her brother, Uli. He was alive. This wasn't a dream. He had his eyes closed and seemed to be unconscious. Karen heard people moving around outside the barn and two figures appeared—the first was a tall, slim blond lady. From her black mini-skirt Karen realized it was none other than cunt extraordinaire Dianne Colder. She had finally caught her man—or rather her men. Accompanying her was a large brute wearing a ridiculous bamboo hat whom she vaguely recognized as a Pigger gangcop. Karen figured he was Colder's driver.

Karen could see their mouths moving, but couldn't hear any words. Colder seemed to be chiding the gangcop, and finally he stormed off angrily, heading to a rusty sports car parked in the muddy yard nearby. Colder was still yelling at him, waving, ordering him to come back.

Though Karen's consciousness seemed to drift around Uli like a feather in the wind, she stayed focused on her brother's slack form, aware that his life was seriously in peril.

With all her strength and ferocity, she yelled: "Wake up now! Wake up! GET THE HELL UP! GO!"

"What?" Uli finally muttered, as though awakening from death itself.

"She's going to torture you!" Karen shouted. "You're going to have one chance and that's it!"

"Help me!" he blurted back to her. She couldn't believe he could actually hear her.

"Where are you?"

"I don't know," he said aloud.

"Is that Oric with you? Is he still alive?"

Suddenly someone was shaking her, and Karen awoke in the now-crowded emergency room at Beth Israel. At least two dozen people, yanked from their own pain, were staring at her.

"You okay, miss?" asked some bruised man.

"Fine." She wiped sweat from her brow.

"You were shouting in your sleep."

"Sorry." Rising to her feet, Karen knew it wasn't just a dream—Uli was being tortured at that very moment, but she had no idea where.

As she hurried out the door, she remembered that there were a couple pigpens in Staten Island and a big one up in the Bronx. But it could just as easily be in outer Queens, where Gallo's mob ran things. In short, Uli could be anywhere.

She returned to her office at 30 Rock, where she spent the rest of the morning checking with outlying precincts, calling in old favors, asking precinct commanders to send gangcops out to the edges of the city, where small farms provided alternatives to the awful shipped-in cans of Feedmore-issued food. She also called Akbar to see if he had been staking out Colder's hotel as he had agreed to, but his phone just rang and rang.

Schuman soon arrived and asked her what was going on. She lowered her voice and confessed that she had been having odd experiences and described a few details from her recent dreams.

"It's probably just regular nightmares," he said.

"I've had dreams my whole life—these images are *real!* They're like . . . what do the Burnt Men call them?"

"Bilocations."

"In the dream I just had," she said, without mentioning that it involved her brother, "some guy was about to be murdered and I know they were at a pig farm."

"Did you hear or smell something that might give some clue as to where?"

"I could only see, but . . ." She closed her eyes and tried to remember. She could see the bamboo-hatted gangcop opening the glove compartment of the sports car and pulling out what resembled a clothespin after being scolded by the lobbyist—it had to be down in Staten Island! "If you could you find me the three largest pig farms in Staten Island, I'd really appreciate it."

When Schuman went into his adjacent office, Karen got on the phone and called Scouter Lewis in Brooklyn to check in. She learned that the head of the antiwar organization had personally contacted Mayor Shub's office, and the mayor's commissioner of events had overruled her decision and was allowing them to have their POW convention back in Fort Greene Park.

"He said it was an election year and the leftists vote so he can't afford to go against them."

"But if they have it up there," Karen said, "they're going to get hit."

"Which is why, roughly an hour ago, I went to the only body that could override the commissioner's decision—the city council's Committee of Event Permits. The bad news is, I was just informed that my request was denied."

"Denied? It's a security risk! Who's on the committee?"

"Four people. It requires a majority vote and two people said no."

"Who voted against?"

"Karen, I'll only tell you if you promise not to do anything stupid."

"I promise."

"A Crapper city councillor named Tony Pagan and a Pigger administrator named Bachus Leiberman. The good news is, they've given us a nice big budget so we can use unlimited council cops to guard the event."

Karen replied that she'd prefer using Crapper gangcops because they tended to have similar liberal political views as those who would be attending the rally.

About ten minutes later, Schuman returned with a list of the three largest pig farms on Staten Island: the BigPig Farm on the western edge, the Oink-Oink Corral down in the Burnt Men area, and the Calypso Pig Farm on the "eastern shore," along the shit canal.

Although she had some jurisdiction as a council cop, the protocol when dealing with another borough was to work with that borough's gangcops to make the arrest. And she knew that if she explained that she was acting on a dream, it would make the case a very low priority at best. Although she didn't like her brother very much, the idea of him being tortured by Dianne Colder was more than she could bear.

So she decided to drive down there herself and asked Schuman to join her. He grabbed a map of Staten Island in order to navigate. Soon they were in her car heading downtown. When they crossed 23rd Street they felt a slight tremor, then sirens erupted from all sides.

Smoke was rising from the low buildings to the southeast. Schuman's walkie wasn't working so they followed a speeding cop car. Karen immediately suspected the worst—that car bombs had indeed exploded around the Onion Square peace rally. But a minute later they passed the square and sailed down Broadway toward 8th Street where the thick black smoke was filling the sky.

"Oh shit!" Schuman groaned as they turned a corner. The three stories of the Cooper Union building, which housed the Crapper political action center and the offices of Manhattan's city council members, had been completely destroyed. It had pancaked into a smoldering pile of rubble. As the dust settled, passersby were digging into the debris with their bare hands. Gasping in horror, Karen parked among a group of emergency vehicles. As soon as she opened her door, she coughed out a mouthful of toxic smoke and took shelter back in her car. Schuman pulled his shirt up over his mouth as an improvised gas mask. She did the same.

In the crowd of people, Karen recognized a secretary from Dropt's office. The woman was covered in dust, sucking oxygen from a tank as a medic treated her cuts in an improvised triage center.

Karen approached. "Where's Mallory?"

"No one knows anything," the secretary replied through her oxygen mask.

Karen was able to get one of the gangcops on the scene to use his car radio to patch her through to Scouter Lewis, who was back at the Williamsburgh Building. He had just heard about the bombing.

"Has anyone checked to see if there are any unexploded bombs in the vicinity?" he asked.

"I don't know."

"I just sent a team, but again, you're the first on the scene. Check the place out and make sure it's safe."

"Hey, you just assigned me the Rock & Filler bombing."

"All I'm saying is, if you see anything suspicious, block it off until my crew arrives. Gonzalez is in charge. He'll be there within the hour."

"This must've taken a crapload of explosives. You should send a car down to Scat Island to check their shit farm. Rafique should be brought in on this."

"No, Gonzalez announced last night that half a ton of fertilizer was missing from his stock in Hoboken," Lewis said. "They must've taken it from there."

"I don't know, Fen said he thought a new explosive was being used here." Until he'd been blown up, Fen, her boyfriend, had been the closest thing Rescue City had had to an ordnance expert.

"Did he find some kind of sampling of this stuff?" Lewis asked.

"I don't think so, but—"

"We still have Fen's little lab here, and he trained that technician to identify trace levels of explosives, so if you're up for it, feel free to try to collect anything remaining and tag it for the lab."

With Schuman trailing behind, Karen cautiously walked around the collapsed, smoking wreckage. If she hadn't squeezed out all her tears the night before after the Midtown car bombing, she knew she'd be weeping now—Mallory had to be in there somewhere. As

they moved around the piles of rubble, Karen identified the four circular inclines on each side of the building where the truck bombs
had apparently been detonated. Not only had the ground been blasted
outward, but the buildings along the far sides of the street had also
been scarred in the apparently coordinated attack. Karen searched for
bomb fragments.

With regard to Lewis's requests, she also kept an eye out for anything else suspicious, like potentially unexploded bombs, but the area
appeared clear. All the vehicles that had been parked adjacent to Cooper Union had been blown back by the explosions. As Karen inspected
the vicinity, she tried to think of what Fenwick would do. Among
other things, his old bomb reports had chronicled the radius of each
attack and the subtle differentiations that he had referred to as the
bomb signature.

When Fenwick had been blown to smithereens, it was labeled as a
horrible accident. He had died during a simple training exercise along
with both of his protégés. A suspicious event like this was the exact
reason they were rarely allowed to work together—so that if one died,
the others could carry on.

Karen and Schuman carefully searched the site until they came up
with three blackened and twisted pieces of metal that were presumably parts of one of the detonated trucks. Except for one section of a
truck door that had the scratched-up stencil *edmore Road Rep*, most of
the pieces were tiny—further attesting to the strength of the blast. By
the time they sealed them in plastic bags and loaded them into the
trunk, Gonzalez's full team was busy investigating the scene.

Karen and Schuman drove together back over the Brooklyn Bridge
to the Williamsburgh Building. Before they could park, they heard a
loud, persistent honking outside the guarded plaza.

Karen recognized the rusty sports car, but didn't know from
where. As they approached, she realized it was none other than Akbar
Del Piombo behind the wheel, and the car was the one she'd seen in
her pig-farm dream the night before.

She discreetly nodded at Akbar, then turned back to Schuman,
who was carrying the three bagged pieces of metal from the blast. She
instructed him to take them down to the lab in the basement.

She approached Akbar alone. There was a big moist bloodstain on
the passenger seat next to him.

"You're an idiot for showing up in Colder's car."

"Sorry, I finally caught her being driven back to her hotel, but it wasn't what I expected."

"Where is she?"

"I waited across the street from her hotel and some dude drove up with her strapped to the roof and some fatty in the front seat bleeding all over the place. The guy driving the car went inside, so I grabbed it—made it look like a robbery, like you said."

"How many people did you kill?"

"Her and a clerk. Just like you said."

"I asked you to find out about her mission with my—"

"Yeah, she said he was supposed to kill Dropt, but something went wrong."

"You killed half a dozen people in Rock & Filler!" she yelled. "And you missed the *only* target!"

"You just gave me a time and place with no chance to prepare. I set off the biggest charge I could find."

Karen took a breath. "What happened to Karove?"

"Who?"

"The fat fuck in the front seat."

"He was dead when I found him."

"How?"

"I don't know, but he had an awful hole in him, looked like they tore into him."

"What did you do with him?"

"Pushed him in the river," Akbar replied.

"So who drove him to her hotel?"

"Some guy."

"Handsome, middle-aged?"

"Oh shit! Yeah." Akbar realized that it sounded like his earlier target.

"You sure you didn't kill him too?" she asked nervously.

"I actually tried, but no."

"You tried how?"

"He pulled up in front of her hotel, but before I could make the hit, he went into her place. I saw him run up the stairs. When I tried to pursue, the clerk stopped me, so I . . . which was why I did him."

"Christ, Akbar."

"Look, the guy grabbed me. I didn't want to. After that I just stole the car with Colder still attached to the roof."

Karen let him go. Although it would've made things easier for her if he had killed Uli too, she was glad he hadn't. Still, her key reason for

interrogating Akbar, something she had never done in the past, was
to make sure he'd had nothing to do with the Cooper Union bombing.
This was a huge relief.

5

There was little doubt that the primary purpose of the Cooper Union blast had been to eliminate the popular mayoral candidate James Dropt—all the other dead council members were incidental. The next morning, while Schuman analyzed the explosive fragments in the basement lab, Karen headed up to the top floor of the Williamsburgh Building. From the expression on Tatianna's face, she knew Lewis still hadn't gone to the bomb site. She walked into his office and confirmed her fears: he was already totally shit-faced.

"Bombsin's a fuggin mess," he slurred.

"This is just one more reason why I really think we should move the POW convention as far from Queens as possible," she said.

"Not now!" He tried to stand up. "I can ony hanel one fuggin crisis at a time."

She waited until he collapsed back in his chair. Another minute and he was passed out, facedown on the blotter. She switched off his lamp and, on her way out, told Tatianna that he would need at least an hour to detox, and then she could bring him a cup of coffee, although a jug of water would be better. It was then she noticed that the secretary had tears in her eyes.

"I-I'm sorry," Tatianna stammered, "my boyfriend worked at Cooper Union."

"Go home," Karen said.

"If I do . . . I might kill myself. How's Dropt? Is he . . . ?"

"The word here is *hope*."

Without any adversary to run against, Karen knew that Horace Shub was going to win yet another election. Though he was undoubtedly a scumbag, in all his years—to her knowledge—he had never done anything this shitty. This had Dianne Colder written all over it. She had seemed far less worried about Shub losing the election than anyone else. *I should've had her eliminated years ago*, Karen thought to herself.

"Gonzalez keeps asking for help," Tatianna said.

Karen called Schuman in the lab: "Keep an eye on things here and I'm going to head back."

As she drove over the bridge to the bomb site, Karen noticed a dull yellow vehicle bobbing in her rearview. Its color was a little conspicuous for undercover work, so she thought that maybe they were both just going to the same location. Based on her brief talk with Mallory, Karen realized that if Uli was planning to bring Oric back to her—even if Oric had been killed—he still might have returned to Cooper Union alone.

Although there was no clear point when the rescue mission became a search and recovery, that's what it had become. Gonzalez had thoroughly sealed off the perimeter and helped coordinate four teams, each group delicately excavating the smoldering debris, painstakingly searching for bodies. He had also worked up a list of probable victims. When Karen saw Mallory's name at the top, she wondered if Uli could be with her.

"Was anyone out sick yesterday?" Karen asked Gonzalez, who directed her to one of the few survivors—a security guard sergeant who had just gotten off duty.

"Dr. Adele was sick. They already sent someone to his house to check on him."

"Did you recover yesterday's visitor sign-in sheet?"

"Not yet," the sergeant replied, "but they did find something odd that one of the visitors left behind." He went around the corner and brought back a bucket with a hypodermic needle and a small oxygen tank.

Karen put them both in a plastic bag to run them for fingerprints. "You didn't see the guy who left this?"

"No, but . . . Charley!" the sergeant called out to another guy, who promptly trotted over. "Charles had door duty yesterday morning. Speak to him."

"Yeah, I was on duty yesterday morning, why?" said Charley.

"Do you remember Mallory having any visitors?"

"One guy," he replied.

"Middle-aged, handsome?"

"Yeah, but the guy didn't even know his own name."

"I don't suppose they found his body?"

"No. In fact, I saw him working with one of the rescue teams."

"You saw him alive?!"

"Yeah, why? Is he a suspect?"

"Is he still on the line?"

Charley led Karen around the wreckage, which was still smoldering, and they checked out the four rescue teams, but they didn't spot him. Afterward, Charley escorted Karen over to the hastily erected canteen and rest area along 7th Street where she checked out the tables and cots—still no Uli.

Next they quickly interviewed some of the bucket passers and other volunteers, asking if any of them had seen a handsome guy named Uli on the line.

"I remember a guy named Huey," said one volunteer. "Marky and I worked with him."

"Yeah!" said his buddy next to him. "He didn't even know why we were all out here."

"Out here digging through the rubble?" she asked.

"No, out in the middle of the Nevada desert. I had to give him the whole rundown on the New York attack."

"Where is he now?"

"I think he just left."

"And you have no clue where he went?" Karen prodded.

"Nope."

Some other volunteers put fresh pots of coffee on the tables. After everyone had refills, they were ready to return to work.

Utterly exhausted, Karen lay down on one of the empty cots in the rest area and passed out.

A sudden commotion woke Karen. She jumped to her feet and went out to see that the southern rescue crew had found something. She walked over to a crowd of people swarming into the restricted area as an ambulance pulled up.

"What's going on?" Karen asked Charley.

"They found her!" he said joyously.

Karen assumed *her* referred to Mallory, and dashed around the corner where she was held back by gangcops assigned to crowd control.

"She's alive!" she heard someone shout, and a number of people cried out.

A moment later Karen watched as Mallory's dust-encrusted, unconscious body emerged from the narrow passage that had been carefully scooped out of the rubble over the past day. There was an IV bag attached to her. It took Karen a moment to realize that something was wrong with Mal's right arm; there was a tight tourniquet wrapped around it. It took another moment before Karen recognized that her hand and arm were completely missing below the elbow. After the initial shock and sadness, Karen couldn't miss the irony. Mallory had lost her right index finger ten years earlier during the accidental bomb blast in Greenwich Village. Now the entire arm was gone in a second blast.

"She was huddled in the basement under the stairway," Charley said, as the ambulance sped off.

"Amazing she didn't suffocate," Karen commented.

"They said she spent the night sucking air through a clogged drainage pipe—smart lady."

Karen learned they were taking her to St. Vinny's, as Beth Israel was overwhelmed with the bodies of the previous bombing.

At about six, a functionally sober Scouter finally arrived on the scene. Karen was grateful to finally be relieved. But instead of going home, she drove to the hospital. Mallory was still in the middle of surgery, so Karen went to grab a cup of coffee from the vendor out front and sat down in the lobby where she quickly fell asleep until the aroma of something delicious woke her up.

"I still have some *lahmajoun* left, if you're hungry," said a voice next to her. It was her dear friend Mr. Bob Aardvarkian, the restaurant owner.

"What are you doing here?" she asked, stretching.

"Brought Mom some food, but she can't keep anything down."

"I'm sorry," Karen said. She saw that his eyes were bloodshot; clearly he hadn't slept in a while. "Is she here?"

"This is the only hospital in Rescue City that claims to offer treatment for cancer," he said. "But all they do is give her something that tastes like Kool-Aid, and I don't think she has much longer."

"I meant to come visit her earlier," Karen lamented.

"The Turks tried to kill her, but I think all those atomic bombs they tested out here finished the job. She was in great shape when we arrived, but she loved going for walks in the desert—said it reminded her of the old country."

"She really is a survivor."

"If you have any idea where I can get painkillers, that would be a great help. Sometimes it's just too much for her."

"How many does she need?"

"Not many, she doesn't have long."

"I got it. Where exactly is she?" Karen wondered if the place had a cancer ward.

"Gen pop." He pointed to the double doors at the rear of the lobby.

"Do you know the bed number?"

"Fifteen seventeen. She's been asking for you."

"Give me just a sec and I'll be right over."

Karen dashed upstairs to the guard on duty, flashed her ID, and informed him that she was going to be visiting a patient in lot number 1517. "Can you or whoever replaces you come get me as soon as Mallory is out of surgery?" The rooms upstairs were reserved for those who could afford them.

"Sure thing," the guard replied.

Karen went back downstairs and saw that the cook had fallen asleep with the pot on his lap. She passed through the rear doors into the giant outdoor tent that had originally been the hospital's parking lot. Over the years, as the need for more bed space increased, this vehicular area had become the new charity wing for most hospitals in the city.

Karen trotted through the ward, noticing that being outside had little effect on the foul stench. Though "surrogate doctors" still made the rounds, nurses and orderlies rarely came out here. Only loved ones and family members consistently attended to the patients down here—if anyone at all. Each patient's partition was roughly four feet wide by six feet across, divided by a network of crisscrossing ropes that were draped with torn and stained sheets. Karen focused on the fading numbers stenciled on the pavement. Parking spot 1517 held the army cot where Dora Aardvarkian lay, slowly dying.

Karen took a seat on an old wooden crate that someone had brought in as a seat. After a moment, the elderly woman opened her eyes.

"Thank God you're here!" Dora said in her native tongue.

"Sorry I didn't come sooner," Karen replied in rusty Armenian.

"It's not that. Before I die, I need to . . . talk to someone who isn't family . . ."

"Do you want a priest?"

"No god, so no priest," Dora said simply. "In the late 1940s, when I first read about how the Jews were being marched into the gas chambers that were disguised as showers, I envied them. Not until that final moment did they know for sure that they were going to die. Unless you've marched for days with those you know and love, and when

they can't keep up you see as they slowly get their brains beaten in
. . . Well, we knew we were going to die, but we kept walking anyway. My mother, aunt, friends, neighbors, all forced to walk slowly in
those thick Victorian gowns. We put on our best clothes, thinking we
were going to be hosts of the state. But marching under the hot sun,
everyone was killed at their own pace . . ." The elderly woman fell
silent, nervously running her fingers along the scars down the sides
of her face.

"Your son knows all about this," Karen said softly. "We all do."

"What he doesn't know—what no one knows, what I kept to myself all these years—is that I was married before I met his father. We
had two beautiful children: a little boy, Dikran, and a little girl, Anash.
At least my father and husband didn't have to see what happened. On
the first day the soldiers came, they marched the men into the woods
and killed them. They made us assemble with the other mothers and
their kids, then they brought over the elderly. And they said they were
moving us for our own protection."

Karen listened as Dora described, partly in Armenian and partly
in English, the horrific caravan of villagers—women, children, and
elderly—who were forced onward and prodded south toward Iran.
After a couple of days, many of them were dead, and there were only
about thirty of the heartiest who still managed to stagger forward.
Two soldiers were in the lead; one brought up the distant rear. The
next day and each day afterward, the soldiers were replaced because
they were in bad shape and couldn't keep walking without a rest.

Karen tried not to react, to just allow the older woman to release
all her suffering and pain.

"We were passing by this steep hill and it must've had a landslide
because I remember this pile of rocks and boulders. None of them
noticed, but I saw movement—I knew whatever was going to happen
would happen there.

"These fat little heads with their beady eyes were peeking out
at us. They were so stupid they didn't even seem to realize that we
couldn't run. Actually, there was one guy with an eye patch, he finally
stepped out in front and waited. He knew. When we finally reached
the bend in the road, the whole gang came charging out, maybe five
or six young men.

"Two of them grabbed my neighbor's daughter. She was just a
teenage girl, and they grabbed her as if she was a kitten they could
snatch. She kicked the first one in the shin, but the second one slugged

her across the jaw and started dragging her away. That's when her mother, Ani—an old friend of mine—jumped forward and scratched him across his face with her nails. She called my name, but I couldn't help, I had two children to protect."

"Absolutely, your life wasn't yours to lose," Karen said softly.

"One of the other guys came up from behind with a dagger and slit Ani's throat. She fell, and the guy with the scratched face started kicking her until she was unconscious, then urinated on her. When another young mother began begging for mercy, they beat her up. Then the soldier in charge started yelling at the man for injuring the women instead of killing them, so they took out their knives and began stabbing them, in the neck and chest, making a game of who could spurt the most blood."

Karen tried to stop listening and just focus on her breath.

"That was the good part. See, I thought they were done. I still had my kids and hadn't given up hope that somehow I could find somewhere to hide them. But as we passed the bend in the road, one of the men leaped forward and grabbed Anash. Dikran screamed, but I wouldn't let go of her. Someone came up behind me and hit me over the head. I felt dazed and when I stood up my shirt was torn off. I saw my Anash was being carried off like a sack of rice. That's the last thing I remember before blacking out. I'll always wonder about my little girl. Did they kill her? Is she still alive today?"

The silence became so severe that Karen asked, "What then?"

"Dikran's screaming woke me up. And we were alone. Everyone had walked on ahead. They left us behind—that's what you did. When other people we had known all our lives fell, or were attacked, or were taken by Kurds, we kept going and tried not to look back. We'd just think, *Thank God it's not us.*"

"So at least you were free?" Karen tried to sound positive.

"An unaccompanied Armenian mother and child alone in the Turkish countryside—we didn't have a chance. Bad as it seemed, at least I still had my son. So our only chance was trying to catch up with the rest of our village. We struggled down the road and soon we saw them in the distance." She paused for a long moment. "It was the old guy with the eye patch, walking down the road behind us, looking for stragglers. Did I mention that he had this big walking stick?"

"No."

"I tried to walk faster, but a moment later he grabbed my hair. I had a long braided ponytail, and he yanked me backward. Dikran threw a fit. Watching his sister getting carried off affected him deeply. He went crazy, attacking the old guy, kicking and flaying his arms at him. The eye patch man didn't fight him, he just threw his arms up and stepped back. I remember seeing Ani's scratch marks on his face. Even though she was dead, she had scarred him. I think Dikran thought—we both thought—it was over, that he'd let us go. We took a couple steps forward and next thing I know I heard an awful crunch and little Dikran was on the ground gagging. The guy had lifted his big stick and brought it down on my son's little skull. A moment later, he whacked him again. I fell on top of my poor baby. Next thing I know, the old Turk has me by my hair, coiling it in his hand. I tried hitting him, but he just started dragging me away from my boy. I was covered in blood, watching poor Dikran, his arms and legs flailing, as he died." The elderly woman cried quietly.

The memory was so painful that poor Dora hadn't wanted to share it with anyone, but she felt she owed her stolen daughter and murdered son the service of keeping their memories alive—so unfortunately, by default, Karen had inherited them.

As she imagined a young Dora being led away by the man with the eye patch, an image flashed before her of a distant desert. It was as vivid as if she were looking at it with her own eyes. But it wasn't in Turkey or even the Middle East—it was right here in Rescue City. She could make out several familiar geological details. The perspective was so clear it could only be from one place, the area known as the Goethals, in the southwestern tip of the reservation. The image had to be coming from Uli, which suggested once again that he was alive. He must be with the Burnt Men, the pseudo–Native American hippie tribe encamped at the bottom of Staten Island.

As much as she wanted to leave the pain of the moment and drive down there to find her brother, she couldn't abandon Dora, who went on to describe how the eye-patched man had brought her to his hut where he and another man had abducted half a dozen young women from various villages. After a few days of being raped, the string of young women were tied together, shoved into an oxcart, and driven to the outskirts of a town four days south. There they were sold to Akmed Mohammed—a gigantic round man wearing a fez and a diamond pinkie ring, who ran a brothel in Ankara. He didn't waste any time. The next day, he had all his new girls delicately branded on their faces, his insignia of ownership—two curly lines on the sides of her cheeks—an advertisement for their new profession.

"When I heard about the tattooed numbers on the arms of the survivors at Auschwitz, I was shocked by how they all do the same thing," Dora said. "Even if they're going to kill you, they need to brand you, to make you their trophy first."

Exhausted and unable to talk any further, the old woman clenched Karen's hand until she passed out.

Karen stayed next to the sleeping woman until Bob finally came by. She gently released Dora's frail little hand and the two stepped outside the sheet-draped partition.

"Stop by the restaurant when you can."

"I always do."

"Captain!" she heard—it was the gangcop watching Mallory. Karen saw him pinching his nostrils, unprepared for the stench of the gen pop tent. "There was an incident."

"What happened?" Karen asked as they returned to the hospital building.

"She's out of surgery, and they put her in the special security ward on the top floor along with the eight other survivors from the Cooper Union blast." The guard followed her up the steps. "She's stable, but some orderly was about to inject her with some kind of poison."

"Where's the orderly?"

"We got him upstairs, but he appears to have no idea that—"

"He's lying," she said instantly. "He's obviously trying to assassinate her."

"But he was the one who saved her."

"The orderly?"

"Yeah. When he came in with the drug, the guard on duty asked him what he was about to inject into her, and he was the one who read the chart and said it was the wrong medication. He could've just as easily injected her. Someone else had written the script on her chart."

"Why the hell would anyone try to assassinate an already injured election commissioner?" Karen asked.

Together they went up to the top floor, past the second guard on duty.

Karen located another gangcop who was helping other victims and reassigned him to Mallory's security detail. She then dashed to the nearest telephone and called the Williamsburgh Building.

"For some bizarre reason, someone just tried to kill Mallory," she said to Schuman.

"Oh, the poll!" he said.

"What poll?"

"Everyone is talking about it here, but no one took it seriously. Don't you remember? A poll taken in September throughout all five boroughs asking what politician people trusted most, and Mallory came out as number five—that's why she was appointed to the Election Commission. Now, with the Cooper Union bombing and most of the Crapper councilpeople wiped out, she's the most popular Crapper figure still alive."

"Oh God."

"And Shub just rejected a formal Crapper request to delay the upcoming mayoral election due to Dropt's death. So without any time to launch a new candidate, Mallory's probably the best hope to beat him, and they know that."

"Life just keeps getting better," Karen said.

"We're trying to get an ambulance."

"Why?"

"It'd be easier to protect her if we move her back to the Williamsburgh Building."

"Did you speak to her doctor?"

"No, but—"

"She's still in recovery after losing an arm. It's a miracle she's even alive. We'll check, but she probably can't be moved yet."

The doctor recommended keeping Mallory in the hospital for at least forty-eight more hours. On her own authority, Karen cleared the wing of the top floor of all other patients, assigned more gangcops to her security detail, and had the adjacent break room converted into a sentry post.

When the hospital administrators contacted the mayor's office to complain, the call was routed to Lewis. He too had just heard that Mallory was now the most electable Crapper candidate in Rescue City.

"If she does agree to run, we can't afford to have a second Crapper candidate assassinated. Forget the Rock & Filler Center bombing and just watch her until she's well enough to be moved," he said when he reached Karen.

"Fine."

Within thirty minutes, a Crapper sergeant named Remington had brought a dozen trusted Crapper gangcops to relieve those on duty, and turned the eastern half of the top floor of the hospital into a small fortress.

The building was swarming with gangcops and the situation seemed to be secure. During a lull, Karen was finally able to make a phone call to Staten Island. The switchboard put her call through to the borough president, Adolphus Rafique, whom she had known for years.

"I know this sounds odd, but you haven't met a middle-aged man who goes by the name Ulysses, have you?"

"Not since reading Joyce," Rafique replied succinctly.

As Karen politely ended the call, Remington made a frantic gesture in front of her: Mallory had just woken up.

She was still quite groggy when Karen entered her room. A nurse had just increased her dosage of painkillers.

"What the hell happened?" Mallory asked, recognizing her friend and trying to raise her bandaged stump.

"I'm sorry, Diana," Karen replied softly. "You lost your hand."

"Diana's dead," Mallory snapped back. "Don't ever call me that!"

"Cooper Union was blown up," Karen started to explain.

"I remember. Is Dropt . . . ?"

"Killed—along with almost everyone else."

"Shit! They've actually done it." Mallory's eyes went watery. "How many survived?"

"Eight in addition to you," Karen responded. "Almost the entire city council and most of the senior staff and secretaries are gone."

"I was in the basement, trying to get the janitor to fix my door, when the explosion went off. I had barely gotten out of the stairwell when I saw the building come down around me."

"Thank God you were down there."

"I had just seen your brother," Mallory said.

"You're kidding! Did you tell him I was searching for him?"

"No, because I thought you were wrong in what you're doing. The guy is clearly not right in the head. I'm not going to just let you kill him."

"I'll give you my word that I won't touch him, but can you please tell me where he is?"

"I sent him away for his own safety. I asked him to do me a favor and go down to Staten Island."

"I knew it!" Karen didn't mention the vision she'd had of him in the Goethals.

"Listen to me. I don't know if they can find it, but he . . . he left a tank of oxygen and a full hypodermic of the escape drug. Just let him take it and go."

"But there is no escape drug," Karen said.

"Then let him die believing there is."

"All right, fine. But I have something to ask of you, and it's big."

"What?"

"As of today, you are officially the most viable member of the Crapper Party."

"Lucky me," Mallory said tiredly.

"Believe it or not—according to that recent straw poll—you have the best chance of winning the upcoming mayoral election."

"That's ridiculous. I know at least half a dozen Crapper candidates—"

"All dead," Karen interrupted. "Look, the odds are probably against you. I mean the election is five days away, but right now you're the most popular figure in the party. The bad news is that others know this, because there's already been an attempt on your life since you got here."

"Shit." Mallory was too exhausted to really even think about it. She needed more sleep.

"You have to decide right now," Karen said, trying to squeeze in all the information before Mallory passed out. "'Cause there's a million details. Are you on board?"

"All right. Call my office and have Jenny put out some kind of release."

Karen was about to break the news that Jenny, her beloved secretary, had been killed in the blast, but Mallory had already passed out.

Karen called her own office at 30 Rock & Filler and instructed Schuman to check with the election headquarters in Queens on which forms were required to get Mallory's name on the ballot. Next she called Bill Clayton, Mallory's paralyzed and estranged husband, to see if he could help with his wife's campaign.

"Don McNeill was running Dropt's campaign," Clayton said. "He knows where all the resources are, he'd be the one to tap. But I think he wanted to run himself. Thing is, he has zero recognition."

Donald McNeill had been a *Village Voice* reporter back in Old Town, and had also been one of Mallory's closest friends. Karen called and made an offer: if he managed Mallory's campaign, Karen would guarantee him a prestigious posting, and she'd back him in any subsequent elections. Realizing this was the best deal he could get, McNeill immediatly accepted the terms.

"As I see it, with only a few days before the election, this campaign will be little more than letting people know she's the other name on the ballot," he said to Karen. "Even the Piggers are sick of Shub. I know I can get a bunch of people to campaign for her while she's in the hospital. It's actually a great angle: the candidate they can't kill."

After Karen got off the phone, she dozed alongside Mallory's bed. Almost immediately she found herself locked in another weird dream, a bilocation. She was looking into the face of a beautiful woman with an olive complexion, pressed up next to her—was Uli having sex again? He seemed to be getting more action in the past couple of days than she had in the past ten years. When the scene faded, the vision of the Goethals returned and lingered in her head. She knew Uli had to be around there.

Karen spent the morning in the hospital. In the afternoon, making a surprise inspection of Sergeant Remington and his garrison, she felt so confident in him that she decided to hurry home, take a shower, and grab a change of clothes.

She drove back to Brooklyn and snagged the last available parking spot in the guarded lot. When she stopped at Stamos's Stamps on the plaza, intending to pick up some snacks, she saw that they were selling Staten Island nose clips, and that was it—she decided to go. Whether her brother was a friend or a foe, she had to know. She bought one clip, along with a large bottle of water, and went right back to her car. It wasn't until she started over the Zano Bridge that she spotted it again—the dull yellow car she had noticed the other day on the Brooklyn Bridge. Someone was definitely tailing her.

6

At several points along Hyman Boulevard, the central road which ran the length of the pungent borough, the pavement vanished under desert sand and streams of wastewater. Forty minutes into Karen's drive, when the road forked in various directions and tapered in the distance, she had to take a compass out of the glove compartment to try to navigate. Rumor was that the Verdant League limited the number of signs in order to deliberately confuse possible invaders, and she was inclined to believe it. At one particularly ambiguous fork she came to a dead halt. After sitting there for about twenty minutes, a caravan of supply vans from JFK whisked past her. Karen waited until the last one passed and followed it south for fifteen minutes until she reached the old ferry building, then she parked and asked the guard at the door if she could meet with Rafique.

"ID, please."

Karen showed both of her badges, one as a Crapper captain and the other as a captain for the city's council cops.

The guard got on the phone and called upstairs, muttering. "He's on his way," he said without looking at her. "Please wait outside."

Karen thought this was rather odd, until a few minutes passed and four security officers raced out of the building and grabbed her. She was thoroughly frisked, and once they found her two knives, her hands were cuffed behind her back.

A moment later Adolphus Rafique, leader of the territory, stepped out of the large building. One of the young cops flanking him had a nose pin over his nostrils like Karen, but the others didn't. She assumed those were the long-term residents who had gotten their sinuses cauterized.

"What the hell is this?" she asked immediately.

"You're an upper-echelon city council official working for an administration that has repeatedly attacked my borough," Rafique responded.

"I'm not coming here as an official," she countered.

"You called and asked me if someone was here, and I told you no. Now, if there's someone hiding out here who has broken the law in Brooklyn or Manhattan, we have an extradition agreement that we uphold, but we also agreed that we all go through our own police forces. This is Police Chief Loveworks." Rafique pointed to an older man with pigtail braids.

"I am here as an American citizen who is looking for her brother, who as far as I know hasn't committed any crimes. And unless I'm mistaken, one of the freedoms of the US Constitution is the ability to travel," Karen argued.

"Actually," Rafique said, "the word *travel* doesn't appear in the Constitution in any context, but it has always been presumed, so we accept it here. However, in the interest of protecting the rights of my citizenry, I will politely ask that an escort accompany you."

"If I agree to this, can I also expect some assistance?"

Rafique turned to Police Chief Loveworks.

"It's not a negotiation. Any assistance will come at the discretion of your official escort," Loveworks replied, pointing behind Karen. "Meet Theodore, the bear."

A large, hairy, heavyset man in his midforties, with a big round face, long hair, and a strange Amish-like beard, stepped forward. He wore glasses and had an unlit cigarette hanging from his lips. Rafique excused himself and returned inside with his entourage in tow. Chief Loveworks walked off toward some nearby trailers.

"Call me Ted. Ted Berrigan," the large man introduced himself.

"You're not related to the Berrigan brothers, are you?" Karen asked nervously, remembering the debacle at the funeral.

"No relation, but I greatly admire their work," the man replied calmly, lighting up the cigarette.

"Well, Ted, I was wondering if I could stroll around a bit, try to find my brother."

"Sure, my time costs a quarter-stamp."

She obliged.

"You lead, I'll follow," he said as she began walking toward the Burnt Men colony. "So you're a Crapper gangcop, are you?"

"Yep. What do you do?"

"Other than working for the city ten hours a week—usually in some kind of policing capacity because of my scary appearance—I'm a poet." They hiked toward the settlement along the banks of the flooded airfield. "So is my wife Sandy. We figured that coming here would be a great opportunity to work on our art."

"Like a two-year sabbatical at Yaddo," Karen smiled. She remembered that this was how the Rescue City project had presented itself in the brochures as an attempt to lure artistic types.

"'When Something Looks Too Good to Be True.' That was the title of my very first poem here."

Karen continued walking through the assembly of hippies, staring into their faces.

"So who exactly are you looking for?"

"My brother, and I know exactly where he is."

"Where?"

She pointed southwest over the foul stench of the flooded airfield. "Over there."

"The Goethals," Ted said. "Why do you think he's there?"

"I had a vision," she said. "Only in Staten Island could you say that without getting laughed at in response."

"A vision, huh? I've met people who've sworn they've had them, but I've never believed they were real—and I'm a hippie poet."

"If you can get us a canoe, I can prove it."

"When exactly did you have this vision?" the poet asked suspiciously.

"Last night."

"How clear was it?"

"It was definitely a bilocation," Karen said, anticipating why he was asking the question. Prophecies were much fuzzier, usually filled with surreal images and infused with dreamlike qualities; whereas bilocations were crisp and clear, like watching something on a television.

"As I understand it, bilocations occur in real time," Berrigan said. "And there's no settlement out there. Nowhere to stand, lie, or sit. So even if he was out there, he's probably returned by now."

"Uli is middle-aged, with rugged good looks and Mediterranean features. See anyone matching that description?" Karen asked.

"Sounds like most guys here. Got a photo?"

She shook her head no.

"Doesn't ring a bell, but frankly, I don't live around here. I got kids, so I live in the upper west side of Staten Island."

Soon they came upon an old baseball diamond that was ringed with makeshift lean-tos and improvised shacks—the epicenter of the Burnt Men tribe. Nearly one hundred hippie types in various states of undress made up the community; chickens, dogs, and other semidomesticated animals mulled about, squawking, mooing, and barking amid the chatter of humans. While walking around this clutter of life, Karen asked her escort, "So what kind of poetry do you write?"

"Wanna hear my last poem?"

Karen reluctantly agreed.

He took out a small cube of paper and unfolded it until it became a large, ledger-sized sheet, then he cleared his throat and slowly read, "*Post . . . morpho . . . genesis.*" He then began refolding it deliberately.

"That's your whole poem?"

"That's it. It took me three years to compose," he said as he transformed it back into a tiny cube.

"This one word took you three years?" She wasn't sure if he was kidding or not.

"It's nothing like the poems I used to write, but being here has had a profound effect on me."

"Three years?"

"Let me put it this way: it took a year to realize what was happening, it took another year to give it meaning, and it took a third to reduce it from ninety pages to a single word. You have to understand that words take on a life of their own. They start out like babies, moving awkwardly, slowly learning to walk, and frequently they stretch out to handle new interpretations and uses. Siring a new word is not as easy as it looks. Getting it on its feet, for people to use it—that's even harder."

"What exactly does *postmorphogenesis* mean?"

"It's all in the word."

"Can't you just give me the quarter-stamp version?" Karen was still roaming around looking for her brother.

"*Post* means after, *morph* means shaping, *genesis* means creation. So the gist of the word is *shaping after birth*."

"Wouldn't that be just *metamorphosis*?"

"I wanted to emphasize how a thing shapes itself beyond its original intention."

"Wouldn't that be *postmorphomortem*?"

"It's not dead yet. It's still very much alive, it's—"

"Can't you just say *corrupt*, or *degradation*, or *transformation*?"

"Maybe, but my point is . . ."

Before the poet could continue to defend his word, Karen spotted something and sailed through the crowd. Fearful that she was trying to lose him, Berrigan lumbered behind, doing his best to stay on her tail.

Karen stopped before an attractive woman about her height. "You know him!" she exclaimed.

"Know who?" the stranger asked.

"Uli!" Karen was almost yelling.

"You're nuts!"

"You screwed him." Karen stepped forward. "Last night! I saw you!"

The woman turned to Berrigan. "I don't know what she's talking about."

"Bullshit!"

"Okay, that's enough bilocating," Berrigan said, stepping between them and gently nudging Karen back.

"She's lying."

"Fuck you!" the woman shouted.

"I saw you with him!" Karen insisted.

"Where'd you see us?"

"She's looking for her brother," Berrigan explained, then turned to Karen. "I'm sorry, but I'm going to have to ask you to leave Staten Island."

The woman, Bea Moses-Mayer, was about to ask the strange outsider to prove she was Uli's sister, but she could see the similarity in her face. She realized that asking for proof would reveal that she knew who Uli was, and implicate her—even though they hadn't actually had sex.

"This is such crap," Karen protested as Berrigan led her away. "Your sacred Verdant League has all this holier-than-thou bullshit about civil rights, so that I can't even talk to some dizzy Lizzy."

"You can talk to anyone here who'll talk to you, but she doesn't wanna talk," the poet replied as he walked his charge back to the ferry building.

"Get a little tough and all you hippies turn into marshmallows!"

"We like to play a little game here," Berrigan said, attempting to distract her and return to the former state of pleasantry. "It's called: *What would our lives have been like if it wasn't for the Wall Street bombing?*"

"I play that every day," Karen responded glumly. "I probably would've been happily married by now to some Waspy stockbroker, with a bunch of adorable kids, living on the Upper East Side."

"And the answer is . . ." He mimed flipping over an imaginary card. "You would've had four kids from two men; you'd be living in Peekskill and working on your third marriage to a Belarusian."

"Hey, you're that council copper," interrupted a security guard as they approached the ferry building.

"Lucky me," Karen said tiredly, not sure which of them she was replying to. The guard handed her a shoebox with her knives and other personal effects.

"I just got a message from one of our northern precincts that heard a Crapper APB at the hospital where they brought all the injured from that Cooper Union attack."

Karen felt her bowels clench up. "Get any details?"

"Just a call for help to all available officers."

As Karen dashed back to her car, Ted Berrigan waved and yelled his final salutation: "Postmorphogensis!"

Twenty-five minutes later, Karen's car slowly crossed the slightly swaying Staten Island Ferry Bridge and passed the sandbags along Lower Manhattan. When she arrived at St. Vinny's Hospital on 12th Street, dozens of official solicars were parked out front. It looked just like Cooper Union, the aftermath of a disaster. Off to one side she saw it parked—the yellow vehicle that had been loosely following her for the past day or so. Within a few minutes she had rushed past the armed gangcops posted about the perimeter and made it up the stairs, before she was stopped just below Mallory's floor by a gangcop she didn't recognize.

"Where's Remington?" she asked.

"Holy shit, you're still alive!" she heard someone yelling down to her. It was Scouter Lewis, standing on the top landing, drenched in sweat, desperately needing a shower. He waved her up.

When she reached the top floor, she saw that it was covered in blood. Bodies of gangcops and hospital staffers were scattered about, marked by knife wounds and bullet holes.

"What the hell happened?" Karen carefully moved around the pools of blood to Mallory's room. Seven bodies, including poor Sergeant Remington's, were lying dead on the floor being photographed. "Where's Mallory?"

"This scene is all of three hours old," Lewis said softly. "So just take some deep breaths. Apparently, an assault team of six men dressed as hospital staff arrived during the shift change. They entered Mallory's room without any alarm and pulled out handguns and machetes."

"How many were killed?" Karen asked.

"All of our people and two of theirs. We thought they took you too."

"What do you mean *took me too?*"

"Well, where the hell were you?"

"I went home and took a nap," she lied, knowing that her vision of her missing brother would never wash. "Where the hell is Mallory?"

"They grabbed her. You're supposed to be dead on the floor, fighting alongside your men!" Lewis shouted. "Why did you abandon your post?"

"Remington had everything in control. Unlike you, I didn't tie one on and have to sleep it off. I've been working nonstop and I needed a shower and a change of clothes."

"First of all, you clearly didn't shower and your clothes are filthy. Secondly, in my experience, when there's a lone survivor, he or she is usually the one who betrayed the rest."

"You're right. I was up for the past two days and didn't even shower, I just—"

"You're fucking lying to me again!" Lewis's face was beet red, spit flying from his mouth. "The very first thing I did was send someone to your house."

"Mallory was my best friend!" she yelled back. "We came to this shithole together!"

"Then you're a lousy friend, because some crazy motherfuckers are probably torturing the crap out of her!"

"Go fuck yourself!"

"You abandoned your post," Lewis said simply. "You're suspended from duty. Go home and wait till I call you."

Infuriated, Karen walked out of the blood-splattered room, pausing in the corridor to inspect the two dead members of the assault team who were dressed as hospital attendants. She didn't recognize either of them. She was about to exit when she remembered something. Going over to the nurses' station, she peeked out the window, then turned and approached the head nurse.

"I'm Captain Sarkisian." Karen flashed her badge.

"I remember," the nurse said. Most of the hospital staff were acutely aware of the woman who had cost them valuable stamps by clearing the paying patients from the top floor.

"I need a hypodermic needle filled with something that's not lethal."

"I can probably get you a syringe with B12."

"Fine."

When the nurse left her station, Karen spotted a container of purple pills that she recognized as morphine tablets. She was able to count out six before the nurse returned. The woman handed Karen a syringe with a cap over the needle. Karen discreetly looked out the window again, trying to get a fix on the person sitting in the yellow solicar.

"Thanks again," she said to the nurse, then headed downstairs and out the rear exit to the gen pop ward.

When she reached Dora Aardvarkian's partition, the elderly genocide survivor was asleep, but her son was sitting next to her reading. When he glanced up, Karen put a finger over her mouth and handed him the six purple tablets, mouthing, *Morphine.*

"Thank you," he said softly.

She hurried out. While circling the block, she spotted a loose fire hydrant cap sitting unchained on the curb. The small, cast-iron object had to weigh at least thirty pounds. She lugged it around the corner and slowly approached the yellow car that had been tailing her. Some bristle-haired guy in his twenties was sitting inside alone, eating a banana, listening to an Elvis song on a portable cassette player. Every few minutes he'd steal a glance at the hospital's main entrance.

Karen lifted the hydrant cap above her head and slammed it through the driver's window and onto his head, pitching him forward into the steering wheel. She pulled the door open, grabbed the stunned youth by his shirt collar, and swung him out, plopping him facedown on the ground. Karen jumped on his legs, took out a plastic band, and looped it around one wrist, then the other, securing his arms behind his back.

"What the fuck!" he moaned, bleeding from a gash on the side of his head.

"I'm just going to ask you once: who do you work for?" Now he was starting to look familiar.

"I . . . I was just waiting for my wife."

"You've heard of the steel yarmulke . . ."

"They don't do that unless someone is dying," he said.

Karen sat on his back and took the hypodermic with the B12 out of her jacket. She held it for him to see and quickly injected it into his arm.

"What is that?"

"You're going to be unconscious in a minute. Then I'll just extract the information out of you before you die."

"Wait, no, please!"

"Count to ten backward."

"I'll tell you whatever you want!"

"Who are you working for?"

"Deere! Deere Flare!" Karen realized that this was the white-bread lover she had thrown out of Deere's boarding room in Downtown Brooklyn the other day.

"Why the fuck were you following me out to Staten Island?"

"I-I didn't—"

"What's your name, asshole?"

"Tim Vey!"

"How'd you meet Deere?"

"In DT!"

"What's that?"

"Domination Theocracy!"

"Where the fuck is Mallory?"

"I have no idea, I swear!"

"Did they grab her?"

"No! Not to my knowledge. I only know I was supposed to follow you and report back to Deere, that's all!"

"Let's go report then." She helped Vey to his feet and pushed him into the passenger side of his car. She knocked out the rest of the broken driver's-side glass, placed the hydrant cap next to him, and slid behind the wheel.

"So, I know I'm heading up to the Bronx," she informed him as she sped uptown, "but you're gonna have to tell me exactly where I'm going."

"But Deere's in Brooklyn."

"You're taking me to the Domination Theocracy headquarters."

"They meet at different places." He sounded increasingly distressed.

"You're going to tell me where to go before we reach Harlem."

He let out a deep sigh and remained quiet until they crossed 96th Street, at which point Karen prodded him: "Nothing, huh?"

He stayed silent. As he looked idly away, Karen hauled the iron hydrant cap down squarely on his knee. He let out a scream.

"Tell me everything you know about DT, right now!" she shouted. "Or you're going to get amputated by a hydrant cap!"

"We believe God put us on this earth and that His lessons should guide us here," he finally rasped through the pain.

"Does that allow for homosexuality?"

"Hell no!"

"I walked in on you fucking Deere the other day."

"DEERE IS A BEAUTIFUL WOMAN!" he screamed violently.

"Sure she is, and I'm not going to hit you again." She slammed the cap down on his knee again.

He groaned in pain as Karen drove over the bridge into the Bronx, past the Yankee Stadium Civil Headquarters, and up beyond the empty zoo. After entering the last residential area in the north end of the borough, Karen started tensing up.

"So how many people are in this DT group?"

When Vey didn't respond, she lifted the hydrant cap into the air.

"Ten! There are ten of us in my cell," he said quickly.

"And how many cells are there?"

"Just one!"

"Where is it located?"

He didn't say a word. Karen stopped abruptly at the next corner and the cap dropped under her seat. She took a box cutter out of her purse, which finally compelled Tim to grunt out directions.

They drove for another ten minutes and eventually parked outside a peach-colored house in the Pelham Bay section of the Bronx. It was a typical Pigger dream cottage.

"This is the place," he said. "But they had nothing to do with Mallory, I swear it."

"Who took her then?"

"I don't know, I just know it wasn't DT. We simply don't have the manpower. We couldn't go up against that armed garrison you had protecting her."

"Who is the head of your God squad?"

"Erica. Erica Allen Rudolph."

"What does she look like?"

"A much-maligned woman," he said simply.

Karen started the car again and sped around the corner, then cursed, turning off the engine. "Shit, I got a flat!"

"I didn't hear anything," Tim said as she got out of the car.

"Come on, I could use your help."

Since his wrists were still bound together, she had to help him out. She led him to the rear of the vehicle and popped open the trunk.

"I can't do anything with my wrists cuffed."

"Turn around, lean forward, and I'll release you," she said. But instead of cutting the plastic tie, she reached down and grabbed her prisoner by his ankles and flipped him forward into the deep trunk.

"What the hell?!"

She pushed his legs in sideways and slammed the trunk down on him.

"What are you doing? I'll suffocate!"

"It's ventilated. I'm just going to be a moment, but give me any shit and you'll be in there a lot longer."

Karen sprinted around the block and up to the peach house. Creeping up to one of the windows, she took out a small compact mirror from her purse and ducked below the sill, using the mirror to periscope inside. No one appeared to be home. She continued circling the house until she finally spotted someone—an attractive middle-aged woman just like Vey had described. That was confirmation enough.

Karen headed back to the car and started driving. At a traffic light she heard thuds coming from the trunk but she ignored them until she made it safely back to Manhattan.

Harlem housed the nearest Crapper precinct. During the entire thirty-minute drive to the station house, she could hear muffled shouts and thumps coming from the rear. Once she opened the trunk, the still-handcuffed Vey immediately started shouting: "Goddamnit! You told me I'd be out of there in a few minutes! I told you everything you wanted to know and now my arms feel like a pincushion! . . . Wait a second. Where are we?"

"Think twice next time you tail me."

Apparently he'd had some wiggle room in the trunk because as she reached down to pull him out, he punched her in the stomach. When he swung at her a second time, though, she caught his arm, pulled him out, and threw him to the ground. Before he could get back up, she jumped on him and put his neck in a vise. Vey reached back and grabbed her by her hair, yanking her head.

"I NEED SOME HELP OUT HERE!" she shouted as two gangcops exited the precinct. When Vey tried to run, she tackled him. In a moment, he was getting cuffed again. In another moment, he was getting tossed into a holding cell in the precinct basement.

"Listen," she said to the watch commander, an old friend named Jerry Howard, "can you hold him until I call you?"

"Do you want us to arrest him for assault or something?"

"No, no paper trail, I'm doing a quick investigation, but if I cut him loose he'll notify his people, so just sit on him till I say otherwise."

"Will do."

Since Scouter Lewis had put her on leave, Karen knew she had a few days before he would calm down and lift the suspension.

Karen borrowed a pair of binoculars from the precinct, then grabbed some food and a couple gallons of bottled water. She sped Vey's yellow solicar back up to the DT headquarters in the Bronx.

While she scoped out the peach-colored house, three men and the one woman came and went. She wasn't sure if Mallory was being held there, but she knew that if she called the police in for a raid, she wouldn't be able to extract any more information from the little cell. During her surveillance, aside from when she dozed off several times, she also kept an eye on several adjacent houses. One next door, which appeared empty, would offer a clean view into the DT's upper floors. If Mallory was inside, she'd probably be upstairs because the place clearly had no basement.

Over the next twenty-four hours, she used her binocs intermittently to check out all the upper windows. Even though she couldn't get a clear view of every room on the top floor, she was able to sort through the garbage left out back and finally decided that Mallory probably wasn't there.

During the second night, when Erica Rudolph finally hit the lights to go to sleep, Karen went to a nearby stamp shop, where she grabbed a snack and made some calls on their pay phone.

Her first one was to Don McNeill, the councilman who had taken charge of Mallory's campaign. Despite the fact that Mallory was still missing, her flash campaign had hit the ground running. Taking it upon himself, McNeill had come up with a list of campaign issues that would make Mallory popular with the moderate Piggers—he knew she already had the Crapper vote.

The first hurdle was just getting her on the ballot. With the help of a brigade of young Crapper volunteers who were energized by the recent tragedy, McNeill was trying to collect enough signatures to qualify Mallory before the deadline.

"Thing is, if she actually wins the election, I don't know how long we can hold an office if there's nobody to fill it."

"I'll free her by Election Day," Karen vowed.

By the time Karen returned to the peach-colored house, she had come up with an idea of how to flush Rudolph and her cronies out of their hole. She snuck in back with a large screwdriver, jimmied the phone box open, and pulled out a few of the wires.

Just out of sight around the corner, she waited. Sure enough, around noon the next day, the door opened. For the first time since she began to surveil the place, Karen got a clear look at Erica Allen Rudolph as she exited with a large brutish man, who escorted her to a car across the street and acted as her chauffeur. Once Karen established that the house was indeed empty, she raced back to the yellow car and pursued them.

Their vehicle cruised slowly through the Bronx and then crossed over to Manhattan, where Karen was astonished to see a variety of freshly slapped-up *MALLORY FOR MAYOR* posters on nearly every corner. Based on whatever material they'd been able to quickly pull together, Don McNeill and his little election campaign cadre had done a fairly impressive job. Just seeing such an immense effort encouraged Karen all the more to rescue her abducted friend.

She had worried that Erica and her henchman would head to some remote location in the outer boroughs, where her presence would stand out and things would get dicey. So she was grateful when they eventually pulled into a parking lot in Midtown, just a few blocks from her Rock & Filler Center office.

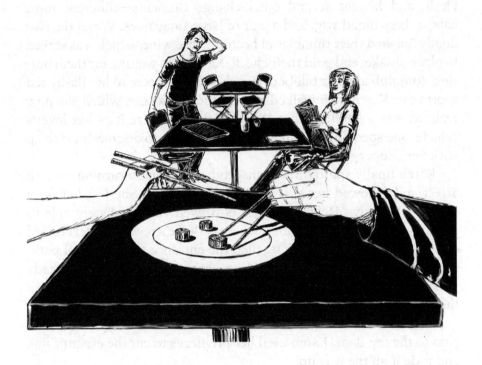

7

Kira Sushi didn't mean *Dirty Fingers* in Japanese, but that's still what everyone called the place—because that's what all the sushi there tasted like. At least everything *looked* appetizing. In the moment one grabbed his or her chopsticks and picked up the tight rolls, tapping them into the shallow dipping bowls just before dropping them on his or her tongue, a patron could forget that all the food there was either frozen, dried, canned, or boxed, and consisted of the lowest-grade nutrients that the Feedmore Corporation could find. Once the sushi hit the palate, the bubble burst—the food tasted awful. Still, it was a hair better than the competing Asian restaurant across the street, commonly called the Great Strands of China due to the balding cook.

Karen sighed when she saw Erica Allen Rudolph sitting at a corner table with none other than Deere Flare. Although there were billions of people in the world, when you washed out all the human ore and detritus, only a few chosen nuggets really sparkled. Still, Mallory was an integral part of all their secret pasts so Karen simply refused to believe that Deere had a role in her abduction.

Because Deere was wily and perceptive, Karen knew she needed a disguise. During the half hour that Deere and Rudolph were eating and talking, Karen hurried over to a nearby clothing store, Dress Your Flesh, and bought several quick-change garments—different tops, hats, a dirty-blond wig, and a pair of large sunglasses. When the two finally finished their thimbles of heated white wine, which was served in place of sake, and paid their check, Karen was waiting for them outside. Rudolph and her tall bodyguard escorted Deere to her flashy red sports car. Karen then walked over to the yellow car, which she now realized was a liability since Deere might recognize it as her lover's vehicle. She sped down Fifth Avenue attempting to discreetly catch up with her slippery friend.

Karen finally spotted the transgender mercenary turning on 14th Street and followed her over the Brooklyn Bridge. She lost her for a while in Brooklyn Heights, as her borrowed car was barely able to reach twenty-five miles an hour, whereas Deere's newer model cruised at a cool forty. When Karen reached the entrance to the official parking lot at the Williamsburgh Building, she saw that Deere had already parked. Only after she watched her enter the building did Karen park the yellow jalopy around the corner and go in.

She learned from the security guard that Deere had just gotten a pass to the top floor. Karen used her privileges to cut the elevator line and rode it all the way up.

Deere was good friends with Dianne Colder. Karen wondered if maybe she'd come here to see the lobbyist, not yet aware that Colder had been killed. When the elevator finally reached the top floor and the door slid open, Deere was standing there waiting.

"Perfect synchronicity," Deere said. "I was looking for you, was just about to leave, and here you are."

"You came here to see *me?*" Karen said.

"You asked me to keep an eye on that prayer group up in the Bronx."

"Okay." Deere must've known she was being followed.

"You said you'd cut someone loose in exchange for some info."

"What do you have for me?" Karen asked nonchalantly, leading Deere into her office.

"Fenwick told you that some new explosives were being used here, and you asked me to check out this fanatical religion, remember?"

"And what did you find out?"

"They don't have Mallory, explosives, or anything except Jesus. End of story."

"How do you know?"

"I just know. Now I need a favor."

Karen stared silently at her for a moment, wondering what the hell was going on. On one hand, she did ask Deere for information about DT, yet she'd also found Vey following her after Mallory had been abducted. And in fairness to the sect, after surveilling their safe house she'd seen no signs that they were holding Mallory. By all available evidence, Vey was telling the truth—they simply didn't have the manpower to undertake an operation as resourceful and well orchestrated as the bloody Cooper Union assault.

"I know this is an odd question," Karen began, "but ten years ago, back in Old Town, how exactly is it that you came to join the Weather Bureau?"

"Are you kidding me?"

"No."

"It's a little late to worry about me being an informant now, isn't it?"

"Indulge me for a minute and I'll do you your favor."

"I was living on the streets of the Lower East Side, hustling for drugs in trashy joints and bars. I was sleeping in Union Square Park— until I met Terry Robbins."

"Where?"

"In Max's Kansas City."

"Then what?"

"Then nothing."

"Why did you want to join the Weather Bureau? I mean, we were all radical college kids, you never fit that bill."

"You're right. My father threw me out for being a fag. What can I say? The war, all the lib movements, the psychedelic shit. I guess the real reason I joined is I just had nowhere else to go." Deere smiled. "But I do now, don't I? I've done pretty well here."

"I wonder why they let you in."

"Well, why the hell did they let *you* in?"

"Actually, they approached me. They needed *me*."

"So what the hell are you saying?"

"I just want to know why you wanted to join. I mean, you have to admit you don't fit the profile."

"You'd have to ask Terry about that."

"Terry was blown to pieces ten years ago," Karen replied.

"I know exactly why he let me in," Deere said. "'Cause when he told me to do something, I did it. I didn't mind getting arrested, or stealing, or getting beaten up."

That made perfect sense. Deere always got the job done, and back then, the Weather Bureau was probably the only organization that would have him. Now, though, here in this ruthless little gutter in Nevada where rats ruled, Deere was getting the job done for whoever paid top dollar.

"You promised me a reprieve in exchange for information, and I gave you the information. You know I wouldn't lie about that."

"Who?" Karen asked.

"He's being held in Kew Gardens."

"What for?"

"Car theft."

Karen flinched. She couldn't help but think that Deere knew she had stolen her boyfriend's car. "Was he pleabagged?" she asked calmly.

"Yeah, they're taking his left hand."

"What's his name?"

Deere handed Karen a card that had *Vito Rizzo* scribbled on it. "Not to reinforce ethnic stereotypes, but he's part of the Gallo tribe," she said. "He's coming here tomorrow to put his hand on the chopping block."

Karen plucked the card from her fingers. "I thought Gonzalez was their inside man."

"I'm scheduled to work the recruitment table downstairs for Pure-ile Plurality on Jay Street tomorrow afternoon. Feel free to pop by if you need me," she said with a smile.

When Deere left, Karen knew she had reached a dead end. Her best friend Mallory had been kidnapped, her brother Uli was still missing, and she had no clue where either of them were. The only thing holding her together was the fact that they were both probably still alive. If they wanted Mallory dead, it would've been infinitely easier to just kill her in the hospital instead of dragging her off somewhere. And if Uli was dead, she knew she'd feel or see it.

In her office the next afternoon, Karen called Kew Gardens and learned that earlier in the day Deere's mobster had been transferred to the Williamsburgh Building, where the small surgical unit was located. Within the next hour he was going to be prepped for a left hand amputation. This was the first time Deere had ever requested that an amputation be commuted, which was strange enough, but the fact that Mallory was still nowhere to be found compelled her to check out this clown.

Karen called downstairs and asked if the prisoner had been anesthetized yet.

"Not yet, why?"

She asked them to postpone until she came down to interview Mr. Vito Rizzo.

Twenty minutes later, Captain Sarkisian took the elevator down four flights and met Rizzo, a vainly handsome fellow who had been in lockup for six days and was in desperate need of a shave and shower. Karen requested that he be escorted to conference room six, the only one with no one-way mirror, just two chairs divided by a small table. His hands were cuffed and the three long bars of bright fluorescent lights were all flipped on when she entered. Karen dropped a file with some papers and a legal pad on the table, sat across from the prisoner, and casually scanned some documents that had nothing to do with this case. After reading them silently for a minute, she finally began: "Mr. Victor Rossi?"

"Vito," the man said in a deep voice, "I'm Vito Rizzo."

"Hold on," she said, reading from her form, "you're not Victor Rossi?"

"No, I'm Vito," he said impatiently. "You here to spring me or what?"

"Sorry." She started collecting the file. "I got the wrong man."

"Now hold on, I'm supposed to get the hell out of here."

"Who told you that?"

"When I did this job, I was told I'd have immunity."

"What job?"

"The job I did. I was told I'd get immunity, or impunity, or whatever it is where they let you off."

"I don't know who told you that, but if you're on this floor, you're going to be put under within the next hour or so." Karen casually checked her watch.

"Who was you looking for?"

"Someone named Victor Rossi."

"Well, sometimes I go by Victor. What do you got for me?"

"I just wanted to talk to him."

"Do you mind my asking what it is you do here?"

"I'm in charge of the council cops' Task Force on Stolen Vehicles," she lied. "We've been losing cars at an alarming rate. Feedmore has stopped replacing them, and I got a notice that Victor Rossi claimed to know something about the thefts."

"I don't rat out no one," he said stubbornly.

Karen considered her next words in silence, then rose to her feet and stepped out into the hallway. She bought two cans of cold lime soda from a vending machine and brought them and a guard with her back into the conference room.

"I'll try to help you," she said.

"If I give you a name, I'm dead. Simple as that."

"I don't necessarily need a name."

She pulled one of the cold cans of soda from her bag, popped the tab, and took a sip. Rizzo stared at the beverage as though it were nectar from the gods.

"Want one?"

"Yeah."

She slid the second can across the table.

He had a bit of trouble opening it, so Karen asked him, "If I free your hands, you gonna try any funny stuff?"

"No ma'am."

She got the guard to remove his cuffs.

"Look, the more you tell me, the less weight you'll lose."

"Then let's see if we can just get my fingernails trimmed," Rizzo said with a flat grin.

"Let me start by saying I'll let you keep one finger if you tell me how many cars you stole."

"One finger?"

"Yep, the other four will still have to go."

"Since I got here I probably stole over a hundred cars. It's what I do."

"And you did this for Gallo?"

"I told you I can't give up no names."

"What do you do with these cars?"

"For another finger?"

"Three questions for your pinkie," Karen said.

"Okay, so I'll have a pinkie and and a thumb."

"A pinkie and an index," she countered. A thumb was worth at least six questions.

"We do everything with cars. Some are rechopped for parts, some are resold to private citizens. Others go to respectable people you yourself work with."

"When you were arrested this time around, let's see, it says . . ." She opened the file and pretended to read it.

"I was stealing a car up in Jackson Heights," he filled in.

"It wasn't a new car."

"No, it wasn't new."

"You can't tell me who it was for?"

"No names." When Karen pursed her lips and looked a little stymied, he offered, "I can tell you what kind of car I was looking for, if that's worth anything."

"Okay. What kind?"

"Something nondescript that could carry a heavy load."

"See, that really doesn't help me."

"Well, what would help you?"

"What would really help me is if you told me who you were getting this car for," Karen said.

"If I tell you that, it's not just me that's dead, it's also everyone I love."

"Okay, well, you've still got two fingers, so if you want to keep the other three digits . . ."

"Yeah."

"I'm not good at playing blindman's bluff. You're going to have to trust me a little."

"I don't trust no one."

"Okay, here it is: you've earned two fingers and I'm willing to let you keep the other three if you can give me one single relevant piece of information. The problem is, I don't even know what that information is."

"If you don't know, I certainly don't know," he replied.

"Fine." She closed the file. "You're a three-finger amputee."

"No!"

"Then quit the bullshit and tell me something I can bring to my boss!"

"Well, my fee is one hundred stamps per car."

"Per car! You mean that's how much you've averaged over the years?"

"Oh no, each job is negotiated differently. Sometimes I get paid in service, sometimes in barter. That fee was just this particular job, which was a multicar deal."

"How many cars were you supposed to steal for this job?"

He chugged down the entire can of soda and let out a low, deep, controlled belch. "I can't tell you that one, 'cause this is still an active case for me and I don't want to incriminate myself."

"Were any of them municipal vehicles?" Karen prompted.

"No, I had nothing to do with the trucks that took down Cooper Union. I'm not insane."

"How many cars were you supposed to steal—regardless of whether you stole them or not? And where were you supposed to deliver them?"

"Okay, so I'll tell you how many, and where I was going to drop them off, but then—"

"And I want to know the deadline for this job," she added.

"That's three questions for all my fingers," he bargained.

"And none of them involve any squealing."

"And then I'm out of here."

"Completely intact."

He cleared his throat, and in a soft voice he said, "I was supposed to grab half a dozen cars within the week and drop them off on 145th and Grand Concourse." That wasn't far from the DT headquarters.

"What do you think they were for?"

"Damned if I know, but that's another question, so unless you're planning on giving me one of your fingers . . ."

"Expensive cars?" she pushed.

"No, just so long as they drove. I looked for cars that wouldn't be noticed."

While Karen pondered this information, Rizzo continued, "I'll throw in one other detail that might or might not interest you—whoever asked for this, they weren't going to chop, paint, or change them."

"Is that unusual?"

"Highly unusual. I mean, we're all stuck here. Odds are someone will spot the vehicle. Hell, I stole one vehicle three times over the years."

"Maybe they were going to customize them."

"Maybe," he said, "but I'll just say I offered them a very good rate to repaint them, so I'd be surprised if they could get a better deal any-where else."

Karen thanked him, told him to sit tight, and went back upstairs to Scouter Lewis's office, wondering why someone might need to steal six cars.

Lewis was passed out on his desk, deep in the post-liquid lunch stage of his day, snoring profoundly. She quietly went through his desk drawers until she located a limb-reprieve form and began filling it in. Under *Limbs spared*, she scribbled, *Left hand*. Under *Reasons*, she wrote, *Informant*. Then she gave Lewis a sharp shake.

"What? What?"

"Sign!" She slipped the form in front of him, barely missing the small pool of drool he'd left on the desk, and stuck a pen in his hand. Without even asking, let alone reading, he drunkenly scribbled on the bottom of the form and went back to sleep.

She added his official stamp, brought it downstairs, and within twenty minutes Rizzo was stumbling exhausted out of the double doors of the Williamsburgh Building.

Although car bombings were frequent, people rarely stole or blew up more than one vehicle at a time. Six cars had to be for a major at-tack, and that could only be from a very committed group toward a specific enemy. Karen, who was still technically in charge of the up-coming POW convention, felt certain this was the target.

That kind of attack would wipe out one of the greatest concentra-tions of domestic dissidents in the US, but it would require more than six vehicles. Regardless, she had to move the convention somewhere beyond any vehicular reach. She didn't know how, but she had to alter the location of the rally. The year before, the annual POW convention had been held in a series of large tents in western Staten Island, far from any roads or car bombs. Rafique had sponsored it, but the smell had been mind-numbing. Attendees found themselves fainting.

But Brooklyn—where they were planning to hold this next convention—was completely vulnerable.

Rizzo's stolen cars were almost certainly intended to be bombs. And the fact that Deere was helping him was scary, because it meant this probably went all the way to the top. Someone powerful was ob-viously planning a large-scale assault.

Although they probably couldn't check every car in the borough, they could check the cars in the immediate vicinity, which was stan-dard practice for public events anyway. But by moving the rally to

Manhattan—the only island in this desert—they could more effectively monitor the vehicles coming into the borough.

"Captain Sarkisian!" Karen heard as she exited the Williamsburgh Building. Turning around, she saw two of the most feared Pigger bureaucrats of Rescue City: the unofficial attorney general, Chain, and the unofficial mayor, City Council President Newton Underwood.

"Hi, guys," she greeted, "I was actually looking for you both."

"Pray tell, why?" Underwood asked with a wide smile.

"The mayor's office has rejected my change-of-location request for the upcoming POW convention, and I was wondering if you could help me relocate it to a safer place."

"We'll get right on that," Underwood said, "if you're willing to tell me where he is."

"Where *who* is?"

"Your dear brother, of course."

Chain just listened without saying a word.

"I heard that he was here; beyond that, I have no clue. In fact, I should probably be asking *you* that."

"We have reason to suspect he killed Dianne Colder," Chain finally spoke.

"Just awful. Not to mention the abduction of the new mayoral candidate Mallory," she replied. "Are you looking for her too?"

"If we find out that you're protecting him or are somehow in collusion . . ." Underwood ignored her.

"We all work together here, councilman. In fact, since the city council is meeting tomorrow, I was hoping you could propose my change of venue."

Underwood started walking away.

"I find you're colluding, my fist is gonna collude with your face," Chain said menacingly, and followed the de facto head of the Pigger Party.

Karen watched as they returned to their car in the lot. Before stepping inside, though, she saw Underwood point at something across the street just out of view. The two men chuckled, got into their car, and drove off. She was curious and took a couple steps backward to see what they had found amusing.

Deere Flare was standing with a group of handsome male Pureile Plurality workers. They had their usual recruitment table set up on Flatbush Avenue right in front of the flow of constant shoppers. Karen went to a burger dive across the street, bought a weak cup of coffee, and watched. Over the next twenty minutes, she saw Deere approach several dozen men. She leveraged her feminine wiles as far as she could, trying to get them to register their names and addresses with PP. All but one simply took the offered brochure and kept walking. What distinguished this table from ones Karen had previously seen was its aggressive political zeal; they were shouting slogans, promoting Shub.

Amid the endless, mindless squawking of countless human animals migrating into one of the half dozen awful eateries along Jay Street, Karen was starting to grow drowsy—until something piqued her interest. A man in a wrinkled PP suit came staggering up to the recruitment table. As Karen focused on him, she jerked forward, spilling the dregs of her coffee. It was none other than Uli, her missing brother. She was so startled to see him that she found herself bewildered as to what she should do next.

Karen remembered that, first and foremost, he was an FBI agent. She casually touched the handle of her knife through her jacket. *I should just kill him now and be done with this shit forever,* she thought. Then she felt her resolve evaporate. A second later she thought, *Whether I kill him or help him, I still have to apprehend him.* Considering he was with Deere, she decided she had better approach cautiously. Since they were standing on the corner chatting, she realized it would be easy to just come up behind him and shove her knife up under his chin and arrest him.

When she circled the block and reached the PP table, she was dismayed to find that both were gone.

"Excuse me," she approached one of the PP recruiters, "I was just here talking with a lovely lady and I was wondering where she went."

"She's gone for the day. But maybe I can help you?"

"Gone where?"

"No one ever knows where or when Miss Flare goes out," the volunteer punned.

Heading back into the Williamsburgh Building, Karen hoped against hope that Deere had brought Uli inside to deliver him to her.

As she stepped into the lobby, she saw Crapper city councillor Tony Pagan heading for the stairs; his office was on the third floor. "Councilman Pagan," she called out, "I don't know if you remember, but Scouter Lewis was trying to change the location—"

"If they want to hold it in Brooklyn, it's not up to us to change it."

"It's a security issue."

"This is America, they have rights."

"And we have a duty to protect them."

"Excuse my candor, Captain Sarkisian, but how exactly are you going to benefit from this move?"

"I'm not benefiting at all. The fact of the matter is that the place is exposed. It's quite close to Queens, and the Piggers have been making constant threats. It's a huge security risk."

"The city council is supposed to be bipartisan. The mayor announced that once we start planning events to exclude each other, we might as well just break the city in two."

"I have reasons to suspect that someone is preparing for a large-scale attack, so I want to put this event somewhere accessible but where we can reasonably protect it."

"It's not up to me."

"From what I hear, you're one of the two people who voted against the move."

"Frankly, I owed the vote to Backdoor."

"Bachus Leiberman?" *Backdoor* was the nickname of the notorious Pigger councilman.

"Yeah, he's the one you want to speak to," Pagan said. "Get him on your side and you can put the rally on the moon if you want."

"Is he here now?" She was prepared to confront him.

"His field office is up in Kew Gardens, but he's rarely there."

"So where might I find him?"

"Well, you didn't hear this from me," he edged closer to her, "but there's a certain godless pier in Queens where Backdoor shows his love quite liberally. If you can find him there at the right time, I'm sure he'd be willing to negotiate with you." Pagan smiled lasciviously, then turned and headed up the stairs.

There's no way I'm going to get backdoored for a change of venue, Karen thought, if indeed that's what Pagan was implying. But she wasn't ready to give up on moving the location either.

Suddenly, a high-pitched siren went off—a sandstorm alert.

The elevator doors finally opened so she headed upstairs and quickly checked for Deere and Uli. No luck. Avoiding Lewis, she made her way to her corner office. On her desk were a stack of phone memos. She flipped through them quickly. One stood out—an urgent message from "Gene," and a long number: 1-12 / 14-21-7-7-5-20.

8

ene was Akbar Del Piombo's nickname, which was ironic as it was
G actually his real name. He had created a simple letter-to-number
code he used when communicating with her: A equals one, B equals
two, and so on. It took her a moment to decode the name A-L / N-U-
G-G-E-T. He was clearing a hit with her. She would only call back if
she objected.

Nugget, a two-bit hood, was good to go.

Over the years Karen had sacrificed friends and foes alike to keep
Akbar as her secret weapon and informant. Only once did she veto one
of his hits—to keep him from killing a pimp whom she owed big time.

But now Gene had screwed up royally—or rather she had. And
she cringed when she thought about the tangled piles of body parts in
front of Rock & Filler Center. She had never fucked up this badly. As
she tore up Gene's coded memo she spotted Hector Gonzalez walking
by her open door. He was an ambitious council cop in charge of the
security of the Hoboken crop.

"Hey, asshole!" she shouted.

"What'd you call me?"

"Your fucking fertilizer blew up my building!" She was referring to
Cooper Union. Tons of fertilizer was stored across the waterway and
used for the choke crops.

"That's bullshit and your boss should have told you so," Gonzalez
replied.

"So it wasn't stolen?"

"It was stolen, but we had an irrigation pipe break so the batch
was soaking wet when they stole it. The explosion happened the next
afternoon. It simply couldn't've dried out that quickly."

She mumbled an apology for the misunderstanding. *Fucking Scouter
is such a drunk, he can't even relay basic information.* Wanting to avoid both
Gonzalez and her boss, Karen closed her door. Before she could sit,
a violent shock spread across her chest, constricting her lungs and
heart. She fell into her chair and was immediately out of breath. It

struck again, with more force, before she could breathe. Just as Karen thought it was over, an intense burning sensation seared through her loins. It took all her strength to keep from shouting out in agony. Through the pain, she inspected her genitals but found that nothing looked different. She closed her eyes and knew something horrible was happening to Uli.

Some time must have passssed, because she opened her eyes and discovered that she'd gotten urgent calls from Don McNeill, Mallory's campaign manager. He'd left his private number. Karen rang him back; it felt as if the pain had never happened.

"The good news is that for a five-day campaign, I think we really have a shot, but . . ."

"What?"

"Tomorrow is Election Day and the Foul Festival ceremony in Greenwich Village."

"I know."

"Well, if we don't have Mallory when they announce her victory, we're going to be celebrating the Day of *Our* Death."

"Relax, we almost have her."

"If she doesn't appear on the podium, Underwood is gonna call the election for Shub. And as her campaign manager, I'll be making her concession speech from Rikers Island."

"I guarantee that by tomorrow at this time, you, me, and Mallory will be at party headquarters watching the votes coming in."

As McNeill went on and on, Karen became aware of some kind of commotion in the hallway. She delicately set the phone down, allowing McNeill to keep venting, and stepped outside where she grabbed Tatianna and asked what was up.

"It just came over the radio. A pair of Pigger gangcops up in Queens found the bodies of Chain and Councilman Underwood."

"But I just saw them downstairs," she murmured.

"Where were they killed?" she heard Lewis yell from his office. The noise had shaken him from his latest drunken stupor.

"Out near the Chrystler Building," someone answered.

"At least that's Queens," another council cop chimed in.

Karen heard Lewis coming around the corner, so she slunk into her office to avoid him. A small bell went off, reminding everyone again of the imminent sandstorm approaching.

". . . so you see why I'm telling you all this," McNeill was still rambling on the phone.

"I do, but we just got a big tip about Mallory's whereabouts, so I gotta go." Karen hung up and quickly located a pair of goggles and a face mask, standard issue for sandstorms. She put them on, walked right past Lewis undetected, and went down the stairs while removing her disguise.

Since it was still clear out and she hadn't eaten in a while, she walked over a block to a Mexican establishment called Hostile Banana and ordered a pineapple burrito and a cactus soda. She ate in the cramped diner as the night sky above grew malarial yellow, swamp green, and then very dark gray. Thick clouds piled higher on the horizon like a tidal wave steadily rising. Eventually, a cold and sandy wind started to pick up. Distant thunder and lightning put on a mystical light show. A sharp boom was followed by an orange flash over Brooklyn Heights.

She knew it couldn't have been thunder; it had come too soon and it was too close—it could only be another car bomb. The sounds of sirens followed soon after. Filled with the fear that Akbar had committed another large-scale atrocity, she tossed her burrito into the trash and headed westward to the Heights.

During the twenty-minute walk to her destination, the breeze grew steadily stronger so she pulled on her face mask. When the wind felt like sandpaper against her face, she slipped on her goggles. As she arrived at the scene, people were still dashing for cover. A car was on fire when she reached Montague Street; a body had been blown forward onto its hood.

Yet the two gangcops on the scene remained seated in their vehicle, apparently waiting for the storm to subside. With his legs completely missing, the vic looked almost like a giant hood ornament. Karen immediately recognized him as Al Nugget, the nickel-and-dime racketeer. Thankfully, Akbar had avoided any collateral damage this time.

Tiredly, Karen plodded back to her apartment on the plaza. Once home, she kicked off her pants and shoes. No sooner did she drop down onto her bed than she was out like a light.

The sun was just coming up when Karen was awakened by rapid knocks on her door. It was Election Day and there was still no Mallory. Looking through her peephole, she saw Deere Flare standing outside looking uncharacteristically distressed. Karen pulled on her pants and unlocked the door.

Without waiting to be invited in, Deere pushed past her into the living room and kept going, first into the bedroom and then into the bathroom.

"Where is he?" Deere yelled, searching the closets.

"Who?"

"Who do you think? Timid Timmy!"

"Who the fuck is Timid Timmy?"

"Tim Vey, my little man. You saw me with him the other day, and now you're holding him somewhere. Don't lie!"

"Well, you just searched my home, did you find him?"

"All right," Deere smiled tightly, "I know that you're the second-smartest person in this dried-out mud puddle, so you've got him stashed away somewhere, but I need him—so I'm willing to make you a trade." After a pause she said, "I'll give you Mallory for Tim."

"Please tell me you're not involved in that."

"Course not. But I know who is."

"Who?"

"First Tim."

"No, first we have to talk about Vito," Karen countered. "Why did I commute the amputation of a man who just stole six cars that are going to be used for bombs?"

"I didn't know that, I just owed Gallo a favor."

"What favor?"

"You seen my new car yet? It's the cutest thing in Shithole City. And it's all legal."

The red sporty number she had followed.

"So if I find your boyfriend," Karen asked, "what do I get?"

"I know someone who was involved in the hospital assault. But you'll probably have to use that cranial corkscrew to yank any information out of him. He's a tough old prick."

"Timid Timmy followed me a little too close, so I had him locked up. Who do you got?"

Deere reached into her handbag and pulled out a crinkled Polaroid, which she handed to Karen. "Scarface."

"I know this jerk." Karen stared at the poor photo, a mug shot. She'd had run-ins with him a few times before. The man had a long, jagged, self-inflicted scar running down the center of his ugly, pocked mug. She remembered him by his alias, *Jewel.*

"Today's the election, so you need Mallory on the podium by tonight, don't you?"

"Any idea where I can find Scarface?"

"I only know he's from Queens."

"There's no way they'd be holding her up there," Karen said, getting a can of soda from the fridge. She had taken to drinking soda recently instead of her morning coffee. "I still can't figure out why they kidnapped her . . . Why wouldn't they just kill her?"

After a moment of contemplation, Deere responded, "I know why."

"Why?"

"I want Tim first, then I'll tell you."

"You've known me since Old Town. Have I ever fucked with you? I'll have him here tomorrow . . . Why didn't they kill her?"

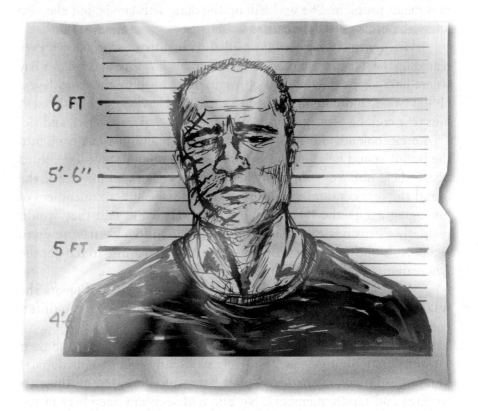

"Operation Sock Puppet is why."

"Sock Trumpet?"

"Sock Puppet—there was a memo."

"Oh shit." Karen did remember it. They were currently looking for candidates—victims with severe but not fatal head wounds—who could be guinea-pigged for a highly experimental operation. If performed successfully, it would turn the poor bastard into a programmable puppet for whatever agenda they wanted to put in them. After the success they'd been having with the steel yarmulke, this was the next inevitable experiment. Clearly the Piggers were hoping to turn Mallory into Mayor Sock Puppet.

"This ass," Deere pointed to her posterior, "had better be getting fucked by Tim by this time tomorrow or I'm gonna be fucking *you!*" She dashed out the door.

Looking out over the Williamsburgh Justice Plaza, Karen realized that this was it: by the end of the day, if she hadn't found Mallory, she was screwed. The fact that she didn't have all her official resources would be a major problem. She was still on the outs with Lewis, but she also knew something else: today was washday.

Twice a week, when Lewis smelled so bad that even his own eyes teared up, he'd have a gangcop drive him to his house in Sheepshead Bay where he'd scrape the crud out of his armpits, wash off the many layers of flop sweat, and burn his ruined clothes. He'd always come in the next morning reeking of Aqua Velva and wearing a new suit, shirt, and tie.

Karen took advantage of his absence today by sneaking back into the building and heading up the stairs to the filing room on the third floor. There she went through the shelves of photo albums until she found the one containing mug shots of Scarface and six members of his ragtag gang—the Boulevard of Death. Their file said they would regularly extort businesses in central Queens and kick a tribute up to Gallo. Now she just had to find one of them and get him to tell her the whereabouts of the others.

She went up to her office, and by calling in a bunch of favors she was able to round up four council cops. She assigned each to a different neighborhood.

Over the next several hours, the cops cruised slowly through their assigned communities—Jackson Heights, Sunnyside, Woodside, and Elmhurst—hitting up bars and pool halls, and checking on thug associates and family members. No one had seen any members of the Boulevard of Death, which to Karen confirmed that the group was probably together, hunkered down somewhere with Mallory.

Karen herself went on the hunt as well. Periodically she'd pass polling sites and see lines of people waiting to vote. As the morning turned into afternoon without any sightings, she decided to drive through the manicured northern communities.

Whoever dreamed up this map system in Queens didn't seem to realize that numbers go on forever, Karen thought as she passed 67th Street, then 67th Road, then 67th Way, then 67th Lane, then 67th Drive, and finally 67th Court, before reaching 68th Street, where the whole process began again. Block by block she drove, occasionally picking up her walkie and checking in with the others. By three o'clock she was exhausted. The hope of recovering Mallory by the time the election results were counted that night was beginning to evaporate. She pulled over at the Kew Gardens police headquarters and waited to see if she recognized any other gangcops who owed her. Soon she spotted a slim, elderly man wearing clothes far too young for him. Backdoor Leiberman was coming down the steps of the building, chatting with a group of other Pigger paper pushers.

She got out of her vehicle and followed him into the parking lot. As soon as Backdoor was alone at his car in the rear of the empty lot, she watched him pause and gaze into the distance as though contemplating some profound moral dilemma.

When she started to approach, she realized what he was doing and began to back away. He heard her and turned abruptly. With penis in hand, Leiberman was still midstream.

"Oh my!" he said awkwardly as a trickle flowed out of him.

"What could you possibly gain from blocking our request for a change of venue?" Karen called out, taking advantage of the moment.

"Who the hell are you?" He was clearly embarrassed.

"Captain Sarkisian with the council cops," she said, showing her ID. "I'm in charge of security for next week's detainee convention, and we don't think it's safe in Brooklyn."

"Look, at my age, I can't just turn my bladder off like a faucet, so would you mind giving me a little privacy?"

She smelled alcohol and sensed he was a bit soused.

"Tell me why you're blocking me from changing the venue and I'll leave," she said simply, stepping to the left so that his sad, shriveled symbol of manhood was fully visible.

"Scouter Lewis told me to and I owe him. Now please fuck off."

The explanation left her speechless. But it made complete sense. This way the son of a bitch had avoided a fight with her, making Leiberman the bad guy. And though he had Pigger leanings, he had always put business over politics.

As she reached her car she could hear Lewis's voice over the squawk box: *"Goddamnit, Sarkisian, come in. Over! Just what the fuck do you think you're pulling?"*

The drunken head of the council cops had somehow showered, changed, and driven back to work all in the same day, where he had discovered that she'd illegally authorized her own private dragnet.

She was too pissed off at him to respond.

"Everyone who doesn't get their fat ass back over here pronto is getting ripped a week's pay!"

And that was it. Her last chance to capture the scumbag who had kidnapped her friend was gone. Karen drove to a stamp shop that offered phone service and called Tatianna at the office.

"You probably know that Scouter wants your head, for starters. He's talking about chucking you from the CCs. Oh, and Don McNeill wants you to call him immediately."

"Anything else?" Karen asked. She knew McNeill would be freaking out.

"A couple car bombs went off earlier at the Foul Festival in Thompson Square Park. Three or four killed, another five or so wounded."

"Typical for Election Day," Karen pointed out.

"The weird part is that supposedly before the crowd could disperse, teams of gangcops blocked off the park and forced everyone to pass through various checkpoints."

"Good for them. Someone's on the ball."

"That's just it, they're not. The Crapper precinct captain said that he ordered no such thing. So some group blocked off Thompson Square Park and made all the festivalgoers pass through three manned checkpoints."

Karen thanked her. *How odd—while I'm up here in Queens looking for someone, there are Piggers down there looking for someone else.* It was too much of a coincidence.

9

K aren ran to her car and sped toward Manhattan as the sun was setting. The Piggers wouldn't have made a brazen move like that, sending a group of their own into the heart of Crapper territory, unless they were desperate. *Maybe Mallory escaped*, Karen thought, but her friend had never been particularly heroic.

After Karen exited the Brooklyn Bridge on 14th, she cruised down to Thompson Square Park looking for Scarface and his cadre. Checking her wristwatch, she realized the polls had just closed. They'd begun to count the votes, and she still had no clue where the Crapper candidate was.

Driving around the park, all Karen found were the three burned-out cars that were the result of the car bombings which Tatianna had mentioned. The Piggers had probably blown up the vehicles themselves to justify coming out in force. Some of the ground around the park was still blotched with drying blood. Karen circled the area. Around seven she stopped at the barren corner of Avenue C and 4th Street. She could hear loud throbbing music coming from the bombed-out brownstone known as the Gathering of Spies, so she parked across the street. Apparently they were in on the Foul festivities.

She watched as a stream of people slowly entered the party. When she moved to get out of her car, a guy who somewhat resembled Uli hurried up the street and slipped inside. Without a disguise and worried about being identified, she continued watching from the safety of her car as more partygoers entered the run-down building. After an hour she saw a taxi pull up and Danny Varholski, the creepy imitative artist, got out, followed by his little entourage.

By nine p.m. Karen was famished, so she decided to grab a bite. She drove over to Odessa, a small diner on Avenue A, and bought a plate of oily potato pierogi in slightly curdled sour cream and a cup of coffee.

When she got back to her car with her food, she figured the count was probably in. Once they deduced that Mallory wasn't alive to declare victory, the head of the city council would declare Shub winner by default. Then it would just be a matter of time before McNeill and his campaign team would start disappearing.

The thought of it all unraveling made her stomach queasy, and the few bites of oily food she'd eaten didn't help. She got back out of her car, walked to the corner, and tossed the remainder into the garbage. From that vantage, Karen could see all the way down 4th Street to flashing red lights a few blocks west. A couple of gangcop cars appeared to be at a crime scene, so she returned to her vehicle and drove down to check it out.

Several cop cars had converged in front of Mamasita's Blah Blah Theater, which had been taking part in the Foul Festival. A small crowd of actors were milling around outside. It turned out they had been pulled off the stage midshow when bodies were discovered in the back of the theater. They were waiting to return to their dressing rooms to retrieve their street clothes.

Karen showed her badge and entered. Two gangcops she recognized were interviewing an elderly man who turned out to be the box office guy.

"This fellow bought a ticket," she heard the senior explain. "He . . . he was the last one, but . . . I guess I fell asleep, so . . ."

Karen walked past to the crime scene at the rear of the auditorium. She gasped when she recognized the naked body of her sometime friend and former compatriot Deere Flare. She and her girlfriend Kennesy had both been stabbed to death.

Although Deere had played every side against any middle and had the scruples of a tick, Karen had come to value her.

"Do you know either of them?" Karen heard. It was Sam McGrew, the only detective on duty that night at the East Village precinct.

"I saw Deere this morning," she said.

"What was she exactly? I mean, what was her title?"

"She stayed behind the scenes. Last I heard, she was a recruitment consultant at Pure-ile Plurality."

"Who's the other vic?" the detective asked.

"That was her girlfriend Kennesy, a deejay with the radio station up in Queens."

"This Deere person looks like a man," the detective said, examining her exposed and flaccid genitals.

"Well, I wouldn't spread that around. Deere had sex with a lot of guys who thought otherwise."

"So maybe one of them did this," the detective hypothesized.

"I would set my sights a little higher. Deere had her finger in a lot of pies."

"Looks like more than just her finger," the detective said, still staring at her groin.

"You know what? This isn't your case. It goes way beyond this jurisdiction." Karen didn't care for his brand of humor.

"Are you saying this is *your* case?"

"No. In fact, I'm on administrative leave. You can take it, but once the Williamsburgh Building learns that she's dead, they're going to send in their homicide team. So if I were you, I'd save myself time and just call them."

Karen returned to her car and drove back to the brownstone on Avenue C, then parked across the street. She got out, took a blanket from the trunk, and climbed into the less-conspicuous backseat. From there she kept an eye on the brownstone, trying to forget poor Deere Flare's bloody end. At least the pressure was off her to surrender Deere's lover.

The rising sun woke Karen the next morning. All was silent across the street, so she pulled the blanket up and tried to keep sleeping, but a quartet of gruff voices drew her attention.

Squinting tiredly, she saw her brother Uli among a small group exiting the brownstone. A tall, strapping man with a huge jagged scar running down his cheek—Scarface—was following two others, who were leading her brother along. Uli had his hands cuffed behind his back. They were walking him westward, and it did not look good. *This is perfect*, she thought. *They're probably going to execute him and it won't be my fault.*

It was hard not to see her brother as someone indirectly responsible for this entire Rescue City fiasco. Yet she also had reason to believe this crew was behind Mallory's disappearance. If there was any chance of rescuing her old friend and giving the city a new chance at freedom, she had to arrest this elusive crew and get them talking.

Picking up her walkie, she tried to get in touch with Crapper headquarters, but the dispatcher seemed to be asleep and wasn't picking up. She switched over to the council cop frequency and said she needed immediate backup.

"*Roger that, Captain Sarkisian. We can have someone out there in roughly twenty to thirty minutes,*" she heard as she lost sight of the little posse.

She knew by then it would be too late, so she was going to have to find some way to do this on her own. She kept a pistol hidden below her dashboard, but when she checked she found that it only had two bullets. She sped west down 4th Street. Turning a corner, she saw them up the block. The two green-shirted men were stepping off the curb in front of Uli, while Scarface brought up the rear. Karen hit the brakes, skidding sideways along a residue of sand. She lined them up and abruptly hit the gas, plowing directly into the two beefy giants leading the group. They bounced off her car hood and onto the ground.

When the vehicle came to a halt, she grabbed her gun, wrapped a towel around her hand, and threw open the door.

"Oh fuck!" she screamed.

"You stupid fucking bitch!" shouted Scarface as he held onto Uli, who was still handcuffed.

"My God," she feigned, "what did I do?"

"Get back in your fucking car!" Scarface yelled.

Karen ignored him and turned to Uli. "Come on. Help me put them in the backseat. We can get them to the Beth Israel Clinic."

"You stupid cunt!" the big gangster barked, and pulled out a giant knife.

"Watch it!" Uli tried to warn Karen, showing no signs of recognition.

Scarface charged toward her.

Since she had a small-caliber bullet, she waited until he was right on her before she shot him once in the chest. He dropped the knife and fell to a seated position, leading her to believe the bullet might have lodged in his spine.

"Fucking bitch!" he mumbled. A moment later he seemed to have slipped into a daze.

"Uli!" she greeted her brother.

He appeared to vaguely recognize her face, but still clearly had no clue who she was. Afraid that one or both of the injured giants would attack, she said, "Let's get the heck out of here! Forget about these Piggers."

"Wait a second! I think he knows where Mallory is." Uli nodded toward the fallen Scarface.

Karen had no idea how he knew she was looking for Mallory, but now was not the time to ask. "You sure?" she said, as she used Scarface's knife to cut the plastic band off of his wrists.

"Yes, come on!"

Since the two other injured men were still moaning on the ground, the brother and sister each grabbed one of Scarface's limp arms and dragged him into the backseat of her car, then raced off.

"I don't want to be rude," Uli said, "but when I met you before—"

"I was undercover as a man," she finished his sentence.

"How do I know you?"

"I'm your sister Karen. You're Uli Sarkisian. Remember?"

"I don't even know my own name. Maybe I came to rescue you," he replied calmly.

"Not likely," she said, and lied further to test him: "You put me here."

"I what?!" He dropped the piece of cloth he was compressing against Scarface's chest.

If he was faking, he was doing a convincing job.

As Karen drove up to 16th Street—and as Scarface kept cursing at them—she told Uli about some of the strange psychic events she had recently experienced.

"*You* were the one who told me to run!" He remembered hearing her voice in his head. "Why didn't you meet me at Rock & Filler Center?"

Instead of disclosing that she had sent a hit man to kill him, she claimed that she had been targeted by the Piggers and was unable to shake them. She added that afterward she'd desperately tried to track him down and thought the DT were holding him up in the Bronx.

"I felt this intense buning pain here and here." She pointed to her own chest and groin.

"I was tortured at Rikers," he replied.

"Here on the reservation, it's not unusual for siblings, especially twins, to have a psychic connection." Some people speculated that it might be due to a drug in the food, or some kind of aerosol that the CIA scientists periodically released into the air.

Uli asked if she could shed any light on why he had been attacked at the Berrigan funeral, so she told him about some of his COINTEL-PRO activity, even though he had never actually admitted, much less disclosed, any of it to her.

In another moment they arrived at the Beth Israel Clinic and dragged Scarface out of the backseat and into the emergency room. After Karen showed her badge, a doctor came to tend to Scarface. Karen asked if she could use the phone at a nurses' station, then dialed a number she knew by heart, and explained that she had an urgent steel yarmulke situation.

* * *

While waiting for the surgical team, a medic started a transfusion on Scarface. But it was only a matter of time—his heart had been severely damaged by Karen's bullet and he was dying.

Ten minutes later, a van pulled up out front and four men in strange costumes got out. They hastily wheeled in a hand truck loaded with their own surgical equipment.

She was trying to remain hopeful—as Scarface was probably her last chance to recover her candidate and old friend. She had seen this experimental operation performed three times, and though they had gradually improved upon it, the results were always dubious. She prayed silently as the lead CIA scientist assessed Scarface's condition, then started prepping and anesthetizing his skull. One of the other surgeons carefully ran a bone saw around his thick crown.

"I didn't know you had neurosurgeons here," Uli whispered to Karen.

"We don't. Technically they're scientists: cleavings, incisions, amputations"—the CIA.

Fifteen minutes later there was a suction sound when they lifted the top of Scarface's cranium off his brain as though it were a hairy bottle cap. She watched as they opened the small wooden box that contained the sacred steel yarmulke. One of them plugged various tiny wires that ran from its metallic top into the back of what appeared to be a small control panel, then carefully lowered the apparatus over Scarface's exposed gray matter.

His vitals were fluctuating wildly, and although the team continued transfusing blood, they couldn't stop the bleeding. He was sedated. It was clearly a race against time to pull that final vital bit of information out of him before he escaped into death. With three men handling the surgery, the last scientist focused carefully on the dials of the control panel.

"Revive the subject," commanded the lead scientist.

After a hypodermic injection, Scarface twitched.

"You can question him now," the scientist said nervously to Karen.

"Where is Mallory?" she asked softly. "Where is Mallory?"

"Be more aggressive," the leader suggested.

"Where the hell is Mallory!"

"Fuck you!" said Scarface haltingly. "I— Fuck you— She—"

"You're not causing him more pain, are you?" Uli whispered to one of the scientists.

"Where is Mallory?" Karen asked.

"No fucking way . . . I . . . gonna tell you shit—"

"Where is she!"

"No, I'm— Stinking-fucking-Island! No!"

"Where?"

"No way! The dumps! No fucking . . . to the dumps. No fucking way . . . The fucking dumps!"

It was astonishing to see someone blurting out information against his own will, as though he were being mentally violated by the session.

"What dumps?" Karen asked.

As the dying man struggled to regain control of his own brain, his confession was accompanied by nervous tics and painful squawks, as though he had developed an acute case of Tourette's: "Stinking-fucking-Island!"

"The city dump?"

Each member of the surgical team attended to his own little tasks—turning dials, readjusting synaptic needles, using an eyedropper to lubricate certain parts of the man's exposed gray matter—steadily hoping to squeeze out more information. Before they could extract anything more tangible, however, the lead scientist announced, "His vitals are dropping."

They frantically tried to save him, but in another moment one of the lesser scientists called out: "And he's gone."

Mallory was being held somewhere in the city dump. And Karen knew that whoever was holding her was not alone—this was probably a large operation. She would have to quickly assemble a small armada and scour the area.

In the corridor outside the operating room, gangcops had collected, hoping that the interrogation might yield Mallory's whereabouts. Karen told them that the subject had passed away before giving them anything valuable. Though there were curses and cries of frustration, Karen suspected that informants were present. "Let's go," she said to Uli.

She decided against calling the council cops—as she was legally obligated to for interborough activity. Because of the informants, odds were that someone would tip off the kidnappers.

"*Shub has publicly congratulated Mallory as the new mayor,*" Karen heard a radio broadcast in the background. "*His concession speech will be coming soon.*"

"Shit," she muttered, realizing that all of Rescue City was probably waiting for Mallory to make a victory speech. She immediately dialed her assistant Chuck Schuman. "Listen! You need to round up every Crapper gangcop you trust right this minute."

"What do I tell them?" he asked nervously.

"Secret mission, top priority, right now!"

No sooner did she hang up the phone than cheers rang out on the hospital floor. The corrupt reign of Horace Shub was over. All seemed surprised to hear how quickly he had stepped down, but only Karen knew that he had done so because Mallory was unable to accept the prize.

Getting in her car with Uli, Karen called Schuman again to work out more details. Within ten minutes, Schuman had pulled together five metal-reinforced police cars as well as ten cops from various Manhattan precincts for the top secret mission—no questions asked. Information would only be available as needed. When Karen told him that this team wouldn't be big enough, Schuman put out more calls and was quickly able to double the number.

Less than an hour after Scarface's death, a convoy of ten cars was slowly heading over the Staten Island Ferry Bridge to an undetermined location near the city dump. Karen didn't want to lose Uli again, so she brought him along; they were in the car leading the convoy. On the drive out there, she gave him a high-speed lecture on the history of Rescue City, beginning with the army's failed attempt to manage the city, through the emergence of endless gangs, and finally the one gang headed by Jackie Wilson—who ultimately gained power by the stopping up of the city's giant sewage, which in turn led to the biohazardous condition of poor Staten Island.

"Staten Island should have become part of New Jersey when they still had the chance," Uli said, thinking of Old Town.

As they made their way through the toxic borough, plowing their armed police cars over streams of sewage, they reached a point where Karen's driver was uncertain of which way to go.

"That way," pointed a gangcop named Caleb Straus riding in the backseat; he had worked for years for the city's Department of Sanitation.

On they drove until they reached the mountains of rotting and burning garbage that were being pushed around by two city tractors. They pulled up alongside a man who appeared to be an on-site sanitation supervisor.

"Have you seen anyone out of the ordinary around here in the past day?" Karen asked.

"Two cars I didn't recognize sped down this road not ten minutes ago," the man said.

"Is there anything down there?"

"A couple of old abandoned buildings."

Karen glanced back and realized that a cloud of dust was rising in the air behind their caravan. It had probably given them away. "Move it! Pronto!" she called out.

10

E ventually they reached a group of dilapidated wooden shacks and buildings that seemed to be some kind of abandoned outpost. Half the vehicles pulled up in front of the largest building. Six gang-cops rushed inside to do a room-to-room search. A few minutes passed before they all heard *pop-pop-pop*—someone had begun shooting down at them from a top-floor window. The cops took up positions around the cars and began returning fire; the gunman had blocked the stair-way with heavy furniture, so they couldn't reach him that way without endangering themselves. One gangcop had already been killed, and another injured.

When no other shooters appeared, Karen deduced that the lone gunman had probably been left behind, a suicidal decoy to hold them all at bay while the real kidnappers were spiriting Mallory away.

"Come on!" she yelled, getting behind the wheel of her car. Three others, including Uli, jumped inside as well.

She drove back up to the main dirt road that was bordered on the left by the rising dunes of the Nevada desert. Five minutes later, Uli pointed out an odd phenomenon ahead of them. It looked like a dust devil, a tiny tornado of sand, just beyond one of the dunes—but no wind was blowing. Karen turned sharply off the road and they sped up toward it. At the top of a sharp ridge, they could see the source of the sandy vortex. A car was stuck and its back wheels were sending up the plume of soft earth. They approached it cautiously until their own vehicle got stuck.

Karen, Uli, and the two other gangcops jumped out and moved ahead on foot. When they were roughly a hundred feet away, Karen could make out four figures. Two men were pushing the rear of the car, another sat in the front, and a fourth was slumped forward in the backseat, wearing what looked like a shower cap. Karen pulled out her gun and raced ahead of the others. One of the guys outside the car opened fire before being shot by the two gangcops. The other, who now appeared to be a teenager, slid into the vehicle momentarily before stepping back out holding a gun. With his free hand, he yanked out the person in the backseat—Mallory. The shower cap fell. Her head had been completely shaved and she looked disoriented.

"Relax!" yelled the kid.

"Just back the fuck up!" yelled the driver, climbing out from behind the wheel. He dumped a flask of liquid over Mallory and held up a lighter.

Her own gun drawn, Karen could tell that this asshole meant business. When Mallory fainted to the ground, the man tried grabbing her. Karen used the distraction to put a bullet through his neck. Dropping to his knees, the injured man clutched his wound and screamed to the kid, "Kill her!"

"Do it and you're dead!" Karen pointed her gun at the youth, sensing he was both scared and intelligent. Even though she knew she could take him out, she didn't want to put Mallory at further risk.

Moving quickly, the wounded man ignited his lighter and tossed it onto Mallory's gas-soaked gown. As the front of her dress went up in flames, she rolled down the side of the dune where the loose sand immediately extinguished her.

While everyone was focused on Mallory, the wounded man snatched the gun back from the skinny kid and started shooting wildly at her. Karen fired four shots into his chest.

"Holy shit!" gasped the kid as his compatriot fell dead. Then he grabbed the gun again and put the trembling pistol against Mallory's shiny scalp. Smoke was still rising from her burned dress.

Karen dropped her gun and in a low, soothing voice whispered, "Look, I know you don't want to kill anyone." She put her hands in the air and tried to reason with him.

"I let her go, they're going to torture the shit out of me and you know it!"

"We can get you out of here!" She told him that she had Mnemosyne—the escape drug.

"Bullshit!" he shot back.

Karen said it was in a bag in her glove compartment. One of the gangcops reached through the window of her car, opened the compartment, and handed her the bag. Karen removed the smashed box containing the syringe that had been recovered from the Cooper Union demolition. She took the hypodermic out and showed it to him.

After some negotiating and the sacred promise of safe passage, Karen finally got the kid to put the gun down.

By this point, the rest of her team had caught up. The young kidnapper, grateful to be alive, explained that there were many more hostiles in the area. Karen had her team place Mallory in her car and the kid in another vehicle. They had to get the hell out of there.

As the caravan wheeled back toward Manhattan, Karen could see that Mallory was not herself and asked her what had happened. Mallory shrugged, but Karen knew—she had almost been turned into Mayor Sock Puppet.

"What did they do to you?" Uli asked cluelessly.

Mallory said they had tried to turn her into a zombie. "I woke up in some hospital room and found that they had cut off all my hair. They were about to operate, but then they discovered they didn't have the right tools or equipment."

At that moment they heard a barrage of gunfire up ahead and screeched to a halt. The entire caravan did a tight U-turn and headed back down the hill they had just come up. Once they were safely out of harm's way with no casualties, they realized that the only road out was completely blocked. To attempt a second assault would lead to a bloody fight with no certain outcome. Caleb Straus, the former sanitation worker who had led them to the dumps, informed them of another way out. He said that if they headed back the way they had come, down the ever-narrowing path, they would eventually reach the bottom of the borough. Although there was no roadway, on foot the group could make their way to the ferry building, and from there Rafique could provide safe passage out.

All were reluctant to abandon their vehicles, but it sounded like the best bet.

The caravan resumed driving, this time south, with Mallory's car toward the rear. Within a minute, an even longer barrage of gunfire rang in the air. This time two gangcops in the front two cars had been hit. Karen and all the other drivers managed to throw their cars in reverse and speed backward to the bottom of the little valley. Now they were boxed in on both sides.

To their great dismay, they realized why the Piggers had chosen this particular glen for their ambush. Due to its depth and angle, none of their walkies were able to transmit or receive any messages.

After weighing the various options, all believed that the enemy gang on the south side of the valley seemed smaller. They agreed to try again to bust out that way—only this time, they wouldn't stop. After further planning, it was decided that instead of trying to send the entire armada up against the unknown force, only two cars would launch the attack. The vehicles lined up side by side to move in tandem up the narrow road. This way, they figured, they would each have one side protected, and their sharpshooters could focus on opposing sides of the road.

As they started up the hill, still about a hundred feet from the summit, a succession of bottles and bullets hit their hoods and roofs—Molotov cocktails set their cars ablaze. Still the cars sped onward like a pair of twin meteors. They slammed into each other, finally veering off to the right side of the road.

From the bottom of the glen it looked like a total catastrophe. Then, to everyone's amazement, one of the men—Danny Silvers, a sergeant from Inwood who had been sitting shotgun—rolled out along the sandy shoulder and returned fire, killing two advancing Piggers and scaring off the others. Quickly he pulled two of his injured comrades out of the burning wrecks and dragged them to a cluster of jagged rocks toward the crest of the little hill. Inspired by his bravery, a third car containing four more soldiers zoomed up to their aid. Other Crappers began running uphill on foot. Silvers picked off a bold pair of Piggers who were shooting at the third car. For a while it looked like their mission might succeed—until the third car started getting inundated with fiery cocktails. Then it too swerved onto the shoulder into a bank of sand. They were stuck—too far away to join Silvers in the cluster and too far up the hill to retreat.

Just as a fourth car was preparing to join the fray, a series of shots rang out behind them. Eight Piggers from the group at their rear began racing down the far hill in a sneak attack, hitting their flank. Instantly, all the men who had carefully inched up the southern side of the gulch had to sprint back down to repel the attacking Piggers.

By the time they pushed them back, three more Crappers had been killed and two others were wounded. Worse still was that the Piggers in the southern front had taken advantage of the diversion and launched a new attack on Silvers and his group. The Piggers were then able to drop Molotov cocktails directly on top of them, setting two of the gangcops on fire and forcing Silvers to run into the clearing, where he too was picked off.

Karen now knew this had been a coordinated attack: Piggers on both sides of the gulch had walkies and were working in conjunction.

The Crapper gangcop force was depleted; they couldn't afford another attack. Karen realized that the best they could do was set up a defensive line and hope to somehow sneak Mallory out during the chaos of the inevitable Pigger surge.

The Crapper soldiers moved their cars into a circle in the middle of the glen so they had complete views of both ridges above them. Next, they started digging trenches by hand in anticipation of the final assault, which would probably occur that night. One gangcop stood guard outside Mallory's car while she reclined in the backseat, sleeping off the last of the pharmaceuticals that were still in her system.

Schuman did an inventory of pistols and bullets. One courageous gangcop snuck into the gulch and recovered three guns from fallen comrades. Even with these, they were dangerously low on artillery.

Before they were done digging, a shot rang out, then a rapid succession of others. Though it wasn't even dark yet, they scrambled into their half-dug ditches expecting the worst. No Piggers appeared, but they could still hear rounds being fired and people yelling desperately. When one Crapper sergeant slowly hiked up the hill to see what was happening, they were all amazed that no one fired upon him.

Two fat Piggers in cowboy hats began running down the hill— not attacking but apparently being pursued. Then one of them fell forward, tumbling down, and went limp. The second was knocked over, and two half-naked savages suddenly appeared behind him. One brandished a bowie knife and plunged it into the man's neck, then began scalping him. Other scantily clad men appeared up over the ridge.

"Holy crap, those are Tim Leary's people!" Uli exclaimed.

A dozen Piggers appeared from the south side of the glen, also racing down toward them, seemingly to the aid of their compatriots, but Karen then spotted a swarm of the semiclad men above them as well. Crapper gangcops took this opportunity for revenge, shooting the Piggers as they came into range. The wild-eyed Burnt Men were screaming ecstatically as they carved up enemy soldiers, baptizing themselves in their hot blood.

"Wow," Karen muttered.

"I always figured the VL were a bunch of peace-loving pussies," Schuman said.

"Me too." Karen was shocked by the savagery.

It was over. The glorious Burnt Men tribe rose with their trophies— recovered weapons, boots, ears, noses, one warrior even held up a disembodied set of genitals—and began marching proudly downhill toward the grateful Crapper enclave. No Pigger prisoners were visible. At the top of the hill all recognized Adolphus Rafique, escorted by his own squad of bodyguards. His infamous aide Tim Leary, oddly wearing a green-and-white football helmet, was at his side.

"Welcome to Greater Staten Island!" Rafique called out to Mallory. They were in the city dump, technically outside of his domain. "I heard you died."

"If you came here an hour or so later, that probably would've been the case," Mallory said, now thoroughly sobered up.

While Mallory chatted with Rafique, Karen watched as Uli went over to the tall, attractive woman who she had confronted down in Tottenville just the other day. Karen wanted to introduce herself and put that unfortunate event behind them.

Before she could, though, Uli inexplicably tackled the woman. No sooner did they hit the ground than Karen heard the crackle of a lone gunshot. Adolphus Rafique—who was standing a couple yards behind her—suddenly flew backward onto the scrub and rocks. A rapid succession of other shots followed and gangcops and Burnt Men alike dropped to the ground.

It was the beginning of twilight. Darkness shrouded nooks and crannies while the long light of the setting sun blinded them. No one could see where the shots were coming from. Luckily, someone had pulled Mallory safely out of range. A moment later all was quiet—presumably the shooter was out of ammo. Karen quickly assembled a team who raced up the hill with pistols drawn. Almost at the top, they found a hot pistol, but no shooter. They peered out beyond the crest, but in the copper light they only saw the desert spreading before them. Rafique was on his back with blood bubbling out of his chest.

Karen began: "Let's get him into a car and—"

"He's not going to last that long," Leary's second-in-command whispered.

"Actually, he's not bleeding that badly," said an old fellow who looked like a medicine man. "The bad news is it looks as if the bullet shattered his neck."

While they all solemnly stood around, not wanting him to die, yet afraid to move him, Karen took one of Rafique's lieutenants aside. "You guys have a shortwave?"

"Yeah, in my car up on the ridge. Why?"

"Turn the band to 117 hertz. That's the channel the CIA operates on."

"Hell no!" barked Loveworks, the VL's chief of police, as he approached them. "Do you have any idea the horrors those monsters have perpetrated on our people here?"

"Yeah, but their policy is to experiment on anyone who is perceived as dying," Karen replied. It occurred to her that this must be the real reason they hadn't operated on Mallory. What Mallory had said—that they hadn't brought the correct instruments—sounded unlikely.

"So what?" Loveworks countered.

"They've been looking for a severed-spine guinea pig for possible reattachment," Karen explained.

"From what I hear, the vast majority of their experiments are failures," Loveworks said.

"Yeah, but they still have a medical team and can stabilize him. And he's not bleeding to death."

Loveworks raced up the hill to the radio in his car.

Karen could see Leary chatting with the mayor-elect. "More than anything," she heard him saying, "he wanted you to see the blocked sewer. Fixing it was his greatest wish." Although Rafique was still alive, Leary was already leveraging the tragedy to further the VL agenda. He was trying to convince Mallory to make a short detour to the blocked sewer.

"Hell no! It's way too dangerous," Karen said emphatically.

Mallory vetoed Karen's concerns. Now that she was mayor, and since she figured she would never want to return to the giant drain after today and the imminent danger appeared to be over, it was a short trip worth taking.

Karen hastily herded all the wounded Crapper gangcops into one car, and all the dead bodies of their colleagues were piled into another.

Among those killed, she saw the body of the skinny young Pigger kidnapper to whom she had promised safe passage. Since they were short on space in the vehicles, Karen had him buried right there in one of the shallow trenches. Then, because the wounded needed immediate medical attention, she ordered them back to Manhattan as fast as they could drive.

Except for Leary, who joined Mallory, the Burnt Men all marched back up the ridge to their own vehicles out of view. The remaining Crapper gangcops divided into the last of the cars and again the caravan resumed driving southward.

The conversation in Mallory's vehicle developed into a debate on whether or not Uli should chance this syringe with the mystery escape drug that offered a possible way out of Rescue City. Because no one had ever come back to report, none could attest to its veracity. Uli was clearly willing to take the risk rather than spend another day in the desert prison.

Karen remained mostly silent during this conversation. She knew that she was essentially sending her brother to his death, but also knew that Uli deserved it a thousand times over for what he had done to his country. She found it pathetic that so many people effortlessly believed that some ridiculous snake oil—from who knows where—had been created that allowed people to go into stasis while their bodies were submerged a great distance.

When Uli searched his sister's eyes for her opinion, she simply said, "You don't have to go if you don't want to. It's your choice."

"It's the wrong choice," Leary cut in, "but he's going anyway." Then he started with some mumbo jumbo about a great mystical god whose name sounded like *Revoker*. Apparently the god had informed Leary that Uli would be taking the Mnemosyne and that was why he had brought his prized football helmet. At that point Karen tuned out the nonsense and simply stared out the window at the strange scenery.

The sewage overflow soon appeared to their distant left, and as the road descended toward it, the smell grew much worse. Even though everyone rolled up their windows, the severe sulfuric odor made their eyes burn. Gradually, as the roadway narrowed even more and paralleled the open trench of filth, the landscape transformed into a surreal hell. The sewer gave rise to a phosphorescent fungus that arose from the waste crusted along its bursting banks. Steadily, more and more skeletons of decomposed animals littered the waterway.

After five minutes, they came to a spot where the vehicles could hardly traverse the road, which was now more of a marshy path. All the cars parked. The Crapper gangcops got out, pinching their nostrils with one hand and holding their pistols with the other, and surveyed the area. No sounds of birds or signs of any other living things were evident. Leary said that this was the northern rim of the sewer drains, walking distance from the hole. He then presented several engineering proposals to Mallory that Rafique and his brain trust had developed over the years, requiring the labor and resources that only a mayor would even have a remote chance of mustering.

"Of course it'd require scuba gear to go into the water," Leary pitched, "but we have people who are trained to do that. The first part would be building a cofferdam around the blocked area. Tunneling into the clogged area wouldn't be too hard—our engineers believe it could be done in just a couple years. We already have an aboveground drainage canal. Just think of it: we'd drain the swamp and this whole area would be restored to its former pristine state!"

Mallory was clearly trying to act mayoral and receptive—she was intent on paying back the debt that she owed Rafique for saving them.

As it seemed Uli had firmly decided to attempt the insane escape, Schuman popped open the trunk and took out some supplies: a can of car grease, a sleeping bag, and a few other items to prepare him for his fantasy trip. The group then set out to find the hole. Silently, they navigated the putrid marshland, making their way uphill.

"So how did Rafique know we were in trouble?" Karen asked Leary.

"I told him."

"How'd *you* know?"

"Wovoka told us."

"Too bad he didn't mention that Rafique was going to be murdered," Uli said, trying not to sound overly sarcastic.

"Actually, I told him there was a good chance it would happen." Leary continued chattering in his mystical lingo, explaining that Wovoka knew all things.

Karen listened as Uli informed Mallory that he knew of some woman named Patricia who had been falsely accused of assassinating Daniel Ellsberg. "She's mentally incapable of pulling off that crime," he said.

"I'll look into it," Mallory replied tiredly.

As they made their way, Leary spoke of the blighted landscape as though giving a tour. Years earlier, the stopping of the drain had restored democracy to the reservation, but it had also turned Staten Island into a fetid swamp, a vile corruption.

Eventually, they encountered a mass of rising rocks, and Karen supported Mallory as they hiked up. At the peak lay a cluster of giant boulders. When they reached the hole, they paused and looked down. It seemed like a bottomless drain fashioned by pickaxes. Leary explained that if the hole had been cut at a lower ground level, the water would have spewed out across the landscape.

All were eager to get the mayor safely back to town, so Uli stripped off his clothes and slathered his flesh with the grease that Schuman had provided. Karen pulled out some masking tape and attached the small oxygen tank to his back.

Leary removed the football helmet he had been wearing, revealing his cottony white hair. He showed Uli two small hypodermic needles stored inside the helmet's Styrofoam padding. Once Uli had reached his destination in the sewer pipe, he was to inject himself with the needles.

This made little sense to anyone, since they basically expected Uli to drown and eventually get flushed out into some giant river or waterway—but then again, not much of what Leary ever said made a lot of sense.

Uli hugged Karen, and a moment later she injected him with the Mnemosyne. He stepped inside the sleeping bag, becoming a one-man submersible.

"I haven't seen my big brother in ten years," Karen said, largely because she knew all those around her were waiting for some sort of maudlin monologue. "And now he's gone again." She taped his nose, ears, and mouth shut, then secured the football helmet on his head and a pair of goggles over his eyes.

Schuman signaled the two gangcops, who grabbed the short ropes that were secured to the top of the sleeping bag and carefully slipped Uli down into the cool craggy hole that had been cut into the rocky hill. They counted to three and released him.

In that instant, Karen felt certain she had just killed her only brother. Sad as it was, justice had been served—the world had one less enemy of humanity. Uli deserved it for what he had done to this nation: destroying real freedom in the name of fake freedom.

Schuman gestured to the large, beautiful moon that had just risen on the eastern horizon. Mallory nodded and pointed out that she had to be at City Hall to claim her rightful title, so they started walking down from the peak back toward their respective cars.

"Can we drop you off somewhere?" Mallory asked Leary.

He said that the ferry terminal was just an hour's walk and thanked Mallory for her time.

"I'll carefully consider everything we talked about," she assured him. Karen was amused to hear Mallory's first great lie of her term. Leary thanked the mayor-elect and started his hike home.

Each vehicle turned around carefully so as to not get stuck in the stinking muck that surrounded them. One of the drivers said that his solicar wouldn't start because the sun had set. Broken electrical gauges were standard in Rescue City, and when the other drivers checked their batteries, they too realized the cars hadn't been properly recharged. It took another hour for them to unscrew the batteries from the six cars and squeeze all the remaining passengers into the three best vehicles, with additional batteries just in case. Despite the fact that many of the gangcops were either dead or wounded, they had successfully rescued the new mayor of the city.

Karen looked over at Mallory and saw an odd smile on her pale face. "You okay, Your Honor?"

"I just can't believe that after all we've gone through, from that first unbelievable day we met—that now *we* are the powers that be," Mallory said softly.

"Yeah, too bad this isn't Washington."

On the long drive north, Mallory began making notes for her victory speech.

When they arrived back in Manhattan an hour later, instead of heading to City Hall, they drove up to the Manhattan Administrative Headquarters at Rock & Filler Center, which Mallory said would serve as the new central office for her term. She also decided to establish her residence on the upper floors of the building.

She immediately called her first official news conference. The single television channel on the reservation sent a reporter, as did the one radio station. A reporter for the *Daily Posted New York Times* came as well. Mallory was checked by a doctor and found to be surprisingly fit; her amputated arm was healing nicely. She had quickly located a nice dress and a tasteful hat to cover her shaved skull. Although she made a couple of oblique comments about Shub's dubious reign, she didn't say a word about her recent kidnapping. This in turn prompted Shub to make a magnanimous concession speech roughly twenty minutes later from Kew Gardens. And that was it—Rescue City officially had its fourth mayor.

* * *

Instead of the usual two-month delay, the transition was set to happen in a mere seven days. Mallory scrambled to swiftly pull together a solid administration. After hearing about all the tireless and risky work of Don McNeill, she appointed him as deputy mayor; he would succeed her if anything should happen. She also asked Karen what position she would like.

"Are you appointing an attorney general?" Karen inquired.

"I'd rather not create a new post, I'm all for less government."

"Then give me the council cops," Karen said.

When Karen showed up at the Williamsburgh Building early the next morning, she was greeted by Scouter Lewis. Her boss stopped her at the door of his office and loudly chastised her for commandeering a team of cops and initiating the unauthorized search for Mallory's kidnappers.

"I had a significant lead," Karen said. "What I don't understand is why you lied to me."

"Lied about what?"

"You were the one who opposed my moving the antiwar rally to Manhattan, and you had Leiberman take the fall for it—why?"

"'Cause it was a bad idea!" Lewis shouted. "I didn't have the energy to fight with you!"

"So why did you even put me in charge of the project?" she asked angrily.

"Look, Karen, you're a great police officer, and you'll still be a gangcop captain, so I'm sure we'll work together again, but we're just not on the same wavelength any longer."

"What are you saying?"

"You're out of the council cops."

"Actually, I hate to say it," Karen leaned in so that only he would hear, "but you're the one who's out. The mayor-elect just appointed me the head of this unit."

Without making any calls to confirm what Karen had just told him, Lewis grabbed his jacket. Before he could leave his office, which was now her office, she said, "Look, we've been dear friends for years, and I've never done anything to betray that friendship."

"Okay."

"I need you here. I really do."

"Karen, you know better than anyone that I'm just an old drunk.

My liver's shot, my health is wrecked. Half the time I'm here I'm passed out on my desk."

"This city is very divided. Half the council cops are Piggers, and they respect you."

"And?"

"Take my old job. I'll run the place, and you'll be my deputy."

"Tell you what," he said. "I'll stay if you keep the rally here in Brooklyn."

"Convince me why that's a good idea."

"Sometimes you have to sacrifice a limb to save the body."

"What does that even mean?"

"I just know in my gut that if you move it, really bad things are going to happen."

"Unless you know something specific that I don't—"

"I know the way things work," Lewis said.

"The only thing I intend to do that you haven't done is change the location of that event."

"I'm going home to give you a day to think about it, 'cause this is a deal breaker."

Lewis put on his jacket and left.

Although many Rescue City citizens celebrated Mallory's victory, the happy occasion was quickly tempered by a rumor coming out of Staten Island that Rafique had died while assisting in Mallory's rescue. A second rumor had it that, in compliance with Rafique's wishes, his body would be cremated so there would be no formal service. Despite all queries, no Verdant League administrator would confirm or deny either rumor.

12

By the end of Mallory's first week in office, Karen had persuaded her to override the Committee of Event Permits and change the location of the upcoming convention from Brooklyn to Manhattan.

It was agreed that the event would be held at the Federal Reserve Theater, a large venue in Lower Manhattan. Mallory further agreed to let Karen put roadblocks on all the bridges coming into Manhattan that weekend in order to screen for car bombs. Additionally, Karen assembled teams of rowboats to monitor the narrow waterways to make sure none were smuggled into the borough.

The first weeks of Mallory's term as the new mayor were surprisingly calm and smooth. As the leader of a divided city, Mallory put all her initial efforts into trying to reconcile with the Pigger boroughs. She paid a much-publicized visit up to Kew Gardens and met with the newly elected head of the Pigger Party, Borough President John Cross Plains of Queens. Mayor Shub seemed to have retired without a trace.

When Mallory sat down with Plains and other prominent Piggers, she began, "I don't know how things got so messy over the years, but I'd like to try to put it all behind us. We need to work together."

"We've always strived for that," Plains responded pleasantly.

"Good. If you're willing to pull your gang out of Brooklyn and Manhattan, I'll get the Crappers out of Queens, and we can try to stop with these ridiculous back-and-forth invasions and elections."

"That'd be great," Plains said. "But the Crappers will have to withdraw first."

Within twenty-four hours, the local militias of blue- and red-shirted men had vanished from the borders between the Crapper and Pigger boroughs. A few days later, Mayor Mallory gave what came to be called her Pax Rescue City speech: "We are no longer Crappers or Piggers, but former New Yorkers and current citizens, working together in the Nevada desert, trying to keep each other alive so we can get back there . . ."

An unanticipated by-product of the new peace manifested in the near-overnight settling of the previously vacant border communities between Brooklyn and Queens. For years these areas had constituted a buffer zone of ghost streets, but once the gang patrols vanished, young people—many of them from outer Staten Island—started moving into the long narrow strip of vacant land. Mallory consulted her cabinet as to whether this new occupation should concern her.

"This isn't a military occupation, so I'm inclined to think it's not a problem," Hector Gonzalez opined. "Particularly 'cause it's mainly VLers, as opposed to Piggers."

"I'm more inclined to think of them as defectors," Karen said. "Plus, the more citizens we're able to woo into our borough, the stronger we become."

Over the next few weeks, Karen and the other Crapper officials monitored the arrival of the new immigrants to the empty north Brooklyn streets of Williamsburg, Bushwick, and East New York. Of more concern was how the Piggers were reacting.

Regarding Scouter Lewis, although he refused to formally accept the demoted position, Karen wouldn't acknowledge his resignation. Not wanting to lose his pension benefits, which included his house and car, he finally just began calling in sick.

Karen hoped that maybe his "sickness" might end when the eighth annual POW convention was over.

The opening day of the convention was beautiful. So many hippies and old-school leftists marched in over the Staten Island Ferry Bridge that it began to wobble. Due to the heightened security, Crapper gangcops frisked people before they could set foot in Manhattan. By six p.m., when the rally was about to officially start, pedestrian traffic from Staten Island was being diverted to the Zano Bridge due to crowding. Only cars and buses could proceed over the Staten Island Ferry Bridge.

Old-timers in Brooklyn marched over the Brooklyn Bridge; some citizens even walked down from the Bronx and Queens just for the entertainment value. No one wanted to miss it. Since the weather was nice, thousands unrolled sleeping bags and camped out in the streets. A nonstop lineup of bands, the best of Rescue City, was set to play in between the many speakers. Medical stations, lines of porta-potties, and food and water booths were all allotted enough space to handle the massive encampment.

Mayor Mallory, who had always been a staunch activist against the Vietnam War, agreed to launch the convention with a speech on the first night. Since Shub had always steered away from the annual event due to his broad base of Pigger support, the new mayor's attendance helped draw the biggest turnout for any public event in the history of Rescue City. People flooded the streets so that Mallory had to stand on the steps of the Federal Reserve Theater behind a phalanx of gangcops. After thanking everyone for supporting her, she took a mic in hand and said, "Putting aside all partisan bickering, let this night be a new start for us here. Just as North and South Vietnam should peacefully put their citizens above their own agendas, so should the northern and southern boroughs of our great city."

Before the applause had even died down, the mayor was rushed out through the back of the theater and driven back up Broadway to her office in Rock & Filler Center.

The key event of the rally was scheduled to occur on the second night. At exactly nine o'clock, some of the most celebrated antiwar detainees— Abbie Hoffman, Allen Ginsberg, and others—would perform a "Give Peace a Chance" sing-along. Then, over the course of the first hour, each of them would talk about some aspect of the peace movement, as well as the fact that long after the government had promised Rescue City residents their return to Old Town, they were still being held in exile.

"All they were supposed to do was rinse down the streets," Hoffman ranted that night. "I mean, after ten years of rain, I can't believe motherfucking nature hasn't already done the job!"

Afterward, there were plans for fireworks and festivities. Word spread that Mallory had promised to return for the finale.

Karen had intended to arrive for the opening ceremony but had spent that day bogged down at the Williamsburgh Building instead, just calling the various supervisors to make sure everything was running smoothly. On the second night, nervously chewing down half a box of saltines for dinner, she finally felt confident that everything was calm enough for her to leave Schuman in charge and run out to the event for an hour or so. Before she was able to leave, Tatianna informed her that Sergeant Giles, who was in charge of the roadblock at the Brooklyn Bridge, was on the walkie.

Giles said that he had just discovered what appeared to be a possible car bomb under the bridge near Cadman Plaza.

"Did you evacuate the area?" Karen asked.

"Not yet, but the area's relatively empty so I don't really think anyone's at risk. It looks like it was just abandoned here."

She instructed him to cordon off the perimeter, sit tight, and wait for her. If there was no immediate risk to anyone, she wanted to see it for herself.

When she arrived twenty minutes later, Giles told her that they'd found that the old car was packed with fertilizer and had a fuse that hadn't been ignited. Karen quickly deduced what had probably occurred: Some Pigger or terrorist had intended to bomb the rally, but upon seeing the long line of traffic going into Manhattan that was being checked, the guy must've realized that he would be caught at the roadblock and therefore took the last exit in Brooklyn before the bridge. Then, by the time the would-be bomber exited, the sun had probably set so his solar panels no longer fueled his old jalopy. Supporting Karen's hypothesis, they had discovered that the battery didn't work, so the driver had presumably been forced to abandon the vehicle.

"This vindicates me," she said to the Brooklyn Heights gangcop. "If the convention had been held in Fort Greene—as it was supposed to be—this would've been detonated."

"Yeah," the cop replied flatly, uninvested in her victory, "so we'll dispose of it."

"Do you have a camera?"

"Yeah, we got the old Polaroid, why?"

"Take a couple photos of it just in case. And leave it on my desk, I want to see if it looks like it came from Gonzalez's pile in Hoboken."

Karen listened tiredly to an argument between the tow truck operator and Sergeant Giles as to whether they should tow the vehicle or roll it a block and a half to the waterway and move it by barge, thereby minimizing the risk of it detonating en route.

"It's already hooked to your truck!" Karen snapped at the driver. "Just move the damn thing!"

"You're the boss," he said, starting his engine.

As he nervously hauled the vehicle forward, a distant flash of green lightning was followed by a quick succession of low, muffled thuds, and then the earth trembled.

"Oh fuck!" a gangcop shouted, pointing at the waterway before them. Whitecaps were emerging at the southern tip of Manhattan. Karen suddenly realized that the river below her was flowing the wrong way.

"What the fuck," muttered Giles.

In a panic, Karen raced up the pedestrian ramp of the Brooklyn Bridge with a group of gangcops on her heels. Once she reached a vantage where she could see Lower Manhattan, her body clenched as her worst fears were confirmed—street and building lights were blinking, accompanied by distant screams and what looked like black sludge flooding northward in the darkness, like a giant black marker redacting the Manhattan streets.

The ever-rising mountain of sandbags, which was supposed to hold back the basin of black water, had initially been intended as a temporary measure for a possibly unfixable problem. Largely the result of the giant clogged drain down in the south end of Staten Island. Now, after all these years, the sandbags had finally been breached down in the Battery. The vast pressure of the polluted great swamp of shit had brushed aside the remaining barriers and let loose an enormous, toxic tide which flooded right into Lower Manhattan where thousands of people were crowded together, celebrating peace. Karen now realized that the exact location of the rally, which had appeared to be the most insulated spot, also happened to be one of the lowest points in the borough.

As some of the few remaining lights continued to flicker, Karen's brain percolated one single thought: moving the convention to Manhattan had been all her doing. It never even occurred to her that such an attack was possible; Mallory had backed her decision. Whoever blew up the sandbags not only wanted to wipe out all the lefties at the convention, but also clearly aimed to torpedo Mallory's newly launched mayoralty.

"Fuck," Karen whispered to herself. If this calamity didn't bring the Piggers back into power, nothing would. *Scouter knew*, she thought as she tried catching her breath. *The old prick knew this was going to happen!* Hell, he had even tried to tell her, and this was why he had fought to keep the event in Brooklyn. In fairness, she also sensed that this was way beyond anything the Piggers could've dreamed up. Bigger forces had to be at work. Still, first and foremost, she had to find and interrogate Lewis.

Although some gangcops were weeping, while others were shouting questions and comments, Karen simply returned to her car and drove back to the Williamsburgh Building.

The Manhattan precincts were handling all of the rescue efforts. This largely consisted of assembling as many inflatable rafts as they could find, and paddling back and forth up the flooded streets, picking up those trapped in upper floors. Although they encountered a lot of floating bodies, they were instructed to focus on the living. Queens Borough President John Cross Plains called Mallory and offered to help on behalf of the Piggers. Gonzalez warned that the two groups working together could erupt in bloodshed, so the mayor politely declined. Karen then told Tatianna to call in all the council cops immediately and commence with a full investigation.

Based on preliminary information, it appeared that the point of attack had been the Staten Island Ferry Bridge, specifically the last stretch just over the thick wall of sandbags, which was now blown away. *How the fuck were they able to get a car bomb that big through the roadblock?* she wondered. She sent a pair of gangcops down to Sheepshead Bay to collect Lewis and bring him back to the office at once.

The next morning, the gangcops reported to Karen that they had found that Lewis's house had been tossed and he was missing. They also discovered fresh drops of blood on the floor of his study.

"It looked like someone grabbed him," the lead officer explained.

"You think it was a hit?"

"If they were going to kill him, I think they would've just left his body there as a message."

Eyewitness accounts of the terrorist flooding reported that the initial black wave had rushed up Broadway and slammed head-on into the brick walls of the Federal Reserve Theater, sending the roof collapsing down on the 1,500 antiwar participants inside. Many who weren't killed by the fallen roof drowned in the liquefied shit. The few who had made it out were shivering with fever, due to the intense toxicity of the water. In a single masterstroke, not only were most of the famous radical luminaries of Rescue City extinguished, but almost all of the city's left-wing activists were either dead or gravely ill.

Karen learned later that due to the heavy volume of traffic, instead of checking cars on the roadway leading up to the bridge, the Crapper border guards had been inspecting the vehicles lined up on the Manhattan side of the Staten Island Ferry Bridge, just prior to entering the borough.

"It was still a good distance from Lower Manhattan where the convention was, so we figured it was safe," said a sergeant.

In short, no one had suspected that someone might target the bridge. When the vehicle—or vehicles—exploded, it happened directly above the sandbags, allowing the water to burst through.

Rescuers were still plucking survivors by boat from rooftops; they were triaged along the sloping avenues above 14th Street.

Mallory held an emergency news conference, calling the attack a heinous act of terrorism and detailing all the planning that had gone into trying to make the POW event secure.

Every major Pigger politician except Plains called for Mallory to step down. Bachus "Backdoor" Leiberman was the first to bring up the fact that he, the organizers, and the Pigger city council had all fought to keep the event in Brooklyn—but that Captain Karen Sarkisian had pushed for it to be moved to Manhattan. Mallory refused to fire her and Karen refused to step down.

A terrorist operation this powerful couldn't be kept a secret. Karen put out a large reward for any tips as to who could be behind this catastrophe, but nothing came back. It was the first time that she really found herself missing the knowledgeable Deere Flare, whose information usually offered a great starting point for an investigation.

Over the course of the next week, displaced Manhattanites whose homes were contaminated in the flood swelled the dry streets and avenues with their tents. Slowly, before the Crappers could come up with housing alternatives, they began migrating over the bridge to the vacant communities between Brooklyn and Queens. Most of these survivors had lost everything.

One day, Schuman dashed into Karen's office. "I just got a strange call . . ." he began. "From Scouter."

"Scouter Lewis? You're kidding!" He had been missing for over a week and was presumed dead.

"He said he had tried to get through to you, but he was nervous that everyone thought he was a turncoat."

"Where is he?"

"Scouter said he knows who did the sandbag bombing, and he's got him trapped down in Staten Island."

"Sounds like bullshit."

"Maybe. But he claims he's got some guy who you falsely imprisoned, and that your brother murdered his girlfriend."

"My brother and I never worked together on *anything*."

"Hold on, he said the guy's name is . . ." Schuman looked at a scrap of paper. "Tim Vey?"

"That was the guy Deere was fucking," she remembered. She'd had him released from the Harlem jail cell after Deere's death. "What exactly did he say?"

"Scouter said he followed the guy all the way down to the drain."

"But there are no phones or cell service down there. How did he get in touch?"

"I don't think he was there yet. He said this Vey fellow got ahold of that wacky escape drug, and he knows he'll be caught and killed if he stays here, so he's planning on escaping down the hole."

"How could one guy do something of this size?"

"Scouter said he was part of some religious group. He also said you already knew about them, and that if we want to capture this guy we have to head down there right now."

"Okay, let's get a team together."

"He advised traveling light."

"Maybe we should call the VL and let them handle it."

"Do you really think that's a good idea? I mean, since Rafique's death there's no telling how they'll respond to this."

"I've racked up way too many screwups lately," Karen said, grabbing some items. "If Scouter's down there, odds are he's drunk and this whole thing is a load of bullshit. Still, we have to check."

The two of them took the elevator down and headed over to the parking lot where they got in Karen's car. Because the Staten Island

Ferry Bridge was largely destroyed, they waited for several hours in traffic. When they finally made it over the Zano Bridge, their vehicle was inspected for explosives, then they were allowed to proceed into the toxic borough. They loosely retraced the route they had followed when they went to free Mallory. After nearly an hour of navigating the unmarked washed-out roads, as the sun slowly began to set, they drove through the bottom of the sandy glen where the desperate standoff had occurred—passing fresh graves and shreds of garbage and clothing that had been abandoned after the fight.

As they made their way down the narrowing path along the fecal canal, which was now lower than usual due to the flooding, Karen put on a nose clip and said, "I still don't understand how he was able to call us if he's pursuing this guy alone."

"Maybe we should call for backup."

"I just hope he's not drunk," Karen said, driving faster. Soon they saw the red taillights of another car in the darkness. Sure enough, Lewis's vehicle was parked at the end of the stinking road. Karen pulled her pistol from its hiding place and silently scanned the area. There was no one around in any direction, and the sun was starting to set.

"I think he said he'd be up there." Schuman pointed up to the jagged rocks in front of them, highlighted by the long slanting rays of refracted sunlight.

"Why don't you go around and come up the other side, just in case anything is wrong," Karen proposed.

They both held guns and flashlights and headed up different sides of the steep incline. It took them a few minutes to reach the jagged crest.

Karen spotted a bulky figure hunched on the edge of the hole, like an overweight condor. As she approached she saw that her old boss, true to form, was drinking from a liquor bottle.

"Karen," he said softly.

She scanned the surrounding hilltop carefully with her flashlight. The landscape was bare; there was no visible threat.

"You know, I'm actually glad to be out of the council cops," Lewis slurred, taking a final swig before tossing the bottle into the long black chute before them.

Karen stepped up toward him. He reeked of liquor and had never been particularly strong or agile, so she felt it was safe to holster her gun. She closed her eyes and leaned into the cool breeze blowing up from the deep well before them.

"I always looked at the job as penance for what I did back in Old Town," Lewis mumbled.

"We're all paying for our sins from Old Town," she responded.

"I'm not saying that job was the reason I drank, but it didn't help."

"Well, this might be an opportunity to work on that," Karen said gently.

"Maybe." Lewis slowly bent forward and got on his feet. He stumbled forward a bit. Karen had to grab him before he could trip into the bottomless pit. Up close, she noticed fresh bruises and scars along his forehead, face, and chin.

"What the hell happened to you?" she asked, shining the flashlight on his face.

"Oh, nothing."

"I sent people to your house after the sandbags were blown up. You weren't there and we found drops of blood, so naturally I was concerned."

"If you must know, after you fired me, I went home, got drunk, and fell down a flight of stairs at home. So I'm fine."

"Good. So what's the deal? Is this Tim Vey guy supposed to meet you here?"

"Actually, you just missed him."

"Missed him?"

"Yeah, but you'll catch your man, you always do."

"Relax, Scouter."

"I *am* relaxed, but I don't think the thousands of people who drowned in that Manhattan toilet are . . . Well, can you imagine their final thoughts while they were sucking down a lungful of shit? So many people dying like that, it really makes me feel just awful. That's why I'm shit-faced right now."

"Are you blaming *me* for that?"

"I begged you to just leave well enough alone, didn't I? Just let the fucking rally happen in Fort Greene, but you couldn't do that, could you?"

At that moment, something cracked her across the back of Karen's skull. Before she could tumble down the back of the little mountain of rocks, Lewis caught her arm. She looked back to see Schuman behind her holding a billy club.

"You promised we'd . . ."

She could just barely hear them talking.

Lewis took something out of his pocket. As Karen wiped blood out of her eyes, she felt a sharp prick on her neck. She snatched the needle out of Lewis's hand and slashed the tip along his flabby right cheek.

"FUCKING BITCH!" he cried out, clutching his face.

She tried to roll down the rocky incline to escape but Schuman grabbed her. Slowly her motor and nervous systems seemed to give way. She couldn't move, but she could still see and hear, and for an instant she registered some kind of fight breaking out around her.

"You said we'd give her a chance!" Schuman snapped.

"There's no chance, it's a lot kinder just to kill her."

"No fucking way! I won't let you!"

"Well, where's all the stuff!"

"Down in the car. I couldn't find an oxygen tank, but—"

"It won't matter, just move it!" Lewis yelled, sending his partner in crime scurrying down the rocks.

Karen tried to talk, but all she could do was watch. Lewis was still holding his fat cheek where she had cut him with the needle.

"When I first met you, I was afraid you might recognize my voice," Lewis said to her. "Hell, I only remembered you because of your scent—it's a wonderful fragrance and I've never smelled it before or since." He lowered himself down to just above her face and sniffed her deeply, then gazed into her eyes. "See, I lost all those memories when I arrived here, but I've managed to regain a few over the years. And one thing I do remember is that my name is Dwight. Remember, I was the guy who sold our old friend Gene—what's his new name, Akbar?—I sold him those alleged bomb fuses that got us into this whole shitstorm in the first place. Then you sold that old man the bag of spark plugs, which were actually more like miniature Geiger counters, sensitive to radioactivity. What harm could they cause? I have to hand it to Paul Moses, we never figured anyone would've been able to rig those pieces of crap into something useful. Oh, and yes, we know that Mallory Levine was KIA, and the woman who now calls herself Mallory is actually Diana Oughton. We figured all that out before you even arrived here. The only reason all this hasn't come out earlier is because it leads right to the top." He shook his head. "Oughton, who doesn't even look Jewish, had the good sense to drop her last name and just be Mallory, but you and the others never even bothered to change your names. I mean, you guys were amateur hour from the get-go."

Rendered utterly inert by whatever he had injected her with, Karen wondered if she was hallucinating. Everything he said sounded so incredible—all her darkest fears laid bare by a man who had just revealed himself as a mortal enemy in her previous existence in Old Town.

"You might be thinking, *How could this man, who I was close friends with all these years, who I took care of when he was drunk in his own puke, how could he do this to me? This man is a monster, the lowest of the low.* Well, I just want you to know—I might be a monster, but I probably couldn't do this to you, someone who I really do have deep feelings for, except for one thing: you did it, didn't you? I should've deactivated that fucking thing myself, but Hoover wanted to keep it completely intact for seven more days. It was supposed to be his big Exhibit A. Of course, you had to go in a week before his most handsome agents could bust through with the press corps in tow, and take credit for uncovering the most sinister plot on our soil since Pearl Harbor—the destruction of Wall Street— just as Congress was preparing its annual budget so he could request comprehensive funding for his new National Security Act."

Lewis paused; Karen felt something on her cheek. It took her a moment to realize that he was weeping over her.

"So we both fucked up, and in case you ever wondered, that's what attracted me to you in the first place. That's why I chose you and partnered up with you and protected you all these years. We were both played, hon."

The fact that this old drunk, an FBI asshole, had managed to use her from when she first arrived here, and that Schuman, her trusted second-in-command, had viciously betrayed her, made her feel as though she truly deserved the pitiful death that was about to come.

"It took me a few years after I got here to realize that I hadn't been in an accident—my brain had been scrubbed. My bigger memories started slowly returning, and I don't mind telling you that remembering you and eventually finding you and others here triggered a lot of the little memories."

"Hey!" she now heard through the darkness. Schuman had returned and was climbing up the rocky incline, huffing and puffing with a knapsack over his shoulder.

"Christ! It took you forever. I gotta take a leak." Lewis stopped his monologue and climbed down.

Karen's consciousness was slipping away into blackness. Schuman had pulled out masking tape and was preparing her, as if wrapping a mummy for its transition into the afterlife. He delicately taped her eyes, ears, and mouth shut.

"Karen." She could barely hear her assistant. "Karen, I'm really sorry. I'm not trying to kill you, I'm doing all this 'cause I really want you to make it out alive. I taped two syringes to your leg. I'm not sure what they're for, but just like we told your brother, everyone says you'll need to inject yourself as soon as you wake up or—"

"There's nothing down there, son," Lewis called out as he struggled back up the rocky path. "Look at her, she's stopped breathing and we have a long drive back. Now let's do to her what she did to her own brother and go."

"Goddamnit, I need more time!" Schuman yelled back. He pulled out a sleeping bag and a small container of grease from the knapsack—the same shit they'd used on Uli.

As Schuman began to unravel the sleeping bag, Lewis shoved Karen's body toward the hole that was as narrow as a coal chute.

"Wait a sec!" Schuman barked.

Karen heard a strange swooshing sound and realized she was falling, falling, into the dark abyss from which no one ever returned. Was she dead? If she was still alive, she was lighter than air, just a feather on the wind. Wasn't she supposed to hit water and drown? She had to be dead underwater. She felt herself bending, speeding through the convolutions and manifolds of her own brain, faster than the speed of light, breaking through the time barrier into the past . . .

. . . into a youth she once inhabited, to growing up, diametrically opposed to her brother, who was the patriotic north to her radical south. His desire for power, for strength and authority, to control, to lead her, as she learned how power was false and authority was anything but . . . and freedom falling blindly down a bottomless pit . . . In a strange way she was on the path to undo his, right up until she got accepted to Barnard College at Columbia University . . .

13

In the spring of 1965, six years before she arrived at the newly established federal housing program in Nevada, Karen Sarkisian was accepted into the prestigious Barnard College, the sister school to Columbia University. Ironically, it wasn't the college she was attracted to but the street culture surrounding it. A year earlier she had visited the area with her parents. The pictures in the brochure showed a deceptively sprawling, beautiful campus, but driving down Broadway, she saw all the tattered awnings and filthy canopies over dark hole-in-the-wall shops and Latino ma-and-pa bodegas, along with endless run-down tenements. It was a study in irony—an Ivy League tower smack-dab in a squalid banana republic.

They parked on 112th Street near St. John the Divine, and walked nervously past rows of bricked-up brownstones with garbage-strewn courtyards and rat-filled lots. They hurried past small gatherings of chubby uninviting men playing dominoes and listening to salsa music, conversing in Spanglish. While she found it inexplicably enchanting, her parents were visibly tense. The locals were mostly first-generation Puerto Ricans and Negroes, the great-grandchildren of slaves and sharecroppers. It was like attending a college in an exotic third world country. Despite the fact that it was a major North American city, shirtless, lawless, bongo-playing, domino-clicking, utterly uninhibited men and tough women had turned Manhattan into the Caribbean's most northerly island—assimilation be damned!

Back during her first year in high school, Karen had known she wanted to be a lawyer. It seemed like the best vocation to help correct society's vast structural inequities—which she envisioned almost as some kind of giant farming apparatus; a huge machine that automatically categorized people by race and divided them into hoppers of salary, culture, and geography. Her mother swore that Karen got her social sensitivity from her grandparents, who had barely escaped from genocidal Turkey.

During her first semester, Karen had a full prelaw schedule with six classes, not to mention study groups and lab work. Her two most rigorous classes were in poli-sci and history, where she first met Mallory Levine.

When they talked about LBJ's Civil Rights Act, Mallory told Karen that Johnson did nothing more than exploit the many Freedom Riders and civil rights marchers who had fought the real battle. "And his War on Poverty is a goddamn joke," she went on. "It gives crumbs to starving people. Worse, it kills their outrage, which would've gone toward making a *real* revolution in this fat-ass country."

"Absolutely!" Karen replied—trying to keep up and afraid to disagree.

"You sure you're a revolutionary?" Mallory asked suspiciously, after Karen detailed her own family history.

"What does that mean?"

"It means you hate your brother because he's some jarhead FBI agent, so maybe you're just saying all this 'cause you really hate what he stands for."

"Huh?"

Since she had just finished reading Freud, Mallory added, "Maybe you're attracted to him, and all this is sexual tension."

Karen assured Mallory that this couldn't be further from the truth. Until she met Mallory, she had still believed that change might be possible within the existing system. But after hours and weeks of coffee, wine, and passionate late-night talks, and hearing Mallory list detail after detail of how the system had corrupted those upstart termites within it, Karen was convinced it all had to go.

Mallory Levine talked, ate, and breathed radical politics—she swore that she was ready to die for what she believed. Karen immediately developed a crush on this sexy, fast-talking Jewish girl.

Politics aside, Mallory was everything Karen wasn't. She had always seen herself as a bit of a wallflower, and for the first time she found herself enjoying popularity by association. Just hanging out with Mallory got her noticed.

The two complemented each other physically as well: where Mallory was voluptuous and feminine, Karen was tall and lean. She had always thought of herself as too masculine to ever attract a man. The fine spread of body hair all over confirmed her abundance of testosterone. Intellectually, too, whereas Karen always felt she was inadequate in her leftist reading list, Mallory seemed to have digested every Marxist tract while still at Brooklyn Technical High School. The periodical she coveted most was *New Left Notes*, the newsletter put out by

Students for a Democratic Society, which she read as soon as they hit the shelf.

"Who exactly started the SDS? What are they all about?" Karen asked early on.

Mallory filled her in on the progressive student organization that espoused participatory democracy, and how they opposed so many things that held this country back—all the discrimination, imperialism, and fascism that cloaked itself under the term *capitalism*. Karen learned about the Port Huron Statement, which was the organization's declaration of independence, and how over the past five years or so they had built themselves up into the nation's largest student organization for change.

"The revolution is going to happen, and our generation will usher it in," Mallory often said. She had an unflagging sense of purpose and righteousness along with a selfless commitment to make America a fair and just place for all, and Karen was in constant awe.

Conversely, Mallory was attracted to Karen's quiet strength as well as her physical prowess and general fearlessness. She always listened attentively. And though her eyes lit up, she barely laughed or reacted during political discussions, only asking questions to elucidate the more complex points or subtle ramifications.

From time to time, Mallory would watch Karen practice karate moves in her tiny room. Though they were amusing, she didn't grasp their practical application until one night when they were leaving the 110th Street subway station and some drunken asshole started making vulgar remarks. Then he grabbed one of Mallory's breasts. Karen caught his wrist, twisted it high behind his back, and shoved him to the pavement. Both young women dashed away before the man was able to get up. The entire time Mallory was thinking that if the guy hadn't been drunk, Karen probably would've gotten her ass kicked. She was only a green belt.

When Karen's brother Uli had joined the FBI during her junior year in high school, she enrolled in Karate for Teens, a class that was offered at the local YWCA. She didn't care for the instructor, who seemed to have control issues, but she'd been immediately taken by every other aspect of the discipline.

Karate was both hierarchal and traditional: black belts were at the top, white belts at the bottom. At the onset of every class, the students lined up according to their rank and went through the elaborate process of greeting each other and the instructor in Japanese before they paired off to spar. Although it had a militaristic sense of order, she had liked the fact that the matches were only based on competition and growth. As her combat skills increased, she steadily worked her way up the ranks.

When she initially took lessons at the Y, her full schedule of classes, along with the fact that she didn't really like the instructor, kept her from getting past a green belt. But she intended to continue pursuing her practice.

One day after her first year at Barnard, while passing St. John the Divine, Karen stumbled upon a small home-style dojo oddly named the 111th Street Dojo for Outer Self-Esteem and Inner Self-Enlightenment Through Physical and Mental Discipline and Training. The bottom of the sign said: *If you're broke, but seriously want to learn, come inside! We swap lessons for labor.*

It was just a few blocks from her apartment. When she looked at the name of the owner and operator, she was surprised to see that he was Armenian: Hrag Jingjanian. She went in and saw a short, wiry, iron-haired man in what appeared to be pajamas.

"Can I help you?" he asked, wiping off his forehead after just finishing a match.

"Hi, I'm Karen Sarkisian and I'm interested in taking some classes."

"A fellow Armenian?" he asked.

"Yep, and I'm enrolled at Barnard."

He gave her a spontaneous embrace, reserved only for fellow countrymen. Although she really didn't care to press up against his sweaty flesh, she didn't want to be rude. She asked how he had come to be a karate instructor.

"After the war I was stationed in Okinawa. I was still in my twenties and there was this dojo that had been there for hundreds of years."

"Wow!"

"It was more of a church, with generation after generation of practitioners." He explained how he'd been utterly fascinated by it. Hrag would discreetly sit and watch them practice, mesmerized by the grace and concentration of movement. Eventually, after repeated requests, he was permitted to study along with a handful of other American servicemen.

Hrag demonstrated some of his basic moves for Karen. She was struck by his strength and agility. He could kick his legs at a ninety-degree angle in any direction without losing balance.

"So you came back to the States and started a dojo?"

"Heck no." He did what every nice Armenian boy was expected to do: married his high school sweetheart, finished school on the GI Bill, and became an actuary. Then he took an office job and tried to raise a family.

"What happened?"

"Sterility—at home and at work. It was my fault, the bullets weren't firing in either place." By 1959 his wife had divorced him for a more fertile partner, and in 1964, after being fired from his job which he had come to hate, he took his modest savings and did a block-by-block search of sheet-metaled, cinder-blocked buildings in Harlem. Although he had a lot to choose from, he finally located a sturdy old tenement that had been abandoned to the city in 1951. The place was six stories tall, with six units per floor. As part of the city's new homesteading program, he was able to file papers and take over the building. The program allowed for eight tax-free years, giving him the time to slowly do the renovations and hopefully bring the place back on the city's shrinking tax rolls.

His first move was to immediately fix up the ground floor, and he hung a small shingle with the wordy hand-painted sign. He would hold karate matches in the big bay windows, and in the same way he had been drawn to the martial art, many kids in the area came and watched. Before the end of the second year he had over a hundred of the local kids throughout the neighborhood coming in for one of his six classes a day. Two fast learners who hastily moved up from elementary to intermediate levels were a Peruvian named Manuel and a large Mexican kid named Carlos.

Since a sensei needed a staff, he hired the two of them to teach the introductory classes as a way of paying off their more advanced lessons. Many of the other young practitioners worked off their karate tuition by periodically helping with demolition and restoration of the empty units upstairs. Despite the rats, mice, and roaches, and with limited heat and hot water, Hrag was able to live out of his office in the back of the ground floor.

Karen immediately admired the man. Following the city's epoch of white flight, long after the bottom had dropped out of the real estate market, buildings couldn't even be given away. Whole communities, including parts of Harlem and the South Bronx, were all but abandoned. Hrag was one of the few people who had come into the area by choice and put his shoulder to the rusty wheel of the impoverished city.

She signed up for his intermediate classes, becoming one of only three females in the dojo. As they got to know each other and Hrag infused more Armenian terms into their lingo, he took her under his wing.

By the summer of '66, even though she'd make it a point of frequenting the dojo five days a week, she still hadn't progressed to the next color belt.

"Everyone else is advancing more quickly than me," she complained one afternoon.

"Yeah, 'cause you're special."

"What the hell does that mean?"

"Look," Hrag said, "only time and work make you better, not clothing dye. When you leave here you're going to be so much more qualified than any of them."

"But I'll be graduating in a few years," she said—not mentioning that she was planning to go to law school for three more years after that.

He nodded his head silently. Still, she never felt better than when she was in that dilapidated storefront, strong in spirit and body, practicing karate with every muscle in her body. By day she studied hard, trying to be on the right side of the otherwise sleazy legal profession and to become an adopted member of a neighborhood in need. In the evenings in the dojo she grew more skillful with each sparring session, and despite her gender began steadily winning on the mat. Karen felt more autonomous, like she was slowly becoming the person she wanted to be.

"The same strength and solace that my parents gained in their faith," Hrag once told her, "I acquired in my practice."

In August 1966, Hrag's little labor force had finished renovating the first two studios on the ground floor of his tenement. He invited Carlos and Manuel to move into the new units. When he mentioned that two other apartments would soon be available, Karen asked to take a look at them. She was sick of living with whiny white children of privilege and having to clean up behind messy, stuck-up roommates. With new Sheetrock and clean linoleum floors—although there were still mice and roaches—it was the nicest building she had seen above 96th Street and it was directly above the dojo, which had become like a second home. The rent was a little steep, but when she mentioned to Mallory that there was a second bedroom, and that they'd be the only whites on the floor, her friend jumped at the offer.

In November, because Karen didn't want to go home for the dreaded holidays, Mallory invited her to stay at her aunt Estelle's home in the Kensington neighborhood of Brooklyn from Hanukkah through New Year's. Since Estelle was a serious drinker and saw no reason the young women shouldn't partake as well, it was whiskey sours and Brandy Alexanders until they passed out. Karen learned that Mallory's parents had died in a car crash when she was four. She had been raised by her maiden aunt, who had been an unrepentant communist since the 1930s. Because of this Estelle had been blacklisted, and unable to teach, for several years in the early 1950s. During Mallory's formative years, her aunt became a radical mentor.

Since there was only a single bed in Mallory's room, the two of them spent the night snuggling together. "Ever smooch with a boy?" Mallory whispered one drunken night.

"No," Karen whispered back.

Mallory suggested that maybe they should practice. After a bunch of kissing, it turned into heavy petting, and they both had their first sexual encounter.

Karen was firmly a part of Mallory's circle of SDS friends. Among the regulars were Alvin Rich, who wore thick glasses and dark turtlenecks; Sharon Stein, a skinny girl who was moved by "the Negro plight"; Sam Gunderson, an intelligent blond kid from Minnesota; Henriette Lipsky, who wrote for the school paper and intended to go into journalism; Oliver Cohen, with a deep thunderous voice and who did everything in a grand theatrical manner; Larry Epstein, who by contrast rarely said a word but when he spoke everyone listened; and Evelyn Peabody McCready, who went to church twice a week and would've become a nun except that she didn't care for "the patriarchy."

14

K aren and Mallory began attending SDS meetings together so regularly that many came to think of them as a couple. The big thing that so many students rallied against was the war in Vietnam. As members of the SDS, they worked at putting up flyers and getting word out on campus about the national rally at the UN that coming April—on tax day.

On the day of the rally, the entire city stopped. School buses were packed with protestors, and marchers from all over converged on First Avenue in the East 40s. That night Mallory, Karen, and the rest of their comrades felt victorious when they heard on the news that it was estimated that between a hundred thousand and a quarter of a million people had attended. On campus, SDS started becoming hip—not just the smart kids were joining.

Around the same time, when a student stumbled across a relatively obscure detail in a university library, the war in Southeast Asia really hit home. A rather bookish senior, Bob Feldman, had been at the school library doing research for a term paper. He had scanned an odd document in the law library written by a mysterious group called the Institute for Defense Analyses, or IDA, which claimed to be affiliated with Columbia University. Feldman learned that they were a "weapons research think tank" associated with the Department of Defense—with a presence right there on campus, yet it seemed that no one had ever heard anything about it.

Feldman made photocopies of the document and handed them out to everyone at that week's SDS meeting. Mark Rudd, the charismatic president of the group, immediately grasped the implications. This was Columbia's imperious participation in an unjust war.

"We don't have the power to end American participation over there," Alvin Rich argued, "but if we can't stop this here, what good are we?"

On behalf of the SDS, Mark sent a letter to the president of Columbia University, Grayson Kirk, requesting that the college cut ties with the IDA immediately. Every member signed it and Mark hand delivered it to the president's secretary. One week, then two and three weeks, went by. When they got no response, one of the students learned through an office aide that Kirk had refused to even open the letter, much less discuss the matter. A week later, a petition table was set up on campus. It was soon followed by a teach-in, educating the students on the college's culpability in America's imperialist war. Still the president refused to comment.

Slowly, as summer approached, another issue started brewing: the university was finally planning to break ground for a new gymnasium that it had been planning for years. The school had secured the rights to build the gym smack in the middle of Morningside Park, which many saw as an infringement on the economically challenged Harlem residents.

In a gesture of good faith to give something back to the community, Columbia was offering the local residents use of the ground floor of the gym, but that was it. They'd have no access to the upper, more luxurious floors, which were strictly for their students. As this was during the height of the civil rights movement—while footage of black citizens being hosed down and attacked by Southern law officers was being played out on the nightly news—the student body began referring to the Columbia University project as "Gym Crow."

The Student Afro-American Society, or SAS, formally came out against the planned structure. In an effort to rally the support of the entire student body, the SDS joined them. At their pamphlet table on 116th Street and Broadway, SDS students vocally protested the school's two controversial issues—IDA and Gym Crow.

The problem was that even though many of the young soldiers being drafted to serve in Vietnam came out of American ghettos, the SAS didn't seem particularly interested in the IDA issue, with the exception of one older student named Eugene Hill. He was a handsome, light-skinned Negro who was a former *Snickerer*, as they called all SNCC members. Even before the gym issue he would sometimes stop by the SDS table on Broadway, holding a mysterious cigar box and a clipboard, usually speaking with various female members of the SDS into the late afternoons. It was actually Karen who first took a liking to him. When Mallory told her that she had seen them talking, Karen shared that every other Columbia boy she'd met was "a spindly wimp."

"We still don't know much about IDA," Karen heard Mallory telling Eugene Hill the next afternoon. "We don't even know why Kirk joined it."

"Actually, I might know more than you," Eugene replied. He explained that Grayson Kirk had been appointed by none other than the former supreme commander and Columbia University president Dwight Eisenhower. "Kirk joined the think tank to prove to Eisenhower that he had a pair of balls."

"Is that true?" asked Mallory, making all these naive and feminine expressions that Karen had never before seen.

"Oh, it's true, but I can't reveal my sources."

"Can you tell us why you always have a clipboard and that cigar box?" Karen inserted, half kidding.

"I drive a cab. And I usually see you guys when I'm about to go on shift."

"How about those dog tags?" Mallory asked, reaching out and touching them. They were hanging out from under his dirty T-shirt.

Gene quietly confessed that he had completed a tour in Vietnam just a year earlier. "But please don't tell anyone," he whispered, tucking them back into his shirt. "I was drafted, and every time someone finds out, they look at me like I'm a baby murderer."

"Then why do you still wear them?" Karen asked.

"I know it sounds odd, but I think it's important to embrace your past—even if you hate it. It's still a part of you."

"Very true," Mallory agreed.

"Are you sorry you served?" Karen pressed, hoping for some hint of contrition.

"For starters, I was drafted, so it wasn't really my call. Ultimately the jury is still out. I mean, if the commies win and all that was for nothing, I'm going to deeply regret it."

It wasn't quite what Karen was hoping to hear, but at least he was straightforward.

Over Gene's next few table visits, Mallory started to look at him as something more than just a novelty. He could discuss the current Supreme Court as fluidly as he could delve into the latest experimental works by contemporary French writers such as Alain Robbe-Grillet and Jean-Paul Sartre. He said he loved whatever Grove Press published, and never saw a foreign film he didn't like.

"Fellini is better than everything that has ever come out of Hollywood put together," he told her.

Although Karen felt it was a little bitchy of her friend to just move in on Gene without talking to her—after all, she had met him first—she didn't say anything. She also started noticing little things about him that she found odd. Sometimes he was stylishly dressed and talked euphorically a mile a minute. At other times he was reticent, disheveled, and barely able to make eye contact.

After a while she thought that she had better share these observations with Mallory. It was then that Mallory did a little checking and quickly solved the mystery of his mood swings. He was always broke, and every waking minute that he wasn't in school he was driving a cab. Since he usually did this at night, he'd pop bennies to stay up and then take downers to get to sleep in the morning.

Unlike anyone else on campus, he actually lived north of 125th Street. Mallory learned that he had an apartment somewhere up "in the valley," a term that some used for Harlem. That detail, along with the fact that he was black and a Vietnam vet, made him special. He was a part of what Mallory thought of as the "real world," something she couldn't wait to join.

One warm afternoon in June of '67, when Mallory had to spend a weekend in Brooklyn with her aunt Estelle, Karen was working at the SDS table alone. Just as she spotted Gene approaching, some letterman passing by shouted, "Go back to Russia, you damn pinko!"

"Just keep walking," Karen muttered, compelling the jock to stop.

"I'm not going to keep quiet while some barnyard bitch is stabbing my country in the back."

"Our country is stabbing itself by doing something illegal and un-American," she countered.

"Only the president has the right to decide that, which is why we elected him."

"The war is wrong and it's killing people who never did anything to us—"

"You don't know shit!"

"Why don't you let her finish, man?" Gene interjected.

"Who the hell asked *you* anything?!" the guy barked.

"Have a good day," Karen said just to be rid of him.

The jock glared at Gene, who stood by her, then walked off.

"You know, I appreciate the support, but in the future it'd be best if you just stayed out of it," she said.

"I was trying to—"

"I know, but it just makes me look like some kind of helpless little lady."

Gene sighed and headed off.

Karen stayed another couple hours until sunset when some SDS friends finally arrived to fold the table up and bring the flyers back to the office. Then they all went to the West End Bar, where they chatted about world politics and tossed back a few beers. When Karen started feeling light-headed she knew it was time to head home. Grabbing her textbook, she left the back room where they customarily hung out. At the end of the long bar in front of the establishment, she spotted Gene, who had apparently just finished a beer and burger and was paying his bill.

"Hey, I'm sorry about earlier," she said. "I was embarrassed and pissed off by that asshole."

"No problem." He put down a fiver and walked out with her.

"So, you served in 'Nam, huh?"

"Yep."

"What was it like over there?"

As they walked south down Broadway, he relayed several poignant vignettes that he typically used to dramatize the place. He didn't expect all her follow-up questions: "What were the Vietnamese people like?" "Did they comprehend the bigger issues surrounding them?" "How could the American GIs distinguish between the locals and the Vietcong?"

Gene soon realized that she was more interested in forming questions than hearing answers—which he attributed to her drinking. He let her ramble on until he heard someone squawk up ahead. Half a block up the empty street he saw a large black man, who yelled out, "Will you look at this, a preppy nigger!"

Karen, who didn't hear the comment, continued asking questions as Gene tried to navigate around the giant man who was closing in on them.

"Brother found himself one sweet-ass ride, didn't he now?" the large man scoffed, pulling Karen out of her thoughts.

"Why don't you mind your own business," Gene said.

The guy smacked Gene hard across the mouth. As Gene spun around trying to maintain his balance, Karen slammed the spine of her textbook into the man's Adam's apple—a karate move she had practiced until it became a reflex.

The goliath fell backward, gagging. Gene grabbed Karen and the two started running down Broadway, taking a left on 111th Street. She led him into her apartment building a few blocks away and raced up the stairs. At the second-floor landing, she looked back and saw that

Gene seemed to be hiding his face as he struggled to catch his breath.

"Are you okay?" She noticed some blood coming from his nose.

He nodded yes, but was still unable to speak. She opened her door and led him into her living room, where he collapsed on the sofa. Karen went into the kitchen and got him a cup of water and some tissues. When she returned, she saw tears in his eyes.

"It's okay," she said softly, handing him the glass.

"He just came out of the blue, and I froze up," Gene whispered. "But you—what are you, a black belt?"

"God no, I just got my purple."

He abruptly buried his face in her chest, but not in a sexual way. She sensed that he was experiencing shame.

"It's okay," Karen whispered into his ear.

"I'm sorry," he said, slowly regaining composure. "It really took me by surprise."

"I feel that way myself at times." Looking into his eyes, she could almost see the little boy through the large, hard exterior. He seemed so vulnerable, and she felt an odd maternal instinct.

"Did anyone ever tell you that you kind of look like Harry Belafonte?" she asked softly.

That remark seemed to shore up his failed confidence: Gene leaned in for a kiss and Karen didn't block it. *What the hell?* she thought as he slipped his tongue into her mouth.

He kissed better than any of the other guys she had been with, and as his hands moved under her shirt and along her back, she found that his massage skills were unsurpassed. The fact that she had downed several beers and felt like she had rescued him made her feel more powerful than usual. The whole evening had caught her off guard, and she usually wouldn't allow anyone to move this quickly. For that matter, she usually wouldn't even let a man into her apartment at night. By the time he was fumbling with the button on her pants, Karen had decided that it was high time to finally be rid of her virginity.

It wasn't until the next morning, while lying in bed with a snoozing Gene, his head on her chest, that she realized the full ramifications of what she had done: she had slept with her best friend's chosen man.

"Hey," she murmured, feeling too anxious to stay in bed a minute longer.

"Yeah," he said, waking up slowly.

"This is a little embarrassing, but I—we—shouldn't've done this."

"Why not?"

"Mallory likes you."

"And I like *you*."

"And I like you too, but not this way."

"Oh, I get it. But you like me as a friend," he said, rooting around in the sheets for his boxers.

"Mallory is my best friend. What I did with you is a betrayal. Normally I don't do things like this."

"Betrayal of what? You make it sound like Mallory and I are dating or something—we haven't so much as kissed. You didn't betray anything."

"Technically you're right. You didn't do anything wrong. But if you care about someone . . . and I love Mallory, you know—so I have to consider her feelings."

"Well, I have no intention of ever dating her," he said coolly.

"Gene, try to understand this: I think you're a nice, intelligent, honest guy. And I think you've got a great body and you're a terrific lover. I was happy to give you my virginity."

"You're a virgin?"

"Well, I *was*, but the point is, even if you're the best guy I will ever meet, I can never sleep with you again. Mallory is my best friend. She's like the sister I never had, and she has officially expressed an interest in you. That means, in my world, you're the only guy I *can't* sleep with, because it would hurt her. If she knew we did this she'd be destroyed. And you don't hurt people you love, do you?"

"Even though I have never slept with her and have no intention of *ever* sleeping with her?"

"*Especially* if you have no interest in sleeping with her, because then it would be that much more painful for her to see me marching around with you."

"So you're putting her ahead of me."

"Unfortunately, yes. I mean, she was my best friend before I even met you."

Though he was frustrated, horny, and still tired, he had to respect Karen. It was just too clumsy a move to be anything but earnest.

She insisted on making him coffee and offered him eggs. He declined, but took a slice of toast to show that he wasn't mad. She carefully buttered it and put out jam, so he could see that she was trying to make amends, trying in some little way to show she was sorry.

"Listen," he said after finishing his coffee, "I really like you, and

I'm hoping someday you'll reconsider—but until then, this can just be our little secret. You don't have to worry about me, okay?"

"You don't know how relieved that makes me."

Although he knew she didn't want him to, he kissed her full on the lips before leaving. And that was the end of it.

15

When Mallory returned from Brooklyn she was none the wiser. But the incident made Karen realize that she did want a boyfriend, something she had never really thought about before. Still, she hoped for someone a little less complicated than Eugene Hill, more manageable. She had her eye on a skinny freshman named Link, short for Lincoln, who was also prelaw. He resembled one of the SDS leaders whom she had a crush on, John Jacobs. Although J.J. was always nice to her, she knew she was too low on the social pyramid to ever be truly noticed by him.

As luck would have it, Link was from Newton, Massachusetts, near Watertown where she was from, and they were both planning to return to New England for summer vacation.

A few weeks later on the summer solstice, the longest day of the year, Mallory bumped into Gene at a newsstand on the northeast corner of Broadway and 110th Street. At first when she said hi, Gene only nodded back. But Mallory waited for him with a big smile and they started walking in tandem.

Gene knew it wasn't Mallory's fault that Karen had dumped him. He quietly endured her rhetoric as she went on about the latest Gym Crow protests. Clearly she had no clue that anything had happened between him and Karen. As she talked, he noticed for the first time that she had a beautiful figure. Wondering if Karen was telling the truth about Mallory's crush on him, he found himself turned on by the possibility of having sex with a pair of Barnard coeds—best friends no less.

"Want to grab dinner?" he asked.

She said no, she wasn't particularly hungry.

"Want to catch a flick?"

"Which one?"

"Trust me," he said. Grabbing her hand, he led her down the steps to the IRT local, which they took to 86th Street. Then he whisked her up to the New Yorker Theater on Broadway and 88th where they caught a special showing of *The Battle of Algiers*.

Afterward, enchanted and inspired by the notion of a successful revolution, of a world in which they could be heroes, they bounced lightly up Broadway, a walk she never would have chanced alone at that hour. The entire time Gene kept an eye out for the big motherfucker who'd jumped him. With a blade in his pocket, he'd be ready this time. When they uneventfully reached Mallory's apartment, she invited him up.

"Do you think Karen's home?" he asked nervously.

"Probably, but she won't care."

Gene said it was such a nice night that they should stay out, so they headed over to Riverside Park where they sat on a bench. Gene leaned in to kiss her, and they started making out. Soon he tried slipping his hand up under her shirt. Mallory wasn't opposed to fooling around, but insisted his hands stay outside the bra. Unlike Karen, she was playing hard to get, but he kept pushing until she grew tired of resisting.

She didn't say anything as his strong fingertips flipped up her bra wire and caressed her ample breasts, massaging her large nipples until they were taut. When he walked her home at three in the morning, her panties were soaking wet. Although Gene knew she wanted him to come upstairs, he kissed her good night at the door and headed off.

It was the very first time Mallory had any kind of sexual encounter with a Negro, though she thought he could also pass for Algerian—like one of the freedom fighters in the film.

The next day Mallory told Karen all about the previous night's adventure. Karen bit her lip and said she was happy for her friend. Link, the young man Karen was now focused on, was turning out to be a cold fish—apparently not all young men were horny. Link seemed far more concerned with being right than getting laid.

Soon it was time for Karen to head home for part of the summer break. She packed her bags, counted out two months of rent, and cautioned Mallory about moving too quickly with Eugene Hill.

"He's a nice guy, but he's older than us, and he's gone through a lot more than you or I can begin to imagine. You shouldn't assume you can just corral him like most of the guys around here." The last thing Karen wanted was to sabotage their relationship, yet she feared she had already done exactly that.

"I'll be just fine," Mallory replied confidently.

The first night Karen was gone, Mallory invited Gene over for dinner, but almost as soon as he entered things got hot and heavy. Clothes came off and they spent the entire night screwing.

By late June, the vast army of Columbia University students had evacuated, leaving a skeletal crew behind. Mallory and a number of the other SDS members were able to get altruistic internships throughout the city while living on or around campus. Alvin Rich, who also intended to go into law, got a job with Legal Aid; Sharon Stein worked for the once great, now beleaguered congressman Adam Clayton Powell in his Harlem office; Sam Gunderson was a student teacher at PS 116; Henriette Lipsky got an internship at the *Village Voice*; Oliver Cohen and Larry Epstein worked for various community-based organizations in the transitional neighborhood of Park Slope, Brooklyn; and Evelyn McCready volunteered for the Catholic Worker down in the Lower East Side.

For her part, Mallory got a job working for Allard Lowenstein as a part of the Dump Lyndon Johnson campaign—an effort to deny him a second term due to his intractable stand on Vietnam. Lowenstein himself seemed to appreciate Mallory's tireless work, constantly giving her words of encouragement.

In the evenings she spent her time with Gene. Through a succession of foreign films set in exotic places, they went on a cinematic vacation around the world. During the hottest days they'd hit every small theater around town—the Bleecker and the Little Carnegie were their favorites—smoking joints in the cool air-conditioning, catching as many double features as they could in those small black rooms. Afterward they'd wind up talking about the movies at the West End Bar over a nightcap. There, along with most of Mallory's fellow travelers, they'd drink beer, listen to music, and discuss politics. It was always about "the revolution"—which all were certain would happen before 1976. Occasionally they'd stagger over to the university, eluding campus security, and she'd give Gene head in one of the little culs-de-sac. By late July, at his prompting, Mallory would hike up her long sundress, which she wore without panties, and she and Gene would do it doggy style against trees or posts. They'd rarely make it all the way without someone passing by, and would usually have to change location several times.

One evening in early August, Alvin mentioned that he'd read that

Columbia had to begin construction on the controversial gym by August 29 or the school would lose its permits.

"I'm sure they're just going to get some kind of extension," said Henriette, the frizzy-haired redhead.

"They've been talking about building it for the past seven years," Evelyn pointed out. "Maybe they'll just let it lapse."

"No, they're doing one of two things," Sharon, who was particularly knowledgeable on the subject, speculated. "Waiting for all the controversy to blow over, or they want to expand and make it even bigger."

"Sounds like the space program," Gene joked.

"Why would you think they'd expand?" Mallory asked Sharon.

"They've doubled their initial budget five times. It went from six million to thirteen million in the past two years alone."

"Wow, what's Kirk the Jerk doing with all that cash?"

"Maybe he's making a pentagon-shaped gym, combining the IDA with phys ed."

Everyone at Mallory's table started pitching strategies to force Grayson Kirk's hand on the new gymnasium—legal maneuvers, future rallies, and other ways to publicize their cause. With each suggestion, Gene just chuckled and rolled his eyes.

"What's bugging you?" asked Oliver.

"A different time and place," he smiled dismissively.

"What a wise old man you are," Sharon teased.

"Yeah, share with us," Mallory nudged him.

"Believe me, you don't want to know."

"Don't wanna know what?" Oliver probed.

"When I was still in 'Nam, I was part of a special-ops team that searched out staging areas for the Vietcong and . . . we'd blow them up." Everyone stopped talking. "No petitions, no rallies, none of this talk-till-you're-blue-in-the-face bullshit—just a couple of grenades and the problem is solved."

"Are you frigging kidding me?" Henriette finally broke the silence.

"See, I told you you didn't want to know. But before y'all call me a baby killer, let me just say: the tunnels we blew up were always empty."

"What tunnels?" Oliver asked.

"There were more tunnels under the jungle of Vietnam than subways in New York. We'd lob a couple of fragmentation grenades in them and it'd all come tumbling down."

"So you think we should just lob some bombs at the gym?" Evelyn McCready said sarcastically.

"I don't care what you do, I'm just telling you something effective that we did."

"Do you happen to have a spare fragmentation grenade?" Oliver asked.

"You can easily get sticks of dynamite out in Jersey."

"They haven't even broken ground on the gym. What are we supposed to do, blow up the Bethesda Fountain?" said Henriette.

"That's the beauty of it! Now's the time to strike, before anyone or anything can get hurt."

"What are you talking about?" Mallory said.

"Do a symbolic act of destruction, something that gets noticed immediately. That should be enough," Gene explained.

"Actually, that's not a bad idea," Oliver said. "I mean, if we get caught, what are we going to get charged with—blowing up dirt?"

"They'll just keep building it," Evelyn said.

"Not if the explosion is big enough," Gene said.

"But not big enough that someone gets hurt."

"Right, but we have to make it clear that it's directed at the gym."

"They'd still just ignore it," Evelyn muttered.

"Want to make a bet?" Gene shot back. "The trustees aren't going to gamble thirteen million dollars on a building that's getting targeted before it's even built." Henriette glared at him, frozen, until he continued, "Look, I've been hearing y'all talk about this for months."

"Although I'm not accepting this notion, I'm not rejecting it either," Sharon declared. "But I know Mark and the others would go nuts if they heard us even talking about this."

"Look, I'm not trying to upset Chairman Mark, let alone hurt anyone, but I've gone to more than my share of protests and stood out there with the rest of you collecting signatures up the wazoo. And for what? Kirk won't even meet with us. He's watching us out of his office window and laughing!"

"I agree," Mallory spoke up, eager to finally be a part of something real and decisive.

"Hypothetically, how much do you think this . . . operation would cost?" asked Sam Gunderson, whose father was a big corporate executive.

"Not that much," said Gene.

"How much?"

"Well, if they start construction in two weeks, I suppose you could get the dynamite for under a hundred bucks."

"Hold on," said Oliver, "I don't mind pitching in money, but I'm not about to handle dynamite."

"Me neither," said Larry.

"Well, I'm not even in your TNT group," chuckled Gene.

"But this is your idea, Gene, and you're the only one who has experience with explosives," Mallory said.

"Besides, it's nothing personal," Alvin chimed in. "This is really a cause for the people up here in Harlem—your people."

"My people?"

"That's true," Oliver said. "Mark has let the SAS handle this one."

"You are the only one who's actually *from* here, sweetie," Mallory tried to appeal to Gene.

"So I'm the only one taking the risk?"

"You know this is a . . . a symbolic act, right?" Oliver said. "I mean, we're just blowing up the ground."

"What's your point?" Gene asked.

"Well, I was thinking we could just use cherry bombs, but I guess that wouldn't make the paper."

"Yeah, we'd need at least one stick of dynamite so they'd know we're serious," Alvin said.

"I can buy a stick of dynamite," Mallory whispered.

Gene knew she had no clue where to find such a thing. "Tell you what—you guys put up the cash, and I might consider helping you out, but this would be *your* deal, no going to Comrade Mark and his central committee. I'll tell you right now, the way people get caught is by talking. So we have to be in it together, and if anyone talks we all go to jail. Otherwise we just drop it now and forever."

During the ensuing silence, Mallory envisioned a loud explosion disturbing a quiet, empty street, shaking the dust off of the teacups and crystal decanters. It would leave a monstrous crater in the center of Morningside Park, as though an asteroid had hit. She could see the headline the next day in the *New York Times*: "COLUMBIA UNIVER-SITY GYM PROJECT CANCELED" Columbia president Grayson Kirk himself would announce that they had decided to discontinue it; the police investigation would reach an abrupt dead end. And even if arrests *were* made, without property damage or any injuries, the worst that could happen would likely be probation. The fantasy emboldened Mallory in a way she'd never felt before. The black man from Harlem,

Eugene Hill, was going to lead them from their candy land of discussion into the real world of action.

"Do you really believe you can do something like this for a measly hundred bucks?" Sharon asked.

"I'll put in twenty dollars, provided you do it *first*," said Oliver before Gene could reply. "I'll pay when the job's done."

"Yeah, I'd be more comfortable paying after the job is done too," Alvin said.

"Doesn't this beat all!" exclaimed Gene. "A bunch of Caucasian students hiring some colored lackey to enact their big revolution for them. Then they'll tip him afterward."

"I-I didn't mean it that way," Oliver said.

"I know how you meant it. You're all goody-goody liberals, but none of you want to get your little white asses stuck out there when things get messy. Well, I might've come up through the ghetto and fought in that muddy war that y'all are protesting against, but guess what? I don't want my black ass hanging out there neither."

"Why don't we take it one step at a time," said Larry calmly. "First we can see how much it costs. If it's affordable, maybe we can take it to Mark."

"Fuck this!" Gene said.

"Yeah," Alvin said, "Gene's right. Do that and everyone will know about it. And Mark will just veto it anyway."

"Let's table this for right now," Mallory suggested.

Gene put down his beer, looked at his wristwatch, and said that he had to run. Mallory said she was beat as well and asked if he'd walk her home. He agreed, and all the SDS members thanked him profusely for his stimulating input.

When Gene and Mallory got home, they quickly had sex. Unlike fucking Karen, sex with Mallory was just too easy. It was almost like masturbation, which made it harder for him to come. For the first time while screwing her, Gene found himself thinking about twitchy Karen—specifically her enticing reluctance.

Afterward, Mallory was surprised to see Gene quietly lacing up his boots. "Are you leaving?" It was the first time he wasn't going to spend the night.

"It's just that I'm supposed to take the cab out tonight."

She let out a long sigh, so he stopped buttoning his shirt; he realized he was being kind of a prick.

"Actually, if I can use your phone, I'll stay."

"You don't have to." She was already feeling hurt.

"No, I want to. I guess I'm just a little nervous about work."

She followed the phone line under her bed and handed the telephone to him. He called the garage, explained that he wasn't feeling well and wouldn't be driving tonight. Then he pulled off his shoes and pants and jumped back into bed. Staring into her large, moist eyes, he saw how beautiful she truly was. And unlike Karen, who simply seemed to tolerate him, Mallory was really into him. A moment later they were having sex again. Only this time he made more of an effort, giving her head before entering her.

16

Karen called Mallory two days later from Boston and told her that she had gone on two nonproductive dates with "Skinny Link," but the third one was the charm. They had finally done it.

"You're kidding!" Mallory shrieked in faux excitement, believing her roommate had finally lost her virginity. They timidly took turns exchanging their "passage into womanhood" stories, as Mallory jokingly put it.

Karen talked about how Skinny Link was paralyzed with fear—evidently he had been a virgin. Mallory's mind wandered and she recalled Eugene's proposal to bomb the gym site in the park. She had to use all her self-restraint not to mention it.

When Karen finally stopped chattering, Mallory felt compelled to reciprocate, delicately mentioning her first time with Gene. "We had been drinking beer all night, so when I finally lost it—I lost it." She burst out giggling.

"Oh God, did you pee?" Karen asked.

"A little," Mallory confessed.

"Me too." She hadn't, but had read that some girls did so during their first orgasm.

A few days later, when Eugene called Mallory to ask if she wanted to join him for dinner, she said she wasn't available—she had already made plans to hang out with her friends at the West End. She asked if he wanted to join them, but he declined.

"Come on, Gene, they love you."

"Yeah, 'cause I'm one of the brothers."

She asked if he was serious about blowing up the gym site.

"Sure I'm serious," he replied. "But I have no idea why you or any of them would be."

"What's that supposed to mean?"

"Just what they all said. You're all white kids, not even from here. Some of you guys are even rich. Why should any of you risk your futures for some low-class niggers?"

Feeling strangely aroused by the tone of his voice, she asked if he wanted to come over.

"Now?"

"Right this very minute!" she said as lustfully as she could.

Ten minutes later Gene was unbuckling his pants as he was coming up the stairs of her tenement. Mallory met him on the landing, wearing one of her loose hippie dresses and no panties. Instead of even going into her pad, he pushed her against the wooden railing in the hallway, hiked up her dress, and did her doggy style right there. When she started moaning, he clamped his hand over her mouth. She tried to oblige, focusing on not making a sound. She had never felt so stimulated in all her life.

He stayed at her place the following three days, not even going home to change clothes. Over the next week, as the temperature climbed, Eugene continued crashing there most nights. She eventually grew suspicious and asked him if he was living out of his taxi.

"I wish. You'd be terrified if you saw my place," he answered.

"Then I definitely want to see it."

"It's an unbelievable mess."

"I'll help you clean it up."

"Some messes can't be cleaned."

Adding it all up, she figured that he must still be living at home with his mom and was just embarrassed about it.

Since Karen was still gone and she liked having Gene around, she had a key made for him. He thanked her and told her he'd be a good roommate, but she quickly discovered a couple quirks about him: instead of brushing his teeth at night, he would smoke a joint and knock back a beer; unless she reminded him, he'd fall asleep with his pants still on; he also loved playing Karen's stereo cranked all the way up. When she finally, gently asked him to lower the volume, he said, "You know, you're only young until you act old."

During the second week of his stay, she came home one night to find that he had invited some friends over without asking permission. Although they seemed pretty hip, they too played loud music, hung out on the fire escape, drank beer, and smoked pot. They also emptied out the fridge and created a big mess.

Yet there was something festively la dolce vita about it all. Gene had a point—you weren't young forever. Mallory suppressed her bourgeois urge to lower the music, but still tossed everyone out by two a.m.

Trying to keep a lid on Gene's cohabitation ended when Karen called one night and Mallory answered the phone: "Black Panthers Headquarters." Karen realized her roommate was intoxicated. In addition to the sounds of male voices, Motown was blaring in the background, and it was nearly midnight.

"Quit pretending you're black, throw everyone out, and go to sleep!" Karen instructed her.

The next evening, Mallory and Gene shared a bowl of oxtail stew and a dozen beers at La Rosita, an inexpensive diner on 105th and Broadway. As they were leaving, Mallory asked if they could spend the night at his place.

"Trust me, you don't want that."

"If you live with your family, I just want to meet them and I'll leave."

"I don't live with my family."

"Oh God, you're not married, are you?"

"Hell no!"

"Then where do you live?" she asked, suddenly fixating on the idea that he had a wife and six babies at home.

"I have a place *way* down in the valley. Over on Seventh Avenue."

"I'd love to go for a night walk," she said, trying to be romantic.

"Girl, Harlem is a dangerous place even for a black man, and you're a white girl."

"So we'll hail a cab."

"Cabs won't go there. Hell, I won't even drive *my* cab there."

"Then let's walk, I'll take my chances."

"No way."

"'Cause you're married with children."

"That's ridiculous!"

"Then prove it!" The alcohol had loosened her tongue.

"Okay, you asked for it. But let me warn you, this trip is really going to test your mettle," he said.

"Just worry about your own mettle," she replied flippantly.

As Gene led Mallory up Broadway, white people and students began to vanish. Once they were below the elevated local train at 125th Street, he turned right, passed several tired hookers and a few men passed out on the curb or leaning up against the rotting buildings. They continued on to Eighth Avenue, and then Seventh, until the streets were empty and large chunks of pavement were cracked apart, as though the area had suffered an earthquake.

While Gene led her down broken sidewalks where burned-out

streetlights had not been replaced—past empty lots and blocks of dilapidated and bombed-out buildings—Mallory started feeling increasingly vulnerable. Both of them maintained a suspenseful silence as if afraid of awaking angry dormant spirits.

Occasionally they'd pass rusty abandoned cars missing doors, wheels, and other vital parts, their axles balancing on cinder blocks. Soon, Mallory found herself resisting unfounded fears, and began to take comfort that she'd be able to tell Karen all about this experience on the phone the next day.

When a group of teens appeared out of nowhere, Mallory walked behind Gene, hoping that his large black frame would hide her smaller white one. As the group approached, one of them nodded to Gene, who nodded back. When the small gang had vanished from sight and Mallory asked who they were, Gene just shrugged. Periodically they'd walk past piles of garbage and rats would scamper out.

Finally they arrived at what must've once been a luxury apartment building, with soot-covered friezes with inlaid cherubs and beautiful old columns framing the windows of the lower floors. Along the ground level, cinder blocks sealed up the doorways and windows. It was the tallest building around for blocks, with little more than rubble stretching in all directions. Eugene casually led Mallory around the back.

"Where are we going?"

"Home sweet home," he said as he pulled aside a heavy metal grate. He crawled through a basement window where the cemented cinder blocks had been carefully chiseled out. Once inside the dark cool space, he struck a match, found a previously burned newspaper lying on the ground, and rolled it to make a smoky torch.

"Are you . . . is this . . ." She was too nervous to form a sentence.

"You wanted to see my house—well, here it is," he said as he led her up the marble stairs. She was too petrified to make a peep. In a moment they were in a derelict lobby that smelled like prehistoric urine. In the light of the quivery flame, she could just make out an incredible vaulted ceiling still lined with some of the original mosaic tiles. Wires dangled from where a grand chandelier used to hang.

A filthy mattress shoved in a corner suggested that the place was a flophouse for addicts. From under a long radiator, she heard some squeaks that could only be coming from rodents. Against the far wall were four rusty doors for the elevators that must've stopped working ages ago. The brass arrow dials indicating the floors had long since been snapped off. Eugene silently led Mallory farther up the large, dusty marble staircase that forked into two smaller staircases at the next level.

"See how ritzy this dive was? It was only built fifty years ago, so you can see how quickly Harlem declined," Gene said softly as they moved upward. "Though they blame it on Negroes moving into the area, that also happens to be when bankers stopped giving folks home-improvement loans and when police, firemen, and sanitation became almost nonexistent here."

"You actually live here?" she finally managed to say.

"Just stay close."

They could hear the whispery echoes of voices above them. Looking up, Mallory could see that a few of the floors had flickering candles burning on the landings. *People must still be living in some of these apartments,* she thought, and she futilely searched for any other signs of life. Instead she saw only empty frames where the doors had been removed. The building seemed to be watching her, and with every added step she had the sense that she would never leave here alive. By the time they reached the fifth floor, Mallory wished she had never asked Gene to see his place. When they got to the seventh, she asked if he worried about rats.

"Long as you don't bring food, they don't go this high up," he whispered, then suggested they remain quiet till they reached his apartment.

As they arrived at the next landing, she heard a huddle of voices coming from a dark corner. A deep baritone voice said, "Looky here, Sergeant New York's back and he caught himself some white-tailed deer." Chuckles followed.

On the top floors the length of the hallways grew shorter, suggesting that either the building was narrowing with height or the apartments were getting larger. Eugene finally brought Mallory through a doorframe and into a huge empty room. He seemed to have X-ray vision in the darkness. "Watch it here, there's a board loose . . . Don't step in the shit there!"

She still couldn't see a thing.

A heavy old door was leaning up against a wall—Gene pulled it to one side. Behind it he slid open what looked like a shuttered window but turned out to be an old dumbwaiter chute. He lifted his legs and climbed into the blackness, causing her to gasp—she wouldn't last a second alone there. Gene quickly flicked his Zippo, illuminating the square shaft. Mallory watched as he climbed up a couple feet and pulled out a thick, coiled rope from behind a board, which he dropped into the darkness below. Then he snapped his Zippo and all went black. She could hear him scurry down the tight shaft, until he flicked his lighter back on. Gene had slid one flight below, where he pulled a knife out of his pocket and wedged it into the dumbwaiter door. Mallory was acutely aware that it would take him at least several minutes to climb back up if she were suddenly attacked. She watched tensely as he was finally able to catch a latch and pop open the chute door.

It took him a little while to work his way back up the rope and out of the narrow chute.

"You just have to climb in there and down one flight," he said to her.

"Are you kidding?"

"Believe me, it's a lot easier than it looks: you just press your feet against one side, your back against the other, and don't let go of the rope. You'll shimmy right down."

"Suppose I fall?"

"Don't fall, just lower yourself slowly and crawl along the wall.

You'll see, it's not that far. I've got to lock the chute behind us so no one else can get in, so I'll be right behind you."

Mallory was grateful that she had worn old jeans and sneakers that day; she never could've done this in a dress. She took a deep breath and reached into the dark space, feeling for the rope. Gene helped her up through the little frame of the dumbwaiter and watched as she slowly angled her ample backside against the rear of the narrow shaft, pressing her feet against the other side.

"There's little rings you can lodge your feet into," he explained. "Just don't move until you're secure."

She carefully lowered herself downward, all the while trying to forget that if she let go of the rope and pulled her limbs in, she would plummet seven floors to her death. When she was halfway down she heard Gene climb into the tight space above her and lock the dumbwaiter door behind them. In another moment she was struggling through the open frame of the floor below.

When she finally landed, she felt like she had entered the set of an Edgar Allan Poe tale—an old ballroom with equal parts grandeur and squalor. The vaulted ceiling rose up nearly twenty feet, with scooped-out pedestals in two corners intended for statuary. Through a set of collapsed wooden doors was a large balcony looking east over Harlem, beyond the glassy river to the South Bronx. Grabbing a flashlight from the mantelpiece of a defunct fireplace, Gene flipped it on and handed it to her.

"Welcome to the Hill Manor," he said. The front door was blocked with so much large debris that it would require a battering ram to open it. Gene led her down a corridor where she could see from the moonlight shimmering through that the apartment was nearly a full city block in length. She peered into the passages shooting along both sides of the building. Each large and empty room had big, beautiful window frames, but the glass in all except one was broken or missing entirely. Pigeons roosted and cooed. In addition to a couple of closets and foyers, she counted four different bedrooms as well as two bathrooms, neither of which had toilets. Clearly there was no running water.

"I'm not even going to ask what the rent is," Mallory joked.

"Only suckers pay rent," Gene said, trying to keep the mood light.

The hallway ended at a massive dining room, and they passed through one of two pairs of double doors into more darkness. He lit an old railroad lantern that was stashed behind the door, revealing a large kitchen with beautiful built-in cupboards and a great antique stove. Gene used the kitchen as his bedroom, which made sense as it seemed to be the most insulated room in the building. She saw that he had cleaned the floor, painted the walls, and amateurishly replaced the kitchen windows.

Cool air passing through the doors was a welcome relief, but it compelled her to ask, "What's the place like in the winter?"

"Well, last winter when it got below twenty degrees, I stayed with my cousin in Bed-Stuy, but this year I'm planning on going to the army surplus store down on Third Avenue and picking up a kerosene heater."

Water damage streaked the old walls, bubbling and peeling the wallpaper and plaster, except for in the kitchen. Likewise, the parquet floors were buckled, and in some rooms, large swaths were missing entirely. On the upper, most out-of-the-way shelf of one customized kitchen cabinet, which had presumably once held fine china, Gene stashed all his belongings.

"How did you find this place?" she asked.

"I was walking by here back in '59 with my aunt, just before she died. She told me she worked here as a maid in the 1920s for some Jewish gangster, when the neighborhood was still mixed. Said it was like a palace. Then, right after I got back from the army, I checked it out for myself. It was loaded with addicts but they didn't mess with me. Once I found the old dumbwaiter and realized that the junkies were too lazy to come all the way up seven flights and too weak to climb down the rope in the chute, I sealed off the doors and took it over. "

"Wow."

He pulled out a bottle of Jim Beam and poured her a drink. Together they got sauced, and then, upon an old twin mattress with springs poking out, they made sweet love. Afterward, when she said she had to go to the little girl's room, Eugene led her to a secluded room and pointed to a shiny bedpan and roll of toilet paper.

"When you're done, just dump it out the window."

"I don't want to hit anyone," she said nervously.

"It's just an empty courtyard; everybody does it."

Back in bed, she asked him what it was like growing up in Harlem.

"When I was a little kid, just after the war, it was a nice, hard-working community where most everyone knew each other. Of course that all changed in the early fifties when the drugs started coming in.

That's when it really got dangerous. What was it like growing up in Brooklyn?"

"The only drugs there were laxatives," she said. "How did you wind up going into the army and attending Columbia?"

He described how he had always been a good student in high school, and although the schoolwork was easy, the other students made it tough. While he was at the top of his classes, the other students frequently called him a faggot, a mama's boy, or an Uncle Tom. "When they used to give the test papers back, I'd grab mine and hide it before anyone could see what I got." Eugene was accepted into Hunter College but he couldn't afford the tuition, so when he was drafted, he figured it was an opportunity to take advantage of the GI Bill.

They talked until he began nodding off. He slept like a baby, but Mallory just lay there, fearful and vigilant. Every little sound and bump from the large, derelict building sounded like a junkie trying to break in. She didn't sleep a wink.

The next morning Mallory was so exhausted she didn't know how she was going to climb back up the rope in the dumbwaiter.

"You don't have to," Eugene said.

He walked her to a balcony, where he looped a rope around one of the bars lining it. Then he tied the ends together and dropped it down.

"Oh God, not another climb," Mallory murmured.

"Just one flight, to the balcony below."

Eugene went down first, twisting the two ropes together into a single spiraling strand, then he signaled for her to follow. Slipping downward without having to move more than an inch at a time in a narrow shaft had been much easier. Once she was on the lower balcony, Eugene untied the twirled ropes and pulled them to one side to make sure no one would climb back up. In a moment they both exited through the vacant, much filthier apartment. Because it was bright outside, the indirect sunlight made it all much less scary. Heading down the stairs, they passed a group of men who were quietly walking up—no words were exchanged. Five minutes later they went through the basement window, and were safely back in the daylight of the Harlem street.

Eugene walked her up the hill to a breakfast spot where she was the only white person present. As their eggs were served and the hazards of the previous night faded away, Mallory started to think of the evening as nothing less than a scintillating adventure; at that moment, Harlem seemed as romantic as Paris. More so, it was like some enchanted yet forgotten land, a Negro Brigadoon.

After the meal, Eugene led her back to the Columbia campus. Then he had to run to the garage to collect his cab, so she gave him a kiss and they agreed to meet at her place that night.

17

When Mallory got home that morning, she called Karen and told her she had spent the night in Eugene's illegally occupied Harlem apartment.

"Does he live in the projects?"

"Hell no. It put me in mind of some forgotten palace, like the abandoned city of Angkor in Indochina. I mean, so much of Harlem is just forgotten property. He took over an old luxury apartment from a different age. It was run-down and all, but it was absolutely romantic." Mallory neglected to report that she had been so fearful of being raped or murdered that she never actually fell asleep, and that she didn't plan to ever return there again.

Karen felt a strange sense of envy. Through Eugene Hill, Mallory had been given access to the bizarre and mystical kingdom of the economically challenged. Even so, Karen told Mallory that she'd taken a big risk spending the night in an abandoned apartment building in the middle of a slum.

"Relax, he would've protected me," Mallory said.

"How about the police, ever think of that? You were trespassing."

Mallory ignored the comment. "God, I don't remember the last time I felt so alive! My heart was thumping so fast. I mean, everything about Gene is so . . . well, he's so *focused!*"

"Focused?" That wasn't the word Karen was expecting.

"On getting results."

"What kind of results?"

Mallory didn't mean to divulge anything, but since Karen was her closest friend, she decided to spill. "If I tell you something, will you promise to keep it to yourself?"

"Sure."

"Promise me."

"I promise."

For the next twenty minutes, Mallory relayed the conversation their SDS confederates and Eugene had had about setting off a small bomb at the new construction site in the middle of Morningside Park.

"Are you out of your cotton-picking gourd?"

"Think about it: it would basically just be a symbolic explosion, yet it would absolutely scare the university from proceeding with the construction."

"Hmmm." Like Mallory, Karen had been frustrated by the SDS's lack of progress in achieving their goals.

"You're not even supposed to know about this."

"I won't say anything," Karen assured her, "but anyway, Eugene's not even in the SDS."

"I know. But it was his idea and he's got experience with ordnance." She was obviously excited to use military slang. "He's the one taking all the risks."

"So he's agreed to do it?"

"Sort of," she replied cheekily, "he just doesn't know it yet."

A few days before the August 29 construction deadline, the SDS crew learned that the university's lawyers had gotten an extension on their construction permit—the project was now slated to begin in February 1968. While talking over beers and burgers that night at the West End, the "SDS in Exile" group, as Oliver called them, discussed their next move.

"Now more than ever we should be supporting Eugene and trying to get him to implement the plan," Mallory asserted. Then she revealed that she had told her roommate about the idea.

"What did Karen say?" Alvin asked.

"She said that this is a historic moment for us alone—the summer SDS students," she lied. "The others will have to find their own moment."

Alvin looked up at Sam, who was biting his lip, all levity gone. Henriette simply turned away, but Oliver was nodding thoughtfully at the notion, staring over at Evelyn, who grimaced and finished her tea.

Even though Eugene had refused to go back to the bar—or to even speak to the group, resenting their treating him like a servant—Mallory kept pushing the idea. That night she told him that they had all talked about it, and even though they were still scared, they admired the pacifism, dogmatism, and simplicity of his plan. Likewise, she spent the following days alone with each member of her little group, trying to persuade them that this was the only way they were going to achieve their collective goal.

By the end of August, five of the original seven other students agreed, at least in principle, that they would like to play a noncombatant part of the plan. Only Henriette and Evelyn refused altogether. They argued that by committing a destructive act, even a symbolic one, it would take them down a slippery slope, which would endanger the entire struggle.

When Mallory finally reported back to Eugene that she had won a majority, he immediately asked, "So there's a minority?"

"Henriette and Evelyn are opposed to any form of violence."

"Prissy bitches—figures," he replied.

"To their credit, they promised to remain silent, provided no one gets hurt."

"They're hypocrites! They preach change, but when we make a real plan they shy away."

"So exactly how much money are we going to need to do this?" Mallory wanted to move on.

"Let me think about it."

She could tell that Gene's initial excitement had fizzled. He'd probably be content to let it all just fade. Mallory knew that if there was any chance of this ever happening at all, it was up to her. Thinking back, she remembered that what had originally motivated Gene was the energy of the group.

Two days later she convinced the five sympathetic members to meet at another bar, Cannon's. She knew that Gene sometimes grabbed a beer there on his way to her place after a night of hacking.

After dropping his cab at the garage, Gene popped in to Cannon's around ten p.m. As he ordered a beer at the bar, he heard familiar voices in the background.

"What are you guys doing here?" he called out.

Mallory and her pals acted surprised and found a seat at their table for him. Mallory asked how his shift went.

"Oh God," he began, "I had this one fare from the airport . . ."

As he talked, Mallory ordered a pitcher of cold beer and made sure to keep it coming. Although the conversation didn't touch on the project, she could tell they were all happy to see him, and after a night of isolation in a cab, he enjoyed their company. An hour later, Mallory's bladder felt like it was about to burst and she went to the bathroom.

When she returned, she heard Gene energetically explaining, "Shit, I'd handle it like any other military mission—everyone would have a specific role and we'd prepare for different contingencies, so regardless of what happened we'd know who was in charge of what and we'd have a plan in place."

"I thought we were just going to throw some explosives over the fence and run," Oliver said.

"If I'm going to do this, I don't want people to dismiss it as just some kids chucking fireworks at Daddy's car, you dig? We have to show professionalism."

"So how exactly would you handle it?" Mallory asked, fueling his energy.

"For starters, we're not tossing anything. We can either climb over their fence or cut it, but I want to place the bomb where it counts."

"You know the gym is supposed to go in the middle of the park, so it's a bit of a hike," Alvin pointed out. "If we're going to climb the fence and set that thing, we'll need enough time to get out before the explosion goes off, particularly if they got security guards or guard dogs watching the site."

"That's true," Sharon said.

"We need some kind of timer," Sam said.

"Where the hell will we get a bomb timer?" Alvin asked.

"Can we use some kind of slow-burning fuse?" Larry asked.

"No one uses that shit anymore," Eugene said. When they all silently looked to him, he added, "Let me just think about it."

"What exactly are you thinking about?" asked Sharon.

"We need some kind of delay fuse, and I think I know where we can get it."

"Where?" Sharon pressed.

"A dude I served with who was assigned to the quartermaster's office. He was the black market guy at the base."

"The army surplus store on Third Avenue might have it."

"They don't sell detonators," Gene said. "These ones are all stolen from the army so they're going to cost."

"How much?" Mallory asked.

"No idea. The dynamite is probably going to be cheaper than the timer, but if we can get some timers it might not be a bad idea to lay down more than one bomb."

"More than one?" exclaimed Oliver.

"I'm just saying that the difference in cost would be negligible, but the results will be significant."

"Significant how?"

"It'll scare the living shit out of them," Larry said.

"What if there's a security guard?" Oliver asked. He was the most hesitant of the remaining group. "Remember, you said no one is supposed to get hurt."

"There's no way they're putting a security guard on that site right away," Gene assured him. "They just put up the fencing."

"Maybe we should wait till they bring in some of the heavy machinery," Oliver suggested.

"That's actually not a bad idea!" Gene set down his empty mug. "They're probably going to have a couple bulldozers parked around the area."

"So we'll target their equipment," Larry resolved.

"When are we going to do this?" Alvin asked.

"When we get the timers, I guess," said Sharon.

"First I need to call Dwight," Gene said, "and he's not an easy guy to locate."

"Didn't you say he was still in the army?"

"I don't know for certain. I have a phone number for him, but last time I called it, it just rang and rang."

"He should get an answering service," Alvin kidded.

"Then they'd be able to track him," Gene said. "I always figured he found a bank of public phones in Penn Station or somewhere, a place where no one's around."

"Which is probably why it's so difficult to reach him," Mallory said.

18

A few days later, when Karen returned from her summer break, Mallory delicately asked if she'd mind very much if Gene slept over from time to time.

"So long as he doesn't eat my food, monopolize the phone, or leave a mess, we should be fine." Karen still felt guilty about her indiscretion with Gene, but she did her best to hide it. She was now officially dating Lincoln, who was so fearful of commitment that he refused to even bring her back to his dorm room. "What became of your little plan?" she inquired.

"Proceeding slowly," Mallory said simply.

That night, Mallory let Gene know that she had told Karen about the Gym Crow plan and her best friend was fine with it.

"You know, when you do that, you put us all at risk," he said. "The cops are going to ask questions, and if she doesn't know, she can't lie."

"She wants this to happen," Mallory replied. And though Gene nodded his head in disatisfaction, he was silently pleased that Karen knew and respected what he was doing.

Soon afterward he took them both out for dinner where, over the course of the meal, Karen told him that if they needed another hand for their little mission, she was always available.

Mallory smiled and glanced at Gene, who didn't make a sound.

A week later registration began for the fall semester at Columbia. Then classes kicked in and everyone became fully immersed in their studies. The gym construction was still slated to begin in February, which was months away, so there was little urgency to the SDS planning. Because Karen had chosen an accelerated bachelor's program, it was her senior year. And while she was anxious about entering law school, Mallory still wasn't sure about what to do with her own future. Her thoughts were fixed on life after the revolution. Why would they need lawyers? The laws were about to change. Redistribution would immediately ensue, tribunals would be formed, and the fascists and monsters would be put on trial. Although knowledge of political science, history, philosophy, and mass psychology would all be helpful, Barnard College simply didn't offer a major in revolution studies.

One night toward the end of November, Karen told Mallory that a hoarse-voiced guy named Dwight had just called and left a message for Gene.

"Dwight? What did he say?"

"He left a number. He said Gene should call him back at three o'clock tomorrow afternoon."

Mallory told Gene when he showed up after a shift. He snatched the number and thanked her. The next day, when Mallory went off to class, he stayed home and made the call.

"It's about the detonators, right?" Mallory asked when she returned in the afternoon.

"He offered me a box of grenades, but they're too much money and not right for what we're trying to do."

"What now?"

"I told him we're looking for slow-burning fuses and he said he'd call when he got some."

Early the next morning, Karen saw Eugene coming out of the shower with a towel around his waist; his chest and stomach glistened with muscles. When she tried to ask about the message from Dwight, he just walked right by her into Mallory's room and closed the door. Later that day, Karen found them sitting silently in the kitchen and asked what was up.

"Just preparing for classes," Mallory said.

Trying to be friendly, Karen asked Gene what courses he had registered for that semester. He made a joke and changed the subject. Later, when Karen was alone with her friend, she asked again what was going on with them.

"Nothing, why?" Mallory said defensively.

"His eyes looked red and he seemed a little pale."

"Oh, just 'cause he's black you think he's stoned all the time?" Mallory said dismissively.

By early winter, Karen's dubious boyfriend Skinny Link had become so tense and frazzled, she actually feared he was going to burst into tears whenever she came over. The responsibility of a relationship for him seemed to drain all the pleasure out of it. One day she simply stopped visiting, and he never called her again.

Karen then found herself home more than usual. That was when she realized that Gene, too, always seemed to be there. In fact, he was around even when Mallory wasn't. Without paying a red cent, Gene had basically moved in. Although he was usually a decent guy and respectful, not eating her food and staying out of her room, he did one thing that drove her nuts: he'd always answer their phone. To avoid a confrontation with him and Mallory, Karen found herself spending more time downstairs in the dojo.

This was well timed because in January, shortly after the Christmas break, Hrag caught a serious case of the flu and couldn't seem to shake it. At his request, Karen led some of the beginner and intermediate classes. She also started collecting monthly membership fees and making sure others who weren't paying either fulfilled their work commitments or at least performed some of the endless little tasks around the place, like cleaning up.

"You're much better at this than Hrag," Manuel said one day, seeing some of the kids washing the windows and noticing how clean the dojo had become recently.

"Thanks."

"No, I mean it. You're a really strong person," he said earnestly. "When you talk to the students, they actually listen."

His remarks gave her the confidence to have a talk with Mallory about either asking Gene to contribute to the household expenses or asking her to stay at his mysterious place some of the time.

When Karen arrived home that night after her karate class, though, she could hear them celebrating, talking excitedly about something.

"What's up?"

"Gene got the call!" Mallory said.

"What call?"

"From his connection!"

"My army buddy," Gene elaborated. "He finally called to say he got ahold of some really top-notch detonators—space-age shit."

"What's this?" Karen had forgotten all about their little project.

"It'll allow us to blow up the gym site and get away scot-free," Mallory reminded her.

"Oh, right."

"He's giving me a bunch of them for three hundred dollars. I'm supposed to meet him at twelve thirty on Saturday afternoon. The downside is they're a little more money than I thought they'd be, so we're going to need everyone to kick in a few extra bucks."

"Three hundred is a lot," Karen said slowly.

"We need the detonators to do this right," Gene said.

"Maybe it's time to go beyond your summer group and bring this to Mark's attention," Karen suggested.

"No way!" Mallory responded. "We can come up with the money ourselves. The more people we tell, the greater the risk of someone snitching."

"It's a lot of money," Karen repeated.

Mallory declared that she would personally call everyone from the summer group and ask them to contribute more.

"Fifty bucks apiece should do it," Gene said.

"Fifty bucks apiece—wow!" Karen said.

"And keep in mind that I'm going to need the cash by Friday," he said, stressing the urgency of the situation.

Without wasting a minute, Mallory opened her address book and got on the phone.

The next day she stayed there, calling and calling until she reached each of the summer SDSers. She argued, cajoled, and guilted them into committing to some of the cash. In terms of the actual handoff, she asked that they all meet her at Cannon's late on Friday evening, the night before the actual transaction was set to occur.

On Friday, before Mallory went off to class, Gene stopped her at the door, gave her a long kiss, and said, "I want you with me tomorrow."

"You mean for the detonator deal?" she asked nervously. "Why me?"

"I need someone to watch my back and you're the only person I can trust."

"Okay, but would you mind *not* going to the bar tonight?" She knew how volatile he could get if he felt people were being stingy. "I should deal with everyone one-on-one."

He agreed and she left.

That evening when Alvin arrived, he found Mallory sitting at the bar nursing a Coke.

"You know, I'm willing to just let the summer dreams go, along with all the beer we consumed," he said by way of a greeting.

"What's that supposed to mean?"

"Just that this thing with Gene is a pretty tall order, and in the light of day I just think—"

"Are you backing out?"

"I actually thought I was letting your boyfriend off the hook. He's taking all the risks."

"Every time Columbia University tears another chunk out of this neighborhood, he's on the hook, so I don't think he's worried about saving face in front of a bunch of privileged white kids." Mallory took a sip of her soda.

"Where is he?" Alvin glanced around anxiously.

"He's working."

"Maybe that's for the better, because over the past few days we've all talked."

"We who?"

"You know, our little group."

"You talked with who?"

"With everyone, and frankly, we just think this is kind of unfair."

"Wait, what are you saying?"

At this point Oliver arrived and saw Mallory's confused expression. He sat down at the bar and said, "So Alvin told you."

"Told me what?"

"We're nervous, Mal."

"Look, this gym has to be stopped and Gene can do it."

"Mal . . ."

"He simply wants us to hold up our end and put in some cash so he can buy the stuff tomorrow."

Sharon entered next, along with Sam and Larry, and the three came over just in time to hear Alvin say, "We're terrified of getting caught."

"You're not going to get caught!" Mallory fired back.

"We just don't think it's worth going to jail over a hole in the middle of the park," Sam chimed in quietly.

"You mean you don't think!"

"Sorry, Mal, but me neither," Sharon added.

As Alvin rose from his chair, Mallory said, "You don't want to take any risks—that's fine. But are you really turning away from your beliefs?"

"What are you talking about?"

"No one will know how much you donated. The guy who's going to do this isn't even here, so he can't say who gave what. And I won't tell him, so you're protected!"

Letting out a sigh, Alvin pulled out his wallet, removed two twenty-dollar bills, put them on the tabletop, and said, "This is for the beer."

Sharon reached into her purse and fished out a five and seven singles and likewise said, "For beer."

To his credit, Oliver said nothing about beer and confirmed that he was good for forty, but he didn't have it on him. Larry gave Mallory fifty-six dollars and then she tabulated the cash, trying to figure out if she had enough.

Sam, the richest kid in the group, said, "Let me know how much you're short and I'll try to help."

"Guys, I don't want to sound ungrateful," Mallory said, "but we need cash up front. This is happening tomorrow morning and I don't have the money to make up the difference."

Sam said that if she came by his dorm room early the next morning, he should be able to come up with more. Then he, Larry, and Oliver headed off.

As Sharon and Mallory walked out of the bar, they heard someone yelling out Mallory's name—it was Gene, waving at her from down the block.

Sharon said she had to get home, so Mallory waited for him alone. Gene caught up, and instead of reprimanding him for not staying away from the bar, she simply said, "It's all done."

"What's all done?"

"I got the money."

"Fuck money, I want them to come with us tomorrow."

"Come with us?!"

"Of course! What am I, the lawn jockey?"

She could see by the jerky way he moved and his facial expression that he was on something, probably uppers.

"That's not what we agreed," she reminded him. "They put up the money but they're scared, Gene."

"I'm scared too!"

"Look, at least they're putting up the cash. You, me, and Karen can do this."

"No fucking way! It's out of the question!"

He started marching along Broadway toward 109th Street. Mallory followed him quietly with her head hung low, hating that she had to deal with him when he was being this way. When they got to the apartment building, he stopped and simply stared off into the distance.

Mallory walked past, took out her keys, and opened the front door, but then realized he wasn't budging.

"Coming?"

"No, I came over to tell you that I'm doing a double shift."

"But you've been working all day."

"I'm fucking broke, bitch!"

"What time do you get off?" she asked wearily.

"Tomorrow at noon. I'll be at the corner of 116th and Broadway."

"But you won't be able to . . ." She realized he was working the shift in order to deliberately sabotage the mission. He'd be too exhausted to close the deal. "Look, this is your neighborhood. Even if those fucking kids are afraid, we're not the ones from here."

"All right, I know. I'll do it. We'll meet at noon, get the stuff, and do this our fucking selves."

"See you then," she said, skipping her usual kiss good night.

Lying in bed ten minutes later, Mallory's eyes popped open. She felt guilty. It wasn't fair that she was pressuring Gene to do this. She knew that the reason he was popping uppers and driving all night wasn't just because of cash, but also because he was freaked out by this whole operation. He was a nice guy and she was steadily pushing him into doing an ugly, dangerous deed. Still, she really believed that if Gene just hung on a little longer, they could actually pull it off. And it needed to be done.

19

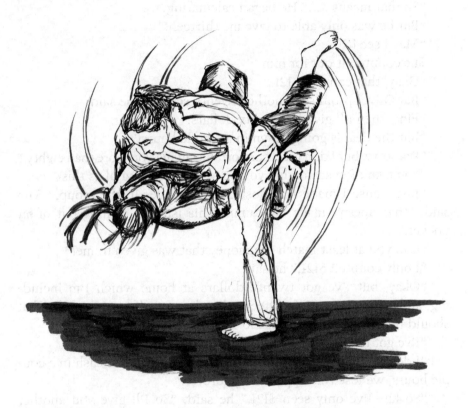

E arly the next morning, just after Karen had left to go teach a beginner's karate class downstairs, Mallory woke up, dressed, and
went off to the Columbia campus. First she stopped by Oliver's dorm
room. He had committed forty bucks in the bar, but could only come
up with thirteen until the bank opened on Monday.

Sam had suggested that he'd make up the difference of however
much they were short, so Mallory decided to simply ask for $150.

"Are you kidding? I don't have that kind of money on me!"

"What do you mean?" she said. "I told you I'd need it today."

"Who committed how much money exactly?"

Mallory took a deep breath. She had never been good at math and now she had to come up with an itemization with a shortfall of $150. "You saw that Alvin gave us forty—"

"Then Sharon gave you twelve," Sam prompted.

"Right, which comes to fifty-two. Larry gave us fifty-six and Oliver committed to forty."

"Let's see it."

"You heard him say it!"

"So that means . . ." He began calculating.

"But he was only able to give me thirteen."

"May I see it?"

She counted it out for him.

"Okay, that comes to 121."

"But Oliver promised another twenty-seven," she said.

"Fine, then I'll give you eighty dollars."

"But the deal is going down in a couple hours!"

"I'm sorry, but I don't feel comfortable giving you more than eighty."

"You think I'm scamming you on something as vital as this?"

"Just 'cause I made the most generous offer in the group," Sam said, "that doesn't make me dumb. This isn't all coming out of *my* pocket."

"Can you at least match the money that was given to me?"

"I only counted $121," he said.

"Okay, but I've got twenty dollars at home which I'm including, and Gene's putting in fifteen when he gets off his cab shift. That should bring it to a little over 150."

"I've got to see it," he said, almost paternally.

"I don't have time for this! And if we don't have the cash in a couple hours, we lose this opportunity forever!"

"So far, I've only seen $121," he said. "So I'll give you another eighty."

"Fine," Mallory said, even though that left them short. As he counted out the money, she added, "So when Oliver comes up with the balance of what he promised, you'll donate the rest of the money?"

"If you want to wait to execute the plan until he's paid you, that's fine, I'll match the balance at that point. But I'm not going through this a second time."

She realized he had her over a barrel. "Okay, just give me the goddamn money."

"And there had better be some kind of explosion," Sam said. "I do not intend to be conned here."

She rolled her eyes silently, then raced back to her apartment and scrambled through her drawers in an effort to bring the total to three hundred dollars. She was only able to find twenty-eight dollars, which included ten quarters, three dimes, and four nickels. When she looked up at her clock, she saw that she was late and still shy seventy-one dollars. She put every penny she had into her handbag and dashed outside and up Broadway until she spotted the old yellow cab parked in front of a hydrant on the northeast corner of 116th Street.

When she opened the car door, she saw Karen's red, contorted face. She was sitting in the backseat as Eugene profanely lectured her on the importance of punctuality.

"Sorry I'm late," Mallory said, winded, "but I'm a little short."

"Oh, do not fucking tell me that!" Gene snapped.

"How short?" Karen asked.

"Seventy-one bucks. There's more coming, but right now that's all I have."

Opening her shoulder bag, Karen counted out every cent she had—forty-seven dollars.

"All we need is twenty-four more bucks," Mallory said to Gene, who had just come off a long shift.

"No way! I don't even want to do this anymore!"

"We'll pay you back," Karen said.

"My money is all pre-spent."

"You really want to quit now? *This close?*" Mallory asked as she stepped into the car. Eugene snatched up his clipboard with his cabbie's log before Mallory could grab it and see how much he had made last night.

He angrily turned the car key and started speeding down Broadway. "You told me that they would at least come up with the motherfucking cash!"

"In fairness, I told them after the banks had closed for the weekend. This was all they could come up with right away."

"This is what happens when you put your faith in whitey!"

"What color are we—blue?" Karen shouted back as they sailed through a red light.

"Take it easy, you're going to get a speeding ticket!" Mallory yelled.

"We were supposed to be there ten fucking minutes ago. He's probably gone by now!"

They sped in silence over to Amsterdam and West 88th Street, where Gene parked his cab ten feet away from a phone booth.

"Okay, this is how he works," he said. "I'm going to drop off the money. He's watching from somewhere around here. When he counts it and is satisfied that it's all there, he's going to call on that phone." He pointed to the booth. "Karen, you're going to get behind the wheel of my cab, and Mallory, you're going to get in that booth and pretend to be on the phone, but keep your finger on the thing so the lines ain't busy when he calls."

"What do I say when he calls?" Mallory asked nervously.

"Don't say a word. He'll tell you where the detonators are."

"Are you kidding? I thought this guy was an old friend."

"No, my old friend actually gave me this guy's number. I don't know him. And by the way, if a cop comes by," Gene turned to Karen, "just drive around the corner and wait for me back here in front of the booth."

When Mallory started to exit the cab, Gene said, "Where the fuck are you going?!"

"You said—"

"Give me the cash and stay with Karen."

"Where exactly are you going?"

"The drop-off is in the backyard of that bombed-out building," he said, pointing to an abandoned structure on the south side of West 88th Street.

Mallory gave him her handbag and told him to be careful. He transferred the cash into a paper bag and slipped it down the front of his pants.

He walked stiffly across the street and through the litter-strewn courtyard of the building. Then he crawled under a gate that enclosed a small alley in back.

During what had to be the most nerve-racking ten minutes of her life, Karen stared in the rearview looking for a cop. When they finally heard the muffled ring of the corner phone, Mallory jumped. Gene had not yet returned.

Without waiting for Mallory to collect herself, Karen grabbed a pencil and paper and sprinted to the booth and picked up the phone.

Mallory watched her cradle the phone in her neck and scribble.

"What's going on?" Gene asked through the window when he came back, wiping dirt off his pants and shirt.

Before Mallory could reply, he scooted behind the wheel of the cab where Karen had been sitting. As he started the ignition, Karen jumped into the backseat and said, "We're going to 164 West 88th Street. He said they're in the garbage outside."

"How did it go?" Mallory asked.

Gene didn't respond.

"Let him focus on driving," Karen answered for him.

Gene sped east on 88th Street. "What's the number again?" he asked.

"One sixty-four," Karen replied, searching for the addresses on the buildings.

In another moment they spotted it—a splotchy brownstone with most of its front stone steps eroded away. Off to the side was a small sunken courtyard strewn with garbage and dented metal cans. Gene parked in front of a hydrant across the street and barked, "Stay in the damn taxi!" He got out, leaving his door open. After a minute, he beckoned to Mallory from across the street. She stepped out and joined him down the steps in the small front yard.

Several banged-up metal garbage cans had rubbish piled up over the top. All of them were missing their lids. Wet brown paper bags of rotting trash fell apart as he searched through them. Bits of spaghetti sauce, cigarette ash, and gunk of all variety quickly covered his fingers and hands. Behind one severely mangled can he spotted a heavy black garbage bag. Opening it, Gene found that it was crammed with clean, square white boxes. Popping one open, he discovered a small metallic object inside.

"Thank God!" he said, holding it up to the sky. Silently, he slung the large garbage bag over his shoulder and hurried across the street, with Mallory quickly following. Once back inside his cab, he started the engine.

"Is that them?" Karen asked.

He didn't say a word as he sped along 88th Street, watching his rearview more than what was in front of him to make sure they weren't being tailed. "Yeah, I got them," he finally replied when they reached Central Park West. "I shortchanged him, so I was a little worried that he might catch on."

"You're kidding!" Karen exclaimed. "After everything we went through, you gambled all our money just to save a few bucks?"

"Hey, do *you* want to take a fare out to JFK in the middle of the night? *That's* a gamble!"

"You should've just put your cash in," Mallory said. "I would've compensated you on Monday."

"He's not coming after us for that little."

"But you didn't need to take the chance," Karen said.

Gene didn't respond. Glancing at her in the rearview mirror, he saw that she had taken one of the little boxes out of the bag and was examining the detonator. "Careful with that, it might explode."

"It looks like something out of a science fiction flick," she said, holding it between her thumb and index finger like a butterfly.

"Pass one up here." Mallory was curious.

Karen handed a second box to Mallory, who was immediately impressed by how compressed and complex the device was. "Modular palpability," she said, weighing it in her hand. It truly looked like something from the brilliant future. Still, it had no timer or fuse connected to it.

"How do they work?" Karen asked, looking for instructions.

"How the fuck would I know?" Gene responded.

"We'll figure all that out when we get back home," Mallory said.

Gene then suggested that they put them back before they blew up West 110th Street. After all the tension, they started making jokes and the mood shifted; soon all were laughing.

"I'm going to drop you guys off at home," he said, "then I've got to return the cab to the garage."

When they pulled up to the building, Karen swung the garbage bag onto her back and the two women headed upstairs. Mallory told Karen to place the bag right on the dining room table.

"Man, I can't believe we actually pulled it off," said Karen.

"I know! I love this guy. He really gets things done, doesn't he?"

Opening the garbage bag, they carefully stacked the little boxes neatly one on top of the other, like wooden blocks. Mallory counted them aloud. She stopped at 103. Then she opened the very last box and studied it a moment. When Karen looked to see what she was doing, Mallory handed the small mechanism to her. Between the two of them, Karen was the more mechanically inclined.

Nervous that the strange little detonator might somehow explode, Karen brought it into the living room away from Mallory and sat under a bright lamp. Prior to this moment, she had envisioned a time-delay fuse as having a dial on one side, like an egg timer, and a flint element on the other side that ignited the fuse, like a cigarette lighter. This tiny contraption had none of that; no moving parts. And though she could make out a screened section and some tiny screws, she didn't dare try to remove them. When she finally returned the mysterious detonator to Mallory, she confessed that she didn't have a clue about how it worked.

"I'm sure Gene knows all about it. Just put it back with the others and don't mention that you were looking at it," Mallory said.

Nearly an hour passed before Gene strolled in. Still euphoric from the success of their transaction, Mallory greeted him with open arms. He dodged her and snatched one of the little detonators off the dining room table. After staring at it for a minute, he glanced around nervously.

"What are you—"

"The bag they came in . . . where is it?"

"I threw it in the trash," Mallory said. He started rummaging through the garbage. "It was empty, what are you looking for?"

He picked the bag up and looked carefully at it. "Instructions."

"Didn't you use these in Vietnam?"

"Hell no, we just had grenades—pull the pin and throw."

"Maybe there's a pin on it somewhere."

Mallory watched as Gene took the detonator into the living room. He sat in the same chair that Karen had, scrutinizing the device. Mallory wanted to offer him a magnifying glass but was afraid to interrupt him. A moment later, when he asked her for one, she immediately handed it to him. A few more minutes went by and he asked for a steak knife. Then he asked if she had a pair of tweezers. Finally, without asking, he got up and located a single pin from the kitchen cupboard.

Mallory sensed she was making him anxious by looking over his shoulder, so she went into her room and tried to keep busy. Soon, though, a steady stream of curses was flowing from the living room. Karen's door was shut. Apparently she too feared the worst. Mallory peeked into the living room and saw that Gene was desperately trying to dismantle the little mechanism. His motley collection of tools appeared to be steadily proving themselves useless. Moments later he hurled the detonator across the room and shouted, "We've been shafted!"

After several minutes of loud screaming, while Mallory stayed silently out of his way, Karen opened her door. She waited for Gene to calm down before saying, "Just call him and ask for your money back."

"Are you fucking stupid? I don't even know who this guy *is!*"

"Please calm down," Mallory said.

Covered in sweat, Gene took a deep breath before regaining a modicum of composure. "There's no deposit and no returns in this business, you dig?"

"You can at least try," Mallory said. "You still got his number."

Both of them could feel Gene's silent rage.

* * *

That night, Sharon called to ask how things went with the pickup.

"All's well," Mallory said succinctly.

"So when's this going to happen?"

"Do you want to be arrested?" Mallory pushed back.

"No, but . . ."

"Unless you want to join us and risk being sent to prison, you guys are officially *out*."

"But—"

"Would you like to join us?"

"No, but I just want—"

Mallory slammed the phone down.

20

O ver the next couple of days, as the other benefactors called and inquired about their investment project, they all had similar conversations with Mallory.

"I just assumed that the amount of money I donated would earn me a little information," said Sam.

"I'm doing this for everyone's protection, understand?"

"So it's all going well?"

"It's going fine, but if there are any more conversations like this, we'll all end up serving time upstate, and we can't have that."

"Fair enough."

"Good. And I'd appreciate it if you'd explain that to the others. You'll see the results in the newspaper when everything is done." Mallory hung up, and that was the last of the interruptions. Although she'd see the different summer SDS members on the street and in class, she'd only talk about things not pertaining to the project.

All the while, though, Mallory sensed that the inquiries were not coming from their commitment to social justice. As time ticked on, she imagined that the other students were growing fearful that their donations had simply been stolen.

For the first two days after the pickup, Gene returned to the detonator again and again, always starting calmly, ending angrily, and never extracting anything new. Though tiny, the detonators might as well have been an insurmountable wall, inscrutable as a sphinx. He lost sleep; he purchased larger magnifying glasses and smaller tools. He finally tried using a hacksaw—nothing.

On the third day, Gene snatched up the phone and dialed the mysterious Dwight's number. It just rang and rang.

On the fourth day, when Mallory found a calm moment to ask if he might consider trying to get his money back, he informed her that he had called and no one had answered the phone.

"I'll keep trying," he assured her, knowing that she had to answer for all of the missing money.

He called again later that night, and one last time before he went to sleep at four a.m. Each time there was no answer. It had taken them months to reach Dwight the first time and set up this deal.

"You know," Karen said, trying to soothe Gene and Mallory, "it's not like the guy was *trying* to rip us off. I mean, whatever the hell those are, they ain't cheap."

"That's a good point," Mallory said, also hoping to calm Gene.

After a moment, he conceded that perhaps he hadn't been conned intentionally. "Maybe this is all a misunderstanding. I'm going to stay on the guy till I at least get a response."

For the next week, Gene called about once a day, usually late at night. It was Karen who pointed out that the more they called, the better their chances were of reaching this mystery man. She came up with the plan to share the work—each of them could call at different times. Gene said that though he appreciated the offer of help, if Dwight heard from anyone else he'd automatically hang up. He promised that he'd get results. But after a few more days, he started forgetting to call at all. When Mallory reminded him one night that she was still accountable for the cash, Gene's guilt intensified.

The next morning he sat down with the roommates over coffee and together they wrote a memo that focused on the four key points that they needed to bring up if any of them actually reached Dwight. First and foremost, if Dwight called and Gene was at home asleep, they should immediately get him to the phone. If he wasn't home, they should politely introduce themselves as "associates" of Gene. When Dwight asked what they wanted, they should sound grateful for being provided with such a sophisticated product—but the problem was, as hard as they tried, they couldn't figure out how the darn things worked. Third, if Dwight could either provide the instructions for the detonators or at least swap them for detonators they could use, it would be much appreciated. Lastly—because it was highly unlikely that Dwight would swap the detonators—they should ask if Gene could sell them back to him for only two hundred dollars, still giving Dwight a profit of nearly a hundred dollars. No one should bring up or even acknowledge the fact that Gene had actually shortchanged the guy during the original deal. If Dwight brought it up, they could simply act ignorant and apologize.

It was nearly two and a half weeks later when Karen called late one night and someone picked up. A hoarse male voice answered.

"Hi," she said, completely flustered. "One second, please!"

"Who is this?"

"Gene!" she shouted into Mallory's bedroom, where he was sleeping.

"You're Gene?" she heard.

"No, I'm calling *for* Gene, I'm not Gene. Is this Dwight?" Karen could hear the song "Groovin'" in the background.

"Who the fuck's this?"

"Gene's on his way."

Groggily, he stumbled into the living room in his boxers and Karen handed him the phone.

"Dwight?"

"Who the fuck is this?"

"It's Gene. Dwight, is that you?" The voice sounded different.

"What can I do for you, Gene?"

"Those detonators you gave me—"

"They're a very expensive item."

"Yeah, I know, but I can't figure out how the hell they work. What exactly are they?"

"One hundred and fifty microspring release switches." It sounded like he was reading the name off some shipping manifest.

"There's no manufacturing stamp," Gene said. And they only had 103, but he didn't correct him.

"They were made in Italy for some weapon." Again the mysterious speaker seemed to be reading something: "Project Cobrahead. It sounds like a missile."

"How do they detonate?"

"Says they're," he paused, "triggered by tiny radiation sensors."

"Dwight, I never asked for radiation sensors."

"You asked for detonators, and it said *detonators* on the crate."

"I'm very grateful," Gene said, "but I can't use them. I need the conventional ones, something I can use."

"I don't have nothing else, and I don't give refunds."

"Fuck, Dwight. I'm in deep shit if I can't get my money back."

"Tell you what: if I get another buyer asking for that item, I can give them your number and you can do business directly. That's the best I can do."

"Can't you just give me two hundred bucks?"

"I never even had your money, I'm just a middleman. I take a small cut from the supplier."

"I'm going to get so screwed here," Gene lamented.

"All I can do is give your number to someone if they want what you got—yes or no?"

"How about a hundred bucks?"

"I told you, I don't touch the stuff. But if you just sit tight, someone will pay you. They always do."

"Okay," Gene said dejectedly. He was intent on not offending the only person who could possibly help him.

"It might take a little time, and I don't know when it's going to happen, but eventually you're going to get a phone call. And those detonators aren't cheap, so be prepared."

"Prepared how?"

"Find two drop-off sites just like you did with me. One where you can get the cash and another where he gets the merchandise. And put any price tag on it that you want."

"You mean I could say a thousand bucks?"

"I mean like a million. Usually I handle the negotiation and take my fee up front, but because this is a return, it'll be all up to you."

"If it's worth that much, why don't you just give me a hundred bucks and—"

"I don't know you, man, and you don't know me, understand? For all I know you're the fuzz, so I'll help you, but I ain't gonna touch this."

"So what do I do, lie to them?"

"Don't lie or you'll regret it in the end." Then Dwight, or whoever he was speaking to, said he had to go and abruptly ended the call.

When Gene hung up, he turned around and saw that both Karen and Mallory were staring at him silently. "Well, there's good news and bad news. First, that stuff is the real deal. It's part of some bullshit missile program."

"Wow!" Mallory exclaimed.

"So is he taking them back?" Karen asked.

"No, no refunds, but he says he can connect us with a buyer and we can get more money than we spent."

"Did he mention that you shortchanged him?" Mallory asked.

"No."

"Do you think he's just screwing with us?" Karen asked.

"I don't think he'd waste his time with the phone call if he was."

"So what now?"

"Now we do as he says and wait for a customer."

"A customer!" Karen was alarmed by all the complexity.

"What do we have to do?" Mallory asked.

"Set up a drop-off for the buyer to place the cash and a pickup where he can get the merchandise, like we did before."

"Wait a second," Karen said, "you aren't afraid that this is all a setup?"

"What kind of setup?" Mallory asked.

"I don't know, maybe the FBI is behind all this?" Karen said, never forgetting her brother.

"Then they would've arrested us when we did the first deal," Mallory replied.

"Not necessarily," Karen said. "This might make the charges more severe. We could go from buying stolen goods to espionage."

"Look, this deal probably isn't even going to happen," Gene said. "But if we actually get a call, let's be ready for it. So we pick a place for him to drop the money, and somewhere else to leave the detonators."

"So he can drop the cash off on Broadway and 108th and pick up the stuff on Amsterdam," Mallory proposed. "Simple as that."

"No," Karen said. "We shouldn't have the rendezvous anywhere near where we live."

"Why the hell not?" Mallory asked.

"'Cause I for one believe that this is a total setup and we're all going to get arrested."

"That's ridiculous, Karen. If they were going to arrest us—"

"No," Gene cut in, "she's right. Selling these nuclear-weapon parts must carry a much bigger sentence than buying them. We got to be really careful here."

"Maybe we should just take the loss, pay off everyone ourselves, and dump that crap in the river," Karen said.

"That's bullshit." Gene had never been burned for that much money in his life and refused to accept the humiliation.

"So where do you want to do this?" Mallory asked him.

"Away from campus," Karen said instantly.

"We'll do it down in the Village somewhere," said Gene. "So the buyer will think it was one of those goddamned NYU brats."

That weekend, the three of them took the number 1 train downtown and walked around Washington Square Park. They carefully scoped out a location where they could tell the prospective buyer to drop his cash.

"We need to let the guy walk a healthy distance, so that when he actually gets the stuff we'll have enough time to count his cash and make sure he didn't shortchange us," Gene said.

Fearful that they'd encounter the other summer members who had donated money toward the useless detonators, both Mallory and Karen decided to avoid the West End Bar until things got straightened out. But four days after their trip to the Village there was a weekly meeting of the SDS at Columbia. Since none of the others knew anything about the secret "Gym Crow" explosion plan, which had been partially financed by several students within their summer group, Mallory said she felt it was important for them to keep up appearances by going to the Thursday meeting. Karen said that she had a time conflict, so Mallory went alone.

Mallory showed up late and was surprised to see that not a single other member of her summer group was present. Mark Rudd discussed the usual items on the agenda, but toward the end of the meeting, he asked if he could have a word with her alone.

He led her into a corner of the big classroom that had been fashioned into a private office by freestanding partitions.

"Did you know that the SDS is now on most campuses throughout America? We have over a hundred thousand students nationwide. And they all talk each week—each day, really. Do you know why?"

"My guess is—"

"They try to come up with a comprehensive platform that will make this country both a fair and just place to live—and we do it together, as one. Annually, the different SDS chapters meet and debate the planks of this platform, and then we try to come up with strategies that will enact our goals."

"I'm aware of that, but—"

"And the college allows us to use their space, and we're able to persuade other students to join us, all because we subscribe to the rules of law and justice as dictated by our society at large. But that isn't always easy, is it? I mean, when we encounter injustices, like the school gym project, or the IDA program, we take our case to the campus to try to convince other students to join us, but they're usually reluctant. Attaining justice is never easy. In fact, it's a long, hard struggle—I'll be the first to admit it."

When he paused, Mallory knew she was in for it. She also knew he just wanted her to shut up and listen, so she did.

"It was brought to my attention that you were a part of a small band of confederates who planned to detonate a bomb in Morningside Park at the site of the new gym. Is that true?"

Mallory stared dead ahead and wondered if he knew of Karen's involvement.

"Is this true?" he asked again.

"We talked about it, yes." She wondered which one had squealed.

"I heard the ringleader was that black guy who isn't even a member of our group."

"Eugene Hill," she said. "It was just talk."

"I heard that you all pitched in money."

"Yes, most of us did."

"How much did it all come to?"

"A little over two hundred bucks."

"So you all got ripped off," Mark said.

Mallory didn't want to give the whole humiliating story of how they ended up buying some sophisticated component that they could never use.

"Renegadism, that's what it is!"

"I'm sorry," she said.

"I know you all tried to do something good—I believe that. But the bottom line is, none of you had any authority to do this. And the only reason I'm not expelling you from our chapter is because nothing came of it. You all got screwed, and now I'm assuming it's all over and you learned your lesson."

"It's definitely over," she lied.

"It really comes down to the notion that the few have no right to jeopardize what the many have painstakingly built, not to mention endanger the lives of others."

"Yes sir."

"I've talked about it with the executive committee, and those of you who are responsible for this are officially on probation. Understand?"

"Yeah." She deduced that Rudd must've already spoken to all the other summer members, which was why they weren't present now.

"After a year, if there are no other incidents, you'll be a full member again and all will be forgiven, clear?"

"Yes."

"Then we're done here."

Mallory rose and exited the little partitioned zone, rejoining the area where the rest of the group was mingling.

Following the meeting, she went home and told Karen and Gene about what had happened. She also called Oliver to ask how he had been disciplined.

"Rudd called us into the office last week and told us we were on probation."

"Why didn't you warn us?" Mallory asked.

"He asked us not to," Oliver replied. "And after all, it wasn't like anything awful happened. We all just got a slap on the wrist." He informed her that Larry, Alvin, Sam, and Sharon had also been dressed down for their transgressions. The general belief was that one of the two naysayers—either Henriette or Evelyn—had ratted them all out.

"Let's get a little retribution," Gene suggested after Mallory ended the call.

"No! We don't know for sure," Mallory said, "and they didn't go to the police, so no real harm was done."

"I guess they figured that since I wasn't in the summer group I wasn't a part of it," Karen speculated.

"Lucky you," Mallory grumbled.

Weeks later, toward the end of February, Karen found herself running the SDS table just off campus by the 116th Street subway exit on Broadway, along with Mark Rudd and some of the more militant members of the group. Someone made a joke about Mallory and her sect's plan to try to blow up the gym site—which still was empty.

"Hey, at least she tried," Karen snapped. "What'd *you* do?"

"I knew it! You were in on it too!" one of the others exclaimed as Mark stood there silently.

"You're goddamn right I was! At least we did something."

"Yeah, well, we're trying too," another student remarked as he handed out flyers.

"If I'm not mistaken, we've been out here for nearly six months, and how much closer have we come to accomplishing our goals?"

"If Gandhi and Martin Luther King can use nonviolence, so can we," yet another student said.

"They used civil disobedience. If you people were any more obedient, you'd be building the fucking gym for them!"

Karen was about to walk off when Mark finally spoke up: "She's got a point. Maybe she's right, maybe it's time we shake things up a bit."

"How?"

"If you're going to bring this to the committe—" Karen began.

"Anyone who is worried about consequences, like being expelled or arrested, is welcome to stay here," Mark cut in. "Whoever is in, please follow me back to campus. I have an idea."

One rather reserved student named Oscar said that he would remain and watch the table, his polite way of declining. Another freshman said he would stay and help Oscar.

"What exactly are you going to do?" someone asked Mark.

"Nothing crazy," he assured them without elaborating.

Mark led Karen and four others across campus into Butler Library.

Inside, Karen saw them—rows and rows of apathetic drones who walked past their table every day without so much as looking up, let alone engaging with the issues that carried the fate of the world. Here they were, with their heads obsequiously shoved in their little books, quietly doing their homework until they graduated. From there on to top jobs attempting to sidestep the vast injustices of the world. Mark brought the little group to the center of the giant reading room. He stepped up onto an empty desk and yelled out, "Everyone—may I have your attention for a second, please?"

The tone of the room went from a soft, general murmur to a stark silence.

"Through a think tank financed by the Defense Department called IDA, our university is actively participating in an unjust war! Is this what you want? 'Cause we refuse to collaborate in the destruction of thousands of innocent lives, and we think maybe some of you do too. Maybe we can't stop our government from bombing a tiny, helpless country off the face of the earth, but if we work together we can at least stop these bastards from spending our tuition money on coming up with new methods to slaughter them."

Scattered applause broke out. Mark stepped down from the table, but before he and the other SDS members could leave, two campus security guards approached the group and asked to see their IDs. After showing them, the six students were escorted to the office of the dean of student affairs.

"It's our right to protest!" Karen spoke up when they arrived.

"Outside, yes. You have your table, and we've respected that," the dean replied sternly. "However, protesting inside a Columbia building is a direct violation of school policy, young lady, and I think you all know that." He then informed the students that they were all officially on academic probation.

Afterward, feeling a strange sense of elation, Karen went home

1036 ❦ Arthur Nersesian

and woke up Mallory from a nap. "Guess what? Now we're both in trouble."

"Mark finally got you?"

"This afternoon we went to the library and Mark jumped on a desk and made a public statement against the IDA."

"In the library?"

"Yep, and security guards escorted us all to Dean Connor's office."

"You're kidding!"

"Nope, now we're all on probation. Mark too." At that instant, it crossed Karen's mind that this might prevent her from being admitted to Columbia Law School.

"Wow! Why didn't you tell me this was going to happen? I would've joined you!"

"It was done on impulse," Karen explained.

21

That night, Mallory and some other SDSers joined "the IDA six" at the West End Bar on Broadway. Everyone lifted a beer mug to Mark's spontaneous activism.

"It really is high time," said one student.

As people toasted the probationary six, Mallory realized that their little act sort of vindicated Gene and the summer bombing project. "Nothing is going to get done until someone makes it happen," she said to Karen. "The days of protests and petitions are over!"

When they got home late that night, Gene was happy for them, and together with a six-ounce bag of pot and two six-packs of Budweiser in the fridge, they kept the celebration going. They were all sitting around in the living room an hour later, chatting, laughing, and flying high, when the phone rang.

Gene snatched it up in a drunken, expansive mood. "Yeah?"

"I was told you had explosives and a detonator," an older male voice said.

"Let me save us both some time, Mr. G-man," Gene kidded. Then he realized who and what the call was, and his face paled.

Who is it? Mallory mouthed. Karen lowered the record player and looked over at Gene.

"The only merchandise of that sort I have is around 150 microspring release switches." Gene tried to sound sober, but because he wasn't, he added, "But we don't know what the hell to do with them."

"Who's he talking to?" Karen whispered to Mallory, who shrugged.

"What are they?" the person on the other end asked.

"A thousand bucks a pop is what," Gene pulled the price out of thin air. He couldn't remember the name of the missiles they were a part of.

"Are they detonator caps?"

"Nothing on them is explosive," Gene said, growing paranoid. "Hell, I don't even think they're illegal."

"They work on a timer?"

"Nope, they're an Italian make, triggered by a tiny radiation detector."

"I don't understand. How can a radiation detector trigger a release spring?"

"Beats me. I think they were produced to fit into something else, but for the life of us, we don't know what."

"Can I see one?"

"Sure, for a thousand bucks."

"How about two hundred?"

That one sale alone would nearly cover their loss, but Gene was intent on making a profit. "Eight. And that's the bottom-barrel price."

"Look, I just want to see if I can use it. If I can, I'll buy more."

"Eight hundred for one detonator. One hundred and fifty of them for ten grand. It's a wonderful deal." The room started spinning; holding the phone to his ear, Gene slid to the ground as the booze and grass kicked into high gear.

"How about eight hundred for one, and 102 additional detonators for five thousand?"

"A thousand for one and six thousand dollars for the rest," Gene countered.

"Okay," the voice finally relented. "I'll test one out and if it works I'll buy the rest."

Gene informed the buyer that he wanted the thousand dollars in small bills. He was to put the money in a white paper bag and drop it in the public trash can on the southeast corner of Washington Square Park at eight the following night, then continue walking east along 4th Street to a pay phone on Broadway, where he would be instructed on where he could pick up the detonator.

"How can you guarantee you won't steal my money?" the guy asked.

"Just do it or don't!" It was the plan that the three of them had prearranged in anticipation of this surreal moment.

Suddenly the line went dead. Gene looked up to see that Karen had clicked down on the receiver.

"What the hell!" Mallory said as Gene burst out laughing.

"Gene's too stoned," Karen said. "I hung up before he could queer the whole deal."

"Shit! I didn't even get his damn number," Gene said, no longer laughing. "We're fucked, we can't call him back!"

"Hold on," Mallory said, "you made plans with him. Let's just go there tomorrow night with the stuff and see if he drops off the cash."

As the night progressed and they all grew increasingly paranoid from the pot, Gene started freaking out and talking about going to jail. Mallory decided that the phone call had gone on too long and was convinced the FBI had traced the call. She kept looking out the window for strange movements outside. Karen said that maybe they should quit while they were ahead and just let it go.

Early the next morning when they turned on the radio, they learned the news that the National Liberation Front—or the Vietcong—had coordinated major counteroffensives throughout the south, killing over 230 American GIs and countless South Vietnamese. Over the past weeks and months, LBJ and the Pentagon had been announcing that the NLF, with their dwindling numbers and paltry training, were all but defeated, so this news definitely came as a shock.

"Shit, if rice farmers in black pj's can pull this off," Gene announced, "so can we!"

All three felt a renewed sense of confidence, not just in being able to push the deal through and recover their cash, but that they could turn a sizable profit. They would then use that money for their very own guerrilla operation targeting Columbia University's war against Harlem's indigenous population.

They broke that night's deal into three major parts, in which each of them would play a key role: Mallory would stay in the apartment by the phone; if the buyer called to change the deal, she would coordinate a new plan with the other two. Gene would stay by the garbage can on the southeast corner of Washington Square Park to verify that the buyer had dropped off the cash, then he'd count it and call Karen at a pay phone to confirm. Because of her karate skills, Karen was trusted with the final task—she would be at the drop site, and upon Gene's confirmation call, she would leave the single detonator a few blocks away at Broadway and 4th Street.

They were all anxious. Gene arrived at seven p.m. and paced in circles, trying not to be conspicuous because the area was empty and he'd be easy to isolate. A little before eight o'clock, he noticed a tall, elderly man scoping out the park. When the coast was clear, the senior citizen walked over to the garbage can and dropped a white paper bag into it, just as described. What occurred next startled Gene. He watched as the man immediately started sprinting eastward. Instead of checking to make sure he wasn't being watched, Gene rushed over, snatched the bag, and hastily counted the cash. Then he went to the pay phone on the south side of the park and called Karen to give her a description of the guy who was currently speeding toward her.

"Give him the thing! I repeat, give him the thing!"

"Will do. Tell him the detonator is in the white garbage can directly to his left," she said, and hung up. She set the bag with the detonator in the garbage can and watched as the old bird came huffing down 4th Street.

Gene called the same pay phone again, this time to tell the buyer what she had said.

Karen nearly brushed shoulders with the old fellow as he hurried to answer the ringing phone. She watched as he listened to the instructions and scanned the area until he saw the bag. He hung up, grabbed the bag, and looked inside. Apparently he liked what he saw—he stepped into the gutter, hailed a cab, and a moment later was sailing down Broadway.

Instead of being happy that they had just quadrupled their original investment for only a single item, all Karen could think was, *Who the hell was that old fart? Why did he just shell out a grand for some useless device?* She headed over to the park and met up with Gene, who couldn't stop smiling. He waved a stack of ribboned twenty-dollar bills—a thousand dollars total.

"Holy shit!" she exclaimed, dumbfounded at all the money they had just made. Together they walked over to Sheridan Square and caught the 1 train for the slow ride back up to Columbia University. On the way home, Gene picked up three quart-sized bottles of Budweiser and some cold cuts—salami, bologna, and ham.

"Where is it?" Mallory asked when they arrived at the door, grinning. Gene counted the money again as she watched incredulously.

"This is amazing!" Karen said. "We just made over seven hundred dollars and we still have over a hundred of those little widgets left."

"All I really care about is that I can pay everyone back now."

"That's not a bad idea," Gene said, finishing his first quart of beer and popping the top on the second. "Then we can just do this ourselves, the right way."

"Hold on now, maybe this whole thing was kismet," Karen mused.

"Kissmet my ass," Gene punned, guzzling his beer.

"What do you mean, *kismet?*" Mallory asked.

"Six students, including me and Mark Rudd, are on academic probation. I mean, it's not like nothing good came out of this. We made money and the SDS is finally getting more aggressive."

"It's still not going to stop the school from building the gym," Mallory said.

"Maybe not, but neither is bombing dirt," Karen argued. "And now the word is out—everyone would know it's us."

"So they know—good! Jail doesn't scare me," Gene said. He belched deeply. "This is still *my* fucking neighborhood! *My* home!"

"She does have a point," Mallory said. "Look, Gene, I love what you tried to do. And for accomplishing this, I want you to have the lion's share of whatever's left over."

"I don't want no lion's shit, I want them to stop building the—"

"Gene, we're not in jail or injured due to some explosion mishap," Karen said.

"And now we even have some cash," Mallory added, holding up the wad of bills.

"I can't believe I'm hearing this shit." Gene shook his head. "I just can't believe it."

"We really tried. I think we should be proud of that."

"And we *still* don't have detonators or explosives," Karen said.

Gene didn't respond; he simply finished his second beer and went right on to the third.

"We just have to know when we're licked, Gene," said Karen.

"I got an idea: why don't you two lick each other's honky assholes." He grabbed his jacket.

"You need to apologize this instant!" Karen shouted.

"Or whatchu gonna do? Karate chop me?"

"You can't talk to my sister that way!" Mallory shouted.

"Sister, huh? Your *sister* fucked the shit out of me behind your back!" he yelled, then stormed out.

Mallory stared at Karen, who was blushing, staring tensely at the floor. "Soon after we first met him," she said after several moments of silence elapsed. "It was before you guys dated . . . We were together."

"How could that happen? Why didn't you tell me?"

"I'm sorry, I really am."

"What the hell happened?"

"I bumped into him one night and we left the West End Bar together, we were chatting, and . . ." Karen went silent.

"And you fucked him?"

"No. I mean, we left the bar and were walking down Broadway, and he was going to go to his place and I was about to go to mine, when some crazy man came out of nowhere and just punched him in the face."

"Is this another lie?"

"I swear it's the truth!"

"When exactly was this?" Mallory asked, choking back tears.

"You were in Brooklyn with Estelle."

"I can't believe what I'm hearing!"

"We were literally chased over here; I thought we were both going to get attacked. I locked the door. He was in such a distraught state that he cried."

"So you fucked him."

"We had both been drinking, we were in a weird state, drunk and frightened. It never would've happened otherwise."

"But you went out on a date and had drinks with him?"

"Not at all! I was with some SDSers in the back of the West End; he was alone at the bar. We saw each other as we were leaving the place."

Mallory sat down on the couch and grabbed her head. "I can't believe this. I think I'm going to throw up."

"The next morning I knew I fucked up. I told him we could never . . . we'd never be together and it was a big mistake."

Mallory started crying, shaking her head.

"It was before you were ever even . . . together."

"You know, in all the time I've known you, you barely even had sex with that one Link guy. I mean, I never thought you were a threat!"

"This was before that."

"You mean you lost your virginity to Gene?"

"Yes, but—"

"So you lied to my face."

"Because I knew how much you liked him and I didn't want to screw things up for you."

"But you did!" Mallory shouted. "You completely loused everything up!"

"I didn't mean to. He just kept pushing it and it just happened."

"*He* wasn't my best friend! *You* were!" Mallory dashed to her room and slammed the door behind her.

Karen stood in the hallway. "I'm really, really sorry," she called through the door.

The sound of Mallory's weeping filled the emptiness. Karen waited in the living room, hoping that after a good cry, her friend would emerge. But an hour later Karen fell asleep on the couch.

She was awakened in the middle of the night by more of Mallory's weeping, which seemed to have intensified. Karen found herself sitting up, listening to the wailing for a while longer, until she drifted back to sleep. She awoke again a short while later, this time to the sounds of bumping. The weeping had ceased, but she could hear clunky movements coming from Mallory's room. Karen waited again for her to come out but eventually closed her eyes and drifted back to sleep.

22

When Karen got up the next morning, Mallory's door was ajar. She looked inside and saw an oddly empty room. Some of Mallory's clothes and toiletries were gone, though not all. Her toothbrush was still in the bathroom, but when Karen looked in the closet, she found that Mallory's large suitcases were missing.

Oh my God, I just ruined the most important friendship I've ever had, she panicked. Karen wondered what she could possibly do to make things right. Without a clue of where to begin, she tried to calm herself down. Time would heal everything. She then tried to treat the day like any other: she went to her afternoon classes, to the library where she did schoolwork, then to the dojo for her karate practice. She spent much of the evening exhausting herself by preparing for her upcoming brown belt exam.

When she came home that night there was still no sign of Mallory. Karen figured she could have gone to Brooklyn, but she also knew that in recent months her friend's patience with her eccentric aunt had dwindled.

The next morning when Karen awoke, she walked into Mallory's bedroom again to find it was still empty. *Just keep calm, her anger will pass*, Karen told herself. But Mal didn't return the next day either. With each morning throughout the week, Karen would leave for classes and when she returned to the old tenement, she would find herself praying as she walked up the stairs that she'd open the door and see Mallory sitting in the living room, waiting to yell at her. Karen was thoroughly prepared to make amends or grovel in some way. When she'd go to sleep she'd still find herself hoping that she'd be awoken by her friend's angry return. But no Mallory.

After that first week, Karen went into Mallory's room and carefully checked to see if there was any indication that her roommate might've come by at some point while she was away. As far as she knew, Mallory had simply left that night and had not returned since. She found herself plagued with visions of her friend jumping in front of the 1 train or off the George Washington Bridge. But she knew that if this were the case, her body probably would've been discovered by now. She was alive, just removed. It was as if Mallory were in a coma. All Karen could really do was wait and pray that Mallory would come out of her anger and find some way to forgive her.

After a week and a half, Karen woke up one morning with an idea. She dressed and raced over to Mallory's English lit class, figuring that her friend wouldn't jeopardize her own academic standing just to get back at Karen. When she arrived the class was already in session.

Peeking inside the large, wood-paneled amphitheater, Karen saw the professor talking about the Romantic poets; she scanned the faces until she spotted one she recognized: Sally, a large girl with frizzy red hair who was one of Mallory's smarter friends. Karen began waving to try to get her attention, but then spotted Mallory taking notes two seats behind Sally. She ducked out of the doorway and found herself gasping for air. She considered waiting after class for Mallory, but realized that this was a bad idea—Mallory would resent being ambushed. Karen just had to wait for her best friend to find the forgiveness in her heart.

But she decided to start preparing for the opportunity in order to make it as smooth as possible. Over the next few days she cleaned the apartment until it was spotless and bought a large Hallmark card that said, *Sorry*, in beautiful embossed cursive. She also purchased an expensive bouquet of long-stemmed red roses that she put in a large plain vase in Mallory's bedroom.

Karen also realized she had to issue some kind of statement—a mea culpa of sorts—which would initiate the forgiveness process. She considered the admiration that she had for Mallory, how much her friend had inspired her, and she thought hard about any possible subconscious motives she might've had for what she had done with Gene.

Frailty, she decided. *I did this as an act of frailty*. Now she had to find a better way to phrase it. She grabbed her pen and tried to organize her thoughts. After producing a great jumble of rhetoric, she ironed it out through logic and reduction. Finally she stumbled upon something that sounded both sincere and yet forgivable, with a psychological twist that would lead to a fight and then ultimately forgiveness. On a blank page she wrote: *What I did was an act of anger, brought on by subconscious feelings of jealousy, combined with a sense of abandonment.*

She read her words aloud, so she could hear how they sounded: "*I felt that you were drifting away from me and looking elsewhere. Maybe I even resented the fact that I met him first, but you immediately staked your claim. Either way it wasn't about him, but rather my feelings toward you."*

These were words she felt confident Mallory could understand and forgive. But she also knew she hadn't gone far enough. The words were there, but the feelings were missing. It wasn't that she didn't feel awful about what had happened—she truly loved Mallory. But instead of emoting like most people, Karen instinctively shut down when sad or hurt. She needed to connect with the deep pain she felt and express it outwardly.

She sat in front of a mirror and began repeating her statement of regret, glancing up at herself, but it wasn't working. She wasn't getting any more emotional. Karen knew she had to do something that really wasn't in her nature—she needed to cry, the more intensely and humiliating the better. The only problem was, she simply wasn't a crier. Even when her favorite uncle had died and she felt his emptiness in her soul, nothing came out of her tear ducts.

Over the next few days, Karen resolved that she simply *must* learn how to cry. She listened to sentimental music and drank cheap wine, but she only fell asleep. Then she tried watching sappy movies. During the mawkish scenes, instead of dismissing that subtle welling sensation in her heart, which seemed to be incipient feelings, she attempted to encourage them. At one point she released a kind of animalistic moan, the beginning of a wail, but instantly felt silly and feared that a neighbor might've overheard her. She carefully studied daytime soaps and paid special attention to how the actors cried, trying to hone the sounds and the subtle vibrations of her body. Soon, she had developed a decent, if not banal, lachrymose performance. All she lacked were real tears.

While cutting across campus one day, her fellow SDSer Alvin stopped her in front of Kent Hall. "Where the hell did you guys vanish off to?" he asked.

"What guys?"

"You and Mallory. You two were last semester's radical lesbians and now that we're finally getting things together, you're nowhere to be seen."

"We just needed a break."

"Well, you couldn't have picked a worse time. We're planning two big rallies and we could really use your help."

"Rallies for what?" Karen hadn't attended the last couple of meetings.

"All the usual shit."

"When are they?" She realized it might serve as a way of approaching Mallory.

"One is later this month and an even bigger one is in April; other groups are working with us on them."

"I'll see what we can do," Karen said softly.

"Hey, what's wrong with your old pal Eugene?" he asked.

"Nothing, why?"

"When I said hello to him yesterday, he told me to stop calling him by his slave name. He said his new name is Akbar."

"Akbar?" She found it funny, but didn't laugh.

"Yeah, and when I asked him what was up, he said he could no longer be seen talking with white devils."

"Gene called you a white devil?" This didn't sound like him at all. She wondered if she was a white devil now too.

"Yeah, then he just walked away."

Karen didn't know what to say. It was all falling apart. This entire debacle of the bombing and its aftermath had obviously changed all of them for the worse.

A few days later, during the second week of March, Karen came home from her constitutional law class and noticed Estelle double-parked in front of the dojo. She dashed up the stairs to find Mallory packing up the rest of her belongings.

"Mallory, you've got to listen to me!"

Mallory kept steadily folding and boxing her stuff without looking up.

"I need to tell you why! I mean, I think I owe you that much . . . ." The fact that her friend's pace neither hastened nor slowed made her nervous as hell. "When I saw that you were in love with . . . what's his name, I . . . I just felt so rejected. I felt . . . I felt like you were dumping me, see?"

It was as though Karen wasn't even there; Mallory kept moving.

"Stop for just a second!" She stepped in front of Mallory so that she couldn't ignore her.

"You betrayed me," Mallory said in a monotone, still not making eye contact. "I want nothing more to do with you."

Karen grabbed her and pulled her firmly to her chest. She was as muscular and lean as Mallory was soft and round, so Mallory didn't resist, she just stayed limp. Without even knowing what she was going to do, Karen hugged her tightly. Mallory simply breathed. Karen closed her eyes and made the sounds and body motions of an actor who was starting to weep. Holding her friend harder, she intensified her lamentation, releasing a series of soft, low staccato sounds as she rocked her body stiffly. Still, a key detail was missing, the thing that would firmly establish a provenance for her grief. Reaching around the back of her roommate's head, Karen slipped her index finger between her lips and then swabbed it across her eyes, making them glossy.

Before releasing Mallory, Karen looked dead ahead. Mallory was staring at her through the two mirrors hanging from opposite walls. She could see it was all an act. No sooner did Karen loosen her grip than Mallory pulled away, grabbed her boxes, and walked out the door. Aunt Estelle returned upstairs with her a few minutes later and together the two quickly collected a few more items. Then Mallory left the apartment forever.

Over the next two days, every time Karen felt dead inside, she'd lie down. Although she was utterly exhausted, she was unable to sleep. She constantly felt like crying, but nothing came. Finally, on the third day, Karen decided she was being self-indulgent. In order to regain normalcy, she had to *act* normal. But it was nearly impossible.

In fact, she had been slacking off instead of prepping for her Law School Admission Test and hadn't even thought about her applications for the fall.

Four nights after Mallory left, Karen was finally at the library studying when a big cheer broke out at the far end of the long table she was sitting at. She looked up fearing it was somehow related to her. Back in reality, rumors were spreading that LBJ was preparing to announce that he would not be running for reelection. After leaving the library, Karen stopped by the West End and found a table of SDSers in the rear.

"Isn't it incredible?" Evelyn said as she approached. "I know it's just a rumor, but still . . ."

"I'm as happy as everyone else," Karen replied robotically.

"But you worked on the Dump Johnson campaign. Heck, you probably even had a hand in this," said Evelyn.

Karen shrugged, but someone still bought her a beer.

Mark and the others had reasoned that this announcement would mean the end of the war. Johnson, who was the incumbent, had been the only significant Democrat pushing for it. Almost every other Democratic contender had already come out against the war. Karen now remembered that in preparation for the early primaries for that fall's election, the SDS was staging rallies in March and April.

Hoping against hope to use these events as a final attempt at reconciliation, Karen called Mallory in Brooklyn. After a couple of rings, Estelle picked up.

"Hi, Miss Levine," Karen began, "can I speak to Mallory?"

"Karen," she obviously recognized the voice, "I'm afraid that Mallory instructed me to say that she is no longer speaking to you."

"Can you inform her that the SDS is holding two big rallies on campus, and they're asking me if she—"

"Mallory doesn't care."

"Then can you tell her that her rent is due?"

"Hold on." During the pause, Karen could faintly hear a tense yet hushed exchange in the background. A moment later, Mallory's aunt came back on the phone: "She said she'll send you whatever she owes you, and that you should find a new roommate immediately."

At any other time this would've been a much harder financial situation, but with her cut of the detonator deal, she had enough money to pay for this month and also look for a new apartment.

"Estelle, can you please tell her that I would do anything, anything at all, if she could find it in her heart to forgive me?" Karen said desperately, seeing little left to lose.

"She's not going to," Aunt Estelle said. "But she told me one of her friends is interested in the place. Some guy named Harry, who also goes to Columbia. If he calls, would you like me to give him your number?"

"Do you think she might come by and visit if I rented to her friend?"

"She might."

"Okay." If this was her only possible access to Mallory, so be it.

It felt as if a drawbridge had been lifted. Between the two of them, Mallory was always the popular one; she was always inviting people over for drinks, making the apartment into a home. Now that she was gone, the place felt permanently empty. Karen considered adopting a cat, something warm and alive to come between her and the emptiness.

Three nights later, when she least expected it, the phone rang. Karen froze, staring at it like it was a noisy black mollusk that had intruded in the night. After the seventh ring, she answered.

"Hello?" an unrecognizable male voice said on the other end.

"Harry?" she asked.

"No, I spoke to some guy a few weeks ago. He sold me a gizmo that could be used as a detonator."

"Oh, yeah, sorry. No refunds."

"I want to buy the other ones."

"Really?"

"Yeah."

"Twenty thousand bucks," she blurted out.

"We already agreed on four thousand."

"That guy's not with us anymore," she said. "You want the rest, they'll cost you twenty thousand smackers."

"I only have nine," the guy said.

"Fuck it." She was trying to sound tough. "Nine grand then." It was an absurd sum of money. "You know how we want our bills—small and old." She was sweating and her hands were trembling as she tried to conceal the trepidation in her voice.

"I'll make them small for you, but it's going to be too much to stuff in a paper bag this time."

"And the numbers on the bills can't be sequential," she said nervously. She feared that she was missing some vital detail. "Just drop off the cash at midnight in the same place you did last time."

"Midnight when?"

"Tonight," she answered without thinking, trying to mimic Gene's cockiness.

"I won't be in town for at least three days," the guy said.

"In exactly one week then." She slammed the phone down, remembering that the call could be traced. It wasn't until she hung up that she realized that one week from then was the day of the first big SDS rally—but it didn't matter, this was still terrific news. Mallory wasn't rich and she only got a partial scholarship. With this cash, Karen could pay for her entire year's tuition. Exuberantly, she called Mallory's aunt back and said she had urgent news.

"Well, you better tell me what it is, dear," Estelle said, lowering her voice, "because she gave me explicit orders that she is not coming to the phone for you."

"Can you just inform her that the guy who we sold . . . cigarette lighters to, down in the Village, has called back and asked if he can buy more cigarette lighters."

"Cigarette lighters? Are you crazy?"

"It's a long story, but she'll know what I'm talking about. Please tell her that he's willing to pay nine times as much as he did before."

"Nine times as much, huh?"

"Yeah, she'll know what I'm talking about."

"Hold on." After some muted discussion, then an angry shout, the aunt came back on the line and said, "She asked for you to please not call here ever again. You'll just have to sell your own lighters, dear."

"No, but I need her help. We can make a lot of money!"

"Just hang up the damn phone!" she heard Mallory scream in the background.

"But she's—"

There was a click and then a dial tone.

As Karen put her phone back on the hook, she decided she would pass on the deal. Nine thousand dollars was an enormous sum of money, but it just wasn't worth the risk. And if Mallory wouldn't help, she couldn't do it all alone.

23

The next morning when Karen was instructing a beginner's class of seven young white belts for Hrag, right in the middle of repetitive thrust moves she thought of Mallory and suddenly felt as though the air had been knocked out of her. She told the group to continue and barely made it to the bathroom before she burst into tears. And once she began sobbing, she couldn't stop. She finally covered her mouth to silence herself. It was all she could do to regain her breath. Terrified of being heard over the collective grunts of the practicing students, she pulled the roll of toilet paper from the spool, squeezed it over her mouth, and then squatted in a corner where she let out a wail that came from the bottom of her soul. She felt as if she had accidentally killed her best friend, and realized only at that moment how deeply she had loved Mallory. It was utterly unexpected, like an acute demonic possession, and after several more minutes of trembling she was fine.

That night she felt completely exhausted. Barely had she put head to the pillow when she fell into a deep sleep. Early the next morning she once again awoke with the thought that she had ruined everything. Just as quickly, however, she decided to stop punishing herself: her relationship with Mallory was over, and she had bills to pay.

Two days later, Karen walked into Columbia University's housing assistance office and posted a flyer about the availability of a large bedroom on the bulletin board. Within twenty-four hours, a soft-spoken girl called up, and twenty minutes later Karen met with Dannette Shaw, a shy, pretty girl in tortoiseshell glasses who was majoring in botany and had cash in hand. Karen packed the remaining few items that Mallory had left behind and put them in the living room closet, then gave Dannette the keys.

The first night they had a long talk that culminated in Dannette painfully confessing to Karen that she had been attacked in Morningside Park a few weeks earlier. In addition to being robbed, she had also been molested. Karen remembered reading about a string of recent attacks on a number of Barnard coeds. Lying in bed that night, she came up with the idea of developing a special self-defensive karate program for young women.

Karen realized that since being rejected by Mallory, she had been deliberately isolating herself—and it was time to stop. Even if Mallory was going to be at the upcoming SDS rally, so were her other friends. She wasn't going to be deprived of her social life. And politically, Mark Rudd was finally bringing the protest home and she wanted to support him. She decided to be nice to herself and purchased the Beatles' *Magical Mystery Tour* album. Everyone but her had it. She started playing it nonstop, trying to push away all the bad feelings and just focus on being upbeat.

As she was passing the SDS office the next day on campus, she peeked in and, seeing that Mallory wasn't around, she entered and hung out awhile. At one point, someone mentioned that his girlfriend had been mugged at knifepoint in Riverside Park. Karen said, "I'm thinking about starting a self-defense class for women at my dojo."

"You know karate?"

"I'm nearly a black belt."

The young man asked if she might consider working with the SDS security committee to make sure that protestors followed Mark's instructions during the big rally.

"Do you really think this is going to require a security squad?" she said.

"Mark is intent on getting Kirk's attention this time."

Karen told him that she'd be happy to do her part; the little task would give her a reason to be there. Now she wouldn't feel shamed by Mallory.

The evening before the SDS rally, while hanging her coat in the living room closet, she saw the bag of detonators just sitting back there where she had tossed them. For all intents and purposes, this bag of gadgets was worthless and it would eventually end up in the trash. She decided that she might as well just put it there now. As she picked up the bag, though, she felt her heart beating. Late the following night, for a few hours of frantic, anxiety-generating intrigue, this bag of trash could be converted into the staggering sum of nine thousand dollars. She could live rent-free for three years!

The more she thought about it, the more she decided that to *not* do

the deal just because Mallory had refused was little more than spite—
yet another way of punishing herself for losing her friend. She decided
that she would do it! Even if she had to do it all by herself.

The rally was scheduled to begin at three o'clock the next day,
but since she was going to try to handle the deal solo, she knew she
couldn't exhaust herself, so at ten p.m. she called Evelyn and said she
was feeling feverish and nauseous and therefore would be unable to
help at the rally.

"Oh, that's too bad. We were really counting on you."

"I'm sure I'll be better for the next rally," she responded.

She wished Karen well and told her to rest up.

Once off the phone, Karen realized she had a lot to do. If she had
any chance of pulling the deal off, she knew she had to scope out the
location again. There would be too many people around during the
day tomorrow. Although exhausted, she had to go right now. By
eleven p.m., she was dressed and walking over to Broadway, where
she caught the 1 train down to Sheridan Square. From there she headed
over to Washington Square and inspected the southeast corner of the
park.

During the first deal, Karen had worked with Mallory and Gene,
but now she was all alone. The buyer would leave the money in a
wire-mesh garbage can. Her first priority would be grabbing his cash
before anyone else could, and then she would head down 4th Street to
Broadway. Her big problem was how she would be able to race ahead
of the buyer while carrying a fifty-pound bag of detonators. If that
wasn't enough, she also had to deposit the detonators near the phone
booth on Broadway first, then find a second phone nearby and call
him to tell him where he could pick them up—all without being seen.

Her one big advantage was that she knew what he looked like,
whereas he neither knew who she was nor that she was working alone.

She walked through the area carefully, contemplating various scenarios. She located two pay phones, made sure they worked, then
took down the two numbers. She realized she really didn't have to get
ahead of him because she was basically invisible, so he'd just have to
wait until she got to the drop site. On Broadway, near West 4th, she
made an important discovery: a bunch of black garbage bags that had
been dumped just around the corner from the pay phone.

While heading back to the IRT, she passed a head shop on Mac-
Dougal that was still open. In the window she spotted a twelve-inch
bowie knife complete with a leather sheath for only ten bucks. She

bought it, then continued west to Seventh Avenue to take the 1 train home.

The one detail that quietly nagged at her was what the hell this strange man wanted with these highly sophisticated space-age gizmos. Could they be used for anything other than building bombs? *That's not your concern*, she told herself, *just get the damn money.*

When she finally returned home, to fend off nervousness she held the sheathed knife firmly in her right hand and repetitively practiced her latest karate moves. *Stab, jab, yank . . . stab, jab, yank*, thrusting the blade in and down. Karen rehearsed exactly how she'd react if she found herself walking into an ambush. But if it turned out to be a police sting, she was ready to surrender immediately.

The next day, after a shallow sleep, she feigned stomach pain to everyone she saw during her morning classes. Then she called her SDS head of security and reiterated that she couldn't make it to the event. As the rally was commencing on campus she headed home. She felt guilty, and exhausted from no sleep, so she spent most of the day in bed just resting.

Around eight p.m., Karen put on black slacks, a billowy sweater, and a loose jacket, hoping to look as butch as possible. Then she slipped her hair into a beanie and the knife with its sheath under her waistband.

At nine p.m. she nibbled at some leftovers. At ten she put the bag of detonators into a knapsack, slipped the straps over her shoulders, and marched to the train, which she took downtown. From there she walked eastward over to Washington Square Park. Despite the fact that it was cold, a loose accumulation of dealers, junkies, homeless, and hippies hung out along the western rim of the giant stone fountain just south of the arch. She watched some NYU students playing chuck-a-luck, a dice game, with a large black man for a while, trying to discreetly survey the area. Then she headed southeast, to an area populated by only a few dog walkers and possible muggers.

The emptiness of the area made her stand out—a young woman with a heavy beige knapsack. She slowly circled the area, lingering in front of a library that looked more like a prison. Soon, right on schedule, the tall old man appeared in the distance. He was coming east from NYU's Loeb Student Center and carried a bag—presumably stuffed with the nine grand.

She watched as he crossed the dark street and casually dropped his black plastic garbage bag into the corner trash can. For a minute he just stood there, as though expecting her to magically appear.

Then, just as before, he peeled off. His lanky old body hurried eastward, along the north side of West 4th Street. Karen snatched the bag from the trash; keeping him in sight, she trotted half a block behind him on the south side of the same street, holding the bag of cash in her arms like an infant while the detonators swayed on her back. As he approached Broadway, she dropped her eyes to the pavement and caught her breath. He went to the pay phone where Gene had called the last time. She casually passed along the south side of the street, crossing Broadway. On the diagonal corner from him, she ducked into a doorway where she slipped off her knapsack. Karen carefully pulled out the heavy plastic bag of detonators and placed it on the ground among the wall of other garbage bags that she had spotted the night before. After only a few steps, however, she realized with horror that she was still holding the detonators and she had left the bag of cash on the ground!

"Hey, sweetheart, you taking out the trash?" said a rough-looking Latino youth. He was standing near the garbage bags.

Glancing over, she realized the old guy was watching them. Casually, as though she were meeting up with him, she started walking toward the young Romeo. "Are you talking to me?" she asked with a smile.

"You know I am."

"What'd you ask?" She stepped over so she was right above the trash.

"Just wondering if I can help you."

"Yeah, actually. Would you know the time?"

The old guy turned away.

"Uhhh . . ." As the young man checked his wristwatch in the streetlight, she discreetly stooped down, swapping her bag of detonators for the smaller bag of cash. "It's like twelve fifteen."

"Do you know where Washington Square Park is?" she asked in order to hold him there.

"Yeah, I'll walk you there if you like," he said, pointing west as she slipped her knapsack off her shoulders and dropped the bag of cash inside. "You not looking to score, are you?"

"Score?"

"That's the only reason anyone would go into the park at this hour. I'll tell right now, that shit is pure catnip, girl."

"Really?"

"No worries, Charlie Dee will take care of you here. How much you want?" he asked as they crossed Broadway.

Karen could see her customer on the north side of the street, the old man fidgeting, waiting impatiently by his pay phone. He seemed to be staring at it—waiting, praying, willing it to ring.

"You know what?" she said. "Let me ask my boyfriend."

Karen dashed fifty feet to Mercer Street, where she jumped into the phone booth across the street from the Bottom Line. She slipped a dime into the slot and dialed the number of the other pay phone, which she had memorized. The old guy picked up after just one ring.

"They're in a garbage bag on the other corner," she said clearly yet softly.

"Huh?"

"The southeast corner; the detonators are there."

"Where? What are you saying?"

"Look at the fucking kitty-corner!" she said nervously, as the Latino dealer started approaching her.

"Okay, I'm looking."

"See the garbage bags?"

"Yeah."

"They're in one of those bags."

"You want me to talk to him?" The street sleaze had arrived at her pay phone. She slammed the phone down on the receiver.

"He said to get as much as I can, which is five bucks' worth." She unraveled a five-dollar bill and held it out to him.

He took a rolled baggie out of his pocket and handed it to her.

"Open it up," she said.

"What? You think I'm lying to yous?" He opened the envelope and let her inspect.

She saw a tight clump of loose dried leaf and stem and she gave it a deep sniff.

"Is that good or what?"

"Okay," she conceded.

"And it's strong stuff, chica. That'll make you wet and wild, so tell your boyfriend I just did him a big favor."

"Will do." She grabbed the bag of pot, shoved it in her jacket pocket, and rushed back toward Broadway.

"Hey, hold up, cutie! I put the extra pinch in there so we could toke it together, you know."

She ignored him and kept moving eastward. When she reached

Broadway, the old guy had vanished. Peering north, there was no one in sight. Considering the weight and value of the merchandise, she figured he had probably grabbed a cab like last time, but when she looked south along the eastern side of Broadway, she made out a lone figure striding jerkily down near Bleecker.

The same curiosity was still burning in the back of her mind: *What is this guy going to do with these detonators?* Because she was alone, without Mallory or Gene to answer to, she followed him. The streets below Houston seemed to narrow and darken. By the time she reached Broome, the sidewalks were completely bare. Even though she was carrying thousands of dollars, she needed to know where he was headed. *What the hell is he going to do with those things?* As she walked, she repeatedly touched the handle of the bowie knife in her waistband to assuage her anxiety about getting mugged. Slowly, she closed the distance between them.

After crossing below Canal Street, Karen kept expecting Daddy Longlegs to either turn off down some side street, grab a cab, or at least hop into a subway station. But the guy did nothing of the kind. Slowly and steadily, he just pressed southward toward the Battery. As they crossed Worth, past the stately steps of the courts and the hollow municipal buildings, cruising by the periodic lost souls who were usually so far gone they didn't even camp out with the other homeless, Karen realized she was too close to him—all he would have to do to discover her would be to turn around. Repeatedly she found herself pausing, giving him more space, but as a single white female she was even more of a target than he was if caught alone. By the time they walked by the entrance to the Brooklyn Bridge and passed the rat-filled City Hall Park, it seemed as if only the two of them occupied Lower Manhattan. Each street was so deserted that the echo of both their footsteps was clearly perceptible. At this point, she moved from doorway to doorway, corner to corner. *He's going to Whitehall*, she decided. *He must live in Staten Island.* But before they reached the old ferry building at the very bottom of the borough, Daddy Longlegs seemed to disappear into the night.

She found herself racing back up Broadway and eastward to Broad Street, just in time to spot the stick figure veering into an old, squat building that looked like a throwback to the colonial era. She went to a doorway across the street from the historical landmark, Fraunces Tavern, and there she waited. After ten minutes, she saw the lights of the top floor flip on. *Gotcha!*

She walked a few blocks southwest over to the ferry building where there was a small line of waiting cabs. She grabbed the one at the front and rode it all the way up the West Side Highway with her knapsack of cash. The meter came to a whopping $8.35—she gave the driver the entire ten-dollar bill.

Once she got inside the door of her building, Karen hurried up the stairs and unlocked her apartment door. For the first time she used all three locks on the door. In her kitchen, she dumped her knapsack on the dining room table and started inspecting the money. Groaning audibly, she quickly discovered that over half the cash was strips of newspaper. Instead of the nine thousand dollars she was expecting, the son of a bitch had stiffed her out of nearly five grand! She counted all the five- and ten-dollar bills, which came to $4,100. She seriously contemplated going back over to his house with her bowie knife and confronting him at his door.

After a few days, when Karen reflected that he could've cheated her out of the entire sum—or worse, she could've been killed, arrested, or at least mugged—she decided that she was actually quite lucky. Besides, it wasn't like it was real money. She couldn't keep it, she'd always intended to donate it to some good cause. And if Mallory or Gene asked for any of it, she'd consider them as well. After all, they had come up with the whole screwed-up and convoluted sale to begin with.

24

The next day at school, Karen heard that the rally had been embarrassingly ill attended. Barely anyone besides the SDSers had shown up. Alvin said he was growing disillusioned. "No one stands up to the bullies anymore!" he proclaimed loudly to anyone who would listen.

"It's *our* job to do that," Karen replied, but she knew what he meant. Despite overwhelming injustice and a severely eroded democratic process, apathy was only getting worse.

That afternoon on the way home, she stopped in the dojo and mentioned to Hrag her idea of offering a self-defense class for female students.

"Why can't women take regular karate classes like everyone else? I've never discriminated."

"It's intimidating enough to walk into a strange place," she said. "These coeds are from the suburbs, they won't have the guts to practice these moves with a bunch of ethnic guys staring at them."

"Well excuse me," Hrag responded tiredly.

Karen noticed in the light of day that he seemed more pale and gaunt than usual and asked if he was okay.

"I haven't been sleeping too well. Give me a little more time to think about this class idea."

As the second SDS rally approached, Karen awoke late one morning and turned on the radio just as a panicky newscaster on 1010 WINS radio announced that Martin Luther King Jr. had been gunned down the night before while standing on a motel balcony in Memphis, Tennessee.

"Holy shit!" She went into shock.

Immediately she started to call Mallory, but before she could finish dialing, she hung up. Watching the TV for the next several hours, she saw footage of riots breaking out in the Negro neighborhoods of large cities throughout the country. That night as she walked down Broadway, a nervous tension seemed to run along the streets. When she stopped by the West End Bar, the only talk was about the assassination.

She was available for the SDS rally which was to occur a few days later. But perhaps because she had missed the first, Evelyn said they didn't need help with security.

When she arrived on campus on the day of the rally, she was surprised to see the huge turnout. Most of the student body was gathered, participating in chants, filled with anger and energy. It was as if all the little petitions, marches, be-ins, teach-ins, and one-on-ones with the students at their table had finally culminated in this single event. The students stood mulling about, waiting—it was like watching a pot slowly boiling. It was supposed to be a peaceful rally, but the rage from King's assassination was evident. Students were shouting things like, *"Burn it down!"*

"Go to Low!" Mark Rudd finally rhymed through his handheld bullhorn. Suddenly a flow of hundreds of students started marching across the wide-open campus. Before they could get to Low, however, a scant and unprepared campus security force raced over. They moved quickly, barring all entrances to the stately building.

Hoping to avoid unnecessary violence, and realizing that much of their current support was due to the racially charged gym project, Mark squeezed the trigger of the megaphone and declared, "Let's go to the construction site of the gym in Morningside Park!"

By the time the large, slow-moving body of students wound its way across the campus and down through the streets, it had swelled. They moved down the park paths and surrounded the hurricane fence sheltering the skeletal foundation of what was going to be the new gymnasium. Nearly fifty surly members of the NYPD had mobilized around the spot. When one bold student got too close to the police line, a scuffle ensued and he was quickly thrown to the ground and handcuffed. Sirens were wailing in the distance as more cops moved into the city park. Mark decided at that moment that he didn't want this protest to end with a riot and mass arrests, and that if they returned to Columbia University property they would only have to deal with campus security. So into his bullhorn he announced, "Back to Hamilton Hall!"

Karen moved through the crowd while keeping an eye out for Mallory, but there was no sign of her. She did notice that Mark was speaking to some black students, emphatically pointing across the park.

Five minutes later she came upon her SDS friend Alvin and asked what was up.

"We're having problems with the SAS."

"What problems?"

"Apparently, they feel like we're taking advantage of them."

"How?"

Alvin explained that they felt the Gym Crow controversy was "their issue"—since they were the black students—and yet Mark Rudd was the one giving the orders and taking the lead.

By the time the marchers approached Hamilton Hall, the president of the SAS had sent word to his people that they should break off from SDS and the others in order to establish their independence. Before anything could happen, though, many of the student protestors suddenly broke and ran into Hamilton Hall. It was then that the SAS students chose to occupy the east end of the building. When SDSers tried to join them, they were turned away.

Spotting Gene among the relatively small cadre of black students standing stiffly together, Karen approached him. "What the heck are you guys doing?" she asked.

"You had your chance," he replied, without making eye contact.

"*Our* chance?"

"That's right. Now it's our turn, white woman!"

"Well, in case you can't see beyond your nose, there's thousands of others fighting for this cause, and they're mainly white!"

"Where's Mallory?" he asked, ignoring her point.

"After you decided to blab our little secret, she stopped talking to me."

"Don't put that on me, woman!"

"I'm only wondering what you're doing right now. I mean, we're supposed to work together on this."

"The only reason you people still mention the gym is to attract support for your IDA bullshit," he said, still avoiding her eyes.

"Isn't it possible for people to help each other? Can't we fight for *both* causes?"

"We can stop the gym from being built, but we can't stop the war, and by muddling it up with all this hippie bullshit you're risking something that is really important to our community." With that, he turned and started moving away from her.

"Thanks for destroying the most meaningful friendship of my life!" she yelled angrily, and walked the other way.

When Mark Rudd arrived at Hamilton Hall, he was informed that the black students were not allowing SDS organizers into their part of the building. Karen told him that she had just spoken to Gene and relayed what he had said. Mark thanked her and went to meet with the head of the SAS, Nelson Meeks, with Karen tagging along.

"Hey, brother," Mark said, giving Meeks a hip handshake. Karen noticed how tense the young, bookish black student appeared. "What's the problem here?"

"The problem is that you're using Dr. King's assassination for your own personal agenda," Meeks replied immediately.

"You know full well that we planned this event together, weeks in advance," Mark argued.

"Actually, you and the triple-C came up with it," Meeks said, referring to another leftist organization on campus—the Columbia Citizenship Council.

"What's your point, Nelson?"

"If King wasn't murdered, do you really believe you'd get this huge turnout? You had no right to lead this protest. This is *our* issue."

"Look, if you want to join us," Mark said, "I'll be glad to emphasize that we are doing this together."

"We just want you to leave us alone," chimed in one of Meeks's lieutenants.

Mark made several other efforts to preserve their unified front, but Meeks and his group stiffly walked away. Sighing deeply, Karen followed Mark out of their space without another word.

Since the Kirk administration was hoping to avoid injury to their student body as well as the embarrassment of mass arrests, the school president refused to allow NYPD onto their campus—Kirk seemed to be banking on students eventually growing tired and heading home. Even campus security was instructed to stand down. Realizing this, and seeing that the large swarm of students still supported him, Mark decided that the Low Library—the building with the president's office—was actually a much more powerful symbol for student occupation. Fearing that there were undercover cops maxing among the protestors, he informed only the most trusted SDSers running the show that they were to tell the group to move in exactly one hour's time: an invasion of the Low Library was set for nine p.m. sharp.

It was closer to nine fifteen when Mark and the SDS suddenly shepherded hundreds of students across the manicured walkway and up the courtly stone steps of Low Library, where the doors were still propped open. Karen, who was with a second contingent of students, raced downstairs through the tunnel passage into the basement of the building. The few campus security guards who were on duty upstairs tried to quickly shut the doors to the administrative offices, but they were overwhelmed as students just kept flooding in.

Because she had not attended any meetings in the past two months and had missed the last rally, Karen was not a part of the organizing committee, let alone the defense committee that immediately started barricading the doors. She was impressed as they taped the windows in the event that tear gas canisters were launched. Another well-organized band of students seized a large classroom where they began frantically writing, drawing, and typing posters—an impromptu propaganda committee. Within five minutes they had commandeered several mimeograph machines from various offices and were spinning out fresh leaflets.

"Anyone need any help?" Karen called out. No one even had the time to look up.

In one of the hallways, several SDSers with paintbrushes and sheets were drawing up a list of demands to be draped from the building's tall windows. Another crew of students was feverishly writing slogans on large strips of cardboard. One said, GYM CROW HAS GOTTA GO! Another read, IDA RATHER NOT BE DEAD!

Boxes of food and large cans of fruit drinks were being carried in from Amsterdam Avenue by members of the sustenance committee and stored in a room that was designated as a pantry. When Karen went inside, she found Oliver and a second student guarding the food.

"I can't let anyone inside," Oliver told her timidly.

She said that was fine. "I'm impressed by how elaborate the plans are," she said.

"We had no idea it was going to turn into all this," he revealed, "but once it started happening, everyone's duties were quickly expanded."

"I can almost understand why the SAS is angry. I mean, King's assassination couldn't be better timed."

"Yeah, but they weren't the only organization we included in this. We also got the CCC and a couple other groups involved."

Karen offered to help, but he declined. So over the next several hours she became a self-appointed rover, going from group to group asking if anyone needed anything. Mainly she tried not to get underfoot. She overheard from one SDSer talking to another on a walkie-talkie that mobs of students had taken over a number of other buildings, including the architecture school. When she tried to leave the library to visit the other occupied buildings, she discovered that students had piled up furniture in front of all the doors—entering and exiting was no longer an option.

She bumped into Oliver in the middle of the night and mentioned that she'd heard some of these occupied buildings didn't even have SDS members inside. "Aren't things getting a little out of control?" she asked.

"I personally think things got out of control when students starting literally taking craps in the dean's filing cabinet," he replied, chuckling.

Gradually, as the occupation calmed down, the strange euphoria gave way to nervous excitement. People started stationing themselves by the tall windows, looking and waiting for an imminent invasion.

By ten a.m. the following morning, other than the fact that the phone service had been turned off, there were still no signs of an assault.

* * *

The next night a relaxed, almost festive atmosphere began to set in. Thankfully, the electricity kept working, along with the bathrooms. One student managed to breach the police lines and brought back his portable record player. He started playing 45s in the lobby, which was the site of what seemed to be an ongoing party.

Limber students climbed onto the broad stone window ledge that ran around the first floor of the building, which was only about ten feet above the manicured lawn below. These sexy rebels sat perched like a colorful row of pigeons along the limestone sill. This quickly became the hippest spot in the school: from there all could see and be seen.

By the third day, most of the students were getting hungry and a few were definitely going stir-crazy. They took turns climbing over the sills to enter and exit. The group of SDSers who were manning the phones off campus put out a call for donated food to sustain the protest.

Throughout day four, more supporters were stopping by, tossing up cans of food to those lining the ledge.

Rumor spread that although the NYPD had originally wanted to move in immediately, the school president feared the bad press—he was intent on just waiting the students out.

Attracted by the party-like atmosphere, adventurous students kept breaching the porous police barricade that surrounded the campus, weaving through tunnels and over gates to join the carnivalesque occupation. By the end of day five, some of the faculty stopped avoiding the occupation. The younger, more agile professors climbed up ladders and over the sills with their valises in hand to drop by their offices and pick up papers. Karen spotted them catching up on paperwork, clowning around with some of the students, and asking repeatedly if the occupiers could please be respectful of their private property, before dashing back out.

Although most enjoyed the general anarchy, Mark and the others in the leadership began to grow irate by the casualness of it all—the university simply wasn't taking them seriously.

"Some of this is our fault," Oliver pointed out. "The general levity is undermining the severity of the situation."

"Most of them are here for the party," Alvin said. "We're the only ones who are truly committed to the cause."

Toward the end of the first week of the student takeover, Karen realized that she barely recognized most of the occupiers.

"Some of them are from General Studies, but a lot are just freeloaders," Mark muttered to her.

The latest wave of occupiers were disheveled, unshaven, and smelly, looking like they had just wandered in off the street. The bigger fear was that there were undercover police officers among them.

After a quick conference, several rules were agreed upon: all but four windows to the Low Library were to be locked shut. Though students could keep sitting out there, each window/entrance had to be monitored around the clock by at least one security committee member. These SDS members had the right to expel and deny entrance to anyone who wasn't able to find someone inside who could vouch for them.

Karen, who knew all the key members of SDS, was able to move freely from building to building. She had gradually insinuated herself in the occupation, becoming a messenger and facilitator between buildings. Each morning as she'd make her rounds throughout the campus, she'd discreetly keep an eye out for her former best friend.

She knew this was exactly the sort of event Mallory had spent her whole life waiting for—the political purpose, the constant threat of arrest, the romantic atmosphere of revolution—so how could she be missing all this? They would be having so much fun together. Karen began to keep a list of little things she'd say when she finally ran into Mallory. At one point, peering into Hamilton Hall, she caught sight of Gene wearing strange African robes and hated him for destroying her most meaningful friendship.

25

One SDS organizer, David Shapiro, eventually gained access to the school president's office. Karen walked in on him sitting in Grayson L. Kirk's swivel chair, smoking a thick, smelly cigar. Someone with a camera came in and snapped a photograph.

"Hold on!" Shapiro said, and asked Kim Withers, another SDSer, if he could borrow her customary dark beret so he would resemble Che Guevara.

"Shit, I left it at home!" Kim pulled out a pair of sunglasses instead.

Just after the photo was snapped, someone cheerfully announced that he had just found a stash of dirty magazines in one of the president's filing cabinets.

Another SDS student and feminist, Andrea Egan, decided to make theatrical use of the entire happening. Dressing up as a Native American princess, she and her boyfriend got married right in the lobby of the building. After the wedding, Karen looked out a window and saw a professor across campus conducting his class on a patch of overlooked lawn. A dozen of his students sat around him, calmly ignoring all the crazy shenanigans.

One student informed Mark Rudd that Acting Dean Henry S. Coleman had just climbed through a window and entered his office, closing the door behind him.

"Coleman? You're kidding!" exclaimed Dexter Brot, a sophomore who was the head of the sleeping accommodations committee.

"We've got to grab the motherfucker!" Mark Rudd said, hoping to inflate the drama.

"If we touch him, we're likely to be arrested on criminal charges," Dexter said. "Then they can call the police and shut this all down."

"So let's just barricade his door so he can't leave," Ted Gold suggested.

Mark agreed that this was a perfect idea, and within minutes everyone had gathered outside Coleman's office. Like an army of ants, they quietly lifted filing cabinets, moved sofas, and piled desks and chairs, arranging them so they were propped up across the hallway and against the opposing banister, securing the door from being pushed open. Karen used the time to ask people if anyone knew the whereabouts of Mallory Levine.

"You really should just give it a rest and maybe she'll actually forgive you," Edith Pilsen blurted out. That was when Karen realized that everyone knew all about what had happened. When she pushed Edith further, the young woman said they had all heard how Mallory had come home one night and discovered Karen in bed with her boyfriend.

"That's not what happened!"

"What *did* happen?"

Karen shook her head, too furious to go into it, and besides, the truth wasn't that far off.

Minutes later brought the frantic sound of a doorknob rattling, followed by straining, groaning sounds: Coleman was trying to exit. He hadn't realized that he'd been locked in. It took him a full hour of shoving before the administrator got the door open just enough to slide his lanky arm through and start pulling the furniture away. Soon he was able to completely slide out.

Although Kirk refused to communicate with the students, members of the media who periodically interviewed organizers of the takeover seemed to negotiate on his behalf.

"If the school is willing to sacrifice the gym, would you be willing to relinquish your IDA demand?" was a question asked by more than one reporter.

"Never—both must go!" Mark adamantly replied.

With time, though, as the takeover wore on, the SDS began to lose support. News stories started appearing with quotes from students who resented that they were being robbed of their costly education.

Through some of the younger SDS members, Karen learned that the black student organizers in Hamilton Hall were being regularly visited by Negro activists, not just from Harlem but from various other communities throughout the city. Reporters slowly began to shift the focus to Hamilton.

After the first full week of occupation, Karen slipped out of a window one morning and walked the few blocks home, where she found her roommate Dannette studying with a television blaring in the background.

"Aren't you supposed to be at the student strike?" Dannette asked, without looking away from either her botany book or the TV.

"I'm just freshening up, then I'm going right back," Karen said. "How 'bout you?"

"I guess I support the strike, but I'm dating a Republican and I don't want this to affect our relationship."

Karen showered, changed her clothes, shoved three pairs of underwear in her pocket, and left without saying goodbye. She was able to easily slip back around the tightening police lines and return to the library.

It wasn't until the eighth day of the strike that the occupiers encountered their first real resistance. Instead of the NYPD or campus security, it was a group of the school jocks, headed by several members of the Columbia Lions football team. They had gotten together and decided enough was enough. As the captain of the team phrased it: "The street is for protest, our school is for learning."

Informed that they could be suspended or expelled if they harmed any of the protestors, the athletes devised their own little blockade. When they saw sympathizers carrying bags of food to donate, they'd climb up onto each other's burly shoulders and, using large round trays, make a game of trying to block the supplies from reaching the destination. The SDSers responded by simply telling the donors other locations where they could leave the food unmolested, so it would be forwarded to them later.

It was on the eighth night, in the small hours, that they all felt it—a growing buzz in the background, like an electrical charge in the air. One freshman had just managed to sneak back in through the increasingly tight grip that the police had on the area. He confirmed everyone's worst fears: several city buses filled with helmeted cops sporting huge wooden clubs were lined up outside the law school. They were assembling on Amsterdam and down on Broadway. About an hour later, another student who had sneaked over from the architecture building warned that from the roof they could see that all the traffic on Broadway was being diverted.

As word spread of the impending invasion, the dilettantes and sightseers who had hung out just for kicks discreetly started evacuating.

At precisely five in the morning, the regimented sound of shuffling feet on pavement could be heard all around campus. Moments later, a bullhorn crackled outside: "*This is Commander Keith Hassen of the New York Police Department. You are trespassing on school property. Vacate the premises immediately, or you will be placed under arrest.*" The announcement was repeated once, then came silence.

"This is fucking *it!*" someone yelled out.

The cacophony of battering rams busting in doors was accompanied by the shattering of glass and splintering of furniture. To Karen it sounded like the destruction of a dream. Students retreated to the sounds of more orders crackling through bullhorns. Then the cops came rushing in after them. Some students lobbed rotten fruit and vegetables at the invaders, but Karen joined the majority who instinctively rushed up the stairs and over the furniture that had been strategically placed as obstacles.

When she heard the thudding of shoes behind her, she and all the others continued to climb all the way to the top flight, where they waited to be arrested. Soon, with no cops in sight, a symphony of cries and screams echoed from below. From the banister Karen could make out the second landing. One fat policeman was pressing his nightstick over poor Alvin's neck, throttling him and then throwing him to the stone floor, where he kicked the kid twice in the ribs before cuffing him. More students were scuffling, rushing up and down the steps, with cops in hot pursuit.

Karen turned and very nearly slipped, just catching the banister. Then she remembered that the center of the stairs had been soaped down as a defense tactic and they had been instructed to walk along the outer edges. Two coeds sprinted by her. Before she could get up three steps, she slipped backward, falling directly upon a cop nearly twice her size. After steadying himself, the officer reached around and grabbed her throat. Without thinking, she yanked his arm, pulling him forward into the stone wall.

He grabbed her collar as he went down, slamming her forehead on the heavy wooden banister. As if it were a water balloon, her head split open and blood burst out . . .

Warm blood was gushing freely from her head, and it just kept pouring. More blood than she thought she had, more blood than her entire body could hold . . .

It took a second of gasping and tasting for her to realize it wasn't blood, but dark-brown water. Her limbs were taped to her sides and her body was ensnared in some kind of network of ropes—a giant net designed to catch the human flotsam that flushed down the drain. She was underwater, but for some reason she wasn't breathing. She had no gag reflex, and she couldn't budge. But before she could peacefully drown, she felt the giant net being hauled up against the current into a painful, narrow hole of light. A pair of hands pulled her up into the air. In a moment she was whacked on the back. She coughed and began gasping for breath, struggling with her bonds. Someone freed her from the giant net and dropped it back down into the hole.

Karen now remembered that she had been taped up and dropped down through a chute in the sewage of Staten Island, where she had lost consciousness—or rather, had been overcome by a steady stream of memories—until now. Barely alive, dripping wet, achy, breathing slowly, she took in this strange dark world that was filled with grunts and groans and smelled like shit.

"Got another," she heard someone utter as he clipped the masking tape that bound her arms and legs.

It all flooded back. Instead of being in her early twenties, living in Harlem in 1968, she was in Rescue City, Nevada, and it was now almost 1981. And worse still, she had been utterly betrayed by two of the men she trusted most.

Sprawled on the floor of a giant subterranean cathedral like some amphibious being, Karen listened as the low moans of countless people echoed in the fetid darkness. She glimpsed a flickering line of what seemed to be elevated candles dividing the large empty space. It looked the size of the main concourse of Grand Central Terminal. At least the place wasn't cold.

As she listened to the moans that seemed to be loosely synchronized into some kind of desiccated prayer, Karen narrowed her eyes and stared harder. In the low, flickering lights, she could see rows of gaunt faces, balding, with jutting cheekbones and narrow noses— emaciated gargoyles each perched over their own lost precipice.

Utterly exhausted, she curled into a moist ball. Not realizing that a virus had already infected her brain and was steadily eating away at her moorings to the present, she let herself rise like a balloon back into her vivid memories from a decade earlier.

26

"You better not have any weapons," she heard.

The giant cop, who had just grabbed her on the stairway at Columbia University during the end of the student occupation, ignored her bloody wound. He pulled her wrists behind her back and cuffed her. When she lifted herself up, a stinging sensation along her head and face was followed by a thick trickle of sweat.

Before she could even think, he patted his hands up under her shirt and sweater and started grabbing her breasts.

"Cocksucker!" She kicked at him, compelling him to shove her face forward against the wall.

"I gotta make sure you're not armed, sweetheart."

"Leave her alone, you nazi motherfucker!" another student yelled. He had also just been cuffed and was being led past them. It was only at that moment, when she looked at the stone wall, that she saw it was splattered with her blood.

The cop led her down two flights of stairs and handed her off to another man, who put her in a line of students slowly streaming down the central staircase, the floor of which had not been soaped up.

"Christ, are you okay?" asked Evelyn, who was also cuffed.

Karen tiredly nodded yes. She hadn't gotten much food or sleep in the past week, and was secretly grateful that the siege had finally been brought to an end.

They could hear shouts, cries, and curses reverberating from upstairs, along with the sounds of glass and wood breaking—the battle was still raging. More cops were rushing into the building.

"Where's Mark?" someone whispered.

"What about Judah?"

"Did anyone see Sam?"

Questions were flying; wounds were immediate badges of honor. All the students who noticed Karen and her bloodied forehead seemed impressed; a few asked if she was okay. Since her system was still pumping adrenaline, she didn't feel much pain. One coed loudly announced that they were legally entitled to immediate medical attention. A police sergeant replied that no one was getting any medical attention until the emergency cases were treated first.

Before anyone could ask what he meant, two paramedics raced up the steps with a stretcher—someone had been injured so badly they'd have to be carried out, and all wondered who it could be.

So many students had been rounded up that the morning sun had risen high in the sky before Karen was finally led over to Amsterdam Avenue where city buses doubling as paddy wagons were queued up. A large crowd of spectators, most of whom were nonparticipating students, was gawking at the cuffed protestors from across the street. As Karen walked out stiffly, she finally spotted her, walking past in another line, also being arrested.

"Mal!" Karen shouted without thinking.

Mallory, who looked utterly unscathed, glanced around, but before she could make eye contact, Karen was shoved up into a waiting bus.

"Shit!" Karen yelled. She knew beyond a shadow of a doubt that she would never look more heroic or sympathetic than at that moment, covered in blood.

Soon they were all being ushered down to Central Booking, where she was put in a crowded cell with a bunch of other coeds whom she had just spent the week with. She was fingerprinted and booked, then waited several more hours until she and several other injured women were recuffed and led into a small school bus. Most of the students on the bus were exhausted and in pain as they were shuttled over to St. Vincent's Hospital. There, after a twenty-minute wait, an older nurse cleaned Karen's crusty wound. She was given three tight stitches.

"You're lucky," the nurse said as she bandaged her up, "your scar runs right along your eyebrow, so no one'll see it."

She was cuffed again and had to wait another hour before being driven a few blocks away to the Women's House of Detention on Greenwich and Sixth Avenue. There, with the other Barnard girls, she was held overnight. Her shirt and bra were laced with blood and grime and ruined. She searched carefully and even called out Mallory's name through the bars, hoping she might be in an adjacent cell—nothing.

By the next morning, the national SDS office had finally secured legal counsel and the two hundred or so arrested students were all fined and released on either their own or their parents' recognizance.

Karen exited with a pair of floral Barnard coeds whom she had met in lockup but never knew on campus. While they walked to the subway at West 14th Street, she learned that they were only slumming for adventure, and had overstayed their visit. Now they couldn't stop giggling about their arrests. *It'll be their one war story for decades to come at countless suburban barbecues and drunken pool parties*, thought Karen. She took a seat and closed her eyes. They hadn't given her more than a topical painkiller at the hospital and her swollen forehead was finally starting to sting.

Once home, she took some aspirin. Despite her bloodied clothes and bandaged head, Dannette was too absorbed in a phone call with her boyfriend to give more than a cringing expression and a sympathetic smile. Karen went right to bed and slept until the phone woke her up late that night.

"How are you?" she heard a gruff male voice ask. It was Hrag calling from downstairs. She had told him a week earlier that she was going to be a part of the student strike. He must've seen her come home.

"I didn't mind being incarcerated, but I didn't expect to get injured," she said, and explained what had happened.

"Maybe you should—"

"I already went to the hospital, it's just a small cut on my forehead."

"Christ! You didn't throw the cop, did you?"

"I was about to," she said.

"You should've knocked the bastard on his ass." Hrag could hear how exhausted she was and told her to go back to sleep.

Karen closed her eyes and dozed for several more hours until Dannette came into her room and told her that someone was ringing their bell downstairs.

"I got it," Karen said, hoping that maybe Mallory was stopping by to see how she was doing. She buzzed the person in and opened the door, peering down the stairs until she saw Hrag, bringing her a bag of food: two sandwiches, corned beef and roast beef, both on rye, and chicken noodle soup.

"That's very kind of you, but . . ."

"I actually brought the second sandwich for me," he said, strolling into the dining room.

"You're so sweet," she said, still groggy.

He sat at the dining room table and took the sandwiches out of the bag. She was famished and ate quickly. Hrag only took a few bites of his roast beef.

"So, how are *you* doing?" she asked. He looked tired as well.

"Not great, but I feel a whole lot better seeing you're in one piece."

While inspecting the stitches on her forehead, he told her he had watched the siege on the news nonstop and was worried about her. She said it had been fun until it wasn't. Since he was there anyway, she asked him to replace her bandage.

"This'll probably put your coed self-defense classes on hold," he mused.

"Actually, after what I went through, I want to do it now more than ever."

He could see she still needed more rest, so he left the remainder of his sandwich for her and excused himself to go teach a morning class in the dojo.

Over the next few days, Karen stayed around the apartment and took it easy. She used the time to catch up on things, including her applications for law school and summer internships that would be helpful for her résumé. Toward the end of the week, as her scar healed, she resumed karate practice. Hrag green-lighted her self-defense class, so she sketched an image of a woman in a karate stance and began making flyers. She was able to place free ads in the student newspaper announcing that she was teaching a free self-defense course for women. She told nearly every student she passed on campus about it.

The morning of the first class, Karen swept and mopped the dojo, and even purchased flowers. She was discouraged when only two women showed up that evening. A third student showed up the following week, but she was from City College. On the third week, a pair of morbidly obese women came, and their sheer size turned the class into little more than basic stretching exercises. On the fourth week, when no one came, Hrag could see how discouraged Karen was. He told her that if she wanted to cancel, she could roll over any interested women into the usual karate classes free of charge. She took him up on it.

"You know, I have a lot of work around here, if you ever want a more regular job," he said.

She told him she'd think about it.

27

I n the wake of the siege, despite costly property damage and lost revenue, a number of concessions were made by the school. Grayson Kirk agreed not to expel the students who were already on academic probation, provided there were no further incidents until graduation. Despite her heroic status at SDS due to her head wound, Karen chose to stay away from meetings. She desperately wanted to get into Columbia Law School and knew she was on thin ice.

A month later when Karen was headed to Columbia's cap-and-gown graduation ceremony, she spotted Mallory on Broadway near 116th Street. She was holding a sign, picketing the graduation with the others, protesting Kirk and the IDA. Karen walked by her without saying a word, though she was fairly certain Mallory had seen her.

"Give her here," she heard some female voice, followed by a firm pair of hands grasping the back of her shoulders and dragging her through the stinky darkness. They released her on a moist cardboard mat and she looked around. It was as though she were in the bottom of a large, flat movie theater without seats or a screen, where the walls slowly arched upward. Closing her eyes, she was mercifully pulled away from this dark, foul existence and drawn back into the fertile reverie of re-life . . .

In early June of 1968, Karen got a phone call from Alice Bellows. She had been the supervisor in charge of volunteers for the Dump Johnson campaign.

"How are you doing, Alice?"

"Good, how are you?"

"Fine. I can hardly believe Johnson pulled himself out of the running," Karen said.

"So, Al has just declared his candidacy for Congress, and we're looking for a few hardworking people. We were all impressed by you when you were here. We were wondering if you'd come back."

"That's kind of you," Karen said. "Unfortunately, I'm a little overwhelmed right now. And broke."

"Well, this job pays." Alice was now in charge of putting together Allard Lowenstein's New York campaign staff. He was actually campaigning out in Long Island, but wanted a skeletal staff in Rockefeller Center to focus on fundraising. Alice said she was also hoping to get at least a dozen volunteers, but she offered Karen one of the three modestly paying posts.

Karen asked if she could have the night to think about it—it would involve long clerical hours with little glory and not much financial compensation. With law school on the horizon and no political aspirations, she was really hoping to get an internship in the DA's office.

"I can't guarantee anything because I have other people to call and not much time," Alice said, "but let me know when you've made up your mind."

Karen was leaning toward no. Lately Hrag had been looking drawn and gray; he lacked his usual stamina. It was clear that the years of running the dojo while slowly fixing and renting out the apartments upstairs were taking a toll on him. And he was the only person who seemed worried about her during the student protest and arrest. She thought that with the extra time she had while not studying, she could help him out, share some of the load.

The very next day, though, while picking up a can of black beans at her corner bodega, she heard over the radio that Bobby Kennedy had just been shot in Los Angeles. She put the can down and staggered home, immediately turning on the radio to find that Kennedy had passed away. Everyone she knew had felt that he was the best chance the nation had of ending the mess in Vietnam. The idea that a second Kennedy brother had been killed was incomprehensible. After a night of weeping and feeling miserable, the thought of stuffing envelopes for the Lowenstein campaign suddenly seemed pressing. First thing the next morning, she called Alice Bellows back and accepted her offer.

That summer she divided her time between her work at the Lowenstein campaign headquarters and management and instruction at the dojo.

One sweltering day in mid-July, Karen saw Mallory walking across Broadway with a small band of wild-haired students. She looked as pretty as ever. The group included the more radical members of Columbia's SDS chapter—J.J., Mark Rudd, Oliver, and a couple others.

Karen tagged behind them for about a block, trying to keep out of view, but Mallory suddenly turned and started walking straight toward her.

"There's that fucking bitch!"

Something was coming toward her in the darkness.

"Wait a sec . . ." Karen began.

"You're mine, bitch." She felt a kick in her ribs. She wasn't in New York, she was in the bowels of the Nevada desert. Someone kicked her again, but she stiffly rejected this reality, fearing that by opening her eyes and losing sight of Mallory, she'd never see her again.

"Leave lil' sista alone!" yelled some older woman.

"Shut the fuck up!" the guy yelled back, and grabbed Karen by her hair. He pulled her off her wet piece of cardboard, past the countless stinking human cabbages who filled the smelly patch.

"Mallory!" she called out as he dragged her slowly across the filth-strewn ground. She was burned by hot wax from flickering candle nubs that lined the way, and bumped into several of the feverish automatons, who seemed no longer aware that they were even alive. Only when she reluctantly admitted to herself that both Mallory and Old Town were gone did Karen reach up between her attacker's legs and claw into his testicles with all her might.

"OOOOOH!"

The young man fell to his knees, screaming in agony. Now fully invested in this moment, Karen jumped up and punched him in his Adam's apple, knocking him backward. When he hit the ground gagging, she jumped on his back. He was a slight, bald freak who looked oddly familiar. She hooked her elbow around his thin neck and yanked his head back.

"HELP!" the little shit whined in a high-pitched voice.

She sat back, grabbing his head firmly in her hand, and took a deep breath. Realizing how small he was, she was preparing to snap his neck when she heard: "Kill him and justice will be just as swift upon you—*that* I guarantee!"

A tall, bearded guy who was clearly blind approached, accompanied by a small posse who immediately swarmed her.

"This fucker tried to kill me!" she shouted, and released him. He fell forward, gasping for air. It was then that she realized he was one of her criminals. She had arrested him recently, but couldn't remember how or where.

"An injustice was done unto you?" said one of the posse.

"Yeah."

"We'll take it from here, sister," the blind man said. The group of four guys, who seemed to be the weird beard's deputies, helped the man to his feet but didn't let go of him.

"What are you going to do to him?" she asked as an intense headache seized her.

"Banishment: he goes into the Mkultra." The only direction Karen could see out of the large chamber was a path up a steep incline into a dark crack in the wall.

"I'm not going in there!" the young man yelled, pushing back against those restraining him.

The blind man struck him once squarely on the back of the skull, which caused him to stop struggling. "Either you go into the Mkultra or back down into the sewer. Your choice, rat."

The small guy stopped fighting and the group of men pushed him up the incline and into the hole in the wall.

"If he attacks me again," Karen declared, "I'll kill him." She scuttled back to her former spot on the ground and almost immediately started to fall asleep.

"HEY!" she heard Weird Beard shout. "You hungry?"

"Sure."

"Give her some chow."

A dented cup was thrust into her hand, but she had already started nodding off.

"HEY!" she heard again. "Down it before you drop it!"

"What?"

"Open wide!"

She did as told and felt something being scooped into her mouth that tasted like wallpaper paste. She almost spat it out. "What the . . ."

"It's wet rations, all we got."

She let the paste slide down her gullet and gulped until it was gone. Opening her eyes, she could barely make out faces in the dim light. Among them, she spotted someone wearing a New York Jets football helmet.

"Uli!" she cried out, then got to her feet and staggered toward the guy. She remembered squeezing Tim Leary's helmet onto her brother's head. When she got closer, she realized it wasn't him at all. "Where'd you get that?" she asked the guy. She could now see that he was just staring off drooling, so she simply sat back down and in another moment was staring off herself.

* * *

Due to her involvement with the student protests, she feared she would have to go to the NYU School of Law, which was her second choice. It was therefore a complete surprise when she learned that she had been accepted into Columbia Law; ironically, this was largely due to the strike itself. Apparently, the bad publicity had caused a slump in that fall's student enrollment, so they took her despite the SDS demerits listed on her transcripts.

Toward the end of July, she bumped into Alvin near campus. He informed her that Mallory's beloved aunt Estelle had passed away during the recent heat wave.

Poor Mallory must be devastated, Karen thought. *Estelle was her only family.* She learned from Evelyn that Mallory had moved with a group of other radicals into a huge railroad flat on 120th Street. Karen got a bouquet of expensive tulips and a Hallmark condolence card and went to the apartment. She stood in the lobby but lost her nerve before ringing the doorbell. She left the tulips at the apartment door, but decided to mail the note. It took two days for her to write: *Dear Mallory, I just heard that your aunt Estelle passed away and wanted to let you know how sorry I am. Your old roommate, K.* She included her phone number and address on the bottom, in the off chance that her old friend decided to contact her.

Another two days passed before Dannette gave her a message she had taken when Karen was in class. "Mallory thanks you for the kind note and she'll call you when she gets back."

"Gets back from where?"

"She said she's going to Chicago to get ready for the Democratic National Convention."

. . . Why does the great weight of social consciousness always press so heavily upon me? Karen wondered before awakening to the now-er now and realizing that someone was kneeling on her chest.

"What the fuck are you doing here!"

She was barely able to speak—it was him again. She had reawakened the alternative universe, the darker, older world beneath the surface.

"Get off of her!" screamed the old woman who seemed to have adopted her.

"Fuck off!" he yelled back. "She got me stuck down here. Now I'm getting even!"

Karen tried pulling herself into wakefulness, but it felt like syrup was oozing through her veins, keeping her dopey and drunk.

The only thing that prevented her from lapsing back into memory were the hyperkinetic sensations running through her. It felt as if a bony pair of rats were desperately gnawing through her still-damp shirt and pants, burrowing into her crotch and under her shirt. With her eyes still shut, she felt herself being flopped over onto her stomach. She realized the skinny criminal was going through her pants.

"I'm not turning into one of these zombies. I know you got it! If you came in after me, you musta brought it with you. Now where the fuck is it?!"

Her rabid instinct to fight had been rendered into a vague afterthought.

I can't stop these memories of Old Town, and I sure as hell ain't gonna die in this stinking shit pile! she thought, only to realize that she didn't think it. Rather, *he* had said it.

Suddenly he withdrew into silence. Slowly, like a miniature climber pulling herself up the ridge of her body by clinging onto her clothes, she worked one hand up onto her own face and flicked open the fleshy veil of her eyelid just in time to see the bald prick shooting croak into his skanky little arm. *Wait a sec, that's not croak.*

No sooner did the cocksucker drop the empty syringe than she remembered that Schuman had taped two needles to her leg. She remembered him instructing her that once she arrived down under, she had to inject herself.

As Karen watched him shove the second needle into his arm and press down on the plunger, she mustered all her strength and kicked him in the face, sending his head slamming backward into some kind of large, gurgling tank. When he fell to the ground she tried rising to her feet, but a profound vertigo sent her whirling right back down.

He appeared to be out cold. She rolled back on top of his limp body, grabbed one of the empty syringes, and searched for his jugular with the needle, intent on slicing it before he could awaken. Unable to see very much, she used her middle finger to feel for his pulse, but before she could locate it, she passed out again.

Awakening a moment later, she couldn't find the syringe, and knew she desperately needed a weapon. She no longer had the strength or endurance to break his neck or suffocate him. The little prick was sure to kill her.

She scurried sideways, feeling around like a crab on the slimy floor of the large subterranean chamber. Crawling along the crust of human filth, candle wax, and rags, she felt for stones or anything hard.

Slowly she approached the sound of the primitive chants, which were presumably prayers for salvation. Someone had nurtured a small bonfire, allowing her to see the god-face altar that they seemed to be aiming their prayers at. Up behind them were giant sluice gates that had been sealed in cement—a passage that had long since been blocked. Unable to keep her eyes open much longer, she glimpsed an elderly white-haired lady waving her down.

"Elise, is that you?" the woman asked.

"Yeah," Karen replied, utterly fatigued and forgetting why she had crawled there in the first place. "And I'm sick."

"I'll take care of you, Eli," the woman said, patting the large frayed square of filthy cardboard she was sitting on. "Come right over here."

Karen slid onto the damp rectangle that seemed to serve as the old woman's living quarters. "You don't have any water, do you? I'm so thirsty."

The woman gave her a pot filled with tepid, brownish liquid. Holding her nose to keep from smelling it, Karen gulped it down to moisten her cotton-dry mouth and throat. In another moment, she vaguely recalled that she was supposed to kill someone, but who or why . . . she had no clue. As the elderly woman used a long, bony finger to stroke her oily hair, Karen felt her eyeballs rolling back in her skull and once again drowsed into her memories.

She distinctly remembered the single in-depth conversation she'd had with candidate Allard Lowenstein, shortly after Robert Kennedy's assassination, when she was stuck in a traffic jam alone with him on the Long Island Expressway. This was just after she had picked him up from JFK Airport. He mentioned that he had personally appealed to the former attorney general to run against Johnson, but Bobby had adamantly refused. She commented that it was odd that he would be killed by a Palestinian due to his support for Israel since there wasn't a single presidential candidate who didn't support Israel. The only thing that Sirhan Sirhan achieved by killing Bobby Kennedy was lengthening the war in Vietnam.

"All we can ever judge are the final results," Lowenstein replied without elaborating.

Toward the end of the summer of '68, all of Karen's energy was focused on law school, which she had heard involved endless reading and nonstop memorization. Still, the Columbia campus was abuzz with the upcoming Chicago convention. Hubert Humphrey, LBJ's vice president, was now heir apparent to the Democratic nomination. But Humphrey had been reluctant to come out against the war. And though the Republicans, with Nixon in the forefront, were also promising peace, they kept talking about *honor* and *containing the communist threat*—code words for fighting on. In March, Eugene McCarthy had had a good showing in the New Hampshire primaries. Karen remembered Mallory saying that she liked him for one reason alone: McCarthy had actually taken a meeting with Mallory's heartthrob, Che Guevara, back in 1964 when the revolutionary was in New York.

When Bobby had finally announced his candidacy, along with his commitment to ending the war in Vietnam, hope had risen among the SDSers that this could be their candidate, and their year.

With Kennedy's assassination in California, hope started unraveling. Suddenly McCarthy seemed insubstantial, and Humphrey, perhaps afraid to piss off his boss, still refused to come out against the war. Meanwhile, all the Republicans were tightly lining up behind Nixon, even as public opinion was turning against the war.

But Karen felt that all wasn't entirely lost. If the Democrats got their act together at the Chicago convention, they could turn things around.

Inasmuch as young leftists still felt some hope in shaping the Democratic platform, the vast army of the disenfranchised—including the Yippies, SNCC, and the SDS—all announced their intention to march for peace outside the convention hall. Without compromise, Chicago's Mayor Daley refused to grant a single event permit, under the ridiculous claim that protests were a security threat. In the wake of the RFK murder, he said all other contenders for the Democratic nomination had been given death threats, so he was essentially declaring martial law in the city. Notwithstanding this, the Columbia chapter of the SDS had rented two buses. Though Alvin invited Karen personally, she told him that she would not officially return to the SDS until she had reconciled with Mallory.

"You know, this convention trip would be a great place for you two to get together. A lot of time to talk," Edith Pilsen said, adding that she would be happy to act as a go-between.

"Mal left me a message that she'd call me when she got back from Chicago, and that works for me," Karen answered. She was working at the dojo and with the Lowenstein campaign, so she couldn't really spare two weeks to protest in Chicago anyway.

A few days later, while Karen was stuffing envelopes at campaign headquarters, someone had the radio on and she heard news reports about the police riots breaking out in the Windy City. When she got home that night, she watched the TV in disbelief as thousands of young protestors were savagely beaten by Daley's uniformed thugs. Even though most of the protestors were kids, the son of a bitch had the audacity to call in the National Guard.

The convention ended as quickly as it had begun. Karen bumped into Henriette the next day; she had heard conflicting reports about who got hurt and who got arrested. Soon Karen was told that the charter bus was on its way back from Chicago. Excited by the hope of reconciling, she wanted to greet Mallory as soon as she stepped off of it, but didn't want to overwhelm her, so she stayed at home and waited.

A week passed, and no call. Then a second week passed, and still no phone call. Nearly three weeks later, Karen ran into Edith, who had a fading black eye and a bandage on her cheek. She gave a brutal account of how cops had just waited for opportunities to attack.

"At one point on the second day, we got separated from the main group and they just came after us with the clubs and mace."

"They hit you?"

1086 🌾 Arthur Nersesian

"No, some of the guys protected me, but I fell down at one point
and that's when someone kicked me in the face."

"Is Mallory okay?"

"No one is okay. I mean, we all got injured and arrested. Some of
the guys were attacked several times. Oliver has three broken ribs!"

"Oh my God! . . . But Mallory said she was going to call me when
she got back."

"She was very bitter about the whole affair. I don't think she wants
to see anyone. First her aunt dies, then she gets clubbed and arrested,
then after forty-eight hours in lockup she goes to another protest and
gets arrested again!"

"She was clubbed?"

"Just bruised. The worst of it was spending half the time there
in the city jail. I mean, you're put in this filthy cell with roaches and
really scuzzy people and nothing to do for hours and—"

"Do you think I should call her?" Karen interrupted.

"I would be very cautious."

"But she left a message saying that she would call me."

"Look," Edith said, "she's safely back in the city, but she needs
to unwind. You want my advice? Step back and let her come to you."

"Could you do me a favor?"

"What?"

"If you see her, can you just tell her I asked about her and I really
want to see her?"

"Sure."

28

About two weeks later, when Edith still hadn't gotten back to her, Karen called and asked if she had spoken to Mallory.

"Actually, I did," Edith replied. "Did you have a . . . talk with her recently?"

"No, why?"

"A bunch of us stopped by her place a few days ago."

"Why didn't you call me?"

"Well, we chitchatted a bit, then I told her that you asked how she was and all."

"And?"

"And she simply said she doesn't want to speak to you . . . ever again."

"Why?!"

"Her exact phrase was that you were a *schizo bitch*. And she wanted you out of her life forever."

"What?!"

"You must've said something to her."

"I haven't spoken to her in over half a year!"

"I'm telling you exactly what she said."

Karen sat horrified on the phone, trying to imagine what might have occurred to compel Mal to say such an awful thing. When Edith asked if she was still on the line, Karen said she appreciated her effort and hung up.

Once law school began, she had to resign from the Lowenstein campaign. It was as though she had vanished into a tunnel: every single moment of every single day she read precedents, case histories, judgments, and opinions that required hours and hours of memorization and interpretation. This was followed by endless writing and arguing the fine points of the law.

She no longer had time for the dojo, and in a way she felt grateful that Mallory didn't call, as she wouldn't have any time for her anyway.

She finally emerged for a moment of daylight on Election Day, Tuesday, November 5, only to learn the painful news late that night that Nixon had beat Hubert Humphrey by less than 1 *goddamned* percent of the vote. The war would go on. A slight ray of light was that Lowenstein had won his congressional seat in Nassau County.

After that Karen returned to nonstop studying, which drained her brain of any excitement and turned her into one of the countless human mushrooms shrouded in the dark cave of Butler Library. Whole days seemed to collapse into mere moments under the constant onslaught of cases and arguments. She didn't even have time to feel lonely. Every so often she glanced hungrily at a *New York Times*, but quickly forced herself *not* to read it.

The next flash of light that occurred was when her mother called to ask if she could please come home for Christmas. It was an unusual request, as she'd thought that by going there for some of her summer break, her brother would be obliged to deal with their parents for the winter.

"We wouldn't normally ask, but for once I'd love to see both my children together."

"We only fight when we're together, you know that," Karen said.

"He's only in town for a single evening, it'll be two hours tops. And he's asking all about you. Despite your political differences, you know he loves you."

Since she desperately wanted to wash law school out of her head, and even her shy roommate Dannette was going home for the holidays, she decided to bite the bullet and agreed to her mother's special request. Her train was delayed due to a big snowstorm, so the trip up to Boston was numbingly exhausting. She found herself sitting in a packed car next to a large man who never stopped clearing his throat.

Her mom picked her up from South Station. Then came the thousand maternal pinpricks of how pale she looked, how thin she looked, and how pretty she could be if she simply fixed her hair, put on some nice clothes, and applied a little makeup. "Just because you're studying to be a lawyer doesn't mean you can stop being a young lady! These really are your flowering years—your skin has a luster! Once you start wilting, good luck ever getting a husband." As a painful afterthought, she also commented on how muscular Karen's body was. What had happened to all her sexy curves?

Karen explained that she did a full regimen of karate exercises several times a week.

"Well, if that's the reason you're so thin, I'd say the first casualty of your karate might be your femininity."

Karen looked at her wristwatch and thought, *Another twenty-three hours before I can tunnel back into the dark sanctuary of solitary studies.*

Over the course of the next day, although Karen found her mother's criticism relentless, she also reluctantly admitted that she'd missed being fussed over and loved. In response, she tried to make it a point of complimenting everything, just short of making it sound like parody: the house looked exceptionally wonderful; the tree had so many silver balls and tiny lights that you could forget it was ever a living thing. She pretended to be grateful about the rich assortment of exotic Armenian dishes that she had no plans to eat, and knew that bite by bite, she'd have to find some way to dispose of her share in the neighbors' garbage can out back, so as to spare her mother's feelings.

Initially, while sinking into the gaudily upholstered sofa, she pondered the lives of her female counterparts in Vietnam—squatting in rice fields or muddy trenches, monitoring the habits of self-righteous Caucasians who indiscriminately killed villagers whom they were ostensibly there to free.

"Whiskey sours, anyone?" her mother called out.

"Sure," Karen said, thus commencing her steady intake of alcohol that would make the awkward conversations and nauseating TV shows bearable. Although she brought a couple of law textbooks, she knew that to open them would be sacrilege. So she wasted her time in front of the loud and colorful wood-paneled box. Her mother was looking forward to a ridiculous Bing Crosby extravaganza that seemed to consist of geriatric Hollywood hacks making trademark comments while winking into the camera. Her father couldn't catch enough Westerns; apparently, Native Americans were put on the continent to either be domesticated or shot.

"Cowboys epitomize the American spirit, don't they?" her dad remarked, along with every other cliché—and he was a liberal.

They were the children of those who had survived centuries of Ottoman domination and prejudice, ending with a brutal genocide, and now they were blithely buying into the whole Madison Avenue lie and celebrating the shameless hypocrisy of Christmas.

Somehow, two thousand years of history had corrupted the memory of a communist revolutionary, before the term was even invented, a spiritual rebel who was violently crucified by his government, and whose birthday, instead of marking a day of liberation, had been transmogrified into a joyous and materialistic occasion.

While her parents were pacified by the TV, Karen looked past it, into the yuletide log, where she found a consoling and mystical solace in the notion that everything would eventually perish. Perhaps it was the alcohol, but she saw the fire as a purging, arbitrarily flaring this way and that, like jazz solos of annihilation. She asked for another whiskey sour. The booze brought her to a time before she learned about and grew enraged by all the social and psychological inequities of the society she'd been born into. Hours passed numbly. Her flimsy bubble of bliss finally burst when her monstrous brother walked through the door.

He was clean-cut, with movie-star good looks, and stood righteously erect. As soon as the heir apparent, Special Agent Uli Sarkisian, entered, the tone of the place shifted radically. Both of her parents raced to hug him at the same time—the living trophy of parental success.

Karen smiled to restrain herself as the Constitution hater came over and gave her a merciful and forgiving hug. Checking his wristwatch, he announced that he was already pressed for time. He had to be on an eleven o'clock flight back to Washington, so they went right to the dinner table. With oven mitts, Dad took the pan holding the eight-pound roasted leg of lamb out of the oven, put it on the counter, and immediately started slicing. When Mom went to the stove to transfer the vegetables into serving bowls, Uli leaned in to Karen and whispered, "I hear you've been busy."

"Law school never sleeps," Karen said, trying to remain invisible.

"Cut the crap," he said.

"What do you mean?"

"You were in that fucking riot."

"Along with hundreds of others. What about it?"

"You're officially listed as a member of the SDS, so aside from whatever injury you sustained, you now have a file with the FBI."

"I'm trembling with fear," she replied sarcastically. She grabbed the blender and refilled her whiskey sour, then walked into the living room, collapsed on the sofa, and downed the drink.

He followed her. "Look, I can't help you if you stay with that crowd."

"How does it feel working for the nazis?" she asked, slamming her glass down on a coaster.

"We defeated them, but we're still fighting the commies," he snapped back. Neither of them spoke above a whisper.

Her parents called them to the table for the meal, and all conversation returned to the absurd pretense of the holiday spirit. Although Karen viewed Uli's remarks as a veiled threat, she decided that she wasn't going to give him the benefit of getting angry and then being accused of ruining the charade of a happy family dinner. And he, always duplicitous if nothing else, didn't say a word about her arrest to their parents. But he clearly held it over her.

After dinner, while their parents asked Uli a million flattering questions regarding his glamorous work with the illustrious bureau, Karen kept chugging down the whiskey sours and watching Huntley and Brinkley give their fascist take on the imperialist war. She tried to ignore Uli's annoyingly cloying, tongue-in-cheek remarks that made their parents giggle. Several times when her father asked about specific cases in the news, he stated, "Sorry, sir, that's classified."

"Come on, tell us about the great J. Edgar," their father said at one point.

"Nice chap, nothing like you'd expect."

Karen remained patiently silent, just pretending to listen, until Uli casually let slip that that he had gone to Vietnam last year on a business trip. "Any involvement outside domestic matters is strictly illegal," she spoke up from across the room.

"Calm down, sweetie," her mother said.

"Speaking of which, congrats on law school, sis," Uli joked, trying to gloss over the tension. Another awkward moment replaced the first one. Through a quick exchange of subtle gestures, their parents deduced that Karen was acting up because they were neglecting her. Very quickly, her mother and father overcompensated, taking turns offering infantile remarks about how pretty and smart she was, making her feel all the more ridiculous.

"Well, why don't we start on dessert," said Mom.

A large tray of baklava was served, along with coffee and tea. No time for any smooth segue, Uli looked at his watch and announced that he had to run. Collecting his few things as well as two small Christmas gifts purchased for their portability, he was ready to go. Mom hugged and kissed him, as did Dad. Karen remained seated on the sofa, just waiting for him to slither away.

Uli went over to her and kneeled down like a parent. She glared as he smiled. Softly he said, "You're my baby sis, so I'm bound to love you, and I only said what I said 'cause I don't want you getting hurt."

"If the US government ever presses a single charge against me . . ."

"They don't work that way."

"Oh, I thought this was a nation of laws."

"Not with the shit you people are doing," he said. "You'll never even see it coming."

As he leaned in to kiss her cheek, she sprang to her feet to avoid him. He grabbed her shoulders roughly, compelling her to pull back for a sharp punch to his abdomen. He saw it coming and caught her wrist, twisting it painfully behind her back. Then, almost as a strike, he shoved his lips against hers and plunged his hard tongue into her mouth. To her horror, his tongue seemed to somehow go all the way down her throat, then it recoiled and he released her.

"Come on," Dad called from across the room, not seeing any of this. "Let's see him to the car."

Shocked, Karen let herself be led outside and just stood there, if only to confirm that he was really leaving. Her mother started weeping as he got into a waiting vehicle. In a moment, he was whisked off to Logan Airport.

29

"That guy did your—your hole . . ." Karen heard the old lady say.

"Huh?" Karen realized she was being spoken to in the lesser, dank reality of the cave.

"He just looked at you, then shoved his," she held up two fingers, "in your . . ." She pointed to her mouth.

Karen's impulse was to shush her, because she was still utterly locked onto her yuletide family recollections in Boston. But no memory rushed back. The old woman's words had pulled the plug. It was over, and Karen had returned to this disgusting world below the surface.

"Who put their fingers in my mouth?" she asked as she looked around. No one replied.

Her memory had been corrupted—her brother hadn't tongue kissed her. At least she didn't think he had. Someone here and now must have put something down her throat, but who and why? Jumping up, she remembered that she had forgotten to kill the man who was stalking her. This nightmarish dungeon she was locked in with so many others, it was really happening. It was the *now* world, the incarcerated world her body was aging within. She knew she had to stop thinking and simply find a way out of this fucking prison. She felt a sudden surge of clarity and energy. Moving, just pulling herself away from her thoughts, became a newly acquired skill.

"Where am I?"

"Sunnyside, Queens," said the elderly lady seated next to her, quite matter-of-factly.

"This isn't Queens." Karen realized that the old woman, like everyone else there, was in her own world, acting in her own biopic. "Where am I?" she called out.

"Ask Richie," someone nearby replied.

"Who the hell's Richie?"

"Rich-ard! The blind guy," someone else elaborated.

The blinding headache from earlier had subsided, but when she rose to her feet, it came right back. She quickly found that if she held her head back at a certain angle, the pain was reduced. Karen stumbled to her feet and started walking around, calling out for Richard. She was directed to the rear of the dank cavern, where people were chanting in loose unison. It was there that she spotted Uli, wearing the Jets helmet.

Her brother was sitting, zombied out, in the tight prayer group, just staring straight ahead.

"I dreamed you kissed me," she said as she approached. But looking closer in the flickering copper candlelight, she remembered that this wasn't her brother at all. "Where did you get that?" she asked, gesturing at the helmet.

Evidently, the man's mind had eroded so much that he could no longer talk.

"Is that the same woman who passed out here a moment ago?" she heard. The tall bearded guy, presumably Richard, was approaching with a small entourage.

"Yes sir," said one of his lackeys.

"If I'm not mistaken," said a second, "and I might be, that guy you got into a scuffle with was talking to the football guy too."

"The guy who attacked me was talking about who?" Karen asked, confused.

"He was asking about everyone who came here lately, but he was the only one who came in, so . . ."

"Where'd Uli go?" she demanded.

"*Who*-lee?" asked one of the lackeys.

"Uli, my brother."

"FBI guy," Richard said, "I remember him. Intent on escaping, he ventured through into hell."

A lackey pointed up the incline toward the chiseled fissure in the stone where they had supposedly banished the criminal who had just penetrated her mouth.

"Your brother . . . went into . . . the Mkultra," said another flunky, who spoke very slowly as if each word weighed a ton. "Probably . . . headed for . . . the Sticks."

"What the hell are the Sticks?"

"The Sticks are the farthest edge of this entire installation!" shouted out another guy as though he were on a game show. "Like *out in the sticks*, so now we just call it the Sticks."

"What exactly is it?" Karen asked. "Why isn't everyone escaping through there?"

"They did at first," Richard told her. "Now it's become a maze of maniacs. And believe me, if there was a way out we would've found it. What we did find was enough rations and water to last hopefully till they do find an escape—then they'll come get us."

"*Who* will come get you?"

"Oh, we're well organized. We voted for a very competent leader who hasn't been affected at all by this wretched disease. We've even got a crack team of miners working on the problems."

"Miners, forty-niners, and my darling Clementine!" free-associated a distant voice.

"What miners?" Karen probed.

"A group of miners who are working around the clock digging for our freedom in the Sticks. Eventually someone will find a way out. Our job is to hold the fort until they do."

"Tell me about this disease."

"The disease you're suffering from, where you're stuck in your memories."

"You mean my Christmas memories?" As the words left her mouth, she realized it had gone a lot further than that.

"Eventually your consciousness doesn't return here," the blind man said. "You just get stuck there."

"How long do I have?"

"Who knows?" the game show contestant spoke up.

"One of the theories is that it's not the place, but the Mnemosyne they inject everyone with before they drop them. The ailment progresses more slowly if you just stay put, which is why I suggest you sit tight."

"Between dying here slowly and dying out there quickly while trying to break free, I'll chance the latter," she replied. "But if you can give me some clue of where to go . . ."

"The space consists largely of an abandoned office area called the Lethe."

"Office space?"

"It's as if some great office building fell sideways, but instead of crushing downward, the different floors just lined up side by side."

"What the hell is this place?"

"An abandoned government facility."

"Why is it underground?"

"Designed to withstand a nuclear strike. The place actually has only three levels. When you reach a blockade you have to climb from level to level, up and down, to keep moving forward."

"Up where and down where?"

"There are periodic cracks in the floor and ceiling. You'll see them."

"Which way is forward?"

"No one has ever produced a map or made markings, so I guess it's just straight ahead. There are flickering lights." Richard raised his arms, pointing up the incline. "I'll give you crackers, but in return, if you do find a way out, you have to promise to come back and get us."

"Of course."

"If you get attacked," Richard concluded, "run! Most of those poor bastards are pretty slow."

"Thanks," she said, and began climbing up the incline on the side of the huge basin, through the half-blasted, half-chiseled hole. What she found next appeared to be a large stockroom, consisting of boxes and boxes of crackers and other assorted supplies. Soon she passed through that room into the blackness, with only distant flickering beyond it. She felt as though she were moving into outer space with a million distant stars in the background. After a while she discovered she was walking on a parquet floor. Despite her constant motion, the monotony of her steps was like a lullaby that drew her back to her memories: that Christmas with her family in Boston was the last time she saw Uli, when life could still remotely be called normal. Soon after, New York City would be hit and she'd wind up here—in this toilet bowl.

A few weeks back, when she'd saved her brother's ass on a sandy street in Nevada, he looked terrible, like something profound had happened to him. No longer the bright-eyed zealot, he was prematurely old and used up—like dried shit. The poor bastard didn't even know who he was, much less recognize his sister.

She continued forth in the darkness of the labyrinth until she came to some strange barrier. Through touch, she realized it was a huge wall of tightly linked desks and chairs, a strange blockade made up of broken office furniture. She remembered the blind man's advice to move up and around. She backtracked until she saw it: a rupture above the stacked furniture, as though a small meteor had torn through the ceiling. Scrambling up the desks and chairs, she was able to reach the handholds that others had fashioned from the protruding rebar. Hauling herself up, she advanced to the second level that Weird Beard had mentioned and kept walking . . .

* * *

Without anyone back in New York waiting for her, Karen spent the remaining week of December in Boston with the family, where she became increasingly more comfortable being babied by her mother, and of course enjoying the constant flow of cocktails. By the new year, though, when she found her mother going through her belongings, sniffing her unmentionables, she knew it was time to sober up and leave. She had officially overdosed on parental love, and told them that much as she regretted it, she had to get back to New York to begin her second semester of law school.

She arrived at Grand Central and took the subway back up to her empty, cold flat—Dannette, the baby botanist, was still at her parents' in Jersey for the holidays. Karen cloistered herself in a buttress of law books, lectures, and loneliness. The only break in her self-imposed exile came when Hrag ascended the stairs and knocked on her door. Slightly used mats had just been donated and he was in the middle of teaching a class, would she mind helping? The delivery van was out front.

"Sure." She raced downstairs and helped bring them inside.

While watching him instructing the class, Karen realized that Hrag had injured himself and was unable to make some of the basic moves.

"You need to take it easy and just heal," she said afterward.

"I have three classes a day and no one to help," Hrag replied.

"I'll cover one of them."

Although at first she was worried about falling behind in her studies, after helping with some of Hrag's clerical work and teaching two of the beginner classes, she found her shroud of loneliness slowly lifting.

By the second week of January, several unplowed snowstorms had blocked the streets and sidewalks, leaving a biting chill in the air. Usually Karen went right from law school down Amsterdam to her apartment, but one afternoon when a group of other students invited her to join them for a quick drink, she agreed. Yet when they headed toward the West End Bar, she paused.

"Don't worry, we're just getting a quick coffee, not booze," one of them assured her. She had avoided the place since the fall and didn't feel like talking to any of the SDSers. Barely had she taken a seat when her classmates ordered four coffees. They slurped them down almost as quickly, then each dropped a buck and went out the door—break time was over. As they returned to the law books and tedium, Karen remained at the bar.

Looking toward the rear, she spotted Alvin and four other SDSers. Mallory was nowhere around, so she stopped by.

"So you joined the Young Republicans Club," Oliver kidded. "We didn't want to embarrass you."

"Nixon all the way," she retorted wryly.

Oliver ordered her a beer and insisted that she stay and catch up. Soon Alvin, Edith, and some of last year's graduates showed up—it was just like being back with the notorious old crowd. Karen knocked back a few drinks and was just beginning to feel at ease when the door opened and J.J., Ted, and Mallory entered. As they began to take off their coats and unravel scarves, Karen told everyone she had get back to her studies. She gulped down her suds, pulled on her coat, and suddenly realized that she was on a collision course with her former best friend. The bathroom was between them, so before Mallory could see her, Karen ducked inside.

How the fuck did this happen, that I have to spend the rest of my college years catering to this fucking bitch? she wondered as she stood in the smelly restroom, waiting for Mallory to pass. In another moment she was outside, headed down Broadway.

"Hold on," she heard a male voice call out as she arrived at her building.

Turning, she saw Gene—or Akbar, or whatever the hell his hip new name was—walking toward her. The whole thing felt like an awful rerun.

"Fuck off," Karen muttered, and pointing back toward Broadway, she added, "Your girlfriend's at the West End."

"Look, I just want to apologize."

Karen didn't want to give him the satisfaction and turned away.

"I always knew that Mallory was just using me to get those detonators," he kept talking, "but I also felt pissed. And I'm not saying I didn't get mad about the whole park thing, but I slept with *you* first, 'cause I really did like you, and you rejected me. So I just want you to know that was why I did what I did. And I'm sorry I'm not a stronger man."

"Give me a break!" Karen shot back. "I didn't force you to fuck her."

"That's true, and I shouldn't've, but you rejected me and she was your friend, so I guess I kind of did it out of spite."

"What are you saying? You slept with Mallory as an act of revenge against me?"

"Look, the reason I'm speaking to you now is 'cause I made some big mistakes, but I think you made a couple too."

She stood in the cold in front of her building, neither affirming nor denying his remark.

"So how's law school?" he asked after a moment, trying to push the conversation forward. She saw that he was exhaling into his ungloved hands, trying to keep warm.

"Want to come in?" she heard herself say.

"Thanks, sure," he responded as she unlocked the front door. The thought of another night in her apartment, reading old rulings from uninspired courts gone by, with the TV softly on in the background, was a little more than she could bear. Once upstairs, she offered him a cup of tea.

"Sure," he said solemnly.

She put some water on to boil. Since she didn't talk, Gene filled the silence by reviewing the past ten months of his life. He had discovered the teachings of Allah and had taken up with a devout contingent of storefront militants up on 125th Street.

"So you really dropped out of Columbia?" she finally spoke up.

"I needed a break. I'm reenrolling in the fall. I'm beginning to realize these kids aren't so bad, and the university was actually pretty generous about letting me in."

"I thought you hated the white-o-cracy."

"Yeah, but I learned that I don't particularly like black-o-cracy either," he said with a chuckle.

After talking awhile longer, he said, "You know, I did you a great disservice. Maybe I can make it up to you."

"How?"

"If you want, I can tell Mallory it was all my fault, that I seduced you. Hell, if you want, I can say I raped you."

"No thanks," she said and sipped her second mug of tea. "I don't know what's wrong with me."

"What do you mean?"

"I mean, if she were my real friend she would've forgiven me by now. I mean, if it was *me* I would've forgiven her."

"I honestly didn't think that my remark was going to break you guys up."

"It's just not easy for me to let people in, to trust anyone."

"I'm actually the same way," he said, putting down his mug.

After a moment, he silently reached over and brushed his hand along her arm. When she didn't resist, he leaned in and gently kissed her neck. He seemed to know exactly where to rub and stroke to make her drift off, only to find that his fingers had advanced to her right breast. Despite the fact that she'd disliked him up until an hour ago, it had been so long since she'd been touched that she just basked in the sensations.

They spent the next forty-five minutes kissing and snuggling before Gene finally pulled her T-shirt off. Kissing turned to heavy petting. By the time they got into her bedroom, sex almost seemed like an afterthought. Karen knew she was doing this as a deliberate deed—her final act of revenge against Mallory's heartless abandonment. As Gene grew more aroused, hastening toward his own climax, she refused to utter a sound, which seemed to fuel him onward.

30

As though looking through a transparency, she could see the present through the past, until the present finally rose and blotted out the memory . . . A loud bear-shaped human was huffing ahead. Staying alert, Karen realized that other smaller stealthy figures were circling around from the other direction to intercept him. She ducked behind a desk and held her breath, unsure as to whether she had also been spotted. One, two, three figures were there in the distance, working like a silent pack of dogs to corral the big slow-moving man. From her hiding place she watched while together the trio pounced on the lost soul. As they beat him and he groaned in agony, she made a break for it. Before she was able to get free, however, she tripped into another barricade of mangled, rusty desks and was forced to follow the slight breeze backward. She was about a hundred feet from where the mini wolf pack was taking out the old bear. As she sneaked by, she wasn't sure if they were raping or killing him. The dull sound of thudding was mixed with sharp screams of pain. Within minutes she found a rupture in the floor and climbed back down to the level below. Immediately she saw a tiny glow in the black distance with something hunched over it. When she cautiously approached the flicker, she could smell something burning, and realized with horror what it was: an emaciated man was bent all the way forward and had the tip of his nose charred black, burning in the tiny fire before him.

When she touched his shoulder, he keeled over to the side. He looked to be skin and bones and seemed to have starved to death one calorie at a time.

Next to him was an ice bucket filled with liquid. She thought it was urine but heard a single drip from above and realized there was water slowly collecting in it. It didn't smell any worse than what she had drunk earlier at the basin, so she sipped some from the top until she tasted a lump and spat. Quickly she resumed walking.

Soon, she was aware of a soft scampering around her, too fragile to be human. Glancing around, she noticed a pair of beady red eyes in the darkness. Small rodents of some sort were moving around her. When she stomped they scattered—nothing to be worried about. She continued shuffling slowly through the never-ending darkness until she struck something again—another mini Wall of China made from interlocking pieces of desks, chairs, and conference tables. She tried to force through them, but found them so tightly interlocked that they were impenetrable. She moved along the wall until she felt a slight breeze from above. This time she climbed back up to the wooden floors of the Lethe level where she could see more clearly in all directions. As she marched through the monotonous blackness, she was lulled back to her memories of the winter of 1969 . . .

Even while deliberately cheating with Mallory's ex-boyfriend, Karen knew it was another awful mistake.

Over the next few weeks, when her exams began, Gene would call her repeatedly, always inviting her out for "a quick dinner." He knew better than to invite her for anything as long as a two-hour movie. Each time, Karen would say she was busy. She was hoping he'd eventually think, *Well, I got laid, I'll quit while I'm ahead*, but he just kept calling. She would've told him to fuck off, but she didn't want to destroy the little bridge she'd made with him, and with her once-promising past. By early February 1969, however, he seemed to have vanished into the woodwork. But then, four days after New York City was struck with an epic snow, he called her again and said that no one should be alone for Valentine's Day.

"Of all the bourgeois holidays that our capitalist society puked out, Valentine's Day is the most contemptible," she replied, repeating something that Mallory had once blurted out.

Still he persisted. She once saw him waving from the street as she was practicing at the dojo. She also spotted him walking past the law library when she was studying there one afternoon, and ducked before he could see her. Then he vanished again.

About a month later, on March 21, when she was studying for a big exam later that day, someone rang her doorbell. She ignored it, but after several minutes of nonstop ringing, she finally looked out the window to see Gene waving up.

"What?!" she screamed down to him.

"I just wanted to see your beautiful face!"

"All right, you saw it," she said, about to close the window.

"Can I see it up close?"

"Believe me, the distance helps."

"I just want to give you a small gift. It'll just be a minute, I swear."

Wordlessly, she buzzed him up, unlocked her apartment door, and resumed her studying.

He entered, but instead of joining her in the living room where her books were spread out, he went into the kitchen. She could hear him rattling around while she tried to study.

"What are you doing in there?" she eventually asked. When he didn't respond, she went in to find that he had blanketed the dining table with a white tablecloth. Upon it he had set a bottle of red wine, a wheel of Brie, a loaf of French bread, and a bouquet of flowers.

"Happy spring!"

"I have a big test, I don't have time for—"

"It'll just be a minute, relax!" He put his arm around her shoulder and leaned in to give her a kiss. She quickly moved to the sink for a glass of water.

Each time he even stepped near her, she would hop up like a jackrabbit and move elsewhere. Although he uncorked the wine and poured her a glass, she wouldn't touch it.

After about twenty minutes of not making any headway whatsoever, Gene suddenly grabbed her. Karen twisted his arm and pushed, sending him flying forward onto a chest of drawers. A drop of blood rolled down his cheek.

"I've taken karate for years, so when someone grabs me, I'm trained to react," she warned.

"Really? Are you trained for *this*?" he said, squaring off his fists.

When Karen snatched up a wooden hanger, he stopped and laughed as though he were just joking.

"I get the message. If I can just have my detonators, I'll be out of here."

She realized now that this was all he had ever really wanted. "Mallory took them when she moved out," she said simply.

Gene rose calmly and found a napkin to put over the cut on his upper cheek. She set down the hanger.

"She said *you* had them."

"You spoke to her?"

"I saw her in the West End the other day and asked her about them. She said you mentioned some kind of a deal awhile ago."

"When she left I was desperate to get her back, so I suggested that we try selling them, but she didn't want anything to do with me. She came by after that to pick up the last of her things, and the detonators were in her closet."

"Do you mind if I look around a little?"

Dannette wasn't home, and with nothing to hide, there was no reason to fight. "You can look in the living room and my bedroom, but my roommate is not a part of this."

"But that was where Mallory lived."

"I gave Dannette an empty room."

"I'll just take a peek."

"No! You can't violate her privacy."

Gene let out an audible sigh and carefully searched Karen's room, then the living room closet. When he was done, he quietly took his bottle of wine and left.

On April Fool's Day, Karen came home in the afternoon after classes to find that her apartment door had been crowbarred open. The lock had been splintered right off the jamb. Her place had been ransacked, everything tossed onto the floor. Oddly, though, the only thing missing was her TV; Dannette's newer RCA television had been left untouched. She knew that Gene had come back to look for the detonators without her breathing down his neck. Fortunately, the money she got from the deal—which was the only thing of value she had—was in the bank.

Upon second thought, burglaries were so frequent in the area that she realized it could've been a desperate junkie in need of a fix. Not wanting to spend hours waiting around, she didn't even bother calling the police.

She already had gates on her windows, as did all the tenants in the building. That afternoon, in addition to putting everything back in its place, she invested in a police bar for the door.

The next day, she opened the New York Times and read that Gene Hill, aka Akbar Del Piombo, was indeed up to something: a cover story described a predawn raid in which her misbegotten lover had been arrested with twenty other members of the Black Panther Party. Apparently, they had made plans to blow up the New York Botanical Garden in the Bronx, along with various department stores around town. For a moment she wondered if she should call the police and ask them if they had also found her TV set.

The loud clang of a can or pipe being kicked close behind her in the

darkness brought her back to her senses. Freezing, she heard the patter of footsteps halt a couple hundred feet away. She dashed for cover,
only to stumble over something and fall to the ground.

To her right, she felt something long and tubular, yet heavy
tipped—a golf club, a driver to be exact. She picked it up, but it wasn't
what she had tripped over. Using the club, she prodded into the darkness and realized it was a badly decomposed corpse. She decided to
wait for whoever was out there to make his move.

Gradually, however, her memories of Columbia University started
creeping back in. She smacked herself to stay in the awful here and
disgusting now. *How the fuck could the government permit all these people to be
stuck in this hellhole?* She knew the accusation might not be fair because
this probably wasn't part of the government's plan, but even Rescue
City itself was completely unacceptable.

Who would've ever anticipated that a bunch of crazy escapees
would inject themselves with some snake oil and jump down a sewer
pipe only to land in a nightmarish subterranean maze? She couldn't
believe all these people were surviving on left-behind supplies.

During her short stint in the Weather Bureau, she'd been informed
that the SDS was riddled not just with informers but infiltrators,
members of the counterintelligence divisions of both the FBI and the
NYPD. Undercover officers had gained membership into most, if not
all, the antiwar organizations; they didn't merely gather information,
they also caused internal strife.

When she'd arrived in Rescue City, she knew that COINTELPRO
had to be working here as well. Once the army pulled out, this sealed
community was a termite hill of agents who divided and, maybe not
conquered, but certainly steered the place, trying to make corrections
as problems emerged. All the while they were creating a permanent
atmosphere of paranoia so they could keep control.

Now, down here in this cave, the Mkultra—she wondered if this
place too might have some ghosts. It seemed to have gone on for years;
someone had to be restocking it. *There must be agents who have access to the
outside,* she thought. *I just have to find them and make a deal, then I'll get the
hell out.*

After an hour of waiting for whoever was stalking her, the fear
diminished and her thoughts began to falter. Whoever was out there
was still waiting for her, and she was growing tired. She remembered
seeing a hole in the ceiling nearby, so she decided to take the initiative. Karen retraced her steps, keeping an eye out for her pursuer.

Although she didn't see anyone, she still felt him, so she kept back-tracking until she felt a breeze; scanning the area, she soon spotted the hole in the ceiling. It took awhile to find an old filing cabinet that she could topple over, making a huge racket. She hastily climbed on top of it, jumped up to a rusty piece of rebar sticking through the ceiling, then hoisted herself to the upper level.

She emerged in the middle of what seemed to be a former labora-tory, rows and rows of waist-high marble slabs. The stone tables had sinks and holes where gas pipes and faucets had once fit.

About a hundred of these slabs evenly divided the space. Wan-dering around the immediate vicinity, she found a section of pipe. Returning to the hole she had just climbed out of, she collapsed and waited.

Late in April 1969, Karen came home one afternoon for a quick lunch. She struggled to open the new lock of her apartment door, which had been amateurishly replaced after the burglary. Startled by a sound be-hind her, she turned to see Carlos in the hallway. He informed her that Hrag had collapsed while instructing his morning class and had been rushed by ambulance two blocks up to St. Luke's Hospital.

Karen rushed over to the hospital, where after an hour of waiting and lying—pretending to be Hrag's niece—she learned that he had suffered a mild heart attack. The next day she joined up with Carlos and Manuel; together they were able to visit him.

"I'm sorry," Hrag said before they could utter a word, "I should've told you guys long ago: I have heart disease."

"What does that mean?" asked Carlos.

"Well, the doctor says I shouldn't teach any more classes, or over-exert myself in general."

"Is the condition degenerative?" Karen asked.

"Unfortunately, yes."

"How bad is it?"

"The doctors are giving me a year or two, tops."

Karen leaned over the bed and gave him a gentle hug. Both Manuel and Carlos looked away, their eyes gleaming with tears.

"I can't imagine what we're going to do without you," Carlos said.

"Me neither," put in Karen.

"Look, I don't want to be a burden on any of you, but I've put the last ten years of my life into that place. More importantly, there are almost a hundred young men from the area, many of them fatherless, who come to our dojo. I think that the strength, discipline, and values we teach fill a big void and allow them to grow up and have a chance in this difficult world. You have to promise me you'll keep that going."

The three of them agreed to divide the three classes that Hrag taught, but the real problem was the business end. None of them wanted to deal with the tedious juggling of finances and overseeing the management of the old building.

"I've always been bad with numbers," said Manuel, looking to Karen.

"And you're Armenian," Hrag said, "numbers are in your blood."

"What do I need to know?" she asked, thinking how overwhelmed she already was with schoolwork.

"All the records are in the bottom drawer of my desk. It's like a puzzle." He grinned. "All the pieces are there, they just need to be worked out."

Even though she was behind in her studying, that night Karen went through all of Hrag's monthly bills and checked the dojo's most recent bank statements. Although there was some fluctuation based on membership fees, as best as she could tell, Hrag usually brought in about four hundred dollars each month. However, he owed roughly six hundred a month in expenses.

If this wasn't bad enough, she discovered that Hrag currently had little more than a thousand dollars in his checking and savings bank accounts, but he had more than ten times that much—$11,800—accumulated in debts. For the last six months, he had been periodically paying off just enough to keep the city from putting a lien on the property and Con Edison from turning off the power. The real problem, as she saw it, was that he failed to collect money—most of his tenants were behind in their rent. And he didn't even keep careful records for the karate dues. Karen knew that he would never turn away anyone who showed up for classes. After calculating how many students he had, she realized that if everyone who rented apartments and attended classes actually paid what they owed, he'd have a tidy savings.

By how things were going, she calculated that by the year's end they'd be at risk of losing the building. She went back to the hospital the next day, hoping that Hrag might be able to reveal some hidden assets to buy them some time.

"Oh, here's your mistake," he said, pointing to the staggering tax bill. "We don't pay taxes."

"So we're a not-for-profit?" She was slightly relieved.

"Should be, but no. See, the city's busted and they don't do anything for us, so I just throw out their bills."

"But they're the government," she said, as though referring to the Mafia.

"Yeah, and they've poured millions into fighting overseas while this neighborhood is utterly neglected and rat infested. The schools, the hospitals, our basic services suck. Whenever someone's getting mugged or there's a fire, try calling the police or fire department and see if they even come."

Karen nodded, not wanting him to get riled up, then softly said, "Hrag, they could take the building."

"Look, it's not like I don't pay anything. I give them what they deserve."

"But Hrag!"

"For the past twenty years they haven't so much as fixed the pavement in front of the dojo. We're doing enough of a service to the city just by occupying the space. There's no way they're going to evict us."

"You haven't even opened your mail! They've taken you to court! They're on the verge of taking action."

"Empty threats."

"What about the insurance and utility bills? How are you going to keep the building warm in the winter?"

"We have over a hundred people in our little dojo. We're just going to have to pass the hat and ask people to pitch in. We used to call them rent parties."

Karen went home, looked at his finances again, and thought about it further. The following day after classes, she met with Carlos and Manuel and, without turning against their beloved sensei, she explained that there was a growing debt and that Hrag offered no real solution.

"If it ain't broke . . ." Carlos replied.

"But it *is* broken," Karen said. "We're on thin ice here."

"What do you think we should do?" asked Manuel.

"I think I can enlist some third-year law students to help me file as a not-for-profit, then we can try to use the fact that we have so many underprivileged kids to see if we can get some grant money, but then it'll be run by a board of trustees—"

"Hrag will not let go of this place," Manuel broke in. "This is his bambino."

"Soon he's going to have a *dead* bambino!" Karen fired back. "And it won't just mean losing the dojo. We'll all need a new place to live, because we'll lose the whole building."

"What can we do?" Carlos asked.

"If we all go in and try to explain it, maybe we can persuade him together," she said.

The two men reluctantly agreed.

The next afternoon, a Saturday, they met at the dojo and walked to the hospital. They jointly went to Hrag's bedside where Karen gingerly brought up the looming financial crisis and suggested forming a board of trustees and filing as a nonprofit organization.

"Karen, we talked about this," he said with a grin, "you have to calm down. Everything's going to be okay."

When she tried to explain the severity of the situation, he told her that this was a good opportunity for her to learn to deal with her anxiety. She closed her eyes, breathed deeply, and quelled her immediate impulse to storm out.

As soon as she got home, she sat down in her kitchen and wept into a dish towel. She did her best not to alarm Dannette, who was watching *I Dream of Jeannie* in the next room. When the phone rang, Karen brought it into her room and found herself telling her mother about the community karate center which she was currently managing and how helpless she felt.

"It's okay, dear."

"It's *not* okay! How the fuck did I become a mistress to all these . . . lost causes?"

"Honey, you'll be graduating in two years from a prestigious Ivy League school with a wonderful future before you. It sounds like you did the best you could for those unfortunates."

"I just feel hopeless, like it's all coming apart," she whispered.

"It's just beginning!" her mother said. "You're young, beautiful, and smart. You can get a great high-paying job and, if you fix yourself up a little, have your pick of a husband who will love you."

Karen ignored all the American dream crap; she felt as though she were sitting in a leaky rowboat, just praying to get out before it sank.

During the second week of May, as she was on her way to class, the inevitable occurred: while entering a deli on 110th and Broadway, she literally bumped into Mallory, who was leaving the place.

"Asshole!" Mal screamed.

"What the hell?"

Mallory hurried up the block without saying anything more. Karen raced ahead and blocked her escape.

"Get the fuck out of my way!"

"What the fuck did I do to you!" Karen shot back.

"You know perfectly well!"

"I'm sorry about Gene! It was a total mess, and believe me, I regret it more than anything, but—"

"Not that! What you said to me on the phone."

"On *what* phone? I don't even remember the last time I spoke to you."

"You said the next time you saw me you were going to punch me in my sanctimonious face."

"I . . . *what?*" Karen was utterly confused.

"You threatened me! I should've called the police."

"When exactly did this happen?"

"The night I got back from Chicago, after getting beaten up and teargassed, I was lying in my bed sick with stitches in my scalp and you called me and said that."

"This is totally insane," Karen said with a smile. "I never did any such thing."

"Well, what did you say?"

"Mallory—I didn't say anything, I never called you. Hell, I don't even know your phone number! In fact, I left flowers at your door when Estelle passed away . . ."

"You're lying, I know your fucking voice!"

"Mallory, I will spend my entire life regretting what happened with Gene, but I did it before you two were together, and I sincerely regret not telling you about it immediately. Aside from that, I can honestly say I've never lied to you about anything, ever!"

"Then who the hell called me?!" Mallory yelled. By her tone it was clear that she was beginning to believe Karen.

"I don't know, but I swear I would never say anything like that. I've always admired you, and more than anything, all I ever wanted was for you to forgive me . . ." Karen was surprised that genuine tears were coming to her eyes.

Mallory looked to the pavement as her eyes welled up too. She slowly put her arms around Karen and hugged her. Karen hugged her back, harder than ever before.

Mallory disengaged first—she said she was late for an important appointment. She was supposed to meet up with Ted, J.J., and some of the others at Tom's Restaurant nearby if Karen wanted to come.

Karen clearly remembered Mallory staring deep into her eyes. Yet she seemed to be emerging, rising out of something dark and silent.

"Oh shit!" Mallory said.

"What?"

"Nothing," the man said.

"Well, I'd love to join you, but I have to run," Karen said.

Mallory's voice sounded deeper and her hair was shorter. "Run where?"

"Constitutional law class."

The two agreed to meet for dinner in two days.

31

It wasn't until now, nearly twelve years later, sitting in the darkness below the Nevada desert, waiting for whoever was stalking her, that she remembered what her brother had said during the Christmas of '68 and connected it to Mallory's claim about a threat she never made. Was she paranoid? Could her brother have done it?

Uli had told her that the FBI didn't work as she'd imagined. Could they have located some woman with a similar voice to hers, called Mallory, and threatened to punch her in her face?

Instead of anything as simple as poisoning me, she thought, *they figured out how to turn the only person who I needed against me.*

It was as though the FBI had bound her wrists together. Suddenly, she realized the pipe was no longer in her hand. In fact, she was no longer positioned over the hole, she was on her stomach now.

"Oh my God!" she cried out.

It wasn't Mallory she had just spoken to but her assailant, who had climbed through the hole where she had been waiting for him. He had delicately taken the pipe out of her hand, gently brought her arms behind her back, and tied her wrists together.

"You're not running to any constitutional law class today, hon."

Now he was yanking down her pants.

"You cocksucker, I'll kill you!" She tried kicking him. It was the same skinny bastard who had attacked her in the basin. He pulled down his own pants and took out his prick. Now that she would welcome losing consciousness, she was excruciatingly present and braced for penetration, though one moment bled to a full second, and soon a whole minute passed. She could feel some kind of frantic act, but didn't want to see. Finally taking a breath, she looked behind her. She could see the little man's slim hand frantically jerking, yanking, trying to solidify. Slowly, like a yo-yo, her awareness slipped down from sensory into memory.

She and Mallory had spoken on the phone and agreed to meet at the Symposium, a Greek restaurant on 113th Street. Throughout that day, Karen was plagued by a new fear. If Mallory learned that she had slept with Gene again—when the creep tried to steal the detonators— she'd have a new reason not to speak to her. According to the news, though, Gene had been locked up in Rikers with twenty others, so for the time being she wasn't overly concerned about them reconnecting.

When they met in front of the restaurant, they hugged and Mallory gave her a kiss and said she was famished.

Inside, Karen ordered the moussaka while Mallory had a Greek salad.

Mallory said she was happy that she had given Karen a second chance to repair the damage caused by Gene. "You have to understand, I always kind of thought he was cheating on me. Which was why when he said he slept with you . . . I mean, you were the only person in this entire world who I completely trusted."

"I really didn't mean to; it just happened."

"And I forgive you. In a way, I guess I took advantage of that."

"To do what?"

"Move out and put some distance between us."

"I suppose I had that coming."

"When I saw you last summer I was ready to reconcile, but then that whole fiasco in Chicago occurred and I remembered hearing the rumor about Allard Lowenstein, who you worked for."

"What rumor?"

"He led a whole bunch of protestors *away* from the convention center and everyone said he was an infiltrator. So when I got that call, I just figured you were working for him and the other side."

"What other side?"

"The side that does *this* to someone who has surrendered to the police." She parted her hair and pointed to a scar, resembling vulcanized rubber, running about an inch below her hairline. "This is what a cocksucker with a badge did to me, with full legal impunity."

For an instant Karen contemplated pointing out the scar above her own eyebrow, but she didn't want to diminish her friend's moment of glory.

"I had tear gas burning my eyes and face and was just trying to get away," Mallory went on. "I was literally crawling on my hands and knees, having people stomp and trip over me, and this fat fuck comes after me and whacks me over the skull so hard I was out cold. When I woke I thought I was in a puddle, 'cause my blood had soaked through the pillow on the gurney while I was waiting with dozens of others in some overcrowded hospital hallway."

Karen just shook her head.

"I kept thinking that if Aunt Estelle was still alive, she would've come and rescued me," Mallory said in a small voice, fighting back tears.

Karen rose from her side of the booth and embraced her friend. Mallory wept and hugged her so hard that Karen could feel her nails in her back.

Mallory went on to describe how she had become closer with Mark Rudd, David Gilbert, and the now-infamous radical contingent of the SDS. She was the only female member in their little group. Mallory talked in a near frenzied excitement about her upcoming trip: they were all heading to the national SDS meeting in East Lansing, Michigan, to consider new and more effective leadership strategies and policies. "Why don't you come along? We'll have a blast!"

Karen simply smiled and said, "I have law school."

As Mallory continued rambling, Karen wondered if her friend was okay. When she mentioned that they were planning a coup in Lansing, Karen stared into Mallory's pupils to see if she had taken amphetamines.

"What kind of coup?"

Mallory said that they had been communicating with other battle-weary SDSers at different campuses around the country who had grown sick of the old Progressive Labor Party. The Progressives had held the reins of the national organization for long enough, keeping the SDS within the narrow confines of the Port Huron Statement—the original manifesto of the student organization. She explained that it wasn't the police or the FBI, but the national organization, who was actually the most repressive body.

"In order to truly effect change, we have to take control of the organization ourselves!"

"You're going to revolt *against* the SDS?"

"Apparently they *do* need weathermen to know which way the wind blows."

"Deere was the only one I could do it with," Karen heard someone else say.

It was then that she remembered who her would-be rapist was! He was Deere's lover—that little cocksucker whom she had caught following her at the hospital and had subsequently tossed into her trunk and then a Harlem jail. In a strange way, she felt relieved. Though she would still kill him when she had the opportunity, the guy had a clear motive for abusing her. And perhaps because of his sexual leanings, he couldn't harden up to violate her.

"Let's go," he said, grabbing her by the belt he had secured around her wrists. He pulled her up to her feet.

"Look," she tried to reason with him, "you took the drugs which I needed to survive. I'm already losing it. Can't you just let me die in peace?"

"Let you die in peace? You're my dinner, hon. I plan to cook and eat you. I'll let you go—*through* me."

She pulled up her pants and sat on the filthy ground. "You can kill me, or leave me, but I'm not budging."

He yawned. "What the hell, this is as good a place as any to rest." Fixing a spot on the ground next to her, he lay down, pulling her in and spooning her. She would've fought him, but by that point her memories were whirling around her again, sucking her back down into the maelstrom.

Although Mallory lived only about six blocks away from her, Karen didn't see her again anytime soon.

This wasn't from lack of trying—Karen made an aggressive effort to resume their former friendship, calling several times each week, mainly in the evenings after classes. Usually someone picked up to say she wasn't home, but several times they did manage to chat.

Mallory offered some dates when she could meet with Karen again, but their schedules seemed to conspire against them. Plus, the charming levity her friend had possessed just a few years earlier now seemed to have been replaced by a skittish paranoia. Whenever they talked, Mallory would obsess about how the real danger wasn't LBJ, or even the military-industrial complex, but other backstabbing "pseudo leftists," who were either trying to poison the revolution or hijack it for "some watered-down, sold-out compromise."

During one conversation at the beginning of June, Mallory proclaimed, "The revolution *is* real. Hell, it's happening as we speak! The oppressed peoples of the third world are already fighting against the US, sacrificing their lives to kill the fascist huns. What this country doesn't know is that soon all the blacks locked up in America's ghetto prisons are going to rise up, along with the oppressed peoples of all the Spanish-speaking countries, and then the dominoes will truly start falling. The real question is, who is going to lead them—you dig?"

"You know," Karen attempted to change the subject, "my parents are coming to visit me. They're taking me to the Russian Tea Room for dinner. Would you like to join us?"

One of Mallory's many housemates cut in to use the phone, and the call ended abruptly.

Soon after, Karen received the first notice that Chase Manhattan had put a lien against the dojo, warning that unless a sum of $1,242 was received immediately for a mortgage taken out last year, eviction proceedings would commence against the building. When she checked the latest bank statement, somehow there was now $3,983 in the building's checking account. She had no idea where the extra money had come from, but without asking for Hrag's permission, she wrote a check and paid the mortgage bill in full. The following week, she opened up the mail to find that a second lien for $3,339 had just been filed against the building. New York State had issued this one for unpaid back taxes. Large red letters on the front of the notice said, *EVICTION PROCEEDINGS WILL COMMENCE IN TEN DAYS.*

Karen called the agency to ask if she could work out an installment plan. After being put through to a supervisor, she was informed that she should've called six months earlier when they had sent a first warning. But since then the case had gone to judgment and penalties had been added, dramatically increasing the sum.

When Karen brought the lien to Hrag's attention, he simply crumpled the letter into a tight ball and tossed it into the garbage can. "That's where we file them," he said with a grin.

The next morning Karen went to the bank. Her own savings account held $4,172. All but the seventy-two bucks, which she had gained as interest, were from selling the detonators the previous year. She asked for a bank check and mailed it off to the New York State Department of Taxation and Finance.

July was as sweltering as it was boring. Karen had no social life, but even if she'd had friends or even, God forbid, a lover, she wouldn't have been able to see them. Between summer classes and managing the dojo, she had little free time. She kept putting out flyers asking students to help keep the dojo running—if not by donation, then by fixing up the apartments that were still shoddy and therefore unrentable. She was always needling Manuel and Carlos to pass the old tissue box for donations after each class in anticipation of the next large bill.

One day Karen opened her mailbox to find a mysterious index card–turned-postcard:

July 9, 1969

This place has more leftist splinters than a one-armed windmill: the Young Socialist Alliance, Wobblies, Spartacists, Marxists, Maoists, Trotskyites, and Cap'n Crunchites-Frootloopists. It makes me suddenly aware of how nutty I must've sounded the last time I saw you. Even I can't figure out the difference. (Sorry!) Ted said the only real distraction here is that one group wipes from the ass upward and another group wipes the other way.

It took her a minute to realize the card was probably from Mallory, though her handwriting seemed to have changed, growing tighter and more slanted. Karen figured she must be at that oddball SDS conference in Michigan.

A few days later, she received a second index card:

July 12, 1969

Big news! Today we formed a radical new administration that will be chal-

lenging the PL bastards. Someone named Bernardine Dohrn is running for president—a woman!—along with Mike Klonsky & we're all commies. Goodbye SDS, hello Revolutionary Youth Movement! (RYM).

Then a third postcard arrived:

Guess what? Trotsky was right. The revolution is permanent! As of last night, Dohrn & Klonsky, the two partners in revolution, have parted ways. Now we got the Revolutionary Youth Movements One & Two! Each group has taken over a different room here at the convention hall. Delegates are bouncing back and forth between them. But we know that most of this rally is probably made up of undercover fuzz (and I know you fellas are reading this, so you might as well tell your boys to go home).

That was the last postcard. When Karen was given a phone number for where Mallory was staying in East Lansing, she got five dollars in dimes, nickels, and quarters and made a call from the corner pay phone, only to learn that Mal had just left the city. No one knew—or would disclose—where she had gone.

In early August, Karen finally got a call from Mallory, who said if she wanted to meet, it had to be at that very instant. Karen dropped her studies, pulled on her shoes, and dashed out, meeting her friend on the steps of Columbia's *Alma Mater* statue.

After a big hug, Karen remarked, "You were gone much longer than I thought."

"That's 'cause we pooled our money and went north to Canada. I got a visa and visited Havana!"

"Cuba?"

"It was so inspiring to actually see a former fascist state that had its revolution."

"Yeah, but their civil rights are a little wanting, no?"

"That's a small price for keeping the fat cats down. They're constantly trying to take back the government."

"Let's get a cup of coffee," Karen suggested, steering her toward Broadway.

"I hate to say it, but I really only have," Mallory looked at her watch, "two minutes and fifty-eight seconds."

"Where are you going in two minutes and fifty-eight seconds?" Karen asked, amused.

"Catching a ride back to Chicago."

"Why?"

"That's where the fight is."

"Mal, I respect what you believe, but do you really want this to be your whole life?"

"See!" Mallory let out a deep groan and muttered, "It really wasn't Eugene."

"What wasn't Eugene?"

"The reason I couldn't sustain a friendship with you wasn't 'cause you slept with him."

"What are you talking about?"

"Admit it! You don't care about the revolution."

"I feel very deeply about my political beliefs."

"Oh sure, liberalism la-di-da. You vote for the right candidates and all, but you're not willing to put yourself on the line to bring down the old guard."

"You're really prepared to sacrifice your life for some crazy revolution?"

"Hey, this is 1969! This *is* the future! So yes, my declaration of war is *today*! For the sake of the children, I'm willing to die for my planet and the people on it. I'm willing to fight against the organized greed and legalized selfishness called capitalism." With that, Mallory rushed off.

32

"Is this my past or my present?" she politely asked the stranger who seemed to be helping her.

"Neither. This isn't even happening," he said softly.

When she tried to withdraw her arms, she realized he had just finished tying her wrists to the walls of some kind of dungeon. It was the awful present. She had lost time again. She remembered reading how alligators were commonly put into a trance, allowing daredevils to insert their heads in the animals' great jaws in carnival sideshows. Her unstable attention span was slowly killing her. Checking her surroundings, she realized that she was in an alcove, some kind of utility closet chiseled out of the stone. She was no longer seeing the stone slabs around her; he had somehow led her to another part of the vast chamber. There was nothing anywhere in the area, just floor, ceiling, and open expanse. A few pinpricks of light that could've been candles were flickering in the far distance. The smell was quite putrid.

"Where the hell am I?"

"It's your new doghouse, bitch. It's perfect—out of the way, no one is going to find you. And what's best is that hole over there." The creep pointed to a jagged stone wall across the chamber. She could make out a narrow cut in the stone. "That's the beginning of the Sticks. From what I learned back at Streptococci River, your brother is somewhere in there. The reason you ain't dead yet is because I plan to kill you both together, but not till I do some pretty awful shit."

"Look, I'm sorry for hurting and confining you, but I was investigating the kidnapping of the mayor and—"

"That's nothing! I don't care about that!" he yelled back. "You two murdered the only woman I ever loved."

"But Deere wasn't even a . . ." She wanted to say *woman*, but zoned out before the word formed. "Hold on!" she called out as he started walking away.

"Shush!" he said, moving back toward her. In a whisper he added,

"You still got some meat on your bones. Think I'm bad? You scream and there are ogres out here who will literally eat you alive."

As she watched him moving toward the barely visible opening in the concrete, her brain slowly lapsed . . .

Her parents were proud that she was finishing her first full year at Columbia Law School, and made plans to come down from Boston, rent a Midtown hotel room, and take her out for a night on the town. They had gotten tickets to the hot Broadway musical *Hair*. Karen felt silly getting all dressed up and sitting next to them watching the big, dumb musical about hippies. She knew her parents felt that they were getting a glimpse of her wacky, youthful culture.

Afterward, they walked north to the Russian Tea Room on 57th Street, where after a twenty-minute wait they got a table near the bathroom. Her father immediately ordered a large platter of beluga caviar along with a bottle of vodka in a bucket of ice. Karen had to restrain herself from saying, *Let's not be a cliché*. No sooner had she reached for the tiny bowl of fish eggs than her father asked exactly what she planned on doing once she graduated.

"I don't know," she replied.

"Your brother knew what he wanted to do before he even entered college."

"Yeah, wear a white cowboy hat and live in a world where everyone else is the bad guy. My world is a little more complicated than that."

"As long as you can support yourself, dear," said her mother.

"I've supported myself since I left home."

"It's not just a question of supporting yourself," her father said. "At its best, having a career gives you a higher reason to live. It's what gets you up in the morning and, at times, when all else fails, it's the only thing that keeps you going."

"Thanks, Dad. As if I don't have enough pressure on me."

"What business is your little friend going into?" her mother asked, referring to Mallory.

"She's either a committed revolutionary or a soon-to-be committed schizophrenic," Karen kidded.

"Well, both are very time consuming and neither pays," her father quipped.

"You care about people. How about social work?" her mother said, as if they could get to the bottom of her problem right then and there.

"Actually, I've gotten a couple offers. I'm going to wait and see what's available once I pass the bar."

"Smart," her father said proudly, "go where the money takes you."

When her arms started cramping, she pulled at them, awakening to find that her wrists were still fastened to the wall above her with an old rope. Glancing around in the darkness, she realized that she had been tied to a rung of exposed rebar. As she slid the rope across the steel, she could feel a subtle friction. The rear edge of the metal rung, where the seam of the cast was molded, had a mildly abrasive ridge. She pulled the rope back and forth, back and forth, back and forth, back and forth . . .

That September, Hrag returned home in a wheelchair, but he was unable to do much else other than sit around as Karen, Carlos, and Manuel operated the dojo and apartment building around him. Through Karen's perseverance, they had managed to get some of the students to finish the rough carpentry on three of the upstairs apartments. The problem was that they couldn't afford an electrician or plumber to make the units habitable and earn more much-needed cash.

Instead of congratulating Karen on all her hard work, Manuel and Carlos grew silent around her. She had grown bossy and unladylike in the little dojo community.

In the first week of October, when the dojo received a late notice from the state for that year's taxes, Hrag said to Karen, "See! When we got the last state tax notice they threatened to evict for nonpayment, and did they? No!"

She wanted to tell him that she had paid the bill out of her own savings, but knew it would only make him feel bad and his health was already in clear decline.

That night, Karen called Mallory's number to see how her trip to Chicago had gone. Her phone just rang and rang.

. . . the back-and-forth motion caused something to snap. *Why did it stop?* She held her hands out, slowly realizing that she was free and her captor wasn't around. But she couldn't stop wondering about Mallory. *Why didn't anyone answer the phone . . . ?*

She called Mallory back two more times over the next two days until some unknown party finally picked up.

"Is Mallory there?"

"Who's this?" the male voice asked. Karen told him, and without saying another word, he hung up.

When Mallory got back to her three days later, Karen could tell just by the static and echo of the call that she wasn't in town.

"You're still in Chicago?"

"We're protesting the trial."

"What trial?"

"All the march organizers are on trial. Don't you read the news?"

"Oh, Abbie Hoffman."

"Hoffman, Jerry Rubin, David Dellinger, Bobby, Tom, Rennie, John, and Lee. We've got some *serious* events planned."

"What kind of events?"

"Direct action," Mallory said cryptically.

Karen feared the worst. "Weren't you just arrested last year?"

"What's your point?"

"If you get arrested again, can't they throw the book at you?"

"Two years ago you were ready to blow up the Morningside gym project. Put *that* Karen on the phone, please."

"We were just going to blow up an empty lot without any guards. That's not the same thing as going to a place where you were already injured and arrested and having a direct confrontation with the fuzz."

"People are on trial. Our constitutional right to protest is on trial!"

"You know, I quit the SDS because I didn't want you to feel uncomfortable seeing me there," Karen said, "and I deeply resented it at the time. But you actually did me a big favor."

"What the hell does that mean?"

"It means taking on the responsibility of an unjust world is way too much. Injustice is a constant; it'll never end. And though you clearly think I lack the necessary passion for this stuff, I do care about the world. Every day, in some little way, I do my part."

"*In some little way?* You know what you are—a freedom freeloader. We do all the real work. We get thrown in jail, and you get the liberty."

"I just don't want to get hit on the head and arrested again, I already did that. Other than a sexy scar, what good did it do?"

"In the past year, since Captain Kirk was beamed out of office, they've canceled the gym project, and the IDA is no longer on campus—that's what good it did."

"Mal, after the student occupation, I made a promise to myself: I'd help with the revolution just as long as it didn't involve getting myself injured or arrested."

"What a wimp," Mallory murmured.

"Call me if you're in trouble," Karen said, trying to show she still cared about her friend.

"If I'm in trouble I probably won't be able to call anybody."

"Well, will you call me when you get back to town?"

"We'll see."

"Promise me—please."

The operator came on the line saying that Mallory needed to deposit another fifty cents. Karen called out—

Coming to, back to the real beyond the real, Karen found that she'd blown it. He had tied her wrists back up to the metal rebar in the utility closet. "Shit! I should've run!"

"From what? Are you hungry?"

"Weather Bureau?" she asked him. The first time she'd heard the phrase was in an article sometime late in 1969, it must've been in the *New York Times*, about a mysterious underground organization calling itself the Weather Bureau. They had issued a broad news release declaring war on the imperialist forces throughout the world. Unnamed sources claimed that this group was made up of radical Columbia University students.

The stranger held a cracker in front of her face. She ate it.

"Did Mallory . . . send you?" Karen asked.

"Sure, she told me to come here and feed you."

"I think someone's holding me captive," she said, looking around nervously.

"You're kidding. Who?"

"This creepy guy; he tied me up."

"Where is he?"

"I don't know. He was just here."

"I saw your brother," he said.

"The FBI agent?"

"He's underground here with you in Nevada."

"Hrag's down here?"

"Oh yeah. Hrag's here."

"Well, tell him we finally got the eviction," she said, almost indignantly. The very first eviction notice had appeared on the door of the dojo from the New York City Department of Finance. Hrag had thirty days to pay the sum due or vacate the premises. When Karen brought the notice to his attention, Hrag opened his side desk drawer and took out a stack of bills that he'd been shoving in there for the past few months.

"You should see the little freak child he's with . . . The kid has a tail . . ."

As the man kept chattering, Karen noticed a package of crackers hanging from his pocket.

"Hungry?"

"Yeah."

He grabbed a small handful and put them in her mouth. They were damp and dry, and very old.

Opening the *New York Times* on October 7, 1969, Karen read that a bomb blast had destroyed the Haymarket memorial police statue in Chicago, which immediately reminded her of the bomb that never got planted in Morningside Park. The Chicago explosion shattered windows for blocks in all directions.

She prayed her friend was okay. The next day she read all about the rally that had failed to materialize. The few hundred who did show up were ready to fight. Donning motorcycle helmets and carrying weapons, the protestors had gone straight into a rich section of town—the infamous Gold Coast—breaking store and car windows as they moved along. It was payback for the brutal beating they had suffered at the previous year's Democratic convention. But it was still Mayor Daley's city and his police force. According to the news reports, one of the cops drove a police car right into the mob of protestors. By the end of the riot, only half an hour later, six SDS members had been shot and twenty-eight of Daley's little piggies had been injured. Of course, the cops had the law on their side: sixty-eight protestors were arrested fighting for civil rights, whereas the cops only received citations.

Two days later, on October 9, Karen read about a second, larger rally that attracted two thousand people. Despite its size, it was a peaceful march through the poorer Spanish section of the Windy City.

The following day there was a third and final march of several hundred young people. Again, they were intent on doing damage. The protestors crashed through a part of downtown called the Loop, but this time the police were ready for them. Though it wasn't as violent as the October 8 march, Mallory ended up getting arrested again, along with roughly half the protestors present.

By the time it was over, the net result for the SDS was that most of its membership and leadership had been arrested. The collective bail for them was a little over a quarter of a million dollars.

When she heard this, Karen went to the West End Bar and found some of the SDSers who hadn't made the trip to Chicago. First they passed the hat to help contribute to the bail fund. Then they proceeded to get drunk.

The next day when Mallory made bail, she called Karen to report that at least she hadn't gotten hurt like last year.

"Thank God for that."

"But they're bringing me to trial," Mallory said excitedly.

"When?"

"It better be before December, because the new SDS is having its big meeting in Flint, Michigan, and we're coming up with a war plan."

"Haven't you had enough?" Karen asked, sincerely worried for her. With her prior record, jail time seemed inevitable.

"Have I had enough? A handful of fascists have hijacked our country, and are making laws to benefit themselves. So no, I haven't had enough."

Karen was sitting in the living room with her karate uniform on, as she was scheduled to teach a class. She went downstairs to find twelve students lined up and waiting for her. After going through some routines with them, she demonstrated a standard back kick into the canvas bag hanging from a hook. Then she did it a second time, more quickly. Then again, letting out a loud yell. As her thoughts focused on Mallory going to jail for years, she kicked the bag even harder, yelling louder.

After several minutes she realized all her students were watching her in tense silence as she just kept kicking . . .

She awoke with her arms still bound, getting kicked over and over by the little creep . . .

33

Due to the growing mouse and roach problems in the building, Dannette moved out in early November 1969, compelling Karen to look for her third roommate. Regardless of all the time she had invested, not to mention all the detonator money, the building's debt had somehow managed to climb back up to a staggering twelve thousand dollars.

Her sense of despair steadily increased until Thanksgiving Day, when she bumped into another Barnard student named Gwen Douglas—an oval-faced girl with bangs whom she had met at an antiwar rally. Gwen needed a new place and Karen desperately needed a roommate, so it was a perfect match. The very next day, while stopping by the dojo, Karen found Hrag at his desk, instructing a new protégé on how to teach a class.

"I know you don't believe me," she said to him, "but we're going to get a knock on the door from the city any day now, and that'll be it!"

Hrag reached across the desk and picked up a document, which he then handed to her: a thirty-thousand-dollar life insurance policy. "That'll pay for everything," he said.

The morbid question that weighed on her mind after that was, would he die before the building went into default? It was getting cold out and just the notion of a new fuel bill filled her with dread. When she shared this concern with Carlos and Manuel, they promised to help her out. Carlos started turning off the heat and electricity in the hallways, and took to placing small jarred candles on each floor. But by nine o'clock each night, almost all of them had been blown out by the cold breeze coming under the door and whipping through the hallway. When Karen came home late from the library, she'd have to feel her way up the stairs in the darkness, always fearful that some junkie would jump her.

Something was rippling across the darkness like a fish swimming just below the surface . . . A small kangaroo-like body was leading a man she didn't recognize. As soon as they disappeared, her bristle-headed captor followed them into the distance . . . She was so hungry and thirsty and in pain. Unable to fuck her, he'd just keep hitting her.

In mid-February 1970, while heading to class one day, Karen bumped into Alvin Rich, who was also in his second year of law school. That was when she first learned that the entire SDS leadership, including Mark, David, and J.J., seemed to have vanished into thin air.

"Apparently they've gone meteorological," Alvin said with a chuckle, referring to the Weather Bureau.

Although she knew that they all meant well, what chance did a group of college kids have against the United States government? She figured Mallory had to be among them. "You wouldn't happen to know a way to get ahold of them, would you?"

Alvin shook his head no, and added, "You could ask around."

Over the next few days, Karen cracked open the white pages and began tracking down everyone she had known during her time in the SDS.

"Are you aware that this phone line is probably bugged?" asked Sam. "So if anyone does know how to reach them, you're giving the FBI a way to find them. Is that what you want?"

Realizing he was right, she simply hung up.

On February 21, she saw a news report that the house of Judge John Murtagh in Inwood had just been firebombed. He was presiding over the Panther 21 trial—Gene's case. Maybe Mallory was involved.

The next week, while walking east on 111th Street between Broadway and Amsterdam, Karen heard a female voice call out from behind her: "Karen Sarkisian?"

She turned and immediately recognized Mallory, disguised in cheap office wear and a short dirty-blond wig. She was staring at the ground.

"Oh my God!" Karen said, hurrying over.

"No!" Mallory barked without looking at her. "Just keep walking straight and listen, please!"

Karen did as instructed.

"Walk south for a bit, then circle around. When you're convinced that no one's following you, meet me at La Rosita," Mallory said under her breath, then broke away.

Karen walked across the street into St. John the Divine, where she sat in a pew and prayed, discreetly glancing around the entire time. Then she exited through a side door. After about ten minutes of continually circling and checking, backtracking and rechecking, until she was convinced she wasn't being tailed, she headed west to La Rosita on Broadway. Mallory was sitting in a corner, reading a copy of the *Daily News*, looking like anyone but herself. Aware that Karen was standing there, she gestured to an adjacent empty table. Outside, in the street, Karen could hear some asshole with a crew cut yelling at someone else.

"Will you help me?" Mallory spoke just above a whisper, and didn't turn to look at Karen. A half-empty cup of café con leche was sitting in front of her.

"Help you do what?"

"I'm no longer aboveground and I'm probably being shipped out soon."

"Shipped out where?"

"I don't know. The bureau doesn't think it's safe for us to stay in the city much longer."

When she said *bureau*, Karen first thought that Mallory was working for the FBI—which made no sense.

Sensing Karen's uncertainty, Mallory explained, "We call ourselves the bureau too."

A waiter came over, put a glass of water down, and handed Karen a menu.

Out front, the shouts of abuse got so loud that Karen wanted to ask Mal if they should do something about it. Yet for some reason, against her own will, she just said: "What do you need?"

"On March 1, I need you to go out to Kensington, Brooklyn, to my aunt Estelle's old place. I've been waiting on some checks. They're the last of my inheritance."

"Didn't Estelle pass away almost two years ago?"

"Yeah, but her place is rent-controlled, so I've been paying the bills, waiting for her life insurance and stuff."

"Do you want me to—"

"Just grab the checks from the mailbox and leave. But be careful. I don't want you to look suspicious."

"Are you wanted by the police?"

"At this point, I think I'm only a person of interest. Technically, I'm still out on bail, though I don't want to take any chances."

"Jeez, Mal, okay."

"We'll set up a rendezvous time and place. Keep looking behind you, and don't tell anyone on the phone or anywhere else that we met." Mallory then turned and smiled at her, while placing a sealed envelope in her hand. "Don't open this until the day you go to Estelle's place."

"Are you okay?" Karen asked above the infernal screams outside.

"Never been better. We're finally starting the ball rolling and—"

The asshole outside must've made Mallory nervous, because she stopped talking and quickly put fifty cents down on the table. Before exiting she muttered, "All you need to know is in that letter."

Suddenly the creep with the crew cut dashed inside and yelled in her face, "You've got shit and piss running down your legs! You're too disgusting to even beat anymore! Why don't you just die?!" Turning to the void around them, the fucker yelled outward, "Free meat over here if any of you cannibals are hungry!" He pointed at her—Karen was nearly nude and filthy. "Now I'm going to go butcher your brother, bitch!"

On the chilly morning of March 1, 1970, a day she had much anticipated, Karen woke up early and opened Mallory's sealed envelope: inside were three keys and a letter that informed her how to get to Aunt Estelle's—which trains to transfer to and where to walk once she was out in Brooklyn. Karen felt like a secret agent as she followed the directions, periodically pausing and casually glancing around. Although it hadn't occurred to her to dress at all differently, she realized that she was wearing a bright, fluffy red sweater, and desperately wished she had dressed in a more subdued color. When she arrived at the apartment building, she entered the lobby and had a difficult time just opening Estelle's mailbox, which was packed with letters.

Then, with the bundle in hand, she headed upstairs. She entered apprehensively, but found that the place was safe and relatively clean. By the various items shoved under the door and the perceptible dust buildup, it was clear that no one had entered the place in months. She quickly flipped through the thick stack of correspondence, business and personal. There were a number of consolation cards among them. She only opened the business letters that looked like they might pertain to her mission. It took almost ten minutes of slicing open envelopes to locate three checks addressed to *Beneficiary, Mallory Levine*. They were from two different banks and one insurance company.

Karen gave a quick perusal of the apartment. She saw that in addition to some interesting antique furniture pieces and various keepsakes that looked to be of value, Mallory was abandoning two lifetimes of photos of her family and documentation of her own childhood.

Although it crossed her mind to try to sell some of the items to antique stores—if only to donate the much-needed funds to her dojo—Mallory's instructions were explicit: *Just take the checks.* Karen locked the door behind her and caught the QB train back to the city. The last line of Mallory's instructions to her merely said, *Go home, and keep the checks on your person at all times. Just wait for me.*

Karen did exactly as instructed. Just accomplishing this task had made her happy; it was the kind of favor that signified that their falling out was officially over. Mallory was now in her debt. With each successive day, though, as she waited for her friend to make contact, Karen grew increasingly fidgety and felt constantly exposed. Repeatedly she would glance around, checking for either some kind of law enforcement surveillance or for her old friend to swoop down on her out of nowhere. The fact that neither party was ever visible made her even more paranoid. As each evening approached, she'd realize that she'd have to endure another day of profound apprehension.

Her daily routine was more or less fixed. It always began with either a seven a.m. law school class or a seven thirty a.m. karate class that she taught at the dojo. School and karate were the two poles of her world, with studying and daily chores worked around them. Usually for about a half hour each morning, she'd come downstairs with a cup of tea and chat with Hrag about one financial difficulty or another, occasionally erupting into spats as he always had his own risky way of doing things. Then she'd sit down by the phone in the office and make calls—begging debtors for extensions, renegotiating delinquent payments, or asking building tenants when she could expect their rent, or at least a portion of it.

As March progressed, Karen found herself having an ongoing imaginary dialogue with Mallory, trying to bring her back from the edge.

Despite unrest and widespread social protest, the United States of America was not about to collapse, and the global class struggle was not close to being over. Despite an endless catalog of past and present crimes and injustices to most minorities and the lower classes, millions of people were quite content living humbly in their oppressed state. Whatever sacrifices Mallory and her cadre were about to make, Karen knew that they weren't going to push this country into a civil war. Inevitably, all that would happen is that Mallory would get shipped off to prison. And considering the amount of trouble she was already in, it was amazing that she wasn't already incarcerated.

Certain accusations that Mallory had made kept popping up in Karen's head. That she lacked "the necessary passion," and "refused to make the sacrifice" to be a revolutionary; that all she really had was "sanctimonious indignation."

"I don't lack the necessary passion, asshole!" she yelled aloud one night to her bathroom mirror while brushing her teeth.

"You say something?" her roommate Gwen called out.

"No, I'm fine," Karen called back, and tossed her toothbrush into the sink, embarrassed.

Lying in bed, she decided that she couldn't live with herself if she didn't at least try to pull her old friend back from the brink one last time.

34

Two days later, when she was leaving to go to school, she found an order to VACATE THE PREMISES WITHIN 90 DAYS taped to the front door. The process server hadn't even tried to serve it. She raced into the dojo only to learn from Manuel that Hrag, who was suffering from shortness of breath and chest pains, had been rushed off to St. Luke's Hospital the night before.

As she was walking up Amsterdam Avenue to the hospital, wrestling with the question of whether or not to inform him about this new crisis, she heard someone softly ask, "Did you get the checks?"

Karen turned, thinking it was Mallory, but the woman looked thinner, and clearly older. "Huh?"

"Keep walking," said the woman behind her, peering down. She looked similar, but it definitely wasn't Mallory. Karen knew she had to assume they were both under surveillance, so she kept a safe distance between them.

"Where's Mallory?" Karen whispered hoarsely.

"Just give me her checks. Drop them on the ground and keep walking."

The woman accelerated past her to the corner, then slowed down. Karen also slowed down, taking the three checks out of her purse and casually dropping them on the cracked pavement. She walked past the woman, who looked like a taller, leaner Mallory in a headscarf. Karen didn't turn back as the woman snatched up the checks and headed off in the opposite direction.

Karen was about to continue on her way to the hospital, but spinning about, she caught sight of the woman just as she turned right on West 110th Street and proceeded west toward Broadway. Karen hurried back to the corner and paused. She saw that the woman had pulled off her headscarf and light jacket and now looked completely different: she was wearing a dark-blue sweater and loose slacks, as if ready for secretarial work. Her hair was gathered up in a tight bundle. At a healthy distance, Karen followed her to the 1 train.

The platform was still filling up with late-morning commuters.

Karen plucked a token from her purse, slid it into the turnstile, and passed through. The woman had already walked to the southern end of the platform.

Karen removed her overcoat to alter her appearance slightly and rolled it into a tight ball, holding it under her arm. Just to be on the safe side, she also pulled off her black knit beanie. About five minutes later, a 1 train pulled into the station and everyone boarded. With each stop, Karen carefully looked through the filthy glass panels before yanking open the doors and passing into the next car. She slowly made her way toward the rear of the train.

When she was in the second-to-last car, she spotted Mallory's courier sitting in an end seat with her head back and eyes shut. This woman didn't have a clue that she was being followed. Presumably the only time her radar had been up was when she'd located Karen and gotten the checks from her. The courier finally got off the train at West 14th and Seventh Avenue. Karen followed her as she exited at the 12th Street staircase. She emerged across the street from St. Vincent's Hospital. Karen stayed on her as she walked with stiff determination down 12th Street over to Sixth Avenue, then turned south one block to 11th. A stream of students was flowing out of the New School for Social Research across the street. Karen blended in with them, following the woman as she moved along the south side of 11th, heading east toward Fifth Avenue.

Though it was probably pointless, Karen wanted one last opportunity to try to change Mallory's mind, if only to eliminate her own crippling guilt. Karen was surprised when she saw the courier abruptly turn and disappear into the ground-floor entrance of an elegant town house. The fact that Mallory and her fellow revolutionaries might be hiding in a wealthy person's home was an irony not lost on Karen as she lingered outside. She knew that knocking on the door could be dangerous. Instead she simply waited down the street, hoping to eventually catch Mallory leaving. Over the next few minutes, she arranged her argument: she had to try to convince Mal that life was bigger than this intense moment, or even this politically charged year. If the downtrodden refused to rise up against their oppressors, no one could force them.

Karen felt more than saw the sudden explosion, which shook the entire block, shattering many windows. She turned to the direction of the blast and saw black smoke rising from the windows of the very brownstone she thought Mallory was in—18 West 11th Street.

She raced over and saw that the ground-floor door underneath the steps was open. The courier was bringing out another young woman, who was naked. Stunned, they stumbled across the street where an elderly lady was flagging them down.

"Where's Mallory?" Karen yelled.

The courier was in too much shock to ask how Karen had found her.

"Where's Mallory?!" she repeated, sprinting over to her.

"I think she's dead," the woman mumbled. "She was in the basement with Ted and . . ."

Karen rushed into the smoking building and down a stairway that was slanting precariously as though it were about to fall out of the wall. All the electricity was gone and the place was primarily lit by indirect sunlight coming through the windows. Scattered fires burning around the basement also illuminated the twisted space. "Mallory!" she kept calling to no response. To her horror, she soon spotted a mangled pair of singed legs and a pelvis. They must've been violently torn from the rest of the body. She also glimpsed a bloody, hairy arm; its musculature suggested it had belonged to a man. The rear of the basement, which was covered in smoke and flames, seemed to be the center of the blast. Against the western wall, Karen made out a burning pulp of organs and a section of muscles clinging to bones. Only when she recognized a blue cowboy boot tucked under a broken table, with a bone rising from it, did she confirm that she was looking at the blasted remains of her beloved friend. With the fire spreading, the smoke and heat were too much. Gagging, Karen hobbled back out through the door under the front steps.

On the sidewalk, coughing the black smoke out of her lungs and wiping the tears from her eyes, she heard sirens in the distance.

"Are you okay?" Some guy who looked like Dustin Hoffman was blocking her.

"What?"

"What the hell happened?" he asked frantically. Others were accumulating around him.

"I don't know, I just heard an explosion and ran in. I—" Looking west, Karen spotted the courier leaving a building up the block. The woman was holding her friend's hand; the naked girl was now clothed in a loose billowy dress. Karen pushed past the small crowd of onlookers toward them. In a moment they turned south on Sixth Avenue.

"Hold up!" she shouted.

They ignored her and kept walking.

"Stop!" Karen yelled as they passed the Women's House of Detention on Greenwich Avenue. She was finally able to grab the shoulder of the courier. The other girl took a swing at her, but Karen easily caught her by the elbow and yanked her forward, sending her to the pavement. Since she was already injured, she just lay there. The courier began to run but Karen grabbed her arm, swinging her against a parked car, and shouted: "I was in the SDS too, asshole!"

"What do you want?" the courier asked fearfully.

"Mallory was like a sister to me, and I want to know what the fuck happened, or so help me God I'll have both your asses thrown in jail."

"Okay!" said the courier, holding her hand up. Karen saw that one of her index fingers was missing. Blood was still oozing from a rag pressed against a torn knuckle.

"First we have got to get out of here!" said the younger woman, slowly rising from the pavement. Both were clearly shaken. Sirens were approaching from all directions, and people had started staring at them.

"Let's go," Karen said.

She spent the next ten minutes helping them get to a brownstone that turned out to be the family home of the courier. Once inside, the two introduced themselves. The courier was named Diana, and Kathy was the one who had exited the bombed building in the nude. It turned out that Ted Gold, Mallory, and Terry Robbins, an SDS leader, had been in the basement at the time of the blast.

"What the hell happened?" Karen asked.

"I honestly have no clue," Diana said.

"Me neither," echoed Kathy.

"One moment all was fine. I mean, we were planning on . . . an event," Diana said. "The next moment, the entire building seemed to lift into the air."

Karen sensed that they wanted her to leave, but the trauma of losing Mallory left her in a daze. She couldn't stop thinking that the blast had somehow been perpetrated by the FBI, meaning her brother. If this was the case, she needed to know.

"No," Diana said, after having a bandage taped tightly around her hand, "the FBI would've just arrested us on trumped-up charges. They didn't do this."

"We don't want to be rude, but we really need you to go and not discuss this with anyone," Kathy finally said, returning to the living room in new clothes.

"Actually," Diana said, "we might need her help."

Kathy looked at her strangely.

Karen wrote down her phone number and explained that she had been friends with J.J. at Columbia. She said that she'd help them, provided J.J. himself called her.

"Fine," Diana said, and Karen left. She noted the address of the house just in case, and sadly returned uptown.

When she got off the train, she staggered the two blocks home just thinking about poor Mallory. As she approached her corner at 111th Street, she noticed a somber group of students standing outside the dojo. When she saw Manuel's red eyes, she immediately knew that Hrag was dead. It seemed like too much of a coincidence. Karen realized that if she hadn't followed the courier, she probably would've been with her mentor during his final minutes.

Although his passing was painful, she had been preparing for it since his heart attack a year earlier. With Mallory, the pain was indescribable.

Sitting up all night, Karen found herself wondering over and over how two of the most important people in her life—Mallory and Hrag— had died at nearly the same time. *How much suffering can one endure in a single day?* Something much bigger was clearly at work.

The next morning, listening to 1010 WINS on the radio, the top story was the brownstone explosion on 18 West 11th Street. They listed the names of the three who had died in the explosion: Diana Oughton, Ted Gold, and Terry Robbins. She was much too tired and raw to even care that they had misidentified Mallory's body.

Over the next hour she found herself obsessively reviewing everything unusual that had occurred in the past couple of years. The one detail that she fixated on was the sale of the detonators, specifically the buyer—that strange old man whom she had followed downtown. *What the hell did that guy do with that fucking bag of bizarre detonators?*

Detonators were used in bombs. And a bomb had just gone off, killing Mallory. Somehow she just knew that he had to be connected to this explosion. It couldn't be simply a tragic mishap.

A flurry of distant sounds grew louder and then spliced into strands of tiny voices like a bundle of cut wires. They emerged up from the darkness, coming back, back, back. This time, though, *he* was out in front of a small group; instead of following them, her feeder/beater was leading them. She was hungry, afraid, and thirsty. *Say something!* She waved and grunted, but they were too far away and she realized that she was covered in her own crusted waste and felt too ashamed to move or utter a word. The monster savior was carrying something in his arms. In fact, he and another man were carrying or helping three smaller, strangely shaped people . . . As the group came closer to her, she discovered that she knew the other, older man. Though she couldn't remember his name, he evoked deep contrary feelings of both affection and disdain. She reached out toward his face. *Is this a memory or is this really real?* Karen murmured, or thought, or thought she murmured. Before she could shape sound into signifiers, the entire party seemed to vanish, like a line of cockroaches disappearing into a crack . . .

She remembered the crack she had followed old Daddy Longlegs into—at the southernmost crevice of Manhattan. With Hrag and Mallory gone, she was too filled with rage and grief to just sit at home and study dusty statutes of law. Karen bolted out of bed, dressed, and grabbed Hrag's giant screwdriver from the office downstairs. She shoved it into a shopping bag and headed out. She caught the 1 train and rode it to the last stop, South Ferry, and walked over to Broad Street near Fraunces Tavern.

The front door of the strange buyer's old building rattled as she shook the knob. She rang the three ancient doorbells and wondered if they were even connected to anything. Without wasting any time, she slammed her hip against the front door and it popped open. She turned her grief into steam, climbing the splintery flights two steps at a time until she reached the top floor. Two doors on either end of the landing seemed to lead to different ends of the same apartment. She knocked quickly, and getting no response, she took the large screwdriver out of the shopping bag and wedged it into the wooden doorjamb. After a few minutes of yanking it violently back and forth, just as the tempered-steel edge started bending, she gave one more strong pull and the old wooden frame splintered off.

Karen virtually fell inside the dump. Clearly no one was home. Looking around for clues about what might've caused the explosion, she only saw books and clothes that looked like they would fit the tall old man. No signs of any wife or companion—other than the roaches in the kitchen sink. Karen pulled open the drawers of his cabinets. No visible cash, jewelry, or identification. On his desk were utility and rent bills, old letters, and various snapshots dating back half a century.

A bookshelf revealed a broad array of tomes, ranging from technical manuals on electrical circuitry and radioactivity, to ancient textbooks on engineering and physics. In the next room was a wall of books on politics, philosophy, and history. In the kitchen, in addition to a full shelf of canned and dry food, there was an old steamer trunk filled with a number of unusual tools—clearly the tenant was mechanically inclined. A film of dust coated every surface, including the floor. On the wall was a two-year-old calendar, as well as a three-year-old Christmas card, along with a few scattered pictures and paintings covered with cobwebs. Karen would periodically freeze and listen for any footsteps from the hallway—nothing. She went into each room and tried not to frivolously touch anything. Although the busted doorframe would reveal her intrusion, she was worried about leaving fingerprints. Yet, as the occupant might be a buyer of illicit detonation devices and Lord knew what other contraband, it seemed unlikely that he would call the police.

After about ten minutes, Karen glanced over to one of the unwashed windows and caught sight of something that stopped her dead in her tracks. Screwed garishly on the window's edge was a shiny lead switch with a wooden-edged handle. It looked like it could've been used to electrocute death row inmates. Wires were stemming from it, but as much as Karen studied it, she couldn't figure out what it was connected to. It didn't seem to connect to anything electrical, let alone anything resembling explosives. The only thought that crossed her mind was that the New York Stock Exchange was just a few short blocks north. *Did this crazy old bastard rig up some kind of bizarre device to blow up Wall Street?* she wondered. *Why else would anyone rent this isolated hovel on the edge of Manhattan?* At night this area was utterly dead.

Maybe the switch had already been thrown. Maybe it had blown up the town house. Only one way to find out.

Do it! she heard, as though Mallory's ghost were right there, whispering into her ear. *Give my death meaning!* The profane memory of the bloody pulp of Mallory's body filled her with rage. She remembered her friend's splintered leg bone arising from torn muscle, with bloody skin hanging like a loose sock from her boot—*Mallory!*

Karen yanked the lever all the way down, connecting the circuit, and waited for the *BOOM!* like the one she had heard yesterday on 11th Street. Instead, she only heard street noise continue outside.

Suddenly, a loud creak in the hallway caused her to jump. Karen peeked into the hall, and instantly awakened to the possible consequences of her reckless action. Since the coast was clear, she dashed out of the old apartment, back down the rickety stairs, and onto the street.

After dumping the heavy-duty screwdriver in a corner garbage can, she stiffly walked the few blocks to the Staten Island Ferry Terminal, where she caught the uptown local. Thirty minutes later she was exiting at 110th Street and Broadway.

35

"Mallory!"

"Mallory, the new mayor?"

"Where's Mal?" Karen asked a neatly dressed woman with a bandage over her blackened nose and eyes. The woman was standing directly in front of her, holding what appeared to be a spray can like it was a gun.

"Aren't you . . . You were one of those . . . Garlic Heads. What are you doing here?"

Karen stared at her.

"My name is Root, Root Ginseng. Can you repeat that?"

"Roo . . ." She could barely talk.

"How long have you been down here?"

"I . . . don't . . ."

"It's amazing you can still speak, that's a good sign. Maybe there's still time."

"This is . . . now. Isn't it?" Karen asked, wondering if she was living, remembering, or dreaming.

"This most certainly is now," replied the woman named Root as she slipped the can of mace back into her pocket and stepped closer. She turned on a flashlight and shone it in Karen's eyes. "My gosh, you're the new mayor's associate, aren't you? What are you doing here?"

"I have problem . . ." Karen nervously strummed her left hand in the air, struggling for words. Then, distracted, she pointed to a fresh bright stripe on the ground and said, "I saw some guy paint that."

"Yeah, that's Plato's little pet project. He went rogue and now . . ." Root snapped on rubber hospital gloves. She found a piece of paper on the ground and carefully wiped some of the dried filth from Karen's hindquarters. "Honey, I want you to try to remember how you got here."

Karen could no longer recall any of the events that brought her from New York in 1971. Now she was sick, half-naked, filth encrusted, and all alone. "They . . ." She pointed to the crack in the stone wall where she had seen the strange people go.

"Don't worry about them. Let's worry about *you*."

"Can you help?"

"I can only try."

"Mallory?" Karen asked, without a clue of what she was talking about.

"You mean the new mayor?"

"No, no, the real Mallory."

"What real Mallory?"

"Did you get . . . blown up?"

"Yep, that's me," Root replied politely. After dealing with the memory ravaged for so long, she had learned that it was usually easiest to just placate them.

But Karen knew that Mallory had been blown up, and the new mayor wasn't Mallory—her beloved friend was forever dead.

Karen's grief from losing both Hrag and Mallory was now diffused by a gnawing anxiety about the mystery lever back in the old guy's apartment, which she knew she shouldn't have pulled.

By day, when she wasn't hitting the books, Karen tried to honor Hrag's memory by attempting to collect his Metropolitan Life Insurance policy, a whopping thirty thousand dollars, to pay off the debt on his dojo. On paper it all looked fine, the problem was time. The tax people were anxiously waiting for their revenue, while the life insurance company was taking its sweet time in cutting the check.

One morning as she was leaving her apartment, two men, both in gray suits with black patent-leather shoes and short hair, exited a car parked on the street and approached her. *Either they're process servers or somebody from the marshal's office is finally serving eviction papers,* she thought.

She was startled when they opened their wallets and identified themselves as FBI.

"Mallory Levine live here?" asked the older one, who evidently did all the talking.

"A couple years back," she said vaguely. "Why?" She immediately assumed that they had finally identified her remains. It had taken them two months to figure it out.

"We're trying to locate her."

"Oh yeah, she kind of went off the deep end," Karen said.

"You were also a member of the SDS with her, weren't you?"

"I was, but we sort of split up."

"Split up how?"

"Well, I'm a law student," she said cautiously. "I like to think we can change things within the system."

"When exactly was the last time you saw her?"

"Gee, it must've been around the time she went to protest the Democratic National Convention in Chicago," Karen said with a smile. "And that's a classic example. If we had all simply supported Humphrey, he'd probably be in the White House now."

"Would you please contact us if you happen to see or hear from her?" the agent asked, handing her his business card.

"Of course."

The two men returned to their car none the wiser and drove off.

The morons still haven't identified Mallory's body. Her only close relative, Aunt Estelle, had died, and most of her other close friends were also in the Weather Bureau—to them, Mallory was probably still alive and living as a fugitive somewhere. Since she alone knew the truth, Karen felt that in a strange, macabre way, she finally had Mallory all to herself.

On her way back from class that afternoon, she learned that at Kent State in Ohio a group of students protesting the war had been fired upon by the National Guard. Several hours later she learned that nine students had been wounded and four were killed. Karen seriously considered calling the FBI back and yelling, *Instead of hunting down a dead idealist, why don't you arrest those cold-blooded murderers in the National Guard?!*

She saw photos of the murdered students the next day and grew enraged. *Mallory was right,* she decided, *it's time to fight fire with fire.*

Two days later, while leaving a class, she overheard a fellow law student jokingly say, "The war is finally coming home."

Karen thought the comment had something to do with the Kent State massacre until she stopped in a corner bodega and heard a fragment of what turned out to be a special report coming over a transistor radio: *"Lower Manhattan is currently closed off and officials with protective suits and Geiger counters are combing the area for the source of the radioactivity. Until then, no vehicles are allowed south of Worth Street and people are required to show proof of residence . . ."*

"What's going on?" Karen asked the bodega owner, who shrugged.

That night at home, flipping from channel to channel, Karen was able to piece together the situation from various news reports. Apparently, over the past couple of months, doctors around Lower Manhattan had been reporting an odd spike in nausea cases. The nausea was followed by fevers and headaches. Soon they also noticed an epidemic of skin rashes. One local dermatologist, who had been stationed in Japan just after World War II, saw a cluster of red dots on a patient's wrist and was reminded of low-level radiation burns that he had seen outside of Hiroshima. He called a friend who had an old Geiger counter, and the two went out and discovered abnormally high levels of radiation throughout southern Manhattan.

The doctor contacted six state and federal agencies until one of them finally sent a team out with new Geiger counters, and an hour later they had determined that the background radiation of most of Manhattan was between 140 and 370 rads, which was a moderate risk level. Hardly a fatal dosage for the short term, but health hazards increased with the length of exposure. Eventually they made two more discoveries: that the radiation arose from pitchblende dust, and that it came from not one but multiple sources.

Within a week, they discovered that a large amount of pitchblende had been carried by winds and was dusting the streets of Lower Manhattan. The grains had flowed down sewer grates, been caught up against doorways and windowsills, and been sucked into air conditioner units. It had mingled with the grass in the city parks, dusted along leaves and litter. It slid down subway kiosks into tunnels, and peppered corner newsstands. It had fallen on the wrinkled, threadbare garments of homeless people and the crisp, flannelled cuffs of the rich alike.

It crossed Karen's mind to call the FBI and anonymously report the old bastard who had bought the detonators. Her fear was that if he was indeed the guilty party, then she too would be discovered. By now they must've stumbled across his little bomb factory on Broad Street. Over the ensuing days, she searched the papers for word that they had located his place, but didn't find anything. She kept praying that it had nothing to do with the old guy.

The government's initial response was to cordon off everything below Worth Street, which was primarily commercial anyway. They focused on the fifteen or so intersections where the radiation levels seemed highest. They sent in teams created to deal with materials of a hazardous nature, who sealed up the sewage pipes to prevent contaminated water from flowing down the drains. Then they used high-pressure hoses to wash the streets, and brushes on wooden poles to scrub down buildings. Afterward they carefully ran Geiger counters along the affected intersections again and found that the rads had not dropped significantly.

The radiation was like a phantom that seemed to move around at will, sometimes attacking, sometimes retreating. As revealed by Geiger counters, it continued steadily creeping north. Someone finally made the startling discovery that the main sources of radioactivity were the ubiquitous sneakers, all the same color and cheap design, dangling from traffic lights and lampposts all around Manhattan. In the toe of each of the sneakers, they found small, sophisticated machines that looked like cigarette lighters but were essentially tiny Geiger counters. When the Geiger counters detected radiation, a small switch was engaged that opened one end of a sealed tube. Inside each tube, a radioactive core released dustlike particles that slowly trickled out through prepunched holes in the sneaker's tip. The radiation levels inside the lead tubes were measured at an alarming 520 rads.

It wasn't until Karen saw a photograph of one of the sneaker bombs in the paper that she actually felt nauseous herself: the lighter-like Geiger counter they showed on the news was one of the useless detonators she had sold to Daddy Longlegs. She knew for certain that this had everything to do with her yanking that fucking lever in the old man's loft back in March.

How and why could one miserable old man build this cheap yet highly effective weapon system and simply let them dangle all over New York City until I broke into his crappy house and pulled some antiquated lever?

The whole thing seemed insane. Worse still was the fact that he was out loose and there was little she could do about it. *Who knows what that fucker is planning next*, she thought. That night, Karen stopped in a liquor store and purchased a fifth of vodka to help her get to sleep.

She decided that the old cocksucker must've just been waiting for some kind of deadline—that had to be why he hadn't pulled the switch himself. And Mallory's demise had triggered her to accidentally commit this senseless and heinous tragedy.

"Triggers trigger triggers trigger triggers," she drunkenly murmured. *This would've happened anyway!* she consoled herself. She downed gulp after gulp of harsh liquor until the room started spinning, her anxiety dissipated, and she found herself being sucked down the giant drain of sleep.

* * *

. . . don't make eye contact, you look and they feel threatened, they won't look at you, we have about a quarter-mile walk before I can get us to a safe room, don't say anything, just keep walking . . . keep walking straight ahead and don't say a word . . .

36

36

Television pundits started talking about the evacuation below Worth Street. Shortly afterward, at a news conference at City Hall, Mayor John V. Lindsay declared, "We might not know who perpetrated this, but we can well imagine why he did it. He hoped that we as a city would weaken and we'd abandon our homes. Therefore, my way of thinking is that we shouldn't retreat a single inch more than we absolutely have to."

As a symbolic act, the mayor announced that the Staten Island Ferry would always keep functioning, the FDR would forever remain open, and so would the mighty Brooklyn Bridge. But except for that narrow easterly area, the entire Wall Street area would be shut down. Likewise, work on the rising World Trade Center project would be suspended until the crisis was resolved and the area was officially deemed safe.

Although many remained optimistic, by mid-June the Geiger counter reports showed that radiation had spread like a tumor. A large chunk of Greenwich Village, from Houston up to 14th Street and from Broadway to Seventh Avenue, was now restricted. The streets were fenced off and all residents were given two weeks to leave before being forcibly evacuated.

In hopes of reducing the pitchblende spread, the Environmental Protection Agency, which had been formed only months earlier, changed procedures. Instead of simply removing the sources of the pitchblende, every intersection where a lethal pair of sneakers was found was sealed off. Giant wooden boxes were constructed, some rising as high as twenty feet in the air. Although there was no looting, Governor Nelson Rockefeller called in the National Guard to aid with the crisis as parts of the city were systematically emptied.

On July 3, Mayor Lindsay went on the air to regretfully announce a third expansion of the partitioned zone: it would be moved from 14th Street up to 34th. One was now unable to go west of Park Avenue or east of Seventh Avenue, so everyone living inside that area had to be immediately evacuated. Within two weeks, the new perimeter would be sealed behind a hurricane fence and monitored by National Guard soldiers in special uniforms that protected them from hazardous material. Additionally, temporary housing was immediately made available by the city in the other four boroughs. For nervous residents still living adjacent to the quarantined areas, the city offered thick plastic ponchos, one-size-fits-most, attached to air filters, and goggles that could be pulled down over the face. Since the radioactive dust that had been released in the lower half of the borough was being carried by the wind in all directions, a series of windbreaks, plastic shields, and plywood barriers were erected along various blocks.

Despite all precautions, according to the Geiger counters now fixed at nearly every intersection, the dust continued to spread. On a positive note, other than the initial health reports that had sounded the original alarm, no new cases of illness were reported. But the conversation focused on the long-term hazards of the situation.

"Over the next few years you're going to see cancer and leukemia rates spike throughout the city," warned the city's health commissioner. "Tens, maybe hundreds of thousands, are going to be dead before 1980 unless more people are evacuated immediately!"

Once Manhattan's interior was boxed off, it was carefully scrubbed down. Instead of being reopened, however, the sanitized areas were left sealed. Recontamination became the new concern, so even though it was deemed clean, the Battery Tunnel remained closed. Recognizing its symbolic importance, Lindsay still fought to keep the Brooklyn Bridge open. Subsequently, the government took the preventative measure of cleaning the last remaining artery through Lower Manhattan, the FDR Drive. The *Daily News* called it the "Liquor Store Highway" due to the plexiglass enclosure built around it.

When Karen started her final year of law school that fall, she almost always had a fifth of vodka in her handbag, and frequently maintained the delicate balance between numb and functional.

During the previous spring semester, before news of the contamination, Karen had worked on the school's law review. But in September she went into free fall, easily distracted in lectures, passing out instead of studying when she got home—steadily slipping to the bottom of her class. The general sentiment on campus was that the city was engaged in a losing battle.

"A Poor Man's Hiroshima," announced a headline in the liberal *New York Post*.

"Despite constant warnings of doom and gloom, not a single person can yet be called a casualty in this attack," countered the more conservative *Daily News*.

But over the course of the next month, as the radiation detection continued, Manhattan widened its quarantine zone northward: 38th, 39th, then 40th Street. Lawsuits by different citizen groups were followed by countersuits, moving up from lower to higher courts. Some streets were reopened as Geiger counter needles wavered a few points back. Because nothing like this had ever occurred before, there was no single office designed to handle the crisis. Although the various governmental departments tried to work together, jurisdictional spats constantly broke out between city, state, and federal agencies. At 42nd Street, the city finally held the line in what was now being called the Battle of Midtown.

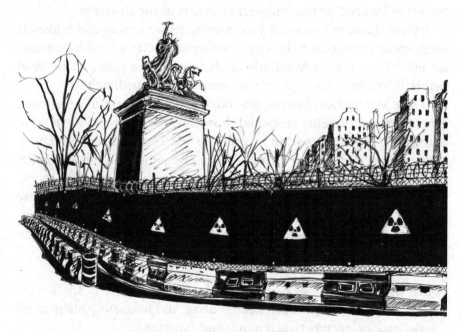

Meanwhile, radiation levels north of Times Square continued to rise.

"Although the levels are far from lethal," said the spokesman for the newly formed Radiation Containment Task Force, "they're still worrisome enough to require further adjustment."

At an emergency news conference during Thanksgiving weekend, it was announced that a twenty-foot fence would be erected along Park Avenue all the way up to 59th Street, then across to Seventh Avenue and south to 49th, then across to the Hudson River.

"Hopefully this will be the final partition," the mayor said.

By the time Rockefeller increased the National Guard presence to enforce the new quarantine zone, the city's emergency housing stock in the outer boroughs began to tap out. A week later, President Nixon gave a nationally televised speech proposing a plan for temporary housing for victims of "the New York crisis." The first area considered for large-scale housing developments was along the eastern edge of New Jersey, from Perth Amboy up through Tenafly, but local community leaders balked when developers with mob ties came forward. Soon various groups lobbied against the Nixon plan, and one little-known organization entitled Band-Aids Don't Work, fearful that New York could lose its role as America's financial center, proposed converting the Rockaways into the new Wall Street.

Nixon put together a bipartisan panel of respected city, state, and federal leaders to come up with other housing proposals for the residents of the city. By Christmas 1970, the first rumors began emerging about the plan for the creation of a large subsidized city where the underprivileged could reside while New York was being properly sanitized, and thus the Rescue City program began to take shape. In addition to planned housing, it also involved a recruitment program for a "volunteer corps" in the medical and legal fields, as well as other technical professionals who could assist in running this new satellite community. For no clear reason, someone nicknamed this group of prospective brains who would run the city the "Garlic Heads."

Since many of the program's applicants were from the lower economic brackets, there were initial plans to include a school system as well as a job-training program, but these services were almost immediately taken off the table because the volunteer program was not attracting the numbers the government was hoping it would. And as the political opposition argued, the focus of the Rescue City program was supposed to be a short-term housing program, not creating an inner-city boarding school.

In an effort to attract more Garlic Heads to run the legal, medical, and administrative aspects of the temporary city, headhunters were hired. Professionals were offered salaried positions, along with good housing opportunities. When the numbers still came up short, the program was expanded to include those searching for draft deferments.

By the first few weeks of 1971, most of the residents who could afford to leave had already moved out of Manhattan. For Karen, if there was any silver lining to the darkening crisis, it was that all legal action against Hrag's building due to his nonpayment of taxes was indefinitely suspended. Likewise, although Columbia University administrators kept classes open, grateful that the campus was at the northern end of the island, attendance declined. While they talked about relocating to a temporary campus somewhere in Queens or the Bronx, much of the faculty felt that as long as the institution was out of the contamination zone, it was their patriotic duty to remain in the city that the institution had been a part of for over two hundred years.

Throughout the blurry, alcoholic fall semester, Karen had barely attended her classes. She knew she would've been tossed out, but due to the tenor of the times, she was getting a pass, along with a stern warning to dramatically improve her performance for her final semester.

"You're limping," said the woman named Root, who stooped down and flicked on a small pencil flashlight, revealing a trail of blood. That was when and how Karen realized that she was still in pain. She had just cut her bare foot on what seemed to be bone shards. The woman silently pulled a large sliver from Karen's heel and tied a clean cloth over her filthy bleeding foot. Then she continued leading Karen through the darkness until they came to a dead end. Moving a board that covered a hole, she helped Karen climb up one level, then another. At one point, when some highly emaciated man lunged at them, the woman sprayed him with mace; he grabbed his face and hobbled away. Finally they reached an empty stretch of corridor, and the woman reached under a tile for a lever that opened a small door.

Root flicked a switch revealing a large, bright, clean room. For the first time since arriving to this subterranean world, Karen felt safe.

"What . . . who?"

"We kind of oversee things from here."

"Crisis management?" Karen blurted, thinking Root was talking about the radiation of Lower Manhattan.

"This facility was never intended to hold people. No one could've guessed that people who jumped down a sewer pipe would find a way out through the water recycling plant, but they came anyway, didn't they? So we try to keep everyone fed. But after they breached the labs, which weren't properly cleaned, it automatically became a quarantine facility."

"Quarant . . . ?"

"This place is contaminated," Root explained, "that's why we can't let anyone out. Of course, try telling that to Plato!"

"What happens if . . . they go?" Karen squeezed out the idea.

"I don't know. We're kind of worried that the EGGS epidemic and Staten Island Fever came out of here, but we just don't know. It's a long story, and we're trying the best we can . . ."

Karen was unable to concentrate on much more than three words at a time, so although Root's basic ideas broke through, she was unable to comprehend larger concepts.

As the kindly lady talked, she helped remove the few remaining strands of dirty rags that were clinging to Karen's body. Once Karen was nude, Root led her into a small bathroom with a shower. She turned the dials until some warm water came up.

"Technically, I'm not supposed to bring anyone in here. But you poor Garlic Heads actually volunteered, so you're on our watch list."

"What list?"

"You're an integral part of the Rescue City apparatus . . . I don't know what you're doing here, but I can't imagine you coming here on your own. You're too smart for that, aren't you?"

Root carefully led Karen into the stream of water. Karen basked in the luxurious warmth as the layers of filth that had been caked onto her skin were gently washed away.

The "contamination curtain," as it was called—the partition between the uninhabited part of Manhattan, which was being scrubbed down, and the still-populated parts of the city—was being moved farther and farther north.

By late January 1971, the curtain had been pushed all the way up to 96th Street on the west side of Central Park, though only to 72nd Street on the east side. Arguments broke out, with some people claiming that the rad numbers had been fudged due to the fact that the east side was full of wealthy whites, while the west side was a neighborhood of low-income minorities. The day after the New York Post ran the headline "Radioactive Racism," Mayor Lindsay called a news conference and announced that by February 6, the quarantine line would run along the south side of 110th Street, directly across the island. There would be mandatory evacuation, from the East River, along the northern edge of Central Park, all the way to the Hudson River, including all highways, bridges, and tunnels.

By mid-February, the hurricane fencing marking the contamination line was only fifty feet away from Karen's building. The brazen, furious act of pulling the lever nearly a year earlier had slowly followed her to her front door. As the city and state worked double time to relocate people to temporary housing in the outer boroughs, the federal government had finally settled upon a spot in central Nevada for the more significant solution, and put all its efforts into making the new Rescue City location inhabitable. In the meantime, as south Harlem went from a low-income ghetto to a ghost town, the real estate in the south and central Bronx boomed. Most of the other residents of the dojo building had already relocated to the neighboring boroughs, but Karen, Manuel, and Carlos continued living under Hrag's roof, along with several other karate diehards. The three of them took turns teaching two largely symbolic classes downstairs. By the last few days of February, the Puerto Rican immigrants who were once the area's principal residents were replaced by the National Guard, who used the grassy field to the south of St. John the Divine as an assembly ground. Seeing the soldiers line up on Amsterdam Avenue each morning and do roll call made Karen feel as though she were living under occupation.

As the first anniversary approached of what was now being called "the attack," it was estimated that over one million people had been drained out of Manhattan. Many in the lower classes had applied and been accepted into the federal government's Rescue City program. But soon a new controversy flared up: the original plan allowed for a light-rail train from Rescue City across the desert to Las Vegas, and Nevada residents were furious. The notion of the world's biggest ghetto being dumped in their backyard was bad enough, but a free shuttle to their largest and most profitable city was simply unacceptable.

Before the Nevada governor could issue a statement, the Rescue City planners withdrew the proposed rail service. Rescue City had to be sealed, with the only way out being through its own airfield back to New York City. That, combined with no guaranteed end date when New York residents would be returning home, started making the place sound more like a penal colony.

Throughout this time, Columbia University had managed to shift most of its undergraduate classes to other campuses out in Queens and the Bronx. The law school remained, though, and Karen continued attending classes during the summer months. She replaced vodka, which she would sip during the daytime, with barbiturates, which she would take only at night, and her grades mildly improved. Throughout the year, her parents had tried futilely to convince her to leave the city. Her mother and father would call separately, quoting daily news reports of the city's hazardous conditions, begging her to transfer to Boston Law or take a leave of absence until the crisis was resolved. She wouldn't hear of it; graduation was within her grasp.

One night, after Karen had taken a couple pills, her mother called to again plead with her to leave.

"Almost there," she muttered as she began nodding off, "almost over."

"Almost where?" her mother asked. "What's the matter with you?"

"Hate life."

"What?"

"Late night, got to sleep." Karen hung up.

All but a skeletal body of students and teachers had transferred or quit entirely. The silent menace of low-level radioactivity in Manhattan created a constant cloud of anxiety for most people. But Karen knew that the real reason she couldn't leave the school and neighborhood was sheer guilt for fucking up so many lives.

Finally at their wit's end, her parents called her brother Uli, who likewise phoned and pleaded with Karen to leave.

"You're not going to wake up one day and just be sick with cancer. It's more insidious than that. In about ten or twenty years, you'll get a lump, and it'll be biopsied, and maybe they'll see that it's benign and remove it. But then soon after, you'll find another one. And that'll be removed. And then the next one will show malignancy, but they'll say that it can be treated—"

"The government," she interrupted, then paused. "*Your* government is saying it's still safe here."

"I'm the first to say that they've been wrong before," he replied.

"Until they say it's a mortal danger, I ain't budging," she said spitefully.

The government had timed it so that Rescue City officially opened on the first anniversary of the event that had devastated New York. Vice President Spiro T. Agnew flew to Nevada to cut the ribbon himself. Shuttle service had begun—an air shuttle in which applicants were brought from JFK to the Nevada desert around the clock. Each person required full processing, which meant housing, food, and some kind of work assignment.

37

In mid-August the inevitable occurred. Mayor Lindsay—whose popularity had skyrocketed since the crisis—announced the good news that the rad levels throughout Manhattan had finally stopped rising. Unfortunately, he added, the Atomic Energy Commission, which had completed a full assessment of the entire city, had found that the rad levels from the southwestern edge of Queens, down through Greenpoint and Williamsburg to the middle of Cobble Hill, Brooklyn, had all risen.

"I'm pleased to report that the levels aren't high enough to require a mandatory evacuation. I know this is very difficult for everyone. My own family was forced to move out of Gracie Mansion, but with this latest news, we're just not taking any more chances. All the citizens of Manhattan, right up to the Harlem River, will have sixty days to vacate their homes for cleaning. Additionally, it is with much sadness that we're asking the residents of Brooklyn Heights south of the Brooklyn Bridge, west of Court Street, and right down to Atlantic Avenue, to also evacuate. We're allowing them ninety days, nearly three months, to do so." The mayor then showed a map detailing how far the new containment borders would extend into eastern Brooklyn, including the coast guard base at Governors Island.

After hearing this crushing news, Karen pulled on her shoes and rushed out the door, heading for the last liquor store still open in the area. In the past week, vodka had reemerged as her primary vice. But as she turned down 112th Street, she spotted a National Guard outfit patrolling the area. Checking her shirt pocket, she realized that she'd left her wallet at home, which would mean being escorted back. She ducked into some bombed-out tenement, hoping to let them pass. Then she heard the door swing open after her and feared one of them had followed her inside. She stopped in the ground-level corridor, trying to act like she lived there.

"Karen," she heard a ghostly male voice whisper behind her.

She turned around, startled, and under an old leather jacket that was zipped up to the collar, she recognized John Jacobs—J.J.—from the SDS.

"Hey," she replied meekly.

"I got a message awhile back that I was supposed to call you."

"Huh?"

"Some *friends* said you were looking for me." He looked at her intensely.

"Oh! That was over a year ago," Karen said, remembering her conversation with Diana Oughton and her friend Kathy on the day Mallory died.

"The FBI has been hunting me down since then."

"Yeah, a pair of them interviewed me."

"They think we had something to do with this whole fucking contamination thing, since it happened just afterward," J.J. said.

"I'm sure they'd be more than happy to pin the whole thing on the SDS."

"Mallory always used to say that you shared our views, just not our commitment . . ."

At that moment, Karen realized this encounter was no coincidence—J.J. must've been following her. "What are you saying?" she asked bluntly.

"You've heard of this Rescue City program that the federal government has set up in Nevada."

"Yeah, it's like Medicaid, public housing, and food stamps all rolled up into one."

"The lower crust of New York has been sliced off and shipped out, while the upper crust is moving to lovely vacation spots."

"The rich get richer and the poor get children, what else is new?"

"The city and the rest of the country are on high alert until they find out who did this."

"So?"

"We're wondering if we can turn Rescue City to our advantage," J.J. said.

"To your advantage?"

"Last year, before all this, we felt that this country was on the brink. All it needed was a strong jolt to move into a new stage of freedom . . ."

"Clearly you were wrong," Karen responded, tired of hearing about the always-imminent revolution.

"Well, we also feel that if there is any chance of this ever happening, our best shot will be in this new settlement in Nevada. I mean, the poorest and most disenfranchised people of this city are being dumped out there for who knows how long."

"What the fuck does this have to do with me?"

"We figured that if we could send in a cell of our own—"

"To blow them up?" she interrupted angrily.

"It's a completely noncombative, no-risk mission. Hell, I don't even think it's illegal," he said. "We're simply hoping to try to use this as a propaganda opportunity to persuade the population while they're stuck in the middle of Nevada."

"Persuade them of what?"

"Soon there will be tens of thousands of poor people out there. We're hoping to use the time there to build recruitment so that when everyone is shipped back here, we'll have a real army."

Karen found herself chuckling.

"Do you know that all the key players of the Russian Revolution met and planned in the czar's prison camps in Siberia? Their prisons became universities for the old Bolsheviks!"

"I repeat: what does any of this shit have to do with me?"

"See, we got three others who are willing to go there as part of their Alternative Service program. The problem is, we need someone legitimate to join so that the program will accept them together as a group. We need someone who the government would really want—you."

"Why would anyone want *me*?"

"You're perfect! You're graduating from an Ivy League law school, with a brother in the FBI, completely above suspicion."

"You're kidding, right? They know I was in the SDS. The FBI came to see me about Mallory."

"They've got many thousands of people out there, and only a very small staff of trained personnel to run the place."

"I was arrested during the student takeover."

"We all were—that was a misdemeanor. Look, everyone going there is a do-good lefty. You have a long history of doing altruistic community work, mostly for that neighborhood karate school. You'd be a shoo-in."

"Who are the other two people going in?"

"Mallory Levine and—"

"Mallory's dead! I saw her body blown apart, so don't bullshit me!"

"They misidentified her corpse as Diana Oughton," J.J. said softly.

"And since charges in Chicago were dismissed against Mallory, and Diana already had a conviction on her record, we decided to maintain the fallacy."

"Diana is going under the name *Mallory Levine?*"

"Along with her boyfriend William."

"Who's the third person in this propaganda brigade?" Karen asked, now slightly amused.

"We got this street-tough sometime crossdresser named Deere Flare. A runaway, hustler type, but she gets the job done."

"What exactly would I be doing once I'm in this . . . Rescue City?"

"Are you kidding? You'd have your choice of jobs! They're suffering from a serious shortage of trained professionals. You'd probably be teamed up with some army official, but the army is just handing out supplies. They want the civilians to run the show."

"I don't think so," she said flatly.

"Just think about it; we really need you. See, in an effort to enlist Ivy Leaguers, the Rescue City program has created this group-package deal, but it's only available if you register through a college, which is another reason we're approaching you—you were in the SDS and you've been at Columbia continuously. They're offering priority housing, top jobs, and salaries, if three or more join up together with an alum."

"You have far more zealous members than me," Karen said.

"At this point, everyone else has either graduated or has a police record, which is an automatic rejection."

"Well I'm sorry, but—"

"Just think it over. You're going to the liquor store tomorrow, aren't you?"

"Why would you say that?" She suddenly felt self-conscious.

"'Cause I've been following you for a while. You've started going there every day. When you go there tomorrow at this time, you can give me your final decision." With that, he slipped out of the tenement and was gone.

"No fucking way," she said softly.

After all I've been through, there's no way I'm wasting a year of my life isolated in some domestic peace corps for ghetto dwellers, she thought as she continued to the liquor store. That night, though, as she started swilling down gulp after gulp of fiery liquid, she considered the radioactive baby slowly crawling northward up Manhattan until it had finally found her—its birth mother. During that long, awful, drunken night, she put herself on trial. Over the past few weeks she'd been unable to sleep or eat, and her drinking was once again spiraling out of control. She had missed so many summer classes that she feared she was going to fail her exams. Throughout the night, as she thought about what she had done, she found herself having a difficult time just catching her breath. Every day she felt squeezed between the guilt of her action and the anxiety of being apprehended. As her panic intensified, she was certain she was going to have a heart attack. She had worked so hard to make herself valuable, goddamnit! Her life was supposed to have *meaning*!

How could she fight for the revolution or oppose the fascist oligarchs who were undermining democracy and enslaving the masses, when she herself had done far worse to the countless poor people living on the fringes of New York City?

She eventually passed out, utterly hammered, as the sun was coming up, and slept through Constitutional Law and Property, her first class. When she woke at noon, instead of rushing off to her afternoon class, she popped a breath mint and headed to the college branch of the Rescue City program in Ferris Booth Hall. There, she found a hunched ladybug of a creature with a name tag that said, *Gretchen, Supervisor*, who was sitting reading a newspaper. When Karen entered, Gretchen rose to her feet.

"So how's this place being run anyway?"

"Being run?"

"Yeah, Rescue City. Is it like a prison with guards and a warden?" Karen asked with a trace of sarcasm.

"These are American citizens with all their rights fully intact. So the government is actually trying to stay out of it. Ideally it'll be governed by the people, for the people."

"Right," Karen said, this time not at all hiding her sarcasm. "What kind of food and supplies will there be?"

"After many bids, the government has awarded the operating contract to a company called the Feedmore Corporation. They'll be purchasing and handling the stock and supplies."

"Where exactly is this place located?"

Gretchen pulled out a brochure that had a tiny map of the US with an enlarged image of Nevada. In the center of the state was a big red dot that said, *RESCUE CITY!*

"Why can't it be in Long Island or Jersey?" Karen asked, although she already knew the answer.

Gretchen explained that this was the only place within the lower forty-eight states that had not put up major resistance to the program. It was a former installation—"a military-situation facility," roughly two-thirds the size of New York City. But its primary feature was the vast buffer zone of public land around the installation, making it difficult to both enter and exit.

"Admittedly, there are no roads in or out of the place, but this is for protection," Gretchen said.

"Protection from what? If no one can leave the place, it's a prison."

"For the record, people *can* leave the place. There are no fences or guards. We'd just rather they didn't."

"Why do you suppose that is? I mean, why can't they just be treated like everyone else?"

"'Cause they're not. Consider this from the native-Nevadan point of view. It's as if an army has invaded their home."

Gretchen had a point. Karen felt this way regarding the National Guard outfits that patrolled her neighborhood five times a day. She kept fantasizing about starting a guerrilla group and fighting these uptown invaders.

"Which leads me to my next question: when's everyone being brought back here?"

"When it's safe," Gretchen said.

"And who gets to decide that?"

The human ladybug took out a different brochure and summarized it: "There are a wide range of estimates, from physicists, environmentalists, and various cleanup managers, each giving their opinion on how long it will take to fully restore a low-level radioactive site the size and contours of Manhattan to an inhabitable high-density area."

"And what are the estimates?"

"Conservative estimates put it at two years."

"And what do the most cautious liberal estimates say?" Karen pushed.

"The most cautious authorities say never. They say the area is an eternal wasteland and should be fenced off permanently."

"So Rescue City could turn into a life sentence."

"Hiroshima and Nagasaki were hit with far worse radiation and they're now reinhabited, but we don't know. I'm not sure how long the Rescue City program will last, but the simple fact is that the rad levels currently aren't safe here. And in two months, everyone in Manhattan is going to leave, either on their own or by force."

"Shit," Karen muttered.

"Can I ask you a little about yourself?"

"I'm a law student, about to graduate."

Gretchen pointed out that Rescue City was already suffering from a severe shortage of professional workers and assured Karen that if she did decide to join the program, she would have a broad selection of top-level management positions, as well as her pick of luxury housing and other top-tier amenities.

Karen glanced at the clock on the wall and saw that she was almost late for her rendezvous with J.J. She thanked Gretchen, said she'd think about it, and left.

Karen walked the short distance to the liquor store and looked around. Not seeing J.J., she went inside. Instead of inspecting the vodka bottles that had become the medication to her growing anguish, she found herself imagining how life would be in the Nevada desert, trying to help all those poor people whose lives she had derailed. For the first time in months, she felt a strange sense of calm. She decided right there in front of the wall of liquor that she simply had no other choice. When she finally exited the liquor store, J.J. came hurrying up.

"Sorry I'm late, but I thought I was being followed and I couldn't take any chances," he explained.

"I'm not offering a blank check," she said. "I want no part in any violence or murder, understand?"

He sighed and said they weren't planning anything like that, but frankly they had no idea what to expect.

"I'll do you people a favor to get you in there, but once inside, I'll decide on a case-by-case basis what my participation will be. Take it or leave it."

"We'll take it. Are you ready to go, because the sooner—"

"I need two weeks." She had already thought it all through. "Friday, September 3, at noon, outside Ferris Booth, and we'll all register together."

"We were hoping to do it today," J.J. said.

"Two weeks—take it or leave it."

He nodded yes and she headed home.

Karen called her old pal Alvin Rich, one of the few remaining law students, and invited him for a burger at the West End, her treat.

After a brief game of catch-up, Karen shared her conundrum: she ran a small karate studio with two friends that helped a lot of neighborhood kids. They also owned the old tenement and rented out most of the apartments. Unfortunately, the building had debts and liens against it.

"We're *all* going to be evicted in the next month or so," he said simply.

"What I'm wondering is what can be done when they clean the place up and we return."

"Chapter 11 on the building and turn the karate club into a not-for-profit, apply for grants, and run it that way. The city is filled with cheap studios that you can rent for a song."

"We need to keep the building," she said.

"Look, Karen, I know you're talking about your little storefront where you and Mal lived. She told us how you help those people, and I've always admired that, but painful as it is, you're fighting a losing battle."

"I can't just let this go."

"Then hold it together. File for nonprofit status and set up a board of trustees. Maybe try to get some press, legitimize your membership so it looks more like a community center. When everyone returns to the area, I bet city, state, and local government agencies, along with the private sector, will be offering grants, tax breaks, and low-interest loans to pull people back here."

That made sense. "Do you think *you* can do it?"

"Do what?" he asked.

Karen told him that she was going into the Rescue City program and needed to know that someone would act as counsel for her organization in her absence.

"There's no telling when all the dust will settle on this," Alvin said. "Hell, you'll probably be back here before me. You can do it yourself."

"But I'm leaving soon, and if I don't make it back I want to know it's in safe hands."

"Boy, you're asking one big favor here."

Karen took his hand and looked deep into his eyes. "I run the place with two Central American guys who barely have a high school education. They really need someone who knows the law and they can count on. They're good people, Al."

"Give them my number, I'll do what I can."

Karen hugged and thanked him with a kiss on the cheek. She knew that once he got involved, he'd stay with it. When she got home she called a thrift store in the Bronx, intending to donate her furniture and clothes, but once they learned where she was, they told her they were no longer accepting donations from Manhattan for fear of contaminants.

She then sat down with Carlos and Manuel and updated them on the situation. "While I'm away, a friend named Alvin Rich has agreed to help you with all legal matters."

"What are you saying?" Carlos asked.

"I'm leaving in two weeks to help those in Rescue City."

"Why, Karen?" Manuel asked, seeing the peril in such a decision. He and Carlos had both rejected the Rescue City option.

"This contamination has deeply affected me," she said, tapping her heart. She figured that Manuel thought she meant she'd been affected physically; over the past few months, she had stopped sparring with him and the others. In fact, these days she was only handling business affairs. Since the contamination, her weight had steadily increased. Dark rings had deepened around her eyes, and when they met in the evenings, she'd slur her words and stagger her way up the steps.

"But you know the law, Karen," said Carlos. "What will happen to us?"

She explained that Alvin knew real estate law better than she did, and that he had agreed to help the karate school until she got back, and to stay on if she didn't.

"Poor Hrag," Carlos said.

"Do me a favor and don't tell anyone else about my leaving." Karen didn't want to have to deal with tearful farewells just yet.

38

At the agreed-upon date and time, Karen met with her three young revolutionaries: a tall, handsome blond man named William Clayton, a young, slim androgyne called Deere Flare, and Diana, the woman whom she'd met briefly after the explosion that killed Mallory. Now Diana was using Mallory's name, and other than the loss of her finger, she pretended that the incident had never occurred. After a brief introduction, all four marched into the Alternative Service office at Columbia and signed up with Gretchen—the largest single win the office had had to date.

On the forms, all four wrote that they wanted to serve in the newly formed Rescue City government. They were given appointments for medical checkups, a daylong orientation, and a date to report at JFK for their flight—Saturday, September 11, 1971, at nine a.m., one week away.

That night, Karen called her parents and said she wanted to come visit them in Boston and stay for a night.

"I'll start cooking now," her mother kidded.

When Karen went downstairs, she saw Manuel and three older guys sparring at the dojo. Although she hadn't practiced in a while, she pulled on her old white jacket, belt, and pants, and sparred with Carlos, who was clearly pulling his punches. There were now fewer than ten karate practitioners who hadn't moved out of the area or enrolled in one of the government evacuation programs. They all knew it was just a matter of weeks before the curtain would cover all of Manhattan.

At one point in their match, Karen gave Carlos a hard kick and he responded by throwing her backward, knocking her to the ground. She sat there a moment, holding back tears. Looking out the window toward Amsterdam Avenue, she thought that in a matter of weeks, all this would be emptied, leaving only Hrag's ghost to roam the old building. And who knows what would become of the city once they had scrubbed everything down, possibly years later. What kind of city would it turn into?

"You okay?" Carlos finally asked.

She nodded yes.

Before she returned to the office to deal with some paperwork, she announced to all that she was going to be leaving soon.

"Where?" a young man named Eduardo asked.

"Nevada—I'm joining the Rescue City program," she said, causing him and the others to raise their eyebrows. The majority of Latino immigrants had rejected the offer. If worse came to worst, they preferred to return home. Most white Americans had simply gone back to whatever hometowns they had come from.

"Actually, maybe I'll see you there," Juan said to Karen. "My wife and I are thinking of going. We were told that we'd get a home of our own, and she wants to use the time to start a family."

"Don't you still have another semester or two of law school?" Manuel asked her.

"I do, but they're desperate, so I'm going now."

On Friday, September 10, Karen took Amtrak up to Boston. Her parents picked her up at South Station and drove her to an expensive restaurant outside the city. Her mom said she looked a little puffy and asked if she was okay. *That's because I've been getting sloshed every single day,* she thought, but only shrugged. After they had a delicious Italian meal and dessert, Karen broke the news on the ride home that she had decided to join the Rescue City program and help the displaced New York refugees. She neglected to mention that she would be flying out from New York the very next day.

"Yeah, right," her father said, assuming she was joking.

"Cut it out, hon," her mother said.

"I'm not kidding."

"Well, it's out of the question," her mother said simply.

"I'm an adult," Karen replied. "I have the right to go without your permission."

"Don't you understand?" her father said, clutching the steering wheel. "It's like a prison sentence. The ACLU has already filed a request for an injunction. You could be stuck out there for years!"

"No judge would sign it. Everyone is saying it's probably going to be no more than two years tops."

"That's what the government said about Vietnam!"

"It's about helping people who really need my help."

"What about your law degree?" her father asked. "You haven't completed your final year."

"These people need me more."

"You can get a thousand jobs to help people here!" her mother exclaimed.

"I have to help *those* people."

"Why?"

"I just do." Clearly she couldn't divulge anything more. "And I've made up my mind, so nothing you can say will change it."

They drove the rest of the way in silence. When they arrived home, the discussions began again and quickly turned into a heated argument.

"I've lived among these people for most of a decade," she said. "They've become my community and they desperately need help."

"I don't understand why she's doing this. What did we do?" her mother said to her father in Armenian, as if she weren't there.

"I'm doing this 'cause it's the right thing to do!"

Quickly the evening turned to screams and tears as her parents begged, threatened, and did everything else they could to try to get her to change her mind. Eventually, her father got on the phone and called her older brother.

"No one knows this yet, but Nevada has officially turned into a disaster," Uli disclosed.

Karen's father handed her the phone, hoping her brother might be able to change her mind.

"Karen, listen to me: I know you don't like what I do, and you probably don't like me—"

"Say what you mean."

"It's pure hell over there. You don't want to go."

"I just finished six years in Harlem," she said to him and her parents simultaneously. "Two years in Nevada can't be much worse."

"Two years?" her brother replied, amused. "Even the most conservative estimates put it at five years before Manhattan is anywhere near ready."

"Fine, five years," she said without hesitation.

"Let me ask you something, Karen. It's been nearly six months since they started sending people out there. Have you seen a single news piece on the place?"

"Yeah, I've seen it on the news."

"Those pieces are fake. You haven't seen any footage inside Nevada."

"No, but . . ."

"Do you know why?"

"I'm sure you're going to tell me some insane reason," she sighed.

"Actually, it's a very sane reason. Rescue City is a total catastrophe."

"What does that mean?"

"Rape, murder, pillaging, you name it," Uli said. "It's like being in prison. People are organizing into gangs as soon as they arrive, and they're battling with each other for every inch of the yard. The murder rate is through the roof. And if that's not bad enough, the violence has spilled over and they're beginning to kill soldiers."

"I don't believe it," Karen said calmly.

"I've never lied to you. You know why—I've never had to. And I'm not doing it now. Hey, if you want to leave the country, or piss off Mom and Dad, join the Peace Corps. Hell, go to Vietnam, it's much safer. But stay out of Nevada."

"Why would they kill soldiers?"

"The government found an isolated training base in the most desolate part of the country and spent less than a single year trying to create an infrastructure for one million people. And now, electricity, water, sewage, and lodging are all coming up short. Forget legal and medical services, those people are screwed."

As her brother continued describing the violent and squalid conditions, Karen's desire to go there only increased; she had to help all those whose lives she had ruined.

Over the course of the next two hours, she stopped talking and simply listened to her parents, allowing them to vent. Fearing that they would attempt to physically restrain her if she simply ignored them, she pretended to reconsider.

"Tell us you're not doing this!" her mother implored, as they were all beginning to collapse with exhaustion.

"I'll tell you what," Karen said. "I'll sleep on it and we'll talk in the morning."

"Okay," said her father.

With tears in their eyes, they all hugged and kissed and then went to their rooms. Karen lay down without pulling back the covers and tried to rest awhile. But she kept thinking of what she might've said, might *still* say, to make them understand. After a couple hours, too nervous to sleep, she flipped on her lamp and wrote a note:

Mom and Dad,

I love you both more dearly than you could ever imagine. You've given me a wonderful life, and for that very reason I must do this. Dad, when you came to the city two years ago, when you both asked what I was going to do with my life, I gave some flippant response, and Dad, you said: "It's best having a career that gives you a higher reason to live. Because when all else fails, it's the only thing that keeps you going." It was the wisest thing you've ever told me. And that pretty much describes this situation. Everything in my life, from my commitment to help beleaguered people, to the fact that I have spent years in an underprivileged section of Manhattan with an up-close view of the harm inflicted on those who I have come to see as my people, my village—all this points me in one clear direction. Dear friends who I've made over the years are already there, so I will not be alone. Lately, I have developed a bad drinking problem. The reason is simple: I have been fighting my desire to please you and ignoring my deeper need to help these forsaken people. Quite simply, I can't see myself living out my life without doing this. I only hope you can understand. This might be a selfish act, but I see no decent alternative. To do anything else would be tantamount to suicide. More than anything, I want you to know that this isn't intended as a hostile act against you. Actually, it's a deeply personal mission—a calling, if you will. Maybe the explanation for my motives can be found in our Armenian heritage—seeing minorities isolated by their own government, essentially abandoned. I simply can't turn my back on them. In any case, I'll be fine and I'll see you soon.

I love you both with all my heart and soul,
Karen

Quietly, she called a car service. She instructed the dispatcher to have the vehicle wait for her on the corner. She opened her bedroom window and sneaked out . . .

39

"Side effects . . . understand? This drug has certain side effects. Do you understand?"

"Side?" Karen said, awakening on a narrow metal cot, as the woman injected her with a hypodermic.

"Some have hallucinations; there are also claims of telepathy."

When she started crying, Root thought it was due to the pain from the injection, but it was actually because she was boarding the early-morning train in Boston fearing she might never see her parents again.

She arrived at 125th Street, which was now the southernmost stop for all trains going into New York City. From there she caught a cross-town bus.

Once she reached Broadway, she had intended to stop at home and pick up a few personal items, but she had all her necessities with her. The thought of returning and saying goodbye to everyone yet again, particularly after abandoning her parents, was more than she could take. Instead she found a secluded bench near where the bus would pick up those headed to JFK for the shuttle to Rescue City. She lay down for a rest.

When she awoke, she realized the airport bus had already arrived and was now packed. The only available seat was in the back, away from the counterfeit Mallory and their two other companions who were seated in the front. No matter; she was simply grateful to be leaving.

On the plane, the front few aisles were reserved for the Garlic Heads. She was seated between a doctor who had lost his license and an electrical engineer who had been given the choice between two years in jail or Rescue City—he wouldn't tell her what crime he had committed. It turned out that most of the professionals on the plane were either religious types or people with legal problems. Even the usual altruistic liberals were missing.

After the food service, a US Army officer named Captain Rose stood in the aisle and gave a talk on what could be expected of the volunteers and the tasks that awaited them up ahead.

"I won't lie to you, the job is formidable. Rescue City is still in turmoil—we simply haven't had enough time to finish building it—but we should be finished over the next six months, and once we get a steady infrastructure in place, along with police, sanitation workers, and representatives who can voice people's concerns, things should calm down. And a lot of that is going to be your job . . ." As he continued detailing the endless tasks in a positive way, trying to inspire the Garlic Heads, Karen dozed off.

She woke up to screams—gunshots had been fired right up through the fuselage of the plane. Apparently they were flying over their destination.

As soon as they landed, she knew that her brother wasn't exaggerating. Colonel Bull Premer, who was in charge of trying to assemble a civilian government, was in way over his head. While they were driving through the place, Karen was impressed by how developed this strange little city was. Far from being some kind of giant Red Cross encampment, the place had streets, avenues, and a budding infrastructure that included electricity, public transportation, and a solid sewer system.

"NewYorkCityland," Diana/Mallory aptly called it. The place felt like an odd interpretation of the original crusty city in the spirit of a lighthearted Hollywood musical.

When they got their housing assignments, they were updated regarding some of the as-yet-unreported problems: First and foremost was an unknown disease, which had already killed a number of pregnant women. Although they still hadn't given up the hope of trying to tackle the problem, this was a huge setback for the new community. Countless young couples had come to Rescue City with the express purpose of raising a family. Another significant problem, in the wake of the guerrilla fights that were constantly breaking out, was the lack of so many basic staples. The Feedmore Corporation was simply unable to match affordable supplies with rising demand. Like every other part of the program, they just hadn't had enough time. *Things will get better—just give us time!* was the slogan printed on nearly every billboard Karen saw. Yet supply planes were still landing filled with superfluous gadgets and items no one wanted. Cans of cranberry chutney, tins of pickled octopus, boxes of staple removers, lint brushes, strings of Christmas lights, and inner tube patching kits were piling up unopened in plane hangars, while thousands hadn't eaten fresh fruit in weeks.

The members of the newly arrived Weather Bureau cell—Karen, "Mallory Levine," Bill Clayton, and Deere Flare—had all requested work in "legal services," and were startled to discover that no official legal system had been established yet. Apparently, since there wasn't a functioning police force, there was no need for a criminal justice system. So Bill and Mallory were reassigned to administrative jobs in the nascent government, which still hadn't been formally accepted by the people. Day after day, week after week, they'd sit around in the conference rooms making small talk with each other while watching fires rage in the city around them.

Two months after their arrival, a bomb went off in the Williamsburgh Savings Bank Building, killing six of the Alternative Service workers, five of whom were doctors. In a single attack, a fifth of Rescue City's doctors had been wiped out.

"The real problem is that we're on the wrong side," Deere opined. "We should've just come with everyone else, not in this elite fucking program, 'cause now we're targets. *We're* the system!"

"She's right," Bill chuckled. "We're on the brink of the revolution—and we're the establishment."

Three months into their stay, the army discovered that the locals down in Staten Island had already developed a grassroots system to create explosives. Although initially there had only been fighting between emerging gangs, over the past few months the American soldiers who were acting as an interim police department as well as handling food dispersal had become a primary target. Initially the purveyors of violence who were apprehended had been deported out of Rescue City, but for each one removed, ten more seemed to take his or her place.

Each week more soldiers were flown out in body bags. To top it all off, instead of sending in more reinforcements and taking out the gangs, the US government seemed to be backing down. Budget overages had proven disastrous.

In the first week of January 1972, Colonel Bull Premer was able to patch together a fragile mosaic of truces and treaties with the larger gangs. A frail coalition finally seemed to be emerging. Simultaneously a rudimentary health care system, consisting of three infirmaries, was set up. Both Karen and Deere became administrators in the budding civilian police department, but it still lacked the manpower to patrol much beyond the three square blocks of the Williamsburgh Justice Plaza. For brief stretches things seemed to stabilize. Five months after they had arrived, and nearly a year after the first wave of the experts had landed in Rescue City, a group of them prepared a petition demanding that they be released from their contracts in Rescue City:

> *Conditions here are deplorable. We have seen our colleagues, friends, and loved ones die. And we are still unable to provide the specialized services we were brought here to perform.*

Nearly every Garlic Head signed it.

Furious, Premer refused to meet with them. He reported that he was too busy. A month later, with a delicate house of cards in place between gangs and the emerging police force, the US Army abruptly pulled out. Every single soldier, gone, most leaving clothes and personal effects behind.

It wasn't the gangs that reacted first, but the hundreds of workers in the Alternative Service program. When they realized that the military had evacuated, Bill, Mallory, Deere, Karen, and a bunch of other Garlic Heads piled into solicars and headed in a caravan over the Zano Bridge. They all sped down to the chained gates of the Staten Island military air base, where they cut the locks and hurried inside. There, with utter shock, they found that they had indeed been completely abandoned in the middle of a war zone.

"What the hell are we gonna do?" asked the acting head of the education department, who had enlisted to start an adult literacy program.

"What *can* we do?" replied the head of the nutrition council. "We're stuck."

"Back to Williamsburgh Plaza!" called out Newt Underwood, the self-appointed head of the Rescue City police department.

All quietly drove back to the complex, where they did their best to fortify the surrounding area in the event of a possible attack.

As the citizens of Rescue City started to realize what had happened, a stream of cars came over from the Bronx, Manhattan, Brooklyn, and Queens, breaking open storage lockers and hangars and ransacking the Feedmore field office in Staten Island. A looting race broke out. Valuables, vehicles, and anything else that wasn't nailed down were snatched up by mobs of greedy hands. Next, the more established gangs stepped in and began drawing up boundaries between various territories.

Everyone started to realize that the closest thing they'd had to an administration had abandoned them, and the skies were clear blue. For the first time since the opening of the reservation, not a single supply plane was landing or taking off. Only impassable hills and arid desert surrounded them. People waited, combing the horizons, expecting something. Some hoped there might be a newer, larger offensive. But three days passed, then four, then five, and there were still no signs from the outside world. All began to fear that they were going to starve to death. Eight days after the US Army pulled out, the very first plane appeared in the sky. There was a nervous uncertainty in the air. What could a single plane offer? After it landed and taxied over to a big supply warehouse, the large bay door of the craft slowly opened and there it sat. Robert LaCoste, the leader of the biggest gang in Rescue City, who had taken over the Staten Island airfield, stepped up onto the plane with his younger brother Anthony and two of his armed lieutenants. Inside they found it to be unmanned and neatly packed with supplies strapped onto wooden pallets. Near the entrance was a printed notice:

1. *IF YOU WANT MORE SUPPLIES:*
2. *USING FORKLIFT, REMOVE ALL SUPPLIES ON BOARD.*
3. *AFTERWARD, IF ANYONE REMAINS ON THE PLANE, IT WILL NOT TAKE OFF.*
4. *IF IT DOESN'T TAKE OFF, NO OTHER SUPPLY PLANES WILL LAND.*

5. *ONCE THIS PLANE IS IN THE AIR, THE NEXT PLANE, ALSO STOCKED WITH SUPPLIES, WILL LAND.*
6. *THE SOONER YOU EMPTY EVERY PLANE AND THEY TAKE OFF, THE MORE SUPPLIES WILL BE IMPORTED.*

The three biggest gangs quickly agreed to a new truce: each would provide an equal number of staff to run the airport and everyone would comply with the instructions. Then they emptied the plane, allowing it to take off. Sure enough, within thirty minutes a second plane landed, thus allowing more food and supplies to flow back into the city. In the meantime, the gang leaders began dividing the stock among their own people.

"They've been waiting for this all along!" the new Mallory declared that very afternoon. She was the first in the cell to have this revelation.

"Waiting for what?"

"The government has been waiting to turn this place into a big Automat."

"She's right," Bill said. "Think about it. This isn't Vietnam, they don't need to end hostilities. All they have to do is keep us here until the old city has been wiped down."

"Fuck!" Deere screamed. "We fell into their trap coming here!"

"Actually, we might be in luck," Mallory said. "If there's no military here, we're not going to be facing any resistance. We'll have free run of this pla—"

The earth itself gave a sudden shrug. Smoke and dust filled the tight chamber and a bolt of consciousness shot through Karen's body, awakening her to the moment. She was lying in a clean single bed, naked, sweaty, and utterly exhausted. She looked around at the dimly lit room. It wasn't a prison cell, but its lack of windows created a sense of captivity. Sure enough, when she tried to move, she found that her wrists were restrained.

"Help!" she screamed out.

"Nothing to worry about," she heard as the door opened and Root appeared.

"Earthquake?" Karen whispered.

"No, a gas main erupted above us."

"Let me the hell out!"

"You still have to be redacted."

"What?"

"We need to erase some of what you experienced here, but the good news is that you should be fine."

"I'm fine now!" Karen yanked at her wrist restraints.

"You're experiencing hyperawareness. It will taper, and then you're going to have memory problems again. But your brain will slowly balance out as it repairs itself."

"Please . . . let me . . ." Her words trailed off as Root gave her an injection.

"This is a very mild tranquilizer to help you rest. Just take it easy . . ."

Because the US Army had pulled out and no single gang had prevailed, for the next six weeks survival was a day-to-day matter. The Garlic Heads bound together, camping out in the lobby of the Williamsburgh Building in constant fear of being attacked. Fleets of brand-new sanitation vans, minibuses, ambulances, and patrol cars all sat unused in various garages around Rescue City.

New York gangster Joe Gallo, who had written the name *Willy Loman* on his application, had been accepted into Rescue City early in the process. Once inside, though, he had immediately reached out and reconstituted his gang in northeastern Queens. He implemented a zero tolerance policy, drawing others looking for safety. Gallo was the first to establish an unofficial eye-for-an-eye approach to justice, which proved very effective.

At Gallo's invitation, Underwood, Chain, and several of the shadier Garlic Heads now settled in Queens, where under Gallo's largesse they were given a vacated complex of buildings in Kew Gardens and permitted to initiate mini police, fire, and sanitation departments that only served parts of Queens. Gallo named his new organization the We the People Social Club, which was soon nicknamed the Piggers.

Other gangs began carving up Rescue City as well, while Karen, Mallory, Bill, and Deere remained stationed in the Williamsburgh Building under the protection of a "justice collective" that went by the deliberately scary name Dead Pharaohs.

Eight months after the US Army split, just as the bigger gangs were beginning to solidify their control, a small-time hood named Jackie Wilson emerged from Hell's Kitchen in Manhattan. Somehow he had gotten ahold of several cases of automatic weapons that the US government had left behind. Though Wilson had only a small number of followers, they were highly motivated, fiercely loyal, and well trained. Instead of the scattered attacks and drive-bys of other gangs, Wilson's crew studied their rivals carefully. They began systematically assassinating charismatic leaders and lieutenants, forcing the large gangs to divide into smaller factions.

Despite their initial success, they were still a small group and couldn't hold territory, so no one thought they'd ever get much beyond Manhattan. Gallo was the only major gang leader who insulated himself and remained all but invisible. After initial attempts to kill Wilson failed, the larger gangs started simply ignoring him. That ended one night when Wilson's crew stole six new trucks, filling them with explosives, and six small tractors from a hangar in the Staten Island airfield—no one knew where they'd gotten them—and drove the vehicles to the giant spillway at the tip of Staten Island where the polluted waters of Rescue City drained. They proceeded to blow up the trucks around the large retaining walls, plugging up the giant drain with blocks of concrete, then used the tractors to shovel in tons of surrounding sand. Within three days the toxic sewage waters had risen dramatically, overflowing the banks of Staten Island. The sewage then flooded south, into the low-lying airport only a mile or so away. Soon after the airport flooding began, an emptied drone plane cut a giant wave in the rapidly rising water, barely able to get off the ground. After it vanished on the horizon, all flights in and out of the government facility once again ceased.

Three days later, the first drone landed in the former US Army airfield on the outskirts of Queens. Anger turned to amazement when people realized that not only had Wilson's small band effectively closed down the old airstrip, they had simultaneously fortified the new airfield, which was now the only place drones could land.

The Piggers and three other major gangs quickly drew up a new agreement to join forces and wipe out Wilson's group. But by this point, Wilson had managed to capture more stockpiles of Rescue City's remaining artillery, and ammo in the rest of the city was becoming scarce. He was also recruiting countless new members of smaller gangs, promising them a place at his table.

Despite a concerted attack, the gangs were repelled by Wilson's strategically placed fighters with their limitless supply of ammo. His team was hunkered down along Rockaway Boulevard, with gunmen stationed in the windows of the cluster of buildings to the southwest of the airfield that was to eventually become the Pure-ile Plurality complex; more were positioned across the Rockaway Beach community to the east; still more lined Jamaica Bay to the south so they couldn't be outflanked.

Yet two days after that first lone drone landed in the Queens air-field, no one had unloaded it. And as supplies dwindled, signs of desperation emerged in the city. Guarded warehouses filled with stock that no one would have ever dared to touch the week before were being looted. Three mornings later, Joe Gallo had his men launch a full-scale attack on the new airport from all sides. Jackie Wilson's renegade force simply mowed them down as they sprinted forward across the open field. When Gallo's few remaining men waved white flags hoping to recover their wounded, they were shot down as well.

. . . in and out of a dream, and like milk in coffee, she felt her consciousness traveling up through dirt and stone, and she could see her brother. He was about a hundred feet below her but was climbing upward. When he looked up some long, narrow shaft at her, she yelled, "HELP ME, ULI!"

"How'd you get up there?" *he called out to her.*

"Help me! I'm stuck!"

40

Furious, perplexed, and completely stymied, Joe Gallo could only have his nanny take his boys back to the house. He didn't want them to see hundreds of dead and dying men who were crying out, perishing in the hot sun, and there was absolutely nothing he could do. Though Jackie Wilson's gang was greatly outmanned, the airfield had wide-open spaces on all sides—it was easy to hold.

Hunger loomed over Rescue City, compelling the Manhattan and Brooklyn gangs to reach out to the Piggers. Gallo was finally forced to do something he swore he never would. He had an emergency pow-wow with his rivals and finally agreed to undertake one more coordinated assault two nights later. What they lacked in bullets they would make up for in numbers.

Setting up smoke screens on all sides, all three gangs simultaneously charged at exactly ten p.m. Wilson turned on floodlights and the men were mercilessly shot down until their bodies piled up like sandbags, allowing subsequent waves to retreat behind them.

By dawn's light the next morning, with the field crowded with dead bodies, large birds from the distant hills started streaming down from the sky to strip the corpses. None of the gang leaders had any doubt that it was over, but still Wilson didn't have the men to move forward, so they all just sat. As the stench of decomposing bodies intensified, Rescue City was beginning to starve. Gang leaders were forced to withdraw their surviving soldiers back to their home turfs to quell uprisings in their own communities. Gallo and his Piggers soon evacuated completely. Finally, Bill Clayton from the Weather Bureau, representing the Dead Pharaohs, came up with the only solution he could think of. He took a single white bedsheet and in large red letters he wrote, *WE SURRENDER!*

After driving to the airfield, he alone marched out over the bodies now covered with flies. When he'd made it about two hundred feet across the field holding the sheet in the air, all heard the crackle of a megaphone.

A voice informed him that Joe Gallo and the other two major gang

leaders were invited to discuss terms of surrender. They were further instructed that they could approach but must do so only in their
shoes—they couldn't wear a stitch of clothing.

An hour later, the gang leaders arrived. All three men stripped
down naked and slowly marched over their dead, across the bloody
field into the fortified airstrip, where they were given gowns and led
into an office. There, a tall black man named Jackie Wilson offered
them food and beverages.

"What are your terms?" asked Robert LaCoste, the head of what
was now the largest Manhattan-based gang. Gallo and the head of the
most powerful Brooklyn gang silently let him take the lead.

"We're stuck here," Wilson began. "This is it. The army is done
with us. We're the whole world."

"So what?"

"So killing each other is what they want."

"You're the only one doing the killing," LaCoste pointed out.

"And don't you fucking forget it."

"So we have to join your gang?"

"The gangs are done. From here on in, we're political parties."

"What do you mean?"

"Put up your best underbosses and run them as candidates."

"This is bullshit, I'm not doing it," shot back the Brooklyn gang
leader.

Wilson pulled out a pistol and shot the man in the forehead. Then he
explained that he would remain at the airport and control the landings
and dispersal of food. For their part, he wanted them to hold local elections and find representatives from each neighborhood; they would come
together as a council—a city council—and decide things as a group:
majority rule. He also expected them to cooperate on city services.

"Exactly how do we do that?" asked Gallo.

"You need to get busy: they gave us minibuses, so we should start a
transit system. There are dump trucks for garbage, buildings designed
as hospitals, and we still have whatever's left of the Garlic Heads if
you didn't kill them all. You each have gangs—have them work as a
police force that puts out fires and collects trash."

"One crucial thing we don't have is a prison," LaCoste said.

"Figure it out. We're all going to either live or die here."

"So you'll be the boss of the city council?" asked Gallo.

"Once we get a city council up and running, we'll have a mayoral
election. If I decide to run, I'll let you know."

After they had all tentatively agreed to his terms, Wilson immediately told some of his men to unload the lone drone, and under armed guard he allowed the gangs to retrieve and bury their dead. Then he made arrangements so that a certain number of trucks from different boroughs would come in each day to collect shipments of food and supplies.

Over the ensuing weeks, as drones began coming and going on a regular schedule, the quantity and quality of the stock improved. Wilson would put letters in sealed envelopes in the rear of each truck, assessing each gang's progress and issuing orders on how they should proceed. Two things quickly became apparent: first, that Wilson had informants everywhere; and second, that the shipments to each area became rewards or punishments depending on respective gangs' efforts to enact his fiats. Within one month, the citywide pact had evolved into a budding central government. Joe Gallo quickly realized that the more work he did at organizing the new bureaucracy, the more reputable he was becoming, and the more Jackie Wilson seemed to be backing off. It was then that gang leaders started rounding up the fugitive members of the Alternative Service who had been hiding in different parts of the city. Gallo had them all driven up to a warehouse in Ozone Park, Queens, where they arrived to find a buffet of decent food waiting for them.

After they ate and drank and relaxed, Gallo spoke to them: "We need a city government, and supposedly you people have taken some courses in city governmenting. Not that I have any faith in college assholes—but since Washington put all this money into suckering you fools over here, and I have a lunatic who is holding all our food hostage, we'll start with you people."

"By city government, do you mean the various departments and agencies, or are you referring to elected officials?" a former ambulance chaser named Horace Shub spoke up.

"The whole enchilada," Gallo replied. "From mayoral and borough president elections, to garbage collectors and sand sweepers."

"For starters," one young city planner said, "if we were off this reservation, the ballpark price tag for what you're talking about would be between ten and fifteen million dollars a year."

"When you say *off this reservation* . . ."

"This isn't even communism, this place is just a gift to those here. But you can't pay people with a gift they already have."

"Then I guess we'll have to take it away from them," Gallo said. "Create some form of currency, hire a workforce."

"What's our budget?" Bill from the Weather Bureau cell asked.

"Okay, asshole, let's try this again," Gallo said. "You people have two weeks to come up with a list of every job we need to make this shithole work."

"We're talking about police, firefighters, sanitation—"

"Some hospitals, and didn't someone say we have a fleet of mini-buses for a bus system?"

"I think there are also boats for dredging the harbor."

"And we found some trucks for road-repair crews."

"Fuck!" Gallo shouted, pounding his desk. "Get as many people as we can and have them break open every lock on every hangar and garage in this shithole place, and get me a full inventory of what we have. Then, based on that, we'll decide what departments we can put together and the staff we'll need."

The next week became a scavenger hunt for resources, a compromise on possible major departments, and a survey of the potential manpower Rescue City had to fill several projected hiring scenarios. As the resources came to light, various police precincts, which were also fire and sanitation battalions, were established, and plans were put on the table for two hospitals in Manhattan, another in Queens, and a clinic in Staten Island. A muscular minister named Rolland Siftwelt, also a Garlic Head, put forward that Rescue City needed a spiritual center, and requested the use of a large abandoned building in Lower Manhattan for his ministry—the Federal Reserve Theater.

"Yeah, religion's good window dressing, but let's keep it as far away as we can," Gallo responded, and he granted Siftwelt the group of vacant buildings to the south of the Queens airfield.

The major gang leaders approached Gallo and said each gang wanted to be their own political party.

"That will be chaos," Gallo stated simply. "Two parties, just like Washington."

"You don't need to do all this," said one of his underlings. "Hell, Wilson is letting trucks into JFK without doing the same sweeps that he initially did. Let's blow him the fuck up and just take this all back."

"Hell no," Gallo replied. "He was right! Before, we were able to only get whatever crap the government gave us. Now, with this system, we can actually get all these people to work for us. He's right, we're going legit, but we're keeping it within our control—two parties."

Over the following months, as Gallo and the others worked at transmogrifying the gangs into political bodies, the Garlic Heads helped assemble and organize all the resources for four major city departments: gangcops, firefighters, sanitation workers, and bus drivers. They also worked on a job hierarchy, from department heads to clerical workers, and figured out the number of people they would need to run each department.

A key problem that the Garlic Heads couldn't resolve was a justice system. Newt Underwood put Chain and his aide, Karen Sarkisian, in charge of drawing up plans to convert the Williamsburgh Building—the tallest structure in Rescue City—into a prison. They also drew up a comprehensive job tree, mapping out the shifts of guards and supervisors, totaling approximately four hundred workers. Karen sketched out a probationary system, which added another hundred people to the job force.

When Joe Gallo saw the elaborate plans for a skeletal criminal justice system, specifically the staff requirements, he said that they simply lacked the resources. Karen remarked that this was the most conservative plan they could come up with, and Gallo smiled. He turned to his former employee, Chain, and said, "Why don't you tell this fine young lady what we do up in Queens."

"Up there we employ Mr. Hammurabi's Code," Chain said simply. "Eye for an eye. Some asshole does something, we take that part of them so they can't do it again."

"But who among us has the power to decide that?" asked Karen, her idealism peeking through.

"I do," Gallo said. "And at this point we already need three thousand people on the city payroll, which we can't afford. No way can we add another five hundred to pamper criminals." With that, he left the room.

"They actually do the amputations humanely," Chain pointed out to Karen, hoping to win her over. "They use anesthesia."

Up until that moment, Karen had intended to use her education as a lawyer to guide her work in this new city. But there was little if any need for legal services, and the notion of sentencing someone to a judicial amputation was unthinkable. So she tendered her resignation from the criminal justice team. It was easy to see that any real opportunity for justice could only be found in the police department. Due to the ongoing distrust and tension between the gangs, a unit called the "council cops" had just been created. Karen was offered a dual post—with both the largest Brooklyn gang, who were now calling themselves the Crappers, and with the new citywide force, where she was supposed to serve under a former police officer named Scouter Lewis . . .

"I have no idea how far Rescue City is from here," Root muttered to her, assuming Karen was no longer understanding anything she said. "So even if I could get you out, we're surrounded by desert. This drug has a blotting agent and you're going to suffer some acute memory loss . . ."

The word *desert* was like a hook that Karen hung onto. She linked it to the scene at Dora's deathbed not long ago. She remembered the Armenian restaurateur's mother telling her about how . . . how . . . the men . . .

. . . Everything is going to be okay, but you won't remember things for ███████████████ *but eventually most will come back to you.*

The Turkish soldiers marched ████████████████████████

██

██

██

██

██

██

██

██

██

██

██

██

██

██

██

██

██

██

██

██

She remembered the men staying behind. That way the villagers did all the dirty work, butchering them. It was the women, the elderly, and the children who were marched out of the village where they had lived for centuries. She took her little boy and little girl, one in each hand, and walked them along the dirt roads, southward through the hills. When a few people cried, others yelled at them to shut up. Two gendarmes, probably from Ankara—a kid in a baggy uniform and a fat old man in a tight one—had rifles slung over their shoulders.

"What do you remember?" a female voice asked.

"I remember my daughter being taken away." Dora started crying. "Where did they take her? She was just a little girl."

"Probably to one of the Turkish families. She was probably raised as one of them."

"I hope so," Karen said in her rusty Armenian.

"I didn't know you spoke another language," the woman said. "Can you speak in English?"

"What do you want?"

"I want to know what you remember from Rescue City."

"There was no rescue. And when I was finally brought to the city, I was sold into slavery . . ."

"Karen, don't you remember coming here to the Nevada desert with the Weather Bureau group?"

"I remember red-hot steel pressed to my face—I was branded. I remember human pigs, fat disgusting old men, shoving themselves into me. Wearing rags, doing things to other Armenian girls, and we couldn't look each other in the eye for all the shame we had to contend with. One of the johns called us 'God's whores,' and he was right. We had prayed and obeyed all our lives, only to have these pigs shove themselves between our legs and smack us, or sneeze in our faces, sweat on us—for what reason . . ."

"And after that?"

"When we lost our luster, none cared 'cause we were used up. Our pride, our bodies, our youth, all gone . . ."

"Then what?"

"A ship to Athens, then steerage to America."

"Then what?"

Dora remained silent. Time didn't always move forward . . . She started coughing.

41

Coughing, coughing, she opened her eyes and realized the little room was filled with thickening smoke. For some reason she thought she was a kid and that her brother Uli was with her.

"Help me, please!" she yelled. "Help me, Uli! Please!"

Karen touched her head and found it bandaged. She got up from her cot and fumbled around the room, unable to breathe.

"Where are you? What's the matter?" she heard him asking.

"Smoke! I can't breathe, there's smoke everywhere!" She thought he was in the room with her. "We're trying to get out!"

She heard him call her name and yelled back, "Help me! Help me, Uli!"

"Hang on, Karen, I'm coming!"

He was nearby, around here somewhere. But she wasn't at her parents' place in Massachusetts. She was in a tight space, like a submarine. She hobbled down a little corridor and stepped through a side door into the Mkultra. She glimpsed a glow in the distance, a yellow-greenish line, and since that was all she could see, she followed it. The bright paint along the ground was like a lane in outer space; it led her to the margins of the colossal emptiness. But soon she started seeing the outlines of others. Their brain roots were drawn to the phosphorescent paint, pulling them to the edge of the darkness.

Smoke everywhere, smoke without flames. If she wasn't medicated and they weren't mentally impaired, panic would be widespread. The sound of coughing grew as more people appeared. Banging into things, stepping on sharp objects. Ghostly figures coming in and out of the smoke through the haze and darkness. Then bright lights started shining, pointing the way. The crowd bottlenecked into the narrow staircases, twining, twisting, plodding up up up . . . Soon, feeling a breeze, she heard generators groaning—giant fans started sucking the smoke upward. The fires had to be burning *inside* the walls since no flames were visible. The ragged, skeletal crazies, though together, were still alone. The haze was sucked up into the faint glimmer of bright baby-blue sky high above them, bringing them back to life. Gradually, as if they were awakening, screams and shouts increased.

In another moment she was outside with the pushing crowd, under the expansive azure sky with stars like tiny, asymmetrical eyes staring down at them, with hundreds of others squinting back, ringed by vast desert, wondering which way to go. She heard a female voice calling out: "What you're doing isn't just treason, these fuckers are highly contagious! You're putting thousands of lives at risk!"

"What's the alternative?!" a male voice called back. "I watched thousands get mowed down on the JFK airfield—no more! I can't do it again, Root. I can't watch them slowly rot to death down there for a single day longer, I just can't!"

Utterly exhausted and numb, Karen walked across the stone and sands, past the crowds, until she finally stumbled over a small fold in the earth. There she curled up and fell into an immediate and deep sleep.

BOOK FIVE

THE
COGNITIVE CONTAGION

OF
QUEENS

For Burke Nersesian

So that the generation to come of your children that shall rise up after you, and the stranger that shall come from a far land, shall say, when they see the plagues of that land, and the sicknesses which the Lord hath laid upon it; And that the whole land thereof is brimstone, and salt, and burning . . . which the Lord overthrew in his anger, and in his wrath: Even all nations shall say, Wherefore hath the Lord done thus unto this land? what meaneth the heat of this great anger?

—The Book of Deuteronomy

L ooking over his shoulder, Uli could still make out a faint line of smoke threading upward. It was coming from the eastern edge of Rescue City in the Nevada desert, from the little community of South Ozone Park, Queens, where, after a ferocious night of hand-to-hand combat, Uli and maybe a thousand others had barely managed to escape earlier that morning. They all went south and he went east. In the prairie land stretching miles before him directly below the rising sun, another column of smoke, much farther away, arose—this one from a subterranean military base.

Uli figured he still had at least a six-hour hike ahead of him. He remembered reading somewhere that due to the scrub and vegetation this was known as a *cold* desert, but within a few hours, when the full brunt of the sun was upon him, he had to take shelter in a shady spot. By four o'clock, it was cool enough to resume walking again.

His friend Bea from Staten Island had given him as much as she could for his little mission—six cheese sandwiches and a gallon jug of water. She too was overwhelmed and undertaking a rescue of her own: evacuating the hundreds of wounded and battle-weary survivors who had fled out of South Ozone Park before the Queens gangcops could finish them off. She had to lead them all south around Jamaica Bay into the anarchist stronghold in Staten Island.

As the sun began to set, Uli gulped down another mouthful of warm water and zoned out as he passed sagebrush, dramatic rock formations, and clusters of barrel cacti. Glancing back, he could still make out the very top of the Williamsburgh Savings Bank Building—the tallest structure on the reservation. Just after sunset, when the distant domed top of the building sank from sight, he figured he must be at least halfway to the burning installation that the inmates referred to as the Mkultra.

Months earlier he had escaped from there and found himself lost in the desert. As he'd wandered across the sands, looking for civilization, he kept seeing a mysterious woman in the distant dunes. And though he tried repeatedly to catch up to her, she would dash before him, just out of reach. Finally exhausted, he had collapsed, carrion for scavengers. He had looked up to see a small concrete platform and a water pump. It was Water Station 27, which had saved his life.

Now, his thoughts drifted as the night settled in . . . Actress Liv Ullmann had just announced that Marlon Brando had won best actor for *The Godfather*. The camera landed on a young woman dressed in Native regalia seated in the audience. She rose and walked down the aisle toward the great proscenium of the Dorothy Chandler Pavilion, where she climbed the stairs past Hollywood royalty and went to the mic. She introduced herself as Sacheen Littlefeather. "I'm representing Marlon Brando this evening . . . he very regretfully cannot accept this very generous award. And the reasons for this being are the treatment of American Indians today by the film industry—excuse me . . ." When she paused, a few booed, but most applauded. ". . . and on television in movie reruns, and also with recent happenings at Wounded Knee."

Uli hiked up a sandy incline, and suddenly beheld a water station! Upon a small pedestal of concrete was another hand pump. It was inside a tiny cage of hurricane fencing with a small rusty metal sign that read, *Water Station 30*. It looked identical to the one he had found when he'd escaped months ago. If this was number 30, there had to be at least twenty-nine others out in the desert somewhere. He ran to it. It wasn't locked. After pumping some of the rusty hot water out, it became clear, so he gulped it down. Then he stuck his sweaty mop of hair under the nozzle and let it flow over his feverish scalp and down his itchy back. He ate one of the stale sandwiches and refilled his water jug.

Even with the sun gone, the column of black smoke before him, which he could now smell, was vivid in the moonlight. Though exhausted, Uli took advantage of the coolness and kept walking toward it.

Of all the things to pop into his head, why the hell did he recall the Marlon Brando Oscar moment?

As Uli grew closer, the diffuse smoke from the Mkultra made his throat raw and eyes water. Soon he pulled his shirt up over his mouth and scurried to the left, trying to get away from the billowing fumes. After roughly another hour of coughing and struggling to breathe, the wind blessedly shifted. Soon he spotted a naked, emaciated form standing at the crest of a dune before him. Noticing his sex, Uli called out, asking if the man was okay. He only staggered away. Then a second person appeared—another quasi skeleton.

For the next twenty minutes the ground below Uli continued to rise. When it finally came to a small peak, he looked down under the thick black cloud and saw that dozens of small scattered fires had been set along the scrub. He had arrived. Most of the survivors just stood or sat silently on the parched earth. As he pressed on, peering through the smoke, crowds appeared. Hundreds of scrawny men and women; all looked much older than they probably were. Uli passed by a particularly noisy area, but there were no words being spoken. People were still emerging from the earth, gasping and hacking up sputum as they reached the surface. It was the entrance to the subterranean base.

Sunken faces, haunted eyes, hollow cheeks; even those with dark skin had turned a fish-belly pale. In flashes of firelight, Uli saw that some had wasted away so much that it looked like their bones would tear through their taut flesh.

"Karen!" his voice broke the silence.

Though it was dark, he scouted the vast perimeter for his lost sister. For the first time he realized that not one, but four pillars of silky smoke were streaming out from four different corners of the subterra-

nean base. The entire area had to be the size of at least three football
fields placed side by side. All these desiccated evacuees had climbed
out of one of these four exits. Comforted by the sight of each other,
they slowly merged together in the center.

Uli followed the nearest column of smoke to the northwest entrance; he didn't see anyone exiting from this particular shaft. Taking
a couple of deep breaths, he dashed down the stairs to the top landing. Murky lights were glowing through pulsating waves of smoke. He
immediately started gasping for breath, his eyes clouding with tears
due to the toxic fumes. Staring downward, he could only make out the
ever-narrowing crisscross of rusty banisters vanishing in the narrow
shaft. While trapped inside the Mkultra, there had been no visible
exits. He could only wonder where they opened onto the floors. Soon
he was overwhelmed by the smoke. Even if he had an oxygen tank
and a flashlight, locating her would be like finding a needle in a vast
smoldering haystack. He struggled back up the stairs, collapsing to
the ground once he made it back out into the open air.

"Stay seated here! They'll come for us!" he heard. A man with a
groomed beard was yelling at some of the more active zombies wandering around.

"I'm looking for my sister!" Uli yelled, catching his breath.

"Just don't wander off."

"I understand, but . . . I'm looking for a woman. Maybe you can
help me?"

"They'll come for us!" The man seemed to be a broken record.

Uli noticed a small group that had accumulated just outside the
perimeter. Those who weren't asleep were just staring off like birds.
Those not seated were swaying gently back and forth, from leg to leg.

He walked over and delicately tried talking to them: "Do any of
you know a woman named Karen Sarkisian?"

Those along the fringes glared over at him; those nearby looked
away.

"She's in her thirties, attractive, with short black hair?" he detailed.

The silence was epic. His first thought was that they were all deaf,
but then he remembered the aphasia.

Frustrated, Uli headed over to a second smoky column in the
northeast corner, where he found a large circle of people moving slowly
clockwise. It took him a moment to discover that they were being
driven forward like sheep by some of the groomed beards who seemed
to be in charge.

"Can anyone speak?" he yelled repeatedly as he rushed through the crowded field toward the southeast exit. Although he heard occasional phrases bubble out, no responses were lucid. It took nearly five minutes for him to reach the third smoky pillar, where another concentration had gathered.

"Anyone!" he yelped in frustration.

"Over here!" a faint voice sounded above the occasional groans and moans. As Uli closed in, he finally isolated and recognized the speaker. It was the tall, blind, bearded guy who seemed to be the sheriff of the Streptococci basin, where he had first arrived in the Mkultra. He vaguely recalled that the man's name was Richard, and it seemed to be his group that was running the show.

"My name's Uli," he said as he approached.

"I recall your voice. You were that big shot FBI agent," Richard said.

"How'd the place catch fire? Who let everyone out?"

The blind man quickly explained that it wasn't really a fire. It was actually part of the rescue plan: smoke everyone out of the many levels via one of the four hidden stairways, getting them all up onto the desert floor, then to Las Vegas and freedom.

"I'm looking for my sister," Uli explained.

"Good luck."

Uli thanked him and hurried over to the final column of smoke. By the time he reached it, he was utterly winded and staggering. He sat on a rock to catch his breath. There was a large metal tub of foul-smelling liquid from which people were scooping handfuls to drink. Uli spritzed some of the dirty water on his parched face.

Several hundred people were squatting or lying on their backs, helpless as baby turtles. He passed through them, looking for Karen. A few along the edges were just staring above in amazement. Uli looked up to see the stars breaking through the smoke and he deduced that most of these escapees hadn't seen the sky in years.

As he plodded around them, what Uli found saddest was the fact that they were no more connected with each other than the stars above them.

After half an hour of searching through the various groups, he finally made out a fifth, smaller ribbon of smoke suspended in the distance. As he moved toward a small group of misshapen people gathered around this final outpost, he imagined they might've been born down there, like the poor scorpion boy. They reminded him of the strange marine life that survived around the lava vents in the deepest trenches of the Pacific Ocean.

While searching for a stairway, he quickly realized that this wasn't an exit at all, but rather a blast site. He made out the broken gas pipe that the poor deformed kid had accidentally blown open, leading to Uli's escape. Smoke was now streaming up from the small chasm. Peering down into the abyss, he thought he could make out a body at the murky bottom.

Exhausted and overwhelmed, he headed back toward the first smoky pillar and nearly tripped over a huddled form. A small barefoot figure was curled in a ball, pressed into the sandstone as though he or she had fallen from a great height. It was the radiance of fresh gauze wrapped around the person's head like a halo that drew him close.

Suddenly he froze: it was Karen. The exposed flesh of her body was bruised, and covered in scabs. She had clearly been attacked, reduced to skin and bones.

"Karen," he whispered, "it's me."

When she didn't awaken, Uli put a finger over her lips and nose, quickly determining that she was in fact breathing. But below the undulating moonlight he couldn't check her pupils. He lifted Karen in his arms and felt the warmth of her body. She was as delicate as a baby bird, clearly in need of medical attention. He thought about taking her back to Rescue City, but she obviously couldn't walk, and there was no way he could carry her the great distance alone.

2

As Uli stared down at his kid sister, who was lying nearly comatose in his lap, tears leaked from his eyes and onto her face. He remembered her time in high school when her rebellious nature first arose, getting her into fights with other students. They were both bullheaded. Civil rights and Vietnam were the first big cracks that divided them. Though he always respected her, the rift steadily widened, controversy by controversy. When another FBI agent confidentially informed him that according to the latest report, his sister was officially a member of the Columbia University chapter of Students for a Democratic Society, a student group that had grown increasingly more radical with probable ties to Moscow, he feared they had reached the point of no return. He remembered calling their father, who said he would talk to Karen about it. But there was no change, so Uli reached out to their mother, who Karen was closer to. She explained that Karen had told her all about the SDS and her activism at Columbia.

When the Columbia University chapter was on the brink of turning into an underground terrorist organization, Uli appealed to Karen personally, but she would have none of it. She said that this country had officially turned into a fascist state, and that Vietnam was its latest imperialist victim. It was up to every citizen to try to protect the democratic dream. A few months later, a Greenwich Village brownstone blew up, leaving three Weather Bureau members dead inside. Shortly after that, New York got hit with the dirty bomb. And although the FBI was never able to trace a clear connection, Karen and her group of suspects vanished.

Uli also remembered losing his security clearance and being pulled from active duty because of Karen's constant bullshit. He was sent back to DC and was interrogated up the chain of command. Although they tried to get him to resign, there was no rule on the books against having a subversive sibling. Quite simply, however, no one trusted him.

That was when he got the call from the big guy himself: Old Man

Hoover. Uli had waited outside the director's office for twenty minutes until his prior appointment exited (a black shoe shiner). When he was finally sent in, Hoover was signing some paperwork, and Uli just stood at attention in the doorway like a schoolboy about to be disciplined.

"So, you're the fella whose sis works for Uncle Joe," Hoover finally said without looking up. "What have you to say for yourself, agent?"

"I feel like I have a bull's-eye on my back, sir."

"More like a hammer and sickle," Hoover replied. America had only one real enemy.

Uli said that he had done everything he could to try to prevent it, but he feared that he had only driven her further away.

"So is she a real commie or just a stoolie?"

"Frankly," Uli said, "I'm afraid that she's just doing this to bug me."

"She must be a great disappointment to your folks—a star undergrad student, then Columbia Law . . ."

"I think going to Columbia was what caused it."

"If I had my way, I'd shut down all Ivy Leagues—they're a breeding ground for spies and Reds."

"Agreed."

Hoover was now looking at a school photo of Karen that he had removed from a file on his desk. "Such a pretty girl too."

"We're all just praying she'll spare us further embarrassment." Uli looked down contritely.

Although Hoover had brought Uli in to let him go, he ended up feeling sincere sympathy for the special agent with the suspicious last name. Since the inauguration of the latest president, he too knew what it felt like to be shunned. During this brief meeting, Hoover found Uli Sarkisian a loyal, intelligent, and personable agent. Due to the idealistic hijinks of a hysterical Ivy League coed, everything this young man had worked so hard for had come to naught. Hoover wouldn't force anyone to take him, but decided to give Sarkisian a little time to find something in the private sector and resign with his reputation still intact.

Several weeks later, Uli's phone rang early one morning, waking him up.

"So I heard your sis got your ass in trouble with the teacher."

He recognized the voice of Aiden Zay, an old friend and classmate from Quantico who, despite a drinking problem, had become a popular agent in the Dallas office.

"If you're calling me just to rib me, Aiden . . ."

"CISPES—the Committee in Solidarity with the People of El Salvador," he said with a mock pomposity. "Ever heard of it?"

"Before you say another word," Uli responded, "you should know something about me—"

"About a month ago," Zay cut in, "we got a memo via the agency about a raid that the Salvadoran National Guard launched on a rebel safe house. Inside they found a ton of documents about this new organization that has been expanding throughout the US."

"Kiss Piss?"

"*Siss-piss*," Zay corrected. "Documents verified that it is definitely Moscow backed."

"All roads lead back to the Kremlin, don't they?"

"We just got authorization from the Justice Department to investigate them."

"Who exactly are they?"

"Duped liberals who have set up this bullshit philanthropy to help them."

"Is this part of the Manhattan Bombing Task Force?"

"Not directly. We're starting really small."

"So what exactly are you doing?" Uli asked.

"First we're just looking for violations of FARA."

"Sounds hard to prove." Uli knew all about the Foreign Agents Registration Act. Moscow and other foreign powers were always attempting to manipulate gullible Americans.

"At this point the investigation is covert."

"Sounds like a lot of wiretaps and surveillance."

"Castro's started his own private fifth column in our backyard. He's backing various little rebel groups who are going after all these banana colonels."

"What do you mean *going after*?"

"Well, he already sent Che into South America, and they sent him back in a body bag, didn't they? So this time he's doing it right: sending Russian arms and supplies."

"To who?"

"He's infiltrating Central America, particularly the unholy quartet of El Salvador, Nicaragua, Honduras, and Guatemala."

"I'm surprised they have the funds for something so speculative."

"And that's the problem. See, they've been playing up to all these humanitarians—CISPES," Zay explained.

"Where are they?"

"Everywhere. They have chapters scattered all around the country. They're using these groups to raise cash. But guess what that cash is going to be spent on?"

"More guns."

"Damn right! Hell, this is going to be the first war where the American people have to pay for both sides. And at this point, no one's doing shit about it."

"Wow!" Uli was trying to show enthusiasm—this assignment would definitely bring his career back from the dead.

"It's a whole new type of warfare, boy. A whole cluster of these organizations sprang up overnight like mushrooms. A pile of them out in California alone. And I got a pilot team all set up, but my lead just transferred out and I need someone fast, someone who I can trust."

"What exactly does this involve?"

"Same shit as COINTELPRO. With one twist, if we can discourage these do-gooders, try to stop it before it gets too popular, so much the better."

"How many in the team?"

"You'll be in charge of five other men, but how can I put this . . . It's new for us."

"Sounds like a fishing expedition."

"A stalled fishing expedition into uncharted waters," said Zay, "and your mission, Uli—if you decide to accept it—is to get it going. That's why, even though everyone says you've got the mark of Cain, I'm asking you first."

Both of them knew Uli had little choice but to accept.

Three nights later, Uli landed at LAX and reported for duty at the Los Angeles field office at nine the next morning. A team of five agents was waiting for him. Two were former cops; Dylan McGuire had worked with the NYPD, and Nathan Stevens was briefly with the LAPD. One of them, Opie Dawson, was a lawyer. The other two were fresh from Quantico—Ryan Marks and Ted Jennings.

On a blackboard were basic details on two CISPES chapters they were currently investigating. They did this by surveilling some of the chapter leaders, as well as checking their mail and bugging their offices and conference rooms. They had been at it for three weeks but so far they had nothing.

"Arnie tried his best, but so did Bill," Ryan Marks told Uli. It was only then that Uli discovered that he was the third supervisor assigned to this detail.

"This guy Herbert J. Rosen seems to be the top dog," Uli said, looking at the first CISPES chapter on the big board. "He knows what we need to know."

"We've been on him for a while," said McGuire.

"He's a pretty straight arrow."

Uli grabbed the file on Rosen and handed it Jennings. He announced that he wanted everyone to grab their jackets. He was going to demonstrate some of the techniques he'd learned in COINTELPRO. Out in the parking lot, the six men got into three cars. Uli had Jennings drive, and read him the address of Rosen's CISPES chapter. The two other cars followed.

Two hours later, the three vehicles parked around a small, newly built synagogue in Bakersfield. Uli instructed the other four men to stay in their cars—just watch and learn. The president of the chapter, Rosen, was a Jewish real estate broker. There was a service going on when Uli and Jennings entered the Star of David Temple. The two agents stood out in their cheap gray suits and shiny black dress shoes.

"What now?" Jennings muttered awkwardly as devout Jews glared at them.

Silently, Uli led the agent back out to the parking lot. In the car he checked the file again, and located Rosen's home address.

"Do you know how to get there?" Uli asked Jennings. He did. "Okay, let's move it."

The tiny convoy drove for twenty minutes until they arrived at a powder-blue 1960s house at the end of an empty cul-de-sac. Uli had the other two vehicles park up the block where they were a little less conspicuous. No movement or lights appeared in any of the windows facing the street. Uli and Jennings sat across from the home for roughly ten minutes until Jennings asked, "You don't think it'd be better to come back after dark?"

"Rosen and his family will be home by then," Uli reasoned. "Stay here. If anyone pulls up, you honk like hell."

"Better idea," Jennings amended, evidently relieved by his sudden noninvolvement, "I'll honk once if he enters the front, and twice if he enters the back."

"Fine."

As Uli walked up to Rosen's front door, he spotted a large wooden mezuzah attached to the frame, under it a doorbell. He rang and waited—silence. He tried the knob—locked. He was glad he didn't hear any barking. A well-manicured lawn surrounded the two-floor house. Uli walked around the building, looking through the big bay windows for any signs of life. In the rear was a beautiful new wooden deck that ended at a pair of large sliding-glass doors. Uli was grateful to find them unlocked. He slowly opened one and waited, listening again for any dogs, but only heard wind chimes. A mild thrill filled him as he went down the stairs into the sunken living room and understood the layout—two bedrooms, two bathrooms, a living room, a study. From some of the hippie macramé items and a soft feminine touch of order, Uli sensed that Rosen had a daughter, possibly in college.

In the man's study, Uli pulled open his antique desk drawers and searched through his papers, which were mainly real estate documents. In the bottom drawer he found a dozen letters held together with a strained paper clip. They were all copies of a typed letter asking for donations to his CISPES branch. The appeal detailed how any contributions would be spent largely on medical supplies for the sick and needy citizens of El Salvador—victims of death squads and other forms of government oppression. In the very back of the drawer, Uli found an unsealed legal envelope. It was filled with old twenties in nonsequential order. He counted out $580 before he realized a horn was faintly honking. He didn't know if it was from Jennings or some other passing car. Looking further through the drawer, he found a list of names and phone numbers. Uli was pretty sure these were people Rosen had solicited or actual contributors. Most of the last names ended in -stein, -berg, and -man. They must've been members of his temple.

Suddenly the front door slammed shut. Rapid footsteps compelled Uli to shove the list into his pocket. He took a deep breath and headed downstairs. When he reached the ground floor, he realized that instead of putting the money back and shutting the drawer, he had simply left it on the blotter. Then a trim, middle-aged woman in slacks exited one room and crossed several feet in front of him into another. Uli dashed silently back up into the study, where he slipped the envelope of cash back in the bottom drawer and straightened out the top of the desk.

He could hear the woman on the phone as he padded softly back down the carpeted stairs, through the dining room, and out the sliding doors, which he gently closed behind him. In another moment he was racing around to the front of the house. There he noticed the garage door open, though no one appeared to be inside. He proceeded across the street back to the car.

"Didn't you hear me honking?" Jennings frantically asked.

"I wasn't sure it was you."

"They both came home."

"Both?"

"Here." Jennings handed him a large pair of field binoculars. Uli took them and saw a short, chubby body facing away from him, standing at a workbench in the back of the garage.

"So what'd you find?" Jennings asked.

"I found that I should always bring gloves and a Polaroid camera with me," Uli kidded, and explained that he had a list of names.

"Really? You think if they call the police and they dust—"

"No, they won't know I was there. I mean, I took the list, but I left the donation envelope. Rosen will just think he misplaced it."

They quietly sped off, the two other vehicles following.

"Now we know all their members," Uli gloated, holding up the list triumphantly. Regardless of the illegalities and the validity of the claim, Jennings was impressed.

3

The next day, Uli had McGuire analyze the list. The agent discovered that unfortunately none of the names were suspected CISPES members, just donors. But it was still a good start. Uli called his five-man team into his office and said, "Look, the word I've chosen for the tone of this investigation is *omnibus*."

"Omnibus?"

"Ominous," Uli corrected. He was twitchy, having downed too much coffee that morning.

"Ominous how?" Nathan Stevens asked.

"These people are not like the mob. CISPES doesn't have a head to cut off. It's more like cancer: cells have spread throughout the body; best to radiate them branch by branch."

"Can the US attorney advise us or—"

"I'll level with you. Some sneaky little shit blows a stink bomb right in the middle of the Big Apple and we don't even have a clue as to who or why. I mean, we know somehow this has got to be from Moscow, so we've got a little more latitude here than usual. But Zay recruited you for this because he knows and I know that you'll go the extra mile."

In that moment they all understood why Uli had been brought in.

"If anyone wants out," Uli added, "say so now."

"So you're saying extrajudicial?" Stevens asked. "Is that what you mean?"

"Look at it this way . . . Consider the antiwar movement *before* the war," Uli said.

"But if there's no war . . ."

"But there *will* be one. The commies have been pouring money and resources into Central America. The good news is, we're on to them. You're tracking down people who will someday be the enemy. Does that shed some light on how you might handle this?"

"What exactly do you want us to do?" Opie Dawson inquired.

"We need to work quicker. You've got one week to get the complete membership roster of each branch as well as their leadership structure. I need results *yesterday*."

"We've done surveillance and interviews—" McGuire started.

"That's over," Uli cut him off, then paused a moment before saying, "No more badges or guns. We're officially covert."

"Like the CIA."

"You got it," Uli said. "In fact, if the opportunity arises, I want you to try to discourage them from continuing."

"Discourage who?"

"The CISPES members."

"Discourage them?" Stevens was bewildered.

"Is there a mission statement to this investigation?" asked Jennings, sensing something was off.

"It's still being formulated."

"That makes an already-vague job a lot harder," Dawson said, "and it doesn't sound like anything I've ever heard of in the FBI mandate."

"Look, I'll say it again," Uli shot back, "if anyone wants out, I will be glad to transfer you, no penalties."

"It's not that," Dawson said. "I'm just concerned with keeping a log of our actions that can be subpoenaed and potentially used against us."

Uli nodded; the agent had a good point. "In terms a grand jury can understand, we are searching for any violations of FARA."

"Exactly how far are we supposed to go to achieve this?" Stevens probed.

"Far as you can without getting caught," Uli answered.

The five men looked silently at him in different stages of disbelief. Deciding to let them adjust to the unusual nature of this assignment, combined with the fact that it was now Thursday and the coming Monday was a holiday, Uli divided them into three teams, himself included. Two of the teams were each assigned one of the CISPES branches, and given the mission of finding out everything they could without getting caught. They should only call Uli in case of an emergency.

"We're going off-road here," he concluded.

"Wait a sec," Stevens said. "What *exactly* are we supposed to do?"

"Each team has till Tuesday to crack your branch's identity. Do whatever you need to do to find out who the members are. And discourage them if you can. We'll meet here on Tuesday morning and you'll report your findings."

There was a strange electricity in the air as four of the agents exited.

Ted Jennings nervously asked Uli what their team's responsibility was, since they were once again paired together.

Uli replied, "We supervise."

The weekend passed slowly. The fact that no one had called Uli's hotel room seemed to be a good sign. He used the time to find an apartment and buy a decent used car.

Finally, on Tuesday morning, he entered the conference room where the other five agents were waiting for him.

After a quick greeting, Uli had team one, Ryan Marks and Nathan Stevens, go first. Since Marks was the lead, he explained that using cheap disguises of mustaches and dark glasses and renting a car, they had kept their CISPES office under surveillance for two days until they were suddenly confronted by a tall, well-dressed woman in her sixties named Lenore Watkins, who walked up to their vehicle on Saturday evening and asked what they wanted. They recognized her as the branch's treasurer.

"Then what?" Uli asked, when Stevens fell silent.

Stevens recounted how he got out of the car, shoved her into a doorway, grabbed her by the throat, and told her that she had better quit CISPES at once if she knew what was good for her. Trembling, the woman had said that she was only trying to help people less fortunate than herself.

"I told her that she was actually killing people, and if she kept it up I'd hunt her down and break her legs," Stevens continued.

"Then we split," Marks added.

"Oh my God!" Uli burst out, both amused and awestruck by Stevens, who had struck him as the softy in the group.

"But you guys failed to collect any data about their branch," Dylan McGuire pointed out. He and Opie Dawson made up the second team. Dawson reported that they had encountered some glitches, as their CISPES group met only once a month and they couldn't clearly identify a "titular head," much less establish the hierarchy. Additionally, their stated meeting place was in the basement of a Baptist church.

"Sounds like we did better than you," Stevens muttered.

Since the church basement was also used for AA meetings, McGuire and Dawson had pretended to be a pair of drunks and went inside before a meeting on Monday morning. They'd looked around but found nothing. No filing cabinets, padlocked closets, or even a PO box to break into. McGuire was able to meet with the pastor and, after a quick chat, got the address of one of the founding CISPES members, an older gentleman named Theodore Issel.

"You blew your cover?" Marks interrupted.

"We told them we were interested in joining," Dawson replied.

"But they saw you, so . . . ."

"We wore disguises too," McGuire countered. "Let Opie finish!"

"We located Issel and followed the subject from his workplace last night," Dawson said, reading from his notepad. "Once he reached his parking garage, I drove in front of him, cutting him off. Dylan knocked him to the ground, cuffed him, wrapped his jacket over the old man's head, and shoved him into the backseat."

"You abducted him?" Jennings yelled.

"Briefly," Dawson said without looking up.

"What initiative," Uli mumbled, unsure of how to respond.

Dawson went on to recount how he had driven around while McGuire stayed in the backseat and pulled Issel's wallet out of his pants.

"Did he fight you?" asked Stevens.

"I told him that if he removed the jacket and saw us, we'd have to kill him, so he remained submissive."

"What happened?" Uli asked nervously.

"I made him identify several wallet photos that turned out to be his grandkids."

"Then what?"

"I threatened to kill them if he didn't identify everyone in his chapter," McGuire said.

"You're kidding!"

"You said we had latitude to handle this any way we wanted."

"You were pushing it."

"We didn't leave any marks. We were dressed like a pair of good old boys—we didn't look like agents," Dawson said.

"We even talked with a Southern twang," McGuire said, demonstrating the accent.

"So what happened?" Uli feared that the entire unit would go up on charges.

Dawson explained how Issel had volunteered that CISPES was a charity that helped oppressed people in Central America. The man was sure they were confused and looking for someone else.

"And what'd you say?"

"If you really want to do this, if you really want to scare the bejesus out of a man, you have to go all the way," McGuire answered softly.

"He told us we can't leave any marks," Stevens said.

"Dylan opened his ballpoint pen and stuck it into the guy's neck," Dawson volunteered.

"That's a mark!" Uli exclaimed.

"Maybe just a deep-blue dot," McGuire said. "But Issel began singing like a canary. He gave out the identities of all ten members and everything else he could even vaguely recall."

"Then what?"

Dawson said that he pulled the car to the curb and used the pen to scribble the names of the members in the margins of a paperback book he was reading. They hadn't anticipated gathering so much information so quickly and didn't have a tape recorder handy. After thirty minutes of riding around through the deserted suburb, Issel became convinced that they were going to kill him and he began reciting prayers and weeping.

"Why'd he think he was going to die?" Uli asked.

"We said we were looking for a place to dump his body," said Dawson.

"He swore he'd never go back to another CISPES meeting as long as he lives, if we would just let him go," McGuire added.

"But you didn't need to punch him in the stomach," Dawson said.

"You told me you weren't going to mention that," McGuire sneered.

"Then he uncuffed the guy and shoved him out the car," Dawson said.

"Fink!" McGuire snapped, half joking.

"Threw him out of a moving car? Are you kidding?" Uli said.

"We were only going a couple miles an hour."

"You might've overdone it a bit."

"That's what I thought," Dawson said. "But we monitored the police radio and didn't hear any calls from his area."

"Hey," McGuire said, "we completely fulfilled all three goals: we got information about the branch, we got him to quit the group, and we didn't get caught. Better than Ryan and Nathan!"

The important detail was that no agent's identity had been compromised. As far as they knew, it was all firmly deniable and untraceable. The maiden LA branch of the CISPES task force had just popped its cherry.

Over the ensuing weeks the investigations continued with significant results. Uli and Jennings joined in, doing their share of the investigatory work as well. Although Uli explained that it would be prudent if they didn't discuss their rather unconventional techniques with each other, he knew that the men bragged about their progress. He decided to put their competitive drive to some use. Uli marked up the chalkboard in the conference room with vertical and horizontal lines representing the progress of the investigative teams. A single letter was placed in each of the boxes for each CISPES branch they investigated. The first letter was H, which stood for *harassment*. T represented *threats*, B was for *burglaries*, and O meant *others*.

The teams would travel throughout the state, sometimes spending a couple weeks in a hotel as they worked at taking down far-flung CISPES branches. By the end of that month, based on their accumulation of letters, McGuire and Dawson were in the lead. Over the next few weeks they all honed their investigative techniques as the three teams widened their circumference to include another dozen CISPES branches. At the end of the second month, McGuire and Dawson's team led the competition, with six more harassments and five more threats.

But Marks and Stevens's team had performed more burglaries, which technically produced more information. Uli and Jennings had found the white pages to be surprisingly valuable, and made use of late-night phone calls to harass the growing list of names. For his part, Jennings used the technique of keying branch members' cars while they attended their CISPES meetings.

* * *

Nearly a year after Uli's CISPES work had begun, Aiden Zay called him to announce, "The investigation is overt."

"It's over?"

"No, *overt!* Open."

They had accumulated a good deal of solid evidence, and now they needed to present it to a congressional subcommittee. Therefore, everything had to be aboveboard, by the book. Whenever they investigated anyone from now on, they had to identify themselves as FBI agents.

4

S oon afterward, Uli received the document he had been wondering about since day one—the investigative guidelines for the CISPES case that officially legitimized their work. He read the index:

The index alone went on for many pages.

A month later, Zay called from Washington, DC, to inform Uli that his office would soon be getting a special visitor. Fred Varini would be stopping by the LA field office. He was a valued foreign asset who had provided the original source material that launched the CISPES investigation. He would be arriving directly from El Salvador in two weeks.

"Why is he coming here?" Uli asked.

"Frankly, I thought it would be inspiring. In addition to whatever information he can give you, I wanted your team to meet him, so they can get it straight from the horse's mouth."

Several weeks later, Uli was listening to the radio while stuck in traffic. At the top of the hour, two news stories caught his attention: first, a harebrained organization called the American Indian Movement had taken over a small town in South Dakota called Wounded Knee. This sounded like the kind of mess that would eventually wind up in the FBI's lap. The next story was local yet had international implications: yesterday, someone had lured the Turkish consul general and his assistant into an expensive hotel room in Santa Barbara where he had shot them both to death. A suspect had been taken into custody. Uli noted the suspect's last name—Yanikian.

"Holy shit," he muttered, knowing exactly what this was about.

When Uli arrived at the office, the secretary said that Zay had been calling frantically and wanted to speak with him immediately.

"Your personnel file says you're fluent in Armenian," Zay greeted him when Uli returned the call.

"I guess so—why?" He had learned it while growing up but hadn't spoken it in a while.

"Well, you seem to be the only agent out there who knows the language. And I just got a call that the State Department fears that this assassination of the Turkish consul general might have foreign connections."

"Half a century ago the Turks rounded up and murdered every Armenian they could get their grubby hands on. That's the only foreign connection."

"But that was then and there. Now, Armenia is a republic of the Soviet Union, whereas Turkey is a member of NATO, so there is a concern that the shooting could have Cold War implications."

"You can't find an interpreter?" Uli said tiredly.

"We need a little more than that. Lars Hentersen has the lead." Hentersen was a hotshot also working out of the LA office. "I want you to help him for the next week or so, and use your Armenian-language skills to see if the suspect has any possible commie ties."

Uli figured this was all just window dressing so that the Armenian community, which tended to vote Republican, couldn't accuse the FBI of being insensitive. "Fine," he said. He needed a break anyway. The CISPES investigation had gone on far longer than he had hoped.

He called Marks and McGuire into his office and told them that they were going to be in charge for a couple weeks. McGuire would lead, Marks would assist.

"Where are you going?" Marks asked.

"I'll be around. I'm going to be briefly reassigned to this Turkish homicide case—it's all over the news."

Both men returned to their desks.

Initially, Uli went to the police headquarters, where he found no less than six other law enforcement agents assigned to different aspects of the case. Hentersen was still top dog, though; Uli realized that just being quiet and listening was the best course of action. And since the suspect's English was far better than Uli's Armenian, he realized there was no good reason for him to be there. But because he was privately sympathetic to the man's desire for justice, he stuck around to see if there was any little way he might help the guy.

When he called in late that afternoon, he was told by Marks that the former Salvadoran intelligence officer Fred Varini had had a long lunch with McGuire.

"What'd McGuire say about it?" Uli asked.

"Not a word," Marks replied.

Over the next week, Uli and Hentersen logged nearly forty hours essentially following the same well-trodden path as the LAPD, the INS, and the local DA and US attorney's offices, all of whom were filing charges against Yanikian.

After several officers finished interrogating the suspect one afternoon, Uli asked for an opportunity to meet with Yanikian alone since Hentersen was elsewhere.

He waited in the interrogation room as they brought in the old man, who was still in cuffs. Uli introduced himself in Armenian, explaining that he was an FBI agent.

"You're Armenian?"

"Yes, I am."

Still in Armenian, Yanikian asked where he was born, as well the name of his family and which village they were from in the old country. Uli struggled to keep up with him—his Armenian was weaker than he'd thought. *Sarkisian* was a popular Armenian name, but it didn't keep Yanikian from going through a long list of Sarkisians he had known over the years. Uli knew none of them.

"You understand why I did this, don't you?" Yanikian said.

"Of course," Uli replied.

The man took a deep breath and seemed relieved to tell his story to a fellow countryman. "I pretended to have some rare Ottoman artwork I had acquired and explained that I wanted to return it to the Turkish people."

"They didn't want you to bring it to the consulate?"

"They did, but I said I wanted to speak to them at the hotel first. They were pretty polite. And I thought to myself, *These guys didn't really do anything, and they probably have families.* But I wanted them to know."

"So what happened?" Uli asked.

"I explained that I was Armenian and I had survived their country's slaughter."

"And?"

"I never expected an apology, but they immediately turned nasty, calling me a liar, and said that I had wasted their time. And they just got meaner and meaner. So I pulled out my gun and shot them, like the dirty pigs they were."

"Would you do me a favor and tell me why you, personally, did this?"

"You mean what happened to *me* during the massacre?"

"Yeah."

Yanikian recalled the day the Turkish gendarmes had entered his village. He and another friend happened to be in the woods nearby. As they were returning, they watched from the tree line as their neighbors were rounded up. While the Turks separated the women and children from the men, Yanikian spotted various family members. Once the women and children were marched off, he watched as the gendarmes signaled to the Turkish villagers whom they had lived with all their lives. They were told to bring whatever weapons they could: shovels, axes, knives.

"They were the ones who did the real dirty work," Yanikian said. He showed Uli an oval scar on his right wrist where he had bit off his own flesh to keep from weeping aloud as the town imbecile beat his brother. This was the half-wit who all had regularly fed and clothed over the years. Yet when he was handed a large wooden ax handle, he slammed it against Yanikian's brother's skull and pounded him senseless. He was unable to finish the job, so a Turkish soldier finally came over.

"It was almost as if he wanted to show how little effort it took him to end my brother's life," Yanikian recalled. "He just nicked the tip of his bayonet into my brother's neck; you could see the spray of blood.

I watched as my brother clasped his hand over the cut, trying to stop the bleeding. After about twenty minutes he collapsed and died."

"What did you do after that?"

"My friend and I abandoned the land that had been ours since the dawn of time before the Turks ever arrived. You know, they were originally horse tribes living in the outer plains of Mongolia. They rode into our country."

The suspect went on to describe how he slowly made his way into Russian Armenia and then north to the Russian capital. There, he pulled his life back together and eventually studied engineering at Moscow State University. During World War II, he was a head engineer on the construction of the railroad across Iran—a huge undertaking for which he was never adequately paid. Afterward, instead of returning to the USSR, he immigrated to America, where he tried his hand as an author, publishing several novels that didn't sell.

They chatted a little more, then Uli wished him good luck and left the interrogation room.

After nearly two weeks on this detail, Uli wrote his final report, concluding, *As far as motivation, his stated reasons for the shooting were not only the result of having to personally witness the brutal annihilation of his family and his people; he also patiently waited four decades before he finally gave up hope that the world community might join together and publicly condemn Turkey's horrific act.*

The next day, a Tuesday, Uli got a call from Aiden Zay, who had just arrived in Los Angeles from Washington the night before—he was furious. Apparently, he'd gotten word about an incident that had happened during Uli's brief reassignment. Before Uli could talk to McGuire or Marks alone, Zay arranged for them all to meet in Uli's office.

"I just received a report from someone at the LAPD that a woman, one of your CISPES members, was allegedly abducted along with her infant son by two men. She was blindfolded, driven to a distant location, and sexually assaulted."

"Is she alive? Did she ID anyone?" McGuire asked softly.

"She says that from their accents, she thinks the assailants were Salvadoran. She believes they were members of the government's death squad."

"Well there you have it! And considering Los Angeles is just three hours from the Mexican border, I must say that I'm not entirely surprised," McGuire responded.

"You're not?" Marks chimed in.

"Hell no! In fact, I always believed that one of our implicit functions in this investigation was to discourage these well-meaning people from provoking these psychopaths who could and probably did infiltrate our open borders."

"Is that what happened?" Zay asked, staring severely at McGuire.

"Apparently. Why is that a big surprise? I mean, think about it. The Salvadoran militia probably perceives CISPES as a foreign enemy who is trying to provoke the US into invading *their* country. How do you think El Salvador's going to react to the fear that they might have their very own Bay of Pigs?"

"Spare me the bullshit, I know Fred Varini was in your office," Zay shot back. "Using a foreign agent to do your dirty work, especially on American soil, might fool the press, but you ain't fooling me!"

"What do you mean?" McGuire said.

"Varini's still connected to the Salvadoran militia. There is no way any of his guys could've found this woman without someone in this office steering them toward her."

"I can assure you that none of our agents were involved in this act in any way, sir," McGuire said.

Zay dismissed McGuire and then turned his rage toward Uli: "It was *your* job to keep your dogs in their kennel, Sarkisian!"

"I was out all last week on the Yanikian case," Uli said. Then he asked, "Am I out?"

"I already appealed to the director on your behalf. Long as this stays quiet, you're still in. But you're probably going to South Dakota."

"Huh?"

"They desperately need men in Wounded Knee."

5

Uli was pulled abruptly from his thoughts when a woman raced over and crouched in the darkness on the other side of his sister. Uli grabbed her wrist just in time to prevent her from jabbing a hypodermic needle into Karen's limp arm.

"What the fuck are you doing?!"

"Finishing her course of treatment," the assailant replied, startled.

In the smoky darkness, Uli recognized her. "You're Root Ginseng." He released her arm.

"And you're Uli! I thought you died!"

"You're NSA," he said, remembering something the tall black man named Plato had told him after he'd escaped the Mkultra into the desert.

"Give me a break."

"If she dies, you die," Uli threatened.

"If I wanted to kill Karen," Root said, inserting the needle, "I would've just left her alone down there."

"What did you just give her?"

"The same stuff you and everyone else who survived this place took."

"I thought you had to take it beforehand."

"It's a lot like syphilis. Symptoms appear, but if you take the meds soon enough, you can still stop it from becoming fatal and hopefully even reverse the damage. I should add that I'm not a doctor, so it might be too late for her. I don't really know."

"You don't work for the government?" Uli asked.

"Actually, if memory serves, aren't *you* the one who is FBI?"

"How'd you get down here?" he changed the subject.

"Through the sewer pipe like shit, along with everyone else."

"Who was the first person to get here? How'd all this start?"

"I don't know," Root said. "Ask the trimmed beards."

"What do you remember?"

"Six years ago, after being pulled out of a manhole onto the floor of the basin, I remember going into that concrete maze, then slowly just losing it. Next thing I know, I'm sitting in my own waste and some guy is giving me injections and cleaning me off."

"Who was he? What did he do?"

"He walked me through the place and said that there were benefits—places where supplies were stashed. Safety zones."

"Did he show you these stairs?" Uli pointed to the nearest smoking exit.

"No, just places to find stock and hide. In return, I'd have to be a 'trustee' and try to help the others stay alive. I remember him saying that help was on the way, but it never came. I was stuck down there with everyone else."

"And you're the only trustee here?"

"No, there's also Plato."

"And all these years you did nothing?"

"Look at all these people here. I helped as many as I could. Plato was the one in charge of finding a way out."

"Why didn't you give *everyone* that serum?" Uli asked, pointing to the needle.

"We only had a few bottles. I gave most of it to the basin dwellers, which is why they're able to organize this. But either I underdosed them or I gave it out too late, 'cause none of them fully bounced back. However, they're not as far gone as all the others who went into the offices, so it seemed to slow the advance."

"Of all the people lost down there, why did you give it to *her*?" Uli nodded to Karen.

"I recognized her. She was a Garlic Head and a part of the founding group that organized the Crappers. She was briefly the ranking female administrator of the criminal justice system."

"What a crock of shit!"

"Why would I lie?"

"Because you and this Plato guy are part of whatever agency runs this shithole."

"You really think the government would permit this?"

"No, this is some giant snafu, but you two are in charge of containment—that's what I think."

"Look, you're partially right. That guy who picked me was probably in on it. But there isn't enough money in the world to stay trapped in this underground toilet for six years of my life. I would rather have spent the time in a maximum security prison. And as far as Plato goes, if he was a part of some covert plan, do you think he'd be busting everyone out?"

"I think he probably waited for the government to intercede. He only did this when he realized they wouldn't."

"I'm telling you, we do not work for the government."

"I still don't believe you. You've probably never even been to Rescue City. You probably leave here every two weeks and there's a new shift of a dozen other operatives stationed in Vegas."

"Do you know Emmett Grogan?" she asked. "He was detained in '72, we both were."

"Yeah, I spoke to him just recently."

"Recently? How'd you get here?" Root asked.

"I walked from Rescue City yesterday—followed the smoke."

"Overground? You're kidding . . . Six years in this toilet bowl and we're only a day's walk from that fucking place? Shit!"

"We'll be lucky if we make it back to Rescue City." Uli looked down at his sister.

"I'll help you with her if you take me and my girls."

"I don't trust you."

"Take me back and Emmett can vouch for me," Root said. "He'll tell you when we came here and how I escaped—or thought I was escaping."

"Actually, that's not a bad idea," Uli mused. "Rescue City is basically in a state of civil war right now, and the Piggers are paranoid. They see a group like this approaching and they'll shoot first and ask questions later."

"Are you serious?"

"The only place that a group of this size can even hope to enter without being immediately attacked is Staten Island, but that would add a lot more distance to get down there. And frankly, I don't see how this crowd is going to make it even halfway there. The best point where we might be able to discreetly bring people in is through Grogan's methadone clinic in Little Neck."

"You better discuss this with Plato. He's in charge."

"My sister needs immediate medical attention, so I'm leaving as soon as she can walk," Uli said.

"We have to wait till the quarantine's over. Plato wants us all to remain for two weeks to let this sickness pass."

"She'll be dead by then."

"She's not that bad," Root said. "And because of the serum, she shouldn't be contagious—no fever, no cold, just acute amnesia."

"I hope."

"If you let me come with you," Root said, "I'll be glad to appeal to Emmett personally."

"Can you get my sister a decent pair of shoes?"

"Yeah, but only if I can bring along the six women I picked up over the years. People who I remember from the old days. I injected them with the serum, so even though they're impaired, none of them are contagious."

"The sooner we leave, the better."

"I still need to clear it with Plato," Root said, then ambled off, presumably to locate the mastermind behind this giant jailbreak.

Uli lay back down on the sand next to Karen and closed his eyes.

Throughout the night, as smoke streamed from the Mkultra below them, the brotherhood of basin dwellers, like border collies, was busy rounding up loose stragglers, trying to direct everyone into the central field.

By the first light of day, Uli was able to clearly survey the disaster zone, which looked like a bloodless battlefield: hundreds of naked or near-naked casualties covered the earth, sickly pale from sun deprivation, befouled, and terrifyingly bony. Many were either shying away from or squinting at the unfamiliar orange ball of fire on the horizon. Though a warm wind was blowing, many were still trembling. Uli sensed that in addition to whatever else they might've caught down there, they had to be suffering from either typhoid or dysentery. Though many appeared to be fast asleep, he knew they were either dead or close to it. The rest were vacant shells. Their attachment to the present had been steadily chewed away by the Alzheimer-like virus, rendering their existence a repetitive series of moments that burst before them without a past.

One group of groomed basin dwellers was trying to erect a line of sheets with ropes and poles to protect as many as they could from the heat of the rising sun. A second group slowly went around passing out C-ration crackers and cups of black water. When one of them finally came to him, Uli took some crackers and thanked the bearded man, then tried to wake up Karen. She could barely open her eyes, much less eat.

By early afternoon, Uli observed a third group of the brotherhood checking the sleepers to see who had died in the night.

"What? Where?" Uli heard someone mumble.

"Karen!" His sister was stirring. "It's me, your brother!"

"From . . . Boston," she slowly muttered. And she was glaring at him.

"I'm your brother Uli."

"You're with them!" she snapped.

"No, I'm with you now—just you," he said with a smile.

She looked puzzled. Uli still had two squished stale cheese sandwiches that he had brought from Rescue City. He offered her one. Karen smelled it timidly. Then, like a scared cat, she stared at him as she nibbled at the corner of it.

"Can you walk?" he asked.

When she looked at him blankly, he gently helped her to her wobbly feet and, holding her knobby shoulder, assisted her in taking some practice steps.

"Hurts," she said, squatting back down.

"Hon, we have a big walk ahead of us, and we have to go soon. So it's vital that you get your legs working again, understand?"

Karen struggled back to her feet. Uli used the opportunity to lead her across the dusty field, away from people coughing nearby.

He led Karen in circles, hoping to tone up her atrophied muscles, walking her until he heard a commotion nearby. The tall black man who had masterminded the escape had finally entered into the vicinity, escorted by a small entourage. Uli recognized Plato immediately and remembered the famous quote by Erasmus: *In the land of the blind, the one-eyed man is king.* Hopefully Plato's mental flame was still able to guide them. As the group came close, Uli saw three semifunctional aides handling his commands as best as their herniated brains could.

"Remember me?" Uli called out as Plato passed by.

The handsome leader's mouth fell open when he saw Uli. "When those bastards failed me," he said to one of his sidekicks, "this wonderful man salvaged my rescue plans! And now he's back! How did you know we'd need you now?"

"I didn't, I just saw the smoke and walked here."

"Where did you walk from?"

"Rescue City."

"Damn," Plato grumbled, "I was hoping you'd say Vegas."

"I wouldn't have found this place if it weren't for the smoke."

"Anyone else see it?"

"Not to my knowledge."

"How long did it take to walk here?" Plato asked.

"About twelve hours at a steady pace."

Plato grimaced. "That's too far."

Karen suddenly started vomiting, so Uli attended to her.

"How did he salvage your rescue plans?" inquired the most alert of Plato's three bearded attachés.

"A few months ago, when I finally had everything in place," Plato said, "I dredged up a team of six semifunctionals who consented to take an experimental drug and venture out in all directions of the compass. But once I brought them up to the surface, they turned into cowards and rushed back down into the Mkultra like mice." Pointing to Uli, he went on, "This happened just as he busted out. He was the only one who agreed to take the injection and make the hike."

"I remember a lake of fire," Uli said.

"Oh, it was just a chemical storage vat. It all burned off."

"You gave me a flare gun, some food, and water."

"Frankly, I didn't expect to see you again."

"What exactly was in that syringe?" Uli asked.

"Some experimental drug that supposedly heightens intuition. Found it in the experimental labs on the second level—it hadn't even been tested. You should probably be dead."

"That explains the hallucinations I had of some woman leading me through the desert."

"After our meeting, I'd climb up and check out the sky at dusk in all directions. Two days later I spotted your flare," Plato explained, pointing due east. It was opposite of the direction Uli had come from. "I was going to have everyone walk that way. What exactly did you find there anyway?"

"A water station. At least that's what it said. It was numbered, so I suspect there are a line of them."

"What's a water station?" another of Plato's entourage asked.

"The two I've seen were small reservoirs of water underneath a concrete base that you can pump and drink from. There's one a few miles from here."

"How far did you walk to get there?" someone else piped up.

"I actually wandered in the desert for miles, going every which way. It was a miracle I survived. The safest way out of here, the only tested way, is *that* way." Uli pointed west, back toward the reservation. "And I located one water station only a few miles from here. After that, it's probably about twenty more miles till you reach the western edge of Rescue City."

"That's probably to discourage any unauthorized evacuations from the Mkultra," Plato surmised. "Hell of an escape plan."

"These people will be lucky if they can even make it back there," Uli said.

"We hardly made it out of sight of Rescue City." Plato sounded discouraged.

"It makes sense," Uli ruminated. "Considering that all these people took some drug causing them to stop breathing for a while, plus the water pressure that thrust them out here. I mean, beyond this point people probably started trying to breathe and drowned."

"Well, we managed to bring up enough C-ration crackers and water for a while. I imagine Root told you that I want to hold these poor folks here for at least two weeks?"

"I don't understand why. They've been sick for years."

"This is a new thing, with different symptoms."

"After two weeks of sitting in the sun without medical attention, at least half these people will die here," Uli said.

"Probably," Plato admitted. "But what choice do we have? I mean, if we bring them back to Rescue City, they could have a full-scale plague on their hands, and they got a lot more people there."

"That's fine, but I'm here for my sister and she's definitely not going to last two weeks out here."

"Root told me she's been giving her the treatment," Plato said. "She also has her little group of spinsters who she wants to bring back with you. I want you to do me a favor."

"What?"

"First, when you get back to Rescue City, don't mention us. That way I can keep up the quarantine and protect them."

"Fine."

"Second, on your way there, I want you to clearly mark the trail so that when we are ready to leave, we'll know where we're going. That should dramatically reduce people getting lost."

"Mark the trail, huh?" Uli hesitated. "See, the only problem with that is I'm going to have a difficult enough time taking my sister back; I don't know how I'm going to have the strength or energy to also make a path."

"We have a couple large buckets of yellow paint that you can use," said one of the entourage.

"And we can send the two brothers with him! They can do all the work," another said to the boss.

"Perfect," said Plato. "So you'll have two more scouts to add to your hike."

"That will be fine," Uli said, remembering that the walk was filled with large stones and cacti that they could paint upon.

Root reappeared with a group of six women in tow and quietly slipped a pair of worn leather sandals onto Karen's filthy feet.

"Speak of the devil," Plato said, then turned to one of his aides, a slim bald man. He instructed the guy to fetch the two brothers to escort Uli and to help him prepare for their hike back to Rescue City. "I have to dash, but Jorge here will take care of all your needs."

"See you in Rescue City," Uli said, and Plato and his entourage were quickly gone.

A moment later, Jorge hurried over with a pair of short, chubby, bearded men who looked like Tweedledum and Tweedledee.

"Pair paints path," Jorge said.

Each man was holding a gallon-size bucket of canary-yellow paint. Uli greeted them but was met with silence—both were obviously aphasic.

Before Jorge could rush off, Uli grabbed him and pointed out that their little group would now consist of eleven members and each of them needed at least half a jug of water for the walk ahead. They would also need two paintbrushes for the trail markings.

Jorge took a stick out of his pocket and seemed to try to write Uli's request down on the palm of his grimy hand. Intent on wasting no more time, Uli scurried through the settlement and was able to snatch three empty plastic jugs, which he filled with the black liquid that brutally passed as water. He couldn't find anything resembling a paintbrush, but found two long sticks that would do in a pinch. It was time to go.

"Okay, folks," Uli announced to his little group, "if we're lucky, we should just make Rescue City by sunrise. And if you're sick of drinking that awful sludge, hold out for the next hour or so until we reach the water station, and you'll be able to get some fresh water."

Only Root appeared to understand him. Uli's little band of eleven consisted of himself, Root, her six older women, Karen—who was probably in the worst shape—and the two portly men with their buckets of paint. Slowly, under the darkening sky, they stumbled through the field of dead and dying. It took a full ten minutes before they were out in the open desert.

6

As Uli marched back into the scrublands leading his groggy group, he found himself trying to remember more about his past. Though his amnesia seemed to be lifting a bit, it wasn't like the clean unspooling of thoughts that he had experienced when he found himself reliving the life of Paul Moses. His memories seemed buried under ice: sometimes whole slabs of time suddenly came loose; other times he had to chip away at each little detail.

He clearly recalled when the shit hit the fan in LA and he lost his command. He alone was banished to the wilds of South Dakota as a punishment. It was a little less than a year after J. Edgar Hoover died. That was when he first learned that the United States had nearly three hundred federally recognized Native American tribes living within its white Christian borders. Each tribe elected its own chairman and voted on an extended council.

Justice on these reservations was technically under the jurisdiction of the BIA—the Bureau of Indian Affairs. Uli remembered that one particular tribe, on a reservation in South Dakota, was run by a former plumber named Dick Wilson, who was only part Native American. Supposedly, by bullying some, relying on the apathy of others, and bribing a few in the middle, Wilson had essentially managed to hijack the post. Since the area had almost no economy, and jobs were few and far between, Wilson—or "the Plumber," as the FBI nicknamed him—had given all the paying administrative posts to his deadbeat buddies and their trailer trash families. Instead of navigating the subtle hierarchy of tribal elders, the man ran roughshod over tradition and had managed to piss everyone off.

When the locals protested the Plumber's thuggish style, the situation quickly spiraled out of control. That was when the long red arm of the Kremlin was extended all the way to South Dakota.

Blacks had fought for their civil rights. Women demanded equality. Even gays were pushing for rights. J. Edgar Hoover had warned that this would happen: once you opened that freedom door, you'd never be able to shut it. Now it was the Native Americans' turn. The American Indian Movement had become a magnet for hip, young "engines." For about six months, it seemed as though nearly every young Native American joined AIM. In fact, so many kids had signed up, the leadership was quickly overwhelmed.

"Just consider this," Uli's new supervisor commented, "after a hundred years of being the most silent minority in America, this tiny group only came into being *after* Moscow money had provoked and funded the coons, lezzies, and queers into rebelling. Naturally, redskins were the last to be invited to the party."

Although the two tubby trailblazers were able to splatter paint, by the time they finally reached the water station, Uli was worried. They weren't using enough paint. For the first time he realized that approaching from the east, the water station was located in a sunken patch, and unless people knew what they were looking for, they might walk right past it. So while the others rested, Uli backtracked for about a mile with one of the paint buckets and clearly routed the trail into the dunes.

When Uli rejoined the group, he guzzled down as much clean water as he could pump up. While Root divvied up some of the crackers, Uli discreetly pulled out his last stale sandwich and divided it between himself and Karen.

After they all finished eating, and before they could start nodding off in the darkness, Uli rose and they resumed their hike.

Around ten at night, Root pointed out a bright star, low on the wavy horizon. "I think that's Neptune or Jupiter," she said.

A few minutes later, Uli confirmed his suspicions that it wasn't a star at all, but rather the very top of the Williamsburgh Building.

Though occasionally startled by snakes, lizards, and assorted nocturnal creatures, the little group made slow and steady progress. As the sun eventually rose in the east, the tip of the Williamsburgh Building grew higher in the west. Instead of steering directly into Brooklyn, Uli wanted to circle around and approach Rescue City from the north—via northern Queens. Hoping to navigate a discreet passage to Emmett Grogan's clinic in Little Neck, he spotted a pile of gigantic boulders in the distance. Five minutes later, Uli scaled the tallest rock and got a decent visual sense of where they needed to go.

He directed the brother who was not suffering from heat rash to paint a large, clear arrow to indicate that this was where the route turned sharply.

Uli soon spotted a narrow gulley. As he headed down into it, he discovered that it was a man-made spillway intended to drain off any flash storms that might hit northern Rescue City, a rarity at best. As the group proceeded down the dried-out channel, Uli was glad to see that it stayed roughly six feet deep, just below the sight lines of the residents of the nearby area. Moving along for roughly a quarter mile, they could make out the occasional solicars speeding along the road that bordered the desert's edge. Occasionally they could also hear faint voices. At one point, an excited dialogue from at least a half mile off gave way to a woman's shrill laugh. Uli wondered if there was any chance that the bulk of the Mkultra survivors could survive this hike, let alone make it into the city without being noticed.

With sulfur fumes filling the air, they reached a swampy patch filled with cacti and other vegetation marking the beginning of Little Neck. In another twenty minutes, Uli spotted the rear of the Lotus methadone clinic elevated before them. It was located on a narrow strip of land; on the far side was the waterway where Rikers Island was located. As the morning sun rose, he led his tired band up the slope and around from the backyard to the front of the ranch-style house where they joined a line of six people waiting for their morning dose of methadone.

"You guys okay, man?" one young man asked, seeing their frayed rags and the hollow eyes in their flinty, skeletal faces.

"We're fine," Root replied.

"Let them go ahead of us," the man called to the others in line, obviously concerned about their severely emaciated bodies.

They stepped ahead to the tall receptionist stationed out front.

"Do you have an appointment?" she asked Root politely.

"If you could tell Emmett that Root Ginseng is back, he'd greatly appreciate it, as would I."

"I'm sorry, but Mr. Grogan is unable to take any unscheduled appointments. He's in meetings all day—"

Root marched right into the house, down a corridor, pursued by the woman, who yelled out as Root flung open a variety of doors, finally reaching the one she was looking for.

"What the hell!" Grogan was sitting at the head of a table with four others.

"Hi, Em," Root greeted.

"My God! I thought you'd be back in New York by now!"

If Root had been posted in the Mkultra by some nefarious government agency, they had created one hell of a cover story, Uli thought.

"I'll tell you all about it later, but first we have a huge problem," Root said. "We desperately need your help."

Grogan gave her a hug and kiss and asked for a moment to wrap things up. They waited as he adjourned his little meeting.

Uli explained that a large number of people who had tried escaping Rescue City over the years had found themselves incarcerated in a subterranean complex about twenty miles outside the city.

"While trapped in there, many have been infected by some unknown virus and are suffering from dementia," Root said.

"Not to mention severe malnutrition," Uli added.

"Exactly how many people are we talking about?" Grogan asked.

"Maybe five hundred," Root said.

"Holy shit!" Grogan snatched up the phone. "I'll call Plains and he can notify Mallory."

"Hold on now, Em." Root gently took the phone from him. "They won't arrive here for a while. The leadership is holding them for a two-week quarantine."

"You're saying that up to a thousand people are dying in the desert and you want to wait?"

"After what just happened in South Ozone Park," Uli spoke up, "the two parties seem to be violently opposed to newcomers."

"That was different. They felt that their land was being stolen."

"Do you really want to gamble hundreds of lives on the Piggers' sense of hospitality?" Uli said.

"What do you suggest?" Emmett asked.

"They won't be coming for a couple weeks, and when they start arriving they'll probably do so in small groups over time."

"Our hope is that maybe we can settle them here, below the radar," Root said.

"How?"

"For starters, they can camp outside in the rear of your building, and we can bring them into the city slowly," she elaborated. "Maybe quietly attempt to locate their families and friends."

"I really think we should notify the authorities right now," Grogan said sternly.

"I just think that the Piggers are in a heightened state of alert, and all these sick people might wind up getting herded into the Bronx Zoo," Uli said.

"We just need a place to temporarily hold them," Root said.

"The clinic doesn't have those kinds of resources." Emmett shook his head. "And everyone will see them coming."

"Not true. The path here is sunken through a dry marsh," Uli pointed out. "And your backyard can't be seen from the street."

"Our little center can barely hold fifty people max."

"The temperature at night is seventy degrees right now," Root said. "They can camp outside—"

"Look," Emmett cut in, "one call and I can get all the city services here in minutes. If they are sick, they'll need help."

"I've seen what happens when Kew Gardens feels threatened," Uli pushed back, not mentioning that he had been tortured by the Piggers and had come dangerously close to getting his hand judicially amputated.

"I'd like to talk alone with Root," Emmett said, turning away from Uli. He led her outside, closing the door behind them.

Uli could hear their muffled voices as they talked heatedly for a few minutes, and then Root returned alone. She explained that Emmett was simply overwhelmed with his own problems. He was late on submitting his annual budget for the upcoming year and had to work nonstop to finish it by the deadline extension.

"Is he going to turn us in?"

"He said that against his better judgment, he'll let us handle things. Oh, he also said that we could help ourselves to whatever stock we find downstairs. A few of us, including you, me, and Karen, can stay inside the clinic. They have a few empty rooms with cots we can sleep on."

In the basement they grabbed blankets, hospital gowns, and other surplus supplies. There was also a large but rarely used kitchen in the rear of the building. Root said that once Grogan was done with his paperwork, he would call around and try to procure other supplies without alarming anyone.

"Sorry about accusing you of being government," Uli said to Root, duly impressed.

She smiled, then got back to the business at hand. "We better check and see what sort of food he has," she said, opening a little pantry in the kitchen. They found a dozen large cans of pinto beans, as well as a fifty-pound bag of white rice. Hopefully that would be enough to handle the first hundred survivors as they started arriving.

Inside a box marked *Xmas Supplies*, Root also found strings of Christmas lights with extension cords that Uli suggested they run from the house out over the backyard. Coils of gardening hose could also bring water outside to the weary travelers.

As the two began making dinner for their little group, a small sense of relief settled in. While Uli spoon-fed his sister, he silently congratulated himself on not just saving her, but playing a major part in rescuing the others as well.

7

When the formerly abandoned neighborhoods of Greenpoint-Williamsburg, Bushwick, East New York, and South Ozone Park—an area briefly known as Quirklyn—became inhabited by squatters who soon afterward declared themselves an independent city, the two gangs of Brooklyn and Queens worked together to force them to vacate. The settlers resisted.

After repeated threats, it had all come to an end just days earlier when the gangcops of both boroughs attacked the occupied areas. Following a fierce battle with many casualties, the survivors fled late at night to an ancient Native American settlement that had been unofficially renamed Rockville Centre. Their reclaimed and repaired homes were burned to the ground as they were driven eastward into the desert. Under the leadership of Bea Moses-Mayer, hundreds of them hiked south around Rockaway Beach and the Jamaica basin, then down below the giant testicular-shaped borough of Brooklyn, where vats of water had been placed by aides to Adolphus Rafique, the wheelchair-bound mayor of Staten Island. Then the refugees hiked through the garbage dumps, crossing the toxic waterway that bordered the eastern edge of Staten Island, until they finally arrived in the southernmost borough.

A team from the Verdant League—Rafique's party that governed the borough—had a dozen minibuses pick them up and shuttle them to the borough's municipal center, the Staten Island terminal building. Once there, VL workers brought the injured Quirklyners to a makeshift infirmary outside the building. The rest were ushered to the large cafeteria in the basement for their first meal in many hours. Barely able to keep her eyes open at that point, Bea Moses-Mayer had passed out on a cot. During that first night, except for the occasional outburst of grief for lost loved ones killed in the fight, all ate in a mournful silence.

After a cup of coffee the next morning, Bea was about to go visit her father Paul Moses when one of the security guards informed her that she had to immediately report to Adolphus Rafique's office.

She was frisked, escorted upstairs, then offered a seat at a long table across from the politician.

"I'm truly sorry about my indiscretion." Bea was still guilt-ridden with the notion that her odd love affair with an official from Pure-ile Plurality had somehow sparked the attack on Quirklyn.

"It was going to happen anyway," Rafique replied. "The good news is, I just learned that three of the Warhol Superstar councilpeople are still alive."

Though Ondine had been killed during the initial invasion, Jackie Curtis and Candy Darling had been grabbed during the Crapper blitz across northern Brooklyn and were currently being held in the Williamsburgh Building.

"What about the survivors?" Bea asked, peering out the window at the nebula of somber Quirklyners who were mulling around among the wounded in the outdoor infirmary.

"Eventually we'll find housing for everyone," Rafique explained. "I asked you up here to tell you some bad news . . . about your father."

"What about him?"

"I'm sorry to say that he died yesterday morning."

Bea gasped.

"It was an accident. He fell and hit his head."

"Fell?!" Tears filled her eyes. She couldn't speak.

"Police Chief Loveworks investigated it himself."

"Investigated *what?*"

"Loveworks initially had a suspect, but the guy had a solid alibi, so he was let go."

"Roger Loveworks is a fucking moron!"

"Trust me, he's not as dumb as you think."

"Who was the suspect?" Bea demanded.

"Some old guy who showed up two days ago claiming to be your father's brother."

"My father's only brother is Robert Moses."

"That's him, unless he's an impostor, and he doesn't look it," Rafique said. "We're holding Robert Moses in custody, though it's not for your father's death."

"But he's like one hundred years old!"

"Ninety-two."

"Hold on. He was with my father when he fell, but you don't suspect him of being guilty?"

"Well, he's guilty of *something*. Otherwise Jacobs wouldn't be preparing charges."

"*Jane* is preparing the charges?" Bea had befriended the short community activist when she worked for her briefly back in Old Town. Jacobs had organized the protests against her uncle's proposed Lower Manhattan Expressway back in the midsixties, but Bea had never revealed that she was Moses's niece.

"A lot of people here were displaced over the years due to his highway systems and building projects." Rafique paused a moment. "But frankly, Jane is pissed at me for the whole Quirklyn debacle and I think she's using your uncle to stick it to me."

"He killed my father—he should be up on criminal charges! I want to interrogate him myself," Bea said.

"Out of the question."

"I've worked for the Department of VL Security since it was formed. I've interrogated prisoners before."

"Not someone who might have killed your father."

"Are you afraid I'm going to attack him?"

"Obviously."

"Fine, you can have someone in the room with me. You can have me handcuffed if you like."

"I'll make you a deal," Rafique countered. "I'll let you interrogate him, but if he persuades you that he's innocent, I want you to consider helping with his defense against Jacobs's charges."

"Defense! Seriously? Why me?"

"You're his niece, and you're popular. You'll bring local sympathy to bear. And you're smart. You know his work from back in Old Town."

"Yeah, 'cause I opposed him with Jane!"

"That battle was fought and won. It's nearly twenty years later. Even *you* can see that this is just vindictive."

"Even if he didn't kill my father, this man uprooted my family home. My mother died and my father fell apart. All because of that bastard's Cross Bronx Expressway."

"Just consider it. That's all I'm asking."

"Fine, I'll interrogate him and try to get him to plead guilty. But," she rolled her eyes, "if I miraculously somehow happen to find he's innocent—and if I somehow find myself growing sympathetic toward the man who ruined my life and destroyed my father—I'll consider defending him. How's that?"

"That's all I ask." Rafique then muttered something to one of his aides, who led Bea one flight below to the private suite where they were holding their prized prisoner.

Harry Blumenthal, the head of security at the terminal building, escorted Bea into a classroom that had been converted into a living room and sleeping quarters. Two men were sitting by the window. Parked solidly in a comfortable recliner was a battered, very old man. With a black eye, split lip, and swollen cheek, Robert Moses had clearly taken a beating. Bea dismissed her instinct to feel sorrow—he was still the old prick who had probably killed her father. Police Chief Loveworks was sitting across from Moses.

"So," Bea jumped right in without introducing herself, "a couple days ago you arrived here out of the blue." Looking closer at the subject's swollen eyes, she realized Robert Moses was fast asleep. "HEY!" she yelled.

The old man woke up, startled. "Is it time?"

"It's time we talk," she snapped.

"Of course," he yawned. His long fingers began massaging his wrinkled face, as if affixing a mask that officially made him Robert Moses.

"You're in the Nevada desert, understand? It's 1981!"

"I see."

"Two days ago you were caught here after murdering your brother Paul."

"That guy! I told the other guy I was trying to free him. He fought me. Look what he did to me!" Moses pointed to his bruised face.

"Still, you're alive and he's dead," Bea argued.

"I didn't get a single punch in. He fell down and next thing I knew . . ." Moses's mouth fell open, then looking up at Bea, he squinted his eyes and asked, "Who precisely are you again?"

"My name is Bea Moses, and you murdered my father."

"Paul? . . . My brother Paul was your father?"

"He was."

"But you don't look . . . I mean, you look different than my brother . . . in some ways."

"My mother was black," she said bluntly.

"Paul married a colored girl?"

"Yes, and I was their mixed-race baby."

"Well then, I'm your uncle." He slowly rose to his feet and extended a hand. "Pleased to meet you."

Bea slapped him hard across his loose face. "You killed my father!"

Blumenthal rose, but Moses held out his large hand motioning him off. "It was an unfortunate accident, dear. He tripped and hit his head, I didn't lay a hand on him. And that's the truth."

Her slap had reopened a cut on his lower lip. The sight of blood running from the old man's mouth only made her feel awful. He looked so much like her dad that she had to turn away so he wouldn't see her distress.

"You know what life is?" Moses began. "It's playing against a stacked deck, with overwhelming odds and unbelievable pressure—and that's it, dear! You get a couple good hands until you lose, and life's over. I tried like the dickens to work with that dope. No offense, but he was my brother long before he was your father. We fought every step of the way, until I tried just avoiding him."

"His life was miserable because of you."

"Oh brother! I only tried to keep him out of my hair, and I tried staying out of his way. That sounds pretty awful for two brothers, I know. But it was the best we could do."

"It wasn't we, it was you!"

"I beg your pardon, young lady, but it was we," Moses replied. "He wanted things done his way, I wanted things my way—we couldn't work together."

"You never even tried."

"We grew up fighting. Hell, the last time I saw him when he was at the hospital, I thought it was rather considerate of me to pay him a visit. I gave him my book. He had fallen down a flight of stairs, and I wanted to see if there was anything I could do for him. You know what he did? He slammed the spine of the book into my face, broke my nose." He pointed to the crook in his narrow nose. "Hell, I came here to rescue him. I mean, I figured he'd finally agree with me on this. What'd he do? He literally fought me tooth and nail. Now he's dead and I'm probably never going to get back to my wife and kids. So believe me when I say that I gave up everything for him!"

With the last of his energy burned out for the day, Moses slumped back in his seat, and in a moment had lapsed into a shallow sleep. Bea glared at him and tried to remain angry. Unable, she stormed out of the room and returned upstairs. Rafique was just ending a meeting, so he allowed her in.

"Why in God's name do you care about defending an asshole like Robert Moses?" she yelled as she entered his chamber. Rafique's anti-establishment record was legend, whereas Robert Moses epitomized the entrenched, smoky, backroom dealings of a great corrupt machine.

"In any other context I'd probably be glad to crucify the old bastard," Rafique said. "Only in this instance, I know Jacobs. She wants to use the Moses trial to catapult her own public profile, 'cause she wants to challenge me next year."

"It really doesn't sound like Jane."

"So you're not going to help with your uncle's defense?"

"I'm not a lawyer. I mean, what exactly do you want me to do?" Bea asked.

"This is really just going to be a big shouting match, so you don't have to worry about procedure. A panel of judges will decide whatever they want at the end, I just think it'll humanize him if his popular Verdant League niece is sitting at the table."

"*Humanize* him?! That man totally fucked up my life. He indirectly killed both my parents!"

"Bea, I'm sure this is unfair of me, but I have to admit I have a begrudging respect for the old bastard. My feelings aside, this whole thing stinks to high heaven. This incompetent old guy somehow wanders into this tiger cage and he's suddenly grabbed and put on this show trial."

"Why don't you stop it?"

"That would be political suicide." Rafique let out a sigh. "Look, if you feel you dropped the ball in Quirklyn with your little lesbian tryst, then this is a chance to set things right by me."

Before either could say another word, Rafique's secretary announced that his final appointment of the day was waiting for him. Bea was hastily escorted out of the office.

She went downstairs and returned to her father's nearby bungalow. She lay down on his cot and when she inhaled deeply, she was still able to smell his presence.

8

After a late dinner the following night, Bea was approached by a guard from the Verdant League. He informed her that she had an urgent phone call in the terminal building.

Fearing it somehow concerned her Quirklyn refugees, she dashed over to the administration building and grabbed the phone at the front desk. She was surprised to hear Uli Sarkisian's voice: "A supply drone didn't crash in the desert like you thought."

"Did you find your sister?" she asked, knowing he was referring to the column of black smoke they had both seen in the distance.

"Yeah, Karen's here with me." He took a deep, shaky breath. "Did I tell you about where I was trapped after I went down the sewer?"

"Yeah," she said. "Where are you calling from?"

"The Lotus methadone clinic in Little Neck, Queens, and we're in deep shit."

"Were you arrested?"

"No, the Piglets don't even know we're here. But the problem is that over the next few weeks we're going to be getting literally hundreds of sick and delirious people coming in from the desert. We barely have supplies for a fraction of them, and we need help."

"As you might recall," Bea said, "we are flooded with wounded and homeless Quirklyners. We're tapped out down here."

"Do you think that in a few weeks' time things might get easier? 'Cause that's when the shit is really going to hit the fan."

"What exactly do you need?"

"Food, meds, and ideally somewhere to evacuate these refugees to." As Uli explained the situation, Bea closed her eyes and tried to stave off a growing headache. She had assumed that once she'd reached the safety of Staten Island, the worst would be over. Now a second wave of refugees was waiting in the wings.

"If I come across any unexpected stockpiles, I'll call you," she said wearily. "But keep in mind that at least half of those people who you've saved are probably Piggers. And they've got the most housing and supplies by far. Why don't you try to get them on board?"

"Because they kill first and ask questions later."

"If those people are really sick, I can't imagine the Piggers perceiving them as a threat. At worst, they'll expel them—"

Suddenly the phone went dead.

Uli tried calling Bea back, but a recorded announcement said the phone lines out of Queens were overloaded. *"Please try your call again later."* Since it was late, he decided to get some shut-eye and consider more options tomorrow. He went to their temporary bedroom, lay down on a cot next to Karen, pulled a thin blanket over himself, and was out like a light.

In what seemed like the next moment, Root was shaking him awake. "They're here!" she yelled. "They're here!"

"Who?"

She grabbed his arm and led him out of bed, not even giving him time to pull on his shoes. He followed her down the stairs and onto the porch overlooking the vast backyard of the clinic; this was the only house in the area that had a view of the dry spillway. Standing out back, some squatting, others revolving in slow circles, were at least a dozen newly arrived, bedraggled, skeletal, blank-eyed people. Uli saw that most of them were roped together with strands of filthy cloth. They could only have come from one place.

"Holy shit!" He ran down the steps to start checking their health. Sure enough, they were all sweaty, sniffling, sneezing, coughing—a walking plague.

"I heard them banging around out here," Root said.

"Didn't Plato tell us that he was quarantining them for at least two weeks?"

"Yes, but here they are! And we can't send them back."

Uli isolated the two members of the new group who appeared to be in charge, both with the telltale cropped beards. They were only marginally more alert than those they were leading. Uli asked them why they were here. Through grunts and gestures, they tiredly conveyed that they had been given jugs of water and told to lead the group, which had been tied together.

"How'd you know where to go?" Root asked the one who seemed most lucid.

"They said, *Follow the yellow*," the man replied.

Uli brought them all inside the rear of the clinic. Root was surprised to find that the last man's rope had been cleanly cut.

"Did you leave anyone behind?" Uli nervously asked one of the two basin leaders.

The man nodded yes.

"How many?" Root asked.

He held open both hands, showing ten fingers.

"Where are they?" Root asked.

The man pointed out toward the open desert.

"Why?" Uli exclaimed.

"They stopped and wouldn't . . . start."

"You were supposed to *lead* them!" Root barked.

"They're okay. They just needed a nap. They'll get picked up by others."

"What others?" Uli prodded.

"More a-coming," the other bearded man spoke up.

Uli and Root stared at each other.

"How many more?"

"All."

"Are you sure?"

One shrugged and the other looked off.

Uli and Root weren't prepared to handle the dozen invalids that had just arrived, let alone hundreds more. They huddled off to the side and spoke quietly.

"Hold on now," said Root, breathing slowly. "Before we start to panic, these guys aren't exactly reliable."

"What are you saying?"

"Is it so difficult to assume that this one tiny group saw us leaving and broke away from the herd, and this is all there is?"

"God, I hope you're right," Uli said. "But if you're wrong, we could be wasting valuable time."

"You scrounge up some food for them," she said. "I'll try to clean them up. If no one else comes in by morning, we'll go out and see if we can find any of those left behind."

Uli went into the kitchen and put some rice and beans on the stove while Root got a bucket and hosed the newcomers down one at a time. After they fed them, they set them up with blankets out in the backyard and let them sleep.

No sooner had they gotten things under control, and Uli had returned to his bunk, than he heard Root yelling. He jumped back to his feet and headed to the porch, where Root was standing. He followed her line of vision into the darkness and soon saw the faint swaying outlines growing closer. Disheveled men and women, like ghosts, slowly filed down the empty gulley toward them. Their worst fears were instantly confirmed. Instead of coming in two weeks, the refugees were trickling in now.

"This is far beyond our capacity," Uli said.

Without responding, Root dashed upstairs and knocked on Grogan's door. When he answered wearing his boxers and a T-shirt, she explained that all the Mkultra survivors were probably on their way right now. And it was more than they could handle.

Uli reached the door as Grogan was saying, "Then there is only one thing I can do, and that's call Kew Gardens."

"Do it," Root said.

Grogan replied that it might still take awhile, so they should try to handle the situation as best they could until help arrived.

Uli and Root went downstairs and started an immediate triage, sorting the critical from the serious.

Twenty minutes later, Grogan rushed downstairs to say that help was on the way. "I spoke to the director of the emergency medical services and told him these people had been out in the desert and weren't a threat, so they aren't treating this as a police issue."

"Thank God," Root said.

Grogan assisted Root in bringing some of the worst cases into the house. Again, the new guides—also barely communicative—said they had abandoned some of their slower charges out in the desert.

Twenty minutes later, the first emergency vehicles screeched to a halt in the driveway. They shone their headlights toward the desert and onto the crowd gathering below. The Piggers started shouting orders to each other, pulling out floodlights and medical gear. When Root came back outside, the most critical refugees were being loaded into minibuses.

"Hold on! Hold on! These people need to be quarantined first!" Uli heard Root warn the emergency workers.

"Calm down, lady. We'll handle things from here."

Uli told her to relax, clearly relieved that he was no longer in charge. Instead of the militia, only medical personnel arrived, providing immediate first aid—laying many on the ground, bandaging some of them, while others were given much-needed water. All the survivors were severely dehydrated. Uli felt bad that he had underestimated the Piggers. He was touched by their general care and sensitivity.

Over the course of the next hour, as a steady stream of Pigger officials arrived, Uli and Root tried to explain the situation at hand. These people were all sick with some unknown ailment. Hundreds had been stuck out in the desert for years.

"I don't understand," said one of the deputy mayors from Kew Gardens who had just arrived. "What the hell are hundreds of people doing out in the middle of the goddamned desert?"

"And how exactly did they all get the flu?" asked a thin, bald gangcop with a goatee and a fresh scar down his face. Uli recognized him as one of the planners of the attack on South Ozone Park; he had seen him at Pure-ile Plurality.

"You must've all heard that insane legend about an escape route through Staten Island," Uli said.

"What are you talking about?" questioned the deputy mayor, who had somehow never heard the rumors.

"You get injected with a mystery drug," Uli responded, "then you lose consciousness and get dropped down a hole in the southern tip of Staten Island that leads to a sewer pipe."

"And you drown?"

"No," said the bald, goateed gangcop. "It's supposed to be a miraculous way out of here."

"I heard you drain out to the Colorado River," said a Pigger paramedic.

"The truth is, if you don't drown, you wake up in a net in this huge underground chamber about twenty miles that way." Uli pointed eastward. "This is not something anyone could've predicted, but over the years all these people accumulated out there like lint in a drainpipe."

"This all sounds like a huge pile of horseshit," said the deputy mayor's assistant.

"Hike out there and take a look for yourself," Uli said. "Just follow the smoke rising in the east."

"I'm Captain Ramsey Farrell," the freshly scarred gangcop introduced himself. "Let me explain something to you. We just had a violent altercation with a group of anarchist squatters who tried to occupy parts of southern Queens." Uli saw that it was more a wound than a scar. It looked like someone had dug a dull knife into the man's smug face. "They killed a bunch of our men."

"This has nothing to do with that," Uli said emphatically.

"A bunch of these clowns escaped into the desert. And you're telling us that this mysterious group who coincidentally came *out* of the desert have nothing to do with them?" Farrell was getting angry.

"Go look for yourself!" Uli said. "A lot of the Quirklyners are pretty young. These people are older. They're emaciated and they're not wounded, but they're feverish. They're very sick. And if they don't get immediate attention, many of them will be dead by tomorrow."

"And who the fuck are you?" asked Farrell.

"Just someone trying to help," Uli said.

"I want your fingerprints."

"All I care about are those people," Uli said, nodding to the survivors.

"We're sending a scouting party out right now," said one of the other senior gangcops. There were only officers around, none of the rank and file. "In fact, if you'd like to draw us a map, that would be very helpful."

"I'll take you myself," Uli offered.

"No, I want to speak to you alone," Farrell said, then pointed at Root. "She can go with the scouts."

Uli watched as tables, cots, medicine, and food were carried out from the back of the arriving trucks.

Before he could ask Root to help keep an eye on his sister, Farrell and another gangcop shoved Uli into a car. For the second time since he had arrived in Rescue City, he was being driven to Rikers Island.

Once inside the gates of the awful jail, Uli started breathing quickly, remembering the last time he'd been there, when he had been sadistically tortured by Newton Underwood. He was finding it increasingly difficult to focus as he was fingerprinted. A moment later he was brought into a private room where the angry Captain Ramsey Farrell was waiting for him.

"Uli Sarkisian—it says here that you were arrested for assaulting a Pigger gangcop. You were supposed to lose a hand, but you were pardoned for some reason. Mind if I ask why?"

"I honestly don't know," Uli replied. He was relieved that there appeared to be no record of his earlier torture, and the fact that Chain and Underwood had been murdered during his escape.

"This is actually an intelligence dossier," Farrell said, holding up the file. "It says you were given the prestigious assignment of revamping the Crapper gangcop force, specifically in prepping them on how to build legal cases and work within their newly implemented criminal justice system." He opened the file and showed Uli surveillance photos of cars that had been dragged out of New York Harbor after the horrific flooding of Lower Manhattan. "I'm guessing that you were pardoned in exchange for your service."

"If you like, I can do the same for your gangcops."

"What exactly were you doing three days ago, during the Quirklyn battle?"

"Exactly what you just said. If you check the court records in Brooklyn, you'll see that while all that was going on, I was in the Williamsburgh Building, in charge of overseeing their new, aforementioned procedures."

"The Quirklyn occupation of Queens was planned and executed by the anarchist Adolphus Rafique, who installed a mentally imbalanced lesbian named Valerie Solanas in our neighborhood of South Ozone Park. Ever met her?"

"Probably." Uli was surprised to hear Rafique's name, and realized now that the VL head must have survived his seemingly fatal gunshot wound.

"Probably, huh? That doesn't sound particularly enthusiastic, considering you boned a Ms. Bea Moses."

"Bea?"

"She was the alleged dyke posing as Valerie Solanas. But if you nailed her, I guess she wasn't too alleged."

"Where are you getting this crap?" Uli asked. "'Cause I'll tell you right now, that's what it is."

"I'd bring in our intelligence officer who contributed this info, only she was mysteriously killed. Deere Flare was her name."

"And how does this connect to the Quirklyn uprising?"

"Why did you cease working for the Crappers?"

"I completed the job."

"Wrong again. You were supposedly dismissed for trespassing on their sacred Hoboken crop—a charge that later led to your collusion with the Quirklyners."

These people had kept surprisingly close tabs on him. It made Uli wonder if the Piggers and Crappers were sharing information. At that moment he realized he should've grabbed Karen and fled before the officials had arrived in Little Neck. "I was dismissed, but I wasn't charged with any wrongdoing," he snapped back. "You can confirm that with the Crappers. Now, unless you're charging me with something . . ."

"I believe that you were a key player in the Quirklyn occupation," Captain Farrell said.

"Even if I was, what would it matter? The place has been burned off the face of the earth."

"We lost the cream of our police force on the Aqueduct Dog Track. I personally lost my brother and two of my dearest friends. Hundreds of those assholes got away."

"Look, you can torture me all you want, but I honestly don't know anything."

"Well, you're in luck because we don't torture anyone here. We will patiently wait, and when you do remember something, we'll be there to listen."

Farrell then signaled to the guard, who handcuffed Uli and led him out to a small holding cell that was packed with petty criminals from the shadier sections of Queens. After a couple of hours, when they couldn't fit anybody else in the cage, the twelve men and three women were handcuffed together and led out to a minibus and driven across a bridge to another familiar location—the former Bronx Zoo.

Uli was quickly processed, given a cautionary lecture by the dreaded warden Polly Femus—who fortunately didn't recognize him from his prior conviction—then shoved into another overcrowded cell and forgotten.

9

A week and a half after Uli was locked up in the Bronx, a call came into Mayor Mallory's office from the mayor of Rescue City North. Mallory was informed that there was an impending crisis involving every resident of Rescue City, and Mayor John Cross Plains urgently requested a three-way conference with the mayor of Staten Island, who had come out of hiding.

Five minutes later all three city leaders were on the line. Mayor Mallory had Attorney General Schuman listening in as well.

"Over the years," began Mayor Plains, "I'm sure we all have known people who took that allegedly magic injection and went down the rabbit hole in Staten Island, hoping to escape this place. Well, guess what? It was just a sewer, and most probably died. But many found their way to an underground facility roughly twenty miles east of here in the middle of the desert, and they put up nets and started saving others."

"Twenty miles away?" Rafique said skeptically.

"If you think I'm lying, we can take you out there."

"When did all this happen?" Mallory asked.

"It was first brought to our attention a little over a week ago. We started sending teams into the desert and rescued as many as we could."

"Exactly how many did you rescue?" Rafique asked.

"Many have died, but we still have about four hundred or so."

"Four hundred!" Mallory exclaimed. "You expect us to believe that within a matter of days you were able to retrieve four hundred people from some isolated desert locale twenty miles away?"

"A few years ago, Mayor Shub funded a secret program in Queens to convert a dozen solicars into off-road vehicles in an attempt to drive across the desert."

"What exactly is an *off-road* vehicle?" Rafique asked.

"They were able to patch together giant tires, drop the axles, put in larger engines, and make slow-moving dune buggies to move across the sands." Most of the standard solicars were little more than high-speed golf carts with narrow wheels that only ran on pavement.

"So we're talking about severe malnutrition?" Rafique asked in his clipped, mechanical cadence.

"Yes, but many seem to also have some bizarre illness that affects their memories."

"Why did you wait a week before telling us this?" Mallory inquired.

"Once we'd retrieved them all, we realized it was more than we alone could handle."

"So you want more supplies?" Mallory said.

"Actually, we were hoping you could each take a fair share of these people—since they are from all over the reservation."

"How much is a fair share?" Rafique probed.

"Well, Adolphus, you're getting nearly a quarter of all the supplies that come out of JFK. You have some medical and housing facilities. How about 150?"

Rafique sighed. "What a coincidence this is. I'm guessing both of you must've heard about the thousand hard-luck cases that you pushed out of your already-empty neighborhoods. They've swung around Jamaica Bay and are now illegally squatting in my borough, exhausting our limited stock of food and housing."

"I think I can speak for Mayor Mallory when I say that we'll be glad to send our gangcops down and finish them off for you," Plains offered.

Neither Mallory nor Rafique responded to this.

"Do you know what boroughs these people initially came from?" Mallory asked, referring to the Mkultra survivors. "Any proof of residence?"

"Unfortunately, most of them have lost the power of speech," Plains said, "though we believe this is only temporary."

"So you want us to babysit invalids?" Rafique scoffed.

"Many who survived the initial wave of sickness appear to be improving. Our in-house gerontologist, Amy Wong, came up with an inventive idea that we'd be glad to share with you. Instead of dumping them in a home or an empty warehouse, we're offering stipends to all families who will adopt a refugee for one year, much like fostering a child. This hands-on approach provides the best chance for recovery, and it's cheaper than simply creating a new branch of bureaucracy."

"We can't handle more than seventy-five," Rafique said bluntly, trying to end the negotiation.

"I was hoping you'd come closer to one hundred."

"How do we know that you're not sticking us with the worst cases?"

"You're welcome to come up and pick your own patients."

"We'll take ninety people—and we still get to pick," Rafique countered.

"That leaves us with about three hundred invalids in need," Plains said. "Mallory, if we divide that in two, that's 150 apiece."

"We're still recovering from the Manhattan flooding," she replied. "We'll take one hundred."

Plains didn't quibble.

"So where exactly are these people right now?" Rafique asked.

"We're holding them in tents out in Flushing Mud Park. If you like, we can bring them to you."

"Actually, I'd rather send my minibuses up there."

"Me too," Mallory said.

"That's fine; the sooner the better."

"We'll need three days to prepare shelters," Mallory said, reading off a piece of paper Schuman had scribbled on.

"We could use three days as well," Rafique piggybacked.

"Fine. We'll have them ready for transport on Thursday," said Plains, then thanked them both and said that although they all had political differences, he was pleased that they could come together to address this common crisis.

Rafique hung up before Plains could finish or Mallory could respond.

10

One ritual that occurred at the end of every week in the Bronx Zoo facility was the opening of the monkey house ward. This was now a jailhouse devoted entirely to the surviving prisoners from the Quirklyn conflict. Although Uli had never acknowledged being a part of this group, he was eventually thrown in with the rest of them.

First, all the men were told to strip. Then, bare-assed, they were marched out across the courtyard and told to grab the back wall as hoses were brought out. Their cage was washed out and new straw was laid down just as it had been when primates inhabited the cell years earlier. Before being marched back inside, the prisoners themselves were hosed down.

The second time that this happened after Uli's arrival, while they were standing there wet and shivering, he called out for towels. A few seconds later, he heard an invisible female reply, "Uli, is that you?"

He immediately recognized the voice. "Root Ginseng!"

"Yeah," she said softly through a barred window somewhere above him.

"You were arrested too?"

"When I was no longer useful to them, that Captain Farrell prick tossed me in here. He said the only reason I wasn't sick was because I was an agent." She groaned. "Everyone thinks I'm a goddamn government agent!"

"Oh my God! Is Karen with you?"

"No, Emmett protected her. She was taken down to Staten Island." Uli now saw that Root was talking through the bars of the cat house, where she was locked up with other female prisoners.

No rags were available so the men were all marched, still dripping, back to the monkey house.

Once inside, they found a three-limbed thief waiting in their cell since the elephant pen was now too crowded. Occasionally other prisoners were tossed in as well.

During the third week of Uli's incarceration, a new inmate was tossed into the cell and fell face forward into the filthy hay. He didn't budge. The Quirklyners just ignored him.

Seeing that the man was four-limbed and ten-fingered—no prior amputations—Uli asked him if he was okay. No response.

Uli could see that he was shivering. He turned the guy over and found that he was soaked with sweat and weak as a newborn. Uli raked together a clump of surface hay for him to rest his head upon.

"What are you in for?" Uli said—it was a question rarely asked.

"Tried to . . . get some . . . antibiotics. Not for me . . . for my wife."

"Isn't medicine free?"

"Yeah, but the shortage and all."

"Shortage?"

"I offered them many stamps."

"Why did they arrest you?" Uli asked again.

"They were giving them to gangcops first . . . so I followed one home and broke into his house."

"Why are they out of antibiotics?"

"Something's going around. Lots of people who got into that damn program, like my wife and me, are sick! The biggest mistake ever . . ."

"What program?"

"You know, that Adopt-a-Refugee." The man started coughing hard.

"What's that?"

"All those people they found out in the desert . . . they figured they just needed assistance, so they gave additional food stamps to families if we adopted one of them . . . But it backfired and we got sick."

The man's name was Preston. The next day during lunch distribution, Uli grabbed him a cheese sandwich and a cup of water, and he tried to feed the poor guy, but he kept coughing everything up. Over the next few days, as Preston's health continued declining, Uli asked a guard if he could get some medical attention.

"We're chopping off arms and legs. Do you really think we give a shit that he's got a cold?" the guard barked.

"Can you at least move him outside? It would give him a little more space."

"We got half a dozen sickies in the elephant pen," the guard rasped. "Why do you think we threw him in here?"

By his fourth night in the cell, Preston was as white as a sheet and unable to catch his breath. His lips moved but no words came out.

When Uli awoke the next day, Preston was missing. Uli learned that he had been carried out that morning for amputation—apparently, he had lived just long enough to be punished.

"That was nice of you," said one of the Quirklyners who had noticed Uli's efforts to help the dying stranger.

Though Uli was cordial, he didn't respond. He knew that the reason he had been put in the monkey house was to trap him. It was an old trick, tossing a suspect into the same cell with suspected collaborators. Usually the cell was bugged. Then the guards would just wait for the accused to utter something incriminating. But the Piggers had nothing new on Uli, and he was careful to keep it that way. Since there was no habeas corpus, however, he feared he could be waiting forever.

Several days later, when the inmates were marched out for another chilly hosing, Uli called out Root's name until he heard her respond, "Uli, are you out there?"

"Yeah, how you holding up?"

"They said I was guilty of treason and sentenced me to lose an arm, but they haven't done anything yet, so maybe they forgot about me."

"I hope so," Uli said.

"It's been almost a month since they rescued everyone from the desert. The Mkulties have been mixed in with everyone here at the zoo. I don't know about your group, but here in the women's block, most of the new inmates look a little piqued."

Suddenly Uli was knocked to the ground.

"Shut the fuck up!" A guard had caught him.

While on the ground, Uli brushed up against something hard, a large nail about six inches in length. He wedged it between his fingers as he rose naked to his feet and was marched back inside.

One evening a few days later, Uli realized that of the six guards who typically made up the day shift, two were missing and two others looked pale and sweaty.

During the next cell hosing, when his group was brought out to the courtyard, standing naked and wet, Uli called up for Root at the cat house once again.

"She got stamped-and-amped a few days ago," a hoarse voice called back.

Throughout the evening, when Uli wasn't lamenting the mutilation of poor Root, presumably now healing with only one arm, he began to think about the possibility of dying in the prison from the spreading epidemic.

The bars of the monkey house were solidly grounded. And the fact that it was indoors gave the place a secondary level of confinement. He remembered from his last incarceration here that the concrete framework of the elephant cage outside was far more worn down.

He pondered the question of how he could get transferred out to there. Though you could bribe guards for little favors, this was a big one, and he had nothing of value to swap for it.

Over the next few days, he watched the other prisoners in his Quirklyn cell closely and took a silent inventory of all their valuables—three rings. That was all that the prisoners had managed to keep from the guards. One problem with his plan was that he genuinely admired his fellow inmates. He vividly remembered that final night in South Ozone Park; even when outnumbered and facing superior weapons, they had refused to give an inch. So many of them had sacrificed their lives in a diversionary battle as their neighbors, wives, and loved ones escaped across the airfield and into the desert.

One of the inmates, a young man named Jonas, wore a large gold wedding band on his bony index finger. He was still healing from two gunshots he'd taken so that his wife and kid could escape.

At dinner one evening, instead of consuming his single-slice bologna sandwich in the corner where he customarily ate, Uli edged toward a small cluster of Quirklyners, including Jonas. When several of the men glared at the intruder, Uli quietly explained, "I wasn't completely forthcoming with you all when I was first put in here. I was out in Queens just above the airport that night when the Piggers attacked."

"Don't fuck with us," one of the bigger men warned.

Uli spent the next few minutes recounting details of the event that only those who were there would have known.

"Why didn't you get rounded up with the rest of us?"

Uli explained that since he was technically a Crapper gangcop at the time, he had provided the Quirklyn militia with secrets about the Crapper invasion and subsequently fled across the top of the JFK airfield.

"So where'd everyone go, anyway?" Jonas asked.

Uli knew he was being tested. "We set up a defensive position, just outside the city."

"Defensive how?" someone else asked.

"It looked like an old Indian ruin on the edge of the desert."

"What did they do then?"

"The next morning, Bea led everyone around Far Rockaway, outside the waterway, and down to Staten Island."

"Aunt Bee from Mayberry?" one of the men mocked.

"Valerie Solanas," Uli corrected himself. Everyone here still knew her as the former Warhol Superstar.

"You've been locked up with us for all this time, and you're only *now* telling us this?" said Jonas. "How do we know you're not a Pigger spy?"

"They weren't able to grab me till a few days after the incident. They're holding me here on suspicion, waiting to see if I'll fraternize. So I figured my best chance of getting out was by not associating with you."

"So why are you associating with us now?" someone chirped.

"The reason I didn't go to Staten Island with the rest of the Quirklyn refugees is because the morning after everyone evacuated, I saw some smoke out in the desert. So when everyone else went south, I headed east . . ." Uli proceeded to tell them about the discovery of the sick and dying Mkultra survivors, and their all-night desert trek back to Rescue City, and how the Piggers then found him. "Those people were in isolation. Very sick. They should've been kept in a lengthy quarantine."

"Like us," one quipped.

"So you're saying this place is experiencing an epidemic?" said Jonas.

"Haven't you noticed that some of the regular guards have been out sick lately?"

There was a solemn silence—they had noticed.

"The way I see it, a plague breaking out in Queens is a wonderful thing," piped up an elderly Quirklyner.

"And if what you're saying is true," Jonas said, "you're probably too late to warn anyone anyway. Best bet is probably just lying low here."

"If a plague starts in Queens, it'll be just a matter of time before it spreads."

"Good, let the Piggers and Crappers die together. There's no difference between any of them."

"Eventually it'll reach Staten Island," Uli said. "That's where your loved ones are. If I can break out of here and make it down there, I can warn them to seal their borders." He told them that he had a better chance of escaping if he could somehow be transferred to the elephant pen.

"And how do you hope to do that?"

Uli finally revealed that he was hoping Jonas would give him the wedding ring to use as a bribe with one of the guards.

"That ain't happening," Jonas responded plainly. "But I'll tell you what I can do—I can get you thrown out of here."

"How?"

Jonas told Uli that in two days, when the straw in the cell was being changed, he'd pick a fight with Uli, and all the other Quirklyners would join in.

"Why don't we just do it now?" Uli asked.

"They don't have the manpower at the moment. They'd just let us beat you to death."

"A bribe would be far more effective in guaranteeing I get placed in the right cell," Uli said. Even though the elephant cage was the biggest one in the zoo, there were half a dozen smaller cages along the perimeter that made up the penal zone.

"First of all, that's not true," Jonas said. "I've seen these guys take bribes and call them gifts. Secondly, my wedding ring is the only thing that keeps me alive. It ain't coming off while I'm breathing."

"Just cover your face," said one of the other men, "and we'll pull our punches. You'll be bruised, but nothing serious."

Without recourse, Uli took a deep breath and agreed to their plan.

* * *

The next morning, when the people of Rescue City walked out of their homes, they were greeted by large, freshly printed posters plastered along the sides of various buildings.

CITIZENS OF RESCUE CITY

GOOD NEWS! New York City has officially been sanitized! The radiation count has returned to pre-attack levels and it is now safe for reinhabitation.

BAD NEWS—a contagion has inadvertently been released here into Rescue City, which, even as you read this, is spreading across the boroughs and could eventually ravage the entire population.

Therefore, we will formally be ending the Rescue City housing program. Please start making preparations now! Within the next two weeks, events will unfold that will signal your hasty departure. When this occurs, please be ready. We are asking each of you to prepare a small travel bag, preferably a knapsack, containing your most precious objects, which you should be prepared to carry for a long hike.

When it is time to leave, all residents must evacuate eastward into the desert. At that time, you will see signs with instructions and directions. In order to successfully complete this arduous journey home, please prepare at least six sandwiches, and bring canteens for water.

YOUR PROVISIONAL GOVERNMENT WILL CLAIM THIS POSTING IS A HOAX—IT IS NOT! DON'T BE A VICTIM OF THEIR ARROGANCE. PREPARE FOR EVACUATION WHILE YOU STILL HAVE TIME!
—The Rescue City Evacuation Task Force

The announcement was reprinted in the *Daily Posted New York Times*, along with a variety of questions regarding its veracity.

Though it indeed seemed like a hoax—some even suspected it was a conceptual art piece—the three different police agencies investigated it in their own jurisdictions and conferred among themselves as to who could be behind it. Using the Rescue City radio station, the council cops issued a plea to the entire population: "*If you saw ANYTHING regarding these postings, please say something to ANY of your local gangcops.*"

While a number of people did come forward stating they had indeed witnessed some of the posters being put up, all described the culprits as white middle-aged men with black beanies, some with mustaches and sunglasses. In short, there were no helpful descriptions.

11

Although Robert Moses never had much regard for public opinion, Adolphus Rafique, whose office was one flight above him, couldn't stop secretly admiring his impressive list of bulldozed and steamrollered accomplishments: housing projects, public parks, cultural and judicial institutions, bridges, beaches, and so on. Moses sometimes worked *against* popular opinion, and on rare occasions, nearly without funding, he still drove vast, frequently compromised public works through to completion. Although Rafique had managed to launch a lot in his little borough of Staten Island, Nevada, the one major project that he'd been unable to accomplish was unblocking the city's massive sewer pipe that had turned the entire place into a biohazard. He imagined that if anyone could've gotten this fixed, it would've been a young Robert Moses. It left him in envy of the decrepit old man now under house arrest just below him.

The borough leader asked the head of the Moses security team, Harry Blumenthal, to inform the cook about any dietary restrictions the geriatric might have. Then he told Blumenthal that instead of bringing Moses his usual meal, he was to simply escort the man upstairs to dine with him tonight.

At seven p.m., when Rafique was informed that Mr. Moses was waiting for him, he told his assistant to show the old man in.

"You mean into your chambers?" asked the assistant. Rafique was rarely allowing anyone in for face-to-face meetings these days, for fear of contamination.

"Yes." He wanted to finally meet the legend in person.

In a moment, Blumenthal slowly led the old bureaucrat into his large study.

"Good to see you, sir," Moses said in a deep, commanding tone, then grabbed Rafique's limp hand and gave it a firm shake, oblivious to the fact that he was paralyzed. "So the reason I'm here, as you well know," he continued, before Rafique could say a word, "is . . . I'd like my old job back."

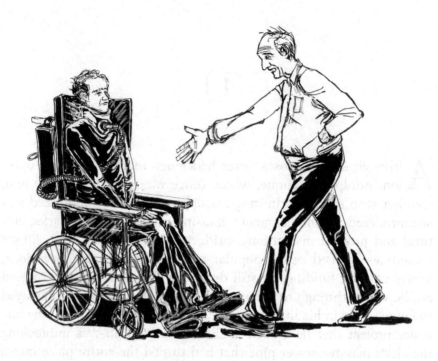

"Your old job?"

"The highway commission."

"The highways here?"

"Absolutely. For starters, I think I did a darn good job downstate, but up here in Albany, I think there's a lot more to be done . . ." Moses went on at some length about other projects he had completed decades earlier.

Rafique realized that the old man seemed to be confusing him with Nelson Rockefeller, who as far as he knew was still the sitting governor of New York State.

"Mr. Moses, it's 1981 and you are in Rescue City in the middle of the Nevada desert."

"Huh?"

"Yes sir. You tried to rescue your brother."

"Oh! Paul." Moses slapped an open palm against his shiny forehead and took a seat at a table facing Rafique. "That guy always screws me up. I tried to help him and . . ."

"His daughter Bea is going to be helping you with your defense, remember?"

"I don't need any goddamned help!"

At that moment, a cook wheeled in a cart of appetizers. He opened a TV tray before Mr. Moses and set down a bottle of red wine and a platter of clams casino.

"You might want to consider your legal defense, sir."

"In due time," Moses replied. Apparently the clams were easing his guilty conscience.

"Did you have a good meeting with your niece?"

"I don't have a niece." Moses began filling his gullet with the heated canned delicacy.

"Bea Moses is a very fine and passionate young lady."

"Let's talk after dinner," Moses said with his mouth full. "They probably want us out of here soon."

The next day, a few hours before the inmates were scheduled to be marched out of the monkey cage, four guards came by with lunch: a box full of bologna sandwiches. Each prisoner reached through the bars and grabbed one. With only two sandwiches remaining, before Uli could get to the bars, Jonas snatched both for himself. When Uli tried to grab the extra sandwich out of his hands, the others in the cell went nuts. Everyone shouted and yelled as they seemed to stomp, kick, and punch Uli. The guards were right there, so they quickly opened the cell door and went in with their nightsticks. The prisoners' blows were fairly light, and before the guards could get to him, Uli sliced open his forearm with the tip of his nail. He quickly smeared the blood over his eyes and screwed up his face in agony.

"Get the fuck off of him!" yelled an obese guard as they reached the injured Uli.

"I can't see," Uli shrieked as they yanked him to his feet. At the last moment, he felt Jonas shove something into his pocket. The guards flung him out of the cell. Once they closed the gate, Uli was escorted into the courtyard.

"Thanks for saving my life," he repeated over and over to the stout guard. As they led him past the elephant cage toward the old lion house, he politely asked, "Can you dump me in the aquarium?"

"We don't have an aquarium, asshole."

"No, I just heard—"

"Actually," interrupted an older guard who was bringing up the rear, "there is a fish house in the back, but it's not a part of the prison."

"How about in there?" Uli asked, pointing to the large outdoor cage. "The sunlight will dry out my scabs."

"I ain't a bellhop," the guard replied.

Without knowing what Jonas had shoved in his pocket, Uli pulled it out—a single wrapped stick of Juicy Fruit gum. He held it up.

The old guard snatched the gum. Not noticing that Uli was holding the large nail in his left hand, the other guard patted him down.

In a few minutes Uli was back in the pachyderm pen that he had occupied not long ago. Nearly half the inmates in the enclosure were coughing, sneezing, or feverish. He was also horrified to discover, while inspecting the pen, that they had screwed four shiny new bars along the top, sealing up the escape route he had taken last time he was here. Fortunately, the concrete at the foundation of the very end of the old cell was still corroded and cracked.

Later that afternoon, Uli watched from a distance as the Quirklyn veterans were pulled out of the monkey house, hosed down, and returned to their cell.

During feeding time that evening, when the guards tossed a box of sandwiches into this new cell—an event usually followed by a stampede—Uli was surprised to see that at least six of the prisoners were too sick to budge. He spotted one lanky, motionless body against the rear wall. He thought the man was dead, but then noticed that he was still shivering. It took another moment before Uli realized it was none other than Plato: the great liberator of the Mkultra.

Uli pushed over and whispered, "What the hell are you doing here?!"

"Stay away," Plato wheezed.

Uli grabbed a sandwich from an inmate who had taken the spares and went back to Plato, who tried to push him away.

"You're going to catch this fucking thing," the pale black man warned him.

"Relax, I've been inoculated."

"So was I."

Uli fetched him a cup of water. After helping him drink, Uli dragged the man to an empty dry spot in the pen.

"How did this happen?" Uli asked.

"Some fucker named Farrell . . ."

"No, I mean, why didn't you stick to the plan? I thought you were going to quarantine everyone in the desert for two weeks."

"I screwed up. I went on a hike the other way. I put Richard in charge."

"Who?"

"The blind guy. He must've got confused."

"Why the hell did you go on a hike? You never should've left them alone."

"After you mentioned the water station in the other direction, I wanted to see if I could find it."

"That's insane."

"What's insane is that we're all dying out here in the middle of nowhere. I was hoping that once everyone got their health back, we could hike east and finally get out of here forever."

"So what'd you find?" Uli asked.

"I got there! The spot where you flared: Water Station 27. Then I came back." Plato smiled weakly.

"You should've just kept walking."

"When I returned to the Mkultra field, they were burning the dead. When I asked where everyone was, some Pigger gorilla grabbed me and next thing I know I'm being tortured at Rikers until I confessed to being in the NSA. Then I was thrown in here."

No sooner did he say this than poor Plato passed out. Uli used the opportunity to grab some shut-eye himself.

Roughly six hours later, both of them were awakened when a new shift of guards filed into the yard.

"I wonder what became of poor old Richard," Plato said.

"I didn't see him here, but I heard Root. They had her in women's detention."

"Root," Plato echoed. "Is she sick too?"

"I don't think so." Uli decided to spare him the fact that she had probably suffered a judicial amputation.

"Poor Root, we knocked heads over the years, but she's good . . ."

"Knocked heads over what?"

"You know, her boss Sandy . . ."

"Sandy Corners?" Uli remembered the poor headless corpse.

"Yeah, she was the first one to say that Rescue City was another botched government commission and the Mkultra was its greatest sin of omission. She was initially even more of a government cog than the rest of us. By the end she said it was our moral duty to torch the place."

"That wasn't *your* idea?"

"No, it was hers. In fact, she pointed out that due to all the leaks and condensation, it would only smoke and the ventilation fans would blow it all out. For years Root and I disagreed with her, waiting for a

remedy. But when you see your own kid grow up with physical defor-
mities, well, one day I had enough. When I told Sandy that I was on
board, Root freaked out."

"She opposed it?" Uli asked.

"Well, let's just say that Sandy died mysteriously soon afterward."

"You think Root killed her?"

"Who knows?"

In another moment, Plato had drifted back to sleep.

Over the course of the following week, Uli would spend each night
at the far side of the cage where the concrete base was dried out and
crumbling. With the head of the large nail cushioned by a piece of
cloth in the palm of his hand, he'd dig the pointy end into hairline
cracks in the concrete, slowly chipping out shards no bigger than a
thumbnail. Periodically, he'd glance over at Plato, who was steadily
growing sicker. One night Uli heard him yelling in his fevered sleep:
"Not until every gangster has put down his weapons do we open the
airport!"

"Shut the hell up!" one of the other slumbering prisoners shouted
back.

Plato yelled out again, "Blow it the fuck up!" Then, "Fire at will!"
Other odd and violent exclamations followed.

"You shut him up, or I will!" cried out one relatively healthy
inmate.

When Uli finally shook Plato awake and told him what he had
been saying, the black man sighed. "God, I hadn't thought about that
in years. Now I can't think about anything else."

"Think about what?"

"My violent rotation in Rescue City. It just keeps rotating in my
head like a broken record. At least that was successful."

"When did you rotate here?"

"Almost ten years ago. Came here as military, undercover. Did my
tour, then I was supposed to be extracted."

"Extracted?"

"The bloodiest tour ever. And once done, instead of getting a medal,
they gave me an even uglier mission—they were desperately short-
handed. After six months they offered me a big promotion and an
out, but that's always been my character flaw: I can never leave a job
undone. And when I realized it was undoable, I went renegade."

"Renegade?"

"A person has only so much strength. You're young, strong, and you think you're right. Things you do righteously at twenty wind up haunting you for the rest of your life. The Mkultra became the penance for what I did here as Jackie Wilson."

"You're Jackie Wilson?"

"Jack Wilson was a Paiute Indian leader from Nevada who died here about fifty years ago. His followers regarded him as a kind of messiah. I took his name to win the support of the Staten Island flakes. They believed he had come back from the dead."

"So what was this whole gang battle?"

"A military mission."

"Figures," Uli said. "Another government snafu."

"Actually, it was an attempt to *fix* the snafu. This place really did begin with the best of intentions. When you ship the poorest segment of a destitute city somewhere, you're also going to include a very real hardened criminal element who naturally like to take their cut and run the show. Why no one saw that coming, I don't know."

"I thought this place was initially run by the army."

"They were more like social workers in fatigues," Plato explained. "None of them ever served in a combat zone. No one was armed. And in all fairness, the place was really lacking. The resources weren't coming in. Shortages were widespread. Nothing was working. So of course the gangsters exploited these shortcomings by turning the people against us. They galvanized this us-versus-them mentality. We needed a government to form from within."

"You couldn't just back the best horse?" Uli asked.

"What do you do when you need a charismatic, altruistic leader who, once he has established himself as top dog, is willing to set up some balanced system of government and just vanish?"

"But it was more than just Jackie Wilson, wasn't it? I mean, it sounds like you had a trained band of Green Berets who killed everyone who got in your way."

"A lot people don't know this, but we were actually able to abduct, extract, convict, and imprison a lot of gang leaders. We left charred remains behind so no one would know. But they all had power-hungry lieutenants eager to take their place. So it did get messy."

"More like a slaughter from what I heard."

"We were ordered to hold our positions," Plato said, "which is called self-defense. And we wounded rather than killed when possible. And it's amazing how no one seemed to notice that we were able to slip in a drone full of army medics who vanished after most recovered. We weren't aiming for a body count, but we got a serious number. I'm still waiting for an investigation. Eventually, I'll probably be arrested for it."

"Maybe that's why I'm here," Uli said, thinking about his years with the bureau.

But the only response was a snore. Plato had abruptly passed out again. Uli wondered if the man had become delirious. In his sleep, Plato continued intermittently shouting out strange commands.

Uli went back to chipping out the base of the bars.

12

After nearly getting caught one evening, Uli changed his work schedule. Around four a.m. every night a lone guard would do a quick head count. Uli would steadily chip away into the old concrete with his spike nail, only pausing when his hand cramped. He'd stop at first light. During the daylight hours, when he wasn't assisting poor Plato, Uli would sleep. In the afternoons he'd revisit his own slowly returning memories.

After he was transferred to work on the AIM case in South Dakota, he soon realized he was basically in the same fix he had been in with CISPES. Both jobs could be summed up in the classic saying: *The enemies of my enemies are my friends*. What troubled Uli more and more were the constant compromises: his old underling, the zealous FBI agent Dylan McGuire, had most likely imported members of a Salvadoran hit squad to the States to carry out the revenge rape in LA. In South Dakota, the FBI had found themselves in bed with a corrupt two-bit thug who had somehow been voted into the tribal presidency of the Pine Ridge Indian Reservation. This plumber named Wilson acted more like a mob boss than a Native American leader. And instead of being checked by the local DA or attorney general, this leftist group AIM was pushing back. Now they were being threatened, beaten, even killed, while the FBI casually sided with the local tribe and looked the other way.

Locked in the elephant pen, Uli was becoming friendly with two of his fellow inmates: a carjacker named Lectro, and a Native American arsonist named Burny Moondog. Uli slowed his pace for a week until two of the more obnoxious convicts were stamped-and-amped, fearful that they might compromise his breakout.

It was a full two weeks before he had carefully cut away enough of the corroded concrete. In the middle of the night, he politely asked for some of the sickly inmates to slide aside. Then he sprinted the full length of the elephant cell and planted a solid kick right onto the thick bar that he had been undermining. It rattled a bit. Plato was fast asleep, but a couple of the healthier convicts looked at Uli as though he had gone nuts—the bar was very thick and it rose over ten feet up to the top. Again, Uli dashed the entire of the pen, jumped up, and gave the bar a second flying kick. Although he slammed to the ground with the third kick, the bar slid nearly three inches down the pre-scored concrete slot that he had been carefully digging out. A fine mist of dust rose in the air.

"Holy shit!" yelled Burny. "You kicked the fucking bar loose!"

"Just keep watching for guards," Uli said.

Instead, Burny proposed a more effective idea. The two of them lay on their backs and took turns kicking the bar forward like a pair of human pile drivers. After half a dozen kicks, the bar had moved several more inches. Uli stood up and yanked it back. Then, using his nail, which he had worn down to a nub, he cleaned out the compacted concrete particles that blocked the slot. Burny pulled the bar upright again and they resumed their rapid kicks.

"What the fuck do you think you're doing?" asked a sickly ampu-tee whom they had awoken.

"Breaking out," Uli said without missing a kick.

"Even if you do it," a one-armed, one-legged prisoner chimed in, "they're gonna catch you, and when they're done pruning you, you're gonna be a wiggling pair of snakes."

"Well, I'm up for a leg this time," Burny replied, "and as you prob-ably figured out, these things work best in pairs, so if they're gonna take one, they might as well take the other."

Over the next hour, Uli and his accomplice pressed on while their fellow inmates watched speechlessly.

"Hold it!" Uli said to his partner when he saw that the spider cracks along the base had nearly broken through the cement encase-ment. "I just realized something."

"What?"

"They still haven't done their four a.m. body count. After that we'll have a couple hours to run before the morning shift."

"Hey," Uli heard behind him. It was Plato, who he'd thought was comatose.

"What's up?"

"Can you take me with you?" Plato asked, barely breathing.

"I really appreciate all you've done," Uli said, "but I doubt that even I can make it out."

"Just drag me into the courtyard. I'm not going to be alive much longer, and I don't want to die behind bars."

"Okay," Uli answered, unable to refuse the last wish of this great man.

Within twenty minutes, one of the late-shift guards appeared and mindlessly did his four a.m. head count. It was then Uli grasped that if anyone alerted the guard, that inmate would get an instant reprieve, while Uli would likely be executed by Polly Femus herself. Thankfully, no one made a peep.

When the heavyset old guard finally meandered back inside the large brick guardhouse, Uli slid off his filthy shirt and strapped it around the bottom of the loose bar, which must've weighed at least a couple hundred pounds. He instructed Burny to kick the thick bar down the growing slot, then he rapidly pulled it back, wedging it through the ever-widening ridge. All waited with bated breath for the dramatic moment when the giant bar would finally clang to the ground—terrified that the sound would alert the guards. But it never happened. After twenty more minutes of excavating, they deduced that the top of the bar was welded tightly in place.

But the bottom of the long bar was angled out just far enough for Burny to slither through at the base. As Uli went over to reawaken Plato, he was surprised to look back and see other inmates squirming out as well.

"Plato!" Uli shook him awake. "We have to move quickly!"

"Right," Plato said, befuddled and feverish. "Let's go."

Uli helped him up, and by the time they made it to the bars, all but one of the other prisoners in the cage had slithered out of the elephant pen.

It took a full five minutes for Uli to laboriously pull Plato out through the bent bar. By then, the others had all sped across the open yard and were struggling one at a time up the gnarly tree whose branches were within jumping distance of the narrow brick wall—just as Uli had done during his first jailbreak. The only advantage to being last in the group was that some of the others who had gone before had sacrificed articles of clothing to the rusty coil of barbed wire. Just as had happened during Uli's earlier escape attempt, everyone who dropped over the twelve-foot wall landed on the other side with a bruising thud. Then they started their mad rush down Crotona Boulevard, the hopelessly long street without houses or lights to guide the way. Uli remembered that there was simply nowhere to hide on Crotona—that was how he had gotten caught the last time.

Once out in the courtyard, Plato tried his best to keep up with Uli, who didn't have the heart to abandon the weakened and gangly man. What little strength Plato had left was expended when he climbed up the tree. Uli scampered up the trunk after him and was able to help pull Plato up onto a higher branch where the two could slowly edge outward.

"There's one jump," Uli coached him, "and you've got to make it."

"I will," said the liberator of the Mkultra, trembling with sweat and exhaustion.

Uli watched as Plato squeezed with all of his concentration into a ball and pitched forward. Uli stared down Crotona Boulevard and could still make out the silhouettes of the last of his fellow fugitives as they ran madly into the eternal distance. In that instant, Uli sensed why the gnarly tree, with its low branches, had never been cut. It deliberately allowed this possibility of escape, because in the capture the Piggers could relinquish all pretense of mercy or justice. He knew that they'd all be rounded up soon enough. He also knew that if there was any real chance of him and Plato getting away, it would depend on whether the single strand of information, which Mallory's aide had casually imparted to him months earlier, was actually true. Maury Hotchkiss, a young liaison to the Crapper government, had mentioned that supposedly there was an old tunnel underneath the fish house, which was why Uli had asked the guard if he could be put in the aquarium. The guard had said that the aquarium was beyond a far wall inside the compound. This meant that if they had any prayer of getting away, they had to break back *into* a different part of the prison.

Regardless, Uli dropped down off the wall, landing next to Plato.

"I'm sorry," the tall black man said, laboring for breath. "You can go now."

"Just try to stay with me," Uli encouraged him, holding onto the man's long arm.

"Shouldn't we be heading the same way as those guys?"

"It's a trap," Uli said. He walked Plato along the brick wall, past the perimeter where the actual prison ended, toward the western corner of the complex. A giant wooden gate marked what appeared to be a nonsecure section of the facility.

Suddenly, loud wailing sounds seemed to awaken a large cyclopic eye that popped open, blasting a white light over the two men's heads. The burning spotlight illuminated every inch of Crotona Boulevard. A series of smaller sirens filled the air. Before Uli could even think about hiding, the giant wooden gate he was hoping to breach swung wide open, releasing a succession of five solicars that burst forth and sped right past them, soaring down Crotona to reclaim their mischievous orphans.

"Stay put!" Uli whispered to Plato.

After catching his breath, Uli waited a moment to make sure no guards were lingering inside the driveway. Then he helped Plato into the gated lot. Hustling past the guardhouse, Uli could hear shouts and responses. In the shadows, he counted four large dilapidated buildings behind the main administrative center. The smallest one in the far corner seemed to be a custodian's shed. Plato collapsed to the ground as Uli sped ahead to figure out where this mysterious aquarium was located.

"FREEZE!" he suddenly heard from the darkness directly before him. "Hands up or I'll blow you away!"

The old guard who had done the final head count just thirty minutes earlier was walking toward him, aiming a rifle. A moment later, a second chubby guard appeared, wielding a giant pistol. The two men, both old and overweight, had clearly been left behind to hold things down at the complex.

"My God, this moron is actually breaking back *into* prison?" the older of the two remarked with a chuckle as he holstered his gun and pulled out his handcuffs. Although Uli knew Plato was lying somewhere in the darkness, he hoped his companion would see what was occurring and take cover. As the older guard approached, Uli raised his arms in the air as though ignorant that the man wanted to cuff his wrists together.

"Behind your back, asshole!" the man shouted at Uli as Plato slowly stumbled into view.

The guard with the rifle swung around and emptied his barrel into Plato. Uli quickly yanked the pistol out of the other guard's holster and shot at them, hitting both men in their chests. Both collapsed to the ground. Uli rushed over and cradled Plato's head in his lap, confirming that he too was gone.

The crackle of an old radio inside the guard station quickly brought Uli back to the moment. His only hope was to stay focused. He hurried around to the rear of the compound and could barely make out a clump of neglected machinery that had been left to decay in the unlit periphery. He could hear sirens growing louder. Some of the cars were returning and he felt increasingly hopeless as he stumbled farther into the yard. The outlying region appeared to have become an unofficial dumping ground. Behind a row of broken and rusty solicars, Uli ventured past some utility sheds and gardening shacks.

His heart began to race when he finally glimpsed the faint stone relief of a dolphin cut above the filthy limestone structure that resembled a large mausoleum. An old chain encircled the tarnished brass handles on the door, unified with a big rusty lock. Although some of the old glass panes were shattered, the windows were all about eight feet up, too high to reach—much less look through. Amid the garbage and debris, Uli located a couple of weathered but sturdy boards. Leaning them against the side of the building, he managed to wedge his foot on the edges and he slowly shimmied up. Using his shirt to cover his knuckles, he punched out the already broken glass and unlatched one of the windows, hoisting himself up and over the large sill. The moonlight peeking through a dirty skylight revealed a small empty pool, roughly ten feet wide by twenty feet in length. Looking down the walls of the tiny natatorium, he couldn't make out the bottom. Unless there was some kind of exhibition gallery below, the design of the place made no sense. Other than the Loch Ness Monster, Uli could only wonder what kind of sea creature would occupy a tank that was deeper than it was wide.

The sheer walls of the concrete basin didn't reveal any rungs or crevices. He frantically looked around the small building for a hose, or maybe a buoy with a rope attached—something that could be used to climb out of the pit if needed.

"Holy shit, they've fucking killed Geoff! And Stu—Stu's dead too!" someone yelled in the distance. A patter of footsteps started approaching the little building. Flashlight beams bounced through the shattered glass along the skylight.

Uli grabbed the edge of the pool and slowly lowered himself into it. He just hung there for a moment, conflicted as to whether to let go or hoist back up.

"Line up the escapees!" Uli heard a harsh female voice outside. "I want them to see why they're going to be executed!" It was the merciless Polly Femus.

Someone began rattling the rusty lock, causing Uli to release his grip and begin sliding down the side of the steep, narrow pool. When he hit the bottom, he rolled onto his back. As he rose, he felt grateful he wasn't injured. Looking up at the skylight, he could now see that this wasn't a pool at all, but some kind of chute that had been sealed with a wooden platform. Judging by the sagginess of the floor under him, it seemed to be rotting away. Uli kept expecting rays from a guard's flashlight to shine down on him at any moment, but soon realized that they weren't even trying to enter the odd building. He had slid down there for nothing! In the darkness, he extended his foot like a cane and tapped on the narrow space around him. Feeling something sharp and crunchy, he reached down and to his horror felt the unmistakable form of a corpse, decayed to its skeletal form. He wondered if this was another escaped convict from yesteryear.

"Shit," he muttered, understanding that he had dropped himself into the black hole of the Bronx. He should've simply clung to the edge till they passed. Then he could've lifted himself back up and just waited till things cooled down before trying to escape.

Before he could attempt to scale back up the grimy sides, he heard someone shout, "FIRE!" followed by synchronized gun blasts—a firing squad. His cellmates were dead. It took another ten minutes before he accepted that his only hope was heading farther downward. Twenty minutes later, using only his fingers, he was able to pry up the

softest, most rotten board below him. A chilly sulfuric stink rose upward from the cool blackness. Pulling up the second and third boards
was much easier.

Uli lowered one of the broken boards into the new black hole,
hoping to hit bottom and find out how far down it went—but it just
dangled. He dropped it and almost immediately heard it hit. He slid
into the narrow passage and lowered himself down, hoping to touch
some kind of ground with his feet—nothing. As he began to hoist
himself back up, the rotten edge of the board that his right elbow was
balanced on splintered away, and he dropped helplessly into the hole.

He fell about eight feet before hitting a slanted stone incline, then
tumbled forward another five feet. From there Uli felt his way down
a tight tunnel until the walls narrowed. In the darkness, the walls felt
strangely scalloped. Using his fingertips, he slowly made out that he
was standing between two giant cast-metal coils. Undoubtedly water
was meant to rush through at some point. For the first time, he grasped
that this was some kind of gigantic heating or cooling mechanism.

Without any other alternatives, he wedged himself between the
two coils into the tightening angles, fearful that he might get stuck in
this claustrophobic nightmare or that it might lead to a dead end. Uli
breathed a sigh of relief when, after taking several steps, the shrinking conduit slowly began to open up into some kind of chamber that
ended at what felt like a thick, circular, tubular object. When he took
it in both hands, he knew it was the release wheel of a hatchway.
Inasmuch as this was clearly designed for water, Uli wondered if by
turning the wheel he could be opening a giant faucet that might flood
the dark chamber and drown him in the process. He pounded on the
heavy metal portal. The resonating ring instantly reassured him that a
million tons of water weren't pressing against the other side. Slowly,
he twisted the wheel counterclockwise. A loud creak followed as Uli
pulled the portal open on its squeaky hinges, and a cool breeze rushed
out.

Uli squeezed through the opening—all the while in complete darkness. When he called out into the void, he could tell from the distant
echo that it went on for a great distance. Reaching out to his left, he
was able to touch one wall, and then a few steps over he touched the
other wall at his right—the passage extended roughly five feet across.
As he proceeded, he was astounded to find that it was covered with
dried-out cobwebs; even spiders couldn't sustain life down here. He
began to wonder if this was a discontinued sewer. As he continued-

along, his intuition told him he was heading north. The problem was that both Manhattan and Staten Island were to the south. While he walked, he weaved left and right with extended arms and hands, hoping to increase his chances of discovering a ladder to freedom. After twenty more minutes, he began to hyperventilate and had to slow down to catch his breath. Nearly an hour later, he passed through another circular hatchway. He took a few more steps before he tripped over something. No sooner did he catch himself than he tripped on something else and slammed headfirst into a solid wall.

"Oh God!" he blurted, fearing the worst. The little corridor had finally come to an abrupt end, deep underneath the earth. *I'm fucked!* Uli thought.

In an effort to stave off panic, he started strategizing: *I just need to turn around and walk back to where I started. If worse comes to worst, I can slowly scale my way back up into the zoo.*

He turned around to begin his long walk back, but after a single step he tripped again. Then once more.

"What the fuck!" he yelled aloud, and reached down to find a cold, sharp protrusion, nearly a foot high, very smooth, and cut directly across the floor of the little corridor. Then he located a second protrusion: there were two cold, narrow ledges that ran parallel to each other. *They're train rails.*

He had stumbled into some kind of train tunnel under Rescue City. Trying his best to remember the trains that ran up to the Bronx of Old Town, he wondered if this was intended to mimic one of the old IRT lines. He listened a moment for the vibration of a subway. Nothing. He had to somehow decide which way to go . . . left or right? Running his hands carefully around in the darkness, he found that there was a two-foot clearance, a narrow walkway along the inside of the tracks. Since he assumed he had been walking north, he decided that he had a better chance of escaping if he turned left, thereby walking away from Queens and the Piggers.

Though puzzled by what he had stumbled into, he also felt a renewed sense of hope that he might still get out alive. As he walked, he continued running his right hand along the left side of the walkway in search of some sort of ladder.

Finally, after what seemed like hours in the darkness, and gradually increasing his pace, he painfully slammed his shin against something and fell forward in agony. On his hands and knees, he felt around until he found it: a long metal rod of some kind had blocked his path.

Feeling around further, he realized there was something riding on the track. When he gave it a shove, it inched forward. As he delicately felt the dimensions, he realized it was an old-fashioned hand-pumped trolley, a light vehicle with a lever that could be driven along the rails. It occurred to Uli that the reason it was left here was probably because someone had exited in the general vicinity. In the blackness, Uli began scouring the walls of the tunnel, trying to find those vital ladder rungs.

"Where the fuck are you?" he shouted, and listened to the echo.

Hungry, thirsty, cut off from all humanity in pitch-black darkness, he genuinely feared for his life.

So he carefully climbed onto the flat bed of the little trolley. Immediately he grabbed the handles—a seesaw bar—which he worried would be rusted shut. But when he pulled it upward, the cart slowly proceeded in the direction he had just come from. He brought the vehicle to a halt and fumbled around in the darkness for a switch that had to be somewhere around the base of the pump. Finding one, he flipped it up, then pumped the bar again. Sure enough, the cart creaked in the direction he had been moving—westward, he hoped, away from Queens. The clanging of the vehicle filled the narrow tunnel and seemed to grow louder as he kept pumping it.

The electrifying sensation of the wind rustling through his hair was the closest thing he had to a speedometer. He thought he was hallucinating when he noticed a yellow cloud just in front of him, but as the cloud brightened and spread, he realized the trolley had a small light generator. The dark, narrow tunnel had a heavy jumble of giant cables slung along the top. Although this odd infrastructural detail looked like it had been conceived to carry water, it appeared to have been repurposed into a giant conduit for electricity. Glancing behind him, he discovered that two small headlights were shining from either end of this one-person vehicle. As Uli pumped faster, the light grew brighter and he could see deeper into the tunnel, which angled gently leftward.

After twenty minutes, he passed something that startled him—a small half-dome opening at the base of the left wall. Uli let the trolley wind down and stop, plunging him back into darkness.

Hand over hand, moving along the wall, Uli backtracked the twenty feet or so from where he had seen the aperture. Fumbling along where the left wall met the ground, Uli located the opening, like a large sewer entrance across from the track.

No wonder I couldn't find the fucking exits; I was searching along the upper walls while these openings are burrowed into their base.

Uli slipped down under it and, sure enough, he finally found the rungs that he had been searching for. He climbed up the narrow tube that ran vertically for roughly fifty feet, farther than he expected. Uli soon bumped his head and, feeling around, realized he was directly under a manhole cover. A large steel wheel locked it into place. He was able to turn it, then he tried to push the heavy metal lid up. It barely budged. He put his back into it, shoving upward over and over. Gradually, sand started pouring down over him. After what felt like a hundred pounds of sand had showered into the hole, he was able to heave the immense steel lid up along a hinge where it stopped at a ninety-degree angle, allowing brilliant reddish sunlight to slant in like water.

Without even realizing it, Uli began laughing. As he looked out of his dank hole, he saw the dramatic splendor of the new sun that seemed to have just been born in the eastern sky. Although he was famished, thirsty, and utterly exhausted, all cares instantly vanished. The day looked so stunning that tears came to his eyes. *This same sun is shining over New York, Paris, and London. It's shining on the white-sand beaches of the Caribbean, and reflecting on the icy tundra of Siberia. Its rays unify at least half of us at any given moment.*

Looking behind him, he saw rows and rows of robust marijuana plants evenly spread out. Their dark green leaves rose toward the sun in full bloom. To his left was scrubland and desert. Uli put his location at the eastern edge of the Hoboken fields. Although he had escaped the tunnel, he feared that if he climbed out now, it would just be a matter of time before he was nabbed by the Crapper gangcops—just as he had been when he had paddled out there searching for the "secret weapon" on the eve of the Quirklyn invasion.

All he could do was go back down. He pulled the heavy manhole lid back over him. It wouldn't be very long before the constant winds and sands would once again hide the manhole from all those who didn't know where to look. *If I can't find anywhere else to climb out, I can come back here at night and try to escape this way,* he thought.

He spun the lock wheel closed and worked his way back down the tube through the narrow portal—now covered in sand—and along the tunnel floor. In another moment, he was back on the manual rail cart in the pitch darkness. Taking the metal pump in hand, Uli hoisted it up and down, resuming his journey.

Soon lost in the monotonous motion, Uli found himself once again remembering his recent years in the FBI, specifically in South Dakota . . . When it was discovered that Doug Durham, the head of AIM's security force during the Wounded Knee siege, had been turned into a double agent, Durham fled and everything changed radically for the organization. Overnight, their idealistic youth was torn away when they grasped that the enemy had breached their defenses and was inside the perimeter. What the bureau had failed to comprehend was the level of paranoia that this revelation would unleash within the group. The intense suspicion was only exceeded by the movement's hatred for the FBI. In retrospect, Uli wondered if they hadn't just been waiting for that day, for what they saw as an opportunity for justifiable revenge.

On June 26, 1975, two FBI agents were driving through the back roads of the Pine Ridge Indian Reservation searching for someone named Jimmy Eagle, when suddenly their vehicle came under heavy fire. Their own .38-caliber handguns were useless against well-positioned, high-powered rifles. Wounded, one of the agents was able to call for help, but the backup officers who responded found themselves pinned down some distance away. It was clearly a coordinated ambush. When the supporting team finally broke through, they found that the two agents in the car had been killed by multiple gunshot wounds.

Now speeding through the dark tunnel, Uli was unable to recall the names of those two men, but he clearly remembered their faces. More specifically, he remembered their death photos. One of the agents must've held up his hand while begging for his life, because a bullet had severed his digits at the knuckle and then blown his brains out.

The following day, orders came down from the very top: "We've got to get these bastards at any cost!"

Uli's anger and frustration at seeing his fellow officers' bullet-riddled bodies fueled his pumping of the little trolley until it became like a crazy dance between man and machine, speeding through the dimly lit tunnel, moving faster and faster until—

The sensation of being catapulted into the darkness lasted only a moment. Uli awoke to several flashlights bouncing around in the darkness and a muffled voice: "Fuck! He could've set it off!"

Before he could even figure out which way was up, hands were pinning him down. In another moment Uli felt something pressed over his mouth and then he faded into the surrounding blackness.

13

Ninety Mkultra survivors were bused down to Staten Island in accordance with Rafique's agreement with Plains and Mallory. Despite the fact that all twenty-three health care workers wore rubber gloves and face masks, five of them began exhibiting flu-like symptoms within a week. Staten Island immediately dropped their own plans for an Adopt-a-Refugee Program and put all the survivors under tight quarantine. The invalids were confined to a single large infirmary in the Smug Harbor area of Staten Island. Over the next two weeks, nineteen of them died. The majority remained in the same state as when they arrived: Plains must've exaggerated the results in an effort to hastily unload the burden. Sixteen did show modest signs of improvement. The one miraculous exception was Karen Sarkisian. Largely due to Root's treatment regimen that she had initiated back in the Mkultra, Karen was soon speaking full sentences. To avoid her being reinfected, Karen was separated from the others and moved to a ward entirely her own.

Two days later, Bea Moses-Mayer tied on a mask, pulled on gloves, and paid her a visit.

"You don't need that," Karen said when she entered. "I'm not sick."

"We still have to take precautions."

"I'm a police captain. Why wasn't I returned to Brooklyn?"

"Luck of the draw," Bea said. "Rafique's people counted out ninety survivors and brought them back here. And the doctor says that when you arrived, you were barely able to grunt."

"Not true. I was speaking, just not in full sentences; now I'm fine."

"Well, some of the hospital staff have been coming down sick, so all the other Mkultra survivors, except for you, are in quarantine indefinitely."

"Where is Uli?"

Bea said that according to the latest intel, her brother was locked up in the Bronx Zoo, but no one had seen or heard a word from him.

"Locked up?"

"By the Piggers. Who else."

"When exactly was the last time you spoke to him?" asked Karen.

"He called me from the Lotus clinic up in Little Neck, Queens, regarding your fellow refugees. He asked if we could spare any food and supplies. I told him that we were low. When I tried calling him back a few days later, I spoke to Emmett, the director up there. He said that everyone who stayed in Queens had either been arrested or shipped to one of their medical facilities."

Karen glanced nervously out the window and asked if Bea had been able to send anyone out to look for him.

"Uli is one of the smartest and most self-sufficient people here. He's also well trained in self-defense and survival. I'm sure he'll make it back as soon as he's released."

"Why would he come *here*?" Karen asked. Brooklyn or Manhattan seemed like more logical destinations.

"While you were away, a battle broke out from Williamsburg to South Ozone Park. Long story short, he's a fugitive up there. Staten Island is the only place that he won't get in trouble, and he knows it. Have faith!"

Bea quickly departed. She had to use all her available time to aid with her uncle's legal defense.

Although another week of bed rest would've been wonderful, Karen was skeptical. She knew that if she was going to help her brother, she had to work quickly. He had walked all the way into the desert to rescue her—it was her turn to help him.

Over the next week, six new patients from Staten Island were admitted to the isolation ward, and the newly appointed director of the facility, Abe Levitol, the former head of the New Dope methadone clinic, was growing concerned about the severely limited space. Then he was informed of their one miracle case, Karen, who occupied a small ward all by herself.

Levitol pulled on surgical gloves and a mask and gave Karen a general checkup himself. Finding no fever, swollen glands, or problems in cognitive behavior—in short, no symptoms—he deemed her fit for release and signed her discharge papers.

"Is there anyone you can stay with?" he asked her.

Karen explained that she hadn't been in the Mkultra very long compared to most of the others. In fact, she had reason to believe that her old apartment and job in Brooklyn might still be available. All she needed were five stamps to get back home. Happy to free up the ward, Levitol gave her the stamps and wished her well.

The next morning, still unsteady on her feet, Karen pulled a poorly coordinated outfit from a pile of donated clothes and was on that day's minibus, slowly creeping up the length of the smelly borough. She awoke from a nap as they were passing over the Zano Bridge, but something was off. The skyscraper panels were missing. She then remembered that Mallory had them dismantled when she took office.

As far as she knew, no official in Staten Island had notified anyone in the Crapper administration about her reemergence in Rescue City. So, as her bus finally approached the Williamsburgh Building, she briefly entertained the thought of surprising everyone with her Lazarus-like return—but she figured that this wouldn't be wise. She didn't remember exactly how she had wound up going down the sewer, but she knew someone had dropped her down there. Karen decided that until she fully recalled what had happened, it would be best to remain dead.

In Downtown Brooklyn she transferred to a northbound bus. Everything looked normal to her until they came to northern Brooklyn, passing through carbonized streets—she realized that this was the former war zone of Quirklyn that Bea had mentioned. When they reached the final stop in Williamsburg, she was the only person left on the bus.

"I need to go to Queens," she said to the driver as she exited.

"You know they're experiencing a plague, don't you?" the man replied.

"I don't care."

"Cross the Newtown Creek bridge, there's a bus stop just on the other side." The driver looked away from her as he spoke. "Can't miss it." He closed the door, executed a tight U-turn, and sped back south.

Karen passed a group of men in lab coats standing around—Crapper health officers. Before leaving the borough, she asked one of them if she'd be able to return to Brooklyn.

"After we inspect you—yes."

"Do the Piggers have health inspectors?"

"Nope, they're *all* sick."

Karen sighed and crossed the bridge. Once on the far side, she saw the banged-up minibus idling. As she climbed aboard, Karen held out a quarter-stamp.

1084 ¥ Arthur Nersesian

"I ain't touching nothing," the driver said, sucking air from the small window to his left.

Karen took a seat and peered out the window as they rolled toward Maspeth. Three, five, then ten blocks passed and she still hadn't seen a single soul on the sidewalks. People seemed to have vanished. Finally, an older woman wearing what appeared to be a World War II gas mask and dishwashing gloves boarded in Elmhurst. After riding a few blocks, Karen asked her only fellow rider where all the people were.

"Where *you* should be," the muffled voice snapped back, "home!"

As the vehicle picked up the pace driving through the barren streets, it bounced constantly, and Karen began to feel nauseous. When they finally reached Jackson Heights—the last stop—the driver threw open the doors and rushed out ahead of the two passengers, gasping for air.

Karen stumbled out the door and immediately vomited due to motion sickness. Then she crossed the street and waited with two others for a connecting bus to bring her to the far-flung community of Little Neck. She noticed that one of the people had a kerchief tied over her face. The other simply kept looking away, breathing in her own exclusive direction.

Altogether it took a total of three hours—almost half of that time spent waiting for buses—for Karen to reach her destination. From the bus stop it was a short walk to the Lotus clinic. When she arrived she was startled to see a mountain of stinking and soiled blankets, mangled tents, and boxes with empty food cans which had been hastily discarded on the front lawn next to a big sign that said, *CLOSED*. It took a full ten minutes of knocking before someone finally shouted through the door, "We don't got no methadone! We're closed for repairs!"

"I'm trying to find someone!" she called back.

"They're all gone. Plains set up some kind of puppy adoption program; that's why we're in this fucking mess!"

"What fucking mess?"

"Are you blind?" The outline of a woman came closer, yet she refused to touch the door. "Everyone's sick with desert fever."

"Do you remember the lead guy who wasn't sick? He brought them all here. Can you just ask what became of him?"

"Emmett's not doing well, he's sick too."

"I came all the way from Staten Island and I need to find my brother."

Karen grabbed the doorknob and rattled it. "And I'm not leaving until I do."

The woman didn't respond.

"In a minute, I'm breaking the glass and coming inside," Karen pressed.

"All right, I'll ask him, but then you got to go. No matter what he says. Promise me!"

"Fine!" Karen shouted back.

In the ten minutes that followed, Karen paced to the end of the wraparound porch and examined the small gulch behind the house. Her time there was less like a memory and more like recalling a weird dream. She had nightmarish images of being hosed down back there, then spoon-fed by Uli.

"Are you still there?" she heard.

"Yeah," Karen responded, running back to the still-closed front door.

"He said they were both arrested."

"Both? You mean just Uli."

"There was a woman with him as well. The cops grabbed them both."

"Can you find out the woman's name?" Karen asked.

"No! Emmett's passed out, and that's all he knows! And those god-damn people got him sick, so I hope they get what's coming to them. Now fuck off!"

Karen checked her pocket—she still had three food stamps but no weapon. She had worked up a variety of Pigger connections during her council cop years, so she decided to try her luck at Kew Gardens. If she could find the right people, she thought, she could call in a few favors.

After an hour of waiting for a bus with no luck, she was finally able to flag down a car with the backseat chopped into a mini truck bed. For a half-stamp, she got to sit in the back and was driven all the way down to Queens Boulevard. After a twenty-minute walk, she found herself across the street from the Pigger police headquarters.

There, she spotted a secluded bench near the parking lot where she could wait and watch as patrol cars from the Bronx and Queens came and went. It was already late in the day when she arrived and she knew things would only be getting slower. After an hour of watching younger gangcops whom she didn't recognize, she finally saw some-one she knew: a short, hunched man with large knuckles who walked like a caveman—Sammy Greenberg, a Pigger sergeant from Jackson Heights. Years ago, she had helped him catch a serial murderer hiding in Red Hook.

"Sammy!" she called as he walked toward the headquarters.

When he spotted her, his jaw dropped. "Everyone said you were dead!"

"Hey, I'm not a ghost."

"Well, I don't want to be rude, Captain, but you look like you just crawled out of a grave." Karen hadn't considered the fact that aside from being feverish and anemic, she hadn't dyed her hair in six months. Instead of her customary short black hairdo, it was long and grayish with white bolts running through it. Additionally, during her time in the Mkultra she must've lost at least forty pounds, and she'd never been heavy to begin with.

"I need your help. I need to find my brother. His name is Uli, U-l-i—"

"Everyone knows about your brother," Sammy interrupted. "He's the most wanted man in Queens."

"What?!"

"He recently orchestrated a huge jailbreak from the Bronx Zoo. Plains said that if the Crappers hadn't already listed him as persona non grata, he'd have invaded Manhattan to find him."

"Holy shit!"

"Captain, if I were to arrest you right now, I'd get a medal. The best I can do for you is tell you to walk three blocks south, catch the Q60, and get the hell out of Queens, pronto!"

Karen thanked him. Twenty minutes later, when the empty Q60 minibus pulled up on Queens Boulevard, the bus driver was wearing a gas mask. Karen offered him a quarter-stamp, which he waved off. The lone passenger, she took a seat in the rear. As they headed west through Long Island City, she was able to count the pedestrians they drove by on one hand. Soon, two more passengers got on.

When the vehicle finally reached a bridge, traffic entering the borough was almost nil. They crossed over the narrow waterway and stopped on Second Avenue in Manhattan. Upon getting off, Karen and the other two riders were greeted by masked health officials who took their temperatures and carefully examined their eyes and throats before allowing them to pass into the Crapper borough. Karen then transferred to another bus heading over to Fifth Avenue and down through Midtown.

She spotted the elevated stone garden beside the Rock & Filler Center and the mayor's office, and couldn't help but think of her old friend Mallory—not the calm, apt politician who was pretending to be Mallory, but the real Mallory Levine, the wild-eyed revolutionary who had lured her into radical politics before getting blown up in Greenwich Village. After reliving her memories in the Mkultra, her long-lost friend was now fresh in her mind.

It was getting late and Karen had nowhere to sleep. At 14th Street, she decided to transfer to a minibus going back over to Brooklyn. During the trip she racked her brain, trying to recall what had happened during her last night in Rescue City before she was flushed down into the hell of the Mkultra.

Trying to remember was like peering at dark forms through a murky scrim. Outlines were visible, but all the fine points were washed away. As her bus rattled along the Brooklyn Bridge, she looked over the waterway south to Staten Island and a single detail clicked into focus: she had gotten a tip that someone she wanted was down in Tottenville—but she couldn't remember who, or why she was pursuing him. Schuman would probably be able to shed light on the situation. Knowing him, he would've launched an exhaustive investigation into her disappearance; he must've turned up something.

When she finally arrived at the Williamsburgh Savings Bank Building just before six p.m., she witnessed her own resurrection through the eyes of the others. As she introduced herself to the downstairs security team—most of whom she had known for years—they all just stared. Before letting her pass, the sergeant in charge quizzed her on a detail that only she would know: "Who did you regularly have lunch with on Tuesdays?"

"Deere Flare." As soon as the name left Karen's mouth, she realized Deere had something to do with her disappearance, but again, she couldn't remember any additional details.

"You know you were officially declared dead," the sergeant told her.

"If only," she replied wryly.

He waved her through.

When she got out of the elevator, Tatianna, the department secretary, dropped the forms she was holding and screamed. People she barely recognized shrieked and embraced the air next to her, a gesture of affection during a time of plague. The news of her return quickly spread throughout the building. A wave of cops, secretaries, security guards, and others swarmed in.

Finally Schuman peeked out of his office and gasped, caught his breath, and fixed a nervous smile on his pale face. When she moved in to hug him, he broke down weeping, and told her that things hadn't been the same since she vanished.

"So what happened?" Schuman asked through his tears.

"No idea. It's all a blank." Karen told him that all she remembered was being stuck in a large subterranean maze known as the Mkultra. Since the spread of the epidemic in Rescue City, reports of this hellish place in the middle of the desert had become the talk of the town, taking on mythic proportions. And most of the healthiest of its survivors could barely grunt, much less describe the place.

"So how exactly did you wind up down there?" he asked.

She said that she was hoping *he* might be able to help fill in the blanks on that. Schuman led her into his office and took out a thick file labeled *Karen Sarkisian*. Mallory had made her disappearance a priority. Schuman himself had led the investigation. Although there were still no clear suspects, there were many people of interest, most of whom came from two groups.

First, there was the mob. Over the years, Karen had arrested and amputated various capos and soldiers of Joe Gallo's family. The other parties of interest were shadow members of Domination Theocracy, the relatively new fanatical religious organization once headed by the late Erica Rudolph. They also suspected the involvement of some of the more zealous members of Pure-ile Plurality who were sympathetic to DT. Though several hundred hours had been logged on the case, they were no closer to an arrest.

"If you don't mind," Karen said, "I'd like to take a stab at my case. As you can imagine, my own attempted murder is very important to me."

"I can team you up with—"

"I'd rather go at it on my own," she cut in. "Easier that way."

"Whatever you like," Schuman said awkwardly. "I guess it's what Mallory would want."

"Actually, I don't think she knows I'm back yet."

"That's something I can't keep secret," he grinned.

"I know."

"Actually, before you start working on the case, we have to officially bring you back from the dead."

"What do you need to know?" Karen asked.

"I only have one question: do you remember anything about this Mkultra place?"

"It was nightmarish," she replied, and added that it was just one big dark, stinking blur.

"Mallory is under the weather," Schuman said, "but as soon as she calls, I'm sure she'll be ecstatic to learn about your resurrection."

Karen asked about her old apartment. She was informed that her brother had been living in it—until he was officially deemed a turncoat.

"Fortunately, since that wasn't long ago," Schuman continued, "I doubt anyone has emptied the place, so it probably still has all your things."

"I hope you're right."

"I haven't let anyone take your office. But I do think people have been using it." Schuman said that if she wanted to cross Williamsburgh Plaza to her old building, he'd tell Tatianna to ask the superintendent to give her a new key. Since it was nearly seven p.m., and she could barely keep her eyes open, she happily said yes.

Fifteen minutes later, she was back in the privacy of her old home. She discovered that although Uli had added some possessions of his own, he hadn't tossed out any of her stuff. Karen was so faint and feverish she was barely able to kick off her shoes and fall into bed.

When she awoke nearly twelve hours later, she found that her sheets were sopping wet. Unsure of whether or not she was still sick, she showered and changed into her own clothes. Until she was finished with all the red tape, she was still not officially back in her department. She decided it was best to keep resting.

She returned to the Williamsburgh Building the next day. While alone in her office, clearing out the litter so many had left behind, she found her spare handgun, which she hid in a compartment in the back of her desk. Schuman had personally advanced her fifty stamps and secured a temporary laminated ID for her. He also got her unlimited use of a solicar from the lot downstairs, though he couldn't officially assign her a weapon or a shield until the papers went through.

Later that afternoon she received a handwritten message from Mallory that read, *Just heard that you're back from the dead! I'm a little sick myself, but once I'm hale, let's have lunch and celebrate. Your pal, Mal.*

She then received a phone call from an old friend, Lieutenant Jerry Howard, formerly of the organized crime division. He couldn't believe she was back.

"I'm dying to find out who killed me," she said with a chuckle.

Howard told her that he had a snitch who had informed him that a ranking council cop had been routinely using the Staten Island sewage hole as his murder weapon of choice.

"Who?"

"Your old buddy Scouter."

It was like a word on the tip of her tongue, and as soon as Howard said it, she remembered—the old reptile had finally turned on her.

14

Despite feeling out of sorts, Karen immediately drove out to Sheepshead Bay while she still had the element of surprise. She had to get to Lewis before he could learn of her return. During the ride, she tried to figure out what it was she was originally investigating when she was dumped. As she headed southeast on Flatbush, she started feeling light-headed. She cut west then drove the final stretch to Lewis's place along the water's edge. Knowing what a sneaky shit he was, she took the precaution of parking a block away. After removing her revolver and checking the bullets, she staked out his place for forty-five minutes before cautiously approaching his study window. No signs of life.

Karen headed to the rear of his dilapidated little house and entered through an unlocked window in his bedroom. Holding her gun out before her, she moved from room to room until she was convinced that the place was empty. A thick layer of dust led her to believe he hadn't been home in weeks. There were no signs of any struggle, nor was there any indication that he had packed his bags. Maybe— hopefully—someone else had already killed him. She found a sealed can of deviled ham in his kitchen and had a quick meal. She examined the medicine cabinet in his bathroom: a lot of antibiotics and some other meds that she had never seen on the reservation. Then she sat down in his old recliner and, without intending to, dozed off.

When she awoke with a start, the sun was almost down. The desert sky was syrupy with wild pastel colors. She decided that she had better get home before it got too dark since streetlights no longer worked out there. As she reached her car, she started experiencing another bout of light-headedness. She was barely able to get into the driver's seat when someone who must've been squatting behind her vehicle leaped forward. The barrel of a large old pistol was shoved squarely in her face.

"Fucking hell!" She braced herself.

But nothing happened. She took a deep breath and looked beyond the weapon. Akbar Del Piombo stared at her in awe.

He lifted the muzzle up in the air. "They said you were dead!"

"Fuck!" If she hadn't just relieved herself at Lewis's place, she would've pissed right there.

"I was instructed to take out some lady who had just broken into that house," he explained, holstering his weapon.

"You're fucking kidding me! Scouter paid you to hit me?"

"No, it wasn't Scouter. I've known him since I arrived and he always does his own kills. Doesn't trust anyone else." Then he smiled grimly and said, "Welcome back."

Struck by the recent flood of memories of her time with him at Columbia University, Karen suddenly wrapped her arms around Akbar—formerly Eugene Hill—and gave him a big hug.

"Wow!" he exclaimed. "If I knew I could still get a hug from someone, I probably would've killed fewer people—but not many."

"I'm not hugging you out of gratitude," she said, still holding him. "It's actually for . . . other reasons."

"What other reasons?"

"Actually, maybe it is gratitude," she amended. How could she put into words the fact that she was just getting over a near-fatal illness that had disconnected her from the present and had catapulted her years backward?

Being flushed down that drain was like being sucked into the past itself. It felt as if she had just experienced this strange relationship with this intelligent black kid named Gene, a young veteran who had recently completed a tour in 'Nam and was desperately trying to find a place for himself in the turbulent America of the late sixties.

"Who hired you?"

"It was done anonymously, but I think I know who it was. I guess he doesn't know that we're pals."

"Who doesn't?"

"Your old assistant, Schuman."

"What?!"

"And once he discovers that you're not dead, two more contracts are going out right away: one on you and a second on me."

"That's insane, he would never . . ." She lapsed into silence, but she knew he was right. She instantly remembered the strange act of mercy Schuman had performed when Scouter had drugged her. Schuman had taped two syringes filled with the Mkultra-virus antidote to her leg. Unfortunately, once she was down there, they had been stolen from her. "Fuck!" she cried out. "We gotta kill him."

"He's the fucking AG now! We'll never get away with it."

"He was the one—him and Scouter. I'm not sure why Scouter did it. I always knew he was some kind of agent here. But Schuman must've done it out of personal ambition—to get out from under me. He hired you and he'll hire someone else."

"Don't you live in Williamsburgh Plaza?" Akbar said.

"Yeah, his apartment is right across from my kitchen window."

"Can you visit him tonight? All you have to do is get him by the window. If I can get my rifle and go into your apartment, I'll take him out from there."

She was going to suggest that an up-close hit would be better, but then realized that outside of his office, Schuman might have body-guards these days. At best, Akbar would get killed in the process.

"Shit," she muttered, unable to think of a better plan.

He said they had to stop by his place in East New York and pick up his rifle and bullets. She followed his car there. An hour later, he went up to his cinder-block compound and brought the gun down, wrapped in a blanket. She was startled to find that instead of some relatively new sharpshooter rifle, it was a nicked-up M1 carbine from World War II—it looked like it belonged in a museum. Even worse was the fact that he could only find three old bullets. Pessimism filled her car like a fart as they silently drove together back toward the Williamsburgh Justice Plaza.

"You know the security's going to spot that at once."

"Right. Stop here!" he barked, compelling Karen to hit the brakes just as they passed a household supply store with a big sign out front that read, CAPETS & RUGS CHEEP! "Give me a sec." He walked briskly into the shop and a moment later exited with a small plaid rug which he dumped into the backseat. While she resumed driving, he carefully spooled it around his rifle.

A few minutes later she stopped the car. This time she dashed into a stamp store. When she exited, she was carrying two large suitcases.

"You going on a trip?" he asked.

"It'll look suspicious if you're coming in with me just holding that. You should be carrying bags. And make them look heavy. I'll carry the rug."

Ten minutes later, Karen parked at the official Williamsburgh Building parking lot. When they stepped out of the car, Akbar held the bags, while she fumbled with the rug. They trotted past the plaza security guard and up into her building, where the evening doorman, Marco, who was seeing Karen for the first time in about half a year, gasped and congratulated her on being alive.

"Yeah, I'm a survivor," she muttered, trying to keep the rifle from slipping out of the rolled-up carpet.

Once she closed her apartment door, she asked Akbar if he was hungry. He said he was a little thirsty, so she filled a glass with water and led him to her kitchen window. She counted out the floors and windows of the adjacent building roughly two hundred feet away.

"It's that window with the gray curtains. Do you think you can hit someone in there?"

"It would have helped if I could've gotten some target practice," he said as he tried clicking the trigger of the empty rifle. "But I guess that ship has sailed."

"If I go over there and start talking to him, I need to know that you can take him down. We're only going to get one chance here."

"I know, I know, but long-distance kills aren't exactly my forte. I'm only doing this 'cause both our asses are on the line." No matter how hard he pulled on the trigger, the hammer wouldn't release.

Karen reached over and flipped off the safety. "You're supposed to be a fucking assassin!"

"Who do I look like—Lee Harvey Oswald? I work up close. Bullet to the head and I'm gone. Couldn't we just get him when he's heading home? I can come up behind him while he's crossing the plaza and put one in his ear."

"I'm sure he'll have at least one cop escorting him. And the plaza has armed guards on every corner. You'll never get away with it."

"Shit! By tomorrow, if your body isn't found, we'll both be hunted like dogs." He loaded his three bullets into the cartridge.

"I can try to turn on a lamp once I'm in there," she said.

"I just hope I don't kill *you* by mistake." He squinted, trying to make out where his target would be.

Karen sighed and explained that once he had done the job, he couldn't leave the gun in her apartment. The plaza security would probably do a unit-by-unit search, so he had to lose it somewhere outside. Also, he should exit by the service entrance in the rear and run as far away as he could, and lay low for as long as possible.

"Do you want to rendezvous afterward?"

It was too much to even consider right now. *What are the chances we're even going to survive this?* she thought. She had gotten Akbar into this situation, but didn't know how else to fix it.

Akbar put his old rifle down, sat across from her, sipped from the glass of water, then poured the rest on his scalp. She watched it trickle along his big head and down his broad back onto her floor. Checking her watch, she saw that it was late, though she remembered from when they had worked together that Schuman rarely went home any earlier than nine p.m. It was time to go and try to position her old friend next to the window. She wished Akbar good luck and exited.

In the hallway, the thought of what was about to happen overwhelmed her. She took a series of long, deep breaths in an effort to steady herself. Then she checked herself in a mirror by the elevator, fixing her hair. She calmly went downstairs and walked across the large and empty Williamsburgh Plaza, which during business hours was usually packed with people. When she reached the lobby of Schuman's building, the doorman stopped her, asking her name.

She identified herself and said that she was there to see Attorney General Schuman.

"He's not home," the young guard replied. "Frankly, he almost never comes home on weekdays. He's been sending his aides for clean clothes. I'm sure he's still at his office."

The security guard pointed to the Williamsburgh Building across the plaza. Karen thanked him and stepped outside. She stared up at the building for a minute, then went to Stamos's Stamps where she bought some wilted greens and several other items and then proceeded back to her place. She walked past Marco, took the elevator up, and opened her apartment door to find that Akbar had created a little perch for himself, resting the rifle on the windowsill, and was sitting hunched behind it in total darkness. She saw that he had taken the liberty of grabbing her nicest handmade quilt and had folded it around the weapon to muffle the sound of the gun blasts.

"What the hell are you doing here?" he growled tensely. He had obviously worked himself up and was dripping with sweat.

"It's too late. He's not coming home, and we're both too tired. No one would find my body at Scouter's place till tomorrow anyway. We'll do it in the morning."

"Thank God," he said, dropping the rifle. "I was barely able to hold that thing—it's like a bazooka."

"The bad news is . . ." She paused and gestured for Akbar to follow her. She led him into the living room and counted out a window in the Williamsburgh Building that was five stories higher up and more than three times the distance away. "You'll have to shoot him in there."

"You're kidding!"

"That's where he is, and it sounds like he's staying put. He might already be asleep up there, so let's plan to do it in the morning."

"It would've been so much easier to have just shot you," he said with a grin.

Karen went into the kitchen and tossed together the vegetables. She had also bought some Staten Island pork chops, which she fried up. While rummaging in her pantry, she noticed a bottle of wine which she hadn't purchased, so it must've been Uli's. She unscrewed the top and was glad to find that it wasn't the worst thing she had ever drunk and only had a mild level of alcohol. She poured them both a glass as they sat silently together. The entire time, Akbar stayed at the window, just glaring at the tiny, well-lit square that was Schuman's office window in the Williamsburgh Building.

Eventually he said, "I can barely make out the window frame, let alone see anyone inside."

She tried not to think of what they had to do the next morning. Just sipping her wine, she gazed off hopelessly.

"Remember that night when we went home from the West End Bar?" Akbar jolted her from her trance.

"You mean when we slept together?" Karen replied flatly.

"I was actually talking about earlier, when we walked home from the bar." He stared at her.

"What about it?"

"That big guy on the street . . . who hit me."

"Oh, right."

"He was a fucking Magilla Gorilla. I really thought I was a goner."

"I remember."

"I was utterly petrified. I mean, I was just waiting for him to stomp the life out of me, like some cockroach, but you! You came right back at him instantly. Didn't even think about it. You took your textbook and rammed it right into his throat. I mean, he went down like a sack of potatoes."

"Then we ran like hell," Karen recounted with a smile.

"That's why you're alive right now. That's when you had me. I mean, you know how many people could've done that? None! Any other person would've either froze, or just left me there and ran. But not you, you snapped into action—went David-and-Goliath on his ass. Over the years here, I've gone through a lot of ups and downs, but I've always remembered that moment. I mean, you were a skinny college kid with bushy eyebrows and you took out a guy twice your age and weight. I know this sounds silly for a war veteran to say, but over the years, those times when I lost my nerve—I've been inspired by that. You saved my ass. No one ever did that for me—ever!"

"Well, thank you."

"Thing is, I need that girl *now*. We both do. We got to snatch victory from the jaws of this motherfucker, and if anyone can do it, it's her."

"I hate to say it, but I think everyone only gets one of those moments. That day, I had spent an hour at the dojo repeating that karate move using the heel of my hand, and with all those beers I had downed, I didn't even think about it."

Akbar put his hand on Karen's and smiled. She leaned over and gave him another hug.

"Can I ask you a personal question?" Karen said.

"Sure."

"That one romantic night when you took Mallory Levine to your home in Harlem . . ."

"You mean the room I subletted or—"

"No, that abandoned luxury apartment where your aunt worked as a maid back in the 1920s."

"My aunt? I don't have an aunt, at least not one I've ever known personally."

"But that abandoned building that you squatted in, you had to climb down a dumbwaiter to get inside."

"A dumbwaiter? Why would I have to climb down a dumbwaiter?"

"'Cause of all the junkies who used it as a crash pad."

"Karen, do I look insane?"

"No, but—"

"Do you really think I'd live in an abandoned building filled with junkies where I'd have to crawl down a dumbwaiter?"

"Wait, you never lived in . . ." Karen froze in horror, realizing that this memory she'd had of him and Mallory while trapped in the Mkultra must've been a figment of her own imagination. "You dated Mallory Levine, didn't you?"

"Of course."

"And you . . ." She paused again, questioning if he had indeed broken into her apartment and later joined the Black Panthers.

"And I *what*?"

"Nothing," she said, flashing a grin, not wanting to distress him before tomorrow's big hit. "Let's get some sleep."

Several minutes later, the two went to different sides of her queen-size bed. All she could do was wonder what she had fantasized and what had really happened.

When they woke up early the next day, they silently washed up and dressed. When they were ready to go, she brought Akbar back to her living room and they once again identified Schuman's window in the Williamsburgh Building.

"In twenty to thirty minutes I'll have him standing right there. All you have to do is shoot those three bullets through it, okay?"

"I also have to kill him," he murmured.

"Just do your best."

Before she could leave, he grabbed her and kissed her so hard it hurt her front teeth. When she finally broke free, he smiled sadly and said, "I love you, Karen."

"I love you too," she replied, though she understood what he was really feeling—that this was probably going to be it. They were probably going to die fighting. He was clearly tense, but ever since she had been freed from the Mkultra, she had felt mostly numb inside. Instead of actually feeling fear now, she only knew she *should* feel it.

He carefully took aim.

"Give me time to get him by the window," she said.

"But I can't even see the window."

"Just do your best."

Without even a final sip of coffee, she moved like a human missile down the stairs and across the nearly empty plaza to the Williamsburgh Building. Glancing up, she saw a single drone in the sky.

The security guard on duty, who had seen her leave the day before, nodded as she flashed her newly laminated ID. She waited with a dozen others for the slow elevator. Five minutes later, the doors opened on the criminal justice department, she walked past Tatianna, and she knocked on Attorney General Schuman's door.

"Hey!" Tatianna called out. "The AG's orders are that he's not to be disturbed."

"Someone is trying to kill him! I have to talk to him right now!"

An armed guard overheard her and rushed over, holding up a baton. "What's up?" he asked.

At that moment the door flew open. Schuman stood there in his stocking feet, pants, and T-shirt. Apparently he had been fast asleep on his couch. Seeing the security guard with the nightstick standing behind Karen, he said, "That's all right, Bob. Come in, Karen."

No sooner did Schuman flip on his overhead light than his office window shattered, and the large slug also knocked a big hole in the map of Rescue City against the rear wall.

"What the hell?!" the security guard yelled from the hallway.

A second round hit the back of Schuman's wooden swivel chair, sending it spinning a couple times before toppling over. Schuman, who immediately grasped what was happening, pushed Karen against a wall, safely out of the line of fire. "Someone's firing at us! Everyone down!" he yelled.

"This is what I came to warn you about!" Karen shouted.

Everyone in the outer office started screaming and the security guard rushed into Schuman's office.

"He's got to be shooting from one of those buildings," Schuman said, pointing out the window.

"I'll get a fix on him," said the guard, who ran back out to a window by Tatianna's desk to try to spot the flash of the gunfire. As soon as he left the room, the third and final shot thudded harmlessly into the rear wall. By this point someone was returning fire from a nearby window.

When the attorney general peeked out his window, Karen pulled out her own revolver, grabbed a pillow from his sofa to muffle the blast, and put a bullet into the back of Schuman's skull. The middle-aged man collapsed back on her. His blood pumped out of his skull like an open faucet, drenching Karen. His arms and legs began convulsing. She shoved the gun into her waistband, dragged his body to the middle of his floor, and let out a bloodcurdling scream.

The guard raced back into the office and saw her cradling Schuman's blood-drenched corpse. "Holy fuck!"

All hell broke loose. Every security guard in the building seemed to scurry into the room. Most had rifles from the arsenal closet. They were lining the windows, taking shots at anything that moved in the distance—including innocent civilians who happened to come into view in and around the other buildings on the plaza.

"Cease fire!" yelled a council cop captain, trying to assess what was going on.

"He was peeking out the window," Karen said, breathing deeply, "and he turned to me, and next thing I know, he's . . . he's down."

Karen was sticky with Schuman's blood and trembling, seemingly in a state of shock. The captain said it looked like she might need medical attention.

"I've got . . . tranquilizers in my . . . desk," she said with difficulty. "If that's . . . okay."

"Go ahead," the captain replied.

Karen slipped into her old office where she was able to stash her pistol back in the hidden desk compartment where she previously kept it. Tranquilizers and almost everything else that she used to keep in the drawers had evidently been tossed out when she was presumed dead. She went to the water fountain in the hallway and washed Schuman's blood off her hands and face.

15

When Uli came to, he felt feverish. The noisiness of his surroundings had awakened him. No longer confined in darkness, he was now in a large white space, like inside of a beautiful cloud, only it was crowded with moaning people in rows of beds. When he tried to move, he realized his right hand was loosely cuffed to the metal-framed cot he was lying on. It took him a moment to determine that he was in a large tent somewhere. In another moment, using a jug of water next to his bed as lubricant, he squeezed his hand out of the cuff. Looking down, he saw cracked pavement and figured he was in a parking lot adjacent to some hospital. These overcrowded and unstaffed areas had become the charity wards for all the hospitals in Rescue City. A ray of sunlight was streaming down through the thick canvas above him. Reaching up, he felt gauze tightly wrapped around his forehead. He pulled it aside and ran his fingers across five little bumps, a tight row of stitches. An IV needle was loosely bandaged into his right arm.

Inhaling deeply, he immediately knew where he was, from that unmistakable stink: it could only be Staten Island.

His shoes were on the floor under his cot. Fortunately, his clothes hadn't been cut from his body. In fact, the upper part of his shirt was pasted to his chest, caked in dried blood.

He didn't know how long he had been out for, but he was thirsty, hungry, and groggy. As he slipped on his shoes, he made out the number 123 faintly stenciled on the ground.

The fact that his hand had been cuffed to the bed suggested that he was yet again under arrest. Fearful of being extradited back to the Bronx, Uli quickly headed for the nearest exit. When he pushed through the tent flap, a gigantic security guard stopped him and bellowed, "No one leaves without a yellow label, or enters without a blue one!"

Uli glanced down and saw the blue label on his shirt. When he tried to ask about the yellow label, the guard closed the flap in his face. Scanning around the hectic tent, he soon spied a probable doctor—a long-legged woman with a surgical mask and rubber gloves besieged by patients and staff alike. He watched her looking down someone's throat using a pen as a tongue depressor. The beds around him were filled with sweaty, coughing snifflers.

Milling around the large tent, surveying the place, Uli noticed a stitched-up tear in the canvas behind a bed with a corpulent comatose man in it. While appearing to be checking the patient, he pocketed a spare shirt from under the man's bed. He made sure no one was watching him, then dropped to the ground, tore open the old rip, and rolled out. Once outside, Uli peeled off his bloody shirt, pulled on the clean one, removed the gauze around his head, and headed to the terminal building.

There, he joined a line of people waiting to gain entrance. He asked a hefty blonde in front of him what was going on inside.

"The Robert Moses trial," she responded.

"Paul Moses's brother?"

"Yeah, the son of a bitch killed him," said a guy in the line puffing on a Hoboken cigar.

"Killed him?"

"Claims it was an accident."

"Actually," another corrected, "that's not why he's on trial."

"Then what's he on trial for?" asked the stoned cigar sucker.

"Turning the homes of the working class into roadways for the rich," replied a redhead as the line started moving.

Uli stayed behind the bloated blonde and watched as three security guards wearing gloves and face masks frisked people, then checked their eyes and throats. Only when they were cleared for weapons and symptoms of the plague were they allowed to enter. For twenty minutes Uli pondered the thought that poor Paul Moses had finally died, and then it was his turn to be examined. Ignoring the fresh stitches on his head, the guard cleared him as healthy and frisked him for weapons. Uli asked a court officer where he might find Bea Moses-Mayer.

"She's working on the trial."

He followed the flow of people into a large multitiered lecture hall that was packed with hundreds of spectators. There was standing room only, in the rear. Looking down at the center stage, Uli saw the ancient New York bureaucrat sitting tiredly in a white chair, like an unflattering statue of himself. His knees were splayed outward and he clutched a cane. Next to Robert Moses was a wiry, wavy-haired man in suspenders who seemed to be his lawyer, and next to him was a well-dressed woman with her back to Uli. When she turned, he confirmed that it was Bea in an uncharacteristically formal dress and a button-down shirt. Far from her usual Calamity Jane look, she appeared to be assisting the defense, which struck him as absurd.

Through bored turtle eyes, Robert Moses watched as Jane Jacobs, a short older woman with a pageboy haircut, slowly climbed up the steps to the stage.

After the judges brought the trial to order and all fell silent, one of them signaled to Bea. In an unassuming fashion she rose to the podium next to a large map of Old Town, and in a soft, simple voice addressed the judges and the assembly: "Ladies and gentlemen, let me begin by saying this is not the Nuremberg trials. Robert Moses, who is seated here with us today, is not a monster. I will present the case that shows that for three decades this nonelected bureaucrat from an upper-crust Connecticut family got to turn New York City into his private Erector Set, giving top priority to cars at the expense of the underprivileged and the working class . . ."

Although Uli had difficulty seeing and hearing at such a distance, he watched attentively as Jane Jacobs kept slapping the large map. It seemed to be the only exhibit offered by the people of the City of New York in the State of Nevada.

Uli angled himself so he was able to get a better view of the giant map, which was vivisected up, down, and sideways by countless lines drawn in various colors. The green marks on the map seemed to denote "safe" projects, where Moses's work had clearly benefited the city, such as the West Side Highway, the Triborough Bridge, the Verrazano Bridge, and the Whitestone Bridge. Yellow lines presumably showed highways where the benefits were dubious, such as the BQE and the Bruckner. But the majority of the lines covering the five boroughs were in deep red, apparently denoting displaced communities, chronic congestion, and redundant road systems that ended up hurting the city's residents.

"Are they going to take into account all the parks and pools he built?" said a balding, bespectacled bulldog of a man standing next to Uli.

"And don't forget the institutions," a woman standing nearby whispered loudly. "He did Lincoln Center, the Coliseum, Shea Stadium—"

"And Jones Beach," chimed someone else.

"That doesn't undo all those awful projects!" added someone else from the peanut gallery. "He moved my family from a spacious rent-controlled apartment on the Upper West Side—with an incredible view of Jersey—into a cramped, crime-ridden housing project in the Rockaways, the Siberia of New York, where it was always freezing!"

A succession of sharp finger snaps from an usher silenced the chatter. Uli listened as Jane Jacobs talked about the "pitilessness of his parkways."

Soon the chief judge mentioned adjourning for lunch, but before he could do so, Jacobs stated that the afternoon had been set aside for "the Belt Parkway Six, who are prepared to give firsthand accounts of how their lives were profoundly handicapped due to Moses's capricious abuse of eminent domain."

When the gavel finally struck, Uli pushed through the crowd, down the stairs of the lecture hall, past an usher, and finally reached Bea.

"Oh my God! Look who's here! Are you okay?" she asked, staring at the stitches in his head.

"I'm fine, but how's my sister?"

"She's okay, though she's not here."

"Where the hell is she?"

"Last I heard, she went to Queens looking for you."

"Shit! I gotta find her!"

"Hold on now, she's a respected council cop—I'm sure she's okay. Don't turn this into a slapstick comedy. I'll tell you what I told her: stay put until she comes back."

"You're probably right," Uli said. Taking a solemn tone, he added, "I just heard about your father, I'm so sorry."

"Did you hear that *he* killed him?" Bea said, glaring over at Robert Moses, who was snoozing in his chair.

"I heard it was an accident."

"Yeah, well, don't ask me why I'm helping him. When Jane saw me at his table she asked what I was doing there. When I told her he's my uncle, her jaw dropped. She probably thinks I was his spy when I worked for her in Old Town."

"Everyone should be forced to defend someone they disagree with at least once," Uli said. "It's the best way to force open a mind."

"Not mine. I'm hoping that I mess it all up."

"I'm really sorry," Uli said again, sensing the pain of her loss.

"If you want to be sorry about something," Jacobs called over, "you should be sorry about bringing that fucking plague down here. I can't believe this place is packed. Everyone's scared to catch it."

"I really am very sorry. I went all the way out there to try to rescue my sister," Uli lamented, "and ended up opening up the gates to hell."

"Actually, there's something you can help with," Jacobs said. "We're very short on people with investigative skills, so you'd be perfect."

"For what?"

"Shortly after this whole Mkultra-refugees fiasco, posters appeared all over town claiming that the Rescue City program was officially over and telling everyone to prepare to evacuate."

"Evacuate?"

"Yeah. A lot of people have dismissed it as a prank, but Rafique has been sitting on a big secret and now he's terrified."

"What secret?"

Bea led Uli out of the courtroom and into a small conference room where she was able to latch the door.

"Do you remember when we first met, down in Staten Island?"

"You said you never had sex on a first date."

"After that, when we paddled over that swamp . . ."

"The Bay of Death," he said. "It's not far from here."

"I won't go through everything that happened, but that was a big no-no on my part. I wasn't supposed to take you out there."

"What are you saying?"

"Do you remember what happened after we paddled across?"

"I remember being chased to the canoe by something, and as I got in, you ran off and I thought you were going to be killed by a wild boar."

"See, we got too close."

"Too close to what?"

"The Fecal Farm," she whispered.

"What?"

"You know how the Crappers have their Hoboken pot farm?"

"Yeah, I almost got killed there."

"Well, we have our own high-security area too."

"A place where they grow pot?"

"Not quite. They use all the piss and crap that flows down here and are able to distill the ammonium and nitrate into crystal sheets. They refer to it as the Fecal Farm—they're manufacturing explosives."

"Wow, that's clever."

"I'm telling you this 'cause you're going to find out soon enough."

"Find out what?"

"They desperately need someone experienced to do a major investigation."

"The VL has their own police department . . ."

"Chief Loveworks is a pothead paperweight," Bea said. "Look, this is in your own best interest."

"How's that?"

"'Cause then you'll be able to live down here—permanently."

"And why would I want that?"

"Because you can't legitimately live anywhere else. And you'll need a permanent place of residence in order to travel through Rescue City."

He didn't have the heart to tell her that he was done with this awful place. After his discoveries about the water stations, his only plan was to pull together some supplies, locate his sister, then take his chances crossing the desert to try to make it back to civilization.

"Rafique could really use your help," Bea added, then excused herself to grab a quick bite before the trial resumed.

Uli decided to stay in Staten Island to wait for his sister to reappear and gather the resources together for their escape. He also consented to helping with the investigation Jacobs and Bea had mentioned. While the prosecution presented their case, Bea led Uli into the defense chambers where she grabbed a phone and put a call through the switchboard to Rafique's office.

Uli overheard her saying: "He might've worked for the Crappers, but he performed investigations long before then, and he's a million times more effective than Love-doesn't-work."

He remembered his brief meeting with Rafique and had the impression that the man was intelligent and trustworthy.

Bea hung up and told him that if he was willing to undergo a full-body search, Rafique's next appointment had just canceled, so he was welcome to head upstairs within the next ten minutes. Another loud bell went off, and she said she had to run.

Uli bid Bea good luck and went to a bathroom. Splashing water on his face, he still felt feverish but also steady. He walked the short distance to the security guard on door duty and explained that he had an appointment to meet with Rafique. The guard called upstairs.

"I understand," Uli heard him say. Then, after the man signaled to several other colleagues at his station, Uli suddenly found himself grabbed and handcuffed.

"What the fuck!"

He was led upstairs into an interrogation room. A few minutes later, an older hippie with a long gray ponytail entered and introduced himself as the Staten Island police chief, Roger Loveworks.

"Why the hell am I in handcuffs?" Uli demanded.

"What you should ask is why you were in cuffs in the hospital ward. The answer is that I put them on you—apparently not tightly enough. My question to you is, how did you get into Staten Island?"

"I don't remember."

"Okay, what's the last thing you *do* remember?"

"Being in an underground tunnel on one of those old-fashioned hand trolleys. It crashed and I slammed into something."

"Someone must've helped you."

"I guess . . . . I don't know."

"How'd you get into that tunnel?"

"I was unlawfully imprisoned by the Piggers and tossed into the Bronx Zoo. I managed to escape into the tunnel from there. You gotta believe me, I didn't do anything wrong!"

"I believe you, but we have a treaty with the Piggers, so we're legally bound to extradite you."

"Give me a break, everyone knows you guys were behind the Quirklyn uprising."

"We had no official ties—"

"If you extradite me, they'll kill me. That prison warden will literally eat my body!"

"Yep. Polly's a well-known cannibal," Loveworks said, fumbling in his pocket for his keys. "If I remove your cuffs, will you give me any trouble?"

"I'll pretend they're still on."

The police chief unlocked Uli's cuffs. "Let me lay it out for you nice and clear. I really don't give a shit about you and the Piggers, but we have a problem and soon it's going to be huge: we had a secret weapon. We had a full rotation of guards watching it. Two days ago, our weapon vanished. Additionally, the entire shift of guards, six in total, were found bound and murdered. We did find one survivor but he was covered in blood."

"That's probably the guy you should be interrogating," Uli quipped.

"I am—that person is *you*." Loveworks took a Polaroid photograph from his pocket and handed it to Uli. Sure enough, the photo showed him lying on the ground next to three dead-looking bodies.

"Where exactly was this?"

"A few miles from here."

"I swear I don't remember any of this."

"I believe that. We brought you to the hospital, where they stitched you up and I handcuffed you to the bed. You were unconscious so I didn't put a guard on you—my mistake."

"I didn't have anything to do with it!"

"Again, I trust you're telling the truth, but clearly someone was trying to frame you."

"So what do you want from me?"

"You know that we're trying Robert Moses?"

"Yeah, I just saw some of the trial. In fact, Bea Moses-Mayer is the one who sent me up here."

"I interrogated Robert Moses as much as you can interrogate any man in his midnineties," Loveworks said. "When I asked him how he got to Staten Island, he said he took a subway."

"Did you ask him where the subway entrance was?"

"I sure did. He didn't have a clue," Loveworks answered. "But he did say a driver picked him up from there and drove him through Staten Island, and that he didn't remember going over a bridge."

"Well, if you're afraid he's going to sneak off and grab the subway out of here—"

"A couple weeks ago, posters sprang up throughout Rescue City warning that things here are drawing to a close."

"That's great, everyone should be returned back home."

"Agreed, but it's not official. Whoever is doing this is doing it because of the plague."

"I don't understand," Uli said.

"We've all assumed it's a prank, but if it's true, if some group is actually planning to force an evacuation, the only thing that would make sense would be to burn the place to the ground. Best-case scenario: thousands will die."

"I've never been a big believer in conspiracy theories."

"We have all heard rumors over the years that outside forces are handling and steering us," Loveworks said, "and I always figured it was true. We tossed the army out, and we had this illusion of autonomy, but ultimately Uncle Sam pays the bills, so Uncle Sam runs the show."

"I don't know Uncle Sam."

"Nonsense—you work for him. In fact, you were just in his house. You know exactly where he lives."

"You mean the tunnel?"

"Very good. Now, you're wanted in Queens and the Bronx, and you're not welcome in Brooklyn and Manhattan. I can grant you citizenship here in Staten Island, but the price is that I want you to take me to this tunnel."

"There must be an entrance somewhere around here," Uli reasoned.

"I'm sure there are a few; the question is where? The only one we know of is where you entered."

"I entered it in the Bronx, but if I get caught there I'll get arrested again. I can draw you a map and give you detailed instructions on how to find it."

"Ever see *The Bridge on the River Kwai*?" Loveworks asked. "You're William Holden. You don't have to do anything, but take me there."

"What exactly do you plan to do once you're there?"

"I have to make an assessment. If the tunnel's relatively small, I can bring in my people. If it's bigger than that, I can approach the Crappers, maybe even the Piggers. I'm guessing it's citywide. But I need more than speculation."

"Here's the only problem: the tunnel entrance is on the prison grounds of the Bronx Zoo facility."

"*Inside* their prison?"

"Sort of—it's around back."

"So it's not heavily guarded."

"No. In fact, I don't even think they know it exists. It was boarded up and sealed."

"So it should be easy to breach."

"Okay," Uli agreed tensely. The notion of going back up to the Bronx terrified him, but he didn't really have a choice. "When do you want to do this?"

"As soon as I get the supplies together," Loveworks replied quickly.

"Let me give you a word of advice: get a folding bike with a light, 'cause you're going to need it in that tunnel."

"I thought you said there's a hand-pumped trolley."

"Yeah, but who the hell knows where it is now. Actually, I can give you a list of things you'll need."

Loveworks handed him a notepad, and Uli made the list: a lot of rope, one or two flashlights, food for several days, a large canteen, a knapsack to carry everything, and the folding bike.

"This should take an hour or so to assemble," Loveworks said.

Uli told him he wanted to watch some more of the Moses trial, so

Loveworks said he'd send for him once all was ready. He also issued Uli a pass so he could skip the long line.

Uli took a seat in the auditorium and watched as an expert witness for the defense read from a schedule of commute times from Great Neck to Fort Lee, and from Bayonne to Ronkonkoma—all to prove how Moses's highway system expedited trips through the entire tristate area, vastly benefiting the city's commerce.

Spotting Bea in the second chair at the defense table, Uli waved to her. She sent a guard to escort him over.

"Did they hire you for the investigation?" she whispered to him as soon as he arrived.

He nodded and smiled, not wanting to say that it was more like extortion.

"They're hitting us with everything from juvenile respiratory ailments related to carbon monoxide emissions to depleted funds earmarked for mass transit," she whispered.

"How about all the public housing Moses put up?" Uli quietly responded. "That's got to be worth something."

"They already smeared his Section 8 housing projects, calling them heartless and mindless."

Peering over at Moses's stoic face, Uli thought the old man looked like one of the semisunken stone Easter Island heads, impervious to time and indictment. But as he recalled the utter disregard Moses showed his own brother over the years, all his sympathy drained away. He returned to his seat

After another forty-five minutes of watching the defense team at work, one of the VL cops nudged Uli—Loveworks was ready to roll.

16

"Would you mind driving?" Loveworks asked. "I want to check the latest intel on the way." In order to blend inconspicuously, the police chief had deliberately gotten one of the older jalopies from the car lot and loaded it up with all the items Uli had suggested. "I made some sandwiches for lunch," he said, "You'll love them, I'm a gourmet of the Staten Island cuisine."

Uli barely touched the accelerator and they zoomed forward jerkily. The car had a hair-trigger gas pedal and the brake was weak, but he quickly figured out how to gingerly tap on one while pumping on the other.

Loveworks used the drive to inspect a map of northern Rescue City that he had just gotten from the VL intelligence division. Two large red marks showed the only places where they could pass over the Harlem River into the Bronx.

"Shit!"

"What?" Uli asked.

"The only way we're entering Piggerland without being checked is if we leave the car in Harlem or Inwood and ride the folding bikes."

Uli sighed. The police chief bringing *two* bikes meant he was expected to accompany the man back into the prison and down into that claustrophobic tunnel.

When traffic started accumulating ahead of them, Uli realized they were approaching the fork in the road that divided cars going to either Manhattan or Brooklyn.

According to Loveworks, since it had recently been repaired, the Staten Island Ferry Bridge swayed dangerously, so Uli turned toward the Zano, but then everything slowed to a halt. Uli could see that the three lanes of cars approaching the Zano were frozen. Farther down, he spotted about half a dozen men with brassards knotted over their right arms. Working in pairs, the men, who had to be Brooklyn health inspectors, were stopping cars that were leaving Staten Island before they could even get on the bridge.

"Traffic's still rolling into Manhattan," Loveworks remarked, pointing back toward the Ferry Bridge, so Uli made a U-turn and steered that way.

Uli figured that they were probably going to have their temperatures checked by Manhattan health inspectors upon crossing the bridge. The good news was he hadn't seen the Brooklyn health inspectors checking anyone's ID. On the other hand, he was still running a slight fever; hopefully he could use the stitches to justify this.

A few minutes later the blockade was in sight. While they queued up, Uli and Loveworks watched as one of the inspectors pulled out a photo album several cars ahead of them. The inspector flipped through it, apparently checking the occupants in the idling car against pictures of wanted men. Another inspector made the driver get out and pop open his hood.

"This is bad," Uli muttered.

"Relax, you're not a wanted criminal in Rescue City South. In fact, technically you're allowed to pass through, you just can't sleep there."

"It's just not a risk I can take." He had been detained twice now and both times had just missed losing a body part—he couldn't chance it a third time. "They're going to see all the supplies we have, get suspicious, and—"

"Hold on, look at that." Loveworks pointed to a cluster of people walking along the narrow pedestrian walkway. "They're not even asking them for IDs. Why don't you stroll through on foot and I'll meet you on the other side, at the Battery."

"Suppose they detain *you*?"

"I'm the police chief of Staten Island. We've always had a cordial relationship with the Crappers. Here," he handed Uli a small cellophane bundle, "this is a marinated pork and avocado sandwich in a mustard and red wine vinaigrette—it's delicious. Savor it, and after they wave me by, you can just walk through. They'll have no clue that we're together. I'll wait for you on the other side."

Since they had already come this far, and the chief was willing to take some of the risk, Uli consented. He grabbed the sandwich, then got out and stretched, trying to calm himself. In the time that it took him to unwrap the food, an inspector waved for Loveworks to approach.

Instead of braking at the giant wooden blockade, the old hippie inexplicably sped past, knocking over a wooden post and plowing his car into the two old planks acting as a guardrail. The jalopy flew up and then speared downward into the water, followed by a splash. Uli dropped the sandwich and dashed forward; the inspector shouted for help. Loveworks had driven right into the toxic brew of the New York Harbor.

"Fuck!" Uli screamed, sprinting past the blockade up to the edge of the bridge. The car was completely submerged.

"Oh my God! Another bridge bomber!" an inspector exclaimed.

"No he wasn't!" Uli shot back. "His gas pedal just got stuck."

Life buoys and ropes were tossed in where bubbles arose. Though it wasn't very deep, none could see through the brackish water for any sign of the car, let alone Chief Loveworks. When one of the bridge guards asked Uli if he knew the driver, he nervously shook his head no and moved away.

He spotted his uneaten sandwich on the ground, picked it up, and brushed off some dirt. He slowly ate the sandwich and tried to think of what he would say to Bea, who didn't even like the police chief in the first place.

Uli looked over toward the Zano Bridge. Since Mallory had removed the panels along the side of the bridge, which were intended as a strange homage to the Lower Manhattan skyline, the handful of old and weathered shacks which had been somewhat hidden below them now stood out.

Seeing the dilapidated little structures, Uli remembered his terrifying encounter while he was working at PP, when he'd been chased into the waterway. That was where he'd been able to climb ashore. When he did so, a Latino gang had grabbed him and seemed like they were preparing to execute him. It was only due to the intervention of baby-deprived Consuela—one of the odd Christian devotees—that they had spared his life.

As Uli now watched members of the gang in the distance, he was amused by their strange uniformity: all of them wore the same black sneakers, blue jeans, and white T-shirts. Additionally, they all had inky-black, combed-back hair, along with low sideburns and mustaches. Though some were a bit bigger and broader, all the men looked relatively fit and appeared to be in their midthirties.

In the several minutes that they were in view, Uli counted as many as twenty gang members. He also realized that although there were several different shacks nearby, virtually all the scary hombres squeezed into only one of them, which didn't look much bigger than a clown car.

Then Uli thought he saw one skinny man's mustache fall off, dropping right to the ground—a disguise!

He had to get a closer look. He noticed a clump of bushes just above one of the shacks. After about ten minutes of carefully edging his way along the rocky cliff toward the shacks, a cloth bag was suddenly yanked over his head. His wrists were grabbed and cuffed behind his back. Two men slipped a rope around his shoulders and started lowering him down the steep incline.

"No point in the pillowcase," said a dispassionate, unaccented voice when they were back on level ground.

The sack was tugged off his head. He was surrounded by three large men.

"What the fuck is going on?" Uli asked tensely.

No one said a word, they just nudged him forward. He was led into the central shack, which turned out to be little more than a wooden alcove covering a manhole with a metal ladder sticking out of it.

Sure enough, it was a tunnel entrance, what Loveworks had died trying to find. The plastic cuff holding his wrists together was cut and he was told to descend down the manhole. After twenty feet or so, a string of lightbulbs confirmed that he was back in a different section of the same tunnel system he had escaped through in the Bronx.

"Are you going to execute me?" Uli asked, turning around to look at his captors.

"If I was going to do that, I would've done it the first time when you climbed up on our shore."

It was the short man with the close-cropped beard and glasses—the guy who had attacked him when he pulled himself onto their little embankment.

"You no longer sound Mexican," Uli said.

"Actually, my name's Patel. Paddy Patel."

"Indian?"

"Indian-Irish. I was raised in Queens where Woodside meets Jackson Heights, so culturally I think of it as the Indian-Mexican border." He smiled.

"Are you the ones who put up those posters saying that this place is kaput?" Uli asked.

The only response he got was the other gang members peeling off their mustaches. Patel's beard, however, was authentic. Uli was gestured into a seat in the back of a small motorized train cart. No sooner did it cross his mind that maybe he should try to flee than one of them tugged his wrists behind his back. As a second man moved to recuff him, Patel said, "Do as you're told and all we'll do is take you somewhere, chat for a while, and set you loose. Otherwise, cuffs and a blindfold."

"Did you guys steal the explosives from Staten Island?" Uli pressed.

Patel nodded to the other man to go ahead and cuff him.

"Okay, okay, whatever you want," Uli relented, eager not to be bound again.

He was seated facing the rear of the cart and driven backward through the cool blackness. As they moved along, he searched the narrow passage in the dim glow of the headlights to try to spot a hatchway near the base, but saw none. Thirty minutes later, the cart slowed down and came to a halt.

Patel pulled out a flashlight. "This way," he said to Uli.

Patel walked him to a small half-moon passageway. They crawled under it and into a shaft where Uli could see a circle of blinding light at the top. Then, hand over hand, they climbed a hundred feet up a ladder until they finally emerged from another manhole. Uli couldn't help but notice that Patel wore brand-new hiking boots.

Once out, Uli immediately recognized where they were—they had arrived in the Long Island City section of Queens, not far from Newtown Creek, which bordered Brooklyn.

The entire nonresidential area seemed to be boxed up, reserved strictly for infrastructure: a giant electric generator plant was spread out along one side; a roadway passed next to it.

Uli heard the crackling of a walkie-talkie. Patel pulled it from his pocket, put it to his ear, listened a moment, then said, "We have to wait here."

"For what?"

"Hungry? Thirsty?"

"Got a Coke?"

Uli's captor led him into an old wooden shed about thirty feet from the manhole. Inside there was a cooler filled with ice cubes and soda. Patel handed Uli a cold can of Pepsi and grabbed a Fresca for himself. In addition to the walkie-talkie, Patel was also carrying a large, clunky transistor radio, which he flipped on. He was able to get the only radio station in Rescue City, which was broadcasting the Robert Moses trial live. The two of them sat back, sipped their sodas, and listened to a warm female voice.

"For decades you wielded your authority—a power that was never given to you by the people! To force project after project down the throat of this city!" Uli recognized the voice—Jane Jacobs.

"I beg your pardon," interrupted the old bureaucrat, *"but every job I was ever tasked with . . . required the approval of countless people . . . This notion that with a wave of my magic wand—"*

"Wave? No! But you bullied, blackmailed, cajoled, and, when necessary, you lied!"

"Wait! I remember you now!" Moses erupted. *"You were that nebbishy housewife who killed my Lower Manhattan Expressway."*

"This nebbishy housewife never forgot you, Mr. Moses," she replied.

"And all the people in Little Italy, Chinatown, and the Lower East Side who have to deal with nonstop bumper-to-bumper traffic remember you!" he countered.

"That's enough of that!" said one of the judges, rapping his gavel.

This was the cross-examination stage of the trial—the big man was finally in the hot seat.

"Did you guys insert Old Man Moses into Staten island?" Uli asked his escort.

Patel smirked. "Believe me, we tried to stop him."

"*Do you think that these people, these victims of your handiwork, are just pretending to have had their homes swept out from under them?*" Jacobs resumed.

"*For starters, they weren't swept. They were usually given six months to a year's notice, and a fair compensation for their properties.*"

"*For meaningless projects that padded your pockets with cash and sucked millions away from vital services like hospitals and schools!*"

"*This is garbage from that book!*"

"*I take it you're referring to my* Death and Life of Great American Cities?" she replied.

"*No, that Robert Cargo kid!*"

"*We suffered for decades at your tyrannical hand, we don't need a book to prove it.*"

"*Look,*" Moses thundered as if suddenly awakened from his decrepitude, "*the value of my projects has proved indispensable to the robust recovery of New York City!*"

"*Robust recovery?*" said the chief judge.

"*New York is the most vibrant and powerful economic force in the world today!*"

"*In case you haven't heard,*" Jacobs responded, "*Manhattan was hit with a contamination bomb that rendered its financial centers useless.*"

"*In case you haven't heard, it was completely scrubbed clean and is already being repopulated. And it's starting to really thrive.*"

"This is what we were afraid of," Patel said. "He promised not to give any updates if he got caught."

There was a heavy pause.

"*Excuse me?*" said Jacobs.

"*New residents throughout America have been pouring back into the great city, and they're not like the freeloading nutcases who took up valuable space before. These people work! They buy property and pay taxes the way you were all supposed to. They're turning New York City into the gleaming city on the hill! New York isn't just recovering, it's coming back stronger than ever. And much of that has to do with the things that I put in place!*"

After another long pause, Uli checked to see if the radio was still on. Evidently, word of Old Town's renewal and repopulation had collectively knocked the wind out of everyone in the auditorium.

Patel burst out laughing. "On the other hand, this is the best radio show I've ever heard!"

"Is he telling the truth?" Uli asked.

"You're FBI, you tell me."

"Are *you* with the bureau?"

Patel didn't reply.

"If Moses is telling the truth," Uli said, "isn't it our duty to try to return these people to their city?"

"*Your Honor, I move to disqualify what Mr. Moses has just said,*" Moses's counsel spoke up. "*It hasn't been verified. And the defendant is clearly unreliable.*"

"*Unreliable?*"

"*I agree with the defense,*" Jacobs said. "*I'm inclined to believe this is the babbling of a ninety-two-year-old tyrant who is falsifying facts to aid in his abuses of power.*"

"*Let's take a recess,*" the chief judge announced.

To save the battery, Patel flipped the radio off. "I used to work in Lower Manhattan, near the courts," he reminisced. "Once a week, on Friday afternoons, I'd take a four-hour walk over the Manhattan Bridge, down Flatbush, left at Tillary past the Brooklyn Navy Yard, then over to Williamsburg via Bedford Avenue, past all the Hasids, then the Polish community, till it turned into Nassau, then into the industrial area near the two giant holding tanks on Maspeth, up Kingsland Avenue, and over that toxic swamp of the Newtown Creek on the John Jay Byrne Bridge into Queens—"

"That's some walk," Uli cut in.

"My heart would start beating when I reached the area around the

Calvary Cemetery," Patel resumed, "where I used to play as a kid, near the Long Island Expressway. With my Latino friends in Sunnyside, I'd sprint across all those lanes of Queens Boulevard—'cause that street is designed to kill you—and under that beautiful concrete aqueduct that holds the 7 train. I'd hike along the trestles up to Woodside, and by all the little shops, bars, and churches into Jackson Heights. I'd stroll even farther toward the crowded streets of Corona and north to the desolation of Shea Stadium and those garages around that canal of College Point, until I finally reached the elevated tracks of the 7 where it burrows into the earth and you come up this hill that seems to be empty, but suddenly you emerge and find yourself in Flushing . . ."

As Patel prattled on, Uli closed his eyes in the desert heat and found himself immersed in his own past.

After Dennis Banks and Russell Means, the two-headed snake of the American Indian Movement, split in different directions, all of the second-tier players emerged. Uli was assigned to follow a suspect, one of thousands he had surveilled over the years. Because of her love of the tropical fruit, several agents had nicknamed her Banana Anna. When he'd first broken out of the subterranean installation in the Nevada desert and began hallucinating, seeing a woman with long black hair, he'd thought she was a survivor of the Armenian genocide. But now that his memory was returning, he sensed it was Banana Anna whom he'd been trying to follow.

She was a short, slim woman with thick black hair whose clothing clearly paid homage to her Native tradition. Those colorful clothes always made her easy to pick out in a crowd.

Her real name was Anna Mae Aquash. When Uli first got her file, it was only a single page long. All they knew was that she was from Nova Scotia, Canada.

"Who gives a shit about this chick?" Uli had asked his supervisor at the time—Corey Spencer.

"Banana Anna—outlaw squaw," his supervisor kidded. "You should be happy. She just moved back to your old stomping grounds, Southern California—you'll winter in LA. Check in with your old office for any resources you need."

"What exactly am I supposed to do with her?" Uli asked.

"Get leverage."

Although this cute Native American woman was clearly low on

the AIM totem pole, she had managed to sleep her way into the inner circle and was the perfect candidate to flip.

When Uli discovered that she was staying at a friend's dive in the Silver Lake neighborhood of LA, he put a bug on the phone and was able to check Anna's incoming mail. Unfortunately, phone calls and letters revealed little. Along with two other agents, Uli spent weeks tailing her, learning everything they could about her. But other than the fact that she was what they called a *slunk*—a slut and a drunk— there wasn't much else.

All that changed one day, just a week before Christmas 1975. Anna had spent the afternoon hitting thrift stores—Goodwill and Salvation Army. Uli saw her buying clothes that were far too small for her and then several dolls. He realized she was purchasing things for children, even though she didn't have any.

That night she carefully wrapped the gifts, clearly intending to ship them in time for Santa. But the next night when she came home with a cheap bottle of wine, she stripped down to her bra and panties and guzzled, steadily losing motor control and growing more emotional, swaying to her stereo. Through his binocs, Uli saw her mumbling quietly, then cursing the air loudly. He realized she was crying.

Suddenly, she tore open the carefully wrapped packages, taking out the clothes she had just purchased, and pulled and bit into the seams of the fabric, ripping them into shreds, until she collapsed into a heap on the floor.

They had to be for her own children, Uli thought—no one else's kids could get someone that upset. Yet none of this was in the file.

Uli contacted the bureau and soon learned that she had indeed kept her kids a secret from everyone. Uli considered some way to use them as leverage—maybe by threatening to take them from her—but since they were already living apart, that wasn't feasible. He was able to sneak into her bedroom window one evening and go through her possessions, and he found several strips of pictures from photo booths. She was smiling with two girls, both around five or six years old.

Instead of notifying his team and asking for support, which he should have done, Uli began taking a greater interest in Anna, following her all by himself off the clock. One afternoon he nearly lost his target when she entered a hardware store and seemed to take forever. He started worrying that the place had a rear exit. He rushed inside, bumping smack into her. She paused before him, stared deep into his eyes, and out of the blue she smiled softly. He quickly turned toward the gardening section.

Uli spent the rest of the day paranoid that she knew he had been tailing her.

During his years in the bureau, he had surveilled countless subjects. Frequently, observing them increased Uli's desire to have them punished. He'd see what assholes they really were; their tiny crimes of omission and commission, nasty personalities trickling through in ugly, petty acts. All seven vices came alive in their daily routines. As he witnessed this, his sense of his own authority had risen and made him feel like an avenging angel for the good people of the United States of America.

Watching Anna, though, was different. He'd see her give money to beggars—only to find she didn't have enough change for the bus. She'd be eating a sandwich and would catch someone watching her and offer them half. He'd see her stop before a garden of wildflowers, just staring at their beauty. One time he saw her trying to comfort a scared German shepherd that was tied to a post and snarling. In disbelief he watched her pet it as it barked and snapped at her. Over time, he noticed how patient she was with strangers who were rude, or polite with guys who obviously wanted to fuck her. It was clear to him that she'd never really had a chance. Life had produced this perfect little sacrifice. The more he saw of her, the worse he felt, knowing that eventually he was going to have a hand in her destruction.

After downing a couple drinks one night, his woozy thoughts began to wander and he found himself fantasizing about her, though not sexually. He was daydreaming about saving her, sweeping her up, finding her kids, and providing a home for them.

What the fuck are you even thinking?! he caught himself.

17

"Hey, *ese!*" Patel called out, employing his fake Mexican accent. "Meeting's over. They're waiting for us."

"Who?"

"You'll see."

Uli expected Patel to lead him to a car, but instead they simply walked through a barren stretch along the weedy southwestern edge of Queens. He followed Patel to the narrow canal where a small, leaky rowboat awaited them. Uli got in front and his escort paddled over the polluted inlet to the neighboring borough about fifty feet away. This section of Brooklyn was a stretch of blackened, burned-out shells—remnants of one of the renegade Quirklyn communities.

For about twenty minutes Uli was led through narrow walkways between piles of burned wood and scorched bricks. The area had once been rows of single-family homes. Finally they came to the remains of a block-long edifice. Uli remembered that this singed structure was once the Quirklyn commune where Paul Moses had lived.

In the backyard, climbing through cracked and splintered pieces of charred wood and scorched concrete which had once made up the rear of the building, Patel brought him to the only structure left standing—a small cinder-block utility shed.

"Where the hell are we going?" Uli asked.

Patel silently opened the metal door of the shed. Inside there were a pair of rusty yet functional bikes. Patel took one, Uli grabbed the other, and they began pedaling.

Together they slowly maneuvered down the main corridor that seemed to unite all these cindered streets and burned buildings. They wove around the assorted ash heaps and carbon-crisp rubbish. The pavement was scorched white in spots, marking the intensity of the conflagration. After about forty minutes of carefully navigating through the incinerated war zone, they came to a single building that had somehow been left untouched by the inferno. When they pulled around to the front of the place, they found a group of solicars parked there. Patel stopped before a squad of nearly a dozen heavyset men who looked like bodyguards and drivers.

The lone building was none other than Aardvarkian's old diner—Little Armenia. The last time Uli had been here, the small yet popular restaurant had been packed with customers.

"He's waiting for you inside," Patel said to Uli before joining the large men guarding the perimeter.

The far end of the place opened into a large booth where a group of three well-dressed men sat, softly chatting. Uli immediately recognized one of them: Horace Shub, the former Pigger leader and last mayor of an undivided Rescue City. He was talking to a handsome younger guy in a wheelchair with his head propped up by a neck brace. This had to be Mayor Willy, Mallory's husband, who had briefly been the second elected mayor of the new city when it emerged from anarchy.

It took Uli another moment to identify the third man. When the guy turned, Uli saw it was none other than Scouter Lewis, whose face looked like it had been pruned down by gardening shears. The last time Uli remembered seeing him, the man had been badly tortured by Joe Gallo's people and was close to death. Now, despite all the mutilation, he seemed to be running the show. Uli watched him passionately explaining something to Shub as a bodyguard came and wheeled Willy toward the door where Uli stood.

"So you guys have decided to burn Rescue City down?" Uli asked the former Crapper mayor as he approached.

"Who the hell are you?" Willy spoke softly, unable to contract his diaphragm fully. Like Rafique, he too had survived an assassin's bullet.

"I'm a friend of your wife, but right now I'm concerned about the people here."

"As are we all," Willy replied.

"Then why do you want to torch the place?"

"Pal," the man said angrily, "a bullet severed my C-4, so I can't even wipe myself."

Uli nodded as the man was wheeled out. Glancing around, Uli realized that Shub, the other former mayor, had just scuttled out through the service entrance.

Scouter Lewis was now sitting at the table alone. A security guard placed a fresh teapot and two empty cups before him.

"It's the absentminded FBI agent," Lewis called out to Uli, who couldn't stop staring at his disfigured face. One of the man's eyes, both his ears, the skin along his scalp, and his lips were all gouged, amputated, or badly burned.

"I'm amazed you're still alive."

"Look, you're an active FBI agent. That, combined with the fact that you saved my life, is the only reason you're still alive."

"Did you guys steal the explosives from Staten Island?"

"I can probably get you out of here—"

"Why did you kill six guards?"

"It doesn't matter. It's all gone."

"What the fuck is going on?" Uli demanded.

"Let's see, a brief history of yet another well-intentioned government program gone awry," Lewis said as if reciting a prayer. "A Republican president tries to do a humane act for a Democratic city in distress. He locates the only place he can situate his NIMBY refugee camp in the most isolated part of the lower forty-eight. Then the private sector figures out how to turn it into their own cash register. One corporation, run by a psycho, underbids everyone else, gets insane concessions regarding security, and supplies the place. The military initially oversees, not anticipating the civil strife that follows. When casualties mount, they pull out and gangs rule, just like in prison. Within fifteen months, nearly a quarter of the population who we're supposed to protect either die from sanitary problems or are killed, 40 percent of the housing stock is burned down, and things keep getting worse.

"Finally, desperate for anything, we implement Operation Jackie Wilson, setting up a mock gang to run things from within. They block the drain, flood the Staten Island airstrip, and take over the new airfield in Queens. We eventually have some minor success and a two-party central government is established. The gang warfare doesn't quite end, but having killed off the most violent criminals with the other violent offenders, we're well past the worst of it. Then a knucklehead FBI agent arrives and gets his brain discombobulated by a power-hungry city council leader–NSA agent who is threatened by him and decides to turn him into an assassin. Next thing we know, the FBI agent unleashes a plague that we've managed to contain for years while searching for a remedy—"

Uli suddenly broke out into a coughing fit. Lewis used his four intact fingers to pick up the little porcelain pot sitting on the table between them and pour some tea into Uli's cup.

"No thanks."

"It's basically liquid vitamin C, makes your engine run a little faster. Keeps you a little hotter, so the virus can't lock in on you."

"I was vaccinated when I was in Staten Island."

"We all were, and we've already lost four agents who got the latest antidote. The epidemic hitting the city is a new strain, much more virulent than the old one."

"Things didn't look so bad in Staten Island."

"Queens is ground zero. Last week they had about 150 casualties. These were mainly people who initially responded to the crisis—the best and the brightest. This week that number is almost tripled and it's rippling out to second- and third-level care workers, which means their frail hospital and police services have been stripped away with no one to replace them."

"If it's mainly restricted to Queens, though—"

"Despite political differences, Brooklyn and Queens are Siamese twins, connected at the hip. Last I heard, they're not letting anyone in or out of Queens without a checkup."

"And you think burning the place down will solve the problem?"

"We're just taking Plato's plan and implementing it here. Instead of hidden stairways up to the desert, we have your water stations to civilization."

"People will die!"

"They *are* dying! We've done everything we can to slow down the inevitable. What do you suggest, Special Agent Sarkisian?"

"I thought Reagan was going to defund this place when he got reelected," Uli said.

"He might. But so far he hasn't said a word. The problem is that this is happening *right now.*"

"Have you notified—"

"Of course we have!" Lewis yelled furiously. "A stack of memos and status reports are teletyped every day. All begging for help. *There's no money in the budget. Do the best you can.* Always the response. Always."

Lewis took a deep breath to calm himself, refilled his teacup, and knocked it back in a single gulp as though it were some magic potion. It inspired Uli to do likewise. The hot liquid tasted like turpentine.

"And the Mkultra mess?"

"We told them when it first occurred—*as* it was occurring."

"And what'd they say?"

"What do you think they'd say? *We're not miracle workers. There's no more money, no more men. It hasn't leaked out to the press so blah blah blah* . . . What are they supposed to do?"

"They must've said more than that."

"Yeah." Lewis grimaced and refilled his teacup. "Feed and comfort as best as you can, which is always the answer. In fairness, over the years they tried. They sent different teams and meds and we'd hand them out. Hell, they probably sent numerous covert teams. Who knows! The right hand doesn't tell the left hand shit."

"What happened when you informed them about the plague reaching the city?" Uli pushed.

"Didn't you just hear the radio broadcast? Moses took credit for restoring New York, but it wasn't 'cause of his bullshit highways. It was because they moved all these fucking deadbeats out. Zero crime rate, uninhabited neighborhoods, a fresh slate."

"So you think that when you burn this place down, they're going to land planes and bring everyone back home?"

"That's the point—they're not bringing us back. Were you a student of history, you'd find that freedom is never given, it's always taken. We're *taking* our freedom!"

"How?"

"*You* showed us! Believe it or not, none of us knew about it. You screwed everything up, but you also gave us the answer."

It slowly dawned on Uli: "The water stations?"

"Which is another reason why you're here right now. I need to know whatever you can tell me about them."

"I've only seen two. They seem to be reserves of water, submerged, I'm guessing, in a concrete drum with a hand pump on top. But there's no way they'll have enough water for thousands and thousands of people."

"You don't know that. We heard reports, solid reports, that there is an underground river that they had tapped into as a water source."

"*Tapped into?* What does that mean?"

"We're about to send a contingent out to hike the distance, aren't we, Patel?"

Uli's escort, who had quietly entered and was listening by the door, said, "We've already staked signs all along the eastern edge of the city."

"We'll find out how much water is there and how far it is to civilization."

"You plan to wheel out there yourself?" Uli asked.

"Patel is a lean, mean walking machine," Lewis said. "He's volunteered."

"You know, Plato felt that walking south from Staten Island was the best route—trying to make it to Las Vegas."

"We don't need *all* these people to walk. We just need enough of them to convince the feds that we do, then they'll have to rescue the rest. But the only way to get people to evacuate the place is by burning it down."

Uli considered Lewis's plan for a moment. "The only way you can burn the entire city down without a lot of gasoline is if you start it during a windstorm."

"We have one more thing to talk about," Lewis said, sharply changing the subject, "and that's your beloved sister Karen."

"What about her?"

"Do you remember the Weather Bureau bombing in Greenwich Village?"

"You mean that brownstone on 11th Street?"

"As you know, Karen was a member of the Weather Bureau."

"So what?"

"They were unable to prove it, but the two events—the brownstone explosion and the Manhattan dirty bomb attack—were linked. Long story short—she triggered it."

"That's insane."

"She didn't know. See, it took several insane cooks to make a cocktail this fucked up—a jealous, brilliant brother, a megalomaniacal FBI chief who was desperately trying to find a way for his estranged president to return him to his days of former glory, and an ambitious young lackey who followed Hoover's crazy orders instead of simply calling the NYPD and ending it immediately. For this awful act, those who aren't dead are condemned to this place. It makes complete sense that we now have Robert Moses—who called in every favor to get his sad senile ass out here, only to be put on trial."

"You're not going to touch my sister," Uli said.

"No, not again," Lewis replied. "See, I was the one who shoved her down that broken sewer pipe in the first place. Believe me, I didn't want to. It took all my strength to do it, yet somehow she returned like Persephone. I don't know who is marked to kill her again, but I'm not doing it."

"*You* did that?"

"I did, but it wasn't easy. I honestly love Karen."

"Then why?"

"Among other reasons, I knew if I didn't do it, they'd send some-one else."

"Then why didn't you just kill her? A bullet to the head!" Uli shouted. "Why'd you drop her into that . . . hell?" He jumped to his feet to find that Lewis was already training a cocked pistol on him.

"Hear me out. What's done is done. Your sister survived, but I want you to understand that there are forces bigger than me who know what I know, and they're not going to let her live. Things have already been put in motion, you see?"

Inexplicably, Lewis set his service revolver on the table and slid it over to Uli, who grabbed it and pointed it at him.

Lewis slowly said, "Walk to Sutphin, catch the Q28 to Fulton—"

"To Dropt's office," Uli remembered. "That's right, then change to the B17 and take it to Dropt's office in the East Villag██████████

███

███

███████████████████████████████

Uli realized *he* was the one saying Lewis's words—it was the chant from when he'd first arrived in Rescue City—but the gun was missing. Uli struggled to his feet with a powerful headache.

"You passed out," Lewis said. Without another word, he pulled a black beanie out of his breast pocket and tossed it over his scalp, concealing some of his injuries. Then he promptly exited with one of his men.

Weak and dizzy, Uli sat there until the throbbing in his skull di-minished. He eventually rose to his feet and staggered outside to find that not only were Lewis and Patel gone, but so were the two bikes.

Without any form of transportation, Uli started hiking south through the scorched streets, down the natural ridge and deeper into the north end of Brooklyn. Although it was late afternoon and some distant cars sped by, there was not a single pedestrian in sight.

Banana Anna's Canadian past meant that no one in the American In-dian Movement had known her prior to her joining the group. It also meant that she had no one to watch her back—no friends or family to come to her aid. Her drinking problem made her unreliable. Her opportunistic promiscuity earned the ire of other women and the frus-tration of some of the men in her little tribe.

The countless hours of wiretaps, the days and weeks of surveillance, confirmed what Uli already knew. She was gullible, pliable, a perfect piece of bait. A simple plan was devised by Uli's superiors: Deposit five hundred bucks into her bank account, just enough to pique the organization's interest. Then one of the agents would be given a crumpled copy of her monthly bank statement. He would turn it over to the tribe's newly assigned security officer, who happened to be clinically paranoid. He in turn would check her bank account and—bingo! No one had that kind of dough unless they were on the bureau's payroll. She'd be chum in the shark tank. After Doug Durham's betrayal, they'd tear her to shreds. The bureau would swoop in, rescue Banana Anna, and start making arrests.

Uli spoke to his supervisor, Corey Spencer, and explained that he felt the plan was a bit rash.

"Rash? How?"

"Suppose they kill her?"

"Doug Durham was head of their security and they didn't touch him. Anna's just a low-level squaw."

"It's too risky."

"Uli, please don't go soft on me now."

"I'm not. I just have a better idea."

"What?"

"Flip her! We put the money in her account, show *her* the statement, and tell her we're going to turn her in if she doesn't cooperate."

"Cooperate how? She doesn't know shit."

"She's slept with a number of them," Uli argued. "She must know *something*. Let's just try."

"She'll tell us to fuck off or she'll run."

"Run where? She's got no one and nothing. Trust me, I've done this before—I did it with one of the SDSers in Berkeley—Anthony DeSandro."

"I'll consider it . . ." Spencer replied.

18

During the long walk through burned and barren Williamsburg and then south to Fort Greene, Uli thought about Lewis's argument and Robert Moses's revelation. If Old Town truly had all its radioactive fallout scrubbed away, it was imperative to return its rightful residents as soon as possible.

When Uli finally reached Jackie Wilson Way, occasional pedestrians started appearing again. Most had kerchiefs tied over their faces and tucked down into their shirt collars—plague chic. Their hands were thrust deeply in their pockets, and their eyes were planted at their feet. Others were wearing heavy coats with hoods, odd for a hot day.

Tiredly looking behind him as he walked down Fulton Street, Uli couldn't spot a single minibus. He tried flagging down a car, since many doubled as cabs, but no one slowed down. He was intending to return to Staten Island to report on poor Loveworks's demise and his own dismal findings. But what was the point? What could he do?

Since the Williamsburgh Savings Bank Building was not far off, he decided to pop in and see if he could glean any news about his sister. If he found her, they could get a jump on the stampede that was sure to follow when the conflagration broke. Together they could fill knapsacks with canned foods and camping gear, and get in front of the impending disaster.

As he approached the entrance to the Williamsburgh Building, he noticed a giant hand-scrawled sign that read, *CLOSED! FUK OFF OR GET SHOT!* When he rattled the locked door, a guard he didn't recognize pointed a rifle at him.

"I'm trying to locate my sister Karen Sarkisian," Uli called out to him.

"Ain't here! Read the sign! We're fucking closed!" the man shouted.

"Where is everyone?"

"We're in the middle of an epidemic! Everyone has evacuated to

Manhattan!" The guard never took his finger off the trigger, so Uli walked away.

Downtown Brooklyn, usually packed with shoppers, was now virtually empty. Almost every business Uli passed was gated or shuttered. Looking into one bodega, he could see canned and boxed food lining the shelves. He was about to toss a cinder block into the plate glass window of a large stamp shop when he spotted a cuchifritos place with the door ajar. The proprietor had abandoned the restaurant in such haste that half-eaten meals had been left on the worn Formica counter. Uli went behind the counter and flipped open the tops of several cold steamer trays: rice, plantains, chicken, baccala—all crusty, but not moldy, maybe a couple of days old at most.

Uli carefully salvaged the most edible items onto a single plate and started eating. The general isolation gave him the creeps, and he wolfed down the food as quickly as he could. When he started hiccuping, he located a warm bottle of Mexican soda and chugged it down. Then he put his empty plate into the big sink and left.

Jay Street was strewn with abandoned merchandise along the sidewalk: endless articles of clothing in boxes. Cheaply made coats, ugly dresses, and tacky suits still on their hangers were swaying in the breeze on wheeled racks. Ubiquitous blue bins of cheap knockoffs blocked the sidewalk. As Uli walked through it all, he searched for a single handheld transistor radio, in hopes of hearing any official news of the plague, or at least catching an update on the Robert Moses trial. Along the ground he saw toaster ovens, blenders, fans, portable record players, and TVs, but no radios.

Out of the corner of his eye, Uli spotted movement. A middle-aged woman with overly teased hair was lying on the ground, still alive. As he approached, he saw that she was dripping with sweat, trying to crawl around on all fours.

"Need help?" he asked, reluctant to touch her.

"Please! A . . . stunning . . . pair . . . rose petal–colored . . . heels . . . saw here . . . yesterday . . . just my size." She spoke just above a whisper.

As he backed away from the plague-addled woman, Uli couldn't help but wonder if the endless flow of chintzy remainders sold over here had any role in shaping the nonmaterialistic counterculture down in Staten Island. Most of the Burnt Men who lived down there prided themselves on rejecting the subsidies—not just the luxury items, but also the necessities of food and medicine. Instead they sustained

themselves exclusively off the local fare. They had melded the homeless urban lifestyle with Native American survivalism, carefully culti-
vating their own homegrown vegetables, hunting and domesticating
the indigenous prairie livestock. So many lively and free spirits, who
back in Old Town would've eventually succumbed to poverty and possibly homelessness, had carved a unique yet self-respecting niche for
themselves in this odd hybrid society.

Uli kept looking up Fulton Street hoping for a minibus southwest
to the Zano, but nothing came. Every few minutes he glimpsed a solicar darting off in the distance. When he got closer to the Brooklyn
Bridge, he came across another person lying on the ground—an older
aproned shopkeeper who appeared to have collapsed, apparently in
front of his own store. He was clenching an old baseball bat, presumably protecting his establishment to the bitter end.

Uli spotted two more survivors turning the corner a couple blocks
ahead, struggling onward. A short, lean fellow was laboring against
a tall, rickety guy. As Uli approached from behind, he saw that the
shorter one was actually a female. She was toiling to support her taller
companion, an older fellow with a gray ponytail. She finally leaned
him up against a signpost.

"I can't go no further," said the lanky man, unable to catch his
breath.

His cute human crutch looked to be around forty years old, dark-
skinned, maybe Latina. Only up close could Uli see that she wore a
pair of latex gloves and a face mask, so presumably the man was sick.
As Uli came up behind, he could see that the guy was wearing worn
jeans, an old, creased ten-gallon hat, and cowboy boots.

"Need help?" Uli asked.

"Yes!" the woman groaned. But when she turned to thank him, she
tensed up.

"Does your friend have the plague?"

"No way! It's just a little emphysema, I swear!"

"Don't ever smoke," the cowboy coughed out.

"Then why are you wearing a mask and gloves?" Uli asked the
woman.

"Just precautions, I swear."

Uli went to the other side of the old-timer, pulled the man's limp
arm over his own shoulder, and, grabbing his hip, got him moving again.

"Obliged," the man rasped. Covered in sweat, he was clearly
feverish.

Together with the woman, Uli helped walk the man several blocks before he spotted a wheelbarrow filled with sand. Uli dumped out the sand, and he and the woman carefully deposited the cowboy into the bucket.

As Uli wheeled the man along, he became aware that the woman walking ahead of them wasn't making any eye contact.

"Do I know you from somewhere?" he asked, trying to discern what her face looked like through her loose-fitting mask.

"Nope," she muttered, still staring straight ahead.

"Hey! You're going to have to push this for a couple blocks," Uli finally said, as she was pulling farther ahead. He dropped the wheelbarrow and the man inside let out a groan. "Sorry, but my arms are killing me."

The woman froze for a long moment before turning around and grabbing the handles. With her head down, she began pushing the wheelbarrow.

"So what's your name?" Uli asked.

"Annie," she said. "Short for Annette."

"Annette, where exactly are you from?"

"New York, along with just about everyone else."

"Were you ever in LA?"

"Sure, who wasn't?"

"Before I came here, I used to be with the FBI," Uli said, and with that she began walking faster. "On the few occasions when I've been recognized, it hasn't always been pleasant."

"I won't tell anyone who you are," she responded nervously as she pushed.

"May I ask who your friend is?"

"Stan."

"Is he Native American?"

"I don't know."

"What about you?"

"Puerto Rican," she answered quickly.

"What's your last name?"

"Rodriguez, Annette Rodriguez."

After another minute of sparse conversation, they began hearing honks and other car sounds. Turning a corner, they saw solicars lined bumper to bumper up the entrance ramp of the Brooklyn Bridge. Everyone was trying to escape the pestilence that had gripped the borough.

Before they could reach the pedestrian walkway, Annette dropped the wheelbarrow, exhausted, and wiped her brow. Up ahead on the bridge, Uli could see foot traffic heading toward Manhattan.

"I'll push it till we get to the top," Uli said, "but once it starts going downhill, you take over."

She nodded, still trying to catch her breath. Uli lifted the wooden handles.

Before they could reach the middle of the bridge, however, the pedestrians started merging into a single line. After a minute the line tightened up and then stopped on the walkway. There had to be at least a hundred people in front of them, most wearing improvised face masks, just waiting to move.

"They're doing checkups in Manhattan," explained a woman immediately ahead who appeared to have a pincushion taped over her mouth.

Not forgetting that he was persona non grata here, and nervous about being detained again, Uli abruptly bid farewell to Stan and Annette.

"Where are you going?" she asked.

"The walkway is pretty much downhill from here," he said for her benefit. "I'm taking my chances back in Brooklyn."

He considered an alternate route to Staten Island where he

wouldn't be stopped. If the Brooklyn Bridge traffic was being checked, the Zano Bridge security would likely be more thorough since it was run by a different government. Passing others coming onto the bridge, he thought, *If I can hitch a ride out to Pure-ile Plurality, I might be able to grab a jug of water and head out into the desert, then spend a day hiking around the river like Bea did.*

As he moved back down Jackie Wilson Way, he glanced back. An older man behind him wearing a face mask and surgical gloves was calmly stepping off the bridge's walkway—a lone commuter from Manhattan.

"Excuse me," Uli intercepted him, "I forgot my wallet, so I'm just wondering if they're checking IDs on the other side."

"No, just taking temperatures," the man said. "'Cause of the plague."

Uli thanked him. By the time he walked back up the bridge and got back on the line, it had grown longer. Annette and the older man had moved ahead and were out of sight. He was now standing behind a guy who looked familiar. Because the line wasn't moving at all at this point, Uli sat down, leaned against the rail, closed his eyes, and quickly dozed off.

When Uli opened his eyes some time later, the line still hadn't moved and the guy in front of him looked even more familiar. He resembled a fellow agent Uli had once worked with—Larry McIntyre. But McIntyre was taller, leaner, and younger. McIntyre was the one who had first told him about the hands.

"What hands?" Uli asked.

"You know, her severed hands."

"*Whose* severed hands?"

"That girl you were assigned to back in LA."

"Oh my God!" He envisioned blood spurting out of Anna Mae Aquash's wrists.

"No, she was dead when they did it," explained McIntyre. "No pain. They just needed her fingerprints, so they could ID her. That's why they sawed them off—to freeze them and send them to Washington."

"Who did this?"

"The sheriff's office in South Dakota."

"They fucking killed her? Spencer told me he wouldn't—"

"No, they found her body on the Pine Ridge reservation a few days ago. Said she died of exposure."

That was how he heard of poor Banana Anna's death.

Although he suspected foul play, this death also made sense: the excessive drinking and crazy behavior. She had probably gotten drunk after a party, then went out into the subzero temperature, passed out, and just froze to death. The thought that she might have died peacefully in her sleep offered Uli some sad relief.

But then a few days later he heard that the medical examiner had found a small hole in her skull and dug a .32-caliber bullet from her frontal lobe. She'd been executed after all.

In that moment, Uli found himself gasping for air and had to sit down. Spencer had lied to him, making Uli an accomplice in Anna's death. *Who's kidding who?* he thought. *They planned this all along.*

They had tricked AIMers into acting as their own executioners. In addition to finally having something to investigate and hopefully someone to arrest, the FBI had gotten a little payback for the vicious murders of their own.

19

Three-quarters of the way over the narrow bridge, Uli looked down and saw that the Manhattan street below had been converted into an outdoor inspection site. He still didn't see the Puerto Rican woman or the sick cowboy.

Among a group of large men were two Crapper health inspectors with face masks, surgical gloves, and official red brassards wrapped around their broad shoulders, holding buckets of sterilized thermometers. They counted out twenty-five people from the line on the bridge and marched them down to the street. The two inspectors then worked their way down the queue, putting fresh thermometers in each person's mouth.

"Do not touch your thermometer! Any attempt to remove it will result in immediate quarantine!" one officer with a bullhorn kept repeating. A few minutes later, the inspectors walked to the front of the new line with a gaggle of guards behind them. One by one they plucked and checked the thermometers. Eventually five people—one-fifth of those tested—were pulled by the guards, cuffed, and escorted to a guarded minibus. The remainder were allowed to pass.

Ten minutes later a second group of twenty-five was marched off and inspected. In this fashion, Uli slowly moved closer to Manhattan.

When Uli's group was finally led forward, he recognized one of the health inspectors—the man was built like a Samoan wrestler and wore a white frock. Nearly bursting out of his undersized surgical gloves, the gigantic officer jabbed a thermometer into Uli's mouth.

A second health inspector appeared and plucked the thermometer out of the first inspectee's mouth. He checked the tiny red line in the tube and comically called out, "Prooo-ceed!" The inspectee walked into Manhattan free and clear. The inspector then checked and cleared the second person, an elderly woman.

Upon reading the thermometer of the third man, the official wordlessly glanced at one of the guards, who quickly grabbed the Brooklyn immigrant by his elbows and cuffed him.

"Wait a sec, I'm as strong as a horse!"

"Nay!" the gangcop said as he steered the man into the quarantined minibus.

A few minutes later, the health inspector finally reached Uli. Snatching the thermometer from Uli's mouth, he looked at it a bit longer than the others, then twisted his lips. Two beefy hands yanked Uli's elbows behind his back.

"Hey! I'm fine."

"You're half a degree higher than fine."

Uli's wrists were tightly cuffed together.

"That's only 'cause I just hiked a couple miles in the sun," he reasoned.

"Calm down," said the thuggish official who was pinning his arms back, "you're probably right. We're just going to have the doctors check you out. They'll let you go."

As he was walked into the minibus, Uli remembered that at Lewis's behest, he had drunk several cups of vitamin C tea. *The prune-faced son of a bitch had to have been aware of the health inspections,* he thought. "The bastard set me up," Uli muttered to himself.

The minibus was nearly packed with other health risks, some of whom were clearly sick. Uli heard a couple behind him coughing nonstop, human petri dishes. As he sat and waited, he could almost see the airborne bacteria, microscopic flying crabs, circulating in the tight space of the vehicle. He tried to inhale downward, away from the others, which he knew was absurd. After a few minutes, he felt a slight vertigo and wondered if he might actually be sick. Ten minutes later, when a few more "above-averagers" filled the remaining seats, the bus started up and all were driven back over the bridge.

As the bus streamed through the barren streets of Downtown Brooklyn, up Jackie Wilson Way, and past the Williamsburgh Building, Uli wondered which hospital they were going to. He was surprised when they finally pulled through the gates of the large chain-link fence that sectioned off the southern end of the sandy field of Prospect Park.

"Last time I was brought here, this was the jail," mumbled the pale guy sitting next to him.

As everyone filed out, they had their plastic cuffs snipped off and were led to a large tent. All the officials had face masks and gloves. To Uli's dismay, everyone was having their mug shots and fingerprints taken—they were also asked to show ID. Most, including Uli, didn't have any documents on them. He feared having his pupils scanned, but soon realized that there were too many people for this lengthy procedure. Uli waited in a line for five minutes before he found himself standing in front of a young man seated before a TV tray. The processor had a new file with Uli's brand-new mug shot glued to the top.

"Name and address?"

Since he wasn't actually wanted, only unwelcome, Uli gave his true name and added that he currently resided in Staten Island.

The man did a quick inspection of his limbs, fingers, and toes—presumably to check his criminal history. Finding him fully intact, he instructed Uli to join the others.

Uli saw that everyone had assembled around a stepladder which had a bullhorn resting on the top. After most of the people had been processed, an older woman in high heels and a laboratory coat carefully climbed up the five steps of the ladder, picked up the bullhorn, and spoke: "Welcome to the Prospect Park quarantine facility. You are not a prisoner, but our honored guest. And in case you haven't figured it out, you were brought here either because you displayed some secondary symptoms, or more likely because your temperature was slightly above normal. If you were genuinely found to be sick, you would've been sent to a hospital. Still, as you all know, we are currently experiencing an epidemic, and one of the key symptoms is fever. Though you're probably not really sick, we can't afford to take any chances, can we? What will happen here is quite simple. You'll be allowed to make a call to a loved one to tell them you're okay. We'll assign you a bed, and you'll be our guest for the next forty-eight hours, at which point you will again have your temperatures taken and be reexamined. If you test normal or show no further symptoms, you'll be released. If you are sicker, you will be treated. Either way, it's a win-win. To get through this process quickly and peacefully, we ask you to follow the instructions of our personnel, but under no circumstances should you touch them or anyone else, as doing so will be regarded as a threat and be treated as such."

A group of six gangcops wearing lab coats, masks, and rubber gloves appeared. The one who seemed to be the supervisor announced, "Please get into a formation of four equal columns and follow us out to tent number 12."

Some of the quarantined "guests" shouted out questions:

"Didn't the lady say we could notify our family members?"

"Could we possibly be allowed out to get our overnight things and come right back?"

"Can you take my temperature again—immediately?"

When they reached their designated tent, the older woman in the lab coat called out, "Everyone will be allowed their single phone call, but nothing will come in or out of the quarantine zone. You'll only be here for forty-eight hours. And we're doing our best to be accommodating, so please help us. This is a serious health crisis and we have to treat it as such."

Forty-eight hours sounded like a lifetime.

Each of the new arrivals was issued a number that showed the order in which he or she could use the single phone. They were instructed on how to hold the phone with one tissue and talk into the mouthpiece through a second tissue. All calls were automatically disconnected after five minutes. After waiting for a full forty-five minutes, when it was finally his turn, Uli called the Williamsburgh Building. When the operator answered, he asked for Karen Sarkisian.

"Sorry, but Captain Sarkisian has disappeared and is presumed dead."

Before Uli could respond, the woman hung up. Although he was technically only allowed one call, Uli was able to dial the switchboard operator at the Staten Island terminal, hoping to reach Bea. Unfortunately, the VL line just kept ringing until finally his time expired and the phone went dead. As Uli returned to his designated tent, he heard a strange monologue over the bullhorn. It turned out that the Robert Moses trial was still being broadcast live. At one point Uli swore he heard Bea's voice in the background.

"What'd that woman just say?" Uli asked a healthy-looking man.

"The defense just went through this whole list of areas that were previously neglected, or used as dump sites or storage facilities in New York City, until Moses turned them into public parks."

"What examples did they give?"

"They focused on one in each borough: Orchard Beach in the Bronx, Mid-Park in Queens, the Lower East Side Park in Manhattan, and Windy Point in Brooklyn."

"Windy Point?" Uli remembered how Lewis had implied that they might ignite the conflagration when a windstorm hit. He saw a ginger-haired health attendant passing by and asked him if he had heard any recent weather reports.

"Blue skies for the next week," the young man replied cheerfully.

Uli headed to his tent and walked through the line of cots looking for his assigned bed. He discovered that across the center aisle was the women's section. That was when he spotted Annette, the woman he had helped in Downtown Brooklyn. She was eating a banana and reading an *Archie* comic book, and she wasn't wearing her face mask.

"I knew I recognized you! You sold me a banana the first day I arrived here."

"You got me! I sell bananas," Annette said. "And they got you too."

"My temperature was half a degree higher than normal. How about you?"

"I was fine, but Stan had the fever after all. So they sent him to the hospital and tossed me in quarantine."

"You recognized me that first day, didn't you?" he said.

"Recognized you?"

"Come on, don't screw with me. You knew who I was even before I did," he said emphatically.

"I saw you at the courthouse, okay?" she finally came clean.

"Which courthouse?"

"The trial of the Catonsville 6," she replied.

"You mean 9. They were the Catonsville 9," Uli corrected.

Annette merely opened her comic book and resumed reading.

It had been the Berrigan trial. Two brothers, both Roman Catholic priests, had been unwittingly recruited by Russian agents who prompted them to steal hundreds of files from the local draft office and burn them. Much like the AIM trial, the liberal judge found problems with the case and the charges were dropped. But that trial was pivotal for the FBI in that it led to the official end of the counterintelligence program.

Uli slept sound as a baby for three hours. When he awoke, he felt slightly congested and his throat was a little sore. But once he took a hot, wonderful shower, his first in a long while, he was fine. He learned that a late dinner was being served out on the big, dried-out lawn: barbecued chicken necks and oversteamed rice with equally overcooked vegetables, exactly like the mushy, tasteless food they served at Pure-ile Plurality.

"Does Rolland Siftwelt cater here?" he asked the ginger-haired attendant.

"Since hospital services are overwhelmed, we've agreed to assist with the quarantine," the man replied. He added that they had sent groups all over Rescue City to aid in the recovery from the epidemic.

Uli inspected the staff, but didn't recognize any of them from his stint at PP. When he returned to his tent, he noticed that the cot near him that Annette had occupied was now empty. By her mildly grouchy nature, he assumed that she'd simply wanted to get away from the FBI agent. He nonetheless asked the attendant if he knew where she was.

"Annette came down with a fever today," the youth replied dolefully. "She was moved to long-term care."

Uli thought that she had seemed fine.

The next morning, the affable redheaded attendant gently woke Uli to tell him that breakfast was being served.

"I'll be up in a moment," he replied groggily, as though hungover. His throat was parched and his sinuses felt cemented shut. Snapping his eyelids closed, he descended backward into a bottomless sleep.

When he awoke shivering, it was nearly noon. His blanket had fallen to the floor. When he picked it up, he realized he was soaked in cold sweat. Feeling nauseous and weak, he closed his eyes.

Two small frozen hands were sliced clean at the wrists as though by a buzz saw. They were sitting on a bright marble slab—somehow he knew that the hands belonged to poor Anna.

Uli had never actually seen these hands so he knew he had to be dreaming. He must've been on a leave of absence when they discovered her body. It had to have been a few months, or maybe even a few years, after the AIM case when things began to sour.

He kept losing his temper over nothing: Blowing up at some kid taking too long at the gas pump. Telling off a barmaid 'cause she screwed up his drink order. Threatening to arrest a checkout clerk at a convenience store for letting someone cut the line. Pulling out his gun at a traffic light when a car tailgated him. All these situations that he would've brushed off in the past now overwhelmed him. Soon he didn't even need an excuse. He'd wake up in the morning absolutely furious. The opportunity to blow some asshole away seemed to outweigh a lifetime sentence in prison. One day he awoke with the acute sense that he had been duped, utterly conned into doing ugly, awful things he never would've or should've done.

He soon found himself obsessing over Anna Mae. She had been a sweet yet troubled kid, and instead of cutting her some slack as he should have, he'd tossed her to the wolves. Was that why he had joined the FBI? Her little girls had been orphaned because of him. All for what? No charges had been brought against anyone for her murder.

Out of the blue one night, he called his old supervisor Corey Spencer at home and cursed at him drunkenly.

A three-day weekend was approaching. Uli decided to take it easy and just use the time to unwind and watch a football game. But it wasn't working. His brain felt like a buzz saw cutting everything in two and he couldn't shut it off. Everything just pissed him off all the more. On Monday morning, he awoke with the image of his sister's face stamped in his skull.

They had never gotten along. She was always a bitch, always stood up to him. But he had a begrudging respect for her principles and an obligatory love for her. When the Greenwich Village brownstone bombing occurred, she went from being a person of interest to more like a fugitive; she had been seen fleeing the scene.

For the first few years after she left, when Uli thought about Karen trapped in that ghetto in the desert, he'd smirk and think to himself that if being stuck in that hellhole didn't change her liberal politics, nothing would. The world was no longer a place for idealists. There were just too many morons multiplying like roaches.

After taking casualties, the army pulled out and supposedly decided to let the inmates run the asylum. They also initiated a program to employ the first generation of pilotless planes to load in supplies. "Flying vending machines," the generals called them.

Soon after, when Ronald Reagan got elected and they essentially turned the whole place into a detention center, Uli stopped smirking at the thought of Karen—she had officially suffered long enough. America was growing visibly more conformist, turning sharply to the right—as if the past ten years of progressive liberalism had never even occurred. Uli wondered how he could've allowed his kid sister to vanish down America's "homegrown Vietnam."

Around then, he found himself unable to sleep and began drinking more and more. Soon he found himself breathing into paper bags to control his panic attacks. During a physical exam, his doctor asked him casual questions and before it was over he confirmed that Uli's main problem was stress at his workplace.

"Is there something you can give me to hold me together for another year or so?" Uli asked. "Then I might be able to put in for a three-quarters pension." Psychological problems were a kiss of death in the bureau.

"Look," said the doctor, "I can refer you to a good psychiatrist who—"

"Fuck it," Uli cut him off, pissed, and started putting all his clothes back on.

"You do have a small ulcer. I can swing you a leave of absence for a week or so."

"That's better than nothing."

Instead of seeking further help, Uli launched into a seven-day drinking binge. During this time, he would carry on imaginary conversations, mainly with Anna Mae and sometimes his sister Karen.

The night before he was supposed to return to work, his doorbell rang. When Uli answered, thoroughly inebriated and wearing only his stained boxers, his new supervisor, Marty Harris, entered. Uli's house was a wreck.

Harris squeezed down next to a pile of unlaundered clothes on the living room sofa. "What's wrong, Uli?" he asked.

Uli rambled incoherently, crying and laughing about his poor kid sister who was probably dead in Rescue City and how it was all his fault.

When Uli woke up the next morning, he remembered everything and was terrified about losing his job and pension. He shaved, showered, and went straight to Harris's office to apologize.

"Uli, that was some pretty crazy shit you said last night."

"I'm sorry, Marty, I guess maybe it's time to pack it in."

"I want to help you, but . . ." He trailed off.

"I can file for a partial pension in six months, but I don't see how I can hold on."

"Listen, I might have something for you."

"I can't go back to Washington," Uli asserted fearfully.

"Go home. Take it easy, lay off the booze. Let me make some calls. We'll meet for breakfast tomorrow—I might have a solution."

When Uli got home, hard as he tried to resist, he downed a few shots of Scotch and sat in front of the TV thinking about how he desperately wanted to be living a different life.

The next day he met Harris at a local diner and immediately ordered a cup of coffee, which he didn't touch.

"Let me begin by saying I made some inquiries," Harris began, "and please don't ask me how I know this, but your sister isn't dead, okay? In fact, she's alive and well."

"Anna Mae?" Uli asked, bewildered.

"No, your sister. You went on and on about her when I visited you. You were intoxicated."

"Oh," Uli said, unable to make eye contact.

"By the way, we didn't even realize she was in there—so thanks for that."

Fuck! Uli thought, realizing that not only had he blown her cover, but he had made himself an accomplice.

"Don't sweat it," Harris said, reading his thoughts. "She didn't even change her name. In fact, we've dropped charges against her, probably 'cause we would've just sent her there anyway. Ironically, according to our reports she's a fairly high-ranking official in Rescue City. She could help us."

"Really?" Uli replied, though he wasn't actually surprised. Karen had always been driven and ambitious.

"There is a short-term assignment that you might be qualified to handle, but you'd probably have to work with her. Can you do that? Or is

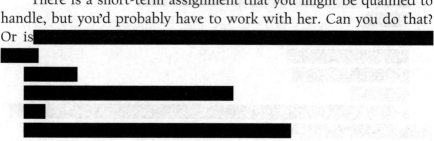

20

Uli glanced around at his strange surroundings and found it difficult to talk, much less focus. Some odd-looking attendant helped
him to his feet. After voiding bladder and bowels into a bedpan, then
slurping down a salty cup of hot liquid, he was sponged down and
rolled back onto his hard cot. He immediately sank back down into a
deep, quicksand-like sleep, utterly submerged.

Eventually, bubbling slowly back up to the surface, he opened his
eyes as the attendant was changing the IV bag dangling over him. He
had a drip in his arm and he saw a tube coming out of his midsection.
While under, he had been catheterized.

"Why the hell hasn't his bag been emptied?" a supervisor was
chastising the attendant.

Uli's eyes took a minute to adjust before he recognized through
her face mask that the tall black woman talking to his male attendant
was Marsha Johnson, his old supervisor from PP. He was being lifted
and moved.

"Uli, how are you feeling?" she asked, seeing him blinking up at
her.

"I was told that I'd be released in forty-eight hours," he said.

"You were in a coma for the last three days," Marsha replied
matter-of-factly. "A big storm's coming, so we're moving you to safer
ground."

"Oh God! They're going to burn the place down!"

"The only thing burning up here is you, with a fever," she assured
him. Uli wondered if she was right. Was it all a dream?

"My sister works for Mallory in the Williamsburgh Building. She's
a captain with the council cops." Karen was the only person he could
trust.

"Pure-ile Plurality really doesn't approve of us dealing with Crapper political officials," Marsha said softly.

"How about Bea? Call her!"

"Bea who?"

"You remember Valerie? Valerie Solanas? Her real name is Bea Moses-Mayer."

Marsha froze and looked nervously away, blushing.

"Please call her! She's a friend. Tell her I'm here, please!"

Marsha let out a deep sigh, clearly uncomfortable with the thought of tracking down her ex-lover. Closing her eyes, she whispered to Uli, "I'll try calling your sister, okay?"

"At the Williamsburgh Building!" Simply transmitting this information had utterly wiped him out. Before Marsha could leave the room, Uli muttered, "She's not dead. She's not!"

He then shut his eyes and his memories began cycling.

Two weeks before he was supposed to report for his new assignment in Rescue City, Uli was summoned back to South Dakota for bureaucratic rigmarole. While there, he bumped into one of the younger agents, Connor O'Riley, who had just been assigned to the team that was investigating the Aquash murder.

"Corey Spencer set her up," Uli confided in him.

"We all know you've been having problems, so I'll pretend you didn't say that."

"You're right, actually—we knew what we were doing."

"What are you saying, Uli?"

"She is as close as I've ever come to killing anyone without pulling a trigger," Uli blurted out.

"Hey, none of us wanted or expected this," the young agent replied, walking to his cubicle. "I mean, AIM isn't the mob. But neither are we."

"So her body was returned to the family?" Uli asked, trailing after him.

"Yeah, awhile ago."

"Who ID'd it?"

"Well, she didn't really have any next of kin, or at least none that would step forward, so I think they did it against her prints. She had some priors."

"Who got the body?"

"She had friends in AIM."

"Is that her case?" Uli asked, gesturing toward a hefty file on O'Riley's desk.

"Yeah, why?"

"Can I look at it?"

"Do you think we're botching the investigation?"

"Course not, I just have a particular interest in this case."

"What particular interest?" the young agent asked.

"I cared for her!" Uli responded angrily.

Without giving verbal consent, Connor silently stepped outside for a smoke.

Uli flipped through the file that contained, among other things, the sheriff's report, witness reports, the photos of the crime scene, and so on. Everything looked in order until he came to an addendum from the bureau coroner who had received the severed hands for the purpose of identification.

His name was Richard Mathis and his report stated, *The hands show strange yet subtle aspects of* ████████████████████████████

Flipping through the file, Uli found a second letter from Mathis which also had large sections redacted. When Agent O'Riley returned a few minutes later, Uli silently closed the file and left.

Two weeks later, while attending a bureau seminar in Minnesota, Uli visited the local FBI-affiliated coroner's office and tracked down Mathis, who turned out to be a senior lab technician. Uli flashed his badge and said he was part of the investigation handling the Aquash case.

"In your report you referred to something *strange yet subtle.*"

"Yeah, don't worry, I took care of it."

"Took care of what?"

Mathis stared at him a moment, then went on to explain that he initially had reason to doubt that the hands he had received were Aquash's at all.

"Her fingerprints didn't match?" Uli asked.

"No, the two hands matched each other. I didn't actually do the fingerprinting."

"What was the problem then?"

"The hands didn't really . . . fit with the description of the body."

"Didn't fit how?"

"Both her hand size, the age, and the complexion of her skin didn't quite match."

"Can I see these hands?"

"They were reunited and returned to the next of kin." Mathis glanced down at his wristwatch. "And my break is over, so if you don't mind . . ." He hustled away.

* * *

A few days later, after he had just knocked back two glasses of Scotch while still waiting for instructions on his new posting, Uli's doorbell rang. When he answered, he was greeted by two agents who identified themselves as internal affairs.

"What's up?" He knew he reeked of alcohol, but he wasn't on duty, so he wasn't overly worried.

"Word has it you were just in Minnesota and spoke to a lab tech, Richard Mathis. You've been snooping around about the Aquash case?"

"Yeah. I worked on it."

"Not on her murder."

"I worked on setting her up, okay? I felt bad about it. Just wanted to know if they had any leads."

"So what did you find?"

"Nothing."

"You're lying," the younger of the two agents replied.

When Uli didn't say anything, the other agent spoke up: "Look, we talked to Mathis. He told us everything, so you can keep your mouth shut and we can bring you before a hearing and dump your drunken ass once and for all—or you can come clean."

"He told me about the severed hands," Uli said. "Big deal."

"It wasn't your investigation and you lied and said that it was, so now that's going into your file."

Uli restrained his urge to punch the man's face and simply said, "We just had a brief chat in the hallway."

"Consider this a stern warning, Sarkisian. If you attempt to ask any more questions on this case, you will be called in for disciplinary action."

The two men stared fiercely at Uli, who stared right back. Finally they retreated to their car parked in his driveway and drove off. Uli knew he shouldn't have asked any questions about Anna, but he still figured internal affairs had better things to do than check out petty bullshit like this.

The next day he finally got summoned by Marty Harris about his rather unique new assignment. Uli spent the afternoon filling out a stack of forms and gave them to Harris, who explained that at noon tomorrow Uli had to report to the military depot in Hawthorne, Nevada. From there he would connect with a pilotless supply plane that would bring him to Rescue City.

"What should I pack for this assignment?"

"Nothing, absolutely nothing. Not even your gun or badge. When you step off the plane, you'll be greeted by the ground coordinator, Newton Underwood, who will fill you in on the situation. He's supposed to put you in touch with someone named D. Colder, who is our liaison officer there. It's all in the file."

"Great," Uli said. Then he casually mentioned that he had been approached by IA.

"The OPR?" Harris asked, concerned that it was about his drinking.

"No, just IA."

"Oh shit! What exactly happened?" Harris claimed he hadn't heard about it.

"I was reprimanded," Uli said.

"For what exactly?"

"I made some inquiries about the Aquash case."

"You mean the ██████████████████████████████
██
██
███████████████████████████

"Is he still alive?" Marsha asked.

"If he is, he's probably a vegetable," said a doctor. "No one comes back from 108 degrees without serious brain damage."

"Poor Uli."

Uli's recollections became vivid: Harris let out a long sigh. "I shouldn't be telling you this, but in a week or so you're going to find out anyway."

"Find out what?"

"There's a quasi–Native American group in Rescue City called the Burnt Men. Some of them were detained just before Wounded Knee, so they have no clue what's been going on out in South Dakota. Many of them knew her before her . . . murder."

"What are you saying?"

"She wasn't killed, Uli. She recovered."

"Wasn't killed?!"

"That's right. In fact, Agent Spencer was at the hospital when Anna Aquash was found. She was in a coma, but still alive. When she got out, he made her an offer: *We can put you in witness protection, but we need the people who killed our FBI guys.*"

"What does this have to do with—"

"Just after the killings, we were able to hold a small but important group of AIMers who we later detained in Rescue City. None of them knew she had fallen out of favor with the organization. She agreed to work for us. We sent her in as a detainee to try to find who shot Jack and Ron. In exchange for any pertinent information toward a conviction, we agreed that we would pull her out of RC, get her kids, and put them all in witness protection."

"I can't believe she's not dead."

"She was close to it when we found her."

"Why the severed hands?"

"Oh, the only corpse we could use within twenty-four hours was a car-accident death who had her hands cut clean off, so we needed a cover story."

"That explains the IA investigation," Uli said.

"The reason I'm telling you this is because she's one of the people you'll be handling when you arrive."

So that was his mission.

"Uli!"

In his feverish state, he saw her lying just a few beds over, also trembling and covered in sweat.

"I don't want to die here!" *Anna Mae said.*

"Don't worry, I'll get you out."

It wasn't until early the next morning that Marsha finally called the Williamsburgh Building and asked to speak to Karen. The switchboard operator explained that unfortunately Captain Sarkisian had vanished and was once again presumed dead.

Marsha thanked her for her trouble and hung up. The task complete, she had done all she felt obliged to do. Before checking in with Rolland Siftwelt and beginning her endless list of daily chores, the face of Valerie Solanas popped into her head. Not the real Solanas, but the woman whose actual name was Bea Moses-Mayer. The brief yet torrid affair they'd had during the Quirklyn occupation still made her heart race. It also brought on a flood of guilt as she had created a major scandal which damaged her good name at PP. In fact, she had taken this risky assignment of helping these highly contagious people as an act of penance to Siftwelt for betraying his sacred trust and for the death of three PP workers. But clearly this was not enough. Of everyone in Rescue City, there must be a reason that Uli had asked her to reach out to one of the only people she was forbidden to contact.

Filled with the strength of God's love, she picked up the one phone in the big quarantine tent and dialed the number for the Staten Island city government at the terminal. After a dozen rings, an impatient voice barked, "VL, what do you got for me?"

"I'm trying to find a Bea Moses-Mayer."

"Hold."

As Marsha waited in the silence, she thought that the next voice she would hear would be the only person she had ever truly wanted to be with. *I should've told her*, she thought fearfully. *I must tell her now!* Still, all that was required from her were the words, *Uli Sarkisian asked me to call you. He's very sick and might die. He's in the Prospect Park quarantine.*

"Bea Mayer here, how can I help you?"

"Uli Sarkisian asked me to call you. He's very sick and might die. He's in the Prospect Park quarantine." Although she desperately wanted to, she couldn't say the other words.

"Oh Jesus!" Bea exclaimed.

Marsha nervously slammed the phone down.

21

After Attorney General Schuman was shot dead in his office, Karen was interviewed at length by one of the only investigators still on active duty in the midst of the plague—a rather lackluster gangcop she had known for years named Ben Davis. He asked about the security guard who had returned fire out the window while Schuman was still alive. Even this dolt knew that Schuman couldn't have been killed by some lone and distant gunman. And though the forensics in Rescue City were primitive at best, the burn marks on the sofa pillow and the small-caliber bullet lodged in Schuman—clearly a different size than the huge holes in the wall—all indicated that it was an inside job.

"Can I see your service revolver?" Davis asked, almost as an afterthought. It would've been the first thing Karen would've seized if she were on the case. And she wouldn't have asked, she simply would've frisked the suspect.

"I wasn't issued a new one," she replied calmly. Everyone had heard of her recent resurrection from the dead, so this was logical and accurate. Her paperwork was still pending.

After thirty minutes of uninspired interrogation, Karen was released. She could have been locked up but Schuman's second-in-command, Kerry Black, was out sick with a possible case of the desert plague, and Davis was clearly nervous about arresting a ranking member of the council cops on his own authority.

When Karen stepped out of the Williamsburgh Building, she seriously considered just hiring a car and speeding back over the Zano Bridge to the safety of Staten Island and hopefully joining her brother. But even there she was far from safe. Schuman, after all, was the attorney general of Rescue City South. Rafique would probably allow extradition. As she crossed the plaza, she figured it was best to just stick it out.

When she arrived back at her apartment, she saw that her trusted hit man seemed to have done a thorough job of cleaning up after himself. She tried to imagine where Akbar might've vanished off to, but the possibilities were endless. Feeling dirty from the exhausting day, she took a quick shower and a long nap.

Karen awoke to a phone call from Tatianna, who alerted her that Davis had been taken off the case and the new lead investigator was Lieutenant Anthony LaCoste—one of the few investigators she had never met, which was probably why he'd been appointed. She also remembered that LaCoste's brother had been a major gang leader who was murdered by Jackie Wilson years ago.

"Should I come in and see him?" she asked Tatianna.

"No. In fact, please don't even mention that I told you. I know you had nothing to do with Schuman's murder so I just wanted to give you the heads-up."

Karen thanked her, ended the call, and decided to try to track down her brother. When she stepped into the lobby of her building on the way out, the doorman was talking to some large guy with bright red hair.

"Oh, here she is," said the doorman.

"I'm Lieutenant LaCoste." The muscular redhead grabbed her hand and squeezed it hard. "I studied with your brother. He was a great teacher."

"And I remember *your* brother," she countered.

"Uli was in charge of the program to train the gangcops for the new trial system."

"I heard," Karen replied.

"Since I've got you here now," he said, "it was reported that you went to Schuman's office to warn him about a shooter."

"True." It was a detail that Ben Davis had completely missed.

After a few more questions, LaCoste fixated on the weakest link of her story: "So you saw someone shooting at his office when you were down in the plaza?" Since it took awhile to get through the entrance and up to the top floor of the Williamsburgh Building, the likelihood that no one else had heard shots was minuscule.

"I know this sounds crazy, but when I was downstairs coming in, I looked across the plaza and thought I saw a gun sticking out the window of one of these buildings."

"A rifle barrel?"

"Yeah."

"And instead of notifying the security guards downstairs—"

"You know how sometimes you stop and ask yourself, *Did I just see that?* And you're just not sure, but you keep thinking about it until you convince yourself?"

"Okay." He sounded as if he might be willing to give her the benefit of the doubt. "So from which building exactly did you see this muzzle?"

Taking a deep breath, Karen stepped outside into the plaza. She peered up at the window of Schuman's office, then turned around, and realized to her dismay that only one building offered a clean shot. "Oh God! Mine, I guess," she finally answered.

"Would you mind if I looked inside your place?" LaCoste asked.

"Go ahead." She handed over her apartment key. "Just give this to the doorman when you leave."

"You were away for a while, weren't you?"

"I was one of those rescued from the Mkultra facility out in the desert," she said.

"So how come everyone who was there came down sick except for you?"

"Actually, I was very sick. And there are others who have recovered as well. You can check."

"Not many."

"You should probably ask a doctor about this. I wish I understood this bizarre sickness, but I don't."

"Would you mind doing me a small favor and sticking around? You know how this works. I have to interview you, and I'd rather get through this quickly and in a friendly way."

"Of course."

Karen asked if *he* would mind if she went to the stamp shop first; she wanted to pick up some food. He said that would be fine, and as she walked away, she saw a team of officers getting out of a squad car that had just pulled up nearby.

She went into Stamos's Stamps. Although the shelves had been mostly cleared out, she managed to find a dusty can of okra, a tin of Spam, and a brick of El Busted coffee. There was no milk or sugar in stock.

When she returned home, she found one officer going through her bedroom while another was working in the living room. She held her breath as she watched a third officer, using a magnifying glass, carefully examining her windowsills, presumably for any signs of gunfire. Gangcops were rarely this thorough. Still, since she was a ranking officer and a close friend of the mayor, LaCoste would clearly need a solid case before arresting her.

She calmly percolated a pot of coffee and offered them all a cup.

They quietly declined. Then she realized that LaCoste was nowhere to be found. About an hour went by before one more officer burst into her apartment holding Akbar's rifle.

"My God!" Karen yelped, genuinely surprised.

"I just found this wedged in one of the chimney pipes up on the roof."

"So they fired it from up there?" Karen asked.

"Maybe," she heard from the hallway outside her front door, "but it doesn't matter. The shooter didn't kill him with that, did he?" La-Coste reentered the apartment.

"He didn't?"

"Come on, you don't need ballistics to know that a shot from that weapon would've taken off his skull. Schuman had a small wound from a weapon fired at close range. Officer Sarkisian, would you mind letting me inspect *your* gun?"

"You're the second person who's asked me that," she replied. "I was still being processed—no gun or shield issued."

"You're going to tell me that after years on the force, you don't have one stashed somewhere?"

"You tell me—you just ransacked my place."

"Do yourself a favor and don't leave the plaza."

During her years in Rescue City, Karen had seen their numbers growing—armless, legless ex-cons at the mercy of strangers to help them carry things, or with bags around their necks. In the bathrooms of some of the seedier dives, where the criminal elements were common, the owners had constructed "protrusion sticks," pieces of wood with toilet paper wrapped around the end that allowed one- and no-armed ex-cons to more or less wipe themselves—truly distasteful and ineffective. She pictured herself trying to use one.

By the time she finally got in bed that night, she sleeplessly thought, *Who am I kidding? If I'm found guilty for Schuman's assassination, I'll be executed.*

For the next two days Karen barely ate or slept. On the third day, around seven in the morning, a loud knock on her door yanked her out of bed. It was LaCoste and two of his henchmen. They marched into her living room without an invitation.

"Here's what I can't figure," LaCoste launched right in. "Schuman was your old number two, wasn't he?"

"You know he was."

"So you vanish suddenly and he's promoted to the attorney generalship." LaCoste plunked down on her sofa. "A job you should've gotten."

"You think I killed him because he took my job?"

"I think you killed him because he shoved you down the sewer hole to an almost certain death."

"I took the drug and jumped down that pipe on my own volition," she said smugly. "Like a thousand others before me."

"Now why the fuck would you do that?"

"We got cajoled into a prison believing it was a sanctuary. Would it sound so unbelievable to say that as opposed to simply killing myself, I took a chance at getting out?"

"You're just not the pipe type," LaCoste rhymed and reasoned. "Most of those people were hippies or deadbeats. You rose up the ranks here; you were part of the inner circle. I mean, this is one of the nicest buildings here. You get full privileges."

"And I volunteered to come here, which makes me even more of a fool."

"Please consider yourself under house arrest," LaCoste politely announced, rising to his feet, and headed out the door. His two silent men were close at his heels.

Returning to bed, Karen stared at the ceiling and thought, *I should've died with Mallory in that Greenwich Village brownstone.* Bizarre how over ten years ago, not politics but love and loneliness had compelled her to stalk her old friend on that fateful day. If she had simply stayed home instead of following the courier, she would probably be working now as a civil rights attorney in her native Boston. *Instead*, she thought, *I'm wasting my life as a glorified trustee, in what is essentially a penal colony for "inferiors,"* as her aunt used to call the underprivileged.

At some point she drifted off to sleep.

When her doorbell rang once again, she figured it was LaCoste coming to take her away. She got up, still dressed from the night before, but instead of opening the door, she just stood there, freezing the moment. The only thought that filled her head was, *This is it, my very last moment of freedom.* When another knock sounded, her eyes swept her living room one last time and she turned the knob.

To her surprise, it was Michael Maloney, the Crapper fire chief, and his second-in-command, Cody Cruiser.

"We just heard that you were still alive!" greeted Chief Maloney. Her two old buddies each gave her a warm embrace.

"And we can't tell you how happy that makes us," Cruiser added.

"I don't have any rotgut . . ." she said, leading them into her living room.

"We're not drinking." Instead of taking a seat, they remained standing.

"Our visiting you, well, we'd appreciate it if you can keep this between us," Maloney said. Apparently the two of them had no clue that she was under investigation for murder.

"We know you're one of the few people who was friends with Mallory in Old Town, and we just don't know who else to turn to," said Cruiser. "You must've heard about the doomsday notices?"

"You mean the end-of–Rescue City hoax?"

"Actually, it's very real."

"How do you know?" Karen asked.

"An abundance of evidence that we were instructed to keep quiet about."

"Like what?"

"Just this morning we found a string of abandoned buildings strategically located along the western edge of Manhattan that were rigged with highly flammable explosives."

"Why couldn't some gang have done that?"

"It was attached to a remote control device that's far more sophisticated than anything we have ever seen here," Maloney said.

"This took time, expertise, and resources," Cruiser said.

"This is so odd," Karen mused. "I used to fear that Russia and the US could have a nuclear war and, isolated all the way out here, we'd be the last to find out. Now it turns out *we're* going to see the end first . . . So why are you telling me this?"

"The mayor is refusing to see anyone," Maloney said. "She's cut herself off."

"And tonight they're forecasting a windstorm," said Cruiser.

"So she doesn't believe it's going to burn?"

"No, she believes it."

"So what's the problem?"

"She wants to go on the defensive," the fire chief pushed ahead. "She's making us throw all our resources at trying to put fires out when they start."

"Good, then she definitely knows it's coming."

"It's the wrong strategy."

"Why?" Karen asked.

"When all this goes down, it'll be way too widespread to put out, and if there's a windstorm—forget about it. We won't even be able to see it, let alone use the hoses."

"So thousands will be incinerated—is that what you're saying?"

"Actually, no. We haven't found any devices near the larger streets. They seem to have left the key arteries open, allowing time to evacuate. Hell, whoever did this was so thorough they even put up signs along the eastern borders of town, like exit doors in a movie theater. The signs trail off northeast through the desert to Lord knows where."

"The only real problem is," Cruiser said, "a few days ago, without telling us, Mallory ordered several precincts of gangcops to venture out into the desert and pluck out as many signs as could be found."

"No!"

"Yep. And apparently the Piggers did likewise."

Karen began to wonder if these guys were part of a ploy to get her to confess to the Schuman murder. The fact that they were coming to her with this problem on the eve of her arrest seemed utterly bizarre.

"In a nutshell," Maloney said, "if instead of fighting the fires, we pull together our limited resources to try and keep the main arteries out of the city open, we'll save far more lives."

"What can I say? If I find the opportunity to speak to Her Honor, I'll certainly plead your case. That's the best I can offer," Karen said.

"Please be careful, she's been a little paranoid lately. We fear we might be running a risk even approaching you with this."

"I'll keep your names out of this," Karen assured them.

Both men thanked her for listening and left.

The notion that a catastrophic event was about to annihilate the little desert community actually relieved Karen's anxiety about getting arrested. Now she found herself once again worrying about her brother's whereabouts. She phoned the Staten Island terminal building and asked the operator to put her through to Bea Moses-Mayer. "It's urgent!"

"She's busy." The receptionist took her name and number and said she'd pass the message along. That was the best she could do.

Twenty minutes later Karen's phone rang.

"Thank God you called!" Bea said. "They're not allowing anyone to enter or leave Staten Island. I tried calling you repeatedly at the Williamsburgh Building, but they keep saying you're dead."

"Morons!"

"I just got a call a couple hours ago that Uli's being held in Brooklyn,"

Bea said. "He's in quarantine in Prospect Park, and they told me he's very sick."

"Oh God, I'll get right over there."

Karen made a few calls and discovered that an old friend, Lieutenant Christopher Bleek, a good man when he was sober, was now in charge of security at the Prospect Park quarantine. While trying to get through to him, the operator came on the line to tell her there was an urgent call for her.

She heard a succession of deep, painful hacks from a congested set of lungs. For a moment she held her breath, fearing it was Uli.

"Comrade Sarkisian?" said a low, wheezy female voice. It was the mayor—Mallory. "On behalf of the good people of Brooklyn and Manhattan, you are under arrest for the murder of Attorney General Schuman!"

"Sorry?"

"How soon can you get your ass over here and turn yourself in?"

"Where?" Karen asked.

"Where the hell do you think? Rock & Filler Center."

"I'm . . . I'm under arrest?"

"Do you really think I'd arrest you over the phone? I'm kidding."

"Hell of a joke."

"Actually, an order for your arrest is sitting on my desk. I'm not signing it, but I want you to get over before this storm hits. Frankly, I'm not doing great."

"I'm under house arrest here," Karen said. "You'll have to call and authorize them to let me leave and take out a car."

Mallory said she would have her assistant make the arrangements and hung up. Five minutes later Karen got a call from Mallory's secretary, who explained that a driver was waiting for her in the guarded parking lot and that she was free to head on over. Karen went down, got in the vehicle, and forty-five minutes later she was dropped off at the Midtown Manhattan office that now served as Mallory's home.

22

The security guard on duty at Rock & Filler Center asked her to wait while he notified his captain. A sturdy middle-aged man named Gaspar Stenson, who had worked with Karen when the Crappers were first founded, greeted her and explained that he was now head of the mayor's security detail.

"It's great to see you alive," he said, and mentioned that he had worked with her brother when he was DAG.

Both remarks had become tired refrains.

"I'm looking for him myself," she replied as he patted her down.

She was directed upstairs, where she was frisked a second and third time before she was finally issued a face mask and surgical gloves for her own protection. She was led to a door where a large, sleepy guard was seated outside. He opened the door but clearly didn't want to risk his health by joining her in the room with the infected mayor.

"It's this fucking plague," Mallory wheezed as Karen entered her chamber. She was lying in bed—frail, pale, propped up by pillows, and soaked with sweat. Her spacious corner apartment high above most other buildings on the island offered a generous view of western Brooklyn, as well as south over Lower Manhattan, all the way down to the northern edge of Staten Island.

"What happened?" Karen asked.

Mallory spoke in clipped and labored breaths: "I made the fatal mistake of grabbing a photo op—to display my willingness to work with the other mayors here. I greeted the busload of those fucking diseased refugees who we adopted from the Mkultra. It was supposed to be a quick in and out. Now I'm fucking dying from a handshake." She reached for an oxygen mask with her only hand. "I wish I had lost *both* my fucking arms in the Cooper Union explosion!"

"At least it's not wiping out your memory."

"Yeah, I only have double pneumonia."

"I'm so sorry," Karen said.

"As soon as I heard you had vanished," Mallory skipped the pleasantries, "I suspected Schuman. The man was too accommodating, as only a weasel can be."

"Look, I was with him when the shooting started—" Karen began her defense.

"Christ, girl, I'm not asking for a confession."

"But I—"

"The rifle shots from outside barely even reached his office," Mallory repeated what she had read in the arrest report. "Schuman was killed at close range with a shot to the back of the head and you were the only one with him, darling."

"What do you want me to say?"

"Was he involved in sending you to the Mkultra?"

"Yeah, him and Scouter."

"Then fuck 'em!" Mallory crumpled up the warrant for Karen's arrest and tossed it in the garbage. "It ends here. I only called you in because the doctor said he doesn't think I'm going to last the next twenty-four hours." Mallory leaned back and closed her eyes. "You and I came here as a team, and you're basically the last living member, so I wanted to say goodbye in person."

"Mallory, people are saying this place is going to be burned down in the next forty-eight hours."

"I will not give in to terrorists!"

"But I don't think these are terrorists. They're not inciting terror. Hell, they're telling people *how* to evacuate!"

"Anybody who makes demands like this is a terrorist," the mayor replied. "We have to fight if we want to survive."

"A lot more people could die if you do that."

"So what am I supposed to do? Trust some secret cabal and just march thousands of people into the barren desert? That's your plan?"

"They are suggesting a way out, freedom beyond the Rockaways," Karen said. "And they're claiming to be the federal government."

"You know as well as I do that this isn't how the government operates. They would send in social workers, the military, the press; they'd undertake an orderly evacuation to the airport, and once everyone was shipped out they'd just deactivate this place. They sure wouldn't burn it down. Hell, they'd probably mothball it in case they needed it again."

"Does it really matter who's behind this?" Karen said. "Shouldn't you focus on protecting your people?"

"I *am* protecting my people—by not abandoning their city and yielding to terrorists!"

"Have you talked to the other two mayors?"

"Actually, we had a conference call about this a few days ago, and we all agreed that instructing everyone to just run into the open plains . . . Well, Rafique aptly referred to it as the difference between a quick death and a slow one. In all the years here, we don't have a single reported case of anyone successfully crossing the desert and reaching civilization."

"I heard that there's supposed to be a windstorm coming through tonight," Karen said. "If they do start fires, it could turn into an inferno."

"I don't need to hear this right now."

"Here's my question: at what point will you stop trying to put the fires out and order an evacuation?"

"Never! I will not order this city to be evacuated until there's somewhere to evacuate them to, simple as that." Spent from the exchange, Mallory started gasping into her oxygen mask.

Karen sat down next to her and soon heard her snoring. The mayor of Brooklyn and Manhattan had passed out. Karen considered quietly leaving, but she was too exhausted; she moved to a larger chair across from Mallory's bed and closed her eyes.

She was awakened a short time later by the whistling of the wind. Looking southward out over the city under bright moonlight, Karen made out what appeared to be a giant black tidal wave approaching in the distance. It was the dreaded windstorm.

"Wow," she uttered aloud.

Mallory's blue eyes popped open and she said, "That's something you can't see from street level."

"You're the leader of these people, and you're responsible for their well-being," Karen reminded her friend.

"And for the record, we've been using our time to conduct rapid-response drills to fight these fires when they do break out. We also have gangcops stationed throughout Manhattan and Brooklyn with orders to shoot to kill should they see any of these provocateurs . . ."

As Mallory continued talking, Karen's eyes remained fixed on the dark line of dust clouds rolling forth over Staten Island. When the storm finally tagged Lower Manhattan, Karen gasped at what she saw. It was as though a Christmas tree were suddenly plugged in. Dozens of small lights seemed to simultaneously snap on in the vast darkness surrounding the city.

"Oh my God! Did you see that?" Karen pointed out the window.

Despite her utter fatigue, Mallory managed to sit up to get a full view.

"They just set off a whole bunch of fires at the same time," Karen said.

"Bring 'em on!" Mallory shouted out, then fell back on the bed, bushed.

In another few minutes, the windstorm had reached their building. Karen watched as the powerful gale fanned the flames that were igniting throughout the city. "Mike Maloney and Cody Cruiser visited me this afternoon," she revealed to Mallory, who was beginning to nod off again. "They said that if they focused their resources on just keeping the main streets open, a lot more people would have a far better chance of surviving."

"They visited *you*?"

"They asked if I'd try to reason with you."

"Treason! What cowards! I'm going to have them arrested, how fucking dare they!" Mallory perked back up and began rambling on about valor and loyalty.

When Karen heard her use the phrase *state of emergency*, she took a deep breath, then snatched a pillow that had dropped to the floor.

She leaped on Mallory, pressing the cushion over her old friend's face with all her might. Mallory struggled, punching her repeatedly with her one and only arm. Karen leaned harder, pushing the pillow tighter over Mallory's mouth and face. Her friend's flailing arm slowly grew heavier and clumsier until it finally dropped. After several more minutes of stillness, Karen rose. She lifted the pillow and saw the gasping expression frozen on Mallory's face.

"Sorry, girl," she whispered. Tears came to her eyes as she delicately stroked her fingers across Mallory's mouth and eyes, trying to relax her taut muscles back to a state of repose. The howling wind was now accompanied by infinite swirling particles of sand drumming against the windowpanes.

Karen carefully squeezed the pillow back under her old friend's head, then reached for the phone next to the bed. The receptionist outside picked up.

"Help, quick! Mallory just stopped breathing!"

In a minute a medical technician dashed in, wearing gloves and a face mask, and began a cardiac massage.

"Shouldn't you be giving her mouth-to-mouth resuscitation?" asked the mayor's personal assistant who followed.

"Be my guest," the technician fired back.

A giant security guard watched as they tried to bring the mayor back to life. After five minutes, the technician looked at her watch and announced the time of death. She advised Karen to wash her hands and face in the private bathroom in case of any contamination.

"What exactly happened?" the large guard asked Karen when she returned.

"Well, we were looking out the window at the storm, then suddenly we saw all the fires spring out at once . . . and she just let out this awful gasp. Hell, we both did. Then she turned to me and said, *We need to evacuate the city at once!* As she reached for the phone, she started dry heaving. She couldn't catch her breath, then she just passed out."

"She wanted us to stay and fight," the mayor's assistant said.

"I don't think she expected to see all those fires. She didn't believe they'd actually go through with it."

"We better call Don McNeill," said the assistant. McNeill was the deputy mayor who, according to the rules of succession, was next in line.

"I think McNeill is stuck up in Inwood somewhere," said the guard.

"Shouldn't you call the fire chief first?" Karen asked. "Let him issue her final order, 'cause this city is going to be a heap of cinders by the time you track down McNeill."

Without giving Karen the benefit of a reply, the assistant dialed Chief Maloney and said that Mallory had just issued an order to evacuate Brooklyn and Manhattan. After the call was made, the room filled with a heavy silence as people adjusted to the notion that, at this crucial juncture when leadership was most needed, the elected head of Rescue City South was gone. Yet considering Mallory's weakening condition, her demise was not entirely a surprise.

From the apartment window looking out over Manhattan, through the thousand veils of yellow, black, and brown sand, Karen and the others could make out bursts of orange and red flames as the fires spread.

"We're so fucked!" said the security guard.

Karen saw tears streaming down the assistant's face. The middle-aged woman's bony gloved hand was resting on Mallory's sunken chest. Her eyes darted between her dead boss lying before her and the ghastly, blurry vision of their city burning down outside.

"Where's the fire command center?" Karen asked softly, finally breaking the silence.

"Down on three," uttered the guard.

Karen excused herself.

23

When Uli awoke, drenched in sweat, he realized he was moving, or rather being moved. He was back in South Dakota. Somebody, some distant tentacle of the Kremlin, had incarcerated both him and Banana Anna, along with many others. In the semidarkness, he could see her lying nearby, unconscious. Her hands were still attached to her body, which confirmed that she had never been murdered—it was all a crock of shit. The commies had erected some vast, open-air prison where they were holding Uli and other freedom fighters. Both he and Anna Mae were sedated, stripped naked, and dumped onto tarps, where they were forced to lie in their own excrement. It made complete sense: the Reds had inserted something into their brains which turned patriots into puppets. Over an indeterminate period of time, falling asleep and awakening intermittently, Uli crawled his way over to her. The mounting, howling winds were now keeping him conscious as the tent structure above him rippled fiercely. People were running around, using ropes and spikes to reinforce collapsing structures. Uli reached up and gave Anna a strong shake.

"Huh?" She was more asleep than awake.

"If you agree to testify against Franks and Beans, I can get you out of here!"

"Huh?"

"Say you'll do it!"

"Just give me some water," she said groggily.

Uli grabbed her under her shoulders and dragged her off the tarp, into the dark, cold desert sands. He searched for surrounding fences, but there were none. The wind and sand just went on forever.

Strategically placed throughout the city, the small fires were mainly ignited on upper floors. At the command center, while identifying the line of outbreaks on a map, Fire Chief Maloney started to grasp what was happening. Whoever was doing this had set their first wave of starter fires in the outermost ring of the city. After the first hour, though, they had ignited fires in larger buildings closer to the center of town. A dozen fires in Gramercy Park, fifteen fires in Chelsea, then in the East Village, LittleHoTown, and so on. To the credit of the pyromaniacs, they had targeted abandoned and underoccupied buildings, presumably trying to reduce casualties. They had orchestrated the line of flames to systematically push people over the bridges, sweeping the residents of Rescue City steadily eastward.

Since Mallory's evacuation order arrived after the storm had begun, many captains were still focusing on the original directive of fighting the fires locally. But the men were spread too thin, and their walkies were nearly useless. Maloney had to send messengers out to tell them to fall back and guard the main thoroughfares.

Information was sketchy, but Karen was hoping for reports that there was still a safe passage through Lower Manhattan and into Brooklyn—she needed to grab Uli. At least she now knew where he was, though she also knew he was incapacitated. When no word came through, she asked if anyone was driving to the Williamsburgh Building. No one was. Throughout the early morning, it was as though the sun were rising a second time in the west. Updates began to come in that Upper West Siders were trapped above Midtown and fleeing by boat across the Hudson to the Hoboken fields.

Karen knew that if she were forced to join those escaping through Hoboken, she'd have little chance of ever seeing her brother again, so she decided to make a mad dash southward.

While leaving Rock & Filler Center, she was able to grab a face mask and a heavy-duty flashlight to get through the sandstorm. When her old friend Gaspar Stenson learned that she was intending to hike to Brooklyn amid the chaos and the flames, he offered her the keys to his own patrol car. She thanked him and said she'd see him again, after the fires were put out.

"Hell yeah, I want my car back," he said.

She put on the siren and sped roughly two hundred feet to Fifth Avenue before she came to a sudden halt. The downsized wooden Brandenburg Gate replica had been targeted. It had collapsed onto Fifth Avenue, blocking all traffic south. When she tried heading down Madison Avenue, she only made it to 34th Street before she found that flaming debris falling from some of the more frail structures had made the narrow street impassable. As she turned her car around and detoured onto a sidewalk, a two-story building collapsed before her, sending an avalanche of brick and mortar onto her hood. She yanked on her mask, abandoned Stenson's half-buried vehicle, and raced back over to Fifth Avenue just as the winds began to taper.

By this point, six fire trucks, stretched out over a couple miles, had been given the impossible task of keeping the avenue open for evacuation. Karen tried flagging down passing solicars, but when one finally stopped, the driver shouted, "Two thousand stamps!"

"The city's on fire!" she yelled back. "Where are you going to spend it?"

"Two thousand—pay or move!"

She waved the vehicle away. When she heard the siren of an approaching cop car, she pulled out her spare shield and was able to get its attention. It was carrying a group of drivers to a fleet of trucks in the Battery to haul supplies out of the city.

"Squeeze in if you can," the driver said.

Her choice was to lie on the hood or across the laps of three huge drivers—she chose the latter. When they reached Onion Square, the gangcop driver stopped. He had to continue south through the increasing flames and offered to let her out. She thanked him and hurried eastward.

As she neared the Brooklyn Bridge, she saw that traffic was at a complete standstill. The walkways were packed with fleeing Manhattanites holding their belongings in suitcases, shopping bags, or bundles on their backs. Fighting stitches along her side, Karen joined others running in the jammed car lanes. From the height of the bridge, Karen spotted beloved places she knew from her first few years in Rescue City—old haunts in the East Village: Kievos on Second Avenue, the Saint Mark's Bookstall, the 11th Street Bathhouse, Cinema Village on 12th Street, Veniero's—all of which were up in flames. Although in the past she'd always disparaged Rescue City and all its quirky shops, now she fully realized how the oddballs had uniquely shaped this forgotten corner of the world, truly making it their own.

Ten minutes later she was peering out over Brooklyn Heights. From there, she heard a series of blasts and witnessed the pyrotechnics firsthand. Explosions erupted along the top floor of a housing project only a few blocks away. Each one was followed by a small concentrated flame. It was like the golden beak of a firebird breaking out of its shell. The winds spread the flames quickly, engulfing the neighboring roofs.

A few blocks up Jackie Wilson Way, barely able to stay on her feet, Karen paid a driver three stamps to squeeze onto the flat bed of an overpacked pickup. As she was hauled along, she saw blackened fire trucks arriving to reinforce others on the route. The driver explained that these new trucks had just been pulled out of their own lost neighborhoods in Manhattan. They were now fighting to keep Brooklyn's widest and longest thoroughfare open.

The streets were slick with water and a gag-inducing smoke filled the air. As the sun rose, the prefabricated city burned.

By the time the truck reached the Fulton Mall, its sprawling walkway was covered in soot. More people jumped in the back of the pickup in a panic, making the already slow vehicle move at a crawl. Karen soon squeezed out, hoping to stop by her complex and grab some supplies. As she neared the parking lot of the Williamsburgh Building, she ducked into a doorway back from the retreating crowds. There she fumbled through her bag for her face mask. Before she could pull it on, however, she caught sight of four court officers at the hidden side of the building. They were rushing nine handcuffed prisoners to the parking lot. When all were hastily uncuffed, Karen watched discreetly as the sergeant checked his wristwatch. As though commencing a race, he shouted, "Go!"

Five thin, full-limbed prisoners started running, followed by two with arm amputations and two with canes, each hopping on a single leg. After a full minute, the sergeant nodded. Karen watched as his four guards, swinging billy clubs, proceeded to chase them. The two one-legged prisoners were the first to go down. Next was one of the single-armed amputees. A swift gangcop even caught one of the full-limbed men. The beating went on until the ground was covered in blood and only stopped when the officers got tired. The prisoners were left semiconscious, bleeding on the pavement. Then two other handcuffed men were led out of the building. But instead of uncuffing them, an obese gangcop escorted them to the rear of a nearby van. Karen thought perhaps they were being driven elsewhere—until she heard two shots ring out.

When the heavyset gangcop returned to the Williamsburgh Building, Karen raced over and looked into the vehicle. To her horror, its floor was piled with bodies.

"What the fuck do you think you're doing?!" she heard. A new squad of jailers was leading another group of prisoners toward the van.

She showed her council cop ID.

"I don't give a fuck who you are!" The largest gangcop started swaggering toward her with his club.

"At ease!" an older gangcop shouted out to him. It was Lefty Cohen, a senior jailer she knew from the old days. "She's with me."

The thuggish cop scowled at Lefty and retreated to his prisoners.

"What the fuck is going on?" Karen asked.

"What do you think, Cappy? The place is burning down. We're clearing out the cells."

"By killing them?"

"Most of the four-limbers get a free pass. If the amputees are back here, they haven't learned yet, have they?" Leaning forward, he whispered, "We've run out of time for ethics, Cappy."

"Do you know if Prospect Park is still holding quarantine cases?" she asked.

"Last I heard, yep."

Karen stared past Lefty and saw two skinny prisoners being led toward the van.

Lefty turned to see what she was looking at. "Hey," he yelled to the guards escorting them, "those are four-limbers!"

"But—"

"Cut the *faygalas* loose."

"These are the Warhol pansies arrested during the Quirklyn riot," one of the guards said. "We were told to . . ."

Without saying a word, Lefty took out his key and uncuffed Jackie Curtis and Candy Darling, both of whom were desperately in need of a drink and a sink. As they scurried up Jackie Wilson Way, Lefty looked sharply at Karen and said, "Are we done, Captain?"

Karen nodded briskly and headed toward her building, which was now spewing black smoke.

"Fuck!" she muttered. Several pieces of gold jewelry and other valuables she might've been able to barter with were now gone. She returned to the traffic jam of Jackie Wilson Way.

After only a few blocks, as she crossed Atlantic Avenue, the smoke started thickening again. The houses in Boerum Hill and Cobble Hill were burning as fast as the wind blew. Karen started coughing and thoughtlessly pulled off her face mask, then accidentally inhaled the toxic fumes. She gagged convulsively.

The rear passenger-side door of a passing car suddenly popped open and an older woman tugged Karen into the backseat.

"That's gonna cost you a stamp," said the driver. Karen nodded yes, gasping the cleaner air inside the vehicle, even though she was flat broke. By the time the car made it up to Seventh Avenue, the swarm of evacuees in the street had brought traffic to a dead halt.

Without a word, Karen pulled her face mask back on and joined the crowd outside. Everyone was bumping awkwardly into each other. The sounds of shouts, coughing, crying, and panic filled the air. Slowly they filtered their way up Jackie Wilson.

As they passed shops and stores, Karen saw widespread looting for the first time. She followed several others into a supermarket and grabbed a bottle of water, which she opened and poured over her eyes. Then she gargled, spat out soot, and drank.

Watching others fighting over food, she snatched several boxes of crackers. Spotting a display of canned sardines in mustard sauce, she dumped the crackers and filled her pockets with the cans instead.

As she arrived at Grand Army Plaza, she started hearing periodic low thuds, as though artillery was being fired into the city. At the crowded smoky entrance of Prospect Park, Karen came across a large trough of cloudy water. She splashed some onto her face and pressed on into the surprisingly empty park—her brother had to be here somewhere. She pushed through some unlocked hurricane fencing and collapsed to her knees on the dry, well-trodden patch of land called the Great Lawn. This was supposed to be a quarantine zone, yet it was completely empty. Past a group of leafless trees, she spotted a row of empty tents flapping in the breeze. Everyone had left. Roaming around, she finally glimpsed a body sprawled out on a tuft of weeds. It was Lieutenant Christopher Bleek.

"Chris! What the hell's going on?"

"Oh, hi, Karen!" He looked dazed.

"Have you seen my brother?" she asked.

As he sat up, he dropped a bag of Hoboken-grown choke, as well as some pills. Bleek's eyes were bloodshot; he was clearly high. "Everyone's been evacuated."

Karen collapsed on the ground next to him. Noticing a tin of sardines in her pocket, Bleek pointed excitedly and she gave it to him. He removed the detachable key from the sardines, but was too stoned to thread the tab into it. Karen took it from him and opened the can.

"Do you know my brother Uli?" Karen asked, handing him the fish. "He was supposed to be here in the quarantine."

"No . . . maybe . . . though I know PP evacuated everyone this morning. They only had three vans, but after about a thousand round trips they were able to move everyone over to their compound."

"So they're up in Queens?"

"Wherever." Bleek took out a single sardine and popped it down, then repeated, licking the mustard sauce from his fingers.

At least Uli was probably safe.

After Bleek finished the can, he stared absently at the black clouds of smoke billowing overhead. As Karen struggled back to her feet, the stoned guard just lay on his back and she bade him farewell. She was hardly able to maintain her balance as she headed northeast out of the park. When she reached Jackie Wilson Way, she sat down on a curb. Crowds rushed past her. Rescue City was steadily becoming hell on earth. Her voyage from Midtown Manhattan to Prospect Park was barely halfway to the Rockaway desert.

Walking once again down Jackie Wilson, Karen could hardly believe it when she felt a gentle sprinkle of water from above. A few steps farther and she realized it wasn't rain at all. Firefighters were posted like sentinels on nearly every block, preemptively spraying down buildings, trying to catch the burning embers shooting north in the wind. Although no buildings had been detonated down here yet, Karen knew that a sudden gale could bring the flames down upon them at any moment.

She had to constantly sidestep an assortment of discarded and dropped objects that had been abandoned by the endless evacuees.

"Keep moving! Keep moving!" she'd periodically hear officials call out.

It's like we're being pushed off the edge of the world, she thought. *What the hell are all these people going to do once they reach the desert?*

For the first time, she began to understand Mallory's reluctance to evacuate. But before she could feel too guilty about what she had done, a new blast of sirens reminded her that there was still no way to stop the flames. Walking amid the ashen flood of refugees, she realized that she no longer thought of herself as alone—she was part of the crowd.

"They can't just let us all die," she overheard someone say, and she knew they all felt the same.

Karen counted down the major streets through the area. The crowd slowed at Cortelyou Road, and again at Ditmas. The mass exodus was finally reaching a safer outer ring of the city. For some of the refugees who had come all the way down from Harlem, Ditmas seemed to mark an unofficial finish line in their marathon of survival. A number of people had dropped to the hot pavement along the way, covered in soot and sweat, gasping for breath. Now, for the first time, city workers were walking around offering cups of water and even oxygen masks to those unable to catch their breath. Many of them were lightly burned, with singed clothes. All reeked of smoke.

Gangcops lined along the street enhanced the notion that they were now officially safe. Using her laminated ID, Karen was able to muscle through a cordoned section where she recognized a number of high-ranking city officials. She soon learned that they were holding the fires in check west of Foster Avenue.

"Dumbo, Bed-Stuy, Prospect Heights, Crown Heights—they're all gone!" a deputy assistant shouted. "The fires will be here soon!"

Karen joined the flow of people walking toward Flatlands. Since the area was still clear of flames, the pace was slower and more relaxed. A car honked at her. Turning, she saw that the vehicle had been customized with running boards completely surrounding its circular chassis and was carrying a dozen people, leaving only the hood open for view.

"You can have my last spot for free, hon!" the driver yelled mercifully to Karen. "It's just outside my door, right near my heart, but don't block my rearview!"

Her feet were swollen and her knees were buckling badly, so she thanked him and wedged in. As they drove eastward toward the Floyd

Bennett Field parking lot, the driver chatted away to any of the passengers who could hear him. He mentioned that only fast-moving solicars dared to drive back into the fire zone, where the fare-gougers were cleaning up.

Karen focused on the mild breeze stroking her feverish scalp. As soon as she closed her eyes, she almost slipped off. She smacked herself across the face to remain firmly awake. When they finally pulled into the Bennett lot, Karen realized that they were at the very bottom of the Jamaica Bay, where the waterway pinched into a narrow canal.

"Last stop! Everyone off! From here I'm going back up to Ditmas!" the driver shouted.

Peering across the long, wide bay, Karen made out the buildings of Pure-ile Plurality in the far distance. If she had any hope of finding her brother, she still had a couple miles to hike. Looking across the canal, to the blankness of the desert, Karen watched a very large tent suddenly arise, then a second, then a third. A crowd of workmen, methodical as the Amish, marched off behind a dune. Karen decided to investigate. That's when she first noticed a shoddily erected wooden bridge that looked like it could barely support two people. It connected Rescue City to the desert beyond. A boyish-looking gangcop was blocking people from crossing. Farther south, beyond a bend in the waterway, Karen was surprised to see what looked like a crowded beach—hundreds of seminaked people soaking in the sun, resting upon a glossy onyx surface, as if waiting for a tide that would never come in.

Most of the sun worshippers seemed strangely immobile. Only a few upright people with gloves and face masks were moving around checking on them. Past the group, Karen could see workers slowly unspooling a giant coil of hurricane fencing, hooking it onto posts that had already been planted. She also saw several small tractors moving busily, their blades cutting through the soft sands.

"What the hell's going on here?" she asked the boy gangcop guarding the bridge.

"Just move along," he replied gruffly.

Karen showed her captain's ID and asked, "Those aren't the quarantined people who were in Prospect Park, are they?"

"Yeah, and beyond that," he waved along the horizon, "Fort Til Then. They're still establishing it."

"What exactly is Fort Til Then?"

"A refugee camp in case things get dicey here."

"Where's the HQ?" she asked, hoping to speak to someone in charge.

"You mean Temporary Metropolis—TempMetro. They're putting it up now." He pointed to the newly pitched tents behind the quarantine area.

As Karen stepped up to the bridge, the guard stood his ground a moment, then acquiesced: "I'll let you through this once since everything's still up in the air. But after this, you'll need higher clearance than a temporary ID."

24

Upon crossing the flimsy bridge and arriving at the far side of the canal, Karen found three forks in the road. The path to the immediate right, which was set back roughly two hundred feet from the embankment of the canal, led to the quarantine zone. Here, hundreds of coughing, sneezing, wheezing men and women were sprawled half naked on the sticky black tarps which were laid out on the sand. The second path was marked by a sign that read, *TempMetro—No Unauthorized Personnel*. It went five hundred feet beyond the new hurricane fence posts to the new administrative tents. The last path led to an area intended to be an encampment for the bulk of refugees who were yet to arrive—Fort Til Then. Here, two small tractors were busy cutting trenches in the earth.

Heading to the giant white tents, Karen searched for someone in charge, someone she knew. Another gangcop stopped her before she could reach the largest tent, from which she could hear a hubbub of urgent voices. When she flipped her captain's ID, the man said that no one entered the executive administration tent without being patted down first. She held her arms out as he checked her for weapons.

Inside, the place was divided by sets of collapsible tables and folding chairs—improvised bull pens. At least fifty people seemed to be on radios getting updates and shouting orders, presumably to those still fighting the fire or handling the evacuation. She recognized a variety of desk jockeys from the Williamsburgh Building, as well as some who had made it out from the Rock & Filler office. Colorful thumbtacks on a large poster of Rescue City, which sat on a tripod, appeared to track the progress of the fire, as well as the number of fire battalions trying to contain it.

"Welcome to the Crapper command center," Tatianna said, intercepting Karen. The judicial secretary pulled out a cigarette and tapped it to pack the tobacco.

"Fancy seeing you here," Karen greeted. "Where's the new mayor?"

"We're praying he made it out alive. Still not here."

"So who's in charge?"

"The only commissioner here is the head of sanitation, Al Shaw." Tatianna lit the cigarette, drawing the smoke deep into her lungs.

"No wonder this is such a mess."

"Actually, he's our savior." Smoke tendriled up from her nose.

"He set up this place?"

"No, this was the fire department's contingency plan. He's the one who put priority on rescuing the stock."

"So most people have made it out safely?"

"God no! Whole pockets of people from Manhattan and north Brooklyn are stuck out in isolated areas, surrounded by flames. Fire-fighters are still trying to reach them."

"Awful," Karen said. Staring off, she could hear the grinding gears of the tractors behind them.

"They're using the time to prepare this space," Tatianna explained. "They're setting up four quadrants—each sector has a dining area, sanitation, general landscaping, the whole nine yards. They initially had a convoy of trucks filled with tents and food, but most of them got trapped in Lower Manhattan."

Karen remembered the carload of drivers who gave her a lift and wondered what had become of them. "What happens once the city is gone? How long can all these people survive out here?"

"That's the other problem. Some of the gangcops and firefighters are saying that whoever these pyromaniacs are, they put up all these exit signs around here."

"I heard, and Mallory supposedly had gangcops remove them. And what about the supply drones?" Karen asked, looking to the sky.

"No one has seen a single one this entire morning."

Someone shouted for Tatianna and she dashed off. Karen noticed one of the new canteens constructed just behind the administrative tent where food was being put out for the workers. Famished, she got in line. Within five minutes she was given a bagged lunch: a liverwurst sandwich, a bag of potato chips, and an apple. She also got a cup of coffee. It was her first real meal in many hours. She carried it to a patch of sand where she sat down and slowly picked it apart like a bird. At some point she leaned back for a moment of rest.

She awoke when someone kicked sand in her face.

"Sorry about that," Tatianna said, out of breath. "I just got an update for you."

"For me?"

"Sort of. Do you remember Anthony LaCoste?"

"What about him?" Karen said nervously. Twenty-four hours ago, he'd been on the verge of arresting her.

"I just heard that he caught one of the coconspirators up in the Bronx."

"That's Pigger territory."

"Word is, he saw the guy ignite a string of fires and chased him from Harlem into the Bronx. And he was trapped up there when the fires broke out."

Karen wondered if LaCoste was a spy—agents and double agents for the Piggers and Crappers were a common problem. "I give him credit for his tenacity." She was still scared that he might come after her for Schuman's death.

"He probably would've just killed the guy," Tatianna said, "but we're desperately trying to find one of them who might know a way out of here—through the desert."

Karen vaguely remembered Uli talking about this when she was still suffering from the desert fever. Something about water canisters placed throughout the desert that allowed passage to civilization. "If I can locate my brother," she said, "I think he might know something."

"Where did you last see him?"

"He was sick. Last I heard, they were holding him in the Prospect Park quarantine."

"Did you check the outdoor clinic?" Tatianna pointed her cigarette just beyond the newly unspooled fence that separated TempMetro from another area.

"The place is packed."

"Ask for Marsha Johnson," Tatianna said. "She's a tall black woman who runs the outdoor clinic for PP. The woman's got a brain like a steel trap. If anyone knows where he is, it'll be her."

"Actually, I might have trouble getting through security."

"Come with me." Tatianna led Karen back into the administrative tent and instructed one of the secretaries to issue her "the red badge." This granted Karen full clearance status.

"Find Marsha," Tatianna repeated. "And if you find Uli and he knows a way out of this place, let us know immediately. Otherwise we're seriously fucked."

Karen thanked her and ran back up to the junction at the little bridge, where two new guards were now stationed. She flashed her red badge, heading toward the outdoor clinic.

"You still need to put that on before you go in there," one of the guards said, pointing to three buckets at the base of the bridge that hadn't been there before. One was trash, the second contained new disposable face masks, and the last had new surgical gloves.

Karen put on the gear. In a moment she was walking among the rows of sickly, nude, sweaty, filth-smeared bodies looking for Uli. The smell was unbearable. Largely because of the shortage of volunteers, conditions were deplorable. The sick were rolling in their own waste. Buckets of water were periodically tossed on or around them. Small drainage ditches along the edges allowed the filth to be partially washed away. As Karen wandered around, some of the more lucid patients brushed their dirty fingers along her ankles and thighs, begging for help.

Karen passed through nearly half the length of the outdoor clinic before she spotted the tall, well-dressed black administrator who was shouting orders to a small entourage of others.

"Excuse me," Karen interrupted, holding up her red badge. "Are you Marsha?"

"Yes—oh my! You must be the council cop sister! I tried calling you from Park Slope. They said you were dead." Marsha turned to one of her aides, a young man with an unruly mop of hair. "Put on a hairnet and help Sam with breakfast in sector two!"

"Yes ma'am," replied the mophead, and duly rushed off.

"Remind me, is your name Anna?"

"No, I'm Karen."

Marsha stopped an older bald woman with a clipboard who was hurrying past them. "Where'd we put Mr. Sarkisian?"

"Who?" asked the lady.

"You know, that guy from the incident the other day."

"Oh! He's still sedated with the veggies."

"What incident?" Karen asked.

"The good news is, his fever finally broke and he woke up from his coma," the bald woman said. "The bad news is, he suffered extreme delirium and lost the power of speech. He was in a very distressed state."

"What do you mean *distressed*?"

"He was doing . . . odd things," Marsha replied carefully.

"What kind of odd things?"

"To a dead body," added the bald woman.

"What?" Karen was appalled.

"Some woman who had died in the night—Uli removed her body from a burial pit and dragged her out into the desert. It took three orderlies to stop him. He fought like the devil. When I finally asked him what he was doing, he said something about rescuing bananas."

"Oh my God! Can I see him?"

Marsha pointed to a smaller tent behind her. When Karen entered, the place looked like a human greenhouse. It had a dozen comatose patients lying naked, side by side like sardines. Karen approached the single nurse on duty, who was working nonstop, cleaning and attending to her patients. Almost all of them had IV tubes hanging over them. Karen let out an enormous sigh of relief when she saw Uli alone in a corner. He appeared to be the only one being deliberately sedated.

"What's going on with these people?" Karen asked, gesturing around at the entire outdoor clinic.

"So far, one out of three are dying, but most of them are actually responding to the meds. The flu symptoms are clearing up. But their mental faculties aren't improving; they aren't showing positive cognitive signs."

"If someone can help me get Uli outside," Karen said, "I'll take care of him from here."

"He put up quite a fight," the nurse warned.

"I'll be fine," Karen assured her.

The nurse detached Uli's IV, ending his sedative drip, then summoned a male staffer to help lift him onto a stretcher. Karen and the attendant carried his body to one of the black tarps near the waterway.

25

Because Uli had been stripped bare, Karen was directed to a pile of donated clothing. She was able to scrounge up khaki pants, a belt, a clean T-shirt, socks, and a large pair of penny loafers that she figured he could at least use as slippers. Tired, she lay down near him and looked at the black clouds now rolling south from the Brooklyn fires.

It was around sunset when she awoke to dull percussion noises that sounded like distant fireworks. All at once, from a mile away, she was shocked to see a synchronized series of luminous jets of orange flames shooting up across a long row of buildings along southeastern Brooklyn, as if someone had turned up a dial on a giant stove. A new breeze had just started blowing.

A general moan went up around her from both the staff and those patients still cursed with consciousness. This new ignition was within the designated safety zone that the firefighters had been valiantly holding. The renewed maelstrom incinerated the remaining hopes many had of returning to homes and buildings. Some began cursing, while others wept.

The conspirators must've decided that enough people have evacuated the city, Karen figured. Now they were finally burning off the last outer sections of the borough.

Still exhausted, Karen drifted off again, only to be awakened late at night by a terrific splash. She opened her eyes to see that the flimsy wooden bridge had collapsed into the waterway. It didn't matter; the canal wasn't particularly deep. In the glow of the distant fires, she could see that the water was crowded with desperate refugees, bobbing heads, half swimming and half walking across it.

As the new fires from southern Brooklyn slowly swept north, hundreds of diehards who had stopped optimistically in the Flatlands, hoping to get first dibs on the unburned homes, panicked.

"No! Go around!" one of the orderlies shouted at people climbing up into the quarantine zone.

"This is a plague colony!" another yelled.

"These people are highly contagious!" cried a third.

In another moment, dozens of frantic evacuees were hoisting themselves up onto the concrete embankment. A few went left or right, along the narrow roadway. But most of the soaked mob, confused and unable to see well in the darkness, started tripping over the stricken bodies lying on the black tarps. When a crowd of refugees came up against the newly erected segregation fence, they started scaling it.

A cluster of gloved and gas-masked gangcops entered the fray with their clubs swinging. Karen watched as a second formation of guards assembled along the canal's bank, blocking other refugees from wading across the canal. They were able to steer the rush around the quarantined section toward the outer encampment. A third group of cops lifted up the fallen fence protecting the quarantine zone.

The next morning when the chaos subsided, Karen heard Uli groaning. The sedatives in his system were thinning out—he was slowly coming to. When he started coughing, Karen went to fetch him a cup of water. He sat up as she handed it to him. He gulped the water down, and looked around, baffled.

"Uli? How are you feeling?" Karen asked tentatively.

Uli just stared behind her. *What's going on?* his brain raced. *Where's Banana Anna? . . .* Peering out into the desert land, he thought, *We're still in the Dakotas . . . Is this Wounded Knee? Why are there flames? . . . We're escaping— trying to escape to the desert—who's burning us down? Who am I? Where am I? . . . I'm an Armenian. Armenia! So it's the Turkish militia. Shoving us south into the Syrian desert to be picked off by the shotas organized by the dirty Ottomans . . .*

After a while, Uli tiredly lay back down, rolled over, and started smacking his lips, which Karen interpreted as hunger. She got up and located the food cart making its way through the aisles. She procured two hard rolls and an apple, then returned to find a thirtysomething black man sitting in her spot. He was quietly petting Uli, who had dozed off again.

When Karen asked him what was up, the man just smiled. It took a moment to realize that, like Uli, he was suffering from memory loss. "Well, bye-bye," she finally said, waving at him, hoping he might leave. When he didn't budge, she squeezed between him and her brother, compelling him to rise and sit back down a couple feet away.

Eventually, one of the PP volunteers, a sweet-faced young woman named Sarah, came over and introduced the impaired man as Woody, short for Woodside, the section of Queens he claimed to be from.

"So he speaks?"

"A little," Sarah said. Squatting down next to him, she asked, "Does Woody want to *vote* on sitting with us?"

"I vote *yay!*" Woody called out, then plunked back down next to Uli.

Sarah explained that Woody was fascinated by the electoral process, and if Karen needed him to do anything, she should just phrase it as a vote.

Karen looked over and saw that Woody and Uli were holding hands like children, which she found both sad and endearing.

* * *

After feeding and cleaning both Uli and Woody, Sarah told Karen that if she wanted to stretch her legs and go for a walk, she would be glad to watch both men. Desperately wanting to remove her face mask and surgical gloves, which were sticky and itchy, Karen thanked Sarah and left the quarantine zone after washing off at the little makeshift sink. She wandered over into the now-crowded encampment area, where she was able to inspect the newly established quarters up close. For the first time she saw that the tractors had cut a series of diversion creeks out of the canal and covered them with metal plates, so that the dirty water from the refugees could drain out into the desert and avoid polluting the encampment.

As Karen looked back toward Rescue City, she saw new refugees marching along, still entering the campgrounds. A squad of gangcops was diverting the newcomers to yet another tent, where everyone had to line up to register. Upon giving their names and other details, they were handed blankets and fifteen food stamps each for meals at one of the canteens. Lastly, they were each issued a number for a designated lot—a twenty-by-ten-foot space in one of the four quadrants that made up the rows and aisles in the prairie land once known as the Outer Rockaways.

In the absence of a mayor, and overriding the sanitation commissioner, the seven Crapper gangcop captains who had made it to Fort Til Then became the ruling council that ran the place. Captain Ronald Korman from Coney Island was put in charge of leading a team of rescue workers along the far side of the canal to assist hundreds of exhausted and injured Brooklynites who had escaped the fires in Red Hook and Sheepshead Bay.

A second captain was sent north, searching for any survivors who had settled in that direction. All they found was a displaced group of Piggers from Ozone Park who were camped out in the desert just east of Jamaica Bay. Members of Joe Gallo's crew had somehow hauled a pool table and a full-service bar to the outer lip of the desert. When the Crapper rescue team asked them to hike back up toward Queens, Gallo's men simply ignored them.

Upon returning from her break, Karen found Woody, Uli, and three others bowing, clasping hands, and muttering some strange lingo. It took her a minute to realize that Sarah, who was no longer wearing a mask or gloves, was leading them all in prayer. Although Karen loathed all religions, she thought the verbal instruction might actually have some therapeutic effects. After the short "service" was over, Karen saw that instead of returning to their former locations, the three new recuperators were making themselves comfortable in her area.

"Would you mind taking them elsewhere?" Karen delicately asked Sarah. "Uli and Woody alone are a handful."

"It's not me, it's Marsha," the young woman said, pointing to one of the smaller administrative tents. Karen could see that a new line of gates had been erected within the quarantine zone. "She's separating all the patients into three groups: those stable or recovering, which includes Uli and Woody; those who aren't getting any better or worse, which is over there; and those who are dying, which is the only group still officially in quarantine."

This explained why none of Uli's companions were exhibiting any flu-like symptoms. Yet all of them seemed to be at roughly the same level of mental impairment. Since they weren't fully cognizant, Marsha had deemed the entire group *noncogs*.

Early that evening, the new settlement witnessed a horrifying event. Throughout the day they had watched as the flames of Rescue City slowly climbed up the distant Williamsburgh Savings Bank Building. Then, a little after sunset, as a musician played a doleful rendition of "Taps," the tower finally collapsed. All fell silent, except for some quiet sobbing.

That night, rows of tiki torches were planted in the sand, creating lanes throughout Fort Til Then. Uli and his new pals had drifted back into slumber, huddled together like cats.

When light broke the next morning, Karen saw that three more companions had joined her group. Since many of the sick had already died off or were stabilizing, the volunteers began heading north back to Pure-ile Plurality. Sarah had chosen to stay and work in the far more demanding Section Two. Behind mask and gloves, she attempted to segregate those who might be getting worse from those whose symptoms were evening out.

At the very least, the noncogs with Uli were mobile, had basic comprehension skills, and were able to use the bathroom and feed themselves.

Karen dozed off for a few more hours, until she was awakened by a cacophonous popping of car engines gradually growing closer, along with some strange repetitive broadcast. When she stood up, she spotted three large-wheeled motorized tricycles which had navigated up along the improvised roadway bordering the canal's outer retaining wall. The drivers were all wearing long, flowing Native American warbonnets—they had obviously come from the colorful borough of Staten Island.

One of the tricycles, which had a bullhorn fastened to its rear bumper, was playing a looped announcement, which became clearer as they approached: "STATEN ISLAND'S HERE TO SHOUT! NO ONE'S PUSHING US OUT! YOU'RE WELCOME TO JOIN US TOO! JUST WALK WEST FOR SOME FOOD!"

Karen noticed Marsha scurrying into one of the administrative tents. Then, before the tricyclists could reach the quarantine zone, two Crapper gangcops sped their vehicles over and stopped the little motorcade. Karen watched as they gestured for the Verdant Leaguers to turn off their bullhorn.

Bea Moses-Mayer, who was clearly the leader of the little expedition, talked quietly to the gangcops for several minutes. Karen watched as Bea was then escorted to the big administrative tent in the TempMetro area.

Bea came out fifteen minutes later and returned to her entourage. The three motorized bikes then continued up the embankment path toward the campgrounds. As they approached, Karen flagged her down. Bea stopped, took off her headdress, and rubbed her fingers through her oily hair.

"I just wanted to thank you for telling me about him." Karen gestured over at Uli, who was awake but staring vacantly into the desert. "How's he doing?"

"His memory's shot. And he can't speak."

"Too bad," Bea said. Then, turning directly to Uli: "I was hoping you could tell us what happened to our police chief, Loveworks. You guys were seen heading north off on some secret mission."

Uli simply stared at her and smiled. *She was an almost-lover who lived among the white engines, then a political lesbian, but all the while she was my little girl, my lost little . . .* He couldn't remember her name, so he just kept smiling . . .

"Look, he recognizes me—don't you, Uli? He's going to be fine," Bea assured Karen.

"Really? How do you know?"

"You weren't that different from him when you were first brought down to Staten Island."

Karen didn't reply that at least she'd had the power of speech.

. . . After burying my poor wife Lucretia, I went home at night with my little daughter Bea. I left her alone night after night and got miserably drunk, and that kindly neighbor Lori would check in on her. I couldn't even clean the place . . . but that wasn't me, was it? No, it was Paul ▮▮▮▮▮▮▮▮▮
▮▮▮▮▮▮▮▮▮▮▮▮▮▮▮

"You're not my daughter," Uli suddenly barked. "You're Paul Moses's daughter!"

"Holy shit!" Karen shrieked.

"Yeah, but my father just passed away," Bea replied tenderly.

"That's the first time I've heard him speak!" Karen stepped closer to her brother.

"Banana Anna . . . would like that," Uli said, pointing to the headdress Bea was holding.

Bea kissed his cheek.

"I remember . . . taking care . . . of you," Uli said slowly and with difficulty, "when you were . . . just a baby . . . up in the Bronx."

"That was thirty years ago," Bea explained, hoping to jog his memory. "Now it's 1981 and we're in the Nevada desert. New York is contaminated, so we're all stuck here."

"I'm sorry . . . about the sneakers."

"What sneakers?" Bea asked.

"The radio . . . snickers . . ."

"Like Snickers candy bars?"

"Sneakers," he mumbled. It felt as though his lips had been tied into a balloon knot.

. . . I found the cheapest sneakers and purchased 101 pairs. I also bought several cones of string. I cut them into four-foot pieces and looped them through the pairs so that the laces were long enough for throwing . . . I poked holes in the front so that it allowed for maximum dispersal of the pitchblende when the panel clicked open . . .

"Uli, do you know where we are?" Karen asked, trying to distract him and derail the strange grunts he was making. She grabbed his hands and pointed out at the desert. "This is Nevada, remember? You went out into the desert to the Mkultra, remember?"

"With Banana Anna," he whispered.

"Do you remember a water station out there?" Karen asked.

painstakinglysolderingthe-littlewirestothespringswitchesofthedetonatorsof101bombs

"Do you remember where you went, Uli?"

After several minutes of struggle, Uli found himself lip locked and unable to squeeze out another word. Bea smiled sadly.

Karen asked her, "So, did they postpone the Robert Moses trial?"

"No, they found hi

thesneakerscouldn'tbespreadmorethantwoblocksapartoth-

erwisetheleveloftheradioactivitymightbetoolowtotriggerthenextbomb ███████

██

"Guilty?" Karen repeated in surprise. "What was his sentence?"

"Oh, they threw the book at him," Bea said. "For significantly distressing the lives of hundreds of thousands of lower- and middle-income New Yorkers, he was sentenced to a four-limb amputation. But considering his advanced age and all, Rafique immediately commuted his sentence to cleaning the dirtiest toilets at the Staten Island terminal."

"You're kidding! How did he react?"

"He was led to the bathroom on the ground floor of the lobby. Jane Jacobs herself gave him a toilet brush and we thought he was going to throw it back at her. But he just rolled up his sleeves and scrubbed the hell out of it. Amazing for such an old man. Then he walked outside just as the winds started blowing. Next thing we know, out of the blue, a guy driving a solicar appeared, helped Moses inside, and took off up Hyman Boulevard. Then the firebombs went off."

"Do you think the bombings were timed to Moses's exit?" Karen asked.

"If it was due to his arrest, it would've made more sense to set the fires when the trial first began, not afterward, right? Frankly, I think the bombers were just waiting for the sandstorm to hit."

"So where exactly did Robert Moses go?"

"A cop followed him for a while at Rafique's request, but lost him in the storm," Bea said.

"How badly did Staten Island get hit?" Karen could see Bea tensing up. "That bad?"

"Compared to you guys, we're fine."

"So what's wrong?"

"They killed Rafique," Bea said softly, holding back tears.

"Holy shit!"

"We don't want to start a panic, but they set off two bombs inside the terminal, and the bigger one was just outside his office. They somehow breached security."

"I can't believe he's gone," Karen said, immediately feeling the loss. Throughout her years in Rescue City, Adolphus Rafique had been the humane eye in a desperately brutal hurricane.

"They hit select homes in every VL community."

"Most of those places are just tar paper shacks," Karen said. "How'd the arsonists manage it without being caught?"

"They basically just tossed Molotov cocktails from solicars. For the most part, we were able to put out the fires before they could spread. It's the only advantage to not having buildings constructed side by side like you guys do."

"Who's in charge now?"

"According to the bylaws of VL succession, Jane is the new acting mayor of Staten Island." Bea paused a moment. "According to Rafique, she initiated the trial to raise her profile for the next election—but I never believed that. She's never been political."

"If I may ask, what exactly are you doing over here?" Karen asked.

"Since I hiked around this area just recently, when we evacuated from Quirklyn, Jane asked me to take this little crew around Rescue City and reestablish communications with the two other governments. Basically a recon mission."

"Aren't you worried about getting arrested up in Queens?"

"Not unless I run into Izzlowski. That guy really hated me."

"Be careful."

"They are more concerned with taking over the whole city," Bea said. "Early reports are that the Piggers actually did pretty well in terms of salvaging most of the South Bronx for resettlement. I just met with your captains who seem to be running this place. I asked if they might be interested in forming an alliance, but they didn't think it was necessary. I hope they're right."

"We need to get going," cut in a member of Bea's entourage. He was worried about the tricycles malfunctioning.

Bea wished Karen well and gave Uli a quick hug, then got back on her tricycle.

"Be safe!" Karen called out as the group puttered off.

"Bye-bye, little girl," Uli said quietly.

"Uli," Karen turned to her brother, hoping to catch some of his fleeting lucidity, "do you know where we are?"

He merely stared off after Bea. Testing a hypothesis that pain would bring him back to the here and now, Karen pinched the soft skin below his triceps.

"Ow!"

"Uli!" She pinched again, this time twisting the skin.

"What!"

"We're in the middle of the Nevada desert, Rescue City. And it's 1981." She dug her fingernails into his arm.

"Ow! Okay!" He pulled away.

"We need to get the *fuck* out of here! Understand? This fucking place is coming apart and we're either going to starve or die!"

Uli's stare fell on some distant point on the eastern horizon and he seemed to hang there.

Karen smacked him across the mouth and he looked at her fearfully. "There's a way out of here and you know it, Uli. Water! Remember the water?" She raked her fingernails hard across his arm, compelling him to lunge forward and backflip her onto the hard sand.

His muscle memory was obviously still intact. She chose not to test it again.

26

During her next break that evening, Karen strolled through the vast outdoor encampment of Fort Til Then. Handwritten signs marked off the key lanes. Although some of the settlers had brought their own pup tents, the vast majority simply had their Crapper-issued blankets along with whatever they had bought, traded, stolen, or found. Many used poles, sticks, and other salvaged items to rig together some kind of shelter, protecting them from the blazing sun. Some of the shelters were just blankets covering shallow holes where people kept their few possessions and rested. But as Karen walked farther out into the fringes, the space loosened up and some people grew more creative, cutting lengthy trenches and building sandcastles.

Soon she circled over to the outdoor mess area in the northeastern sector—rows of improvised picnic tables. A cafeteria-style line was forming around the large open grill. Dozens of people had paper plates filled with what appeared to be tuna casserole and steamed vegetables. Upon being served, each person had to give up an issued food stamp.

When Karen returned to the clinic after her walk, she found chaos. Contagious and critical patients in the first and second divisions of the clinic were moaning and no one was responding. Uli and his group were all alone. Sarah and most of the remaining PP workers had simply vanished.

Marsha Johnson moved alone among the sickly, trying to prioritize her efforts.

"Where is everyone?" Karen called out to her.

"They went back to Pure-ile Plurality."

"Why? What happened?"

"The Piggers forced Rolland to withdraw," Marsha said. "It's always about politics, isn't it?"

"So why are *you* still here?"

"Between belonging to a Christian organization and being a Christian, I chose the latter. I can't abandon these people. They're human beings."

"I'll run over to the administrative tents and get some help," Karen offered.

"I already told them. They said we'll be getting some new people in a couple hours. We just need to hold out till then. I'm going to stay with the contagious section. Just watch the noncogs and try to handle any emergencies until a cavalry gets here."

As Karen moved around the clinic area, periodically cleaning and hydrating her charges, she noticed a middle-aged white woman lingering just outside the hurricane fence, staring suspiciously at her. The woman looked familiar and when she turned, Karen saw she was missing an arm. Whenever Karen saw an amputee she automatically feared that she'd had a judicial hand in their loss. But this woman, holding a green sack in her one hand, just seemed sad.

"You're not one of the new volunteers, are you?" Karen asked as she neared the fence.

"You don't remember me, do you?" the amputee replied.

"Did I arrest you?" Karen asked tensely.

"The Piggers punished me for colluding with the enemy."

"What enemy?"

Glancing around nervously, the amputee murmured, "I was a . . . trustee in the former underground lab called the Mkultra. I found you there."

"Found me?"

"You had been sexually assaulted and beaten."

"Sexually assaulted?"

"I'm afraid so," the woman said.

"By who?"

"Who knows? All I could do was clean you up."

"You just decided to save me out of the goodness of your heart?" Karen asked doubtfully.

"You were completely out of it, so I don't expect you to believe me."

"You know, this area is quarantined but unrestricted—why don't you put on a mask and glove and come over?"

The one-armed woman headed to the entrance, where she put on the protective gear and joined Karen several minutes later. She introduced herself as Root.

"*He* might remember me," she said, gesturing toward Uli with her chin. She dropped her bag and sat down on the other side of him. "How you doing, pal?"

Uli stared at her and smiled. He seemed to recognize her, but didn't say a word.

"How'd this happen?" Root asked Karen.

"He got sick."

"But he was vaccinated."

"Who knows what really happened. There are only a few crappy doctors here. In fact . . ." Karen removed her face mask. "If I get sick, so be it. I can't wear this anymore."

"I was with him when we came out of the desert. Hell, I spoke to him while we were both up in the Bronx Zoo," Root said, also removing her mask but keeping her glove on. "He seemed miserable but I didn't think he was sick."

"Do you know where the water stations are?" Karen asked the only question that mattered.

"You mean that water pump on the way here?"

"Yes! Where exactly was it?"

"Thataway." Root pointed due east.

"Did you just arrive here?"

"Yeah, I was up in Queens still recovering from my amputation when the fires broke out, so I was evacuated with the Piggers, but I left when I could 'cause I didn't want to be with those fucking savages who cut my arm off."

"Why don't you join us?" Karen proposed. "We could sure use the help."

"I'm a useless gimp! They took my fucking arm! I can't even help myself."

"If you were able to survive in the black hole of the Mkultra, you must be incredibly strong and resourceful."

"Please don't patronize me."

"If you were down there, you probably have more experience than any of us in dealing with the mentally impaired."

"We really do need help," Marsha suddenly appeared. "No one has responded yet to our call for volunteers."

Root let out a big sigh and said she'd stick around until others joined them.

Over the next hour two others volunteered, provided they worked in the noncontagious zone.

Karen was able to get Root a blanket to sleep on, as well as food stamps and basic supplies—a toothbrush, a towel, and a change of clothes. She walked Root and the other volunteers through the daily schedule of chores that had to be performed—all patients had to be cleaned, fed, and given some kind of exercise.

"With all due respect, this is nothing," Root remarked when Karen finished with her instructions. "In the Mkultra, I tried to look after hundreds. I never slept more than a couple hours at a time. I was able to turn a group of semifunctionals into a staff."

"Where's your staff now?" Karen asked.

"Lost in the refugee shuffle."

Over the course of the next several days, Root's experience with invalid care more than made up for her missing arm. She was also able to impart little tricks she had learned, such as tying a string to the more functional noncogs' fingers to help them remember little things, like pulling up their pants after going to the bathroom. The overall staff shortage actually had the serendipitous effect of speeding up the rate of death for those already dying and allowing more time for the care of the noncogs.

After three days, however, Root started feeling dizzy herself and had trouble getting out of bed. Marsha realized that the woman was running a low-grade fever and feared that she might've contracted the dreaded plague. But when she checked Root's amputation scar, she saw that it had become infected. Marsha picked up some supplies at the medical tent, including a roll of gauze and a handful of antibiotics.

"Listen," Karen said, as Marsha cleaned Root's wound that afternoon, "tell me again how you get to the water stations."

"I don't know about stations, I only saw the one, but I remember him saying there were others due east."

"So how do we get to the one you saw?" Karen asked. "Didn't you say there was some kind of trail?"

"Uli said he followed the smoke to get to the Mkultra site when the place was on fire. The Piggers would know—they drove out there in dune buggies."

"They went to the water station?"

"No, they went straight to the Mkultra. They just followed the smoke and took a vehicle-friendly route."

"But there's no smoke," Marsha said, peering east.

"Wait a sec." Root paused and scratched her head. "He had those two guys splashing the yellow paint."

"What yellow paint?"

"Plato made that a condition of our early release—to create a path with the paint."

"So where's this yellow trail?"

"Just hike north and you'll probably find it."

"And from there the other water stations just magically line up due east?" Karen asked.

Root shrugged.

That night, three more critical cases died.

Around noon the next day, a wail of sirens sounded from the distant embers of Brooklyn.

"That's them," Tatianna announced, appearing from the other side of the fence.

"Who?" Karen asked.

"Remember I told you that LaCoste caught one of the pyros? Apparently it wasn't one person, but two. He held them up in the Bronx until the fire had all burned out."

All eyes focused across the canal as two blackened and singed minibuses came to a halt. After countless detours, they had somehow managed to navigate a passage through the still-smoking embers of the city. Karen could hear orders squawking over Tatianna's walkie-talkie. In another minute, all the gangcops in the vicinity started converging along the banks of the canal. Some jumped into the shallow waters. Others formed a gauntlet. Twenty men with pistols in hand faced the growing crowd of refugees watching from behind the fencing.

"Does LaCoste really think these two prisoners will tell us a way out of here?" Karen asked.

"The yarmulke will yank it out of them," said Tatianna. "Otherwise we're screwed."

Amid all of the hubbub, Karen, Marsha, and some of Uli's group angled around to the west for a better view. All wanted to catch a glimpse of the mysterious coconspirators who had burned their city to the ground.

The minibuses pulled a few more yards forward and the crowd groaned and shouted curses. LaCoste stepped out of the lead vehicle and opened the back door. Three gangcops from the other minibus helped the two handcuffed prisoners out of LaCoste's vehicle and lowered them into the canal. The first prisoner was a handsome, middle-aged black man, and the second was an older white man with severe facial wounds. The gangcops already in the canal encircled the two and together they all waded in tight formation across the waterway.

Once she got a clear view, Karen's heart sank when she saw that the older man was none other than Scouter Lewis, and behind him was her dear friend Akbar Del Piombo.

When the suspects had crossed the canal and were lifted out, La-Coste growled orders and two lines of gangcops surrounded them. Karen watched as the prisoners were marched over to the heavily guarded administrative sector of TempMetro.

"What do you know about this, Gaspar?" Karen called out to her old friend, a fellow captain, once he had hoisted himself up from the canal.

"LaCoste caught the burners is all I know," he replied. "Held these two out in the desert beyond the Bronx for two days without food or water so the Piggers wouldn't catch him. Then he snuck back into the Bronx, where he was able to hijack some cars and drive back through that giant smoldering ash heap down here." As he talked, Karen followed him toward TempMetro.

"I don't know that black motherfucker, but Scouter Lewis—screw him!" Gaspar Stenson continued. "It makes sense that he'd be a part of this. He was always a slippery shit."

"During the two days that he held them in the desert, did he interrogate either of them?" Karen asked.

"He tried. Neither would say a word. Two tight clams. He's gonna twist the yarmulke onto both of them."

Karen was relieved that Akbar apparently hadn't mentioned her during the interrogation. If he had even uttered her name once, La-Coste probably would've strangled him right there and then come after her.

"Is the CIA medical unit even around anymore?" Karen pressed. They were the only ones qualified to do the yarmulke procedure.

"No, but he's got Olsen, who stole the machinery and says he can do it himself." Ted Olsen, a functional croak addict who had been tossed out of medical school for stealing pharmaceuticals, was the Pigger gangcop medical examiner until they tossed him out for the very same reason.

27

The next day, in an effort to try to help Akbar, Karen headed over to the new penal tent to see if she could find some chain of command above LaCoste whom she could appeal to. She approached Tatianna and asked her who the new AG was.

"McNeill appointed someone, but the guy died in the fires of Manhattan," Tatianna explained. "Right now we have the group of seven precinct captains who are overseeing this place—the Captain Committee."

When Karen asked if she could speak to Gaspar Stenson, Tatianna directed her to an adjacent tent. This large canvas domicile seemed to be the tactical headquarters for the criminal justice division. Before entering she had to get patted down, then she was directed to Stenson's secretary Cathy, a short, stout woman whose hairdo looked like a pile of Brillo pads.

"Sorry, but he's completely overwhelmed," Cathy said, not knowing who Karen was. "Come back in a week."

"It's absolutely imperative that I see him this very minute." Karen flashed her red badge. "Just tell him it's Captain Sarkisian; I guarantee he'll make time."

Cathy pointed to a chair off to the side. Karen took a seat and contemplated how she was going to explain that she knew Akbar was innocent. How could she recount the whole twisted saga of trying to eliminate Schuman and enlisting Akbar's help? In telling the story, she would inadvertently incriminate both of them in the AG's murder.

In the middle of the large tent was a metal cage that served as an armory locker. As a gangcop loaded two guns inside, Karen glimpsed a small shelving unit that held boxes of ammo. At the very end of the shelf, she recognized the wooden box that held the notorious steel yarmulke.

After more than an hour had passed, Tatianna rushed into the crowded tent. Karen saw her pick up a cardboard file box and then head over to the locked cage, where she took a large ring of keys out of her sweater pocket and opened the metal door. Tatianna grabbed the wooden yarmulke box and placed it on top of the file box, then locked the cage behind her.

"Need help?" Karen intercepted her as she was heading out.

"No, I'm fine." Tatianna was instantly suspicious. "What are you doing here?"

"I have a meeting with Gaspar," Karen said. "But I have a few minutes, so let me help you."

"Actually, if you can put these on my desk," Tatianna handed her the bulky file box, "I have to run to the penal area in the back."

As Tatianna set her load on the ground, the keys dropped out of her pocket. Karen stepped forward as though to retrieve them, but tripped over her own feet and kicked the keys under a desk.

As the secretary stooped under the desk, Karen quickly flipped open the lid of the box containing the steel yarmulke and looked inside. At least a dozen colorful hair-strand wires splayed out of the shiny skull-shaped apparatus. In the space of a few seconds, she carefully twirled one of the fine wires around her thumb and plucked it out. Tatianna rose with her keys just as Karen closed the lid.

"Just leave that cardboard box on my desk, if you would," Tatianna said, grabbing the wooden box.

Karen headed toward the administrative tent as Tatianna hurried off.

After dumping the file box on the secretary's desk, Karen returned to the criminal justice tent. She was taken by surprise when Stenson appeared behind her and said, "If this is about my car—don't sweat it, there's no longer anywhere to drive it."

"I know this is LaCoste's big case," she said, sidestepping his humor, "but I worked with Akbar for years. He was one of my best ghosts."

"It's all done. LaCoste is about to bar mitzvah him right now."

"I only hope they get something. I don't know how much longer all these people can survive out here."

"Agreed," Stenson said, then left for his next appointment. Karen prayed that her little stunt would buy Akbar some time.

Back at the clinic, she and Root began preparing meals for Uli's little gang, which had now grown to nine noncogs. As Karen was chopping vegetables, Root pointed out that some older guy was shouting her name from the far side of the fence. Karen glanced over to see Captain Stenson waving at her.

"What's up?" she asked, walking over.

"We're taking you up on your generous offer," Stenson replied.

"To interrogate Akbar?"

"Not quite." Lowering his voice, he said, "The operation did not go according to plan."

"What do you mean?"

"They had just sawed off the top of Scouter's skull when the machine started shooting off sparks and smoke."

"Oh my God!"

"He's still alive, but he's got one hell of a headache. When we try talking to him, he just keeps saying Uli's name. Since your brother's not exactly able to talk, we thought maybe you could speak to Scouter, but we better hurry."

"I'll speak to him, but only if I can talk to Akbar afterward," she said.

"Deal." They rushed to the tent where the prisoners were being held. "Karen, as you yourself have said, we got thousands of people here and it's only a matter of time before we start running out of supplies. We need to know how to get the fuck out of here, understand?"

"I'll do what I can."

A security guard patted Karen down outside the tent. When she and Stenson entered, she saw Scouter Lewis seated at a table with a woman who appeared to be a nurse. She had just finished wrapping gauze around his bloody head. The thin fabric seemed to be all that was holding his skull in place. Sopping wet with blood, the gauze slid down over his dull, unfocused eyes. On the table was the shiny bowl-shaped instrument with wires coming from the top—the steel yarmulke. It was splattered in blood.

"Scouter," she said loudly, sitting down across from him.

"Bea, is that you?" he replied, clearly discombobulated.

Playing a hunch, she softly muttered, "Yeah." Fortunately, Stenson didn't interfere, he just sat there watching the scene unfold.

"Bea, dear, I'm so sorry. I just want you to know that your mom really was the unfortunate victim of a very common accident. She slipped on the ice and hit her head. That's the best we could figure out. It was God's plan." Near death, all scumbags turn religious. The blood was still trickling across his skull. "I feel bad because, well, Valerie Solanas, that woman you asked me about . . . well, that's another story."

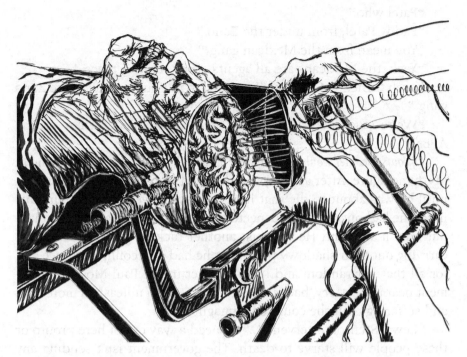

Karen breathed deeply to make him aware that she was still listening.

"See, she was alive when I found her, but in really rough shape from the flood. She was basically unconscious. I knew you were up to something, but I didn't kill her 'cause of that. I did it to put her out of her misery . . . That's the truth. I hope you can forgive me, 'cause I really think *she* forgave me."

"Were you putting *me* out of my misery when you shoved me down the sewage hole?"

"Karen!"

"Are you putting the *city* out of its misery now?!"

"Did your brother tell you—"

"My brother didn't have to tell me anything. I remembered it, just like I remember Schuman with you down there in Staten Island!"

"Since you remember . . . everything so well," he struggled to say, "let me ask you this: do you remember flipping the switch?"

Karen went silent.

"What's he talking about?" Stenson asked.

Karen ignored him. "Scouter, if you want to do one final good thing before you die, this is your chance! Where are the water stations?"

"How the fuck should I know? You think I've been out there? Ask Patel, he's on recon."

"Patel who?"

"Paddy Patel, from under the Zano."

"You mean from the Mexican gang?"

"Yeah, the Mexicans are all agents. They run this place."

Karen turned to Stenson. "You need to put out an APB on the Zano gang."

"We're stuck here in Fort Til Then," he replied. "There are no APBs."

Of course Scouter would leave it to the bitter end, Karen thought, staring at his dying figure. After all the years they had worked together, it wasn't until he was about to die that he'd finally removed his mask. In fairness, she had once openly suspected him and he had flatly denied it—but now it was out. He was just another fucking government agent, carrying out their shadowy plans. But he had also confirmed once and for all that her random and impulsive act inside Paul Moses's apartment near the Battery, back in March of 1970, had unleashed more pain and suffering than she could ever imagine.

"Lew," Stenson intervened, "we need a way out of here pronto or these people will starve to death. The government isn't sending any more drones, do you understand? No one's coming to our aid—we're on our own!"

Lewis's mouth opened slightly, but only shallow breaths came out.

They spent another ten minutes desperately trying to revive the man, but his faculties were steadily diminishing. When an aide came in and whispered something to Stenson, he led Karen out of the tent and told her, "We're fucked."

"Give me time alone with Akbar—I promise I'll get him talking."

"I don't have the authority. He's LaCoste's prisoner."

"What the fuck?" Karen yelled. "LaCoste is a lieutenant, you're a captain!"

"Actually, due to his big arrest, LaCoste was just promoted. He's a captain now too."

"Promoted by who?"

"Mayor McNeill. He just arrived here last night."

"So he knows about this case?"

"This is the only active investigation here. That's why LaCoste got promoted. When I told him that you've worked with Akbar and offered to help, LaCoste said he had proof that you murdered Schuman, and has requested that McNeill sign your arrest warrant. He hates you."

Karen sighed and returned to the clinic, joining the others in the various routines that were required to care for the noncogs.

That evening, as she was putting the last of the noncogs to sleep, Karen was confronted by a breathless gangcop with a skull shaped like a pear. She assumed he was placing her under arrest, but instead he told her to follow him. As she moved behind him past security into the penal tent, LaCoste shoved his way out without even noticing her. Captain Stenson was on his tail and cursing furiously at him.

"What the hell is going on?" Karen asked.

Half a dozen other gangcops were standing around looking over at Mayor McNeill, who evidently had also just entered.

LaCoste suddenly returned inside and, finally noticing Karen, hollered, "This is all *her* fucking fault!"

"Screw you!" Karen yelled back.

"She killed Schuman and probably Mallory!"

"You're nuts!"

"Any more of that and you're out of here!" McNeill scolded LaCoste.

"I might as well go," he fired back, and pointed at Karen. "You people trust a cold-blooded murderer over *me!*" He stormed out of the tent with Mayor McNeill and three of his bodyguards on his heels.

"What the hell happened?" Karen asked Stenson.

He informed her that after Lewis died a few hours earlier, LaCoste had arrived and interrogated Akbar, who insisted that he didn't know anything. LaCoste told him that he had till midnight to give up the route out.

"I asked him to let me call you in to help interrogate, but of course he despises you," Stenson said. "Then I tried to talk to Del Piombo myself. I got him a warm meal and had the guards bring him a bucket of water to clean himself . . . But apparently LaCoste returned when I wasn't there and flipped out, saying we were coddling him."

"What happened?" Karen could feel her heart beating in her chest.

"The steel yarmulke broke so apparently he decided to do it himself."

"Do what?!"

"The interrogation. When I came back a half an hour ago, I heard screams. There was blood everywhere. LaCoste was still with him." Stenson shook his head dismally.

"Did he kill him?" Karen was barely able to breathe. "Is he dead?"

"LaCoste blinded him."

"Blinded?"

"Stabbed him, first in one eye and then the other," Stenson said.

"Is he getting medical attention?"

"Morphine, and we had the medic bind his wounds, but . . . You wanna talk to him?"

"And say what?" Karen asked, unable to hide her tears. "*We blinded you, now tell us what we want?*"

"Look, I think he understands that there are two sides here—us and LaCoste. It might be an opportunity to show that he can either work with us or he'll be at the mercy of that monster again."

"Let's go."

Stenson led her several tents down to the infirmary, where he waved her past the guards. Poor Akbar was lying on a cot, covered in blood, making gasping sounds, trying to manage his suffering. Fresh bandages were taped over his eyes.

"A moment alone?" Stenson asked the guard. Both of them stepped away.

"I'm so sorry, Eugene," Karen whispered.

"Karen . . ." He reached out and hugged her, weeping softly.

"What the fuck were you doing with Scouter Lewis?" she asked.

"The night of the blaze I was awakened by my phone ringing. It was Scouter saying the city was burning down and if I wanted out, I could go with him—he needed a driver. Before I could tell him to fuck off, I looked out the window and realized the whole city *was* burning down."

"What a mess."

"They kept asking me how to get out of here! If I knew, don't you think I would've left?" Akbar was shaky, injured badly, and only lightly sedated. "The fucker handcuffed me. I thought he was going to smack me around a little. Instead, he stuck me."

Karen shushed him, fearing the guard was listening. She took his hand. "They're trying to keep LaCoste away from you for the time being," she whispered into his right ear. "This is what you're going to do. Wait a day or so, until your mind clears, then insist on speaking to the new mayor. They're desperate so they'll do it. His name is Mc-Neill. He's your best shot. Explain to him that you'll tell him how to cross the desert, but you want your life spared. Simple as that."

"And what am I going to say when he asks me how to get out of here?"

"Tell him to walk north from here until they start to see yellow paint."

"There's a yellow brick road through the desert?" Akbar replied with mournful sarcasm.

"They splattered rocks and cacti with yellow paint. Anyone who walks due north of here should eventually come across it."

"North?"

"Go north till they come across the painted path, then follow it due east to a water station and keep heading that direction into the desert."

They spoke quietly for another few minutes before LaCoste and his two henchmen stormed into the infirmary. "You do *not* have permission to talk to my prisoner!" he roared. "Next time I see you here, I'll kill you myself, *capisce*?!"

He had his guards escort Karen back to the clinic. There was no sign of Stenson.

28

Back in the clinic, Captain Stenson stopped by and explained that LaCoste had pulled her red pass, and thus her status. Without any security clearance, she was no longer allowed into the TempMetro zone.

"Did Del Piombo tell you anything?" he asked.

"Yeah, that LaCoste tortured him without even giving him the opportunity to speak. He knows something, but now he just wants to die."

"Bullshit."

"LaCoste isn't a cop, he's a lowlife piece of shit just like his brother," Karen said. "When you give a sadist authority, you create a tyrant. It'll just be a matter of time before he tries to take McNeill's office."

For the next two days, Karen simply took care of her noncogs and patiently waited to see what would become of Akbar.

On the morning of the third day, the gangcop with the pear-shaped skull came to tell Karen that Captain Stenson needed her to report to the mayor's tent at once. She followed him past the guard post and over to the largest tent, where an executive meeting appeared to be in progress. The entire Captain Committee was standing in a circle watching their newest member, Captain LaCoste, scream at the mayor.

"You don't have *any* idea how easy it is to get lost in the desert. You're just a kid!"

"We have compasses," McNeill replied calmly. "Figuring out which way is north and which way is east shouldn't be a problem."

"Okay, let's just take a look at what we see east of here." LaCoste yanked open the tent flap and pointed east. "Oh gee, what's that? I believe it's a giant mountain range."

"Not quite; the path actually cuts just south of it," another captain corrected, looking through a small pair of opera glasses.

"In my day, when we saw a yellow-lined path," LaCoste yelled, "we knew we were following someone with a full bladder! But *you* think it's a way out!"

"Look," the mayor said, "he gave us new information. We're going to test it. Simple as that."

LaCoste glanced over and saw that Karen had entered. "What the hell is she even doing here?" he shouted at Stenson.

"If you have something to say, say it to *me*, asshole!" Karen stepped forward. "You're a torturer and an asshole!" She was hoping to provoke him into throwing a punch, and was prepared to grab his arm and knock him flat on his ass. Before this could happen, however, Stenson stepped between them.

"That's enough!" snapped the mayor.

"This is coming from the guy who's about to let thousands of people die 'cause he's a hothead," Karen accused.

"They'll die a lot more quickly in the desert," LaCoste shot back.

"Bad news, Tony," Karen said. "Now that Rescue City has burned down—this *is* the desert. And we *are* dying."

"We still have water—it hasn't stopped flowing."

"I'd rather starve fighting to make it across the desert than starve here," said one of the other captains.

"Me too," agreed another.

"Here's what we're going to do," McNeill said. "We'll send out an expedition of maybe a dozen armed, fit men. They'll leave at sunset tonight with as much as they can carry. If they don't find this yellow path, which is supposedly fairly close to here, they'll come back. If they do find it, they follow it to one of these wells and send one man back to tell us where it is. And the rest of the team can keep moving forward, leaving a clear path for us all to follow. When they reach civilization, half of them will get help, the other half will return and tell us how to get the hell out. Then we'll follow."

Before any further discussions could ensue, LaCoste announced that he was now embracing this plan—under the sole proviso that he lead the advance party.

Still feeling in LaCoste's debt for his capture of Lewis and Del Piombo, and clearly attempting to show a unified front, McNeill gave LaCoste his blessing as the commander of the expedition.

Over the course of the next couple of hours, Captain LaCoste identified eleven men to join him. He gave them all blue shirts, and had someone write on them in bold print, TEAM RESCUE.

Each team member was supplied with a knapsack packed with

food, a sleeping bag, a fully loaded pistol, and good shoes. The mayor insisted on adding two of his own men to LaCoste's team: two experienced survivalists, Sergeants Philip Kendowski and Caleb Straus.

The group departed quietly that evening so as not to draw attention to themselves.

While serving her people lunch the next day, Karen learned that the mayor's two scouts had just arrived back at camp with startling news: after roughly three hours of longitudinal and latitudinal combing, the group had in fact located the streaks of yellow paint along the rocks, and had followed them to the first water pump. LaCoste had then used the opportunity to eject the only two members of the team whom he had not personally chosen.

Each morning after that, Karen went to see Tatianna in the administrative tent, hoping for updates on the expedition's progress. Yet each day, nothing. Over the course of the next week, Tatianna relayed that McNeill and his staff were growing increasingly concerned. Food supplies were dwindling.

"Is there a plan B?" Karen asked Tatianna on the ninth day after the team's departure.

"They've been talking about sending out a second, smaller team, but what's the point? Best-case scenario, they'll find the first team dead and have to turn back because they won't have enough supplies to keep going."

Two days later, during dinner, the upper west quadrant ran out of canned chicken Parmesan before everyone was served. Within twenty minutes, tables were overturned and garbage was strewn across the dining area.

The following evening, when rice and veggies for the lower west quadrant ran out, the unserved refugees raided the food pantry. All available gangcops were called in to quell the disturbance, resulting in one dead civilian. Six cops and more than a dozen other civilians were injured.

The food riot prompted Mayor McNeill to hold his first public address the next day. Everyone agreed that if nothing else, people needed something to hope for. In the wide expanse before the TempMetro tents, near the entrance to Fort Til Then, a fifteen-foot ladder was installed. At its top was a small microphone. Loudspeakers were placed around so all could hear. At noon, Mayor Don McNeill, wearing a black suit, white shirt, and brown tie, solemnly stepped up the shaky ladder to the mic, which he took in hand.

"For those of you who don't know me, I'm Don McNeill. I was deputy mayor under the late Mayor Mallory. When she died of the desert flu, I legally succeeded her. A couple weeks ago, we learned about a covert plan created by the federal government to allow a large volume of people to pass across a designated path in the desert that is lined with water. It is widely believed that this path is located above an underwater river or aquifer and leads out to civilization. The very night we learned about it, we sent out an elite team to test this method of departure and we have been waiting for the results."

Predictably, some applause went up.

"I'm now asking that you be patient with us and pray, as we have been praying, for that team to return soon with either help or a way out."

An additional smattering of applause followed, but before the mayor could climb down from the ladder, grumblings sounded throughout the vast camp area. After many days of anxiously watching supplies run low, this message simply wasn't enough. Aside from concern about the next big windstorm that might wipe out the exposed settlement, the mayor had failed to explicitly address the food shortages, as well as the looming Pigger threat from the north. Everyone had heard reports of armed Pigger patrols passing within view of the encampment.

The next day, a contingent of the most radical refugees organized a group called Evacuate Now and circulated a petition. Within hours it had been signed by over a thousand encamped refugees.

Mayor McNeill:

It's been two weeks since Team Rescue went out into the desert, and they haven't been heard from since. Food is running out and we can no longer afford to sit idly by.

Ergo, we believe it's time for a contingency plan. This plan should be cautiously extended to those who are physically able to endure the challenging hike ahead. Fit hikers should be stocked with supplies and allowed access to all information about the pathway out. That way, instead of having a single team trying to save former Rescue City residents, we could have multiple teams working toward a common goal, all going at their own risk.

We urgently await your response,
Evacuate Now

The next morning, Mayor McNeill climbed back up the ladder and made another official statement: "To the renegade few who are asking us to open our pantries and let them take to the great plains, I say no! We're not going to freak out and permit our limited resources and our citizens to be scattered across the Nevada desert! We have a crack team out there, carefully selected for their physical prowess, searching carefully along uncharted land, moving faster than most, and they're going to return soon. Either they're going to bring the cavalry back with them or they're going to tell us exactly how to get clear of here as a single unified group. I refuse to let anyone be sacrificed to panic or fear!"

He received some light applause and no one jeered.

Later that day, at the suggestion of one of his advisers, McNeill assembled two squads of gangcops. One was sent back into the smoldering rubble of Rescue City to try to salvage additional caches of food from the ashes. The second group ventured out into the scrubland to set traps and hunt for wild boars. One of the captains also sent the two original group members, Straus and Kendowski, back out to the first water station, so that when any exhausted members of Team Rescue were spotted, they could help them race back with the glorious news. But each new day, as certain foods grew more scarce, new inconveniences mounted. When shampoo ran out, all were fine with soap. Then butter evaporated, but butter was an indulgence anyway. When black pepper ran out, everyone noticed, but that hardly seemed like a reason to riot. They were living in a time of deprivation. McNeill coined a slogan: "If you save something, state something—show your sacrifice!"

Over the next two weeks, however, all the little pleasantries seemed to drain away. One afternoon, the tiny fruit cup that had always been included with everyone's lunch was absent. When someone inquired, everyone learned that the last of the gallon-sized containers of canned fruit in heavy syrup had been consumed.

That night, a small group of hooded men overwhelmed the two guards watching the lower west quadrant's pantry and stole a couple hundred loaves of frozen raisin bread. Teams of gangcops began aggressively patrolling the rows and aisles of the encampment, stopping anyone who was found eating, making them open their mouths, pulling their blankets off of their holes. Tension was growing. Graffiti started appearing with phrases like, *Your job is to protect and serve, not test our nerve!*

A few mornings later, the official ladder and microphone appeared before the giant white administrative tent and speakers were once again put out. The mayor announced that anyone who wanted to leave Rescue City would be given some food. They had to provide their own canteens. "I don't suggest anyone take this alternative, but for those troublemakers who are contemplating violence, I'd rather they go in peace than become a drain on the rest of us."

The mayor knew that Evacuate Now was behind the vandalism, and in an effort to stem the tide of dissent, he and his team figured that when confronted with the real possibility of having to cross the endless desert by foot, with only a bag of food, any sane person would immediately back down and grow docile. The mayor was therefore amazed when he was awakened the following morning with a report that nearly twenty people had arrived at one of the mess tents and were asking for their departing food stock—they wanted out.

At that day's security meeting, a captain from Bensonhurst proposed that every member of Evacuate Now be arrested as traitors, but McNeill said, "No, a promise made is a promise kept."

"Actually, maybe we should get in front of this. It might avoid a larger uprising," said a Manhattan gangcop captain.

"How?" the mayor asked.

"Let's escort them to the first water station. This way we can at least keep people from defecting into the Pigger camp and tipping them off that we're losing people. We can walk them at night when visibility is poor. From the first station we can point them east. That way we get rid of the troublemakers, and we look like good guys to those who remain here."

"And," a third captain added, "if they actually do make contact with anyone on the outside, they'll still be in our debt, instead of feeling like we abandoned them."

The plan was ratified.

At midnight, a group of twenty-two showed up for the first sanctioned departure from Rescue City. Each member was provided with twelve bologna-and-cheese sandwiches, then they were greeted by Sergeants Straus and Kendowski, who proceeded to escort them through the night to the first water station, roughly eighteen miles away. During the hike, Kendowski imparted basic survival tips, such as how to carefully sever the top of a barrel cactus and chew down its pulp for moisture in case of severe dehydration. He also told them about dangerous wildlife in the region, such as wild boars; what to do in the event of a snakebite; and the importance of taking shelter during the heat of midday. Since they didn't have any extra compasses to hand out—another unpleasant surprise—Sergeant Straus, who had studied astronomy, demonstrated how to use constellations and geological markers for guidance in moving eastward. He also explained that the lead group, Team Rescue, was supposed to have left trail markings along the "Freedom Trail." They should all be on the lookout for these signs. They might be stacks of stones or even carefully positioned sticks. At the very least, everyone should always keep an eye out for shoe prints and extinguished firepits.

"Also, others will probably be following you," Kendowski said. "So if you can leave sticks or stones yourselves—anything to mark the path—it'd be greatly appreciated."

The hikers were grateful for the tips, and the next morning, when they finally reached the first water station, they camped out for the afternoon to avoid the blazing sun. The two scouts bid them farewell and began their own march back to Fort Til Then.

29

Three days later, when Fort Til Then officially ran out of the last canned vegetables, Mayor McNeill received a report that another group, this time thirty-two people, had requested their food quota and an escort to the first water station.

"Damn! I knew we should've executed the first group," muttered the Bensonhurst captain.

The pantries were stocked and wooden pallets were loaded with fifty-pound burlap sacks packed mainly with rice, as well as lentils. Thus, a new diet was issued: Each person was allotted two plastic bags, one containing two pounds of rice and one with two pounds of lentil beans. They were also given a small tin of lard, two Sterno cans, and a four-ounce envelope of salt.

As news spread of the defections, it emboldened others with the thought that it was better to die trying than to starve here. Two days later, a third group of fourteen people came forward.

The following day, another expedition left. Then another. After several more defections, a group stepped forward asking for their food quota but adding that they didn't need the escort. They had opted to go west—to join the VL. McNeill issued a public decree that very evening that anyone joining another political party in Rescue City was not eligible for the "water station entitlements."

Without food, the VL defectees left the next day.

More groups flaked off in the ensuing days, until the one-month anniversary of the LaCoste team's departure arrived. By then, people had begun writing them off. What could have happened to a dozen strong, armed men so that not a single one could return?

This is no longer a matter of protecting the rights of the minority, wrote one indignant citizen in an outhouse-posted open letter to Mayor McNeill. *Your generosity is now imperiling the rights of those of us who are staying.*

Five weeks after Team Rescue had vanished, Tatianna came by the clinic to bid farewell to Karen and Uli. She and her family were scheduled to walk that night.

"You're not worried about dying in the desert?" Karen asked.

"We're more worried about dying here."

Karen wished her a safe and hasty passage and hugged her goodbye.

The next morning, over half a cup of Quaker Oats and weak tea, Marsha spoke with Karen.

"I don't want to leave you high and dry, but I just heard a rumor that the pantry is a lot emptier than they thought. And though I don't feel right abandoning you, I don't want to die here."

"What are you saying?"

"I'm going to try to join one of the outgoing expeditions."

"I can't abandon my brother," Karen lamented.

Marsha paused before responding, "They're all ambulatory. We can walk them."

"Really? What chance do you think we'd have taking a group of mentally impaired people for a grueling hike through the Nevada desert? A hike with little food and no end in sight."

"This is when one's faith helps," Marsha said.

Karen let out a deep sigh. The thought of having to take care of everyone without Marsha's help was beyond daunting.

The following day, before the sun arose, everyone at Fort Til Then awoke to a series of massive explosions that rocked the campground near the canal. Four bomb blasts had gone off within minutes of each other. Three of the smaller administrative tents were completely destroyed. When the smoke cleared, six people were dead and twenty-four were injured, some severely. Although none of Karen's wards were hurt, several were temporarily deafened by the attack.

"Are the Piggers invading?" Marsha said, peering about nervously.

"Even they probably don't have those kind of explosives," Karen speculated. She remembered that the VL had a secret ammonium nitrate farm, but just as quickly she dismissed the thought—it wasn't their agenda or style.

By noon, six more had died from their wounds. Repairs were made on the shredded tents and new security precautions were put in place. A squad of gangcops was sent out across the canal to assume forward positions in the rubble and search out any Pigger scouts in the vicinity. Karen's group was told that they had twenty-four hours to pack and move eastward, as the clinic area was now part of the new defensive buffer zone.

Around two o'clock that afternoon, while Karen was packing and preparing her charges for the big move, they heard the *put-put-put* of a single engine coming over from the west. Three nervous gangcops raced down to intercept, but all they found was a lone motorized tricycle arriving from Staten Island. It was Bea Moses-Mayer and some gangly older man sitting loosely behind her. Although she was frisked and escorted to a penal tent, no one said a word to her ancient dozing passenger.

"I'm not trying to stir up any trouble, I just came to speak to Captain Sarkisian," Bea explained to Captain Stenson.

He granted her permission to be in the encampment for one hour, provided she had a supervised escort.

"My uncle is crippled," Bea said. "Can someone loan me a wheelchair?"

A chair was found and, with a guard close behind, Bea wheeled Robert Moses down to the new outdoor clinic. When Karen noticed their presence, it crossed her mind to inform Bea about Scouter Lewis's final confession—that he had killed the real Valerie Solanas, though it had allegedly been a mercy killing. There seemed little point in stirring up anger toward the miserable bastard, particularly since he was already dead.

When Karen and Root greeted them, the old man formally rose to his feet. No sooner was Moses standing than a guard snatched his chair away and pushed it back to the administrative tent.

"All the hospitality seems to have evaporated," Bea observed.

"We had a bombing this morning. Twelve killed, so everyone's on edge," Karen said.

Bea gave her condolences.

"My name is Robert Moses," the old man introduced himself.

"What an honor," Karen said, trying not to grin as the aged bureaucrat kept shaking her hand. When she finally pulled it free, Moses almost lost his balance, so she found him a wooden crate to sit on. The noncog named Woody, perhaps curious about Moses's advanced age, touched his wrinkled face. Moses ignored him as though he were a gnat.

"A steady stream of your defectors are coming down and telling us about an exodus into the desert," Bea said, leading Karen out of the old man's earshot.

"Where else can they go?" Karen said. "And by the way, I thought your uncle had vanished."

"He was found trying to climb down the cliff under the Zano. Someone drove him back down to the terminal and now he's staying with me."

"Lucky you," Karen said.

"He accidentally killed my father. And then Rafique asked me to help defend him, which I did. Now, every morning I wake up missing the hell out of my dad and am forced to take care of the man who fucked up my life. Frankly, nothing would make me happier than to find a large chunk from one of his highways and beat him to death with it. But I know I couldn't live with myself after."

"Doesn't the VL have a home for the elderly?"

"We did, but it's long since been overrun by Mkultra survivors and Quirklyn refugees. Our tiny support system is utterly herniated, and you guys are our only buffer against the Piggers, so we need you to survive."

"How'd your goodwill mission to Kew Gardens go?"

"They gave me thirty minutes to leave Queens. I'm just glad they didn't recognize me, 'cause I'm sure they'd've chopped my limbs off." Looking over at Karen's patients, Bea asked, "Didn't you have more of a staff?"

"The Piggers at PP made them withdraw. Now it's only me and a few others. I see you have your own patient now."

"The reason I'm here is that Uncle Bob is usually lucid for about an hour in the mornings, and a few days ago he said something that

I thought might solve both our problems. I asked him how he had hoped to extract his brother from Rescue City, and he said that some sort of 'agent' was initially supposed to capture my dad for him, but something happened so he came himself."

"Who was he talking about?"

"He gave a tall tale about some guy with a device lodged in his head. He was supposed to find my dad, and then the two were going to go out into the desert about a day's walk from here where a helicopter was supposed to retrieve them."

"Sounds like Uncle Bob's device is missing a few batteries."

"I thought so too, but then he woke me up early this morning and said the guy he needs to find is named Mississippi Sauerkraut. I thought maybe he meant Ulysses Sarkisian."

Karen shook her head in disbelief.

The two women walked back over to the wooden crate where Robert Moses was propped up, chin on hands, elbows on knees. He was fast asleep, snoring like a foghorn.

"Hey, Uncle Bobo!" Bea barked.

Root, who had been keeping an eye on the old man, took a few steps back and remained quiet.

"Sugar with a little milk, please," Moses said.

"Tell my friend here what you told us this morning."

"Tell who?"

"How can we get you out of here?" Bea shouted into his ear. "Across the desert?" She pointed into the great eastern expanse.

"Oh, I have to find this guy named Aloyiusus Supposition."

"Aloyiusus or Ulysses?" Bea prodded him.

"Oh, right, that's it—Ulysses!"

"Ulysses knows the way out?" Karen asked him. She glanced over at Uli, who was sitting nearby staring into space.

"He's got a thing in his head, an electronic type of gizmo . . ." Moses tapped the crown of his liver-spotted skull with a long, bent finger.

"I know this sounds odd," Bea said, "but I remember Rafique telling me that he thought Uli had some kind of implant in his brain. He supposedly had a visible head wound when he first arrived here."

Now they all looked over at Uli.

"What the hell are those stitches?" Bea asked, pointing to his skull.

"Those are fresh," Karen replied.

"We could cut the stitches and look inside," Bea said. It didn't sound like she was kidding.

"And if we do," Karen countered, "am I supposed to drag this fossilized fool and all these mental defectives out into the desert and wait for some kind of flying saucer to come rescue us?"

"You know I was just interrogated by your gangcops when I pulled up, and I told them that through our own intel we know that the Piggers have already sent teams back into the burned-out Kew Gardens to salvage what they can of their arsenal. I assume they're planning to attack your shrinking encampment, then they'll swoop down to take over Staten Island, which currently has the largest amount of usable housing stock. We're preparing as much as we can for an imminent attack."

Before Karen could respond, Uli jumped to his feet, then ran over and tackled Robert Moses, knocking him backward off his wooden box onto the hard, sunbaked ground.

"Assassin! Assassin!" the old man groaned.

"Uli, no!" Karen shouted, jumping on him. She and Bea pulled him off the geriatric, who gasped and twitched.

"What the hell did you do!" Karen yelled at her brother. "Bad!"

"P-p-p," he tried spitting out a word.

"Penn Station?" Bea asked, as someone back in Staten Island had recently pelted the old man with a tomato for leveling the glorious old train terminal.

"Paul!" Uli roared, pointing at Moses. "His fault! It's all . . . his fault!"

"His fault, how?" Bea asked.

But Uli didn't utter another word.

They helped Robert Moses to his feet. His long, narrow beak was bloodied, as was his slouching lower lip. Yet he seemed to have suffered no serious damage.

"Well, I guess we should get going if you're not heading out," said Bea.

Uli sighed loudly and just stared straight ahead. In another moment, however, his lips were moving, though nothing was coming out. His haunted stare was the final straw for Karen. Uli urgently needed medical attention if there was any chance of him ever recovering. That, combined with the remote possibility that the senile bureaucrat was telling the truth, compelled her to rethink her predicament. If there really was a homing device placed in Uli's skull, it might mean that their passage through the desert would be dramatically truncated. Maybe they'd only have to get just beyond the outskirts of Rescue City before a search-and-rescue chopper would lift them all to safety. After a lifetime of dealing with bigwigs and overseeing multimillion-dollar projects, Moses must still have some VIP pull. The notion of finally returning to New York City was as enticing yet unreal as going to heaven itself.

"Funny they named this Rockaway," Bea said, peering up along the stretch of embankment where the reservation bordered the desert. "It kinda looks like the old beach."

"The Rockaways in New York City?" Root spoke up.

"Yeah, the family who adopted me used to take me to Orchard Beach. But that was on the Long Island Sound, so there wasn't any real tide. When I was old enough, I'd go to Rockaway Beach with friends. If you bodysurfed on a breezy day, it felt like you were zipping a million miles an hour. And when the waves tumbled you . . . if you didn't break your neck, you felt like a spirit in a storm. It was as close as I've ever come to feeling like I was meeting God—"

"We're leaving," Karen suddenly announced. "And he can join us, if that's what he wants, but he's going to have to move on his own legs."

"Not possible," Bea said.

"They brought him over here in that wheelchair," Root put forth. "Maybe we can use that?"

"Won't the narrow wheels sink in the sand?" Karen asked.

"The higher you go into the rocks, the harder the ground gets," Bea said, having hiked the area.

"Worse comes to worst, we can always turn around," Root said, then left to tend to the noncogs.

"Do me a favor: when you do get rescued, don't tell them about us in Staten Island," Bea said. Turning to Robert Moses, she stooped over and added, "Godspeed, Uncle Bob."

He nodded almost imperceptibly. Bea turned, only to find herself face-to-face with her former secret lover Marsha Johnson, who had silently approached. The two just stared at each other for a moment.

Karen led Uli away from the old man to prevent another attempted assault.

"You must hate me," Bea finally whispered to Marsha.

"That would be impossible," Marsha whispered back.

"I know it sounds odd, but I really wasn't myself in South Ozone," Bea said, attempting to justify her behavior while on her mission in the once-hopeful city of Quirklyn.

"I never felt anything, I mean I never *did* anything, like that either," Marsha said. "I just found myself way over my head."

"All I remember are my feelings for you, which haven't diminished in the least."

Marsha blushed and looked away.

At that moment Karen reappeared. "Marsha, you might be happy to learn that I've decided we're leaving."

"Really? What made you change your mind?"

"My friend Bea convinced me," Karen said, pointing at her. "Root," she called out, "do you think we're up for it?"

"I don't know," Root called back, "maybe we should try explaining it to the noncogs first. They might want to stay."

Karen agreed, and the two women hurried off toward their charges.

"Are you coming too?" Marsha asked Bea.

"To quote the writer Thomas Wolfe, you can't go home again," Bea replied.

"I was hoping we could spend more time together," Marsha said, extending her hand.

Karen turned to see Marsha whispering something to Bea, which she thought odd as she didn't realize the two even knew each other. Suddenly Bea stepped back and yelled, "Yes! I was an impostor 'cause I had to be, not 'cause I was a fucking coward!" Then she turned her back to the PP administrator and strode back up toward TempMetro, hopped on her trike, and zoomed off.

30

Later that afternoon, Karen went to the criminal justice tent to inform Gaspar Stenson of her decision to vacate Rescue City. She learned that he had been sent north to monitor Pigger activity. Her friend Lieutenant Jerry Howard, who had been working as Stenson's assistant, was now officially in charge of desert departures.

"Let me get this straight," Howard said sternly. "You're going across the desert with that group of zombies you've been taking care of?"

"They're all partially cognizant now."

"Do you really believe they have any chance of walking across what could be hundreds of miles of raw scrubland?"

"They have a better chance of getting blown up here," Karen replied. "The nearest bomb was only a couple hundred feet away. This morning we got covered with dirt from the blasts."

"Karen, no one has come back from the hike! And I don't think it's 'cause they forgot to call. No one's making it to the other side."

"This morning, my people barely got half a cup of cereal and a tablespoon of powdered milk. How much more food do we have left?"

"This is confidential, Karen; what I'm telling you, I'm telling you as a friend." He lowered his voice. "One of my gangcops just returned from the fifth water station, and he said that the Freedom Trail is clogged with a couple hundred people going at a snail's pace. Most have already gone through their rations. They're straying off course—they're ignoring our instructions, and walking during the hottest part of the day. Hell, we just sent a team out to try to rescue the worst of them!"

"I'm willing to take my chances."

Howard pulled out a small square form, made some notes, then signed it. Under *Number in Party*, he had written *16*, even though Karen had told him there were only thirteen in her group, thereby granting her more supplies than allowed. She thanked him.

"If I really cared for you," he said, "I'd deny your request." Checking an appointment book, he added, "The next available slot is next week."

"Next week?" Karen feared that by then she would lose her confidence and change her mind.

"Actually, a party leaving tomorrow just canceled, but—"

"We'll take it."

"Okay, but I hope you truly understand the risk you're taking."

She said she did, then thanked him again and left.

While en route back to her group, Karen stopped by the infirmary to ask about a wheelchair for Robert Moses. When she was told they didn't have any, she explained that she had just seen one being used.

"Oh! That was loaned to us," said a large woman in a floppy sun hat who was acting as one of the camp nurses. "A double amputee took it back."

"You're looking for a wheely chair?" a nasal voice said. Karen turned to see a thin man who was working as an attendant. "'Cause Vivian has an old one, but I think he uses it to wheel stuff."

"Viv the janitor?" Karen asked.

"Yeah, he's got an orange tent in the upper east."

Karen thanked them and roamed the encampment until she spotted a dirty orange tent with an open flap. Peeking inside, she saw that it was packed with assorted lengths of wood, pipes, and old crates containing screws, nails, washers, and so forth.

"Anyone here?" she called out.

"I heard you were worm chow," a familiar voice behind her responded. She turned to see the pockmarked man who had been the chief custodian at the Williamsburgh Building. In his right hand he was holding a penknife, and in the other a pointy stick.

"I decided to die here instead."

"Me too."

"When I saw the Williamsburgh Building come down, I thought of you," Karen said. "You were the real captain of that ship."

"I'm ashamed to say, but I cried like a baby when it collapsed."

She asked if he had a spare wheelchair.

"What do you need it for?"

"I have an elderly guy we're bringing on the Freedom Trail, and he can't walk."

"Put him on an ice floe instead."

"I promised I'd bring him along even if we have to carry him."

"The good news is I have something that might work and I no longer need it; the bad news is it'd never make the trip. A chair like that would require wide, light tires," Vivian paused a moment, "which I actually might have."

"You'd be saving a life," Karen said.

"You're traveling with a group?"

"Yeah, about a dozen."

"That's good, 'cause you're not going to be able to push this alone," Vivian said. "Give me three days."

"Actually, we're scheduled to leave tomorrow."

"Wow! This really is the challenge I've been waiting for." He sounded almost excited.

She thanked him profusely and said she'd see him later. As she was passing the large criminal justice tent, she thought about Akbar, whom she hadn't seen since his awful blinding. She felt a sharp stab of guilt at the thought of abandoning him here, so she decided to try to bid him a final farewell. LaCoste had forbidden her from visiting him, but now he was gone.

As she approached the penal tent, she was surprised that not a single gangcop was stationed outside. Throughout the course of the week, they had been steadily relocated away from the encampment. The lucky ones had been assigned to "path duty," helping those on their way out and now trying to bring the weaker ones back. The less fortunate gangcops had been transferred north and east, to prepare for the threat of a Pigger attack.

"Hello!" she called out when she entered. As her eyes adjusted to the darkness, she was shocked to find the dark-green tent completely empty. She was immediately hit with a foul odor and a cloud of flies. Then, behind a gated door in the rear, she spotted Akbar lying face-down on an army cot. His broad muscular back and thick arms heightened the tragedy of his permanent imprisonment. When he flopped over, she saw how dirty his clothes were. He hadn't shaved or been washed since his capture. His lips seemed to be moving, but no words came out. There was a waste bucket on one side of Akbar's cot and a jug of water on the other, next to a carton of saltines. The crusty bandage over his eye wounds desperately needed changing.

"Eugene," Karen whispered urgently, "what's the situation here?"

"Karen!"

"Tell me quickly, before I get caught."

"The only guard I have is some drunken redheaded dwarf named Ross who's awaiting orders to execute me."

"I didn't want to leave without saying goodbye," she said.

"For God's sake, get me a knife," he pleaded. "I can't even kill myself."

"They might let you go," Karen said.

"I wish I was killed in 'Nam!" He started weeping. "I can't believe how pathetic I am."

"You shot Schuman from a long distance," she lied, trying to bolster him. "No marksman could've done that!"

"Did I really?!" he asked, sniffling.

"Damn right you did. His head exploded like a crenshaw."

"Just find me something so I can finish myself off."

"Hold on." Karen searched across some tables covered with litter and rotting half-eaten sandwiches until she found a sharp pair of scissors, then placed them in Akbar's left hand. He ran the tip of his right index finger along his neck, feeling the pulse of his jugular—it was clear that he was ready to go.

"God, I wish I could've done so much more with my life," he groaned.

The remark hit Karen right in her heart. Without thinking, she blurted out, "Come with us."

"Where?"

"We're hiking through the desert to the water stations."

"I can't."

"Yes you can! No one is here, I'm sure I can sneak you out."

"In my present state, I'd just be a burden."

"I have nine mental defectives, a one-armed nurse, a crippled geriatric, and a Christian. So a blind former Panther should actually be a step up."

Akbar smirked, then sat up in bed, swung his legs out, and reached down for his shoes.

"No need to make this any riskier than necessary," Karen said. "Stay here till we're ready to leave. Try to exercise your arms and legs. The stronger you are, the better. I'll come get you tomorrow night, and be prepared to leave right away." She snatched the scissors out of his hand.

"Leave me the scissors just in case," he said desperately.

"I'd rather not."

"But you might not make it back!"

"Hey, I'm the same girl who dropped Goliath up in Harlem. You got my word."

* * *

Karen used the rest of the day to get ready. A large pile of clothes and shoes, discarded articles from those who had already set out, filled some of the pits around TempMetro. She and Root picked through it all, pulling together enough items to make sure their people were prepared for the chilly desert nights ahead. They divided the clothes and supplies into ten shoulder bags that were then converted into knapsacks. Karen also grabbed gauze and antibiotics to clean Akbar's wounds. Marsha gathered blankets for everyone and packed them into the knapsacks. They were able to secure a dozen bowls, spoons, and cups. Marsha had also managed to find three sharp knives, ostensibly for protection. Karen had Root get the little group on their feet to walk them around Fort Til Then, preparing them for the long trek.

The next morning Karen swung by the small orange tent in the upper east quadrant to find that Vivian had been up all night with an acetylene torch, feverishly converting his former hand truck into a bizarre wheelchair. If anything it looked too heavy, like a cross between a pushcart and a mobile throne.

"What are those things you fastened onto the wheels?" she asked, inspecting it.

"I screwed clamps along the outer edges of the rims, creating mini caterpillar tracks," Vivian explained. "When the ground gets soft, they'll keep it from sinking down and getting stuck. Just try to keep the sand from getting into the axles. Destroy the bearings and that'll be it."

"It looks heavy."

"That's why I modified it so that multiple people can push the chair when the path gets steep." Vivian pulled out one of three steel bars that ran up along the back. He showed Karen how all the bars could be inserted laterally across the backrest so that up to three people could simultaneously push.

"Can't we do that with just one or two of the bars?" she asked.

"Oh, I figured you guys are probably going to be cooking outdoors over those Sterno cans, and I have these two smaller pots here . . ." He demonstrated how to tripod the steel poles and interlock them at the top, then he dangled a small chain down to show how the pots could be hung just above the Sterno.

Karen was impressed—Vivian had also built two small shelves below the seat for storage and modified two large leather saddlebags under the armrests. "I can't believe you did all this in one day," she said.

"For all those years I worked in that building, you were the only higher-up who always said hi. Besides, I got nothing else to do."

Karen hugged and thanked him repeatedly. As she pushed the chair back to her encampment, she was delighted by how easily the large traction wheels clawed the ground and how smoothly it coasted along the bumpy earth.

Karen, Marsha, and Root spent the rest of the morning tying up all the remaining loose ends. In addition to sixteen cans of lard and a full case of Sternos, they also gathered more than ten pounds of rice and beans, and a quarter-pound of salt, which they packed into the wheelchair's saddlebags.

"Hope you don't mind my asking," Root said as they worked, "but do you realize that the hardest job here is going to be pushing that monstrosity?"

"It's actually pretty easy," Karen said. "It's designed for multiple pushers."

"I hope so, 'cause with all the stock, not to mention the old man, it's going to be like climbing Mount Everest with a baby grand."

"We'll be fine," Karen said.

"What I'm terrified of is losing people," Marsha declared. "I mean, I know I pushed for this, but how the heck are we going to get all these people walking together in the dark with no road to follow?"

"Faith," Karen said, trying not to sound sarcastic.

31

By eight p.m., when the temperature dropped down to the midfif-
ties, it was time to go. Karen loaded Robert Moses into the new
wheelchair and led everyone through the recently crowded field now
lined with empty holes and trenches filled with garbage. From among
the debris, Karen grabbed a lengthy coil of frayed rope.

It took about fifteen minutes for everyone to assemble at the
canteen site at the northeastern tip of Fort Til Then. Karen brandished the old rope and suggested tying everyone together like in a
mountain-climbing expedition, one after the other.

"No," Marsha responded, "you want to place each person in a spot
where they are best utilized."

"Sounds like you should be in charge of walking placement,"
Karen said.

Marsha cut the long rope into a number of smaller pieces and fastened one end of each to the chair and the other end to someone's
waist. Those whom she judged to be fast walkers were put in front
and the slower ones in the rear.

Three gangcops, including Lieutenant Howard, eventually appeared and slowly made the rounds, checking everyone's gear to make sure they were marginally ready for the perilous trek ahead.

The mood was almost festive as some of the remaining residents of Fort Til Then gathered to wish the expedition party well. Upon seeing the group's rope system, most either shook their heads or gasped. Nine clearly impaired people surrounded a geriatric who was strapped to a strangely rigged wheelchair. When they finally started moving, Root, Woody, and Marsha did most of the pulling. Indeed, three of the noncogs in the rear missed the concept entirely and began pulling the other way.

Since all were still waiting for the two scouts to arrive and lead them to the first water station, Karen asked Root and Marsha to march their little group along the perimeter, in hopes of turning them into a well-synchronized team.

During these trial walks, Marsha decided to try pushing the chair rather than pulling it, but with the various noncogs stumbling every which way, combined with the tough terrain, she quickly found herself exhausted and frustrated. "How the hell are we going to do this?" she moaned. "I can barely keep this up for five minutes."

"Relax," Karen said with a smile. "They'll get used to it, and I got a good rickshaw driver with a strong back. Just try your best till he arrives."

"Welcome to the twenty-third Freedom Trail orientation!" a man's voice shouted. Karen turned around and saw a short, bald man standing on an abandoned steamer trunk—Sergeant Straus. He clapped his hands together until all were silent. "My name's Sergeant Caleb Straus. I'm taking the front. Sergeant Kendowski is bringing up the rear. You'll be entering the Great Basin Desert. Although the path, which we call the Freedom Trail, might sound broad, the infringing cacti and sagebrush actually makes it pretty narrow. You'll see that at times it splits into two and even three parallel paths. Always try to stay together on the widest path. Regarding desert survival: avoid red leaves, plants with milky sap, or plants shaped like handcuffs. Each person usually requires about a gallon of water a day, but we're asking everyone to use half of that because the heat hasn't been terrible over recent weeks and we're worried about running out of water."

"How far away is the first water station?" Marsha called out.

"The first station is roughly ten hours away. We should reach it before sunrise. You're lucky, 'cause people have been funneling through the path for weeks now, so the road ahead should be clearly marked.

But here's a word of advice: don't dawdle. Either go forward or go back. If you choose to just camp out on the pathway, which people have been doing, you're inviting danger and I'll tell you why . . ."

"If I'm not back when he's done," Karen whispered to Marsha, "just start walking without me. I'll catch up."

"Where are you going?"

"Getting our secret weapon; have faith. I promise I'll join you soon."

Marsha nodded, and as the guide continued with his orientation, Karen slipped away, darting back through the dark encampment, tripping over abandoned items, moving toward the once-heavily guarded TempMetro. Only a handful of gangcops were around, walking back and forth between various posts.

Karen slipped unnoticed into the penal tent. She immediately caught a powerful whiff of choke. On the cot in the corner she saw the tiny redheaded man who must be the guard. He was lying bare-assed on the cot, snoring loudly, passed out cold. Poor Akbar was exactly where she had left him, faceup in his cot.

"You there?" He spoke just above a whisper.

"Let's go," she whispered back. Akbar apparently had been practicing, because without missing a beat, he sat upright, slipped on his shoes, and gently walked right up to Karen as though he could see her. He placed his large hand on the small of her back and followed her out.

"Can you remove your bandage for a moment?" she asked as they moved along.

"I don't think you want to see what's behind it."

"You need to put these on till we get clear." She placed a pair of dark sunglasses in his free hand. He cringed in pain as he peeled off the crusty bandages and put the glasses over his hollowed eye sockets. Karen also handed him an old Yankees baseball cap and assured him that once they were clear of the encampment, she'd change his bandages herself. He kept his arm around her shoulders as they slowly walked, so they looked like buddies.

"I hope you're up for a serious hike. It could go on for weeks," she told him. "No one has come back."

"After all I've gone through, I'm more than ready to die trying."

As they approached the canteen, they found that expedition number twenty-three had already departed. Karen could see the last of her group heading up a moonlit dune with one of the two guides bringing up the rear. To keep out of view, Karen led Akbar along a parallel path on the far side of the dune.

They hiked steadily for an hour until they finally spotted a cluster of people and slowed down. Karen identified the unwieldy wheelchair and her sad group moored around it. Behind the chair, Marsha, soaked in sweat, was obviously in distress as she pushed onward. Root used her one hand to help. The others resembled stray dogs on multiple leashes, occasionally trying to pull away.

"Hold up!" Karen yelled. She was almost glad that Akbar couldn't see them. The sheer amateurishness of this dysfunctional Iditarod would've only discouraged him. Karen hastily introduced him to all the cognizant.

Root and Marsha exchanged suspicious glances when Karen had Akbar take over her spot as the human engine behind the mobile chair. As he began pushing everyone along, Karen explained that he was an old friend from college in Old Town.

"Is that Deputy Uli Sarkisian?" they all heard someone ask. Just off the path ahead of them, Sergeant Caleb Straus was waiting for the group to reach him.

"Yes, it is, but he's a little quiet right now," Karen answered. She noticed that the guide still had the pistol issued to all members of the original Team Rescue. She was terrified that he'd identify the fugitive Akbar.

"He had the fever," Marsha said.

"Oh, don't I know you?" Straus asked her with a grin.

"Maybe. I used to work at PP."

"That explains it," he said. "I used to work the Brooklyn precinct near there."

"How do you know my brother Uli?" Karen asked, trying to act relaxed.

"I once chauffeured him around the city," Straus said.

"Really?"

"Yeah, when he was in charge of the program to bring gangcops up to speed on the new legal procedures. We all had great respect for him. Not many people here are both intelligent and principled. I certainly hope he gets better soon."

"Thanks, I appreciate that," Karen said. She then recalled that Straus had been part of the caravan that rescued Mallory, and had therefore worked with her and Uli before. It felt like a lifetime ago.

Straus and Kendowski stayed put and wished the group well as they continued marching.

An hour later, Akbar was clenching the handgrip and leaning into the wheelchair so forcefully that their group started making steady progress; the little formation was slowly locking into step. Woody, Uli, and two of the sturdier noncogs took the lead. Old Man Moses simply slumped forward against the sashes that strapped his lanky body into the chair. The adjustable leg rests and foot plates had been pulled all the way up to clear the brush and rocks in their path. Karen, Root, and Marsha stayed in front for now. Using the full moon as a headlight, the three women periodically called out obstacles for Akbar to avoid.

After another hour, they finally saw the first splatter of yellow paint.

"Do you remember this?" Root asked Uli, pointing to some of the golden arches that she made out in the darkness. He barely shrugged.

As the terrain rose, and the rocks and soft sand grew tougher to navigate, Akbar began tripping repeatedly as he pushed the heavy chair.

"Halt!" Karen shouted. She adjusted two of the bars fastened along Moses's backrest, allowing for a much wider grip, then tied Uli next to Akbar. As an afterthought, she asked Akbar if he'd talk to her brother.

"I don't talk to no FBI."

"He's also mute, but I think he understands us."

"So what?"

"You're a former Black Panther; I just thought this might be a great opportunity to share your worldview." She saw a grin spread on Akbar's face.

As soon as they resumed walking, Karen listened as Akbar started in on a lecture about how black people had been kidnapped from their homeland and brought to America by the white man against their will and were now amused by liberals who wondered why they were always so arrogant and bitter.

I have to kill Akbar, I have to kill him, Uli thought. *The Turkish soldier next to me pushes the wagon before us, leading me and my fellow villagers away from our sacred Armenian town, which they have just set on fire, and toward the Persian desert, which means a steady draining and a dismal death. They are transporting the final survivors from the southern edge of the teetering Ottoman Empire toward the doomed city of Deir ez-Zor in distant Syria.*

Many hours later, as the sun began to rise, Akbar, covered in sweat, was losing his steam. Still, he kept rambling on to Uli about the plight of the black man in America, until quite unexpectedly Uli let out a yelp, causing Akbar to pause.

"A rebuttal?" Karen said.

"Shut 'em up," Uli replied softly.

Karen smiled hopefully as his true character was finally breaking through.

32

An hour later they started seeing tarps and scattered bivouacs. Then, finally, they spotted it—a small concrete platform with a dozen people patiently sitting around it. When they were within a hundred feet, they could see a large man resting on the platform, using a machete like a paintbrush to cut an image in the dirt. He had to be a gangcop.

As the roped, wheelchaired caravan approached the water station, all stared. The gangcop smiled and said, "And the blue ribbon for the best Thanksgiving Day float goes to you guys."

"Thanks!" Woody chirped.

"Hey, you're Captain Sarkisian," the cop said to Karen, rising to his feet.

"I am," she replied.

"I worked briefly under your command. My name is Tibor."

"Pleased to meet you," she said tiredly.

He shook her hand as he announced the rules: "Everyone gets a free canteen fill, which is about four glasses of water. That should last you until you get to the next water station. I'll also give everyone a cup of water right now—but that's it. If you become fungus, you get just two cups of water per day, so I suggest you take your water and keep moving."

"Fungus?"

"You know how it grows around a leaky pipe?" Tibor grinned as though none of the people sitting around him could understand a word of English.

Karen recognized a couple of the fungi—people who had vacated Rescue City several days earlier. A number of tents were spiked into the hard earth or had blankets hitched to cacti or rocks in the vicinity. It seemed to be a mini settlement. She also saw a large ashen ditch in the center, presumably for a communal fire.

As each member of her group was issued a cup of drinking water and had their canteens filled, Karen asked Tibor if he could tell her what lay ahead.

"The path veers a little north, but it's pretty much what you saw on your way here for about an hour. Then you'll start smelling a really bad odor and you'll come to this big open field. Although the yellow paint leads into it, make a right and go around."

"Why is there a bad odor?" Akbar asked.

"It's the underground military installation where the city's plague started. Most of the bodies were cremated, but some are still around, and from what I've been told, you can still catch the disease from them—so don't stop."

"When do we hit the next water station?" Root asked.

"It's not quite as far as this one, but it's still a good walk. Sleep a couple hours, then eat and start walking. You'll get there by sunup."

"If the next water station isn't due east, how did the lead group find it?" Marsha asked.

"Who knows, but thank God they did."

Karen showed Marsha what Vivian had created, clipping the wheelchair's crossbars together to create a cooking tripod. Marsha filled the two pots with water. Popping the lids on two Sterno cans, she was able to steam the rice and beans simultaneously. As she cooked, another small expedition team arrived at the water station.

After napping a few hours, the rest of Karen's group arose to the mouthwatering smell of rice and beans. All the fungi stared blankly as Marsha divided it into fourteen portions so that everyone in their group had roughly four heaping tablespoons of food. Although the rice was a little soft and the beans were still a bit hard, everyone happily gobbled it down.

At sunset, Karen's group, along with two other small groups, started moving out. The other groups quickly pulled ahead.

Roughly an hour into the walk Marsha, who was in the lead, spotted something. "Praise the Lord, we're saved!" she yelled, pointing toward some relatively fresh tire tracks cutting into their path—clearly, cars had driven down it. Root felt bad when she explained that those treads weren't from the outside world; rather, they were from the customized vehicles the Piggers had driven out here using a different route when they rescued those from the Mkultra.

For a half hour they followed the tire treads, until Root pointed out large ominous birds circling in the distance. Soon they began to smell the stench, which steadily intensified. Yet it wasn't until they rose over a set of small dunes that they were able to see the vast field.

"Shit," Akbar said, "I *know* that smell."

Root grew silent, and started making odd sounds. Karen knew she was suppressing tears as they silently walked past. Rags, debris, C-ration wrappers, and other strange items were littered along the ground and caught up against rocks.

As they rose to an elevated crest, they could see several large ash heaps on the cracked cement that appeared to have served as an outdoor crematorium. They stayed along the southern edge as instructed. It took another half an hour before the pathway finally dipped and the awful place fell from view.

Upon leaving the site, there was a dramatic reduction of wear on the ground. Litter and feces likewise diminished. Over the next few miles, they lost the path a few times before finding it again.

"Where'd everyone go?" Karen asked, bewildered by the abrupt disappearance of the well-defined path.

Eleven hours later they sluggishly reached the next water station, which was also guarded by a large gangcop who Karen vaguely knew. Much like the first station, they came across several smaller groups who had pitched tents there and didn't seem to be in a hurry to move along. Some of them seemed to have been there for days.

After another six-hour sleep, while the rice and beans slowly cooked, all awoke to the sounds of shouts and struggling. Uli was on top of Akbar, strangling him. Root was trying to pull him off of the blind man with her one arm.

"What the fuck is the matter with you?" Karen screamed at her brother.

"They're killing us!" he burst out.

"Who?"

"The Turks!"

"What Turks?" Root asked.

"They're driving us into the desert!"

"He thinks we're in Turkey," Akbar said.

"We're in America, Uli," Karen said. "That was in Turkey. More than sixty years ago. We're halfway around the world. This is the Nevada desert. It's 1981!"

"We're not in . . . ?" Uli looked around. "He's a gendarme!"

"No, this is Akbar, he's an American detainee."

"Akbar is a Muslim name!"

"I was born Eugene Hill," Akbar rasped, rubbing his throat. "I dumped my slave master's name."

The explosion of rage seemed to have a therapeutic effect on Uli, as though blasting away at the calcification separating him from the outer world. He seemed to awaken to his arid surroundings. Everyone was too agitated to go back to sleep, so after Marsha divvied up the rice and beans, they all ate and then set out for the next water station.

They soon passed more people; invariably, they were in worse shape, usually older and heavier. Karen instructed everyone to remain silent, as sometimes those they passed would plead for just a little food or water. All knew that they could no longer afford the luxury of mercy.

When they reached the third water station that night, Karen didn't recognize the gangcop on duty. Still, he was helpful in explaining how the Freedom Trail curved southeasterly up ahead. He also described some upcoming geological details that they should keep an eye out for—a giant mesa marked the beginning of a riverbed where the trail curved again.

After another six-hour nap and a small meal, the group of fourteen set out again at sunrise. Uli no longer wanted or needed to be tied to the chair. Within two hours, they reached the mesa; its slabs of broken shale were collapsed like a gigantic deck of orange and brown cards.

"Look!" Woody pointed. Small creatures darted about.

Uli and Marsha began pulling up rocks where lizards had scampered. Behind a clump of stones, away from the path, Marsha found two stripped decomposed torsos. The genitals were still attached: they were both males. Uli, who had walked farther down the path, let out a ghastly yowl.

Others raced over to the small rock ledge where he was standing, gazing at a badly decomposing head. The eyes had been plucked out and the nose, cheeks, and ears had been torn off, presumably by birds, though they could still make out his closely shorn beard.

"*That's* what made you scream?" Root said, having grown inured to corpses by now.

"That's Paddy," Uli replied dolefully.

"Who?" Karen asked.

"Paddy Patel," he said.

Karen thought she recognized the name.

"NSA, I think." Uli's consciousness had started flooding back. "And this is bad."

"Let's keep moving," Karen said.

Over the miles, as shrubbery began to thin out, the hardened path became easier to follow. As the landscape grew cooler, it was also becoming easier to walk during the daytime hours. When a slight decline presented itself and Root announced that the path was a solid uninterrupted slope, Akbar stepped on the bottom rear bar of the chair, lifting its large front wheels, and slowly coasted it forward, tugging the noncogs along as well. Karen and Uli were unable to keep up.

"Uli, I need to apologize," Karen said. "And thank you."

"For what?"

"I should have stopped you from going down that sewer pipe in Staten Island; I knew that wasn't going to end well. When I found myself down there, I thought it was my punishment for letting you go."

"I should've figured it out myself, I was just so eager to get the hell out."

"How are Mom and Dad?" Karen asked.

"Dad died in '77. Mom passed in '79, a little while before I came here. She always felt awful about losing you."

"So why *did* you come here?"

"I wasn't in a good state of mind. They should've fired me. I'm still not clear what my mission was."

"I know we've disagreed on everything all our lives," Karen said, "but can we agree on one thing right here?"

"What?"

"After years of failing at so many things, watching so many good and beloved people die for no reason, if I . . . if we can just do this one thing, and get this little group through this and back home . . ."

The words stung Uli as he considered so many of his own personal failures. "It'll be the first time we've worked together on the same mission," he said with a smile.

A shrill cry interrupted their pact. Downhill, at the base of the long slope, the entire group had come to a halt and were circling around something. Karen and Uli raced down to find one of the usually fast-paced noncogs on the ground holding his foot in agony—Akbar had accidentally rolled the chair over the man they called Special Ed.

"Root, I thought you were guiding me!" the blind pusher called out.

"You were going so fast that I couldn't keep up."

Although there didn't seem to be any broken bones, Special Ed, who had been lifted back to his feet, now had a significant limp.

"Can you walk through it?" Marsha asked.

The noncog didn't respond as he limped slowly onward. Over the next hour, his condition steadily declined. Soon he was being virtually dragged by his rope.

Marsha untied him. She began walking on Special Ed's right side, while Karen held his left arm, trying to help him along. It took about five hours to make it roughly two miles to the next water station. Karen recognized the gangcop on duty, a gaunt youth named Nathan who asked her if they had passed any other gangcops en route. She shook her head.

"They were supposed to bring supplies and spell me. I haven't eaten in two days."

"Sorry, Nate, we didn't see anyone."

Two small groups were already camped there, one to the right of the water pump, the second to the left.

"I'm sure Ed will be fine after a good sleep," Root said, trying to remain upbeat.

Tiredly they lined up for their ration of water and slowly refilled their canteens. Marsha placed her tripod apparatus in the middle of their camp so no one could swipe their food. She added beans, rice, and water to the pots and lit Sterno cans as everyone spread their blankets out and napped.

When they awoke, Marsha and Root served the rations, while Karen brought a heaping spoonful of rice to Nathan. He hungrily chewed it down. Twenty minutes later, he came over and said he was going to take advantage of the sudden rush of calories and try to make it back to Rescue City.

"Can you tell us anything about the road ahead?" Root asked.

"No, but these two groups came from there—ask them."

"Are there any other gangcops watching the upcoming water stations?" Karen asked as he filled his own canteen.

"I don't think so."

Ten minutes later, Nathan officially abandoned his post.

Karen silently went to check on Special Ed, who had fallen back asleep.

Root timidly approached the four people in one of the other groups; they were staring off in different directions like a small flock of birds. A teenage girl locked eyes with her.

"You're not looking for bugs, are you?" the girl asked nervously. "'Cause we already called dibs on them on this side, see?"

"They're all yours," Root assured her.

"You see any choppers?"

"You mean helicopters?" Root thought the girl was being sarcastic. "No, we prefer walking."

"Then you're in luck, 'cause the stretch ahead is a doozy. We tried to make it to the next water station a couple days ago, but we got lost, so we came back here. Now we're collecting as many bugs as we can, then we'll give it a second shot."

"Is there anything at all that you can tell us about this route?"

"There's this point where you think the road goes to the left, but it really goes to the right."

"Where is this fork in the road?" Root asked.

"Up ahead a ways."

Root thanked the girl and decided to see if she could get anything from the second group. Marsha silently joined her. The apparent leader, a tall, pale man with wild eyes who introduced himself as Peter, said he was originally a part of expedition number fourteen. He explained his strategy—foraging for bugs like the other group, then heading on to the next water station.

"You didn't see any grasshoppers on the way here, did you?" Peter asked Marsha as she approached. "Their legs are yum-yum! A real delicacy in Argentina."

"We just saw human bodies," Root said.

As they walked back to their own camp, Marsha said, "Those bodies earlier today, their arms and legs were sliced off. And they weren't very decomposed."

"You think he might've . . ."

"Who knows?"

"We should get out of here pronto," Uli said.

"No way, Ed needs more time," Marsha replied.

"It's vital we keep pace," Uli said.

"If you guys want to leave, go ahead. I'm spending the night," Marsha said. "Ed will be fine by morning."

33

They put the matter to a vote. The majority agreed with Marsha that a little break was in order. Carrying Ed along the road for hour after hour had tuckered everyone out. Though it was early afternoon, all were soon dozing again.

Ed's moans awoke everyone just as the sun was setting. The group with the anxious teenager had already lit out. Marsha discovered that poor Ed was burning up and his foot was discolored. It looked like he had broken a bone after all. Akbar brought up the possibility of trying to put him in the chair with Robert Moses.

When they tried to shove Ed in the chair, however, the old commissioner repeatedly protested, "Someone's already sitting here!" Finally they stopped.

"That's how we, and probably a lot of others, got stuck at the pumps," Peter said as Marsha and Root passed by.

"How?" Root asked.

"A loved one gets sick, so you wait till they get better. A couple days, maybe a week passes, you use up your resources, then they die. But you're weaker now, aren't you, so you're stuck too."

"What else can we do?" Marsha had grown attached to Special Ed.

"Well, we're stuck here anyway," Peter said without making eye contact. "I guess if you want to leave some food, we can take care of him."

Root looked to Marsha, who quickly said, "No thanks."

Peter nodded and rejoined his little group.

Around midnight Karen, Marsha, Uli, and Akbar were sitting around a Sterno can that was still burning while Ed and most of the noncogs slept.

"I really think it's just a sprain," Marsha said. "I mean, we don't have an X-ray machine, so we don't really know."

"Maybe so," Karen said softly. "But best-case scenario, he won't get well for a few days."

"What are you suggesting?" Marsha asked.

"She's saying we're a group," Akbar replied. "And we're gonna live or die as a group, so we have to decide what's best for the group."

"Odds are stacked against us as it is," Root said. "The same food we've used sitting here waiting for poor Ed to heal, we could've used walking for the past several hours."

"Just one more day, please," Marsha said. "If he's not better by tomorrow . . ."

"Marsha, we're low on food and we're tired," Root reasoned. "And we have everyone here to worry about."

"I would wait for *you* if you were sick."

"Then you'd die," Root shot back.

"Hell," Akbar muttered, "we're probably dead already."

"Relax," Karen said, trying to soothe the others.

"We have to decide on whether to leave Ed here," Uli said, "or wait for him for an extra day."

"If we give up on Ed, how long before we give up on each other?" Marsha said. "I know what it's like to be injured and left behind."

"Let me go on record as declaring that if I ever slow this group down and can't talk," Root said, "my sincere wish is that you put me out of my misery and move on."

"I will not be a party to this," Marsha said, rising to her feet.

"Then your vote will be an abstention," Uli said.

"When you were delirious I cleaned and fed you, even though I could've caught whatever that was!"

"Marsha, you were also the one who was going to leave us back in Fort Til Then when things started getting dicey!" Root said.

"I wasn't sentencing you to a certain death. You were still a part of a community."

"There is a group here willing to look after Ed," Karen pointed out.

"Yeah, cannibals!"

"You don't know that," Root said.

"I haven't seen them catch a single bug the entire time we've been here! And they eat skin," Marsha said, turning to Uli. "Like your friend Patel."

"Shush," Karen whispered, worried that Peter could hear them.

"All in favor of waiting for Ed to get well, say *aye*," Akbar proposed.

"Aye!" said Marsha.

"Aye!" said Woody, mimicking her.

"All opposed?"

Karen, Root, Akbar, and Uli lifted their hands in opposition. Silent tears streamed down Marsha's cheeks.

"While the moon is out, we can still see the path," Karen said. "So I think it would be wise if we departed immediately." No one else spoke.

Akbar was about to go wake Ed up, but Root reiterated Marsha's concern that he was still in pain from the injury and it had taken him a long time to fall asleep.

"Anyone want to join me?" Karen asked.

Marsha refused to look at anyone.

Root accompanied Karen and together they headed over to the glassy-eyed members of Peter's group.

"We'd like to take you up on your kind offer," Karen said to Peter.

"You mean . . ."

"Yeah," Root spoke up. "He's sick, so we decided not to wake him, but when he gets up, we're wondering if you can keep him with you."

"How bad are his legs?" Peter asked.

"His right foot is sprained pretty badly," Root said, not revealing that it might actually be broken.

"You should go ahead. I'm not a doctor or anything, but I'll do what I can for him."

Karen thanked Peter and the two returned to their camp and spent the next ten minutes silently packing.

Marsha kept to herself. Karen noticed her going through the dry grain, but didn't ask what she was doing. Finally, after Karen and Uli tied the noncogs to the wheelchair and Akbar held the grips ready to depart, Marsha grabbed a small bag and Ed's knapsack and walked over to the other group.

"His name is Ed," Marsha said. "We actually call him Special Ed, but that's 'cause he's always sweet and kind, and that makes him very special. These are his belongings." She tried hiding her tears as she handed the knapsack to Peter. "He never really opens it, but he'll know if it's missing."

"Okay," Peter said in a daze.

"I also put aside his share of rice and beans." She handed him the second, smaller bag.

"Okay," Peter said again.

"He's always been very gentle, so if you plan to kill him, please let it be quick and painless. And if you intend to do anything else to him, just . . . keep in mind he is as human as every one of you."

No one in Peter's group said a single word.

Karen called over to Akbar, who started pushing the chair. Everyone else fell in line; Marsha dropped to the rear, weeping softly.

"I think it would be fitting if we said a prayer for the memory of our friend Ed," Karen said after two hours of trekking in silence.

"He's not dead!" Marsha erupted.

"A prayer that he gets better," Karen amended.

When Marsha didn't respond, Root said, "How about a prayer that some goddamn army choppers see that their fucking citizens are dying and swoop down and save our asses!"

"I'll pray . . . to that," Uli whispered.

"Marsha," Karen said, looking back at her friend, "I'm really sorry. Please lead us in prayer."

Marsha slowly recited the Lord's Prayer, one sentence at a time, allowing the others to join in.

"I'm sorry too," Akbar said. "What happened to Ed was my fault."

"No one's blaming you," said Root.

"I felt something under the chair, but I thought we were caught in some bushes and just plowed through, then I heard his screams . . ." He stopped talking and composed himself. "Marsha, I can't tell you how bad I feel."

"It's not your fault," she said softly.

No one said more than a few words as they proceeded through the darkness, occasionally smelling and then passing dead bodies along the side of the path. Periodically, Karen or Root would navigate Akbar, who carefully hoisted the wheelchair around rocks and occasional ruts. After another hour, when they came to a sudden rise, the expedition nearly bumped into a herd of wild horses, brilliant in the moonlight. Startled by the group's appearance, the horses galloped fiercely away, their manes flapping like flags.

"There goes a month of steak dinners," Root grumbled.

"Forget dinner," Karen said, "we could've ridden all the way back to New York."

"If we had just one," Marsha mumbled solemnly, "we could've gone back and gotten Ed."

Silence followed until the red and copper rays of sunlight came up over the distant hills several hours later.

Marsha, who was in the lead, noticed something behind a pile of rocks about a hundred feet off the path. When several of them went over to investigate, instead of the usual discovery of bodies,

Root gasped to find an empty, unmarked crate. Stenciled on the wood was the word *C-Rations*. As they further explored the area, Root came across a scattering of empty wrappers and small containers, yet the labels appeared to have been carefully peeled off.

"This is recent," Uli said, inspecting one wrapper.

"Where the hell did these come from?" Karen said, sniffing another small wrapper. "I never saw anything like these in Rescue City." The bulk food there was usually kept in large cans or boxes.

They resumed walking, until Akbar suddenly stopped thirty minutes later, inadvertently bringing the entire caravan to a halt.

"What's up, cowboy?" Karen said.

"Hear that?"

All listened—no one heard a thing.

By late morning Karen had counted fifty-two bodies since dawn, not including occasional fresh graves. When the group stopped for a break, Woody spotted something billowing in the distance. Karen and Root went to check it out and found a tarp that appeared to have been made from a ripped parachute. Under it were a pair of bodies, two middle-aged women. Nearby Root found a pair of beautiful porcelain teacups and matching saucers. It looked as though they had finished their afternoon tea and biscuits and promptly slit their wrists.

"This explains it," Root said, holding up the parachute.

"You mean the crate we saw earlier?"

"Yeah. It was air-dropped."

"I knew I heard a chopper," Akbar groaned.

Root said, "That's what the teenage girl told me at the last water station."

"What exactly did she say?" Karen asked.

"That they missed the chopper. I thought she was nuts."

"So who would've flown a chopper?"

"The government! Who else?" Uli said.

"Why would the US government air-drop a single crate of food?" Marsha wondered.

Karen found it hopeful. Someone knew they were in need and was trying to do something about it.

Around four p.m., after a short nap, they got back on the path. Three hours later they could see a distant hill ahead laced with strange silver channels. As they came closer they made out nude figures that appeared to be frolicking around. Karen had lost count of the dead at around 220.

They were surprised to find more people camped at this new water station than at any of the more recent stations. Most were indeed
naked. It was the first watering hole without a gangcop. No doubt
because of this, it was a virtual Roman orgy of water, with nude and
seminude people splashing around in the mud and drinking freely
from the spout, almost intoxicated on the water.

Instead of settling in, Karen persuaded everyone that this was
dangerous. These people had lost their marbles. After rehydrating,
she convinced everyone to keep marching and find a place to camp a
safe distance away. An hour later, with no one in sight in front of or
behind them, Marsha and Root set up the tripod bars, lit a Sterno, and
simmered the rice and beans while others napped.

34

Everyone began waking up to the smell of food, only to find that their quota was down to a single tablespoon of rice and beans per person. After eating they packed up and hiked for a few hours, until Karen, who was in the lead, stumbled upon a cold firepit with charred bones mixed in with the ashes. She quickly tried to kick the bones beneath some rocks in the firepit, but some of the others had already seen them.

Within an hour, Marsha spotted another dead body; it had a water jug strapped to its bloated shoulder. "That's the third canteen I've seen today."

"The bodies have canteens?" Akbar asked.

"Yeah, some of them do."

"If we have more canteens and the water pumps are unmanned, we can bring more water with us," he said. Often drenched in sweat from all the pushing, he consumed more water than anyone else in the group.

"Is that really necessary?" Marsha said.

"Absolutely! We don't know if these watering holes are going to get farther apart, or dry out completely. We shouldn't take any chances if we don't have to."

All agreed, and thereafter, every time they came upon bodies, they scrounged around for spare canteens and other water receptacles.

At one point when Uli had ventured a hundred yards ahead of the others, he came upon an unusual party of four corpses tangled together on the ground. He couldn't tell if they were dead or asleep. Sniffing around them, he cringed. They smelled ripe, so he began quietly digging through their surprisingly colorful belongings for their canteens.

Although the group seemed to be mostly male, they had purses and a mix and match of women's wear. One member of the group was obese; another was skeletally thin. When Uli snatched a bright red goatskin water bag strapped around one of the few females in the group, her mascaraed eyes popped open and she snapped: "Come back in five, grave robber!"

"Sorry," Uli said. But then, taking a closer look in the moonlight, it clicked that two of these people were members of the Andy Warhol Superstars who had won the city council seats representing the break-away city of Quirklyn.

"Wait up," the woman said, struggling unsuccessfully to free herself from the interlocked bodies. "Help me, goddamnit!"

"I'm not a rescue worker, we have no—"

"Just fucking help me up! My arms and legs are pins and needles."

The late Candy Darling's arms were flung around the woman on one side, and poor, emaciated Jackie Curtis was pressed tightly against her on the other side. Uli was able to work her limbs free, then gently helped her up. This woman appeared to be the only living member of the group.

"What's going on?" Karen asked, arriving with the wheelchair and everyone attached to it.

"I'm just helping—"

"We can't help anyone!" Root barked.

"These people were heroes who fought for the independence of Quirklyn," Uli explained. Both Root and Karen had been in the Mkul-tra at the time.

"I remember them," Marsha said softly.

"My name's Cookie Mueller. I just needed a little assistance."

"We simply don't have any extra food or water," Karen said adamantly. "We don't have enough for ourselves."

"I still have some rice," Cookie said, struggling to get sensation back into her extremities. "I think I can still walk."

"I'm sorry, but you can't come with us," Root declared.

"If she can keep up and feed herself," Uli said, "then why can't she?"

"We don't know this person," Root whispered, as Cookie stumbled around the bodies of her friends, pulling out some essentials: a blanket, her coat, a sizable bag of rice and beans. She did her best to position the bodies of her friends as respectfully as possible.

"I think Root has a point," Karen said. "We really don't know her."

"Actually, I can vouch for her," Marsha said, remembering some of her amusing campaign antics.

"I'm sorry, Uli," said Karen quietly, "but for the safety of our entire crew—"

"Hold on! We're still a democracy, aren't we? Let's put it to a vote."

"No way!" Root said.

"No, he's right," Karen relented.

"I remember when Cookie was running with Candy Darling to free Quirklyn, and the two gangs came down on them with everything they had," Uli said. "If she can carry her own weight, she deserves a chance to come with us. This is about saving her life without risking ours."

"I remember all that Quirklyn stuff too," Akbar pitched in. "Minority rights—I admired what they were doing."

"Excuse us a moment," Karen called over to Cookie, and they wheeled the chair a little away from her.

"Look," Cookie called back, "I don't want anyone's food, and if I can't keep pace, you guys can just keep going without me."

"That does beg the question," Root said. "If you are able to walk on your own, why were you lying there with your dead friends?"

"We took a suicide pact. They took their pills and I chickened out. I mean, I didn't want to die, but I didn't want to go on alone either."

"All in favor of a new addition to our group, say *aye*," Karen proposed.

All raised their hands except for Root, who abstained.

As long as she could walk, Cookie Mueller was now officially a part of the group, complete with voting privileges. Always eager to gain new information, Karen asked about her ill-fated expedition. Cookie told them that it had been hell from the start. Jackie had been so weak to begin with and Candy was so out of shape that although they had managed to bring a large stock of their own food, they kept camping out for days at a time at the water stations.

"Our only advantage was that we left early on, and people didn't think the path was so long, so they were more charitable."

"Why didn't you eat more?" Karen asked, seeing the leftover dry goods.

"We didn't get Sterno cans. We thought we could just chew it all down, but our teeth are all in bad shape, so it was painful." Turning to Uli, she added, "You're searching for uneaten food from those who starved to death?"

Uli explained that they were collecting abandoned canteens in the event that the water stations weren't being guarded.

"Well, you woke me up," she said. "So I guess I'm lucky."

* * *

They arrived at the next water station around three p.m. to find not a single person around. After they hydrated and erected a lean-to, most of the noncogs crashed instantly. Marsha, who seemed to regularly function on less sleep, set up the poles, but stopped when she opened the saddlebags and realized they were completely empty. She quietly announced this to the group.

"My treat," Cookie said, handing over her bag of rice and beans mixed together.

"That's yours," Marsha said. "And to be honest, we wouldn't've shared our food with you."

"Hey, you voted me in. Thanksgiving Day's on me tonight."

All thanked her.

Root and Uli scouted around and found some beetles in the vicinity. Marsha also found some purple-leafed plant that Karen said was sage. She tasted it. Since it wasn't too bitter, and since after waiting a few minutes she didn't feel dizzy, she tore up some of the leaves and dumped them and the bugs into one of the two little pots. Akbar and Uli worked together to help Robert Moses out of his chair so he could void his bowels and bladder. Then they helped clean him and laid him down on a blanket to give his lower back a rest. Cookie just sat on a rock off to one side and stared off sadly.

"Oh God," Robert Moses groaned nearby, "I can't feel anything below my waist."

Without being asked, Cookie went over and elevated the old man's legs, gently massaging his calves and thighs.

"Oh," he mumbled gratefully, "God bless you, girl." Both of them soon dozed off.

Karen awoke four hours later to the sound of someone scampering about. Marsha had just caught a small blue-belly lizard. She smashed it with a rock, but the other food had already been cooked.

Everyone got a heaping spoonful of rice and beans. Most picked the sharp bits of beetle and stringy vegetation out. When the pot was wiped clean, Marsha spoke the words all were dreading to hear: "We're officially out of food."

"Didn't someone catch a lizard?" Akbar asked.

"A little one. It's like a rubber band," Marsha said, having tried a leg.

"If no one else wants it . . ." He opened his hand.

Marsha gave him the squished reptile and watched as he differentiated the head from the tail, then bit into it and steadily chewed it down—to no one's envy.

"Let's get moving," Karen said.

Over the next few nights, their pace steadily dropped as only their body fat sustained them. They went from reaching one water station per day to barely reaching one every other day. Everything took so much more work as they found it hard to concentrate. The only luxury was the abundance of water.

Robert Moses, who for most of the hike had remained silent in his chair, started asking for food. Soon he would just point to his mouth.

"Sorry, Robert, we're out," Root and some of the others answered time and again. His giant head would slump forward and he'd doze off, releasing a snore that sounded like a broken rattle.

Karen pointed out with dismay that almost all of the corpses they now passed had limbs hacked off.

"Some of them are legitimate amputees," Root responded with a wave of her unamputated hand. No longer appalled by the sight, both she and Uli occasionally rummaged around the bodies to see if they held anything useful. And more than once they found grains of rice and beans in the bottoms of bags or pockets.

On the three-week anniversary of departing Rescue City, the party staggered up to a new station with water still in their many canteens, but starving.

"I have two proposals," Akbar said after a long and grave silence. "For the record, I hate them both, but they'll increase our chances for survival." No one said a word, so he continued: "The first is that we'd make much better time if we jettison . . ." He pointed to Robert Moses, who was snoring loudly in his wheelchair. "In fact, there are a number of people here who probably aren't going to recover anyway. If we put them out of their misery now, it will only help those of us who still have a chance."

"Do you think you'll recover from being blind?" Karen said.

"I've been pushing that chair from day one, and the day I'm unable to push it is the day I'll kill myself. And I won't put that to a vote."

"We're a team," Karen said. "We left as a team, and while every-one can still walk, we'll arrive as a team."

Although Marsha thought of poor Ed, she didn't say a word.

"Vote! Vote! Vote!" Woody chanted as though provoking a fight.

"He's right!" Akbar said. "As a member of this group, it's my right to call a vote!"

"All those in favor of dumping Moses and some of the noncogs, raise your hand," Root said softly, just to shut him up.

Woody's hand flew up, then he grabbed the hand of his nearest fellow noncog and yanked it up too. Unable to see this, Akbar's hand went up, and after a moment, to everyone's surprise, Root's single hand rose as well.

A moment later Uli's hand followed. Then Robert Moses's big hand slowly creaked up like a flag on a pole. Karen and Marsha were aghast to see two other noncogs nervously copycat the old-timer.

"All opposed!" Marsha blurted quickly to stem the tide.

Woody continued holding up his hand as well that of the limp noncog, thus invalidating both their votes. Marsha, Karen, and Cookie's hands all rose.

"What's the vote?" Akbar asked.

"Seven to five, you lose," Karen lied.

Uli shook his head, but no one corrected her.

"My second proposal preserves the life of every member of our team," Akbar said. "Throughout this walk, I've been told that we're passing nutrients that would buy us as much energy and time as we need."

"Please don't say it," Root whispered.

"Maybe it's 'cause I'm blind and don't see them, but we should consider the Donner Party prerogative," Akbar euphemized. "Is that polite enough?"

"Out of the question," Karen protested.

"Maybe it's not for you, and that's fine. But there are people here who would gladly eat whatever is given to them. And they'd also be able to push the chair and keep the rest of us going."

"So you're just looking for human engines, is that it?" Root said.

"Those in favor of . . . . it?" Marsha said hastily.

"Let me just repeat," Akbar lifted his hand, "that it will mean life for us and it won't hurt another *living* being."

Woody again held up his own hand and that of the noncog sitting next to him.

"That's one," Marsha said, ignoring Woody. "All opposed?"

Woody double voted yet again, with gusto. Most of the others simply mumbled, "Aye."

"As these poor imbeciles start dying off, ask yourself if you really had their best interests in mind," Akbar snapped. "Also, keep in mind that this vote might be for the group, but I personally don't accept it. I have a right to survive."

"That's true—if you can butcher a body, it's your right," said Root.

"So even though I don't want to starve with the rest of you, you're going to deprive me of my right to procure food?"

"If it interferes with our rights not to dismember and cook a dead body—yes," Karen said.

"That's unfair."

"He's right," Uli spoke up. "I'll do it."

"Do what?" Root asked.

"I think it's his right," Uli said. "We're starving to death. And the path is lined with sources of protein. He doesn't want to hurt anyone. He wants to live. I think this should be everyone's right, so I'm going to help him."

"All right," Karen acquiesced, presuming to speak on everyone else's horrified behalf, "just please don't do it here."

"Thank you," Akbar said to the FBI agent, who up until that moment he had mostly scorned. "I don't want to push it, but would you mind if we do this posthaste? I'm starving."

"I saw two bodies about five minutes back," Uli said, "but we're gonna need a knife and one of the Sterno cans."

Karen passed them over to him.

"If you get sick on decomposing meat," Marsha warned, "you get left behind! Just like Ed!"

"And when you all grow too weak to walk," Akbar responded, "and when the last one dies, I'll be forced to die with you 'cause I can't see the road. But rest assured, I'll greatly admire your integrity as I chew down your corpse."

Karen refused to part with either pots or a plate, but Uli grabbed a lighter and a canteen of water.

As the rest of the group made camp, Akbar and Uli marched off.

In the distance, the others could hear the two men's voices, which soon gave way to grunts of labor. Then they all smelled the smoke. The aroma of cooked meat wafted through the encampment. Karen, Marsha, and Root looked down, but some of the noncogs were clearly energized by the smell.

"Barbecue?" old Robert Moses muttered hopefully.

"No!" Root responded. "Bad!"

When the two men returned, Akbar was noticeably more lively, and Karen was shocked to see that Uli too had a new spring in his step. "You didn't . . ." she began to ask, but stopped herself.

Uli didn't volunteer anything.

The next day when they resumed their slow progress, Akbar and Uli didn't merely set the pace, they practically pulled all the others forward. Around noon, when the noncogs started tripping and stumbling, Karen suggested that they take a break. As soon as they sat down, Woody and several others immediately fell into a deep slumber.

"I don't want to push it," Akbar said, "but obviously we're running up against an energy discrepancy."

"If you want to carry us . . ." Marsha replied in a whisper.

"What I want is for each of you to carefully reconsider your position on what we talked about. Otherwise, Uli and I might be forced to leave you behind."

35

For the next two days they moved in near silence, with Uli and Akbar leading the way. Although they still came across an abundance of bodies, they were all too far gone for consumption. The frayed rope that held them together seemed to be their only lifeline. Though they plodded on, it seemed as though gravity itself was both increasing and diminishing. Karen feared that if she let go of the bar on the back of the chair, she might just float away.

One evening, they nearly bumped headlong into a ragtag crew of about twenty wild-eyed men and women walking back toward Rescue City. They immediately asked if Karen's group had any food.

"We've been out for days now," Karen said.

That didn't stop a couple of the more aggressive members of the group from poking under and around Moses's wheelchair, opening the flaps of the empty saddlebags and rustling through their sleeping gear to see if Karen was lying.

"If you're out of food, why are you still walking this way?" one of them asked suspiciously.

"What would we go back to?" Root countered.

As the group started to move along, Marsha recognized a man named Harold who had been a member of PP.

"Hi, Miss Johnson," he said respectfully when she greeted him.

"What station did you make it up to?" she asked, always driving for intel.

"I'd guess at least four or five watering holes from here. We got some of the food drop, so we were able to make it farther than most, but—"

"What food drop?" Akbar cut in.

"You know, the food that was air-dropped," Harold said.

"Who dropped it? Where?" Uli asked.

"I don't know, the choppers probably."

"What choppers?"

"I don't know. I only saw them at a distance, down along the highway where they picked up all those people. We got there too late."

"What highway?" Uli prodded.

"Long ways from here. You'll see it, just keep going," Harold said, hurrying to catch up with the rest of his group.

They reached the next water station late the next afternoon. There they found three old lean-tos that had been recently abandoned, as well as a central shitting area and a mound of stones that had to be a burial site.

As most of the group made preparations for sleep, Uli quietly led Akbar farther up the Freedom Trail. Although no one asked them where they were going, Root confirmed that the contaminated knife was missing: they were hunting for more bodies. Before the awful aroma could rise in the air, Marsha and Root went out on a bug hunt.

Thirty minutes later the two men returned, grouchy and still hungry.

"He couldn't find shit," Akbar announced.

"Hey, I looked!" Uli shot back.

"Are you kidding?" Root said. "A few days ago, you could hardly walk ten minutes without stumbling over a body."

"They must all be down there," Uli said, hobbling toward the mound of stones.

"Hold on now!" Marsha rasped. "Finding bodies is one thing, but those people have been properly interred. Don't even think about disturbing a sacred tomb."

"Hey! I've always held human life sacred," Akbar said, despite his years as a soldier and then as a paid assassin, "but these bodies died without any help from me. And I for one would be happier knowing my dead body helped to save another."

"The only problem is that once you eat another person," Marsha said, "you forever lose your soul. And I need mine in the afterlife."

"Okay, enough," Uli said.

Uli and Akbar chugged water and lay down with the rest for some shut-eye. Most of them went out like a light.

Because it was still bright out, Karen had trouble sleeping. As she stared off in a daze and tried to ignore her hunger, she noticed something moving in the distance. It appeared to be a dragonfly buzzing about. As she focused harder, though, she saw that it was actually very far away. Sitting up suddenly, she realized it was a helicopter!

She jumped to her feet and noticed something falling from it. A parachute popped open.

"Oh shit," she muttered.

The light-blue chopper proceeded up the trail toward them just a couple hundred feet in the air. As Karen struggled to think of how to make some sort of signal, two more choppers appeared in the distance—darker, newer models that moved a lot faster. They sped forward like a pair of guided missiles. The older, smaller craft swiveled around and the other two appeared to chase it eastward.

"Holy shit!" Karen shrieked. "Did anyone else see that?"

"See what?" Akbar called out.

"I think I just saw an airdrop!"

"Where?"

Karen pointed to a distant hilltop. Remembering that Akbar was blind, she said, "The next hill over."

"How far?" he asked.

"I don't know, maybe five or six miles away."

"A two-hour walk on a full stomach," he said.

"Yeah."

"Do you think it was food?"

"What else would it be? But it doesn't matter," Karen said. "I can barely get to my feet. And I'm so tired and dizzy, I'm seeing double. Let me sleep and we'll figure it out when I get up." She faded quickly.

Most of the group awoke several hours later to the sound of loud male laughter. Uli kept snoring next to Karen as four lean, robust-looking men emerged along the path behind them. They appeared to be a well-stocked expedition.

"Don't I know you?" the shortest man in the group asked Marsha as they approached.

"I used to be with PP."

"Thought so. We'll give you all the food you can carry if you turn around and head back."

"Why?" Marsha asked.

"'Cause otherwise it's just a waste, isn't it?"

"But the city is gone," Root spoke up from her sleeping spot behind Marsha.

"Just the opposite—it's been liberated."

Cookie sat up, looked over at Karen, and rolled her eyes. The men were obviously Piggers.

"He's right," Karen said. "We're dying here. We just need some food to make it back."

"Here." One of the men pulled a small half-eaten box of raisins from his back pocket and tossed it to Karen. "My name's Nelson."

Karen shook a few raisins into her palm and passed the box to Root, who popped a few into her mouth and handed what was left to Cookie.

"These are tricky times," Karen said. "There's evil all around."

"Don't worry, ladies, I'll protect you," said Nelson.

"Protect us?" Marsha said.

"I'll help you make it back. Let's get up."

Root now noticed that the man had a pistol holstered in his belt. "Hold on," she said. "We ain't going anywhere under armed escort."

Marsha turned the little box upside down and poked her fingers to the bottom—several raisins were still clumped together down there. One of the men tried snatching the box but she pulled away.

"Give it back," Nelson said, pulling out his gun.

Uli, who had been snoring the entire time, pretending to be asleep, lunged up and grabbed Nelson's wrist. Without intending to, the man squeezed the trigger—*click*. The gun was empty. Two other men jumped on Uli, who was able to get off a couple punches before they knocked him to the ground. One of them kicked him in the head and he appeared to lose consciousness. By then Root had entered the fray with a cooking knife, slashing the biggest man across his hand and forearm. Akbar raced over, tripping on Uli's body, but grabbed onto one of the Piggers, who snagged the box of raisins from Marsha; she retreated, overwhelmed by it all. With only one arm, Root was able to do little more than keep the man she had cut from going after

Cookie, who clawed at Nelson, holding him at bay. Although the pistol had no bullets, Nelson finally cracked it across her mouth. When Karen jumped on his back, he flipped her over his shoulder and onto the ground, then whacked the butt of the gun against her kneecap. Cookie leaped on him and sank her teeth into his shoulder. A moment later the Piggers beat a hasty retreat.

"Fucking hell!" Karen shouted, dropping to the ground and grabbing her knee.

"At least we got some stale raisins," moaned Cookie, wiping blood from her upper lip.

"And we still have that crate out there somewhere," Akbar said.

"My fucking knee!" Karen winced. "I don't know if I can . . ." She tried to walk but immediately fell down.

"Oh God, did he stab you?" Akbar asked.

"No, I'm just bruised."

"What crate?" Root asked.

"Karen thinks she saw something air-dropped on a hill," Akbar said.

"God, I feel dizzy," Cookie said, flopping backward to the ground. "Thanks for biting that fucker, I think he was about to kill me . . ."

"Karen, what's this about a crate?" Root pressed.

"Before we all went to sleep, I saw a parachute attached to a box drop from a chopper and land somewhere on the side of a hill farther down the trail."

"A chopper," Woody said.

"Right in the path of those four little piggies," Root said.

"Do you think they were involved with the airdrop?" Marsha asked.

"They probably would've dropped the crate closer if it was intended for those guys, no?" Karen said.

"We have to try to get to the airdrop before they do," Akbar said.

"Out of the question!" Karen responded. "With my knee, and Uli basically unconscious, we're all officially out of commission."

"Exactly how far do you think it is?" Marsha asked.

"At least five miles away," Karen said.

Root closed her eyes. Cookie had already fallen back asleep. Five miles sounded as far away as the moon.

Marsha tried not to think about how close she had come to getting some raisins. She had felt them with her fingers before the prick had yanked the box away. She licked her fingertips and peered over at Cookie, Uli, and Karen, who had all been injured in the attack.

Despite the fact that she was beyond exhausted and aching all over, Marsha knew she was their only chance.

"It's got to be food out there," Akbar said softly, as if reading her thoughts. "If you want to take me along, I'll try to help."

"If I want to take you along?" Marsha said with a weak grin. "How about *you* take *me* along?"

"I'd go alone if I wasn't blind."

"Look, I might make it a couple miles, but that's it."

"You'd make it if you had something to eat, right?" Akbar said.

"Yeah, and those gosh-darn raisins would've been just perfect."

"I got something," he said just above a whisper. He could now hear Karen and Root snoring behind him. Reaching into his pocket, he carefully removed six long strands of jerky.

"That's not what I think it is, is it?" Marsha said with disgust.

"It's life for this entire group!" Akbar urged. "It's fuel, that's all. No one else can do this. I know it's tough, but you can do it. Chew this down and walk up that fucking path. No one but you and me will know."

"*God* will know!"

"Maybe God also put that crate up there. And God made it so that only *you* can save us. Ever think of that?"

Marsha stared at the dark-purple strands of scorched human muscle. "I just don't think I can . . . do it."

"There's no commandment against eating meat in the Bible," Akbar reasoned.

"Yes there is, but even if it said you could, I just don't think I could . . ."

"Then we're all dead here, Marsha. We really are. But if you do this—and I know it's a sacrifice you would be making, and I know that you might not make it back—but if you do, you'd be saving fourteen lives. I know that coming from me it sounds phony, but I really think God would approve of that, don't you?"

Marsha snatched the scabrous strands and stuffed them in her pocket.

"Bring a knife and some water with you," Akbar advised.

Without speaking, Marsha grabbed the supplies and staggered off toward the distant hill.

36

A savage scream yanked most of the group out of their daze. The sun was up and one of the noncogs had been startled by a bedraggled couple who were scavenging through their belongings. At the sound of the shriek, the two skinny figures scurried like a pair of cockroaches down the path in the direction of Rescue City.

Karen scanned their surroundings, now on high alert. She spotted another intruder in the distance hobbling unsteadily toward them from up the Freedom Trail. She grabbed her knife.

"Oh my God, who is that?" Root said, looking up the path.

"Is it Marsha?" Akbar asked.

"Not unless she's seriously bowlegged," Root said.

"Wait a sec." Karen glanced around the campsite. "Where is she?"

The figure waved something over its head. The intense morning light indicated that they had slept for many hours. Cookie and Uli were still asleep.

"It *is* her," Karen said, recognizing Marsha's clothes.

Root led Akbar up the path and the two kept walking until Marsha nearly fell into their arms. Her clothes were wet and filthy. The two of them helped her as she stumbled back between them like a drunk.

As soon as they made their way back to the little encampment, Marsha fell to the ground. She opened her pack and revealed six twelve-ounce cans of tuna fish she had recovered. "How are those guys?" she asked, nodding toward Uli and Cookie.

"Still alive," Root said. "Thanks for saving *our* lives."

When Akbar tried hugging Marsha, she pushed him away. "Don't thank me—thank Jesus!"

"I'll thank him when I see him," Root said.

Not wanting to have any problems with the aggressive scavengers, and since all were slowly returning to consciousness, Karen said it was high time to move on. She proposed that they wait to eat the tuna fish until they had cleared the area.

"I'm sore as hell," Marsha said, rising slowly.

"Hang onto the wheelchair's crossbars when we start moving," Akbar whispered. "I'll pull you."

"We don't have to go far," Root said.

They woke Cookie and Uli and told them that some food awaited them up the path. Soon, Moses was secured back in his chair. The team packed up and pressed on.

"Can't believe this—no sooner did I make it down this awful path than I'm heading back up," Marsha grunted, barely able to swing her legs.

Thirty minutes along, Karen stopped and asked Cookie to watch the route behind them and Root to monitor the front. Using a heavy-duty bowie knife, she pried open the six cans and divvied the contents into fourteen cups as all watched. Even Robert Moses was reaching for a cup before it was filled.

Moments later, after everyone had scarfed down their portion, Marsha explained how the team of Piggers who attacked them had actually helped her. "While heading up this way last night, I just kept moving, one foot in front of the other. But after a couple miles, I started losing steam. Couldn't see the path, and I strayed into the bush . . ."

"And you saw them?" Akbar asked.

"No, heard them."

"But they didn't see you?" Karen asked.

"I was half asleep, but I don't think so."

"You don't think so?" Akbar said.

"If they did, she'd probably be dead now," Root reasoned.

"So what exactly happened?"

"To be honest, it's all kind of a blur. Clouds just covered the sky. But their voices pulled me forward. It was pitch black and I started tripping on everything. So I finally just stayed down in the darkness and let the winds pummel me. I awoke just before sunup and had no idea where I was. That's when I realized I was on the wrong side of the hill. I had to backtrack."

"How the hell did you find the crate?" Akbar asked. "I don't understand how you—" Karen discreetly tapped him on the back, which he understood to mean that he should stop talking.

"Actually, as soon as I got back to this side of the hill," Marsha pointed forward, "I realized that I'd been so focused on the Piggers that I had moved away from it. In retrospect, I don't know how they didn't spot it. The parachute was flapping just off the path, *whack-whack-whack*. Hell, it was all I could hear as I tried to sleep."

"You slept near the parachute?" Root asked, and looked up at Karen. There were tears in Karen's eyes; she was staring at the back of Marsha's pants, where blood had seeped through.

"*Passed out* is more like it."

"Are you okay?" Root asked.

"Yeah, I'm just having my woman's time."

"You know," Robert Moses muttered, holding his cup to his mouth, "this would be really delicious with a little mayonnaise and chopped celery."

"So if there was a whole crate, where's the rest of it?" Root asked.

"I couldn't carry it, so I took what I could carry, ate one can there for fuel, then bundled up the parachute and buried it behind some bushes."

"One of us should've come with you," Cookie said, dried blood still streaked across her face. "We could've helped you carry it."

"It's okay if this is all you got," Karen said.

"You sure you buried it?" Root half kidded.

"I had to! And if I hadn't, how would I have gotten this?" Marsha held up her fingers, showing how her nails were worn down to the nubs. Her hands and arms were bruised and scraped. "What else could I do?"

Root grabbed a canteen, helped Marsha up, and took her behind some rocks to try to get her cleaned up. When they were out of earshot, Karen quietly explained that she feared something awful had happened to Marsha that she wasn't telling.

"Do you think she really buried a box of tuna?" Akbar asked.

"I believe her," Cookie said, fighting back tears.

"Let's give her the benefit of the doubt," Karen whispered. "She sure paid for it."

Five minutes later Marsha and Root returned, ready to go.

"In case I didn't say it before," Uli finally spoke up, "thank you."

After eating real food for the first time in days, and motivated by the notion that more sustenance lay buried ahead, they resumed walking. The path rose steadily, and despite the nourishment, the group was moving slower than usual. Uli's face and head were covered in bruises and lumps from the clash with the Piggers. Cookie's bloodied lip swelled, and Marsha staggered, her thighs throbbing, barely able to remain on her feet. By late that afternoon, the Freedom Trail began to level off and Marsha said they were getting close.

"Welcome to high country," Uli joked.

The winds kicked up. More clouds began rolling over and the temperature started dropping. Before they could search the hillside, it was as if a giant faucet had spun open—a cold, hard rain began beating down, the likes of which they had never experienced in Rescue City. Uli quickly hooked a blanket over a clump of three tall cacti and they huddled around Robert Moses, creating a quasi shelter until the storm passed.

Most remained clustered around the chair for body heat as Karen and Cookie assisted Marsha out into the muddy scrub.

"Just point to where you put it, we'll find it," said Cookie, seeing Marsha wincing in pain.

"Everything looks different now," she muttered, upon returning to the shelter. All the hard edges in the area had been reduced to murky puddles. "I don't think this is the right spot."

"Where do you think it might be?" Cookie asked.

Marsha nodded her head uncertainly.

"Maybe we should just move on," Karen said.

"Move on? After all I went through?" Marsha paused. "You think I'm lying?"

"We know you're not lying," Cookie said emphatically. "Come on, let's find it."

After an hour of scouring the area, Woody spotted a group of people approaching in the distance, maybe a mile away. Everyone feared that it was the Pigger team returning to finish them off. But after counting more than four members and seeing that they were clearly run-down and moving slowly, the group breathed easier.

"Can I stay back here and keep looking for the crate?" Cookie asked.

"Sure," Karen said. She and Marsha headed back to the wheelchair to prepare for a possible attack. Uli and Root had knives hidden yet easy to reach.

Ten minutes later, when the new group arrived, the leader called out, "You're not going to attack us, are you?"

"Of course not," Uli responded. "Why would you say that?"

"Last night, four men on the path gave us some food and told us that a homicidal gang of renegades was behind them and that we should kill them before they kill us."

"Those guys are Pigger gangcops," Akbar said. "They tried to force us to go back."

"That's what we figured, but would you mind showing us your hands?" asked the leader.

Everyone complied. They were surprised to see that this group's raggedy clothes were dry. Apparently the burst of rain had been very localized.

"They gave us enough crackers for a couple of days, provided we return," explained the leader.

"To Rescue City?!" Karen asked.

"Yep," said another member of the new group, holding up a small box.

"Just take the crackers and screw 'em—keep moving forward!" Uli advised.

"Forward to death?" a third member of the party spoke up.

"The Piggers have probably taken over the entire city!" Akbar said. "Hell, they'll probably lock you all up or turn you into slaves."

"Maybe, but the only way you're going to make it any farther is by eating your companions," said the leader.

"Go to hell!" Root shouted.

"Actually, we're *leaving* hell—you're the ones going there."

Before turning away, the leader reached out to hand Root his own small box of crackers. She gasped when he suddenly grabbed her wrist.

"I watched six people in my original expedition die or get abandoned until I was finally left behind at a water post a day past here. There's nothing up ahead."

"Consider how many came this way before us." Root broke free. "Isn't it safe to assume that some of them made it out?"

"I hope so, I truly do, but there isn't a single member of this crew who hasn't tasted human flesh, and we've vowed not to do that again."

Marsha looked away.

"If we run into any help," Root said, unable to look the man in the eye any longer, "we'll tell them about you. We'll send help."

"Same here," he replied. Then his group resumed trudging back toward Rescue City.

"God, I thought they'd never leave," Cookie said, emerging from the bushes.

"Find anything?"

"Yeah, death by a million pricks," she said, carefully extricating needles and burrs from her clothes.

It was too dark now to keep searching for the crate, so they divided up the box of crackers the man had given them, made camp, and slept beside the narrow trail.

* * *

At first light the next morning, Marsha, Root, Cookie, Karen, Uli, and Woody got in a line roughly ten feet apart and walked forward over the rough terrain, carefully checking every bush, cactus, and large rock. After marching out a thousand feet—the maximum distance Marsha said she could've ventured from the road—they turned around and rescanned the same area back to the Freedom Trail.

Afterward, Karen found Marsha silently weeping. "Hon," she said, hugging Marsha, "you saved our asses and got us here!"

"You don't understand," Marsha said. "This happened because of what I did. God took it all back!"

"Over by those rocks there's some long scrapes in the ground," Cookie said. "I hate to say it, but I think someone found the crate this morning and just dragged it off."

"A lot of people have come through here," Root said.

"I saw those scrapes and thought the same thing," added Uli.

Marsha closed her eyes and shook her head sadly.

Abandoning the search, they followed the path up into some foothills until they reached a small rocky plateau that gave view to a new, slightly higher range in the ever-rising mountains. Impassable peaks loomed in the distance. Suddenly, Woody spotted an airplane overhead and they all started waving at it.

"What happened to that electronic signal that was supposed to be in Uli's head?" Marsha asked quietly so that he couldn't hear.

"I guess his battery ran out," Root said with a smirk.

Karen stared at Robert Moses as Uli and Akbar pushed his wheelchair along. She didn't think Bea had deliberately manipulated her, but she wondered if the nonagenarian could have fabricated this little lie to trick her into leaving Rescue City. The man seemed so bleached by time, it was hard to imagine he was still capable of such guile.

As the sun started to set later that day, they heard some hoots up ahead. Karen pulled everyone together and Uli grabbed a knife just in case. It turned out to be another quartet of men who looked more shipwrecked than bedraggled.

"Polly Femus wants a cracker!" screeched a wild-eyed, shirtless man in the lead. His ribs pushed out through his chest. "Got a cracker?"

"We're out," Root said. "What expedition are you?"

"He's thirteen, I'm nine," answered a second man, who looked a little more sane. The two other men, one with a long beard and the other missing an arm, shuffled past. All of them had rags wrapped around their heads.

"How do I know that name?" Uli asked, almost to himself. "Polly Femus?"

"Can you tell us anything about the path ahead?" Cookie asked.

"Sure, give us a cracker and I'll tell you everything," said the survivor of expedition thirteen.

"We're really out," Root said.

"No cracker, no info."

"Please reconsider, we're traveling with invalids," Marsha appealed, gesturing to the wheelchair and the noncogs. "You have a moral duty."

"I ate my moral duty two weeks ago," said number nine.

"I'll tell you this," said thirteen, "turn back now, while you still can."

In another moment, the small giddy pair continued on their way.

Three hours later, the trail led them across a plateau with the next water pump rising in the distance.

"I knew they were bullshitting," Karen said, as she pumped fresh water up. All drank, set up camp, cleaned themselves, then bedded down, hoping to rest until morning.

Although no one was certain, Root proclaimed that six weeks had passed since they had departed from Rescue City. Marsha disagreed, saying it had been no more than a month. As the two argued back and forth, Karen and the others drifted off to sleep.

"Karen Sarkisian, thank God you're alive!"

She opened her eyes to see a haggard and sweaty Captain Gaspar Stenson, whom they had last seen near Fort Til Then. He was standing before her with Jerry Howard, his assistant. They both looked gaunt and were soaked in sweat, panting.

"You don't have any food, do you?" she immediately asked.

"Jerky," Howard replied, "but it's a little stringy." He opened his hand to reveal crusty strands that resembled the stuff Uli and Akbar had been eating.

"No thanks," Karen said. "You've abandoned Rescue City?"

"Actually, we're here on a new mission," Stenson said.

Karen glanced nervously at Akbar, fearful that they had come here to recover their prisoner.

"You used to be a Crapper captain, so I'm appealing to you on behalf of the—" Stenson stopped speaking and collapsed to his knees.

"What's going on?" Uli had woken up and stumbled over, in case his sister needed help.

"Hey," Stenson said from the ground, "you've recovered."

"Not a hundred percent, but I'm getting there."

"We have a serious crisis and we need your help!" Stenson was trembling. Howard, meanwhile, was guzzling water from the hand pump. "A day after you left, a small team of Piggers snuck in and slaughtered six of our border guards. We're still managing to hold them at bay, but they've surrounded Fort Til Then. It's basically a siege. The VL has given us some supplies, but they can't do much else."

"We're done with all that," Karen said softly, fearing he was asking them to return and fight.

"Actually, we're here for your benefit too. In addition to the siege, they launched their little army headed by Ramsey Farrell, a Pigger captain, to head up the Freedom Trail."

"Why?"

"To try to get as many people back as they can."

"Farrell? I remember that prick," Uli said.

"But why?" Root asked.

"They're afraid that the mass Crapper defection will make the government shut the place down for good. So Plains sent out the cream of his force to 'persuade' everyone to return."

"Oh, we already saw them—four guys. Big deal," Akbar chimed in. "They offered us crackers and then threatened us. We fought them off."

"That was their diplomatic corps," Stenson said. "We were behind the army so we've seen their savagery."

"Or," Howard amended, "we've been passing group after group returning to Rescue City."

"We've tried persuading some not to go back," Karen said.

"We did too," Howard said, chewing a red strand.

"Their army is right behind us," Stenson continued. "They're letting the returnees pass, giving them enough food to make it back, but once they return, their plan is to turn them into labor battalions and rebuild the city. They're butchering everyone who refuses them."

"When exactly did you guys leave Rescue City?" Akbar asked.

"Fifteen days ago. We've been popping down amphetamines, replacing the soles in our shoes, walking nonstop, day and night."

"Only a few days ago did we finally catch up to Ramsey's gang," Stenson said. "They had just reached this clearing along the side of a mountain not far from here." Presumably he was referring to the hilltop where Marsha lost the crate of tuna fish. "We watched them sneak up on another group of survivors who were camped there . . ." He paused and let out a deep breath. "We watched them line those poor people up and slit their throats. And they were *returning!*"

"Why?" Karen asked.

"It was as if they were making human sacrifices," Howard said. "We snuck around them and kept moving this direction."

"My God!" Marsha grabbed her mouth—she remembered the pirate crew they had passed.

"Howard and I are beat to hell. We're about to collapse. We need your help."

"To do what exactly?"

"We need to bring the water down on them."

"What does that mean?" Cookie asked.

"We brought eight explosives with us," Stenson said.

"You want us to blow them up?" Karen was growing impatient.

"We just need you guys to march ahead as fast as you can and continue warning everyone you see that there's no turning back—"

"We're doing that anyway," Uli interrupted.

"Farrell's army is less than a day behind us. After they kill all the refugees who they can't turn into worker ants, they're going to return and invade Fort Til Then. Then they'll march down and take over the VL."

"I don't understand how you're going to *bring down the water*," Marsha said.

"Remember the two scouts, Straus and Kendowski? Those two are on their flank right now. They've been blowing up every water station behind them. If you blast three or four stations ahead of them, the entire Pigger force will die of thirst."

"They've been refilling at each station," Howard said.

"The only saving grace to this entire hike has been the accessibility to water," Root said.

"These are the same people who didn't give two licks about chopping off your arm," Karen reminded her.

"But after blowing up this station," Stenson nodded at the pump before them, "we're going to double back around them and make sure the station they just left is blown too."

"That way they'll have nothing to go back to," Howard added.

"If they just have one station—only one!—they'll be able to shuttle water from it," Stenson said. "That's why we need you guys to hurry ahead and hit the other stations."

"We barely made it here!" Karen protested. "We're famished and exhausted."

"You've got to go right now," Stenson urged. "Farrell's army could be less than a few hours away. They're well stocked with food and could show up at any moment."

"How many men do they have?" Uli asked.

"At least a hundred of their best men, all armed with guns," Howard said. "With bullets."

"And they have multiple canteens," Stenson said. "Once they realize the situation, they'll pick their swiftest ones, give them full canteens, and they'll speed ahead."

"They might already be racing here," Howard said.

"He's right." Uli was finally grasping the full picture. "These people are fanatical. They need to be stopped."

A moment of silence served as consent: no one objected.

"Okay, let's move out," Karen sighed. As she and Marsha refilled the canteens, Uli, Cookie, and Root started helping the noncogs get ready. Stenson and Howard kept watch for any dust clouds rising from the Freedom Trail behind them.

Still, everything took much longer than usual. The hunger was now like oxygen deprivation, making everyone slow and dopey. Despite Stenson's constant goading, it was another hour before they were ready to march. At that point, Stenson showed them his secret weapon—six bombs little bigger than M-80s.

"Are you kidding?" Uli said. "Those dinky things are supposed to blow up these concrete water pumps?"

"You tape one to the lever," Stenson demonstrated, taking some electrical tape from his knapsack and spooling a bomb tightly to the cotter pin at the neck of the pump. "It'll blow open the pin holding the handle in place."

He had everyone step back about twenty feet, then lit the fuse and dashed over to join them. After a loud, smoky POP, everyone could see that the coiled pin was indeed broken. Howard took a couple minutes to hammer the pin with a rock and pull it out, sending the large metal lever dropping to the ground.

"Just to be on the safe side," Stenson picked up the handle, "take this with you a ways. Bury it somewhere off the path so they can't find it."

"That doesn't look too hard to repair," Uli commented.

"Try it," Stenson replied.

Uli went over to the water pump and tried to find a way to crank up the water—he failed. Sure enough, the tiny explosion had done the trick.

"It might be a good idea to try to move as quickly as possible for the next day or two, because once they realize what we're doing, they're going to speed up and try to beat you to the next water station."

"We're out of food," Marsha said.

"Please take this." Stenson held out some jerky.

"That's not beef, is it?" Marsha said.

"Pork, from the wild boars," Stenson said unblinkingly.

Uli reached over, but before he could grab it, Karen slapped the disgusting strands out of Stenson's hand. "We're not stupid! That's human flesh. We'll make it to the next station, but there's no way we're eating that shit!"

Howard quietly leaned down and picked up the strips of mystery meat.

"Gaspar," Karen said, "if Kendowski and Straus are behind them, why don't you join us?"

"'Cause I don't know exactly where they are. And once Farrell's army gets here and sees the broken handle, they're going to divide their forces and send a team back to protect their last water source. And if Kendowski and Straus didn't knock out the last station, the Piggers will protect that one. Making sure they have no water is the only way we'll be able to protect Fort Til Then."

They bade farewell and Karen's group dragged themselves back onto the Freedom Trail.

37

That afternoon, evening, and night, the notion that they were on some vital mission to destroy Farrell's army, the strongest of the Pigger gangcops, as well as rescue both Fort Til Then and Staten Island, motivated both Uli and Akbar. They took turns doing cadence calls, and the team moved clumsily forward.

Miraculously, late the next morning, utterly feverish and barely able to stand, they stumbled upon the next water station.

After quickly drinking, washing, and refilling all their canteens, they all collapsed on the ground near the waterspout. Uli convinced them, however, that it'd be wiser to head farther up the trail. Ideally they could rest at some nearby location where Pigger scouts couldn't easily sneak up on them.

No one dissented—most had already passed out. It took another hour to get everyone back on their feet. As everyone else staggered up the trail, Uli carefully taped one of the little bombs to the handle of the pump, like Stenson had demonstrated. Just as before, the small explosion snapped the pin enough to hammer it out with a rock. Uli removed the large handle and slung it over his shoulder like a rifle, then hiked up the hill after the others. It took another two hours to reach a bluff that looked all the way down at the long trail unraveling behind them. Unable to even take out all of the sleeping gear, much less help the invalids get ready for bed, everyone fell into a heap. As Uli dozed off, all he could think was, *Why the hell didn't I snatch up that jerky when Karen knocked it to the ground?*

A couple of hours into their slumber, Akbar, Karen, and Uli began to shiver. The temperature had dropped precipitously. Akbar said it was always much cooler in the high country.

"We're going to freeze here," Uli warned.

"Yeah, this little ridge is way too exposed," Karen said as the wind whipped into them.

The sun was still high in the sky, so they woke up the others and they all got back to their aching feet and resumed walking. Soon, they reached a summit where the path leveled off. Instead of descending, the plateau stretched forward, covered with small trees and thorny brushes.

Akbar pushed Moses for about a quarter of a mile along the plateau until the chair suddenly collapsed forward into a shallow ditch. Akbar, Moses, and three of the noncogs went down, but none were seriously injured. They appeared to be in some sort of sunken hollow, roughly two feet deep by ten feet across.

"Fuck," Akbar muttered, "why didn't someone say something?"

"Sorry," said Root, who was in the lead. She was barely able to keep her eyes open.

Uli helped Akbar pull the wheelchair out.

"Actually, this isn't so bad," Marsha said. "This hole is large and just deep enough to shield us from the wind."

It took them all thirty minutes to pull out the blankets and some of the clothes and properly pad their little hollow. Soon everyone was lying together in the warm nest. It occurred to Karen that, surrounded by friends and family, amid the perfect divinity of nature—this was actually a great place to die. Although it was chilly, it was a beautiful day. She felt oddly ecstatic in her daze, like she had *become* part of the landscape.

The next morning it felt colder still, and though all were rested, only Marsha, Uli, and Root were able to move around. The noncogs just sat there like baby birds with their mouths open. Karen was in pain when she slowly rose. Her feet were raw. Her arches, calves, and thighs were so swollen they felt like they were going to burst open. Cookie said her hips felt as though sand had gotten into her joints and was grinding into her pelvis.

"You know what killed us?" Akbar eulogized. "It was trying to do double time to that last fucking water station."

"He's right," Cookie said.

"They didn't even give us food," Root said.

"They tried," Uli muttered.

"They broke us," said Akbar. "We never should've changed our pace."

"We've always been able to bounce back," Karen said.

The sun rose steadily in the sky as if to mock them. Through a fuzz of thought and a giddy, growing disregard of consequences, everyone other than the noncogs knew in their hearts that it was over.

"Hey," Root said, nudging Uli, "you were muttering in your sleep."

"Sorry," he said. "Just like Plato."

"Plato?"

"Yeah, I was with him during his final days in the Bronx Zoo. You know who he mentioned? Sandy Corners."

"Poor Sandy," Root sighed.

"You know what he said? He said that Sandy was the one who came up with idea of burning the Mkultra down, not him."

"Why are you bringing this up?"

"He said he thought *you* might've killed her."

"If I knew that he was going to act on her idea," Root replied, "I would've killed her before she said it."

"Really?"

"A city that once housed countless people is now a heap of ashes, but not before a plague ravaged it and left thousands dead and dying. This all came out of her wonderful notion of liberation, which Plato, bless his heart, acted upon. Do you think we'd be sitting in a hole starving to death if I had killed her?" Root's angry response woke Karen.

"Well, I'm not going to sit here and starve to death," Uli said angrily, struggling to his feet.

"You're in no better shape than the rest of us," Karen said.

"Maybe, but I'd rather die trying."

"Hold up." Akbar pulled himself to his feet. "Can you lead me somewhere so I can pee?"

Uli walked him about ten feet away before Akbar murmured, "It's all on you, bro. You understand that?"

"I'll do my damnedest."

"Will you really? 'Cause you know Karen never should've turned down that jerky. You know that, right?"

"Yeah, I know. But that bus is gone."

"There's still one more bus, right here," Akbar said.

"What do you mean?"

"We'll all be dead soon anyway. Let my death mean something."

"No way."

"I'll kill myself. All you have to do is—"

"Do it and I'll make sure you get a wonderful funeral, which will only bring us all closer to death."

Akbar wished him luck and followed the sounds back to the earthen nest.

* * *

Throughout the rest of the day, their exhausted bodies slowly burned off calories, growing weaker and weaker. A primary fear had been that a thirsty Pigger force—well stocked with food—was going to catch them. For Karen, though, this soon became a silent hope. It occurred to her that they could use the water they still had to bargain with— since it could just as easily be poured out.

Although everyone remained huddled together, some felt colder than others.

When dawn broke the next morning, Karen discovered that one of the noncogs had died in her sleep. And even though Robert Moses looked dead too, they knew by his faint snoring that he was still somehow alive. For the next several hours, whenever his large, moist eyes opened and made contact with someone else, even a noncog, he'd make eating motions, as if people had forgotten to feed him.

By the third day in the quilted trench, the only time anyone stepped out was to drain bowel or bladder. As everyone weaved in and out of consciousness, they began relieving themselves closer to their nest. By the fifth day, when the water started to run low, most were relieving themselves right where they lay.

On the sixth morning, a second noncog had died. On the eighth day, a third passed. Akbar made some mention about wasted protein, which everyone ignored. Uli was no longer there to support Akbar's barbaric wishes.

38

The next morning, Root checked to see who had died in the night. She put a finger under each sleeping person's nose to see if they were still breathing. She smiled weakly when she determined that no one else had passed.

Karen, meanwhile, was trying to make a game of remembering and replaying folk tunes in her head, sometimes humming them aloud, sometimes thinking she was.

"Piggers," Root mumbled. She saw them, or thought she saw them, slowly climbing up a ridge in the distance.

Karen opened her eyes to glimpse Sergeants Straus and Kendowski holstering their pistols. They took off their packs and started waking people up, handing out crackers—old C-rations.

"Are you . . . ?" Karen began, fingering the space in front of her.

"We're really here," Straus said, smiling.

"Gaspar and . . ."

"We passed their bodies, strung up," Kendowski said. "Not pretty. I'm guessing the Piggers tortured them trying to find the pump handles."

"I hope they didn't talk," Straus murmured.

When everyone took swigs of water, they discovered that a fourth noncog had indeed died.

Following a respectful pause, Straus said that they had to move.

"Where's Farrell's army right now?" Akbar asked.

"When they discovered the first destroyed water station, they sent their fastest men back, while the rest waited," Kendowski said. "We were able to slip around them."

"But they're on their way now, so we have to shake a leg," Straus said.

Robert Moses signaled for a little more water.

"Sorry, old-timer, we're officially out," Straus said, holding his canteen upside down.

"We need to get to the next water station just like you all," Kendowski said. "Drink from it and blow it up, before any of them get there."

"Where'd you find these?" Root asked, munching down crackers, regaining some of her strength.

"Down in that Mkultra military installation," Kendowski said, reaching into his bag. "Oh, we also found some Piggers asleep on the road. We snuck up on them and grabbed these." He opened his knapsack to reveal six cans of tuna fish.

"Tuna! Those are just like the ones we had," Marsha said.

"They must've gotten them at the drop," Karen said.

Within minutes, nearly half of the tuna fish and crackers had been devoured.

With Uli still gone, and the four noncogs deceased, their original party of fifteen, including Cookie, was down to a starving nine: Root, Marsha, Akbar, Woody, Karen, Cookie, Robert Moses, and the two other remaining noncogs. Karen couldn't stop thinking about Uli, wondering if he had made it to the next water station. Although she still wouldn't do it, she'd understand if he had cannibalized again—so long as he was still alive.

With a handful of crackers and a mouthful of water per person, everyone gradually felt their vigor returning. The two scouts kept reminding them that they had to move pronto.

"Too bad we blew up the last water station," Akbar said. "That's only a couple hours behind us."

"Yeah," Straus said. "We were hoping to get there before you did and refill."

"But better safe than sorry," said Kendowski.

"There's a decent chance the Piggers are there right now," Straus surmised, "trying to dig directly to the source."

Within an hour, they had finished packing everything up. Too tired to scoop up the hard earth, they left the deceased noncogs in the trench and covered them with brush before setting off.

Four hours later, Kendowski was the first to spot the lone figure up ahead. Judging by the person's long hair, it appeared to be a large woman leaning on a boulder near a clump of bushes and trees. The scouts took out their guns. It wasn't until they got close that they realized the woman was long dead and was fairly decomposed. Closer still and they saw that both of her legs had been hacked off, and her eyes were missing.

"Holy shit!" Root shrieked. She rushed over and kicked the corpse in the chest, sending up a wave of green flies. She started stomping on the body until Marsha hurried over and pulled her back.

"That's the cunt who chopped off my arm!" Root hissed. "I told her I wasn't one of them . . . When I begged her not to, she laughed and said she was going to eat it for lunch with mustard!"

"I'm sorry," came a hoarse whisper from behind them. They all jerked around to see Uli sitting up against a rock that had obscured him from view.

"You're alive!" Karen raced over and immediately gave him some crackers.

"Are you injured?" Akbar asked.

"Just starving." Uli had a knife clenched in his hand. "I just couldn't do it."

"Looks like someone did to her what she did to everyone else in the Bronx Zoo," Root said, gesturing toward the corpse.

"It was those creepy guys we saw a couple weeks ago, remember?" Uli said. "The guys who refused to give information unless we gave crackers?"

"Oh, right! *Polly Femus wants a cracker*," Root said. "That was her name."

"What the hell is the Pigger prison commandant doing all the way out here?" asked Kendowski.

"She didn't pass us," Karen said.

"And she doesn't really look like she could have walked all this way," Cookie observed.

"What are you guys doing here?" Uli whispered to the scouts. "Where's Gaspar?"

"They got him," Straus replied, then explained how he and Kendowski had met up with Karen and the others.

"God," Uli said, chewing down a cracker, "these things taste like smoke and asbestos."

"We pulled them out of that underground base with all those stinking bodies," Kendowski said.

"You went down *into* the Mkultra?" Root asked.

"Well, when we fled from Rescue City, we barely had a crumb. And we spent enough time at the first water station to know that surviving this hike was all about food."

Within twenty minutes, Uli was on his wobbly feet and roped back to Robert Moses's wheelchair.

As the group made their way up the path toward a steep hilltop, the wind started blowing again.

With the last orange rays of the sun giving way to dark clouds, the path was barely visible. Peering back beyond several overlapping hills in the direction they had come from, Straus caught a harrowing sight—three distinct dots, campfires in the far distance, near where they had found Uli and Polly Femus. It was almost certainly the remnants of Farrell's little army, camped down for the night.

"Holy shit, they're a lot closer than I thought," Straus said.

Despite what appeared to be an impending storm, everyone pushed on. Karen proposed that they try to descend the far side of the hill and keep marching into the night.

"It's too dangerous," Uli said. They could barely make out the rocky terrain shifting below their feet.

Although they were able to detour around several steep inclines, they had to repeatedly hoist the wheelchair off the ground. Near the next summit, the sky suddenly broke and cold rain and hail began to pelt them. Kendowski and Straus, who had scouted ahead, directed everyone to the opening of a shallow cave just below the hilltop. Wet and cold, the group huddled under its blankets, and though there were dried sticks and twigs scattered around that could be used for a fire, all were petrified of revealing their position.

The howling wind, beating rain, and soon the cracking of lightning kept Karen and most of the others up for hours. Finally, when the storm began to subside, one by one they nodded off.

"LOOK! LOOK!" Root's screams woke everyone up. It wasn't even dawn yet, but the edge of the sky was bright enough to illuminate a giant red wave rolling in from the west—a mighty sandstorm was tumbling over the desert floor, crashing right toward a distant orange speck, presumably a single campfire that the Piggers had kept burning throughout the night.

Another minute or so and the orange dot vanished under the sea of red sand.

"God's mighty hand hath smited thee," said Marsha.

"Smited the shit out of thee!" Straus echoed gleefully. "That, along with no water, should buy us some time."

A couple of hours into their trek that morning, the storm blew itself out. As they neared the top of another large hill, Woody began yelling: "There! There!"

Everyone saw it, about fifty feet below and in front of them: a straight line cutting through the brush.

"Incredible," Cookie muttered, "is . . . is that a train track?"

It took another minute before they realized that a bona fide two-lane highway was running perpendicular to their trail. In the ten minutes or so that it took them to scramble down to it, they didn't see a single vehicle pass. When they finally lowered the wheelchair onto the road, they found that it was filled with cracks and fissures; it had to have been abandoned long ago. Up ahead and to the left, the road twisted sharply to the right, hugging along a mountainside.

"Oh my God!" Uli suddenly cried out.

"What is it?" Cookie asked.

"I just remembered that when I first broke out of the Mkultra, I got lost in the desert and I found a highway."

"*This* highway?" asked Akbar.

"I'm not sure. The road was surrounded by sand. But if this one circles back, it could be the same road."

"Was the one you saw still being used?" Marsha asked.

"Yeah. In fact, someone picked me up. So this probably isn't it."

"Who picked you up?" Cookie asked.

"Some kid in a VW Bug. I thought I saw a city—buildings in the distance—but then I passed out."

"What happened?"

"No clue. I woke up back in Rescue City, sedated in a bed up in the Bronx."

"Look at this shit," Karen said, pointing toward a trail of litter as they moved farther down the abandoned highway: old blankets, knapsacks, canteens, torn clothes. The litter increased as they moved along. A couple hundred feet down, they found a pile of burned debris.

"What the hell is this?" Root asked.

"A pickup point?" Uli speculated.

"You think maybe a Greyhound runs down here?"

"No, this road is too pitted, I don't think it's passable," Uli said. "But looky here."

A succession of large, ski-like tracks overlapped each other at one dusty section of the road. The trees on both sides of the area were cleared away.

"Those are chopper pads," Root said, "but not a very big chopper."

"This is what Harold mentioned!" Marsha cried out, referring to one of the people they had passed.

"They left a lot of crap behind, so there must've been a bunch of trips."

"They must've had some kind of airlift here," said Karen.

"Is this where the Freedom Trail ends?" Akbar asked. "Can you see if it keeps going?"

"I think it continues somewhere down there," replied Root, pointing behind her.

"Well, that's where the water is," Marsha said. "So we better find it."

After a few minutes of rummaging around to make sure no food had been left behind, they returned to the spot where they had initially entered the road. Straus had identified a bunch of small stones shaped into an arrow pointing down the incline.

39

They had a tough time picking up the path again. For the first hour or so, the ropes were untied and everyone walked side by side, scanning the earth for any signs. Clearly the airlift had siphoned off many refugees who had helped define the Freedom Trail—without their added footsteps, the route had faded considerably. Uli circled back, raking their path with a branch.

"What the hell are you doing?" Root asked.

"We can't find the path—let's not make it any easier for Ramsey's men."

About forty-five minutes in, Woody pointed out a small brown clump on the ground.

"Looks like deer scat," Uli said.

Others examined it, sniffed it, and snapped it apart. A debate ensued, a vote was taken—the specimen appeared to be shriveled human feces, ergo they were still on the Freedom Trail.

"People who are starving just don't shit very much," Akbar said.

"And a lot of them either died, turned back, or maybe got picked up on the road," Marsha said.

Without any water, all were enduring an unforgiving thirst.

Just as another mountain loomed up ahead, and all felt a sinking of hope, Cookie spotted the next water station. "Halle-fucking-lujah!" she shouted.

Straus rushed ahead and cranked the lever until water began to gush out. Everyone hurried over and started pushing each other aside to suck it down. Robert Moses, who was stuck in his chair, smacked his lips together and shouted, "Mercy! Mercy!"

Straus and Kendowski announced that they could only remain for a few hours before blowing the pump handle off. But Karen and the others put it to a vote and decided to ignore them and spend the night.

"Let me just remind you that we all saw the Piggers from that hilltop just hours behind us, and they do have guns," Kenodowski said.

"They were at least ten miles away," Root said.

"But they're still probably moving much quicker than us," Uli joined in.

Straus gestured to an overhanging bluff that he estimated was only about twenty minutes up the path. "From there we can see anyone coming."

After everyone drank and refilled their canteens, Straus and Kendowski carefully detonated one of the little explosives, then hammered out the pin and removed the handle.

The hike uphill to the bluff took nearly an hour with the chair. When they arrived, it felt much colder. Because of the direction of the wind, they were able to gather sticks and branches and start a small fire which hopefully couldn't be seen from the path below.

Karen awoke in the middle of the night to see Marsha scampering behind some rocks, presumably to relieve herself. But before she could fall back to sleep, she thought she heard soft moans coming from where Marsha had vanished. Concerned about the Pigger threat, she grabbed her knife and stood up just as she noticed Marsha lumbering back. Karen was surprised to see that she was completely naked.

"You shouldn't be walking around like that," Karen said.

Marsha didn't respond and immediately went back to sleep.

A sharp, ragged cry of agony from below woke Karen a second time just as the sun was coming up. Jumping to her feet, knife in hand, she scurried down the incline until she reached the broken water station. Kendowski and Straus had captured two weathered men—presumably Pigger gangcops. Judging by the dozen empty canteens piled nearby, it appeared that they had been sent ahead of their compatriots to retrieve water.

When Karen got closer she saw that the scouts had bound the men's wrists and ankles together and gagged their mouths. One of them had his shirt pulled up and wrapped over his head, so he was unable to see what was going on. Kendowski and Straus were both focused on the other soldier, who was groaning and writhing; their backs blocked whatever they were doing. As Karen approached, she noticed a small bloody pile next to them—fingers, toes, and what looked like an ear.

"What the fuck!"

"Scram, Karen!" Kendowski snarled. "You don't want to see this."

She ignored him and stepped closer, until she could see the face of the bald prisoner they were operating on. There was a bloody hole where his nose had been. He was moaning, though he no longer appeared fully conscious.

"What the fuck are you doing!" Karen shouted in horror.

"A Pigger pleabag!" Kendowski snapped, tearing at something and then holding up a patch of flesh with hair on it. He had scalped off the man's chin with its goatee attached.

"Captain Sarkisian, meet Captain Ramsey Farrell," Straus introduced.

"Yep, that's the prick who dumped me in the Bronx Zoo." It was Uli, who had evidently followed his sister down the hill. He moved closer and looked down at the mutilated gangcop, his former interrogator, who was muttering incoherently.

"Stop this at once!" Karen appealed.

"After the Piggers seceded from Rescue City, this prick was put in charge of the anti-Crapper unit," Kendowski seethed, and jabbed his knife hard into Farrell's right eye, popping it like a grape. "Their true goal was what they've finally achieved—eradicating the Crappers from Rescue City. But that wasn't enough for them!" he shouted into Ramsey's dying ear. "You had to march out into the desert and grab those poor refugees just looking for a place to die, didn't you? You little prick!"

"My God!" Drawn by all the noise, Root was now approaching. "Why are you doing that?"

"That's the guy who sent us to the zoo," Uli said.

Root took a deep breath, turned, and started walking back up to the camp. It was too late anyway—the Pigger commander was nearly dead. But Karen could hear the other one moaning through his gag. She reached over and pulled the shirt off his face.

It was Sammy Greenberg, Karen's Pigger friend who had told her of Uli's status when she was last up in Kew Gardens. Blood was trickling from his nose and mouth. Though they'd roughed him up, they hadn't started cutting yet.

"If everyone could please just let us do our job!" Straus demanded.

"You got Farrell," Karen said, "but I know Sammy, he's a good guy."

"Good guy? Want to know what this good guy did to Gaspar and Howard?" Straus said, grinning menacingly. "These two guys cut off their genitals. Want me to tell you what they did with them?"

"Aren't we better?" Karen asked. "Can't we show a little compassion?"

"Only a victim can pardon a crime—no one else has that right," Straus said. "We only owe them vengeance."

Kendowski took off his own shirt and used it to wipe the blood and sweat from his face. As he did this, Karen leaned down and jammed her knife into Sammy Greenberg's jugular.

"Goddamnit!" Straus yelled.

As blood sprayed out of the man's neck, Karen whispered, "Sorry, Sam, it's the best I could do."

Suddenly, Uli lurched forward with his own knife in hand.

Kendowski pulled out his pistol, but Uli dashed right past them and farther down the hill.

A third Pigger gangcop was crawling on hands and knees toward the broken water pump. Without pause, Uli plunged his knife into the man's back before they could start on him.

Kendowski sighed and holstered his gun.

"Enough blood, please," Karen groaned. "Let's get going!"

40

A fter a five-hour uphill hike, they reached an encampment left by some previous party. Marsha nervously poked through the firepit; the stones were still warm. Inside they found bone fragments and singed strips of fat—cannibalism. Strangely, there were no bodies around.

They hiked uphill for another hour, then down a small dale, then up a steeper hill to another peak. It was late afternoon when they approached the top—a wooded area where Woody began acting frisky, pulling ahead as though following a scent. When the rest of the group arrived at the summit, Woody screamed and pointed at something.

Using a long stick, Root was able to scratch a rusty twelve-ounce can out of some thorny bush. She read the label and yelped, "It's a full can of Spam!"

"Oh my God!" Marsha shouted.

Everyone passed it around as though it were a brick of gold. Inexplicably, Woody took off again, running downhill, away from the path.

"Where the hell is he going?" Karen asked tiredly.

Cookie took the lead as they hiked down after him. "What are those?" she called out. He was standing about a hundred feet away holding something in each hand.

"Oh shit!" Root said, realizing that he had located two more rusty cans of Spam. She looked farther down the path and saw a fourth can peeking out through some leaves. "There's more down here!"

"Dude's a regular truffle pig," Cookie said.

"Hold on," Marsha said, inspecting a can. "These are from Rescue City!"

"Who cares!" Straus shouted out from behind.

Marsha immediately removed the little metal key and rolled open the aluminum top, then quietly divvied up the spongy reconstituted meat.

"Thank the Lord! A miracle!" Marsha chirped, looking up at the heavens as if the cans had fallen from the sky.

"They probably dropped out of one of those choppers," Root said.

"Why would choppers bring them from the rez?" Marsha asked.

Root shrugged.

Reenergized after gobbling down the cans, most took bathroom breaks off the path. Marsha, the most modest member of the group, headed farthest downhill for privacy.

Peering out across the beautiful mountain vista, Karen said to Root, "Why would choppers get food from Rescue City and drop it here?"

"Hush!" Akbar snapped, tilting his head sideways.

Everyone could make out faint screams.

"It's Marsha!" Akbar shouted.

Karen snatched her knife from the back of the wheelchair and, holding it away from herself in case she fell, raced down the side of the mountain with Uli and Root on her heels.

Kendowski had already reached her. Marsha was pointing at something in horror. Breaking through leaves and collapsed branches were four decomposing bodies lying side by side. By his flaming-red hair, Karen immediately recognized Captain Anthony LaCoste with his face partially eaten away. She figured that the three others had to be part of his original expedition—Team Rescue.

"Why . . . How'd they get down here?" Root said.

"Better question is, who did this?" Karen said, glancing around nervously.

"Look." Uli pointed to the nooses still tightly squeezed into the skin around their blackened necks. The ropes had clearly been severed.

"Oh my God," Marsha groaned. "Were they lynched?"

"No," Uli said. Brushing off leaves and dirt, he pointed to the dark blotches on their clothes. Bullet holes riddled their bodies. Although they had holsters, their pistols were missing. Uli dropped to his hands and knees and began inspecting the ground around the corpses.

"Anyone see their guns?" Cookie asked. "Who do you think did this?"

"I'm not really in the mood to dig slugs out of rotting corpses, but . . ." Uli ran his hands through the ground as though looking for a coin, raked back the branches still covering the bodies, then stood abruptly and started walking back uphill.

"What is it?" Marsha called after him.

"Look," Uli said, pointing at a snapped branch, and then another, as he continued uphill. There was a trajectory of small broken branches and heel marks through the humus. The bodies had been dragged down there.

Uli raced up along the path back to the summit where the two other noncogs were waiting with Akbar and Moses. As the others arrived behind him, Uli stared above the wheelchair at a cluster of tall trees. "There!" he shouted, pointing to a particularly tall tree.

Karen could make out three cut ropes dangling from it. A fourth, longer rope twined around the biggest branch. "They were probably ambushed," she said.

"Someone was shot?" Akbar asked.

"The first expedition—the one that was supposed to save Rescue City," Uli explained. "And then they were strung up here."

"What the hell?" said Cookie.

"Wait, who?" Akbar said.

Uli told him that they had just located the remains of the first team. "They were led by Anthony LaCoste."

"That's the cocksucker who poked my eyes out!" Akbar roared.

"Oh God!" Cookie was learning all of this for the first time.

"So the motherfucker walked all this way just to get his ass shot and lynched up here," Akbar said, fully comprehending the situation.

"I didn't see any kill shots, so he was probably still dying when they strung him up," Uli said for Akbar's benefit.

"Leaves the question of who did it and why," Root chimed in.

"The people in one of the newer helicopters killed them," Karen said. She reminded them that she alone had seen the older chopper dropping food and the new ones scaring it off, chasing it.

"Nothing personal, Karen," Root said, "but that just sounds nuts."

"What I wonder is, if they were strung up there," Straus said, gesturing toward the trees, "who went through all the trouble of climbing up there to cut them all down, and why?"

"Maybe later they decided to hide their crimes, or maybe one of the early expeditions from Rescue City that hiked all the way here saw the poor bastards dangling there and decided that they were deterrents to others coming this direction, so they cut the ropes and dragged them out of sight."

"We were pissed when LaCoste cut us from their team," Straus said to Kendowski, "but we were lucky as hell."

Four hours into the next stretch, the group's misfortunes were compounded when they reached the next water station only to find that it had already been destroyed. Unlike their minor explosions that dislodged only the handles, the entire pump head was missing, leaving only a small hole with a pipe sticking out.

"Fuck!" Akbar barked when Karen explained what they were seeing.

"Anyone have a really long straw?" Root asked, looking down the dark hole.

"Thank God we doubled up on canteens," Uli said.

"So the new-helicopter people ambushed LaCoste's team up on the hill," Straus said, adopting Karen's hypothesis, "then they hiked down here and took out the water station?"

"Why here?" Akbar wondered. "I mean, if they're going to knock out our water, they should've done it earlier, at the very first water station."

"And left the bodies there as well," Uli added. "That could've stopped the entire evacuation at the outset."

"Maybe there was some jurisdictional issue," Karen surmised.

"Or maybe they were just dumb," Cookie said.

As everyone started discussing the ramifications of this setback, Karen checked all the canteens. Four still had various levels of water, but only two were completely full. Because of the extra canteens, people had been more indulgent. And though they weren't dry, Karen knew that this upcoming hike was going to be hell.

"I'm beat," said Akbar.

"Me too," said Cookie.

"Let's camp here for the night," Marsha said, collapsing to the ground. The sky offered only a sliver of orange against an expanse of dark blue.

"With the water situation, I really don't think we can afford to," Akbar opined.

"He's right," Uli said. "Unless we want to crawl on hands and knees like those Piggers, I think we have to push ourselves farther. Hell, it's not even fully dark yet."

Karen reluctantly agreed. Some groaned as they tiredly balanced on raw feet and shuffled on.

As the group reached the bottom of a large hill, they fell silent when in the growing darkness they beheld an eerie sight: two very pale white men, embracing like Greco-Roman wrestlers, lying still upon a flat white rock that appeared to be evenly covered in dark blood, almost like a velvet tablecloth—the tableau looked like a marble sculpture.

Root approached and delicately touched one and then the other with her index finger—cold. They were dead, but rigor mortis hadn't yet set in.

"They must be the cannibals from the campfire this morning," said Karen.

Uli used a lighter to inspect their wounds and speculated that one man had slashed the other's jugular, then sliced his own wrists.

"You'd think at least one could've eaten the other," Cookie said with a demented grin.

"The murderer-suicider put the head of the older man on his lap and died hugging him," Uli observed. "No sign of a struggle, only affection. I think it was more of a double suicide."

As they pressed on, the trail rose and the foliage thickened until trees blocked the moonlight. The path grew steeper and harder to find. Straus and Kendowski dipped sticks into a Sterno can and lit them as torches. The two of them spread out, checking the ground for human feces, while Root identified the easiest route for the wheels, leading everyone slowly forward. As the incline steadily increased, the path grew clearer but the chair became harder to push. Uli braced himself against the bars across the back and others joined in. Soon it was more of a climb than a walk. It was the first time that they needed to use all three bars at the back of the wheelchair.

When they finally arrived at a small plateau, everyone was bushed; they took out the blankets and bedded down. Karen set twelve cups side by side and emptied all the canteens, carefully making sure the level of liquid in each was equal. Everyone had roughly half a cup of water. Cookie and Marsha sipped theirs like a fine wine, while everyone else knocked it back like bad Scotch. Woody carefully licked the inside of his cup. The small amount of water only made them all thirstier.

After about four hours of sleep, Karen announced that it was time to go. They had to use what little energy they had left wisely.

"If all goes well," Root speculated optimistically, "we'll have as much water as we want before nightfall."

"And hopefully we'll be more frugal with it," said Karen.

The hill before them didn't look particularly large, but none could clearly make out the top. Although it wasn't quite as steep, the path just kept rising.

In the moonlight, Marsha noticed some green berries clinging to a little bush just off the path.

"Don't eat them unless you know exactly what they are," Uli warned.

"They look delicious," said Cookie. "I'll try one."

"If you get sick, we can't wait or carry you," Karen said.

"*I'll* risk it," Akbar said. "Pass some over here."

Cookie plucked several of the berries from the bush.

Root grabbed her wrist and said to Akbar, "You're the only one who can handle that chair. You get sick and Moses is a goner as well."

"Just give me the berries," he replied, holding open his palm.

"No one's preventing you," Root said. "But we're not obliged to help you either."

An awkward silence followed.

"Uli, will you hand me those fucking berries?"

"Akbar, we've come this far and there are only a few berries on the bush," Karen coaxed.

"Uli!"

Uli sighed, and Karen said, "How about we pick some but we don't eat them till we get to the top of the mountain?"

"How about you give me the fucking berries or I ain't taking another step?!"

Karen took the berries from Cookie and handed them to Akbar. He tossed them to the ground, fumbled for the handle of the wheelchair, and resumed pushing.

Root silently grabbed the bar next to him and helped steer. They continued for another ten minutes before the path once again began to rise steeply, forcing all hands back on the chair. They heaved and groaned and slowly pushed Moses's chair up the hill for about thirty minutes before Straus, who was walking ahead, called out, "Holy shit! Look over here!"

There was a clear fork in the Freedom Trail. The main path seemed to go sharply uphill while a second one looped around some rocks and vanished out of sight. The divergent path, though smaller, seemed more worn and sculpted. When Kendowski checked it out, he found that it maintained a flat gradient as far as the eye could see.

"That side path looks almost like one of those roads made during the Depression by the Civilian Conservation Corps," Root said.

"Up until now," Karen said, "we've been walking directly uphill, and we have no idea where this new path goes—"

"For starters, this isn't a hill," Uli interrupted. "It's a *mountain*. And we're exhausted and haven't had a drop of water in hours!"

"I vote that for once we take the easy way," said Akbar, drenched in sweat.

"We didn't come this far just to get lost out here," Root countered. "I think we stick with the Freedom Trail."

"I kind of agree," said Marsha. She, Karen, Straus, and Root all voted for the uphill march; Akbar, Cookie, Uli, and Kendowski all voted for the other way.

"Which way you want to go, Gramps?" asked Root, hoping to break the deadlock. "Up or around?"

"Always up!" Moses exclaimed. "To the promised land!"

"Up it is," Karen said.

"I love it—the deciding vote is made by a senile rich guy who gets to ride while we push," Akbar grumbled.

No one tried to influence the noncogs.

As they resumed their ascent, Akbar and Uli pushed the wheelchair while everyone else held ropes and pulled from the front. Roughly two hours later, as the trees began disappearing, the moonlight revealed that they were finally nearing the summit. Root pointed out that Moses's breathing had grown noticeably labored.

"We're not high enough for altitude sickness," Uli said.

"He's both cold and sweaty," Root reported.

"We're almost at the top," Karen said. "Should be going downhill any moment now, then we'll hit water." She took off her thin jacket and wrapped it around Moses's large hands. "Just hang on, we'll be there soon."

When the path finally flattened out at the summit, the retired bureaucrat started moaning.

"Keep moving!" Karen instructed as they were met by a steady headwind.

"You wanna rest, Gramps?" asked Root, growing weary of Karen's bossiness.

Moses pointed over to a cliff where the whole world seemed to suddenly drop away. "There!"

As the group moved on, moonlight revealed a phenomenal view of the valley below them. Cookie walked right up to the edge of the cliff. Looking straight down what seemed to be at least a thousand-foot drop, she could make out a dark line that had to be a river.

"The path goes this way!" Kendowski called out.

Straus, who was farther ahead, let out a loud gasp.

Perched just below the mountaintop was the next coveted water station.

"Hallelujah!"

"A station all the way up here?" Uli was bewildered.

But Kendowski then confirmed their worst fear—the metal pump and handle had been entirely removed. As this terrifying reality began to sink in, Straus noticed something round in a clump of bushes back near the cliff. It was a giant metal drum with a spigot fastened at the bottom. The scout raced over and turned the knob. Sure enough, clear, cool water started flowing out.

"This must've been lowered by one of the good helicopters," Uli said. "I mean, no one could've carried it all the way up here. It's gotta weigh a ton."

"We're saved!" Straus shouted, drinking desperately from it.

Everyone lined up. Karen issued a one-cup-at-a-time rule so that it wouldn't turn into a mad rush again. But just like the last time, Robert Moses was overlooked. Slowly he untied the straps around his broad chest. As the others guzzled water, he dropped his granitelike feet and hoisted himself up by the armrests.

"Hold on! I'll bring you a cup," said Root.

"No! I have to take my tablets!"

"Tablets?" Akbar said. "Does anyone have any pills for Mr. Moses?"

Moses shuffled a couple steps away from the path and grabbed what looked like a wooden staff covered with large white leaves. Without saying a word, he yanked one of the leaves off.

"What the hell is that?" Root approached, carrying a cup of water. As she stepped closer, she saw that there were sheets of paper thumbtacked to the pole.

Moses tore one off and handed it to her as she passed the cup to him.

"These are legal documents!"

Karen, Uli, and Marsha hurried over; each tore off several pages from the staff and began reading in the moonlight.

"This one is an order to cease and desist," Uli said. "Though I'm not sure what for."

Marsha read another notice aloud: "*You are hereby trespassing on private property of such and such a longitude and latitude, blah blah blah, latitude, blah blah blah . . . owned by the Feedmore Corporation.*"

"Why are they here? Could they be for us?" Karen asked.

"Holy cow!" Marsha cried out, holding up another page. "This one says, *Appeal pending to the Utah Supreme Court!*"

"Could we be in Utah?" Karen said. "Did we walk all the way to another state?"

"There," Moses spoke again, releasing the staff and pointing down to the valley below. Lights flickered in the distance—it was a town! And two rows of lights were sliding along the distant plane—an active highway.

"Holy shit!" Uli yelled.

For a moment everyone stood in awe of civilization, until Robert Moses suddenly collapsed backward, hitting the craggy ground with full force. Karen and Uli raced over and ran their hands along his ribs, hips, and legs, feeling for broken bones. Root saw that blood was dripping from his large ears—like his brother, he had hit his head very hard on a rock.

"Don't move him," Cookie cautioned.

Root brought out a blanket for Moses. Kendowski, Straus, and the others gathered sticks and in a few minutes a small fire was burning near the old man to keep him warm. Karen gave him more water, but over the next hour his condition steadily deteriorated. After what Marsha calculated was forty agonizing days, it appeared that Robert Moses was finally dying.

"Tell Paul . . ." Moses said in a low, labored whisper, "I never meant to hurt him."

"He was your older brother," Uli said, overcome with feelings of protectiveness toward the deceased sibling. "Why did you treat him so badly?"

"The hardest . . . most thankless thing in the whole world is . . . trying to help others. I tried helping Paul and I killed him . . . I only hope I did better for New York."

With a final exhale, Robert Moses was gone.

Root gently covered his face and upper body with a blanket. Exhausted and chilled to the bone, the cognizant group members agreed to bury him at first light. They barely had enough energy to unpack their own blankets and huddle together. Sleep came quickly and mercifully.

41

Just before sunrise, Karen awoke to the sound of urgent whispering. Marsha's blanket next to her was empty. She scanned the area and spotted Marsha ambling off in her underwear. Was she sleepwalking?

Karen followed her beyond a series of boulders. Someone else was beckoning her in the darkness. Karen moved closer until she saw the outline of a naked man, then realized there were *two* nude men—safely out of everyone else's view. Moments later she realized it was the two scouts. She watched as Straus and Kendowski led Marsha up against one of the rocks and began fondling her. She waited for Marsha to scream or fight; then she could burst forth and save her. But Marsha wasn't making a peep. As Karen edged closer, she stepped on something soft and warm. One of them had left his clothes in a clump just behind the boulders. Poking out of one of his boots was his holster and pistol.

As one of the scouts began to climax, Karen grabbed the gun and fired it once in the air. "Freeze, assholes!"

"Shit!" Straus cried out in surprise.

"Marsha!" yelled Karen. But Marsha remained limp, now locked between the men.

"Just relax," Kendowski said, disengaging. "It's not what you think."

"We aren't . . . raping her," Straus said softly.

"Marsha, what's going on here?!"

Freed from the men, the former PP supervisor sat on the ground, drew her knees up, hung her head between them, and wrapped her arms around them to keep warm.

"What the hell's going on?" Karen heard behind her. Turning, she saw Uli, Woody, and Root lumbering groggily through the darkness.

When Uli noticed that Marsha and the two men were naked, he immediately remembered the odd sex play he had witnessed in the dark warehouse pier behind Pure-ile Plurality. He also recalled how oblivious Marsha had acted when he tried discussing it with her the next day.

"They were attacking her!" Karen said.

Kendowski, who was naked, scurried over behind Uli to a second pile of clothes.

"Freeze!" Karen said, pointing the gun at him.

"I'm just putting on my underpants!"

"Calm down, everyone," Root said, seeing Karen's finger on the trigger.

"This might be a big misunderstanding," Uli began. "There's no need to—"

"NO! These men were raping Marsha!" Karen shouted.

"Marsha, are you okay?" Root asked. "Were you raped?"

Marsha remained silent, her eyes closed with her forehead resting on her knees.

"Look," Uli went on, "I was at PP for a while and I saw this same thing happen one night—it's weird . . ."

"What'd you see?" Karen asked.

"At night people from PP seemed to go into this odd subconscious state, and they all had sex, including Marsha."

"Trance sex," Straus called out.

"You guys don't seem too tranced out," Cookie said. "Why just her?"

"'Cause guys don't have shame," Kendowski replied. "That's what I heard, anyway."

"Can you just put the gun down and we'll talk about it?" Root said to Karen.

"She's neither denying nor admitting anything," Uli said.

"But she's acting very strange," Cookie whispered.

"Get Marsha away from them first!" Karen demanded. "When she's talking again we'll determine what the charges are."

Root picked up Marsha's shirt and covered her with it. As she did this, Straus grabbed his pants, but came up pointing a second pistol. "We didn't do anything wrong!"

"Put it down," Karen said, pointing her gun back at him.

"Did you see Marsha fighting us? Or showing any resistance?" Kendowski pleaded. "It's all her own choice, Karen!"

"There's a big difference between not resisting and choosing," Karen snapped, still pointing her gun. "I'm gonna give you five seconds to drop your weapon, or I'm gonna choose to shoot!"

"Give me the gun," Uli said calmly to Straus.

"All right," the scout said, clearly wishing the standoff would end, "I'll surrender it to your brother."

"Drop it and I'll drop mine," Karen ███████████████████

"Dropt

. . . Uli was on the ground with a sharp, burning pain in his shoulder. *Caleb shot me!* he thought, but looking a few feet behind him, he saw both scouts lying dead on the ground. When he tried to stand, he felt a numbness in his left thigh and left arm—he glanced down and saw that he had been shot twice. Blood was gushing out. His femoral artery must have been hit. He heard moaning about fifty feet behind him. Poor Woody was writhing in the morning light, and Cookie was off at the cliff's edge, shouting down into the void. Root was weeping as she pressed a piece of clothing against a bloody wound on Woody's stomach. Karen was nowhere to be seen.

"My God, what happened?" Uli removed his belt and wrapped it around his arm as a tourniquet, but his thigh wound was much worse. "Where? Who's the shooter?"

"*You* are!" Root groaned through tears.

It was then that he realized for the first time that Cookie was repeatedly screaming his sister's name. "Where's Karen?" he asked, fearing the worst.

"Dead, you fucker!" Root roared. Grasping that he had no idea what was going on, she breathed deeply and said, "Caleb handed you his gun. You froze a moment, then went apeshit!"

It flooded back:

When Uli took Straus's gun, he heard Karen say to the man, "Okay, I'm dropping mine."

Dropping, dropped, Dropt, he held it a moment and then glared at her. She saw the expression on his face and jumped back. The first bullet hit Woody, who was standing behind her.

Karen retreated toward the cliff as he kept firing. "No, Uli!" she yelled. When he hit her in the shoulder, she returned fire, nailing him in the thigh and arm. He dropped his gun.

"Uli!" Karen called out, rising to her feet.

He snatched the gun up and she froze for a moment, staring into his eyes, before he fired twice into her chest. The two scouts rushed him. Thinking his pistol was empty, Uli nonetheless shot at one and then the other, hitting both squarely in their foreheads. Then he fell to the ground.

In the early morning light, he could see the blood trailing off and over the edge. Cookie was still yelling his sister's name. He limped over and looked down into the vast darkness below. As he scanned for Karen's fallen body, he glanced up and saw a spot on the horizon. A lone blue helicopter rose over the edge of the valley and was coming toward him.

"KAA-REN!" Uli shouted down into the valley. The only sound that came back was the helicopter's propeller growing steadily louder.

Within a minute, the chopper was directly overhead. A single beam illuminated the hilltop, revealing the living and the dead. Slowly it descended, sending up plumes of dust as it landed in the center of the flat plateau.

Three soldiers jumped out and came rushing over holding rifles. The middle-aged man who looked like he was in charge called out, "I'm Captain Nesbitt with the Utah National Guard! Please drop your weapons and show your hands if you want help!"

Uli collapsed to the ground, blood still running from his arm and thigh.

"Our only weapon is on the ground over there!" Cookie yelled back, pointing to where Uli had been standing when he was shot.

"We have two wounded and two dead!" Root shouted, holding her hand up.

"*Three* dead," Akbar corrected. "Four if you count Karen."

One of the men checked out Woody while a younger guard dashed back to the chopper to get supplies.

"He needs immediate medical attention," Root said as she continued compressing Woody's wound.

The young guard hurried back with a medical kit and the two men started working to stabilize Woody. They didn't pay any attention to Uli, who now lay at the edge of the cliff.

Peering down into the ravine as the sun rose, Uli could make out the azure line, like a fine blue flame, a river at the base, where his sister had plunged—where he had sent her. The blood from his thigh was pooling around him, and just as he was about to call for help, he heard a distant echo of her faint voice: "Uli!"

"Karen?" he said softly.

"We did it!" she cried out in the distance.

"I'm so sorry!" he shouted down.

"He's over here," Uli heard behind him. One of the medics flipped him over, cut his clothes, and inspected his wounds. "Shit! I need help over here!"

As they started working on Uli, he whispered, "I know what it was."

"Know what *what* was?" asked one of the medics working on him.

"My mission," he moaned. "It was Karen! They didn't want me to take Moses out of Rescue City. They wanted me to take out *Karen.*"

Once they had packed his wounds, they lifted him onto a stretcher. They marched past Root and loaded him into the chopper, strapping him next to Woody's stretcher.

As the chopper lifted into the air and circled downward, Uli peered out into the valley below and muttered, "I'm coming, Karen."

Four more Utah National Guards emerged from the woods below the summit. They were part of a team sweeping westward, hiking up the Freedom Trail, searching for survivors. Together they joined the man already there and soon the area buzzed with soldiers. One group collected Robert Moses and the bodies of the two scouts. Another group started checking the survivors, offering food and medical assistance.

"Have we been rescued?" Root heard. Marsha finally seemed to be coming to her senses. "Where are Karen and Uli?"

"Don't you know what happened?" Akbar said angrily to her.

"Of course we do," Captain Nesbitt replied apologetically, thinking Akbar was talking to him. "As the caravans began to trickle in, we tried our best to help. It just wasn't in our jurisdiction."

Marsha rose and stumbled into the woods, desperately needing a moment of privacy. Unable to find a tree to hide behind, she continued down the Freedom Trail until the noise and pain on the summit dissipated. A few minutes later, she nearly stumbled into another squad of Utah National Guards hiking up the path.

A tall young sergeant approached. "Are you from Rescue City?" A rifle was strapped to the back of his shoulder. His men were unarmed.

"I'm fine," she replied. Pointing behind her, she added, "But there's a bunch of others up on the mountain you can help."

"Where exactly are you going?" the sergeant asked, seeing that she was barefoot and barely dressed.

"Off to freedom, I guess," she said tiredly, not making eye contact.

"May I ask your name?"

"Miss Marsha Johnson."

"Marsha, we set up a big camp with medical care and delicious hot food just down yonder." He pointed downhill in the direction she was walking. "Why don't you stop in and get fixed up?"

"That sounds nice," she said, and resumed hiking.

"Marsha, I'm going to have someone accompany you."

"That's okay, I can find it."

"I'm sure you can. I'd just never forgive myself if you came this far and got attacked by a grizzly or a rattler," the sergeant said with a kind grin, then gestured to one of his men, who barely seemed out of puberty. "Terry is so timid you won't even know he's there."

Without waiting for her consent, the sergeant and his group continued up the hill, while Marsha and Terry headed downhill. As they walked, Marsha tried to outpace the youth, who quietly kept up with her. After about twenty minutes of this, she stubbed her toe on a rock, and grabbed a sapling before she could hit the ground.

"I'm such a klutz," Marsha said, wincing. "My body's never quite fit me."

"This is a hard path," Terry replied as they resumed walking.

"God usually gives us one path and we usually have to take it," she said. "But due to a miracle of modern science, I was offered a second path."

"You started life on a different path?"

"I was a very different person going down a very different path."

"What path?"

"It started at a Howard Johnson's in Times Square and ended at a riot on Christopher Street," Marsha said, then let out a sigh. "Actually, it ended a year later. The end for everyone in Rescue City—that contamination bomb. Around June of '70 they partitioned off my neighborhood, which was the one place in this country that a person like me could be me."

"What did you do?"

"That summer, a wealthy older gentleman invited me to join him in his villa in Sweden. We thought they'd have the mess cleaned up by the fall or winter."

"Sweden?"

"Yes, and I had this little problem, but they had this specialized clinic and they were developing this new experimental surgery, and they needed volunteers, which was good because I couldn't afford the treatment."

"What was the surgery?" Terry asked softly.

"They called it *reassignment*—sexual reassignment." Marsha paused and looked at Terry for a moment, half waiting for a nasty comment. When it was clear that he wasn't phased, she continued: "But I wasn't really reassigned. In fact, God had preassigned me in many ways."

"Preassigned?"

"Through my genes. I mean, I don't have much facial or body hair, and I do have a tiny Adam's apple. He did give me one obstacle, but he also sent down a cure."

"So what happened?" Terry seemed fascinated.

"I was healed from the operations by early 1971, which was good 'cause my visa ran out, so I returned to New York. But instead of finding that the radiation thing had been cleaned up, I discovered it had spread, like cancer. Instead of just the Village, the entire southern half of Manhattan had been cut off. But Harlem was still outside the quarantine zone."

"So you moved up to Harlem?" Terry asked as they continued down the slope.

"To a Christian mission on 145th Street run by Reverend Siftwelt. He said he had gotten God's calling to go out there."

"You joined a religious mission?"

"Yes. See, my mother was very religious. So it really came natural. I understood them. And all I ever wanted was to do good. That's all I

1504 ♥ Arthur Nersesian

wanted from life. And they all lovingly accepted me. Most people in the parish were applying as a group to go out to Rescue City to help people. So I basically had this revelation that this could be my big chance—not just to help people, but to find my place. A kind of second chance."

"Nearly a decade in Rescue City must've been tough," Terry said.

"The trick is turning your disadvantages into advantages, and believe me, Rescue City is a city of the disadvantaged," Marsha chuckled. "If men took advantage of me, they might've thought it was to *my* disadvantage, but I turned it to my advantage, didn't I? They might've thought they were hurting me, but in a way . . . I was hurting them, 'cause they thought I was something that *could* be hurt."

A gloss of tears came to Terry's eyes as he saw the pain Marsha was denying.

"Don't you dare feel bad for me," she said flatly. "'Cause I flipped my disadvantage over into someone else's disadvantage. It's when the things you do to stay alive become the same things that hurt . . . and you wind up killing those who tried to protect you." She stopped and cried out, "I'm so sorry, Karen!"

Terry saw her bring her hands up to her face and weep until she looked like she was going to topple over. He put his palm gently on her arm to let her know he was there, to keep her steady. Soon the distant sound of a helicopter propeller grew close, and two minutes later it landed on the summit above them.

Captain Nesbitt led everyone safely to one side of the narrow plateau, allowing the chopper to land. When the propeller blades finally went silent, Akbar turned to the officer and said, "You understand that there were mass deaths? Killings! Cannibalizing! 'Cause this will all come out! And I guarantee people will be put on trial for this! Government and military officials . . ."

"All I know is Rescue City was privatized a few years back," Nesbitt said. "They had their own security force, ostensibly to protect it from ousiders."

"They bought this land here *in Utah*?" Root asked.

"They only bought the mineral rights here, which is why we were able to enter."

"So you people knew about the starvation going on and . . ." Akbar started.

"We notified the authorities but they got an injunction. We're still fighting them in court. Everything takes time."

"How can you live with yourself?" Akbar growled.

"We were able to make two major evacuations—one at some burned-out military base and another on an abandoned highway. We also made repeated food drops along Death Road." Evidently this was their term for the Freedom Trail.

"They kept filing injunctions and chasing us away," cut in a lieutenant who was listening in.

"Karen was right after all," Root announced. "There were two groups."

"So how many have made it out alive?" Akbar asked. "What's the body count?"

"There is no number yet. The Supreme Court finally overruled Feedmore, so the army is back in Nevada."

"Where are those who did make it?" Cookie asked.

"They've set up tents for the refugees down in the valley." Nesbitt pointed to the far side of the mountain. "A helicopter will take you down there, but I should warn you that Feedmore is still in charge."

"When are we going back to New York City?" Akbar asked.

"I don't know, but I'll tell you this: your city isn't like it once was."

"Probably 'cause they replaced New Yorkers with tourists," fumed Akbar.

Trying not to think about her own culpability in this tragedy, Root sat down next to Robert Moses's body and took in the spectacular view of the morning sun illuminating the endless valley below them.

"Can you take me to where Karen fell?" Akbar whispered behind her.

She held out her arm and carefully led him to the rocky ledge where Karen had been shot. "Watch it," she said, "you're stepping in her blood."

Akbar stooped over and patted the ground with both hands until he felt the sticky liquid. "This is her?"

"Yeah," Root whispered.

Akbar absentmindedly ran his thumb and index fingers below each of his eyes, creating two bloody streaks as he mumbled, "Good-bye, hon."

Root found herself hypnotized by the incredible strata of red rocks with green etched along their tops until Captain Nesbitt came over to tell them that the chopper was ready for them.

"Where the hell is Marsha?" Akbar asked, having not heard a word from her.

"One of our soldiers is walking her to the encampment," Nesbitt informed him.

"This is one of the most beautiful places I've ever seen," Cookie said, awestruck by the vista below.

"That phenomenon where the rocks are layered that way is called an *uplift*," Nesbitt said, pointing down into the valley. "A vertical thrust pushed blocks of the earth's crust from deep below. There are rocks here that go back two billion years, if you can believe it."

"The past just keeps butting into the present," Cookie said. As the men returned for Moses's body, she asked, "And Feedmore purchased all of this?"

"Just the mineral rights. This is actually a national park," the captain replied. "Welcome to Zion."

February 3, 1993–May 3, 2019

Acknowledgments

I would like to thank the following people for their support during the writing of *The Five Books of (Robert) Moses:*

My loyal friend and intrepid editor Johnny Temple, without whom this work would not exist.

Lisa Archigian, whose inspired illustrations periodically lifted my spirits over the long years of writing this work.

My beloved workshop writers, who inspire me every week: Francis Levy, Joseph Silver, Heidi Boghosian, Sharon Jane Smith, Anne Foster, Tommaso Fiacchino, Kevin Lee, and Geoffrey Bridgman.

My brother Patrick.

My thoughtful friend Don Kennison.

My crew at Akashic Books—Alice Wertheimer and Alex Verdan—for all of their excellent editorial contributions. Also Aaron Petrovich, Sohrab Habibion, Johanna Ingalls, Ibrahim Ahmad, and Susannah Lawrence. Thanks so much, guys.

Thanks to my mother's side of the family, the Burkes: Uncle Thomas P., Aunt Geraldine, Chris, Jody, Andrew, Stephanie, Genji Ridley, Nicholas Sunshine Ridley, Uncle Patrick, Marianne, Joseph, Ally Brown, Pat III, Teresa Vance, Patrick IV, Ciara, Uncle Michael, Aunt Patricia, Claire, Michael Dubon, Uncle Richard, Uncle Stephen, Mary, Kate, Kevin, Timothy, and Stephen Jr.

Thanks to my father's side of the family, the Nersesians: Uncle Paul R., Robert P., Paula A., Marie J., Lee A., Daniel A., Diane S., Ian A., Aaron D., Jackson C., Kristi, Abigail R., Cameron R., Courtnie E., Crystal, Joshua, and Beth Miller.

I also need to acknowledge my community, both online and in person, for their influence and support, no matter how small or elusive it might've seemed: Steve Abbott, Abril Books, Arlo Adamic, Johnny Adamic, Nancy Agabian, Sheri Albert, Natalia Alfonso, Mike Alhberg, Pam Papertsian-Van Alstine, James Altucher, Andria Amaral, Lawrence Applebaum, Zachary Aptekar, Penny Arcade, Bruce Armstrong, Meakin Armstrong, Juan Pablo Artinian, Ozzy Aydogdu, Constance Ayers, Sue Bachner, Maura Alia Badji, Summer Athena Bailey, Steph Baker, Diana Balton, Marianne Balton, Melissa Barberia, Kevin Barclay, Delphi Basilicato, Jonah Bay, Stephen Berg, Malin Bergman, Sharon Berman, Anselm Berrigan, Matthew Binder, Ali Birnbaum, Max Blagg, Deborah B. Blake, Ellen Blum, Brian Boehm, Justin Booth, John Bornstein, Terry Boyd, Meryl Branch-McTiernan, Celia Bressack, Jean Brock, Donna Jean Brigitte Brodie & The Writers Room, Eden Brower, Crystal Brown-Ellsworth, Claire de Brunner, Carol Buck, Jack Buehrer, Megan Buehrer, Michael Burnam, Linda Frye Burnham, Brett Busang, Naomi Cabral, Ozlem Cakir, Margret Calas, Rania Calas, Peter Calderon, Phil Paul Call, Dalcini C. Canella, Ajax Caravan, Cynthia Carr, Charles Carroll, Elizabeth Carson, Michael Carter, Laurel Casey, Pam Cash, Lauren Cerand, Jessica Chalmers, Christine Champagne, Colin Cheney, Nastya Chernikova, David Chestnut, Saoirse N. Chiaragáin, Leslie Ching, Erich Christansen, Lonely Christopher, Fred Cisterna, James Claffey, Don Clark Jr., Joe Clark, Marion Cole, Patricia Coleman, Patricia Collins, Paul J. Comeau, Aaron Cometbus, Johnny Commorato, Katherine Olaya Compitus, Steve Connell, Elizabeth Cannoli Connelly, Kate Conroy, Savona Cook, Larry Coppersmith, Anne Briggs Couture, Kevin Crawford, Lyss Crawford, Douglas Cronk, Shane Cudahy, Steve Dalachinsky, Gabrielle Danchick, Kimmie David, Allesandre Davylle, Nicole DeLaittre, Dewey Delle, Aimee DeLong, Wendy DeLong, Marcy Dermansky, Mary K. DeVault, Dewey-Dell, Sai Dholakia, Barbara Dickey, Kenneth Dombrowski, Lisa Dominick, Hanna Doniger, Pamela Donovan, Sean Doolan, the Downtown Bakery Cocina Mexicana (Manny, Oliva, Coco, Marcos, and Tito), Bill Driscoll, Frank Dunn-Roser, Carl Dupree, Tony DuShane, Melanie Edwards, Simon Egleton, Peter Erickson, Kevin Ernest, Jason Erwin, Sean Fairhurst, Mark Farnsworth, Elena Faro, Siobhan Farrugia, Jim Feast, Ande Fegin, Agnes Field, Bonny Finberg, Diana Finch, Martha Fishkin, Amber Flanagan, Cody Flanagan, Elisa Flynn, Mary Forsell, Dan Fox, Fiona Fox, Trevor Fraser, Lisa Freeman, Patty Freeman, Twanda Freeman, Benjamin George Friedman, Dan Frydman, Brown Furlow, Saul Fussiner, Ray Galindo, Jeff Gallashaw, Julian Gallo, Melly Garcia,

Jeremy Gaydosh, Houry Geudelekian, Phillip Giambri, Jennifer Gilmore, Lee Glass, Matt Glaze, Jonathan Glazer, Andy Gleason, Patricia Gomes, Krystyna Goral, Shaynee Lee Gordy, Rachel Goshgarian, Pameladevi Govinda, James M. Graham, Michael Granville, Howard Greenberg, Trilby Greene, Linda Greer, E.V. Grieve, Jennifer Griffith, Luciano Guerriero, Veken Gueyikian, Raffi Hadidian, Gillian Halpin, Cale Hand, Jane Hansen, Sarah Hansen, April Hare, Lance Harkins, F.D. Harper, Trevor Harran, Jerry Brian Hart II, Emily Hatch, Yukari Hayashida, Emma Hayward, Loraine Hayward, Bruce Hazel, K. Latrice Heath, Elena Helgiu, Richard Hell, Thomas Hendrickson, Jessica Safavimehr Hernandez, Scott Hisley, Adam Hocker, Kurt Hollander, Kevin Holohan, Shawn Joseph Hooper, Kenneth Michael Hoover, Blair Hopkins, Ned Horn, Bronwen Gilbert Houck, Ives Hovanessian-Grau, Andrew Hubner, Carolyn Hughes, Anne Husick, Sarah Hutchinson, Derrick Hynes, Gary Indiana, Marjorie Ingall, Joan Hunter Iovino, James Izurieta, Jude Izurieta, Michael Jackman, Meg Jacks, Judy Jackson, Marilynn Jackson, Yoshika Jai, Tasha Jakush, Aris Janigian, Kristen Hemingway Jaynes, Deer Jen, Rich Jensen, Keri Johannessen, Janice Johnson, Noa Jones, Laura Kahn, Ronald J. Kahn, Sasha Kahn, Taleen Kali, Karen Karavanic, Lucille Avakian Karnick, Irene Karpathakis, Nadia Katya, Rachel Kay, Isa Paula Kechichian, Hillary Keel, Sean Keenan, Riley Kellogg, Shannan Kelly, Chris G. Kelso, Greg Kessler, Rachel Kessler, Caroline Kim, Richard Kingcott, Jamie Kirchner, Deanna Kirk, Switchblade Kitten, Andrea Kleiman, Christine Knight, Beth Knobel, Alexandra Koch, Tim Koehler, Ellen Koga, Ron Kolm, Zack Kopp, Lola Koundakjian, Karl Kowalski, Maria Kozic, Marcia Kuhr, Arpi Kupelian, Raphael Lasar, Denise Johnson Layton, Frankie Lembo, Paul Lembo, Tessa Lena, Ian Graham Lesk, Mindy Levokove, Leanne Libert, Kristen Ligocki, Karen Lillis, Jennifer Lilya, Donna Linden, Jason E. Lips, Greg Locke, Tony Loor, Cary Lorene, Thelma Lou, Lavinia Ludlow, Natalie Luna, Maggie Luo, Marvin Hau-bond Luo, Victoria Luther, Billy Lux, Natalia Lyudin, Lana Magnuson, Jennifer Maguire, James Maher, Kevin Maher, David Malaxos, Cy Manis, Tina Manis, Ellen Marello, Matt Marello, Jacob Margolies, Nate Santa Maria, Denise Marie, Sissa Marquardt, Bam Martin, Sam Massol, Luke Matheissen, Christine Matthews, Jen Mazer, Chet Mazur, Jon McCullough, Ben McFall, Tom McGlynn, Mike McGonigal, Marie McGowan, Judy McGuire, Tim McLoughlin, River James McMahon, Rob Meador, Lynne Tenpenny Medina, Lisa Medoff, Anna Meehan-Detrick, Bernard Meisler, Patricia Melvin,

Minolta Mendez, Sharon Mesmer, Jon R. Meyers, Tim Milk, Cynthia Miller, Morgan Miller, Doug Milliken, Stephanie Mittak, Frank Moliterno, Dominik Moll, Michael Montana, Omar Montelongo, Bernie Mooney, Emily Moorefield, B. Michael Morgan, Joelle Morrison, Elisabeth B. Morse, Jeremiah Moss, Kate Moss, Sandy Mullin, Shaheen Nazerali, Karen Nelson, Karen Nercessian, Whitney Van Nes, Alicia Neville, Dayve Newman, Kathy Newman, Lindell Nillo, J. Michael Niotta, Justin Norton, Chris Notionless, Reginald Oberlag, Kevin O'Donnell, Adam Ogilvie, Don Ogilvie, Fan Ogilvie, Henny Ohr, Don O'Keefe, Lizzy Oppenheimer, Fly Orr, Lorcan Otway, Raffi Ouzounian, Garth Owen, Jose Padua, Paechan, Romuloa Paez, Kris Pak, Howard T. Palmer, Christoph Paul, Dale Peck, Glen Perau, Miriam Peters, Katie Tisch Peterson, Danielle Pfeifer, Julie G. Pfrommer, Claire Phelan, Deborah Pintonelli, Lou Pizzitola, Bart Plantenga, Plant Man, Dimitri Portnoy, Roddy Potter, Valentino Povirk, Denise Prescod, Rob Press, Katie Purkiss, Paul Rachman, Ivan Ramirez, Penny Rand, Tara Jean Randall, Jill Rappaport, Mary Rattray, Lise Raven, U.V. Ray, Gerritt Reeves, Jon Reiss, Richard Reiss, Tom Reiss, Sean Revoltah, Anthony Reynolds, Cole Riley, Richard Rivas, Julie Ann Robblee, Matthew Robert, Samantha Robinson, Matt Rodbro, Alicia Rodriguez, Nancy Archino Romer, Beverly Ronson, Jules Ross, Barney Rosset, Astrid Myers Rosset, Lenny Rotali, William Rowen, Alena Rudolph, Garrett Russo, Meaddows Ryan, Susan Ryan, Earl Samuelson, Lauren Sanders, Kelly Sanford, Monte Schapiro, Diana Scheuhemann, Ellen Left Eye Schinderman, Nina M. Schneider, Amy Scholder, Kala Schubak, Garret Schuelke, Sarah Schulman, Kelly Sebastian, Alan Semerdjian, Rami Shamir, Robert Shapiro, Matthew Sharpe, David Shaughnessy, Kelley Shaw, Matthew Sheahan, Aurelie Sheehan, Danawyn Sherman, Michele Sherstan, Eve Sicular, Julie Simpkins, Anil Sishta, Agatha Slagatha, Wendy Slater-Erbs, Dave Slinkster, Jonah Smith, Rachel Smith, Tom Smith, Iris Smyles, George Solomine, Alexis Sottile, Anne Spencer, Shannon Spencer, Kelly Spitzner, Janet Stafford, Janet Steen, Howard Stock, Chris Such, Koko Sugiyama-Burr, Elizabeth Sun, Julia Tanner, Geoff Taylor, Sarah Teti, Eddie Thiel, Laura Thoms, Jim W. Thurman, Lynne Tillman, Susie Timmons, Elizabeth Tippins, Jennifer Tittle, Mina Tittle, Jeffrey Turboff, Julie Turley, Ellen Turrietta, Fred Tuten, David Unger, Seema Upadhyay, Marie Valigorsky, Jeff Conan Vargon, Hrag Vartanian, Vera Videnovich, Alfred Vitale, Margaret Harrison Vitek, Anne Vitiello, Amanda Jane Vogel, Daniela Voicu, George Wagner, Earl Wallace, Julie Walsh, Kevin J. Walsh, Ann

Walton, Patricia Ward, Tricia Warden, Nathan Warden, Desi Warner, Rob Warren, Sherry Wasserman, Carl Watson, Jude Webre, David J. Weiss, Jonathan Welford, Alena Wertalik, Shauna Westgate, Michael White, Jincy Willet, Grace W. Williams, Conrad Williamson, Danielle Winston, Patricia Winter, Erica Wolff, Jonathan Woods, Maggie Wrigley, Lorah Yaccarino, Bernard Yenelouis, Arno Yeretzian, Janine Young, Joel Yudin, Vic Zajac, April Zay, Marti Zimlin, and David Zimmerle.

Last, but most of all, I have to acknowledge my place of birth, New York City. For the first half my life it was cheap, vacant, and vilified. For the second half of my life it was overpriced, colonized, and deified. I've tried my best to adapt with your ever-changing image.

OLD TOWN

(New York, New York)

NOTABLE LOCATIONS

A Maria and Lucretia's House, East Tremont
B Leon Skarcrowski's Scrapyard
C Eugene Hill's Squat
D Columbia University
E Morningside Park
F Karen's Apartment
G West End Bar
H Paul and Robert's Parents' House
J 11th Street Brownstone, Site of Bombing
K Washington Square Park
L Millie and Paul's Apartment

SELECT LIST OF ROBERT MOSES'S ACHIEVEMENTS

1 Co-op City
2 Lincoln Center
3 New York Coliseum
4 United Nations Headquarters
5 Madison Square Garden
6 Shea Stadium
■ Bridges and Tunnels
■ Parks
■ Expressways

Hutchinson River Parkway

Bronx River Parkway

Mosholu Parkway

Saw Mill River Parkway

Major Deegan Expressway

Cross Bronx Expressway

Bruckner Expressway

THROGS NECK BRIDGE

HENRY HUDSON BRIDGE

BRONX

Harlem River Drive

TRIBOROUGH BRIDGE

DOWNING STADIUM

HUDSON RIVER

West Side Highway

MANHATTAN

CENTRAL PARK